- KPSV -

V

EVERYMAN,
I WILL GO WITH THEE,
AND BE THY GUIDE,
IN THY MOST NEED
TO GO BY THY SIDE

THE RAJ QUARTET

THIS IS A BORZOI BOOK
PUBLISHED BY ALFRED A. KNOPF

First included in Everyman's Library, 2007

ISBN: 978-0-307-26397-1 (US)
1-85715-298-0 & 978-1-85715-298-2 (UK)

Book design by Barbara de Wilde and Carol Devine Carson
Typeset in the UK by AccComputing, North Barrow, Somerset
Printed and bound in Germany by GGP Media GmbH, Pössneck

PAUL SCOTT

THE RAJ QUARTET

VOLUME TWO

THE TOWERS OF SILENCE
A DIVISION OF THE SPOILS

EVERYMAN'S LIBRARY
Alfred A. Knopf   New York   London   Toronto
298

CONTENTS

___

THE TOWERS OF SILENCE

To Penny
with all my love

CONTENTS

THE UNKNOWN INDIAN

I

IN SEPTEMBER 1939, when the war had just begun, Miss Batchelor retired from her post as superintendent of the Protestant mission schools in the city of Ranpur.

Her elevation to superintendent had come towards the end of her career in the early part of 1938. At the time she knew it was a sop but tackled the job with her characteristic application to every trivial detail, which meant that her successor, a Miss Jolley, would have her work cut out untangling some of the confusion Miss Batchelor usually managed to leave behind, like clues to the direction taken by the cheery and indefatigable leader of a paper chase whose ultimate destination was not clear to anybody, including herself.

Miss Batchelor, christened Barbara (Barbie for short), knew she had many shortcomings, most of which were due to two besetting sins. She seldom stopped talking and was inclined to act without thinking. She had often prayed to be blessed with a more cautious and tranquil nature but had always done so by falling enthusiatically on her knees and speaking to God aloud, which may have accounted for the fact that these prayers were never answered. Her attempts to reform without intercession were also unsuccessful. When she held her tongue people asked rather anxiously about her health – not without cause because the stress of keeping quiet gave her headaches; and the headaches were not helped by the worry of work piling up if she put any of it off to think about it first. So in the end she was content to bear the burden of her own nature in the belief that God had known best what was right for her. Secretly she was rather proud of her voice. It carried.

Barbie was a believer in the good will and good sense of established authority. If the mission had told her that her furrow was not ploughed, that she was good for a few years yet, she would have squared her shoulders, spat on her palms and pressed on, grateful to be made use of. But the mission said no such thing and she outwardly accepted the situation with her usual bustling equanimity. Inwardly she accepted it with mingled relief and apprehension.

'I shall be glad to slow down,' she said. People smiled. They could not imagine Barbie except at top speed. In putting her out to grass the mission, which always looked after its own, would have provided her with temporary accommodation in Ranpur and helped to establish her eventually in Darjeeling or Naini Tal where they had twilight bungalows. They would have given her an assisted passage home, but the war made that difficult and in any case Barbie said she didn't want it. She had not been in England for thirty years.

It seemed that Barbie wanted nothing except her pension and her freedom to go where and do what she liked. She let it be known that she had plans. She said she did not intend to be idle in retirement. She would find a *pied-à-terre* and devote herself to some kind of voluntary work. She had saved. She was perfectly content, perfectly happy. She would always be available should the mission need her help or advice. They had only to ask and she would come, at the double.

The facts were that she had no plans and no clear idea where to go or what to do. She would have liked to be of use to someone or something but could not visualize whom or what. On the whole it did not matter much so long as being useful left her with a certain amount of time to devote to a personal problem.

Barbie had what her mother would have called a secret sorrow. She had been a fairly competent teacher, especially of small children, because they brought out her maternal instincts, and she had often been rewarded by proofs of her capacity to earn affection and esteem from pupils and their parents. But to Barbie the teaching of reading, writing and arithmetic had never been as important as the teaching of Christianity.

For almost as long as she could remember she had believed in God, in Christ the Redeemer and in the existence of Heaven. They were very real to her. The fate of unbelievers was equally real, particularly the fate of those who were unbelievers through no fault of their own. This was why when both her parents were dead she had given up her job at a Church school in South London, joined the mission and come to India.

To bring even one Hindu or Muslim child to God struck her as a very satisfactory thing to do and she imagined that in the mission it would be open to her to do this for scores, possibly hundreds. Once in India she was disappointed to find that all the emphasis was upon the mission's educational function, that the mission gates were ajar to let Indian children in to learn things that would be useful to them but not wide open in a way that encouraged teachers to go out and bring the children in, as into a fold.

Initially disturbed by this secular attitude and by the discipline imposed inside the mission to discourage its members from excessive displays of zeal, she soon accepted them as sensible measures taken by those who knew best and who were anxious to preserve and hold what had been won rather than risk losing it all in trying too hard to gain more. She discovered that the missions were not popular with the civil administration or with the military authorities and had not been since the mutiny of 1857, which people said started because the Indian sepoys believed they were to be forcibly converted, having first been polluted by the introduction of cartridges greased with pig fat. Moreover, the authorities, both civil and military, seemed to take considerable trouble to enable Hindus to go on being Hindus and Muslims to be Muslims by giving them every opportunity to practise their rites and hold their festivals and by giving official recognition to the communal differences between them.

'Well, one step at a time,' Barbie told herself and settled to the business of teaching Eurasian children whose parents were Christians already, the children of converts and the children of Hindu and Muslim parents who were anxious for their sons, and occasionally daughters, to get a good grounding in the English they had to know if they wanted to get on, but very few of whom would ever be baptized.

Over the years she became inured to this system. The Bishop Barnard schools, named after one of the founders of the mission to which she belonged, had expanded considerably between the wars and in the principal cities become distinguished and proud of an academic reputation that attracted Indian girls and boys whose parents were advanced enough to want to educate them to the standard required for entrance to government colleges and Indian universities. As reputation and supply of pupils increased so did the demand for teachers with the right kind of qualifications. Year by year the religious basis of instruction was chipped away and women like Barbie kept in junior posts or elevated to administrative positions in which neither their missionary ambitions (what was left of them) nor their lack of academic stature could do much harm. With the appointment of Barbie's successor, Miss Jolley, even that preserve of the old guard was infiltrated. Miss Jolley was young, she had letters after her name and her file disclosed her religion as nonconformist, not C of E which in Barbie's day had been a primary requirement.

But it was not in all this that Barbie's secret sorrow lay. It lay in the fact that in recent years she had felt her faith loosening its grip. She believed in God as firmly as ever but she no longer felt that He believed in her or listened to her. She felt cut off from Him as she would if she had spent her life doing something of which He disapproved. This puzzled her because she didn't think He could disapprove. He could be better pleased, but that was another matter entirely and one for which neither she nor the mission was exclusively responsible. One did what one could and it should not be necessary to be a saint or a martyr to feel His presence. She no longer felt it. She could not help blaming the mission just a bit for this and she thought there might be a chance of regaining the joyful sense of contact now that she was retiring. She would not hurt anyone by explaining this but her cheerful expression was not entirely due to her habit of keeping one; although that came into it too because she secretly feared a lonely old age.

The address in the advertisement for a single woman to share accommodation with another, which appeared in the *Ranpur Gazette* a week or two before Barbie's retirement, sounded attractive: Mrs Mabel Layton, Rose Cottage, Club Road, Pankot.

She had never been to Pankot. It was the hill station where most official Ranpur people spent the hot weather and to which a few of them eventually retired. Since Ranpur was the place in which she chanced to be when her career petered out the idea of retiring to Pankot herself appealed to her. She wrote to Mrs Layton at once, giving an account of herself, mentioning the sum she could afford and suggesting that if she took the short holiday she had been thinking of spending in Darjeeling – seeing old missionary acquaintances – in Pankot instead, they could meet and come to a decision.

She assumed that Mrs Layton was a widow and that the advertisement implied means as small as her own. The name of the house, seeming diminutive, rather bore that out. Barbie had long since lost the immediately tell-tale signs of a poverty-stricken lower-middle-class English background and could stand her own in any company as what, in her earlier life, had been called a gentlewoman, but she had remained a little fearful of women born in superior walks of life, especially if they had money to support their position.

Mabel Layton's reply was encouragingly simple and friendly.

'Dear Miss Batchelor, I have had a number of answers to my advertisement but I imagine from your own that we could get on well together. Unless you have changed your mind, in which case please write and tell me, I shall do nothing further about the accommodation available until you have had a chance to see it. If you come to Pankot on holiday perhaps you would like to spend it here at Rose Cottage. Smith's Hotel – a tiny branch of the one you will know of in Ranpur – is rather crowded nowadays and a bit expensive. With regard to a permanent arrangement, should we decide to make one, the sum you say you can afford is ten rupees a month higher than I intended asking, and should expect. Rose Cottage is a very old bungalow, one of the oldest in Pankot. Its main attraction is the garden. It is a little inconveniently situated but after your long and arduous work in the missions I fancy you don't especially wish to be at the hub of things. If you decide to come up just write or telegraph the time of your arrival and I will get my old servant Aziz to meet you and help you with your bags. As you probably know the train leaves Ranpur daily at midnight and reaches Pankot about 8 a.m.'

The kindly tone of this letter offset Barbie's first impression on receiving it. The envelope was lined and the writing paper thick. The address and telephone number were printed; in fact engraved. A smoothing motion of Barbie's fingers confirmed this. She felt alarmed, uncertain that she could live up to such things. But having read the letter she felt only pleasure and gratitude. Out of a number of applicants Mabel Layton had selected her and was actually prepared to keep the vacancy open until she could go to Pankot and see Rose Cottage for herself. This meant, Barbie thought, that although Mabel Layton needed someone to help with expenses the need was not so desperate that she could not afford to wait for the right person. She seemed to be a woman who liked to keep up standards, in important matters such as her choice of friends and in minor ones like the kind of paper used when writing to them.

Barbie sat down to reply.

'Dear Mrs Layton, Thank you for your letter and for your very kind suggestion that I should spend my holiday at Rose Cottage. I accept most gratefully. I hand over officially to my successor here on September 30th. She is very capable and my duties are already negligible. Therefore I can plan to leave without delay. I should be able to come up on the train that reaches Pankot on the morning of October 2nd. As soon as I have made the booking I shall write to you again or telegraph. Meanwhile I can begin my packing at once. I hope you will not mind if I bring with me rather more luggage than might be expected of someone coming to Pankot on a vacation. Conditions here do not easily permit of other people's stuff lying around for long, so I am anxious to leave behind as little as I can even if it means bringing things with me which I do not actually need for a holiday and should have to bring back with me if we do not come to a permanent arrangement. Fortunately I have always travelled fairly light. A long experience of postings from one station to another has taught . . .'

At this point Barbie realized she had set off on a tack that could well have the effect of boring poor Mrs Layton to tears.

But her luggage was a priority. She had wanted to make this clear. The importance of luggage was often overlooked. Barbie had never overlooked it but since hearing officially from mission headquarters in Calcutta that her retirement 'need not be postponed' her luggage had been perhaps overmuch on her mind. At the end of her career the tide of affairs which had involved her was on the ebb, leaving her revealed. And what was revealed did not amount to a great deal, which meant that every bit counted. There was, to begin with, herself, but apart from herself there was only her luggage and of that there was little enough although rather a lot in comparison: bedroll, camp-equipment, clothes, linen, many unread books, papers, photograph albums, letters, mementoes of travel, presents from past pupils, a framed and very special picture, a few ornaments and one piece of furniture. This latter was a writing-table and was the only item that still remained from the stuff she had originally brought out from England. It had legs that folded in and so was portable. Someone once told her that it was late Georgian or early Victorian and had probably belonged to a general for use in writing orders and campaign dispatches under canvas. She was very fond of it, kept it polished and the tooled leather surface stuck down at the corner where it tended to come away. It rather annoyed her to see Miss Jolley using it as if it were mission property and not Barbie's private possession; but so far she had not felt quite up to warning her that when she went the table went with her.

Mrs Layton could not possibly be interested in such things but it was important to Barbie to establish their existence as inseparable from her own and therefore to be taken into account in any plan to welcome her in Pankot. The luggage by itself, with the exception of the table, was merely luggage she knew, but without it she did not seem to have a shadow.

However, commonsense prevailed. She crumpled the letter, began again, determined to put herself into the recipient's place as she had been taught by her earliest mission instructor in the field, and record no more than was necessary to convey the prosaic details of her acceptance of Mabel Layton's invitation and of her intended time of arrival.

This accomplished she sealed the letter and called Thomas Aquinas. Thomas Aquinas was not her personal servant. He went with the superintendent's bungalow. He tip-toed everywhere but banged doors so loudly that sometimes you jumped out of your skin. He also suffered from chronic catarrh and sniffed perpetually. He was called Thomas Aquinas because the Catholics had got him first. She gave him the letter and told him to post it at the Elphinstone Fountain post office and not in the collection box on the Koti Bazaar road which she thought untrustworthy. She did not want the letter delayed. She hoped, as she watched Thomas take it, that she had struck the right note in it.

'Always remember,' she had been told, 'that a letter never smiles. You may smile as you write it but the recipient will see nothing but the words.'

The time was 1914, the man Mr Cleghorn, the place Muzza-firabad. Mr Cleghorn was handing her back the draft of her request to mission headquarters for a special discount on another half-dozen *First Steps in Bible Reading*, a limp-bound book illus-trated by line drawings which the children earned marks for colouring – good marks for delicate tints, poorer marks for bold ones. A little Hindu girl once gave Jesus a bright blue complex-ion because that was the colour of Krishna's face in the picture her parents had at home.

Barbie sighed, got up from the writing-table, opened the almirah and got out a suitcase. At Muzzafirabad she had suc-ceeded a younger, brilliant, indeed heroic woman, and was con-scious of her shortcomings even then. Among them was the tendency to make a ruling without first thinking out its con-sequences. After the Krishna episode she had taken away the blue crayons. And then the children had no way of colouring the sky.

II

When she arrived in Pankot at twelve minutes past 8 a.m. on October 2nd, Mrs Layton's old servant Aziz was waiting at the station looking from one alighting European woman and another to the snapshot she had sent with her second letter as insurance against not being recognized immediately and being left until only she and some strange old man occupied the plat-form and there could be little doubt that each was waiting for the other. She had wished to appear efficient and thoughtful. She had also always had a horror of being stranded. She had just managed to restrain herself from sending two different snapshots by separate posts, realizing in time that these might both irritate Mrs Layton and confuse the servant.

'Perhaps he would like to keep it,' she said when Mrs Layton offered the snapshot back, complimenting her on the foresight which had eased Aziz of some of the burden of his responsibility. 'He was so good with the bags and so helpful about the trunk.'

The trunk, a metal one, was full of relics of her work in the mission schools. It had been her intention to leave it and the writing-table in Ranpur and to send for them later, if she were staying in Pankot. Thomas Aquinas had misunderstood and had the trunk loaded on to the van which preceded Barbie to the station. When she got there the van had gone and trunk, suitcases and cardboard boxes were already crammed into the coupé which Thomas Aquinas stood guard over. She was less worried about arriving in Pankot with the trunk than about leaving the writing-table behind now unaccompanied. There and then she wrote a note to Miss Jolley telling her what had happened and confirming that she would send for the writing-table at the first opportunity. She gave the note to Thomas, with a further five rupees to add to the fifty she had already given him as parting baksheesh.

Mrs Layton's servant, Aziz, had two tongas waiting in the concourse of Pankot station. Seeing the trunk he declared it too heavy for a tonga, took charge of it and left it in the ticket office for delivery by some mysterious agency he assured her he could command. He loaded one tonga with Barbie and her small hand baggage and the other with her suitcase, bedroll, cardboard boxes of odds and ends, and himself. He sat in the passenger seat gripping on to this paraphernalia and indicated that his tonga would lead the way.

On the old two-wheeled horse tongas you rode with your back to horse and driver and watched the ground unravel beneath the footboard, back towards the place you had come from. Driving like this from the station, Barbie had an impression mainly of the rock face which brought the railway to a halt, then of a narrow metalled road with broad strips of kuttcha on either side, steep banks of rocky earth and overhanging trees. The road curved uphill, this way, that way. There was nothing much to see but after the plains the air at this altitude struck her as sweet and welcoming. In a while she felt the strain put on horse and tonga slacken, as if a crest had been reached. The tonga stopped. Twisting round to discover the reason she found the other tonga also halted and Aziz getting down.

'Memsahib,' he called, rather fiercely. 'Pankot.'

He spread one arm towards the panorama revealed on this side of the miniature mountain-pass. She got down to see it better and stood for quite a minute before saying aloud, 'Praise God!'

Down in Ranpur after the rains, in places where there were grass and trees, the green nature of these things reasserted itself. Through so much of the year they showed dusty, parched and brown. But in the plains, after the wet, there was never any green like this. Here, all looked like rich and private pasture. Flocks of blackfaced sheep and long-haired goats, herded by sturdy skull-capped peasants, tinkled down a slope, making for the road down which the tongas would also go: a long straight road that led directly into the valley formed by three hills — on the crest of one of which Barbie was standing. The valley itself was under a thin blanket of morning mist. At its centre was a township: the bazaar, a triangular pattern of wooden buildings, whose upper storeys, decorated in Indian hill-style with verandahs and orna-mental roofs, were clearly visible above the vapour. Beyond the bazaar one hill rose to the left and another much more steeply to the right. She could tell it was to the right that the British had chosen to build. She could see the roofs of many bungalows and buildings, a golf-course and the spire of a church. On this side of the town she could make out the random pattern of army installations.

The crests of the hills were forested. Apart from the receding clunk of the sheep and goat bells there was a holy silence.

'Rose Cottage kiddher hai?' she asked Aziz.

Again making the gesture with his fully extended right arm he answered in English, 'There. On the other side of the big hill.'

She looked in that direction and saw how beyond the hill more distant ranges marched towards a mountainous horizon. Was that snow or sunlight on the farthest peak? She sighed, content to have seen such a vision of beauty even if it was not to be her luck to live out her days in constant sight of it.

Looking away from the panorama he had presented, as if it were in his gift, she found him watching her. She nodded her thanks and made her way back to the tonga with a forthright manly stride.

It was on the long haul up the hill from the bazaar, going past the golf-course and the club, that she felt quite suddenly that she had passed Aziz's test. 'Memsahib, Pankot,' he had said. Like a command. And she had looked and said, Praise God. Even if Aziz hadn't heard, or had heard and hadn't understood, the praise on her face must have been unmistakable.

The snapshot she told Mrs Layton Aziz might like to keep (and which she discovered later he had put in a little silver frame) probably still exists, may even be on display along with other items of iconography on the rough walls of a hut in the Pankot hills, in the distant mountain village Aziz came from. If so one wonders what his descendants make of it, if with the snapshot they have inherited knowledge of the white woman of whom it is a likeness: Baba Bachlev, who had much *saman* (luggage) and much *batchit* (talk), a holy woman from the missions who came to stay at the house with the garden full of roses.

This snapshot (of which she had several copies because it was her favourite) showed the canal network of lines on her parchment skin. The iron-grey hair, cropped almost as short as a man's but softened by attractive natural waves, gave an idea of sacrificial fortitude rather than of sexual ambivalence. Her costume, severely tailored, and made of hard-wearing cloth, did not disguise the rounded shape of her unclaimed breast.

She wore dresses but favoured coats and skirts. With them she wore cream silk blouses or ones of plain white cotton. Always about her neck hung the thinnest of gold chains with a pendant cross, also gold. A present of eau-de-cologne on her birthday gave her twelve months of lasting pleasure as did Christmas gifts of fine lawn handkerchiefs on which to sprinkle it. With these annual endowments the voluptuous side of her nature was satisfied. Like everything else she owned, cologne and handkerchiefs were cherished, but the cologne, although eked out, was in daily use so that she was always pleasant to be near. She washed mightily and sang in her tub: not hymns, but old songs of the Music Hall era about love on a shoestring. Such songs had been her father's favourites.

'My father loved life,' she told Mabel Layton during the period accepted by both of them as probationary. 'I never heard him complain. But then there wasn't any reason to. I mean he only had himself to blame, poor man. He gambled and drank. Champagne tastes and beer income, according to my mother. People said he could have been a clever lawyer but he never qualified. He didn't have the education and could never have afforded to, but he worked for a firm of solicitors in High Holborn and they thought highly of him. Well, they must have done because they had so many little things to overlook. Not, heaven forbid, that he was ever dishonest. But he was erratic and a great spendthrift.'

She wanted to be sure that Mabel Layton knew the Batchelors had been very small lower-middle-class beer. In Rose Cottage there were photographs of Laytons, and of Mabel's first husband and his family (it turned out she had been married and widowed twice) and all of them looked distinguished and well off, very pukka, the kind of people who belonged to the ruling class in India: the *raj*. Mabel, it was true, had let herself go, but in the manner that only people of her upbringing seemed capable of doing without losing prestige and an air of authority.

Barbie's first view of her was of an elderly shapeless woman wearing muddy grey slacks, an orange cotton blouse whose sleeves and collar had been ripped out to afford more freedom and expose more to the sun the brown, freckled and wrinkled arms, neck and shoulders. An ancient straw hat with a frayed brim shaded her face. She had seemed unwillingly distracted from the job she was doing: grubbing out weeds from one of the rose beds, a task she performed without gloves, kneeling on the grass on an old rubber hot-water bottle stuffed (as Barbie discovered later) with discarded much-darned cotton stockings. She did not look up until Barbie, obeying Aziz's gesture of permission and invitation, approached to within a few feet of her and cast shadow on the busy work-roughened hands.

She was in the garden every day of the year, she said. The mali usually did only the heaviest work of digging and keeping the grass cut, and even then under Mrs Layton's supervision. In the wet season she would go gum-booted and sou'westered and macintoshed in search of a job that needed doing. The heavier downpours would drive her in to the verandahs, but these were vivid with shrubs and creepers: azaleas, bougainvillaea and wistaria – and flowers such as geranium and nasturtium. All needed constant attention.

Seeing the garden at Rose Cottage Barbie realized she had always longed for one. She was ashamed of her ignorance of the names and natures of plants.

Built in the old Anglo-Indian style, Rose Cottage was a large rectangular structure with cream stucco walls and colonnaded verandahs at front, back and sides. There were two main bedrooms and a third which was called the little spare. There were a dining-room and a living-room. Central to the rooms was a square entrance hall which had been panelled in the 'twenties by its former owner. On the panelling Mabel had hung a variety of brass and copper trays. On either side of the doorway into the sitting-room stood a rosewood table with a crystal bowl of flowers – usually roses, as on the day of Barbie's arrival. These could be cut from the bushes almost continually from February to November.

Barbie's bedroom was to the right of the hall and Mrs Layton's to the left. Both had windows on to the front verandah and french doors on to the verandahs at the sides. Barbie's room connected to the little spare through a shared bathroom. Mabel Layton had a bathroom of her own. Her bedroom connected to the dining-room which, like the living-room, had views on to the back verandah. Dining- and living-room also inter-connected. In all but the cold weather these doors were left open to give extra air. Behind the dining-room lay the kitchen and storeroom. Here Aziz had a bed made up. The general servants' quarters were reached by a path from the kitchen but were screened from the garden by a hedge.

Mabel Layton said she hoped Barbie would not mind being looked after mainly by Aziz. She had never cared for personal maids and in recent years had done without one entirely. Aziz, she said, was as competent to look after a wardrobe as any woman. The mali's wife came into the house to collect soiled household and personal linen and could attend to Barbie if that was what she preferred. Barbie said she was used to being looked after by male servants and had every confidence in Aziz. It seemed that Aziz cooked too. After her first meal, lunch, she no longer wondered why Mrs Layton, who appeared far better off than Barbie had expected, depended so much on him. The food was simple but exquisitely prepared and served.

'So long as I have Aziz and a mali to do the rough work in the garden,' Mabel Layton said, 'I don't much care to be bothered about servants. I leave Aziz to hire and fire whom he will. That way we get along perfectly. And he's been with me since my second husband died, which makes it twenty-two years next month. I'm not sure how old he is but James took him on in Ranpur the month before he was ill and Aziz seemed quite elderly then.'

Barbie's holiday was originally agreed as one of three weeks' duration. During the first few days there were quite a number

of casual visitors and Barbie assumed that she was being submitted by Mabel Layton to the test of selected friends' approval.

She made a careful note of names and apprehended that they
were in all probability names with which any woman who
deserved to live at Rose Cottage should have been familiar. Mrs
Paynton, Mrs Fosdick, Mrs Trehearne: these were the most formidable. Their husbands were probably all generals or colonels
at least. Mabel Layton was herself what Anglo-Indian society
called Army: Army by her first husband, Civil by her second and
Army again by her second husband's son, her stepson, no less a
person than the commanding officer of the 1st Pankot Rifles
which Barbie had heard enough about to know was a very distinguished regiment indeed, particularly in the eyes of Pankot
people. She was spared a meeting with Colonel Layton and his
wife and the two daughters who had just returned from school
in England, because they were all down in Ranpur. She was
sure that the younger Mrs Layton would also be formidable, the
daughters hard and self-assured.

In fact she was puzzled why a woman like Mabel Layton
should advertise accommodation and go to the length of vetting
such an unlikely candidate as a retired teacher from the missions.
She decided she could cope with the situation best by just being
herself. Mabel Layton had really little of the burra mem in her
at all although obviously she was one. But with the other women
who called in for coffee Barbie felt exposed to a curiosity that
was not wholly friendly.

She admitted to having an indifferent head for bridge but no
prejudice against gambling, in spite of the fact that her father
lost more on the horses than he could afford from his wages as
a solicitor's managing clerk which meant that her mother had
had to earn money herself by taking in dress-making.

'We lived in Camberwell,' Barbie explained, 'and it was a great
treat going with her to big houses in Forest Hill and Dulwich.
I helped her with the pins. She had an absolute horror of putting
them in her mouth because of a story she'd heard of someone
swallowing one and dying in agony. So I used to hold the pincushion. I called it the porcupine. It was filled with sand and
absolutely bristled and was really awfully heavy, but it was
covered in splendid purple velvet with seed-pearl edging and
I used to stand there like a little altar boy, holding it up as high

and as long as I possibly could. I can tell you it was tough on the arms but worth it because I was positively enchanted, I mean by watching my mother turn a length of silk or satin into a dress fit for a queen. I only hated it when she was doing mourning because then we both had to wear black and the houses we visited always smelt of stale flowers. And of course we knew we'd have to wait ages to be paid. Weddings were the big things. We got all sorts of perks.'

After such expositions a little silence used to fall, like a minuscule drop of water from the roof of an underground cave into a pool a long way below, where it made more noise than the scale of the actual situation seemed to merit. And the situation was worsened by Mabel Layton remaining immobile and expressionless as though what she always appeared willing to listen to when she and Barbie were alone, even if slow or reluctant to comment on it, bored her when it was told in front of her friends. It was left to the visitors to respond, which they did in those little silences and in then recalling, as though suddenly reattuned to the realities of life, other obligations and appointments that took them away wearing airs of concentration. There was, after all, a war begun in Europe. At any moment the Empire might be at stake.

'Come on, Batchelor,' Barbie said on a morning she decided there could be no future for her in Pankot at Rose Cottage, 'chin up.' She went to her room because Mabel had gone back into the garden. She sat at the borrowed mahogany desk to write yet another letter on the beautiful engraved paper, supplies of which had been placed in a wooden rack for her convenience. There were as well supplies of the matching purple-lined envelopes with stamps fixed at the inland rate, a mark of hospitality that amounted to graciousness but suggested a limitation of it, there having been but twelve; a generous but perhaps significant calculation of four letters a week for three weeks being enough to meet the requirements of any reasonable visitor.

But there were now only four stamped envelopes left which meant she had used two weeks' supply in one. She was a prodigious letter writer. She believed in keeping up. She once estimated that she wrote upwards of a dozen for every one she received, but the proportion had since changed to her further disadvantage.

'I know,' she said, murmuring aloud, the morning having become unusually still, pregnant with the possibility of her immediate eviction, 'that my own addiction to pen and paper is a form of indulgence. It's also of course a form of praise, I mean praise for the fascination and diversity of life which if you notice it yourself is always nice to bring to someone else's attention. I have written eight letters which means that there are now eight people who know things they didn't know, for instance how beautiful Pankot is and that I have hopes of living here. They know that a Miss Jolley has taken over my job. They know that I am happy and comfortable and looking forward to taking things easy. They know about the ridiculous mistake made by Thomas Aquinas and about Aziz and how helpful he was, and that the trunk is still at the station. They do not know that I am slightly worried about the trunk and the table because it is as unfair to share one's fears as it is right to share one's hopes. I shall share my hopes now with someone else.'

But when she had a sheet of writing paper squared up on the blotter and her Waterman fountain pen poised (it was one that was filled through a rubber top on the ink bottle into which the pen was inserted and pumped with a motion whose faint indelicacy was a constant source of slight embarrassment to her) she was aware of being about to project her thoughts not to one of the many people to whom she was in the habit of writing but into that deep that darkness was once said to be upon.

And suddenly she felt what she had felt once or twice before in Ranpur, the presence of a curious emanation, of a sickness, a kind of nausea that was not hers but someone else's; and sat stock still as she might if there was something dangerous in the room whose attention it would be foolhardy to attract. On the earlier occasions she had attributed the emanation to some quality of atmosphere in the Ranpur bungalow and so it surprised her to encounter it again. She felt instinctively that if the sickness touched her she would faint. And then she might come to with Mabel Layton standing over her telling her that Aziz had found her unconscious clutching a piece of paper on which she had written, 'Dear . . .' and no more.

'And that of course would be the end,' she said aloud in a normal conversational tone so that the emanation could observe that she was not bothered by it. 'Mrs Layton would quite ignore my assurance that there was nothing wrong with *me* and that there was no need to send for a doctor. I'd be off out of here and popped into a hospital bed as quick as winking. But I'm not ill. There's illness in the room but it isn't *my* illness.'

She gripped the edges of the desk and hoped she wasn't due to become a visionary. 'At my age! I mean how awfully disagreeable, not to say inconvenient.' She gripped the edges so hard that her palms hurt. Cautiously she removed her hands and was relieved to find nothing scored in the flesh that bore any resemblance to the stigmata.

'Whatever it is or whoever you are who isn't feeling up to par,' she said, having lost her fear of the emanation, 'I'm awfully sorry but there's nothing I can do for you, so please go away. Preferably in search of the Lord.'

She waited and felt the room return to normal.

'I've seen it off,' she thought. And at once thought of the person she should write to. She recovered her fountain pen, inscribed the date, October 9th, 1939, and wrote 'Dear Edwina,' and then found herself stuck for words, a rare event but an effect that Edwina Crane had always had on her. Edwina was the woman Barbie succeeded at Muzzafirabad and to Barbie she remained the heroine of a quarter of a century ago when alone, with the children cowering behind her in the schoolroom, she stood valiantly in the open doorway, at the height of serious civil disturbances, facing a gang of crazed and angry Muslims who had come to burn the mission down, and told them to be off; which they were (so the story went) in a subdued and silly-looking bunch, whereupon Miss Crane, leaving the door open because it was very hot, returned to the dais and continued the lesson as if she had just said no to an undeserving case of begging; a lesson that no doubt centred upon the picture she was reputed to have put to such brilliant use as an aid to teaching the English language that Barbie had never dared attempt emulation but had introduced instead *First Steps in Bible Reading* and taught from this, almost literally in the shadow of the picture which hung on the wall behind the dais.

This picture, of which she had a miniature copy among the relics in her trunk, a coloured engraving showing Queen Victoria receiving tribute from representatives of her Indian empire, had originally aroused in Barbie a faint dislike which she had prayed to be purged of because she guessed it was not the picture but Miss Crane for whom the dislike was felt, and at that time she had not even met the woman. Edwina had gone from Muzzafirabad before Barbie arrived to take her place. But spiritually she was very much still there, in the picture behind Barbie and in the minds of the little boys and girls who faced her, challenging her to do half as well for them. And Mr Cleghorn had a tendency to make comparisons between Barbie's methods and Miss Crane's.

Miss Crane, she was told, had been presented with a large gilt-framed replica of the picture as a memorial of her Muzzafirabad appointment and heroic stand, which even the civil and military authorities had applauded. When Barbie was posted away south scarcely a year after taking the appointment up she was given a miniature of the same picture, as if it would do her good to have a permanent reminder of her lesser merits. Possibly her expression when receiving it had stayed in Mr Cleghorn's mind and penetrated the mists of mildness in which he normally existed to the clearer brighter region where his deeper conscience lay, because he wrote to her in Madras: 'You had a difficult, perhaps impossible task. It was one Miss Crane envisaged for herself, which is why she asked to be sent elsewhere. She hated to be a heroine. She said the children had stopped giving her their attention, their eyes being on that doorway, anticipating the reappearance of the mob, for her to quell once more with that look, that flow of words. Perhaps I should have explained this to you. Your successor will have a comparatively easy task. The children have lost the sharpness of their adulation of Miss Crane in the process of comparing Miss Crane with Miss Batchelor. And so young Miss Smithers stands a chance of being compared with no one, but of being accepted for what she is. Life will be duller, but we can all get on with the work we are supposed to be doing.'

'I was the guinea-pig,' Barbie thought, with her pen still poised and the letter to Edwina still not advanced beyond the salutation. 'I suppose I resented it, but it was a revelation to know that Edwina had taken her work so seriously that she would not stay in Muzzafirabad. I suppose up until then I'd assumed that she grabbed promotion as her right and went off consciously trailing clouds of glory for me to step on at my peril. The truth was quite otherwise. When I met her at last her modesty was an inspiration to me. She hated being reminded. She has buried herself in her work since and has sought out the most difficult and unpopular, indeed dangerous posts. God is truly with her.'

She wrote: 'It seems ages since we were in touch,' and continued in the rather flat and mundane style that often seemed to impose itself, like a bridle on her thoughts, when writing to Edwina, just as when meeting her every couple of years or so at major mission conferences an uncharacteristic inarticulacy dammed the free flow of her speech. At their last meeting, in 1938, she could have sworn that momentarily Edwina had not recognized her and that when she did their shared recollection of Muzzafirabad was felt by Edwina to be a greater impediment than ever to conversation.

Now, before sealing the letter, she checked her address book and the last issue of the mission's quarterly magazine to make sure she had not overlooked a note about a new appointment. She had not; her address book was correct. She inscribed the envelope: Miss Edwina Crane, Superintendent's Bungalow, The Bishop Barnard Protestant Schools Mission, Mayapore.

Aziz announced lunch.

She went into the living-room prepared to find more guests, casual callers-in whose real purpose was to sum up and later advise Mabel Layton whether her prospective p.g. was up to snuff. But Mabel was alone, presiding over the tray – a decanter of sherry and two glasses. No one had come to lunch. This seemed especially significant as though a point of no return had been reached.

When the meal was over she and Mabel parted, ostensibly to sleep; and for a while Barbie tried. She stretched herself full-length on the bed with her arms at her sides and her eyes shut, counting the tufts of an imaginary dandelion clock which she blew at rhythmically, puffing out her lips in the manner of some-one happily dozing. She often recommended it to friends as an association of ideas more effective than counting sheep; but this afternoon the dandelion clock she had conjured was a tough proposition. Not a tuft stirred. Try (she told it) try to be more co-operative; waft, waft, waft away, as I huff and I puff. She replaced the obstinate dandelion with the image of a yellow rose. She stopped blowing and took in slow methodical lungsful of air and scent and then sat up to guard against being overcome by something inexpressible which seemed to be connected with the whole of her life in India.

The house was soundless and the world outside the window was full of bones.

She left her room and went out to the back verandah.

'Oh, you're up too, Mrs Layton,' she said in her best elocutionary voice. 'I do admire your industry. And how worth while it is.'

She gazed at the potted shrubs on the balustrade and at the garden with its immaculately cut lawn in which oval and rectangular beds of roses were set to provide infinite pleasure to the eye, rest to the mind and balm to the soul. Beyond the lawn and the bordering shrubs where the garden ended the land fell away, and rose again several miles distant in pine-capped hills from which scented breezes always seemed to whisper. And more distant yet were the higher hills and the celestial range of mountain peaks.

She looked at Mabel Layton again but Mrs Layton was still working at a pot of cuttings. Barbie was upset by this unexpected and total disregard. Dejected, she sat on one of the three wicker chairs that were set round the verandah table, kept an eye open and a smile ready for the moment when Mrs Layton abandoned her work and came to join her. She examined her conscience but found no special cause for blame in her behaviour that morning. On the other hand it wasn't Mrs Layton's fault if she found her an unsuitable companion. In her oddly withdrawn way Mrs Layton had been meticulous about arrangements for her guest's comfort. But clearly in Mrs Layton's view theirs were not complementary temperaments. She had probably never had a paying-guest in her life and was bound to find it difficult to open her lovely home to a stranger. It must be companionship, not money, Mrs Layton needed and she probably already regretted putting the advertisement in the paper. She may since have heard of someone more likely to fit in – an old army friend for instance – but felt in honour bound to stand by her suggestion that Barbie should spend her holiday in Pankot. Perhaps – and Barbie felt a sympathetic twinge of understanding – Mrs Layton was steeling herself to say that there could be no permanent arrangement. Barbie was not sure whether to be glad or sorry. When she and Mrs Layton were alone they seemed to get on together well enough and she was already in love with the bungalow and garden, its views of the outside world, and ready to love it more, aware that in coming here she had been afforded a glimpse of something life had denied her but which she was not unfitted for, having prayed for it once in a different form: tranquillity of mind and nature. That, perhaps, she would never achieve but there was a sense of tranquillity here, of serenity, which someone like herself might enter and be touched by, lightly if not deeply.

And watching Mabel Layton busy with the plant pots she had the feeling that Mabel had not entered it yet herself, not fully, but was trying to and finding it difficult to do so alone. 'We could have helped each other,' Barbie thought, 'but I'm a disappointment to her. I'm simply not her kind of person. She must know I'm here on the verandah but is pretending not to and hardening her heart to tell me the room will not be vacant after all.'

She stared hard at Mrs Layton's back, attempting telepathic persuasion to make her turn round and come out with it so that they would both know where they stood and the uncertainty could be ended. She saw Mabel hesitate. The busy probing fingers were suddenly still. For a few seconds it seemed that the fingers and arms stiffened to support weight. Then one hand was removed from the plant pot and placed on her chest near the base of the throat, and for a while she seemed to look at the garden as if struck by an idea about it.

Barbie got to her feet, moved forward a bit, and thought that Mabel wasn't looking at the garden at all. Her eyes were open but on her face was an expression of the most profound resignation Barbie had ever seen.

'Mrs Layton? Are you all right?'

Barbie spoke distinctly and calmly but her object of letting Mrs Layton know that assistance was at hand if needed was not achieved. The other woman stayed in that position of remarkable stillness and slowly it was borne in on Barbie that whatever else was the matter with Mabel Layton that caused her to stand as if waiting for some kind of pain to go away, she was deaf. She hadn't heard Barbie come out and hadn't heard her speak.

'Mrs Layton?'

The other woman glanced round.

'Are you all right?' Barbie repeated, going nearer, involuntarily putting out her hand as if to take Mabel's arm.

'Oh –' Mabel said; then removed her hand from her breast and touched Barbie's arm: a reversal of roles. 'Couldn't you sleep? I don't blame you. It's such a lovely afternoon.'

She hadn't heard or understood the question. But she hadn't been startled. The touch was scarcely more than a sketch of one and she was now busy again with the earth in the pot of cuttings, tamping it down.

'Actually,' she said, talking to Barbie via the plant pot, 'I seldom have forty winks after lunch so don't feel you have to if you find it difficult. I don't suppose you're used to it either.'

She moved on to the next pot and did something expert with a pruning knife. 'I ought to have done these this morning,' she said, 'but we were interrupted again. I suppose it's wrong of me to worry but there aren't usually quite so many visitors. I expect you've realized they mostly come to satisfy their curiosity. We get the Ranpur papers up here and everyone saw my advertisement. What worries me a bit is that after a while when they've got used to the idea there'll be days when nobody comes at all and then you'd think it rather dull I dare say. You're used to lots of people around you, I imagine, and I expect you enjoy it. I'm not and don't particularly. I'd say I've become something of a recluse but of course that's not possible in India, for *us*. Even when we're alone we're on show, aren't we, representing something? That's why I can't stop people turning up. They come to make sure I'm still here and that we're all representing it together. But I go out as little as possible, in company I mean. I wonder if you'll be happy here?'

'Yes, I see. I quite understand,' Barbie murmured.

'What?'

'I said I quite understand.'

Mabel had stopped potting and was staring at Barbie who under the weight of that resigned expression began to feel that she understood nothing. Her smile of assumed cheerfulness made her mouth as awkward to bear as something God had added to her in a fit of creative absent-mindedness.

'Oh, no,' Mabel said, 'I don't think you do. I meant that if you decide to stay I want you to feel that Rose Cottage is your home as well as mine and that you could have as many friends here as you care to make and go out as often as you wish, without bothering about me or whether I joined in or not. I know it's selfish of me to ask someone as gregarious as I believe you are to live here. On the other hand it would be disastrous to share the place with someone as selfish as myself and −' she paused, made a gesture drawing attention to the garden, the bungalow, the whole complex at whose heart this notion of serenity lay, 'I think it could do with sharing, but only by someone who appreciates it. I got the feeling from your letter that you were the kind of person who would. I still think so, but I'd hate you to think it had to be appreciated in my way and no one else's. I'd hate you to feel cut off.'

She glanced at the garden. 'It often strikes me as something the gods once loved but forgot should die young and that there's only me left to love it. I'm not here for ever and I'm not sure I love it enough.'

Barbie said, speaking loudly to make sure she was heard and understood, 'I'd love to stay, Mrs Layton. Actually I shall be glad to slow down and live a quieter life. It's what I hoped for. To have some time to myself.'

Mabel looked at her. She felt the look penetrate, right down to the core of her secret sorrow, and then withdraw, back into its own.

'I'm so glad,' Mabel said, returning her attention to the plant. 'Please ring the bell and ask Aziz to give us an early tea if you'd like it. I think I should. It won't be long before we find it chilly enough to have tea indoors and that always depresses me a bit. And you'd better remind him about your trunk. He's getting a bit forgetful, poor dear. And do send for anything else you've left behind in Ranpur.'

'My writing-table,' Barbie cried; but Mabel merely nodded. She probably hadn't heard. Barbie turned, pressed the bell on the board of switches, some of which lit the verandah and some the floodlights in the garden (these presently were to be robbed of their bulbs to conserve electricity as part of Pankot's war effort). Mabel continued to deal with the pots of cuttings and when Aziz came she left it to Barbie to tell him they would both like tea brought out now instead of at four o'clock. He gave her a sideways nod, accepting that it had become her place to give some of the orders.

'Oh, Lord,' she prayed that night, her knees punished through the thin cotton of her nightgown by the thick woven coarse rush mat at her bedside, 'thank You for Your many blessings and for bringing me to Rose Cottage. Help me to serve and, if it is Your will, bring light to the darkness that lies on the soul of Mabel Layton.'

She prayed for longer than usual, hoping for a revival of that lost sense of contact. But it did not revive. She could feel the prayers falling flat, little rejects from a devotional machine she had once worked to perfection. The prayers hardened in the upper air, once so warm, now so frosty, and tinkled down. But she pressed on, head bowed, in the hailstorm.

III

In a woman with a less well-authenticated Anglo-Indian back-ground than Mabel Layton's what was accepted as eccentricity would probably have been seen as hostility to what Anglo-India stood for, but Mabel's background was impeccable, she criticized no one and seldom expressed any opinion let alone a hostile one. Her absorption in garden and bungalow, her habit of taking solitary walks, her refusal even of invitations it was generally con-sidered obligatory to accept, her complete detachment from Pankot's public life, were attributed to the personal idiosyncrasy of someone who had lost two husbands in the cause of service to the empire, one by rifle fire on the Khyber, the other by amoebic infection; and having thus distinguished herself retired from the field of duty to leave room for others. Her withdrawal was accepted with feelings that lay somewhere between respect and regret; which meant that they were fixed at a point of faint dis-approval, therefore seldom expressed, but when they were, an idea would somehow be conveyed of Mrs Layton's isolation having a meaningful connection with an earlier golden age which everyone knew had gone but over whose memory she stood guardian, stony-faced and uncompromising; a bleak point of reference, as it were a marker-buoy above a sunken ship full of treasure that could never be salvaged; a reminder and a warn-ing to shipping still afloat in waters that got more treacherous every year.

This sense of danger, of the sea-level rising, swamping the

plains, threatening the hills, this sense of imminent inundation, was one to which people were now not unaccustomed and although the outbreak of war in Europe had momentarily suggested the sudden erection of a rocky headland upon which to stand fast, the headland was far away, in England, and India was very close and all about. And as the war in Europe began to enter its disagreeable phases it looked as though the headland had been either a mirage or a last despairing lurch of all those things to which value had been attached and upon which the eye, looking west from Pankot, had been kept loyally fixed through all the years in which the encouraging sensation of being looked at loyally in return was steadily diminished until to the sense of living in expectation of inundation had been added the suspicion that this inundation would scarcely be remarked or, if it were, not regretted when it happened.

The slight disapproval which counterbalanced the respect in which old Mabel Layton was held could probably have been traced to the haunting belief that in spite of everything she was among those people who would not regret the flood. Her whole demeanour was, in fact, that of someone who already saw the waters all around her, had found her boat and did not want it rocked.

A few months after Miss Batchelor's arrival, in answer to the advertisement for a single woman to share, an interesting situation had arisen. In retrospect it looked as if Mabel Layton had anticipated it and for some unintelligible but perhaps typical reason taken steps to protect herself.

This situation was the one arising in regard to accommodation in Pankot for Mildred Layton, the wife of Mabel's stepson, Lieut.-Colonel John Layton and his two grown-up daughters Sarah and Susan whom he brought up to the hill station at the beginning of the hot weather of 1940 and established in the only place now available: a rather poky grace and favour bungalow in the lines of the Pankot Rifles regimental depot, opposite the mess. The bungalow they had occupied for a few weeks in the late summer of 1939 before going down to Ranpur in September had since been appropriated by Area Headquarters as a chummery mess and Colonel Layton failed to persuade the accommodations officer to give it back.

Having settled his family in what comfort he could he returned to Ranpur where the battalion he commanded, the 1st Pankot Rifles, was under orders for abroad. The 1st Pankots sailed for the Middle East a few weeks later, and in Pankot Mildred Layton settled down as a grass-widow in the grace and favour bungalow with her daughters who had got back to India from school in England only in the July of the previous year.

Before 1939, the year of family reunion, the Laytons had not been on station for many years but they were Ranpur and Pankot people. The parents had been married in Pankot and both girls born there. It took no time at all for the Laytons' friends to fit them mentally into Rose Cottage and find that the arithmetic worked. Sarah and Susan could share the second large bedroom currently occupied by Miss Batchelor, Mabel could stay in the room she had and Mildred sleep in the little spare.

Although there were three bedrooms in the grace and favour bungalow down in the Pankot Rifles line, they were small and the whole place had an atmosphere of barracks: PWD furniture, a view at the front of the rear of the mess and at the back of a bare brick wall hiding the servants' quarters. The garden was bleak – weedy grass and no flowers – and one's peace indoors and out interrupted by parade-ground noises. A military wife and her daughters would be expected to pig in there without complaint if it was the best that could be done for them, but its discomforts and inconvenience (the wrong side of the bazaar and twenty minutes' tonga ride to the club), the enchanting prettiness of young Susan around whom Pankot males were already gathering, and the quiet but obvious efficiency of the elder daughter, Sarah, hardened the conviction that Rose Cottage was their proper and rightful place.

Mildred Layton refused to be drawn on the subject but when a question was put to her in any one of several oblique ways whose meaning was simply: Did Mabel discuss her plan to take a paying-guest with Colonel Layton? she left little doubt that the answer was no, and that the first she and John knew about it was down in Ranpur when they saw the advertisement.

Nevertheless relations between Mildred and Mabel Layton seemed perfectly amiable. No abnormal strain was apparent to the inner circle of Pankot women who were in the habit of dropping in to make sure Mabel was still there and representing what had to be represented. Mildred and her two girls were frequent droppers-in at Rose Cottage themselves. In fact for the first few weeks after her arrival from Ranpur Mildred made free of Rose Cottage as if it were a logical extension of her life, which it was, being only a few minutes' drive from the club; and her right, which it also was, because when Mabel died Colonel Layton would inherit the property along with what was believed to be a considerable amount of money.

The girls made free of it to a slightly lesser extent; Sarah more often than Susan who tended to be occupied appeasing as many as she could of the young subalterns who made demands on her time and company, swimming, riding and playing tennis. In the elder sister's case, visitors noted, making free was not quite the phrase to use. Sarah was less volatile than Susan, far less off-handedly possessive than her mother. She seemed very fond of the place, particularly of the garden, and much more communicative with Mabel (whom she and her sister called Aunt). She was also more patient with Miss Batchelor who chattered at her as she chattered at everybody but was given attentive replies to her comments and questions.

Sarah was a quiet girl. According to her mother she suffered badly with her periods, as badly as Mildred had suffered before having her. Mrs Paynton, Mrs Fosdick and Mrs Trehearne, the three women who could claim some intimacy with Rose Cottage's silent chatelaine, observed this well-mannered and presumably sometimes stoic behaviour of Sarah's with sympathy and approval. Colonel Layton's elder daughter was an unassuming and intelligent girl with a face a bit too bony to be called pretty, and obviously took her obligations seriously. Her quietness suggested to them that the perplexity of her English years was still upon her. She probably had some strange ideas because life at home was no longer what it had been, but there was backbone there. The other girl was as clear and uncomplicated as daylight by comparison. England had not touched her except to give her a necessary scraping to detach the barnacles gathered while becalmed in the sea of Anglo-Indian childhood; a ruinous experience if not corrected by schooling in England: all privilege and no responsibility. But here now was young Susan, sharp-keeled from home, clean and eager. It heartened one just to look at her. She seemed to know it, and that could be dangerous, but presently she would settle and the gravity of Anglo-Indian life would touch her pretty face soon enough.

The flush would disappear. The enchanting laugh would give way to the kind that reflected the gratitude felt for anything that still exercised one's sense of humour and kept it from atrophying. The years would play havoc with that rosy skin, tauten the mobile mouth, expose the sinewy structure of the neck that turned so attractively as she looked about her, endlessly responsive to the stimulus of surroundings which woke her adult perceptions as well as her childhood memories.

In the garden of Rose Cottage Susan's gaiety was especially flowerlike. Her bewitching quality was heightened for the other women by their sad awareness that her bloom must fade as their own had done. But not yet. And before then she would be plucked and carried off. She seldom came to the bungalow unaccompanied by young men. If she did she was attended by them later and quickly spirited away, alone or with Sarah who played the chaperone role of sensible elder sister.

With all this Mabel seemed perfectly compliant, although it was apparent that she was not keen on Susan's black Labrador puppy, Panther, who threatened havoc among the rose beds but came at Susan's call and learned the hard way that the garden was not his. This disciplining of the dog (until in going into the garden, heel-tracking Susan's progress in an awkward splay-footed progress of his own, he looked conscious of special dispensation) was – apart from Sarah's more tentative approach to the act of being in Rose Cottage – the one acknowledgement Mildred and Susan publicly made of enjoying little more than a dispensation themselves. The use of a pet as a symbol of that acknowledgement was a guide to the dissatisfaction felt with the arrangements that kept them from living there. The mock-severe tone of Susan's and Mildred's voices and the impatience of the gestures Susan used to admonish the dog, instructing him to be quiet, lie down, come here, stop slobbering, keep his paws off the table, behave properly, were clearly not intended to correct him but to advertise and simultaneously relieve an exasperation with something other than the dog's exuberance.

While Mabel raised no objection to this invasion of her home, allowed it to develop unhindered until scarcely a day went by without a coming and going on the front verandah, a settling in chairs on the back, a persistent tinkling of the telephone, she did not become involved; so it emphasized her detachment, even strengthened it, enlarged its scope. There was now more for her to be detached from. Caught up in the midst of these unusual activities she assumed a protective colouring and merged into the backgrounds of normality which the activities created.

If it was Mildred's intention to force the issue, this capacity Mabel had for creating an illusion of not being in possession of anything anyone could want to take from her or force her to share was an effective deterrent; far more effective than Miss Batchelor's physical presence.

Demonstrably Miss Batchelor had what presumably Mildred desired, but to judge from her reactions she was increasingly self-conscious of the fact, daily more embarrassingly aware of enjoying what she had comparatively no right to, and obviously torn between the conflicting beliefs that she should either make herself pleasant, or scarce.

Whichever course the poor woman adopted the effect on Mildred was the same. Outwardly her attitude towards the missionary was one of unchanging indifference and Miss Batchelor could not disguise from visitors that she was frightened of her. Her inconsequential conversation began to be accompanied by nervous gestures: hand to throat, hand rubbing hand, hand clutching elbow. She jumped up and down fetching things, providing comforts, answering the telephone. Such energy hinted at an overloading even of her remarkable power-house. At any moment a fissure might appear in her structural organization and she would then collapse in fragments and a little cloud of dust; from the sight of which phenomenon Mildred Layton would surely turn, as if this sort of thing were an everyday occurrence and only vaguely to be regretted in the brief instant it would take for her attention to be given to some other evidence of the oddity of Anglo-Indian life.

In company Mabel made no effort to protect Miss Batchelor from Mildred's presence. It became doubtful that the missionary woman could survive and it was not at all clear whether Mabel cared one way or the other. It was just possible that the reappearance of her stepson's wife and her two grand step-children, their proximity, their needs, their standing, would remind her of her own duty to the station.

For there was – let there be no doubt of it – a distinction, a virtue attaching to Mildred Layton which set her apart and gave her a weight quite independent of her actual rank. In that, she was not above Nicky Paynton whose husband commanded a battalion of the Ranpurs, or above Clara Fosdick whose late husband had been a civil surgeon and whose sister was married to a judge of the High Court in Ranpur. She was junior in rank to Maisie Trehearne, the wife of the Colonel-Commandant of the Pankot Rifles depot and junior, naturally, to the wife of whatever officer occupied Flagstaff House.

The special virtue of Mildred Layton was not to be found in the place she enjoyed in the formal hierarchy nor even in the fact that her father, General Muir, had been general officer commanding in Ranpur in the 'twenties, and that she and her sisters had lived at Flagstaff House in Ranpur and Pankot as girls. The virtue was not to be found either in her being the wife of a man whose father (Mabel's second husband) had a distinguished career in the Civil, was still remembered in the Pankot hills and whose portrait hung in the chamber of Government House in Ranpur where the council sat and where before his death of amoebic infection in 1917 he had distinguished himself further.

Her position as John Layton's wife brought one closer to the secret of her virtue but it was a virtue that could have escaped them both, settled on other shoulders. All her history of eminent connection counted once the virtue became attached to her, but the virtue itself was the gift of a condition, the visible source of which was down there in the valley in that random pattern of army installations which Barbie had seen from the miniature mountain pass; its actual centre a low, ugly, rambling brick and timber building: the Pankot Rifles mess.

This building, like a temple, was only an arbitrary enclosure but it was a place in which the particular spirit of Pankot was symbolically concentrated. No more nor less than any other station whose history was inseparable from the history of a regiment, Pankot's pride and prejudice and lore were deeply rooted in its famous Rifles. The gentle roll of the hills, the tender green, the ethereal mists: these were deceptive. There was not a village as far as the eye could see and in the rugged terrain beyond that marched towards a mountainous horizon which was not steeped in Pankot's regimental tradition.

In the ordinary smoke of morning and evening fires the ghostly smoke of old campaigns was mingled. There was always an opacity. Clean and hard and clear as the sunshine struck it seemed to strike gun-metal. On a hot still day the snapped branch of a forest pine resounded like a sniper's shot. A sudden flurry of birds led the eye away from them to the dead suspect ground from which they had risen. There was an air of irrelevancy in husbandry.

The mind could never quite free itself from the hard condition imposed by the military connection. This condition could be mocked but it lay deeper than a joke about the honour of the regiment ever probed. From the curious quality of flatness of their eyes a stranger arriving in Pankot and warned to look out for it might have told which men among several in civilian clothes were Pankot Rifles officers. In uniform this guardedness of eye was even more noticeable; a visible sign of a man's awareness that his virtue instantaneously commanded a recognition which he found onerous to bear but proper to receive. It could be and was accorded by senior officers to juniors of the same regiment but in that case the recognition of virtue was mutual. The real subtlety of the virtue lay in the recognition it commanded in Pankot from any officer however senior of whatever regiment or arm. There was a scale in the condition of life in Pankot in which a Pankot Rifles subaltern, on station, pegged higher than a general who had been less ambitious in his choice of regiment.

And there was a scale within the scale, and here was the secret of Mildred Layton's virtue. The men's virtue fell upon their women and the scale within the scale gave precedence by battalion as well as by rank. A subaltern of the 1st Pankots was a fuller embodiment of virtue than a subaltern of the 4/5th whose cool weather station was in distant Mayapore. Ranging outward and upward through a host of permutations of regimental and non-regimental employment the logical peak of attainment was reached in the supreme active regimental command, the command of the 1st Battalion. An extra glow warmed the peak if the distinction was achieved by an officer whose parent battalion it was – as was the case with John Layton – but no Pankot Rifles officer would willingly accept an appointment however attractive if he had reason to suppose that the command of the 1st was an alternative within his grasp; even though to have held it once did not enable him to bear the special virtue subsequently. It passed like a crown, itself perpetual, the heads it adorned coming and going. Trehearne had held it, a 4/5th man, now red-tabbed and banded, a full colonel; in effect father of the regiment; but the crown was presently John Layton's on whose head it glinted in a middle eastern sun; and his wife Mildred, in the scale of this condition, had more virtue than Mrs Trehearne who took precedence over her in every other way.

Through the 1st Battalion of its Rifles Pankot especially judged itself, felt itself judged, gave hostages to its fortune, sent emissaries into the world. At this level an element of sentiment was allowable but it was a sentiment supported by the condition which only one thing could shake and weaken: the disclosure of a fault in the rock, disaffection, disloyalty. Everything else was forgivable: incompetence, failure, defeat, even cowardice which was a private affair, a personal and not a corporate failure.

So there was Mildred Layton, a still handsome woman whose face quite properly showed not a tremor of the concern she would feel for her husband away on active service in North Africa, and no change as she looked at and through her step-mother-in-law's talkative and intimidated companion in that expression of constantly and perfectly controlled dedication to her duty to withstand the countless irritations to which English women in India were naturally subjected.

If the men's eyes were flat the women's – to judge from Mild-red's – were slightly hooded as though belonging to the weaker sex they were entitled to this extra protection; and the mouths, again to judge by hers, being less allowably firmed than a man's, were permitted a faint curve down at the corners which could be mistaken for displeasure, in the way that Mildred's languid posture when seated could be mistaken for *ennui* (closer observation of her as she was standing or walking suggested that she had probably achieved this economy of movement as a result of a long experience of the need a person in her position had to get through the day with the least trouble to herself).

But in the matter of Rose Cottage her distinction got her nowhere. The elder Mrs Layton remained impervious to it and something of that imperviousness seemed slowly to rub off on to Barbara Batchelor. It was imagined that the missionary must have asked Mabel outright whether she should go and had been asked to stay put and thereafter had girded her loins to the task of staying. The basis of her efforts to make herself pleasant changed, but too gradually for the day and circumstances of the substitution of security for insecurity to be determined.

Subtly she became endowed with some of the attributes of a co-hostess, a member of the family. She enlisted Aziz's aid in fetching and carrying, at first covertly and then openly because he had a habit of coming out and asking her what it was she had asked him to do for the guests. She assumed responsibility for the dog by making a friend of him, throwing his ball in an invisible but clearly demarcated zone within whose bounds he could do no damage, saw him fed and took him for walks when his mistress Susan abandoned him for more adventurous pursuits.

Her attitude to the girls became that of an aunt who knew her nieces had heard her discussed unfavourably but could not help showing her interest in them and some of her affection. Indeed she seemed to acquire something of the thick skin such a woman had to cultivate if her feelings were not to be constantly hurt by inattention to her questions, opinions, and fund of boring anecdotes.

And within a month or two the visits began to thin out as though the holidays were over and more serious affairs demanded attention. The poky grace and favour bungalow showed signs of being grudgingly settled in. It was (Mildred seemed to suggest) rather more convenient for Susan's followers, more convenient for herself whose duties were much bound up in the life of the regiment, for instance in helping Maisie Trehearne keep a matri-archal eye on the wartime crop of young men lucky enough to have got their emergency commissions into it. While suggesting this Mildred's expression did not change from the one which inspired fear in Miss Batchelor. It did not need to because it was an expression for all occasions, the expression of a person who could not allow herself to doubt that she was right, would always do what was right and therefore had nothing to explain even when not done right by, except to people who did not under-stand this and to such people an explanation was never owing.

But expression or not Mildred could not remove from people's minds the notion that she had suffered a defeat. The question was whether she was hurt by it. Later when a certain weakness began to reveal itself in that apparently indomitable armour it seemed likely that she had been hurt more deeply than she may have admitted even to herself.

There was something especially unpalatable about a family quarrel because it could undermine the foundations of a larger and essential solidarity. There was no known quarrel between Mabel and Mildred but family feeling had not been conspicuously shown. Blood had not proved thicker than water. 'Mabel's been like she is as long as I've known her,' Mildred once commented. 'According to John she was like that when he got back from the first war, quite different from the way he remembered her when he was a subaltern. He believes she never got over his father's death.'

This was the only remark she ever made that had any bearing on her stepmother-in-law's refusal to get rid of the Batchelor woman but it confirmed the impression that Mabel and Mildred had never hit it off and it was natural to wonder why, even if Mabel was not a person with whom it was easy to associate the idea of a close relationship.

It was odd that Mabel should squander upon a retired missionary what Mildred had a positive right to and would grace in a way that the Batchelor woman never could. And by depriving Mildred of this right she deprived her of another: trust. It was as if in Mabel's eyes Mildred could not be trusted; which was thought ridiculous at the time and just as ridiculous later even when the weakness began to show.

This weakness, so admirably and typically controlled, had to be put down to a particular cause, a blow courageously sustained – the news in 1941 that the 1st Pankots had been severely mauled in North Africa and Colonel Layton with the remnants of his command taken prisoner by the Italians (an especial wound to pride).

For a week or two after receiving the news Mildred Layton acted with a fortitude she never afterwards lost but which in this initial phase was found exemplary. None of her husband's fellow-officers, killed or imprisoned, had wives living in Pankot but she wrote to all these women offering sympathy and any help that was needed. On horseback and accompanied by the depot adjutant, Kevin Coley, she visited the nearby villages to talk to the wives and widows of the 1st Battalion's VCOs, NCOs and sepoys. Any who came in from outlying districts for con-firmation or interpretation of the news, for help and advice, assurances about pay allotments, and who expressed a wish to see her, she talked to in the lines, on the adjutant's verandah; and once or twice – receiving deputations – in the compound of the grace and favour bungalow.

'It's sad,' she said to her old acquaintance, the newly arrived occupant of Flagstaff House, Isobel Rankin, 'they think John will still be able to look after their men in prison-camp but of course the men will be separated from their officers and I have to tell these women what the position is. Then they ask me to write to the Italian general to make sure that John's allowed to visit them and I have to tell them it's highly unlikely he'll be allowed to but that if he is he'll need no reminder from me, and that seems to satisfy them.'

Thus Mildred conveyed to the new Area Commander and his wife, Dick and Isobel Rankin whose paths she and John had crossed in Lahore, New Delhi and Rawalpindi and with whom they were on Christian name terms, that it did not really satisfy her.

The station concurred. As if the disaster befallen the 1st Pan-kots weren't bad enough, in prison-camp the other ranks would be deprived of their inalienable right to the comradeship, the guidance and unstinted moral support of their officers and the officers of the privilege of giving them. It was a hazard of war but for a regiment like the Pankots situated in a valley from whose surrounding hills its soldiers were traditionally recruited it struck at the foundation of the trust between officers and men.

Was it the act of trying to reaffirm that trust which exhausted Mildred or reaction to the blow she had personally received? Or, in going among the villagers on horseback had she suddenly become conscious of acting out a charade which neither she nor the women she comforted believed in for a minute?

As often as not it is the sense of the unbearable comedy of life that lights those fires which can only be damped down by compulsive drinking. Whatever the cause in Mildred's case the idea of her fortitude as exemplary did not survive the discreet but unmistakable evidence that she was starting on the Carew's gin too early in the day and arriving for bridge, for committees, for morning-coffee, for lunch, with that look and air of being less sensitive than anyone else to the cross-currents of feeling and opinion in the room she entered. Her natural languor, to which everyone was accustomed and which she had worn lightly, like a protective cloak, seemed a degree heavier and her gestures more studied as if they demanded a shade more effort than was usual. At first her expression remained stable, what it had always been, but presently, although still unchanging, it began to lose definition, as though the face which it controlled was gradually slackening.

By then Mildred Layton's drinking habit was too well established in people's minds for it to give rise to much comment; and it was indulged with such style that nothing about her was diminished by it. In a curious way it sharpened her distinction. In her, drink released none of the vulgar or embarrassing traits disguised by soberness in people of softer grain; it gave extra keenness to those edges in her personality that made her a woman no one in her right mind would want to cross. One approached her with the same discretion she displayed in her own behaviour but did so perhaps slightly more aware of the need.

No longer exemplary, aided by drink which it was known she could not afford, there were occasions when her fortitude was felt by those who knew her well to be a fortitude shown not just for her own benefit but for theirs as well, so that the drinking was for them too; a resistance to pressures they were too conscious of not to acknowledge as collective and likely to increase. In the guarded eyes, the faint upcurve of the downward curving mouth, there was the authority of the old order and an intelligence that could calculate odds accurately, interpret them as indications that the game that had never been a game was very likely up.

So Mildred drank; compulsively and systematically; two or more up on everyone when drinking in a fairly hard-drinking community officially began and more than that when a session ended. One became so used to it that really it became part of the manner which with the impeccable background and irreproachable behaviour had always promoted and still promoted the image of her utter reliability. Even the little matter of mounting bridge debts could be seen in a certain light as the exception that proved the rule of her soundness. Her forgetfulness was annoying and embarrassing but whichever way her luck was running, win or lose (it was mostly lose), one could not help feeling that she saw debts due only in the context of larger and more important issues; and then in speaking gently to Sarah (the one sure way of getting paid) one was bound to understand that in that grander context even so sacred a thing as a card debt was enclosed in an aura of irrelevance.

And after all it was not a question of honour alone but of money, and for money Mildred clearly had an upper-class contempt which meant that her attitude to it was one of complaint at not having enough but of this being no excuse for not spending it. Unpaid bills at local stores and overdue mail order accounts at the Army and Navy were not her personal fault. She had standards to maintain and two girls as well as herself to dress, especially Susan who had a perfectly proper streak of what her looks and figure excused – extravagance. With both girls now enlisted in the WAC(1), working as clerks at Area Headquarters with Carol and Christine Beames, the civil surgeon's daughters, spending much of the working week in uniform, the number of new dresses Susan needed was reduced to what Mildred described as less unmanageable proportions, but unlike Sarah, who tended to stay in uniform, Susan changed immediately she got home; which was quite early quite often. There was not a great deal for a girl to do at the daftar if she thought it not her job to look for work and stupid to look busy if she weren't; and in Susan's case working in Dick Rankin's office had doubled her number of escorts. It was her obligation to look fresh and pretty and Mildred's obligation to help her do so.

How often, people wondered, did old Mabel Layton come to the rescue? How many times were bills (which Sarah had helpfully taken it upon her shoulders to see settled before they became an embarrassment) paid with cheques supported at the bank by money Mildred had off her absent husband's stepmother? A half-colonel's pay did not support the style of life to which Mildred was accustomed and which she kept up rather better than anyone else. It was not expected to in peace time. It was ironic to think that so much of the *raj*'s elegance which provoked the Indian temper had always been supported by private incomes. From the Viceroy down the difference between his pay and allowances and necessary expenses meant that a man was usually out of pocket administering or defending the empire. One was used to debt, to cutting down, to the sense of imminent shabbiness in approaching retirement. After a year or two of war the shabbiness was rather closer than that. It seemed to settle like a layer of dust, clouding certain issues, such as the reason for being in India at all. Anything that proved durable and resistant to the dust and retained the bright gleam of a stubbornly clear conviction was precious because it stood out, a challenge to dark and perhaps superior forces, and this meant that if you went down you would be pretty sure what it was you went down defending.

Mildred stood out. Almost disdainfully. The virtue that attached to her as Colonel Layton's wife was crystallized by the other virtues of her family connection with the station. One had (as Barbie had done) only to wander in the churchyard of St John's and see the names Layton and Muir on headstones to realize that in those lichened-over advertisements for souls there was an explanation of Mildred, even a reference to the habit she had acquired in the slightly drunken tilt which age and subsidence had given them but not yet given her.

Nor would they. She would not rest there, one felt, would not want to. Her languor was not that of someone superiorly regretting the passing of the golden age. The illumination of Mildred Layton made by the stones aslant in the hummocky grass was one of contrast; contrast in deductions and expectations from identical premises and identical investment. Mildred's enemy was history not an early death in exile, but neither end was the kind that could have been or could be assumed, and the evidence of cessation which a clear look into the future might reveal did not countermand her duty to the existing order of things if she continued to believe in it.

And there in the picture one might have had of her going to her not-so-secret hoard (the bottle in the almirah to save her the boredom of sending Mahmoud to the drinks cupboard, the flask in her handbag to guard against the tedium of finding herself held up in a dry corner at the wrong hour) the question of her belief was posed and perhaps only ambiguously answered; but the picture is much the same as the one presented by Barbie on her knees in the hailstorm (the sole kind of tempest that the devotional machine now seemed capable of conjuring). If

Mildred had been a religious woman she might have prayed for John, for the remnants of his battalion, for the wives and widows among whom she had graciously gone offering the solace no woman could give to others or herself. At the turn of the year (1941–1942) she could have prayed for the bodies and souls of those who faced, were to fall before or extricate themselves from the destructive tide of the extraordinary and beastly little Japanese: among them, quite unknown to her, her future son-in-law Teddie Bingham who in the early months of 1942 enters the page as it were in the margin, a dim figure limping at the head of a decimated company of the Muzzafirabad Guides across the grain of the hills of upper Burma towards India, temporary safety, Susan's arms, a moment of truth and fiery oblivion. Depressing as Teddie's contribution sounds one can be sure he would have had a generally cheerful idea about it.

But Mildred was not a praying woman; and the drink suggests that had she been she would have prayed like Barbie not for particular favours but for a general one; the favour of being disabused of a growing and irritating belief (which drink soothed) that she had been abandoned to cope alone with the problems of a way of life which was under attack from every quarter but in which she had no honourable course but to continue.

IV

In the old days both the military and civil authorities of the province had spent half the year in Ranpur and half in Pankot which meant that between April and October the hill station had enjoyed the formality of an official season, with the Governor and his wife at the summer residence and the general officer commanding and his wife at Flagstaff House.

The last full official season had been that of summer 1939. It ended on the 1st of October when the Governor went back down to Ranpur preceded or followed by his staff, clerks, files, lorry and train loads of baggage; one day before Barbie arrived by the opposite route with her own encumbrances.

A few weeks later like governors of other provinces in which the Congress Party had taken office after the elections of 1937 he was accepting the resignations of every member of the ministry, headed by Mr Mohammed Ali Kasim, a prominent Muslim of the Congress Party which many English people suspected of being the party of the Hindus in spite of its claim to represent the whole of India.

After accepting these resignations, unconstitutionally forced on the provincial ministers by a party whose leaders had no central duty to the limited Indian electorate and an apparent antipathy towards assisting the British to preserve democracy and show Hitler what was what, the Governor assumed governor's control, as he was entitled to do under the safeguard clause in the Act of 1935 by which attempts had been made to go some way to meet the Indians' insistent demands for self-government; and thereafter ruled the province directly, in the old pre-reform style, from Government House in Ranpur.

In Pankot in 1940 there was half a season. Flagstaff House was open, indeed had never been shut because on the declaration of war the general officer commanding in Ranpur, then situated in Pankot for the summer, elected to stay put, but the Governor and his wife did not manage to come up until May, and in June they had to return suddenly to Ranpur. One of the effects of the Congress ministry's term of office from 1937 to 1939 had been to reduce the scale of the annual removal of the majority of the secretariat to the hills, and although on reassuming autocratic control the Governor would have liked to reinstate this traditional move in full he would have found it difficult to house more than a skeleton of his civil service because by now the army had infiltrated into the complex of buildings where the civil departments once enjoyed the cooler air for six months of the year.

Frustrated in his attempt to direct from Pankot a secretariat largely left behind down in Ranpur and denied his simple need to lead a peaceful life by new viceregal attempts to come to terms with unco-operative Indian leaders after the fall of France, the Governor, choleric and savage, stormed back to Ranpur en route for Simla and, as he put it, further fruitless talks with the Viceroy who would have further fruitless talks with bloody Gandhi and bloody Jinnah in a further fruitless pursuit of the bloody Pax Brittanica, when all that was needed to scare the Indians into toeing the line and getting on with the war was a regiment or two of British infantry and a Brigadier as spunky as old Brigadier-General Dyer who had mown down hundreds of bloody browns in Amritsar in 1919. No one cared to remind him that the Lieut.-Governor of the Punjab who had stood by Dyer both at the time and in the years of Dyer's subsequent disgrace had only this year been shot dead in London by an Indian in delayed retribution, in Caxton Hall of all places. It was felt in any case that the Governor did not need reminding. He was a man of the old school – actually a bit of an embarrassment – the kind who if he could not have peace preferred a row and might even welcome being shot at now or twenty years later. His lady followed him, as pale as he was scarlet, and as talkative as he was taciturn between outbursts of bad temper, leaving Pankot bereft of the two people who most graced its official public occasions.

In 1941 when the choleric Governor's term of office ended and he was succeeded by a new Governor, Sir George Malcolm, there was scarcely a season in Pankot at all (other than the tentative one provided by the energetic new GOC's wife, Isobel Rankin, at Flagstaff House). The Rankins made their presence felt, but in the right sort of way. Malcolm, it was said, was an example of the rather alarming kind of person whom the war was throwing up, people with an immense and exhausting capacity for work and an impatience with any tradition which, like the annual movement of an entire administration from Ranpur to Pankot and back again, put the slightest strain on an overworked executive.

'Sir George will settle down,' people said; and there were hopes of a full season in 1942; but at the turn of the year the war that had seemed so far off was suddenly on India's doorstep. Malaya went first, to the Japanese, then Singapore. Burma followed. With these stunning losses the hope of anything ever being quite the same again faded quietly away into the background. And as if things weren't bad enough with the enemy at the gate there was an increasingly troublesome enemy inside it: Indian leaders who screamed that defeat in Malaya and Burma was a forerunner to defeat in India, that the British had shown themselves incompetent to defend what it was their duty to defend but which wouldn't need defending at all if they weren't there, inciting the Japanese who had no quarrel with the Indians themselves.

The political situation sizzled dangerously from the March of 1942 throughout the summer and finally exploded in August with a violence that set people talking about a new mutiny.

Foreseeable as it had been to anyone with an ounce of common sense and regrettable as it was it was not actually unwelcome. It cleared the air. The policy of placating the Indians and getting on with the war at the same time had failed as it was bound to. Now the question of further Indian advances to self-government could be firmly shelved for the duration. It was felt to be a pity that it had not been shelved at the beginning when Indian politicians proved that there was hardly a man with statesman-like qualities among them.

After the absurd débâcle of 1939 when the Indian Congress Party threw away all the political advantages it had won, by resigning provincial responsibility on points of principle (failure of the Viceroy to consult it before declaring His Majesty's Indian empire at war with Germany, refusal to co-operate in a war whose aims it pretended to be in sympathy with but said should have included immediate freedom to Indians to do as they liked) the more troublesome firebrands (that man Subhas Chandra Bose for instance) were popped neatly into clink under the Defence of India rules, but it was felt that the Viceroy should have made a broader sweep.

The Viceroy in question was Linlithgow; described in Pankot as an odd chap, sound but tactless and as usual not quite the thing because he didn't know enough about the country. Viceroys seldom did and few had the panache of Curzon who had tried to make not knowing a virtue in itself. The Congress-wallahs had put one over on Linlithgow by adopting this policy of official approval of the war against Hitler but disapproval of the means by which they were to be allowed to co-operate in it; and only those who stood up in the market place and opened their mouths too wide found themselves silenced by imprisonment.

If the Congress-wallahs had had any political cunning as well as political stubbornness they would have stayed in office in the provinces as the few Muslim League ministries had done, co-operated so far as was necessary in the war effort, expanded their political experience and power and, simultaneously, their grip on the administration, so that when the war was over their claim to speak and act for the majority of Indians and their right to advance steadily to self-government inside the commonwealth would have been difficult to refute.

But they had thrown their opportunity away and one began

to wonder whether in doing so they hadn't set their cause back to a point where independence would seem as far away on a post-war horizon as it had been on a pre-war one. There were sensible men among them, the ex-chief minister in Ranpur, M. A. Kasim (known popularly as M A K) was an example, but they were all either under Gandhi's saintly spell or too weak-kneed to exorcize it, and the saintly spell of Mr Gandhi had finally been exposed for what it was: a cover for the political machinations of an ambitious but naïve Indian lawyer whose successes had gone to his head.

His demand now that the British should quit India, should leave her to 'God or to anarchy' sounded fine, courageous, desperate and inspired, but it meant that they should leave India to the Japanese who were already on the Chindwin but with whom Gandhi obviously expected to make a political bargain. Unless you were stupid you did not make bargains with the Japanese but war. Even the liberal American Jew, Roosevelt, had been forced to understand this and it was entirely to placate Roosevelt that Churchill (who knew a thing or two, including the fact that the Americans' only interest in India was that the sub-continent should remain a stable threat in the rear to Japanese ambitions in the Pacific) had sent out that Fabian old maid, Stafford Cripps, to do what Churchill knew couldn't be done: put pepper into Indian civilians and politicians by offering them what they'd been offered before, but which a pinko-red like Cripps, unused to office, would see as new, generous, advantageous, a left-wing invention. The farce of this particular confrontation between an English pinko-red and grasping Indian leaders had not been lost on the English community. Its total and inevitable failure had been a smack in the eye to Cripps who went home eating crow as well as his bloody vegetables. Given a chance to show that a modern British socialist could achieve what the old-fashioned Right had never achieved, unity among Indians and political co-operation between Indians and English, he had also been hoist with the responsibility of office; a responsibility which meant, quite simply, having to make things work.

And he couldn't of course make them work because Indian politicians always wanted more if offered anything. Not understanding this he returned to Whitehall with that smile like a brass plate on a coffin and a conviction that while someone had been unco-operative it was not clear who. Once he had gone the Quit India campaign gathered momentum; which was also funny because it made Cripps look as if he had invented it; and early in August the Congress Party officially adopted the resolution calling for the British to leave or take the consequences. For once the government in New Delhi seemed to have been prepared. Within a few hours prominent Congressmen all over the country were detained under the Defence of India rules in an operation of arrest that gathered them in from Gandhi all the way down through the scale to members of local sub-committees in the towns and cities. Even the moderate ex-chief minister Mohammed Ali Kasim was reported arrested.

The country held its breath and then with a fierceness not equalled in living memory the leaderless mobs rose and for three weeks the administration was virtually at a standstill.

V

From the Ranpur Gazette: *August 15th, 1942*

ENGLISH WOMEN ATTACKED

It has just been officially disclosed that on the afternoon and evening of August 9th two Englishwomen were victims of violent attacks in the Mayapore district of this province. In the first case which occurred in the rural area of Tanpur no arrests have yet been made. In the second which took place in the town of Mayapore six Hindu youths are being held. It is understood that a charge is likely to be made under section 375 Indian Penal Code. The prompt action of the Mayapore police in apprehending the suspects within an hour or two of this disgraceful attack will be applauded. The arresting party was under the personal command of the District Superintendent of Police.

In a statement issued to the press DSP said, 'It is not in the public interest to reveal the name of the girl at this time. She worked on a voluntary basis at the Mayapore General Hospital. Her family is one that distinguished itself in service to India. According to her statement she was attacked by six Indian males who stopped her on her way home at night from the place where she also did voluntary and charitable work for sick and dying people of the scheduled castes. She was dragged from her bicycle into the derelict site known as the Bibighar Gardens where she was criminally used.'

DSP confirmed that among the men arrested was one with whom she was acquainted in the course of her work at the poor people's dispensary.

The earlier incident in Tanpur took place in broad daylight. Miss Edwina Crane, Superintendent of the Protestant mission schools in Mayapore district, was attacked by a large mob who obstructed the passage of her motor-car en route from Dibrapur back to her headquarters in Mayapore. Accompanying her was the teacher in charge at the Dibrapur mission, Mr D. R. Chaudhuri. He had left the school to give his superintendent protection from gangs of badmashes rumoured to be roaming the countryside following news of the arrest of Mr Gandhi and other Congress Party leaders.

Mr J. Poulson, assistant commissioner in Mayapore, said he left Mayapore in a police truck at approximately 3.45 p.m. on August 9th to investigate reports that telephone lines had been cut between Dibrapur and Mayapore and that trouble-makers were gathering in rural areas. He stated: 'At Candgarh we found the local police locked in their own kotwali and having released them pressed on in pursuit of the mob who had terrorized them. It was raining. A few miles short of Tanpur we saw first a burnt-out motor-car and then a hundred yards beyond, Miss Crane, sitting on the roadside guarding the body of Mr Chaudhuri who had been clubbed to death. She was soaked to the skin. In attempting to save Mr Chaudhuri from the mob, which had apparently objected to an Indian driving with an Englishwoman, Miss Crane had been struck several times. When she recovered consciousness she found Chaudhuri dead and the mob gone.'

Miss Crane is presently in the General Hospital in Mayapore where her condition although improved still gives some cause for anxiety. Although Ranpur remains quiet, Dibrapur and Mayapore have been the scene of serious riots and in Dibrapur Congress flags have been run up on the court house and the magistrate's private residence. Troops are reported on the way to Dibrapur to deal with the situation and are also standing by in Mayapore in anticipation of a request for aid from the civil power. The senior military officer in Mayapore is Brigadier A. V. Reid, DSO, MC.

The rapidity with which the whole situation has deteriorated so soon after the Congress Committee's endorsement of Mr Gandhi's quit India resolution in Bombay on August 8th, suggests that plans had been laid well beforehand for these acts of insurrection. The scale on which civil disobedience has been offered in this and other provinces, the reports constantly being received of riots, wanton destruction, burning and looting, hardly support the opinion expressed in some quarters that these are 'spontaneous demonstrations of anger by the people at the unjust imprisonment of their leaders'.

The authorities showed foresight in arresting members of Congress within a few hours of the committee passing the resolution. It behoves us all to be equally on our guard. And it is to be hoped that those who are guilty of these vicious and outrageous attacks on two innocent Englishwomen and the murder of the Indian school-teacher will quickly be brought to justice.

This confirmation of rumours there had been in Pankot of attacks on Englishwomen down in the plains produced a full house at the club-meeting. People arrived with their copies of the *Ranpur Gazette* opened and folded at the page on which the report appeared, on the off-chance that someone had not read it. 'I see you've all got your tickets,' one member said. But it was no laughing matter.

The purpose of the meeting, announced several days earlier, was to discuss arrangements to protect lives and property in the event of riots occurring in Pankot. So unlikely had this seemed that provision had been made for only half the number of people who came. The meeting was delayed for a quarter of an hour while more chairs were brought into the main lounge. Eventually it got under way with an address by Colonel Trehearne in his capacity as senior member of the cantonment board. His voice, although musical, lacked power. 'Can't hear!' someone at the back shouted. He was shushed. Older hands knew from experience that Trehearne's contribution to any public gathering bore the same relationship to what followed as an overture did to an opera. If you came in after he had sat down you'd missed nothing.

He was succeeded by two civil officers from district headquarters down in Nansera: Bill Craig, assistant to the deputy commissioner, who assured the meeting that the district was so far unaffected by the disturbances in the plains and expected to remain so; and Ian MacIntosh of the Indian police who confirmed Craig's report and opinion and added that three men from Ranpur, on whom the CID had kept an eye, had just been arrested for disturbing the peace by attempting to harangue the inhabitants of a nearby village. Mr MacIntosh added that he used the word 'attempting' advisedly because the villagers had simply laughed at the men and might have stoned them if a truck-load of constables had not intervened and taken them off to a place of safety: gaol.

The atmosphere in the club which had been rather tense at the start as a result of the reports in the *Ranpur Gazette* now reverted to near-normal. The groundswell of indignation, of determination to stand no nonsense, of fear, of sad annoyance that things should have come to this pass, was checked by the counter-pressure of communal good-humour; hilarity, almost.

At this point an Indian officer from General Rankin's staff, Major Chatab Singh, known affectionately as Chatty (which he was) got on his feet and explained in broad outline civil and military plans to keep control in Pankot and Nansera (which was ten miles down the road, on the way to Ranpur), should the unthinkable actually happen. There were to be collection points for residents who desired to seek refuge from riots and attacks on European property and installations; for example women living on their own, or with children, and women whose husbands were off-station or likely to be in the event of serious disturbances in the area. One such centre would be the club itself. Chatty said he appreciated that these would henceforth be known as funk-holes but hoped that would not put people off using them if the need arose.

He spoke with humour and precision. His handsome wife, who headed the small Indian section of military wives, made precise notes. People laughed at his jokes, which were not too clever. Had they been so the suspicion might have arisen that Chatty harboured bitter thoughts inside that neatly turbanned head.

After a short pause for question and answer Isobel Rankin got up and announced that after refreshments the heads of the various women's committees were to meet in the card room.

These women were co-opted to form the special Pankot women's emergency committee. She said she hoped this would turn out to be both its inaugural and closing session. She referred to the notice in the *Ranpur Gazette* and to the rumours of such attacks which had been current in the last few days, grossly exaggerated in regard to the number of women said to have been hurt.

She did not (she said) wish to play down the seriousness of what had apparently happened in Mayapore but warned against the effects of what she called excessive reaction. Before she left the platform she asked whether Mrs Smalley was present and finding that she was (she could not have been in doubt) invited her to act as secretary to the emergency committee. Mrs Smalley was already secretary to three permanent committees.

'I'm sorry to throw another job at you but you're the obvious choice,' Mrs Rankin said.

'Oh, that's all right,' little Mrs Smalley said, sitting down and, small as she was, promptly disappearing. People smiled. Mrs Smalley would have been piqued if the general's lady had given the job to someone else. She was a glutton for work.

Most stations had their Smalleys; a number of stations had at some time or another had these Smalleys. Because they looked nondescript and unambitious they provoked no envy and hardly any suspicion. In Pankot, where they had been since the end of 1941, they arrived at parties harmoniously together and then put distance between them as if to distribute their humdrum selves in as many parts of the room as possible. Leaving, they did so arm-in-arm, giving an impression that by playing their separate parts in a communal endeavour something integral to their private lives and mutual affection had been maintained.

The Smalleys were slight bores but very useful people: Major Smalley with his expertise in routine A & Q matters at Area Headquarters and little Lucy Smalley with her knowledge of shorthand and patient way with paper: the perfect dogsbody for any committee. Socially they were thought dull but it was always just as well to have some obvious dullness around. The sight of Lucy and Tusker standing arm-in-arm in the porch when a cocktail party was over, looking into the night for the tonga that had once again failed to stay or return for them, brought out the Samaritan instinct in gayer and better-organized guests because this constant breaking-down of arrangements they made for their personal convenience seemed to emphasize the willing efficiency they showed in affairs that affected the community as a whole. The Smalleys always managed to get a lift home.

They lived in Smith's Hotel. They had a suite: a small dark living-room and a smaller darker bedroom. Tusker declared himself perfectly happy with this accommodation (he received a special pay allowance for living out) and while Lucy was often heard to say she wished they could find a little bungalow of their own where they could more easily entertain their friends to dinner, Pankot was happy with the arrangement too. Cocktail parties were one thing, dinners another. The experience of being sat next to either Smalley at an official function – he in the dress uniform he insisted on wearing in spite of the wartime dispensation from such formality and which was tight round the shoulders, and she in her crimson taffeta gown (familiar enough after a while for her to be seen as a struggling little point of patient modest reference in a restless and sometimes greedy world) had helped Pankot to form the sensible opinion that the Smalleys were ideally placed where they were. In fact it became almost disagreeable to imagine them outside the context of Smith's; they went well with the napery and the potted palms; and, residing in an hotel bedroom, they were interestingly endowed with the attributes of perpetual honeymooners even after ten years of childless marriage. In this light their arm-in-armness was not only agreeable to see but satisfactorily explained.

When Lucy Smalley took her place in the card room, notebook and pencil neatly balanced on her neatly arranged legs, she added the final touch to a picture of the female hierarchy to which it can be assumed she aspired – in her shy but persistent way and irrespective of which station she was on – to belong. Her timid glances were more penetrating than they seemed. Content to appear mediocre and dull she looked for opportunities to offer opinions that struck people as just clever enough to confirm them in their own opinion that while she was dull she was not too dull, and mediocre in the right sort of dutiful and helpful way.

Six card tables had been placed together so that the committee could do its work in comfort. Around them sat Isobel Rankin,

Maisie Trehearne, Mildred Layton, Nicky Paynton, Clara Fosdick and Clarissa Peplow, the wife of the Reverend Arthur
Peplow, incumbent of St John's and chaplain to the station. Lucy
Smalley sat a foot away from one end facing Isobel Rankin who
had her elbows on the table at the other. Apart from Isobel's
choice of seat no special order of precedence had been observed.
The omission was probably deliberate. An equality of a kind had
been established.

The meeting was informal. Isobel had made a draft agenda
and out of general chat she formulated every so often a minute
for Lucy to record.

The quietest member was Maisie Trehearne. She was tall,
slender and stately in the way that a woman given to private
preoccupation can be if she has the figure for it. What Maisie
Trehearne's preoccupations were no one knew. There may have
been another explanation for the impression she gave of having
more important things to think about than the matter under
discussion.

There were people who said that her mind was as blank as her
pale patrician face was comparatively and unfairly unlined; but
she never fumbled if asked to comment on a view just given.
She seldom smiled. But she was seldom upset either. The only
thing known about Maisie Trehearne's emotional life was that
she had a fondness for animals and a horror of cruelty to them.
But she expressed both the fondness and the horror in much the
same tones as those in which she spoke on other subjects.

No one had ever uncovered in her the steel core which a military career in India normally required and which was presumably
responsible for keeping her so upright even when sitting down.
Perhaps the uprightness was due to an uncomfortable corset,
but she looked too composed for that. Composure was Maisie
Trehearne's main characteristic. Were it not for the war her
husband would have been coming up for retirement but she conveyed neither pleasure nor disappointment at the postponement
of – as in her case it curiously but suitably was – Cheltenham.

Of the other women only Clarissa Peplow had any kind of
physical affinity with Maisie. Clarissa was also pale although she
was plump with it. She was stately but in her case the stateliness
was that of someone conscious of the dignity of Christ's church
militant. Lucy Smalley excepted, Clarissa Peplow was the least

important woman in the room; unimportant in temporal terms. Her clear-blue eyes proclaimed circumstances in which other terms prevailed.

Opposite her sat the widowed Clara Fosdick, whose sister was married to Mr Justice Spendlove of the High Court in Ranpur. Clara was big-boned and well-fleshed. She had a resonant contralto voice which enabled her to argue convincingly even when it was obvious that she had reached an opinion through a process of emotional reasoning, not logical deduction. She got on well with young men. She conformed in many ways to a young man's idea of the perfect mother. She struck them as affectionate, even-tempered, good-humoured, restful, tough when necessary but blessed with a considerable capacity for understanding and for-giveness in that part of her which at her age and with her build could properly be called a bosom. It came as no surprise to such young men to learn from her friend Nicky Paynton that Mrs Fosdick had lost her only child, a boy, at the age of five, when he died of typhoid in the Punjab.

Mrs Paynton, the most talkative woman at the table and with whom Clara Fosdick shared a bungalow, was wiry, tight-wound, energetic. Her husband Bunny Paynton, the commanding officer of the 1st Ranpurs, was on active service in the Arakan. She had two boys at school in Wiltshire whom she had not seen since her and Bunny's spell of home leave in 1938. She had seen little of her husband too. Only in the frequency with which she introduced the subject of the absent Bunny and the far-away children could one detect how seldom she was not thinking about them. But the references were all light-hearted, in keeping with the discipline the station expected such a woman to impose on herself. She was referring to Bunny now and to the report in the *Ranpur Gazette* which had named a Brigadier Reid as commander of the troops in Mayapore where the attacks on the two English women had taken place.

'I shan't tell Bunny Alec Reid's got a brigade. We never knew him well but always thought him a bit of a duffer. I thought he was still in Rawalpindi which was where we last saw him. You remember Alec and Meg Reid don't you, Mildred?'

'Vaguely.'

'Meg Reid was a bit of a wet blanket too. I can't think why they've given Alec a brigade. He's been behind a desk for years.

If I write and tell Bunny Alec Reid's got a brigade he'll probably blow his top.'

'Shall we get back to the agenda?' Isobel Rankin said.

She tapped her sheet of paper with a pencil. One noticed her knuckles. They looked hard. Her finger-nails were bright red. No languor about Isobel Rankin. She allowed some gossip at a friendly meeting such as this but kept it checked and did not contribute to it. She got things moving in the direction she desired. The slightest gesture – an index-finger adjustment of her reading spectacles on the bridge of her nose – was dynamic.

Concentration of energy distinguished her from the other women at the table, even from Nicky Paynton whose vitality, potentially as great, seemed by comparison to lack purpose. But then Isobel Rankin could not afford to relax as her colleagues could. She bore the burden of command. It could have fallen on several of the other women – on Mildred, on Nicky, on Maisie – and they would have borne it just as capably. The question of which of them sat at the head of the table as the GOC's wife had been settled by their choice of husbands. With a long war and any luck Bunny Paynton could end up not merely with a brigade but with a division, and Mildred's husband would probably have had a brigade by now if his wartime promotional expections had not been brought to a grinding halt in North Africa.

But these were military roles. Dick Rankin would never get an active command. He was a military administrator and young and well-connected enough to anticipate capping his career with military appointments at government level.

An air of power more far-reaching than that of the Army alone emanated from Isobel. She was preparing for the world where things were arranged and matters of consequence decided. A certain secretiveness, dressed as discretion, already hinted at a familiarity with what went on behind the scenes.

Outside the inner-circle of her friends she was of course much misunderstood. Those who thought themselves not as well-used by her as they deserved interpreted her flashes of wit and natural hardness of tone as evidence of malice and her impatience in argument as a sign of mental inflexibility. She was neither a stupid nor a malicious person and was in fact quick to detect stupidity and malice in others. And she was far from being the hidebound stickler for rules which she may have appeared in the eyes of people who, puzzled by the brusque manner she adopted towards the time-wasters, the ignorant and the prejudiced, decided that they had erred socially.

But today, Clarissa and Lucy apart, she was among friends and had she after adjusting her spectacles announced her personal creed instead of the next subject – the special arrangements for Indian mothers and children who came into defended areas for protection from riots, rape and arson – she would have found a measure of agreement, because in her there resided in a highly developed form the animus of declining but still responsible imperialism.

She had an astringent affection for the people and the country in which she had spent so many years of her life, and no personal prejudice against Indians as Indians. As with members of her own race she allowed her instincts to guide her when it came to separating those Indians with whom she was happy to associate from those with whom she officially had to deal or whom she could ignore. She counted quite a number of Indian men and women among her friends but these, like her English friends, were people she felt could be relied upon to preserve for India's sake everything the English and the Indians had done together which could be reckoned of lasting value. She was under no misapprehension about the mistakes made in the past and still being made by her own people in India but if she had been asked to say in what way India had most benefited from the British connection, what it was that could be offered in extenuation of fault, error, even of wickedness, she would have been perfectly clear that it was the example so often given of personal trustworthiness: a virtue that flowed from courage, honesty, loyalty and commonsense in what was to her a single definition of good. She did not see how a person or a country could survive without it.

She was convinced that most of the things that offered some assurance of India surviving on her own resources in the post-war world would reflect the example of personal trustworthiness set by her countrymen in the past. She was in two minds about the benefit that might be had if the connection with England were much prolonged. She accepted the fact that at home her own people had often been indifferent to Indian affairs and that this indifference sprang from ignorance. But in the old days when the code by which she lived had been widely upheld in England this indifference to India had not mattered much, because those who came out to shoulder the responsibility could rely to a great extent on moral support at home. But of recent years, in England, she knew that these values had been eroded and she thought that this mattered a great deal because govern India as one might from Viceregal House, Government House, the commissioner's bungalow, the district officer's court and a military headquarters, the fount of government had always been and still was in the mother country and the moral climate there was bound to influence the climate in which the imperial possession was ruled.

In judging moral climate she took little account of factors usually selected to show evidence of decline. She was a tolerant woman in many of the matters that woke intolerance in others. She held the view that it was a bad thing for society to remain static, a desirable thing for it to be on the move and to divide its rewards more fairly and distribute its opportunities more equitably. She did not feel that there was a conflict between her idea of the way society should change and her conviction that certain principles should be inimical to change. She was aware however of there being that sort of conflict in other people's minds. She was unsympathetic both to the prejudices of stubborn traditionalism and to the anarchic influence of those who often set about destroying it. She believed that through the business of attempting to divest old authorities of power the notion could become current that authority of any kind was suspect. To Isobel Rankin a world without authority was meaningless. There would be no chain of trust if there were no chain of command. She feared that in such a climate there could be a demission of authority in India by her own people that it would be possible only to describe as dishonourable, if by demission one implied as one should a full discharge of every obligation.

She was intent on discharging one such obligation now.

'The problem with mothers and children is that the mothers look after their own to the detriment of community discipline. What we want is a strong-willed woman who's good with kids and can keep them occupied while the mothers do their bit for the community.'

'It's difficult with Indian mothers,' Clara Fosdick said.

'We have to conceive of a hypothetical case, a state of siege lasting say a week,' Isobel went on. 'The teachers at the regimental schools can cope with the boys but I'm thinking of the girls. Mildred, what about that ex-mission teacher your stepmother-in-law has living with her?'

'Barbara Batchelor,' Clarissa Peplow said before Mildred had the chance, presupposing the inclination, to reply. 'I think Barbara would be an excellent choice.'

'But she'd never leave Mabel,' Clara Fosdick pointed out. 'And Mabel wouldn't budge from Rose Cottage if the hordes of Ghengiz Khan were galloping down from the hills.'

'She might have to,' Isobel said. 'Mildred? Any comment? Would Miss Batchelor be capable of controlling a gang of Indian boys and girls?'

'Presumably she's made the attempt in the past. I should think if Clarissa were in charge of her she might be of some use.'

'I want someone capable of running her own show,' Isobel put in. 'Could you take it on, Mrs Peplow?'

'It's more Barbara's line.'

Lighting a cigarette Nicky Paynton said, 'Clara's absolutely right though. She'd never leave Mabel. They'd die together on the verandah of Rose Cottage. Aziz too.'

Lucy Smalley coughed.

'What is it Mrs Smalley?' Isobel recognized the request to speak.

'I'm sure Mrs Fosdick and Mrs Paynton are right and that it would be difficult to prise Miss Batchelor away from Rose Cottage so long as Mrs Layton senior elected to stay there. But there's another reason why I don't think she would be, well, much good at the moment.'

'What reason?'

'She's in a terrible state this morning because the woman who was attacked in Mayapore district is a friend of hers. I mean the mission teacher, the one whose name was given. Miss Crane.'

She had the whole attention of the meeting. One of the advantages of having Mrs Smalley on committees was her more intimate knowledge of the affairs of the lower deck. Isobel turned to Mildred.

'Really? A close friend?'

'My dear Isobel, don't ask me. I know absolutely nothing about Miss Batchelor's connections.'

Isobel looked back at Mrs Smalley and raised her chin inviting further information.

'I wouldn't have known myself,' Lucy said, 'if I hadn't met her in the bazaar a couple of days ago. She was quite worried then because of the reports of things being bad in Mayapore. I didn't pay much attention, well, she does tend to go on. You don't actually need to listen to every word, do you? But when I read the *Gazette* this morning and saw the name of this woman I remembered Miss Batchelor had been telling me about a mission friend of hers called Crane in Mayapore who'd been a heroine in what sounded like the dark ages. So I rang her after breakfast. She'd just read the report too and was hardly coherent. She seemed to think I was someone else, ringing up with *news* of her friend. So I don't think she'd be much good looking after the children if we have riots in Pankot. From the way she was talking you'd have thought her friend was the other poor girl, whoever she is, who's been criminally assaulted.'

'Raped,' Isobel snapped. Lucy Smalley blushed. 'And her name is Miss Manners. Her uncle was governor in Ranpur back in the late 'twenties or early 'thirties. They've been trying to keep her name secret but it's leaked out as it was bound to. Did you know Sir Henry Manners, Mildred?'

'We were in Peshawar and Lahore while he was in office. He was rather pro-Indian wasn't he? I mean politically.'

'Nicky?'

'We were off station too.'

'Dicky says he had a good reputation,' Isobel said. 'His widow is still alive in Rawalpindi, I gather, but nothing's known about the girl. It could be a sticky case, from what I hear.'

Isobel did not say what she had heard. She tapped the agenda again.

'Right,' she said, 'we obviously rule out Miss Batchelor, and I'm not keen on making Chatty Singh's wife responsible for *everything* to do with the Indian community. She'll be over-worked as it is. What about the librarian, Mrs Stewart?'

'My dear, my poor Edwina, (Barbie wrote), I was so shocked to read in the *Ranpur Gazette* about your truly terrible experience.

For an age I wandered about distracted, wanting to help but not knowing how. Mayapore is so far away and even so, what could I do? My good kind friend here, Mabel, coming in and seeing me in this restless state, this state of great, of overwhelming anxiety, and learning the reason, said at once well if you can get through you must ring and find out how she is and leave a message. Practical woman! I followed her advice. It took an age. But I got the Mayapore exchange at last and then the hospital and spoke to a Sister Luke who said that you were quite comfortable, past the crisis, that she would give you my love and of course any letter I cared to send. Past the crisis! I dared not ask of what. Sister Luke seemed to think I would know, though Heaven knows how. Once again it is Mabel who lifts the veil from my uncertainty with her suggestion that after that shock and exposure, waiting, waiting in the rain, you must have been struck down with fever, perhaps pneumonia. My poor Edwina. You must, now on the mend, take care, take care.

'All this was yesterday. I delayed writing to you until today in order to get some sense into my thoughts. The point is that presently when you are better the Mission I am sure will want you to take sick leave to get your strength up properly again. Please take that sensible course. God knows how long these terrible disturbances will last – we aren't troubled by them in this lovely peaceful old station – but we can only hope and pray that they will end soon before more lives are lost. It is they, *they*, poor people who will suffer in the end.

'Well now when you are better, when you are ready, there is a room for you here. It is Mabel's suggestion. She points out that I have never had a visitor. This is true. But it would be so very wonderful to have you, for as long as you are able to spare before buckling to work again as I know you will but must not too soon. I shall say no more for the moment. But let it sink in as an idea. Pankot is a beautiful place. I've been happy here as you know from my previous letters. You can be sure of the friendliest welcome but all the privacy and seclusion you wish, or otherwise. It quickly got round that I knew you and people have been so kind in their inquiries. Today in the bazaar I was stopped many times and asked for news of you. All those of whom I have written before ask especially for their good wishes to be conveyed to you. The Reverend Arthur and Clarissa Peplow, Mr

Maybrick who plays the organ at St John's, Mabel of course and sweet Sarah. I have not seen Susan for a day or two. One feels dreadfully for these young girls, I mean in view of the terrible reports about that other poor woman in Mayapore. Her name was not given in the *Gazette* but we had rumours in advance and now it is freely said by people here who seem to know that her name is Manners, the niece of a one-time Governor of the province. Poor girl, poor girl. You probably know her for it seems she was much involved with charitable work among the untouchables and lived with an Indian lady, a friend of her aunt who is now a widow in Rawalpindi and who must be suffering. One is so puzzled. One senses a mystery, an imponderable – I mean in regard to those who are hurt like yourself, Edwina. Your life too has been so utterly devoted to *them*. I shall write again very very soon. Meanwhile my love and prayers. May God protect you, through Jesus. Sincere, sincere good wishes, Barbie.'

Miss Crane, Miss Manners; Miss Manners, Miss Crane. At times there was a tendency to confuse them; to forget momentarily which of the two victims it was Miss Batchelor knew until a few seconds' thought made the missionary connection; and then a different kind of confusion arose because there being nothing to identify Miss Crane the shortest way to her was through the familiar face and figure of her friend Miss Batchelor. At any given second a fleeting glimpse might therefore be had, as Barbie strode downhill to the bazaar, of the Crane woman doing that very thing for no particular reason unless it were to snatch the observer's thoughts and concentrate them upon a special issue: the safety of women.

There would now enter into the pine-scented and gun-metal air a stiff breeze of the kind that cooled without actually being felt to blow and in Miss Batchelor's, Miss Crane's, wake all kinds of horrors coupled and multiplied and gave her the look of a woman in danger who did not know it, walking in broad daylight, inviting attack, creating conditions in which an attack could take place.

Met face on she had the surprised happy appearance of someone who a few minutes ago had survived assault. It was irritating to find that she had no information; none, that was, that stood the test of sifting from the mine-tip of her inconsequential chatter.

'I am reminded,' she said, 'of Miss Sherwood. Amritsar, 1919. She was a school superintendent too. I never met her, she wasn't Bishop Barnard, but Edwina met her I'm almost certain. She had such a pretty Christian name. Marcella. Perhaps we missionaries are singled out because they see us as agents of the dark, although actually of light. She narrowly escaped with her life. A Hindu woman rescued her, in that awful place, that little lane we sealed off afterwards and made people *crawl* down, on their bellies, in the dust and dirt, to punish them. I sometimes think none of that has been forgiven.'

The word forgiven seemed wrong in present circumstances and the introduction of yet another name, Miss Sherwood, an unnecessary complication. Miss Sherwood was not Miss Crane, neither was Miss Batchelor who after all was merely herself and in no danger except from passing traffic. What she had survived was being in wartime Pankot but not quite of it, three years of comparative obscurity now interrupted by her brief prominence as a friend of the less interesting of the two Mayapore victims.

She was a familiar enough figure though, recognizable from a distance, the length of the bazaar say, whose busy road she had a habit of crossing and recrossing or walking down the middle of at full tilt, narrowly avoiding tongas, bicycles and military trucks; intent on performing innumerable and apparently urgent tasks at bank, post office and shops, in the shortest possible time; shortest in her judgment. The actual economy of method was open to doubt, but presumably old Mabel Layton was satisfied with it. Bit by bit Miss Batchelor had taken over the running of Mabel's household. If Mabel had been looking for someone who would make her withdrawal easier she could not have done better than choose this retired missionary; obviously the kind of person who cried out to be used, like a cow with a full udder moaning for the herdsman to lead her to the pail.

But her yield in information was low and the suspicion arose that she knew Miss Crane less well than had at first been generally assumed from her manner. If the affair of the attacked missionary had not been so serious Miss Batchelor's association with it might have introduced a note of comedy; but it was undoubtedly serious and there were questions it would have been nice to have answers to. For instance was there any significance in the fact that the burnt-out motor-car was one hundred yards away from the dead teacher's body? Had he jumped clear and run back along the road to Dibrapur, attempted to save his own skin, before being caught by the mob? And why after he was dead did she stay with the body and not attempt to seek refuge in the next village? Would she recognize any of the men who had hit her?

Satisfying though it would be to have questions like these settled, the picture of old Miss Crane sitting by a dead body in the road in the pouring rain was of less intense interest than the picture of the other victim, the girl who was criminally assaulted, Miss Manners, whom no one in Pankot knew, of whom no one had ever heard even if the name Manners was familiar to people whose connection with the province extended back ten or fifteen years. That the late Governor Sir Henry still had a widow living in Rawalpindi was a surprise to most people; that he had a niece in Mayapore living with an Indian woman (so the reports had it) was a greater surprise.

Apparently her other name was Daphne which for those who still remembered snippets of classical mythology produced the image of a girl running from the embrace of the sun god Apollo, her limbs and streaming hair already delineating the arboreal form in which her chastity would be preserved, enshrined for ever; for ever green. From her, then, the god could pluck no more than leaves. But this image could not be sustained and the other unknown Daphne stumbled on from antique laurel-dappled sunlight into a plain domestic darkness, dressed in her anonymity, and something simple, white, to suit her imagined frailty, her beauty and vulnerability; now half-sitting, half-lying on a couch in a shaded room with her eyes closed and one hand, inverted, against her aching forehead, speechless in the presence of friends who smiled when they were with her but otherwise looked grim.

And the violence done to her was not over yet. In due course she would have to leave the darkened room, go half-blinded by sunlight (or soaked by rain) to the ordeal of courtroom evidence unless she could be spared that which was not likely, so deeply had the democratic process undermined personal privilege. No closed doors for Miss Manners. The press would make sure of that. And the arrested men would not lack clever Bengali lawyers who would plead without fee, anxious for the publicity and the opportunity to sling mud, to impugn the morals of an English girl. It would be a high court case with a full gallery and the police out in force in the city to discourage the inevitable demonstrations on behalf of the accused. The judge would probably be an Indian. It was hoped so. The sentences of transportation for life to a penal settlement would come better from Mr Justice Chittaranjan than from Clara Fosdick's brother-in-law, Billy Spendlove. And then, only then, might poor Miss Manners fade back into the oblivion from which she had been cruelly dragged.

But her name would be written on the tablets.

The riots spread to Ranpur. Several lorry-loads of British and Indian troops left Pankot, ostensibly on convoy exercises but in fact bound for an encampment outside the city. In Ranpur the city police fired to disperse mobs. The military assisted them on two occasions. An attempt to sabotage the railway between Ranpur and Pankot was discovered in time. The night train up and the day train down now went under armed guard. For several hours the telephone connection was cut. When it was repaired reports came in thick and fast. The *Ranpur Gazette* offices had their windows broken. A mob had penetrated the civil lines with the intention of surrounding Government House. This mob carried banners demanding the release of 'the innocent victims of the Bibighar', meaning the boys arrested for the rape. Scurrilous pamphlets appeared accusing the Mayapore police of torturing and defiling these six Hindu youths by whipping them and forcing them to eat beef. Factories were at a standstill and so was public transport. Life was reported quiet in Ranpur cantonment but there was a sense there undoubtedly of calm before storm. Things were said to be very bad farther afield, particularly in Mayapore and Dibrapur.

Politically in Ranpur it was a difficult time; in Pankot peaceful and, climatically speaking, marvellous: clear skies by day, refreshing rain by night, the perfect combination and a rare one even in the old station which was protected from the streaming and steamy monotony of the southwest monsoon by the very hills that made Ranpur so wet and humid. As Isobel Rankin said – at least the weather was pro-British.

There was bridge at Rose Cottage: the first session for some time. Mildred said she was tired of the club where the Pankot emergency committees had been meeting. Through the open french window came the velvet smell of roses and the marquee smell of cut grass. At mid day Aziz brought drinks out to the verandah and cards were abandoned. Mabel was still in the garden cutting flowers for the house. Miss Batchelor was out shopping in the bazaar. Mildred Layton, Maisie Trehearne, Clara Fosdick and Nicky Paynton had the place to themselves. Presently the girls were due with some of the boys; and there was to be curry lunch down at the club.

But into this idyll, this scene reminiscent of more pacific times, Barbie erupted unexpectedly accompanied by the spectres of broken bloody victims and the Reverend Arthur Peplow's wife, blue-eyed Clarissa, whose expression was one of constant challenge to the devil, an uncomfortable attribute but useful so long as it did not get out of hand, which it had never been known to. Her presence was a kind of corrective to over-optimism, at the same time calming. She had a still clear voice and used it tellingly like a gift harnessed for professional purposes.

'Of course,' Miss Batchelor was saying, 'we weren't at all bound by such things at the Bishop Barnard. Oh, hello. Hello. I was telling Clarissa, that it was teaching first last all the time, well practically speaking, that is especially after the Great War. Miss Jolley is non-conformist which hides a multitude of sins. In my day and Edwina's day it had to be C of E. It's in my trunk or should be. I'll go and look and bring it out and then everyone can see. If I can find it. In spite of one's resolution to be neat and tidy, as my father used to say a human being's no better than a magpie.'

She went indoors. The silence that followed was explicit. Mildred broke it, beating Clarissa perhaps by the shortest head.

'What treat have we in store?' she inquired.

She had her elbows on the arms of the wicker chair and her glass at chest level, held there by the fingers of both droop-wristed hands, and like this seemed to define the limit of her contribution to public interest in Miss Batchelor as the friend of a victim of the riots. Her indifference to her as the sharer of Mabel's kingdom was unchanged. Clarissa, who sat upright on a stool with her feet together and her handbag on her knees, directed her Christian gaze at Mildred but finding no fault unless it were in the large glass of gin and lemon summoned her still clear voice and said, 'It's some kind of picture I gather. One that has to do with her friend.'

'How *is* her friend?' Nicky Paynton asked.

'The question that concerns me more,' Clarissa answered, 'is how is *she*? She has just been acting very strangely on Club road.'

Walking without due care; a danger to herself, indeed to others, up the long stretch from Church road which tongas bowled down or strained up, which no one *ever* walked or if they did walked with accidents in mind, keeping well into the bank on the golf-course side and facing the oncoming horses, bicycles and vehicles; not – like Barbara – on the left-hand side and certainly not in the middle, stopping, starting, drawing her own or an invisible companion's attention to some aspect of the Pankot scene which she must have seen hundreds of times before. And talking. Not in a loud voice. But quite definitely talking. To herself.

'I felt,' Clarissa said when she had described this curious and dangerous behaviour, 'that she imagined herself in the company of her friend, Miss Crane. I made my tonga stop and pick her up and directly she got in she said how kind it was of Mabel to let her invite Miss Crane to Rose Cottage when she is better. And then she started talking about a picture and insisted that I come in to see it.'

One after the other, Clarissa last, heads or eyes were turned towards the garden where Mabel stood motionless except for her hands and arms cutting roses. In the heavy air the click of the secateurs was clearly audible. The sound had a slightly enervating effect but suddenly there were other sounds, voices indoors, all but one of them male. A dog barked and Panther appeared scuffling blackly on to the verandah to greet the company one by one with a sniff of curiosity and a wag of tribute before gallivanting back to the french window, barking and skittering backwards as Susan came out ahead of four affable-looking sub-alterns. 'Nigel you know,' she said, 'this is Bob, Derek, Tommy. My mother, Mrs Trehearne, Mrs Paynton, Mrs Fosdick oh and Mrs Peplow, hello, no Panther come here.'

'I expect there's some cold beer,' Mildred said. 'One of you ring and Nigel we could do with refills, you'll find the trolley indoors. No, don't bother, Aziz has forestalled you, but tell him to bring the beer and if you don't mind making yourself useful get me another of these and anyone else who wants one. Susan you're looking hot. There's some nimbo on the trolley, go and say hello to your Aunt Mabel first while one of the boys gets you a glass only stop Panther going mad for God's sake. Is Sarah coming or joining us at the club?'

'She said she'd join us at the club and may be late. Come on, Panther, come on old boy. Oh don't be silly. It's all right.' She grasped the dog by its stout leather collar and took it down steps it remembered as the scene of chastisement, and just then Barbie reappeared.

'I've found it!' she announced. The men made way for her and each other. She held the framed picture – measuring twelve inches by eight – and was cleaning the glass with the sleeve of her jacket, gripping the cuff with her fingers to make a firm rubbing surface. 'Isn't it extraordinary when you see something you haven't actually looked at for a while how familiar it is. The way the old man holds the alms bowl and the other leans on his staff. If you'd asked me to draw it from memory I couldn't have but one look at it now and one thinks of course! that's how they stood, that's how the artist drew them and left them, caught them in mid-gesture so that the gestures are always being made and you never think of them as getting tired.'

She gave the picture to Mrs Peplow and now stood to one side and a pace behind, both hands behind her back, legs apart (tightening her skirt at the calves) her head tilted, looking down over Clarissa's shoulder.

'You have to imagine it much larger, on the schoolroom wall behind the desk and all the children gathered round just as the people are gathered round the Queen, and Edwina standing with a pointer, not that I ever saw her give a lesson because she'd left Muzzafirabad before I got there but Mr Cleghorn gave me a demonstration and wanted me to try it but as I said, no, no, one must plough one's own furrow. I can see him now, copying Edwina. Here is the Queen. The Queen is sitting on her throne. The uniform of the Sahib is scarlet. The sky here is blue. Who are these people in the sky? They are angels. They blow on golden trumpets. They protect the Queen. The Queen protects the people. The people bring presents to the Queen. The Prince carries a jewel on a velvet cushion. The Jewel is India. She will place the Jewel in her Crown.'

'Yes, I see,' Clarissa said. She was holding the picture like a looking-glass. 'Most admirable. To teach English *and* loyalty. Thank you for showing it to me.'

She handed the picture back. Miss Batchelor caught hold of it, strode across and thrust it at Mildred who had her refilled glass in both hands so that a young man with freckles and dark red hair gallantly reached out and took the picture and held it where Mrs Layton's glance might fall upon it, which fleetingly it did.

'Do pass it round,' Miss Batchelor said. 'It's a copy of a picture my friend Edwina Crane used years and years ago. The children adored it. Pictures are so important when instructing the young. But one has to be careful. Edwina once told me she had a very grave suspicion that in the end the children confused her with Victoria! Isn't that amusing? You must admit the artist got everything in, Mrs Fosdick. Disraeli's there, the one with the scroll and the smug expression. Generals, admirals, statesmen, princes, paupers, babus, banyas, warriors, villagers, women, children. And old Victoria in the middle of it sitting on a throne under a canopy in the open air of all things, really quite absurd but allegorical of course, she never came to India. She looks quite startled, don't you agree, Mrs Trehearne? But I think that's the effect of the reduction in scale. The print on the schoolroom wall was ten times as big and in that I remember – thank you, Mrs Paynton – she looked terribly wise and kind and understanding.'

Receiving the picture back from Mrs Paynton via a young man with a fair moustache she looked at it again herself. 'It always seemed to me to be a picture about love rather than loyalty. Perhaps they amount to the same thing. What do you think?'

She looked at the moustached young man whose mouth was puckered in concentration. He was pulling his left ear-lobe.

'Have you got transport?' Mildred asked one of the men, who said yes they had. 'Then directly you've downed your beers we ought to be getting along to the club.'

There were movements of departure. Two of the men went into the garden to rescue Susan.

'Oh, are you all going?' Miss Batchelor asked in her carrying schoolroom voice. 'Let me just say I do appreciate everyone being so kind, so solicitous for Edwina.'

*

She hammered a nail into the wall above the old campaigner's writing-table and hung the picture. Aziz approved. He would pause in his work to consider it, stand like one of the children of Muzzafirabad grown old but still possessed. She had told him about her friend Miss Crane, that she was in hospital in distant Mayapore hurt trying to save someone who was attacked and killed, and might when better stay for a week or two in the little spare. He nodded his understanding in the Indian way. In Aziz this was a gesture of great economy. He had the dignity of the people from the higher hills who walked shrouded in blankets and secrecy and made excursions into Pankot, involved in mysterious errands whose object escaped her since they came and went empty-handed as if merely to look and reassure themselves that nothing was happening in the valley of which they disapproved.

Mabel, in her solitary walks, went in their direction but nowadays went less often. On her own walks the other way downhill Barbie had become used to feeling like a dove sent out to check the level of the flood. After three years the darkness still lay on Mabel's soul and Barbie felt a bit discouraged. But since the incident on the road from Dibrapur the nature of her outings seemed to have changed and the familiar route had become unfamiliar. She anticipated revelation.

In her mind she too guarded the body. It lay near the milestone half-way up (or down) Club road. Passing the milestone made her light-headed; almost there was a sense of levitation. Edwina's act of guarding the body had been one of startling simplicity and purity which possibly only a woman like Edwina could have had the occasion to perform and in performing it sum up the meaning of her life in India. From the schoolroom door at Muzzafirabad to the place on the road from Dibrapur was a distance measurable in miles, in years, but between the occasions there was no distance. Right from the beginning Edwina had been close to God and therefore to herself. Not teaching but loving. From her plain face, her manner, you might not have guessed this. Only from her actions. And in this most recent action, this guarding of the dead Indian's body, it seemed to Barbie that Edwina had achieved her apotheosis.

Oh how I long, Barbie said, standing still suddenly, having passed the milestone and accepted the sad fact that there was no body there for her to guard, how I long for an apotheosis of my own, nothing spectacular, mind, nothing in the least grandiose nor even just grand, but, like Edwina's, quiet with a still-centre to it that exemplifies not my release from earthly life although it might do that too but from its muddiness and uncertainty, its rather desperate habit of always proving that there are two sides to every question; my release from that into the tranquillity of knowing my work has been acceptable, good and useful perhaps, perhaps not, but performed in love, with love, and humility of course, indeed, humility, and singularity, wholeness of purpose. That is the most important thing of all.

But not knowing what kind of apotheosis this could be she walked on in the direction of the bazaar to settle the accounts at Jalal-ud-din's and Gulab Singh Sahib's, and buy more stamps to write more letters to Edwina who did not reply. No news she said to Sarah who inquired, being also at Jalal-ud-din's querying a bill upon which was writ large the rising cost of living in her father's continuing absence, no news is good news. She hoped for both their sakes that this was so.

She was in love with Sarah Layton and with Susan but more with Sarah who seemed to need it more. She was in love with Pankot and her life there and her duty to Mabel and the wind in winter. She was afraid to be in love with Mr Maybrick who played the organ at St John's and was widowed and retired from Tea, because he was to begin with a man and to go on with a man with a temper and an air of self-enclosure who did not normally invite proofs of attachment even of Barbie's kind, which did not extend to flesh. In any case he had large hands with more hair on the wrists than on his head and when he played the organ his hands looked extraordinarily vivid and enterprising. He lived alone except for his Assamese houseboy in a tiny and very untidy bungalow not far from the rectory-bungalow on the same tree-shaded road. In his bungalow there were many photographs of his dead wife and in most of them she had her hand above her eyes to keep the sun out, a fact which always made Barbie feel outdoors when really in.

On her way back from the bazaar she looked in at St John's to collect his album of Handel which was falling to pieces and which she had volunteered to repair. Mr Maybrick was at prac-tice. She could hear the organ as she approached the church door. Bach. Toccata and fugue.

She sat in a pew and listened. She imagined Mr Maybrick's red face and bald head reflected in the mirror above the keyboards. The mirror was a framed picture. Who is this? This is the Planter. The face of the Planter is reddened by the sun. Here is his Lady. She shades her eyes from the light. She is of the North and ails in the climate. But keeps going. What is the Planter doing? He is showing the coolies how to pick only the tender leaves. As he shows them God sings through his fingers. The leaves are green. When they are dried they will be brown. The music will be preserved in caddies. The Planter and the coolies between them will bring Tea to the Pots of the Nation.

She thought: I shall bring Edwina to St John's to hear Mr Maybrick at practice and on Sundays to hear Arthur Peplow's sermon. And afterwards we shall return to Rose Cottage. And I shall be large again and shapely with intent, so close to Edwina that God will remember and no longer mark me absent from the roll.

The attitude of the old Queen inclining her body, extending her two hands, was then suddenly an image of Edwina on the road from Dibrapur holding her hands protectively above the body of the Indian. Flames from the burning motor-car were reflected in the sky where the angelic light pierced bulgy monsoon clouds.

In this image she had a surrogate for God, a half-way house of intercession, capable perhaps of boosting the weak signals from the rush mat and transmitting them through the crackling overloaded ether which her direct prayers could not penetrate. She knelt with her body upright, facing the writing-table and the picture that pointed the reality of a Christian act, the palms of her hands turned to receive whatever was offered. She exposed her chest well below the gold pendant cross to give the metal room to act as a lightning conductor and sometimes felt it warmed by the reflected light from the burning vehicle; which was a promising beginning. Otherwise everything remained as it had been.

Once a week she visited the club subscription library for Mabel, seldom for herself who found what Mr Cleghorn had called the book of life sufficiently entertaining and puzzling to keep her occupied without recourse to the print and paper of imaginary or refurbished adventure.

Lost between the shelves among which she and Edwina would wander she heard a voice say, 'I'm told the whole trouble is she was infatuated with the Indian. She'd have done anything to save him.' She recognized the voice of little Mrs Smalley, the station gossip, and then Clarissa's saying, 'You can't know that.' To which Lucy Smalley replied, 'It's what people in Mayapore are saying, according to Tusker, and they have been in a position to judge. They say she was always out with him, holding his hand in public places. And now she's threatening to say the most dreadful things against the authorities if the men they've arrested are charged and tried, because *he's* one of them. The police officer who made the arrests is almost out of his mind.'

Barbie emerged armed with a volume of Emerson still open at the page with her thumb on the line, 'Man is explicable by nothing less than all his history,' which a moment ago had caused her to catch her breath. She cried out, 'Of whom are you talking?'

Not, it seemed, of Edwina, but – Lucy Smalley explained, recovered quickly from the nasty shock of Barbie emerging and bearing down like a Fury – of 'the Manners girl', the other victim. 'You didn't think we were talking about your friend, surely?'

Barbie took Emerson home with her. She had not meant to but he was in her hand as she arrived at Mrs Stewart's desk and was marked out to her with a rise of Mrs Stewart's eyebrows because Mrs Stewart, a widow from Madras with a literary turn of mind, was more used to receiving from Barbie her inter-pretations of Mabel's standing order for something light, which generally turned out to be so easy on the mind and lap that Mabel nodded off over it in her wing chair having pronounced it earlier 'just right'.

Presented with Emerson's essays Mabel said, 'Oh, I read those as a girl, I don't think I could bother again.'

'I'll take it back tomorrow,' Barbie promised. 'It was a mistake, or rather absent-mindedness, my attention was taken as it can be all too easily. Well, you know, you know. I *am* sorry.'

But Mabel merely smiled and touched Barbie's arm as she did from time to time as if to make up for all the occasions when she might have failed to let Barbie know she was appreciated.

Barbie sat at the writing-table, opened the rejected book. 'If the whole of history is one man,' she said, 'it is all to be explained from individual experience. There is a relation between the hours of our life and the centuries of time.' She closed the book abruptly and made herself busy in the room, opening drawers and rearranging their contents.

Not taking Emerson back she returned to him daily like a sparrow easily frightened from a promising scattering of crumbs by the slightest noise, with a nagging sense of having more duties than intelligence. It was pretty plain she was not cut out for the philosophical life but through Emerson it impinged on her own like the shadow of a hunched bird of prey patiently observing below it the ritual of survival. The bird should have been an angel.

She began to feel what she believed Emerson wanted her to feel: that in her own experience lay an explanation not only of history but of the lives of other living people, therefore an explanation of the things that had happened to Edwina and to Miss Manners of whom she had only the vaguest picture, the one that had been commonly shared in Pankot of a reclining figure, in white, in a darkened room. But now it had changed. The girl's hand was no longer pressed inverted against her forehead but held by another which was brown like the dead teacher's. The picture shimmered, became fluid. Colours and patterns ran. When Barbie sat at her desk and gazed at the actual picture she was no longer sure of what she saw: Edwina guarding the body, Mabel kneeling to grub out weeds or inclining to gather roses; or herself, Barbie, surrounded by the children she had presumed to bring to God; or Miss Manners in some kind of unacceptable relationship with a man of another race whom she was intent on saving.

From this there emerged a figure, the figure of an unknown Indian: dead in one aspect, alive in another. And after a while it occurred to her that the unknown Indian was what her life in India had been about. The notion alarmed her. She had not thought of it before in those terms and did not know what to do about it now that she had. She could not very well look for him because she did not know where to do that. Aziz for instance seemed content even in his alternative persona of a man from the hills with a blanket and a secret. He did not strike her as being in distress of any kind.

But the dead man in the vicinity of the milestone had moved. Overnight there had been a rearrangement of his limbs as if while it was dark he had sat up. And howled. The hills were hunted by jackals. People would not have noticed. But she thought that she would henceforth be able to distinguish the man's cry from the cries of the animals.

She began another letter to Edwina.

'September 4th. Why don't you write Edwina? I need your letter,' then tore it up and began another sensibly.

'Some people from Mayapore have been here. I didn't meet them but a woman called Smalley who lives at the little Smith's Hotel where these people stayed for a couple of days told Clarissa Peplow that according to these visitors whose name I think was Patterson or Pattison you were reported well on the mend and about to be discharged. How thankful this news has made me. I have not rung the hospital again because of the expense and the delay in getting through and then getting only the briefest official answer to the question. But I have written several times. I hope my letters all arrived. The posts have been badly delayed, indeed disrupted. If you are already discharged no doubt the hospital will send this note round to your bungalow. I shall mark the envelope please forward and shall probably send a separate note to you at home. How glad you will be to be there. I hope, hope that you are truly recovered, Edwina.

'Is there a possibility of your making the journey to Pankot? The invitation still stands. Mabel has asked me to emphasize this and also to say that we should keep you free from the prying and the curious. I do trust that you are not too disagreeably involved with the aftermath of that awful business. It is said officially that the country is returning to normal and that now surely is the time for magnanimity. But one hears the unhappiest accounts and most unpleasant remarks. I am, my dear Edwina, a bit con-cerned for you as a result of something Clarissa said, echoing Lucy Smalley and presumably these Patterson Pattison people. It would be monstrous if after all you have been through you were in the least criticized for stating that you could not either describe or recognize individuals among that wicked mob. It must have been a nightmare and after a nightmare the details are often mercifully forgotten. Only those with vengeful natures would wish to see you drag some detail back into the light, one upon which they could then proceed to act over-righteously perhaps and in all likelihood unjustly. No doubt you feel as I do that God will punish and perhaps has already punished. As Clarissa says, some of the men who hurt you and killed the teacher may since have been killed themselves in the rioting. Divine retribution!'

Here Barbie's pen hesitated as if of its own accord and she could not continue. Divine retribution was all very well. It did not help the unknown Indian who seemed this morning to be crying out harder but still soundlessly, begging for justice and not alleviation. She found it difficult to distinguish between the teacher who died in the attack on Edwina and the Indian who was supposed to have had Miss Manners infatuated with him. Lucy Smalley's opinion was that the Indian boy Miss Manners thought she was in love with must have been some kind of hypnotist. But perhaps love was a form of hypnosis anyway. Had not Barbie been mesmerized herself years and years ago?

My life, she thought, has become extraordinarily complicated. There is more than one of me and one, I'm not sure which, has a serious duty to perform. 'It seems perfectly dreadful (she wrote suddenly, allowing the Waterman pen its now free-flowing head) how within the space of a few weeks poor Daphne Manners has become "that Manners girl".' And she continued for a page or two becoming while she did so a projection of that poor misused creature who it was said was not frail and pretty after all but rather large and ungainly and in need of spectacles, so that the sympathetic transference of Barbie to Daphne and back again was easier to make than it would have been had the idea of Miss Manners as frail, ethereal and beautiful in victim's white turned out to be accurate.

Instead here she was according to reports from people who had been in a position to know, in a rather grubby dress to suit the circumstances arising from her extraordinary behaviour, throwing up blinds, peering short-sightedly and threatening to create a scene, standing in shafts of sunlight which were alive with particles of dust. Barbie understood this image better than the other.

Miss Manners said the men arrested were the wrong men. Barbie wondered how that could be but was impressed by the reported strenuousness of Miss Manners's insistence which everyone else seemed to feel outraged by, just as they were ready to be outraged by Edwina's insistence that she had no contribution to make to the identification of a few men in a large crowd. In those circumstances they all looked alike anyway in their murky dhotis and Gandhi caps and filthy turbans. And the smell. Suffering, sweating, stinking, violent humanity. It was the background against which you had to visualize Jesus working. People did not remember this important thing about His presence. Edwina did. Did Miss Manners? Or was she only intent on confusing the police to save her lover? Apparently she kept changing her story. According to the Pattersons she had threatened to say that if the six youths who included her lover were charged and tried for rape she would stand up and say that the men who assaulted her could just as easily have been British soldiers with their faces blacked.

In that threat, that outburst, which had scandalized her countrymen, Barbie detected what she thought of as the girl's despair and was sorry for her. She would have liked to take Miss Manners in her arms and comfort her. She was not convinced though that Miss Manners was telling the whole truth so she was also sorry for the police officer who had arrested the men and was convinced of their guilt. It was said by the Patterson Pattisons that the police officer had warned Miss Manners about her association with this particular Indian who was handsome if you liked that sort of thing and educated, so he claimed, in England but certainly beyond his real station, and had already been questioned over something to do with political affiliations. On the face of it, Barbie saw, the Indian was as likely to be guilty as not, leading Miss Manners on, laughing at her behind her back as Lucy Smalley suggested, and planning to attack her in the dark on the way home from one of her errands of mercy, in the company of five of his westernized friends, student-types, who came at her from behind, dragged her off her bicycle into the Bibighar Gardens, covered her head with her own raincape, raped her and left her to stagger home in pain, in torment, totally disorientated.

If they covered her head how could she see who they were? When did they cover her head? Only after she had a glimpse (as apparently she began to say), a good enough glimpse of them to be able to insist that they were dirty peasant-types not well-groomed European-style dressed boys of the kind arrested? And there had been some confusion about her bicycle. Had it been found by the police in the ditch outside the Indian boy's house? At first this was what had been said but it had been denied later by the police officer himself. The most damning thing of all had not been denied though. When arrested the Indian boy had been bathing his face which was scratched and bruised. He would not say how; had never said, had refused utterly to talk. The others denied any complicity, any connection with his English girl-friend, pretended they had spent the whole evening drinking hooch in a hut near the Bibighar Gardens where the attack had taken place. They had been arrested in the hut.

Now they were disposed of, all of them, to gaol, without trial, as political detenus. And Miss Manners seemed to have won. But what had she won except disgrace among her own people? And her Indian boy-friend; what had he got away with?

Barbie did not even know his name. She began to have dreams about him, but in these dreams he was the Indian Edwina had tried to save. In this dream his eyes were blinded by cataracts. He had a powerful muscular throat which was exposed because his head was lifted and his mouth wide open in a continuous soundless scream.

VI

It was the element of scornful rejection implicit in every violent challenge to authority which hurt most deeply and blighted the tendrils of affection which entwined and supported the crumbling pillars of the edifice. Upon faces already drawn from the strain of conveying self-confidence and from the slight but persistent malaise suffered by constitutions imperfectly designed to withstand the climate, there would fall – during these periods of pressure – shadows of brooding melancholy, even when the face was expressing scorn or indifference, amusement, wrath; whatever it was that was being felt or assumed. In the cries of shock and outrage with which news of victims was heard and passed on, in the calls for condign punishment of culprits, a plaintive note managed to be struck which corresponded to the melancholy shadow; a note of awareness that the victims must have been people in whom the impulse to show as well as feel affection in the performance of their duty had been stronger than was usual, even than was wise, so that the fates of these people were seen through all the tangle of misfortune and circumstance as sacrificial.

But in the aftermath, as the status quo was re-established, these original victims were replaced by the figures of those who had tried to avenge them and become victims themselves; and then that melancholy shadow was burnt away by fires of irony which, lighting faces, gave them the glowing look of belonging to people who found themselves existing on a plane somewhere between that of the martyr and the bully.

The irony lay in the fact that the new victims were sacrifices offered by one's own side as a placatory measure in restoring order and regaining Indian confidence. It had happened before, it would happen again, but that did not make it any more palatable when it was happening now. As early as the beginning of September when the jails were crammed and the country and administration nearly back to normal it was said that Brigadier Reid, openly accused by the Indians of having used excessive force in putting down the riots, was not receiving the kind of support from above which he had the right to expect. At the end of the month he was reported posted to another command.

Nicky Paynton said, 'It seems to me Alec Reid did damned well. The civil always expect us to be on tap to pull their chestnuts out of the fire but when we do they start complaining that we've burnt *their* fingers.' She was stating what was generally felt to be true. In Reid's case community sympathy for him was strong because although he had used his British battalion in Mayapore he commanded as well a battalion of the Pankots (the 4/5th) and one of the Ranpurs. But this sympathy had been deepened by the news that at the height of the riots in Mayapore his wife died of cancer in Rawalpindi. It was also known that his only son had been captured by the Japanese in Burma earlier in the year, news which could hardly have made Meg Reid's last months any easier for her or Alec Reid to bear. But, called by the civil power to give military aid, he had done so, so far as one could tell, resolutely and effectively. If a larger than average number of Indians was killed or wounded in Mayapore and Dibrapur that was because the riots in those two towns were worse than in any other town in the country and because the civil power had dithered, had been unwilling to call the army in until the situation had got completely out of hand.

It was quite obvious to Army people that the civil authority in Mayapore lacked nous. Apart from the almost criminal negligence shown by the long postponement of a request for troops, the revolting affair of the rape of Miss Manners had been allowed to disintegrate in the most scandalous way. The only people who had come out well of the troubles in Mayapore, in Pankot opinion, were the brigade commander and the District Superintendent of Police who had arrested the suspects in the rape case within an hour or so of the assault. And now, like Brigadier Reid, this officer was said to be in bad official odour.

What was needed of course was some first-hand information and for that one had to wait for people like the Pattersons to arrive from Mayapore. They had been interesting on the subject of Miss Manners but, being civilians, a poor source of intelligence in the matter of the alleged excessive use of force. The first man to arrive in Pankot from Mayapore, a junior officer of a British regiment fairly recently out from home, found himself much in demand. But his mind seemed to be on other things. In regard to the rape, for instance, he said, 'Really, one began to suspect there hadn't been one.' He described the military action taken in aid of the civil power 'like something out of Gilbert and Sullivan mixed up with the last act of *Hamlet*'. The discovery that this young man had been an actor in civilian life and was in Pankot en route for a sinecure in welfare and entertainment in Delhi was made early enough to put his views into proper perspective. He was vulgarly handsome. Probably a chorus boy, Mrs Fosdick suggested.

After the theatrical lieutenant had gone there arrived as many as a dozen men and women who had been in Mayapore at the time of the riots. They said that the number of dead in Mayapore, considered uncomfortably high by the authorities, was accounted for chiefly by people drowned in the river when scattering in panic at the sound of rifle fire and the sight of troops on both sides of the Mandir Gate bridge. In Dibrapur it had been a different matter. There the rebels had used home-made bombs and land-mines. They got what they asked for. Brigadier Reid nearly lost a whole rifle company when it was cut off by a blown bridge; and when you thought of that, and that the company was part of a brigade he was trying to get ready to fight the Japanese and stop them invading India, you had to agree it was inhuman to start crucifying him for showing a bit of sand. In Reid there was obviously more sand than the desk-wallahs thought it right for a British officer to show these days. They were getting ready to dish him. The command of the brigade was Alec Reid's first real job of soldiering for more than ten years. If it hadn't been for the debâcle in Malaya and Burma he'd probably have ended his career fretting at a desk. He'd now been given command of a brigade that was almost ready to go back into the field but it was rumoured that GHQ thought it better to promote him to a job he'd quickly prove he couldn't do than send him meekly back to a staff appointment because the civil in Mayapore had kicked up a stink about him.

There was a rather sordid little joke going round among Mayapore Indians that if you spelt Reid backwards it came out sounding like Dyer who shot down all those unarmed people in the Jallianwallah Bagh in Amritsar in 1919. It never took long for people to home in like vultures on the reputation of a perfectly decent and competent officer. The only comfort to be had from the business was that if Reid did prove himself just too old to command a brigade of more seasoned troops his fate would be better than old Dyer's. He'd likely get a general's hat and even if there was nowhere else to hang it except on a peg in an air-conditioned office the pay while it lasted and the pension when it ended would be some compensation.

The first of the officers who gained Pankot's full attention was the adjutant of the battalion of the British regiment that had been brigaded for training with a battalion of the Ranpurs and the Mayapore Battalion of the Pankots under Reid. This officer was on short local leave. His knowledge of India was infinitesimal but he was a regular soldier and gave a fascinating account of the action in aid of the civil power in Mayapore in the Mandir Gate bridge, following which an unfortunately large number of women and children had died in the river. He knew the departed theatrical lieutenant, of course, but surprised everybody by describing him as a first-rate platoon commander who had won the MM as a lance-corporal at Dunkirk. He claimed to be the originator of the famous comment about that retreat: The noise! The people! To men the adjutant confided that he thought young X was probably as queer as a coot but that if so he had the courage of an Amazon. He was among those who had led a detachment of British soldiers in aid of the civil. He had behaved well but perhaps the experience of firing on unarmed civilians had 'turned him'. The adjutant remembered finding him vomiting in his quarters when going to ask why he hadn't reported to the daftar on his return from aid duty in the city. 'My dear fellow,' the actor-soldier had said, 'I'm being sick because in a properly organized production the extras never actually get killed. The little thing today was wildly under-rehearsed.'

The next arrival was an even more promising source of information. This was Ewart Mackay, the brigade major whom Reid's successor had replaced with a man of his own choice. Mackay was in Pankot for a couple of days. He had broken his journey to his regimental depot in Muzzafirabad in the North West Frontier province, where he anticipated being offered the command of the battalion of the Muzzafirabad Guides that was now being brought back up to strength after limping out of Burma.

Initially he seemed more interested in standing drinking at the men's bar in the club than in answering questions about Mayapore which he deflected with frosty blasts of his Carew's gin and ice-chunk-cooled breath and chilling stares of a keen blue eye. His sandy pranged moustache was kept airborne by constant manipulation of his restless fingers.

But after he had put down what one member swore were twelve burra pegs in the course of two hours he became brisker, informative, and introduced a speculative element into the hitherto clear-cut argument that Reid had been badly treated.

Apparently Ewart Mackay had quite a good opinion of White, the Deputy Commissioner in Mayapore. He said, 'We all knew the Brig's son was a p.o.w. with the Japs and we knew his wife was in hospital up in 'Pindi. But I was the only one who knew she was dying of cancer and I didn't know that until quite late in the day. I think if the DC had known he and the Brig would have got on better because he would have made allowances. As it was I often had to pour oil especially during the time the Brig was pressing him to call the troops out and the DC was digging his heels in and saying the civil police could cope. It's nonsense to say excessive force was used but it could be that if we'd used troops say a day earlier the result wouldn't have been so bad. I think the DC would have called for troops the day before if the Brig had given him more confidence about how they'd be used. Old Alec Reid's a bit of a fire-eater you know. And nowadays the civil distrust us if we look anxious to have a crack. I suppose if your wife is dying and you're stuck in a place like Mayapore with all hell let loose you'd want to get stuck in, but it's never a good thing for the man at the top to be under an emotional strain. All the same old Alec Reid's had a shabby deal. Giving him that other brigade was only a face-saver for him and the army. He won't be keeping it. I know the man who's been told he'll be getting it. Reid will be back in Delhi by Christmas.'

And Miss Manners? No, he had not had the pleasure of meeting Miss Manners. He pronounced her name in mock Scottish as it were with a deliberate skirl of the pipes and a whirl of the kilt. Since that unfortunate affair he had of course learned quite a bit about her. No, she wasn't particularly attractive according to reports. Big and gawky he understood. She was staying in one of the oldest houses in Mayapore, a place called the MacGregor House built by a Scottish nabob in the early nineteenth century but now the property of an Indian woman, Lady Chatterjee, one of the Indians with whom the DC and his wife played bridge. Miss Manners was quite new to India. Although born in the country she had been taken home by her parents while still an infant. She lost both parents before the war and her brother had been killed. She'd driven ambulances throughout the blitz in London but been invalided out. Her closest surviving relative, her aunt, old Lady Manners, widow of ex-Governor Sir Henry, arranged for her to join her in Rawalpindi. There she met Lady Chatterjee. Sir Henry Manners and Sir Nello Chatterjee, a Bengali industrialist, had been old friends and after their deaths their widows had kept the friendship up. Lady Chatterjee was a Rajput, Chatterjee being her second husband. Her first was a prince who broke his neck playing polo. Chatterjee was knighted for founding and financing the Mayapore technical college which produced young Indian engineers, not unemployable arts graduates. Lady Chatterjee was considered okay.

Major Mackay had met Lady Chatterjee once in the course of his social duties. Miss Manners may have been at the same function but he didn't recall seeing her. The fact was she was probably otherwise occupied. After coming to stay with Lady Chatterjee and doing voluntary work at the general hospital she had become friendly with this Indian journalist fellow who was among the six young men the District Superintendent of Police arrested for raping her.

Mackay was offered another drink. He accepted and said nothing more until it reached him. After a couple of swallows he reflighted his moustache and said, 'Curious business altogether. And it made life extra difficult because it gave the troublemakers something special to shout about. I expect you heard the tales that got around that the police tortured the boys and defiled them by making them eat beef to get them to confess, which they never did. A lot of our own people felt that if the tales were true they only got what they deserved. I don't expect they were handled any too gently. Some of these Indian inspectors and sub-inspectors can be pretty ruthless but the rabble were accusing the DSP himself. It got so bad the DC ordered an Indian magistrate to question each one of them but none of them complained of ill-treatment. They might have been scared to. Anyway it made no difference. The crowds were still screaming blue murder. I never cared much for the DSP, he wasn't my kind of chap, but the Brig liked him and considering the crowds were out to get him if they could he acted pretty coolly. I saw him once in the thick of it on horseback rallying a squad of police that looked as if it had had enough. If there'd been one rioter with a shotgun he'd have been a dead man. As it was a bloody great stone missed him by inches. Still, guts don't count if you fail in another direction. He never made the rape charges stick and I don't suppose his department will let him forget it. But that's life. Bring home the bacon and you're forgiven a lot. Don't, and you're sunk.'

One of the other men said, 'From what we hear that wasn't his fault but the girl's. She sounds round the bend to me.'

Mackay glanced at the man, emptied his glass, put it on the counter and ordered another round.

'You think so?' he said.

'Don't you?'

'I just think she was in love. Not round the bend. Not infatuated. Not intimidated. In love.'

'With the journalist fellow?'

'That's right.'

'Even after he and his friends raped her?'

'Forget the friends. The trouble about this case is that nobody's ever been able to forget the friends or start from the simple proposition that Miss Manners was in love and still is with the Kumar chap. And that the Kumar chap was and still is in love with her.'

'Was that his name?'

'There were six names but I think Kumar was the lad in question. Hari Kumar.'

'Harry?'

'H, a, r, i. He was brought up in England. He went to school at Chillingborough.'

'Good God.'

'Quite so. Interesting, isn't it?'

'Well what the hell was he doing working in a place like Mayapore on a local rag?'

'They tell me his father died bankrupt in England before the war and he came back penniless to the only relative he had, an aunt who lived in Mayapore. She was a widow and lived on the charity of her dead husband's orthodox Hindu family. Young Kumar must have had a tough time adjusting himself to *that*. It could be he failed to adjust himself. The police had an eye on him. He was politically suspect. That's the other red herring.'

'Red herring?'

'It introduces complications. It makes it hard to concentrate on the proposition that he and Miss Manners were in love.'

'What's the other red herring?'

'The friends. The police had files on them too. I think you have to forget the politics, the friends, even the rape, and concentrate on this one proposition. They were in love.'

'What do you mean, forget the rape?'

Mackay's glass was empty. He put it on the counter. A man in the group ordered refills.

'I mean forget it because it's irrelevant.'

The word irrelevant came out slightly blurred and Major Mackay lost something of his grip on his audience. But with his next sentence he regained and hardened it.

'She's pregnant, you know. She's gone back to R'l'Pindi pregnant. People say she'll get an abortion. Myself, I doubt it.

I concentrate on the proposition that she and Kumar were in love, still are, he in clink and she pregnant in R'l'Pindi. Having what she thinks is his child. Thinks, hopes or knows. You can't tell. Perhaps she can't either in the way women think they can. The old intuition.'

A man with a red face and sparse hair, a civilian asked, 'What's your theory, Major Mackay?'

'Well yes I have a theory. Glad you asked. My theory's this. If you love and marriage isn't on or isn't easy sooner or later you get round to poking, to put it crudely. My theory is Miss Manners and this Kumar fellow poked in the Bibighar either that night for the first time or that night for the umpteenth but that that night whatever teenth time it was these so-called friends of his who'd not only guessed he was poking her but had found out where, were all lined up waiting for the show to begin and when it was over jumped on him, sat on him and then –'

Major Mackay made an arm.

'Then why didn't Miss Manners say so?'

'Say what? That she and Mr Kumar had been making love at night in a derelict garden doing no harm to anyone when up come these friends of his and say, Okay Hari, move over?'

'Why not? From all accounts she's not the easily embarrassed type. And if what you suggest is true and she and this journalist fellow had made a clean breast of it that part of it might have been kept dark and the other fellows just charged and sentenced.'

'And do you think any of them would have let Kumar get away with that? They'd have implicated him like a shot. They'd have said it was Kumar's idea, to share her.'

'Well wasn't it? The police thought so.'

'Which is where you come back to my proposition. If it had been like that I don't care what kind of act he put up she'd have known and she'd have stopped being in love with him. If you stick to my proposition that they were in love, are in love, everything's as clear as daylight. These so-called friends of his jumped him and beat him up. She may not have seen who they were. If not he told her afterwards and told her what they'd threatened, that they'd accuse him of arranging it if there was any trouble. Well, she wasn't a bloody fool. Everybody in Mayapore knew she'd been going out with him. Neither of them was popular as a result. He wouldn't have stood a chance however much she swore his innocence. So they cooked up a story that they hadn't seen each other for days and they damned well stuck to it, right through. What she hadn't reckoned with was finding when she got home that Lady Chatterjee had already reported her missing to the DSP. It was the night the balloon was expected to go up and she hadn't come home at the usual time. She wasn't at the club or at any of old Lady C's friends and the woman was pretty worried. And when she got home there wasn't any disguising what had happened. Her clothes were torn and she was in a state. Lady C had a woman doctor from the Purdah Hospital up to the house in a brace of shakes. Maybe Miss Manners panicked. But she said she'd been assaulted by a gang of men and that was the situation the DSP found when he called at the house. He had no time for Hari Kumar. He'd had his eye on him. He'd warned Miss Manners about associating with a fellow like that. So young Kumar's the first chap the DSP thinks of. He hares off to the Bibighar, finds Kumar's pals drinking in a hut not far away, arrests them and hares off to Kumar's house and finds him bathing cuts and bruises on his face, the sort a fellow might get if he attacked a girl who fought back. What other evidence did he need? He jumped to the conclusion most people would. And he was right in my opinion except in this one case, the case of Mr Kumar who never did explain how his face got like that and just went on insisting as she did that they hadn't seen each other since the night they visited a temple.'

'What about the others?'

'Oh they played dumb too. They pretended they'd spent the whole evening drinking in the hut. They never changed their story but if Hari Kumar had split on them they'd have taken him with them. There was a pretty odd thing happened about her bicycle. The one she was supposed to be dragged off. First the police said it was found outside Kumar's house and then the DSP said no that was wrong it had been in the Bibighar Gardens near the scene of the rape and put in the police truck that went to get Kumar, and a sub-inspector who came on the scene late thought one of the constables had found it in the ditch outside the house and put that down in a report. Indians said the DSP planted the bike himself and then realized it looked too bloody obvious. My own theory is that these other five took the bike from the Gardens and stuck it outside Kumar's place and that the DSP didn't find Kumar's or any of their fingerprints on it because they'd wiped it clean, and guessed they'd been trying to incriminate him alone. It's just the sort of crazy thing boys like that would do, forgetting that if Kumar was incriminated they wouldn't stand a chance themselves.'

'But that would mean this police chap withheld vital evidence.'

'Messy evidence. Rigged evidence. Without Kumar's prints on the handlebars or the saddle the sort of evidence he didn't want. He wanted Kumar. A jury would have been very wary about the girl's bike being found outside Kumar's house even if wiped clean of fingerprints. I don't think he was very interested in the other fellows. Whenever people talked to him about the case Kumar's was the only name he ever mentioned. I think he disliked the chap because of the kind of boy he is. First-rate British public-school education, but black as your hat and going out with an English girl, and politically unreliable.'

'Was he politically unreliable?'

'A young educated Indian? It's likely, isn't it? On the other hand the paper he worked for was Indian-owned but pro-British. Not that that means anything. The police must have had enough on all six for the civil to decide to lock them up without trial as political detenus when the rape charge couldn't be got to stick, but everyone knows that locking them up like that was nothing more than a face-saver. She wasn't able to stop that. But by God she stopped the charges and she stopped the trial. The assistant commissioner was scared stiff about what she might come out with. They hadn't a hope in hell of bringing the beggars into court with Miss Manners as the only witness for the prosecution ready to swear blind that the fellows who raped her were peasants, and saying God knows what else. You have to admire her. Well. You do if you accept my proposition that Kumar had her but didn't rape her and that they're both bloody well in love.'

'Did the DSP know her well?'

'In a place like that everybody knows everybody as likely as not. If you mean was he sweet on her himself I can't answer. He wasn't married and plain as they say she was she'd have been a good catch for a man like him, but he struck me as a pretty cold fish. Thought of nothing but his job, I'd say. Not a sociable character. Abstemious. Never heard him make a joke. Old Reid liked him though, but then Reid always admired a man for his guts first. Anything else came a poor second. Well, there it is. That's my theory. Who else is thirsty?'

No one was. The theory was peculiarly unacceptable. An hour later when the bar had been closed for some time Major Mackay was lifted off his stool by three servants and carried through to the room he occupied, undressed and tucked into bed. He smiled in his sleep. With that, the troubles could be said to have come to a happy end.

Barbie got up from the rush mat, buttoned the high-necked nightgown and shivered. It was cold enough now to have the electric fire on in the bedroom but she had begun to explore the by-ways of self-mortification and had asked Aziz not to switch it on as he did Mabel's an hour before bedtime. She climbed chilled into bed, turned the lamp off and lay for a while blowing dandelion clocks, each one as useless as the last. The grey-white tufts wafted away almost before her breath reached them, leaving her to hold a limp sappy stalk. And tonight the alternative, smelling roses, didn't work either. They were of a scentless variety and on the turn, bulbous seedboxes with a few overblown petals so precariously attached she hardly dared to touch them. She counted sheep but they were stubborn and the gate too high.

She counted children. They submitted to her calculations with expressions of ill-concealed dislike of such regimentation. She called the roll and crossed names out with a blue crayon. When all the names were crossed out one child remained uncalled: the little Indian girl to whom the blue crayon had belonged. She could not remember the little girl's name. The little girl couldn't remember it either and accused her silently of depriving her both of name and crayon. The little girl would not go away until her name was called. It was an impasse. We are stuck with each other, Barbie said, which is absurd because you have Krishna and I have Jesus. We are separately catered for. Let's shake hands and call it a day. But the little girl had her hands behind her back and kept them there.

Hold it higher, her mother said, so she held the porcupine higher and counted pins going into the place where the neck and shoulders had to be altered. Altared. Her mother was sticking the pins in too deep. Little beads of blood appeared like drops of red sweat on the white satin. The bride continued to smile like the Spartan boy with the stolen fox under his shirt. Observe, her mother said, the advantages of a strict upbringing in a family of rank.

Her father was singing one of his funny songs. I've seen a deal of gaiety throughout my noisy life. Barbie sang it to her mother. Stop that vulgarity, her mother said. So she sang alone under her breath but found she had forgotten everything except the first line. The stairs were always dark and smelt of damp and gas jets and old linoleum. The paper on the walls was brown and patchy. She sang the first line of the vulgar song over and over going up the stairs but still under her breath because the stairs frightened her. She counted the stairs but there had only ever been twenty of them including the landing floor. Twenty stairs were not enough to send her to sleep.

She switched on the lamp. Slowly she was in India again and as she returned to India she became homesick, ridiculously, unaccountably, inexpressibly homesick. The old chaukidar would be asleep on the front porch huddled in his blanket like a tired shepherd. She felt disturbed and then, hearing the weird calling of the jackal packs, lost in an immense area of experience, the whole area that separated her from childhood and young womanhood. She thought of it as an area because the separation seemed to be in space, not in time.

She sat up wrapped in her own arms. The light from the bedside lamp did not reach the farther walls but the glass that protected the picture gleamed faintly. Behind the glass there was nothing. The picture had gone out.

She thought: I have gone out, Thou hast gone out, He she or it has gone out.

She reached for Emerson who had not gone out but had been renewed and renewed to Mrs Stewart's perplexity.

'Each new law and political movement has meaning for you,' Barbie read and was convinced that this might be so because Emerson told her. 'Stand before each of its tablets and say, "Here is one of my coverings. Under this fantastic, or odious, or grace-ful mask did my Proteus nature hide itself." This remedies the defect of our too great nearness to ourselves.'

She put Emerson aside and picked up her pocket dictionary.

Proteus. Changing or inconstant person or thing. Amoeba. Kinds of bacteria. She laid aside the dictionary and recovered Emerson from the bed-cover. She had lost the place but with Emerson that never seemed to matter.

'The world exists for the education of each man. There is no age or state of society, or mode of action in history, to which there is not somewhat corresponding in his life. Everything tends in a most wonderful manner to abbreviate itself and yield its own virtue to him. He should see that he can live all history in his own person. He must sit at home with might and main, and not suffer himself to be bullied by kings or empires, but know that he is greater than all the geography and all the governments of the world . . .'

Suddenly she was aware of the intense stillness of Rose Cottage. Intense stillness and a faint odour as of something singed. She put Emerson away, got out of bed, put on her slippers and her long blue dressing-gown. She wondered whether Mabel had remembered to turn her fire off, whether something was in danger of scorching or bursting into flames.

She left her door open so that she could see her way across the hall. There was a slit of light under Mabel's door. She hesitated. The smell had gone. She went to the door and tapped very gently. She got no answer. She tapped again and said, Mabel. She would have gone back to bed because she realized how silly it was to expect a deaf person to hear and she did not want to open the door and frighten her. But potential alarm was exerting its hollow fascination. She opened Mabel's door until she had a gap wide enough to admit her head and one shoulder.

Mabel was asleep propped on the pillows. The light was still on. Mabel's head had fallen to one side and her reading glasses were low down on her nose and looked as if they might come adrift and get broken and cause damage to her eyes and face. A book was open on her lap. The hand that had held it lay inert.

The fire was off. Barbie went to the bedside. She took the book away, placed it on the table with its tasselled marker between the pages at which it had been open. Next, she very carefully removed the dangerous spectacles, returned them to the leather case. She settled the pillows, drew the sheet and blankets farther up. She wanted to cover Mabel's hands but decided not to in case she woke her up. She seemed to have disturbed her slightly as it was. A sigh came. And then a sound in the back of the throat almost like something being said.

Barbie looked down at her friend. Very briefly she had a ridiculous idea that she didn't like her. At the same time she knew that she loved her. And she knew that Mabel was fond of her in spite of not appearing to be fond of anyone much. It was a curious relationship, like one between two people who hadn't yet met but who would love each other when they did. Mabel had come closer to meeting her than she had come to meeting Mabel. After three years Barbie still knew almost nothing about her friend but even if one discounted facts not taken in because of deafness Mabel must now know almost everything about Barbie because Barbie had told her over and over. Telling Mabel things was part of the job of looking after her, almost more important than doing things to absolve her from household cares and responsibilities. Without the actuality of Barbie's voice incessantly saying things Barbie thought that Mabel would not have appreciated so much the silence in which she seemed to exist. The only thing Barbie had never told her about was her secret sorrow. When she looked at Mabel as she was doing now she believed Mabel knew about it anyway and had known from the beginning.

She thought: In a way my secret sorrow is Mabel. I don't know how much of me gets through. I'm rather like a wave dashing against a rock, the sounds I make are just like that. There is Mabel, there is the rock, there is God. They are the same to all intents and purposes.

Mabel stirred but did not wake. How old she looked in bed, immensely old. Barbie put out her hand to switch off the lamp. The old woman made that noise in her throat again as if disturbed by the shadow of Barbie's arm. She made it again. She was muttering but the sound came from her throat because her lips were too far gone in the drug of each day's little death to come together properly. She muttered for several seconds then paused and then said something which caused Barbie to stand alert and undecided with her finger and thumb on the little ebony key-switch of the old-fashioned brass table lamp, willing the echo of the sound to pause too before continuing on its flight into a state of being beyond recall. She caught the rhythm back first and then the vowel sounds, then the consonants. A name, a woman's name, Gillian Waller.

She watched Mabel's face but could not tell anything from it. There was no more muttering. Mabel had reached wherever she had been going. Beyond Gillian Waller she had found the dark of dreamless sleep.

TRAGIC DEATH OF ENGLISH MISSIONARY

Ranpur, October 29th, 1942

The death is reported in Mayapore two days ago of Miss Edwina Crane, superintendent of the district's Protestant Mission Schools who was roughly handled by a mob during the August riots and narrowly escaped with her life when another teacher, Mr D. R. Chaudhuri, was murdered. Police have so far been unable to apprehend their attackers.

At an inquest held yesterday in Mayapore a statement obtained from Miss Crane's servant was submitted by the police. According to this man his mistress sent him to the bazaar at 3.45 p.m. to collect a package from the chemist. Since her return from hospital he had frequently gone on such errands. On this occasion however the chemist said he knew nothing of a prescription for Miss Crane. The servant then returned home.

Reaching there he smelt burning and saw smoke. A shed in the compound was a mass of flames and servants from neighbouring houses were attempting to extinguish it. One of these men called out that Miss Crane was in the shed.

The police submitted a statement from this other man. Shortly before 4 p.m. he had seen a woman in a white saree in the compound of the mission superintendent's bungalow. Thinking it was someone who had no business there he challenged her. She motioned him to go away. He observed that the woman in the white saree was Miss Crane. Neither he nor her own servant had ever seen her adopt this mode of dress. He watched her go into the shed and then returned to his work. Shortly afterwards he smelt smoke and noticed that the shed was on fire.

The police also submitted a note found in Miss Crane's study addressed to the Coroner. An official in Miss Crane's Mission confirmed that it was in her handwriting. The note which was not read out at the inquest was accepted by the police as satisfactory evidence of Miss Crane's determination to take her own life.

Dr Jayaprakash, consultant physician at the Begum Mumtez

Zaidkhan Purdah Hospital and health officer to the mission schools stated that he had attended Miss Crane for some years. Normally in excellent health she had not regained it since the attack on her in August. After her discharge from hospital he prescribed tonics and advised her to take a holiday. On his last visit about a week before her tragic death she told him she had decided to retire from the mission.

A verdict of suicide while the balance of the mind was disturbed was recorded.

A touching note was struck when Miss Crane's servant who seemed to confuse the proceedings with a legal case asked whether 'Madam was to be released and restored to him'. A colleague of the late Miss Crane at the Mission who led the weeping man from court told your reporter that this man, Joseph, had served Miss Crane since he was a kitchen boy at the mission in Muzzafirabad (NWFP) where Miss Crane taught before the Great War. 'She was a heroine to him. She stood alone at the door of the school guarding the children and faced up to a gang of armed hooligans who threatened to burn the school down.'

The funeral took place later in the day. Waiting outside the cemetery were groups of Indian women, mothers of some of the children who attend the mission schools. After the funeral rites were over your reporter noted that these women entered the cemetery and placed flowers on the grave.

She went into the bathroom and locked the door and the other door that led to the verandah and the door that led into the little spare. She got down on her knees on the cold floor and clasped her hands on the rim of the smooth white porcelain hand-basin, then groped for her damp flannel and stuffed it into her mouth so as not to disturb the house. She reached up and turned the tap on full. The water spashed into the bowl, down the pipe and out into the open runnel that carried it away. She sank lower until her body was almost touching her thighs and let herself sob aloud.

Edwina had sinned. But that was not why Barbie wept. The question of what would happen to Edwina's soul was beyond her power to calculate. It would be settled in limbo which to Barbie was a bleak and incomprehensible but real place chilled by God's breath and darkened by the Devil's brow; barren neutral territory where the dead waited, trembling and naked, incapable of further action to support a claim to either kingdom. To kill oneself was wicked. Her father had killed himself with drink walking with a skinful under the hooves and wheels of a horse-drawn carriage on the Thames Embankment. Her widowed mother had killed herself not with work as people said but with a combination of heartless love and heartless pride better known as keeping up appearances. Their deaths were small sins in comparison with Edwina's terrible act of self-destruction but in their private little despairs of which the drinking and the pride had been evidence she had long since learned to see a glimmer of the devil's face; thoughtful, chin in hand, offering recompense, suggesting anodynes that were not that at all but addictive means of excitation of the ill he did.

Barbie's Devil was not a demon but a fallen angel and his Hell no place of fire and brimstone but an image of lost heaven. There was no soul lonelier than he. His passion for souls was as great as God's but all he had to offer was his own despair. He offered it as boundlessly as God offered love. He *was* despair as surely as God was love.

And that was why she wept. Blinded by her tears, still kneel-ing, she reached out, entering that moment that should have brought her to the centre of the sublime mystery but did not because there was no mystery. She was an old woman like Edwina and the dead body was the one Edwina guarded – her life in India come to nothing.

She wept because the gesture that had seemed sublime revealed an Edwina who was dumb with despair not purified by love. Revelation of Edwina's despair uncovered her own, showed its depth, its immensity. For herself she could have borne the knowledge, would have to bear it. For Edwina it must have been a cruel thing. Edwina had always seemed so strong and sure in God, in God's purpose, so richly endowed that just to be near her was to share her gift and feel one's doubts turn sour for want of nourishment.

And yet Edwina must have felt it too, the ever-increasing tenuousness of the connection, the separation in space as God inexplicably turned His face from humble service He no longer found acceptable but was too kind actually to refuse.

She rose painfully from her knees and soaked the flannel under the running tap, carried it sopping to her face and repeated the process until her face was chilled and only her eyeballs felt hot. Edwina's faith had been of a higher order than her own, she had no doubt, and as a consequence her despair had been great enough to disturb the balance of her mind. But the disturbance could not be offered in mitigation because it was, itself, the work of the Devil. She looked in the mirror that hung above the basin. On the opposite wall there was another mirror. She was multiplied back and front. Frontwards she was Barbie, approaching herself, and backwards another self retreating through one diminishing image after another into some kind of shocking infinity.

She felt her skin freeze and harden as warmth went out of her blood. The bathroom was suddenly rank with the nausea, fetid and foul, but there was in its foulness a sense of exquisite patience and desire. She clutched her abdomen and her throat, leant over the bowl and was sick. She retched and gasped. The tap was still on and the running water carried the horror away. Now she supported herself gripping the porcelain basin. She let the water run until the whiteness sparkled again. Her whole body felt clammy. Slowly its warmth returned.

She rinsed her mouth over and over and then turned the tap off. When the last gurgle had died away there was a silence such as might follow a sigh.

'Poor creature,' she said. She shut her eyes. 'I know who you are and I know you are still here. Please go.'

She waited, then caught her breath at the sound of a slow ungainly winged departure as of a heavy carrion bird that had difficulty in overcoming the pull of gravity. She waited for a few minutes and then fastidiously washed her face and hands, but – still dissatisfied – unlocked the door to her bedroom, collected clean clothes, returned and dropped each discarded article into the dhobi basket until she stood naked. Redressed and cologned she went back to her room and tidied her hair.

Beauty is in the eye of the beholder, her mother had said but she had not said who might behold.

PART TWO

A QUESTION OF LOYALTY

Notices in the Times of India, *May 1943*

Births

MANNERS. On May 7th at Srinagar. To Daphne, a daughter, Parvati.

Deaths

MANNERS. On May 7th, at Srinagar, Daphne, daughter of the late Mr & Mrs George Manners, beloved niece of Ethel and the late Sir Henry Manners.

Forthcoming Marriages

CAPTAIN E. A. D. BINGHAM and MISS SUSAN LAYTON
The engagement is announced between Captain Edward Arthur David Bingham, Muzzafirabad Guides, only son of the late Major A. E. D. Bingham, MC (Muzzafirabad Guides) and of the late Mrs S. A. Hunter, of Singapore, and Susan, younger daughter of Lieut.-Colonel and Mrs John Layton, of Pankot.

I

THUS TEDDIE enters already marked by a fatal connexion.

Sarah Layton, subsequently describing him as a man who didn't grow on you, as one you soon got to the end of, initially gave a lone but vivid impression of vacuity, albeit cheerful vacuity. At the time, his future mother-in-law, Mildred, complained that there wasn't much to go on and although she was thinking in severely practical terms (what to tell Colonel Layton, now transferred from an Italian to a German prison-camp, which made it seem more imperative to make an efficient and detailed report about the man his daughter Susan intended to marry), the idea of not much to go on coupled with that of his not growing on you at first led one inescapably to think of him as a person who conformed in every way with the stock idea one might

have of a young man with nothing between his ears, a set of
trained and drained responses and a cheerful complacency that
would see to it he did nothing outstandingly silly and nothing
distinguished either.

How close he came to being jolted out of complacency in the
first few months of 1942 in Burma was possibly indicated by his
demeanour when he turned up in Pankot a year later, on Dick
Rankin's staff, 'rather disappointed' with the immediate result
of his attendance at the Staff College in Quetta but 'hoping for
something better' in the future. Presumably he had been rather
disappointed too to discover that the Japanese had proved 'more
useful in a scrap' than the British and Indian armies together
and, as he trudged through the jungle back to India with the
remnants of his unit (because that was the direction everyone was
going in who still could) hoped for an improvement presently.

One could picture him marching out, tired, dirty and hungry,
carrying more than his quota of small-arms (to relieve a couple
of exhausted sepoys of their weight), keeping *on* and smiling
because being personally blameless for what he supposed had to
be summed up as a stunning defeat, a complete disaster, there
was no call to look miserable and every reason to give an example
of how to keep going, even when every limb was attached to
the trunk by things that felt like loose hot rubber bands.

Between this picture of Teddie leaving Burma and the one of
him arrived in Pankot a year later there is a gap, but it is one
of many and it plays a perfectly proper schematic part in an
account of him because to Teddie himself his whole history
seems to have been a series of gaps linked by a few notable events
if one is to judge by the extraordinary difficulty Mildred had
in getting anything out of him except a few bare and not very
encouraging bits of information and a slight frown of concentration, which could have been the effect had on him of his
realization that between them he and Mildred had a duty to do.

'I do have an uncle,' he said, and added, 'In Shropshire actually,' as if this made the uncle more lively and identifiable. Teddie
had lived with the uncle when sent home from India to school,
just as Sarah and Susan had lived with their Aunt Lydia, Mildred's
elder London-based sister. Teddie's father had been in the
Muzzafirabad Guides which was why Teddie was in them now
but had broken his neck hunting when Teddie was fourteen. His

mother married again, a commercial chap called Hunter (which was odd when you thought of the cause of the first husband's death). They lived in Singapore until Hunter died. 'I don't mind telling you,' Teddie told Mildred, 'people said she had a rotten time with him.' She died suddenly in Mandalay on her way back to Muzzafirabad. All this was before Teddie came back to India himself to join the regiment. In due course he went to Burma, tried but failed to find her grave and worried a bit about it until he remembered she'd been cremated. In due course the Japanese arrived in Burma too and presently Teddie marched out.

And that was about it. He had red hair and sandy eyelashes (which Clara Fosdick said she thought a sign of untrustworthiness). He was twenty-five but had that elongated bony English look of not yet having completed the process of growing-up and filling out which meant that in a few years he would suddenly appear middle-aged as well as beefy because to men like this everything seemed to happen at once round about the age of thirty; everything except white hair which was reserved for retirement and was equally sudden and the only sign that old age had arrived.

School, military academy, regiment, baptism of fire, staff-college: the next logical step was marriage so that the process could be repeated through a continuing male line. Arrived in Pankot Teddie metaphorically cleared his throat, put up his head and looked round for a girl with whom to take it. It could not be any girl. The choice had ideally to be made among girls in the range labelled Army which more or less knocked out Carol and Christine Beames whose father Colonel Beames was in the civil branch of the IMS. It knocked out several others whose fathers' regiments did not in Teddie's opinion match the standard set by his own, the Muzzys, to which none of course was superior but with which one or two might claim equality. This opinion was one Teddie's father had held and Teddie had acquired it in much the same way that he had acquired a bit of private property in the shape of an unearned income, although the capital from which the income came had been filtered to him through his mother and therefore been diminished somewhat by the commercial chap Hunter, who fortunately died of drink before his mother died of what Teddie always assumed had been shame and sorrow, otherwise he might never have seen a penny of it and have been forced either to go into some sort of business or join an inferior regiment, which would have been pretty awful he supposed. He doubted that his uncle would have 'stumped up'. He believed that his uncle hadn't liked his father. His uncle had been the elder brother.

'I suppose you'll get money from your uncle eventually,' Mildred said. She believed in coming to the point and came to it stylishly, using her languid but abrasive first-two-drinks-of-the-day voice.

'Oh, I shouldn't rely on it,' Teddie said. 'He's a bit of an old skinflint. I'm not looking beyond the six hundred a year. And my pay of course.'

'Well it will be years before Susan gets anything from us,' Mildred warned him. 'So you'll just have to buckle to and rise to dizzy heights.'

'Yes. Rather.'

'Have you a photo or a snap?'

'What of?'

'Of you. So that I can send it to John in prison-camp. I think he'll want to know what you look like, don't you?'

'I'll get one done, shall I?'

'That would help.'

'Full length or head and shoulders?'

Teddie had a practical turn of mind. It made up for his lack of imagination. He would never have thought to offer Mrs Layton his photograph but knowing that she wanted one and suddenly understanding why he saw that it was important to get it right. In uniform or mufti? Postcard size for easy handling or something larger? With or without his cap? Since he seemed to have no personal vanity the questions had to be taken seriously. He couldn't be palmed off with a casual reply such as, 'Oh anything so long as it looks like you.'

He had the kind of thick skin which managed to fall just short of suggesting insensitivity. Mildred became bored with the photograph long before the details were agreed. Teddie did not notice she was bored or that she drank too much. Perhaps he did not really notice people. There were times when he did not seem to notice himself. For instance he didn't appear to be at all put out by what another man might have thought of as the delicacy or awkwardness of his position in a household where he constantly bumped into Sarah. Before he took up with Susan he had taken up with Sarah and shown every sign of not being aware of the younger sister's existence. His attentiveness to Sarah now suggested he might at any moment explain why he'd cooled off her in spite of the fact that Sarah had not encouraged him sufficiently to make his cooling off actually require an explanation. His attentiveness would have struck an outsider who knew nothing of their history as the kind a man felt he had to show the girl whose sister he was about to marry; anything apologetic in it being an apology for taking Susan away not for giving Sarah up. Perhaps that how he saw it too.

There were several explanations given in Pankot, though, of his defection, change of mind or change of heart. Had he known about one of them he might have been surprised (at last) because it is unlikely that 'fickle' was a word he would ever expect to hear used to describe him. Had he known about the other two explanations he would have agreed with the first of them, that he had finally been unable to avoid seeing how pretty Susan was and unable to resist the strong emotion with which the sight suddenly affected him. The other explanation he would probably not have understood at all and he certainly would not have cared to hear it.

Little Mrs Smalley had described Sarah Layton in terms which were sufficiently accurate for the inaccurate conclusions she then drew from them in regard to Teddie's defection to be accepted as coming close to the mark. But Teddie would have made nothing of the Smalley image of Sarah. He surely never felt that she didn't take him seriously as a person; never felt that she took none of 'it' seriously ('it' meaning India, the British role in India, the thing the British were in India to do); never felt that she laughed at 'it' and consequently at him; never felt, being a man and therefore much more serious about 'it' than a woman had to be, that Sarah was the kind of girl who although admirable in every other way lacked the attitude which men thought it important for a girl to have underneath everything else and that this explained why after a bit men felt more comfortable in the company of the younger sister. He might have agreed with Mrs Paynton when she gathered all these potentially damaging Smalley threads into a single sensible one and declared that what Sarah needed was to settle down and that she would be all right then, being fundamentally sound and a veritable rock so far as Mildred was concerned.

Getting Sarah to settle down as Mrs Bingham was exactly what Teddie had first hoped for. For him the question of her sound-ness never arose. Seeing her come into his office at Area Head-quarters with some confidential files he had asked his friend and fellow-Muzzy, Tony Bishop, Dick Rankin's ADC, who the WAC(I) corporal with the fair hair and slim figure was. The answer was tremendously satisfactory to him one assumes. Failing a Muzzy Guide girl a Pankot Rifles girl would do very well, in fact rather better because Teddie probably thought that there was something vaguely incestuous about marrying into one's own regiment. His father had done it and it really hadn't turned out at all well. If fate had at first disappointed Teddie, bringing him to a static headquarters as a mere captain when it might just as easily have sent him to an active formation perhaps as a G2, it now looked as if in bringing him to Pankot it had done so with the sole and excellent purpose of introducing him to this girl from the station's favourite regiment.

Chasing or wooing would be the wrong words to use about Teddie's activity in regard to Sarah Layton. He applied himself to her as he applied himself to any task that fell within the area of his competence. But because he was unable to think of more than one thing at a time he appeared to everybody to have mounted a frontal attack on a girl who had caught his eye and awoken feelings in him of a tender and passionate nature.

This was the light in which if he gave it any thought he must have appeared to himself and he must have given it thought, and found nothing amiss. After all chaps fell in love every day. There was nothing peculiar about it. And she was awfully nice. His father would have approved.

The most interesting gaps, perhaps, in Teddie's history are those through which one could have traced the progress or lack of it of his relationship with women. At twenty-five one assumes some heterosexual experience, but the questions – with whom? in what circumstances? – are impenetrable enough to leave about him a pure aroma of cheerful male virginity tainted only by traces of something more pungent, the odour of voluntary or involun-tary nocturnal emission, which does not alter his expression but does emphasize the underlying shadows of modest perplexity.

Tony Bishop had no recollection of Teddie ever having been 'mixed up' with a girl before he applied himself so wholeheartedly to the business of being mixed up with Sarah Layton. Bishop knew him before Burma and after Burma but not during Burma, so his recollections did not cover a possibly important phase of Teddie's development. He had the unit-image of him rather than a private one. The Muzzy Guides (so Bishop said, fondly mocking) was one of those regiments which not only had a rule about never mentioning women in the mess but stuck to it with such iron resolution that an outsider could have been persuaded to believe that its young subalterns not only stopped mentioning them but stopped thinking about them too until a certain age was reached and they came face to face with a situation that called for a tricky decision: whether to remain a bachelor or get married. This question was usually settled by another of the regiment's unwritten rules which was that an officer had to have a wife before he was thirty unless he wished to enjoy a reputation for unseemly frivolity.

Since Teddie was deeply attached to his regiment – it was the one thing he may be thought of as taking seriously – the regimental aura of ambiguous monasticism probably explained Teddie's own aura of either never having sown wild oats or of having sown them so far out of range of the regimental eye that they didn't count as his but as those of someone whose body he had borrowed for the purpose. Whatever the reason for this aura, it shone behind his approach to Sarah which was that of a man whose physical appetite had never bothered him before but promised to be really rather adequate, as if it knew all about itself.

What it finally came to was that Teddie was in pursuit of an idea. The idea was initially embodied in the person of Sarah Layton. After three weeks he was close enough to her to feel that all he need do next was pop the question and settle the matter. He had, one imagines, few doubts about the outcome. She had been awfully amenable and absolutely available. He hadn't kissed her yet but he had held on to her hand and made other gestures claiming physical possession. They had played tennis, gone riding, swimming, dancing, to the pictures, the Chinese restaurant and Smith's Hotel for supper. He had called for her at the Club, at the grace and favour bungalow and once at Rose Cottage where an elderly woman (something to do with missions) had talked rather a lot about Muzzafirabad but not about those aspects of its life which he knew. Sarah and he had walked together, shared tongas, and the front bench of a staff car when he had been able to log it out as on official duties and get rid of the driver.

The next step was therefore clear. He must arrange for them to be alone so that he could put an arm round her, kiss her and say something like You know I'm most awfully Fond of You? which sounded a bit dull but was certainly the truth and once he had said it he could logically follow it up by suggesting they might Sort of Get Engaged If She Felt Like It; which was as far as one needed to go because once one had gone that far everything else surely fell into place of its own accord.

At first (Sarah says) she thought Teddie Bingham no different from other young officers who assumed that because she was there and they were there something should be done about it. But after a while she realized he was different. He had been wound up and wouldn't stop and she wasn't sure what she could do about it except hope that he suddenly ran down or noticed Susan as so many other officers had. She did not find him unattractive but this was somehow proof of what she thought of as his negative transparent quality; he was not unamusing, not unpleasant to talk to and not uninteresting up to a point which was soon reached.

When the moment came she knew instinctively that it had and was in as great a state of uncertainty as ever about how to deal with it. He encircled her and kissed her and became rather elaborately excited. She noticed that he smelt of Pears' soap. This heightened her impression of him as being transparent because suddenly he was not, having worked himself into a lather. His excitement was a bit embarrassing because he failed utterly to move her to any kind of response and she wondered whether this was his fault or hers. She had very little fear of Teddie attempting anything more serious. Apart from his lips which were glued to hers he was not actually doing anything to any part of her with any part of him which he could not have done in a ballroom or would be ashamed of in the morning.

She thought, too, that his excitement was caused less by the effect kissing her had on him than by the feeling he had of breaking out, to the degree that was allowable, from the strict confines of his normal pattern of behaviour. But a man like Teddie didn't kiss a girl as he was kissing her just for the hell of it. At any moment, she thought, he would make a declaration. She considered this imminent event as calmly as she could. She had no intention of accepting a declaration from Teddie Bingham but for an instant she understood the awful ease with which the whole business could gather momentum and overwhelm them both. If she had not been cursed with a mind that questioned everything she could at this very moment have been within an inch or two of becoming the future Mrs Bingham because she couldn't think of a single practical reason why things should not take this course, providing one discounted the question of whether they loved one another, which wasn't a question anyone seemed to take very seriously.

In any case Teddie on the face of it was doing well enough on that score for the two of them. Or had been doing well. But Sarah realized she was bored and had been bored ever since he began and suddenly she felt that he was bored too. She would have understood his becoming depressed or cross at finding his amorousness was not infectious but she had a distinct impression of his boredom. He kept the kiss going but it had taken on a remote and pointless quality, like a breath-holding contest, which it was to some extent. She had a stubborn inclination not to be the first to give in.

Just as she decided she couldn't go on he came unstuck and breathed deeply. They stared at each other in the dark of the motor-car. Surprisingly it was a serious, even tender, moment and she was afraid that in spite of everything he would make his declaration; but he didn't. For Sarah it was as if they had both drawn back in the nick of time from being involved in an association neither of them wanted but which Teddie had thought they ought to want.

Presently he resumed a proper sitting position behind the steering-wheel, looked at his luminous watch and said, 'I say, I think we ought to be getting back.'

Two days later he turned up at the grace and favour at a time when she wasn't there but Susan was. And that was that. He was still wound up, still working. She thought he would run down and disappear like Susan's other young men whose numbers remained more or less the same while their names and faces altered. But within a month he was engaged to Susan to be married. It was this that so surprised Sarah. One day he had been just one of the crowd round her sister; the next he was the only one. Susan seemed to have put out her hand and picked out the toy she decided she liked best. Sarah had a picture of Teddie held upside down with his wheels racing and the spring whirring, his eyes closed in the ecstasy of being singled out and taken to Susan's heart for ever.

But in real life Teddie was upright, on his feet, and his eyes open, alight with the pleasure if not the pain of being in love – or what passed for it in his opinion; and his opinion was the only one that could matter to him and was in this sense as good as anyone else's. Allow him that happiness, and the illusion that it sprang from Susan and not from an idea. The moment in the car with Sarah could possibly have been a turning point but the effort of making it would have been tremendous, virtually impossible. It would have involved treachery to his upbringing, a complete rearrangement of the ego, a thorough breaking-out, an entry into an unknown and rather frightening world. Besides it is better to accept the explanation that lies nearest and easiest to hand: that Sarah's lack of interest eventually got through to him as a failure of physical response, as a personal rebuff, not as a general pointer to the boring artificiality of the situation that could have prodded him alive to the fact that to date his life had been one protracted grinding experience of boredom after another because he never did anything, never would do anything, except according to the rules laid down for what a man of his class and calling should do and for how and why he should do it.

There was of course that little gap (characteristic) between getting Sarah home and turning up a couple of days later to take up with Susan. Perhaps the gap in this case represented a dark night of Teddie's soul (a whiff of that pungent odour?), a battle between a disturbing new instinct, only half felt, and an old safe and happy one which was familiar and reliable and inevitably the victor. In that case the spoils were Teddie, not Susan.

'I'd rather they waited,' Mildred told Sarah. It was apparent that she had in mind a long period; waiting until Colonel Layton was restored to them, in other words until the end of the war. But Susan would not wait. Neither would Teddie. Together they seemed to recognize a sense of urgency as if they wanted to abide by the rules while the rules were still there to abide by. The announcement of their engagement appeared on the same day as those other two announcements which advertised the fact that one of the rules had already been broken. It was the first coincidence and perhaps it was significant. This was in the second week of May. Mildred agreed to put the notice in *The Times* because Susan insisted and Mildred saw no harm in putting in what could easily be taken out by a second announcement of the cancellation she expected at any moment – for instance when Teddie produced the photograph and Susan looked at it and imagined herself left with that and nothing else after Teddie had gone back to the war as he was bound to eventually.

But the photograph turned out surprisingly well. Teddie's smile was rendered down to a quirky upward twitch of one corner of the lips which gave the lower part of his face a look of even-tempered manly resolution. The stilted professional studio lighting had for once worked on a fortuitously inspired level and produced a sort of subdued halo that was reflected again by a dreamy look in the eyes, so that his face was amazingly that of the soldier-poet, the man of action capable of making sensitive judgments. When Susan saw it she at once demanded a cabinet-sized copy and had it framed for her bedside table. Towards the end of May, publicly acknowledging that there was not another thing she could do to delay matters, Mildred announced that the wedding would be shortly after Susan's 21st birthday, which fell in November. It was the most she could do to relate the affair to circumstances beyond her control. She wrote to her sister Fenny in Delhi who came up at once to inspect Teddie. Aunt Fenny thought him 'rather sweet'. Apart from Susan she was the first person, perhaps, to see anything below the surface.

II

Before making the necessary imaginative readjustment to see most of the rest of the short life of Edward Arthur David Bingham almost entirely from Teddie's point of view one minor and possibly irrelevant aspect of his behaviour is to be noted. His experience of combat conditions had coarsened his vocabulary.

In certain circumstances in male company he nowadays permitted himself to use words he had seldom found it necessary to use before going with the first battalion to Burma. The standard of vulgarity he reached never rose above that acceptable in an officer of his type and standing and he would never have dreamed of swearing in the mess let alone in front of women. The Muzzys had been as strict about bad language in the mess as about references to the weaker sex, if anything stricter. Damn was allowed, in fact it did not count, but bloody was frowned upon if used by anyone below senior field-rank. Teddie therefore found the conversation in the junior officers' mess at area headquarters alarmingly and disagreeably lax. He was quite shocked. Regular officers from good regiments could still be relied on to do as Teddie did – reserve bad language for private or office occasions – but this mess was full of curious unmilitary fellows with emergency commissions and civilian habits. Fortunately as he thought it he seldom had to eat there. He and Tony Bishop together with an officer of the engineers and a gunner lived in a chummery a few bungalows down the road from Nicky Paynton and Clara Fosdick. In the chummery mess he maintained formality of manner and speech and once rebuked the gunner for the terms in which he expressed an opinion about the origin of the woodcock toast.

But in private, the bedroom he shared with Tony Bishop and in the daftar, Teddie's otherwise predictable statements and responses were enlivened by certain rich images and expletives often enough for Bishop to have marked them down as something new in Teddie dating from the Burma experience, indicative of the kind of wildness even a cheerful and level-tempered fellow like Bingham would have found bubbling up in him when (as he now described it) the shit hit the fan and he had to duck.

Bishop went so far as to see two Teddie Binghams: the one who stood upright encased in the armour of the mystery of being a Muzzy Guide and the one who in moments of office crisis stepped out of the armour's support with no warning whatsoever and emphatically but unvehemently announced his opinion that the situation was balls-aching, only just short of a fuck-up, and that he had no intention of being buggered about.

*

The signal ordering him to a place called Mirat to take up a G3(O) appointment at the headquarters of a new Indian division had originally been sent to Muzzafirabad. The delay and confusion caused by this administrative error led to a further signal, peremptory in tone, which managed to give the impression that Teddie was to be blamed for not being where he was not and must make up for it by leaving for Mirat immediately.

This second signal which was the first Teddie knew of his default was brought round to the chummery by special messenger on an evening in the middle of July*. There was a thunderstorm in progress which lent the occasion an apt touch of flashy drama. Teddie was lowering his long ribby body into the tin tub in the ghusl-khana. It was 6.15. He had had a hard day at the office. He was due at the grace and favour at 7.30 to take Susan to the Electric Cinema and had just bitten his bearer's head off because the dhobi-wallah had failed to turn up with his second suit of khaki-drill. Allah Din had gone grumbling into the storm. Meanwhile the bhishti had heated the bathwater above the degree Teddie enjoyed, had left no tin of cold and was presently nowhere to be found.

As Teddie's buttocks made contact with the steaming water his thighs came out in goosepimples to compensate. His knees smelt of leather, which reminded him of when he was a boy having a hot bath after a game of football. He completed his submersion and breathed out slowly. He reached for the Lifebuoy soap (Pears' was for face and hands) and just then Tony Bishop walked in with the fatal signal and the messenger's pad for Teddie to sign.

Teddie had one sterling military quality. He never panicked. The word immediate had no galvanizing effect on his intellectual machinery. Immediate meant as soon as possible because nothing could be sooner than that. In the past year he had become aware that there were people in positions of authority who pretended otherwise. They put texts up on their office-walls and issued directives advocating the strangest beliefs: for instance that what was difficult could be done at once whereas the impossible might take a little longer.

Teddie thought this showy and undeserving of serious consideration. He was inclined to blame the Americans, who mistook

*1943.

activity for efficiency, and those civilian elements in the wartime army who were naturally anxious to get it over and done with and go back into commerce where they belonged. Between them the Americans and the civilians were trying to dictate the pace of army operations and run them like a business. And they were being encouraged in this by the careerists and odd-men-out in the regular army who saw the war as an opportunity to promote themselves and their eccentric ideas.

Teddie distrusted anything to which the word flamboyant could be applied. On the other hand he admired what his Shrop-shire uncle called style. Not knowing quite what style was he sometimes had difficulty in distinguishing it from flamboyance and thought his uncle must have been right when he said style was on the wane and went unnoticed in an age in which vulgarity was admired more often than it was deserted. Teddie took pride in having some style himself. At the moment it meant sitting on in his bath for at least five minutes after Bishop had opened and read the signal, after he had dried his hands to read it himself, sworn, signed the book and sent Bishop away.

Quite unfairly behaviour like this gave rise to an idea that Teddie was a bit slow-witted. His confidential report at Quetta, while paying tribute to his cheerfulness and capacity for work, had mentioned lack of 'verve'. The phrase had caused him no lasting pang.

Actually Teddie grasped all the implications of the posting at once. Where the slowness came in was in the method that came most naturally to him of considering them one at a time in a roughly ascending order of priority; for example: where exactly was Mirat? How long would the journey take? Should he take his own orderly with him? Did he really want to in view of the fact that the fellow couldn't organize his laundry? Who was the divisional commander? Had he heard anything at the daftar about this particular formation? Would he be able to get leave in August to join Susan and her family on the late holiday they were planning to take in Srinagar? Would he be able to get leave later in the year to come back to Pankot for the wedding? Would Susan kick up a fuss about changing the arrangements if a change was necessary? Since the posting did not bring him any promo-tion would it be worthwhile having a word with General Rankin to see if it could be cancelled? Did he want it cancelled? Was it fair to marry a girl when it looked as if he was in for another dose of active service? He had thought of that before but had she? Should he ask her whether she would like to be released from their engagement?

The prospect of her saying she would suddenly looked very likely to him because it would bring his world in ruins about his head; and there on that July evening in the tin tub Teddie – one may fancy – could not rid himself of the idea that he might be turning out to be the sort of man around whom things collapsed, not noisily but with a sort of slithering, inexorable, folding-in and -over movement. He scrubbed his back vigorously to kill this notion but stopped when he found that in getting rid of it he had got hold of another. The friction of the bristles was making him feel randy. This feeling was persistent. It continued after he had put the brush down. It had in fact been pretty persistent on and off for some time, ever since he had set his heart on getting married.

Teddie was a firm believer in cold water. He yelled for the absent bhishti. Unexpectedly the old boy staggered in with two full cans. Teddie camouflaged himself with a sponge, swore at the bhishti for not having been available earlier and told him to leave the cans near the tub. Alone, Teddie stood and dowsed himself. There was no significant change. In fact the cold water had a setting-up effect. He shut his eyes and said, 'Oh, Christ', stepped on to the duckboard and wrestled himself dry with a towel.

Susan was an absolute brick. Kissing him in front of Mildred and Sarah she had said, 'Congratulations', as if being a G3(O) in a new division was something pretty terrific. For a while he felt it was. On their way to the cinema he had an ugly but exciting thought about the journey home. He felt heroic and felt that she felt he was heroic. He didn't understand the film but became physically alert each time the girl with the enormous tits got manhandled which was every few minutes. At the end of one scene there was almost nothing left of her dress. There hadn't been much of it at the start. The other ranks down in the body of the hall whistled and stamped. The film ended with her disappointingly fully clothed kissing the fellow with the jaw who was lying on the steps of a church riddled with bullets. For some reason it was also snowing.

In the tonga Teddie held Susan's hand – the ungloved one –
and surprisingly she let him and even seemed to want it. His
thoughts stopped functioning in anything like a logical order.
Normally when they were alone the chaste kisses and affectionate gestures Susan allowed in public were somehow made
difficult as if she disapproved of what they might lead to.

'We could have coffee at the chummery,' Teddie said.

'Aren't we going to the Chinese?'

'I mean after.'

'Oh,' Susan said. Then: 'Yes, we could.'

Like that. Teddie's neck prickled. They had never been in the
chummery alone. His hand and hers were clammy. He did not
dare squeeze in case it frightened her. His heart was pumping
nastily. It took only two minutes to get from the cinema forecourt to the restaurant. All the bazaar shops were open and
brightly lit by electric bulbs or naphtha lamps. The street was
full of British Other Ranks. Some were lounging against the
pillars of the arcade in a slovenly manner with their hands signifi-
cantly in their trouser pockets talking to Eurasian girls in white
high-heeled shoes. In one shop a radio played Indian film music.
The tonga stopped outside the restaurant.

Teddie got down. Susan's face was coloured faintly by the
lights. She looked marvellous. But she wasn't looking happy.

'Teddie, I'm not awfully hungry.'

'Oh.'

He climbed back in. A muscle in his left cheek twitched of
its own accord.

'Just coffee then?'

'Yes.'

He twisted round and spoke to the wallah. The tonga was
turned in the street, causing trouble to other vehicles. The wallahs
shouted at each other. For a while all the tongas were stationary.
The wallahs waved their arms. Teddie felt put out because he and
Susan were at the storm centre. He hated scenes but in any case
this one was like having everything advertised.

He hit the wallah on the shoulder and told him to get moving.

The wallah obeyed but continued to exchange insults with
each of the wallahs in the line of tongas whose free passage he
had blocked. And the driver of the tonga immediately behind
their own, coming in their wake, shouted insults too, presumably

at their driver but in effect at them. The damned fellow was grinning too, as if he knew.

They did not hold hands. When the tonga left the lighted area they continued not holding them. There were puddles at intervals reflecting the infrequent street lamps. Between lamps the night was promisingly dark and humid. On other occasions when he had invited her to the chummery she had always managed to work the conversation round to the question of who else would be there before accepting. It was becoming clearer and clearer to him that tonight she had no intention of asking and that she anticipated finding exactly what she would find: nobody. Tony Bishop was dining at Flagstaff House. Bruce Mackay, the engineer, was down in Ranpur, and Bungo Barnes, the gunner, had gone round to see the QA sister, Gentleman's Relish. He would not be back until the small hours. Teddie had seen Gentleman's Relish only once. Her other name was Thelma and he thought her extremely unattractive and alarmingly common for a girl who ranked as an officer. Since Bungo had a reputation for never wasting time on a girl who – as he put it – didn't, Teddie assumed that Gentleman's Relish did, and more often than seemed reasonable because Bungo had been out every night for two weeks and looked washed out at breakfast. Where they did it he had no idea. He disapproved of Bungo Barnes. He also envied him.

When they reached the chummery he envied Bungo more than ever because he knew that the whole thing was hopeless. Susan wasn't that kind of girl. Her trim little body was protected by some sort of absolute statement about its virginity this side of the altar. She might wish otherwise but that was how it was for her, for him. As usual lights were on in the porch, entrance-lobby and living-room. Prabhu, Bungo Barnes's equally lascivious servant, came out pander-like from the dining-room to see what was happening.

'Oh, you're duty-wallah are you, Prabhu? We'd like coffee.'

'May I change my mind and have tea?' Susan asked. She stood in front of the screened fireplace dealing with her gloves and handbag in that stunning way girls had.

'Anything you want, old thing,' Teddie said. 'Matter of fact I thought I'd have a peg. Would you prefer that?'

'No, tea is what I'd like. I've got rather a head.'

'Oh, Lord, you'd better have an aspirin.'

'No, I don't want an aspirin, Teddie. Just tea.'

'Strong or weak?'

'Just as it comes.'

'It usually comes like dishwater in this place.' He told Prabhu to bring tea but make sure that the water boiled.

'I say, do sit down or something.'

'I will in a minute.'

They stood, apart, smiling at each other. The room had always struck Teddie as a bit chintzy for an all-male establishment. He thought it awfully nice tonight because she was in it. Her dress had white and navy-blue flowers on it.

'I say is that new?'

'Yes.'

'It's awfully nice.'

He had not noticed it at the grace and favour because he'd been worried about how Susan would take the news. After that it had been dark most of the time. He reached out, stroked her shoulder. Her flesh was warm and cushiony under the thin silky material. The neck of the dress was cut square. He could just see the beginning of the division between her breasts. The skin was dotted with tiny little freckles. Her arms were freckled too. Delightfully. He slid his hand down the arm to the soft flesh on the inner side of the elbow.

He said, 'It's rotten going away, leaving you.'

'I know.'

Since he touched her shoulder she had not looked at him. Her eyelashes were wonderfully long. The tips curled up. There were a few freckles near the bridge of her nose. He felt tremendously moved and protective. Her beauty was so simple, so artless. She glowed with health. The freckles came out because she was always in the sunshine. She was made for a clean, healthy, simple and loving life. He clutched her suddenly, pressing her to him. Her hair smelt sweet. It tickled. He kissed her forehead through it. She was awfully tensed up. Her whole body seemed to be a skull. If he kissed and kissed her she would melt. Through their clothes their bodies would flow into each other. He kissed her again and again until he had the most shamefully majestic erection. He didn't care. She was still protected by that absolute statement. The erection was a statement too and just as absolute but in a negative way.

'Su, I love you so much.' He clasped her head, kissed her closed lids. Soft, marvellous, living warmth. The melting would begin here. 'So much, honestly, honestly.'

He heard the tea-things clunking like monks' sandals and broke away, turned his back on her and the approaching Prabhu and walked, sweetly bitterly crippled, to the drinks cabinet. When he heard the tray set down he said without looking, 'Thank you, Prabhu. Just leave it, will you.' He opened a bottle of Johnnie Walker and poured a stiff measure. His eyes felt hot and hollow. His limbs were steady but felt as if they were not. He wasn't sure if there was enough blood in the soles of his feet. His knees were awkwardly placed in his legs, a shade out of true. He didn't really want soda but wasn't yet ready to face around to things so popped a bottle and poured a long one. He thought therapeutically about liquor; of what it could do to your liver. His mother's second husband, Hunter, couldn't have had any liver left.

When he came away from the cabinet Susan was sitting on one of the chintzy chairs staring at the tea-tray which Prabhu had put down on an ornate and untrustworthy mother-of-pearl encrusted table. It was maddening how easy it was to get worked up, how difficult to do anything about it if you cared about things like marriage and doing right by each other. She looked pretty pale. He hadn't yet asked her if she'd prefer to be released from their promise and come to an understanding that they weren't actually bound to each other while he was away; and now didn't dare, not because she might jump at the chance but because it would be a damned insult after the way he'd just pressed up against her. When she suddenly reached for the teapot, using both hands, the little cluster of engagement diamonds glittered balefully. The line between self-sacrifice and acting like an unspeakable cad seemed perilously thin.

He sat on the sofa at the end near her chair and watched her perform her womanly little tasks. A lifetime of tea-trays stretched ahead of them. Or might. With luck. He felt a draught as of a premonition that he'd drawn a dud chit out of luck's hat and had been given Susan either briefly to make up for it or to give him a sniff of what he was going to miss. He was on the point of declaring an intention to talk to Dick Rankin in the morning about pulling strings to keep him in Pankot when to his great relief (because the intention was a callow quivering hand with a sleek shiny white feather in it) Susan said:

'Of course it was bound to happen, this proper job I mean. I hoped it wouldn't happen so soon which was silly of me, but it doesn't make any difference does it?'

'Difference?'

'Difference to us.'

'What difference could it make?'

'I thought you might think we should wait, not make definite plans. Settle for a long engagement.'

'Do you think we should?'

She glanced into the pot to check how full it was. 'No,' she said, 'if necessary I think we should speed things up.'

She raised the cup to her lips and Teddie raised his glass. They were both trembling. Teddie couldn't think why but it seemed touching and very serious. Just then they heard a car on the gravel and in a moment Tony Bishop came in looking done up. The Rankins had been entertaining visiting top brass but Tony had been able to mention Teddie's posting-order. General Rankin said Teddie's new commander was a fire-eater by all accounts, a youngish man with a reputation for unorthodoxy.

Teddie groaned. 'I suppose I'd better talk to the movement people first thing tomorrow,' he said.

'There's no need, it's all arranged. Mirat was on the blower asking where you'd got to. They said to get you down to Ranpur tomorrow and out to the airfield at Ranagunj and they'll fly you down to Mirat tomorrow night.'

'Fly? But I've never flown in my life! Supposing I'm sick?'

'I think you'll have to get used to it. Your new general's tremendously keen on his officers flying whenever they can. He's air mad.'

'What about my kit? Aren't they awfully strict about weight?'

'Pretty strict. You'd better go as light as you can and I'll send your trunk on directly you tell me to.'

'What about Allah Din?'

'Sorry, no personal servants. We'll get him back to Muzza-firabad.'

'What am I going to do without Allah Din?'

'You'll probably share an orderly. I'm afraid you're in for a rather Spartan existence.'

'It's indecent. I mean hang it all Mirat's only another military station. We might be there for months. It's not like buzzing off to the Arakan.'

He felt hollow again and indignant. The new general probably had a text on the wall saying: Do it Yesterday. This turned out not far from the case. Actually it said: Do it Now.

He took Susan home in the car which Bishop had been using to ferry the Rankins' guests and had efficiently kept waiting as soon as he saw a tonga at the chummery and guessed whose it was. Unlike the tonga-wallah, who complained at being deprived of the fare back to the grace and favour, the lance-naik driver was quite happy with the arrangement. He was obviously one of those Indians who was tireless when behind a wheel and didn't care how late he worked so long as an officer signed for the journey. Teddie and Susan sat in back-seat comfort. They held hands. Teddie had stopped feeling randy and started to feel emotional but chipper too because they were together in the same emotional situation: last night out for some time to come, last few minutes, probably, of being alone together.

'It might be fun, flying,' he said.

'Yes, it might.'

'I'll tell you what would be.'

'What?'

'Flying back, for the wedding.'

'You'll tell them directly you get there, won't you?'

Practical Susan!

'Of course. I'll speak to the Gee One first thing.'

'What will happen if the division's going away almost at once?'

'It's pretty unlikely. If we do it'll be for working-up. Anyway, they'd always give an officer leave to get married. Don't worry.'

'I'll try not to.'

He cuddled her. She was still very tense. But what a girl! No scene, no shilly-shallying. Just tremendous pluck and determination. As the car turned into Rifle Range road a cold night breeze blew in through the lowered window from the open spaces of the Pankot Rifles lines. It flirted a lock of her hair against his cheek. Behind the southern ridge of the hills the sky was suddenly illuminated. Down on the plains the monsoon was loose like an electric beast.

His uncle in Shropshire always said that a thunderstorm made the milk go off in the pantry. It occurred to him that his uncle was rather a lonely sort of chap being able to notice things like that.

III

The other, empty, bed in Teddie's room had begun to make its presence felt. A plain wooden charpoy like his own, its mosquito net, folded up, was taped to the four bamboo poles tied to its legs. Three biscuit mattresses and a ticking pillow were piled at its head. Otherwise the bed was bare to the cords, awaiting an occupant.

In Mirat the rain was incessant. Violent storms were nightly visitors. They woke Teddie up. The empty bed seemed lit by St Elmo's fire; it rode the night rock-firm, half-ship, half-catafalque. In the peaceful early mornings its message was simpler but still to be reckoned with.

Ten nights after his arrival the electric beast lay quiet and he enjoyed uninterrupted sleep but woke before the orderly Hosain came in with the chota hazri. His eyes recorded the fact that the other bed was fully shrouded by its mosquito net several seconds before this struck him as new. He raised his head from the pillow and stared through the mesh of his own net. The other bed was occupied. He raised the net. How awfully odd. He thought back over his sleep and dreams but could recall nothing which the presence of the recumbent figure explained. His sleep had been wholly undisturbed. It was as if the figure had slowly material-ized during the night and had now reached a stage of total conviction about itself and its surroundings. Teddie frowned. He was unused to thinking in imaginative terms. He glanced towards the window.

His own clothes were in their usual place: jacket thrown care-lessly over a chair back, trousers on the seat, under-clothes on the floor. The other chair held clothes too but these were neatly arranged. Nearby stood a large leather suitcase and a bedroll which had obviously been opened to remove sheets and pyjamas then rolled up again but left unstrapped. The chap couldn't have done all that in the dark. And he must have had an orderly to help him, if not young Hosain.

Teddie reached for his slippers, automatically tapped them by

the heels on the floor to dislodge any lurking scorpion gone into
hiding during the night, set them side by side, swung his legs
out and slipped his feet into them. The bed creaked. The other
chap must have moved like a cat. Obviously a considerate sort
of fellow. Teddie grabbed his robe. The humidity was high. The
ceiling fan was whispering round at its lowest number of revs a
minute. He clicked the dial a couple of notches higher and was
rewarded by a faint and regular blowing on his forehead. Leaving
the switchboard and going to stand under the fan he inspected
his new companion's jacket. Captain's rank. Punjab Regiment.
But a green armband hung over the chair back. Intelligence.
Scholarly sort of fellow probably; not a real Punjab officer at all.
The uniform and the pips looked new. The luggage looked very
old though. Teddie twisted his head to find a name on it. The
bedroll was set in such a way that any stencilled name on the
canvas cover was hidden from view. The suitcase was more
revealing. But initials only. R.M. There was no tin trunk. Like
himself, RM had travelled to Mirat light. By what method
though?

The writing-table caught his eye next. Set out upon it with
noticeable precision were a briefcase, a field-service cap and a
leather-bound swagger cane. The cane was parallel to the base
of the briefcase and the cap lay between them with its badge
facing front, squared up on an invisible line parallel with the
other two. The three items were placed on the left of the blotter
as if marking out that side of the desk as the new arrival's, to
correspond with the placing – on the left-hand side of the room
facing the window – of the chair with the new occupant's clothes
on it and the bed in which he was asleep. A white line drawn
from the middle of the window to the opposite wall would have
defined the area which seemed to have been meticulously but
silently claimed in the small hours.

But on the blotter on Teddie's side of the line there was an
intruder: a piece of paper tucked into one of the leather corners.
Teddie recognized it as a page torn from a Field Service Notebook. In clear rather tight handwriting it read: 'I hope I didn't
disturb you. The man who helped me find my quarters said our
orderly is called Hosain. I should be grateful if you would ask
him to wake me with tea at 08.30 but not before as I did not get
in until 03.00. The train was badly held up. I'm told breakfast is

between 08.00 and 09.30 but I shall skip it. I look forward to meeting you later in the day, perhaps at lunch if we are messing together. Meanwhile my thanks and my apologies for any noise last night. Ronald Merrick.'

In this note Teddie thought there was as much self-assurance as consideration. He went to the mess and on to the daftar by push-bike. At 11.30 he was back in his quarters hastily packing his bedroll – Merrick was not there – and at midday was driving with the G1, Lieut.-Colonel Selby-Smith, to the airfield. At 12.30 he was airborne in an RAF Dakota for Delhi where he would meet the divisional commander for the first time. He was away for six days. When he returned, feeling run off his feet but happy to have come daily under the general's eye as the 'young Muzzy officer who wants to get married', he found that Captain Merrick was away on a course. In the interval Teddie's tin trunk had arrived from Pankot; so had Merrick's, from somewhere else. Merrick's was just as old and battered as Teddie's. The rank of captain was freshly painted in, however, and a band of new black paint obliterated something that had been written under-neath the surname.

Teddie, who never gossiped to servants, only just managed to resist the temptation to ask young Hosain what Captain Merrick Sahib was like. He noticed that the boy took considerable care with the things Merrick had left behind and he resented this in an ill-defined way that made him feel generally at odds with his domestic arrangements.

He was feeling similarly at odds with his work. There was a looseness as yet about the organization of divisional headquarters which made it difficult for him to grasp what was going on. In Delhi the general had talked a lot about what he called fluidity and about the fellow Wingate who had recently been behind the enemy lines down the road in Burma with a specially trained brigade, trying to play havoc with the Japanese lines of com-munication and being supplied by air. Teddie thought that this operation sounded like a costly and showy variation of the old cavalry role of sometimes penetrating enemy-held country, beating up their baggage trains and galloping back home: useful, an antidote to boredom, but hardly a pukka strategical operation of war. And the supply by air thing had reportedly become a fiasco once Wingate's troops were out of the jungle and into the plains and having to move so fast to escape being trapped that stuff was dropped to them long after they'd had to leave the place they'd asked for it to be dropped to them in. Which meant the Jap got it. Worst of all, Teddie thought, when the operation petered out Wingate had told his chaps to split into groups and get the hell out by any means they could. From Teddie's point of view this was like an officer abrogating his responsibility at the very moment when he was most responsible. That it had been the wisest thing to do only showed how unmilitary the whole affair was.

Even so, the casualty list had been alarming. More alarming, to Teddie, was the way his own general talked about the Wingate expedition having provided the key to the problem of defeating the Japanese. Teddie had a professional soldier's contempt for anything that came under the heading of guerrilla tactics. He did not want to swan around in the jungle with a beard and a bag of rice blowing up bridges. And now he was not sure that he much wanted to play messenger-boy in a top-brass outfit like Div. HQ. He missed the comradeship of his old battalion. He missed the good feeling of knowing every sepoy's name, the name of his village, the number and ages of his children, the state of health of his wife, all the things that turned the fellow from a number or a statistic in an order of battle into a man whose personal welfare was a prime consideration.

But then Teddie thought of Susan, of the dizzy heights advocated by her mother, and accepted his present status as an essential trial and testing of his ability to rise to them. A chap, worse luck, couldn't remain a cheerful subaltern or company commander for ever.

'Delhi was pretty hectic,' he told Susan in the first of the bi-weekly letters which his return to Mirat enabled him to resume. 'I didn't manage to drop round to see your aunt and uncle, Major and Mrs Grace, until the last evening. I told them it's clear there isn't any hope now of my joining you all in Srinagar either in August or September. Naturally I'm disappointed but we didn't really expect it, did we, darling? As for the wedding the form here seems to be that we go ahead with the plans already made but stand ready for a rearrangement perhaps without much notice. It was nice to see your Aunt Fenny again. She got rid of the cold she caught in Pankot as soon as she got down into Delhi again. I also enjoyed meeting your uncle Arthur. He said he was glad to have the opportunity of seeing the chap he's going to give you away to. He gave me the name and address of the houseboat contractor who's fixing you all up in Kashmir so I can send a letter to await your arrival. You'll have a lovely family holiday, I wish I were coming too but I'll be too busy to mope, so don't worry. I'm enjoying Mirat and beginning to feel my feet. I still haven't met the man I'm sharing quarters with. Please thank Tony for me and tell him the trunk's arrived safely. Now I can settle in properly. The rain's been terrific here but there's a lull at the moment. If my letters become a bit irregular you'll know it's only a matter of business before pleasure.'

He had been about to write: 'You'll know it's only because we're out and about on schemes and exercises,' but even news about training was useful to spies. Teddie had been fairly security-minded ever since in Burma his battalion (he could have sworn) had been infiltrated by fifth columnists.

Through the curtain of rain the distant fort looked like a stranded battleship. The general's artillery had been pounding its walls for two hours with 5.5. In four minutes when the barrage lifted his airborne commandos would parachute in to the south to establish a perimeter, cut off the garrison's flight, block advancing enemy reinforcements and mop up pockets of local resistance. The tanks would advance from the north in the van of lorry-borne infantry. Two battalions had already moved in a wide arc to launch an attack from the left and another was holding the right flank.

The general stood, wrist cocked, eyes on watch, rain dripping from the peak of his red-banded cap. Inside the command lorry the R Toc crackled. Suddenly the general's arm dropped, he turned his face up into the rain and after a few seconds smiled beatifically. A score of officers, including Teddie astride his motor-cycle, looked up into the sky. A vicious fork of lightning ripped across it. Teddie winced, blinded by the flash and deafened by the explosive bounce of thunder. When the thunder had gone tumbling and rolling out into the deep field where old Jove had thumped it, he heard a more homely sound which the general's sharper ears had caught earlier: labouring aero engines. A lone Dakota appeared out of the monsoon clouds, roared overhead

low enough for them to see the figure of a man standing in the
open port; the air liaison officer presumably; and then flew back
into them.

'Well, gentlemen,' the general said. 'I think we may safely
assume that we've taken Mandalay. Let's go home.'

Teddie muttered, 'Good.' They had been out on the ground
for two days. He looked forward to a hot bath and a man-size
scotch in the mess. As Div. HQ sorted itself out into its several
kinds of rough-country transport Teddie kicked his machine
into life and went bumping and slithering down the muddy track
to make sure that the general's staff car was waiting at the
crossroads. A couple of officers representing the reserve brigade
were standing miserably under thin branched trees. The fort at
Premanagar had vanished entirely behind the curtain of rain.

It was dark when Teddie got back. A light in the window of his
room showed that the servants' quarters had been alerted and
that Hosain was prepared for him. He entered unbuckling his
rain-sodden equipment, yelled for the boy and then, dropping
his belt, holster, straps and pack on to the floor paused – observing the signs of renewed occupation: a row of highly polished
shoes, fresh underclothes and socks – not his own – already laid
out on a chair for the morning, both beds with lowered nets and
pair of slippers within foot reach; and on the other officer's side
of the writing-table a pile of books and pamphlets.

There was something else on the table on Teddie's side: a
round chromium tray, a jug of water and a glass each with a
beaded muslin cover – a tray such as could only be got from the
mess bar by signing a chit and sending an orderly over with it.
He heard Hosain at the back calling for the bhishti. There was
a note under the tumbler. He slid it out. 'I would have waited
and joined you for dinner but I have an appointment. In view
of the kind of weather I hear you've had on the scheme I thought
you'd need this as well as a hot bath. R.M.'

The tumbler held three fingers of whisky.

'I say,' Teddie said.

What an extraordinarily decent thing to do. He sniffed the
whisky and drank some of it neat then yelled for Hosain again
and sat in a wicker arm-chair with his damp legs stuck out. The
boy came in with a newly pressed suit of KD.

'Well done, Hosain,' Teddie said. But the suit was Captain Merrick's. Teddie had to wait until it had been hand-flicked and hung in one of the almirahs before he could get Hosain to come and unlace his boots. He'd had them on for thirty-six hours. Relieved of them his feet felt alternately hot and raw, cold and raw. He smoked, drank and listened to the swoosh of water as the bhishti poured it from cans into the tin tub in the adjoining bath-house. He picked up one of Merrick's books, opened it and stared at the incomprehensible Japanese text on the right-hand page. On the left-hand page there were questions in English and, underneath, the same question in phonetics to show you how it would sound if you asked it in Japanese. What is your army number? What is the name or number of your regiment? In what division is your regiment? Tell me the name of your divisional commander. What unit had the position on your unit's left flank when you were captured?

'Some hopes,' Teddie said aloud. If you ever got close enough to speak to a Japanese soldier one of you would be dead a second later. That was how poor old Havildar Shafi Mohammed had been killed, reporting a wounded Jap lying out in the open and volunteering to bring him in. The Jap had had a grenade in his tunic. He must have pulled the pin surreptitiously when he saw the Havildar get within a few paces. They both went to Kingdom Come. Merrick was wasting his time learning a bit of Japanese.

Teddie turned the page and displaced a piece of square-ruled paper which must have been marking the place Merrick had got to. In the tight neat handwriting was written: Lecture Note. 1942, approx. 10,000. Berlin, Tokyo, Singapore, July '43. Mohan Singh. Bangkok Conf.

'Sahib,' Hosain said. He motioned shyly in the direction of the bath-house. Teddie replaced the marker in the book, carried his whisky into the next room and began to shed his clothes.

He came back from the mess early. He was too tired even to write to Susan. He scribbled a note and pinned it to Merrick's mosquito net. 'Thanks for the drink. Have one on me tomorrow.' He left Merrick's bedside lamp burning, turned off his own, climbed inside his net and was asleep almost at once.

Hosain woke him at 07.00. He brought only one tray of tea. Hosain indicated Merrick's huddled form, put both hands to his cheek, inclined his head, shut his eyes. Teddie scratched his head, understanding himself requested to be quiet, and went off to the WC. When he left for the mess at 08.00 Merrick had still not moved.

It is possible, perhaps, for death to come slowly, even gently, civilly, as if anxious to make the whole thing as painless as possible. One thinks of death at this juncture because Merrick represented Teddie's. Coupled with the civility and consideration a certain reluctance could be detected, almost as if Merrick knew and kept giving Teddie a chance to pack his bags and go before a meeting actually took place. A final opportunity occurred that morning because Teddie saw Merrick and heard him talking for a good twenty minutes before the moment came to claim acquaintance and establish the specific relationship. But there was nothing in Merrick's appearance that caused Teddie to feel uneasy.

After his schemes the general held post-mortems behind locked doors in the Garrison Theatre. During his career Teddie had sat through countless hours of what in common with other junior officers he called prayers. He found that what distinguished the general's prayers were brevity, deadly earnestness and the presence – among the hybrid ranks of divisional, brigade, battalion and supporting arms officers – of VCOS and senior British and English-speaking Indian NCOs, who were seated not quite under the general's eye but in constant danger of attracting it.

One of Teddie's jobs, he discovered, was to make sure that the NCOs from the British battalions did not sit in stiff-necked seclusion but were properly mixed up with their Indian colleagues. According to Selby-Smith the general had a bee in his bonnet about mutual trust and also about making the ordinary soldier feel he had a 'share in the company'. Teddie thought that mutual trust was a matter of respect for each other's achievements in the field more than of sitting next to a chap you didn't know and hadn't got time to get to know, and he wasn't convinced of the value of the share in the company business when it involved the risk of an officer giving a silly answer to the general's questions and making a fool of himself in front of non-commissioned ranks.

The post-mortem began at 11.00 hours. Since one brigade

headquarters was stationed twenty-five miles to the east of Mirat and another twenty miles to the north and some of their battalions farther away still, most of the officers attending had had an early start. Some of them had stayed in Mirat overnight and looked the worse for it but neatness and formality of dress were among the things to which the general seemed to attach little importance. The general himself was wearing a set of cellular cotton overalls cut to look like battle-dress jacket and trousers and made in the new jungle green material that was not yet on general issue. His feet and shins were encased in black dispatch rider's boots. This morning to Teddie's horror he had a Paisley patterned scarf at his neck.

He spoke from notes at a lectern on the stage. His aide and an NCO from the intelligence staff produced beautifully drawn giant-scale sketch maps which they pinned efficiently to the blackboard one after the other to illustrate the points the general was making. After a while Teddie had to admit that everything began to make sense to him. For the first time he fully understood what the scheme had been about. He was even aware that it had a kind of beauty. Formless, almost shapeless, the beauty consisted in the subtle cohesion of what seemed like disparate parts and in the extraordinary flexibility of each arrangement made to bring them together.

Suddenly withering in his mind were the stiff and predictable patterns that made traditional military affairs so easy to grasp on paper, so difficult to put into operation when the real thing was all about you. His blood stirred momentarily with a new sense of excitement in his occupation. The general, direct and thrusting, was filling Teddie's mind with poetry. Teddie sat physically composed as usual, wearing the rather blank expression of a man not naturally receptive to any idea which took time to be expounded. Had the general noticed him particularly and glanced at him every so often to judge what sort of impression he was making on the young man he might have thought he was making none and so made a note to tell the G1 to replace him with a more alert and aggressive officer, in which case he would have done Teddie an injustice because Teddie's soul, uncommitted a short while ago, had risen to its feet and was gallantly attempting to expose itself totally to the revelation.

If recognition of talent had been the same as having it Teddie might have blossomed under the general's eyes. When the general threw the meeting open to questions Teddie's soul sat down, finding itself dumb, unwilling to expose itself further, but it had planted a hopeful flag. Teddie had been won over, to what he was not sure, but the boots and the Paisley scarf were now part of the man whose man he felt he could become. You couldn't call the boots and the scarf stylish but they were not really flamboyant, Teddie decided. They were idiosyncratic marks of identification.

The post-mortem was wound up by the general with a quick but comprehensive summary of the main lessons learnt and a look into the future from which Teddie got a fleeting but satisfactory glimpse of his own as one that involved no immediate move from Mirat. The formation was still in the process of working-up exercises. These would lead to a period of intensive training for jungle warfare.

'I think you may assume,' the general ended, 'that our role will be there, to the east. Some of us are familiar with jungle conditions. My advice to you is to forget them because we knew them at a bad time. We have the wrong picture. Fortunately I don't think any of us is affected by the myth of Japanese invincibility. Man for man there's no problem. That's all I have to say this morning but I ask you now to give your attention to one of my junior officers, a man recently appointed to my Intelligence staff. If any senior officers wonder why they should stay to hear what a mere captain has to say they may restrain their natural impatience if I explain first that what he will tell you is confidential and of importance to the picture we need of the enemy we may expect to meet, and secondly that he has been in the service of the Indian government for longer than quite a number of the officers present today. He is something of a rare bird, an officer of the civil authority who has managed to persuade his department to let him into the army for the duration of the war. Captain Merrick's civilian rank was a senior and responsible one. I scarcely believe him when he tells me that there was so little going on in his district that even his superior officers agreed he might be more usefully employed. I do believe him when he tells me he first applied to join the armed forces as far back as 1939 and has continually renewed his application and I suspect it was not a case of nothing much going on but of his department deciding that if they wanted any peace they would have to let him come to the war. The kind of work he was doing meant that the most suitable branch for him to serve in was intelligence and his civilian rank would have qualified him for a more senior army rank than the one he holds. I happen to know, and I have no wish to embarrass him, in any case he is now stuck with what he's got, that he had a choice between this appointment and one elsewhere which would have given him more glamorous epaulettes. He chose the more active role and the lower rank because it was an active role he was looking for. I am glad to welcome him to this formation. I repeat that what he has to tell us is confidential. There should be no general discussion of the subject inside units and certainly not outside. Although Captain Merrick will perform the ordinary tasks of a G3 this particular subject is likely to become one of his special interests and he will continue to keep in touch with brigade and battalion intelligence staffs in regard to it and to the level at which it remains a restricted subject. Brigadier Crawford, Captain Sowton and I will not stay to listen to his address because he gave us a full and detailed account last night after dinner. Thank you gentlemen. No standing if you don't mind, it only makes for disruption. Colonel Selby-Smith, will you take over please?'

The general came down from the stage, was joined by Crawford and Sowton, and left by the main aisle. From the foyer on the other side of the doors came the sound of boots stamped on the tiled floor as the men on guard duty came to attention. Selby-Smith got up and now made a gesture of invitation. On the far side of the right-hand second row of seats Teddie saw his elusive room companion rise. At first sight he looked younger than the general's reference to seniority had led Teddie to expect. Tall, fair-haired, slim and well-built, he moved with a sort of snap that Teddie would have expected in a smart cadet or a young hard-case sar'major. But once on the platform, behind the lectern, in stage-lighting, the fairness of the hair faded and the used quality of the face was revealed. He could have been any age between thirty and forty.

The hall was remarkably quiet. The general's recommendation and explanation had alerted an old instinct to dislike on sight anyone about whom there was a faint mystery, a difference, anyone who was not fully defined by rank, occupation and regiment, who appeared to have an obscure but real advantage over his fellows. Teddie was aware of this because he felt a prick of resentment himself. *I would have waited and joined you for dinner but I have an appointment.* Dinner with the general. How and when had that been arranged? The general would have got back in his staff car from Premanagar two or three hours before Teddie spluttered in on his motor-bike after playing messenger-boy over several square miles of bloody awful country and then helping off-station officers to find accommodation in Mirat for the night. The three fingers of whisky represented something ambiguous like the postcards his mother used to send from Singapore saying 'Miss you' while all the time she was having a high old time with that chap Hunter.

For the first few minutes of Merrick's address the silence persisted, but during these minutes it lost density, became riddled with receptive channels drilled one way by Merrick's strong and resonant voice and the other way by the audience's growing interest in what the voice was saying until the two sides met like tunnellers who had worked from opposite sides of a mountain and come face to face at the centre point of a clear uninterrupted passage. As if he knew that contact had been made Merrick now made a dry joke and was rewarded by more laughter than the joke deserved. Thinking about it afterwards Teddie believed that most men would have attempted a joke right at the beginning to break down the unfriendly atmosphere. Merrick must have been conscious of the critical silence that greeted his appearance on the platform. But he ignored it, simply started to speak, standing at the lectern removing his papers from his briefcase then dropping the case on a nearby chair and sorting out his notes, apparently in no hurry to look like a man giving a lecture but already giving it.

'In December 1940 an eminent member of the All India National Congress whose extremist views had become something of an embarrassment to other members of the Congress High Command, not to say an annoyance to ourselves, escaped from India, so far as we can ascertain through Afghanistan. His name was Subhas Chandra Bose. Although arrested early on in the war he had been released to his home after staging a hunger strike in captivity which the Indian Government feared might lead to his death. In spite of rigorous surveillance by the police and CID of the house he now lived in he managed to get away presumably in some sort of disguise and make his way to Kabul where it seems he was in touch with the German consulate. Thereafter, quite logically, he turned up in Berlin with the declared intention of carrying on what he called India's fight for freedom from there. There are two points worth noting about this situation. The first is that a man who has such a high opinion of himself and his talents as to believe that single-handed he might achieve what the Congress as a whole has not managed to and takes the trouble to put such a great distance between himself and his jailers, is in all likelihood suffering to some extent from delusions of grandeur. The second point to note is the direction of his flight and its final destination. Berlin. The two factors, the kind of man one may think Bose is and the place he went to are not incompatible as factors in our assessment of the meaning of the situation. Indeed, all this makes a perfectly sensible pattern. Hitler, Ribbentrop, Goebbels, Subhas Chandra Bose.

'At this stage of the war of course, in 1940, Mr Bose might have been excused for believing that the Germans were going to win it anyway and that his mission was a merciful step taken to minimize any suffering Indians might have undergone following a British defeat. One can quite see that the appearance of Mr Bose as Gauleiter of India could have militated against the excesses of storm-troopers in cities such as Delhi. Once again one learns the lesson, that historically a man's actions – however questionable they appear at the time – can usually be satisfactorily explained away afterwards as altruistic. No doubt Mr Bose has been sacrificing himself in the interests of his country. His is an odyssey that deserves to be better known and no doubt will be because it is not over yet. Like many great adventures it has its marginally amusing elements. I am assured on the best authority that although Mr Bose stumbled most of the way through Afghanistan on foot he effected his entry into Kabul in a tonga.'

The laughter swept the hall at this point. Teddie laughed too. He was not sure he knew just who Subhas Chandra Bose was. There were so many Indians called Bose. His interest in Indian politics and politicians had always been minimal. He had a generally comic idea about them. The picture of a portly chap in dhoti, shirt and Gandhi cap bumping up and down in the back of a rickety horse-drawn two-wheeled trap on his way to meet the German consul struck him as perfectly splendid. Teddie folded his arms, always a sign of his contentment. This Merrick fellow certainly knew his stuff even though his voice, confident and carrying, was – well – not quite pukka, a shade middle-class in the vowel sounds.

'Nothing I've said so far is confidential. The business of Bose's escape and activities in Berlin, although soft-pedalled by Government, is known to many people – perhaps better known to civilians than to army personnel and to Indian officers better than to British. Civilians have more time to gossip and read the minor items in the newspapers. Indian officers are probably more interested in what an Indian politician gets up to than their British colleagues are. But by and large the Bose situation is treated more as a joke than a threat. He has broadcast from Berlin and has made as little impression as the Anglo-British commentator Lord Haw-Haw. Men like Bose tend to appear to live, publicly, in isolation from what we are inclined to think of as the realities. What he actually did in Germany may therefore come as a surprise to some of you. With Hitler's permission, to assist Hitler in fighting us, he raised a unit of battalion strength from Indian prisoners of war who presumably volunteered for this distinction.'

The temperature in the hall seemed to drop perceptibly. For an instant the barrier between audience and speaker fell again. Teddie looked at the necks of the two Indian officers in front of him and wondered what on earth it felt like being one of them.

'This unit,' Merrick continued, 'is first reported as officially in existence in January 1942. In other words it took Mr Bose at least a year to find eight or nine hundred men to accept the bait of ostensible freedom from prison-camp and to form a group which no doubt he described as the nucleus of a great army of patriotic Indians whose quarrel was with the British and no other nation. Whether Hitler was disappointed at the feeble response or was merely amused to have his views of Mr Bose confirmed we do not know. The unit does not seem to have survived as a fighting force or even as a coherent one. It is reported scattered around Hitler's Europe, particularly in the Low Countries, doing the odd spot of beach defence, police and guard duties.

But before we criticize these men, remember that as prisoners-of-war forcibly separated from their company and battalion commanders, and very far from home, they were deprived of the one thing the Indian Army has always been especially rightly proud of – the high level of trust between men and officers which is based on the real concern shown for the men's welfare by those officers, be those officers British or Indian. It is clear that Bose's failure in Germany stems from the fact that he simply couldn't find enough Indian King's commissioned officers to help him in his work of suborning cold, hungry and miserable Indian sepoys.'

There was an appreciative murmur from the front row where the most senior British officers sat.

'Bose was still in Berlin when the Japanese launched their lightning attacks in the Far East, on Pearl Harbor, Malaya and Burma. Intelligence reports reveal that he was in touch with the Japanese ambassador in Berlin and it takes little imagination to work out that one of the things he must have suggested to that gentleman was that the Japanese should encourage the raising of similar forces from Indian prisoners of war to assist them in their operations in the Far Eastern theatre. But now we come across yet another gentleman with the name of Bose –'

Teddie smiled. There you were. Common as Smith.

'– Rash Behari Bose, an old Indian revolutionary living in exile in Japan. Rash Behari Bose also approached the Japanese with a scheme of this kind. He was unsuccessful in his first contact, with Field-Marshal Suguyama, who took the practical soldier's view that since India was part of the British Empire Indians could never be anything but enemy subjects. He had more success with the Japanese war ministry. Rash Behari was already head of a thing called the Indian Independence League in Japan. With the backing of the Japanese government he was now in a position to extend this as a going concern in all the invaded territories. A branch of the Indian Independence League, or IIL, was set up for instance in Bangkok and it sent representatives with the Japanese forces that invaded Malaya. You see which way the wind begins to blow. Mr Rash Behari Bose probably makes great play with the fact that the IIL saved Indian lives and property during the period of hostilities. Indeed there are many instances reported of Japanese soldiers having approached Indian civilians in Malaya asking them if they followed the Mahatma and leaving them unmolested when hearing that they did.

'But the dividing line between saving innocent civilian lives from Japanese bestiality and suborning Indian troops was very thin. You could say it was non-existent. At this stage of our story there emerges I'm afraid not a cold and hungry sepoy but an officer, Captain Mohan Singh of the 1/14th Punjab Regiment. Captain Mohan Singh was captured in Northern Malaya very early in the campaign in, so the report we have states, Alor Star. The next thing we hear about him is that he is head of a small group of Indian officers working with a Japanese intelligence officer called Fujiwara. Fujiwara also had with him a representative from the IIL in Bangkok. Consequently one can trace a direct line from Rash Behari Bose through Bangkok and Fujiwara to Captain Mohan Singh. Mohan Singh proceeded to organize captured Indian soldiers into small fighting groups which accompanied Japanese forces during the rest of the Malayan and Burma campaigns.

'Here again evidence exists of lives of Indian soldiers and civilians having been saved. But to what end? The answer comes to us unequivocally in the extraordinary event which took place in Singapore in February last year on the occasion of General Percival's surrender to the Japanese commander. Contrary to normal procedure Indians – that is to say Indian officers – were separated from British officers as well as Indian troops from British. The Indian officers and troops were congregated in Farrer Park and there publicly handed over by the Japanese commander – to whom? To none other than our old friend, no longer Captain, but General Mohan Singh who thereupon addressed these troops, blamed the British for losing the battle and deserting their Indian comrades, announced that the days of British imperialism were over and that it was the duty of every patriotic Indian to form an army to help the Japanese drive them out from India for good and all.'

For the first time Merrick paused and glanced at the audience as if to judge its temper.

'Circumstances ideal for both the Boses' purpose now obtained, a potential – numbered in thousands – of well-trained and experienced Indian soldiers who only had to be persuaded to abandon their allegiance to a regime which appeared to have been utterly, perhaps one might say disgracefully defeated, and muster into a force of the kind envisaged by Rash Behari in Tokyo and Subhas Chand in Berlin, the army of new India, of free India. The Azad Hind Fauj. The Indian National Army. An army that would march alongside the Japanese not as traitors and stooges but as patriots and men of destiny. I think we should be clear about that – about the emotional feelings that lie behind an act of what in strictly legal terms must be defined as treachery. I have named Captain Mohan Singh. There were others with him whose names are also known. Perhaps it is unfair to single him out and his subsequent actions do not all contribute to the portrait of a man without a sense of honour, a man on the make. He has in fact suffered what we call vicissitudes. But history must name him as the King's commissioned officer who stood on the wrong side of the rail at Farrer Park and accepted a gift from the Japanese, the gift of command over men who were prisoners but still soldiers of the King-Emperor.

'We don't know how easy or difficult it was for Mohan Singh to come to the decision he obviously came to back in Alor Star at a time when even if a British defeat looked likely it had not yet been suffered. The timing of his transfer of allegiance and its apparent swiftness are rather damaging as I'm sure you will agree, but one must not forget the presence of that man of Rash Behari Bose's, the civilian representative of the IIL from Bangkok. Surely a persuasive fellow when talking to Indian officers taken prisoner. Possibly though, Mohan Singh had been brooding for some time on the situation he was in as an Indian who held the King's commission. He may finally have felt that incompatible with his nationalist ardour. Information come to hand shows that during his time as head of the Indian National Army he made great play with allegations that in Malaya the Indian KCO had always been treated as a second-class officer with a lower rate of pay and fewer privileges than his British comrade, that British officers arrogated superior status to themselves as members of a ruling class on whom the security of India mainly depended, that during hostilities with the Japanese and quite apart from the so-called gross incompetence of the high command, British officers panicked and thought of nothing but their own skins, in short got the hell out whenever they could and

left Indian officers in the lurch by putting them in command of
rearguards covering retreat.

'Since Mohan Singh's own British battalion commander is
known to have been captured with him at the same time and in
the same place, his views are not in this instance notably supported by the evidence. Nevertheless, I think we must say that
Mohan Singh had decided to be disenchanted, to believe that the
Malayan catastrophe destroyed for ever the myth of the *raj*'s
supremacy and therefore its right to remain even a day longer in
control of India's future, and furthermore to believe that it was
now his duty to think only of how best to serve his country and
his countrymen.

'Here in India in some Indian nationalist circles there has been
as you know a curious and to most of us naïve argument that
the Japanese have no quarrel with India and Indians, that it is
only the British presence and the use of India as a base for armed
operations that forces Tokyo to adopt a threatening attitude to
the sub-continent. It was a Gandhian idea and it lay behind the
serious civil disturbances of twelve months ago.

'If Mr Gandhi can believe this about the Japanese and make
millions of Indian civilians believe it, Captain Mohan Singh presumably had no tremendous difficulty in making thousands of
naturally apprehensive Indian prisoners of war believe it. Perhaps
the remarkable thing is that for the many he seems to have persuaded as many – indeed many more – have remained uncon-
vinced. I say remarkable because the consequences of resisting
persuasion cannot have been, cannot be pleasant. In front of the
eyes of your stubborn prisoner, officer, NCO or sepoy, things
doubtless happened which made the decision to remain a
prisoner and loyal to the crown a difficult one. Additionally they
saw erstwhile members of the *raj*, the white sahibs, submitted to
all the indignities we now know the Japanese are adept at devising. Add to the sight of these indignities the threats of hunger,
thirst and physical coercion and it obviously requires a special
stoutness of heart to resist the blandishments of men who yesterday were your leaders and comrades and who offer to be leaders
and comrades again in an enterprise which is projected as patriotic. A prisoner is always homesick too and here is Captain
Mohan Singh, supported now by many other Indian officers I'm
afraid, promising to lead him home in a particularly glorious

way, to a home from which the British have gone for ever, to a home where the old national leaders, many of them worn and thin from prison, will greet him as a hero, as a liberator, as a true son of the India they too have fought for.'

Again Merrick paused.

'The question of what loyalty is isn't easily answered.'

The remark only deepened the silence. Merrick referred to his notes.

'The Indian National Army under Mohan Singh consisted of approximately 10,000 ex-prisoners, officers and men, but according to our information little more than half of them had arms. However, if there had been arms and equipment readily available that number of ten thousand would have been considerably increased. Broadly speaking, Indian prisoners of war fall now into three categories – those who have so far resisted all persuasion and continue as prisoners, those who have not resisted but have indicated readiness to serve, and those who have actually been mustered in. This information is restricted. As you will appreciate when bearing in mind that figure of 10,000, and official Indian government comment and counter-propaganda, the policy is to deflect attention from this situation by minimizing its importance and ridiculing claims made by the enemy. But enemy broadcasts are regularly listened to by those civilians in this country who are rich enough to have wireless sets capable of receiving them. Foreign broadcasting is of course the one form of communication upon which Government cannot place an embargo. There have been instances of Indian families recognizing the voices of relatives who were officers in the Indian Army but who are now officers in the INA and who give stirring accounts of the great things which the INA will presently do.

'The question is, will they? I mention vicissitudes. Right from the beginning there appears to have been not unexpectedly an element of Japanese contempt for the Azad Hind Fauj matched by an element of Azad Hind suspicion of Japanese intentions, and some resistance to Japanese attempts to treat the INA as a mere appendage of their own imperial army. Under Mohan Singh the INA was theoretically the military arm of a civil independence movement headed by Rash Behari Bose, and after a conference in Bangkok this movement dedicated itself to take actions which would be wholly in line with the nationalist policies adopted here in India by the All India Congress.

'From February to August 1942, you'll recall, the Congress in India was demanding that the British quit India, that they should leave India, in Gandhi's memorable phrase, to God or to anarchy. What would happen if the British didn't quit was left, on paper, not very clear. But that is by the way. What did happen was clear enough.

'What I think important to bear in mind is the effect the news of Congress's demands, and of the outcome of those demands, must have had on Indian prisoners of war in Malaya and Burma, particularly upon those who had now committed themselves to the INA. It must have seemed to them that India was about to rise and throw the British out, that great events were afoot, that history was making their decision for them. True, their technical allegiance was to King and Country but if the mother country did not want the King and was about to get rid of him that left them with the country alone. They certainly belonged to that. It was their country after all. But apart from the matter of the British there was the matter of the Japanese. What truly were their intentions? Would they really leave India alone if the British were got rid of? INA officers have openly said to their troops that whereas the troops must be ready to fight the British – even their own old officers and comrades – they must be just as ready to fight the Japanese if the latter showed any signs of substituting the Rising Sun for the Union Jack. And there was another great INA uncertainty. Would *Congress* really approve of the Azad Hind Fauj?'

Merrick stopped to give the question time to sink in, it seemed. Perhaps that was his prime intention but suddenly he looked down at Colonel Selby-Smith and said, 'Sir, I believe the No Smoking signs are intended to apply only to the period of discussion about the scheme. I expect quite a number of people would appreciate it if you felt inclined to give permission to smoke.'

Presumably Selby-Smith nodded because Merrick glanced up and nodded to the hall, which now came stealthily alive. Teddie opened his own case in nervous gratitude. In a few seconds the hall looked like an Indian bazaar during the festival of Divali, but the business of lighting up was completed with unusual rapidity. In less than half a minute the hall was quiet again.

'This was the question. Would Congress really approve of the Azad Hind Fauj? Would they give their blessing to an operation that might lead to a bloody meeting between a rebel nationalist army and the regular Indian army? The INA assumed that upon its appearance on Indian soil the Indian army proper would disintegrate and its sepoys join hands with their rebel brothers. But even if Congress also assumed this could they accept the INA as a legal instrument of their own policy of achieving self-government?

'Quite apart from the views of the moderates and constitutionalists, the kind of Congressmen who had thought their fellow Congressman Subhas Chandra Bose an extremely dangerous man, there was the other Gandhian principle of non-violence to consider. To find out the answer to this question then, it was decided to send a group of INA officers into Burma, well-equipped with means of radio communication, to infiltrate secretly into India and contact Indian political leaders. This was done in August 1942. The enterprise was a total failure because one of the chosen officers took the first opportunity to abandon the group and to contact us and thoroughly spill the beans. The rest returned to Malaya disillusioned and the officer who reneged on them brought with him very useful documents and information. This officer is not named, but he is a bright spot on a somewhat dark horizon. It is his belief that more than a few officers and men joined the INA with the same intention as himself of either wrecking it from within or of coming back to their loyal duty directly contact was re-established with the Army to which they really belong. In other words it is suggested that they used the INA as a rather specialized means of escape from prison-camp which as we all know it is a soldier's duty to try to effect.'

An officer at the front said, 'Hear, hear.' Someone clapped. Merrick waited. He kept his eyes on the lectern and turned a page of his notes. Resuming he said:

'The spot on the horizon would be brighter however if all the officers in the infiltrating party had done precisely the same thing. We must have fairly deep reservations about the extent to which this joining up as a preliminary to returning to duty represents a significant factor in the constitution and motives of the INA. Nevertheless in any future confrontation with INA units and formations in the field it must obviously be borne in mind that not all INA soldiers on the other side of the wire, so to speak, are necessarily intent on attacking us. Some of them may be looking only for an opportunity to come in with their arms to turn them against the Japanese. Just how many we shall have no way of knowing until the time arises – if and when it does.

'But there will be a natural tendency among Indian sepoys and among other ranks in British battalions to resent these apparent deserters and traitors quite intensely, a tendency not to extend to them those military civilities we are required to show in the field to the fallen, the wounded and the captured.

'One of the main purposes of this talk is to establish certain facts and to provide what is hoped will be useful background knowledge so that we can avoid the worst effects both of minimization and exaggeration of the problem presented by the existence of this army. My own view is that whatever one's personal reactions, corporate judgment must certainly be suspended until all the facts are known. Meanwhile the restricted information presently given can settle quietly in our minds and may help us to exert a steadying influence on the men under our command if and when this division finds itself in action against units or formations of the INA. I will end this survey with an account of what has happened since the failure of the infiltrating party.

'There's no doubt that political events in India in August 1942, culminating in the severe riots that followed the detention of members of the Congress Party committees and sub-committees, had at least a potentially vitalizing effect on recruitment of prisoners of war into the INA, but the INA itself seems to have suffered a fairly severe crisis of confidence, in regard to Japanese intentions and in regard to its own. The major question whether the Congress Party would approve had gone unanswered and with all Congress's influential policy-makers in jail there was now no hope of getting it answered.

'Captain Mohan Singh was naturally at the storm-centre of this crisis of confidence. Without going so far as to say that he personally agreed with the stand the Azad Hind Fauj was making he was as its head inevitably identified with it and we may give him the benefit of the doubt here, credit him as I hinted earlier with a certain stubborn adherence to what may be called honourable principles. The main stand that seems to have been made was over areas of responsibility. What the INA was saying was that it and it alone must deal with India. Correlatively it was saying it would have nothing to do with Japanese operations elsewhere – for instance against Burmese nationalist guerrillas. To those people in the Japanese Imperial army who thought contemptuously of the INA as a mere appendage this attitude was totally unacceptable and we can assume that considerable pressure was brought to bear on Mohan Singh to conform, to put his forces at their disposal without reservations. Equal pressure was doubtless brought to bear on him by INA officers who stood by the policy of working only according to Congress principles and who saw these as integral to the principles of action and thinking in the INA. One has a picture here of the whole organization of the INA trembling on the brink of disruption.

'In December last Mohan Singh was arrested by the Japanese. The actual reasons remain to be discovered although it is believed that Rash Behari Bose was at the bottom of it. As a politician, Rash Behari presumably had a talent for bobbing like a cork on the stormiest waters, for his own position was not immediately affected. But for the first six months of this year the Azad Hind movement and the INA had a look of being something of a broken reed. It needed a strong man to mend it, a man talented enough to satisfy both sides, the Indians and the Japanese, with his views, policies and capacity for leadership.

'Who else but Subhas Chandra Bose? But he was in Germany. *Was* in Germany. Just a few weeks ago in June this ubiquitous gentleman turned up in Tokyo. The information we have is that he came out by submarine – a typically glamorous, apparently hazardous enterprise – but, let it be marked, not one he could have embarked on without the approval, indeed the wishes, of the government in Tokyo. From Tokyo he has broadcast speeches which leave no room for doubt that he is in his own eyes the man of destiny whom the Azad Hind movement and the Japanese have been waiting for. In Singapore last month he was elected President of the Indian Independence League, the other Bose – Rash Behari – having resigned to make room for him. So there we have it: Mohan Singh a prisoner, we believe in Sumatra, and Rash Behari gone into the retirement which is the reward of failure. In their place, Subhas Chandra Bose.

'He has not yet formally assumed command of the Azad Hind Fauj but that can only be a matter of time. We can indeed expect Mr Bose to claim authority over all Indian nationals in the Far East and manipulate a kind of legality for the entire proceedings by the establishment of a form of free Indian government in exile, recognized on paper anyway by the Japanese and their allies in what they call Asian co-prosperity. He is that kind of man. His qualities of leadership must not be underestimated. These were qualities that frightened several senior Congress politicians off him in the past. He was thought by them to have the makings of a dictator. One feels inclined to agree.

'This survey ends, therefore, on a note of some assurance about the continuity and enlargement of the INA as a machine of war that it would be as foolish to underestimate as it would be to allow its existence and inevitable growth to distract attention from the principal and still very dangerous and highly ambitious enemy, the Japanese. It seems to me to be very unlikely that even under Bose, who will almost certainly enjoy outwardly cordial and co-operative relations with the Japanese high command, the INA will ever slot anything but uncomfort-ably into the Japanese military machine and this may well contribute to its downfall. The other contributory factors to this likely downfall are of course its logistic problems and the mixed psychology and motives of its members. In terms of its capacity to equip itself either in co-operation or competition with the Japanese it must rank as a low-priority organization. In terms of its psychology and motivation it must rank as something less than an army capable of achieving a high and durable morale. How much less capable will depend on the magic of Mr Bose. But even the most skilful magician cannot sustain for long an illusion of common purpose when the purpose itself is so riddled with complexity. This will emerge as an important factor when Indian soldiers of the INA – intent on liberating India – come face to face with Indian soldiers who are under our command and are loyally determined to defend it from whomsoever dares set foot on Indian soil aiming a rifle at them.'

Merrick picked up his notes and had retrieved his briefcase before the audience quite realized he had finished. Although the applause broke out before he actually left the platform he did not remain to receive what might then have looked like a personal ovation, and was down the steps and returning to his seat when the applause was at its peak.

Selby-Smith rose and climbed on to the stage. As he stood at the lectern he clapped his hands about four times to demonstrate his own approval and to give a lead in the matter of bringing the ovation to an end. When he stopped clapping he seemed to be requesting silence and quite quickly got it.

He said, 'Although this meeting has now gone on for longer than many of you anticipated, what we have just heard so ably and interestingly presented was certainly worth staying to hear. I think there is no disagreement on that score. On your behalf I thank Captain Merrick for the trouble he has taken to present a clear picture of this rather sticky subject. In bringing the meeting to a close I would firmly reiterate that the subject of the INA is not one that the divisional commander wishes to have generally or casually discussed among you. In other words keep what you've heard this morning under your hats. Junior officers and NCOs have a particular responsibility to be alert for gossip and rumour among the men and to report its existence without taking steps to squash it until they've had advice on the line to take. That is all, gentlemen.'

A bit stunned by what he had heard Teddie did not seize the opportunity that now presented itself to meet his room-companion. He found it easier to go with the stream making for the doors than against it down to the front where Merrick stood alone doing up the straps of his briefcase. At the foyer doors which had been swung open and latched back by the guards Teddie nearly changed his mind because the idea of Merrick standing by himself made him feel he was not being as friendly as he should be, but someone spoke to him and when he next thought about Merrick he was climbing into the back of the 15 cwt Chevrolet – the last man of a party of five. The driver put up the tailboard and in a moment or two the truck was entering the queue for the exit from the forecourt.

In B mess he sat with two other officers in the anteroom and ordered beer. At five to one he saw Merrick come in. This time he wasn't alone. An Indian and an English officer accompanied him, guests from one of the brigades. Again he hesitated but just then Merrick's glance fell on him and seemed to stay. Teddie stood up and went across and offered his hand.

'I'm Teddie Bingham,' he said. 'What'll it be?'

For a second or two he had a feeling that Merrick was wondering whether he should find the name familiar. His hand came out rather tentatively as if casual physical contact with someone not intimately known was ordinarily unwelcome. The hand-shake failed as such. Teddie was about to explain who he was when Merrick said, 'We meet at last then.' He still had Teddie's hand and suddenly, unexpectedly, exerted grip, then quickly broke contact.

Between the man on the platform and the same man close to Teddie found a kind of discrepancy. When he thought about this afterwards he decided it was the same sort of discrepancy he'd noticed years ago in London when he was about twelve and his mother took him to a matinée and backstage afterwards to meet a man who'd played one of the character parts and still had his make-up on but spoke in an ordinary voice and seemed shy, but made up for it when they left by putting his arm round Teddie and giving him ten bob.

'Whisky or gin?' Teddie asked. 'Or are you a beer only man at tiffin?'

'It's very good of you,' Merrick began. Teddie now noticed that the blue of the fellow's eyes was made particularly vivid by the steady way he considered you with them. 'But I'm rather pressed. I'm supposed to be somewhere else at two o'clock so I'll have to go right in. Could we make it this evening?'

'Yes, of course –'

Merrick nodded. 'Good. It's time we got to know each other.' He smiled, turned, then turned back again. 'By the way. Congratulations.'

'Congratulations?'

'Hosain tells me you're getting married soon.'

'Oh. Did he? Well yes, I am. Thanks.'

He watched Merrick steering his guests to the dining-room, ushering them through the doorway with a guiding hand on each of their backs in turn. The bearer brought Teddie's beer. The man standing next to him was the adjutant of the British battalion of the brigade up near Premanagar.

'Interesting that, this morning,' the adjutant said. 'No idea anything like that going on but then I've only been in the country six months. What was he, do you know? I mean in the Indian government?'

The chap meant 'in the Civil'. Amazingly ignorant. Teddie said he had no idea which should have been good enough but apparently wasn't.

'A sort of spy do you reckon?' the adjutant asked. He had a plebeian voice and manner. He was the sort of chap one found in the bars of Tudor-style roadhouses back at home in the vicinity of Kingston-on-Thames. The fellow actually winked as such fellows did. The vulgarity of modern English life suddenly overwhelmed Teddie. It was flowing into India, blighting everything. He smiled distantly at the adjutant and murmured an apology for leaving him. He intended to swallow his beer and go into mess but, warned by a mild but sudden sensation of inner instability, put his glass down and made his way across the room to the door that led to the lavatories. Secluded there he discovered that his normally healthy and regular motions had become unpleasantly loose, untrustworthy. His forehead came out in a sweat. He felt rather unwell. The thought of food didn't much appeal. He must have picked something up.

He left by a side entrance and entered the complex of covered ways that connected B mess building to the junior officers' huts. The whole place had a temporary feeling about it. The last occupants of these particular lines had been members of the staff of a chemical and psychological warfare school. They had left a smell of gas capes and propaganda. Teddie had heard someone say that. It struck him as apt. Reaching his own room he found the door padlocked. Hosain was on mess duty. Teddie cursed his present domestic arrangements. He fumbled for his key and then paused, having noticed something extremely odd. Leant against the wall under the window there was a push-bike, or rather the remains of one. For an instant he thought someone had been in the room, taken either his own or Merrick's bicycle, removed one wheel and buckled one of the mudguards for a joke. But that wouldn't account for the rust. And then, the wreck under the window was without a cross-bar: a woman's bicycle. Nevertheless he hastened to take the padlock off the door and open up.

Bicycles were kept inside rooms because of the danger of theft.

Both bicycles were where they should be. He went out for another look at the useless and mysterious object and in doing so noticed something else: chalk marks on the floorboards of the verandah, decorating the threshold. Some sort of design. The effect was cabalistic.

He sniffed the air for the lingering scent of an ill-wisher, wondering whether he would be able to isolate such a smell from all the others to which he had become used. He could not. He stepped over the chalk marks and went to the verandah rail. There wasn't a soul; just a perspective of doors like his own, each with its padlock, and beyond the hut a space and in continuing perspective another hut. Straight ahead across the bare earth compound the prison-camp-style wire fence divided the lines from waste ground. Nobody could get over the wire but nobody needed to. The lines were always full of unexplained people. They came in at points where the PWD had either got fed up with erecting the fence or run out of material. It was not a security area. It might once have been someone's intention to make it one.

He reconsidered the broken push-bike. Perhaps Hosain had found it dumped and placed it there to show that he was an honest boy. He could have got a few annas for it from the cycle-shop wallah in the cantonment bazaar. But there had to be a connexion between the bicycle and the chalk marks. The marks could have been made by Hosain. If the boy had been a Hindu Teddie would have more readily believed that this was the explanation; that the bike and the chalk marks were some odd form of puja or offering for the welfare of the rooms' occupants to ensure them a safe journey, wherever they were going, through intercession with some modern addition to the Hindu pantheon: the god of mechanical transport.

But Hosain was a Muslim. It was unlikely that either the bhishti or the sweeper took sufficient interest in any of the officers they served to make such a well-meaning gesture to one or two of them. Besides which the marks had an inauspicious feeling to them. Teddie hesitated, controlling an urge to obliterate them. His bowels began to move again. There was a griping pain in them and the sweat broke out on his forehead. He stared down at the cabalistic signs which suddenly seemed to be responsible for the disorder in his guts, for the disruption of his life which he now felt the whole morning had somehow plotted to bring about. He scuffed his rubber-soled shoes across the marks, blurring the outlines. He continued scuffing and scraping until only an ashy smear was left. He felt better.

Back in his room he found a letter from Susan on his side of the desk. He ripped it open. It was dated five days ago. 'Dear Teddie, Tomorrow we're off to Kashmir. Aunt Fenny and Uncle Arthur will meet us in Delhi and then we'll all travel together up to 'Pindi.' They would be in Srinagar by now. He stuffed the letter into his jacket pocket and went round the back to the privy. Things were no better but he had stopped sweating. He hoped he was not going to be really ill. He read Susan's letter right through. When he returned to his room he lay down on the bed hoping to catch forty winks. After ten minutes, still wide awake, he sat up and lit a cigarette and read Susan's letter again. Srinagar would be full of officers on leave. He saw the danger he was in of losing her to some fellow with more to offer, a fellow with talent and money, a fellow who had the measure of things as they were, the kind of fellow who would understand everything Merrick talked about this morning and be able to believe it without feeling that if it was true nothing was sacred any more and nobody could be relied on, that everyone was living in a bloody jungle.

Teddie got off the bed and stubbed his cigarette. He felt emotional but couldn't work out what he felt emotional about except the prospect of being jilted or of hearing that the whole of the Malayan battalion of the Muzzys which had been captured near Kuala Lumpur had gone over to that Bose character. What he did work out was that everything that was wrong for him was really the fault of that bounder Hunter who had drunk away his mother's money and then her vitality and when he was dead hounded her to her own grave. Except that there wasn't a grave. He would have felt more settled knowing there was a grave.

It was raining again when he was ready to go back lunchless to the daftar. He couldn't face putting on a sweaty cape and cycling. He stuck his cap on and padlocked the door behind him. The ruined bike struck him as ridiculous. He walked through the covered ways until he got to the front of the mess where he was able to whistle up one of the cycle tongas whose drivers congregated outside the main gate.

IV

During the afternoon Teddie forgot about the bicycle and the chalk marks but remembered them at six o'clock on his way back to the hut. Hosain was squatting on his hunkers outside the room, whose door was open, latched back against the outer wall leaving the mesh screen exposed. The orderly got to his feet when he saw Teddie coming up the steps. He had been sitting on the spot where the chalk mark smear was. There was no sign of the bicycle.

Teddie asked where it was. Hosain indicated the room, entered ahead and pointed at the two serviceable machines. Teddie explained about the broken bicycle. Hosain went outside, looked and came in saying there wasn't a bicycle.

'I know,' Teddie said. 'But there was. What time did you get back from mess duty?'

Hosain said he was back at 14.30 but had gone straight to his own quarters, changed and gone to the bazaar for Merrick Sahib. He came back from the bazaar at 16.30 and opened the room. There hadn't been a bicycle then. If there had been a bicycle earlier someone must have taken it, probably the person who left it there in the first place. He would ask some of the other orderlies and the bhishti. But what was the good of a bicycle with only one wheel?

'Quite. That's the whole point.'

Teddie felt cross because Hosain was looking at him as if he thought Teddie was trying to cause trouble for the servants over something he had only imagined seeing. Suddenly Merrick called from the bath-house. Hosain shouted, 'Sahib!' and went with alacrity. It wasn't Merrick's fault but, no doubt about it, since his arrival Hosain had given Merrick preferential treatment. It was ridiculous having to share an orderly. Come to that it was bloody stupid having to share a room.

Teddie sat in his armchair with his legs stuck out in the shoe-removing position. Presently he heard Hosain laugh and a warm friendly sort of noise from Merrick. Less than a minute later he heard the back door being unbolted and Hosain shouting for the bhishti and then Merrick clomped in wearing unbuckled chappals and nothing else but a towel tied round his middle. He was rubbing his head with another towel.

Teddie's immediate reaction to the sight of Merrick was admiration shot darkly through with envy because Merrick had one of those bodies in which every sinew was clearly and separately defined, properly proportioned and interlocked. The fellow didn't seem to have an ounce of fat on him. You could count the pads of muscle that made up his abdominal wall.

'Ah, there you are,' Merrick said. 'I'm sorry about lunchtime.' He stopped rubbing his head and stuck the towel round his neck. 'We seem to have been Coxing and Boxing for days one way or another. I didn't see you come into mess, by the way.'

'As a matter of fact I got rather taken short.'

'Oh. Mirat tummy?'

'Sort of. But I think it's gone off.'

'I have some stuff that will settle it if it hasn't. I expect you've been sitting under the fan or drinking too much iced beer. Take a dose anyway to be on the safe side. Hold on and I'll get it.'

Teddie felt reluctant but grateful. It was like being jawed by an older boy about looking after your health; like being taken to the San because someone had noticed you were suffering in silence. Merrick came back with a small bottle and a spoon. Hosain followed him in. 'I'll pour,' Merrick said, 'because it tends to come out in a dribble and then in a rush.' He poured a couple of drops. The drops were followed by a dollop. It was brown and looked nasty. Merrick leant forward and obediently Teddie opened his mouth. The stuff tasted like very strong cough mixture. It seemed to grip his throat all the way down.

'It cements you up,' Merrick explained. 'If you have another dose in the morning you'll be right as rain.'

'Thanks.'

Merrick made a gesture at Hosain who knelt and untied Teddie's shoes. He took the medicine bottle and spoon back to the bathroom and returned rubbing his head with the towel again.

'It must be the humidity,' Teddie said. 'Not used to it recently. I've been stationed up in the hills the past few months.'

'Well you'd notice it then. Actually the humidity's fairly low here. Ever been in Sundernagar?'

'I've never even heard of Sundernagar.'

'It's where I was before they let me into the army. Your shoes go green overnight. I had an inspector who swore he was getting webbed feet, and *he* was an Indian.'

'An inspector? Were you in the Indian Police then?'

'Yes. I was DSP Sundernagar. Most of it's tribal area. Pretty boring for anyone who isn't an amateur anthropologist. My predecessor was. He was desperate to get back. I was just as keen to get out.'

'Were you there long?'

'Too long.'

Teddie nodded. DSP meant superintendent, the top man in a district after the collector and the judge. He was glad Merrick wasn't ICS. The few ICS men he'd known had been remote clever fellows, too intellectual for his tastes. The police were different, easier to get on with. Some of them envied you if you were Army. Merrick was now satisfactorily placed and explained and in spite of his high police rank Teddie felt pleasantly superior to him in occupation as well as in type, background and – as was clearer the longer he listened – in class. The police weren't always quite as particular as the other services.

He forgot about the bicycle and chalk marks until he was in his bath and then he had a flash of inspiration about them. Having arrived at an explanation that connected the whole incident to Merrick rather than to himself he was reluctant to mention it but decided he ought to, for security reasons.

Returning to the room, already dried and wearing clean underclothes under his robe, he said, 'I say, Merrick –' and then stopped, struck by a sense of having intruded upon a situation between Merrick and Hosain which he could not describe but which seemed full of potential for an intimate kind of anger or violence. Hosain was looking sullen but also tearful. He went out. Merrick now fully dressed, appeared momentarily distracted, deprived by Teddie's entrance of the opportunity to press home some kind of point that a moment ago had been important to him to make.

Merrick said, 'I'll see you in B mess in a few minutes then. What will you drink?'

Surprised, Teddie said, 'No, it's on me –'

'Well, we'll see.'

Merrick went. Teddie looked round the room expecting to see something that explained what he found inexplicable. He shrugged, called Hosain and began to dress. When he got to the shoe putting-on stage he called Hosain again. Putting on and taking off his own shoes and boots were activities at which he drew the line if there was a man available to perform these services. He had learned to draw the line in Muzzafirabad where his first CO, Colonel Gawstone, advised him never to stoop if he could help it. The climate wasn't right for it. Mrs Gawstone had stooped to pick up a glove and keeled right over and never got up. They had buried her the next day.

'Everything comes suddenly in India, Bingham,' Teddie remembered old Hooghly Gawstone saying. 'Sunrise, night, death, burial. Nothing keeps in the heat.' And in Shropshire in sultry weather the milk went off. Extraordinary chain of thought. He had forgotten why Gawstone was called Hooghly but vaguely remembered a story involving an elephant and the floating body of a dead sadhu. Or was that another story? Even two stories?

He went to the door and looked out. Not a soul in sight. The chalky smear was indiscernible because the light was going and the glow of the lamps in the room pushed his shadow across the place where the smear was. A man appeared suddenly round the corner of the hut. It was Merrick. He came up the steps saying, 'I left something behind.'

It sounded rather feeble. Something. What? Key? Wallet? Why not say? Had he come back to find out whether Hosain was telling Teddie what the row had been about? If it had been a row. There'd been no sound of a row.

'Did you send Hosain on another errand?' Teddie asked.

'No. Isn't he here?'

'No, he bloody well isn't. He's just buggered off.'

'Anything special you want?'

'Only for the little blighter to put my shoes on for me.'

Teddie went back in, sat down, and began to slip his feet into the clean pair of shoes.

'Here,' Merrick said, and threw him a long tortoise-shell shoe-horn. It made the job easier but Teddie was too irritable to mutter more than an almost inaudible 'Thanks.' It irritated him to have to do the job himself and irritated him to have Merrick watching him. At one point in his exertions he could have sworn the man was about to come and help him. The idea made him nervous. He fumbled with the laces. He went into the bathroom to wash his hands. When he returned to the room Merrick was standing in the open doorway as if looking for someone but presumably just waiting patiently for Teddie to finish.

'I'm ready now. Did you get what you came back for?'

'Yes, thank you.'

'We'd better lock up at the back too, I suppose. The whole thing strikes me as a bit bloody much.'

'What does?' Merrick asked Teddie when Teddie had bolted the bath-house door from inside and the door connecting bath-house to living quarters and rejoined him at the doorway on to the front verandah.

'What does what?'

'Strikes you as a bit much.'

'Having to put on your own shoes and lock up your own room. The little blighter has practically fuck-all to do. I've a good mind to boot him in the arse when I see him again, buggering off like that.'

Teddie wanted to get out of the room now into the open air and over to the mess to have a couple of burra pegs; but Merrick was standing in his way. There was an expression on his face which Teddie interpreted as disapproving. Perhaps Merrick was one of those chaps who had moral objections to strong language. Teddie wasn't very happy about it himself but there were pressures building up inside him these days which he didn't understand and using words like that helped to reduce them; or did if they weren't silently rejected, crammed back down your throat by someone like Merrick. Perhaps the fellow was religious.

Merrick said, 'I think I'm to blame for Hosain making himself scarce. I had to tick him off. It was the first time and he got quite a shock.'

'And what was the ticking off about?'

'A small enough thing.'

It may have been the way Merrick looked at him (in that manner Teddie would have called calculating had it not been for the tentative friendly smile) but now he felt exposed to the accusation he believed Merrick had intended to spare him. He said, 'Was Hosain complaining about me?'

Merrick seemed in so little hurry to reply that the answer became unnecessary. Merrick dressed it up, though. He said, 'I got the impression he found working for two officers – onerous.

I wasn't conscious of anything so strong as a complaint against one of us in particular.'

'But that's what it came to.'

'Only if you assume it's more natural to raise the subject of overwork with the one officer you'd be willing to go on serving. But the natural way isn't always the one they choose, is it? He may have been making a subtle complaint about me, to my face.'

'I wouldn't call Hosain a subtle sort of chap.'

'All Indians have subtle minds if you put it like that. Often I prefer the word devious for uncultured fellows of Hosain's stamp. I'm sorry if that offends you. You regular army people are rather touchy on the subject of army personnel, aren't you? But I'm afraid my experiences as a police officer have blighted any enthusiasm I ever had for the idea that the simple fellow from the village is eager to prove his devotion to the *raj*.'

'Oh.'

There seemed to be nothing else to say. On the other hand Teddie did not feel as shocked or unhappy as he guessed he ought to be. In the back of his mind there were crammed scores of case-histories which showed the relationship between white man and Indian in a holy, shining light; but none was pre-eminent, none actually came pushing through to the front to make him articulate in defence of this relationship. Merrick stood aside and Teddie hesitated, then went out on to the verandah. In any case Hosain was not a good example of the kind of man he wanted to be thinking of. He waited while Merrick closed and pad-locked the door.

'That was interesting, what you were talking about this morning,' he said.

'I'm glad you thought so. One courts a certain amount of unpopularity with that kind of thing. Myth breaking's a tricky business. To make the facts at all palatable you have to leave people with the illusion that the myth is still intact or even that you've personally restored it.'

Teddie hadn't the least idea what Merrick meant. He fell into step.

'For a moment,' Merrick said, ' – towards the end – I was made to feel I had the honour of the Indian Army in my hands entirely. The relationship between a man and his subject is very close. People tend to confuse them. It was impossible to leave the facts to speak for themselves. They had to be presented in the most charitable and acceptable light. Not necessarily so that people would leave the hall thinking well of me in spite of what I'd told them but leave it thinking optimistically about the future. One has to produce a positive response not a negative one. And the facts about the INA are a negation of most of the things the army, people as a whole, have believed in as a code of *possible* conduct.'

'I can't help feeling,' Teddie began, and because he hesitated Merrick put a hand on his shoulder, to guide him. They had reached a radial intersection of the covered ways. It was quite dark now. They steered by instinct, usage and the star patterns of lit buildings. Continuing along the correct path to B mess Merrick allowed his hand to remain.

'What? What can't you help feeling?'

'Well. That ninety per cent of the chaps who've joined the INA intend to come back over at the first opportunity. As you suggested.'

A moment or two elapsed before Merrick said, 'But I suggested no such thing. You heard what you wanted to hear. You've proved the point.'

'What point?'

'That the facts aren't as important as the light they're presented in. What's chiefly interesting about all this is that a lot of those men may persuade themselves they joined the INA because they saw it as the quickest route back to base but I doubt very much whether that's the true reason in more than a handful of cases.'

'What do you think is?'

'Herd instinct. Self-preservation. At the top among men like Bose it's a combination of herd-*leader* instinct and self-aggrandizement. Patriotism doesn't come into it. So neither does the question of loyalty. It will end up as a simple matter of two opposed views of legality, and even that's going to be settled on a purely theoretical basis.'

'How?'

'You can't hang ten thousand or more traitors.'

'You can shoot the officers.'

'Or just Bose? To encourage the others?'

'Perhaps they'll save us trouble and shoot themselves.'

'Would you?'

'Good God, yes. It would be the only way out, wouldn't it? I mean if I'd done that and got recaptured.'

'Even for a man who thinks himself a patriot?'

'You said that didn't come into it.'

'I don't think it does, but a lot of them will think they are patriots.'

'Well, I'm sorry. But there are still a few things one just doesn't do. I don't blame the other ranks so much but I find the idea of King's commissioned officers leading their men – our own men – against us utterly unspeakable.'

'Beyond the pale?'

'Yes, beyond that. Whatever it means.'

'It means outside,' Merrick said, taking him up rather too literally. 'Pale, fence, boundary. Where you draw the line between one thing and another. Between right and wrong for instance.'

'The line's already there, isn't it? We don't have to draw it.'

'There was a British officer at Farrer Park too,' Merrick said. 'He told the Indian prisoners that from now on they had to obey the Japanese as they'd obeyed the British. I don't think he meant obey in quite that sense, but it's something that may cause trouble when the legal rigmarole begins, which it will, when the war's over. Assuming we win it.'

'A British officer?'

'A senior British officer.'

'You didn't mention that this morning.'

'I thought it wiser not to.'

Teddie nodded. He felt oddly light-headed. He had a sensation of not being quite himself and at the same time of recognizing Merrick as one of the most unusual men this other self had ever met. He felt himself being drawn out, enlarged. This was dangerous because if you were enlarged there was more of you and the world was still exactly the same size. It didn't get bigger to make room for you.

The anteroom of B mess was almost empty. It was not a place in which you would ever feel at home. Its atmosphere was transitory like that of a waiting-room. Teddie was glad to have Merrick with him. He ordered scotches and sodas and thought it would be pleasant to get mildly drunk. Or even quite drunk.

'When is the wedding?' Merrick asked.

'December, or earlier.'

'Earlier, surely? We'll be gone from here in a couple of months. Once that happens you're unlikely to get an opportunity.'

'I thought sort of of leave during our jungle training period, or just after it.'

'I shouldn't count on it. If you've really decided to marry I'd advise going ahead as soon as possible. Here in Mirat, for instance. There's a hill station called Nanoora not far away. You could go there for the honeymoon. If you're lucky you might get a second honeymoon about Christmas or just after, but my guess is you won't.'

'You seem well-informed.'

'Well-advised. You've talked to Selby-Smith presumably?'

'Oh, yes. Well, I've raised the subject. He knows and so does the General.'

'I'd press it if I were you. Ask for a clear statement. Of the situation.'

He emphasized the last two words. They began to repeat themselves in Teddie's head. The situation. The situation. What situation? Getting married was the simplest thing in the world. All you needed was the girl, the ring, a padre and a few minutes to spare; and that was it. The catch was in getting the few minutes and in extending them to hours, days, a week or two. The situation was one of time; not having enough of it to be able to call any of it your own, except by arrangement, by permission. Your whole life was subject to permission one way and another.

Teddie frowned, gulped his scotch and soda. Everyone's life was lived by permission. Whose? There were plenty of people around whose permission you had to seek but to give permission they had to have it themselves from somebody else. Where the hell did it all lead? Where was the highest, the final authority? One ought to know because logically it was this highest final authority that was creating the situation that made a simple thing like marrying Susan so damned difficult.

He called the bearer over again, ordered two more burra pegs, smiled aside Merrick's attempt to make the second round on him.

He said, 'I suppose one's wedding should be the most important day of one's life. To other people it's a sort of irritation, isn't it?'

The belief that he had made an unexpectedly profound statement about the comparative unimportance of the individual in
the wider general scheme of things pleasantly aggravated the
notion he had this evening of not being quite the man his friends
would recognize. Merrick, he thought, was looking at him with
the intense regard of someone more finely attuned than most
to another person's potential. He felt encouraged to further
profundity but found the way down to it blocked. He said, 'Are
you married, Merrick?'

Merrick was drawing on a cigarette. He took his time, inhal-
ing and exhaling. 'No, I'm not.' Each word was marked by a
wreath of ejected smoke. Teddie was left with an impression of
a sad history in this respect, of what they called a torch being
carried. Perhaps the heat of the torch explained the cool bright
blue of Merrick's eyes. Everyone had his defence. He supposed
cheerfulness was his. Recently he had found the smile on his
face a bit on the heavy side. Underneath it there were these
pressures. Mostly sexual, he imagined. He recollected the soft
flesh of Susan's inner arm, just near the elbow. He signed for the
second round, raised his glass and said, 'Cheers.'

Unaccountably the second whisky went straight to his head.
Denied physical intimacy with Susan who at this moment represented all women he craved the substitute; intimate accord with
some man, here represented by Merrick who sat admirably composed, self-possessed, with all those hidden muscles relaxed but
doubtless reassuring to him, sources of self-confidence as they
were of Teddie's envy and grudging respect. It occurred to him
that Merrick was – how could he put it? – a mystery that
attracted him. He found himself telling Merrick about his
parents, about Hunter and the abortive search for his mother's
grave in Mandalay. On Merrick's clear, handsome but experienced face he saw an expression that encouraged him to feel
more in control of his affairs, more intelligent about the significance of a history which it surprised him to discover he had
rather a lot of. Talking to Merrick made him feel that he'd almost
made a contribution to the totality of the world's affairs. He
believed that Merrick cottoned on to this and was assessing the
contribution accurately and appreciatively. It pleased him that
Merrick continued to look interested and to ask him questions
because this suggested to him that Merrick didn't dismiss the

contribution as negligible. With his third burra peg, which Merrick signed for, Teddie acquired a certain self-conscious tenderness towards him.

He also felt sick; rather suddenly. The medicine had cemented him up at one end perhaps but not at the other. He wondered whether the feeling would go away if he ignored it. He embarked on a description of Susan and said what a marvellous girl she was, what a lucky fellow he was. The more he thought about it (he said) the luckier it seemed to him he was. Pretty girls were usually frivolous, weren't they? She was damned pretty but terrifically sensible as well as fun to be with. 'I'd like you to meet her,' he said. 'You will if we do what you suggest and get married here.' That sounded like a good idea: to show people in Mirat what a fine girl he'd got hold of. His forehead was damp.

'Are you feeling bad again?' Merrick asked him.

He said, 'It'll go off in a minute. It had better because I've decided to get pleasantly pissed tonight and that always takes me a fair time.' He signalled the bearer for two more scotches but Merrick said, 'Not for me. I'm not a great drinker. In fact there was a time when I hardly touched it. It used to amaze me how much some people could put away. It was Sundernagar that got me into a regular habit. But two in a row is still about my limit before eating.'

'My uncle actually taught me to drink,' Teddie began, remembering himself at seventeen and the evening session in Shropshire with the decanter and his uncle's dedicated but critical eye; but then stopped short of explaining why: that his uncle said that a good head for good liquor was one of the few things that still distinguished a gentleman from others. But Merrick appeared to cotton on to that too. He said, 'Mine was the kind of family that never kept drink in the house except at Christmas and then it was port.'

'My uncle's a port man,' Teddie said, intending to encourage. 'He's always talking about putting some down for me, but I'll be surprised if he does.'

Merrick smiled. 'This was the sort that doesn't get put down. Australian port *type*. When I was a boy I thought all wine was port and that all port came from Australia. It's the sort of thing that makes life difficult for clever children from humble families. One suffers disproportionately. The young are extremely unkind to each other and their elders aren't always free from prejudice. I doubt there's a more unattractive sight than that of a schoolmaster currying class favour by making fun of the boy in his form whose background is different from the others. It's the kind of situation in which it's as well to be tough as well as clever. Fortunately I was both.'

'What school was this?'

'A grammar school. But my natural element would have been the local county. I got into this other place on a scholarship and my people were very proud of that. They weren't exactly poor but they were poverty-stricken in comparison with other parents. And lower-middle-class. By those standards. I took up boxing and found my own level.'

'Do you still box?'

It was the only thing Teddie could think of to say.

'No. But it was my athletic skill as much as my academic achievement that got me into the Indian Police. Those and the interest taken in me by the assistant headmaster. He taught history which happened to be one of my best subjects. I owed him a lot. We kept up a correspondence after I came out, right up until the time he died.'

'I was an awful duffer at school,' Teddie confessed. Like his confidential report from Staff College, recollection of his scholastic stupidity and only average capacity at games caused him no regret: certainly no shame. School, after all, was only part of the adult arrangement to keep children out of the way while they were growing up. He supposed it was different for people like Merrick's parents, but he imagined there was a similarity somewhere. In any case here they were, the two of them, arrived on the same sofa in the same place with the same rank and the same privileges, sharing the same room and the same servant who, as it happened, preferred Merrick who hadn't been born in a world where servants figured and port got put down.

At once he remembered the bicycle and the chalk marks and the idea he had had that these were a message to Merrick, a warning to Merrick by an INA sympathizer who had found out that Merrick was taking a detailed interest in the subject and perhaps that he was lecturing on it that morning. But just what a bicycle and cabalistic signs had to do with either the subject or Merrick's involvement was a mystery.

He said, 'Does a bicycle have any special significance for you, old man?'

He had never seen such a change in a fellow. At least, he couldn't remember seeing one. It was brief but – there was no other word for it – electrifying. The tingling sensation communicated itself to Teddie. For a moment Merrick looked as if he had been made by a machine and was waiting for someone to come and disconnect him so that he could collapse back into his component parts because there was no possibility of his being galvanized by the vital fundamental spark. Subsequently what puzzled Teddie was that he should have thought about the change in Merrick in such terms. He wondered whether he was becoming over-sensitive, whether he had picked up something that had attacked his nervous system, speeded up his reactions and sent his imagination out of control. Something odd had been happening to him ever since he arrived in Mirat. There was that peculiar fancy he had had about the spare bed as a burning ship or catafalque. Perhaps he had been affected by the aeroplanes. The height had hurt his ears and after each flight it had been a day or two before his hearing was really clear again. That sort of thing could upset your physical balance so there was no reason why it shouldn't upset your mental balance too.

'A bicycle?' Merrick asked. 'What do you mean, special significance?'

'Well I don't know. Is it a sort of symbol of the INA?'

'Not that I'm aware of. Why?'

Teddie told him.

'Just that?' Merrick said, when he had explained. 'A broken bicycle?'

'Well there were these chalk marks. I'm afraid I scuffed them out.'

Presently Merrick said, 'What a pity.' He sipped some of the scotch remaining in his glass. 'Do you remember the marks in any detail?'

'I'm afraid not. I say, do you think I was right?'

'About what?'

'The INA.'

Merrick did not reply for a while. He was inspecting the palm of his left hand. He said, 'Possibly. Have you told anyone else?'

'I asked Hosain. He didn't know what I was talking about. I expect the beggar thought I was accusing him of something.'

'I see. Well that explains that. He did say or at least imply you'd questioned his honesty. But I never listen to complaints from servants about other officers. That's why I was ticking him off. Have you mentioned the bicycle and the marks to anyone else?'

'No.'

Teddie, sensing a secret, felt privileged.

'Then I shouldn't.' He looked at Teddie's glass. 'Let me get you another of those before we eat. To kill the bugs.' He called the bearer over. Ten minutes later when they got up to go into the mess Teddie felt euphoric. At dinner he drank beer. Afterwards he drank several brandies and Merrick drank one. Without Merrick to guide him he might have lost his way in the maze of covered walks. By the time they got back to their room Teddie was satisfactorily several over the eight but still on his feet. He protested when Merrick helped him take off his shoes. He did not remember getting into bed.

He woke with a thick head when Hosain roused them at half-past seven with morning tea, and recalled a dream that had been so vivid it hardly seemed like a dream at all but obviously was because it couldn't have happened that he woke in the middle of the night and saw an Indian – a Pathan in a long robe – standing in the middle of the room.

When he pressed the subject of his marriage, as Merrick had recommended, he was unable to ignore a moment longer its grand irrelevance to the position in which he and every other officer at divisional headquarters were placed. He found himself having to treat it with the same sympathy and impatience that Colonel Selby-Smith showed (wrinkling his face and tempo-rarily detaching his mind from the main stream of his multiple concerns) so that it was not until Teddie was alone in his room that he fully appreciated the fact that he was none the wiser but somehow committed to panic-action. He had no idea how to conduct his affairs on such a basis, nor how to break it to Susan and her mother. He wished he had left the subject unpressed but at the same time realized that to have done so might have been disastrous. His feelings towards Merrick were now ambivalent.

He was grateful to him for the advice but couldn't help identifying him with the unsatisfactory result of taking it.

Between mid-October and Christmas, Selby-Smith had said,
there was now no likelihood of getting away because the serious
business of working up would be done during those few weeks,
probably in one of the stickier areas of Bengal. After Christmas,
leave was anyone's guess. Selby-Smith's own was that there
wouldn't be any. The battalion and brigade leave rosters were at
the tail-end stage. With the exception of Teddie every officer
at divisional headquarters had had leave before joining. The
general had been very keen to establish what he called a pattern
of full working continuity once the division was formed. He
would be adamant about not granting leave to any officer unless
the circumstances were exceptional. Selby-Smith promised to
have a word with him at lunch because Teddie's circumstances
were, if not exceptional, at least different. In the afternoon
Teddie received the general's ruling. He could either postpone
his wedding until after Christmas and risk not having it at all or
he could get married in Mirat at any time he wished between
now and the third week in October and have seventy-two hours'
leave to enjoy the consequences.

At first he felt bucked. Cycling home from the daftar he saw
Mirat through the honeyed eyes of an ardent young husband,
but suddenly its strangeness imposed itself on him and he could
not picture her there. All kinds of practical details about the wedding presented themselves for consideration and for once he
found it impossible to deal with them one at a time. He arrived
at his quarters incapable of coherent thought and wondered how
best to get hold of Tony Bishop whose job it should be, as best
man, to do his thinking for him. Hosain brought tea and he
began a letter: Darling Susan –

The blank paper only emphasized the immense distance she
was from him and it was a distance he did not feel he could cover.
He abandoned the letter in favour of a List which began after an
entry or two to look suspiciously like a staff officer's note to the
Q side. He had just written the word accommodation which was
all right as an idea – in fact as such essential – but the ramifications
of the word now began to be exposed; the names and faces of
people requiring accommodation sprang up argumentatively
claiming attention, comfort, indeed some reasonable degree of

luxury. The bride; the bridesmaid (Sarah); the bride's mother; the matron of honour, Mrs Grace (Aunt Fenny); the chap to give the bride away, Major Grace (Uncle Arthur); the best man. It would be simpler for him to go to Pankot. But that would take forty-eight of the miserable grudging allowance of seventy-two. There would hardly be a night he could call his and Susan's own.

He yelled for Hosain, told him to tell the bhishti to get a move on with the bath water. A thunderstorm broke. For fifteen minutes the electricity was off. He fanned himself with the writing-pad. The solution came to him dressed in its own perfect grey and respectful logic. There would be no wedding until after bloody Christmas and bloody Bengal. There would probably be no bloody wedding. He went out to the closet and sat miserably hunched, resting his forehead on both fists.

As a boy in his first year of English exile, in the house of his Shropshire uncle, he had often retreated to the unfriendly privacy of the cold English lavatory to consider the extraordinary miseries of life. His eyes blurred in sympathetic remembrance. It was several seconds before he realized that the most shameful thing was happening. He was blubbing.

Darling Susan, he began again a few days later when this unusual and useful man Merrick had solved the problem for him. And broke the news to her. With enthusiasm. 'As for arrangements here,' he continued, 'they're simple enough. Rather exciting in fact. Can't remember whether I mentioned that Mirat is a princely Indian state' (he hadn't; the fact had escaped his notice; Merrick had told him). 'The palace and all that sort of thing are on the other side of the lake' (he'd hardly noticed the lake either), 'but it seems the old Nawab has a guest house there that he's made available to the station for special visitors who can't get decent accommodation. I've had a word with the SSO and the guest house is available for the October dates I suggest. I've booked it anyway because I can always alter it if you can't manage it. There's tons of room for all of you, apparently, including Aunt Fenny and Uncle Arthur. The SSO says it's very comfortable, even luxurious. And apart from the commissariat which one arranges oneself it's all free as air. It seems the old nawab likes having English people there. It's in the grounds of the palace but quite separate and of course guarded, so don't worry. It should be fun. There's a nice old church in the cantonment, which is where it'll be, and afterwards we can shoot up to the Nanoora Hills in just a few hours. . . .'

He stopped, gazed at the rain outside, living the eternity after the word hours, or trying to. Not having been to Nanoora he found it difficult to conjure a background to Susan's hair which he could see and smell. The background to her hair kept coming out as Pankot. Nanoora might well do so too, in fact. One place looked much like another once you were used to it. He bent over the desk again and wrote: 'I'll drop a line to Tony Bishop but perhaps you or your mother would too. I'm sure General Rankin will give him long enough leave to accompany you all down, even if you come a week before the wedding. I can get him a room at the club. So don't worry on that score. Darling Susan. Enjoy Srinagar. How I wish we could have been there together. But it was not to be.'

One other thing was not to be either. Five weeks later, a week before the wedding party was due in Mirat, Susan rang from area headquarters in Pankot to divisional headquarters in Mirat, got put on to Teddie personally and told him that Tony Bishop was in hospital with jaundice and had to be written off as best man. Teddie felt disturbed, less by the news and the problem it presented than by the business-like and utterly unromantic tone of Susan's voice which he had not heard for a long time and which quite clearly commanded him to take firm steps to ensure that there was no other hitch.

Teddie's desk was endways on to a window that looked out on to the main verandah of the Ops block. Susan was saying, 'So Teddie, you'll have to detail someone at your end to hold your hand in Tony's place,' and just then Ronald Merrick walked past.

Teddie smiled. 'Don't worry, old thing. Easy as wink. I'll probably get the fellow I share quarters with. He's a helpful and willing sort of chap.'

Coda

I've got a terrific favour to ask old man he had said but really it had been the other way round the favour being done to Merrick who as a boy could not have dreamed ever of supporting an

officer of the Muzzafirabad Guides as best man at a wedding: a
dignity not to be taken on lightly and certainly not to be repaid
like this with a cut cheek and a piece of sticking plaster, an
impediment to the tender conviviality of skins.

Shaving, the sensation of having been taken advantage of, of
having had a casual friendship presumed upon, settled like a claw
between his shoulder blades (which were otherwise unscarred,
unmarked by the talons of physical desire. Her fingers had conveyed a reluctance which he supposed was a degree better than
distaste.) Teddie dabbed his cheeks and chin with a towel, cut a
fresh piece of sticking plaster and applied it to the wound.

Merrick's wound. Teddie had borne it with an equanimity
that disguised incredulity. This morning however the face in the
mirror was that of an acquaintance well enough known, taken
enough interest in, to make an explanation of what had happened at the wedding obligatory and, in advance of getting it,
unconvincing, in fact unbelievable, part of an especially sly confidence trick. The face in the mirror was that of a man Teddie
felt he couldn't trust. The eyes were too narrow, shifty under
sandy lashes. The cheeks were drawn, as by some vice lately
attempted and come to nothing. The bones shadowed them with
a mixture of shame and unaltered intention.

Yesterday they had arrived in Nanoora. Tomorrow they must
return. Their one complete and uninterruptible day had begun.
The hours were almost too many for him to hold because the
whole weight of them seemed to be on his back. It was as if he
had invented the day for his own convenience. He went back
into the bedroom where Susan lay, crumpled, asleep or wishing
she were. He couldn't be sure. She appeared discarded, not by
other people but by herself. The curtains were still drawn across
the too large window which was bordered by breaking and
entering bands of vagrant sunshine. The room was otherwise still
part of the private revelations of his wedding night and would be
until the bearer brought morning tea and pulled the curtains
back: an event that was not due for another forty minutes.

Showered and shaved he was conscious of thirst and hunger.
But there was this other more insistent appetite; so intense it
seemed that it would never be satisfied. He could never get
enough. The mere sight of her sharpened and hardened him. His

genitals ached but were totally in command again, engorged. His mind was frozen. He stripped and clambered in, without making a sound; it felt to him nevertheless as though he had whimpered. His arms trembled, anticipating exertions. She was night-scented, a warm aromatic combination of breasts and thighs and rucked transparent nightgown which gave his spoiler's hands no rest but racked them with endless exhausting domineering tensions.

She cried out softly, apparently rudely awoken. With an abrupt gasping acquiescence she opened her legs but not her eyes; offered what assistance she could think of, but the duality of their enterprise did not connect them. Only his flesh did that and there was an improvement in her in that direction, the only one that mattered for the moment, having been earned, worked for with a kind of tight-lipped patience. The contest over, detumescent, he lay licking her wounds with kisses.

Later he drew her bathwater, poured in generous handfuls of sweet, silly pink salts. For half-an-hour he sat by the bedroom window, considering the unknown prospect of Nanoora which was surprised in its own daylight. He drank tea and listened to the irregular but confirming sounds of the sponge dipped and squeezed. He tried to believe that the bathroom was not her refuge but a place of preparation for the business of giving and sharing and taking up her part of the day which somehow had to carry a whole future in its mouth – like a mother-beast with her cubs, to a place of safety.

What had he done? Hurt her physically? Shocked her with his carnal approach? Had he been while exercising consideration and patience inconsiderate in showing vigour, making no attempt to hide this extreme of happiness? His own shock had been the shock of joy that was legitimate, endorsed, blessed, with nothing murky or restricting perched on its shoulder. He had discovered a private area of freedom inside the stockade. She had not entered it with him. He must be at fault. He had failed to arouse her. He had a miserable impression that she did not like him. His body ached for her affection.

PART THREE

THE SILVER IN THE MESS

I

BARBIE HAD never known the wilder secrets of life nor held the key to its deepest sensual pleasures. The mystical element in a wedding was therefore real to her. She observed with pleasure the grace and stillness which became Susan's chief attribute the moment her engagement was announced. The girl was different. Her realization of her love had driven everything else from her mind and left her body in repose. Where once she had worked so hard at being the centre of attraction she was now, as of right, at a centre and stood there smiling out at the world; even that part of it which Barbie inhabited.

Barbie watched Sarah closely and was satisfied that there was no broken heart. She had not believed Teddie and Sarah well suited in the few short weeks they were going everywhere together. She thought of these girls as her own girls, born of her womb, dramatically separated from her but now living near her in ignorance of her maternal claims. It was a harmless act of self-deception and hurt nobody, except perhaps herself.

It was a great disappointment to her when the Laytons returned early from the family holiday in Kashmir and announced that the wedding was not to be in Pankot in December but as soon as it could be fixed, in Mirat where Teddie had been posted. She had intended to be at the church even if Mildred had not found it in her heart to invite her to the reception. She had persuaded herself that she would in fact receive an invitation and had ordered through Gulab Singh's a set of twelve Apostle teaspoons for the wedding gift. She planned to have a new costume made in some festive colour. She inspected bolts of cloth at the durzi's. A heliotrope caught her eye. She believed in planning early but said nothing to anyone. Her fear was that in spite of the instructions she had given him the durzi would turn up at Rose Cottage and scatter all these colourful materials on the verandah and so give away her hopes and expectations.

Which is what he did, on the evening of the day the Laytons got back from Kashmir and, uninvited, assembled at Rose Cottage with Clara Fosdick and Nicky Paynton to discuss the problems of the sudden change of plan; so that at first it appeared to them all that the durzi had heard the news and was prompt off the mark, anticipating an urgent order for a trousseau as yet only half-heartedly bespoken.

'Full marks for information and method,' Mildred told him. 'Show us what you've got.'

He set the white-sheeted bundle down, but at Barbie's feet, and opened it, perplexed by so large and interested an audience, and revealed bolts of woollen cloth in colours and patterns that would have killed every woman there except one: who stood exposed. The durzi twitched the heliotrope material between thumb and finger and said, 'Pure.' He said it to Barbie.

'It's a material I've been looking at,' she told them. But the truth was all too clear. She never wore 'colours'. The material was for a special winter occasion. 'I can't make up my mind and he's trying to do it for me, the wretch. What do you think?' She took refuge in the dog. 'Panther now. What do *you* think?' She got a desultory wag. In this climate pets faded even quicker than women.

'The question is, could I carry it? That's what my mother used to say to her clientele. I doubt you can carry it, or, It wouldn't do for everyone but you could carry it. I always imagined a difficult material as an immense *load*.'

Which it was. She would have liked to lighten the load and at the same time obliterate the embarrassing scene; and saw how this might be done – by swooping on the bolts of cloth and throwing them like huge unwieldy paperchains until the verandah was heaped in heliotrope, electric blue, bilious emerald and garish pink. She grinned in frustrated exultation.

'I suppose it *is* somewhat festive. Christmas Day perhaps or would that be carrying it too far?' She laughed at her unintentional pun, turned, looked down at the durzi. 'No, take it all away. Some other time perhaps but this is not the place.'

'Aziz,' Mildred said, 'tell him to call at the grace and favour tomorrow at eleven.'

Aziz did so. Satisfied, the durzi did up his bundle, salaamed and was away; an old bent man ever ready to exercise his skill at both sides of his trade – selling and stitching. His cloth was better and cheaper than the stuff at Jalal-ud-din's. At night in his open-fronted shop he sat cross-legged on his platform under a naphtha lamp and an oleograph depicting the Lord Krishna fluting maidens by moonlight. He wore half-spectacles on his nose and looked up at you from above them and smiled, pressing his palms together, as if in a predominantly Muslim bazaar it required alertness and good manners as well as predestination to be Hindu. Barbie pictured him spread-eagled under the bundle, strangled on the way home by *thugs* as a sacrifice to the Goddess Kali; his bloated tongue the colour of the rejected cloth, and listened in now to Mildred talking to Clara Fosdick and Nicky Paynton.

It seemed that in Kashmir, at Mildred's insistence, the house-boat had been moved from its original site – a noisy berth between two others that were rented by American officers who played portable gramophones until the early hours and had Eura-sian girls draped on the sundecks under awnings. They had tried to involve Sarah and Susan in these late-night parties.

Mildred ordered the boat taken to the remote spot where she and John Layton had spent part of their honeymoon, and moored it one hundred yards from someone who had got there sooner but whose boat seemed quiet, hardly to exist in fact; muted to the point of creating its own illusion of itself as though at any moment it might break up into component parts of air and light and water.

Or so Barbie conjured it, absorbing all the separate pieces of information from Mildred's account and reassembling them. To begin with she had never been to Kashmir and had to imagine this entirely for herself, helped out by recollections of pictures in books and on postcards. She thought of Kashmir as snow and apples at the same season and a deep lake into which the snow melted and the apples fell. In spring there were sheep from which the fine wool shawls came; and then in autumn the smell of carpentry. The water was always placid but grey and misty. At night there were stars and heaven looked very far away, far behind the stars, as it did in places where there were mountains. For the first time, listening to the story, she admitted the actual quality of colour and sunshine so that the water now looked green as well as deep, shaded by willows whose fronds brushed the ornate fretted wood of houseboat roofs.

And in this long warm sleeping afternoon a cry came, across the one hundred yards of water, a cry of a child, which seemed odd. Only an elderly woman, apart from servants, had been noted. To this woman, after discussion, cards had been sent and the cry of the child at first sounded like the ambiguous answer and continued to do so until the arrival of the tiny reciprocal rectangles of pasteboard with that name in copperplate, engraved.

Lady Manners.

The lake was still placid; no ripple. Distantly the mountains still erected sharp outlines. Shade remained dark like indigo velvet. Butterflies hemstitched this tangible material, and Barbie – living it – watched them and heard the cry repeated, felt the fascination of the situation before she understood the predicament created by the proximity, the awful nearness to the untouchable condition that attached to that name, Manners, which was the name of the woman and, with her inexplicable permission, of the child whose father was any one of six disgusting hooligans. There she was, the old woman, once distinguished, once elegantly in occupation of Government House in Ranpur and the now virtually disused Summer Residence in Pankot, at ease upon the sundeck of a houseboat; isolated from the world her niece and now she had scandalized.

The girl, the Manners girl (poor running panting Daphne) had paid the price of her folly by dying, bearing the tiny monster of the Bibighar that should have been destroyed in the womb and, it was once suggested, thrust down the throats of the culprits or their bloody priests. Miss Manners had not had, surely, religious scruples about abortion? More likely a conviction that she knew the father. The implications of this conviction were almost too astonishing to imagine, as were the old woman's motives in announcing the death, the birth, to a world that thought it better to forget.

Of course, Mildred said, it wasn't possible to follow up the ritual begun in ignorance with the exchange of cards. She let her slightly hooded eyes stray explanatorily towards the garden where the girls innocently played with Panther in that permitted

zone originally marked out by Barbie. But, she added, there had
been odd moments of hiatus: shikaras setting out from both
houseboats at the same minute, or unable to avoid what only a
few yards of water stopped from being an actual confrontation,
but close enough to demand an inclination of heads, since the
occupants of each had met by pasteboard and they could not
accept the burden of uncivilized pretence that this had not
occurred, could not assume that they were total strangers, even
if it were tacitly agreed there should be no development of an
acquaintance from which neither side could benefit, and from
which one side (that of the girls, playing there with the ball and
the dog, those appendages of unsullied English life) could only
incur positive harm.

'What did she look like?' Nicky Paynton wanted to know.

'One couldn't see. We were never, thank God, *that* close, and
even under the shikara awning she wore an old topee and a veil.'

Teddie's letter about the new arrangements for the wedding
had been almost a relief, giving as it did a conscientious reason
for ordering the boat away (even if it looked like embarrassed
retreat) back to its original mooring to be closer at hand for
unexpectedly early last-minute shopping and the making of
arrangements for an early return to 'Pindi by cars, to Delhi by
train (where Aunt Fenny and Uncle Arthur became detached),
and on to Ranpur, back to Pankot, and the excitement as well
as the slight hysteria of bringing the wedding forward and somehow transferring it to Mirat: a place of palaces, mosques and
minarets.

Guests of the Nawab! Barbie's visions were now coming to
her through the fretted stone screens that embellished so much
Moghul architecture. Through these she peeped at lawns and
lakes and fountains and saw Susan, standing in her new-found
stillness, in bridal white, her veil lifting in rose-scented breezes
that had blown across deserts.

Quite quickly she detected a mystery about the book but put it
down to the curious evasiveness Sarah had brought back from
Kashmir with her, like something caught and not yet shaken off.

The book was an elegant affair of dark red leather, gold tooling
and paper in which you could see flecks of the wood from whose
pulp the paper had been made. The text was printed in the

Arabic script which Barbie, fluent in spoken Urdu, had never learned to decipher. But she could see it was poetry.

The book was to be the Laytons' thank-you present to the Nawab of Mirat in whose palace guest house they were to stay. Mildred mentioned the book and now Sarah had brought it up to show to Mabel. She unwrapped it and offered it as if it were a gift she had received not one the family were to give.

'It was a bit of luck really,' she said.

'Why luck?' Mabel asked, hearing.

'Luck to discover the connexion.'

'Connexion? Who are the poems by?'

'Gaffur.'

'Oh!' Barbie interrupted. 'Gaffur. He's a classic Urdu poet. I used to know several quotations. What connexion do you mean?'

'He was court poet to a Nawab of Mirat in the eighteenth century. A relation. The same family as the present Nawab. A Kasim.'

' "It is not for you to say, Gaffur," ' Barbie suddenly recalled, ' "that the rose is God's creation. Howsobeit its scent is heavenly." Oh, how does it go on?'

'Yes,' Sarah said. 'How?'

Her face was very pale. This was unusual.

'I don't know. But I do know that in each poem they address themselves by name, just once, I think. Not their real names. Their pen-names. I didn't know Gaffur was a Kasim.'

She hesitated, held up one finger. 'It is not for you to say, Gaffur, that the rose is God's creation. Howsobeit its scent is heavenly. Something something something. It's quite useless. I've lost it. Is there a connexion between the Nawab and Mr Mohammed Ali Kasim the politician?'

'Yes,' Sarah said. 'The Nawab and he are kinsmen as well, but fairly distantly.'

'How extraordinary, and well – fraught. I mean, is that the word?'

'What are you saying, Barbie?' Mabel asked. Barbie answered from her abdomen, a schoolroom trick that did not strain the throat. Her whole body acted as a sounding board.

She said, 'The Nawab of Mirat is related to Mohammed Ali Kasim who is presently in gaol.'

'Oh,' Mabel said. 'Is he?' So that it was not clear which he she meant or which condition – the relationship or the incarceration.

'The Congress ex-chief minister in Ranpur,' Barbie emphasized.

'I know,' Mabel said. 'My second husband was once a colleague of *his* father.' She turned to Sarah. 'Who thought of the book?'*

'Someone we met in Srinagar.'

'What was their name?'

A pause.

'The idea just emerged in conversation. We met so many people,' Sarah eventually said.

As Sarah took the book back into her hands Barbie remembered the old parlour game in Camberwell. I open the book. I look at the book. I close the book. And I pass the book along. The catch had been to cross your legs as you passed the book to the next player otherwise you were out. It was a game which like others of its kind scared her until she was old enough to think it silly, and even then the icy little hand would touch her low down on the back of her neck, the hand of the invisible guest, the demon-spirit of the party who knew the answers to all the conundrums and puzzles and who presided over the gathering with a thrilling kind of malice, totting up the scores and marking down for ridicule, if not worse, special victims: the foolish aunt, the sickly cousin who cried when Barbie's father did his grotesque babes-in-the-wood act, sitting in a tub, under the table, with only his bare knees showing, and on each knee a grinning face sketched with burnt cork, the eyes closed.

*It is not for you to say, Gaffur
  That the rose is one of God's creations,
  Although its scent is doubtless that of heaven.
  In time rose and poet will both die.
      Who then shall come to this decision?
        (Trans. Edwin Tippitt, Major. I. A. Retd)

You oughtn't to say, Gaffur,
  That God created roses,
No matter how heavenly they smell.
    You have to think of the time when you're both
      dead and smell nasty
And people are only interested in your successors.
      (Trans. Dmitri Bronowsky).

Sarah, having taken the book, looked at it herself. Her grace was a different kind from Susan's. If grace was the right word then Susan had the look of imminent entrance to it, Sarah the look of being born there, of merely having to wait for it visibly to form itself around her, when she and it would exist in a state of mutual recognition. It had not happened yet, but something had happened, in Kashmir, which had heightened the other look she had always had of taking very little on trust, of preferring to work things out for herself; heightened the look and presumably her realization that it was far from easy. It then occurred to Barbie that Sarah could have seen the child, talked to Lady Manners, taken one of those opportunities when characteristically alone to pay the visit her family steered clear of.

Barbie pictured it: this young girl and the old woman, and the child somewhere in the vicinity. I came, the girl was saying, because I couldn't go without saying hello. So said hello and talked and later was shown the child. One of God's creatures. Although, as Gaffur for some reason would have it, that was not for one to say. The idea of the book could have come out of this visit because the conversation could have turned upon the imminent journey to Mirat, and the reason for the journey. It was the kind of thing the old woman would know: the connexion between a poet and a prince and an imprisoned politician.

Convinced that she had hit upon the solution to the mystery of the book Barbie gazed at Sarah with awe and curiosity; fear for her toughness and temerity. Sarah had her father's dignity but it was committed in a different cause, or seemed to be; committed to discovering where she would feel it earned, where her duty was. On the score of duty her father obviously had no questions. His dignity was therefore unqualified. It was this difference in dignity that people saw and in Sarah misinterpreted; people like the Smalley woman who saw the difference as something perilously close to 'unsoundness' – a condition which led to an inability to retain the affection of suitable and dignified young officers. Barbie thought: More fools they, Sarah's worth ten of most of them; lucky the man who gets her but he will have to be pretty special. She looks at my old fond and foolish face and sees through it, I think, sees below the ruination, hears behind the senseless ceaseless chatter, sees right down to the despair but also beyond to the terrific thing there really is in me, the joy I would find in God and which she would find in life, which come to much the same thing. But if she's not careful she'll find herself not living, just helping others to. Perhaps that's all I've ever done. If so it isn't much, it isn't enough I don't suppose. Especially if I ask myself: How many of those children did I ever truly bring to Jesus?

Sarah glanced at her.

'What did you mean, Barbie, fraught?'

'I suppose I meant odd, difficult, to be the guest of a man whose kinsman we've put in clink, but India is full of oddities like that isn't it and perhaps the Nawab disapproves of his politi-cian kinsman. Or if he doesn't he obviously doesn't disapprove of us. But then the princes like us better than the rest of them do, don't they? We've bolstered them up and some of them one gathers hardly deserve it. One of my friends belonged to what's called a zenana mission and she once spent a year in a palace of a tiny state in Rajputana. Actually I forget but I think it was Rajputana. Her job was to try to give the rudiments of a modern education to the ruler's wives and daughters who were all in purdah or going to be in purdah. She adored the children but said there were times when she actually went in fear of her life, not that it was ever threatened but she heard such terrible things, quite barbaric. But I'm sure Mirat's not like that.'

'No, I'm sure it isn't,' Sarah said. 'I must go.'

She got up, leant and kissed Mabel who thanked her for bringing the book of poems. Barbie went with her to the front where the tonga was waiting.

'She did appreciate it. She would have liked to be at the wedding, but Mirat's so far. Too far. It was awfully nice of you to come up specially to show the book. Shall you invite the Nawab to the wedding?'

'I expect so, Barbie. You would have liked to come too wouldn't you?'

'Oh yes. But I couldn't leave Mabel. Has Captain Bishop been given permission to accompany you?'

Now seated in the back of the tonga Sarah looked down at Barbie. 'Well he was, but he's just been taken to hospital. We believe it's jaundice. Mother's gone to see him this afternoon to find out.'

'But whatever will you do?'

'If it's jaundice Susan's going to ring Teddie and tell him to find another best man quickly.'

'But what about the journey?'

'We'll be all right. We're meeting Aunt Fenny in Ranpur and all going on together.'

'And your Uncle Arthur, Major Grace?'

'He can't get away from Delhi until the Thursday before the wedding.'

'All that way, with no man to look after you?'

Sarah smiled. 'I'm sure there'll be lots of officers on the train. We shall be quite safe. Don't worry.'

There are these spoons, Barbie wanted to say. The twelve Apostles. They came today. My gift to Susan and Teddie. Twelve witnesses to love of the sublimest kind. But having got them she was at a loss how and when to offer them. She watched the tonga turn and waved to Sarah's retreating figure. Sarah sat holding on to the struts of the hood with one hand and on to the book on her lap with the other.

It is not for you to say Gaffur that the rose is God's creation, even if, though, its scent, its scent is of Heaven, heavenly. 'My memory,' she said aloud, turning back in, 'Is not What it Was.'

She wondered what happened to all the thoughts which once having had you stored up, and especially what became of those that seemed to be lost which you couldn't put your hand on. She stood in the middle of her room, one repository inside another, and was filled with a tiny horror: the idea of someone coming to claim back even one item of what was contained in either. The idea was horrifying because if you allowed the possibility of one claim then you had to allow the likelihood of several and then many of them, and finally of thousands; so that the logical end to the idea was total evacuation of room, body and soul, and of oneself dead but erect, like a monument marking some kind of historical occasion.

II

The disappointment people had felt at missing an event that would have added some necessary glitter to life was lifted a bit when the Laytons got back from Mirat and it became known that the wedding had been dogged by a series of minor misfortunes.

Mildred's initial attempts to dismiss these as being of no importance only succeeded in making the misfortunes seem major and presently the word disaster entered people's heads and was actually used on several occasions.

If Susan herself had looked downcast the idea of disaster would have gained currency; but, as if making up for what Pankot had missed, she glittered for it, trailing the absent ceremony and reception behind her like a diaphanous shadow that sparkled in the pure late October light, a shadow which was a degree or two darker than was really fair but causing her no trouble, a fact that attracted the kind of new regard to which she was entitled: a girl who had left Pankot pale and beautiful and come back flushed, happy, quite her old self, but with this extra dimension of having entered the honourable company of grass widows, with the bloom of the orange blossom still on her cheeks and her husband already gone on the first leg of the journey back to the front to fight for the preservation of the sterner world she now inhabited.

And when the misfortunes had been pieced together in some sort of chronological order, when they were looked at calmly, then even the stone that had broken the glass that cut Teddie Bingham's cheek on the way to the church could be seen as an acceptable symbol of the attacks to which people who merely tried to get on with the job in hand were only too well accustomed.

The stone, it seemed, had not been meant for Teddie but for his companion, the last-minute substitute for Tony Bishop, an extremely interesting man whatever way you looked at it, a man who had apparently incurred such intense dislike among Indians of a certain kind that they persecuted him, kept track of him wherever he went and then chose a moment to embarrass or harass him. On the day of the wedding it had been two moments: on the way to the church and on the platform of Mirat station just as Susan and Teddie were about to wave good-bye from the window of their honeymoon compartment.

Between these two moments there had been another for which Captain Merrick was hardly responsible unless you expected a best man to think of everything in addition to the groom's state of nerves; but from the point of view of the wedding this middle incident had been the worst, or very nearly. In a way nothing could be worse for the bride than to be told within a minute or two of leaving for the ceremony that there had been a hitch which meant a half-hour delay, and then, on coming up the aisle at last, see her groom standing at the head of it, pale, smiling lopsidedly, with a large piece of gauze padding stuck to one cheek with sticking plaster.

'You have to admit,' Lucy Smalley said, 'that it has its comic side,' but no one else was prepared to admit that it did when a Layton girl and a Muzzy Guides officer were the central characters in the affair.

It was the involvement of a Layton girl and a Muzzy officer that weighed most heavily against the substitute best man, an otherwise virtuous target for despicable attack. He ought to have made it clear to Teddie who he really was.

Mildred said that after the wedding was over he had admitted persecution of one kind and another ever since leaving Mayapore for a dreary backwater called Sundernagar, where he had continued in his police rank as District Superintendent until making his escape into the army for the duration. It would, she supposed, have been rather difficult for him to anticipate a demonstration against him on the day of the wedding, but if he had made it clear, if he had said to Teddie right at the beginning, Look, I'm the policeman who was made to seem to have put up a black in that ghastly Manners case, the fellow who actually arrested those blighters, then even if he hadn't added, And I'm still being tracked down and messed about by Indians who think I arrested the wrong men and treated them in some sinister sort of way; even if he hadn't added *that* useful bit of information, then when the stone came sailing through the window of the car taking Teddie and him to the church, he would have been able to say, That was meant for me, and explained why then or later. And boring as it would have been, a perfect bloody nuisance, everyone would have known what was up and Teddie wouldn't have been able to say he'd never been warned that his best man was someone who'd been unpleasantly in the limelight. Teddie had always had a horror of being mixed up in vulgar scenes, apparently. He thought at first that the stone was meant for him because he was a British officer or that it had been chucked by someone demonstrating against the Nawab because all the cars used at the wedding were lent by the palace and had crests on the doors. And in either case, of course, it made him feel perfectly miserable. Not to mention his poor cut cheek.

And there, in regard to the stone, Mildred left it with a sound of shattering glass and an impression of Teddie making just a little bit of a fuss, and of Mr Merrick having failed by a perceptible margin to act quite like an officer and a gentleman; an impression which she hardened by reporting him by no stretch of the imagination out of the top drawer, so that it had seemed almost a special kindness to have chosen him for best man, an unconscious repayment to him for the poor way the authorities had treated him in the Manners affair, after all he had done to try to solve and settle it.

After the stone there had been the incident at the club, and it was reasonable to suppose (Mildred suggested) that if there had not been the incident of the stone nothing dire would have happened at the club.

The Nawab and his party had been refused entrance to the reception by the British military police who were stationed at the front. The MPs were a last-minute precaution, only there in case there were further untoward or unexplained incidents. Assuming that no Indian was persona grata at the Mirat Gymkhana, they stopped the Nawab, his chief minister and his social secretary from crossing the threshold, which could have caused troublesome diplomatic repercussions if the club secretary hadn't got wind of it and personally rescued them, personally conducted them into the reception. It was the wedding group's first meeting with the Nawab and his chief minister, Count Bronowsky, *émigré* white Russian who now looked like one of those dessicated Muslims of the Jinnah stamp. The two had been away on a visit to a neighbouring state. The social secretary was a different kettle of fish, perhaps a tricky one. He was Ahmed Kasim, the younger son of the ex-chief Congress minister in Ranpur, M. A. Kasim. Heaven knew what he thought of everything. If he thought badly he'd disguised it well. He'd made himself very useful during the week – you couldn't say charming, he'd been too formal and correct for that. He accompanied Sarah riding one morning and she had no complaint about his behaviour, which Aunt Fenny had been worried about. He never mentioned his father or the fact that he was in prison. He had not struck one as in the least politically minded which may have been why his father had packed him off to work in a princely state as a hopeless reactionary case. When it came to M. A. Kasim's sons, the old Congressman had probably had to swallow political pride and disappointment, because the elder was a King's commissioned officer currently a prisoner of war in Malaya and here was the younger working for an Indian prince and looking after the comfort of visiting members of the *raj*.

'It was Susan,' Mildred said, 'who really saved the day. When the old Nawab finally arrived on the lawn, still bristling from the insult, she went forward and dropped him a curtsy, which wasn't protocol but made all the difference.'

Glances went admiringly to where Susan stood, or sat, wherever she was on the two or three occasions Mildred re-created this picture of her, on a lawn, in sunshine, in her wedding veil and dress, holding together a situation that had threatened to fall apart. Admirable girl. The Nawab must have been immensely flattered.

It was the third incident that most concerned and puzzled Barbie because it seemed to her from what she could understand of it that it was of a different order, one that reached outside the wedding and cast innumerable patches of light and shade. The patches of light revealed nothing because the light did not fall on anything, rather it pulsed on and off so that the patches were like mysterious glowing areas attempting to burn their way out of an imprisoning mass of darkness. They did not move; and, coming on, they had gone out before you could fix their positions or even their relationship to each other.

'What was it,' she asked Sarah, 'that actually happened at the station?'

They were walking in the garden of Rose Cottage; or rather Sarah had been walking and Barbie had come down to her. It appeared that they were together but Barbie did not feel that this was the case. She was wary of the girl. She had an idea that it might be unwise to touch her. The Nawab had been pleased with the volume of Gaffur's poems, Mildred said. Sarah had not mentioned them again. She had not mentioned Mirat, or going riding with the Kasim boy, Ahmed; an excursion which Barbie would have liked to hear about. It was as though she had never been to the wedding or had been and not come back but sent only her reflexion home. She looked at Barbie now from that sort of distance.

'At the station? No more than you've already heard.'

'But I heard it without understanding it.'

'I think that's how we all saw it at the time. Without understanding it. But it was very simple really. Just an elderly Indian woman pushing through us and kneeling at his feet.'

'Captain Merrick's feet?'

'Yes.'

'Beseeching him?'

Sarah paused with her hands behind her back, looking down at her own feet as though she could see the woman there.

'Beseeching him,' she agreed. 'Yes, that's a good word.'

'But who was the woman?'

'The aunt of the Indian boy Miss Manners is supposed to have been infatuated with. The boy who was the chief suspect. He's still in prison.'

'Poor woman. What was she like?'

'Grey-haired. Dressed in a white saree like a widow.'

'In a white saree?'

'Yes.'

'And that was all that happened?' Barbie asked after a while.

'That was all. She pushed through the crowd and fell at Mr Merrick's feet and had to be taken away. Then the train was going and we were waving good-bye to Susan and Teddie.'

'It couldn't have made much sense.'

'It didn't, at least not then.'

'When, then? When did it make sense? When you knew who Mr Merrick was?'

'Oh, we knew that by then. It came out during the reception. He was embarrassed because it made it look as if he'd tried to hide it but according to him he was just trying to forget it. I suppose he wasn't really lying when people asked him what he'd been in the police and he said DSP in Sundernagar.'

'No, that's true. How did it come out?'

'Count Bronowsky remembered his name.'

'Who is Count Bronowsky?'

'The old Russian the Nawab has as his chief minister. He was talking to Aunt Fenny. He said how well the best man had dealt with the stone-throwing incident, making sure they knew at the palace that the reception would be delayed. When Aunt Fenny told him Mr Merrick had been in the police and was used to dealing with a crisis he identified him at once as the DSP in Mayapore. I gather the case had interested him or perhaps he just had an exceptionally good memory. He went to find Mr Merrick and they had a long talk on the terrace but Aunt Fenny had the news well broadcast by the time they came back in. Teddie was awfully cool with him which was a bit unfair, but I think someone had already suggested that if Mr Merrick was the DSP in Mayapore at the time of the Manners case then the stone had probably been thrown at him and not at the Nawab's car. And the thing that happened on the station capped it. But still without making much sense. I didn't really get the hang of it until that evening when Mr Merrick came over to the guest house to apologize to Mother.'

Barbie thought: Mildred never mentioned an apology.

'But I was the only one up,' Sarah went on. 'All the others were still resting. I was waiting for the dark and for the fireflies to come out. So Mr Merrick and I sat and waited for them together. He was going that evening, leaving Mirat for the new training area in Bengal. He told me quite a lot of things. He seemed to want to talk about it now that it had all come out. He explained who the woman in the white saree was. He said he was sorry for her because she was what he called an ordinary decent person who had done everything for her nephew, the one who's in prison. He'd not seen her since he was in Mayapore but he'd always known he was kept track of by the kind of people who tried to make out he'd arrested the wrong men and ill-treated them, the people responsible for what happened to spoil the wedding. He said they were exploiting the woman, using her as part of a scheme to make him feel like a marked man. It all seemed a bit far-fetched to me, but I expect it's the only explanation.'

'Did he remember my friend, Edwina Crane?'

'I'm sorry. I never thought to ask.'

'Well, I don't suppose he did. Although as DSP in Mayapore he'd have known all about her being attacked. But I expect one of his juniors dealt with that. He had his hands full with that other awful business, didn't he? Does he still feel he was right, or does he think he might have made a mistake after all, arresting those boys? Miss Manners seemed so positive they weren't the ones, if we're to believe all we heard.'

They had reached the shade of a pine tree that stood near the very end of the garden. From here there was the view to the farther hills and the mountains. In a week or two the snow-capped peaks would be obscured by cloud as often as not. Sarah sat down. Barbie followed suit.

'He feels he was right,' Sarah said. 'He sounded very sure. Very sure indeed. But the more he talked about it the more I felt he'd got it all wrong. And that would be terrible, wouldn't it? If he had got it wrong but is always going to believe he didn't. Do you see what I mean? I know it's terrible in other ways, for the boys who have gone to prison and for – well – but she's dead, and that's another question, another sort of terrible. But to have got something wrong, and never see it, never believe it . . .'

Sarah dug her hand into a cushion of pine needles, sifting them, considering them. Suddenly she went on: 'He said that he was once attracted to her himself, in love with her perhaps. He made it sound like a confession, like a determination to be honest about every possible aspect but all the time I felt it wasn't. I don't know why I felt that. But everything he said sounded rehearsed. And while he was saying it you felt him watching for the effect, even knowing what it was going to be.'

'You didn't like him.'

After a while Sarah shook her head.

'No. I don't think I liked him at all.'

Perhaps, Barbie thought, because you had seen the child and talked to the old woman, and had seen the other woman, the woman in the white saree, and felt the presence of the unknown Indian. And wonder how in all this complexity guilt can lie alongside innocence and whether it might not have been in Mr Merrick's power to separate them.

She continued to sit in spite of getting cramp because Sarah did not move and she did not want to leave her alone.

'What did you say?' Sarah asked, coming back into herself after what seemed a long time.

'I wasn't talking.'

Sarah stared at her for a moment or two and said, 'I'm sorry, I thought you were,' and then Barbie wondered whether she had been.

For years she had had real and imaginary conversations with people, with herself, with God, with anyone who was there to listen or not listen. But an imaginary silence was something new. If you didn't know you were talking then you didn't know what you were saying. She tried to remember exactly what she had been thinking in case she had spoken some of her thoughts aloud, but her mind appeared to have been blank after the image of Sarah sitting with the old woman and the child, pondering the question of guilt and innocence and the part Mr Merrick had played or not played in attempting to establish them.

'You seem to be haunted by it,' she said, 'I mean by that awful business. First in Kashmir, being so close to the houseboat, and now in Mirat, with Captain Merrick.'

'Someone should be haunted by it,' Sarah said.

And then Barbie was sure she was right: Sarah had visited the woman and seen the child. She had a concern to hold the child, to take it to St John's and see it baptized.

'Yes,' Barbie said. 'Perhaps we should.' She got up. 'Stay here. I've got something for you to take to Susan.'

She went into the house, returned with the box of Apostle spoons and the note she had written. She knelt again and offered them.

'They're a combined wedding and twenty-first birthday present. Nothing very much. A set of teaspoons. I'd be grateful if you'd take them to her.'

'Thank you, Barbie. That's very kind.'

Sarah put the box on the cushion of needles and looked at the envelope on which Barbie had written, 'Mrs Edward Bingham'.

'I may be leaving Pankot,' Sarah said.

'Oh, Sarah, why? Where?'

'Just to do something more useful. Nursing perhaps or what I'm doing now only in a place where the war's a bit closer. Do you think that's selfish?'

'Why selfish?'

'Because of leaving Mother and Susan. With Daddy a prisoner it's always seemed to be my job to help look after things.'

'Susan's a married woman now.'

'Yes. That's why I thought I could go.'

'I should miss you dreadfully, well we all should, but it would be wrong to hold you back. *That* would be selfishness.'

Sarah glanced up. For a while they looked at each other gravely. 'I wish I could see things clearly enough to be positive like that,' Sarah said. 'But I never can. I must go –'

Abruptly she rose.

'Thank you for Susan's present. Please don't bother to see me off.'

She was gone before Barbie could get to her feet. She watched her until she was out of sight and then followed slowly.

Mabel was not working in the back or on the verandah which must mean she was either at the front or gone for one of her increasingly rare but still solitary walks.

I must explore, Barbie thought; and then spoke aloud: 'I must explore this mystery of the imaginary silence,' and as her voice continued she found that she could detach herself from its sound so that it seemed to go drifting away, or she to go drifting away from it, until she was left in a state of immobility or suspended animation, surrounded by what she could only describe as a vivid sense of herself as new and unused, with neither debit nor credit to her account, no longer in arrears with any kind of payment because the account had not been opened yet.

This was very clear to her but she guessed it wouldn't be when the immobility was cancelled. She thought: Emerson was wrong, we're not explained by our history at all, in fact it's our history that gets in the way of a lucid explanation of us.

She began to enjoy the sensation of her history and other people's history blowing away like dead leaves; but then it occurred to her that among the leaves were her religious principles and beliefs, and – observing the solemn evergreen stillness of the wood-capped hills – felt reassured and wisely reinstructed.

An imaginary silence should not be used to destroy contact but to create it. She went round to the front to find Mabel but the garden was empty. Mabel's stick was on the front verandah so she was not out walking. She went inside, knocked on Mabel's door and opened it.

Mabel was sitting on the edge of her bed watching Aziz removing the contents of an old press and placing them carefully on a blanket spread on the floor.

'Hello, Barbie,' Mabel said, looking up. 'We're sorting out some winter things.'

Barbie had never watched this ritual at Rose Cottage but she

knew that it took place. She came further into the room fascinated as she had been since childhood by the prospect of viewing
someone else's possessions; for these had a magic quality of
touch-me-not that belonged in fairy tales and in such tales
dispensation was possible but not inevitable and every invitation
to come nearer was a sugared gift.

'Oh, no, Aziz,' Mabel said, as he opened layers of tissue to
show the coat of a grey costume.

'Hān,' he insisted. 'Bond is-street.'

Mabel smiled. 'I bought it in London the last summer I was
there,' she explained to Barbie, 'the summer John's grandfather
died. Susan was only ten or eleven then so you can tell how out
of date it is. But every winter Aziz tries to make me bring it out,
because of the tag.'

'Bond is-street,' Aziz repeated. 'Pukka.'

The whole costume was spread out now. It had the simple
elegance of all expensive clothes.

'You could shorten the skirt,' Barbie suggested. 'It wouldn't
spoil the line.'

'Wouldn't it?'

Encouraged by Barbie's interest Aziz said, 'Hān. Shorten
is-skirt.'

'Perhaps. If I can still get into it.'

Mabel reached down and pulled the costume towards her,
twitched at it, and Barbie wondered how easy or difficult it
would be to make her take an interest again in things outside
Rose Cottage: in clothes, in visits, sprees. The two of them could
have a holiday, a short one, not far away. They could go down to
Ranpur to do some Christmas shopping. She would take Mabel
round the Bishop Barnard and introduce her to Helen Jolley.
For such a holiday she would have the heliotrope.

'Very well, Aziz,' Mabel said. 'Put it on the pile.'

Aziz nodded. He rearranged the costume, folded it with
reverence, replaced the dried sprigs of lavender whose scent
mingled with that of sandalwood and mothballs. The tissue-
wrapped costume was put on the smaller of the two piles. Suddenly he reached into the chest and said to Barbie, 'Memsahib!'

'No, no,' Mabel said. She made a gesture as if to stop him but
it was ignored. He was intent on revealing a treasure. He lifted
a package out and removed the top layer of tissue with a flourish.

'Sarah bachcha,' he said. Barbie went closer. A wedding veil? No, a complete garment. She could see the neckline and tiny sleeves folded across its front. Sarah bachcha. Sarah as a baby. She got down on her knees. 'Oh, it's a christening gown. Was it Sarah's?'

'Hān. Sarah Mem.'

Aziz linked thumbs and flapped his splayed fingers. 'Batta fye,' he said, and laughed at Barbie's puzzled expression. He put his hand in under the creamy lace from which the gown was made. As he did so Barbie exclaimed. The hem of the fine lawn under-garment was edged with a band of seed pearls. But there was more enchantment to come. 'Look,' he said, and fluttered his hand. The lace came alive. Butterflies palpated his pink brown palm. Three of them. Five. Seven. A dozen. More than that. The whole gown was made of lace butterflies.

'Oh, but it's beautiful,' Barbie said. 'Did Susan wear it too?'

Mabel answered. 'No. Susan had something new.'

Now that the lace was exposed Mabel seemed willing to acknowledge it. But putting out her hand to touch it Barbie felt that she was encroaching upon one of the many parts of Mabel's hidden history. She drew her hand back.

'No, do take it out,' Mabel protested. 'It's beautiful lace. My first husband's mother gave it to me for when we had children, but we never did. There's a full length of it still unmade up. Enough for a shawl. Aziz, show Barbie Mem the piece.'

Aziz reached into the press and lifted out another tissue-wrapped package. He opened it and unravelled the lace as the durzi unravelled bolts of cloth. The lace cascaded across his and Barbie's knees. The butterflies hovered, settled, rose, settled again. Some of their wings were folded, others only partly folded. Some displayed the full spread.

'It's exquisite,' Barbie said. She hardly dared touch it. 'So delicate and alive.'

'It's rather remarkable when you realize that the old woman who made it was blind.'

'Blind!'

'Not from birth. But for many years. She sat in a room in the top of a tower of an old French château that belonged to my mother-in-law's family. She called the butterflies her prisoners.'

Barbie put both hands under the lace and raised them. The

butterflies quivered as in a taut web. They were part of the web.

'Yes,' she said. 'They are caught, aren't they? How carefully you've looked after it.'

'Aziz sees to that. Would you like that piece?'

Barbie let the lace free. 'It's very kind of you,' she said, 'but it's much too beautiful. I wouldn't know what to use it for. And besides it's precious and it's family.' She thought of the wedding and its possible consequences. 'And now it may come in.'

'What?'

'If Susan and Teddie have children.'

'There's Sarah's dress already made up and there if wanted. Are you sure?'

'Quite sure. But thank you very much for the offer.'

III

Mrs John Layton, the card began, Miss Sarah Layton and Mrs Edward Bingham, request the pleasure of your company at the Officers' Mess, The Pankot Rifles. The date was for two weeks ahead, the time midday. On the bottom right-hand side it said Buffet Luncheon and on the left RSVP. Two cards were delivered to Rose Cottage.

In the envelope containing Barbie's there was a note from Susan. 'Dear Barbie,' she had written, 'thank you so much for the beautiful set of Apostle teaspoons. I'm writing to Teddie who I know would wish me to say thank you on his behalf as well. I heard from him a few days ago and he says he is very fit but of course working very hard. Mummy and I have decided that she should give a little party here to make up for having to have the wedding in Mirat and that it would be a good idea to have it on my twenty-first. A lot of our wedding presents were to cover both occasions. I do hope that you and Aunty Mabel will both be able to come. Mummy says it's years since Aunty Mabel visited the Mess and a lot of the young officers who have heard of her but never met her are dying to because really she is quite famous, not just because of Daddy but because of all the silver her first husband presented and which is used on special occasions. We shall have the wedding presents displayed, by the way, and your spoons will look awfully nice in their blue-lined box. With Love, Susan.'

'I expect you'd like to go, Barbie,' Mabel said.

'Only if you do.'

'Well I shall have to but I'd want to come away before they start eating. I can't bear eating standing up or eating in crowds. But Mildred knows that. She won't mind. If I put in an appearance that's all anybody will want, but you stay on and have a good tuck in.'

'Eating in crowds gives me indigestion too. We'll go and come back together. We'll arrange to slip away.'

I shall have the heliotrope, she decided. When I look in the mirror and see my grey hair I know I can carry the heliotrope.

She went down to the bazaar towards evening which was the time she liked best, especially in November when it was quite cold and there were braziers and early lanterns and the smell of charcoal and incense. She stood at the entrance to the durzi's shop. A chokra beckoned her in, dusted a chair and invited her to sit and then went through the curtain which presently parted again to admit the old man and the chokra who was carrying the bolt of purple cloth.

'Ah, so you know what I've come for,' she said. He unravelled three or four yards and held it up. She gazed at it, testing for the edge of an old uncertainty and found it gone. 'The name heliotrope,' she said, 'comes from the Greek words helios, meaning sun, and trepo meaning turn. Heliotropion. A plant that turns its flowers to the sun.'

'Memsahib has decided?'

'Yes. And you have my measurements. The usual style, the skirt straight, box pleat at the back, the coat with pockets on my hips, deep enough and roomy enough for me to stick my hands in. As in the last suit, the grey one. I leave the choice of lining to you, it is always perfectly matched. When shall I come for the fitting?'

The fitting was a formality. Year by year his scissors and needle were wielded with precision, year by year she gained, lost, nothing in weight nor changed shape in any way. He had only to refer to his figures that were filed away either in a drawer or in his mind under the name Bachlev, Baba; the holy woman from the missions. The fitting was arranged for one week from that evening and the finished garment promised for delivery the morning of the day before the party. He gave her a snipping of the cloth. She put it in her handbag. It would be useful if she wanted to match up shoes, gloves and handbag, or to consider the tones of the blouse to go with it or of one of her sprays of velvet flowers for the lapel.

'How nice you look, Barbie,' Mabel had said. 'What a happy colour,' and had seemed almost eager to be off; but half-way down Club road she had suddenly turned as if she had changed her mind and would tell the tonga-wallah to take them back. In the lapel of the Bond Street costume a small diamond brooch glittered, a miniature of the Pankot Rifles badge. She wore no other jewellery. The brooch had been a gift from her first husband, who died on the Khyber. Her face was shaded by a grey felt hat with a wide brim. In place of a ribbon a fawn chiffon scarf was tied round the base of the crown. The free ends hung behind to shade her neck. Her legs, too often hidden by shabby gardening trousers, were still slim and well-shaped. Seated, the shortened skirt revealed them to the knee; to just below it when she stood. Fawn gloves covered the work-roughened hands.

We could go to Ranpur, Barbie had said the night before. To do some Christmas shopping. 'Oh, I shall never go to Ranpur again,' Mabel replied, 'at least not until I'm buried,' which had seemed to Barbie an odd sort of thing to say until she remembered that her friend's second husband was buried there, in the churchyard of St Luke's; and the way she now twisted round as if to tell the tonga-wallah to go back seemed like a momentary confusion, as if what was uppermost in her mind was the idea of going to Ranpur for that macabre purpose and the understanding that the time hadn't yet come and that the journey downhill must be cancelled, or anyway postponed. And then her eye had been reattracted by Barbie's heliotrope costume and the real object of the journey had again become clear. So that she resumed her position and watched the road unravel beneath her feet, and said nothing, but listened, or did not listen, while Barbie talked –

– or talked and was silent. God, she felt, had waited a long time for her to see that she could ignore the burden of her words which mounted one upon the other until they toppled, only to be set up again, and again, weighting her shoulders; a long time for her consciously to enter the private realm of inner silence

and begin to learn how to inhabit it even while her body went
its customary bustling way and her tongue clacked endlessly on:
as at present, keeping time with the clack of the horse's hooves
as the equipage, avoiding the bazaar, dropped down through
Cantonment Approach road, making for the military lines.

'We're late,' she heard herself exclaim. In the world where she
talked, where everybody talked, time was of peculiar importance. In Rifle Range road there were no other vehicles. They
passed the end of grace and favour lane and in a moment or
two turned left into Mess road. The geometrically laid out huts
showed black against the green and the green itself was sparse,
trodden. Distantly, in groups, sepoys drilled. A board painted in
Pankot Rifles colours and with a huge gilt and coloured replica
of the badge marked their destination. They turned at right-
angles, crossing a culvert into a compound, approached the long
square-pillared portico, and drove into it. When the tonga
stopped Barbie could hear the uneven drone of voices inside.
Servants stood at the entrance, dressed in white tunics and floppy
white trousers. The ribbons in their pugrees, and their broad
cummerbunds, were woven in horizontal stripes of the regimental colours. One of the servants, tall and thickly built, elderly,
moved forward and saluted and stood offering his arm to Mabel.

'Memsahib!' he said.

Mabel had automatically put her hand on his wrist but the
note of urgency in his voice arrested her. Her body seemed to
stiffen with uncertainty or alarm. The servant spoke again and
Barbie listened carefully so that she could tell Mabel louder and
in English what he was saying.

'He says he wonders if you remember him now that he's old
and has a beard.'

'What?'

Barbie repeated it but was not sure Mabel understood. She
was looking down at the man, her hand still gripping his wrist.

'Is it Ghulam?' she asked at last. 'Ghulam Mohammed?'

The old man nodded and for a while they stared at each other.
Then he turned his wrist over so that his palm touched hers.

'You are well, Ghulam Mohammed?' she asked in Urdu.

'I am well. Is it so with you?'

'It is so.'

'God is good.'

'Praise God. Ghulam, this is my friend, Miss Batchelor.'

'Memsahib.'

'Now we must go in,' Mabel said in English. He made his arm into a crook and helped them down, and then up a shallow flight of steps into the dark interior.

'Thank you,' Mabel said, and added – as if to impress the name on a memory she could not trust – 'Ghulam Mohammed.'

The hall was pillared. The voices came from a room on the left whose double doors were open. Barbie could see Mildred in a flowery hat, Colonel and Mrs Trehearne, and Susan looking younger than twenty-one talking to Kevin Coley, the depot adjutant who had lost his wife in the Quetta earthquake, was now the oldest captain in the regiment and said to be content to remain so. Barbie always thought he had a face like a medieval martyr; one of the unimportant ones who went to the stake in job lots.

And then, as they approached the doors, there was a change of rhythm in the voices, a slowing down, and a quietening; what Barbie recalled ever afterwards as a hush which spread back through the room and brought people's heads round to watch Mabel's arrival, her return after a long inexplicable absence to the place she had first entered longer ago than anyone else present, which meant that her presence now had a mystical significance. In her there surely reposed the original spirit of the hard con-dition, the spirit that belonged to the days of certainty, self-assurance, total conviction?

With several paces yet to go Mabel hesitated as if she would draw back and suddenly Barbie wished that they both could. But – 'It is very crowded,' Mabel said and then moved forward indomitably as Mildred came out to receive her. The brims of their hats forced distance on their embrace, but Mildred looked genuinely pleased and even grateful to Barbie whose trembling hand was taken in a gesture that implied there was greater affection than the social circumstances allowed Mildred to show. 'You both made it,' she said. 'How nice. Mabel, there are some young boys who are dying to meet you but scared stiff so go easy on them for God's sake. There's one called Dicky Beauvais whose uncle was a subaltern under Bob Buckland. I know he's particularly hoping for a word.'

'Hello, Aunty,' Susan said. 'It's so nice of you to come and thank you for the marvellous present.' She kissed her aunt and then surprisingly kissed Barbie too and said, 'What a nice colour,' and led them into the still hushed assembly where the distance between Barbie and Mabel began subtly to lengthen because the Trehearnes interposed themselves and guided Mabel gradually towards the Rankins while the Peplows claimed Barbie as their own. Mabel looked over her shoulder, bewildered, but the already tenuous link was snapped by Mildred's obtrusive hat and Kevin Coley's crucified shoulder and Barbie felt herself forced away from the centre to the periphery. I never understood, Mrs Stewart was saying, your sudden interest in Emerson. I do not wish to talk about Emerson or indeed about anything, Barbie said, but only from inside that area of privacy and silence. Her voice was saying something quite different. Is Sarah here? she was asking Clarissa. She wasn't at the door unless I missed her, how awful if I did. No I have not met Mrs Jason, how do you do?

There were glimpses to be had of the felt hat and the chiffon scarf. They formed a point of reference. Her eye continually sought it. The room, dark-panelled and Persian carpeted, was uncomfortably warm and close. Half-lowered tattis on the porti-coed verandah kept out the glare. A bearer offered a tray and she took a glass of sherry to occupy her hands. She had not reckoned with this separation and it occurred to her that it had been engineered, arranged beforehand by Mildred with the innocent connivance of Clarissa Peplow who seemed to have assumed the duty of making sure that Barbie was kept entertained, refreshed, introduced and out of certain people's way. She began to be afraid that when the time came for her to help Mabel slip away she would be unable to find her, which was ridiculous since there was only this one room in use and the verandah on the other side of the long buffet table, where the windows were open, letting in some fresh air. She looked for but could not see the display of wedding presents. Neither, now, could she see the hat with the chiffon scarf. The room frightened her.

'What a nice suit, Barbie.'

It was Sarah. Barbie clasped her hand. 'Is she all right do you think, in this crowd? I feel I ought to be with her but there are so many claims on her attention.'

'They've got her a chair,' Sarah said. 'Over in the corner there. You can't see her from here but she's all right.'

'We're slipping away, you know, before the buffet.'

'Yes, I know. Barbie, you know Tony Bishop, don't you? He's been posted to Bombay. Isn't he lucky?'

'We met once at Rose Cottage but you may not remember me from among all those young people.' She offered her hand to the ill-looking man who had been Teddie Bingham's friend. 'Are you quite recovered from the jaundice?'

'Thank you, yes.'

'It is so debilitating, well so I gather, never having had it, only heard. I've always enjoyed excessive good health which I suppose is rather indecent, a sign of diminished sensibility perhaps, a certain coarseness of constitution no doubt inherited from my father whose life was terminated by the wheels of a hansom cab or bus on the Embankment I forget which in fact I was never quite sure but everyone expected him to go from cirrhosis of the liver which given the same intake any ordinary man would have contracted. Did you change your mind, Sarah, I mean about the presents? Susan told me they'd be on display but perhaps it proved too difficult, I mean they'd need guarding wouldn't they?'

But the presents were on display on the verandah, guarded by a naik and two sepoys who stood stiffly in the at ease position not catching the eye of any guest because it was not the guests of whom they had to entertain suspicion but intruders or con-tractors' servants coming too near the sparkling array of cutlery, glass, tea and coffee sets, trays, table-lamps, vases and carved boxes. A kind of queue had formed, as for the rite of passing by a bier Barbie thought when fifteen minutes later she accompan-ied the Peplows and Mrs Stewart to inspect the remains of the wedding. The verandah was crowded too.

Trees partially screened the view across to the grace and favour bungalow which Barbie had never been inside because she had always declined Sarah's invitation to go in when – as they some-times did – they shared a tonga from the bazaar and Barbie went out of her way to bring Sarah home. She thought she could hear Panther barking. There were cries from the parade ground. But the verandah of the mess seemed to lack conditions in which an echo could exist. Voices, sounds, had a brazen hollow quality. 'Wavell's the first Viceroy we've had who knows anything about the country and then of course he's a soldier,' someone told her but when she glanced round the speaker's face was not turned to her but to another man and she did not know either of them. When they reached the loaded table she could not see the spoons.

'Absolutely splendid, I agree,' she said, taking Clarissa up, 'a splendid display.'

After a while she abandoned her feverish attempts to find the spoons and carefully, slowly, quartered the table from edge to edge and from front to back. She longed but did not dare to ask Clarissa, 'Do you see my little Apostle spoons anywhere?' She wondered if she had a wrong impression of what they looked like in their box and looked twice at pastry forks and for any box whose lid was not open; stooped to see whether they were placed where the eye could not fall on them easily from a standing position. 'Excuse me,' someone said, and straightening quickly to let a woman pass behind her had to steady herself with a hand placed too quickly and heavily on the table so that for an instant she feared being the cause of a shameful and unforgivable incident. 'Oh, Barbie, be careful,' Clarissa said. 'I think we'd better stand back.' 'It wasn't my fault,' she said and then came away to be out of danger and free of the risk of other people's anger.

It was humiliating to think it might be realized what she had been looking for. But the spoons were not displayed and that was humiliation enough and one from which she could not retreat. The line of escape from the toppling towers of her words was blocked. 'There's such a crush,' she said, 'and I've forgotten how to cope with crowds. Also I can't hear myself think, not that I suppose you imagine I ever can.' She grinned at Clarissa who was looking worried. With such a look Clarissa would observe the good Samaritan at his work.

'Do you know,' Barbie went on, 'I have never been in a Mess before. I mean Mess with a capital M. Isn't that odd, or don't you think so? I suppose the room in there is the anteroom, is that the correct nomenclature? Where the officers forgather before going in to dine and toast the King-Emperor and throw their glasses into the hearth, or does that only happen in kine-matograph pictures?'

Oh, and I could throw my glass into a hearth, she said (but saying something else to Clarissa and so finding her way back into that blessed privacy where words actually spoken didn't matter) – dash it into a thousand sharp fragments, so that the sound would attract attention and He would say, What troubles you? What is your name? When did we last talk? Because it is to be talked to that I want above anything. I want to create around myself a condition of silence so that it may be broken, but not by me. But I am surrounded by a condition of Babel. To this, all my life, I have contributed enough for a dozen people. And He stops His ears and leaves us to get on with it.

She moved, prompted by Clarissa's charitable hand and Christian heart to re-enter the maelstrom and was granted a curious vision, fortuitous and short-lived. By chance, and people's movements, a clear channel was opened and she saw at the end of it the felt hat and the chiffon scarf and Mabel seated on the leather armchair, enthroned thus, and young men arrested in postures of deference and inquiry, one – an Indian – leaning forward while Mabel's hand was raised to her deaf ear and then folded again with the other on her quiet lap, and young men's smiles which were not as fully understanding as hers but ready to acclaim some imminent discovery; of what, only they could tell. Barbie could no longer see them because the vision was shut off again by barriers of fleshy faces, arms, bosoms, chins and epaulettes; the bark and chirrup of the human voice manufacturing the words which created the illusion of intelligent existence.

Behind this mass of people Mabel also presumably continued to exist but she would have liked proof of it and contemplated forcing a passage, gathering her friend in possessive and protective arms.

'Are you all right?' Sarah asked, reappearing. 'Can we get you another drink? Have you met Captain Beauvais? Dicky, this is Miss Batchelor, Aunty Mabel's companion.'

'I suppose companion is the right word. How do you do? I see you're Pankot Rifles too.' Captain Beauvais looked very young to be a captain. He had a shiny pink skin and a little fair moustache and the enthusiastic expression of mediocrity which Barbie had learned to recognize from years of looking in a mirror. 'Have you met Mabel yet? You *are* the one Mildred mentioned who hoped to speak to her because of someone called Bob Buckland?'

'Yes, that's right, and I have,' Captain Beauvais said. 'Was it sherry?' He detained the bare-foot bearer. 'His feet,' Barbie said, 'in this crush!' And received a fresh glass which she sipped from immediately. 'Do you know Muzzafirabad?' she asked. 'I was there centuries ago but of course there's no reason why you should because you're not a Muzzy.'

'Well actually I do. Are you connected?'

'Not with the Muzzys. I was Mission not Army. Are you on Dick Rankin's staff or with the regiment?'

'I was with the regiment but Area collared me to take Teddie Bingham's place.'

'But you know Muzzafirabad. I expect it's changed. Teddie knew it but we seemed to be talking about two different places. I was Bishop Barnard, but only the infant school. A mere shack. Well, very small. The children came mainly for the chappattis. There was so much hunger. And disease of course, the two go hand in hand. And still do. One is appalled, appalled and thinks – well, can nothing ever be done, is it truly a hopeless task? The love of God can't fill an empty belly and when it's full one seldom thinks to thank Him.'

'We accept some pretty skinny fellows nowadays, but they soon fill out.' His eyes snatched at avenues of escape. 'Talking about food, I think there's some beginning to come in. May I get you something?'

'That's very kind but we're slipping away before the buffet.'

She retreated, backing away from Captain Beauvais, slightly spilling her sherry. She begged someone's pardon, put the sherry down and turned, found the crowd moving inexorably forward, pressing her back towards the table on to which salvers and tureens were being placed by the contractor's scruffy servants who were coming in from the verandah in what looked like dozens. Excuse me, she said, but I must get to Mrs Layton senior. Excuse me. I do so beg your pardon. Retreating from the crowd, from the cold consommé, the pâté, the chicken and turkey and ham, the salmon mayonnaise and Beauvais's skinny recruits with the army beef already thickening their stick-thin arms and legs, and from the nameless little girl; the unknown Indian. To find Mabel. Who had retreated from all these things long ago as if she knew the whole affair was doomed and hopeless.

The channel was open and she broke through into it and saw

the chair, empty, abandoned. She looked round but there was no sign of the felt hat with the chiffon scarf flowing from it. Nearby on a leather sofa two young Indian women sat in their best sarees smiling into a middle-distance, waiting for their husbands to resume responsibility.

'Have you seen Mrs Layton, Mrs Layton senior?' she asked one of them.

'Oh, no.'

'The lady in the grey hat and scarf who was sitting in the chair.'

'Oh, no. She went I think.'

She cannot have gone, Barbie said, unless she was never here and it is all a dream; and pressed into the crowd again trying to make her way back to the place she had been standing in before in case Mabel had noted it and gone there to find her and tell her it was time. Perhaps she had made for the verandah to find her and see the presents. She would not have left by herself.

She was not on the verandah.

Having walked its length Barbie re-entered the anteroom through the open door used by the contractor's servants. From here she had a clear view of the still empty chair. She moved through the narrow passage between the straight line of the wall and the uneven line of backs and elbows. The noise was deafening. She looked for a familiar face but on this side of the room there seemed to be none familiar enough. The mouths in the faces had forks going into them. She marvelled that there should be such a volume of conversation. She became hungry both for food and chat and mercy and felt faint and then a bit sick, put her hand out to steady herself and saw that her hand rested on a door. At waist level there was a brass knob that looked gaunt. She grasped it, turned and thrust. The door was very heavy. Passing through the opening she pushed it to behind her and was surprised to find it lighter in the closing than the opening. It banged.

The sound echoed down the long corridor in which she now stood. When it died away there was a profound silence. The noise of the party was miraculously shut out. A door at the other end seemed a great distance away, as far, as unattainable as the landing at the top of the frightening stairs in the gloomy

little house in Camberwell. She considered the grace which
levitation would bestow but setting out on her journey in search
of Mabel found herself denied it, as earthbound as ever. The
corridor was filled with aqueous light from the murky fanlight
windows whose long cords were looped on their hooks with
military precision, their free ends hanging at what looked like
equal measured lengths. Between the cords were mounted
trophies. Ranged along the opposite wall stood heavy marble
busts, rock-firm on stout tapering plinths. Through these she
must walk the gauntlet, dare the waxen and sightless faces of
Mabel's forbears, the tusks and glaring eyes of their guardian
beasts: the hunters and the hunted, now voiceless and immobile
but met in a permanent conjoint task of terrorism of strangers
and intruders.

The floor was tiled in lozenges of black and white but down
its centre lay a Persian runner which smothered the sound of
footsteps. She paused in the centre of one of the blue and crimson medallion designs. A few paces ahead, on her left, there was
a wide arched recess with a pair of mahogany doors set in it. One
of them was half open. She was still some distance from the
closed door at the end of the corridor. The closed door had a
look of Mabel not being in the room it led into. The half-open
door on the other hand suggested her recent passage through it.
She strode the last few paces, pushed the door further open and
entered.

Immense. Shadowed. A long room, the length of the corridor
but higher. The main windows were shuttered. Again light
entered only through the fanlight windows. In the centre of the
room a vast mahogany table reflected two great epergnes that
floated on the dark unrippled surface like silver boats on a glassy
midnight lake. On opposite banks chairs, awaiting occupants,
were placed arm to arm in close formation. The walls were
panelled in dark-stained wood to the height of the tall shuttered
french doors. Above this level they were whitewashed. Fixed
to them as thickly as butterflies to a naturalist's display board
were flags, some worn as thin as mummies' rags; standards and
heraldically disposed weapons of war: swords, sabres, lances,
muskets. Between the windows were sideboards and dumb-
waiters heavy with plate. At both ends of the room were monumental fireplaces and above them gilt-framed battle landscapes.

Against the wall on the corridor side of the room there were three glass-fronted display cabinets. The light slanting down through the fanlights was reflected back by the silver contained in them. In front of the furthest cabinet stood Mabel.

Barbie opened her mouth to speak but did not. Mabel stood in front of the cabinet like someone in the presence of a reliquary. She had become untouchable, unapproachable, protected by the intense and chilling dignity of the room in which (Barbie felt) some kind of absolute certainty had been reached long ago and was now enshrined so perfectly and implacably that it demanded nothing that was not a whole and unquestioning acceptance of the truth on which it was based.

Still unaware of Barbie's presence Mabel turned and went to the nearer fireplace, stood and gazed up at the dark picture in which Barbie could make out a white horse with a dim uniformed figure declamatorily astride against a backdrop of clouds and cannon puffs. Like the representation of the crucifixion above an altar the picture held the room in silent celebration of the mystery of its governing genius.

I have lost her, Barbie thought. Mabel had not wanted to come but having done so she had been unable to resist the impulse to enter the inner sanctuary of the world from which she had cut herself off and, having entered, the associations had proved too powerful. Yes, I have lost her, Barbie repeated, but come to that I have never really found her.

Mabel turned round and Barbie wondered if she had spoken her thoughts aloud. Nervously she touched her cheek with her gloved hand. For a moment neither of them said anything but faced each other across the length of the inhospitable table until Barbie had the distressing impression that Mabel's first words would be accusing and dismissive.

'Is it time for us to go, Barbie?'

She nodded. If she spoke she guessed she would not be able to stop and it seemed imperative for their future that she should hold her tongue in this place.

'I'm sorry if I've worried you, wondering where I'd got to,' Mabel said. For a few seconds more she surveyed the table, the walls, the cabinets of silver, then she walked towards Barbie and when she reached her grasped her wrist as she had grasped the bearded old servant's.

'We can go out the back way through the cloakroom at the end of the corridor. If you're ready.'

'Oh, yes,' Barbie said. 'I'm quite ready.' She turned her hand round so that her palm was pressed encouragingly in her friend's. But Mabel stood immovable. Suddenly she said:

'I thought there might be some changes, but there aren't. It's all exactly as it was when I first saw it more than forty years ago. I can't even be angry. But someone ought to be.'

Barbie unhooked the dangerous spectacles and placed them near the table-lamp. She settled the pillows, adjusted the tops of the sheet and blankets so that her friend's hands were covered. And then sat for the customary ten minutes before turning the light off. In the morning at breakfast Mabel would not say: It's very strange, I went to sleep over my book but woke in the morning without book or spectacles, is it Aziz or you who tucks me up? Barbie knew she would say nothing because she had said nothing on all the previous occasions.

Tonight there was no muttering, not even a movement of lips. Barbie stood up, switched off the light and waited until she was sure that Mabel still slept. Back in her own room she approached the penitential area of the rush mat but found herself reluctant to attempt communication through that medium. I shall have an imaginary silence, she said; and sat at the writing-table, opened Emerson – her own copy, bought to replace the borrowed one – and proceeded to read aloud to the class from his essay on self-reliance.

'Society is a wave. The wave moves onward, but the water of which it is composed does not. The same particle does not rise from the valley to the ridge. Its unity is only phenomenal. The persons who make up a nation today, next year die, and their experience with them.'

And some are buried here (she thought, as her voice droned on through the essay and then off into inaudibility as her imaginary silence took hold) – some are buried here in the churchyard of St John's and some in the churchyard of St Luke's in Ranpur, as Mabel's second husband was, the one who was not a soldier and died of disease not wounds. By his side it is her eventual wish to rest because she says I shall never go to Ranpur again until I'm buried. But who were Bob Buckland, Ghulam Mohammed and Gillian Waller?

A voice replied: Does it matter?

She clutched her throat in alarm. The voice had spoken so clearly. It was not her own voice. Her own voice was still droning on through the words of Emerson. Scared, she tuned back into it. 'In the will work and acquire, and thou hast chained the wheel of Chance, and shall always drag her after thee. A political victory, a rise of rents, the recovering of your sick, or the return of your absent friend, or some other quite external event, raises your spirits, and you think good days are preparing for you. Do not believe it. It can never be so. Nothing can bring you peace but yourself. Nothing can bring you peace but the triumph of principles.'

She cried out involuntarily, stood up, pushing back the chair. She went towards the mat and then began to tremble because she could not quite reach it and in any case her knees would not bend. She seemed fixed in this proud and arrogant position. Her jaws were locked too, her mouth still open as if to allow the cry to come back in. She could not remember what her principles were.

A few weeks later Mildred announced that Susan was going to have a baby and that Sarah, who had put in an application for posting to a forward area, had dutifully withdrawn it.

IV

Romeo, if dead, should be cut up into little stars to make the heavens fine.
(Emerson's essay on Love)

Nowadays she communicated with the world outside Rose Cottage by writing letters to Helen Jolley. She had never known Miss Jolley intimately. There was the right amount of uncluttered distance between them. Miss Jolley had sent only one reply and Barbie did not expect to hear from her again so had ceased to post her own letters or write them on notepaper. She wrote them in old exercise books taken from the trunk of missionary relics. Many of these were only partly filled and had a useful number of blank pages in them. There was a considerable saving in the cost of stamps and stationery; and an ease of reference back.

*

December 24th, 1943

My Dear Miss Jolley,

On this special night you would do well to pause in your administration of the Bishop Barnard and ask yourself as I do what gifts our mission has brought to the children of India, and if – among them – has ever been the gift of love. I do not mean pity, I do not mean compassion, I do not mean instruction nor do I mean devotion to the interests either of the child or the institution. Love is what I mean. Without that gift I doubt that any can be, could have been, brought to Jesus. After many years of believing I knew what love is I now suspect I do not which means I do not know and have never known what God is either. Do you? Do not be deceived by my self-assured expression. Reject the evidence of my confident stride. Shut your ears to my chatter. They are all illusory. I question my existence, my right to it. This is not I trust despair. While you are about it by the way (prayer I mean, if indeed you submit to that discipline busy as you are with so many other things) you might pray for the soul of Edwina Crane. My own prayers are not guaranteed reception. Her need though is greater at the moment than mine or yours. On this night, especially. Most sincerely, BB.

March 8th, 1944

Dear Helen,

It is all right. About Edwina. Let me describe it to you while the detail is fresh in my mind. Ever since the news of the enemy's invasion of Indian soil we have been alert. This morning when I rose I knew that something of vital importance to our safety had happened. I called Aziz but got no answer. I knocked at Mabel's door and went in expecting to find her still in bed because it was early. Her bed had been slept in but was empty. I searched. She was nowhere to be found. She and Aziz had gone. The servants' quarters were abandoned. It didn't take me long to work it out that everyone was making for the railway station and that a place would have been reserved for me on the train alongside Mabel. In fact I remembered that this had been carefully planned beforehand in the event of Pankot falling in danger of enemy attack.

I packed a few things, closed and bolted all the doors, windows and shutters, and let myself out. Imagine my relief when I saw a tonga waiting. The wallah flourished his whip and warned me to step on it. I thought, 'I may step on it but can the horse?' It looked more like an ass than a horse but I thought it would embarrass the driver to have this pointed out. 'You'd better jump in,' he said, 'because they're coming and everyone's gone ahead to catch the last train out.'

I stopped trusting him. He observed my hesitation and in a different tone of voice said, 'What are you waiting for, Barbie? You'd better buck up.' It was Mr Maybrick in disguise. He had piles of his organ music tied up in untidy bundles in the back. I scrambled in, made room for myself. Off we started. The horse wasn't lame as I'd feared. We made excellent progress. I felt elated, as in those days when my father took me on a spree and I had to hold my hat on. (It had a wide brim with artificial flowers Mother made out of coloured scraps of velvet.) As we bowled down the hill past the golf-course I thought there were people there all wearing hats like this but then realized they were holding up umbrellas, coloured ones, made of paper. Mr Maybrick told me they were fifth columnists and that the golf-course was the rendezvous. We were in danger of being cut off and there was no time to catch the train. We would have to seek refuge in St John's Church.

It was at this stage that everything became weird. You say I dreamt. But what is a dream? Everything 'happens' in the mind whatever the source of the event. Now four-in-hand, first Mr Maybrick and then I whipped the horses down Club road making for the haven of the church. My short grey hair flew black and long and I was filled with joyful longings and expectations. I was not myself.

I felt capable of dealing with every eventuality, calm in anticipation of the Lord's help. We arrived at the site of St John's but a change had come about. It was not the churchyard which I and Mr Maybrick (now back in his ordinary clothes but with a dog-collar like Mr Cleghorn) were standing in but the compound of the mission school in Muzzafirabad. My servant Francis was calling the children to school by tolling the bell. He tolled it eleven times. We had a view across the golf-course. The number of paper umbrellas had increased and the fifth columnists had now been joined by the Japanese. We could see their yellow faces and the guns they carried in place of golf-bags. Mr Maybrick also had a gun. He looked at me and said, We must save a last bullet each. I did not believe such a terrible step would be necessary. When I looked again I did not see the enemy but troops of children marching to their lessons. I called out, wishing to hurry but not to frighten them. Francis whispered to me that the danger had not passed. I was afraid his expression would show how desperate he felt so I smiled and said to each group of children as they passed through the school doorway, 'It's quite safe now.'

At last all the children were inside. Mr Maybrick and I went to join them. And then I was Edwina no more but myself and the schoolroom was the church after all and I was alone. Mr Maybrick was at the organ playing. The church was otherwise empty, still, safe, happy. I knelt in a pew to give thanks for our deliverance and as I did so the most benign thought entered my mind. A voice said to me: I'm all right now. I knew it was Edwina. She wanted me to know that God had forgiven her that mortal sin and received her into His everlasting peace and mercy.

This was a form of communication, wasn't it? From Him, about Edwina. Which means I am not abandoned, although I think that now Edwina has gone from me in this life for ever I am not unlonely. But this is a loneliness I can support.

April 28th, 1944

Dear Helen,

Do as I have done. Go to the window when it is dark and look at the night sky and ask yourself this question: Are the heavens finer than they were?

Teddie Bingham is dead, killed in action. The house still rings with Susan's single cry of anguish and on the edge of my bed remains the imprint of her body where she sat afterwards in stony silence, cut off from all human correspondence. My poor Susan. Heavy with child. Weighed down by her loss. Scarcely more than a child herself. In front of the other women here I couldn't restrain my tears.

I shed tears at my father's death. I felt he had died through some fault of mine. I was so plain and gawky and not clever in the ways a little girl is meant to be. Over the seams I sewed, for instance, my mother pursed her lips, and blacking his boots

I fumbled so badly his socks became smeared and he said, Heavens, child! but the Heavens were not open to receive me and shield me from his forgiveness. His funeral as is the custom among the London poor was more splendid than his life. So many flowers! A crowded church. Men I had never seen in the house, stiff in black and with the formality of respect for a life gayer than it should have been but now gone and leaving wisps of secret masculine camaraderie behind it that had no business either in our family or the house of God. And there was one young woman, in passing whom on our way out my Mother sparked with ebony lights and an electric stiffness in that corset which made her waist a tower of strength but not particularly of affection.

At home in the midst of ham and stout she placed her hand warningly under her heart and thus announced the approaching years of her martyrdom and her patient claim on my body, soul and memories, and I was aware of the peculiar poetry and diversity of life and its intricate loyalties which left me bereft and determined to arrive at a source, as it were at a conclusion, which the mirror announced in advance of the event. God, anyway, would have me; therefore I yearned for Him. But was it He who answered?

I look at the night sky where Teddie is scattered and am awestruck at this kind of immensity. Unthinkable distances. Surely no prayer can cross them. I am humble in the face of such sublime power. But in the next instant I try to imagine what existed before it was created. I try to imagine no universe. Nothing, nothing. Try to imagine that. In all that terrifying blackness try to imagine no blackness, nothing, not even vacuum, but nothing. Nothing even as a thought. Space deprived of space in which to exist. Draw in the billions of light years of space and stars and darkness, compress and compress until all existence, all space, all void is the size of a speck of dust.

And then blow it out.

The mind cannot conceive of this situation. The mind demands that there be something and therefore something before something. Is the Universe an unprincipled design? Does God weep somewhere beyond it crying to its prisoners to free themselves and come to Him? If it is all explained by chemistry, that chemistry is majestic. It can only lead to the most magnificent

explosion, to which God will harken while we burn and disintegrate and scatter into pieces.

I am worried about Mabel. She talked once not about God but
about the gods as though some kind of committee were sitting,
one before which she had become weary of giving evidence. At
night she falls asleep over her book with her spectacles on her
nose at a dangerous angle. I have nightmares in which I see her
turn into the pillow, crushing and splintering the lenses, cutting
herself, bleeding slowly from closed eyelids so that she appears
to be crying blood. She waits with Spartan fortitude for her life
to run its course. Her days are spent in celebration of the natural
cycle of seed, growth, flower, decay, seed.

One day she said to me, 'No flower is quite like another of
the same species. On a single bush one is constantly surprised by
the remarkable character shown by each individual rose. But
from the house all one sees is a garden, which is all there is to it
anyway in the long run.'

Perhaps that is how she sees the world. She puts her hand
on my arm and I am imprisoned by her capacity to survive. A
sentence of life, suffered with patience and forbearance and with
small pleasures taken by the minute, not the hour. Is that tranquillity? She is not so tranquil in sleep. Bygone things press on
her then.

The fighting in Manipur has been very fierce but it looks as
if we shall drive them back, doesn't it? There will be no paper
umbrellas on the Pankot golf-course. As Mabel said, everything
will be just as it always was.

June 5th, 1944

My Dear Miss Jolley,

Shortly after the Memorial service that was held here for Captain Bingham a mysterious event took place. A name appeared
in the visitors' book which is kept at the gate of Flagstaff House.
The person signing gave no indication of her whereabouts in
Pankot, contenting herself with the word Rawalpindi after her
signature, as if to leave no room for doubt while withholding
opportunity for contact. It was as though she wished to say: I am
here in your midst, think about it.

But no stranger has appeared. No one has seen her or seen anyone who might be her. Yesterday evening I raised the question

discreetly with Sarah, suggesting to her that since they were so close to her in Kashmir they would recognize her; but Sarah said they would not. I did not think it a good idea to press her, to face her directly with the question whether in Srinagar she had visited the woman, spoken to her, seen the child.

Is the child here too? Unbaptized? You will know to whom I refer, whose signature it is that has appeared in the book. You will not know, none of us does, why she is in Pankot or where she is staying. Unless the signature was a practical joke, as has been suggested, she must be hidden away in the area of West Hill where there are summer residences that belong to rich Indians from Ranpur, an area which people from East Hill never visit. Her arrival and simultaneous disappearance serve to emphasize the stark division there is between our India and theirs. She has made herself one of them. The division is one of which I am ashamed. I have done nothing, nothing, to remove it, ever. My poor Edwina sat huddled by the roadside in the rain, holding that dead man's hand. That, I continually see, was significant. For me that image is like an old picture of the kind that were popular in the last century, which told stories and pointed moral lessons. I see the caption, 'Too Late.'

Sarah came to the cottage yesterday evening to say goodbye. She went to Ranpur today to catch tonight's Calcutta mail. Only for a short visit, but for a special reason, and for Susan's sake, to see and talk to a Captain Merrick who is in hospital there, having been wounded – Susan believes badly – in the same action in which poor Teddie was killed. It seems in fact that he was with him on that occasion at the height of the fighting on the Imphal plain and performed some sort of heroic act whose object, although it failed, was to save Teddie. An officer from Teddie's division wrote to Susan and told her of Captain Merrick's bravery, since when she has had a letter from Captain Merrick himself, in hospital, but not in his handwriting. This weighs on Susan's mind. If ever she blamed him for the disturbing events that spoiled her wedding day she is determined to forgive and forget and in any case, as a soldier's daughter, sees it as her duty to extend the hand of gratitude to her dead husband's comrade. She has asked Sarah to ask him if he would stand as godfather to the child, when it is born.

For this I am thankful. In the past few weeks she has been,

many of us feel, dangerously withdrawn, lying here on the verandah at the cottage day after day, as she used to before Teddie's
death when her pregnancy curtailed her activities, but without
that look of living inwardly. I heard a woman here, Lucy Smalley,
say that poor Susan reminded her of the daughter of a woman
called Poppy Browning, but she shut up when she saw I was in
earshot; and tonight I asked Sarah who Poppy Browning was.
She did not know. Nor does she know who Gillian Waller was,
or is, for I was silly enough to ask that too and then had to
explain, to expose myself as a stupid old woman who tucks
another old woman up, one who mutters in her sleep.

A little while ago I mentioned to Susan the existence of the
lace and when Sarah and I had done talking tonight she went in
to Mabel and received that exquisite christening gown to take
to her sister. The child is due next month. In Calcutta, Sarah is
to stay with her Aunt Fenny and Uncle Arthur. They have
moved from Delhi. He is now a Lieutenant-Colonel. I longed
to go with her, to have a chance to see our old headquarters
again and to see the wounded man, who perhaps knew Edwina.
Will Sarah remember to ask him this time?

Yours,
Barbara Batchelor.

She scrawled the signature, closed the exercise book that had
belonged to a little girl called Swaroop. She undressed, put on
her gown and opened her door to listen and judge the state of
affairs. It was past midnight. She crossed to Mabel's door, opened
it silently and stood arrested. Mabel, propped against her pillows,
must have watched the door opening.

'Can't you sleep either?' she said; and Barbie recalled the day
nearly five years before when she had gone out to the verandah
and found Mabel working there, the day she had expected to be
told she must go when her holiday was over. Can't you sleep
either? Mabel had said. I don't blame you. It's such a lovely day.

Mabel had already put her book aside and replaced her spectacles in their case, and Barbie felt pleased with her as she would
have been pleased to find that a pupil had learned a difficult
lesson well.

'Oh, I haven't tried yet,' she said. 'I've been writing letters,
catching up, and time just slipped by. Can I get you anything?'

'No, thank you, Barbie. There's nothing I want. I'm not sleepy though. It's rather close, isn't it?'

'Just a bit.'

Mabel nodded, apparently glad to have her impression confirmed.

'It won't be long before the rains get here,' Mabel said. She glanced at the curtained windows as if through these an approaching rain might be discerned. 'Did I tell you it was raining the first time I came to India? I remember being very disappointed. I'd expected brilliant sunshine and it seemed such a long way to come just to get wet and see grey sky. But then I'd not experienced the heat. So I didn't appreciate the contrast.'

'It's not so marked up here.'

Barbie went further into the room and then to the bedside, checked the muslin-covered water jug even though she could see that the tumbler hadn't been used.

'Stay and talk to me,' Mabel said. The request was so unexpected that for a moment Barbie wondered whether Mabel was making fun of her. But her friend's face betrayed no irony.

'Talk? What about?'

'Anything. About when you were young. I always enjoy that.'

'Do you? Do you?'

She sat on the edge of the bed. She could not remember, now, ever being young. And then did. 'I was always a bit afraid of going upstairs to bed. So I hummed a song which I fear Mother disapproved. That is to say the first line of it. I don't mean she disapproved only of the first line and of course I don't mean hummed because you can't hum words, but I sang it under my breath over and over. And in the end I couldn't ever remember the rest of it and never have. Isn't that strange? I've seen a deal of gaiety throughout my noisy life.'

'Throughout what?'

'Throughout my noisy life.'

'Oh.' Mabel smiled. 'One of your father's comic songs.'

'He was passionately fond of the music hall. And often promised to take me but of course never did, he was afraid of what my mother would say if she found out and anyway he was always short of what he called the ready. There was the Christmas when he lost the presents for my stocking on the journey home. As white as a sheet when he came in at the door and very very late, but not drunk, that's what Mother said years later when she told me, when he was dead and she had forgiven him, and told me there wasn't any Father Christmas anyway. I never knew I once nearly didn't get a stocking. I don't remember a Christmas when there wasn't something in it. Mother said that when he came home and said: I've lost the stocking things, poor Barbie's stocking things: they set to and turned out drawers and cupboards looking for odds and ends for hours so as not to disappoint me and that I said it was the nicest stocking ever. But perhaps that's only how she remembered it. But it showed they loved me. I adored Christmas mornings. I always woke while it was still dark and worked my toes up and down to feel the stocking's weight and listen to the rustle and crackle. And then I'd sit up and sniff very cautiously to smell the magic, I mean of someone having been there who drove across frosty rooftops and had so many chimneys to attend to but never forgot mine.'

'Yes,' Mabel said. 'I remember that – the idea of a strange scent in the room, but I don't think I put the idea into words.'

'I don't suppose I did either. It's how I describe it now. As children we accept magic as a normal part of life. Everything seems rooted in it, everything conspires in magic terms.' She laughed. 'Even the quarrels in our house had the darkness of magic in them, they were strange and incomprehensible and threatening as magic often is. I expected to find toads hopping on the staircase and misshapen things falling out of cupboards.'

'Poor Barbie.'

'No! My life was never dull.'

'Is it very dull now?'

'Now least of all.'

She had a sudden strong desire to lower herself gently and be taken into the older woman's arms and to lie there in peace and amity until they both fell asleep. She would be content then not to wake but to dream for ever, enfolded, safe from harm, and for an instant it seemed to her that if she sought harbour in this way it would not be closed to her; that Mabel would accept her and go with her happily into this oblivion of cessation and fulfilment.

But Mabel slowly closed her eyes as if shutting that avenue of escape and said very quietly, 'I can sleep now thank you, Barbie,' and Barbie got up, smoothed the top of the sheet and was careful to make no disturbing contact with her friend's hands. She whispered, 'I'll deal with the light,' and when Mabel nodded reached for the ebony switch and turned it. She felt her way in the dark back into the hall and her own familiar room and circumstances.

A meditation. St John's Church. 4.30 p.m. June 7th 1944

i

You said: Stay and talk to me because I can't sleep. So I stayed and talked. I told you about the stairs and a Christmas stocking and after a very short while you said: I can sleep now.

The next time I saw you was in the morning. You were on the verandah drinking a cup of tea and you apologized for having had breakfast without me. I never thought to ask Aziz what you had eaten. Perhaps he would not have told me because you'd already instructed him not to in case I said: That's no sort of breakfast. And began to fuss and bother. As it was I sat down and drank tea too and said nothing because I had noticed nothing.

This was yesterday. I must search for clues to moments when you may have been on the point of making an appeal like that of the night before. Stay. Talk to me. Those few moments on the verandah drinking tea were not one of them. When Aziz called me to breakfast you said nothing. You resumed reading a seed catalogue. But you were still there when I came back. I thought that you were absorbed, planning next year's garden.

I said: I'll do the accounts this morning. If you do the cheques after lunch I'll take them down to the bazaar and settle them on my way to Mr Maybrick's.

I had to repeat it. But that wasn't unusual. In case you had forgotten I reminded you that I'd promised Mr Maybrick three days before to go to his bungalow for tea and mend his volume of Bach. You said: Oh I thought that was tomorrow. So I said, No, it was fixed for today, the sixth of June.

Is that the date? you said. And looked towards this year's garden.

I went inside and sat at your bureau and began the accounts for May. After a while I heard you stirring and saw you through the window putting on your straw hat and going out into the sunshine with the pannier. At eleven Mildred came with Susan and shortly afterwards Mrs Fosdick and Mrs Paynton arrived.

Aziz was worried. He said to me: Memsahib said nothing about lunch for so many. I assured him that only Susan was staying for lunch, that presently Mildred and the others would go down to the club and be there all day playing bridge, and that Mildred would return at about six o'clock to take Susan home.

He said: Memsahib, when will *you* be back?

I thought of the volume of Bach and of the difficulty I always had persuading Mr Maybrick to let me get on. Perhaps seven o'clock, I said. Or seven-thirty. But certainly by eight, in time for dinner.

When the others had gone I went out to where Susan lay. Her smock was taut over her swollen stomach. I said: Did you like the christening gown? She said yes, it was beautiful. So I told her the story of the blind woman who made the lace, of how she called the butterflies her prisoners. After a while Susan said: I like things that have stories to them, somehow it makes them seem more real: and then closed her eyes to show that she wanted me to go away. I returned to the bureau and finished the accounts. I made out the cheques so that all you had to do was sign them. We had another visitor then, Captain Beauvais, who brought Susan a book. Aziz gave him a drink and Susan and he talked in low voices. He had gone before you came in from the garden at lunch-time.

At lunch you said: When will Sarah be back? And Susan laughed and said: Oh, Aunty, she's only just gone, she was only due to reach Calcutta this morning.

You said: So she'll be gone for a few more days.

After lunch I helped Susan to settle on the verandah again. I tried to get her to walk for a bit in the shady part of the garden but she said she was tired. I found you at the bureau signing the last cheque. You said as you always did: Thank you for coping with all this. I took the cheques and the bills and went to my room. I lay down for a bit. At three o'clock I asked Aziz to send the mali's boy for a tonga. Then I tidied myself for Mr Maybrick and looked for you to tell you I was off. You were in the garden, but not in the shade. I said, 'Aren't you awfully hot?' You said, 'No, I like the sunshine.' And then, 'Will you be long?' I said, 'I should be back soon after seven.' This seemed to puzzle you. You'd forgotten again about Mr Maybrick. I had to remind you. You said, 'Oh yes, so you are. Have a nice time.'

When I looked back you were watching me. And lifted your hand. Which wasn't usual. But pleased me. I waved back. I went round the side of the house so that I wouldn't disturb Susan.

Isn't it very close? Stay. Talk to me. Is that the date? When will Sarah be back? Will you be long?

These were your appeals. Which I did not hear. I did not hear Aziz's appeal either. When will *you* be back? He saw the sunlight and the shadow and in his heart interpreted them correctly. But followed your mood and example. When I left in the tonga he made Susan some tea. No one knows what he did after that. The kitchen was neat and tidy. He always kept it so.

ii

Mr Maybrick waves his arms in the air. Pages of Bach fly from his hands, swirl, swoop, drift, fall. His face is contorted by the anguish of a man who requires order but cannot keep it. We stand erect in this tempest of paper music. Then I turn, pretending to go; having only just arrived. He waits until I am at the door and cries, 'Come back!' I am no longer even a little afraid of Mr Maybrick but I obey because it pleases him to act the martinet. I can see him terrorizing coolies who grin when his back is turned because he never harms them. I can see him ordering his wife about, before she began to ail, and see her, one hand shading not just her eyes from the light but her smile with which she commences to perform what he demands but in her own way and to her own satisfaction, which she knows will be to his as well.

What a pickle you are in, I tell him, and sit on the one chair that is not cluttered with things that have no business on chairs. We are ankle deep in Bach. The situation looks hopeless, more hopeless to him than to me because the pages are numbered and it only requires patience and application – qualities he does not normally possess – to restore them to their proper order. The problem will be the rebinding. He complains about the quality of the gum I used last time, about the quality of the original binding, about having no room nowadays to store things properly, about the climate that makes things fall apart anyway, about the decline in standards of workmanship, about the fact that, as he says, nobody gives a damn any more; and finally –

the rub, because it explains why he has scattered the pages in a
childish rage – about a double sheet that is missing.

'Have you looked in the organ loft?' I ask. He declares that
the missing sheet cannot possibly be in the organ loft. He says,
'It's no good sitting staring at it, what are you waiting for?'

I tell him: Tea. I tell him I require a cup of tea first and that
after that I will walk down to the church and look in the organ
loft while he makes a start clearing up the mess he has made.

On my way to St John's I see suddenly what a vast improvement my time in Pankot has wrought in my character. Application I had, and patience, but of a questionable kind. Confronted
in the old days with the ruins of the Bach I would have fallen
avidly upon the scattered pages and somehow contrived to make
greater confusion than before. And I would not have dared insist
on Tea.

I see that I have acquired qualities of leadership and command.
For a moment my pride in this achievement is disproportionate
to its degree. I feel a deep glow of satisfaction. I lengthen my
stride. Although it is a very hot day I have on the heliotrope.
The sun is lowering towards West Hill. I turn my face to it. I am
happy. I have, I feel, always done my utmost and now enjoy my
reward on this earth whose beauty is serene towards evening.

As I turn into the churchyard the clock strikes the half hour
after five. I enter and go straight to the organ loft. The light is
not good. I crouch down, searching, convinced I shall find the
missing sheet. And I find it in a corner. It bears the dusty imprint
of Mr Maybrick's shoe. I smile. And then I hear a sound, the
sound of the latch lifted on the little side door through which
I too have just entered, the slight squeak of the hinges, the sound
of the door closing. Mr Maybrick has followed me.

I stand up and cry 'Eureka!' and look down to where he should
be. But there is no one. The church is empty. I call again, less
boldly. No answer. I have the missing sheet in one hand. With
my other I seek my neck, automatically, and then the chain, the
pendant cross.

I leave, unhurriedly. I tell myself my entrance must have disturbed someone at private devotions, someone whom I did not
see when I came in and who has taken the opportunity of my
climb to the organ loft to leave unnoticed. Slowly I follow this
solitary worshipper out and down the path past the gravestones,

but he – or she – is still invisible. I walk back to Mr Maybrick's.

I find him sitting on the floor, the scattered pages all around him untouched. He is listening to the news on the wireless and shushes me when I begin to protest at his idleness. Resigned, I throw things from the chair which has now become cluttered. He shushes me again. I subside. For a while I do not listen to the news but then do so and become aware that it is important. I cannot pick up the thread, though. It ends. But the announcer repeats the opening and this is followed by martial music.

It seems that British and allied forces have invaded Normandy. They have opened the second front. Mr Maybrick shouts for his bearer and then heaves me out of the chair and does a little jig. His enthusiasm is infectious. Poor Bach is in danger of being trampled underfoot. Mr Maybrick tells his boy to bring sherry. He says that when the Germans are defeated the whole weight of the Allied armies will be thrown against the Japanese and then we can all live civilized lives again.

'And all the prisoners in Germany will be freed!' I cry. 'I must phone the cottage –' I go into the hall, pick up the receiver and wait impatiently for the operator to answer. I am anxious for Susan to know, because of her father. I ask for the number and continue to wait. The operator tells me the number is engaged. Crestfallen I go back to the living-room. I work it out that Mildred has heard at the club and is already on the phone to Susan. We drink sherry. Ten minutes later I telephone again but the operator says there is still someone speaking. Mildred is probably back at the cottage and ringing all her friends. I resign my role as the bearer of good tidings. Come, I say to Mr May-brick, let us begin on poor Bach.

iii

'Perseverance,' Barbie said, 'which was incidentally one of my father's favourite words if not one of his virtues, unless you count perseverance with the bottle and the cards, perseverance – Mr Maybrick – wins the day.'

She slapped the last page of Bach, straightened her bent back and cried out partly from the pain of easing the ache and partly from astonishment at Mr Maybrick's firmly planted kiss. Only on the forehead. Nevertheless. She felt her face and neck grow hot.

'Angelic Barbie,' he said. 'Ham-fisted with glue but angelic. What would you say to mutton curry and rice?'

'I should say no.'

'Is that all?'

'Had you been more complimentary about the glue I should have added thank you. You may help me up.'

'I will if you say yes. It was planned. Mutton curry and rice. For two.'

'Planned by whom?'

'By me.'

'Mr Maybrick, you have been overdoing the sherry. At your age it is ill-advised.'

'You've not done so badly yourself. You can knock it back.'

'Two glasses are all I've had.'

'Refilled occasionally without your noticing, between fugues.'

'I see you are determined to be difficult.' She got up un-assisted. Her joints were very stiff. She looked at her watch. It was seven fifteen. She had been crawling across the floor and kneeling sorting pages for over an hour. Mr Maybrick had been more of a hindrance than a help.

He said, 'If you stay to supper you could start the binding afterwards.'

'If I stayed to supper I should do no such thing. The binding will have to wait. Meanwhile I should be obliged if you'd send Kaisa Ram for a tonga. I'm going to tidy myself and when I come back I'll expect to hear that a tonga is on its way.'

'You've become a hard woman, Barbie. I'd set my heart on it.'

'Then you should have said so three days ago and not left it to chance and your powers of persuasion. And if I said yes you know very well you'd have to dash into the kitchen and tell Kaisa Ram to throw some more meat into the pot, and that he'd complain, that you'd shout at him and that you'd have a burnt supper, bad temper for the rest of the evening and indigestion all night.'

She turned to the door that led through the single bedroom to the bathroom.

'It'll take fifteen minutes for Kaisa Ram to get a tonga,' he said, 'but only five to cut off another chop.'

'And an hour for it to cook properly. So please send him down to the stand. When I come back I'll have another sherry. I don't believe a word of your story of surreptitious refills.'

She left him but caught the flicker of the smile he was doing his best to disguise. The bedroom, crammed with the monumental furniture of his spacious tea-planting days, was even more untidy than the living-room and overpowered by the majestic bed that filled the central space. As always, this bed was shrouded by the regal canopy of a faded white mosquito net. In Pankot there was no need of one and if there had been Mr Maybrick's would have been inadequate because it was full of holes and rents which Kaisa Ram neglected to mend. But Mr Maybrick said he couldn't sleep in a bed that had no net. She sympathized with this peculiarity, remembering that whenever she had moved from a mosquito-ridden area to a cool and airy one she had always found the absence of a net initially alarming, a source of apprehension, of fears of falling out at least, at worst of attack by night-intruders.

The bathroom was cheerless. A single unshaded bulb illuminated its dingy whitewashed walls and concrete floor. In one corner there was a cubicle and in this an ornate commode of which Mr Maybrick was very proud. The commode, fortunately, was always spotless but the bathroom itself was grimy. There tended to be cockroaches.

Normally, when visiting Mr Maybrick, she hurried through the business of tidying herself. But tonight she found herself slowed down, struck by the significance of her surroundings, the reality of this ordinariness, this shabbiness, this evidence of detritus behind the screens of imperial power and magnificence. The feeling she had was not of glory departing or departed but of its original and continuing irrelevance to the business of being in India, which was her and Mr Maybrick's business just as much as it was the business of the members of the mess in whose inner sanctum she had stood last year, intimidated by the ghostly occupants of those serried ranks of chairs.

She paused between soaping and rinsing her hands, riveted by an image of the captains and the kings queuing to wash their own hands in Mr Maybrick's bowl after relieving themselves in Mr Maybrick's mahogany commode with its rose-patterned porcelain receptacle, and finding no fault, nothing unusual, feeling no hurt to their dignity; and going back through the unholy clutter of Mr Maybrick's bedroom without a glance at the half-opened drawers festooned with socks and vests and shirts that wanted mending, because the one thing to which the human spirit could always accommodate itself was chaos and misfortune. Everything more orderly or favoured was a bonus and needed living up to.

She closed her eyes and was back in the Camberwell scullery and then in the dark hallway, taking the first rise of the stairs, with all the captains and kings behind her waiting to do the same. Why, she said, the mystery at the top of the stairs is where we're all headed, willy-nilly, which is what my father but not my mother understood. She opened her eyes. The lather had begun to encrust her hands with a creamy rime. She rinsed and dried them on the week-old roller towel. She dabbed her wrists with cologne from her handbag phial and resprinkled the fine lawn handkerchief. Chaos, misfortune. Punctuated by harmless escapes into personal vanities. She clicked her handbag shut. The click was as satisfactory as a decision.

'Mr Maybrick!' she called, re-entering the living-room.

He came in from the hall.

He said, 'Oh, there you are, Barbie. Arthur Peplow is here. He has something to tell you.'

iv

'I said, I will take heed to my ways: that I offend not in my tongue. I will keep my mouth as it were with a bridle; while the ungodly is in my sight. I held my tongue, and spake nothing, I kept silence, yea, even from good words; but it was pain and grief to me. My heart was hot within me, and while I was thus musing the fire kindled and at the last I spake with my tongue; Lord, let me know mine end, and the number of my days; that I may be certified how long I have to live.'

v

Where the rime had been was Arthur Peplow's hand. In the pause between the word 'stroke' and the words 'it was very sudden', she heard down the road the chime of the half-hour after seven.

Mr Peplow said, 'I think we must believe that she felt no pain, but went very peacefully. Susan was tremendously brave. The poor girl was quite alone. When she realized what had happened she rang Colonel Beames at once, and then her mother. She couldn't find Aziz anywhere. Have you any idea where he could have gone?'

'Aziz?'

'Never mind. In a moment or two Clarissa and I want you to come down to the rectory. Captain Coley's going to spend the night at Rose Cottage to look after things there for Mildred. Clarissa's having a bed made up for you.'

'I have a bed,' she said. And removed her hand from Arthur Peplow's to take the glass of sherry from Mr Maybrick's hand which was shaking. She held it, but did not know how to deal with it. Some of the deep brown liquid spilt on to the heliotrope skirt. 'I don't want it,' she said. 'After all.' Arthur took the glass. There was nowhere for him to put it down.

'The thing is,' he said, 'we all think it best if you stay the night with us. You can come straight away. If you don't mind borrowing some things Clarissa can lend you what you need. Beames or Travers will look in later with something to help you sleep. I asked Beames myself, I thought it would be wise. You'll need a good night's rest.'

'It's very kind of you, Arthur. But I must go home at once. If someone will fetch a tonga.'

She watched Arthur Peplow get up. Some of the books and magazines which he had pushed aside to make room on the sofa for the two of them slid back into place. She observed the glance he exchanged with Mr Maybrick before parking the glass of sherry on top of the grand piano. Glad of the momentary relief such a prosaic detail provided in the mountingly oppressive nightmare, she recalled that the piano was badly out of tune because it had not been played since Clarice Maybrick's fingers were last upon its yellowed, mottled, keys. Another thing she remembered Mr Maybrick telling her was how Clarice always took her rings off before playing and placed them on the ebony ledge at the bass end of the keyboard.

Arthur Peplow went out into the hall. She heard the ping that accompanied the lifting of the receiver. You could not get a tonga by ringing the exchange. Suddenly the door between hall

and living-room closed, which meant that Arthur didn't want
her to hear what he was saying or know to whom he was saying
it. She stayed where she was, readopting an old habit of mind;
that of believing in the good sense and good will of established
authority; although the waves of rebellion had already risen and
were – she guessed – only temporarily subdued. Mr Maybrick
came to the sofa and sat beside her, pushing the books and magazines to give himself room. He sat with his elbows on his knees
and his hands clasped in the space between and looked down at
the worn bit of carpet.

'When I left this afternoon,' Barbie said, watching the door
that led to the hall where Arthur's voice had begun to drone, to
vibrate, to punctuate longer periods of silence, 'she watched me
and waited for me to look round, and then lifted her hand to
wave.'

Mr Maybrick nodded but said nothing.

'You do understand, Mr Maybrick, that I can't possibly sleep
at Arthur's and Clarissa's or anywhere but at the cottage. There
will be no need for Captain Coley to be there. In fact I find
the idea quite unacceptable. Aziz and I will manage everything.
I quite see that Mildred can't stay. She'll have to take poor Susan
home and look after her. But Captain Coley's presence is not
necessary. I am prepared to wait here for a bit but eventually, no
– quite soon, I must go back.'

'I'll come with you if you like.'

'Thank you. That would be kind. So long as it's understood
that I stay there.'

She grew rigid with impatience. There was much to be done.
And quickly. In India these things were always done quickly.
They had to be. And the problems of making special arrangements were likely to be many. She herself must be prepared for
the journey to Ranpur. Packing was something that would
occupy her.

'And I must pack,' she said. 'I must be ready to leave tomorrow. The man at St Luke's in Ranpur used to be the Reverend
Ian Wright and still may be. Arthur will know.'

Again Mr Maybrick nodded. She did not know whether he
was listening but his mute agreement was encouraging. The door
opened and Arthur came back in smoothing his head with one
hand. He asked Mr Maybrick whether Kaisa Ram could produce

some tea or coffee. Mr Maybrick got up and went out saying he would see. Directly they were alone Arthur said, 'That was Kevin Coley at the other end. I told him you want to go up to the cottage and he's had a word with Mildred. She's still there with Susan and I think she'd be grateful if you'd let her get Susan away first, because the girl's in pretty much of a state. In fact she's suffering badly from reaction. Colonel Beames left about an hour ago and Susan was fairly all right then but he said he'd have a word with Travers because it's Travers who's been attending to her during her pregnancy. Well, they've been waiting for Travers to turn up and Coley's trying to get him on the phone now. Mrs Fosdick and Mrs Paynton are there helping Mildred cope. There's nothing you can actually do, Barbie, and frankly I think the best thing is for you to wait here a while and then if you feel you must just go up and collect some things for the night. I'll take you.'

'Mr Maybrick has promised to do that.'

'Well, that's fine. Coley said he'd ring me as soon as Mildred's got Susan away. Please don't misunderstand. Mildred knows how upset you must be and that you can only be more upset the moment you set foot in Rose Cottage. Just now she has her work cut out keeping poor Susan on an even keel. The danger is premature labour brought on by shock. And you *do* appreciate how much of a shock it was, don't you?'

'Yes, Arthur.'

'Coley says Aziz is still missing. It's very odd. When I mentioned it before I don't think you took it in. But he's not been seen since he brought Susan out her tray of tea. She had a cup and then noticed it wasn't yet four o'clock so she dozed off again and was only half awake when Mabel came and sat down and seemed to nod off.'

'What time was that, Arthur?'

'About five. Beames got there at five-thirty.'

'More than two hours ago. I don't understand. I don't understand why I wasn't called at once.'

'No one knew where you were.'

'Aziz knew.'

'But Barbie –'

'I'm sorry. I keep forgetting. But Susan knew.'

'She said she only knew she'd seen you making out cheques and imagined you'd gone down to the bazaar to pay them.'

'Yes, I see.'

'Clarissa was out when Mildred rang and asked me to go up. Otherwise we might have traced you sooner. She rang me at the cottage when she got home at seven and found my message. She said she thought you might be here with Edgar. So I came straight away.'

That was very kind of you, Barbie intended to say; but she could not because it was being borne in on her that Arthur Peplow was deeply implicated – even if he didn't realize it – in a plot to keep her out of the way, to stop her from going to Rose Cottage. She could not judge whether punishment or kindness was intended. If punishment, then Mildred was probably at the bottom of it. If kindness, then Mabel's death could not have been the quiet and peaceful passing Arthur had described.

She saw her friend with blackened face, protuberant tongue, and limbs stiffened in the final gesture of total and absolute terror; and Susan backing away, clutching her swollen belly, shrieking for Aziz, getting no answer and then – with space achieved between her own body and the horror – scrabbling at the tele-phone and shouting incoherently for help, making for the door, running down the gravel drive to the rockery-bordered exit to Club road, clasping the pillar of the open gateway and screaming until the whole of Pankot echoed and trembled.

But this was not the way it had been, nor the way it ever could have been. The convolutions of the petals of this rose are dissimilar to the convolutions of this, Mabel must have said; and, leaning towards it, to examine more closely the miracle of its individuality, become aware of a corresponding shadow leaning over her, so that she straightened carefully to absorb the shock and leave the rose to its freedom and perfection; and turned, holding the basket, walked cautiously towards the short flight of wooden steps to the verandah. Here there was a promise, briefly kept, of continuation. A figure sleeping. Within it another; patiently achieving its human shape. Briefly too, a green leaf, one of many sprouting from stems in pots on the balustrade, adumbrated the shape and texture of its successors to fingers still occupied by love and custom.

But again the shadow leans and the hand that touches the leaves is arrested by another which is more grandly and fearfully informed. And a voice – the same that said: Does it matter? – says, That's all, that's all.

She sits. The favour granted to someone like her. A rock. The seas pound. One wave scarcely distinguishable from any of the others puts out the faltering spark. But in that place there is no visible difference between sleep and death. She had nodded off. And out. The dear indomitable body remains. Marking the place.

I have a concern, Barbie thought, to see if the eyes are open. She felt that they should be but didn't know why except that in Mabel's case this would somehow be seemly.

'Barbie,' Arthur said, taking her hand to his cold but well-intentioned comfort. 'Don't try so hard not to cry. You loved her and cared for her. You did it well.'

'But not today. She wanted me to be there. But of course she would never have dreamed of asking. If she could have made it back to her room she would have, for Susan's sake.'

'There, there. That's better.'

'Forgive me.'

But before she could disgrace herself she became free of the encumbrance of Arthur Peplow's sympathy. She got up, grabbed her handbag and went into Mr Maybrick's bedroom and shut the door. The physical exertion closed the gate on useless grief. From what appeared to be a considerable distance away she saw Mabel waiting. She achieved levitation and floated without trouble through the apex of the regal canopy of the mosquito net and left the room filled with the dark bat-wing flapping of the ghosts of her sorrow. She longed now only to escape and destroy the distance between the terrible little bungalow and Rose Cottage.

She switched on the light in the bathroom and closed the door, crossed, reached up and unbolted the side door. Warm night air stroked her cheeks. She stumbled, surprised by an un-familiar dimension – a high step – and saved herself from falling. She pressed on through an opening in what appeared to be a trellis. There was a sickly odour of sweet jasmine in the night and charcoal fumes from the outhouse where Kaisa Ram was cooking mutton curry. At the front of the bungalow she moved cautiously but, gaining the road, planted her feet firmly.

She hastened past the rectory bungalow, squat behind its partial screen of trees, showing but one lighted room, and walked down the hill, past St John's. Where Church road joined Club road she would with luck find an empty tonga making its way back from club to bazaar, but reaching there she found the road deserted and, having no time to waste, set off on the uphill climb. Presently two tongas went past, both laden; and then she had to stand still and hide her eyes from twin glares that loomed and roared and went past leaving dust and petrol fumes and echoes of singing male voices. At the milestone she paused to rest. She heard the clock of St John's strike eight in another world. She got up and plodded on.

Captain Coley was in the front porch, waiting, which meant that Arthur and Mr Maybrick had discovered her escape and telephoned a warning.

'We're waiting for Travers,' he said. 'It's Susan. We think she's started.'

'Then she should be got to hospital.' She glanced into the lighted hall. Already the place had the look of not belonging to anyone. 'They should have taken her home long before this,' she said. 'Colonel Beames should have insisted. Where is she?'

'With Mildred in the spare bedroom.'

She went into the hall. Just then Susan cried out. At the same instant from some quality of sound and echo Barbie realized that the thing she had come to look at wasn't in the house. She turned, intending to raise the question of where Mabel's body had been taken but was forestalled by Mildred calling Captain Coley's name and then appearing in the living-room doorway.

Barbie noticed that Mildred's hair was still immaculately set. She would have expected something of the last few hours to have left a mark of itself in the form of disarrangement however slight. She noticed the hair because its groomed perfection set the tone of Mildred's whole appearance. She searched for signs of wildness in Mildred's face and in doing so realized that for a perceptible count, even if only in fractions of seconds, she and Mildred were staring at each other like old enemies who knew that the truce by whose terms they had both faithfully abided was now officially over.

'I'm sorry to have arrived before you've got Susan home,'

Barbie said. 'But I won't get in anyone's way, unless of course there's something I can do.'

'Thank you,' Mildred replied. 'But I think we can cope. Providing Travers gets here pretty soon. What's the form, Kevin?'

'The form is he should be here any minute now. Probably with an ambulance.'

Mildred nodded, made to go back in but paused. She looked at Barbie. She said, 'Have you any idea where that bloody man can have got to?'

'Which man, Mildred?'

'Aziz,' she said; and repeated it. This time the sibilants struck like snakes. 'Aziz.'

'I think, yes, I'm sure it was for today, he had permission to visit a relative in one of the villages.' The cautious lie came pat. But Mildred wasn't fooled.

'A sick relative, I suppose. No. I don't think so. The other servants know nothing about it. Well, if and when he ever shows his face again, Kevin here's promised personally to boot him in the rear.'

'I don't think you understand, Mildred. I don't think you understand at all. About Indians like Aziz.'

'I understand only too well. My God, I understand! He knew what I presume none of us knew. That she was ill. And bloody well funked it. Let's see how far he gets. I've asked Beames to have a word with the police.'

'The police! Whatever are you saying?'

'– not that there appears to be anything noticeably missing. But there hasn't been time for a proper check.'

Another cry from Susan cut her off. For an instant her eyes closed and one hand gripped the jamb of the doorway. A voice which Barbie recognized as Clara Fosdick's called Mildred's name. Mildred went back towards the little spare.

Behind Barbie Coley said, 'Terribly upset. Don't take police business too seriously. No one really suspects the old chap of pinching anything but it's a necessary precaution, at least until Beames is satisfied about the cause of death.'

She faced round to Coley upon whose martyr's face there already seemed to be the reflection of flickering flames.

'What do you mean?'

He looked pained by so direct a question.

'Only a formality. Feels he should have a pathologist's report to confirm his opinion that it was a stroke.'

The sound of an engine revving, of a driver changing into a low gear to negotiate the entrance to the drive, rescued him from further explanation. He went quickly out to the porch. Barbie hesitated, then approached Mabel's bedroom. She grasped the handle of the door and had confirmation that it was locked. In the dining-room she repeated the process. The door between Mabel's bedroom and the dining-room was locked too.

And there was something new and peculiar about the dining-room itself. It took Barbie a few moments to pin it down. The few pieces of silver normally kept on the sideboard were no longer there. Aziz, Aziz, she cried out silently; but almost immediately knew that Aziz had had nothing to do with it. She tried the cupboard doors in the sideboard. These were locked too. Doubtless the silver was inside.

She heard Travers's voice, and Coley's, and stood erect and still while the voices moved from hall to living-room and to the spare bedroom. Then she opened the french window on to the verandah which was illuminated by the light cast from dining-room and living-room and little spare. Susan's lounging chair was there, with its cushions. The book brought by Captain Beauvais lay unopened on the floor together with another book and a copy of the current issue of the *Onlooker*. A tray of tea on a low stool was on the other side of the place where Susan had lain dozing, and several paces beyond on the other side of the french window into the living-room, but near the balustrade, another chair: upright and empty, with the pannier-basket beside it.

She moved closer to it and then stooped and picked up the basket. It contained secateurs, dead rose-heads, a hand fork to whose tines particles of earth clung. She touched all these things, assuring herself of their existence; consequently of her own.

Then she saw lying on the floor where she supposed Beames had let it drop after removing it the old frayed-brim straw hat. She stooped and picked this up too.

'But it can't have!' Susan cried out. Barbie heard her clearly. 'It can't have started. The baby isn't *finished* yet.'

Barbie moved into the shadow but saw through the uncurtained open window of the little spare. They had Susan on her feet. Travers held one arm and Mildred the other. Clara

Fosdick had her own and Susan's handbags. Nicky Paynton held open the door into the living-room. The girl seemed to be a dead weight. Travers said, 'Come along, Su, you don't need the stretcher. Just keep on your feet. We'll have you right as rain, you'll see.'

Her resistance went. Meekly but cautiously as if every step she made was an opportunity for the baby to make a dangerous bid for its freedom she let Travers and her mother lead her out.

When they had gone Barbie waited, giving them time to get out to the ambulance. Then she moved into the area of light and went back to Mabel's chair, still holding the basket and the straw hat.

She sat down.

But there was no way in.

Presently she was aware of a shadow fallen across her feet and she felt the little shock-waves of someone's fear or agitation. She glanced up. It was Kevin Coley. He thought he had seen a ghost.

He said, 'Mr Maybrick's here to take you down to the Peplows for the night.'

'Very well, Captain Coley. Thank you. I'll pack a few things.'

In the living-room she realized what she carried that was not hers and what was missing that belonged to her. 'I think I left my handbag on the sideboard in the dining-room. Would you look? There are some things in it which I ought to hand over.'

He came back with the handbag held high, as men held such things. She put the pannier and straw hat down, took the bag, got out the receipts and crossed to the bureau. The lid was locked and the key missing. She stood until the flush of humiliation had come and gone and then turned and offered the receipts to Coley saying, 'Will you see that Mildred gets these?' Coley took them. Leaving hat and pannier behind she went into the hall where Mr Maybrick was waiting.

'Barbie –' he began.

'No recriminations,' she said. 'I'm going to pack an overnight bag. I take it you have transport of some kind outside.'

'Only a tonga.'

'That will suffice. Do one thing for me first. Find out from Captain Coley where they have taken Mabel.'

In her bedroom she collected nightgown, slippers, dressing-gown, a change of underwear and toilet articles. She crammed

these into an old fibre suitcase whose handle was mended with
string. Back in the hall ten minutes later she found Mr Maybrick
and Captain Coley standing several feet apart and not talking.

'If Aziz should come back, Captain Coley, you will tell him
where I am, won't you? And you will treat him with the same
courtesy he and Mabel always showed one another, I trust.'

Coley looked hunted. And then she realized that he was a
coward, and always had been, in spite of that uniform, that precious insignia. She turned the screw.

'Well? I have your word? The word of a British officer to an
Englishwoman?'

Coley flushed, aware of her mockery, and – with his fingers
tainted by keys and valuables – of its justification; that she
mocked him not only for himself but for the whole condition.
She did not care. The charade was finished. Mabel had guessed
the word years ago but had refrained from speaking it. The word
was 'dead'. Dead. Dead. It didn't matter now who said it; the
edifice had crumbled and the façade fooled nobody. One could
only pray for a wind to blow it all away or for an earthquake
such as Captain Coley's wife had died in. Barbie saw how perhaps with one finger she might topple him, because there was
nothing to keep him standing except his own inertia.

But she had other things to do. She decided not to wait for his
reply; and in any case the silence that followed her demand
revealed how little she would be able to count on any promise that
he gave. She marched out to the tonga with the fibre suitcase.

'What was the answer?' she asked when Mr Maybrick
joined her.

'We should go to the general hospital and inquire there.'

'Then please tell the wallah.'

'I'm bound to say Coley didn't think there would be much
point.'

'Naturally. Captain Coley sees little point in anything. He
should have died in the rubble of Quetta. In most ways he did.
The Lord alone knows for what purpose the remains are
preserved.'

She waited in the reception hall of the general hospital seated
on an uncomfortable highly polished bench, watching Mr Maybrick making things difficult for one of the girls at the inquiry

desk, a fair-skinned Eurasian who kept on lifting the receiver of her telephone, presumably trying yet another extension at Mr Maybrick's insistence. After ten minutes something definite seemed to be decided and the girl suddenly looked impressed and helpful. Mr Maybrick came over to the bench. He sat down.

'Beames is over at the nursing home annexe. If we go across now he'll have a word with you. The nursing home is where Susan's been taken, and Mildred will be there too.'

'My business is only with Colonel Beames. I'm sorry you're being put to so much trouble, Mr Maybrick. If you want to go home to your supper I can manage on my own.'

He stood up, grabbed the suitcase and said, 'Come on, we can walk it, it's not far.'

They came out and followed directional signs along the asphalt path. They both knew the nursing home well. They had visited Clarissa there the year she was ill with pleurisy.

The reception hall was less forbidding than the one at the main hospital. There were rugs and bowls of flowers. The woman behind the desk was a VAD. Her grey hair was blue-rinsed.

'Miss Batchelor?' she asked, ignoring Mr Maybrick. 'Colonel Beames is engaged but won't keep you long.'

Barbie and Mr Maybrick sat together on a leather sofa. The blue-haired woman made notes on a file of papers with a very sharp-looking pencil. Whenever she answered the telephone she said, 'Pankot Nursing Home, can I help you?' She had a miniature switchboard on the desk with red and green switches on it which she manipulated with dexterity and self-assurance. Once she banged a bell and was answered by an Indian porter to whom she gave a folded note and a brisk instruction. Ten minutes later another VAD came through the hushed swing doors.

'Miss Batchelor?'

Barbie stood up. She followed the woman through into a polished corridor and round a corner into another where they stopped at a white painted door marked Private. The woman knocked, opened and stood aside after announcing Barbie's name. The room was carpeted. The civil surgeon got up from behind a large desk and crossed the carpet silently. In the few years they had passingly known each other they had exchanged not many more words. He was a tall man with a nose and eyebrows and jaws that looked as if they had champed bones.

'I'm sorry to have had to keep you waiting,' he said. He pulled a leather chair close to another, waited for her to sit and then sat himself. He subjected her to a kind of remote scrutiny. His was a face that accepted nothing and gave nothing. 'It will perhaps have been an even greater shock for you than for any of us. I am so sorry. But I do now have my pathologist's report which confirms my assumption of cerebral haemorrhage. I suppose one must be thankful that it wasn't the kind of stroke that would have left her paralysed but alive. Had she complained of feeling unwell lately?'

Barbie shook her head.

'Well if she felt out of sorts I don't suppose she'd have said so or called any of us in. She was very much a law unto herself wasn't she? I'm sorry that there had to be this very slight delay in giving the certificate but in the circumstances I really had no alternative. I've told Mildred – Mrs Layton junior – the result of course. She's here with young Susan, as I expect you know. You're staying the night with the Peplows?'

Barbie nodded.

'Mrs Layton has phoned Arthur Peplow and given him the all clear to go forward with the arrangements. It's unfortunate Sarah's in Calcutta. Mrs Layton is going to telephone her sister but even if Sarah starts back first thing in the morning she won't be here until the day after tomorrow. I'm afraid Susan's in for rather an arduous time from what Travers says, so her mother won't be able to see to the other business personally. Fortunately Arthur Peplow and Captain Coley have undertaken to deal with it.' He brought a small envelope out of his pocket. 'I want you to take the two tablets in this packet with some warm milk when you go to bed tonight. To give you a proper night's rest.'

She accepted the envelope. She said, 'Thank you, Colonel Beames.' She would not take the tablets. 'That is very kind of you, and very practical. There is a great deal to do and one must be on one's feet to do it.'

'Well, yes, but it's all being done. Don't worry. Sleep is the best thing for you.'

'Can you tell me anything about the arrangements, for instance about the arrangements for transportation?'

'Transportation?'

'To Ranpur. I imagine there will be a service here at St John's, especially as Mildred won't be able to leave Pankot while Susan is having her baby. And perhaps some kind of brief ceremony the next day at St Luke's. But I'm concerned about the transport. You see, I should wish to accompany.'

'Did you say St Luke's?'

'Yes. St Luke's in Ranpur. That's where the actual burial is to be. At St Luke's in Ranpur. She wished to be with her late husband, Mr James Layton. Hasn't Mildred mentioned that to you?'

'No.'

She waited for him to say more. But his face had gone out entirely. The heavy jaws were clamped shut.

'Then I had better see her and remind her,' Barbie said.

'Are you sure those were the elder Mrs Layton's wishes?'

'Quite sure.'

'I see.' Beames paused. 'Then I'll mention it to Mrs Layton junior. Interment in Ranpur is not among the impressions I have about the arrangements but possibly I haven't a complete picture. I do know that a service at St John's late tomorrow after-noon has been talked of.' He looked at his watch. 'I have to leave now for Flagstaff House but I shall be coming back later to see Mrs Layton. I'll mention it to her then.' He stood up. 'We've given her the room next to Susan's and she's resting on my orders. She's had a very trying time which would explain why she might overlook a point such as the one you've raised – if she has overlooked it. I'm sure that she'd know about it if it is an established wish or a definite instruction. You may depend on my letting her know what you've told me.'

She got up. She had no intention of depending upon Colonel Beames, but that, she thought, need not concern him. She allowed him to lead her to the door.

'Are you accompanied?' he said.

'Mr Maybrick is with me.'

'Good. And have you transport?'

'We have a tonga.'

'It's curious about the servant, isn't it? But I knew of a similar case. I suppose it's a kind of sixth sense coupled with this odd fatalism some of these old fellows develop. But it's not proof of unfeeling.'

'The opposite,' she said. 'Quite the opposite.'

They stood at the open door now.

'I wish to see her, of course,' Barbie said. 'Can I do that now?'

He observed her without reacting visibly to what he saw. She felt the same expression moulded upon her own face.

'I'm afraid not. But if you ring the general hospital in the morning and ask to speak to Doctor Iyenagar or to his assistant I'm sure it could be arranged, should you really wish it.'

'Doctor Iyenagar?'

'Or his assistant. Extension 22.'

'Thank you, Colonel Beames.'

He made as if to accompany her but she assured him she could find her way. She walked back along the corridors to the waiting-room. Mr Maybrick stood up. She went to speak to the blue-haired woman at the desk.

She said, 'Colonel Beames tells me that Mrs John Layton is staying the night. I may want to telephone her in the morning. Is that fairly easy?'

'Yes, there's a telephone in every room.'

'What extension should I ask for?'

The vicious-looking pencil ran delicately down the list.

'Extension eight. Mrs John Layton.'

'Is that also the room number?'

'That is correct. Her daughter Mrs Bingham is in number seven.'

'Thank you so much. Goodnight.'

'We should have left the case in the tonga,' she said as they walked back along the asphalt path.

'And let the fellow run off with it,' Mr Maybrick replied. As if it contained things of value. 'He's probably gone away. It's not like the old days. They'd wait all night to get paid what they were owed. What did Beames say?'

'It was a stroke. So nothing need be delayed. They can go ahead with the arrangements.'

'That's a blessing.'

'What *are* the arrangements, Mr Maybrick? Did Arthur tell you?'

'He was hoping everything could be ready for a service at five o'clock.'

'And then?'

'Then? The interment.'

'In St John's churchyard?'

'Yes. He was relieved Mildred didn't insist on cremation. So many people do nowadays and he doesn't really hold with it. But she asked him to go ahead and select a site himself.'

'Are you absolutely sure?'

'Oh, yes. He was quite relieved. He hasn't had a burial there for some while.'

They came to the end of the path. 'I'm afraid it will have to be stopped, Mr Maybrick.' She halted and held his arm. They now stood on the broad asphalt area in front of the main entrance to the general hospital. The tonga-wallah called to them and then the tonga emerged from the dense shadow of a clump of trees whose branches overhung the drive.

'What do you mean stopped? Aren't you satisfied with Beames's opinion?'

'It isn't that.'

'What then?'

'The burial has to be at St Luke's in Ranpur. I told him so but I'm afraid that might not be enough. I must see Mildred. I think I must see her tonight. Either she's forgotten or Mabel never told her. She couldn't deliberately disregard a wish like that, could she?'

'What wish? Whose wish?'

'Mabel's. She wished to be buried next to her late husband James Layton, at St Luke's in Ranpur.'

'And you said so to Beames?'

'Yes.'

'What did *he* say?'

'He said he'd mention it to Mildred tonight when he gets back from Flagstaff House.'

'Then he will. If it's all that important you can tell Arthur when we get back and one of you can ring Mildred in the morning to check whether Beames kept his word. Come on. You need some food and something warm to drink and to get to bed and try to sleep.'

He swung the case up beside the tonga-wallah.

'I'm sorry to be a stubborn nuisance to you, Mr Maybrick, but —'

'For God's sake!' he said. 'Call me Edgar, can't you, after all these years?'

'Yes, all right.' She nodded her head. 'Edgar. Edgar.' She began to laugh and covered her face. She could not stop. She laughed for her sorrow and for his name because it didn't suit him and presently she was laughing for Mabel because the alternative to laughter was shriek after shriek of wild and lonely despair because Mabel had gone and she had lost her occupation and she saw that was how it was and would always be for everyone.

'Barbie!' Mr Maybrick (Edgar) was saying; he had her by the shoulders but she could not allow herself to be enfolded, admonished or cherished. She forced her body away and began walking towards the steps that led to the glass doors through which shone the lights in the main entrance hall of the hospital. She scrabbled in her handbag and found her cologne-scented handkerchief and dried her cheeks and eyes.

'Now where are you going?' he called.

'It's all right. You go back home.'

He caught up with her as she placed her foot on the first step. 'Barbie, what are you doing?'

'I have to see a Doctor Iyenagar.'

'A doctor what?'

They were at the door now, each pushing one immaculate sheet of framed glass, so that the arrival had all the force of an important emergency. The Eurasian girl glanced up, startled. Barbie went to the desk without hesitating. The spirit of the hard condition had entered: an inspired visitation.

'Colonel Beames will have rung,' she announced in a penetrating voice. 'Please tell Doctor Iyenagar I am here.'

'Oh, but Doctor Iyenagar has left.'

'Then his assistant, Doctor whatever his name is. Extension twenty-two.'

The girl swung round in her swivel chair, fumbled with plugs. She said, 'It's Miss Batchelor, isn't it?'

'Yes. I am to see Doctor Iyenagar or his assistant in connection with the death this afternoon of Mrs Mabel Layton. Colonel Beames should have rung before he left for Flagstaff House.'

'Yes. I see. I don't remember –' She responded to a voice in her ear. 'Get Doctor Lal, please.' She looked up at Barbie. 'Doctor Lal will come. Please sit down.'

'Is he on the other end now?'

'Not yet. I will tell him.'

'There's no need for him to come. Just tell him I'm here as arranged by Colonel Beames and then be good enough to have someone show me to his office.' She turned to Mr Maybrick. 'Edgar, why don't you go back to the rectory bungalow and tell Clarissa I'll be there in half an hour. You could send the tonga back for me. It oughtn't to take me half an hour but if there's any snarl up here I'll have to get on to Isobel Rankin and ask her to get Beames to sort it out from that end.'

'I'll wait,' Mr Maybrick said, then added, 'You may need me if you have to deal with people called Iyenagar or Lal or whatever it is.' He glanced at the Eurasian girl who looked at him as if she agreed. He looked back at Barbie. His face was redder than usual, but grave. He understood.

'Doctor Lal?' the girl said. 'I'm sending Miss Batchelor to your office in connection with the late Mrs Mabel Layton. It is arranged by the civil surgeon. Please see her urgently. Thank you.' She removed the plug and banged a bell. A chaprassi came. She gave him an order.

'Doctor Lal will be waiting, Miss Batchelor,' she said.

'Thank you.'

She followed the chaprassi through into a corridor and found that Mr Maybrick was accompanying her.

'Barbie, what are you doing, for heaven's sake?'

'Something I have to,' she said. The chaprassi indicated a flight of steps leading to basement level. On the half-landing there was a directional sign. It said: Mortuary.

Mr Maybrick grabbed her shoulder. 'Barbie, you can't!' But she shook him off. The basement corridor was low-ceilinged and very hot. She glanced back up the stairs and saw Mr Maybrick leaning against the wall holding his elbows. He shook his head. His mouth moved. She did not think badly of him. Because of Clarice. Who had ailed in Assam. And died slowly. And been unrecognizable. According to Clarissa. Who knew.

The chaprassi opened a door. A thin young Indian in a white coat got up from a stool at a bench littered with white enamel trays and large glass jars. The walls were of whitewashed brick. In one corner a fan whined on a chromium stand. There was a smell of formalin.

'Doctor Lal?'

'Yes, I am Doctor Lal.'

'I was expecting to see Doctor Iyenagar but I'm told he's left.'

'Oh, yes. Half an hour since.'

'Then you are in charge.'

'Yes. You come from Colonel Beames, isn't it?'

'Yes, I do. Obviously Doctor Iyenagar told you to expect me. Upstairs I was afraid there'd been a tiresome lack of liaison. May we please proceed without further delay, Doctor Lal? I should have been at Flagstaff House ten minutes ago.'

The young man looked tubercular. His eyes were enormous. He had studied too hard. He had not eaten enough. He had his qualification. Which should have opened a world to him. But the way into that world was blocked by Beames and his fear of Beames upon whose good opinion his career depended. Contrasting his delicate night-animal's features with Beames's bone-fed face she felt instinctively that he had no sanguine expectations of that opinion.

'Oh, yes,' he said. Did his lower lip tremble? Necessity made him frank. 'Proceed with what? I am sorry, but Doctor Iyenagar –'

'What about Doctor Iyenagar? Are you saying you've no instruction in this matter? If so we'll waste no more time. Ask the switchboard for Flagstaff House. I'll speak to Colonel Beames and ask him to repeat to you what he's already said to Doctor Iyenagar.'

For a moment she feared that a habit of acting upon the last order given would send him to the telephone. But almost at once he said, 'It should not be necessary if you tell me what is the problem.'

'It's not a problem. Or at least it wasn't. It's a question of identification.'

'Identification? Of what, please?'

'Doctor Lal, you're making this extremely painful and tedious. The business is bad enough without prolonging it. I have to see and identify the body of the late Mrs Layton.'

He looked relieved. And then puzzled. He said, 'Oh, yes. But no one mentioned to me this necessity. Are you a relative?'

'Yes.'

'One moment.'

He went towards a door, then came back, moved a chair a few inches from the wall. 'Please sit.' She did so. He opened the door and went through. She closed her eyes to pray for grace, for the continued suspension of Doctor Lal's disbelief. And abruptly opened them, warned by the blankness behind her eyelids. She got up, opened the door he had gone through. The corridor on the other side of it was narrower and lower than any she had been in this evening. But chill. At its end there were closed double doors flanked by fire extinguishers. In each door there was a circular window.

The corridor floor was covered with tiles of some kind of rubber-like composition. She walked silently to the doors and opened them upon an enclosed winter that hummed faintly on a high note so that she seemed to be both deafened and de-sensitized, projected into a season of frost, a landscape and a time unknown to her. Entering it she became inhuman, like Doctor Lal, like the two white rubber-clothed figures who seemed to be chafing the naked body in a farcical attempt to bring it back to life. The body was on its side with its right arm raised, held by brown hands. There was a yellow pigment in the arm and in the shoulders. It ended just above the pendulous white breasts but spread upwards across the face which was framed by tousled grey hair. The eyes were open and looking directly at the door-way. The mouth was open too and from it a wail of pain and terror was emitting.

'You should not have gone in!' Doctor Lal shrieked. 'It is most irregular. Please go back and wait.' He stood guarding the doors through which he had just pushed her with feverish hands, back into the corridor. 'Nothing is ready yet. Doctor Iyenagar is saying nothing to me about identification. I am telling the men. But suddenly you come in without permission upsetting every-thing. It is not allowed. And now you are in a state. Please, please you must sit somewhere and wait and be patient. Why should I be blamed for this?'

The wall supported her. She felt its hardness against the back of her head. She closed her eyes and breathed in deeply through her mouth.

'No one is blaming you, Doctor Lal. No one will blame you.

I shall say nothing. You would be wise to say nothing too. I've seen all I need. Just forget I was ever here.'

She went up the corridor and through the still open door into the laboratory. When she got out into the main corridor she saw Mr Maybrick sitting on the bottom step of the flight that led up to the ground floor. Their glances met. She felt that they were people who had known each other a long time ago, too long ago for either of them to presume upon an old acquaintance by speaking first. They ascended silently: he from his reminder and she from her first authentic vision of what hell was like.

The blue-haired woman was still on duty. Barbie approached her alone. Outside, in the tonga whose driver had been persuaded to come by the narrow asphalt path prohibited to vehicles, Mr Maybrick sat, still speechless from the shock of that word: Mortuary.

'I'm afraid an emergency has arisen that makes it imperative for me to see Mrs John Layton at once. It's in connection with the death this afternoon of Mrs Mabel Layton.'

'Oh yes. Well, now.' She glanced at her watch. 'Mrs Layton isn't a patient so I expect it can be arranged. I'll have a word with Sister Page.'

'You'd better tell her I've come on behalf of Captain Coley and the Reverend Arthur Peplow. It's really extremely urgent. It affects the funeral arrangements and of course Mrs Layton has to be informed at the earliest possible moment.'

The blue-haired woman nodded. She had already lifted the phone, pressed one of the red switches and turned a little handle. She asked to speak to Sister Page. It seemed that Sister Page was with a patient. The blue-haired woman gave a careful message, repeated everything that Barbie had told her but had to say names twice. She waited. While she did so the box buzzed. She manipulated switches and said, 'Pankot Nursing Home, can I help you?' And then, 'Just a moment.' She pressed more switches, turned the handle, listened and then presumably switched herself off from the conversation and back to Sister Page's extension.

'Hello?' she said. She listened. 'Well, will you do that? Meanwhile I'll have the visitor brought up.' She replaced the receiver, banged a bell and said, 'Sister Page is with Mrs Bingham but Mrs Layton hasn't gone to bed yet. A porter will take you to the second floor. If you wait at Sister's desk in the lobby, Sister Page or Sister Matthews will meet you there and then take you to Mrs Layton's room.'

She told the porter who had come in answer to the bell to accompany Memsahib to Wellesley. Barbie said, 'Thank you,' and followed the man. They went up by lift.

Sister Page's desk was unoccupied. It was surrounded by vases and baskets of flowers taken from the rooms for the night. A clock on the wall behind the desk showed ten minutes to ten. To the right, painted in black, was the legend: Rooms 20−39; with an arrow. To the left a similar legend pointed the way to Rooms 1−19. Barbie turned left along the broad corridor. As she turned a corner into a narrower one a nurse came out of a room half-way down it and walked towards her. She had wide hips and thick legs.

'Sister Page?' Barbie asked.

'No, I'm Sister Matthews. Are you lost?'

'I don't think so. I'm here to see Mrs John Layton. They told me downstairs to come up.'

'Oh.' The girl looked put out. But then smiled. 'I understood it was a Captain Coley with a message from a Mr Peplow.'

'Then they've got it slightly muddled. It *is* a message, and a very urgent one, which concerns Mrs Layton, Mr Peplow and Captain Coley.'

'Yes, I see. And there I've just told Mrs Layton it's Captain Coley. Well never mind.'

'How is her daughter, Susan?'

'Mrs Bingham's just as well as can be expected.'

'It isn't a false alarm?'

'No. But the pains have settled down a bit. I'm afraid it's not going to be an easy delivery, she's so tense. But who can blame her? We've been trying to get her mother to take something to get a good night because Captain Travers says it won't be until morning at the earliest from the look of things. But Mrs Layton's awfully anxious to get on the phone to her sister and other daughter in Calcutta. We've been through once but a dense sort of servant answered, so we're trying again at eleven tonight. I expect they're all out celebrating the second front, which is what I should be doing if we weren't so short-staffed. I'll take you to Mrs Layton.'

'Don't trouble. I know the room number.'

'No trouble.' She turned to lead the way but as she did so a door opened and another nursing officer, coming out, said, 'Oh, Thelma, thank God, come and −' and broke off, seeing Barbie. 'Be with you,' Sister Matthews said and then knocked at room number eight, thrust the door open, glanced round and called loudly, 'Your visitor, Mrs Layton,' and stood aside for Barbie to go in.

The room was filled with a cheerless festive odour. From what was obviously a bathroom Mildred called, 'Come in, Kevin. There's a fresh glass on the dressing-table. Pour yourself one and freshen mine, will you? I'll be with you in a minute.' A tap was turned on for a few seconds. 'What's happened?' Mildred asked. 'I warn you I can't stand much more today. Bring mine in, will you? There's an angel. I'm going barmy in this bloody place. I've been phoning Calcutta like mad but there's nobody at Fenny's except some half-witted Bengali bearer. Since you're here you might have a go and see if you can get any sense out of him.' A pause. 'Kevin?'

Another pause. The bathroom door swung wide open. As she caught sight of Barbie Mildred seized the edges of her open dressing-gown and quickly covered her nearly naked body.

For a moment she stood quite still.

Then she said, 'You bloody bitch.'

'Mildred, no. Please don't. Don't talk to me like that. We mustn't let any unfriendliness come between us and what we have to do. It's much too important. I'm sorry if there's been some kind of confusion. But it's not my fault. I had to mention Arthur's and Captain Coley's names because it *does* concern them and I knew you'd never see me just on my own. But you must realize it's not my fault if the message was wrong by the time it reached you. Do I look like someone called Captain Coley? It's pure nonsense, and very wrong of you. But I don't care. You can call me anything you like afterwards, punish me in any way you like for anything you've ever thought I've done to you or done you out of. But you must listen to what I have to say and you must do it, you must. Otherwise she'll never rest. Never. Never. I've seen her, so I know. She'll haunt me, she'll haunt you, all of us. She's in that terrible place and in anguish because she knows you've forgotten your promise or aren't going to abide by it.'

Mildred had gone to the dressing-table, and refilled her glass. Now she said, 'I've no idea what you mean. What promise and to whom?'

'The promise to Mabel to bury her at St Luke's in Ranpur.'

'What on earth are you talking about?'

'It's what she wished. She told me. She must have told you.'

'At St Luke's? In Ranpur? I know absolutely nothing about it and it's quite out of the question. If you don't want the humili-ation of being asked to leave by a member of the staff you'd better go now.'

'Why is it out of the question? There's a telephone on that table. All you have to do is ring Arthur and tell him to get on to Mr Wright in Ranpur, tell him this simple thing, that it was her wish to be buried next to her second husband, your own father-in-law, at St Luke's in Ranpur. Arthur and I will do every-thing else that's necessary. But the instruction to cancel the arrangements for St John's must come from you.'

'What you will do is leave this hospital at once and stop inter-fering in matters that aren't your business. I find your suggestion utterly obscene. It is June. Perhaps you've noticed it's warm even in Pankot. Quite apart from the question of the cost of the ice, I have no intention of having my husband's step-mother trans-ported like a piece of refrigerated meat to be buried after several days' delay in a churchyard that so far as I recall hasn't been used for burials since the nineteen-twenties. And especially I have no intention of doing so at the whim of a half-witted old woman. Even if there were an indication of such a wish in my step-mother-in-law's will, or a subsequent written instruction, I should have to override it.'

'I know nothing about a will, I only know —'

'But I do know about the will. I've had a copy of it ever since my husband went abroad and copies of subsequent codicils. She had a horror of people having to grub through papers. In fact she was most meticulous and thoughtful about sparing her family unnecessary bother and anxiety. The gruesome little convoy you seem to think she wanted us to become involved in is quite out of character. After five years of living on what one presumes were fairly intimate terms with her I'm surprised you didn't know her better. On the other hand –'

Mildred sipped her gin, put the glass down. And smiled.

'– I'm not surprised. You were born with the soul of a parlour-maid and a parlour-maid is what you've remained. India has been very bad for you and Rose Cottage has been a disaster. I imagine you're paid up either to the end of the month or the end of the quarter. This month it comes to the same thing. I'd be glad if you'd be out before then. As quickly as possible in fact. I'd see that you got a pro-rata refund.'

'Mildred –'

'How dare you call me Mildred! To you I'm Mrs Layton.'

'No, that is ridiculous. That's just spiteful. Mildred is your given name, your Christian name, given when you were bap-tized. I *shall* not call you anything else. Not in His hearing –'

'Oh, God,' Mildred said. She covered one ear and bent her body as if to ward off a blow or to ride with the flow of a physical pain. The movement brought her in direct visual contact with the table and the telephone. She moved forward and reached for it. Barbie lunged; grabbed her wrist and found herself off-balance, forced heavily and painfully to her knees. But she grabbed Mildred's other wrist and hung on, imprisoned by her own violence in this penitential position. She shut her eyes so that the surge of her strength would not be interrupted. It flowed through her arms and into Mildred and they were united in a field of force, an area of infinite possibility for free and exquisite communication.

Tears of wonder, of love and hope and intolerable desire flowed from beneath Barbie's parchment-coloured lids. For a moment she could not get feeling into her lips. They would not come together to help her form the beginning of the required first word of supplication. She had to dispense with it and begin with a confession.

'I am sorry,' she said, 'sorry, sorry. I am what you say but I loved her so much and it seemed she was my chance, my gift from God to serve Him through her when everything else had been no good hadn't come to anything and just now she was trying to say help me help me. Please, Mildred. She asked for so little but she did ask for this. Why should I ask for it? Why should I make up a story? I'll do anything everything you say but please please don't bury her in the wrong grave. Not that, not that.'

She felt Mildred's wrists force themselves free and knew the answer. She opened her eyes but could not make anything out clearly. The shock of an impact stunned her. For an instant she thought that Mildred had hit her face with her open hand. But then she felt the coldness of water soaking into her blouse and as her eyes cleared she saw the empty carafe which Mildred held.

Without water there was no ice, no frosty particle, no storm of hail. The devotional machine had come to life in the shape of Mildred and a handy jug. The bathos of this situation shocked Barbie into a perilous composure. She felt capable of killing in cold blood, of burying Mildred alive along with Kevin Coley, a pile of empty gin bottles, some silver from the mess, and one of the mummy-rag-thin flags on top to mark the place.

She held an edge of the table, getting purchase to rise which she did without dignity but perhaps honourably. Who could say? She did not know. Dignity and honour were not inseparable. At times, and this was one of them, they seemed far distant for both of them.

Without another word she retrieved her handbag from the floor where it had fallen and left the room. She closed the door gently. In the corridor she realized that limp strands of hair clung to her forehead. The front of the heliotrope jacket was blackened by water. Her chest was icy cold. She put her head up and strode past Sister Matthews and another nursing officer, said good night to their open-mouthed faces and clumped down the stone stairs that entwined the lift shaft. On the ground floor the blue-haired woman was busy on the telephone and smiled absently when Barbie called good night. She was spared the shame of a direct encounter.

Mr Maybrick was asleep. He had reclaimed the fibre suitcase from the driver's seat and sat nursing it, with his head on one side. She climbed in gently and spoke in undertones to the tonga-wallah. When the vehicle jerked forward Mr Maybrick woke, alarmed. She clutched one edge of the suitcase and he another to save it from disaster. And like this they swayed and bucked through the benevolent night guarding her possessions.

vi

Four young officers of the Pankot Rifles took the weight of the
coffin on their shoulders. A scratch lot they could have been
better matched in height, but the angle of their burden was
maintained step by faltering step at a degree several notches
above a level that would have led to a bizarre accident. She
recognized the pink face of Captain Beauvais, pinker from the
exertion of this funereal regimental duty, and wondered whether
on his way out he felt the additional weight of a recollection of
Bob Buckland, whoever Bob Buckland had been or was. The
shortest of the four, he had the right front station and so the
coffin had an inclination downwards and moved upon a line that
drove logically into the ground beyond the open door to the
hastily dug hole for which the woman immediately behind the
cortege was responsible.

Beside Mildred walked Kevin Coley; behind these two Isobel
Rankin and Maisie Trehearne, and then Clara Fosdick and
Nicky Paynton and Clarissa. A thin scattering.

For some time after the coffin had been borne out and the last
mourner had followed it through the open door Barbie remained
seated in the shadow of a pillar far back in the church, and in
the denser shadow of her own bitter and terrible conclusions.

There (she thought) went the *raj*, supported by the unassailable criteria of necessity, devoutness, even of self-sacrifice
because Mildred had snatched half an hour from her vigil to see
the coffin into the hole she had ordered dug. Presently she would
return to the hospital where Susan was still in labour. But what
was being perpetrated was an act of callousness: the sin of collec-
tively not caring a damn about a desire or an expectation or the
fulfilment of a promise so long as personal dignity was preserved
and at a cost that could be borne without too great an effort.

And so it will be (Barbie thought) so it will be in regard to
our experience here. And when we are gone let them colour
the sky how they will. We shall not care. It has never truly been
our desire or intention to colour it permanently but only to make
it as cloudless for ourselves as we can. So that my life here has
indeed been wasted because I have lived it as a transferred
appendage, as a parlour-maid, the first in line for morning
prayers while the mistress of the house hastily covers herself with

her wrap and kneels like myself in piety for a purpose. But we have no purpose that God would recognize as such, dress it up as we may by hastily closing our wrap to hide our nakedness and convey a dignity and a distinction as Mildred did and still attempts. She has a kind of nobility. It does not seem to me to matter very much whether she appears half-dressed in front of Kevin Coley. But I think it matters to God and to the world that she rode with him into the valley and offered matriarchal wisdom to women older and as wise or wiser than she. For that was an arrogance, the kind which Mabel always set her face against, because Mabel knew she brought no consolation even to a rose let alone to a life. She brought none to me in the final count, but what distinguished her was her pre-knowledge that this was anyway impossible. So she probably forgives me about the grave and closes her eyes. It was not everyone who saw that they were open.

'Those are for her, aren't they?'

It was Edgar Maybrick's voice. He gathered the bunch of flowers from where it lay on the pew at her side.

'They've all gone now,' he said. 'Is that your case?'

'Yes,' she said, and rose, letting him reach down and pick the suitcase up as well. He led her out. When they reached the place – a blur of fresh-piled flowers – she took the bunch from him and standing well away from the shape of the dark hole that should never have been dug cast it in.

She returned to Rose Cottage alone. As the tonga pulled up at the porch she saw the figure of an old man come from the side of the house and stand waiting. She got out and paid the fare. The front door was open, as were the windows of her room. She and the old man watched each other for a while and then she called to him, 'Will you come and help me, Aziz? I'm very tired and should like a cup of tea.' She went up the steps and entered the hall. Behind her she heard the clunk of his sandals as he cast them off on the verandah before following her in.

PART FOUR

THE HONOUR OF THE REGIMENT

I

SUSAN WAS delivered of a healthy male child, that looked absurdly like poor Teddie, at five o'clock in the morning of June the eighth, three hours before Sarah, hurriedly summoned home from Calcutta, arrived in Pankot on the night train from Ranpur and thirty-three hours after Susan had cried out 'But it can't be! The baby isn't finished yet.'

For a while Susan did not look at the child. She averted her head no matter what her mother said or Travers said and the nursing staff said. It began to look like a classic case of rejection. It was not until Sarah took the child in her arms and impressed on Susan that there was nothing wrong with it, that it was as lively as you liked, in fact pretty obstreperous and not in the least pleased by anything or anyone it had seen so far, that Susan turned her head and looked at Sarah and then at the child and said nothing but let Sarah put the screaming bundle where she could get a view of its purple face and groping miniature hands.

Accepting the child in her own arms her reluctance to examine it closely was obvious. She said, 'Is it whole? Is it?' and took some time to comprehend the evidence, revealed detail by detail by Sister Page, that there was no doubt of this. The effort exhausted her and she cried a bit but smiled and touched the baby's cheek; and slept and woke; and when the moment came applied herself to the primitive task of giving suck with a frown of spartan concentration which gradually eased and left upon her brow a radiance that was too old, too heavy for her face. But no one noticed that.

Presently her milk failed which Mildred said was just as well because one ought not to become so physically involved. It was bad for the child and the mother, unhygienic and potentially a bloody nuisance for everyone concerned. She had advised against it and had been surprised by Susan's insistence that at least she should try. Well, not surprised. The poor girl had done her damnedest to do everything right. She'd been a brick.

'After all,' Mildred said, 'one can't imagine more trying circumstances.' She gave up the room next door to the one auspiciously numbered seven, took herself back to the grace and favour but still spent most of the day with Susan. Isobel Rankin saw to it that a telegram was sent to Colonel Layton through the Red Cross. Letters were written. The slight unease felt about the welfare of prisoners of war in Germany now that Europe had been invaded was not openly admitted; instead it was suggested to Susan that her father might be home for Christmas.

'How lovely if he were,' Susan said. 'For us anyway. But it seems a bit unfair, doesn't it? All he'll want is peace and quiet and looking after and what he'll get is a screaming baby that gets all the attention.' She smiled and added, 'But I don't suppose he'll mind because it's a grandson,' and then closed her eyes so that the visitors lowered their voices for a while and thought of the need there would presently be for Susan seriously to consider getting married again to give the boy a father; preferably to Dicky Beauvais who was attentive and in every known respect an excellent choice.

Like other young men in the past Captain Beauvais had originally seemed interested in Sarah; but in his case it would have been impossible to show interest in Susan because when he arrived in Pankot she was a married woman and then a pregnant married woman. He had assumed a brotherly role and it was only since the news of Teddie Bingham's death that the brotherliness had begun to wear thin which it did in a way that suggested to some people that it had never been more than a disguise for the warmer feelings he had always had but tried to reserve and express for Sarah only.

Again it had become necessary to subject Sarah to scrutiny. There seemed to be something wrong with the girl, something complex which was not going to be put right by a simple antidote like the safe return of her father or getting her married off to the right sort of officer, or allowing her to abandon her family responsibilities in Pankot to do a more exciting or exacting job of soldiering closer to those areas where the shooting was. Neither did that hint of little Mrs Smalley's at the time when Teddie

Bingham transferred his affections to young Susan – that Sarah was perhaps just a little unsound in her views – really seem justifed. All that could be said was that her behaviour was a degree less than admirable because it lacked either enthusiasm or spontaneity.

'She thinks too much,' Nicky Paynton said. 'And say what you will men don't like it when it shows. She should learn to hide the fact which shouldn't be too difficult because she already knows how to keep her thoughts to herself.'

But that was before the crisis brought on by Mabel's death and Susan's premature labour, both of which events Sarah missed by going to Calcutta. The journey back to Pankot must have been tense and exhausting. She had been fond of her aunt and tireless in her efforts to jolly Susan along after the blow of Teddie's death. Fate had deprived her of the opportunity to help at a time when her help was most needed, but she was at Susan's bedside within an hour of reaching home on the night train from Ranpur. Both her sister and her mother were asleep but she stayed in Susan's room and nodded off in a chair beside the bed, with one hand on the counterpane where Susan could reach it when she woke.

Travers, who found the sisters like this, was touched, and related how the relief that Sarah must have felt at finding her sister well and the baby safely born, had caused her to smile as she slept. The same look of happiness was on her face on the occasion she held the baby and persuaded Susan to accept it, and it occurred to Nicky Paynton who was present that at last something like an enthusiasm could have entered Sarah's life, even if it were second-hand: an enthusiasm for her sister's child. The important thing, Mrs Paynton thought, was that the soil should be tilled. Sarah, she thought, had spent long enough unconsciously making up to her father for not being a boy. At that moment the situation became clear to Mrs Paynton and so did the future which ceased to be worrying. The solution to Sarah was simple after all. What had been repressed was nothing other than a highly developed maternal instinct.

'Sarah, did you manage to see Captain Merrick?' she asked – remembering on the way out of Susan's room what Sarah had gone to Calcutta to do.

'Yes, I saw him the afternoon of the day I arrived.'

'How was he?'

'Waiting for an operation.'

'Anything very serious?'

'I suppose in medical or surgical terms it was quite straight-forward. They were going to cut off his left arm above the elbow. Excuse me a second.'

Sarah went to Sister Page's desk and spoke to the girl who was sitting there. Clara Fosdick and Nicky Paynton waited near the liftgate and looked at one another. When Sarah rejoined them Mrs Paynton said, 'How very upsetting.'

'What?'

'About Captain Merrick. Does Susan know?'

'Yes, Captain Travers thought it better to say straight out because she had an idea he might have no arms at all. The letter he wrote us from hospital in Comilla was dictated.'

The lift came. Inside, the cramped conditions discouraged conversation but enabled Nicky Paynton and Clara Fosdick to study Sarah's face and agree later when they were alone that there was an uncharacteristic hardness and decisiveness in its expression, a look of impatience which made the tenderness shown for her sister and her sister's child more noticeable.

Coming out of the lift into the reception foyer Mrs Fosdick added, 'Did he agree to be godfather?'

'No. He was grateful for the suggestion but didn't think he'd make a good one.'

'Because of his arm?'

'I expect that came into it.'

'What happened to him? Did he say?'

'He pulled Teddie and a driver out of a burning jeep and got them under cover. He got bullet wounds and third degree burns. He saved the driver but was too late for Teddie. He'll be getting a medal.'

'I should think so too.'

'The police's loss was obviously the army's gain,' Nicky Paynton said. 'But I'm sorry Captain Merrick's said no. He'd have been a godfather for any boy to be proud of.'

'Later on, perhaps,' Sarah said. 'When the boy was old enough not to be frightened. His face was burnt too.'

'Oh, dear. Badly?'

'I couldn't tell. There wasn't much you could see through the bandages except his eyes and the mouth. But Sister Prior said his hair would grow again and he might even look human.'

'What an extraordinary thing to say.'

'She said it to relieve her feelings. She didn't care for my Lady Bountiful act. She's the sort of nursing sister we describe as a bit off, the sort who wouldn't be an officer at home but is because she joined the QAs and came out here. I think she blames people like us for the fact that there's a war on at all. She thought it was scandalous giving badly wounded men medals. She thought money would be more to the point. But she's on the wrong tack there with Ronald Merrick. He's not interested in that kind of payment or in the kind of people who'd suggest it.'

'I should think not.'

'He says he blames himself for Teddie being killed. Dicky Beauvais promised to be back with the staff car. Can we give you a lift? I'm going to the daftar so it's on the way.'

'That would be nice,' Nicky Paynton said.

'I'll see if he's here.'

Sarah went into the forecourt and presently returned and reported the car coming up the drive. While Captain Beauvais took a rupee from Mrs Fosdick to pay off their waiting tonga-wallah the three women got into the back of the car.

'Why does Captain Merrick blame himself?' Mrs Paynton asked when they were settled.

'I don't think he does really. It's his way of putting things. He'd gone forward to collect a special prisoner and Teddie went with him, although there was no need. I think Teddie was interfering, I mean not trusting Ronald Merrick to deal with a situation in the way he thought it should be handled. After they'd talked to the prisoner Teddie took the jeep when he shouldn't have and went further forward still, and took the prisoner with him because the man said he had two friends in the jungle who wanted to give themselves up too. Ronald didn't know he'd gone and when he found out he had to go after him.'

'That's okay,' Dicky Beauvais said, getting in the front. He signalled the driver to start and sat with his arm over the back of the front bench to take part more comfortably in whatever conversation was in progress.

'Sarah's telling us about Captain Merrick and poor Teddie.'

'Oh, yes.'

'But isn't it very unusual,' Mrs Paynton said, 'for Japanese soldiers to give themselves up?'

'Oh, they weren't Japanese.'

'What then?'

'Indian soldiers from Teddie's old regiment.'

The car slowed at the end of the drive and then moved smoothly and comfortably, well sprung and upholstered, out on to the road that led to area headquarters.

'Muzzys,' Sarah went on. 'Not Teddie's lot. From the other battalion that was captured in Malaya. Now fighting with the Japanese against us. They belonged to the INA we hear about but aren't supposed to take seriously. Captain Merrick says there are far more of them than is allowed to be supposed but that they're badly led and armed and half-starved because the Japanese don't think much of them, especially not of their officers. Anyway he followed Teddie in another jeep and then they found themselves being mortared and shot at by the Japs *and* the INA. The man driving the jeep Ronald was in turned it round to get back where he belonged, so Ronald jumped out and went the rest of the way on foot. When he got to Teddie's jeep it was burning and the prisoner had gone, so he pulled Teddie and the driver out and dragged them under cover, which is when he got shot up himself as well as burned. I haven't told Susan all this because although Ronald Merrick didn't actually say so I think everyone felt Teddie had been wrong and silly. I don't suppose he could bear the thought of leaving two old Muzzy Guides hiding in the jungle, waiting to be recaptured. I gather the divisional commander was rather brassed off, losing two staff-officers and a jeep as a result. But of course the *regiment* would be pleased by what Teddie tried to do, wouldn't it? Don't you think so, Dicky?'

Dicky nodded, but glanced at the driver and then warningly at Sarah.

'After all,' Sarah said, apparently not noticing, 'he was doing it *for* the regiment. Ronald says that when they were talking to the prisoner and the prisoner realized Teddie was a Muzzy officer the poor man broke down and knelt and touched Teddie's feet. So it makes you wonder how many of the men have joined the INA without knowing what they were doing. It's different in the case

of the officers. Ronald said Teddie thought INA officers completely beyond the pale. I gather the same thing nearly happened
in Germany, but on a much smaller scale. Isn't that so, Dicky?'

Dicky said nothing.

Again Sarah seemed not to notice his reluctance to discuss the
subject in front of a lance-naik driver, but her next comment
might have been taken as an oblique criticism of this attitude. She
said, 'I can't think why there's so much secrecy about it. It makes
it look as if we're afraid of it spreading, but Ronald Merrick said
it was difficult in Imphal to stop our own sepoys shooting INA
men on sight even if they were trying to give themselves up.'

'The best thing for them,' Nicky Paynton said. 'It'll save
rope later.'

'Did you hear the news on the wireless this morning?' Sarah
asked, as if changing the subject.

'You mean what Dickie Mountbatten says about carrying on
operations through the monsoon? I thoroughly agree. Bunny
said ages ago that downing tools directly the monsoon set in was
military suicide if you were fighting the Japanese, but perhaps
now that Mountbatten's said it we can press on and push the
little horrors right back across the Chindwin and not sit on our
bottoms for three months waiting for the rains to let up.'

'I didn't mean that. I meant the news about ex-chief minister
Mohammed Ali Kasim being released from jail and taken to
Mirat.'

'Oh, that,' Clara Fosdick said. 'Well the poor old man's ill and
there never seemed much point in locking *him* up. My brother-
in-law Billy Spendlove always had a high regard for him. In fact
he expected him to tell the Congress to take a running jump
when there was all that nonsense about ministers having to resign
in 'thirty-nine. Billy said that in 'forty-two the Governor gave
Mr Kasim an opportunity to disown Congress policies because
he knew he'd disagree with practically everything Congress
did from 'thirty-nine onwards but the old boy refused and said
he preferred to go to jail. And it's not a pukka release, is it?
He's obviously got to stay in Mirat in the Nawab's custody. At
least until he gets better. It's so embarrassing when they start
getting ill because the people automatically think a political
prisoner's ill-health is due to bad treatment.'

'But,' Sarah said, 'someone said at the daftar this morning it's

mostly eyewash about him being ill. The real reason is because
the elder son who was an officer in the Army and was a prisoner
in Malaya has just been captured in Imphal, fighting with the
INA. The government thinks Mr Kasim's the kind of man who
won't try to make excuses for his son turning coat, and that by
being nice to him now he'll be very helpful to us after the war
if other Indian politicians start calling INA men heroes and
patriots. Which they're bound to.'

'Why bound to?'

'Because of there being so many. If there were only a few
isolated cases of Indian officers and other ranks going over to the
Japanese then they wouldn't be worth bothering about and we
could court-martial them without anybody either noticing or
caring.'

Nicky Paynton cut in. 'It seems to me that what's good for
one is good for as many as there are.'

'But that's looking at the thing from the point of view of the
principle that's involved. We shan't really be able to afford to
do that.'

'We should damn' well try.'

'Then we'd make fools of ourselves, wouldn't we, Dicky?'

Dicky smiled bleakly. He gave the driver instructions to turn
in at the next compound.

After the staff car had left Mrs Paynton and Mrs Fosdick at their
bungalow, Nicky said, 'Do you know, Clara, Sarah hasn't once
said anything to me about her Aunt Mabel's death, has she to you?'

'She said thank you when I told her how upset we all were.'

'That's all she said to me, too. I thought she was probably
too cut up to say anything else but now I'm not sure. I think
Mildred's going to have trouble with that girl. Perhaps Lucy
Smalley was right. She seemed to want to provoke Dicky
Beauvais just now.'

'How, provoke?'

'Well, Clara, let's face it. Dicky's an awfully nice chap but he's
not particularly intelligent is he? I got the impression she was
trying to provoke him to come out with the kind of remark she
could have a private little laugh at. In fact she was provoking us
too. It makes one wonder –'

'Wonder what?'

'Well, put it this way. She's always had guts. Suddenly she has nerve. It makes one wonder what happened to her in Calcutta.'

'Perhaps it's just the wrong time of the month.'

'No. You can usually tell when she's having one of her bad periods because she goes quieter than ever. She wasn't quiet this morning. In fact Dicky Beauvais was dying to tell her to shut up because the driver was listening. That's why I took the line I did, about shooting them now saving rope later. But I expect she's right. If we ever do win this bloody war we might hang Bose and one or two of the bigwigs but the rest will just have to be cashiered or dismissed with ignominy. Only by then we'll probably be on our way out in any case and the bloody Indians will have to deal with them in their own bloody way, and they'll probably bloody well make heroes out of them.'

'Nicky!'

'Well, it's true.'

'But there can't be all that many.'

'Can't there? There can be and are. We all know it. But we try to pretend it's not so. But it is so. The bloody rot's set in. When I think of Bunny sweating away in the bloody jungle –'

She went to her room to calm herself and wrote a letter to her husband who had got a brigade at last. 'Darling Bunny, Hope you're in good form,' she began and looked at the latest snap of the two boys in Wiltshire, grinning into the sun with the innocence of youth. 'Mildred's younger daughter, Su, has just had a baby boy.'

II

When Mildred pronounced Susan 'a brick' Travers concurred. Seeing Susan come through, as he put it, he said this showed how wrong people had been who had thought her dangerously withdrawn like that poor girl of Poppy Browning's; and was then taken aback by the hardening of Mildred's jaw, her snapped demand and explicit rebuke, 'Who said that?' and thought it better not to mention it had been Sarah who, in case it was something he should bear in mind when treating her sister, told him what the missionary had said.

'I think it was Miss Batchelor.'

'That woman!' Mildred exclaimed. 'What can she know about Poppy Browning or her daughter?'

Poppy had been Ranpur Regiment, with a daughter married into the cavalry, a young girl six months pregnant when her dashing husband was killed in Quetta by a roofbeam collapsing on his back and on both arms of the Indian girl under him whose open mouth was choked with plaster and who was also dead, suffocated by lover and rubble, when rescuers arrived and disentangled them from the ruins of the bungalow and each other's bodies: a situation which Poppy Browning's daughter had celebrated by smothering her baby two days after it was born. The affair had been hushed up, which was one of the reasons why the daughter was now never mentioned by name but referred to as Poppy Browning's daughter, and a clean clear image preserved of Poppy herself, whose life and record and those of her husband had been unblemished. The sad scandal that brought their Indian career to a premature and obscure conclusion, no longer being spoken of directly, had elevated them to a special place in the minds of people who recognized the value of selfless service, hard work and cheerful dispositions. Poppy and her husband had been mixed doubles champions three years running, back in the 'twenties when they were in their prime and their daughter still at school in England.

Ever since the Quetta tragedy the name Poppy had blown gently, frail but hardy like the flower, brave among the stubble of the reaped field of human experience. But this section of the field was private. The name Poppy Browning was scarcely known among the younger generation and it was certainly not one to be bandied about by a retired missionary, an interfering woman whose tiresomeness had reached its apogee and was no longer to be borne. So Mildred implied. But her habit of leaving her disapproval to speak for itself, of making exclamatory denunciations rather than explanatory criticisms, as if these were sufficiently informative, left the actual details of Barbie's bad behaviour unclearly set out in the minds of people who felt their sympathies were due to Mildred and indeed assumed by her to be offered; anything else being unthinkable if the appearance of the order of things were to be preserved.

'Some wild idea,' Mildred said, 'that Mabel wished to be buried in Ranpur. Can you imagine anything more grotesque?'

Imagine, no. But imagining the grotesque was not necessary when it got about that there had been a macabre and unauthorized visit to the mortuary, a visit which had involved a Eurasian receptionist and a Doctor Lal in serious trouble.

Daily, Miss Batchelor was seen aboard a tonga, clutching a bunch of roses, on her way to the churchyard, a visit prolonged beyond the time it took her to place the flowers on the grave by (it was said) a lengthy vigil in the church itself. Presently in addition to the roses she was observed to clutch a suitcase, the one in which bit by bit she was transferring her belongings from the cottage to the tiny room in the rectory bungalow where Arthur and Clarissa Peplow had offered her temporary refuge.

Neither Arthur nor Clarissa was to be drawn out on the subject of the grotesque idea Miss Batchelor had apparently had about her dead friend's wishes and on the whole people refrained from asking them because merely to do so raised the question whether Mr Peplow had buried Mabel Layton in the wrong place. Neither were many questions asked on the subject of the offer of temporary refuge which Clarissa described as the most practical way out of an unhappy situation and a Christian duty but not to be thought of by anyone as a preliminary to a permanent arrangement being come to. The room was too small.

'I am already worried,' Clarissa said, 'about the amount of stuff with which Barbara seems to be encumbered. If there is much more she will have to speak at Jalal-ud-din's about temporary storage.'

Alive, old Mabel Layton had been precariously contained; but her gift for stillness, the sense that flowed from her of old and irreversible connections, had made the task of containing her less difficult than her detachment implied it could have been. She should no longer have been a problem but a once slightly disruptive pattern that now dissolved and faded into the fabric. But, dead, she emerged as a monument which, falling suddenly, had caused a tremor which continued to reverberate, echo, in the wake of Miss Batchelor who, bowling down Club road in the back of a tonga, now guarded the fibre suitcase as if it were crammed with numbered pieces of the fallen tower that had been her friend, and as if it were her intention to re-erect it in the garden of the rectory bungalow or even in a more public position, in the churchyard perhaps or at the intersection of Church

and Club roads where – imperfectly reassembled – it might lean
a little and dominate the whole area with a peculiar and critical
intensity, make it impossible to go past the spot without having
one's confidence further impaired and one's doubts increased by
this post-mortem reversal of roles. For whereas one had been in
the habit of looking in on the eccentric elder Mrs Layton to
satisfy oneself that the purpose and condition of exile were still
understood (however idiosyncratically by her), furthered and
supported, now she would look down from an eminence upon
the purpose, upon the condition, accusingly, still silent; but silent
like someone who knew that events could speak for themselves
and would do so.

On cue, the clouds of the southwest monsoon, thinned by
the overland journey across the parched, open-mouthed, plain,
appeared in the Pankot sky and spilt what moisture they had left,
establishing the wet-season pattern of sudden short showers, of
morning mist which could be dispersed by the sunshine or give
way to a light persistent drizzle. When the sun came out there
was a strange mountain chill that did not make itself felt upon
the flesh but in the nostrils, mingling there with the pervading
scents of hot mud and aromatic gum. But this year these familiar
manifestations of a Pankot summer contained an element,
difficult to analyse, but unmistakably felt, of something that acted
as an irritant.

As if aware of a special necessity, Mildred Layton now took a
day off, put on jodhpurs, and accompanied by Captain Coley set
out on horseback on a day's trek to the nearest villages to thank
women who had sent little presents and messages of goodwill to
Colonel Sahib's younger daughter and baby; to discuss with
them the now excellent prospects of the early return of the long-
absent warriors from across the black water. It became known,
through Coley, that Mildred had gallantly drunk cup after cup
of syrupy tea, eaten piping hot chappattis, a bowl of vegetable
curry, been soaked in a sudden shower between villages, held
squealing black babies, patted the shoulder of an ill-favoured
looking woman who was weeping because since her husband
went away she had grown old and fat; discussed the crops with
village elders, more intimate problems with the wives and
mothers, the hopes of recruitment with shy striplings pushed
forward by their old male relatives to salaam Colonel Memsahib,

and returned exhausted but upright through one of the wet season's spectacular sunsets which turned her white shirt flamingo
pink and the shadows of the horses brown.

There was a glow, but it was external to the affair; a bit too
theatrical to penetrate to the mind where it was needed. It gave
the performance qualities of self-consciousness which made it
look as if Mildred's main achievement had been to draw attention to an undertaking whose only claim was a nostalgic one
upon the fund of recollected duties and obligations which time
and circumstances were rendering obsolete; as obsolete as
Teddie's gesture, of which the division had taken a view of a
kind it would not, in better days, have taken, but with which
one somehow could not argue – considering the cost of a jeep
and the shortage of equipment, not to mention the escaped
prisoner, the burnt sepoy-driver and Captain Merrick's lost left
arm. The price of regimental loyalty and pride seemed uncomfortably high.

The circumstances surrounding the death of Teddie Bingham
were better not discussed but it was circumstances such as these
which were speaking, louder than words, sustaining the illusion
of Mabel Layton grimly looking down from the eminence
whose site was shifted according to the whim of Miss Batchelor,
who sometimes seemed uncertain what to do with the contents
of the suitcase and was seen once to get as far as Church road
and then order the tonga back up the hill to the cottage, which
she had now received official notice to quit by the end of the
month.

Perhaps at the height of this piecemeal removal from cottage to
rectory Clarissa had put her foot down. 'She'd better not,' Nicky
Paynton said, 'otherwise where will the poor old thing go?'

A comic but horrifying thought took hold: of old Miss Batchelor, homeless, seated on a trunk in the middle of the bazaar,
surrounded by her detritus, unpacking and rebuilding the
monument there, to the amusement of Hindu and Muslim shopkeepers who would interpret such a sight as proof that the entire
raj would presently and similarly be on its uppers.

'She's writing to the mission,' Clarissa said, 'or so she assures
me. One hopes but has doubts that they'll soon find something
for her, either in the way of voluntary work or permanent
accommodation. But everything points to the advisability of her

leaving the station. In view of everything that's happened she could never be happy here again.'

It would have been different if over the last five years Miss Batchelor had entered more into the spirit of things; for example, Clarissa hinted, she could have done more for the church in Pankot. But shortsightedly she had subordinated all her private interests to those of the elder Mrs Layton, had become over-wrapped up in that peculiar woman's solitary affairs, 'against, I often felt', Clarissa said, 'her true instincts which were to say the least of it for having as many fingers in the pie as possible if I'm any judge. But I'm afraid it's too late for her to revert to type. Which is a pity because Barbara was born to serve. And then there is this attitude of hers to that old man which isn't going to help her patch things up with Mildred. I mean the man Aziz. She says only she and Mabel would really understand his behaviour which is as may be, but Mildred says that if it hadn't actually happened Mabel would have invented it, if necessary beyond the grave.'

Aziz's extraordinary perhaps sinister disappearance had gone counter, utterly, to the case law, the accumulated evidence that justified a deep and affectionate belief in the dependability of old and faithful servants. In the welter of conflicting and often unsatisfactory responses of Easterner to Westerner, one simple rule had stubbornly persisted, the rule of loyalty to the man or woman whose salt had been eaten. It was an ancient law but it had lived on and been honoured countless times. Men had died for it, not only in their youth on the battlefield fighting the sahibs' wars but in their age and infirmity on the steps of veran-dahs in defence of their masters' women and children. Women had died for it too, ayahs for their infant charges, maids for their mistresses. The rule, uncodified, was written in the heart and in old men like Aziz could normally be assumed to have passed across the line of law and custom into the realm of personal devotion.

Well, so one might have thought; so it had seemed, as it would seem for Mildred and John Layton with their Mahmoud, Nicky Paynton with her old Fariqua Khan who wrote monthly progress reports to Brigadier Paynton; countless others, in Pankot, in Ranpur, the length and breadth of India, wherever master, mis-tress and servant had grown used to and fond of one another, had jointly experienced good times, bad times. A sahib's, a mem-sahib's death left such old bearers inconsolable and the death of a Fariqua or a Mahmoud could bring tears to eyes accustomed to the discipline of staying dry in public.

But Aziz had not conformed, he had not been inconsolable. He had not wept, he had not got in people's way while doing his touching best to shoulder his share of sad and necessary duties. He had not shouldered them. His desertion – no matter what the civil surgeon said about having known a similar case – smacked of unfeelingness. His return and refusal to explain himself was like a declaration of an absolute right to answer to no one for his actions, to opt out, if he wanted to, from any situation in which there were established and desirable lines of conduct for him to follow.

So that queer thing Mildred said about Mabel inventing Aziz's disappearance if it had been necessary to do so was clear. Mildred saw Aziz's brief defection as a gesture made as much by Mabel as by him and which summed up, reflected, Mabel's long-sustained and critical detachment from the life and spirit of things. Mildred – whom it used to seem that Mabel didn't trust – had obviously never trusted Mabel, and for better reasons. While the old woman was alive Mildred had held her own criticisms in check, for John's sake, the regiment's sake, the station's sake, and even now could not descend to anything so crude as a direct attack.

Instead there had been a faint shrug of the shoulders when Kevin Coley reported Aziz unassailable, protected by Miss Batchelor's assertion that he had returned to serve *her*, that she would require, indeed insisted on, these services for the few days remaining to her at Rose Cottage, would herself pay his wages from June the first until the day of her departure for the rectory and his for his village and retirement. Mildred shrugged her shoulders too when people questioned Aziz's right to receive the small pension Mabel had made provision for in the will.

'One must respect a will,' she said. The impression she gave was of blaming Mabel, not Aziz, and of declining to take any tiresome action that would draw attention to the fact that one was living through a period in which general moral collapse seemed imminent, a collapse for which Mabel was as much to blame as anyone.

It was remembered how on the day of the wedding party the old woman had sat, deafer than ever, making things difficult for young officers who were anxious to pay their respects, notably difficult for young Beauvais whose uncle had been a subaltern under Bob Buckland who, in turn, had been a fellow-subaltern of Mabel's first husband and whom she had known, been fond of and consoled by between her husband's death and her marriage to James Layton.

It was remembered too how she had left the party without a word, and apparently by a door at the back of the mess, 'feeling unwell and not wanting to be a skeleton at the feast', according to Mildred's later explanation of an absence which, without causing any special concern at the time, had certainly made itself felt through the empty chair, like a criticism too subtle to be interpreted easily or accurately.

The truth could no longer be avoided. It had been a criticism of the foundations of the edifice, of the sense of duty which kept alive the senses of pride and loyalty and honour. It drew attention to a situation it was painful to acknowledge: that the god had left the temple, no one knew when, or how, or why. What one was left with were the rites which had once propitiated, once been obligatory, but were now meaningless because the god was no longer there to receive them. Poor Teddie! His was an end of an expository kind, like a last sacrificial attempt to recall godly favour. If there were still a glow to be had it would have spread from there, but it did not. Nor did it spread from the action of the man Merrick as once it would have done because nothing could obliterate the image of Merrick as an earlier victim of changed circumstances, of the general loss of confidence, the grave shifting of the ground beneath one's feet as the layers of authoritarian support above one's head thinned and those of hostile spirits thickened.

Somewhere along the line doubt had entered. Even on a sunny day it lay upon the valley, an invisible mist, a barrier to the clearer echoes of the conscience. A rifle shot would no longer whip through the air, slap hard against a hillside and bounce, leaving a penetrating and convincing smell of cordite, sharpening senses and stiffening the blood. It would go muffled, troubled, and its message would be garbled; and the eye would not dart alerted, Khyber-trained, to the hillsides for the tell-tale flick of a mischievous robe, but shift uncomfortably, to observe the condition of the lines, for signs of mutinous movements on the parade grounds where the Pankot Rifles went through the motions of training another generation of candidates for the rolls, acolytes for the temple.

And presently – not suddenly but with an increasing persistence – Mildred's personality began to stand out, a reminder to people of what life had meant, been like; so that an interesting counter-image to the one of Mabel began to emerge – an image of Mildred, also made of stone, splendidly upright, and revealing her true distinction through her refusal to compromise either her upbringing or her position by allowing what was irresistible to move her or what was expedient to take precedence over what in her judgment was right.

And so after all a glow came, even if it did not spread. The glow was Mildred. The famous expression shone. It could not infect but it could remind. And when she said, 'What Teddie tried to do was worth the whole bloody war put together,' it was realized that with her unerring instinct she had gone straight to the heart of the matter, cutting through such irrelevancies as divisional annoyance, the cost of a jeep, the loss of a prisoner and Merrick's arm, leaving one with Teddie's blameless death, his praiseworthy sacrifice for a principle the world no longer had time or inclination to uphold.

From the rear of the compound of the grace and favour bungalow smoke rose, between showers, as Mahmoud directed the burning of the stuff Mildred was beginning to throw out, the unwanted accumulation of the years of pigging-in which were now over; over too late, of course. Rose Cottage would certainly be more comfortable, more convenient for most things, but the station had been deprived for ever of any significance that might have attached to her presence there. Now she seemed to wish it to be recognized that she was merely claiming what had become her husband's property; not, as once could have been the case, acquiring an appropriate and proper setting for her virtue. She would live there and hold it in trust for him.

'Susan has decided to give the baby all Teddie's Christian names,' she said. 'So there'll be another Edward Arthur David Bingham. On the whole I approve.'

It was the continuity, logical and unsentimental, to which she responded, the idea that in this matter of a name Teddie would endure long after the acrid smell of the lost jeep had died away and the bloody accountant-general had finished reckoning out the amount in rupees. Dick and Isobel Rankin had agreed to be godparents. Sarah would be the younger godmother and Dicky Beauvais the second godfather. The child would be well endowed. Mahmoud's widowed niece, called Minnie because her real name was unpronounceable, had gladly accepted the duties of ayah. The christening would take place at St John's, a week after the day fixed for Susan to leave the auspiciously numbered room in the nursing home.

'We shall have the christening party here,' Mildred said, meaning the grace and favour. 'I want to get it over before we move up to the Cottage, and get Su used to the idea of having the baby at home. The last time she was up at the place wasn't the happiest occasion.' At the cottage, she said, she herself would have Mabel's room, the little spare would be an excellent nursery. Susan and Sarah would share the other room, the one Miss Batchelor was in the process of vacating. Even sharing, they would have more space each than they had in the tiny bedrooms of the grace and favour.

'I should have liked to do some redecoration, but I think that will have to wait,' Mildred said. 'I'll have to keep the mali on but I've told Mahmoud to keep an eagle eye on him. It's time the mali earned his keep. You can't say that with Mabel he was exactly overworked, can you?'

She glanced down at her half-empty glass. For a while after Teddie's death, the drinking habit had been less frequently indulged, but then resumed as if she had decided that giving anything up was a sign of weakness. Now that she could afford it, with the whole of Mabel's money coming into Colonel Layton's possession, there was no reason left for anyone to question the habit at all. For a hard-drinking woman who had recently had a great deal to cope with she was comparatively abstemious. And remembering the time when it seemed as if she drank for the station's sake as much as for her own, people felt there were many good reasons, few of them identifiable, why she should actually drink more than she did. It was as if, anticipating more reasons to come, she deliberately held back, in order to be in good form for the occasion.

III

Her flesh had hardened. It had the toughness of metallic substance. When she walked she sensed her body's displacement of
the air. Between herself and Aziz there was a magnetic field of
force. They spoke seldom. It was not necessary. In their brief
exchanges there was an undertone of parable.

'There's very little more,' she told Clarissa after several visits
to the rectory bungalow; and edged out of the narrow space
between the bed and the wall, catching the nailed feet of an
imitation ivory crucifix with her sleeve, so that the Lord was
tilted sideways as He would be if the cross weren't planted firmly
enough or were lowered into the wrong hole, one too wide
for it.

She straightened the sacrificial figure and turned to face Clarissa's forgiveness which was conveyed through a swift averting
of the eyes as if from the sight of a near accident of an ominous,
sacrilegious kind.

From the rectory she went to St John's, visited the grave and
then sat down in the shadow of the pillar, in the same pew as on
the day of the funeral, so that Mabel might find her without
difficulty. This was a vigil she kept every day between four and
five, bringing roses cut from the bushes with Aziz's help. It
interested her to discover how much he seemed to have learned
about the way to cut blooms without weakening the bush or
spoiling its shape. She did not understand the principle but
guessed there was one and allowed him to guide her by silent
indication or a sudden gesture of restraint.

Returning home she faced daily the mounting evidence of
what seemed like improvidence. Could one single woman have
acquired so much, have needed so much? The drawers in the
Rose Cottage chests were deep. Sometimes she thought of them
as comically bottomless, yielding up one item more for each item
removed and crammed into a suitcase.

And shoes. In serried ranks. On tip-toe along parallel brass
rods at the base of the almirah, each pair polished and cared for
by Aziz and the mali's boy.

'I am fond of my shoes,' she said, newly discovering this
attachment. She took the favourite pairs to the rectory but found
the base of the almirah an unwilling repository. There were no

brass rods and in any case the skirts of her suits and dresses hung
too low, right down to the bottom of the cupboard. In one angle
of the wall there was a curtained recess. She placed the shoes on
the floor but the curtain did not conceal them. The shoes looked
like the feet of old people eavesdropping. Nowadays tears came
unexpectedly. 'Crying in a happy home,' Clarissa had warned
her, 'is like untidiness in a neat one, and is a worry to God.'
Barbie dried her eyes and looked round belligerently.

The room was dark as well as small. She peered through the
single window, craning round the side of the miniature dressing-
table to see what was to be seen. The view, on to the side of the
bungalow, was blocked by creeper. She pushed the window open
to let in some air. There were bars on the inside, a protection
against thieves. The creeper sighed and shook. Tendrils of it, in
possession of the sill, groped stealthily forward, probing for a grip
on the interior. She hit and pushed them away, closed the window, found one tendril trapped inside and growing. She nipped
it off. It was tough-skinned like herself. Its sap was odorous. Two
kinds of death she had always feared: by drowning and by suffoca-
tion. She would need to be wary of the creeper. It was an understanding enemy.

Returning along the gloomy but sanctified passage to the hall
she looked for Clarissa to say good-bye until tomorrow. Clarissa
was no longer speaking on the telephone as she had been when
Barbie arrived and sought and received nodded permission to
take the suitcase through to the place of temporary refuge.

She said 'Clarissa?' and, leaving the suitcase on the floor,
parted the old-fashioned bead curtain that hung in the archway
between hall and living-room. The living-room was crowded
with leather chairs and wicker-work. There were exhausted
indoor ferns in brass pots which filled the air with a green
spiritual miasma. An oval mahogany table covered by a bobble-
fringed bottle-green cloth stood roughly in the centre of the
room. By this table Clarissa was waiting, with her hands laced
in the long string of sandalwood beads she wore in the afternoon
but for some reason never before lunch and never at dinner.

'Clarissa, I am just going to the grave and then home.
I brought a few pairs of shoes.' She clutched a bunch of roses,
yellow ones whose strong sweet scent Mabel had loved best of
all. Clarissa did not reply, except by nodding.

'Is something wrong, Clarissa?'

Slowly Clarissa flushed.

'Yes. At least. I have something I find it painful to say. But must say. I hope there has never been anything except total frankness in our relationship. I mean other things as well, a mutual respect and recognition of common Christian intention, but always frankness. You will have to forgive me, Barbie, but it would be totally – a totally false *position* for me if we went ahead with our arrangement without my saying what I have to.'

'What is it Clarissa? Is it the amount of luggage? It *is* a little more than I thought.'

'It is not the amount of luggage although speaking of that I am afraid you've already brought more than I can adequately provide room for and still leave the servants space to keep order. I don't wish to be unthoughtful or unimaginative but if there is anything more to come than a caseful the day after tomorrow – providing we reach that stage – I think you'll have to speak at Jalal-ud-din's about storage. They do offer some facilities.'

'That won't be necessary, Clarissa. I should not want my stuff mouldering in a native storehouse.'

'Let us say no more about luggage. Personally I always try to keep in mind the fact that we bring nothing into this world and can certainly take nothing out. Ever since childhood I have firmly rejected the tyranny of possessions, thanks to a proper upbringing in this regard. And Heaven knows that those of us who serve in India soon learn how transient our experience of home and hearth is, don't we? I doubt that we shall remove from this station before Arthur's retirement, but there is very little in this room that has been with us in other places or would go with us to our next. One is sure of but one thing, the strength and love of God.'

The scent of the roses became overpowering. Barbie supported herself with one hand on the bottle-green cloth. Its texture was harsh and scratchy. Like a hair-shirt. The flush had left Clarissa's face and neck. She was now pale as from a sense of eternity and the will to earn her place there.

'I have strayed from the point,' she said. 'The painful point.'

Barbie moistened her dry teeth with the tip of her tongue. The sandalwood beads began to clack through Clarissa's suddenly animated fingers.

'I was at the club this forenoon,' Clarissa began, still in the pedantic way she had of speaking when delivering herself of an oration or an opinion previously formed and rehearsed. 'Not alone, but with others, people whom I respect and whose good opinion I value, people whom you know but whom I shall not name. It happened, it so happened, that the question of your temporary refuge here arose, and it was said by one, it was said, well, what a pity it was that after all these years some way could not have been found of allowing you to remain at Rose Cottage to help Mildred, if only for a while, with the enormous burden she will bear at least for a time, with Susan and the baby to look after. What a pity, and how useful, what a help you might have been since you know so well the details of the running of that house.'

The beads ceased clacking for a moment, having been gripped by Clarissa's plump white fingers, in one of which the gold wedding-band was countersunk. But then the fingers fluttered again and the clacking resumed.

'It was of course an impractical suggestion but well-meant. But then it was said that quite apart from it being impractical it would be most, most, unsuitable. Unsuitable especially, it was said, with two pretty young girls in the house. And I could not, no I simply couldn't believe my ears, so much not believe that the moment, the opportunity, to challenge it, to discredit it, had gone before I fully understood exactly what had been implied. But having understood what was said, what was implied, in the hearing of several, I must convey it to you otherwise my position would be intolerable both in private and in public. For should I ever hear this thing repeated I must challenge it. I do not propose, Barbara, to refer to it again of my own accord, inside or outside this house, but I require, for my own peace of mind, under this roof, I require – from you – some word –'

Barbie was confused. She could not take in a clear notion of the matter, which seemed to be a special failure since obviously it excited Clarissa considerably. 'If I knew what word, Clarissa,' she said.

'A word,' Clarissa repeated, jiggling the beads in agitation, 'a word of refutation, of assurance, assurance that there are no grounds, no grounds, for such a wicked implication.'

Clarissa had flushed again with the effort of her demand, her appeal, whatever it was. Suddenly she let go of the beads and placed one hand under her heart, so that thinking she was unwell, perhaps overcome by the humidity that often accompanied the onset of the rains, Barbie took a step towards her, but stopped, because Clarissa had taken a simultaneous and involuntary step back. And, alerted by this evidence of apparent physical revulsion, Barbie began to grasp what had been said and a flush of anger began to darken her yellowed cheeks and old throat, spreading in unison with the electric surge of intelligence that awakened a desolate withered capacity for needing affection in return for giving it.

'Yes, I see,' she said. She thought for several moments before continuing. 'You naturally wish to be reassured. But what can I say? If it were true I should probably deny it because at the moment I've nowhere else to go and if this is going to be said about me I should find it difficult to go anywhere in Pankot. It's a difficult thing for an elderly spinster to refute. But for what it's worth, Clarissa, so far as I know my affection for Sarah and Susan is not of an unnatural kind, unless it is unnatural to feel maternally to them, to take pleasure in their company and care what happens to them.'

'Thank you,' Clarissa said. And then, exhaling, clapped her hands to her cheeks and sat down on a bandy-legged stool.

'Is that all, Clarissa?'

Clarissa's mouth was still open. The tips of each of her little fingers held it in that exclamatory shape. Her eyes were closed.

'Oh!' she whispered. 'It was wicked. It was wicked.'

'Am I expected, Clarissa? As arranged? The day after tomorrow?'

Clarissa opened her eyes but did not look at her. Presently she nodded her head and Barbie turned and left the room, leaving her friend to recover the sense of deep Christian repose to which she was accustomed.

Without touching the other withered wreaths and faded cards she tidied up the green tin vases that held her own offerings, removed prickly stems from which the last petals had fallen and placed the yellow roses in a vase of their own. The hump of clay would never settle. When she had finished she noticed it was raining. She went inside the church and sat by the pillar; and as usual prayed that there would be no letter for her from the mission in answer to her hasty request, or that if there were it would be couched in negative or unoptimistic terms. But half-way through the prayer she retracted it and, remaining on her knees, opened her eyes. She thought: I do not see how I can stay, I do not see how I can face it.

And not seeing how, she understood the depth of need and desire to stay which had been forming in her mind and heart ever since the day that Mabel was buried in the wrong grave; to stay for as long as it took to right the wrong that had been done, even if that meant waiting for the return of Colonel Layton who might be moved to listen to the truth. It was Colonel Layton's father by whose side Mabel had wished to rest.

She had begun to regret the letter to the mission, her offer of voluntary services in any capacity however menial in return for a roof. She had begun to feel that bit by bit she and Clarissa could become used to and of use to one another. She had even begun to imagine the possibility of patching things up with Mildred. All for Mabel's sake. All to achieve for Mabel's soul the repose that depended on the proper repose of Mabel's body. She had believed that she should not leave Pankot while there was hope. She had felt no horror at the idea of opening the grave and taking the remains to Ranpur. The idea had filled her with a sense of the quietude that would follow.

But she felt horror now; the horror of her own shame. In front of her hovered the pale shape of Clarissa's face with hands pressed against the cheeks. She wanted to put immense distance between herself and her life. How can I face it? she repeated. How can I walk about in the bazaar or sit here on a Sunday in the middle of the congregation, knowing what has been said, what has been hinted? The shape of Clarissa's face changed into that of Mildred's and the hands were not at the cheeks but droop-waisted below the chin, holding a glass, the downward-curving lips quirked at the corners in a dismissive smile.

'How can I face it?' she asked aloud. And the face became that of yet another, chin in hand, regarding her with that com-passion and patience, that exquisite desire. She trembled and leaned for support against the pillar, hiding in its shadow. She longed to be transported back to Rose Cottage. Outside the cottage she had become utterly vulnerable. When she left the cottage for ever she would enter an arena of defeat from

which she could see no exit. There was beauty in the quiet formality with which the trap had been set. Already she felt the onset
of the last, the grand despair, the one that was awaited. Mabel,
she whispered. Mabel. Mabel.

Abruptly she was cold because she had heard the sound of the
latch, as on the day of Mabel's death. Far down the church the
little side door had been opened and closed. The sound echoed
faintly. She clung to the pillar, listening to the light-falling footsteps coming up the aisle to the back of the church. They were
a woman's. Her skin prickled but her eyes suddenly brimmed,
in gratitude, and awe, and loving terror. She remained kneeling,
pressed against the pillar and dared not look up. Her nostrils
quivered, fearfully alert for the sweet odour of the ghost, the
compound of flowers and formaldehyde that must attach to the
newly dead. I am here, she muttered, here, here. Bound to this
pillar, to this life.

She covered her face. The stone of the pillar chilled the bare
knuckles of her right hand. The footsteps had ceased, having
come close. There was a faint creak, and then silence. She did
not have the courage to move. But presently, astonishingly, she
became peaceful, comforted. She thought, 'I can face anything
if I try.' She withdrew from the shadow of the pillar. The air was
cool on her overheated forehead. She glanced along the pew but
could see nothing. She inclined her body backwards, bringing
into her range of vision the pews in front, and caught her breath,
shocked by the visible presence of the seated figure. Involuntarily
her hand covered her mouth.

It was not Mabel. It was not any woman she knew. The head
was covered by an old-fashioned sola topee with a veil swathed
round the brim. After a while the woman became restless as if
she had become aware of being watched. Upright in the pew,
staring at the stained-glass window above the altar, the woman
touched her throat and turned slightly, looking to left and tight.
Reassured, she resumed her still and silent vigil, and stayed thus
until there was one of those mysterious adjustments, a small shift
of the empty building's centre of gravity, as of a momentary
easing of its tensions and stresses which created an illusion of
echo without traceable source, so that to Barbie it seemed that
the church's guardian angel had half-opened and then closed one
of his gigantic wings.

The unknown visitor rose, stepped into the aisle and walked down it towards the altar. She was elderly and moved with the care of a person conscious of a duty to carry her years with dignity. Before turning towards the side door she placed a hand for support on a pew and with lowered head bent one knee. Going out, she opened and closed the door gently. A little later Barbie caught the sound of a motor-car starting up, not on the Church road but on the West Hill road side.

As the sound faded, as the car took the woman away in that revealing direction, she realized who it was who had sat a few feet in front of her, but she was slow to respond. What might have been curiosity or superstitious fear of such close proximity was muted by the stronger current of an emotion which warmed her body and kept her kneeling, one hand on the pillar and the other still upon her mouth.

Within that little complex of events, the expectation of the ghost, the shock of seeing the woman, the echo from an unknown source high in the roof (above all, within that) she wondered if there had been one other thing, no more than a faint disturbance, a rearrangement of the sources from which she received impressions. Fleetingly, it seemed to her, her presence had been noted by God. She stayed very still. The impression was not enlarged, confirmed in any way, but it was not destroyed.

Well, I am going now, she told Mabel. She waited. There was no answer. Carrying the empty fibre suitcase in which she had transported shoes, she left the church. Outside she put her head up and went in search of a tonga.

When she got back to Rose Cottage she filled her largest suitcase with things taken at random from the stuff remaining in her room, left space in it for her nightwear and toilet things and then emptied the drawers on to a sheet spread on the floor. Without looking at what she must leave behind she knotted the sheet, making a bundle, and called Aziz, asked him to have it removed because she wanted none of the contents and did not wish to see the bundle again. He returned with the mali's boy and the sweeper girl who between them dragged the bundle out on to the verandah and out of sight.

Directly it had gone she felt reduced, already cut off from the source of energy and power residing in the bungalow. She glanced at what remained: the suitcase, the writing-table and the metal trunk of missionary relics which this morning Aziz had helped her pull away from the wall between dressing-table and almirah into the centre of the room. She knelt on the rush mat in front of it, as at an altar, as at her life. The once-black paint was scored and scratched with the scars of travel and rough handling; and the name, painted in white roman capitals – Barbara Batchelor – had faded into grey anonymity of a kind from which a good report might be educed by someone who did not know her; a chance discoverer in a later age.

'Poor trunk,' she said. She touched the metal. It was warm like an animal, one that relied on her, dispassionately but assuming certain things about their relationship. 'There is no room,' she said, 'no room at Clarissa's.'

She considered alternatives. One was to ask Mr Maybrick to give it temporary shelter. But it would not survive, neglected amidst all that chaos. Nor would it survive in the alien Muslim shadows of Jalal-ud-din's. She caressed the lid. Beneath it lay the proofs of her failures and successes, evidence of endeavour. Gazing down at the name it seemed to her that the trunk was all that God need ever notice or take into account; that she herself had become unreal and unimportant.

An idea began to exert itself, persuasively; to flow up from the trunk through her arm like a current; an idea that the trunk should be left at Rose Cottage where she had been happy. But where? Where Mabel could see it, or sense it, or even touch it, groping blindly for a familiar or friendly object to give her troubled spirit momentary relief in its wanderings between the cottage and the alien grave?

The brass padlock with its key was in the lower ring of the main hasp. She had but to lever up the two side hasps to raise the lid; but the prospect of looking through the contents dismayed her. She unlocked the padlock and transferred it to the securing ring, clicked it shut and used the key to lock the two smaller clasps. She put the key aside to place it in her handbag, but continued kneeling.

From behind her Aziz spoke. 'Memsahib. Sarah Mem.'

She looked round as startled by the interruption as she would have been if caught in an act of private devotion. In the open doorway she saw the two faces, Aziz's and Sarah's. The colour came into her own. She got unsteadily to her feet as Aziz stood aside for Sarah to enter. Since the evening of the day Sarah got back from Calcutta, the day after the funeral, she had not visited the cottage, and that single visit had been brief, cut short by their nearness to Mabel's death, their reluctance to talk about it and inability to find other subjects of conversation. The girl had rung subsequently to ask if Barbie was all right, opening the way for an invitation. She had now come of her own accord as if there were matters that could no longer be laid aside, but Barbie was afraid of being alone with the girl because of what had been said.

'I must look a sight,' she said, pushing back a stray lock of her short-cropped hair. 'I've been clearing up, trying to get some sort of order into things, some sort of sense. It's quite a task.'

'I'm sorry,' Sarah said. She did not say what about. 'Is there anything I can help with?'

Barbie shook her head. Sarah was in uniform. She had probably come straight from the daftar. She looked soldierly. But womanly. Perhaps Mildred genuinely suspected something 'wrong' with the girl, and 'wrong' with Barbie. There had been a book once, of arcane reputation, which she had never read; but she remembered the title. Well, Barbie cried in herself, to herself, to the quiet room, the ancient walls; *I* am lonely. Lonely. But God help me my loneliness is open to inspection. It's here in this place beneath my breast. Between Sarah and myself, between myself and any woman, there is nothing that there should not be. I have been slandered. Spitefully. As punishment. For my presumption.

She went into the bathroom, washed the grime from her hands and splashed her face, to cool her skin and the anger that hardened it and made it smooth. She chafed her wrists with cologne, combed her grey hair and called to Aziz.

'Tea! Tea outside, or –' returning to her bedroom, 'sherry?' And stopped. The decanters were locked in the sideboard and Kevin Coley still had the keys. Sarah, arms folded, turned from contemplation of the view from the front window.

'I should love some tea, Barbie.'

'Aziz has probably anticipated. Have you not? Aziz? Aziz!' In the hall her voice rang beating against the gongs of brass trays on the panelled walls, rebounding from the implacable wood of the locked door of Mabel's bedroom. From the region of the kitchen he shouted back in simple confirmation of his presence. She led the way through the sitting-room, unbolted the french window and went out on to the verandah. The sky was clear again but the areas of sunlight were evening-narrow, the shadows long. The garden scent was heady, heightened by the dampness in the air. The chair in which Mabel had sat down to die had not been moved. Fallen rose-petals lay ungathered on the lawn.

'One full day more,' Barbie said, standing by the balustrade. 'Early mornings and from tea until dusk – those were always my favourite times.'

She heard the creak of a chair as Sarah sat and presently the click of a lighter. She waited for the aroma of cigarette smoke to reach her and then turned round.

'I shall be out of here after breakfast the day after tomorrow,' she said. 'Aziz will be ready to go too. I don't know what his travelling arrangements are. He and I will say good-bye here but if he's required to do so he'll wait until someone arrives to take over his storeroom keys. Mahmoud or Captain Coley. Otherwise he'll lock up and leave the keys with mali.'

'Yes, I see. I'll tell Mother.'

Aziz brought tea out. When he had gone Barbie said, 'Will you pour?' Then she sat down and took her cup. She asked how Susan was. Susan was well, Sarah said. They were taking her back to the grace and favour. The day after tomorrow. Minnie, Mahmoud's widowed niece, who had never had children of her own and was scarcely more than a child herself, was excited but also fearful of her new responsibility. For a while Sarah would have to help her.

If there was a feeling of constraint between them, Barbie thought, the fault was her own. The girl's manner was if anything less indrawn than it had been in the past, and beneath the pallor, the marks of strain, there was a faint flush, a look of contentment in the flesh of the face as if she had reached a firm decision about the situation she was in.

'Clarissa told me your news about poor Captain Merrick,' Barbie said.

'Yes, I didn't mention him last time I was here. I meant to tell you that he talked a bit about Miss Crane. He didn't know her very well, I'm afraid.'

'I imagined their paths were unlikely to have crossed.'

'He knew her by sight of course, and visited her in hospital after she was attacked. They weren't able to talk much because she was so ill, and afterwards one of his assistants dealt with it. By then he was involved in the other business of Miss Manners.'

'And later still? When Edwina took her life?'

'Yes, he dealt with that. He was at her bungalow. That's what he remembers. He talked quite a lot about an old picture he found there. From the way he described it I think it must have been the one you had a copy of and showed to people.'

'It would have been that one, I expect. I still have the copy in my trunk.' Barbie thought back to that day on the verandah nearly two years ago. 'I don't remember your being with us when I showed it.'

'I heard about it.'

Barbie nodded. She had made an exhibition of herself over the picture. She said, 'Why did Captain Merrick talk about the picture?'

'He seemed to see a connection between the picture and Teddie. Has Clarissa Peplow told you how Teddie was killed?'

'She said he was trying to bring in some Indian soldiers who'd deserted. I'm afraid I didn't listen very hard.'

'Man-bap,' Sarah said, after a pause, but abruptly.

'What?'

'Man-bap.'

Man-bap. She had not heard that expression for a long time. It meant Mother-Father, the relationship of the *raj* to India, of a man like Colonel Layton to the men in his regiment, of a district officer to the people of his district, of Barbie herself to the children she had taught. Man-bap. I am your father and your mother. Yes, the picture had been an illustration of this aspect of the imperial attachment; the combination of hardness and sentimentality from which Mabel had turned her face. If Teddie had died in an attempt to gather strayed sheep into a fold she saw why Captain Merrick might remember the picture. But Sarah's reasons for referring to it were otherwise obscure to her. And she did not wish to probe. She did not want to talk about Edwina, or about Teddie and the ex-police officer who had lost an arm and whom Sarah had never liked.

But – 'It's interesting about Ronald Merrick,' Sarah began. 'He'd like to be able to sneer at man-bap but he can't quite manage it because actually he'd prefer to believe in it, like Teddie did. If he did. Do you think he did, Barbie?'

'I don't know.'

'Did Miss Crane?'

'Why do you ask that?'

'Because Ronald Merrick thought so. He talked about her sitting at the roadside holding the dead Indian's hand. He thought that was man-bap. Was it?'

'No.'

'What was it?'

'Despair.'

For a moment Sarah looked stricken by the bleak word as if it was the last one she had expected; but then she smiled briefly in recognition.

'Yes,' she said. 'That makes sense.'

Again they became silent but it was the silence of matched temperaments.

'What happened between you and Mother, Barbie?'

'If you don't know I expect it means she'd prefer that you shouldn't.'

'She said you had an idea that Aunt Mabel wanted to be buried in Ranpur.'

'Then you know all there is to know.'

'That's all it was about?'

'That's all.'

'What about Aziz?'

'That wasn't a bone of contention. Although your mother can't have liked my saying she didn't understand.'

'No, she wouldn't like that.'

'I didn't really understand myself, in the sense of being able to explain it. But I didn't feel the need and your mother did. That was the difference. I'm sorry for any annoyance I caused her. She had a great deal to attend to. I had only this – one thing.'

Sarah nodded. She put out her cigarette. Barbie thought she would get up, make an excuse to be off home; but she settled back in the wicker chair.

'How were your aunt and uncle?' Barbie asked her.

'Very well, thank you.'

'You can't have seen much of Calcutta.'

'No, not much. A bit. I was taken dancing at the Grand, and then to a place where they had Indian musicians.'

'By Aunt Fenny and Uncle Arthur?'

Sarah smiled. 'No, by one of the officers who attended the course Uncle Arthur's running. He and Aunt Fenny live a much gayer life than they used to in Delhi. They have one of these large air-conditioned flats and it's usually full of young people, mostly these young men who do the course.'

'What kind of course?'

'About how India is run in peace-time. It's supposed to attract recruits for the civil service and the police among men who've liked India enough to want to stay on after the war.'

Barbie tried to consider this. But she was giving Sarah incomplete attention. The image of the trunk was superimposing itself on the image of the verandah, the tea-table, and Sarah on the other side of it smiling as if waiting for her to smile back.

'Is the course a success?' she asked.

'I suppose one or two of them might be tempted. Having them back to the flat is part of the attracting process. You know. The ease and comfort of lots of servants but in modern surroundings, the kind they have to admit are pretty decent. But I should think they're more likely to try for one of the business firms where the future's more secure and they can get transferred home to the London office when it begins to pall or if they want to get married and have a proper family life. Otherwise I get the impression they think the course is rather quaint.' Sarah paused. 'They were the kind of young men I was just beginning to get to know before Su and I came back out in 'thirty-nine. My sort of people. The sort of people we really are. There's such a tremendous gulf, I mean now. More so from their point of view than from ours.'

'Well,' Barbie began, intending to say something about Sarah's sort of people, her own sort of people, but she could not apply herself to the subject. She said, 'I'm glad you had a bit of fun.' She recalled Sister Matthew's explanation of the solitary presence of a Bengali bearer in the Calcutta flat on the night Mildred had tried to ring her sister from the nursing home: that everyone must have been out celebrating the second front. She wondered at what hour the news of Mabel's death and Susan's premature labour had reached Sarah; and pitied the girl, imagining her returning to her aunt's place, flushed with the excitement of a night in the city in the company of those young men, men of her own kind, men whom she understood or had once understood and now envied because they were part of 'home', and her aunt saying: Sarah, your mother rang, it's bad news I'm afraid. Had the girl's thoughts immediately turned to her father, far away in prison camp?

Had the Layton girls missed a 'proper family life'? What did that mean, anyway? Was it important to have one, significant if one missed it? As in other Anglo-Indian families the discipline of separation of children from parents had presumably marked Sarah's childhood. With such a separation Barbie had never had to contend. The separation she had suffered had been permanent and presumably more tolerable as a consequence since there was no arguing with death: her father's and then her mother's. But she was full grown when she came out and she came out as a treader of new ground, not old, and in her own behalf and, so she had thought, in God's, and had never married, never had children.

Knowing Sarah and Susan was the closest she had ever been to knowing what it felt like to have daughters. If they had been her own children, could she have borne the separation? Would Susan eventually have to bear it, or would the whole condition of life in India for English people have changed by the time the child had reached the age of seven or eight, which brought the first, the childhood, phase of Anglo-Indian life to a conclusion? It was not many years ahead. But the condition would well have changed by then. The child might be lucky.

But not its parents. Not Susan. Nor Sarah. Nor young Dicky Beauvais whom Clarissa Peplow hoped Susan would marry. Looking at Sarah Barbie felt she understood a little of the sense the girl might have of having no clearly defined world to inhabit, but one poised between the old for which she had been prepared, but which seemed to be dying, and the new for which she had not been prepared at all. Young, fresh, and intelligent, all the patterns to which she had been trained to conform were fading, and she was already conscious just from chance or casual encounter of the gulf between herself and the person she would have been if she had never come back to India: the kind of person she 'really was'.

Reaching towards the table to replace her cup Barbie hesitated, completed the movement with conscious effort, to keep her hand steady, and then leant back in her chair. There had been a disturbance, another quick displacement of air, but this time a faint whiff of the malign breath, of the emanation. Alert, she watched the verandah and then the garden which was in sharp focus but seemed far away, hallucinatory, dependent on the human imagination rather than on nature for its existence, wide open to the destructive as well as creative energy of mind and will.

She heard herself say to Sarah, 'I have what I think nowadays you call a problem in logistics,' and then stopped, hearing as well a gentle exhalation which presently she decided must have been her own sigh of relief, of renewed patient anticipation.

'My little room,' she said, 'I mean of course my little room at Clarissa's. It has its limitations. Quite serious ones. And Clarissa has said there cannot be, apart from myself, more than another suitcase. Which leaves two items. Important to me but not to anyone else. To begin with there is the writing-table.'

She looked at Sarah who looked back at her without the concern and commitment suitable to the occasion. But then Sarah was still very young. She would not have learned as yet to understand the grave impediment to free movement which luggage represented in one's affairs.

'Well my writing-table,' she went on, 'in a way, yes, that can be managed because it folds. Like a wing. It is portable. It can stand against a wall, go under a bed. I think I can get my writing-table past Clarissa. And quite apart from a silly affection I have for it I also have use. I expect I shall conduct quite a heavy correspondence. And I can unfold it, sit on the bed and write without worrying whether Clarissa's room is put out of shape, because its shape can be quickly restored, but the trunk —'

She paused, collected her ideas.

'The trunk is a very different kettle of fish. Unlike a writing-table, unlike one's clothes, one's *shoes*, it is of no *use*. But it *is* my history. And according to Emerson without it, without *that*, I'm simply not explained. I am a mere body, sitting here. Without it, according to Emerson, *none* of us is explained because if it is my history then it is yours too and was Mabel's. But there is no room for my trunk at Clarissa's, no room for my explanation.' She grinned. Sarah's brow had become creased. Barbie could not blame the girl for being puzzled. The situation was very complicated and she was not sure she understood it herself.

'I had thought,' she continued, 'of asking permission to leave my trunk in care of the mali, until I can send for it. It could be put in the shed in the servants' quarters where the gardening implements are kept. But –'

'But what?'

'But if I asked permission of the person fully qualified to give it – asked permission of your mother – it would certainly be refused. Would honour be satisfied if I were to ask it of you?'

'I should think so.'

'If I asked should I obtain?'

'I'll look after your trunk, Barbie. It can stay in the room. Susan and I are going to share it but it can stay in my half.'

'That is kind. Very kind. But if you are to share the room with Susan you can't also share it with the trunk. Let the mali have it. Let him keep it in the shed. Then there should be the mini-num of fuss for all of us. The alternative is Jalal-ud-din's. Clarissa has already mentioned it. But I should not be happy to think of my trunk in a heathen storeroom. The trunk is packed with relics of my work in the mission. It is my life in India. My shadow as you might say.'

Sarah nodded, readjusted the hold she had on her own arms, then said, 'You'll let me visit you at Clarissa's, won't you, Barbie?'

For several seconds Barbie did not reply. Then, 'It might be better if you didn't,' she said. 'At least not for a while. Not until I've found my feet. The room is too small to be a suitable place in which to receive guests and I am myself merely a guest, albeit a paying one. You may of course always visit Clarissa and antici-pate seeing me as well but I do not want, as the saying is, to push my luck. I do not want to incur Clarissa's wrath by filling her house with wild and extravagant parties. I shall have to learn, have to learn, yes, to be as quiet as a mouse. Which won't be easy. Clarissa does not hold the key to imaginary silences. Shall you tell Aziz about the trunk now, Sarah? So that he can tell the mali? And it will be official?'

Sarah nodded and Barbie called the old man. When he came Sarah spoke to him. Presently he went away and returned with the mali and Sarah spoke to the mali too. When they had gone and Barbie had thanked her Sarah got up to go. The light was fading quickly.

'There is one thing else,' Barbie said. 'Mabel once told me that she had made provision for Aziz in his old age.'

'Yes, she did.'

'And it will be – respected?'

'Yes, Barbie.'

'Forgive me for mentioning it. I feared perhaps she may have meant to make provision, meant to remember him, but failed to put it into words.'

'No, she remembered Aziz. She remembered you too, Barbie.'

'What?'

'Only in a little way. A small annuity. To help out with the pension. You should hear from the bank in Ranpur soon. Although of course they always seem to take ages.'

'Yes, I see. She should not have.'

'Why not?'

'She should not have. It's taking it away from the rest of you. And I didn't expect anything. But it was very kind. Very kind.'

'Oh, Barbie, don't.'

'Kind,' Barbie repeated. 'So kind.'

She felt in her jacket pocket for the cologne-scented handkerchief. She blew her nose.

'My mother,' she said – laughing – 'was always terribly impressed by the word annuity. She thought it a mark of true gentility. It's odd how these things come back to one. She would have been very proud. My daughter, she would have said, need never concern herself about money because she has her annuity.'

That evening before supper she sat on her bed and watched Aziz and the mali measure the trunk for its shroud of stitched gunny-sacking, which the mali said his wife would cut and help him to sew round it. Later, holding a lantern, she followed the *cortège* round to the mali's shed and saw the covered object stowed in one cleared corner. As she left, holding the lantern high, she heard the clink of the spades and forks as the mali carefully replaced them.

On the morning of the day she left Rose Cottage she woke early, before Aziz brought the pot of tea, the banana, the thin slice of bread and butter which usually made up her chota hazri. The previous night she had drawn back the curtains in order to be able to distinguish between a clear morning and a grey one. It was scarcely light but she could hear the whisper of fine steady rain. She rose and walked bare-foot to confirm it and saw the hunched blanketed figure of the chaukidar who at night guarded Rose Cottage and the next bungalow down the road, patrolling between the two but usually to be found asleep on their own front verandah. The rain was dripping from the verandah roof but there was a lightness in the shadows of the garden that indicated a clear, perhaps sunny, morning later.

She turned back into the room, gazed at the rush mat and then impulsively knelt to say a morning prayer. The prayer turned out to be as full of information as requests. Thank You for Your many blessings and for the years of Rose Cottage. Please guard this room where my two girls are to sleep and admit to Your kingdom the troubled soul of my friend Mabel Layton. I have left my trunk in the shed. I am going to Clarissa's. It is not far.

Rising she inspected the roses gathered yesterday. She had meant to cut many more but a further and final visit from Sarah had interrupted her, put her off her stroke. Seeing the girl crossing the lawn in the late afternoon she feared she had come to cancel the arrangement about the trunk. But she had not.

Barbie had kept the roses in her bedroom all night; young buds, because she had wanted them to begin to unfold and absorb the substance of her dreams and waking meditations, so that they could express upon the grave a special love and particular gratitude. Leaning close to them now it seemed to her that they had absorbed little, perhaps nothing; that each bud was merely a convoluted statement about itself and about the austerity of the vegetable kingdom which was content with the rhythm of the seasons and did not aspire beyond the natural flow of its sap and the firm grip of its root. The bushes from which these roses came had been of English stock but they had travelled well and accepted what was offered. They had not wished to adapt the soil or put a veil across the heat of the sun or spread the rainfall more evenly throughout the year. They had flourished.

'You are now native roses,' she said to them. 'Of the country. The garden is a native garden. We are only visitors. That has been our mistake. That is why God has not followed us here.'

Like a departing guest she opened the drawers in dressing-table and chest just enough to show that they had been dealt with and were empty. For a similar reason she opened the almirah, took out her travelling costume and left the door ajar. After she had bathed she found the chota hazri tray on the bed-side table. She sat in her underwear and dressing-gown and sipped and munched, kept glancing at her watch, already alert for the sound of the taxi which Mr Maybrick had guaranteed to send up not later than eight o'clock. She had told Aziz that she would not wait to eat a proper breakfast.

At a quarter to the hour she began her final preparations. At five to she called Aziz. Between them they upended the writing-table which she had locked the night before and folded the legs in. He carried it into the hall and came back for the suitcase. He brought newspaper in which to wrap the roses; and then gave her a key.

'What is this, Aziz?'

He told her he had found it on the floor, that it must be the key to her trunk. She recognized it now. She put it in her hand-bag and then sat alone until she heard the car arrive.

The rain had stopped. Outside, below the verandah, the other servants stood. She had tipped them all the night before for the last time. Now she shook hands with the mali and his wife, ruffled the boy's hair, smiled at the sweeper girl who kept in the background. Last in the line was Aziz. He had on his fur cap and carried a shawl over one shoulder, ready for his own journey.

'Good-bye, Aziz.'

'Good-bye, Barbie Mem.'

'Have you far to go?'

He indicated a direction, his arm straight and stiff, the hand open, pointing vaguely towards a mountainous distance. A day's journey. Two days'. More than that? She did not know. The name of his village and district written for her in uneven block capitals on a scrap of paper had meant nothing to her. One day she would borrow a large-scape map of the area and search for the name among the contours that showed the greatest heights.

'God be with you,' she said.

'And with you,' he answered. Briefly their hands met and clasped; and then she entered the taxi whose door was held open by the mali's boy.

IV

On the first Sunday after Barbie's arrival at the rectory bungalow
Arthur Peplow conducted the morning service as one of thanksgiving for the defeat of the Japanese attempt to invade India at
Imphal, for the news that the last Japanese soldier had been
driven from Indian soil, and for the continuing good reports
from France of the allied offensive against the Germans. Having
announced that this should be their theme in all their hymns and
prayers he said that they would begin with a rather more intimate
kind of thanksgiving. He moved towards the front pew where
Susan sat with her sister and mother.

'Forasmuch as it hath pleased Almighty God of His goodness
to give safe deliverance to this our sister, and hath preserved her
in the great danger of childbirth, We shall give hearty thanks
unto God and say: Except the Lord build the house: their labour
is but lost that build it. Except the Lord keep the city: the watch-
man waketh but in vain.'

As if blissfully unaware that several members of the congregation (the Smalleys for instance) raised their eyebrows at his inclusion of the form for the churching of women in a service
attended by Other Ranks and young and impressionable officers,
he announced hymn number 358; and it may have been that
towards the back of the church where a group of young British
soldiers on church parade got noisily to their feet, one of them
glanced at the elderly woman next to him, on the other side of
a pillar that rose between pews, alerted by a strangled sound such
as might be caused by a sudden constriction of the throat. If so
he must then have been reassured. No incident was reported.
And the service got off to a rousing start with Bishop Heber's
missionary hymn: From Greenland's icy mountains: which
everyone knew and could sing happily without bothering much
about the words.

The hymn chosen to close the service was Onward Christian
Soldiers. People felt that Arthur Peplow had done the station
proud.

Outside, shading her eyes from a splendid burst of Sunday
sunshine, Nicky Paynton said that there was nothing so cheerful
as a good rollicking morning at church. It set you up for the
day. Ahead lay an equally cheerful session in the club bar and a

luncheon there of Madras curry guaranteed to bring cleansing tears to the eyes and an overall feeling of well-being. In the evening Clara and Nicky were dining with the Trehearnes. They asked if they could stop in on the way and see the baby. Mildred assented. Kevin and Dicky were dining at the grace and favour. They could all have a drink together before Clara and Nicky went on to Maisie's.

'The baby will be asleep,' Susan warned them. 'I shouldn't want him woken. He falls asleep as soon as he's had his six o'clock bottle. It's his best time.' She plucked at her mother's sleeve. 'We ought to be getting back. Has Mahmoud brought the flowers?'

'I'll check,' Dicky Beauvais said and walked off briskly down the path through the lingering groups of worshippers.

'We sent Mahmoud up to the cottage,' Mildred explained, 'to get some roses for Susan.'

'For Aunty Mabel's grave,' Susan said. 'Because I missed the funeral.'

Dicky was coming back, self-conscious with a large bunch of roses. Presumably Mahmoud had been waiting outside the churchyard gate. Susan went to meet him. She looked slim and pretty and very young. Dicky took her round the side of the church to place her offering on the grave Arthur Peplow had chosen for Mabel's resting place: a secluded spot. It was plucky of Susan to come to church so soon after her return from the nursing home, Clara Fosdick said; and thoughtful of her to arrange for the flowers.

'But she's anxious to get home now,' Mildred said. 'Minnie's not been in sole charge before. But it seemed wise to start as one means to go on. Minnie's quite capable of making sure the brat comes to no damage even if she's hamfisted with the paraphernalia. And Panther's taken a shine to him. He growls if old Mahmoud goes near. He knows the ghastly thing belongs to Su. He doesn't mind Dicky taking a peep because Dicky brought them home. But he took an unpleasant interest in poor Kevin's ankles last night, didn't he Kevin?'

'One can protect ankles. Throat's what you have to watch out for.'

Susan and Dicky came back but were detained within earshot by Lucy and Tusker Smalley.

'Lots of congratulations, Susan,' Lucy said. Tusker added, 'Rather.'

'Thank you. And thank you for the lovely flowers you sent. I'm afraid I haven't yet written to everybody.'

Lucy said, 'I hear you're calling the baby Teddie.'

'No, not Teddie. Edward. It's very important to get it right. I've got not to care for nicknames and diminutives for men.'

She glanced at Lucy's husband. 'Why do they call you Tusker, Major Smalley?'

Smalley indicated his regimental insignia, the Mahwars: a bull-elephant from whose back, howdah-like, sprang a tuft of toddy-palm.

'Mahwars. Tuskers, regimental nickname.'

'Yes, I know that. But why do they call *you* Tusker?'

'Bit of a long story.' Tusker looked modest but pleased.

'– after all,' Susan continued as if he had not said anything, 'we never called my husband Muzzy Bingham. Nor daddy old Pankot Layton.'

There was a pause. A breeze riffled the skirts of the women's dresses.

'Which regiment will you want little Edward to belong to?' Lucy Smalley asked. 'That will be quite a decision, won't it? Between the Pankots and the Muzzys. You'd have to be making it now if you could put a boy down for a regiment like you have to for a school.'

Mrs Smalley's voice drifted away, caught by the tail of the breeze and chased by the stronger following gust that whipped through the churchyard and prompted Susan into action. She appeared almost to be spun round by it, so that no one could have said that she turned her back on the Smalleys nor that she pushed through the group headed by her mother, but there was what amounted to a convulsive movement, a rearrangement of positions, a making way for her whch was ended abruptly by her touching her sister's elbow as if finding base and going off then slightly ahead of her, down the path at a pace quick enough for Dicky to have to start off rather fast and lengthen his stride to catch up with them.

'The children are having tiffin at home,' Mildred said, 'and they have their own tongas.'

'Is Susan all right?' Nicky Paynton asked.

'Susan is fine.'

She anchored the group round her by not budging until the Smalleys approached. And then, turning her back, snubbed them as if so far as she was concerned Susan had been perfectly behaved until they managed to upset her; Lucy by mentioning Teddie's name and Tusker by saying the word regiment which was the very thing Teddie had died for; and then slowly led the way down the path between the ancient gravestones: a woman making a point, one that was less well defined than it was felt – the point, perhaps, that if Susan's behaviour could be seen as a further demonstration of how time was running out for people like Mildred then anything like a scramble was vulgar, too tiresome to consider let alone join.

The next time Mildred walked along that path would be for the christening, the admission as a lively member of holy church of little Edward Arthur David; and that would bring to a formal close a difficult phase of the responsibility she had shouldered during her husband's absence. From things she said it was gathered that there could be no question of Susan marrying Dicky Beauvais or anyone until John Layton came home. The implication was that the same must apply to Sarah. One dead and never-seen son-in-law, one live grandson, and two still healthy daughters were sufficient evidence of life having gone on for Colonel Layton to come back to and not feel that things had fallen apart for want of a firm hand. Now Mildred was digging her heels in. She would not be rushed again. She had been rushed once and the result had been pretty disastrous or nearly so. Real disaster had been averted by Susan not letting the baby die on her or herself die on the baby.

According to Nicky Paynton, Mildred's off-hand manner towards the child, her use of a word like brat, did not disguise the fact that she was bucked at the prospect of having a grandson to hand over to Colonel Layton when he resumed his position as head of the family. The boy was half a Layton. John must have often regretted having no son of his own to bear his name, though he had been proud and fond of both his daughters. And he had been pleased about the marriage, quite taken, so Mildred said, by Teddie's photograph. How stoically he received news of Teddie's death wasn't known. His letters took a long time to reach Pankot and there was proof of letters going astray in both directions. It was possible that he would get the news of the child's birth and not know that his son-in-law was dead. It was possible that he was ignorant of both events. They had heard nothing for some time and with the opening of the second front they perhaps had to be prepared for a period of silence and uncertainty.

But they were inured to both and Mildred without dropping her characteristic guard infected her friends with a spirit of optimism. The christening party to be held at the grace and favour after a quiet family ceremony at St John's promised to be a jolly affair, rather like a picnic amid (Mildred warned) the packing crates that were already being filled as the process of separating Layton private possessions from stuff belonging to the army and public works department got under way.

When it was all over there would be little left to delay the move up to Rose Cottage. The christening party had its valedictory aspect. In spite of all its drawbacks the grace and favour bungalow had served its turn and deserved a good send-off. The accommodations officer was already nagging for possession so that he could turn the bungalow into a chummery for officers of the new emergency intake and relieve pressure elsewhere. From being full of women it would become (Mildred said) 'full of chaps' and presumably they wouldn't object so much to being woken at the crack of dawn by bugles opposite or, if they did, would have less cause.

And (at the club during midweek) Mildred smiled, directed the bearer's attention to her glass and said, 'Although I'm afraid Edward's going to be even more effective than a bugle. He seems to have an instinct for getting everybody on parade at six a.m. prompt. Doesn't he, Su?'

'Most children wake at six,' Susan said. 'I used to wake at six at Aunt Lydia's in Bayswater and at great-grandpa's in Surrey. They never had bugles.'

'But then you're Army,' Nicky Paynton said.

'Yes,' Susan said. She sat very upright on a club chair watching the clock and everybody who came in and went out. She had not been inside the club for months, not since she had begun, as she put it, to 'show' and took to smocks. This morning her mother had persuaded her to put in an appearance, to take up the reins of a proper routine.

'Relax, darling,' Mildred said. 'You simply must learn to trust Minnie. And you ought to change your mind and have a drink, even if it's only a nimbo.'

'All right.'

The bearer brought her a nimbopani. She sat holding the tumbler in both hands and used both hands to raise it to her lips. 'Are you cold?' her mother asked. It had been raining hard all morning and the temperature had dropped. No, Susan said, she wasn't cold.

'I thought you shivered,' Mildred went on. 'I hope you're not sickening for something.' No, Susan said again. She was quite all right, she wasn't sickening for anything. She put the glass on the table and made an effort to take part in the conversation by giving her attention to the person speaking; but after a while her glance strayed to the clock again and to the people coming in and going out and back to the clock and then to her wristwatch. She reached for the glass one-handed, lifted it and then lost her grip.

The glass fell, wetting her skirt and legs with the nimbo, and broke into sharp fragments on the floor at her feet. She stayed seated. There was a hush in the room, then talk was resumed. A sweeper was sent for. Clara Fosdick examined her stockings and pronounced them unladdered and only a bit damp. On the other hand Susan, she said, was soaked.

'Well,' Mildred said, 'that *was* clumsy of you, wasn't it? You'll have to change when you get home. Are you madly uncomfortable?'

'No, Mother.'

'Perhaps you'd better go to the cloakroom and mop up with a towel. Then come back and have another nimbo. There's loads of time.'

'I shan't want another nimbo.'

'Well go and dry off.'

'I'm more comfortable sitting still.'

The sweeper came with brush and pan. Mrs Fosdick, without getting up, shifted her chair and gave him room to get at all the splinters but Susan did not. She watched him sweeping gingerly round her feet. After he had gone Mildred ordered another drink but the conversation lagged and Susan had not looked up again. Irritably Mildred said:

'Darling, what on earth's the matter with you?'

'Nothing's the matter. I'm relaxing.'

She smiled and suddenly leant back with her arms folded. She asked Nicky Paynton whether she had heard recently from the two boys in Wiltshire. Nicky said she had. The elder was looking forward to being eighteen, finishing with school and joining the RAF of all things. 'But I expect we can talk him out of that,' she added, 'unless he's really set on it as an alternative career to the army and it's not just the temporary glamour of the boys in blue at home that's attracting him.'

'And what about the other?'

'Oh, it's the Ranpurs for him. But then he's still at the stage of thinking his father's the cat's whiskers.'

Susan had not stopped smiling but the others were aware of the avoidable subject having once more cropped up and conjured Teddie's shade. Again their conversation lagged and presently Mildred looked out of the window, finished her drink and said, 'It's stopped. We'd better get you home and out of that damp frock.'

'Yes, I should like to go home now, if you don't mind.'

But she waited until the others had got to their feet before rising herself. She walked, arms still folded, behind her mother and her mother's friends, past the pillars and the potted palms –

– and into her inner life, her melancholia; an inexplicable business, worse than that of Poppy Browning's daughter because that girl had had a certain justification for what she did: an unfaithful husband dead in the arms of his Indian mistress. But Susan's husband had died gallantly and tragic as the circumstances were then and later in the matter of the premature birth she was surrounded by love and devotion and the child was surely a lively reminder to her of this fact and of the duty she had to cherish him, show him at least as much affection as she herself had been shown.

And she had done so. Therefore the incident that occurred at the grace and favour bungalow on the afternoon of the day before the christening ceremony was even further beyond anyone's ability to understand than it would have been had she continued to show signs of rejecting the child. But the rejection had been of brief duration. Her subsequent concern for the

child's welfare was both charming and touching; a bit exaggerated but no more so than the other traits and characteristics that
went to make up the bright little personality in whom there had
always seemed to reside a spirit of particular determination to do
the right thing, but with style and youthful freshness; no doubt
drawing attention to herself in the process but also to the purpose
and condition of a life based upon a few simple but exacting
ideas.

Now through a single action she shattered her own image as
a child might destroy its own carefully constructed edifice of
bricks. Indeed there was in her behaviour a disagreeable element
of play, of wilful destruction of a likeness of the adult world
she inhabited. At first her action was said to be one that had
endangered the child's life but once the facts were known the
idea of tragedy narrowly averted was replaced by a suspicion that
if mockery had not been intended it had been accomplished;
and this suspicion proved as strong as the pity felt for a girl in
the grip of such a deep post-natal depression that there was little
to distinguish it from madness.

But the word madness did not help. If she had gone off her
head presumably she had done so because she found everything
about her life unendurable. Meaningless. It did not help either
to remember that she had not only fitted in but had been seen
to fit in. She had tried. Trying should not have been necessary.
Apparently it had been, for her; and suddenly she had stopped;
not only stopped but symbolically wiped out all the years of
effort by her extraordinary gesture.

On the afternoon of the day before the christening when her
mother was at Rose Cottage supervising the measurement of
new curtains, and Sarah had gone back to the daftar and so left
Susan in sole command, she sent Mahmoud to the bazaar to buy
some blue ribbon for the christening gown – Sarah's old gown
which Mabel had kept in a trunk for years and only handed over
a day or two before her death. She made Mahmoud take Panther
who she complained was getting fat and lazy through lack of
exercise. Ten minutes after he had gone, dragging the reluctant
dog, she called Minnie from her task of sorting sheets and pillow-
cases for the dhobi and told her to run after him and tell him she
wanted white ribbon, not blue.

So Minnie set off, but turned back. Questioned about that

later she said that in spite of all the little offerings she had made since the little Memsahib became a widow, the bad spirits had not been appeased, they had not gone elsewhere, they still infested the bungalow and the compound, and this particular day – the day before the alien rite of christening – was especially inauspicious. And from certain things the little Memsahib had done – taking out the christening gown, smoothing it, holding it, talking to it; looking at the baby but not touching him as if afraid to – she believed the little Memsahib was also aware of the bad spirits. She had turned back at the gate partly because she was afraid of what might happen if she deserted her post and partly out of curiosity. She thought little Memsahib intended to make a special Christian puja of her own.

Although, like her uncle, Minnie professed the Muslim faith, the rigours of that austere religion lay lightly on the people of the Pankot hills. Wayside shrines to the old tribal gods were still decorated with offerings of flowers and here and there in places believed to be inhabited by bhuts and demons – a tree, a cross-roads – there might sometimes be found dishes of milk or clarified butter. For some time now in secret places of the grace and favour compound Minnie had prepared and kept replen-ished such tokens of appeasement. It would interest her to see how little Memsahib might go about a similar enterprise.

She returned to the bungalow but stayed hidden and was rewarded by the sight of Susan, seated now on the verandah, dressing the child in the lace gown, talking to it to reassure it and then – the dressing completed – continuing for a while with-out speaking and looking not at the child but straight ahead, so that Minnie assumed she was engaged in some kind of silent incantation.

And then quite abruptly Susan had risen and carried the child down the verandah steps and across the grass towards the bare brick wall that divided the garden from the servants' quarters. Minnie thought that perhaps there were a number of magic paces which mother and child had to take together and automatically she began to count. The alarm she might have felt when Susan suddenly stopped and placed the child on its back on the damp grass was momentarily stilled by the fascination exerted by the whole strange process, for there could be no doubt now that she was the spectator of a ritual which no other Indian had ever witnessed, otherwise she would have heard tales about it. When Susan walked away from the child, along the wall, towards the place where the wall ended, again Minnie counted the paces taken, and when she bent down, picked up a can and walked back, it was the whole action that exercised Minnie's imagination and not just the can, the reason for the can, which she recognized as one full of the kerosene Mahmoud found handy for lighting his bonfires of accumulated rubbish. Kerosene was oil. Was it holy oil to people like little Memsahib?

Susan's next action was the most fascinating of all. She walked round the child in a wide circle tipping the can as she went and sprinkling the oil. Then she put the can down near the wall, approached the circle again and knelt. With the can there must have been matches because she had a box in her hand and was striking one and throwing it on to the kerosene. Flame leapt and arced in two directions, tracing the circumference until the two fiery arms met at the other side, enclosing the sacrifice.

Minnie did not understand but she had stopped trying to work it out because she understood the one important thing. She understood fire. Crying out, she snatched a sheet from the dhobi's bundle and ran. The grass inside the circle was too wet for the flames to catch hold and spread towards the middle where the child gazed at the sky and worked its legs and arms. But Minnie did not understand that either. She acted instinctively, flung the sheet over the flames which were already turning blue and yellow, dying; and used the sheet as a path to reach the child. Picking it up she backed away calling out all the time to little Memsahib who continued kneeling and gazing at the centre of the ring of fire where the child had been. She seemed not to notice that the child was no longer there and that Minnie was crying out to her.

She was still there when Mahmoud got back from the bazaar and found Minnie on the verandah hugging the now crying child, not daring either to approach her mistress or let her out of her sight. She was still there when, summoned by Mahmoud, Mildred returned. She ignored all her mother's orders and entreaties to get up. When Travers arrived she ignored him too. She stayed where she was until Sarah, driven home by Dicky Beauvais, went out and talked to her. She let Sarah take her indoors and presently into the ambulance that Travers had called

to take her back to the nursing home. In all this time she had
looked at no one, spoken to no one, but smiled as if happy for
the first time in her life.

In servants' quarters up and down the station the tale spread
quickly. It reached the bazaar and the nearer villages that same
night before the last fire had been damped down and the last light
extinguished. The little Memsahib was touched by the special
holiness of madness and her melancholy cries could be heard in
the hills, scarcely distinguishable from the howling of the jackal
packs that disturbed the dogs and set them barking. The sound
could be heard all night but faded out as morning came leaving
a profound, an ominous, silence and stillness that seemed to
divide the races, brown-skinned from pale-skinned, and to mark
every movement of the latter with a furtiveness of which they
themselves were aware if their aloof preoccupied expressions
were any guide.

Certainly an air of furtiveness hung over the ceremony of
christening which Arthur Peplow at Mildred's insistence conducted as arranged at eleven o'clock in the forenoon, ushering
the participants in and speaking to them in a whisper as though
the ritual were forbidden and every one of them a potential
martyr, fearful of God but also of discovery. The child's feeble
cries were a constant threat as were the nervous coughs, the
scraped feet, Arthur's mumbling, their muttered responses.

There was no party afterwards. Mildred had cancelled it. How
she managed to attend the ceremony was considered a marvel.
Outside the church the Rankins, having done their duty as
godparents, thoughtfully went back to Flagstaff House leaving
Mildred to be taken home by Sarah and Dicky. To the innermost
circle gathered for lunch, Isobel reported Mildred composed
but uncommunicative except in one matter. 'What was that
bloody woman doing in church?' she had asked, meaning the
Batchelor woman who had been observed by all of them seated
as far away from the font as it was possible to get, in the very
front pew where she had never been seen to sit before; and on
her knees praying as if her presence were going to make all the
difference between a christening that 'took' and one that didn't.

'But I'm really not sure,' Isobel said, 'that Mildred hasn't
become over-obsessed by Miss Batchelor.' Asked by Nicky

Paynton just what she meant she showed some reluctance to answer. Things were bad enough, she said, bad for the station, without their being aggravated by criticism and gossip. But in the end she revealed that Clarissa Peplow who like Isobel herself had called at the grace and favour the previous night to see if there were anything to do to help had been forced by Mildred to take a box of teaspoons which the old missionary had given to Susan as a wedding present. Clarissa had tried to get out of it but Mildred became 'extremely agitated'. She swore that nothing had gone right since Susan received them and said she didn't want them in the house a moment longer. Clarissa could throw them away if she couldn't face giving them back but she must take them with her. All of which, Isobel said, suggested that Mildred had got it into her head that Miss Batchelor was a bad influence and to blame for everything.

In fact (Isobel went on to say) Mildred had come as near as dammit to accusing Barbara Batchelor of deliberately turning Mabel against her family. She said that if Mabel hadn't been cosseted and flattered by Miss Batchelor right from the start she would have got rid of the damned woman and moved into the spare and let Mildred and the girls take over the rest of the house and that if that had happened Susan would probably never have married Teddie Bingham who had been a decent enough chap but not the husband Susan deserved. He would probably never have risen above junior field rank. Pigging in at the grace and favour had distorted the girl's outlook, it had got on her nerves, completely unsettled her, until suddenly she had seen marriage as a way out, chosen Teddie without thinking properly and married him only to find herself back where she started, a grass-widow, then a widow, and then a mother with a fatherless child. And now God knew what was to happen to her.

'According to Travers, Susan hasn't spoken a word to anyone but just sits in the room they've given her staring out of the window and *smiling*,' Isobel ended.

It was this that seemed so appalling: to have done what she had done and yet to smile. But what had she done? The more one thought about it the more incomprehensible it became. Even the mechanics of the act – let alone the motive – were meaningless until one of the men, Dick Rankin himself, said it reminded him of the kind of thing kids did to scorpions to watch them sting themselves to death rather than be burnt alive. 'It's not true, though,' Rankin pointed out, 'if you pop a scorpion into the middle of a ring of fire it arches its tail and looks as if it's stinging itself to death but it's only a reflex defensive action. The blighters scorch to death because in spite of what they look like they've got very tender skins which is why they mostly come out in the wet weather. In the hot dry weather they hide under stones.'

But God knew why the girl should use the child as a kid might a scorpion. She must be completely off her rocker. Perhaps in her deranged state she had been trying to re-enact the circumstances of Teddie's death, which had been by fire. But why the carefully described circle? When you looked at it logically the child had never been in danger except of catching a chill which the little ayah had taken the first opportunity to ensure he didn't, by bathing and wrapping him up warmly.

'Well,' Rankin summed up. 'I suppose the psychiatrists will make something of it. You can't apply ordinary logic in a case like this. But it's damned embarrassing for the station.'

And back you came to the smile and through the smile to the uncomfortable feeling that Susan had made a statement about her life that somehow managed to be a statement about your own: a statement which reduced you – now that Dick Rankin had had his say – to the size of an insect; an insect entirely surrounded by the destructive element, so that twist, turn, attack, or defend yourself as you might you were doomed; not by the forces ranged against you but by the terrible inadequacy of your own armour. And if for armour you read conduct, ideas, principles, the code by which you lived, then the sense to be read into Susan's otherwise meaningless little charade was to say the least of it thought-provoking.

V

'I am sorry, Barbara,' Clarissa said, having given her the spoons. 'I know it was wrong of her. They were not her spoons to return. But I had no choice and have none now. Dearly as I should have liked to refuse, I felt I could not. Dearly as I should like to hide them and forget them, I cannot. I hope you will take the exceptional circumstances into consideration and forgive her.'

'Blessed are the insulted and the shat upon,' Barbie said. 'For they shall inherit the kingdom of Heaven, which is currently under offer with vacant possession.'

. 'What did you say?'

Barbie did not repeat it. She said, 'Forgive me. The circumstances are indeed exceptional. I am not myself. Mildred is not herself. Thou are not changed and God is not mocked.'

Clarissa's mouth hung open. She clutched the rosary of the afternoon sandalwood beads. Barbie put the box of spoons by her side on the bed. With Clarissa in the room there was scarcely sufficient space for the two of them to stand. From the bed she could see the old people concealed behind the curtain in the angle of the wall.

'I had a letter from the bank in Ranpur this morning, Clarissa. The annuity Mabel has left me will amount to one hundred and fifty pounds a year. It will take some time for the first quarterly payment to reach me because it all has to be done in London. But it is considerable additional security. It means I can afford to pay you more for my board and lodging.'

'For a temporary arrangement I am adequately repaid,' Clarissa said. 'Your suggestion is generous but I cannot accept it.'

'I had another letter too, Clarissa.' She opened her handbag, got out the letter and gave it to Clarissa. It read: 'Dear Miss Batchelor, Mr Studholme in Calcutta passed your letter to me because he himself had no suggestion to make in regard to employment in the Mission on a voluntary basis. But he asks me to tell you to write to him again if the matter of accommodation remains unsettled at the end of the year. He says that he has no immediate solution to offer because during the past five years there have naturally been other retirements and the continuing difficulty of arranging passages home has led to more demand for places in Darjeeling and Nan Tal than there is a supply. However the main reason for his passing your letter to me was the possibility he thought there might be of our having a suggestion to make at this end both about accommodation and employment. Unfortunately we have none. I hope that you will soon find somewhere suitable to live. It is very kind of Mr and Mrs Peplow to take you in meanwhile. I trust you are well. Yours sincerely, Helen Jolley.'

Clarissa gave her the letter back, said nothing and began clacking her beads.

'I called at Smith's Hotel after the christening this morning,' Barbie continued. 'Because the annuity means I might have afforded their price for a while. But they have no vacancies and the accommodations officer has what the manager calls a lien on any room that falls vacant.'

Clarissa released the beads and turned to go.

'What news is there of Susan?' Barbie asked, not wanting her to.

'There is no news. She looks out of a window and smiles.'

'Smiles?'

'Smiles.'

'Why then she is happy.'

'Happy? How can she be happy when she is out of her mind?'

'Perhaps she has entered it,' Barbie said and then raised her voice because Clarissa had gone. 'Perhaps that's why she's happy and why she smiles.'

She lifted the lid of the box and stared at the twelve rigid identical apostles. One of them, Thomas, was said to have reached India and to have preached near Madras at San Thome which was named after him. Which spoon was Thomas? She wondered what she would make of them and they of her if they were suddenly made manifest and stood before her, laughing and lusty; simple hard-working men, good with nets and boats, swarthy-skinned, smelling of sweat, of fish, of the timber-yard; men who worked with their hands, most of them. 'You'd get short shrift in Pankot,' she said. 'I wouldn't give tuppence for your chances, least of all if you tried to get into that place where the silver is and asked permission to sit at that table and break your bread and drink your wine.'

She began to shut the lid but stopped, held by the picture she had just conjured of the apostles in the mess and by the fact that the spoons were silver, solid silver. They had cost, in her terms, a lot of money and had been given with pride as well as love. She realized that Susan had probably looked at them once, written her thank-you letter and forgotten them, making it easy for Mildred to ensure that they were left out of the display of presents. She did not blame Susan but she could never offer them to her again, she would never be able to say to the girl, Your mother sent these back, don't you want them? It would be for

Mildred to tell her should she think of asking where they were. It would be for Mildred to tell the truth or to lie.

She did not want to keep them herself but they were too good to throw away. She could hardly offer them to Clarissa. The home they must find should at least be appropriate and she believed she had hit upon the most appropriate of all.

She shut the box, dragged the writing-table from its place against the wall, unfolded the legs and set it up by the bedside. Having unlocked the drawer she took out some crisp blue writing paper and matching envelopes which were lined with sky-blue tissue.

Dear Colonel Trehearne,

I am sending today *via* the adjutant a small gift of silver teaspoons which I should like to present to the Regiment for use in the Officers' Mess, in memory of the late Mrs Mabel Layton. I hope that this small gift will be acceptable to the regiment.

Yours Sincerely,
Barbara Batchelor

Dear Captain Coley,

I have written today to Colonel Trehearne to say that I am delivering to you this box of silver spoons which I am presenting in memory of the late Mrs Mabel Layton for use in the Officers' Mess.

Yours Sincerely,
Barbara Batchelor

Before sealing the letters she considered carefully whether she should bother with Coley. She could deliver the spoons direct to Commandant's House without involving him; but she wanted to involve him because she wanted Mildred to know where the spoons were going before they actually got there and she was sure that Coley would tell her and that if he did she would try to make him send them back. And this he would be unable to do if he knew about the separate official letter already on its way to Colonel Trehearne. He would have no alternative but to pass the spoons on. She believed that even Mildred would be afraid to arrange for them to be lost in transit and would shy away from asking Trehearne to be so ungallant as to decline them.

In the hall she checked the address of Commandant's House in Clarissa's directory. She looked for Coley's too but could not find it. There was a telephone number with the words 'Adjs, Office' written in beside it. She would have to go to the Pankot lines and inquire. Back in her room she sealed the letters and addressed Trehearne's and at half-past two set out stoutly shod, macintosh over her shoulder, stick in one hand, the box of spoons and the two letters in the other.

In the bazaar which she could reach within ten minutes of leaving the rectory bungalow she bought stamps and posted the letter to Colonel Trehearne. As the letter disappeared into the box she thought: No going back now! Nothing for it now! March! To the barricades! She strode facing the oncoming traffic which seemed uncommonly heavy but with next to nothing going in her own direction so that she began to feel like someone moving against the flow of columns of refugees. The shouting tonga-wallahs, the bobbing head-load carriers, the gliding cyclists and the lurching soldiers in the open backs of uncovered trucks and lorries might have been calling: Wrong way! Wrong way! The notion exhilarated her. For the first time since leaving Rose Cottage she felt strong and free because the intense vulgarity of Mildred's gesture in returning the spoons had released in her a vulgarity just as intense but of greater splendour. I, Barbara Batchelor, she declaimed, daughter of Leonard and Lucy Batchelor, late of Lucknow Road, Camberwell, am about to present silver to the officers of the Pankot Rifles. And as my father used to say, storming out into the night or into the morning, bugger the lot of you.

Half way down Cantonment Approach road she transferred the remaining letter and the box of spoons to her macintosh pocket because her palms were sweating in the humid afternoon. The cloud level was low. There was no rain as yet but the light was strange: bright under a dark sky and then dark under a bright one as if there were a single band of luminosity which bounced, throbbing, between earth and heaven. She did not mind if it rained. She had her sou'wester in the other pocket of her mac. The umbrella, her mother used to say, take the umbrella. Horrid umbrella. Black cotton cave. Dead bat. God is weeping for the sins of the world, her mother said. Laughing, you mean, her father replied, laughing fit to bust. But rain was only rain: sea sucked up and sprayed on the parched land by the giant elephant, the elephant god.

She paused opposite the main entrance to the grounds of the general hospital. The nursing-home wing was hidden from view by trees and the lie of the land. She walked on attended by a faceless wraith whose Susan-pale arms opened the way for her, parting misty curtains, one after the other, as if insisting on a direction, an ultimate objective, a sublime revelation at the end of a tricky and obscure path.

The light became apocalyptic. Puddles in the road shone white reflecting a purity whose source was not visible. The landscape was now bleak, the ground on either side of the road waste: areas of windshorn turf broken by rifts and channels. The last refugee had gone by and she was alone, resolute in alien territory, entering Rifle Range road that ran straight full-tilt across the valley towards the hills. Suddenly, as if they had cracked under their own weight, there came a report and then another before the echo of the first had spent itself; and yet another, as many as a dozen. The air shifted under the duress of a wind of panic from the hills and the first drops of rain began to fall. The panic did not touch her but the rain would. She put on her macintosh and sou'wester, patted the pocket where the box of spoons nestled, and strode on past the entrance to grace and favour lane with scarcely more than a glance in the direction of the bungalow to make sure it was still there. Presently she turned into Mess road. It was the day of the wedding party. We could go to Ranpur, Barbie had said, to do some Christmas shopping. Oh, I shall never go to Ranpur again, Mabel had answered, at least not until I'm buried. But on that day it was sunny. Coming from the shade of the portico into the glare the white of the servants' uniforms dazzled the eye and the emerald leaves of glistening plants in terracotta pots shone like scimitars and cast razor-sharp indigo blue shadows. Is it you, is it you, Ghulam Mohammed? Mabel said. And Barbie knew for whom she might ask. She walked into the mess compound. The pebbles in the path gleamed in the rain. Ahead, level with the entrance, there was a parked military truck and as she gained the shelter of the long portico a group of young officers came out laughing and began to climb up over the tailboard while one stood smoking and calling to the absent driver.

Turning, he saw her, and two of the other three now settling in the back of the truck and slapping wood and metal with boisterous good-natured impatience saw her too. She filled her old schoolmarm's lungs, grated her Memsahib's voice into gear, and called: 'Good afternoon. Can one of you help me?'

Close to them she noticed that their faces were tight and youthful. Their single subaltern's pips looked painfully new. None of them could have been at the party eight months before. She guessed the thought stiffening their necks and minds: Careful – You never know who she is.

'Do you know if Captain Coley is in the mess?'

'Coley? The adjutant? No, I don't think he is.'

The officer who had been shouting for the driver glanced at the three in the truck who shook their heads. One of them said, 'He wasn't in the daftar this morning.'

'Oh, dear. How dreadfully inconvenient.' She smiled, mimicking the bright brassy manner of women like Nicky Paynton and Isobel Rankin which she had noted tended to make men put themselves out and do things without actually being ordered to.

'I'll ask,' the young officer said and began to go inside but remembered his manners in time and invited her to precede him into the building. Inside, his newness and uncertainty were even more apparent. There was no one about and he seemed unsure what to do next. Barbie said, 'It's my own fault. I ought to have rung. But I was coming this way and thought I'd kill two birds with one stone. The trouble is I've never visited him in his quarters and have no idea where he hides out. Have you?'

'No, I'm afraid I haven't.'

She got it then: the unmistakable London accent. It came out in the word afraid. It warmed her heart. So did the rather overgreased black hair, the stubby plebeian but not unhandsome features beneath it. As a soldier he must be confident and efficient otherwise the regiment would not have accepted him even at this stage of the war when regiments were taking the best they could get, which she had heard was very good, but having to close their eyes to social shortcomings. As a gentleman he obviously fell short of the Pankots' traditional requirements, and knew it, was far from happy in this silent mausoleum.

'The fact is we only got here from OTS last week,' he said. A bearer crossed the hall, carrying a tray. The subaltern stopped him and asked in inaccurate Urdu whether Captain Coley was in the mess. He didn't understand the bearer's reply but Barbie did. Captain Coley would not be in mess until after the week-end. She asked the servant if he knew where Captain Coley lived because she wished to see him quite urgently. He gave her directions but they were very muddled and she did not understand the references. She said, 'Is Ghulam Mohammed here?'

The bearer said he did not know Ghulam Mohammed. There was no Ghulam Mohammed in the mess.

She asked him how long he had worked in the mess, and the answer was disturbing. Since last November.

'Ghulam Mohammed was here then,' she insisted.

No, he had never worked with a Ghulam Mohammed. If Memsahib wished he would ask the head steward.

'It doesn't matter.' She turned to go. The officer followed her. He probably hadn't understood a word. She was glad. Her hold on things had begun to be undermined.

All the same he grasped the situation. 'No luck?'

'No, none. But I think I'll be able to find it.'

'The driver will know, won't he?'

'Oh, I'd forgotten the driver. How clever of you. The driver's bound to know.'

When they got outside, the driver had turned up and was waiting by the cab door. Asked if he knew where the adjutant sahib lived he said nothing but inclined his head to one side and kept on doing so in answer to every one of her questions.

'He knows?'

'He knows.'

'Can we take you?'

'How kind. But shan't I be making you late for a parade?'

'It's only the munshi.' He led the way round to the passenger seat, warned her about the height of the step.

'Adjutant Sahib bungalow,' he told the driver after he had slammed the door shut for her. A few seconds later he knocked on the back of the cabin and shouted, 'OK.' As the truck engine started she thought she heard men's laughter. She smiled. The cabin smelt of petrol and other peculiar metallic odours. The truck, one of the snub-nosed variety, gave her the feeling of riding in a tank. It bucked and growled. The windscreen wipers swung like metronomes but squeaked on the glass. She expected it was against the rules for a civilian to ride in it. She wished she had insisted on getting into the back. She would have liked to gossip to the young officers and to have found out where they all came from and what they thought of India. Were they the kind of young men Sarah had met at her aunt's and uncle's in Calcutta? If you're ever stationed in Cal, she might say, watch out for a man called Colonel Grace, he'll be after you to sign on for *ever.*

She glanced at the driver. Thin cheeks. Hawk's nose. And a skin so sunburnt that the usual Pankot copper-colour was, in this light, blue-sheened. There were minute red veins in the whites of his eyes. She was startled by the clarity of her vision. He smelt powerfully of garlic. His khaki was immaculately starched and pressed. His marbled brown legs were covered by fine dark hairs above and below the knee, between the tops of the socks and the hem of the knife-edged shorts. Tucked above the windscreen was a faded postcard, a photograph of a chubby wide-eyed smiling beauty with a caste-mark between her thick eyebrows; an Indian film star, she supposed. She imagined a smell of jasmine, a thin nasal voice. How remote his life from her own. But he could have come from the same village as Aziz, or Ghulam Mohammed.

She had never asked Mabel who Ghulam Mohammed was. Now he had gone, like Poppy Browning's daughter, like Gillian Waller, with Mabel to the grave, the one that should not have been dug: crying out soundlessly like the unknown Indian on the road from Dibrapur and the girl in white whom she imagined running in the dark from a martyrdom, or from something unimaginable, which might even have been love. She thought: Perhaps I should have given the spoons to the old woman in the veiled topee, have waited in St John's for her to arrive, and kneel or sit staring at the altar unconsciously sharing my vigil, and called to her softly: These are for the child. And given her the twelve little apostles. But perhaps she isn't in Pankot any longer. Perhaps she was never here. In any case it's too late. I'm presenting the spoons to the mess.

She clapped her hand against her pocket. Yes, the box was still there. She gazed out of the streaming windows. The speed of the truck made the rain seem heavier. All this area of Pankot was new and strange to her. It looked unwelcoming. Rows of huts, squat and dark, parade grounds, basket-ball pitches. Distantly, clutches of figures silhouetted against the white light running for cover. It was very hot in the cabin. The window in the door on her side was misting up.

At a cross-roads marked by military signposts the driver turned left. This road after a while became tree-lined. They were going past bungalows up a slight incline and then down into a dip at the bottom of which the driver stopped. There was no bungalow visible, only a dirt track leading off to the left through a kind of copse.

'Adjutant Sahib,' the driver said and pointed at the track. She noticed a square white board on a short post aslant in the hedge, but could not read it. The young officer appeared and opened the door. 'Is it far up the track, do you think?' he asked. 'The truck could get up there. It's muddy to walk.'

'Oh I don't mind. Not in the least. I'm dressed for it.'

'What about when you leave? I've not been this end before. Do you know where you are?'

She asked the driver how far she would have to walk to get a tonga. He indicated ahead and said half a mile. She thanked him and got out. She put her sou'wester back on but did not bother to tie the strings under her chin.

'It's been very good of you. I hope I haven't made you late for the munshi.' She offered her hand. Before shaking it he took off his cap. She could hear the others talking. 'My name's Barbara Batchelor, incidentally. At present I'm staying with the Peplows, that's at the rectory bungalow next to St John's church. Arthur Peplow's always glad to see new faces. People sometimes look in for a beer after Sunday-morning service, before going up to the club. So don't forget. And good luck to you all, if I don't see you again. Don't get wet. I'm all right. Well protected.'

She went and stood at the end of the dirt track. The door slammed. She waved, watched the truck turn in the road and waved to the men in the back when a full view of them was presented by the truck's manoeuvres. When it had gone out of sight she turned and studied the board.

A foot square, two feet off the ground, it had been painted white some time ago. The paint was peeled, the black letters had faded and the first letter had come off with its background. The notice read: apt. K. Coley. Under the name an arrow pointed up the track or would have done so had the board been straight. Its tilt directed the arrow downward into the mixture of gravel, pebbles, earth and mud and tyre-marks which made up the track's surface.

From the path there was nothing to be seen of the bungalow where Coley lived. It was an appropriate setting for a man whose military ambitions were said to have been smothered ten years before in the tumbled bricks and masonry of Quetta. One could imagine him choosing it for its isolation, its proximity to the lines and to the office he was content to occupy for the rest of his working life. He stirred himself, Barbie had heard, only when threatened by promotion and posting to another station. There was nothing he did not know about the running of the regimental depot. Successive commandants had connived at his schemes to stay put.

At the entrance to his hidden retreat Barbie felt a pang of remorse. She could never like Coley but the air of melancholy emanating from the faded tilted board and from the whole area persuaded her to make allowances, to forgive him for behaviour that perhaps had not been natural but forced on him by Mildred. Perhaps he had been afraid to resist her, fearing the power she potentially wielded. Mildred's husband – if he survived prison-camp – was Trehearne's likely successor as depot commandant. Or so Coley might anticipate. And presumably he had only a slender stock of pride. Most of it would have gone with his ambition. If acting the part of the dog at Mildred's heels secured his future, he would play it.

The track curved and came to an abrupt end: a corrugated-iron shed, a garage. To the right a gateway without a gate opened on to steps of rough-hewn stone that led up into the copse.

She climbed the stone steps. What she entered was a compound planted with hedges, shrubs and bushes that had grown wild among trees. She identified rhododendron among other more exotic leaves and could see that the path had originally been laid out with an eye to withholding for as long as possible a view of the bungalow that lay at its end; so that the revelation of what was ordinary and ugly stunned her for an instant into acceptance of it as rare and beautiful. Walls, windows, roof, verandah – entirely commonplace, mean even – moved her with the austere poetry of their function. Here a man sheltered from and diminished the horror and vulgarity of the world by the simplicity of his arrangements for living in it.

The path had brought her within a few feet of the front verandah steps. The verandah was narrow. From where she stood she could see the padlock on the hasp of the closed doors. Eden was unoccupied. But perhaps round the back she would find a servant capable of being roused from mid-afternoon torpor. As she moved a gust of wind blew leaves upward. At the back of the bungalow she found a small grassed compound, a servant's hut, also closed and padlocked, and an open-sided byre in which a tethered goat was munching vegetable stalks.

The rain was still not heavy. She hesitated before climbing the steps to gain the temporary shelter of the back verandah, then went up stealthily, conscious of trespass during the occupier's and the servant's absence. This verandah was deeper than the one at the front and was furnished in the familiar way with wicker chairs and table. The windows were shuttered. There were no french windows; only plain narrow doors, also closed.

She prepared to wait for the rain to reach its peak and die out or settle into a persistent Pankot drizzle through which she could walk in search of a tonga without getting too wet. The darkness of the sky suggested a heavy fall. Already the air seemed thick with mutterings of storm and the distant warning murmur of tempestuous forces gathering in the hills to strike through the valley.

But after that single gust of wind no other came and the rain continued to fall modestly. Nothing in nature confirmed as real the restlessness in the surrounding air. She clenched her fist and put it against her chest; her heart was not pounding, but there was a pressure round about her, a pulsing. She turned and stared at the shuttered windows and then at the narrow doors which when not closed would be hooked back to the outside walls. The hooks hung loose. But the hasps were not in position. The doors were not locked. Cautiously she tried the handle on one of them. It opened without a sound and the screen of wire mesh yielded to a touch.

'Captain Coley?' she said, and cleared her throat, meaning to call again, more loudly, but the interior was dark and so hot it seemed to suck the breath out of her lungs and at the same time to whimper with relief like a creature deprived of liberty who

sensed release. 'Captain Coley?' she repeated. The words came
out unsteadily and made no impression on the creature's distant
incoherent supplications, its scarcely audible gasps and cries.
The mesh screen swung back; she was not aware of pushing it.
'Captain Coley?' she said again and something folded her in its
sticky arms and drew her into the interior; not the creature but
its keeper. It held her for a moment and then was not there and
the illusion of hot darkness was splintered. Her flesh tightened,
attacked by frosty particles of fear, the shuttered bungalow was
filled with subterranean light and at its centre the creature was
imprisoned in a room divided from the one she stood in by swing
ornamental shutters that filled no more than the central space
of the open doorway. It was like being back again in that chill
corridor approaching other doors that gave a view through oval
windows. She was drawn to them by the creature's moans and
cries until she stood in a place where over the top of the shutters
she saw in the gloom the creature herself, naked, contorted,
entwined with another, gaunt and male and silently active in a
human parody of divine creation.

It was not the stark revelation of the flesh that caused Barbie
to gasp and cover her mouth for in her own body she guessed
the casual ugliness that might attach to a surrender to sensuality.
What filled her with horror was the instantaneous impression of
the absence of love and tenderness: the emotional inertia and
mechanical pumping of the man, the cries coming from the
woman who seemed driven by despair rather than by longing,
or even lust. It was as though the world outside the subterranean
room was dying or extinct and the joyless coupling was a bitter
hopeless expression of the will of the woman for the species to
survive.

Turning, groping, Barbie regained the verandah, closed the
door and leaned on it, head back, mouth open like a swimmer
breaking surface; and then fearing she must have been heard
made for the steps, stumbled in going down them and blundered
round the side of the bungalow, terrified of discovery, of turning
and seeing Mildred and Kevin Coley bearing down on her,
naked, raw-eyed, determined on her destruction as the sole
witness of their act of adultery.

She ran down the path and – misjudging the twists – was
whipped by twigs and obstructed by branches. Going down the

rough-hewn steps she misjudged again and wrenched her ankle, falling. Scrambling up she ran down the track. It seemed endless. When eventually she came out on to the lane she turned left into the unknown.

The ankle did not begin to hurt until, after walking for fifteen minutes without coming upon a landmark or a wider road that might lead her back to familiar surroundings, she stopped, knowing that something was wrong. She felt in her pocket – but the spoons and the letter were still there. The wrongness was in the other pocket. There was no sou'wester but it wasn't on her head either. Her hair was sopping wet. She turned, intending to go back to look for it but at that moment became aware both of the pain in her ankle and of the futility of such a search. The sou'-wester must have been torn off her head by the overhanging branches in the garden. She could not remember that happening. But then she could not remember either whether she had taken the hat off on the verandah and left it on the table. Her name was written in indelible pencil on the white lining of the headband.

Limping, punishing the stick, she struck out again through what had become a downpour, not daring to stop and shelter in case her ankle seized up and she found herself unable to move, marooned in this inhospitable region.

PART FIVE

THE TENNIS COURT

I

MISS BATCHELOR was taken to the civil wing of the general hospital on the day Nicky Paynton heard that her husband had been killed in the Arakan.

For three days Clarissa had sent meals into Barbie's room, spoken to her from the doorway but otherwise kept clear in order not to be infected by the awful cold the old missionary had caught as a result of walking about in the rain, without a hat, getting lost, returning home like a drowned rat and then refusing all advice and offers of hot balsam.

But on the fourth morning, alarmed first by the sight of Barbie's flushed face and the fact that she opened her eyes but seemed unable to speak or rouse herself, and then by the feeling of hot dry skin under her own cool hand, Clarissa rang Doctor Travers who, after a brief examination, sent for an ambulance.

'How long has she been like this?' he asked while they waited. Clarissa confessed that she hadn't actually seen her since before lunch on the previous day when she thought she looked better but not as well as she insisted. 'I made her promise not to get up and she said she wouldn't. After that I was busy all day but the boy said she ate all her meals, except her supper. She was asleep when he took it in. She hasn't touched her night drink either.'

Travers said, 'I wish I'd known sooner. Actually it's risky moving her but I don't think we could save her here. I ought to warn you it's ten to one against her making it. She's got broncho-pneumonia and the heart's pretty weak. What on earth's the poor old thing been doing?'

Clarissa said she didn't know but described the state Barbie was in when she came back into the house on the afternoon of the day of the christening. They went back to the room and for a moment Clarissa thought Barbie had gone in the few minutes she and Doctor Travers had been talking in the hall.

He sat on the bed holding Barbie's wrist and then listening to her chest again through his stethoscope. 'I suppose she's quite alone in the world?' he asked presently.

'Until she came to Pankot she lived only for the Mission,' Clarissa said. 'She talks about getting back into harness but of course she's past it. I think it was the letter she had from them saying they wouldn't have her back that did it.'

Travers looked round, surprised because Clarissa Peplow's voice sounded very unsteady. He had always assumed her to be emotionally dehydrated.

'Will *you* have her back, Mrs Peplow? That is, if the question happens to arise?'

Clarissa nodded.

'I ask because it could be important. I mean if we get her over the pneumonia. People don't die only of diseases, you know.'

At that moment the telephone rang and thinking it might be the hospital warning him of a delay Travers got Clarissa's permission to answer it. It wasn't the hospital but Clara Fosdick, asking for Clarissa. She said she was glad to be speaking to him, however, because Nicky Paynton had had this telegram about poor Bunny being killed in action and Clara had already thought of ringing Colonel Beames to suggest that he should look in. Clara said she thought Nicky was taking it too well and being over-conscientious about not breaking down in front of people. Nicky and Bunny had absolutely adored each other and it was awful, Clara said, to see Nicky going about the house as if nothing had happened and even trying to get ready to go to the club to play bridge in order not to let Isobel and Maisie down, because with Mildred temporarily dropped out it was difficult to make up a four at short notice if, as she had last night, Isobel indicated that she had a free afternoon and wished to play.

'I'm not sure whether I should cancel it or not,' Clara said. 'I mean I know I should. In fact must. But she seems set on keeping her promise. She says Bunny would have understood.'

There was of course no bridge. But neither did Nicky Paynton ever break down in front of anyone. She adopted a manner that made her in the eyes of her friends curiously immune from their sympathy although not from their admiration. After sending a telegram to her friend Dora Lowndes in Wiltshire (who was married to the boys' housemaster and looked after them during

the holidays) and then following the telegram up with a letter
to the boys themselves, she continued her daily routine, not as
though nothing had happened but as though it had and was over
and wasn't to be mentioned because it concerned no one except
herself and her sons.

Bunny's death, she implied, was entirely her private affair.
Even from the start, although still referring to him and saying
his name, she used the past tense, which made people feel he
had been dead for years and that her widowhood had been the
determining factor in her personality for a long time – the one
everybody had missed noticing before and had to get used to
quickly if they were to stand a chance of remaining on friendly
terms with her.

Everybody agreed that it was an astonishing performance; the
best ever put up in a society that prided itself on being able to
do exactly what Nicky Paynton was doing if the need arose. That
it was also a farewell performance was understood. It could only
be a matter of time before Nicky announced that she was packing
up and going home by the quickest means available, to be with
her sons. No one else had any claim on her. With one stroke
India was finished for her and although she would probably
assure her friends that she'd be back, this was one of those crystal-
clear cases of a woman leaving and knowing that her chances of
seeing India again were slim enough to be non-existent. She
would never be able to afford the fare. If either boy eventually
came out she might be tempted to scrape together enough to
come and visit him and renew old acquaintanceships, but she
would be foolish to do so. It would be unbearable.

Already you could see her looking at things as if trying to fix
them sharply enough in her memory to carry away indelible
impressions of them; and then beginning not to look at all
because she was only making it worse for herself, knowing she
was looking for the last time.

Nicky had had the worst kind of luck. If the children had been
grown up or if there had been no children the decision to go
home could have been postponed at least until the end of
the war, even indefinitely. Perhaps – as in the case of her friend
Clara Fosdick – the question would never have arisen. All her
closest friends were in India. They would have rallied round as
Clara's friends – Nicky and Bunny in particular – rallied round

when Freddie Fosdick died of cancer in his own hospital back in '36, leaving no children but a wife rather younger than himself; although not young enough to have further expectations, even if she had had the inclination to marry again, which she had not. As it was between Nicky and Bunny so it had been between Clara and Freddie.

Clara knew that Nicky's loss affected her as much as anyone because the moment Nicky packed and went she herself would be homeless. The bungalow they shared was occupied officially by Nicky as the wife of Colonel Paynton of the Ranpurs. Clara was merely a paying guest. The obvious solution would be for her to go to live in Ranpur with her sister and brother-in-law, Mr Justice Spendlove, but she didn't care much for Billy Spendlove and her sister knew it and stuck up for him whenever she thought he was being criticized. They usually managed to quarrel during Clara's short visits.

And so, stoically but without being able to disguise her inner preoccupations, Clara waited for Nicky to make the inevitable announcement.

She made it at what was from Clara's point of view an unsuitable moment; at Rose Cottage and to the company assembled there as in the old days on a sunny Saturday morning.

Mildred's sister Fenny had come up from Calcutta to be at Mildred's side during Susan's illness and to help with the move to Rose Cottage; a move finally achieved a few days after Nicky received the telegram – if anything so piecemeal, so incomplete, could be reckoned an achievement. It was piecemeal because spread over several days and incomplete because Susan's things were in Miss Batchelor's old room along with Sarah's, and Susan's baby and the ayah were in the little spare; but there was no Susan. And Panther had escaped twice from Mahmoud's custody and twice been found outside Susan's old room at the temporarily empty grace and favour bungalow, his head resting on one of his two outstretched forepaws, too far gone in his animal misery to keep up the whining and whimpering which in the first few days of Susan's absence had made Mildred lose her temper and say that the wretched creature would have to be put down.

After the second escape during which he seemed to have torn

his hindquarters on what the vet thought was barbed wire
Mildred ordered the dog to be tethered in the servants' quarters
of Rose Cottage. He turned vicious. None of the servants dared
approach. It was Sarah who risked being bitten, trying to calm
and feed him and bathe his wound. She left water and a meaty
bone within his reach. He did not touch them. It looked as
though he intended to starve himself to death to prove his loyalty
to Susan. His deterioration was frighteningly rapid. The tether
became pointless. He hadn't the energy to stand. No longer
capable of snapping and snarling he trembled when Sarah stroked
his head. She fed him warm milk and brandy through a pipette
given to her by the veterinary officer from the old Remount
Depot, Lieutenant Firozeh Khan. Lieutenant Khan said that the
kindest thing would be to have the dog destroyed. It hadn't acted
like this when Susan was away having the baby. It was possible that
the dog thought Susan had been taken away and the baby left in
her place as a substitute. It might be dangerous to have it around.

'No,' Sarah said. 'That's pure imagination. Panther's got to be
saved. Captain Samuels says Panther may be important to my
sister when she's a bit better.'

Samuels was an RAMC psychiatrist attached to the military
wing of the hospital. He hadn't been in India long and was used
to dealing only with men, chiefly British other ranks. Mildred
had already said she didn't see what good he could do since most
of his work was confined to treating slackers who thought they
had nervous breakdowns because they were deprived of fish and
chips. Her friends agreed that perhaps there was something disagreeable about Susan being talked to, questioned, by a man;
particularly by a man like Samuels who might be considered
clever at home where psychoanalysis was fashionable, but who
was after all a Jew. But the alternative was the Hospital of the
Samaritan Mission of the Sisters of Our Lady of Mercy in Ranpur, a mental home staffed by Catholics; Eurasians and Indians
mostly; the same ghastly kind of place with a small wing for
Europeans such as poor Poppy Browning's daughter had ended
her days in, screaming obscenities at her mother who used to go
home from her weekly visits and wash in Lysol because they'd
given up bathing the girl forcibly, except once a month, and
Poppy used to touch and hold her close in an attempt to show
her she was still loved.

Susan, thank God, was reported quite the opposite; clean, well-behaved, silent. She had said a few words to her mother and to Sarah and presumably more than a few to Captain Samuels who told Mildred her daughter was 'beginning to adjust' whatever that meant. Adjust to what? Mildred had apparently not bothered to ask. She distrusted the whole psychiatric process and had no time at all for the jargon. She said Travers had acted precipitately, sending Susan back to the nursing home. There was nothing wrong with the girl that a good rest, a change of air and the company of young people wouldn't put right. She wasn't getting any kind of rest at the nursing home with Captain Samuels visiting her sometimes twice or even three times a day. Mildred managed to make these professional visits sound as though something unwholesome was going on.

'I'm sure Millie is right,' her sister Fenny said on this particular Saturday morning when Mildred had gone indoors in answer to Mahmoud's announcement that Captain Coley Sahib was on the telephone. 'I think it would be a good idea for her to come and stay with me in Calcutta and bring both girls and ayah and the baby. There wouldn't be room in the flat but Colonel Johnson and his wife who are friends of ours have a simply huge old eighteenth-century John Company house and would gladly put them up. Or we could spend October in Darjeeling with old Dogra friends of Arthur's and come back down to Cal in November when the weather's really nice. Sarah would benefit as much as anyone. In fact I've suggested she and I could go down to Calcutta together quite soon. She's been up two nights with that dog as well as making sure ayah looks after little Edward properly and she visits Susan at least once a day, *and* still reports to the daftar whenever she can in spite of Dick Rankin telling her she can have extended station leave for as long as she wants. She's gone there this morning.'

'How *is* the dog?' Maisie Trehearne asked.

'Sarah says it's on the mend. She's got it in the mali's shed. I haven't looked myself. I can't bear the sight of sick animals but then I'm no good in a sick-room of any kind which is why I never visited Sarah's friend Captain Merrick, although the hospital's practically visible from the flat. But I did ring before I came up to Pankot and they said he was fine and quite cheerful considering he's lost his left arm.'

Fenny stopped and conscientiously avoided looking at Nicky
Paynton, presumably in the belief that the subject of wounded
officers was to be avoided. Fenny had become stouter since her
last visit to Pankot at the time of Susan's engagement, when she
pronounced Teddie Bingham 'rather sweet'. She filled the chair
she was sitting in, which happened to be the one Mabel died in.
The others wondered whether she knew but supposed she didn't
in view of her confessed inability even to visit someone who
was ill.

And she was smarter than they remembered. Arthur Grace's
belated elevation to a Lieutenant-colonelcy and appointment in
Calcutta seemed to have given her a sort of cosmopolitan gloss.
She belonged, as though in default of having arrived sooner
at a desirable peak, to a new order of Indian authority and had
apparently, as a result, absorbed and smothered a multitude of
sins. For Rose Cottage she was slightly over-dressed. Of the
three women sitting with her, Maisie, Nicky and Clara, only
Maisie remembered her as the youngest and prettiest of the three
daughters of General Muir who had lived in Flagstaff House in
the years immediately following the end of the 1914–18 war.
Lydia, the eldest, had been cold and rather snooty, very intelligent and not at all enamoured of Anglo-Indian life. Her fiancé
had been drowned in the Atlantic by German submarine action,
a loss that had brightened the northern, arctic, gleam in her
critical eye. She had gone home, got married and settled in
Bayswater. Fenny in those days had a reputation for charming
silliness, Maisie recalled, and in spite of being chased by scores
of personable and promising fellows had married a man who
turned out something of a failure. But all three knew well
enough the Fenny to whom in middle-age an air of portly dowdiness had attached; a dowdiness she had combated by being
vigorous in her opinions. Which had been comfortingly conservative. The vigour remained but now suited her. Fenny was
particularly welcome just now. She radiated self-assurance.

'I'm so glad to have got Millie out of that poky little bungalow,' she said, making a sign to Mahmoud to replenish glasses.
Mildred was still on the telephone indoors. 'I don't mind telling
you I had to prod her a bit. At the last moment she said she didn't
want to come. But she didn't want to stay in the grace and favour
either and anyway she no longer had a choice. She said that if it

wasn't for the girls she'd ask Dick Rankin to pull strings and get the air-force to fly her home to wait for John there.'

She looked over her shoulder to be sure Mildred was still indoors. Then lowering her voice slightly she said:

'She's awfully against that missionary woman, isn't she? She told me she's been going through Mabel's papers because the money looks like being less than she expected. I thought she meant Miss Batchelor had been cooking the books and feathering her nest but she said there wasn't any sign of that, only of what she calls influence.'

'What sort of influence?' Clara Fosdick wanted to know.

'Payments to charities. *Indian* charities. Orphanages, famine relief funds, child-widows, that sort of thing, and always *anonymously*. There are all these letters from the bank in Ranpur, dating back *years*, acknowledging her instructions to make anonymous donations to this and that – hundreds of rupees at a time, and advice notes about transfers of sterling from London which means she was selling securities at home as well as having the interest sent out.'

Maisie said, 'I don't see where the influence comes in if it's been going on for years. Unless you mean only five. Miss Batchelor came here at the end of 1939.'

'I know. But according to Mildred although Mabel had been giving money to Indian charities for ages, long before Miss Batchelor came to live with her, it almost doubled afterwards, especially in the last couple of years. And there was one donation to the Bishop Barnard Mission which isn't an Indian charity but does help to educate them. Not that I'm against it, any of it, but Mildred says the Bishop Barnard was the mission Miss Batchelor worked for, which proves it –'

'Proves what?'

'According to Mildred, that Mabel was influenced to dish out all this dough *by* Miss Batchelor. On top of which the estate has to fork out to buy an annuity for the woman and if she dies soon after it's bought it's hundreds or thousands of rupees wasted.'

'Perhaps she won't live long enough for it to be bought at all,' Nicky said. 'Clarissa Peplow told me Captain Travers doesn't expect her to pull through.'

'But she's been in hospital well over a week, nearly two, and she hasn't popped off yet. Don't tell Mildred, for Pete's sake, but

Sarah's been over to the civil wing once or twice to see her when she goes to talk to Susan. Sarah says she only seems semi-conscious but reckons she's a tough old bird and will get over it. But whether she does or doesn't Mildred says the idea of an annuity could only have come from *her* because it's a typical lower-middle-class idea of upper-class security and respectability.'

'Isobel Rankin says Mildred is over-obsessed by the idea of Miss Batchelor as an eminence-grise,' Maisie Trehearne said. 'I don't know whether that's true or not but if it is we oughtn't to encourage her. The whole situation is becoming very – unhappy.'

Particularly in regard to spoons; about which Maisie's husband had received what he called a charming and touching letter from the old missionary, but not, as yet, the spoons themselves, which had puzzled him until he heard she had gone into hospital. It still puzzled him a bit. Maisie did not know what to tell him. For some years he had lived in an old-fashioned chivalrous world of his own. If it hadn't been for the war he would have retired in 1942. Sometimes, she thought, he acted as though he *had* retired. He had become fond and foolish and sometimes querulous. He couldn't understand why Coley insisted he'd received no spoons but only a sou'wester, and he inquired every day after Miss Batchelor's health. The position was not an easy one for her to support. He lived for the regiment. Silver for the mess was as much an obsession with him as Isobel Rankin said Miss Batchelor was an obsession with Mildred Layton. When it came to choosing between Mildred's and her husband's obsession there was no question which side she would support. He wanted the spoons. She hoped no one would tell him the spoons were originally Susan's and that Mildred had returned them in a fit of the extraordinary pique that generally possessed her nowadays. Another puzzling feature was that Mildred had said nothing about the spoons. Presumably Kevin Coley hadn't mentioned Miss Batchelor's intention to present them. But Maisie thought this strange too because Kevin and Mildred were so thick. Perhaps he was telling her now, on the telephone.

'Of course,' Fenny went on, 'I've told Millie there's absolutely no proof and certainly no reason why Mabel shouldn't have forked out all that money without prompting. Millie seems to have forgotten, but I don't suppose you have, Maisie, I mean about Mabel's attitude to Jallianwallah.'

'Attitude to whom?'

'Jallianwallah. The General Dyer business in Amritsar in 1919.'

'Well I have forgotten. What was her attitude?'

'Don't you remember how we all collected money for Dyer when Government should have stood by him but didn't and issued that report that he'd exceeded his duty, firing on the unarmed mob in the Jallianwallah Bagh, and the poor old boy was disgraced and retired on half-pay?'

'Well of course I remember that. We were down in Mayapore at the time. There was a lovely ball at the old Artillery Mess and we collected about four thousand rupees just from that.'

'Oh well, if you were down in Mayapore you probably didn't know, which isn't surprising anyway because I had to remind Millie how Mabel refused to give anything. It was very embarrassing for John. After all Mabel was rich in comparison with most of us. She got simply loads from her father, the Admiral, and quite a packet from her first husband, the Pankot Rifles chap who gave all that silver to the mess. And she simply wouldn't give a penny for Dyer.'

'But that means you're saying she was mean –'

'Only about Dyer. At the time we all thought he'd saved the poor old empire and ought to have been given a peerage not the sack. Of course since then people have blamed him for turning Gandhi against us. But the point is, and I was awfully embarrassed because I thought Millie must know if *I* knew, but it seems John never said a word to her, only to me. He told me in strictest confidence, or rather it slipped out and he asked me not to say anything to anybody, he told me Mabel sent money to the funds the *Indians* raised for the widows and orphans of the people Dyer shot. She *told* him she'd done so. I think he said she sent it to that old Muslim, M A K's father, the man who was on the Governor's Council down in Ranpur at the same time as John's father. Sir Ahmed Kasim, wasn't it? She told John she'd done it but had asked Sir Ahmed, if it was Sir Ahmed, to pay it over anonymously because she didn't want to harm John's career. John told me it was a hundred pounds. In 1920 that was a hell of a lot of money.'

'It still is,' Nicky said. 'Do you think Sir Ahmed paid it over?'

'Nicky!'

'Perhaps he gave it to his son, M A K, to swell the Congress Party Funds?'

Fenny said, 'But Sir Ahmed was pro-British. People said he was awfully upset when his son joined the rebel faction of Congress, as we used to think it.'

'Rebels run in the Kasim family,' Nicky said.

'Oh, I'd hardly say that,' Fenny objected. 'M A K's own son, the young Kasim boy we met in Mirat at the guest house, struck me as rather sweet for an Indian. And you couldn't call him a rebel, working for an Indian prince. As a matter of fact it was in Mirat I found out Millie didn't know about Mabel giving money to the Jallianwallah Bagh orphans and widows, because I asked her if I was right thinking she'd sent it via this young Kasim boy's grandfather and she simply didn't know what I was talking about. So I thought I'd better shut up. Mabel was still alive then. But she remembered and asked me last week when she was hot on the trail of these other donations.'

'I wasn't thinking about the Kasim boy you met in Mirat,' Nicky said. 'I was thinking about the other one, the one who got the King's commission and has been captured fighting against us in the INA.'

'Really?' Fenny said. 'I didn't know about that.' She looked doubtful as if Nicky had said something in bad taste. 'All I know is what everybody else knows, that M A K himself is ill and has been released to go and live with the Nawab on some sort of extended parole.'

'He's not ill,' Nicky said. 'He's being cosseted by Government and a fat lot of good it'll do. The Nawab's probably anti-government as well and M A K'll be the first to call his officer son a bloody hero. It's double standards all the time. It makes me sick. But that makes it easier bidding it all a fond farewell.'

There was silence. Even Fenny seemed pre-warned of Nicky's inevitable announcement and to recognize that the moment for it had arrived.

'It's a salutary thought,' Nicky said after a while, 'that Bunny may have been killed by a one-time officer of his own regiment. After all why not? I've been checking up. A Lieutenant Sayed Kasim was commissioned into the Fifth Ranpurs. He was the first Indian the Ranpurs ever took. There were plenty of others but he was the first. Bunny always took immense pains with his own Indian officers. And I took pains with the wives. God knows it was sometimes a hard grind. And you wondered at the time whether it was worth it. It seems it wasn't. It's a bloody bore because you end up distrusting everybody. Sometimes I even look at old Fariqua and try to work out what it would take to make him do the dirty on me even though he's gone around red-eyed ever since I told him Bunny had bought it. Incidentally, Clara, Fariqua lives in a village outside Ranpur. If you go down to your sister you might help find the old boy a job. He has so many spare wives around there he'll need the money and have to go on working until he drops.'

'Are you really going home, Nicky?' Clara asked when she could manage it.

'Yes.'

'Have you decided when and how?'

'The answer to when is as soon as I can. As to how, I'll do what Fenny says Mildred would have liked to. Scrounge a lift with the air-force even if it means being stuck in somewhere like Cairo for a bit. I'll auction everything off and just send a trunk or two of odds and ends by sea. And if the boat's sunk it won't matter much. There's really nothing of value to take back with me.'

Clara said:

'I'll miss you dreadfully.'

For an instant Nicky seemed ready to crumple. But the iron will was not to be broken.

'Oh well, I'll be back in a year or two I expect. When the boys are off my hands. Do you know, there are loads of things I've never done out here? When Bunny was alive he always promised we'd go down to the Coromandel coast one winter, but we never managed it and we never got to Goa either. And then it would be nice to see the Taj again. Bunny thought it terribly overrated but I must say I thought it rather splendid. And of course I'd like to see Gulmarg again, and Ooty, and even dreary old Simla.'

Her friends said nothing. They nodded encouragingly but absent-mindedly. The dispiriting fact had not escaped them. Already Nicky Paynton was talking like a tourist. It was this that drove home to them the terrible bleakness – thinness – that settled upon and somehow defined anyone whose connection had been severed; and then as their glances mercifully fell from her one by one and turned upon the garden Fenny cried out:

'God, what's that?' She jerked out of her chair, startling them. 'What? (one of them shouted) What is it Fenny?' Her alarm was infectious. Her plump ringed fingers were crossed at her throat. She had become speechless and was staring, horrified, at a patch of petal-strewn grass, a corridor between long rectangular beds of rose-trees, bush and standard, vagrant-looking with green reversionary shoots pale and erectile, already sucking the life out of the roots. Along this path the creature crawled, slunk, towards them; a black spectre of famine worn to its hooped rib cage and the arched column of its backbone. A thin dribble of saliva hung from its open mouth.

'Millie!' Fenny called, and then turned and went into the house still calling her. The others stayed where they were, watching the apparition approach the verandah steps slowly, dragging one leg, pausing every few paces to rest, droop-headed, before struggling on, its eyes upturned and fixed on the objective, showing blood-shot whites.

'How can she?' Nicky exclaimed. 'How can Sarah have let it suffer like this? She ought to be ashamed.'

'But Nicky, it means it's getting better,' Maisie said. 'It's looking for her.' Even Maisie could not manage to say the animal's name. She went to the head of the steps cautiously and called down to it, 'Sarah? Where's Sarah, then? There's a brave old soldier. There's a brave old boy.' And got gingerly down on one knee and extended invitation through an outstretched arm and placating fingers which the animal observed from below, raising the iron weight of its neck a fraction of an inch and then lowering it again and standing there at the bottom of the steps as if unable to work out the complicated problem they presented.

Mildred was not on the telephone. Fenny thrust open the door of Mabel's room which she and her sister were sharing. Neither Mabel's old bed nor the charpoy she herself slept in was made up yet. Fenny thought this unforgivable of the servants but blamed Mildred for not controlling them better. However she held her tongue.

Mildred was sitting on the edge of Mabel's bed, topping her glass up from her private bottle.

'Millie, that dog's got loose and is crawling about the garden.'

Mildred put the bottle back on the bedside table.

'What did you say?'

'The dog. It's got loose. I can't bear to see it. It looks as if it's come out to die.'

The corners of Mildred's lips twitched and then curved down in the characteristic smile.

'Lucky dog,' she said.

'Oughtn't we to ring Sarah and get her back here quickly? She can't let it go on like this, Millie. I know she means well but it's not fair, it's not kind.'

'She'll be back any moment now.'

Fenny looked at her watch. It was barely twelve.

'But she never gets back from the daftar before one when she goes in on a Saturday and if the vet isn't rung before then we probably shan't get him until this evening.'

'I said she'll be back any moment.'

Mildred took a drink then looked at Fenny.

'Sarah passed out at the daftar. Only we're not supposed to know. Dicky Beauvais found her in what he calls a fainting con-dition in the map room. She got him to promise not to tell me. But apparently it's the second time this week and he thought I ought to know. He decided honour would be satisfied if he rang Kevin and left it to Kevin whether to tell me or not. He'll be back with her in about ten minutes I should think, with some story about the daftar being slack.'

Fenny sat heavily on the charpoy. 'There! Perhaps she'll listen now and stop being so silly. It's ridiculous her going into the daftar at all.'

'Is it?'

'Millie, you can't let her go on like this. She can't go round fainting all over the place. If you don't speak to her I will.'

'Haven't you spoken to her already?'

'What do you mean?'

'What should I mean?'

'I don't know but if you're not going to do anything I shall have to tackle her myself.'

Mildred got up and stood with her back to Fenny, arms folded but still holding her glass, looking out of the window which gave on to the verandah at the front of the house.

'Directly Dicky Beauvais has gone,' Fenny continued, 'I'll talk to her then. I suppose we'll have to deal with the business of the poor dog first, but one of us must talk to her.'

Mildred said nothing.

'I've been thinking, Millie,' Fenny said. She had always been a bit afraid of her sister. 'You don't honestly need me here much longer. And if Sarah doesn't get a holiday soon she'll crack up. Why don't I do what I suggested the other day, take her back with me to Calcutta, in say a couple of weeks' time? Minnie's perfectly competent with the baby and I can't see Susan being allowed home just yet. When she is we could all meet in Darjeeling for a few weeks and be together in Calcutta before Christmas. Even *for* Christmas. Let's face it Millie, Pankot's awfully dull for two young girls like Sarah and Su.'

'You used to say what a jolly little place it was.'

'Well it's not any more.'

'No,' Mildred said. 'And compared with Calcutta it's got nothing to offer, has it?'

'Very little.'

'No madly handsome young officers fresh from the jungle or about to go into it and ready to tear the place apart?'

Fenny laughed, relieved by what looked like Mildred's change of mood. She said, 'Oh, we have our share of those!'

'So I should imagine. Can you wait two weeks?'

'Oh, Millie. All I ask is for you to give it some serious thought. It would do Sarah the world of good.'

'You think so?'

Fenny hesitated before speaking her mind. 'I know it's been difficult for you without John all these years. Now don't misunderstand, Millie, but it's always seemed to me a great deal of the weight of *your* burden has fallen on Sarah's shoulders. It's in her nature, I know, to take on responsibilities, but it's not right, not for a young girl. And it begins to show and then it's difficult. I mean – with men. We don't want Sarah on the shelf, do we? I know she could have married several times, certainly once. There was Teddie wasn't there, before he switched to Su? But that's the point. If she isn't careful, a girl like Sarah begins to look sort of discarded or second-best choice. And she isn't. You should have seen her just in that very brief time she was with us.

She looked stunning. The boys we had in certainly thought so. One in particular –'

Mildred swung round. 'Don't tell me any more, Fenny! I don't want to know. Just get on with it. Take her to Calcutta. The sooner the better, I imagine.'

'Well you might sound more enthusiastic! Don't you want Sarah to have a good time?'

Mildred laughed. She picked up the bottle, sat on the bed, filled her glass again. And laughed. Then she clattered the bottle back on the table between the water jug and the table-lamp. She took a hefty swig. But the gin didn't compose her. Her eyes glittered under lids which were for once wide open.

'A good time?' she asked. 'She's *had* the good time, hasn't she?'

'Millie, what on earth's wrong with you?'

'Oh, stop putting on the act. It's very good but it's beginning to irritate me. I don't want to talk about it and I don't want to know any of the details. Not any of them. Now or ever. But you can stop treating me like a bloody fool because I know exactly what's going on.' She took another drink. 'I'm even grateful to you for trying to cope with it without my knowing, although it's the least you can do considering you're bloody well to blame. If you want Sarah to go on thinking she's fooled me that's up to you. But you're my little sister. You were always silly and it would be bad for my morale to let you imagine *you'd* fooled me.'

Fenny did not reply at once. She looked at the glass.

She said, 'You're drunk, Millie. That's all I know. So you must be right. If it's any consolation I'll admit I'm silly. Dense. I haven't the slightest idea what you're talking about.'

'Oh?' Mildred drank most of the rest of the gin in her glass but did not top it up. 'Let's forget it then. Let's pretend everything in the garden is lovely and just do what seems best for Sarah. Since you're so concerned about her why don't you ring Captain Travers or Colonel Beames and ask one of them to drop in after lunch to give her a check-up?'

'Well, yes, we could do that. Isn't it a bit out of proportion though? They're both busy men and what can either of them say except what I say, that's she's been overdoing it and needs a holiday?'

'But supposing she's really ill? I'm surprised you haven't

thought of that, Fenny. I tell you what. I'll ring Travers now myself. I'll do it right away.'

'Well. If you think so.'

Mildred finished her drink. 'I think so,' she said. She waited for a moment as if challenging Fenny to stop her and then smiled and went into the hall, leaving the door open. Fenny heard the ping of the bell as the receiver was lifted and then several rapid pings as Mildred impatiently jerked the hook up and down to wake the dozy operator. Sighing, Fenny got up and went into the hall too.

Mildred was at the telephone but the receiver was back on the hook. She was not ringing anybody.

'You were really going to let me!' she exclaimed.

'But it was your idea. Why should I stop you?'

'Haven't you honestly the least idea what I'm getting at?'

'No, I haven't.'

'Then you'd better come in here.'

Fenny followed Mildred into Sarah's and Susan's bedroom. At the wall opposite the foot of one of the beds was a chest of drawers. Placed centrally on its top among neatly ordered lacquered boxes stood a photograph of Sarah's father. Fenny gazed at it fondly for a moment. Mildred went to the chest and opened the second of three long drawers.

'Look,' she said. She turned back piles of neatly laundered underwear. Fenny looked. There were two pudgy blue-wrapped packages, both unopened. Mildred covered them up again and shut the drawer. She went out of the room and after a few moments Fenny went too. She found Mildred back in their own room pouring herself another drink.

'Shut the door, Fenny.' Fenny did so. 'Do you want a gin too?' Fenny shook her head.

'The one thing I've always done for Sarah,' Mildred began, 'and perhaps it's the only thing, is make sure she's got plenty of sannies when she's due, because like I used to be she's as regular as clockwork but has an absolutely ghastly time, worse even than I did before she was born. She was due a week after she came back from her visit to you in Calcutta. I gave her one of those packets then. She was due again last week and that's when I gave her the other.'

'Millie, what are you saying?'

'That according to the evidence in that chest of drawers she's missed twice and hasn't told me. I thought perhaps she'd told you. I thought she might have had to. To make you help her get hold of the bloody man you so kindly introduced her to, or get rid of the thing in Calcutta.'

Suddenly Mildred rounded on her.

'And isn't that the truth, Fenny? Isn't that what your cosy little trip to Calcutta is all about? To fix things up with some snide little emergency officer or fix them up in a different way with a shady Calcutta doctor or pop her neatly into an expensive clinic as a Mrs Smith requiring a d and c?'

'No! No, Millie! Oh, no.'

'Well, that's what you're going to have to do. Get the bloody thing aborted. My God, I could murder you. You have charge of her for just twenty-four stinking hours and she's in the bloody club.'

Fenny sat down, with her hands at her cheeks, her eyes shut. Mildred sat too, facing her.

'What are you doing? Working out which one of your and Arthur's adoring and adorable panting bloody boys it was? Or isn't there any doubt in your mind? What a stupid woman you are. In Mirat you made that ridiculous fuss about her riding in broad daylight with the young Kasim boy. Was it wise – isn't that what you asked me? Wise! A pity you didn't ask yourself if it was wise before you chucked her into the arms of some randy little English officer from God knows where. What was he? All strong white teeth and bloody prick? Did you fancy him yourself? Did you get a kick out of handing him Sarah? Because that's what you did and I never intend to forget it. Never. Just as I never intend to be told who the little cheapskate was. It hasn't happened. Look at me, Fenny. It hasn't happened. You'll take her to Calcutta and between the two of you *deal* with it. Get rid of it. I don't want to know how or where or how much it costs. You can get the money from your husband because he's equally to blame. But *I* don't want to know anything more about it. And if anything goes wrong it's on your head, not mine. Because I can't stand any more. I can't and I won't.'

The sound of a car entering the drive arrested her. She got up.

'Now,' she said. 'Pull yourself together. When everybody's

gone you can start worming it out of her. Pretend I don't know if you like. But *deal* with it. Do you understand?'

'Millie, you don't *know*. You're only guessing. You don't *know* anything.'

Mildred leaned over her, lowering her voice but speaking vehemently and distinctly. 'Two missed periods? Fainting at the office? For God's sake what more do you want? And today's not the first time I've wondered what was wrong with her. I am her mother. A bloody bad one, but I am *that*, and I *know, I know from the look on her face.*'

She went briskly to the door, opened it, and in her ordinary abrasively cheerful voice said, 'Dicky! What a nice surprise. Aren't you both rather early? Well, all the better. You'll stay for lunch, won't you Dicky? I'll tell Mahmoud. Sarah dear, you're looking exhausted. Why don't you freshen up and get out of that boring old uniform? Dicky, use my bathroom, but go through the dining-room. My sister's in the bedroom powdering her nose. But literally.'

There were several kinds of footsteps going in different directions away from the hall and presently Fenny heard a man's in the adjoining bathroom and the click of the bolt on his side of the door. She heard Dicky beginning to urinate – a splash followed by a murmuring silence as he considerately redirected the stream away from the water to the porcelain.

She got up. There was no one in the hall. Sarah's door was ajar. She tapped and went in. She could see the compact shape of his body, uniformed, and smell its assertive masculine odour. She wanted to hate him but could not. Dimly she had always seen that he represented the kind of force that would make the world safe for her and Arthur while laughing at them. For an instant she entertained the absurd idea that he might be forced to do the right thing. But he was gone, as such men always were – involved in apparently lighthearted but in fact complex affairs that had to do with the world as it really was. For him military status was merely part of a game of the compulsory kind. And in her heart she knew that Sarah had used him as he had used her. But had been less expert. Meanwhile there was the question of the dog. She could not remember the dog's name but now that it had come into her mind she could not get it out because it was a living thing whose destruction Sarah had opposed with a significant and dangerous passion. Oh God, she thought, let me be wrong, let Millie be wrong.

Just then through the half-open doorway into the bathroom she caught sight of Sarah standing by the handbowl, grasping the side of it with one hand, reaching for the tap with the other. At the same instant in the little spare on the other side of the bathroom the child woke and cried and Minnie's voice came through quite clearly, speaking to him soothingly. Sarah raised her head, not to look towards the child's room but straight ahead of her into the mirror above the basin as if the source of the cry were there in her reflection. Then she lowered her head again and twisted the tap on and watched the water running in and away.

Dicky Beauvais was kneeling on one leg by the dog's side stroking its head. The others watched from the safety of the verandah. The dog sat on its withered haunches. It swayed when Dicky stroked it.

'What do you think, Captain Beauvais?' Maisie Trehearne asked.

'I don't know. The poor old boy looks pretty much a goner.'

'But don't you think his coming out means he's feeling better?'

'Maybe. On the whole I'd say it's too late. It'll be rotten for Sarah.'

'It's suffering,' Nicky insisted. 'It's dying on its feet. I should have thought anyone could see that.'

Mildred alone was seated, holding her drink under her chin. When Fenny came out ten minutes later Mildred glanced up but Fenny did not look at her. She went to the head of the steps.

'Dicky, I've told Sarah about Panther. She leaves it to us.'

'Oh.' Again he stroked the dog's head. The neck was arched down, the jaws open. 'Poor old fellow.'

He stood up. 'I'd better ring the veterinary officer hadn't I, Mrs Layton?'

Mildred said nothing. He looked at Fenny.

'Isn't Sarah coming out to see for herself?'

'No.'

'Perhaps if I could get the dog round to the gharry it would be better for me to take him than bring the vet up here.'

'I shouldn't if I were you,' Mildred called. 'He could have a fit

and you could end up driving over the khud and killing you both.
Take him back to the mali's shed if you can. It's not the most
elevating sight, is it? Or better still get Sarah to do it. After all she's
responsible for keeping the wretched thing alive and for it ending
up in this state. She oughtn't to be allowed just to opt out.'

'I'll get him into the shed, Mrs Layton.'

Dicky bent down again.

'Come on, old boy. Come along. You can make it.'

The servants had gathered at a safe distance. Dicky tried to
direct the dog's attention to them.

Mildred spoke to Fenny who was watching Dicky.

'Have you persuaded Sarah to go to Calcutta with you?'

'Yes,' Fenny said, without looking.

'Come on Panther, old son,' Dicky said. 'Come on. Rabbit.'

Its tail moved once, a slow-motion scything movement across
the grass and Maisie Trehearne exclaimed, 'He wagged his tail!
I told you. He's feeling better. It's awful to talk about destroying
him now, after all Sarah's done.'

Then she added, 'We owe so much to dogs,' and Mildred
started laughing: a clear fluting laugh of genuine amusement that
made everyone except Dicky down there on the grass turn to
look at her in astonishment. Only Dicky noticed the effect that
the sounds Mildred was making had on the dog. It lifted its head
and snapped at the air or at Dicky's hand which he jerked out
of reach. It began to tremble. It went on snapping as if the peals
of Mildred's laughter were coming at it in some visible form:
small predatory birds or maddening insects. Dicky backed away
and shouted a warning to Mrs Layton but she did not hear. Her
laughter seemed to have become uncontrollable and suddenly
the dog twisted its body and began dragging itself round, still
snapping at the air, making no sound but moving away from the
steps and increasing the width of its circular chase until it was
blundering through the nearest of the rose-beds shaking the
bushes and scattering petals.

The servants also scattered. Dicky stood, alarmed but on the
defensive at the head of the steps with only his bare hands to
fight off an attack if the dog took it into its head to go for any
of them. But the impact with the rose-bushes had disorientated
the animal. It no longer traced a circular pattern but a random
one, staggering from bed to bed with a high-arched back and

low-slung head, wreaking havoc, putting distance between itself and the inhospitable verandah. Suddenly it emitted a stream of pale yellow liquid excreta and then began to drag its hindquarters as though it were dying from that end up. It came to the path between the two rectangular beds and fell on its side. For a while it moved its forelegs, dreamily dog-paddling the air; then it twitched and was still; twitched again and was still again. The intervals between spasms became longer.

Fenny said, 'It isn't rabies, is it, Dicky?'

'No. I've seen rabies.'

They waited for a further spasm that didn't come.

'That's that,' Dicky said.

He went down the steps and called up to Fenny.

'Perhaps as I've handled him I oughtn't to come back into the house though. Would you phone the vet-johnnie, Mrs Grace? I'll get something to cover him with. I expect the servants have some sacking.'

He went off towards the servants' quarters.

A few minutes later he reappeared with a length of gunny, approached the dog's body from behind and then put the sacking over it.

'Dicky, what's all this about not coming into the house?'

Mildred's voice carried strongly. She came down into the garden. He waited for her. She joined him. The dog's body was between them. 'Of course you must come in. You're staying for lunch.'

'Mrs Grace is afraid it might have been something like rabies. It wasn't but I don't want to risk anything.'

'There isn't any risk. It was just a fit. But if you prefer to stay outside until the vet comes by all means do so. Fenny's been on to him and he's coming right away. And you must stay to lunch. I'll need you to cheer Sarah up. Kevin rang me, incidentally. I know about her not feeling well at the daftar. I'm grateful to you for tipping me off.'

'I felt pretty shabby because she'd made me promise not to mention it in case of worrying you. But I thought her health more important than my word.'

'Absolutely right.' She looked down at the heap of sacking. 'I expect this will be the last straw. But we've been cooking up a scheme for Fenny to take her down to Calcutta and get her out of it for a bit. I shall ring Dick Rankin this evening and tell him she oughtn't to go into the daftar between now and then. Come along, Dicky. Don't let's stand here. I'm not feeling so hot myself.'

She moved away. In a moment or two Dicky was walking at her side.

'There's something I've got to tell you, Mrs Layton. And something I want to ask you about. I was going to tell Sarah this morning, that's why I was looking for her and found her – like she was.'

Mildred had stopped. She smiled. She said, 'I hope it's nothing unpleasant.'

'Not unpleasant exactly. I mean – I've been posted. The order came this morning. I've got to report to the military secretary at Fourteenth Army.'

'When?'

'I must leave tonight. There's some transport going down to Ranpur. I'm flying from Ranagunj tomorrow morning.'

'To Comilla?'

'Yes.'

'Is it promotion?'

'I've no idea what's entailed. My guess is I'll be in Imphal inside a week.'

'I won't commiserate,' Mildred said. 'I expect you're glad. No young officer wants to be stuck in a place like this for long. But we're going to miss you. You've been an absolute brick. Like part of the family.'

Dicky blushed.

'You've been very kind to me,' he said.

'You had something to ask me about.'

'Yes. I'm sorry because it seems the wrong sort of time.'

'But it's the only time you have, isn't it?'

'I don't quite know how to put it. Probably you guess. I mean, you have a right to. I've taken up a great deal of your daughters' time – Sarah's *and* Susan's. What you said, about being part of the family, that's what it's been like for me. I was terrifically pleased being asked to be godfather to Susan's baby. The thing is, one day I'd like really to be part of it.'

Dicky's blush had deepened. But he kept his eyes manfully on hers.

'I know there can't be anything offiical,' he continued. 'I mean, in the circumstances. But I didn't want to leave without telling you what I feel and asking if you think there's a chance, and of course if you'd approve.'

'Are you saying you'd like to be John's and my son-in-law, Dicky?'

'Yes.'

Mildred put a hand on his arm.

'My dear chap. I can't actually think of anything nicer. That's all I *can* say. But you've already appreciated that. I'm sorry you have to go without being able to say anything to her, but perhaps it's as well. I made up my mind some time ago that all questions of this kind would have to wait until my husband comes home. But an understanding – not necessarily binding – but an under-standing between the two of you would have been a different matter. You've thought hard about it, haven't you Dicky? It isn't just a case of your feeling sorry for her?'

'Sorry? No, why should I feel sorry –?'

'People exaggerate so. But it's only a temporary set-back and she's getting better every day. She's had the most ghastly luck when you work it out. Later on she'll need someone like you, Dicky, but I wouldn't want you to take it all on unless you were absolutely sure. I must confess I was rather hoping for something like this to give her back a feeling of stability. I'm sure it's all she needs. That, and someone she can lean on, really depend on in the future. Personally, I couldn't be happier. I think the form is for me to talk to her, when that's possible, and to let you know what sort of reaction I get and then for you to start writing to her to tell her a bit of what you feel, but not too much. She needs time as well as reassurance.'

She tapped his arm. 'Now come along in and have a drink. I suggest we keep this entirely to ourselves, at least for the time being, but you and I will know what we're drinking to.'

'Mrs Layton –'

'What, Dicky?'

'I'm afraid I must have made the most awful mess of it –'

'Mess? What do you mean?'

'You were talking – you were talking about Susan.'

Mildred let go of his arm. She studied his face. The blush had gone. He looked quite pale, for Dicky.

'Weren't you?' she asked.

He shook his head. Briefly she touched her own, tracing the outline of her left eyebrow, and then put her hand to her throat, linking the little finger into the string of seed pearls. She smiled but her eyes showed no amusement nor for that matter embarrassment at having jumped to the wrong conclusion.

'I'm so sorry. I'd no idea you felt like that about Sarah. Has she?'

'I hope, a bit. But I don't know. I was going to speak to her today.'

'Yes, I see. Of course there was a time when I wondered. But then when Teddie was killed I thought you realized it had been Susan all the time.'

She moved away from him, a pace or two; but stopped and said, 'It's up to you of course, but my advice would be to say nothing just yet.'

'Would you tell me why, Mrs Layton?'

The pearls had become twisted. But this was the only sign of agitation.

'I shouldn't want you to leave Pankot with your hopes completely dashed.'

'I'd risk that. And it might be otherwise, mightn't it?'

'Perhaps. But I don't think so. I don't get the impression she's fond of you like that. I must take your word for it that so far as you're concerned the scales have finally gone down in her favour. You *have* been thrown together more by Susan's illness. I should be surprised if she feels the same about you but – let's say I'm wrong. Then I'd have to tell you I have reservations about your coming to any kind of understanding. I'm sorry if that sounds unfair or illogical. But what could have been a good thing in Susan's case, a good thing for you both, wouldn't necessarily be in Sarah's and yours. With Susan there's the element of dependence, the question of the child, the need she has to feel wanted again, which is why I asked you whether you were sure, absolutely sure, about taking it all on. But Sarah's very independent. She's about and around, if you see what I mean. I'd hate you to go off to Burma or wherever, feeling chipper, and then get a letter saying she's met someone else.'

'Is there someone else, Mrs Layton?'

'Someone adored from a distance?' Mildred smiled. 'I simply

can't say. Sarah's never taken me into her confidence. She's always been the quiet introspective type. But she's pretty determined and she can be impulsive. Susan's the one who feels the need to settle down to an orderly kind of existence. I was never absolutely happy about her choice of Teddie and I'm pretty sure she ended up regretting it. But they both rushed into it and I think a lot of her trouble is that she's feeling guilty about him.'

'Guilty?'

'I believe that when you turned up she realized what a mistake she'd made. Perhaps she feels it showed in her letters to him.'

'Did she ever say anything to you, Mrs Layton?'

Mildred had folded her arms but still played with the necklace. The movements of her fingers were more assured.

'No, Dicky. And don't run away with any ideas. It's all much too complicated. You seem to have made your choice anyway and apparently it's not Susan. Let's go in. I'm dying for a drink and I'm sure you are. At least we can drink to your safe return. *That*'s the important thing.'

The verandah was now unoccupied. Everyone had gone indoors to avoid the sight of the heap of sacking. Weeks later, sitting on an empty upturned ammunition box and resting his pad of paper on his knee, Dicky ended a letter to Sarah: 'There was a lot I wanted to talk about that last afternoon in Pankot but somehow everything conspired against it. My fondest love to you. And to Susan. And of course to my godson.'

II

She woke to the strong sweet smell of roses and did not need to open her eyes to know that they were yellow. In any case if she opened her eyes the scent and the roses would almost certainly go away, dismal proof that she was only dreaming them. She turned her head and slowly let the white room come into focus. The scent was fainter but it had not gone and she guessed she was not alone.

She looked round into the massed pale yellow velvet petals of the flowers which Sarah had placed on the pillow and was holding there with her left hand.

'Hello, Barbie. Are you feeling better? I've brought these from the garden. I remembered the yellow were your favourite.'

Barbie smiled and nodded.

Her voice, of which she had been proud, had become a humiliation. It was weak on the consonants. It cracked on the vowels. When she spoke she could feel the vibrations in the tight drum of her chest.

'Thank you, Sarah.' She tried to whisper it but the first vowel betrayed her. One had to face it. 'My silly old voice,' she said in two registers at once. 'It seems to have packed up on me. Some will think it a blessing if it keeps me quiet.'

The roses trembled as the fractured sounds hit them.

'You've been here before, haven't you?'

'Once or twice. But you were very sleepy.'

'You were in uniform. You brought me a bottle of barley water. I still have some. Would you like a glass?'

'No, but I'll give you one.'

'It would oil the cogs.' She watched from the pillow-bower of roses while Sarah poured barley water. Helped into a drinking position she could feel her own backbone against Sarah's hand. Her wasted body filled her with revulsion; in the room it alone lacked the security of shape and form and definition. It was like something the bed had invented, got tired of and left half-finished to fend for itself.

'I shall be glad to get out of here,' she said when Sarah had resettled the pillows to support her in the half-upright position the nurses were always trying to keep her in, in an unequal struggle against the gravitational pull of the foot of the bed and the mattress under her bony buttocks. 'There is something about a hospital bedroom that drains one of self-confidence. One feels anonymous.'

'You have your name on the door.'

'Have I? That's handy. It minimizes error. Was I in this room when you came before?'

'No, in one with three other beds but only one was occupied. By a Mrs MacGregor whose husband was an engineer.'

'I remember curtains round the bed with sprigs of forget-me-nots and scarlet pimpernels. And a horrible thing like a bomb. But it was only the oxygen. Why have I been moved to a room on my own?'

'Captain Travers thought you'd like it. You've got a private balcony. When you're better you'll be able to sit out and not be bothered by people.'

'People have never bothered me. It's been the other way round. Was I very ill?'

'You had pneumonia.'

'I know. But Edwina had pneumonia. She wasn't in hospital more than three weeks. I've been that already.'

'A little over.'

'Shall I be here much longer?'

'A week or two I expect. You're much better today. You'll make strides now.'

'Was Clarissa very cross?'

'What could she have to be cross about?'

'Cross with me for being ill.'

'She visited you. She wouldn't visit you if she were cross, now would she?'

'I don't remember her visiting me. I only remember you.'

'I expect you were asleep.'

'Will she have me back?'

'Of course she will. There isn't any question.'

'I thought Dr Travers might be keeping me here because he knows Clarissa's *had* me.'

Sarah smiled. At the turn of phrase presumably. It was what soldiers said. I've had it. You've had it. It was very expressive.

'And she knows the mission's had me too. I showed her the letter.'

'You mustn't worry about Clarissa.'

'Is my trunk still safe?'

Sarah nodded.

'Still in the mali's shed?'

'Yes, still there.'

'Does your mother know?'

Sarah shook her head.

Barbie looked at the roses. 'It was wrong of me getting you to hide it. But Clarissa would have drawn the line at the trunk. It had better go to Jalal-ud-din's. If we could move it one day when your mother's out.'

'Mother's unlikely to look in the mali's shed. Anyway it's

doing no harm. Whenever you want it it's there. You only have
to ask me or mali.'

'No. Your mother will get to know. And you'll be in trouble.
There are some little toys in it. Things the children made for me.
If I give you the key you could get them out. The baby could
have them when he's older. The mali could keep the trunk.
Everything else in it can be thrown away.'

'You said the trunk was your history.'

'Lying here one has no history. Just each hour of the day.' She
grinned.

'Yes you do. And you needn't worry about the trunk or about
Clarissa having you back. Just concentrate on getting well.'

'Is Susan getting well?'

Sarah nodded.

'And the baby is all right?'

'The baby's fine.'

'Is Susan quite near me?'

'You can see the nursing home from your balcony.'

'Then I'll sit out there and transmit prana to her.'

'What's prana?'

'The goodness in the air. You breathe it in. And out. Like
smelling roses. Like blowing dandelions.'

'Like what?'

'Blowing dandelions.'

It was one of the more difficult words. It came out so distorted
she doubted that Sarah would understand. Her eyelids felt heavy.
She let them close just for a second or two.

When she opened them Sarah had gone, the roses were in
a vase and the lights and shadows in the room had rearranged
themselves as they did in theatres to denote the passage of time.

The red hospital blanket round her knees and chest reminded
her of Christmas. Seated in the wheelchair at the open doorway
between room and balcony she might have been surrounded by
shiny pink-and-blue-wrapped parcels and by children waiting
for their turn to climb on her knee and whisper secret longings
and desires. She could smell pines. Through half-closed eyes she
could transmute the gold of sunshine on the leaves of the trees
into snow and ride the sleigh of the chair high above the roofs
of the hospital and the carved balconies of the bazaar and the

spire of St John's. Santa Barbie: leaving a lingering glittering frosty scent of her own magical intrusion.

We could go down to Ranpur she had said to do some Christmas shopping. Oh I shall never go to Ranpur again Mabel answered at least not until I'm buried.

The reply had begun to trouble her with its vagueness, its curious subtlety. Its element of prophecy.

She opened her eyes fully and through the balcony rails saw the girl walking in afternoon sunshine along the tarmac pathway from the nursing home. Sarah with roses. The girl looked up. The red blanket had caught her eye. She waved and came on. It seemed a long time before Barbie heard the door open in the room behind her and the little Anglo-Indian nurse say, 'You have a visitor.'

'Hello, Sarah,' she croaked. 'You see. I'm on the mend except for this wretched voice. If you wheel me in we can see each other. There's only room for one on the balcony.'

Roses descended upon her lap and she felt the chair grasped and tip up as Sarah began to negotiate it back into the room. When they were settled, seated together at the window, Barbie said, 'You've been visiting Susan. How is she?'

'Much better. Captain Samuels thinks she can come out quite soon. And incidentally Captain Travers seems very pleased with *you*.'

'Have you seen him?'

'On the way in. He thinks about another week will do it. Perhaps two to be on the safe side.'

'Did he mention my voice?'

'No. Why are you worried about your voice?'

'That's what Doctor Travers says when I ask him. But listen to it. It gets no better.'

'It's only a bit hoarse. You'll be all right when you're on your feet and walking in the fresh air.'

'I hope so. It would be awful to lose one's voice. For me, like a painter to lose his sight, a musician his hearing. It was never a singing voice of course, but it carried in the schoolroom. Mr Cleghorn said it had a note of command which he advised me to develop because it was very important for a teacher. When I was a girl I took elocution. I called it electrocution. My mother paid for me to have the lessons to help me in later life and in her decline she often asked me to read to her. You put such expression into it, Barbie, she used to say. It was the best of times, it was the worst of times. She died half way through *A Tale of Two Cities*.'

She lifted the bunch of roses to smell them. Sarah took the opportunity to speak.

'Barbie, I shan't see you again for a while. I'm going back with Aunty Fenny to Calcutta to stay with her. We're going tomorrow. When Susan's okay she and Mother are going to join us so that we can all go to Darjeeling, probably some time in September.'

Barbie let the roses fall. Her body seemed to have reacted of its own accord in advance of the sense of dismay, of loss, which was slower, only just now taking hold of her.

She said, 'What about the baby?'

Sarah gathered some of the dropped petals from around the bunch on Barbie's lap.

'Well of course they'll bring ayah and the baby with them. Captain Samuels thinks it would be better for Susan not to go back to familiar surroundings right away, so tomorrow after we've gone Mother's going to close Rose Cottage and move into Flagstaff House until Susan's discharged. Then when Captain Samuels gives the word they'll come down to Calcutta.'

'Close Rose Cottage?'

'Only until we get back. Perhaps for Christmas. We're sending Mahmoud on leave but the mali and his wife will look after things.'

'Who is this Captain Samuels?'

Sarah paused. 'A very intelligent man,' she said.

'But the journey, Sarah, with a tiny baby.'

Sarah dropped the petals into a wastebin.

'I don't think the baby will come to any harm. He's quite a tough customer. And I think we can depend on Mother to travel in the maximum comfort and with every available amenity.'

'I'm sorry. It's none of my business. I was looking for objections. Because I don't want *you* to go.'

'I must be going in any case. I've promised Aunt Fenny.'

'I didn't know your Aunt Fenny was in Pankot.'

'She came up to help Mother. You know what some families are. In trouble they close the ranks and stick together.'

'Wouldn't it be better for her to wait? Until you can *all* go, with Susan?'

'She can't be away from Uncle Arthur any longer. Well. That's one answer. But I'm the culprit really. They've decided I need a holiday.'

'Are you ill?'

'No, Barbie. Do I look ill?'

'No. No, you don't. You look tired but that's not surprising. Oh, I should be glad for you, shouldn't I? You liked Calcutta.'

Sarah nodded. She was looking at the roses, still touching them, making sure all the loose petals had been gathered.

Barbie observed the pale gold lights in the girl's hair. She felt possessive in her love. She moved a hand to make contact, but Sarah misunderstood. She must have thought the movement of her own fingers among the petals had begun to irritate the invalid. She took her hands away, folded them in under her arms but stayed bent forward in the chair, her knees almost touching the red blanket.

'Will you visit Captain Merrick when you're in Calcutta?' Barbie asked.

Sarah shook her head.

'He's probably gone anyway. To somewhere where they fit artificial limbs. I believe they get on to it quite quickly nowadays.'

'But he's only just had the amputation.'

'It's two months ago.'

'I've lost track of time,' Barbie said. 'What will happen to him?'

'I suppose they'll find him a job somewhere either in the police or the army. He wouldn't be the only officer around with a disability. Why?'

'I've been thinking about him.'

'Have you, Barbie?'

'Lying here one has little to do but think. I've been thinking about something you said after you'd been in Mirat. Do you remember? We were sitting under the pine tree and you said you thought Captain Merrick had got it all wrong about the men he arrested in Mayapore, the ones who were supposed to have attacked Miss Manners. You said it would be terrible not just for them but for him, to have got it wrong. but never see it, never believe it.'

'Yes, I did, didn't I? What made you think of that?'

At last Sarah looked up from her study of the roses. But her eyes were not lit by more than polite inquiry. Perhaps it hadn't been her interest in the question that made her look up but her arrival at the end of an earlier train of thought which enabled her to.

'I've been wondering whether *I* was wrong, about Mabel, about Mabel's wishes,' Barbie said. 'And if I were whether it will be more terrible knowing it than not knowing it. Wouldn't it be more terrible for Mr Merrick to *know* he'd got it wrong?'

'Perhaps, for a moment. But better in the end surely?'

'Better to know and to say, I got it wrong? But everything that happened as a result of him getting it wrong would be on his conscience for ever wouldn't it? There's nothing he can do now to put it right, is there? Even if those men have been released from prison since.'

'Wouldn't that be better than having *no* conscience?' Sarah looked down at the roses again. 'Don't let's talk about Ronald Merrick. Let's talk about what's bothering you.'

'It's connected really,' Barbie said. She could observe the fair head again without disguising the depth of her feeling. 'Everything seems to be. Even spoons. I think it's this room. It addles my mind. The walls are so white and bare.' If she shut her eyes she could feel how everything depended now on the pumping of her old heart and the strange electrical impulses of her brain which switched from one picture of her life to another, encapsulating time and space, events, personalities. 'I saw her,' she said. 'I was very frightened because I heard her first and mistook her for Mabel. When she left I heard the car. It went towards West Hill.'

She had closed her eyes. Now she opened them and found Sarah watching her.

'People said it was a joke, didn't they? When her name appeared in the book. They said it must be someone playing a joke in bad taste. But I saw her. It couldn't have been anyone else. The way she talked and stood, genuflected. You could see she had held a position of importance in public life. I wished I could have seen her face. But there was this veil and the old-fashioned topee with a wide brim. And she sat in front of me. When she looked to this side, that side, there was just a shadow of a face.'

'Who are you talking about, Barbie?'

'Miss Manners's aunt, Lady Manners. You met her in Srinagar. Your houseboat was moored close to hers. Everybody else was embarrassed, because of the child being there. But you –' She stopped. Sarah was looking at her in the oddest manner. 'Have I only imagined it?'

'Imagined what, Barbie?'

'That you crossed the water and talked to her. And saw the child. Yes, I'm sorry. I remember now. It seemed to me the sort of thing you would have done, so I imagined you doing it. The picture was very vivid. All that hot sun and deep green water. Fronds of a kind of willow hanging above the roof of the houseboat. And the child crying. Motherless, fatherless child. But it had Krishna as well as Jesus. I think Miss Manners must have been rather a special person. She could have got rid of it. I mean before it was born. People would have praised her. And her aunt would not now live in obscurity. But –'

'But what?'

'Obscurity or not she was very proud. You could tell. Not of herself, of her niece. My father once said to me, Barbie, there is a conspiracy among us to make us *little*. He was tipsy at the time of course. There was a stage of his tipsiness between the initial release and the final moroseness and anger when he sang and talked and said things like that. My mother told a neighbour whom she wished to impress with our superiority, "My husband has a lot of the poet in him." After that I used to watch him hard. I imagined the poet in him as an unborn twin, one that could be cruel to him as well as kind. Like the demon spirit of a party. After he said that about there being a conspiracy among us to make us little I thought of the demon spirit or poet as a giant bottled up inside him and turned into a dwarf by a spell which only liquor could break.'

Still gazing down at the fair head, bent above the roses, she continued. 'My father's life was full of anomalies but so was my mother's. For instance she was a great church-goer. Her piety on Sundays inspired me as a little girl. It was through her local connections that I got into a church school and stayed on as a pupil-teacher. But when I was grown and told her I wished to serve God in the foreign missions, the missions to India, she was very shocked. Oh, Barbie, she said, not among heathens!

She made me feel my ambitions were wrong, almost sinful. Perhaps they were. Even when she was dead and I'd summoned the courage to apply I went to my first interview as if I knew I was doing something to be ashamed of. I huddled into myself. I walked through the streets hunched. I made myself small. To slip through the mesh of people's disapproval and not to be noticed. When I sailed for India I thought: Now I can be large again. But that has not been possible. One may carry the Word, yes, but the Word without the act is an abstraction. The Word gets through the mesh but the act doesn't. So God does not follow. Perhaps He is deaf. Why not? What use are Words to Him?'

Encouraged by Sarah's quietness she touched the girl's head, smoothed the soft helmet of hair. Almost indiscernibly, but unmistakably felt by the hand, the girl inclined her head briefly into the caress.

'I shall never see you again!' Barbie cried suddenly. 'Don't go to Calcutta!'

Sarah laughed: a girl embarrassed by a foolish and importunate elder. 'Oh, Barbie, I'm not going away for good!'

'No.'

There are these spoons, she wanted to say; and began to – but mercifully her voice gave out and she was saved the indignity of rambling on about such nonsense. Apostle spoons! She grinned and shook her head. Her voice came back. 'You'll write to me if you have time, won't you? And if you meet a Mister Studholme . . . but that's unlikely. Very unlikely. He's Mission. Although very important.'

'I don't think Aunt Fenny knows any mission people. I'll try to write though.'

Barbie began to tell her about the mission headquarters in Calcutta but as she did so she tuned out of her voice and into the soundless echo of the white room.

There is a letter in my handbag from Colonel Trehearne, the echo announced for her. The walls shone with an extra purity as if they had absorbed the simplicity of Colonel Trehearne's kindness and the clarity of Clarissa's eyes. There was a letter for you, Barbie, Clarissa had said standing by the bedside like a caryatid supporting the weight of a celestial esteem which might have weighed a lesser person down. I brought it with me. On the back of the envelope there was an engraving in shiny blue ink of the Pankot insignia. My Dear Miss Batchelor. Two huge epergnes floated across the room. Empty. Awaiting a cargo of apostles. 'There is your sou'wester too,' Clarissa said, 'but I didn't bring it. Captain Coley found it in his driveway.' 'They were out,' Barbie whispered. 'They?' 'He and his servant.' Clarissa did not ask why Barbie should visit Captain Coley. Probably she knew from Colonel Trehearne. But spoons were not mentioned by either of them.

The spoons and the note to Captain Coley must still be in her room at the rectory bungalow locked in the drawer of the writing-table where she had put them after getting home soaked. 'It was kind of Captain Coley to return my hat,' she said. Clarissa said, 'Why should he not? Your name is in it.' Enclosed by white walls she was aware of risk: her own, not Coley's, not Mildred's. The return of the sou'wester had been a master-stroke. She would never again be able to put it on her head without feeling the pressure of Mildred's contempt. They had seen the signifi-cance of the sou'wester and coupled it with the mystery of the missing spoons. They must have known they had not been alone. Coley might care. Mildred did not.

'I must go now, Barbie,' Sarah was saying. 'Is there anything you want?' She shook her head, thinking: I want you to help me find Lady Manners so that I can give her the spoons as a present for the child. I want us to sit together in St John's and wait for her and for you to say, Lady Manners, this is my friend Barbara Batchelor, a holy woman from the missions. Or to go with me into the region of West Hill where the rich Indians from Ranpur have summer houses in which they live for a few months of the year without being bothered by us or with us and are seldom seen in the bazaar, having their own sources or sending servants into ours for the products of the West. We could go into West Hill (curiously named) and search and ask. But you are going to Calcutta. And in any case haven't met her after all, it seems. Or have you? This time you didn't comment.

'Good-bye, Barbie.'

'Good-bye, Sarah.'

The girl bent and kissed her. Barbie put up her arms. Sarah submitted to the embrace. Then she rearranged the blankets.

'Shall I wheel you back to the balcony?'

'Please. Then I can watch you go down the path.'

'I don't go that way, Barbie, I'm afraid.'

'Is Captain Beauvais waiting for you with a car?'

'No. I'm getting a tonga.'

'Oh, but I was forgetting. Clarissa told me Captain Beauvais has gone.'

'Yes, and now I must.'

She felt the girl's head close to her own again and breath coming against her cheek as though she were an old yellow candle being blown out very gently. Some time later she was surprised to see the girl on the tarmac pathway, having walked out of her way to wave, and waving, and then coming back towards the building to follow the path round to the front where a tonga would take her on the first stage of the long journey to Calcutta.

She looked at the familiar panorama and after a while pulled the blanket up to her throat and tucked her chin in. The sun dipped below the overhanging roof of the balcony and shone through her eyelids. The little Anglo-Indian nurse had never left her on the balcony so long. Perhaps she had forgotten her.

She pictured herself abandoned there, until dark, and beyond; for many days, through the changes of season, from one decade to another, while the building slowly crumbled round her, leaving her isolated, high up on a pillar of jagged but stubborn masonry, enthroned, wrapped in the scarlet blanket, with a clear view across the uninhabited valley to the ruins of the church of St John.

III

Isobel Rankin's generosity to Mildred in allowing her to move into Flagstaff House and close Rose Cottage did not escape criticism. Lucy Smalley, more or less indistinguishable nowadays from the potted palms and stained napery of Smith's Hotel, said it was a bit odd that a place could be closed, however temporarily, and yet escape the net of the accommodations officer who she swore slept with requisition orders under his pillow in the hope of being woken in the middle of the night by one of his spies and tipped off about a bungalow that had been left empty for a day or two, so that before daylight a notice could be tacked to the door denying entry to its rightful owners.

'I heard about Nicky Paynton's decision to go home within a few hours of her making it,' Lucy complained, 'and I rang him at once, because Tusker wouldn't, and he said he had a waiting list and had already made provisional allocations. He was barely civil.'

But Lucy Smalley's disappointment did not prevent her turning up several weeks later at Nicky Paynton's auction party, wandering from room to room in the place she had briefly visualized herself and Tusker moving into, and wanly watching the auctioneer – Nicky Paynton herself – hammering down the familiar detritus of an Anglo-Indian career.

The most prized items were those which had practical use, scarcity value and a comparatively short life – a radiogram, a refrigerator, a portable wireless set, an electric iron and an ironing board, two electric fires, an electric fan. After these, for which the bidding was on a tense but modest level, Nicky had success in getting rid of crockery, cutlery, glasses, two alarm clocks, blankets, sheets and pillow-cases, a picnic basket, camp equipment, and assorted thermos flasks which were a godsend on the trains packed with ice or filled with decent drinking water. Lowest on the list of desirable things were the ornamental coffee tables, the Benares trays, numdah rugs, vases and ornaments which for most of the people who could find room for them would be replicas of those they already had.

Finally there was the stuff which in other circumstances might have ended its days in a modest house in Surrey, and still might, although not in the possession of Colonel and Mrs Paynton. The Payntons themselves had bought it at an auction in Rawalpindi. It had spent quite a number of years in storage, and on loan, during the periods when Nicky and Bunny were moving too frequently from one station to another for it to go with them. A mahogany sideboard, elegantly proportioned, a mahogany dining-table (with two leaves) and a dozen imitation Georgian chairs, plus two armed servers, were the chief items on this particular list. Supplementary to it were two wing chairs covered in rather murky but genuine tapestry – one man-size and the other woman-size. These chairs, Nicky announced, had belonged to the late General Sir Horace and Lady Hamilton-Wellesley-Gore and one of them had been sat in by the Prince of Wales when he toured India in 1921.

'They were snitched from under my nose at the 'Pindi auction,' Nicky explained, 'by a simply frightful chap with pots of money. He turned up next year at the same beano in Gwalior and without telling me Bunny played him for them at poker and the next thing I knew they arrived on the doorstep. So what am I bid? No reserve price. Going for a song.'

Maisie Trehearne called out a figure which her husband didn't hear. He called out a lower one and under the screen of the ensuing laughter Clara said to Nicky, 'I want the chairs.' She doubled Maisie's figure.

'You must be mad,' Nicky said. 'But I'm not saying no.'

The chairs were knocked down to Clara Fosdick. Her sister in Ranpur wouldn't be pleased – she already housed some of Clara's and Freddie's old furniture – but these were chairs Clara and Nicky had sat in, many a winter evening, over a pine-log fire listening to the news.

When the auction was over the dining-room furniture was still unsold, but Nicky's farewell party got under way merrily enough. In the next few days the stuff that had been auctioned off would be collected and removed, leaving the two women bereft of most of the things that made the bungalow into a home. But that was all to the good, they felt. Their departure from a place in which nothing belonged to either of them would come as a relief and with luck (from Clara's point of view) they would have a few days together in Ranpur, perhaps more because although five days was all the notice Nicky would get of a flight from Ranagunj she had to be prepared for postponements. Her final departure might be a relief as well. Already, at the height of the party, they were both on tenterhooks, and old Fariqua had obviously been at the rum bottle.

For the party he had put on the white trousers, tunic, Ranpur sash and head-dress that he used to wear to go in to mess when Bunny dined there, but the pugree was indifferently swathed and the fan of muslin which should have been as perky as a cock's comb had flopped over. As he got drunker he grew lugubriously into the role of skeleton at the feast, chief mourner at the wake for Bunny Paynton, the only one with a long face, sodden with the liquor that buoyed other people up.

'To look at Fariqua,' Lucy Smalley said, with what was becoming after the years of her social frustration an unerring sense for saying the right thing at the wrong time, 'you'd think Nicky was going to invite bids for him as well.'

She was saved the rebuke that Maisie Trehearne might have administered by the arrival of the general's lady, Isobel Rankin, to whom all heads turned, like compass needles to a magnetic north. There was nothing unusual in this ritual observance, this metaphorical doffing of caps and bending of knees, but this morning a special intensity attached to it, because of certain rumours that had been taking shape and seriously disturbing the station's sense of balance and proportion and were now contributing a ground-swell of uneasiness to the determined light-heartedness of the occasion.

Nicky had announced her decision to go home in mid-July. Thereafter, slowly and quietly she had made her dispositions, settled her affairs, transferred money to London, paid her debts, written to Dora Lowndes to warn her and to advise her to say nothing to the boys until she got a cable from Clara Fosdick confirming her departure. She had also written to her friends in India and given them Dora Lowndes's address. By the middle of August she was ready to take the last step. The air-force liaison officer on Dick Rankin's staff told her he would start pulling strings the moment she said the word. For a week she did not say it and it began to look as if she might change her mind at the last moment. But it was during this week that the rumours were first heard and by the end of it there seemed little doubt that there was more than a grain of truth in them. If Nicky had been wavering her mind was now abruptly made up again. She rang Wing-Commander Pearson and asked him to pull the first string on the last day in August. She announced her auction and fare-well party for that same day.

The rumours which had encouraged Nicky to stick to her decision to go home had begun at area headquarters as a result of the circulation of curiously worded documents from higher authorities about reallocation of areas of military responsibility; innocent enough on the surface and apparently without refer-ence or application to the military hierarchy established at Pankot. This hierarchy was still in effect the old Ranpur Com-mand whose authority, in spite of erosion here and there, extended over large stretches of the province's territory.

But between the lines of the documents' oblique phraseology casual references acquired dangerously direct meanings. Among the senior members of Dick Rankin's staff the junior officers detected signs of that alert fascination which people in high places cannot disguise when first glimpsing a future upheaval which they know they are personally too distinguished and secure to be adversely affected by.

What had emerged was an image of Pankot stripped of a proportion of its powers as a central seat of military control and administration. How large a proportion could only be guessed at but since it was human nature to adopt a pessimistic view of any rearrangement from above the guess was that for 'a proportion of' one had to read 'most of'. Once such a guess had been made the rumours proliferated, some of them disagreeably backed by mounting evidence that the guess was correct: rumours that the old Ranpur Command was to be hacked up into several areas and redistributed on a geographical rather than a viable military basis between Central and Eastern Commands, that Pankot would be separated from Ranpur and become a training and rest centre with a Brigadier as its area commander; that a new OTS was to be established, most of whose cadets would be Indian; that the old Governor's summer residence which dominated the height of East Hill and had been closed throughout most of the war, was to be reopened – not, as Isobel Rankin had often proposed, as a convalescent home for wounded British and Indian officers of all three services, but as a leave centre for American troops of non-commissioned rank. Only in the bazaar where the rumours were quick to penetrate was the latter news greeted with enthusiasm. One or two ladies swore there had already been a rise in prices to prepare people for the new era of native prosperity.

'We shall all have to get used to walking,' one of them said, 'because the cost of a tonga up the hill to the club, should one manage to find one not already loaded with GIs, will be quite beyond *our* pockets.' But on second thoughts, she went on, one would probably stop going to the club because it would be crowded with American officers – those in charge of the leave centre – and perhaps with top-sergeants, whatever species *they* were. If the cinema was any guide even the sergeants in the American army seemed to get saluted and to call officers by their

Christian names, so they would all be at the club with their hands in their pockets, their bottoms hanging out of their shiny trousers and cigars in their mouths, getting drunk, breaking the place up and bringing in Eurasian girls.

Moreover, she said, with Pankot's military role downgraded there would be fewer and fewer *young* British officers doing a stint on area headquarters staff between regimental and active staff appointments. From area headquarters as it now existed the top and junior levels would be creamed off and the men would be off to brighter places. Probably only men like Major Smalley could expect to survive from the old to the new regime, if such a thing could be called survival. And Flagstaff House would be occupied by some doddery dugout Brigadier. In Mildred's father's day, the Ranpur Command had carried a Lieutenant-General's hat. It still carried a major-general's.

Which brought one to the Rankins. What glamorous appointment would fall into their laps? Already people had it on good authority that they were for Mountbatten's staff and the fleshpots of Ceylon; that they were for the India Office and home; for Washington on a military mission, for Moscow, for Cairo, for Persia; Simla at the very least. Two days before Nicky's party Dick Rankin had been driven down to Ranpur to be flown to Delhi. When he got back perhaps he would have fuller details of the station's fate and of his and Isobel's brighter prospects.

And here was Isobel, arriving too late for the auction, alight and vibrant with both power and discretion, giving nothing away which was only comforting if it could be assumed that she had nothing to give and was as ignorant of what was in store as the least among those present.

She embraced Nicky in the centre of the crowded living-room, apologized for being late in a voice that carried above the resumed conversation and then without lowering her voice said, 'Where can we have a word?' which caused a tremor of delicious apprehension, a pause in the flow of talk. Nicky led her into the dining-room where the unsold table, chairs and sideboard already appeared to have lost their sheen.

'Nicky, I'm late because I waited for Mildred to get back from visiting Susan, but she rang and asked me to come along on my own and to warn you that she's bringing Susan with her.'

'Oh.' The two women looked at each other straight. 'Is Susan allowed out then?'

'It will be the first time.'

'A noisy party? What an extraordinary choice.'

'She wanted to come. She asked this Captain Samuels chap and apparently he said it was a first-rate idea. He hopes it's all right if he looks in too. I think he'll take her back, to save Mildred doing it.'

'I must say that's a bit cool, isn't it? I don't know Captain Samuels and it's a private farewell party not a therapy session. Is she really fit enough? I should hate a scene. That's why the trick-cyclist wallah insists on coming, isn't it? To be on hand if Susan throws a fit or does something odd.'

'He says she's well enough. In fact he's letting her out in a day or two. She'll be coming up to the House, so I can only assume he knows what he's doing. He thinks a party would be a good ice-breaker. Do you mind?'

'As long as it's only ice. Does she know about Bunny?'

'Yes. And she knows you're going home. That's why she wants to come. It's very sweet really.'

'I hope she's not going to be condoling,' Nicky said. She looked feverish.

'The thing to do is tell everybody before she gets here and prepare them to look as if they're acting naturally. Did you sell this dining-room stuff?'

'No.'

'Mildred may want it. Try to persuade her. She has a lot of plans for the cottage. In any case she could store it. I'd have it myself but God knows how much longer we'll be here or where we'll be going. What about getting Jalal-ud-din's man along? He might sell it like a shot to one of his rich Indian clients.'

'I'll see.'

They went back to the living-room, separated and passed the word that Mildred was bringing Susan and that Captain Samuels would be looking in, to take her back to the nursing home to save her mother going all that way herself when the party was over. Prepared for important general news this struck the guests as an anti-climax and it took a while for it to sink in and to be recognized as important too, important to the old Pankot if not to the one currently in a state of derangement of its own, which one had to hope would turn out to be as temporary as Susan Bingham's had proved. Curiosity and nostalgic affection began to flow out to her in advance of her arrival. Heads kept turning towards the door through which she would enter.

As she did, within ten minutes of the first warning, un-announced by any sound of tonga or car wheels that could have hushed the sound of talk and laughter; a step or so ahead of her mother, wearing a simple full-skirted dress of white with navy blue polka dots; to all appearances unchanged, a pound or two heavier perhaps but as pretty as ever, prettier if anything, and with that familiar flush on her cheeks which suggested some special happiness anticipated or re-encountered.

To look at her, as she greeted Nicky and her mother's other friends, was to doubt the truth of the accounts of her bizarre behaviour and to guess that no explanation of it would ever be had. It was as if it hadn't happened. No unhappy memory seemed to live behind her face. Her smile was not the smile of someone with a secret life. She was looking at the world as it was.

She said nothing, did nothing, that could be reckoned odd or interpreted as an indication that her mind was still clouded in any way by her illness and misfortunes. There were omissions, but were they significant? She did not mention the baby, but that could as easily be put down to a regard for other people's feelings as to anything sinister or threatening. She was punctilious in thanking Isobel Rankin for the invitation to Flagstaff House and said how much she was looking forward to it. Since the baby and the ayah were already installed there with Mildred one could surely assume that by 'looking forward' she meant glad to think she would see the baby again as well. In any case, Captain Samuels would not let her out if he had doubts about her attitude to the child.

She said she was also looking forward to the holiday in Dar-jeeling and Calcutta. She said she missed Sarah's visits but had had postcards and letters to make up for them. Out of Nicky's hearing she told Clara Fosdick how sorry she was about Briga-dier Paynton, about Nicky's decision to go home and about Clara herself leaving Pankot to go to live in Ranpur. She said she hoped Mrs Fosdick would come up to spend holidays with them at Rose Cottage.

Her mother had briefed her well. She knew about the rumours

of change and said it all sounded rather dreary. She asked Clarissa
Peplow how Mrs Batchelor was and seemed surprised to hear that
although much better she was still in hospital. Clarissa assumed
that in the case of Miss Batchelor's illness, Sarah – not Mildred –
had been Susan's informant.

She did not mention the dog, Panther. Maisie found the
opportunity to ask Mildred whether Susan knew the dog had
died and Mildred said she had had Samuels's permission to tell
her and had done so, without the gory details, and Susan had
taken it well but not referred to it again. If there were any forbidden subjects they were the dog and the baby. Was Dicky Beauvais
a third? Apparently not. She said, 'I had a letter from Dicky the
other day. He sounded a bit browned off. After all that rush he's
still stuck in Comilla waiting for a posting. I must remember to
tell Sarah because the letter was to us both.'

She moved gracefully, freely, perfectly at ease. She sipped her
drink as if she intended to make it last and had accepted it only
to be sociable. When Lucy Smalley suggested she should sit, not
tire herself standing, she laughed in a friendly way and said she
had sat enough in the last few weeks and needed exercise. She
went from group to group, watched but not shadowed by
Mildred who had shown only one sign of the strain she must
have been under when at a first attempt to raise a full cocktail
glass to her lips she spilt a few drops and waited (Clara Fosdick
noticed) for at least a minute before raising it again.

'How relieved Mildred must be to have Susan her old self
again,' Maisie Trehearne said.

'I wouldn't call it that,' Nicky replied, blowing smoke to one
side, holding her glass high to minimize the risk of her elbow
being jogged. 'Susan used to take up a position and let people
swarm round her. I've never seen her mingle in my life. But
that's what she's doing now. I'm half inclined to think the Jew-
boy trick-cyclist is cleverer than Mildred gives him credit for.'

What Nicky had observed, perhaps because she was more alert
to the shapes and patterns of her last party than any of her guests
could be, was true. If a change in Susan were to be noted it
would be this one: the free-ranging movement and presentation
of herself within the tableau. Before her illness she would have
stood herself at its centre, receiving tribute. Her new mobility
suggested that she was offering it, reaffirming her commitment

to a society she had lived in since childhood and had now returned to, after a brief but inexplicable withdrawal.

Interest in the unknown Captain Samuels, the Jew-boy trick-cyclist, mounted. Apart from Mildred no one at the party had ever met him and no one had been inquisitive enough to investigate him since hearing his name in connection with Susan. Mildred's attitude had summed up all one needed to know or feel about an RAMC analyst. The job was not one which could normally be taken seriously. No man who fitted the picture conjured by the name could be recalled from among the welter of new or itinerant faces at the club. Samuels probably kept himself to himself. Neither Beames nor Travers – who might have expressed professional if not personal opinions – had turned up. Both had been invited, but it was obviously a busy morning at the hospital.

Someone, perhaps its new owner, put a record on the radiogram: a selection from 'Chu Chin Chow'; but the record was so worn that only people close to the machine could make much of the tunes. Fariqua and the cook-boy Nazimuddin were bringing in plates of bridge sandwiches and canapés. Nicky called out, 'Food everybody. There'll be more in the dining-room in a minute so everyone just help themselves.' Several guests went through to relieve the crush in the living-room where there was a gradual rearrangement of groups which left Susan temporarily unattached. She took a sandwich from the plate offered none too steadily by the spectral Fariqua and went to stand a little apart by a window that gave her a view of the front verandah and compound.

In an instant her mother joined her and by chance or design interposed herself between her daughter and Lucy Smalley who had seen that Susan was alone and was approaching her. So even Lucy who was close to them was unable to say how Susan's cocktail glass fell out of her hand and splintered on the parquet floor. Later, considerably later, Lucy said she had always felt Susan dropped the glass deliberately. She couldn't say why she thought so but her intuition told her that this was what had happened. Mildred had been talking perfectly naturally to Susan, saying, 'Are you all right, darling? Not too tired?' and Susan had said also quite naturally but a bit testily, 'I'm fine.' And the next thing was the sudden sound of the breaking glass and a little cry from

Mildred; no sound, Lucy recalled, from Susan, but Mildred saying, 'Did I jog you?' And then the incident – if it could be called
an incident – was over.

There was a stain down Mildred's skirt. Susan stooped and
picked up the unbroken base of the glass and started to gather
the fragments. She handed them to the cook-boy who came to
help her and then stood up. 'My fault,' Mildred said, while Susan
apologized to Nicky for the mess.

Susan declined the offer of another drink and went to talk to
Mrs Stewart, Clarissa Peplow and Wing-Commander Pearson,
leaving her mother with Nicky who said, 'D'you want to sponge
that skirt?'

'It won't stain.'

'Then come into the dining-room and see if you want this
furniture.'

On their way past Susan Mildred spoke to her.

'I'm going into the next room for a moment. You'd better
keep an eye open for Captain Samuels. I don't think he knows
anybody.'

'Is this him now?' Clarissa asked. They turned to look.

Susan said, 'Oh, yes. That's Sam.'

Nicky Paynton threaded her way back towards a door that
stood open to the side of the verandah. 'Come in,' she shouted
when still a few feet away. 'I'm Nicky Paynton, the one who's
throwing this shin-dig.' She pushed her hand out at him and kept
it there until he relieved her, as it were, of its weight. The noise
in the room had begun to subside directly it became clear why
Nicky was making her way towards this part of the room. Here
was the stranger: the Jew-boy trick-cyclist. The noise diminished
to such a degree that the sounds of merriment in the dining-
room seemed to belong to a different party, almost a different
world; one safe from such an intrusion. Astonishment more than
curiosity caused the hush accentuated by the continuing drone
of a male voice which, finding itself solo, ceased for a few seconds
and then resumed, nudging the general conversation slowly back
to life.

Captain Samuels was slender, fair-haired. He looked down on
Nicky from above average height. He did not smile. When she
let go of his hand he did not let it fall but lowered it carefully.
He did not attempt any of the opening gambits which a guest

might have used in the special circumstances which had brought him to the party. He did not appear to have spoken at all. He gave the impression of being a man who had dispensed with casual physical responses as time-wasting.

The image of the Jew-boy trick-cyclist was completely shattered. He was remote, patrician; in the opinion of most of the women present disturbingly, coldly handsome. It was a shock to see, on closer inspection, how young he must be. His youthfulness made the attention he instantly commanded seem, to those who were giving it, as disagreeable to them as a personal affront would be: the more so because he did not appear to be conscious of any obligation to conduct himself with that air of apology for *being* young which was usually considered part of a young man's charm when in the company of his elders.

Theoretically, Nicky might have been said to lead him into the room. In practice she went ahead to prepare a way for him to use. At the end of it stood Isobel Rankin. He took his time reaching her.

'May I introduce Captain Samuels?' Nicky said. 'Captain Samuels, Mrs Rankin, the wife of our area commander.'

They murmured how-do-you-do to one another.

'Are you related to friends of ours at home, Myra and Issy Samuels?' Isobel asked him, after he had declined the drink which Nazimuddin offered on a tray.

He observed her very closely.

'Sir Isaac Samuels?'

'Yes.'

'No. He is no relation.'

'But I gather you know him.'

'Professionally. I've met Lady Myra at Chester Square.'

'If you've met Issy professionally does that mean you're interested in tropical medicine too? If so you're in the right place. How long have you been in India?'

'Since the middle of May.'

'And in Pankot?'

'Since the end of May.'

'Really? As long as that!'

Listeners, hitherto fascinated by the social connection through mutual friends of the general's lady and the young army-doctor, now recognized a rebuke. Captain Samuels had neither

sent in his card nor signed Isobel Rankin's book outside Flagstaff
House: an essential step for an officer to take if he wanted to be
considered officially on-station. In the old days for an officer to
have been on-station since May and not to have signed the book
by the end of August would have been unthinkable. Nowadays,
with so many people coming and going and holding only temporary appointments the ritual was not so strictly observed, but
for a man appointed to the staff of the hospital not to have
observed it was still a serious omission, the result either of sheer
ignorance or, which was worse and presumably the case here,
indifference.

'I know absolutely nothing about psychological medicine,'
Isobel continued when it was clear that Captain Samuels had no
comment to make. 'I don't suppose Guy Charlton does either.'
She referred to the chief medical officer, Beames's military counterpart, who was new on-station himself. 'So I imagine you
pretty well run your own show. Are you a Freudian or a Jungian?
Isn't that what one is supposed to ask?'

For the first time Captain Samuels allowed himself a flicker of
emotion: it seemed to be amusement.

'People do,' he said. 'Personally I find Reich's ideas on the
subject of considerable interest.'

'And what does or did Mr Reich say?'

'Any answer I could give would be an over-simplification.'

'That would be the only kind I would understand. So do
tell us.'

Again he studied her. But Isobel Rankin had never yet been
quelled by a look and wasn't now. He glanced at Nicky, at
Colonel and Mrs Trehearne; briefly at Lucy and Tusker Smalley
who had joined the group; either sizing them up or politely
including them in the conversation.

'One must draw a distinction between analysis and treatment.
Whatever the cause of a neurosis the psychotherapist is concerned with a patient's ability to relax, physically. This is a
simple extension of Reich's belief that the human orgasm is
a major contributory factor to physical and mental health, but
the corollary need not be that all neuroses are rooted in sexual
repression.'

Several seconds went by before Tusker Smalley went red in
the face and said, 'Good God!'

Isobel Rankin glanced at him as if to stop him from making an issue of an officer having dared mention such things in front of women. The smile on her face was perhaps a little set, but she directed it again at Captain Samuels.

'What particular branch of tropical medicine interests you?'

'The amoebic infection of the bowels known as amoebiasis.'

'Oh, yes. What interests you so much about it? Surely it's of relatively minor importance? It's easily cured I gather. Is it one of Issy's pet subjects?'

'I wouldn't say so. But then I've come to the conclusion that in general English physicians aren't as interested in it as perhaps they might be, considering how large a tropical empire we have. And I would disagree with you, Mrs Rankin, when you suggest it is easily cured. Since coming to India it's struck me that even diagnosis is a very hit and miss affair. I should say that quite a fair proportion of my psychiatric cases are suspect of chronic infection, but it is very difficult to arrange for a convincing check.'

'What are the symptoms, a permanent kind of gippy-tum?'

He smiled. 'It's rather different from amoebic dysentery. Unfortunately it can be contracted and carried for years until it eats through the walls of the bowels and invades more vital organs. At least that is a theory a few people have. Without a convincing check it tends to go undiagnosed and the symptoms aren't alarming. A general air of languor, as lassitude. A tendency to concentrate the mind rather obsessively in one direction.'

'Why is a convincing check so difficult?'

'I think I should not explain why. I shall get a reputation for indelicacy. I apologize if my earlier remarks caused any offence.'

He looked at his watch.

'Not at all, Captain Samuels. I asked a question and you answered it. I see you are pressed for time.'

'I have quite a full afternoon ahead.'

'Then I expect you want to ask Mrs Bingham if she's ready to leave. But you must come up to Flagstaff House one day and tell me about these theories of yours. I'm always interested to hear a young man talking on his subject. I'll ask Guy Charlton to bring you along.'

Samuels made no answer. A slight inclination of his head towards her was his sole acknowledgement of her invitation.

Several people in the group round them were astonished that Isobel Rankin had made it.

But having made it she ended the conversation by moving away. The group dispersed. He took the opportunity to look round the room. He did not appear to be interested in meeting anyone else. Eyes were averted if he chanced to look into them. Hints of extraordinary behaviour were already reaching people who had not heard the conversation. As soon as he saw Susan he went through the crowd towards her.

'Hello, Sam. Is it time?'

'If you're ready.'

She said she was. She introduced him to Clarissa, Mrs Stewart and Wing-Commander Pearson.

'I must say goodbye to Mrs Paynton,' she said. 'Will you come with me, Sam?'

He put a hand on her shoulder. The gesture, although brief, struck those who saw it as unnecessarily possessive. Susan belonged in the room. Samuels did not. But he was taking her away. She was allowing it; at least, the girl in the polka-dot dress was allowing it and it now occurred to the watchers that in a subtly disagreeable way the girl was not the Susan they knew at all but a creation of Captain Samuels, or a joint creation of the two of them, a person who had emerged from a secret process of pressure, duress, insinuation, God knew what. And God knew what they talked about, or whom they talked about, when they were alone during sessions of analysis or whatever it was called. As Samuels followed her his glance fell here and there upon faces as if he were looking for evidence of mental and emotional dis-orders of the kind he had presumed to uncover in *her* but blamed *them* for. He bore himself like a man taking someone out of an area of contagion.

'Mrs Paynton,' Susan was saying, 'thank you for letting me come to your party. I'll only say au revoir if that's all right.'

Holding glass and cigarette in one hand Nicky used the other to give her the half-embrace which had become part of her farewell party armour.

'Au revoir it is then, Susan. Probably true too. It could be ages before they pop me on to a plane.'

She nodded at Captain Samuels.

Mildred was waiting at the open doorway.

'Are you off now then, darling? Would you like me to come round this evening?'

'No, there's really no need. You must be bored stiff coming down every day, there's no reason to do it twice.'

That much was heard. Mildred went out with Susan and Captain Samuels. For a minute they stood talking on the veran-dah, then Samuels and Susan went down into the compound and climbed into the tonga that had been waiting. Mildred came back into the house, not through the doorway they had left by but through the main entrance. It was some time before she re-appeared in the living-room and by then the party was beginning to break up.

When Isobel's car arrived to take her and Mildred back to Flagstaff House she said to Nicky, 'You and Clara come back with us. There's nothing as depressing as an afternoon surrounded by the remains. We could have a rubber or two and wind down.'

'Fair enough. I'll get rid of the late-stayers.'

She did so by announcing that she was shutting up shop. Within ten minutes the house and compound were clear. Lucy and Tusker Smalley were the last to leave. Their tonga, they said, was missing.

'What bad luck you do have,' Nicky said. 'Shall I send Nazimuddin for one?'

'We can pick one up on the road, I expect,' Tusker said. Lucy had her eye on the Rankin car but Tusker waved to Nicky and started off down the steps and presently Lucy followed.

'Pankot *must* be changing,' Nicky said, coming back in. 'Poor Lucy and Tusker failed to cadge a lift. I'm sorry really. It spoils the shape of my last Pankot party.'

A limousine such as could be hired in Ranpur to drive leave and summer parties up into the hills and down again was coming along Flagstaff road which turned and twisted and was not easy for two large cars to negotiate if they met head on. But for them to do so was rare. Only Flagstaff House traffic used the road. In any case the general's car always took precedence over local traffic. Assuming this the naik-driver taking Isobel and her guests home was prepared to glide on and up and give the minimum of room to the limousine which he expected to pull over and come almost to a halt.

On the limousine's roof there was a luggage rack, piled high and covered by a rainproof sheet. Perhaps this extra weight gave the limousine's civilian driver the strange idea that his vehicle was the more important of the two, even though the furled flag on the bonnet of the general's car proclaimed that this was not the case. If he saw this symbol of the car's status he ignored it. He came on. At the last moment the naik-driver called a warning to his passengers and slammed on the brakes. The limousine sailed past. The general's car quivered under the pressure.

'My God!' Isobel said. 'The raving bloody lunatic. Who was it, Clara? Did you see?'

Clara had the offside window seat in the back.

'There were blinds down at the window, so I couldn't.'

'*Blinds?*'

The naik-driver had got out with squared shoulders and bunched fists. He thought the other driver would stop to apologize or argue. He looked forward to telling him off and earning a good mark in the Burra Memsahib's book who it was known liked men to be sharp on the draw. But the limousine sped on. It was already rounding the corner. He did not even have time to get its registration number.

'What do you mean, blinds, Clara? What was it? A damned hearse? What was it doing on Flagstaff road if it was?'

'Not a hearse. Just a car with blinds down.'

'Was there a crest?'

'I didn't see one.'

'The only people who drive with blinds down are Maharajahs.'

'Or their wives. Mostly their wives.'

'Well, if we've had a call from a spare maharajah and his harem he's got off on the wrong foot. Unless of course it was old Dippy Singh. *He's* as mad as a hatter. All right, Shafi. It wasn't your fault. Let's get on.'

At the end of the road the tarmac broadened, providing a turn-round outside an imposing iron gateway. There was a sentry. The guard-commander was also present as if he had recently been disturbed.

'Shafi, stop at the gate and ask guard-commander about that car.'

He did so. The sentry was already presenting arms. He

clattered. The guard-commander ran forward, came to attention and saluted.

Shafi spoke to him. Presently he said, 'He says the car stopped and a lady got out.'

'Yes, I heard.' She called over Shafi's shoulder in Urdu. 'What lady?'

'An English lady, memsahib. An old lady. She wore a topee. She came to sign the book, memsahib.'

'Thank you.'

She got out, went to the other sentry-box where the book was kept, on a shelf, chained. She was there for a few seconds and then came back and got in.

'Carry on, Shafi.'

As the car moved into the grounds she said, 'The first time wasn't a practical joke then. She's signed out. "Ethel Manners, *pour prendre congé*." '

There was a silence. Then Nicky Paynton laughed.

'That,' she said between gusts, '*that* has made the day for me. *Pour prendre congé*!'

She was still laughing when the car stopped under the great portico in front of which, in the centre of an immaculate lawn, in a circular bed of white chippings, stood the tall white flagpost, moored to the ground by ropes, like the mast of a ship. From this eminence great stretches of the Pankot valley were visible. Early-afternoon sunlight shone upon it. Before going inside Nicky Paynton stood for a moment, still shaken by spasms of laughter, and gazed. Then, turning her back on it, she opened her handbag, got out her handkerchief, dabbed at her lower lids and joined her friends for what might be their last game of bridge together.

It was. Nine days later, aching in every bone and deaf in both ears, she stepped out of a Dakota on to the tarmac of an RAF aerodrome and into the amazing unreality of the Wiltshire countryside.

IV

When October came Barbie stopped taking the spoons to the church with her. The old lady must have gone. She packed the spoons up, wrote a letter and asked Clarissa if one of the servants could take them to Commandant's House. Clarissa agreed. She had become solicitous. The next day Barbie had by hand a letter of acknowledgement from Colonel Trehearne. He asked her if she would do him the honour of dining with him on Ladies' Night in November.

For a day or two she did not reply because she knew she would not accept but while her letter of apology and thanks remained unwritten she was able to enjoy the pleasure the invitation had given her. Ankle-length black velvet, she thought; a brooch, no other jewellery. A special cropping of the hair and a set to add lustre to the soft natural waves on the crown of her head and forehead. Black slippers and a glittering black evening bag. Perhaps a velvet rose – crimson or purple – instead of a brooch. No. The brooch would be more distinguished. A gossamer-thin black silk chiffon stole to warm but not hide completely the marble of her arms and shoulders. For the journey there a cloak of the same black velvet as the dress but with a warm scarlet lining. Perhaps a gilt or silver chain for the clasp at the throat. Elbow-length gloves. White, these. Or black? White, if she wore the brooch. Black for the coloured velvet flower. And a fine lawn handkerchief sprinkled with cologne.

When her letter pleading unfitness had been sent she studied the reflection of her wasted bony body and the lank straight hair that needed cutting. In such a dress all you would see would be the wild untended head, the gaunt collar bone and corded wrinkled neck, the scarecrow arms, the tombstone teeth that were too big for her mouth. And hear what had once been a voice; a hoarse grating sound alternating between a crackling whisper and an uneven cry.

She put Colonel Trehearne's letter in the drawer of the portable writing-table where there already lay the letter from the bank and the letters and picture postcard from Sarah in Calcutta and Darjeeling. The letter from the mission which had arrived on the morning of the christening and the undelivered letter to Captain Coley she had destroyed. The picture postcard from Sarah showed the headquarters of the Bishop Barnard in Calcutta and was postmarked September 6 which was the day Mildred had left Pankot with Susan, the baby and the ayah, and the day before Captain Travers had let Barbie come back to the rectory bungalow.

'You'll recognize this,' Sarah had written on the back. 'I hope you're better. I'm better too, fit as they say for human consumption again. Love, Sarah.'

Like so much that had to do with Sarah the postcard was an enigma. Normally the only place you could buy the card was at the headquarters of the mission itself. But Sarah did not say whether she had been there.

Walking, she found it difficult to go further than St John's in one direction and Mr Maybrick's bungalow in the other. For the bazaar she sent out for a tonga and did not get down from it until it returned her to the rectory bungalow.

In the bazaar she had the wallah stop outside Jalal-ud-din's. The first time she did this a minute or two by before a ragged little chokra came bare-foot in search of an errand and an anna. But nowadays she was met at the outskirts by a dozen or more who ran behind the tonga advertising their prowess, willingness and honesty.

At first her own little boy had joined the opposition but, re-assured of her loyalty, now waited outside the store until she arrived. To reach her he had to fight his way through a thicket of limbs mostly sturdier than his own. She gave him a list and money and clear instructions. While she waited she distributed sweets to the others. If there was a list for more than one shop she gave him one list at a time. The other boys lost interest once they had had the sweets but her own little boy ran to and fro from shop to tonga, tonga to shop, rendering a meticulous accounting between each visit. The purchases were mainly Clarissa's. When there were a lot of packages the chokra rode back with her to the bungalow, sitting at the driver's side, and helped her to carry the packages up to the verandah. Out of her own money she gave him a percentage of the total expenditure. She hoped that he got commission from the shopkeepers. She did not always specify which shop he should go to and sometimes he was gone for quite a time. Invariably, then, he came back with a bargain. Clarissa was pleased.

They conversed in a mixture of Urdu, Pankot hill dialect and English.

His name, he said, was Ashok. His parents had died in Ranpur. He had come up to Pankot to look for work. He had no relatives.

He did odd jobs. He slept where he happened to be when finishing the last job of the day. He was eight years old. It was his ambition to work in the elephant stables of a maharajah.

'There are no elephants in Pankot,' Barbie pointed out.

No, he agreed. But in Pankot a boy could earn rupees. And then he could go to Rajputana. There were hundreds of maharajahs in Rajputana. Each one of them had a thousand elephants.

At home, Barbie said, most little English boys of his age intended to be engine drivers. He said to be an engine driver would be all right. Providing there were no elephants.

'Do you have to be a special caste to be a mahout or even to go near the elephants?'

He did not understand. He said his father had worked for the Ranpur municipality. Ashok did not say in what capacity. She decided he was a Harijan, a child of God, an untouchable. The elephants were his dream. Perhaps in Rajputana he would be allowed to clear away their droppings. But there was probably a caste for that too. She did not know. Hinduism, Mr Cleghorn had told her, is not a religion but a way of life. So, she replied, should Christianity be. He had given her an old-fashioned look.

'What am I?' she asked Ashok.

'You are Sahib-log.'

'No, I am a servant of the Lord Jesus.'

She sat on the verandah steps of the rectory bungalow and offered her hand. Ashok looked at her seriously.

'Come,' she said, 'I am your father and your mother.'

He came. She clasped his thin shoulders.

'You don't understand,' she said in English. He smelt musky. 'It is all too long ago and far away. The world you and I live in is corrupt. I clasp you to my breast but you conceive of this in terms of an authority unbending. I offer my love. You accept it as a sign of fortune smiling. Your heart beats with gratitude, excitement, expectation of rupees. And mine scarcely beats at all. It is very tired and old and far from home. Ashoka, Ashoka, Shokam, Shokarum, Shokis, Shokis.' Somewhere she had got that wrong.

He laughed. His eyes were luminous.

'Chalo,' she said.

She put a silver rupee into his tiny hand. He salaamed and ran. At the gate he turned. They waved to each other.

'*Tu es mon petit Hindou inconnu*,' she whispered. '*Et tu es un papillon brun. Moi, je suis blanche. Mais nous sommes les prisonniers du bon Dieu.*'

'It's uncertain how much longer I shall be able to visit you,' she told Mabel. She had begun to think of a grave as a closed entrance to a long tunnel, dark and tortuous, which you had to crawl through on your belly if ever you were to reach that area of radiance at its end. For a while, she supposed, you might kneel huddled against the blocked entrance getting up courage to begin the journey. There were days when she thought Mabel had gone and others when the sensation of her nearness was strong. Today she seemed very near. 'I'm sorry there are so few flowers. There aren't many in the rectory garden. I don't like to cut them without asking permission and don't like asking too often.'

When next she saw Ashok she asked him to buy flowers. He came back to the tonga with both hands full of stemless marigolds and jasmine. She scattered these on the grave. Thereafter he had flowers ready for her daily: some wild picked from hedges, others (she suspected) stolen from gardens. For such flowers he usually refused payment.

'Do you know what the flowers are for, Ashok?'

Yes, he knew, they were for puja. For worship.

'They are for my friend.'

Ashok looked troubled.

'I am your friend,' he said.

'Yes. I mean for my other friend?'

'Where is your other friend?'

'In Pankot.'

'Where in Pankot?

'She is everywhere.'

Ashok looked round. Was she here now? Yes, Barbie said. Her other friend was watching them. His eyes swung this way and that.

'Is she my friend too?'

'Oh, yes. But you won't see her.'

'Can you see her?'

Barbie shook her head.

He accepted this.

From an edition of the *Onlooker* she cut out a picture of an elephant bearing a howdah-load of sportsmen. It was a small picture. She fitted it into the mica envelope in which she had kept her subscription library ticket and gave it to him.

'My friend asked me to give you this, Ashok.'

He stared at it for some time. Next to one of the sportsmen in the howdah there was a lady with a topee.

'Is that your friend?'

Barbie examined it. The face of the woman was out of focus. 'No,' she said, 'but it is like her.'

Pictures were important to a child.

'When are you going to Rajputana, Ashok?'

Ashok shrugged.

'When you have enough money?'

He did not answer.

'Have you changed your mind?'

He nodded.

'But there are no elephants in Pankot. Why aren't you going to Rajputana?'

'I will go if you go,' he said.

That night, saying her prayers, she wept.

For quite a long time after Clarissa gave her the envelope with the mission's name on it and a Calcutta postmark she did not open it but sat on the edge of her bed observing how still the old eavesdroppers were.

She knew without reading it that the letter was from Mr Studholme and that the only reason he could have for writing to her was to offer her a place in one of the bungalows the mission kept in Darjeeling and Naini Tal. Someone had died and left a vacancy. She did not want to fill it. In such a place she would die herself, unwanted. She would have to go but it would take courage. She picked the letter up and considered the consequences of destroying it unopened. But she could not cheat Clarissa like that. Was it good news about accommodation −? Clarissa would ask at lunch. And then she would have to lie.

She went into the bathroom and brushed the taste of the lie out of her teeth.

She returned to the little room of which she had become

almost fond because Mabel knew she was in it and she had survived to come back to it; Clarissa had become amenable and the creeper outside the window had not entered. An extra tack kept the crucifix straight when she brushed past it. Each toe-nail she had discovered, was beautifully wrought. The old people behind the curtain were enemies but were kept at bay. After she had read the letter they would part the curtains, advance on her and smother her. An act of mercy.

She cut the envelope with a sandalwood paper-knife whose upper edge was carved in the shape of a string of tiny elephants. Mr Maybrick had given it to her to welcome her back to what he called the land of the living. He hated hospitals. Which was why he had not visited her. It was quite a long letter. It was signed by Mr Studholme.

November 20th, 1944

My Dear Miss Batchelor,

First let me say that this unfortunately is not to give news of a vacancy at Mountain View in Darjeeling or at The Homestead in Naini Tal. However rest assured that I have your situation well in mind.

I write to you for two reasons and must in fact apologize for not having written weeks ago when I was told that you had been rather unwell but were recovering nicely. We oldsters are not so easily laid low. After years in the country I think we develop a special resilience. (Lavinia Claythorpe, up in Naini Tal, is eighty-eight this month.)

My informant about your illness and recovery was a Miss Sarah Layton whom I had not had the pleasure of meeting before but who called one day while staying in Calcutta with relations. Well that is the first reason for writing, to say I hope you are now perfectly fit again. I heard how indefatigable you had been looking after the poor lady whose death left you in some uncertainty about a permanent home. The second reason I write is really to test the ground for asking a particular favour. I am encouraged to do so by your earlier offer of voluntary services.

You will appreciate that since the beginning of the war the flow of recruits to our mission has been severely curtailed. Young men and women at home have had to answer other calls. Increasingly we have been hard put to it to fill teaching posts effectively and there is one area in which for a variety of reasons this difficulty has become temporarily rather pressing.

I am sure you will remember Edwina Crane? She was superintendent of our schools in Mayapore district, amongst which is the little school on the outskirts of Dibrapur. Since the death both of the Indian teacher there and of Miss Crane the Dibrapur post is one we have found it not at all easy to fill.

Fortunately, six months ago, we were able to place a Miss Johnson, a Eurasian Christian, who has been very successful and whom we hope will continue as teacher in charge of Dibrapur for some time to come. However, Miss Johnson recently announced her engagement to be married and has asked for a month's leave from December 12th in order to solemnize the union and go down to Madras province with her husband. To this request, naturally, we have acceded. What has proved more difficult to arrange is for a teacher to take her place while she is away. The Dibrapur school is an infants' and junior school, most of its pupils come from nearby villages, not from the town. Unlike the senior schools in the towns it is normally closed for a few days only at Christmas. There is a bungalow nearby where the teacher in charge lives. Mayapore, I'm afraid, is 75 miles distant. One is rather cut off. The town of Dibrapur is not salubrious. But the troubles that affected that area are long since over.

The question is, would you consider filling in for Miss Johnson? We should be most grateful. A telegram saying one way or the other would settle the matter. If your answer is in the affirmative I will at once instruct Miss Jolley in Ranpur to arrange your transportation from Pankot to Mayapore on, I suggest, December 5th, which would enable you to reach Mayapore on the 6th or 7th and have a couple of days with Miss Johnson in Dibrapur before she departs. The superintendent in Mayapore is Mrs Lanscombe whom I do not think you know. She would undertake all the arrangements for your reception and transportation at the Mayapore end. If you are agreeable I will ask Miss Jolley to telephone you at the rectory bungalow as soon as she has effected all the necessary bookings so that she can give you the details. Meanwhile my sincere good wishes: Cyril B. Studholme, MA.

*

She read the letter twice before folding and returning it to its envelope. On the second reading she knew what Sarah had done. She had visited Mr Studholme to disabuse him of any idea he'd got hold of that the old warhorse was past it. She had done this subtly, so that he had not realized it and had even forgotten to write a letter of good wishes on her recovery from her illness. With this gesture of Sarah's, practical, unobtrusive, Barbie felt that their relationship had been sealed in a way that touched her more deeply than any open declaration of esteem could have done.

She put the envelope in her handbag. Again, as at the time of Colonel Trehearne's unexpected invitation, she wanted to be enclosed in the world of her private happiness so that she could experience it fully, exist for a while at its tranquil centre which was not a fixed point in space but a moving one gliding across a flat landscape in the long straight line which, in her imagination, was the road to Dibrapur. She shut her eyes and in the dim room turned her face to the enormous white sky and the scorching oven-breath of the sun that baked the earth and the body to a holy exhaustion.

India, she thought. India. India.

India, she whispered.

She said aloud, 'India. India. India.'

The children laughed. Say it again, Barbie Mem, they choroused. India, she cried. The first syllable was inaudible and the second seemed to spring shrieking from her throat, hover, then fall like a bird struck dead in flight. She lowered her voice and spoke in the breathy tone adopted for talking to Arthur, Clarissa, Edgar Maybrick and little Ashok. I must conserve my real voice, she said. Conserve it for use in the schoolroom at Dibrapur.

But her real voice had gone. Would the warmth of the plains restore it to life and vibrancy or was it permanently damaged? Would a Pankot winter of cold nights complete its ruination? These questions were rhetorical. The damage to her voice in spite of Travers's assurances was a punishment whose sting she only truly felt this morning. If she accepted the mission's invitation she would be doing so under false pretences.

She could only pray and having prayed decline, because prayer had long since become a matter of form, of habit. She did not even bother to kneel. Oh, God, she said, give me back my voice.

*

When she reached the hall she said loudly, 'Clarissa!'

The bead curtains merely shivered. They should have opened.

With the letter from Mr Studholme firmly held in one hand she parted the beads with the other and clattered through into the sea-green incorruptible room. And stopped.

Captain Coley rose.

Clarissa said, 'There you are, Barbara. I was just going to send to see if you had a moment.'

'Oh, I have plenty of moments.'

The old crone, cracking jokes. There had been a night when she felt she could have toppled this man over merely by placing a finger on his chest. Was there hair on it? She knew nothing except the prone view from above. They were looking everywhere but at each other. Mostly they looked at Clarissa who gleamed under this concentration of light.

Clarissa spoke: an oracle with questions instead of answers. With Coley present Clarissa had reverted. She no longer looked solicitous. She spoke as she might to children from whom it was her duty to prise secrets.

'There is some mystery,' she said, 'about a trunk in the mali's shed at Rose Cottage.'

'No mystery,' Barbie replied. 'The trunk is mine. Is it required to be removed?'

Clarissa silently referred the question to Captain Coley. Apt Coley. Barbie turned to him. His face (that martyr's face) was red and, she could have sworn, stippled with sweat on the anguished forehead, although the daytime November warmth had not come into Clarissa's room with him.

'Be appreciated,' he said.

Clarissa explained. 'Captain Coley is keeping an eye on things while Mildred is away, you see.'

'Including the gardening implements?'

'Not exactly,' he said. 'Spot of bother. Between the mali fellow and old Mahmoud.'

'Is not Mahmoud on leave?'

'Came back. Going to Calcutta tomorrow to join Mildred. Mrs Layton.'

Apt Coley did not use many words. After a decade and more as adjutant of the depot words were probably meaningless to him.

Since his routine did not vary from one week to the next, year after year, he must use the same ones every day of his life.

'What was this spot of bother between the mali and Mahmoud?' she asked him.

'Suspected theft.'

'Why on earth should Mahmoud suspect theft? My name is clearly printed.'

'Covered. Trunk covered.'

'But didn't mali explain it was mine and that he had it only to look after for me?'

'That's why I'm here. Check his story.'

'But you still want it removed.'

He looked round the room as if looking for a place where it might go.

'Be appreciated,' he said eventually.

'When? Today?'

'Heavens, no.' For a moment he was almost stung to articulacy. Perhaps he feared one thing as much as a posting he couldn't get out of. The word Urgent. 'They'll be home for Christmas. Twentieth actually. Loads of time. Month in fact.'

'But you'd like to tell Mahmoud before he goes to Calcutta tomorrow that he can forget the trunk because it will be gone?'

The telephone rang.

Clarissa got up. 'That will be Isobel about the prizes for their farewell dance. Are you going, Captain Coley?'

'On duty that night, I'm afraid.'

Barbie knew that by farewell dance Clarissa meant the first and most important. There would be several others, in descending order of priority, with smaller bands, ending with a quartet. The Rankins were not going until after Christmas. No one knew where. They pretended not to.

'What a pity,' Clarissa said. Passing Barbie she added, 'Captain Coley is such a lovely waltzer.'

When they were alone the tension between them soared to a peak and then quite simply and quietly died as if they had survived an act of God and found themselves stranded and non-combatant.

'I danced too as a gel,' Barbie heard herself croaking. The 'gel' interested her even as she said it. It was a pronunciation a man like Coley might feel happy with. 'Which may surprise you. We danced at a place called the Athenaeum. Not *the* Athenaeum, naturally. I think its real name was the Athenaeum Temperance Assembly. Every year there was a church charity ball. I loved the mazurka. My father taught me to dance when I was a child. He hummed the music. Once he danced me all the way down Lucknow Road.'

'Lucknow?'

'Lucknow Road. Camberwell.'

'Oh.'

'When will it be convenient?'

'What?'

'For the trunk?'

'Oh, that. I'll send it down.'

'Don't trouble.'

'No trouble.'

'There wasn't room, you see. For the trunk. But it's different now.' She waved the mission's letter. 'I'm back in harness. Going Dibrapur.' Coleyism was catching. 'Clarissa won't mind about the trunk because it's only a week or two before I go. After that, who knows? If I do well Mr Studholme will be pleased with me, won't he? And I can stay in Mayapore for a while afterwards. Edwina's buried there. My friend, Miss Crane. I expect you remember. And then I'll be quite content to go to Darjeeling or Naini Tal. With all my luggage. I can always *write* to Colonel Layton when the war's over. I can leave it to him to decide where Mabel should have been buried. But I should like to see Rose Cottage just once more, Captain Coley. Preferably after Mahmoud's gone to Calcutta.'

'Going first thing tomorrow. Got him on a convoy to Ranpur.'

'Then second thing tomorrow would be fine. Say eleven a.m.?'

'On duty tomorrow, I'm afraid.'

'Oh but that doesn't matter. Just tell mali. There's no need for you to be there.'

Coley inclined his head. There was a childlike grace about him which she suddenly understood and found pleasant. She felt that somewhere in the background he kept a box of bricks. She went with him to the hall where Clarissa, smiling and talking to the telephone, raised her hand in august farewell.

On the steps of the verandah Barbie said:

'Thank you for sending back my sou'wester, Captain Coley. That afternoon I tried to deliver the spoons there was no one there. I must have lost it running – running in the rain.'

His face reddened slightly but the martyred look had gone, briefly, as it might have done centuries ago if a man from the bishop's palace had galloped up to the place of execution waving a paper that quenched the fire before it could take hold. He offered his hand which she took.

'Thank *you*,' he said. He hesitated. She feared a more intense declaration.

'Regiment most grateful. For the spoons.'

He turned, went down the steps putting on his cap, thrusting his little cane under his left arm, making for a battered old Austin 7 which they both knew had been in the locked corrugated shed on that particular day.

V

She told the tonga-wallah she required his services for the entire morning and made a bargain. He was an enclosed dilapidated man with a curved nose and predatory sleeping eyes, a starved bird with folded wings.

'Is your horse strong?' she asked. 'Strong in the bone?' The three of them had bones aplenty. The horse was strong he said. She told him to drive her in the direction of Pankot railway station.

At the crest of the hill where the road led out of the valley through the miniature mountain pass she ordered him to turn round and stop. She got down and stood for several minutes. She could not see the celestial range of sunlit peaks. There was cloud there to the northeast, cloud that brought snow to the mountains and sometimes if the winds could carry them so far cold rain to the valley. But the late-November sun was strong and the valley clean, bright, sparkling.

She pictured Aziz, arm extended, offering Pankot to her. She put out her own arm in conscious imitation and ordered the tonga-wallah to drive her back to East Hill and when he got there up Club road. He gave no indication of having heard but when she got back in set off. No doubt he thought her mad.

Twenty minutes later they were passing the milestone half way up Club road. There was no body lying there. All the bodies were buried but the jackal packs had multiplied; men ran with them on all fours, ravenous for bones. The tonga-wallah sat hunched letting the horse make its own pace.

At the entrance to the club it began to turn in as if this were its nature. 'No,' she called. 'Further, further.' Horse and man struggled for supremacy. The tonga lurched back on to its route.

They continued on and up past the familiar entrances to the bungalows between the club and Rose Cottage. She felt no pang. All this had been in another life. It seemed strange that it still existed. Staring at the road below her feet she counted the horse's paces and then said, 'Stop!' and glanced round. The equipage was outside the gates which the mali had left open, presumably because Captain Coley had told him to expect her. She imagined that most of the time while Mildred was away the gates were closed and padlocked. She told the tonga-wallah to drive in.

The first thing she saw was the trunk. It was uncovered. It had been placed conveniently on the front verandah at the head of the steps. The main door behind was shut and barred. The mali must be in the servants' quarters. She thought it lax of him to leave the trunk unattended and the gates open. Anyone could have come in and removed it. But he may have thought it too large and heavy for a casual thief. She went up the steps and tested the padlock. It was intact.

The trunk certainly looked bigger than she remembered. She had imagined it roped easily in the back of the tonga and herself up front sharing the driver's seat for the return journey. She glanced at the stationary contraption, the droop-headed horse, the drooped old man. He would need help, persuasion probably.

'Wait,' she said. The man said nothing. He was already waiting.

She edged her way round the trunk to gain the front verandah. Again she felt no pang to be standing on familiar ground. The unkempt plants on the balustrade looked confused by some rearrangement that was not clear to them and to which they would never get used. There was an element in the atmosphere that was neither warm and friendly nor yet quite cold and hostile. The window through which she could have seen into her old room was shuttered. She paused in front of it and had an impulse which she restrained to rap on the wood and cry: Is anybody there? and then to put her ear to the crack between the shutters and to listen for the sounds of the years she had spent there scattering in panic at the stranger's voice. She moved on round to the side where her old french window used to be. It was still there but was also shuttered. Again came the impulse to knock and again it was restrained, just in time. Her hand was already a fist, the knuckles resting against the wood which her forehead was almost touching. She stood like this waiting for the impulse to go away. When it had gone she felt hollow with her history, so long unused. She uncurled her fist. There seemed to be webs of new-grown flesh between her fingers.

She moved from the door and then stopped, arrested by a conviction that she was not alone. She glanced towards the corner of the bungalow where the rear verandah began, the verandah on which Mabel had died. It was coming from there, the sense of a presence, of someone in possession and occupation, of something which made the air difficult to breathe. She put her hand to her throat and felt for the gold chain with its pendant cross and then walked forward, turned the corner and gasped – both at the sight of a man and at the noxious emanation that lay like an almost visible miasma around the plants along the balustrade which had grown dense and begun to trail tendrils. The man stood as she had once seen Mabel stand, staring at the garden as if struck by a thought about it but also beyond it to the hills and where the mountains lay behind the impenetrable formations of sunlit cloud: a lean tall Englishman, dressed in civilian clothes and a soft tweed hat, his right shoulder towards her, his right arm extended and hand flattened upon the rail, gazing as from a height, upon a world spread out before him.

Fighting the sickness she called out, 'I beg your pardon. But would you please explain what you're doing here?'

Some ten yards separated them. He heard her voice but probably not the poorly articulated words. His sharp glance in her direction was not accompanied by any movement of his trunk or limbs.

'You,' she called again. 'What are you doing? This is private property, not a public right of way.'

She went to confront him. He let go of the balustrade, clutched the tweed hat at its crumpled crown and began to raise it; and then the nausea and her apprehension faded, scorched out of her by this courteous gesture. She had a wild notion that the man was Colonel Layton, released and restored and come home to find his family absent.

But she had seen Colonel Layton and the hat was now fully off, revealing a head and an unshadowed face, one half of which, the left, was branded under a lashless and uncanopied blue eye with a pink and white spider web of puckered flesh. There, on that side of his head, the man had been burned.

He put the hat back on.

'I'm sorry,' he said – and the apology served a dual purpose. 'My name's Ronald Merrick. I came to see the Laytons but the mali tells me they're in Calcutta. He invited me to stay while he made me a cup of coffee.'

He had moved round to face her. His left arm hung un-naturally stiffly. His right hand was bare. The left was encased in a black leather glove, the fingers and thumb of which were moulded to hold something invisible and useless.

'Oh,' she said. 'I do apologize. Of course. Captain Merrick. My name's Barbara Batchelor. I was *Mabel* Layton's companion. I used to live here.'

She put out her hand and at once wished she had not; not because by doing so she broke one of the stuffier rules but because the arrangements he had to make to reciprocate were compli-cated. Taking his hat off again, revealing once more the raw geo-graphy of his face, he inserted the hat into the black leather glove, clamped its fingers and then put his one warm living hand in hers.

'How do you do? Miss Layton mentioned you to me when she visited me in hospital. It must have been in connection with a Miss Crane. Is that correct?'

'How clever of you to remember.'

'Not really. Sarah told me her aunt Mabel's companion had been in the missions and often talked about Miss Crane.'

'Edwina and I were old friends.'

'Were you in the same mission?'

'The very same. The Bishop Barnard schools.'

'They are highly thought of. Were you in Mayapore?'

'No. I was in many places but never there. When I retired in 1939 I was superintendent in Ranpur.'

'That must have been a very responsible post.'

She realized that she was trying to look at the right side of his face and the right eye and ignore the left. His short stubby colourless hair was stippled with grey on the left side and looked patchy. Had he been handsome? It was difficult to tell. She would have liked to touch the scarred side of his face and she had an equally strange desire to touch the gloved artificial hand and feel up the arm inch by inch to discover where the wood or metal ended and the flesh began. She thought she remembered Sarah saying it had had to be cut off above the elbow.

And she recalled then that Sarah had never liked him. Loving Sarah and believing in her though she did, she could not let herself be prejudiced in advance. He had acted with great physical courage; perhaps with moral courage too. His voice was wonderfully distinct; every word clearly enunciated. A man's voice.

She turned to where the chairs should have been, intending to invite him to sit. The verandah furniture was gone. She had not noticed it consciously until now. 'Oh, dear, they've taken away the chairs. We sat out almost every day even in December and January when it can be quite chilly in the shade even at midday. I suppose the chairs are inside. Mildred and Susan have been away since early September, and Sarah longer than that. She went to Calcutta with her aunt. Did she come and see you?'

'I left the hospital there in mid-July.'

'When did you reach Pankot?'

'Yesterday.'

'Are you here for long, for a holiday?'

'No, only for a week. I'm at the hospital for tests and fittings. But it's a kind of holiday. I'm allowed a lot of freedom so long as I keep the appointments with the medicos.'

She glanced at the hand. Perhaps it was new and painful.

'How disappointing for you that the Laytons aren't here. And *they'll* be sorry to have missed you. Especially Susan. She was tremendously grateful to you, for what you tried to do to save Teddie.'

Her voice had hit a patch of special roughness but she had also been hit by the terrible consequences for Captain Merrick of his heroic act, hit as never before because she hadn't known the man or been able to imagine in detail the ruined face and the awful artificial arm.

'My voice,' she croaked, and hit her chest as if to dislodge an obstacle inside, and wished it were in her power to heal them both. 'I had a very bad cold a little while ago and this is the result.'

A movement caught her eye.

'Mali!'

She went to meet the man who had appeared on the verandah carrying a tray of coffee. Directly he saw her he set the tray on the ground and salaamed and then took both her proffered hands. His boy came up behind.

'Are you well, mali?' she asked in Urdu. 'And your wife? And the chokra. Oh! I can see he is well.'

All were well, the mali said. 'But look, Memsahib –'

He led the way past the high-grown plants on the balustrade to the steps where the view was not interrupted. She looked. And did not believe it.

All the central beds of rose trees had been dug up and turfed over. Lines of string and limewash mapped the place where a tennis court was being prepared. The roses in the beds that were left had been pruned down to bleak little skeletal bushes.

'Tennish,' mali said. There were tears in his eyes.

She turned from the sight of desecration and found Captain Merrick smiling at the mali's boy because the boy's eyes were fixed on the black-gloved hand. He looked up at her.

'Have there been changes?'

'It's unrecognizable.'

'I was thinking just before you came what a fine garden it is, but I could see some work was being done.'

'It was once a mass of roses.'

'It must have been beautiful.'

Beautiful was an unusual word for a man to use except about a woman. She was grateful to him for using it now. Her father had used it in similar contexts. Because of the poet in him.

The boy had taken up the coffee tray and the mali was un-padlocking the louvred shutters in front of the french windows of the living-room. He swung the shutters back and then went round the side of the house to the kitchen entrance.

'Would you like to see inside the house, Captain Merrick?'

'Only if you'd like to show it to me. I'm content in the fresh air.'

'Then let's stay here. He'll be bringing out the chairs.'

The french windows were being unbolted from inside. With a creak one swung open and then the other. The mali came out with a chair she did not recognize; a dining-room chair. He set it down, went back in and came out with another. On his last journey he brought a basket-work teapoy which, like the chairs, must have come from the grace and favour. The chokra put the coffee tray down on this.

'Thank you, mali. I don't recognize the chairs.'

The chairs were from Brigadier Paynton Memsahib's house. Brigadier Paynton Memsahib had flown home to bilaiti.

'Yes, I know. What happened to our old table and chairs?'

The old table and some of the chairs were in the hall. The old sideboard was in the main bathroom. The rest of the chairs were in the mali's shed taking up room. All the old stuff might be sold. It was because Mahmoud had put the chairs in the shed that he had found the trunk and caused trouble. All the living-room furniture was being re-covered. The verandah furniture was in the bazaar being repaired and relacquered. The Indian carpet in the living-room was to be put in the young memsahibs' bedroom and a fine new Persian carpet had been ordered from Bombay.

From his expression Barbie saw that the mali, loyal to the old order, was nevertheless impressed by the new. In time he would be impressed by the tennis court. Perhaps he already was and had only been upset for her benefit. That was very Indian. The tears in his eyes had been genuine but that was part of being Indian too.

They settled in the strange but elegant chairs and she dealt with the coffee. None of it mattered. For her Rose Cottage had ended with Mabel's death. She could not see the future that Mildred apparently saw for it. A Persian carpet was a wild extravagance. Or perhaps it was simply an investment. The boy brought out another cup and saucer and a plate of rather soggy-looking biscuits.

'Roses or tennis balls,' she said suddenly. 'Which would you choose, Captain Merrick?'

He did not reply but took the cup of coffee in the one hand capable of dealing with it and which might still hold a racquet.

'I'm sorry,' Barbie said, choosing forthrightness. 'Were you a good player?'

'Pretty fair. I shan't miss it though so long as I can ride. I'm teaching myself to get up on a horse from the wrong side. I'm hoping to get a mount tomorrow. You need an arm with feeling and control in it to get up, don't you, for the horse's sake as much as your own, but the rest's a question of one sensitive hand and a couple of strong knees. Once I've mastered that there's no reason why I shouldn't train myself to play patball too.'

'I think that's very brave.'

'Not at all. One's scale of priorities and comparisons changes, that's all. Actually it's rather like being born again. Even drinking a cup of coffee presents unexpected problems.' He smiled. 'But it tastes better when you get it.'

He stuck the saucer between the black leather thumb and forefinger, clamped them, picked up the cup and drank.

Having drunk he set the cup back in the saucer, reached over, lifted the plate of biscuits and offered it to her. After she had declined he put the plate back on the tray, chose a biscuit, settled back and began to nibble at it. The cup and saucer were retained in that rigid grip. She noticed that he had taken the opportunity at some time to dispose of his hat by folding and placing it neatly into the right-hand pocket of his misty Harris tweed jacket. His trousers were fawn cavalry twill; the shoes chestnut brown with the high glassy polish of old shoes originally expensive and since well cared for. His flannel shirt was open at the throat. He wore a green silk scarf inside it.

Her eyes, taking all this in, now met his. He did not seem in the least embarrassed to be the object of such close scrutiny but met it with what she thought of as a manly composure. Nevertheless she was ashamed of herself. She had been examining him as though he were not real. He had finished the biscuit and now drained his coffee cup. She wondered, thinking of the liquid going down, what intimate problems he also had to resolve, and looked away, saddened rather than embarrassed, and uncertain whether to offer him another cup. She sipped her own coffee.

'How are the Laytons?' he asked.

'Fine, I'm glad to say. I hear from Sarah sometimes. They've been in Darjeeling with Mildred's sister.'

'Mrs Grace. I met her at the wedding. Was the baby born successfully?'

'Oh yes, didn't you know?'

'I saw Sarah in June but I've heard nothing since. The nurse who specialled me told me Mrs Grace rang once to inquire how I was. I believe she was coming up to Pankot and that was early in July if I remember right. The baby was due about then, wasn't it? I suppose Mrs Grace was coming up for that?'

'No, the baby was born prematurely. In June. A little boy.'

'A boy? Teddie would have been pleased. And Susan?'

'Susan was pleased too.'

'I meant was she all right?'

'She had a difficult time but she came through. She was very brave. She was here on the verandah and Mabel was working in the garden. I was out. There was no one else here. Susan saw her die. She acted marvellously. Ringing for the doctor first and then her mother. But the shock brought the baby on.'

'Mrs Layton senior's death was very sudden then?'

'Very sudden.'

She looked at him. His good arm was bent, the elbow resting on the arm of the dining-chair – a carver's chair, she supposed; her own had no arms – the good hand supporting his chin, one finger resting on his right cheek.

'She died the day Sarah was in Calcutta.'

'Yes.' He moved the finger from his cheek to the corner of his mouth and then tucked it under the chin. 'Sister Prior saw the notice in the *Times of India*. She thought it might be Sarah's mother. She knew Sarah's name was Layton and that she'd come all the way from Pankot to see me, and Sarah said she might come again after the operation but she never did. Sister Prior thought she'd had to rush back here. She kept it from me. I wasn't shown the *Times* notice for a couple of weeks. Of course I realized at once who it was who'd died. I meant to write. But never did.'

'Didn't Sister Prior see the notice of the baby's birth a few days later?'

'I think she only looks at the deaths and marriages.' He smiled. 'Is there another cup of coffee?'

'I'm so sorry. Of course. No – leave it there.' She stood, poured the coffee. The cup and saucer were at a slight angle. She was careful not to fill the cup too full. She helped him to milk and sugar, then sat down.

He said, 'You're probably wondering how I knew to come to Rose Cottage.'

'Why should I wonder that?'

'Because the last time I was in touch with Sarah they were still at the Pankot Rifles address.'

'Oh, I see. Well. I suppose someone at the Pankot hospital told you they'd moved.'

'No.' He glanced at the palm of his good hand. 'I've not talked to many people at the hospital yet. But Teddie mentioned Rose Cottage quite a lot. Susan usually wrote to him from here, didn't she? She used to put the Rose Cottage address on the flaps of the envelopes. He liked that. He liked to think of her in this setting. He said her father would inherit it when her Aunt Mabel died. But I'd forgotten that until I got to Pankot yesterday. I meant to get in touch with them at the other address or look them up in the telephone book. But as soon as I arrived I remembered about Rose Cottage and wondered if they'd moved in.'

'So you came up to see.'

'No, I came up to the club to sign on as a temporary member but the secretary was out. They said he'd be back about midday so I took a walk up the hill. As soon as I started passing bungalows with names like The Larches, Rhoda and Sandy Lodge I was pretty sure I'd come across Rose Cottage. I thought I was out of luck after I'd passed the last place. But suddenly here it was. So I came in. The mali was working at the front.'

'You were fortunate to choose today. Mali was expecting me. Otherwise you'd have found the gate shut and padlocked. I came to collect my trunk. I expect you saw it.'

'Yes, I noticed a trunk. Where are you living now?'

'At the rectory bungalow. You saw the church spire? Well, it's just behind there. You must visit us. And there will be lots of other people here who'll be anxious to meet you.'

'Thank you.' He looked at his black glove. 'Not too many, I hope.'

'I'm afraid so. You're famous. Not only because of what you tried to do to save Teddie but because of your connection with the Manners case.'

He continued to regard her.

'She was here you know,' Barbie said.

'Here? Miss Manners?'

'No, no, the aunt. Lady Manners. She came to Pankot this summer.'

'Oh, yes. Sarah told me the name had appeared in the Flagstaff House book. She said no one had seen her though. I never met Lady Manners myself.'

'I saw her. In the church. I knew it was her. It couldn't have been anyone else. But she must have gone. I've never seen her again. Forgive me, perhaps you prefer not to talk about it. After all, if it hadn't been for that awful case you'd probably still be DSP in Mayapore or something even more important like a Deputy Inspector General.'

Chin back in hand he continued to regard her. Briefly she found the situation disturbingly familiar, as if they had sat like this before in another life. Now he removed the cup and saucer from the smooth black glove and replaced it on the tray. He took out his cigarette case.

'Why do you say that, Miss Batchelor?'

'Isn't it true? People have always said that your superior officers failed to stand by you.'

He offered her a cigarette. She declined but asked him to smoke if he wished. She glanced round. The mali's boy was watching from a corner of the bungalow. She told him to bring out an ashtray for Captain Merrick Sahib. Merrick had selected a cigarette, returned the case to his inside pocket and taken a gold lighter from another. The live-hand had great dexterity. He blew out smoke. The mali's boy came with a brass ashtray. Merrick looked at him gravely then pointed at the gloved artefact. With a frown of concentration the boy tried to place the ashtray in the palm. Merrick reached over to help him secure it between the finger and thumb. The boy stood back, arms behind him, prepared to watch.

'Chalo,' Barbie said. When the boy had gone Merrick smiled at her.

He said, 'The curiosity of children has a great therapeutic value.' He blew out smoke again. 'Reverting to that other subject. I ought to correct any impression people have that my department failed to stand by me. It was an impression we were quite willing that the Indians should get. Nothing takes the steam out of the opposition more effectively than appearing to remove the cause of conflict or complaint. But I always imagined our own people understood that.'

'But weren't you sent to a rather unpleasant area?'

Merrick was regarding her again. The eyelid from which the lashes appeared to have been burnt looked fixed. She found herself watching it to see if it blinked.

'Only with my full approval,' he said, 'and on the understanding that the department wouldn't stand in my way, if I renewed my application for a temporary commission in the army. I applied originally in 1939 and they sat on it then. And subsequently.' He paused to take in another methodical lungful of smoke and then let it escape in puffs with each of his next words. 'Actually you could say the army was my reward for my handling of the Manners case.' The smoke had gone. 'But probably only my Inspector General appreciates that fully.'

He noticed how her glance fell on his ruined arm.

'I hope you don't interpret this elegant monstrosity as payment deferred for having made a tragic mistake.'

'Oh no.'

'They were guilty, you know. The I.G. agreed.'

When he put the cigarette to his lips this time she thought for an instant that his fingers trembled slightly but she must have been mistaken. The live-hand now hung free, unsupported except by the forearm on the arm of the chair, and the cigarette looked as steady as a rock.

He said, 'One in particular is guilty. The ringleader. He is guilty for the rest of them.'

He gazed at her through wreaths of smoke.

'His name is Kumar,' he continued. 'The worst kind of western-educated Indian. With all the conceit and arrogance of the Indian whose family owns or once owned land, plus the arrogance of the most boring and unprincipled but privileged English lad who believes the world belongs to him because he was taught at a public school to think he should rule it by divine right instead of by virtue of a superior intelligence. It's difficult to see why she fell for it, but of course he spoke and acted like an English boy of that type.' He blew more smoke. 'And he was extremely good-looking.' He had not stopped regarding her. He said, 'Well, enough of that. I can see you find the subject painful. I do too. As a reasonably conscientious police officer it's rather gone against the grain to see six criminals comfortably put away as mere political detenus.'

'Painful yes. One must find it that. But that doesn't mean we should hide it away or pretend it never happened or that it's over.'

'Oh, it's over. The girl's dead.'

'The child's alive.'

He smiled. 'I mean the *case* died with the girl. I agree, the child's alive. His child, presumably. At least one presumes she imagined so.'

'You told Sarah you were fond of the girl yourself. And yet you sound so bitter. About her.'

He seemed quite undaunted. 'I *was* fond of her. I had to take that into consideration. But I think I stopped being fond of her when I realized which way she'd jumped. So it was never a serious impediment.'

She thought: What a curious word to use. Impediment. And – jumped. That's a curious word too. Sexual jealousy? Racial jealousy?

She found herself suddenly unwilling, unable, to consider the matter. She felt drained of imaginative energy. She stared at the embryo tennis court. It meant nothing. It was simply a place to pat a ball to and fro, to and fro.

Between their feet the woman in the white saree abased herself. Beseeching them. 'We are gods,' she thought, 'and this was our garden. Now we play tennis. It's easier to beseech against a background of roses.'

That flash of inspiration had come, unexplained, unattended. But there seemed no more to come. She looked at him. Again he was regarding her. His chin was in his hand. He had stubbed the cigarette. It lay dead, bent double, on the little brass tray that had come from Benares on the banks of the Ganges where bodies were burnt and the ashes cast to float, float on, float out to an unimaginable sea. Her old trunk of missionary relics with them. Bobbing, lazily twisting, under a copper-coloured sun. Immense crowds came to the festivals on the banks of the holy river. Greater crowds than came to any church. The air was heavy with the scent of jasmine, decayed fish, human and animal ordure. In the trunk Edwina's picture sailed to a far horizon.

She said, 'I am your mother and your father.'

'What?'

'Man-bap. It wasn't that for Edwina. It was despair. But I suppose Teddie felt it.' She realized that in an oblique way –

in his remarks about Kumar and a certain type of Englishman – he had been referring to Teddie, to men like Teddie, but she could not fathom his deeper references. The arm he had lost for Teddie span away too – on the swift current of the holy river: garlanded.

She had slumped forward, knees apart, feet splayed, her skirt stretched, elbows on her knees, her hands clasped.

'Tell me about my friend, about Edwina Crane. Was there much left?'

There was a long pause. She did not look at him. She stayed in that ungainly position.

'Enough to identify.'

She nodded. And to bury. She had never thought of that before. Never thought of the possibility that the coffin was light with a few scorched bones shrouded in fragments of burnt saree. 'And the letter?' she asked. 'What did she say in the letter, the one that was never read out at the inquest?'

'I'm afraid I don't remember except that it satisfied the coroner.'

'And satisfied the police. You remembered the picture. You must remember the letter. The letter was much more important to a policeman.'

'Is it important to you?'

'It might be.'

She glanced up. His chin was still resting on the live-hand, but he was looking at the garden.

He said, 'Well, it was a sane letter. Personally I should have recorded a simple verdict of suicide.'

'What did it say?'

'Simply that she was resolved to take her own life.'

'There must have been more.'

'You mean something to support the verdict of suicide while the balance of the mind was disturbed?'

'Yes, was there?'

'Personally I don't think so.' He seemed in a way to regret that Edwina had gone to hallowed ground. He added, 'But she did end the letter with the kind of statement that satisfied people she was off her head. The kind it was thought better not to read out. I can't think why.'

'What was it?'

He turned his head towards her, using his hand as a pivot for his chin.

' "There is no God. Not even on the road from Dibrapur." '

An invisible lightning struck the verandah. The purity of its colourless fire etched shadows on his face. The cross glowed on her breast and then seemed to burn out.

' "Not even on the road from Dibrapur?" '

He nodded.

For a moment she felt herself drawn to him. He offered recompense. He looked desolated as if Edwina's discovery were a knowledge he had been born with and could not bear because he had been born as well with a tribal memory of a time when God leaned His weight upon the world. He needed consolation.

She became agitated. She felt for the gold chain and found it but it seemed weightless.

He smiled. He said, 'How serious we've become.' He shot the sleeve of his good arm and looked at the dial of a watch which he wore with the face on the inner side of the wrist. 'And I ought to be getting back to see the club secretary.'

She got up. 'No, wait. I want to give you something.'

She bent down and retrieved her handbag from the ground near the leg of the unfamiliar chair.

'Come, you can help me. The locks may be stiff.'

She waited until he had got to his feet and then led the way round the verandah to the front, walking several paces ahead of him. The tonga-wallah sat hunched, half-asleep, his head at the same angle as the horse's. She saw to her horror that the horse had deposited a neat pile of manure between the shafts on the sacrosanct gravel of the drive.

She edged round the trunk and knelt on the first step, then scrabbled in her handbag for the key. The padlock clicked open easily, so did the left-hand clasp. The right-hand one had always been a brute. But it gave. She flicked the hasps up.

'Now,' she said. She raised the Pandora-lid, stared and cried out. From rim to rim the trunk was filled with the creamy white butterfly lace.

'But this isn't mine!'

She snatched at the lace and pulled it out. Beneath it were her relics.

'How did it get in here?' she wanted to know. 'I never put

it in here. I've not seen it since the day Mabel showed it to me.'

She held the lace in both hands and then looked up to appeal to Captain Merrick. But the lace was before his time. She had a desire to show it to him. 'Look,' she said, and threw one end. He caught it deftly. She drew her arm back. The lace hung between them. The butterflies trembled.

'Isn't it beautiful? The woman who made it was blind.' She stared at and through this lepidopterist's paradise-maze but could see no further than the old woman's fingers. 'Mabel wanted me to have it for a shawl.'

He offered back the end he had. She gathered the lace in and then flung it over her shoulders.

'Can I carry it?' she asked, laughing. The lace smelt of camphor, lavender and sandalwood. These were the scents of Mabel's and Aziz's gift. 'She must have given it to Aziz, and he to me. During that time he had the key to my trunk.'

She pulled the lace off her shoulders. 'I'm sorry, Captain Merrick. You haven't the least idea what I'm talking about. No matter. I opened the trunk' – she picked up the picture – 'to give you this.'

She held it up to him. He made to take it.

'No,' she said. 'The other hand.'

She reached up and helped to insert the picture into the rigid glove.

'It's small, but much bigger than an ashtray. Is it too heavy?'

'I don't think so.'

The black glove, his good hand and one of her hands held the picture. Slowly they each withdrew the support of their living flesh.

'There, you can do it. You can *carry* it.'

There was perspiration on his mottled forehead. He gazed down at the awkwardly angled gift.

'Oh, this,' he said. 'Yes, I remember this. Are you giving it to me?'

'Of course.'

One eyebrow contracted in a frown. The other – vestigial – perhaps contracted too.

'Why?'

She thought about this.

'One should always share one's hopes,' she said. 'That represents one of the unfulfilled ones. Oh, not the gold and scarlet uniforms, not the pomp, not the obeisance. We've had all that and plenty. We've had everything in the picture except what got left out.'

'What was that, Miss Batchelor?'

She said, not wishing to use that emotive word, 'I call it the unknown Indian. He isn't *there*. So the picture isn't finished.'

A drop of sweat fell from his forehead on to the bottom left-hand corner of the glass that protected the picture.

'Let me relieve you of its weight, Captain Merrick. I'll ask mali to wrap it in some paper for you. Meanwhile' – she began closing and locking the trunk – 'would you be so kind as to ask my tonga-wallah there to put the trunk in the back of the tonga? I'll ask mali to help him and also for some rope to lash it in. But I think it will require a man to order him to take it.'

'The trunk? In the back of the tonga?'

'What else?'

'I should have said it's much too heavy.'

'Oh, nonsense. It only contains my years and they are light enough.'

She strode round the bungalow calling the mali.

The trunk was roped, upended like a coffin on its foot, one edge resting on the footboard of the passenger seat, the other within an inch of the canopy above. The shafts of the trap were at a high angle. The bony horse looked in danger of elevation. The morose tonga-wallah stood at the horse's head, keeping it down.

She placed the lace shawl over her head like a bridal veil. Captain Merrick was examining the lashings and knots with a man's expert and wary eye for such things. At her approach he said, 'I don't advise this. Have you far to send it?'

'Just down the hill. To the church.'

'It's very steep. I think the fellow is right.' He jerked his head at the tonga-wallah. 'It's too great a load.'

'But I shall pay him well. He's an old man. The competition is very severe nowadays. The young drivers dash hither and thither, getting all the custom. It's a kindness really.'

'How do you intend to get back yourself?'

'In the front, of course.'

Captain Merrick said nothing.

'Do you disapprove of that? Of my driving hip to hip with a smelly old native?'

'The weight will be impossible.'

'But *I* shall balance the trunk. You see? We shall tip forward on to a splendid even keel. Are you walking to the club?'

'It was my intention. Mali says it may rain. Don't you think –'

But she interrupted. 'Where will you be going when you leave Pankot, Captain Merrick?'

'Simla.'

'For a holiday?'

'No. On army business.'

'We must talk again. There are many things I should like to discuss. I'll ask Clarissa Peplow to ring you at the hospital. At the military wing, presumably.'

'That would be very kind.'

She turned to the mali. She gave him twenty rupees. She ruffled the head of the mali's boy.

'Can you understand what I say?' she asked the boy in Urdu. He nodded. She smiled. In Dibrapur it might be all right.

She offered her hand to Captain Merrick. The mali had the packed picture ready for him.

'You won't forget the picture, will you? Will you help me up?'

They moved to the tonga. The footplate was very high. She felt his good arm take some of her weight. He had been a strong man. As she arrived under the canopy she was enclosed by the sadness of that. She stared down at him.

'Does it hurt?'

After a moment he smiled. 'A little.'

'Poor boy,' she said. Suddenly he seemed like a boy. A boy without bricks. 'You were going to be decorated. Did it come through?'

'Yes.'

'An MC?'

'A DSO for some reason.'

'But that is very distinguished, congratulations. Have you been invested yet?'

'Not yet. Next month I gather.'

'Where? In Simla?'

He nodded. She smiled at him compassionately. Simla meant the Viceroy. She felt that this would please him particularly.

'I'm sorry you missed the Laytons,' she said again.

'There'll be other opportunities,' he said. 'Shall I tell the fellow to get up?'

'If you would.'

He went to the horse's head. The old man came round, mounted, untied the reins from the rail and picked his whip out of the stock.

'Au revoir, Captain Merrick.' She adjusted the lace veil and raised her hand.

The equipage moved slowly and creakily out of the compound of Rose Cottage. As it turned into Club road she saw the valley lay under a thin blanket of cloud and felt the first spots of a chill November rain.

She had not even noticed the sun go in.

The tonga gathered momentum. The old man began to apply the brake. Once or twice the horse slipped. Barbie could feel the weight of the trunk at her back: her years pressing on her, pushing her forward, pushing her downward. She pressed her feet hard against the curved footboard but her legs had little strength.

There is no God, not even on the road from Dibrapur. But then (she argued) I am taking the road *to* Dibrapur, not from it. The tonga-wallah shouted at the horse which had stumbled. 'You mustn't shout at him,' she said, 'he's doing his best.' For some reason she longed to have the picture back. The rain was coming down quite hard. As they passed the club there was a flurry of tongas coming up the hill and about to turn in there. The old man's hands were knotted in the reins. One of the other wallahs shouted an insult.

'Hold your tongue,' Barbie shouted back. In turning her head she became more fully aware of the lace. Her head was a nest of butterflies. They were caught in the lank grey hair. She shut her eyes. Twenty stairs, including the landing floor. She began to sing. 'I've seen a deal of gaiety throughout my noisy life.' She opened her eyes.

Behind the equipage a peculiar light glowed on and off; winter lightning. Something troubled her. The lightning brought it closer. It was Mildred's face, eyes hooded, mouth turned down, quirked at the corners; glass held under chin in droop-wristed hands.

The horse slid, stumbled, righted itself. It raised its tail. There was a smell of stable. The horse stumbled again. The old man jerked the brake on harder. She thought she smelt burning. She glanced at him. His eyes at last were wide open. He looked at her for an instant before redirecting his own troubled gaze at the road ahead and at the trembling flanks of his old horse; and Mildred's face was there again just for the split second it took for it to dissolve and re-form and become the face of the man who regarded her, chin in hand, thoughtful and patient, so purposeful in his desire for her soul that he had thrown away Edwina's.

She began to tremble. She pressed with all her strength against the footboard. Below, Pankot lay shrouded by the mist of the winter rain which had left its snow on the summits. They were passing the golf-course. People were running for cover under coloured umbrellas.

Sometimes although very rarely, these cold showers – penetrating the warmth of a Pankot November day – troubled the atmosphere and produced an imbalance, a rogue element of electric mischief that shattered the silence like a child bursting a blown-up paper bag containing flashes of paper fire.

There was just such an explosion now, as the rickety old tonga entered the steepest part of Club road. It blared across the valley, jerking alive the unliveliest members of the club, comfortably cushioned in upholstered wicker, and was accompanied by the brightest amalgam of blue and yellow light ever seen in the region: an alert such as even the combined rifles of Pankot and its tribal hills could not have achieved by sustained fusillade.

The horse screamed; its eyes rolled; it reared, thrashing the space between its hooves and the greasy tarmac and then achieved both gravity and momentum, dragging and rocking the high-wheeled trap with its load of missionary relics.

Why! It is my dream! Barbie thought, hanging on to the struts with both hands, shutting her eyes to contain the blessing of it. Her hair flew long and black and she was a child dancing spinning down Lucknow road and racing up the stairs and holding the pincushion high to her mother who held her black bombasine sides laughing to hear her father sing it:

I've seen a deal of gaiety throughout my noisy life,
With all my grand accomplishments I ne'er could get a wife.
The thing I most excel in is the PRFG game, a noise all
    night,
In bed all day, and swimming in champagne.
For Champagne Charlie is my name,
Champagne Charlie is my name,
Good for any game at night my boys,
Good for any game at night my boys,
Champagne Charlie is my name
Champagne Charlie is my name
Good for any game at night boys,
Who'll come and join me in a spree.

On the long downhill sweep the equipage gathered speed, out of control of the crazed horse. The wheel spokes span counter to the rims. Sparks from the burning brake and spray from the wet surface formed bow-wave and wake.

She opened her eyes and saw the toy-like happy danger of human life on earth, which was an apotheosis of a kind, and she knew that God had shone his light on her at last by casting first the shadow of the prince of darkness across her feet.

Careless of the shawl of butterflies she reached for the reins to help the old man resist the gadarene pull of the four horses. He tore at the monstrous membrane that blinded him and which blinded Barbie too like a great light followed by a giant explosion, a display of pyrotechnics that put the old November Crystal Palace shows to shame.

Ah! she said, falling endlessly like Lucifer but without Lucifer's pride and not, she trusted, to his eventual destination. My eyeballs melt, my shadow is as hot as a cinder – I have been through Hell and come out again by God's Mercy. Now everything is cool again. The rain falls on the dead butterflies on my face. One does not casually let go. One keeps up if one can and cherishes those possessions which mark one's progress through this world of joy and sorrow.

I remember (Sarah said) Clarissa Peplow telling me how Barbie suddenly marched into the rectory bungalow covered in mud and blood but still on her feet and said, 'I'm afraid there's been some trouble at the junction. Perhaps someone would kindly deal with it. I have seen the Devil. Have you a spade?'

The driver survived too. But the horse had to be shot.

Coda

Lines from the Hospital of the Samaritan Mission of the Sisters of Our Lady of Mercy.

Ranpur. December 1944–August 1945

'Good morning, Edwina,' Sister Mary Thomas More said. She had bad teeth. She smelt of garlic and of galloping corruption. 'Or are we Barbie, today? What are we looking at?'

Miss Batchelor wrote on the pad: The birds.

'I see no birds, Edwina. Aren't we speaking today, either? Is it a day of silence?'

Miss Batchelor wrote: It is the same as all days.

'Not all days can be the same. There is the one which we all await and ought to fear.'

Miss Batchelor wrote: Bugger off. Or bring me a spade. Suit yourself.

After Sister Mary Thomas More had pursed her crypt-like lips, Miss Batchelor added a postscript: And bugger the Pope.

There was bread and water.

It was the only food she liked. It was clean.

Sarah said, 'Barbie? Barbie? Don't you know me?'

Miss Batchelor could not hold the pencil because she could not see it and both her hands had been severed. When Sarah had gone they took away her shoes because of the tramping sound.

'Good morning, Edwina. Or is it Barbie? You don't know me. My name is Eustacia de Souza. I'm new. I mean I visit. You're my first. You must tell me all about yourself otherwise I shan't know what to do to help, shall I, and Mother Superior will be upset.'

Miss Batchelor wrote: You may tell me about the birds.

Miss Batchelor liked the look of Eustacia de Souza. Eustacia de Souza was as black as your hat, several shades blacker than Sister Mary Thomas More. Eustacia de Souza was not a nun.

Miss Batchelor added to her note: My name is Barbara, not Edwina. I am under a vow of silence.

'I understand, dear. At least I understand that part. I'm not sure I understand about the birds. Which birds do you mean?'

Miss Batchelor pointed through the barred window. Eustacia put on her glasses and peered.

'I can't see any birds, dear, apart from a few crows. You can't mean crows, can you? India's full of bloody crows.'

Miss Batchelor drew a picture of the horizon and a middle distance. She sketched a point of reference. A minaret.

'Oh, a heathen thing.'

Miss Batchelor shook her head. She struck the minaret through with her pencil and then drew a line and a ring. And made angular strokes, playfully. Like birds flying.

'Just a moment, dear.'

Eustacia clung to the bars like a helpful monkey. She was very ugly. Her bottom stuck out of a print artificial silk dress. She had white shoes and high heels. She stank under the armpits but it was the stink of hope.

'I don't actually see any birds there, Barbara dear. Are you sure they're still there?'

Miss Batchelor looked. She wrote: No – but they often are.

Eustacia sat on the spare stool and smoked and talked. About peculiar things. 'We've got them in Mandalay, dear. We'll be in Rangoon like a streak of piss before May's out. Cast not a clout. Old Billy Slim could screw me any time he asked, dear. Better'n my husband. Small as he is I'd put the flags out for Billy any day.' Eustacia frowned. 'Have you ever thought about length, dear?'

She did not look as if she required an answer. She looked at Miss Batchelor who sat contained by her dignity and desire.

'Do you have the least bloody idea what I'm talking about, love? Do you know where this is, dear, I mean what town for God's sake?'

Miss Batchelor wrote: Ranpur, looking west.

Eustacia de Souza smiled and nodded. Then frowned again. 'West?' she said. She looked. She nodded. She smiled very wide. 'That's where it is,' she said. Miss Batchelor was reminded of a melon. She felt thirsty.

She wrote: You must go now. It is the dangerous hour.

Mrs de Souza's face turned a nasty purple. When she had gone Miss Batchelor broke the tea-cups and waited for the relief of cold water and winding-sheet. She screamed and struggled because that was the way Sister Mary Thomas More liked it. At the end the nun's coif was limp.

The landscape had changed because the light had altered. It was very hot. She wrote: Calendar. They brought her one. It said June 6th. She destroyed it. Next day they brought her another because Father Patrick was visiting. It said June 7th, 1945. She put it on her bedside table, and when Father Patrick had gone, under her mattress. But they did not take it away.

'How are you, Barbie?' the girl with the fair helmet of hair said.

The calendar said, June 30th, 1945. She wrote: I am in good health.

'Is there anything you want?'

She wrote: Birds.

'Birds?'

She wrote at length:

From the window, beyond the minaret, there are birds. Smudges in the sky. Not necessarily now. But there are birds there often. You can hardly see them but they circle, as though there is a nest there. There is a hill. Trees, I think.

She watched the girl reading the note. She put out her hand to touch her. The girl looked momentarily startled. Miss Batchelor withdrew her hand not wishing to frighten her. But the girl then reached out and held her.

'It's all right, Barbie. Let's look at the birds.'

They went together to the barred window.

Miss Batchelor tried to articulate. Her throat rattled. 'It's all right, Barbie,' the girl with the fair helmet of hair said. 'I understand. Where now, beyond the minaret?'

Together they watched. Distantly where the land folded there was a haze. Above it, birds.

'Yes, I see. I don't know why they're there. I'll find out. They must be quite big birds, mustn't they?'

Miss Batchelor nodded. She was proud of her birds.

She wrote to the girl: Do you live in Ranpur?

The girl said, 'No, in Pankot, at Rose Cottage. I'm only in Ranpur for two days. I'm going to Bombay to meet my father.'

Miss Batchelor held the girl's hand. She felt that she had to say something important but could not remember what.

The girl came the following morning. She said, 'The birds belong to the towers of silence. For the Ranpur Parsees.'

Then she wrote it down on Miss Batchelor's pad as if she thought Miss Batchelor might forget it.

Miss Batchelor wrote: Yes, I see, Vultures. Thank you.

She looked round the room. She shook her head. She wrote: I have nothing to give you in exchange. Not even a rose.

For some reason the girl put her arms round Miss Batchelor and cried.

'Oh, Barbie,' she said, 'don't you remember anything?'

She nodded. She remembered a great deal. But was unable to say what it was. The birds had picked the words clean.

Often now she was left alone. Sister Mary Thomas More had used the word incorrigible. She sat at the window watching through narrowed hungry eyes the birds that fed on the dead bodies of the Parsees. At night she blew dandelion clocks and continued to blow them long after they had become bereft, deprived. To blow them to the bone was the one sure way she now had of sleeping, sure in the Lord and the resurrection and the spade.

A young Madrassi nun, observing her thus, and thinking old Miss Batchelor's hour had come, ran out into the darkling inter-mittently lit medieval corridor and brought the stark night-sister, who, standing in the traditional pose, with shriven fingers on patient's pulse, and uncommitted eyes, merely firmed her lips in imitation of the daylight brides, and then made a high mark on the bed-bottom board that charted the old missionary's journey across the hilly country of exodus.

Asleep, Barbie no longer dreamed. Her dreams were all in daylight. Do not pity her. She had had a good life. It had its comic elements. Its scattered relics had not been and now can never all be retrieved; but some of them were blessed by the good intentions that created them.

One day after such a dreamless sleep, she woke, rose, knelt, prayed, splashed water on her parchment face from the rose-patterned bowl that sat like one half of a gigantic egg in an ostrich-size hole in a crazy marble top, dressed, had breakfast and marked off the calendar of the fair-haired girl's absence.

It was August 6th, 1945.

The date meant nothing to her. No date did. The calendar was a mathematical progression with arbitrary surprises.

She took her seat at the barred window. Today it was raining. She could not see the birds. But imagined their feathers sheened by emerald and indigo lights. She turned away and rose from the stool. And felt the final nausea enter the room.

She stood, swaying slightly, in the ragged heliotrope costume which was stained by egg and accidents with soup, and then holding her naked throat, padded slippered to the secure refuge of her bed and sat, leaning her shoulder casually against the iron head.

She strained at the rusted mechanism of her voice and heard its failing vibrations in her caved-in chest.

'I am not ill, Thou art not ill. He, She or It is not ill. We are not ill, You are not ill, They are all well. Therefore . . .'

She raised a questioning or admonitory finger, commanding just a short moment of silence for the tiny anticipated sound: the echo of her own life.

They found her thus, eternally alert, in sudden sunshine, her shadow burnt into the wall behind her as if by some distant but terrible fire.

Appendix

'I find myself uncertain which of two recent events – the election of a socialist government in London and the destruction of Hiroshima by a single atomic bomb – will have the profounder effect on India's future.'

Extract from a letter dated in August 1945 from
Mr Mohammed Ali Kasim to Mr Mohandas Karamchand
Gandhi

A DIVISION OF THE SPOILS

To Doreen Marston
with my love and regard

CONTENTS

BOOK ONE 1945

AN EVENING AT THE MAHARANEE'S

I

HITLER WAS DEAD, the peace in Europe almost a month old; only the Japanese remained to be dealt with. In June the Viceroy left London, flew back to Delhi, said nothing in public for nearly two weeks and then announced a conference of Indian leaders at Simla to discuss proposals which he hoped would ease the political situation, hasten final victory and advance the country towards her goal of full self-government. To enable all the leaders to be there he had to issue several orders of release from imprisonment.

The conference opened on June 25 and did not break down until July 14, an unexpectedly long time in the opinion of many English officials for Congress and Muslim League views on the composition of a new Indianized Executive Council or interim government to prove irreconcilable. The Viceroy, Lord Wavell, admitting failure, blamed himself and begged that there should be no recriminations. Subsequently, in press conference, the leader of the All-India Congress Party, a Muslim, blamed the leader of the Muslim League for the unbending nature of his claim for the League's right to nominate all Muslim members of the proposed Executive Council and blamed the British Government for not having foreseen that the conference would break down if one party were given the right of veto on nominations and therefore the opportunity to hold up the country's progress to autonomy. The leader of the Muslim League spoke disapprovingly of a combination of Hindu interests supported by the 'latest exponent of geographical unity' – the Viceroy – whose plan in his opinion was a snare for Muslim interests. Mr Nehru described the Muslim League as mediaeval in conception, and warned that the real problem facing a free India would not be communal and religious differences but economic backwardness.

The members of the conference then left Simla to consider the situation in private. Among the first to go was Mr Mohammed Ali Kasim, a Muslim Congressman and ex-chief minister of the pre-war government of the province of Ranpur, who, if Jinnah had his way, could expect no portfolio in the higher council. Like several other prominent Congress politicians Mr Kasim had not been seen in public for nearly three years. Guarded from reporters by a small but efficient entourage headed by his younger son Ahmed, he ignored the questions shouted at him as he left the Cecil Hotel and concentrated on helping Ahmed to support a frail old man later identified by onlookers as his aged and ailing secretary – Mr Mahsood. Safe in his car at last he snubbed the young man from the *Civil and Military Gazette* who got close enough to the window to say, 'Minister, is Pakistan now inevitable?' by commanding Ahmed to put up the glass and pull down the blinds.

The lowering of the blinds caught the imagination of an Indian cartoonist who portrayed the car (identified as that of the ex-chief minister by the initials M A K on one of its doors) with all its windows, including the driver's, shuttered and making off at high speed (smoke-rings from the exhaust) from a once impos-ing but now crumbling portal inscribed 'Congress' towards a distant horizon with a sun marked 'Hopes of Office' rising behind a broken-down bungalow on whose rickety verandah the leader of the Muslim League, Mr Jinnah, could be seen conferring with several of his associates.

The cartoon annoyed adherents of Congress. They objected both to the inference that Mr Kasim was about to betray them and join the League and to the representation of their party as a derelict doorway with nothing behind it. Similarly, Muslim Leaguers objected to the portrayal of the Qaid-e-Azam as the occupier of a squalid little property such as the one depicted.

By the time the cartoon appeared (two days after the end of the conference) the liberals and middle-of-the-road men in Indian politics – who might have protested at the lampooning of a man whose legal skills and political integrity had commanded wide respect for a quarter of a century – could not help wondering whether Mr Kasim had after all shown himself as capable as men of lesser merit of acting with an eye to the main chance. What else, they asked, but an intention to shift his allegiance to the League, in the hope of securing his political future with a party that had grown strong enough to wreck a viceregal conference, could better explain his subsequent mysterious behaviour?

Between Delhi and Ranpur Mr Kasim seemed to have succeeded not only in evading the journalists but in disappearing together with his entire entourage. He was not on the train when it arrived in Ranpur and he never turned up at the old Kasim house on the Kandipat road. This house had been closed since Mr Kasim's wife (and then Mr Mahsood) had left it in the middle of 1944 to join him after his release from the Fort at Premanagar in the protective custody of his distant kinsman, the Nawab of Mirat. The reason given for that release had been Mr Kasim's reported ill-health, but it was Mrs Kasim who, some six months later, died.

The journalists who waited outside the still-locked gates of the house on the Kandipat road to greet the distinguished Muslim Congressman on his return home after three years' detention and restriction, found themselves joined, towards evening, by colleagues who had waited just as uselessly at the station, and then by a growing crowd of spectators who eventually tangled with a truck-load of police sent to disperse them. A running battle developed between the lathi-armed constables and the quicker-tempered of Mr Kasim's admirers (students). The peaceful pleasures of families taking the air in the Sir Ahmed Kasim Memorial Gardens opposite were disturbed. A number of arrests were made and rumours then spread through the Koti bazaar and out to the suburb of Kandipat that Mr Kasim had been arrested by the British on the train from Delhi, had been abducted by Hindu extremists, had been murdered by the communists, had succumbed to poison administered by agents of the Viceroy. The shop of an unpopular merchant, a Hindu who gave short weight, was broken into and looted and that of another, a Muslim, ransacked in retaliation. The following day students of the Ranpur Government College demonstrated in the area of the Civil Lines carrying placards asking 'Where is M A K?' and hartal was observed in the Koti bazaar by Hindus and Muslims alike for fear of riot, arson and the consequent loss of profits.

At this stage it was discreetly leaked by the Inspector-General of Police to the Municipal Board that Mr Kasim was alive and well and back in the Nawab of Mirat's summer palace in the Nanoora Hills, and this information was simultaneously confirmed by a telephone call from a correspondent in Mirat to his editor in Ranpur. It seemed that Mr Kasim and his party had left

the Delhi–Ranpur train at a wayside halt some miles outside the
provincial capital and had then been driven to another wayside
halt where the Nawab's private train awaited him and carried
him back to the scene of his protective custody, although in this
case it had to be assumed that his return was voluntary and caused
by nothing more sinister than the need to sort out the detritus
of the year he had spent there under government restriction.

The news inspired the same cartoonist to a further interpretation of Mr Kasim's evasive behaviour. Mirat was a princely
state whose territory was contiguous to the province, whose
inhabitants were predominantly Hindu but whose ruler was of
the Islamic faith. In the new cartoon M A K was shown sitting
cross-legged at a low table in the company of the Nawab and Mr
Jinnah. The table, heavily spread with a feast, was labelled 'Islam'.
Beneath it, only head and arms visible, was the struggling body
of Free India. From behind a pillar the puckish face of Winston
Churchill peered, the head sporting a Jinnah-shaped fez to depict
the English leader's alleged preference for Muslims and sympathy
with their aspirations, the face smoothed by an expression of
satisfaction at the thought that the Princes, those loyal Indian
supporters of the Crown in two world wars, and the Muslim
League which had refused to have anything to do with the non-
co-operation tactics of the Congress Party, would together – for
whatever different reasons – now so bedevil every move the
Congress made to force the issue of Indian independence to a
conclusion favourable to themselves that British rule could comfortably be extended far enough into the future for the phrase
'indefinitely if not in perpetuity' not to seem inappropriate.
Another cartoon on the following day depicted Mr Churchill
receiving an ovation from a moronic (or badly drawn) and
adoring British public, to whom he was about to appeal for re-
election, holding in one arm a baby labelled 'Victory in Europe',
with the other arm extended presenting its hand in giant
perspective and the famous V-sign, but with the two fingers
raised the wrong way round. One of these fingers was labelled
'Jinnah' and the other 'Princely India'. Clenched in the curled
fist below the fingers was a limp body representing Indian unity
and nationalism. Thereafter, as a result of a visit to the editor's
office by a representative of the CID no cartoons by this particular artist appeared in this or any other newspaper for some time.

The news that Mr Kasim had gone back to Mirat caused a similar influx of journalists into Nanoora to that of the previous year when he had been let out of the Fort; but although there were now presumably no restrictions on his movements or activities the journalists again failed to obtain an interview and this time did not even receive official messages of regret from court officials that Mr Kasim had no statement to make. Several abortive attempts were made to enter the grounds of the summer palace; a costly business since it involved bribing servants and officials, and a dangerous one because there was the risk of arrest for trespass, even (it was said) of summary imprisonment in one of the Nawab's dungeons. One by one the journalists departed, filing imaginative copy, until only a handful remained in the rambling little hill town, drinking in the coffee and liquor shops, discussing the interesting rumour about Mr Kasim's elder son Sayed, which their editors dared not yet print, and visiting the brothels, for private entertainment but also in the hope of meeting Mr Kasim's younger son, Ahmed, who was said to be a drunkard and a lecher, an incorrigible wastrel who had come near to breaking his father's heart before being packed off to Mirat in the Nawab's service, to womanize and drink himself to death if he wished.

But there was no sign of Ahmed Kasim either. A story that he was being treated for venereal disease in a room in the private residence of Dr Habbibullah, chief physician to the Nawab, sent the remaining journalists from the Nanoora Hills down to the city of Mirat and then a rumour that M A K had initiated the story of his younger son's illness to get rid of the press and leave Nanoora unnoticed sent some of them rushing back and others out of the State altogether, back to Ranpur and British India. The latter found the Kasim house on the Kandipat road still closed and the former were no more successful than hitherto in establishing through the evidence of their own eyes whether the elusive Congressman was in fact in residence at the summer palace.

Journalists in other parts of India thought they detected in the attitude of members of the Congress high command more pious hopes than firm convictions of Mr Kasim's continuing allegiance to the twin cause of freedom and unity which he had supported throughout his political life, and a characteristically enigmatic comment by the Mahatma (not spoken, but written down, it being his day of silence) did little to remove the suspicion that during the Simla conference there had been private differences of opinion between M A K and his distinguished colleagues. Asked if he could throw any light on Mr Kasim's apparently self-imposed security screen, Mr Gandhi wrote: 'God alone throws light on any matter and in this light we may from time to time perceive the truth.'

With this the two journalists had to be content because the Mahatma indicated that the interview was over. They departed, leaving him to bathe and have his massage.

A few days later public interest in Mr Kasim's political intentions was temporarily extinguished by the unexpected news that the British electorate had voted overwhelmingly for the Socialists and, in doing so, relegated the arch-imperialist, Mr Churchill, at the moment of his triumph, to the post of Leader of His Majesty's now numerically harmless Tory Opposition.

The story that three senior members of the Bengal Club promptly died of apoplexy, although not without a certain macabre charm, proved to have no foundation in fact; but there was no doubt that for several days relations between many British officers and the rank and file of conscript British soldiers serving their time in India, who had voted by post and proxy, were a little distant, and in one reported case demonstrably strained and only saved from escalating to the point where they would have formed the basis of a very serious affair of conduct prejudicial to good order and military discipline by the presence-of-mind of a sergeant-major who stood between his captain and a lance-corporal who had admitted 'voting for old Clem' on the railway station at Poona and said, 'Sir, I think we have a little touch of the sun.' It was raining at the time.

The rifle company of which this captain was in command formed part of a British infantry battalion that was on its way to Kalyan, near Bombay, to join the forces gathering there for the invasion and liberation of Malaya, in an operation known as Zipper. The battalion reached Kalyan on July 30 and settled itself in to a section of an immense hutted encampment that looked and proved dreary. The wet monsoon was at its peak. The Churchillian officer and most of his colleagues managed to travel frequently by jeep to find solace in Bombay, in whose roads part of the invasion force of shipping had already anchored in preparation for the embarkation of the troops, but the rank and file were less fortunate.

There was Housey-Housey, a camp cinema, and Indian prostitutes who were cheap but out-of-bounds. There was mud. It was a bleak terrain that it took some effort of imagination to see as once having been part of the background to the romantic and exotic affairs of the Mahratta kings in whom a fair-haired and well-spoken British Field Security sergeant – with a degree in history from Cambridge – attempted to interest a bored and restive group of captive Cockney, Welsh, Midlands and Northern Englishmen who had to be forgiven for wondering what they were doing in Kalyan getting kitted up for the Far East when the real war (the one in Europe) was over and the lights had actually gone up in London, in every sense. Accounts received from home of VE night celebrations had already eroded what little sense of India's attractions they had acquired and since this had in any case never been lively enough to nourish in them any kind of curiosity about her history or her future, the Field Security sergeant, whose name was Perron, was soon left in little doubt of his audience's indifference to the political machinations and territorial ambitions of Mahdaji and Daulat Rao Sindia. Since he had embarked on the lecture with neither enthusiasm nor optimism, the audible appeal to wrap it up for ****** sake caused him no surprise and scarcely a pang. His closing description of a lady-warrior said to have reduced her male rivals to a state of military impotence, by admitting them to her chamber one after the other on the night before a battle, brought the lecture to an end in an atmosphere of near-hysteria. 'Bring 'er on,' the same voice cried, and the room then resounded to whistling and the stamping of hundreds of ammunition boots – a noise that greeted the Welfare Officer as he arrived to see how Sergeant Perron was getting on and which seemed to encourage him in a belief that such lectures were a good thing; a belief of which Sergeant Perron did not disabuse him because he had decided quite early in his military service that for life to be supportable officers had to be protected from anything that might shatter their illusion that they knew what the men were thinking.

Knowing himself incapable of reaching the required standard

of self-deception in this, and other matters that came under the heading 'Leadership', and believing that life in the ranks would provide him with a far greater measure of freedom and better opportunities to study in depth human behaviour during an interesting period of history, he had politely but stubbornly res- isted every attempt made to commission him. Only one set of the batch of uncles and aunts who had taken it in turns to bring him up thought this short-sighted. The others approved of his decision. They thought it agreeably eccentric, quite in keeping with the radical upper-class tradition which they liked to feel distinguished them as a family.

'It obviously went down well,' the Welfare Officer said, toning down his North Country accent and matily accompany- ing Perron from the lecture hall. 'I must say I had doubts, but a chap who really knows his subject is more likely to pass some of his enthusiasm on than not. You must do some more, sergeant.'

'A good idea, sir.'

'These waiting periods are damned difficult. There's a batch of airborne blokes due in soon. Now that the show in Germany's over they'll be itching to get started and give the Jap a knock. They'll be a handful to keep occupied and entertained. I know you've got your own special security job to do but I'd be grateful if you'd spare half an hour to talk to them one morning on this Indian history thing of yours. I'll try and come myself. Learn a bit too. Extend my range beyond the Black Hole. Never too late for that, eh?'

Perron said, 'Actually, if you don't mind, sir, I think they're more relaxed without an officer present.'

Captain Strang looked relieved. To reassure the officer that his interest was appreciated but that his friendliness would not be taken advantage of and made an excuse for slack behaviour, Perron slapped up a particularly smart one when they parted and would have stamped his feet had they not been standing in a puddle. Perron had cultivated a formidable parade-ground style and soldierly manner not only to preserve that encouraging image of discipline and efficiency which heartened officers but also (after a tiresome experience with a Seaforth Highlander captain in the map-room of a camp on Salisbury Plain) to minimize the risk of his BBC accent (as fellow-NCOs called it) and his cultural interests giving them the impression that he was a pansy.

*

The sight of the armada gathering off Bombay – a city to which
Sergeant Perron's field security duties now began to take him
fairly regularly – appearing, disappearing and reappearing as the
curtains of monsoon rain and mist rose and fell with sinister effect,
did not usually depress him. In four years of service he had learned
to look upon the entire war as an under-rehearsed and over-
directed amateur production badly in need of cutting. In this light
the low grey shapes of the troopships and escorts could be seen
as figments of the imagination of an unknown but persistent
operational planning staff whose directives had caused them to
appear. The same imagination could just as easily dispel them.
Nothing in the army was absolutely sure until it happened and he
did not intend to worry about Zipper or the danger he might be
in until the ships weighed anchor with himself on one of them.

But on the afternoon of Sunday August 5 as he drove past
the Taj Mahal Hotel in a brand-new jeep that had been lent in
temporary exchange for the motor-cycle he had left at the
motor-pool for water-proofing for the sea-borne landings in
Malaya, he observed that the armada had increased in size since
his view of it a couple of days before. Perhaps it was the sense
of futility lingering from his previous day's lecture on the Mahrattas that chiefly contributed to his unusual feeling of disquiet,
of there being something in the air that boded no good and
moved him to nostalgic thoughts of a world where peace and
common sense prevailed.

Being early for his appointment with a Major Beamish he
stopped the jeep and gazed at the brown-grey waste of Bombay
water. Without ever having taken any other personal avoiding
action than that of co-operating cheerfully over the deferment
of his call-up to enable him to sit his finals and obtain his degree,
he had managed to get through the war so far without coming
any closer to a violent end than half a mile away from a bomb
off-loaded by a Heinkel over Torbay after a night visit to Bristol.
But he had always assumed that his turn for danger would come.
Posted to India in 1943 he had expected it to come quite soon
but, of course, any apprehension that he felt in regard to that
was combined with the excitement of finding himself after
several years' scholarly absorption in Britain's imperial history
actually in the country in which so much of it had originated.

In the first six months the luck of the draw of postings had given him opportunities to visit Cawnpore, Lucknow, Fort St George, Calcutta, Seringapatam, Hyderabad, Jaipur and Agra, and if he had felt some disappointment in these places as relics of old confrontations he had always managed to suppress it before it grew strong enough to undermine his academic confidence. 'India', he wrote in his notebook, 'turns out to be curiously immune to the pressures of one's knowledge of its history. I have never been in a country where the sense of the present is so strong, where the future seems so unimaginable (unlikely even) and where the past impinges so little. Even the famous monuments look as if they were built only yesterday and the ruined ones appear really to have been ruined from the start, and that but recently.'

Occasionally he was tempted to blame the war for his inability to relate the country he saw to what he knew of its past and at such times he thought how interesting it would be to come back or stay on when the war was over, to examine India undisturbed. But this afternoon, looking at the unfriendly vista of the Arabian Sea which as a boy he had thought the most romantically named ocean in the world, he felt more strongly than ever how perilously close to losing confidence the actual experience of being in India had brought him; and he wanted to go home – not (like the men to whom he had lectured) merely for home's sake or to enjoy the first fruits of a new political dispensation (for which he too had posted his vote by proxy through his Aunt Charlotte) – but so that he could regain lucidity and the calm rhythms of logical thought. These, he knew, depended upon a continuing belief in one's grasp of every issue relevant to one's subject and India seemed to be the last place to be if one wanted to retain a sense of historical proportion about it.

He got out his notebook with the intention of writing something down that might clarify his thoughts and expose as baseless his nagging doubts about the value of work he intended to do in pursuit of certain ineluctable truths but just as there seemed to be no connection between the India he was in and the India that was in his head there was no connection either between paper and pencil and the page remained ominously blank. This depressed him so much that he wrote out in a determined hand: 'Tell Aunt Charlotte that Bunbury is deteriorating rapidly?'

*

'This is Captain Purvis, sergeant,' Major Beamish said, indicating a thin-faced, mousy-haired, ill-looking man who was dosing himself with brown pills which he washed down with water without quite choking. 'You an' 'e are goin' this evenin' to a party.' Beamish, like so many elderly regular officers, spoke a kind of upper-crust cockney.

'Yes, sir,' Perron said, keeping his thumbs in line with the seams of his trousers.

Beamish was in a bad temper, either as a result of a thick Saturday night or of lingering resentment at being made to work on a Sunday. He said, 'Fer God's sake sit down. It's too bloody hot fer parade-ground manners.'

Perron, who stood over six feet in his socks, chose the deepest of three available chairs in deference to Major Beamish whose trunk was short in proportion to his legs and who therefore sat lower at his desk than seemed either fair or suitable for a man of his domineering temperament. Satisfied that his eye-level was now a flattering few inches below Beamish's, Perron met the officer's gaze with soldierly frankness.

'D'yer have yer civvies with yer?'

Before Perron could answer, the other officer – who was now sitting with his eyes closed and his arms folded – broke in. 'Shouldn't advise civvies in this case.'

'I have my Army Education Corps gear, sir,' Perron said.

'Those'll do,' Purvis said.

'You fill 'im in, Purvis, or shall I?'

'Would you? I'll interrupt if I don't think you've got it right. Could we have that fan on more?'

Perron got up and went to the board of switches and turned up the dial that regulated the ceiling fan. Irritably, Beamish reallocated weights to keep the papers moored to the desk top, then lit a cigarette but did not offer the tin.

'It's about security fer Zipper and loose talk here in Bombay,' he began. Perron listened attentively for the ten seconds it took Beamish to pass from the informative to the opinionative mood and then tried to tune in what he called his other ear: the one that caught the nuances of time and history flowing softly through the room, a flow arrested neither by Beamish's concerns nor his own sense of obligation to further them by putting himself at

Beamish's disposal. Glancing at Purvis he wondered whether that officer also heard the whisper of the perpetually moving stream or whether the expression of concentration was due to the compelling effect of the brown pills. When Purvis's brows suddenly contracted he decided it must be the latter.

'Are yer still with us, sergeant?'

'Yes, sir.'

'Right. Tell 'im about the party, Purvis.'

For a moment Purvis neither spoke nor moved. Then he opened his eyes.

'God!' he said, got up and went out of the room.

'Feller's got squitters,' Beamish explained.

'Who is Captain Purvis, sir?'

'Damned if I know. Brig didn't say. Never met 'im in me life till half an hour ago. Seems a bit of a wash-out ter me. Chap should be able to keep 'imself fitter than that!'

A chaprassi came in with a foot-high pile of folders tied up in pink tape and put them by the side of a similar pile on the In side of Major Beamish's desk. There was a single file in the Out tray. The chaprassi took this with him when he went. Beamish poured himself a glass of water then took the top folder from the nearest of the two piles.

'Smoke if yer want ter,' he said. 'While we're waitin'.'

Perron murmured his thanks but did not do so. Beamish read the note in the file, initialled it, flung the folder in the Out tray and reached for the next.

Ten minutes later Purvis came back. Beamish was reading the minute in the last folder of the second pile. Without glancing up he said, 'Feelin' better?'

'Frankly, no. I think the sergeant will have to come back to my billet. I'll put him in the picture there. In any case he'll need somewhere to change and freshen up for this evening.'

'All right, sergeant, get along with Captain Purvis. Are yer goin' back ter Kalyan ternight?'

'That was my intention, sir.'

'Ring me from there in the mornin'. We'll decide if there's anything ter follow up.'

Perron stood, put his cap on, stamped to attention and saluted. As he turned he caught the tail end of a wince on Captain Purvis's face.

'Shoes, sergeant! Have you got *shoes*?' Purvis asked.

'In my pack, sir. With the uniform.'

'Thank God for that. What are you on, a motor-bike?'

'I've got a jeep today, sir.'

'We'll dump it at my office.'

Outside in the corridor Purvis maintained his distance a couple of paces ahead. They passed a long bench on which a line of chaprassis dozed, like figures on a frieze in bas-relief, awaiting employment. The building – currently at the disposal of the army and navy – belonged to the port authority and smelt of rope, gunny sacks and the dust on old bills of lading. Through the immense windows in the main corridor into which they turned came that other pervasive dockyard smell of oily water: Bombay, Bom-Bahia, an island swamp, part of the dowry brought by Catherine of Braganza to Charles II which it took the British five years to persuade the Portuguese Viceroy actually to hand over. Perron stemmed the stream of thought before it could disorient him, apart from which Purvis walked very fast and Perron didn't want to run the risk of losing him in the labyrinth. He concentrated on Purvis's back and noticed that the officer's shoulders were hunched – probably against the ringing sound of Perron's studded boots on the stone floor.

Descending by a broad stone staircase they reached the main entrance hall on whose marble flags stood a profusion of poles on heavy plinths which bore directional signs. None of the officers and NCOs passing to and fro glanced at the signs and Perron wondered how long it would take for the place to be reduced to a state of hopeless confusion if someone ever took it into his head to move the signs round. Perhaps no one would ever notice.

He smiled and at that moment Purvis stopped and faced him. They nearly bumped into one another. Whatever Purvis had intended to say he forgot.

'Something amusing you, sergeant?'

'No, sir.'

'I mean if there is, do *share* it.'

Perron told him his thought about the signs. Purvis glanced at them. Without another word he led the way into the open: a forecourt normally crammed with vehicles but today fairly empty. In the minute or so since they had left Beamish's office the sun had come out. The heat struck Perron's eyelids.

'Where's this jeep of yours, then?'

Perron indicated it.

'No driver?'

'Only me, sir.'

Purvis went down the steps. 'Mine's that fifteen hundred-weight Chevvy. Follow me and for God's sake keep up. Right?'

Jeep-borne, Perron followed the truck through the archway which was blocked at night by a white pole but at present open to all comers and goers under the eye of a stick-guard who was supposed to inspect identity cards but was taking people on trust. They drove along a road parallel to the docks. At the end of it Purvis's truck turned left. Caught in the midst of Bombay's traffic – buses, cyclists, hooting taxis, overladen trucks, horse-drawn doolies and jay-walking pedestrians – Perron concentrated on not losing contact. The truck braked sharply to avoid an obstacle Perron couldn't see. He slammed on his own brakes and stopped a foot or two short of an impact that might have snapped the tether Purvis seemed to be near the end of. Possibly the nest of spies, fifth-columnists and loose-talkers Perron gathered Purvis thought he'd uncovered was totally illusory. Driving on, but allowing more distance (and noting that the cause of the abrupt halt had been a handcart piled high with crates of live fowl, hauled by a half-naked coolie) Perron decided that so long as Purvis wasn't at his elbow the entire evening, hissing warnings, the party might be supportable; or even enjoyable.

Purvis's billet turned out to be a flat in one of the modern blocks opposite the Oval – that elegant, coconut-palm-fringed rectangle of open, grassed, space; or *maidan*; brilliantly green at this wet time of year. They reached the block in Purvis's truck, having left Perron's jeep in the courtyard of a house several streets away which was guarded by sentries but otherwise unidentifiable as a military office. Purvis had instructed the guard-commander that Sergeant Perron was to be readmitted on production of his identity card at whatever time of night he returned, in whatever kind of clothing or uniform, and be allowed to collect and take away his jeep; but – short though the journey was – the route then taken from Purvis's office to Purvis's billet seemed to Perron, in the back of the truck, so complicated that he had doubts about finding his way back to his jeep unaccompanied.

This had not bothered him much because he assumed they would go to the party in the fifteen hundredweight and be brought back from it by the same means, after which he would be taken to retrieve the jeep; but when they dismounted in Queen's Road Purvis signed the driver's log book and dismissed him until morning.

'Is the party being given nearby, sir?' Perron asked as they approached the entrance to the block of flats. Purvis didn't answer. He was in a hurry. Reaching the two steps that led to the open doorway and a dark hall he stumbled up them, bumped into and almost knocked down a servant who was coming out ahead of a young English woman.

'For God's sake look where you're going!' Purvis shouted.

If he was aware of the girl he gave no sign of it. He brushed past the two of them and disappeared into the dark.

'I do beg your pardon,' Perron said to the girl.

'Why?' she asked.

'I'm afraid the officer isn't well. He couldn't have seen you.'

She studied his uniform briefly, taking everything in at a glance as young English women in India were trained to.

'It wasn't me he bumped into, it was Nazimuddin. But thank you for apologizing for him.'

He waited for her to add ' – sergeant', but she smiled instead, an ordinary friendly smile, then put on the hat she had been carrying. The movement released a little wave of delicate scent. She came down the two steps and made for the pavement and the road where the ill-used bearer was flagging down a cruising taxi. She was a bit thin, a bit bony, but she walked well. He judged her to be in her early twenties but found it difficult to place her. Accent, style of dress, forthrightness: these proclaimed her a daughter of the *raj*, but her manner had lacked that quality – elusive in definition – which Perron had come to associate with young memsahibs: a compound of self-absorption, surface self-confidence and, beneath, a frightening innocence and attendant uncertainty about the true nature of the alien world they lived in. They were born only to breathe that rarefied, oxygen-starved air of the upper slopes and peaks, and so seemed to gaze down, from a height, with the touching look of girls who had been brought up to know everybody's place and were consequently determined to have everybody recognize their own.

Waiting until she had completed that movement – charming in a girl, especially in her – of climbing into the taxi, he shouldered the pack containing his Army Education Corps disguise, went into the building and through the gloom to an inner only slightly better lighted hall where there was a lift shaft and a flight of stone steps leading up. A notice, askew on a piece of string suspended from the handle of the trellis–work gate, informed him that the lift was out of order, but in any case he would not have known which floor to go to. There was no sound from above of Purvis climbing. The door of the flat immediately to his right had a dark–stained strip of wood above the bell with gold-lettering on it saying Mr B. S. V. Desai. To the left a similar notice read H. Tractorwallah. Both these doors seemed unlikely ones for Purvis to be on the other side of and neither had the look of having been opened recently.

Perron ascended. On the next floor the two flats were occupied respectively by a Lieut.-Colonel A. Grace and a Major Rajendra Singh of the Indian Medical Service. The Indian medical officer's name seemed to have been painted on its strip of wood longer ago than Colonel Grace's. Perron hesitated, but then, deciding that if Purvis was billeted on this floor one of the two doors would have been left open, started on the next leg up and as he did so heard a voice above call, 'Sahib?'

Purvis's servant, he supposed. The man salaamed, stood back as Perron reached the next landing, and indicated the open door of the flat above Rajendra Singh's. As he entered he heard a groan. The servant closed the door and went quickly down a corridor to a curtained doorway. The groan was repeated. A tap was turned on. Perron put his pack down, went in the opposite direction to the one the servant had taken and entered a dining-area. This was separated from a living-room by a wide un-curtained arch. The living-room was elegantly furnished, filled with aqueous light of sunshine filtered through a set of louvred shutters. On a wall behind a long settee hung a series of what looked like paintings from the Moghul period, which upon close inspection Perron identified as genuine. He was still admiring them when the servant came in and invited him to go along to Captain Purvis's room.

This room, although large, was barrack-like by comparison. Apart from an almirah and a wooden table littered with books, papers and some discarded shirts, there was nothing else in it except a rush-seated chair and the camp-bed on which Purvis was lying, one hand over his eyes, the other hanging free, almost touching the floor. But an open door afforded a glimpse of a well-appointed green-tiled bathroom.

Purvis said, 'I'm not going to be able to make it, sergeant. You'll have to go by yourself or forget the whole thing. I wish to God I'd kept my mouth shut. It's all an utter waste of time. Every bloody civilian in Bombay knows where Zipper's going and why it's going and how it's going. We're the exceptions. We know where. But they know where better. They can even name the damned beaches. It'll be a shambles, a complete and unholy utter bloody cocked-up shambles.'

Suddenly Purvis uncovered his eyes and stared wildly at Perron.

'You *are* Field Security?'

'Yes, sir.'

'Beamish isn't. What the hell is he?'

'He has certain responsibilities for liaison between intelligence and operations.'

'But he's not your officer?'

'No, sir. My officer is in Poona at the moment.'

Purvis shut his eyes.

'Poona,' he said, almost under his breath. 'It scarcely seems possible.'

'Poona, sir? Or that my officer is there?'

But Purvis didn't say. Outside the barred but open window there was a sudden piercing contest of crows and then a human voice below in the courtyard raised in what to an untutored ear must sound like a protracted cry of pain but which Perron knew was only the call of an itinerant tradesman. Purvis groaned and turned on his side, the side away from the window. At that moment the sun went in and the sluice-gates of the wet monsoon reopened. Purvis's lips began to move but Perron could hear nothing above the noise of the rainstorm.

The bearer parted the curtains and came in with a tray of tea for two. Perron assisted by clearing a space on the table and when the bearer had gone he looked at Purvis intending to say, 'Shall I be mother, sir?' but the officer's eyes were open, fixed and unreceptive – in fact, glazed. For a moment Perron thought he was dead, extinguished by the single clap of thunder that had heralded the arrival of the tea.

Refreshed, bathed and now disguised as a sergeant in education, Perron walked – shoe- instead of boot-shod – along the tiled passage to the living-room where he found Purvis standing on a balcony that had been revealed by the folding back of shutters and windows. It was now a beautiful evening with a sky the colour of pale turquoise. The coconut palms framed a view of the Law Courts and clock tower on the other side of the *maidan*.

'I appreciated the bath, sir. I'm afraid I used some of your Cuticura talcum.'

Purvis had a glass in the hand that rested on the balustrade.

'Help yourself to a drink, sergeant. You'll find everything on the tray.'

There was, if not everything, a generous selection: gin, whisky, rum, several bottles of Murree beer and various squashes and cordials. The spirits were country-distilled so Perron – not caring much for rum of any kind – chose the gin which he found more palatable than Indian versions of Scotch. He added lemon-squash and – luxury for him – a cube of ice from a zinc-lined container.

'Cheers, sir.'

'I'm an economist,' Purvis said, irrelevantly to everything except his private train of thought. 'It's enough to send you round the bloody bend.'

He came in from the balcony, refilled his glass with rum and lime and sat on the long settee under the priceless paintings. After drinking a stout measure he shuddered, closed his eyes and put his head back.

'Can you guess how long I've been ill, sergeant?'

'No, sir.'

'Since I got off the boat. And that's three months, two weeks and four days ago.'

'Bad luck, sir.'

Purvis raised his eyelids a fraction and looked at him. Perron was standing with his feet apart, one hand behind his back, the other at waist level holding the tumbler steady.

'How long have you been in this bloody country?'

'Since 'forty-three, sir.'

'And in the army?'
'Since 'forty-one, sir.'
'Before that?'
'Cambridge, sir.'
'Doing what?'
'I rowed a bit. And read history.'
'What was your school?'
'Chillingborough, sir.'
'How the hell have you avoided getting a commission?'
'By always saying no, sir.'
Purvis shut his eyes again. His face began to contort.
'I'm sorry,' he said, 'but that is extremely funny.' He did not
say why but took another long drink, set the glass on a low table
in front of the settee then leant back with his hands clasped
behind his head.

'The party,' he said, changing the subject and ploughing
straight into the new one, 'is in the apartment of an Indian lady
living on the Marine Drive. I'll write her a note, so you'll have
the address on the envelope. There should be no difficulty about
your going in my place. I was there the other night and she
doesn't seem to care how many people turn up or whether she
knows them or not. You'll see what I mean when you get there.
Judging from the other day there'll be a lot of non-commissioned
men so you won't feel out of place. The fact is, it seems to be
the kind of flat where officers and men fraternize, not to mention
white, black and in-between. Sexually I'd say some of the company was on the ambivalent side.'

'Yes, sir.'
'Will that worry you?'
'I don't think so, sir.'
'You may even be taken for a special sort of friend of mine.'
'I think I shall be able to cope in the event of a misunder-
standing arising, sir.'

'Not that I care a fig about my own reputation. I shan't go
there again. In any case you'll find lots of girls, if you can sort
out the ones who're only interested in men.'

Perron finished his drink but retained his glass.

'Apart from unambivalent girls, sir, what precisely should
I look out for? Any special person or group of people?'

'So far as I'm concerned, sergeant, you can just go there and get stoned or laid, as our American allies so picturesquely put it. I *told* you. The whole thing's an utter waste of time. You're not going to arrest anybody. At least, not for spying.'

'Major Beamish seemed to think otherwise about it being a waste of time, sir.'

'Think? Think? He's a professional soldier. They're all alike and worse out here than back home. Totally automatic. Touch a button by accident and they go into action. I'll tell you, Perron –'

Perron was surprised to find that his name had registered.

'– how this bloody farce you're up to the neck in started.'

Three days ago Purvis had encountered, in circumstances not clear, an old friend – obviously a breezy, hectic sort of man – who had whisked him up from whatever he'd been doing, dined him at the Taj and taken him off to the apartment in Marine Drive which Purvis's friend had described as 'always good for a lark'; as indeed it had proved, in so far as an uninterrupted flow of drink, food and merrymaking was concerned. Although Purvis did not say so, Perron understood that the larkiness had been infectious enough to make Purvis forget his chronic inter-nal disorder and become expansive with his hostess to whom in a weak but hospitable moment he had promised one of two remaining bottles of whisky he'd managed to get hold of in England and bring out to India for personal consolation. She had declined but he'd insisted and then been invited to come to another party with or without the bottle on the evening of August 5.

'I could have forgotten the whole damned thing,' Purvis said, 'if I hadn't stupidly made a casual remark next day to the bloody fool officer I work with about the amount of careless talk going on in Bombay. He said – where for instance? And instead of shutting up I said "Well, take this odd party I was at last night where the Indian civilians were actually telling *us* that the Zipper invasion fleet wouldn't sail for Malaya until the end of August because of the tides on the beaches around Port Swettenham," and the next thing I knew the bloody man had reported it and I was hauled in front of that Brigadier Whatsit and congratulated on keeping my ears open. When he heard I'd been invited to the same flat tonight he was like a cat with two tails and before I knew where I was I was under strict security routine and told to say nothing more until I had instructions, and that was this

morning when I was ordered to report to this Beamish fellow
of yours. When Beamish told me I had to go to the party with
a Field Security chap in disguise I thought he was joking. I tried
to tell him you can hear that kind of talk anywhere in Bombay
but he wouldn't *listen*.'

Perron put his empty glass on the drinks table.

'Are we landing on beaches near Port Swettenham, sir?'

'How the hell do I know? I've got no personal interest in
Zipper. I'm not going, thank God. Are you?'

'Yes, sir.'

'Oh.'

Purvis noticed Perron's drink was finished. He said, 'Help
yourself, sergeant.'

'Thank you, sir. But I think a clear head might be advisable
this evening.'

'Advisable? In this country?'

Purvis became restless and Perron momentarily allowed himself to stop thinking of him as an officer with an officer's responsibilities for getting the war over and done with and think of him
as a man, one whom in other circumstances he might even like.

'Well if you're *on* Zipper,' Purvis said, 'I suppose you have to
take all this incredible lack of security seriously. I don't suppose
you want to be shot out of the water by the Japanese before
you've even set foot in the damned country, especially at this
stage in the war.'

'I should prefer not to be, sir.'

'Does it bore you to call people sir?'

'No, sir.'

Purvis got up. He refilled his glass.

'What is your actual job, sir, if I may ask?'

'You may well ask. I've given up asking. I've even given up
asking myself. Three times in my life the phone's rung and the
fellow on the other end has said, "Can you get down to see me,
Purvis? I've got something special for you." And each time it's
ended like this, with me wondering not what's special about it
but what it *is*. The first time was 'thirty-nine. I'd done a few
papers that were well thought of. I'd got a good lectureship. And
then the war started and the phone rang. "Purvis," this fellow
said, "if you can get here in twenty minutes I've got something
that will interest you." I was there with three minutes to spare

and an hour to wait. And that led to a folding chair behind a deal-table in an attic without heating and a telephone that never rang. I thought I was supposed to contribute some original thinking to the problems of distribution of goods and services as between high and low priority demand sectors, or in layman's terms, the problems of trying to stop the army wasting what could be saved and what the civil population could bloody well make use of. I even drafted a paper and this chap rang up cock-a-hoop and said it was just what he wanted but if that was so I must have been under a misapprehension about what he wanted it for. I was in that attic for eighteen months. Then the phone rang again. Same chap, "Purvis," he said, "I've got some-thing I think will get you out of that dead-end you're in." I arrived half an hour late, deliberately, which put him in a filthy temper because he'd promised to ring this colonel chap that very morning and tell him if I was interested. He sent me off to one of those anonymous areas somewhere near Stanmore which always strike me as vaguely sinister. When I saw the colonel he struck me as sinister too. He said, "We've read your paper" but hedged when I said I'd done several and which did he mean.

'The trouble is, Perron, I used to be the sort of man who couldn't bear to embarrass another by making it plain I saw through him and knew he was talking cock. So I let it go and just concentrated on trying to find out what I was supposed to *do*. I never did from him. But then they sent for me from the War House. This time it was a mere major. Awfully pleasant chap. He'd actually read my paper on high and low priority demand sectors. I don't say he'd understood it. But he'd read it. And he called me *Mr* Purvis. He was even articulate about the job. Wrong. But articulate. He made me feel the inspiration for the special joint services advisory staff that he said was being got together to liaise with the various ministries and industry had been my paper and that I'd be one of its kingpins. "One thing," he said, "we'd want you in uniform. An immediate commission, naturally." '

Purvis's complexion suddenly went grey, either as a result of acute recollection or of acute physical discomfort. He downed the rest of his rum and poured another.

'I said I couldn't see what use a commission was. I'd signed the official secrets thing when I went to the attic. Well, as I said, he

was an awfully pleasant chap. We didn't argue, and I went back
to the attic and waited. I waited three weeks. When the summons
came it wasn't to the War House but to the office of my benefactor. He congratulated me on making such a good impression
on the people he'd recommended me to. He described my new
job as the opportunity I'd been waiting for to exercise my talents
as an economist for the country's benefit, an opportunity not to
be thrown away on the totally irrelevant issue of what style of
dress I exercised them in. I said, "You're right. Irrelevant is the
word. So why the fuss? The army isn't me. Neither is officer
status." '

Purvis sat down; he'd got up to get more lime-juice. He sat
crouched, elbows on knees, head lowered and eyes hidden by
his free hand. His shoulders began to shake.

'I'm sorry, sergeant, but it's so bloody funny. What you said
about always saying no to a commission brought it all back.'

He straightened up.

'I'll tell you what this fellow said. "Purvis," he said, "in this
country only a man born and bred *in* the officer-class can decline
a commission without running the risk of having his integrity
and future usefulness doubted." '

'Was that some kind of threat, sir?'

'Threat? It was a bloody ultimatum. Get into uniform or
get out of the department. Not just out of the department but
out of line for anything half-decent going after the war. Not to
mention the immediate danger of ceasing a reserved occupation,
getting called up and wasting the rest of the war as a highly
inefficient and underemployed squaddie.'

'And subsequently, sir? Were your experiences as an officer on
the advisory staff as unsatisfactory as those in the attic?'

'Oh no. No, I couldn't say that. Not unsatisfactory. Nor
satisfactory. You see, Perron, there never was an advisory staff.
I mean there was never *that* one. Plenty of others. It took me
several weeks to realize that ours didn't actually exist. I used to
go to these meetings. At first I thought I'd missed something
important about its inauguration, because of the Gas course.'

'Gas course?'

'The day I reported to the War House disguised as an acting
captain and war substantive lieutenant, the nice major said, "Oh,
Purvis" – he'd dropped the mister, you see. "Purvis," he said,

"d'you mind awfully, there's this boring gas thing come up, but I suppose you might just as well learn how to use a WD mask since you've now got to carry one." So I went down to Salisbury Plain.'

'An interesting part of the country, sir.'

Purvis looked at him, as though testing for sincerity.

'I didn't find it so. I expect you had some rudimentary military training at that public school of yours. Isn't it one of those places with a long record of turning out the future soldiers and administrators of Empire?'

'I wasn't in OTC, sir. It wasn't compulsory.'

'Well I had no military training whatsoever. My progress to my current distinction was from elementary via secondary to grammar school and to the earnest heights of the London School of Economics. Walking about with three pips up and no faintest notion of how to salute let alone whom to salute can be a highly embarrassing experience. I was glad when I got back to the War House and they sent me to this quaint little establishment off the Marylebone High Street where a retired Guards sergeant-major taught a batch of poor fellows like me how to dissemble sufficiently to avoid being put under close arrest as nuns parachuted in from Stuttgart. I almost wished, Perron, yes almost wished I'd scrubbed the whole career thing, been called up and gone into intellectual hibernation for the duration. There was something soothing about Sergeant-Major Bracegirdle. He was so pleased with us when we got anything *right*. In a way nothing is more restful than to stand in the ranks and do what the man says. The whole thing is definitely erotic, a sort of communal wet-dream without the discomfort but with that same sublimated asexual quality of purely involuntary obedience to a dominant force.'

Purvis caught his breath, placed one hand on the left side of his abdomen and then slowly breathed out. Inflammation of the colon, Perron decided. Amoebic in origin, almost certainly. Perron had become interested in the effects of tropical environment on temper and character. At home Purvis might well have been, as he had intimated, the most mild-mannered and considerate of men. Of strong constitution himself, Perron – who had not maintained his health in India without an almost valetudinarian attention to the medicinal needs of his body – had even so not been free of the shortness of temper that was one of the side-effects of an overworked and easily discouraged digestive system.

The insight this had given him into the possibly important part played in Anglo-Indian history by an incipient, intermittent or chronic diarrhoea in the bowels of the *raj* was one of the few definite academic advantages he felt he had gained by coming to India.

'Shall I freshen your drink, sir?'

'Oh, God, would you?'

Perron did so. Purvis now sat back, one arm stretched along the top edge of the settee, his face turned towards the window and the view – now fading – of the coconut palms.

'Have you ever felt it too, Perron? That the only way to survive a war is to treat it as totally unreal?'

'The thought has struck me, sir.'

'But have you ever succeeded?'

'From time to time.'

Purvis was silent for a moment.

'I envy you,' he said. 'I've tried. But I don't seem to have the capacity to pretend.' He looked at Perron. 'Six years! Six years' criminal waste of the world's natural resources and human skills. History, you said?'

Perron nodded.

'Seriously, or just as a way of spending the years of gilded youth?'

'I intend to continue.'

'Well, it's different for you, Perron. If you make a study of history you make one of human folly. But sometimes I believe I simply shall never be able to *forgive* it. I had a breakdown, you know.'

'I'm sorry to hear that, sir.'

'They sent me to this place full of human wrecks like myself, but I did my own therapy. Bloody fool me. I'd had a lot of spare time in the three years I was on the non-existent advisory staff. I'd been thinking about the long-term deleterious effect of imperial possessions on the economic viability and creative drive of the country that held them. Now I really got down to it. I did a paper and sent it to a chap I knew who published it. But how my benefactor in Whitehall got hold of it, God knows. I suppose he still received the journal it came out in and read it because my name was under it. Otherwise he'd given up serious reading in 1938, I should say. Incidentally, he's probably right now in the process of landing himself a plum job with Attlee's crowd. He was a Marxist when I first knew him, a Liberal Edenite anti-Municheer under Chamberlain, a high Tory under Winston, so why not a milk-and-water Socialist under Clem? But that's by the way. Let me tell you what happened.'

'The phone rang again, sir?'

'Same man, of course. "You've had a raw deal, Purvis," he said, "no one knows it better than I but it wasn't my fault. When you're out of that place come and see me. I think I can really help you this time if you make it soon." Has it ever struck you, Perron, that there is nothing more gullible in the whole animal world than a human being? One has this hysterical belief in the non-recurrence of the abysmal, I suppose. One always imagines one has reached the nadir and that the only possible next move is up and out. And then, of course, there was the magic formula – third time lucky. Why not? I placed the most inordinate confidence in that third ring of the telephone, so much so that the trick-cyclists thought I'd had an unprecedented overnight recovery and congratulated themselves no end. Directly I got down to London I rang this fellow and arranged to meet him. This time it was lunch at the club he'd been bucking to get into for years. He was already veering left again because he didn't see Churchill lasting long after the war. He introduced me to some of his new friends – I knew one or two of them myself and there was one in particular I respected. I thought, God, something's going to be done at last. I was right, but wrong about what. Something was being done. Von Rundstedt's attempt in the Ardennes had collapsed and all the signs were that the Germans were on their last legs. What was happening was people sniffing the peace and jockeying for position, but I was too stupid to see it like that at the time. I swallowed the whole line this fellow shot, about things now swinging the way of what he called "our sort of people" and how necessary it was to spike the guns of the old reactionary gang who'd be happy to let the war with Japan drag on and on and how our sort of people were determined that shouldn't happen. I ought to have seen through it when he started waffling about the Singapore-mentality that had come within an inch of bringing us to our knees in '42 and still existed out East in spite of all the efforts of men like Slim and Mount-batten to blow the cobwebs off the whole imperial-military apparatus. But I didn't. I just said, "Where's all this leading?" He said, "You mean what's in it for you?" That's the way he thought. "I'll tell you," he said, "that Indian paper of yours. It's really made an impression." I'd never thought of it as an Indian paper and I told him so. I told him it was a paper dealing in philosophical terms with an aspect of imperial economies and India came into it simply as an example, which didn't make me an expert on India. I shouldn't have said that. It gave him the line he needed. "But Purvis, experts on India are the last thing we want in India. We only want clear thinkers who'll help men like Bill and Dickie cut through the Singapore mentality and put ginger up the backsides of all those curry-colonels sitting in the Bengal Club in Calcutta and living in the nineteenth century." So I said, "Is that where you're sending me?" And he said it would be more likely Delhi where the real damage was done because GHQ India was still a vital link in Mountbatten's chain, *the* vital link, upon which the whole thing depended logistically, from the supply of men, arms and ammunition to the last piece of string and bamboo. Moreover, he said, if I wasn't an expert on India now I would be within a few months, at any rate in my own specialized field, and since the Indian empire was simply not going to survive in the kind of post-war world he knew he and I both hoped to see, my personal experience of it should prove invaluable to whatever government had the intricate job of transferring power to the Indians and advising them during a period of transition. "And that, Purvis," he said, "is the kind of little tree on which CBEs grow for the plucking. After which you can pretty well write your own ticket. Continue in public life or retire, suitably rewarded, to the blessed groves of Academe." '

A flash of monsoon lightning lit the darkling flat.

'Has he risen much himself, sir?'

'Oh yes. You mean since '39? Immeasurably. He might with questionable luck for the nation be a future Chancellor of the Exchequer. He wasn't permanent establishment. I shouldn't be surprised to hear he's resigned his appointment and contested and won a safe Labour seat in the recent election.'

For a while Purvis sat without speaking or moving. Then he said, 'I must admit that as a man who can see the way things are and the way they are going, he's always left me standing. Academically it was the other way round and I don't expect he's ever forgiven me for that. People don't, do they? Inside every successful man there's often a disappointed and envious one, wouldn't you say? Moaning and groaning and plotting and planning. You see, Perron, I know the score now. He's got me out of the way deliberately. So that no nice little plum should fall in my lap.' Purvis again suffered a spasm of pain. 'I suppose you wouldn't be so kind as to give me another refill, sergeant? I have an idea it would be dangerous for me to move.'

Perron again performed this duty. While he did so the servant padded barefoot into the dining-room area where he clicked two or three switches which turned on some of the wall lights in the living-room and a well-shaded table lamp. The effect was pleasant.

The bearer told Purvis his bath was ready.

Purvis waved him away. The bearer went.

'Is the entire flat yours, sir?' Perron asked, handing Purvis the refilled glass.

'No. Thank you, sergeant. No, I wish it were. I'm only billeted here. It belongs to a senior British bank official, his ghastly wife and his beastly simpering daughter. They're on leave in what they call Ooty, which I gather is Anglo-Indian for Ootacamund. As you can imagine, he and I don't get on. We don't see eye to eye on the subject of the creation and distribution of wealth. He thinks England has just committed suicide and thinks I'm mad when I point out that it's not a socialist government but capitalist, simply substituting labour for finance. He tells people I'm a communist. Politically he's a bloody fool.'

'Are those paintings his, sir?'

'What paintings?'

'Those eighteenth-century paintings in the Guler-Basohli style. Behind you.'

Purvis didn't look. 'They may be part of the fixtures and fittings belonging to the bank for all I know.'

'I wonder whether he realizes their value.'

'Are they valuable?'

'Yes, sir.'

'Then obviously he doesn't. His lady-wife locked up all the Sheffield plate before going to Ooty. Frankly, I personally wouldn't know a work of art from a bee's arse and I fail to see any valid reason why one bit of pigment-daubed paper or canvas should be worth thousands and another worth sod–all, unless you fix the value of such things on the comparative basis of size of canvas and amount of paint actually expended.'

Perron stopped thinking of Purvis as a man and concentrated on the image of Purvis as an officer. Apart from inflammation of the colon, Purvis was suffering from paranoia. The man ought to be treated.

'What do the doctors say about your illness, sir?'

'I haven't seen any doctors.'

'Do you think that wise, sir?'

'Yes, I do.'

'You were taking some pills in Major Beamish's office, sir.'

'Oh, those. Our banker friend's lady-wife recommended them when I first arrived and she saw I'd already got the trots. They're supposed to cement you up. Sometimes they do. Sometimes they don't. The only thing that really helps is liquor. No wonder the sahibs have always gone around half-cut. If I report to the army doctors they'll either prescribe the same treatment or send me into dock for a check-up and I can't afford to be in dock, Perron. Not for a day. Not for an hour.'

'Why, sir? You gave me the impression that your duties here aren't onerous.'

'That's because I'm not even supposed to *be* here. I'm supposed to be in New Delhi. We're all supposed to be in New Delhi.'

'All?'

'The six of us who formed the para-military mission sent out to liaise with and advise the Indian Government, heads of services, and the Government at home, on – I quote – "all matters relevant to the anticipated increase of military forces requiring to be based in India as a consequence of a cessation of hostilities in Europe and the continuance thereof in South-East Asia, with special reference to the supply/demand factor as it will affect the existing ratio between civilian and military claims on the Indian economy". End of quote.'

'It sounds very distinguished, sir.'

'Quite. I should have smelt a rat. And I should have smelt another when I saw the names of two of my fellow missionaries, including that of the head, and another when we were sent out before the war in Europe was quite over, although in the latter case I could be forgiven for noticing no alarming odour, except that of uncharacteristic forethought.'

'Where are the other five members of the mission?'

'Disposed, singly, by the cunning Indian Government to various parts of the country. Only the head of the mission has managed to get to Delhi. So you see, Perron, why I must stay on my feet. I must be where the head of the mission knows where to find me. I must be instantly available to join him.'

'Have you heard from him recently, sir?'

'No.' Purvis again shut his eyes. 'No. *No.* I can't bear to let myself think it but I believe he's ratted on us. I believe he's comfortably esconced in some niche he's found that just fits him and no one else. I used to send him reports. I suppose the others still do. But when I began to suspect that he was collating them, falsifying them, and sending them back to Whitehall as an account of the mission's collective activities, I stopped. Childish, I suppose, but necessary, to flush him out or persuade him to flush *me* out. And, of course, I've nothing to report except a state of total chaos far worse than ever I encountered at home.'

He opened his eyes again but only for as long as it took him to drink the rest of his rum and lime.

'I used to think, Perron, that on the day we started handing the colonies back to the bloody natives we'd all be able to look the twentieth century in the face at last. But if India's an example the only way we'll be able to do that and stay sane is by wearing blinkers and dark glasses and forgetting such places actually exist, and leave them to stew in their own juice except during their inevitable periods of acute financial crisis when we'll have to pour money into them to stop a chain reaction of bankruptcy bringing any half-civilized economy to its knees.'

'What makes you think that, sir?'

'For heavens' sake, sergeant! You've been in India for what's it, two years? It's taken me no more than three months to write it off as a wasted asset, a place irrevocably ruined by the interaction of a conservative and tradition-bound population and an indolent, bone-headed and utterly uneducated administration, an elitist bureaucracy so out of touch with the social and economic thinking of even just the past hundred years that you honestly wonder where they've come from. Not England, surely?'

'Perhaps it's the enervating effect of the climate, sir.'

'It's nothing to do with the bloody climate. The fact is places like this have always been a magnet for our throwbacks. Reactionary, unco-operative bloody well expendable buggers from the upper and middle classes who can't and won't pull their weight at home but prefer to throw it about in countries like this which they've always made sure would remain fit places for them to live in. They've succeeded only too well. The most sensible thing for us to do is get rid of it fast to the first bidder before it becomes an intolerable burden.'

'Wouldn't that be rather unfair, sir? Historically, we have a moral obligation, surely?'

'I couldn't disagree more. Moral obligation! What next? It's disastrous *ever* to feel a moral obligation for other people's mistakes.'

It was in Perron's mind to say that he'd always been under the impression that certain material benefits had flowed from the imperial possession, enriching Britain if not demonstrably impoverishing India (but somehow widening the gap in the two standards of living?) and that moral considerations could surely not be totally ignored by economists and accountants. But he thought it better not to aggravate Purvis who in any case would almost certainly be a member of the school of thought which held that the flow of benefit had petered out several years ago and a law of diminishing returns set in so that now the flow was operating in reverse. He compromised.

'All the same, sir, and though I do appreciate what you say, I should hope to see the transfer of power accompanied by some indication of our continuing interest and concern.'

'I'm sure you'll be gratified then, sergeant. The demission will certainly be accompanied by such pious assurances. But they won't mean what it will be hoped they're thought to mean. Labour capitalism is no more generous than finance capitalism. Incidentally, we talk about transfer of power, demission of power, getting rid of it, whatever phrase you prefer, but that's going to be easier talked about than done.'

'Do you think so, sir? Some people say that once it's appreciated that we sincerely mean to go the Indians will sink their differences and agree how to work together.'

'Then personally I think some people are absolutely wrong because the Indians are utterly demoralized at the very thought of having to take the ghastly mess over and run it themselves. We'll have the devil's own job off-loading it. And, God! one says "it" as if it's a single transferable package which it isn't, never has been and now never will be.'

'A fact for which we're partly to blame, sir?'

'We? Don't sell me that divide and rule stuff. The bloody place was divided when the sahibs first came and will be divided when the stupid sods go because they've always been content to sit on their bums in their bloody clubs and interfere only when the revenues were slow coming in. The place is still *feudal*, Perron. And so far as I can see the only man of influence who's warned about that is whatever the chap's name is, Nehru, but he's a Brahmin aristocrat and can hardly speak any language but English, and against him you have to set the Mahatma and his bloody spinning wheel. Spinning wheel! In 1945. For God's sake, what's the man *at*? In the past twenty-five years he's done as much to keep the country stuck in the mud with his village-industry fixation as the whole bloody *raj* put together.'

Stung as much by his feeling that there was something in what Purvis said as by the sense of the unfairness of such casual elimi-nation of any consideration that didn't automatically fall within the economist's habitual terms of reference, Perron said:

'Your sponsor in Whitehall was right, sir. You've become an expert on India in a very short time.'

Purvis stared at him.

'Most Indian economists I've met happen to agree with me.'

'Yes I see, sir. Then perhaps that is a reason for optimism.'

'I doubt it, sergeant. It is in the Indian character to complain, but not to contest if a job depends on a posture of acquiescence. I'd better write you that letter. Bearer!'

While the letter was being written, Perron waited on the balcony and gazed across the Oval to the dark bulk of the Law Courts. For a moment – perhaps under the influence of that sym-bol of the one thing the British could point to if asked in what way and by what means they had unified the country, the single rule of law – he felt a pressure, as soft and close to his cheek as a sigh: the combined sigh of countless unknown Indians and of past and present members of the glittering insufferable *raj*; all disposable to make the world safe for Purvis. And other men like Purvis. (And, I suppose – Perron thought – for men like me.)

Purvis called him over and handed him an envelope. It was addressed to a Maharanee. Perron glanced at Purvis, mildly surprised, but the man was leaning back again, eyes closed. To Purvis, Maharanees were probably two a penny.

II

At seven-thirty Perron arrived by taxi at a block on the Marine Drive which according to the address on the envelope bore the name Sea Breezes. The driver he had flagged down in the Queen's Road translated this after several movements of uncertainty as Ishshee Brizhish, a place known to him. Armed with the envelope and a square package which contained the bottle of whisky, Perron entered the building and went up in the lift to the floor indicated by the board which gave flat numbers and the names of the occupants.

The décor in hall and landings was reminiscent of that in houses and apartments built in the ultra-modern style of the late 'twenties and early 'thirties, but it achieved a severe and bleak rather than a severe and functional effect. The cream-painted walls were dingy and the chromium rails bore the patina of years of contact with the human hand. The door of the flat at which he now stood was pea-green like those he had seen at successive stages through the latticework iron gates of the lift shaft and was well finger-marked round the keyhole.

He pressed the bell. No comforting sound of having got it to ring reached him and no hum of party conversation either. He wondered whether Purvis had the date right and then whether someone had tipped the Maharanee off about Security's interest in her circle of friends so that she had cancelled the party and would be found curled up with a good book. Wondering this he next considered the possibility that she had taken a fancy to Purvis and planned to lure him back to the flat with or without the bottle of whisky on a night when she knew they could be alone together. He could not assess the power of Purvis's sexual attraction. In such matters women had their own unassailable scale of values and judgment. But, having arrived at this possible explanation he now wondered how old she was and, if young, how well-favoured. The evening suddenly seemed full of an unexpected kind of potential.

The door was opened abruptly by a young Indian girl of gazelle-like charm. 'Hello,' she said. Clearly she had none of that creature's timidity.

'Hello. I've got a note and a package.'

'For me?'

He gave her the envelope. Her beautifully architectured eyebrows contracted. 'Oh, it's for Auntie. What a jolly shame. But do come in.'

'Thank you.'

Perron stepped inside and let her close the door. Her scent was too cloying for his taste but welcome after the smell on the night breeze blowing in from the Bombay foreshore which Perron was convinced was used as a lavatory. Indian insistence that it was just the smell of the sea and the seaweed had not yet made him change his mind.

In the hall – the top end of a long wide passage with doors leading off from either side of it and cluttered with solid but poorly assorted furniture, including an ornately carved black Chinese settle upholstered with velvet cushions – the girl took the package from him and put it together with the envelope on an ebony table on which a heavy and thick-ankled Shiva danced in his petrified ring of fire. She said, 'Come and have a drink why not?' and led the way into a living-room.

Around the walls sofas and chairs were set in the solemn and rather hostile manner of the segregational East. The tiled floor was uncarpeted – perhaps for dancing. There was no balcony but the windows were wide open. The lighting was less successful than in Purvis's flat. From the centre of the ceiling hung a cluster of bulbs in a cruciform wooden chandelier of the kind that at home was *de rigueur* in rooms that sported fake beams and parchment lampshades with galleons stencilled on them. But these bulbs were unshaded. A few wall-lights in glass and chromium brackets added to the glare but did nothing to eliminate the harsh shadows. Near the window was a cocktail cabinet of impressive vulgarity, and to this the girl had gone. She turned round.

'You're a sergeant, aren't you? Auntie says all sergeants drink beer but there was one the other night who asked for a White Lady.'

'Were you able to oblige him?'

'One of the officers got it for him but it took them ages because of the glass having to be put in the refrigerator.'

'A straightforward gin and lemon squash would suit this sergeant very well. Shall I make it myself and get you a drink too?'

'Oh, no. I'm supposed to do this sort of thing. Auntie says it's good for me because it helps me not to be shy. I used to be very shy. But if you like to hold the bottle and help to pour it would be nice because I find the bottles so heavy, and once I dropped one and Auntie trod on a piece of the glass and was very cross.'

Perron joined her at the Wurlitzer-style cabinet. At a rough estimate he thought there were about fifty glasses of different shapes set ready, none of them as clean as they might have been. Gravely he uncapped a bottle of Carew's and held it above the glass she presented. She put her hand on his and canted.

'Is that enough?'

'More than generous.'

'May I leave you to do the rest? I must take Auntie the letter and parcel. Oh −' She half-ran to an occasional table and returned with a cigarette box and a lighter. After he had taken a cigarette he had to hold the box because she insisted on lighting the cigarette for him and needed two hands to produce a flame.

'There. Please excuse me now. There are plenty of ashtrays.' At the door she again remembered something important. 'What is your name? If there were a lot of people it wouldn't matter but since there's only you it would look rude not to tell Auntie who it is, wouldn't it?'

He told her, and added, 'But I'm sure it's mentioned in the note.'

After she had gone Perron went to the window. For all his doubts about its present source he had long since learned to appreciate the sensuousness of the warm smell of the East and how it could set mind and body at ease. He enjoyed a sensation almost of tranquillity and continued to enjoy it for some time, in fact until he became aware of the riding lights of a section of the anchored Zipper-destined flotilla out in the roads. And then a ludicrous but slightly worrying image presented itself, of the Maharanee standing at this very window, observing the scene in daylight through a telescope and dictating notes for the girl to record (in invisible ink) about the class and tonnage of each ship as it arrived and dropped anchor.

'Auntie says will you come through?'

The girl was standing in the open doorway. He stubbed his cigarette and followed her into the long passage and down to a door at the end which, if closed before, now stood half-open upon a room so dark that at first he thought there was no light on at all and hesitated to enter when the girl indicated that he should do so.

'It's all right. Auntie has been resting but she's finished now.' Inside, he saw that there was a light, but this was from a table lamp in the far corner of the room whose shade was draped with a square of what looked like heavy crimson velvet. A hand, in silhouette, crept over the cloth and removed it; and in the now brighter but still deep rosy glow of the lamp the Maharanee was revealed, recumbent on a Récamier couch. Her saree was also red, but of what shade and intensity Perron could not easily judge because the material obviously took colour from the lamp shade. She seemed like an ember that might at any moment pulse brilliantly and dangerously into life. She wore no jewellery. Her skin was pale but darker than that of the Parsee ladies of Bombay. Her hair, cut and set in a style that obviously owed more to what she thought suited her than it did to any fashion of the day, was black, unoiled, parted in the middle, and fell, in corrugations of the kind obtained by using hot tongs, just short of her shoulders, framing a classic Rajput face of prominent cheekbones, full red lips, a hawklike but beautifully proportioned nose, and eyes whose luminosity was accentuated by cunningly applied kohl. Between her black brows she had painted a red tika one-quarter inch in diameter. She looked about thirty and was probably forty. She wore no choli and both arms, one shoulder and part of her midriff were bare. Perron, half-convinced he also saw the thrust and outline of a nipple, found her seductively handsome.

'Auntie,' the girl said from behind him. 'This is Sergeant Perrer. Sergeant Perrer, this is my Auntie Aimee.'

Perron bowed.

'Have you come to my party?' the Maharanee asked in a high-pitched but slightly hoarse voice. 'I'm afraid you're on the early side. Aneila opened the door to you because all the servants are resting. I make them rest because sometimes my parties go on for a day or two. Aneila, what is wrong with you? Why is our visitor still standing?'

'I'm sorry, Auntie.'

Perron turned to help her but the chair she chose was very small and presumably almost weightless. She managed it easily, placing it two feet from the couch.

'Now you had better go to start rousing everybody.'

'Yes, Auntie.'

'Tell them the guests are beginning to arrive. Do sit down. Have we met before?'

'I've not had that pleasure, Your Highness.'

'Please call me Aimee. Pandy and I are divorced. I keep the title because it is useful and servants and shop people like it and Pandy's new wife doesn't. Are you a friend of someone I know?'

Perron explained his mission and drew her attention to the package and envelope which were on the table, propped against the lamp where Aneila had presumably left them.

'Captain Purvis?' she asked, reaching for the letter. 'He must be one of Jimmy's friends. When Jimmy is in Bombay he brings so many people.' She opened the letter. The paper it was written on seemed to displease her. She held it between the tips of two fingers whose nails were elegantly manicured and varnished. 'Leonard?' she said. 'Leonard Purvis?' And presently, 'Whisky?' The note although short called for concentration. 'Chillingborough and Cambridge? Why does he tell me this? Why shouldn't you have studied at Chillingborough and Cambridge? So many Englishmen do. Who is Leonard Purvis?'

'A member of an economic advisory mission to the Government of India.'

'Are you also in this mission?'

'No, I'm concerned with army education.'

'What does the mission do?'

'I don't think it does anything.'

'And what do you do?'

'Very little.'

'What a relief. People are always dashing about. What is your first name?'

'Guy.'

'Have you another?'

'Lancelot.'

She frowned.

'There's also Percival,' he said, and added, 'but I'm not keen on it.'

'Names are a terrible problem. It is best to make them up. Will you stay to my party? It may be boring but it is difficult to tell in advance. It depends on who comes. If it is too tedious I just come back to my room and tell the servants to lock up the drinks and go to bed. It is the only way to get rid of people. Anyway tonight I will be optimistic because it has begun well. Where are you staying?'

'In a place called Kalyan.'

'Oh, then you are on Zipper. Nearly all the military people who come here nowadays are on Zipper.'

He thought it wiser to let this pass.

He said, 'It's very kind of you to invite me to stay and I do have an evening off duty. But if I'm too early shall I come back later?'

'Oh, no. Other people will be here in a minute. If not ask Aneila to entertain you. Ask her to play the gramophone, and then you can dance. She is a very good dancer but needs practice with men. She loves it when I bring her to Bombay. Her mother is so strict with her. Her mother is my sister, the one who married that business man and has become very serious as a result. Before you go would you be so kind as to ring the bell?'

Perron stood up, touched the button on the wall which she had indicated, murmured his thanks and took his leave. On his way out he had an urge to turn back and explain who he was and why he was there. He had never enjoyed the part of his job which involved deceiving people and tonight deception seemed irrational. He believed that if he confessed his true identity and purpose to the Maharanee she would probably be amused, for the few seconds it took her to forget and concentrate again on her own affairs. But, leaving the room, closing the door and facing the long cluttered passage of more closed doorways he re-accommodated himself to the masquerade because Aneila was in the act of greeting more guests, let in this time by a servant. Again there had been no sound of a bell. A woman servant was hastening down the corridor to the Maharanee's room. Perron wondered whether he was going deaf or whether the bells rang on a note that only members of the household had learned to detect; but before he could become more than passingly interested in the subject his attention was taken by something of potentially more serious consequence.

Among the new arrivals – the only one he automatically took notice of – was a girl, an English girl; but not just an English girl, *the* English girl; the one to whom he had had to apologize for Purvis's discourteous behaviour at the entrance to the block of flats on the Oval. Remembering the penetrating glance she had given him he could scarcely doubt that she would recognize him when they came face to face. The question was whether she would notice his miraculous change of employment or whether the fact that he was in off-duty khaki drill and not in jungle green would be sufficient to distract her from any previous impression she had gained that education was not at all his line. The other question, of course, was whether if she recognized that a transformation had taken place she would thoughtlessly comment on it to him in the hearing of others, or sensibly put two and two together and keep mum.

There was only ten yards' distance between them and no way of lengthening it. In fact it was already shortening because Aneila had waved the men in the party towards the living-room and was now bringing the girl to a room in which presumably women-guests could make themselves comfortable. This room turned out to be the one against whose door Perron was standing. No confrontation could have been more direct.

He stepped aside, smiled at Aneila and then at the girl. He thought it best to take the initiative. 'Good evening. We meet again.'

'Oh,' Aneila said. 'Do you know each other? I'm awfully glad because if not I would have to introduce you and I'm so bad at remembering names.'

'Perron,' Perron said, to both of them.

'Sarah Layton,' the girl said. Rather shrewdly, he thought, she said it to Aneila.

'Please join the guests in the living-room, Mr Perrer. Auntie says men can always introduce themselves if there is no one around to do it and I must show Miss –'

'Layton.'

'– Miss Layton where to powder her nose.' She opened the door. Sarah Layton nodded and started to go through. He caught the moment of hesitation, the slight frown, that followed the brief fall of her glance upon his left shoulder tab. Expecting the glance then to be redirected upwards to meet his he prepared to meet it as frankly as possible, but she followed Aneila into the room without looking at him again.

He continued along the passage and re-entered the living-room where a bearer was presiding over the cocktail cabinet and where he had another and rather more devastating shock.

Perron had been stationed in the Bombay Presidency for nearly three months but before becoming involved in operation Zipper he had visited the city only once. The reason for that visit, made in the company of his officer, had been the arrival of a ship that had sailed from Bordeaux in June bringing several hundred Indian soldiers, ex-prisoners of war captured in North Africa, who had succumbed to the temptation to secure their release from prison-camp by joining a Free India Force which its leader, the revolutionary ex-Congressman, Subhas Chandra Bose, at that time in Berlin after escaping police surveillance in India, had hoped to put into the field to fight alongside the Germans.

In England, Perron had learnt quite a lot about this embryo army and its failure to cohere into a fighting force. Details of it had been among items of classified information it had been his job to study but say nothing about. Because of the tremendous pride the British had always taken in the loyalty of their Indian soldiers, and in the Indian Army's apolitical nature, this evidence of a flaw in its structure had interested him, both then and later when he heard of the numerically far greater and infinitely more serious defection among Indian soldiers taken prisoner by the Japanese. They, it seemed, had formed themselves into operational fighting formations, at first under an Indian King's commissioned officer and then under Subhas Chandra Bose (translated by submarine from Berlin to Tokyo) and had accompanied the Japanese in their attempt in 1944 to invade the sub-continent through Manipur. Some of these, recaptured in the recent successful British campaign in Burma, had, he understood, already arrived in India and were being held in special camps where presumably the contingent from Europe would join them. Many more would follow after the end of the war in Malaya and the Far East.

His duties in regard to the boatload of disgraced Indian

officers, NCOs and sepoys from Bordeaux had not been exacting. Neither he nor his officer was sure where their responsibility began or ended. So far as they could tell their main job was to keep an ear to the ground and report to the military and civil authorities anything that might give cause for suspicion that a popular movement was afoot in Bombay to storm the docks and whisk the prisoners from under the noses of those in charge of them off into the bazaars or into the hills where in the past many a band of irregular Mahratta horsemen had melted away to live on and fight again. But of this there had been no sign at all. Bombay went about its business and the military quietly got on with the job of transferring the boatload by trainloads to a destination Perron understood to be in the vicinity of Delhi and the Red Fort.

On only one occasion had he had the opportunity to observe the process, and this was at dead of night when he found himself standing with a group of military police on the dockside at a point where a file of the men in question straggled past, in oddly assorted uniforms, in the imperfect lighting of well-spaced and high-pitched arc-lights which left him with no more than an impression of the vacuity that falls upon the human face when a peak of incomprehension has been reached. That they were home at last they could not doubt. The smell of home must have been unmistakable. But what this might mean to them they obviously could not judge. After the last man in the batch had gone by and the cordon of armed military police had closed in and hidden them from view, Perron had found it difficult to assess the significance of what he had just seen. There was, on this scale, surely no parallel to the situation in the whole of Anglo-Indian history? No such gathering of Indian soldiers (and the present one represented no more than the tip of the iceberg) had surely ever gone abroad across the black water to fight in the Sahibs' wars and come back as the Sahibs' prisoners?

He was still testing the situation to find a weakness in his estimate of it as one that was historically unique when his officer sent a message calling him over to the shed from which the security side of the operation was being conducted and there introduced him to a British officer, a major in the Punjab Regiment whose face had been burnt badly, on the left side. The left arm had been damaged too, although it had taken Perron rather

longer to realize this and to appreciate that the glove hid an
artificial hand. Several ribbons decorated the officer's chest, the
foremost that of the DSO.

Perron was introduced by his own officer as 'the sergeant I was
telling you about'.

'You'll appreciate this, sergeant,' he said and began a story he
said he'd heard earlier that evening. Perron assumed he'd already
told it to the Punjab officer because the man glanced at a wrist-
watch which he wore with the face on the inner side of his right
wrist and then turned his attention to a wall-map of the dock
area. The story was about the boatload of prisoners. In Bordeaux, hearing that they were to be shipped *en masse* back to
India in a boat reserved exclusively for them, they decided it was
the British intention to take them out to sea, disembark the crew
and scuttle the ship. They refused to go until a sufficient complement of British soldiers had been taken on board to insure against
the execution of such a diabolical plan.

'Don't you think that's rich? I mean you have to give them full
marks for an undiminished sense of self-preservation, don't you?'

The Punjab officer broke in.

'I'm told you speak fluent Urdu, Perron. Will you be able to
follow a brief interrogation in that language?'

'Yes, sir.'

'Good. I have a few questions to ask one of the prisoners,
none of special importance but I prefer to have independent
witnesses in case the man says anything I consider valuable. If he
does I shall tell you what it was and you will then treat it as
restricted and highly confidential information.'

'Yes, sir.'

'Whatever he pretends, this man will be very apprehensive at
being singled out for immediate questioning. The MPs who'll
bring him will remain in the room but they're British and won't
understand what is said. I want you to place yourself behind my
chair and keep your eyes fixed on him, for the psychological
effect. It would help if you could manage to look not in the least
sympathetic.' He turned to Perron's officer. 'I should like you to
sit at the table with me. Have you a file you could be looking at?'

'A file?'

'Or an official-looking book. It's always helpful if the man
sitting next to the one asking the questions appears to be

absorbed in some task of his own which the prisoner finds it difficult to connect with the proceedings.'

Perron's officer laughed nervously. 'I could always play patience.'

'A file or a book preferably.'

'Why is it helpful?'

'It increases the prisoner's sense of isolation and weakens whatever resolve he may have to withhold information from the one man in the room who is speaking to him. He should be here any moment. Shall we take up positions?'

They did so. The table at which the two officers sat was the ordinary trestle type, covered by an ink-stained army blanket. It had been cleared of the papers and trays that were on it when Perron visited the hut earlier. A briefcase, a spare glove, a swagger cane, marked the Punjab officer's place. One-handed he opened the case and withdrew a file of papers and a fountain-pen. Perron's officer, having rummaged about on another table, now joined him, bringing with him a notebook and a thick folder of assorted cyclostyled memoranda.

The room was the inner one of the two into which the hut was divided. It was poorly lit by a single electric bulb. The trestle table faced the connecting door through which the prisoner would have to come after passing through the outer room which was used by MPs and dock police but at this hour of the night, morning rather, occupied by just one sleepy corporal. It was this corporal who presently knocked on the door, looked in and announced the arrival of prisoner and escort.

They came in in file. The MP in front, a burly sergeant, halted about three paces from the desk, saluted, put a folded note on the desk, took a pace to his right and one to the rear, while the MP at the back took one to his left and then a pace forward, a manoeuvre that revealed the man they guarded; a thin, stoop-shouldered Indian in denim fatigue trousers the bottoms of which flopped over ill-fitting-looking boots, a long-sleeved khaki pull-over and, beneath it, a khaki shirt whose shoulder tabs were thrust through the slots made for them in the pullover. The man wore no belt. On his head there was a forage cap without a badge. The taller of the two MPs removed this roughly enough to jerk the prisoner's head to one side. There was nothing on his sleeve to denote rank. The clothes had obviously been issued in Europe, perhaps in Bordeaux. He appeared not to have shaved for a couple of days. His thick black hair was over-long. A strand of it lay across his forehead. He stared from one officer to the other and finally at Perron who had been shocked to see that the prisoner's hands were manacled. It was as if everything had been done to make him look and feel unworthy of any uniform whatsoever.

The Punjab officer asked the escort to remain in the room but to retire to the door. So far he did not seem to have looked at the prisoner but when he spoke to the MPs the man looked at him with close attention and took no notice when the two policemen moved. The Punjab officer (again so far as Perron could tell, having his eyes more or less dutifully fixed on the prisoner) still did not look up. After a while, perhaps as long as ten seconds, the prisoner glanced at Perron's officer who was uselessly busy with pencil, notebook and the folder of papers, but almost immediately had his attention taken again by something the Punjab major was doing.

Perron glanced down. One-handed, the major had taken out a tin of cigarettes and a lighter. He opened the tin, selected a cigarette, lit it, closed the tin and then with the good hand reached across to the left arm which hung straight, grasped the wrist of the gloved artificial hand, raised it and placed it on the table. Having taken a draw on the cigarette he inserted it between two of the gloved fingers and left it there: an erect white tube with smoke curling from the tip.

As Perron switched his glance back to the prisoner he caught the burly MP's eye. The MP winked.

'Tumara nam kya hai?' the Punjab officer asked suddenly in a low voice. The prisoner put his head on one side as a man might who recognized a language but could not identify it beyond doubt. *What is your name?*

Without waiting longer for an answer the officer continued; again in Urdu –

It says in this paper that your name is Karim Muzzafir Khan. Havildar Karim Muzzafir Khan, 1st Pankot Rifles, captured in North Africa with the other survivors of his battalion. With his comrades. With his leaders. Colonel Sahib himself also being captured. Is this so? It says so in this paper. You recognize the emblem on the paper? Does the Sircar make mistakes?

The man seemed bewildered. He looked at Perron, as if for

help. Perron stared at the bridge of the man's nose. The man looked down again at the officer.

Well?

Yes, Sahib.

Yes, Sahib? Yes? What is the meaning of this answer?

Karim Muzzafir Khan, Sahib.

Karim Muzzafir Khan, Havildar, 1st Pankot Rifles?

Yes, Sahib.

Karim Muzzafir Khan, Havildar? Captured with his battalion in North Africa?

Sahib.

Karim Muzzafir Khan, Havildar. Son of the late Subedar Muzzafir Khan Bahadur, also of the 1st Pankot Rifles?

Sahib.

Subedar Muzzafir Khan Bahadur? VC?

Perron was aware of his own officer looking up, alerted.

Well?

Sahib.

The Punjab officer removed the smoking cigarette, drew on it, tapped the ash into a tray, slowly exhaled and replaced it between the rigid gloved fingers. He turned a page of the file. The prisoner's head was lowered. He was staring at the cigarette and the artificial hand as though they exerted for him the special fascination of an object or arrangement of objects which, properly interpreted, might help him to understand precisely what it was that was happening to him. Perhaps this was what the Punjab officer intended. He continued to study the new page in the file. He was in no hurry. Perron kept glancing at the cigarette. If left to burn right down would the artificial fingers react? Unexpectedly the officer removed his cap and sat back. The prisoner stared at the scarred face, then looked away at the other officer's busy pencil and then at Perron and after a moment shut his eyes.

Are you fatigued?

The prisoner opened his eyes.

Sahib.

You are not getting good sleep?

No answer.

Why? Why are you not getting good sleep?

No answer.

*Something troubles you? What? What will happen? This troubles
you? What will happen to you? What will happen to your wife and
children? You have a wife and children?*

The man nodded.

*What they will say? That this is a matter of great shame? Is that
what troubles you? What your wife and children will say? What the
people in your village will say to your wife and children? Is that what
you are thinking? That your wife will not hold up her head? That this
will be so because of all the men in the battalion who were not killed but
captured only Havildar Karim Muzzafir Khan was not true to the salt?
Only Havildar Karim Muzzafir Khan listened to the lies of his captors
and of the enemies of the King-Emperor whose father rewarded his father
with the most coveted decoration of all? Only Havildar Karim Muzzafir
Khan brought shame to his regiment and sorrow to the heart of Colonel
Sahib?*

A pause.

How long is it since you saw Colonel Sahib?

No answer.

*Where do you think he is? At home in comfort? You think perhaps
on the day he and the other officers were released from prison-camp in
Germany that he got into an aeroplane and flew home to his family in
India? This is not so. It is you who are in India first, ahead of him,
ahead of all your comrades of the 1st Pankots. Like you they had not
seen Colonel Sahib since the day of their capture when the officer sahibs
were taken to one camp and the men to another. But on the day Colonel
Sahib was released he said, now let me go to my men. I shall not go back
to India without them. Come, let us find the men, let us go to the prison-
camp where the men are. Let us go to the camp and collect all the men
together. Let us wait in Germany until every man who was still alive
after the battle and was taken prisoner has been accounted for and then
let us sail back to our families in India, as a regiment. And so it has
been. And only one man of the 1st Pankots has not been accounted for,
one man who was not killed but who was not in any prison-camp. He
had deserted his comrades to fight alongside the enemy. We do not know
why. We shall find out why. Where you are going you will be asked
many questions. You will be asked many questions by many officers. You
will see me again also. I also shall ask you many more questions. Tonight
I am not asking questions of this kind. I speak to you only of the shame
and sorrow you have brought to Colonel Sahib. I do not know Colonel
Sahib but I know Colonel Memsahib and I know the two young*

memsahibs. Susan Mem and Sarah Mem. I was in Pankot four weeks ago. They had a letter from Colonel Sahib. Be patient, he wrote. I am making arrangements about the men. So, they are patient. All Pankot is patient, awaiting the regiment's return from across the black water. In Pankot they do not yet know the story of Havildar Karim Muzzafir Khan who let himself believe in the lies of Subhas Chandra Bose. But soon they will know. And they will be dumb with shame and sorrow. The wild dogs in the hills will be silent and your wife will not raise her head.

The Punjab officer spoke a resonant classic Urdu. It was a language that lent itself to poetic imagery but Perron had heard few Englishmen use it so flexibly, so effectively, or to such a purpose. Throughout the speech the prisoner's eyes had grown brighter, moister. Perron thought he might break down. He believed this was the officer's intention and he was appalled. He would have understood better if the officer and the prisoner were of the same regiment because by tradition a regiment was a family and the harshest rebuke might then be ameliorated by the context of purely family concern in which it could be delivered and received. Then, if the man wept, it would be with regret and shame. If he wept now it would be from humiliation at the hands of a stranger.

But he managed not to weep. Perhaps the years in Europe had eroded his capacity to be moved – as Indians could be – by rhetoric. Perhaps he suddenly realized that nothing except full bellies would keep the wild dogs of the hills silent, and was astonished that a British officer should use such high-flown language. Perron thought that for a second or two a flash of contempt was discernible in the moist eyes. Certainly, they dried, and were directed again at the burning cigarette.

There was silence for perhaps as long as a minute. 'I have finished with this man,' the officer said suddenly. Karim Muzzafir Khan understood English. He drew in a deep breath and glanced round, awaiting the MPs who, put off their stroke by the abruptness with which the interview had ended, made a somewhat patchy job of coming forward, saluting and leading the prisoner out.

When the door shut, the officer picked the cigarette out of the artificial hand and sat smoking and making notes on the file. The episode, to Perron, seemed pointless. His own officer obviously thought the same because he pushed away the file he'd pretended to work on, leant forward, rested his forehead on his right hand and watched the other man's note-taking; clearly inviting comment.

At last the Punjab officer spoke.

'I wonder whether your sergeant would ask the corporal next door to get hold of my driver and tell him I'll be ready in about five minutes? The corporal will know where to find him.'

'Oh, I'll do that myself. I need to take a leak.'

Perron's officer got up and went into the other room. He left the door ajar. Perron collected the notebook and folder and took them back to the other table. The Punjab officer stubbed the cigarette and began to repack his briefcase.

'Were you able to follow every word?'

'Yes, sir.'

'What did you make of him?'

'He looked fairly harmless, sir.'

The officer closed the briefcase. He leant back and looked at Perron. 'His name has cropped up several times in depositions made in Germany in connection with the coercion of sepoy prisoners-of-war who were unwilling to join the Frei Hind force. In fact it has been linked with that of an Indian lieutenant suspected of causing the death of a sepoy in Königsberg.' A pause. 'But I grant you the harmless look, and, of course, he may be innocent of anything like that because a lot of these fellows are going to be only too ready to accuse each other to save their own skins.'

He put his cap on.

'Incidentally, your officer was singing your praises before you arrived. I gather you have a degree in history and are particularly interested in the history of this country. Have you studied Oriental languages too? I mean, systematically?'

'Not awfully systematically, sir. Naturally I became interested in Urdu and learned some during vacations and had some practice in conversation with a fellow-student during term.'

'An Indian fellow-student, at university?'

'Yes, sir.'

'If you followed every word you've become very proficient. Have you taken Higher Standard out here?'

'Yes, sir.'

'It's not much use, of course, except in the army. It's nice to be able to speak it. In my old job I generally had to use a mixture of bazaar Hindi and the local dialect of whatever district I happened to be in.'

'What job was that, sir?'

'The Indian Police.'

Perron was surprised. Neither the ICS nor the police had been in the least co-operative over pleas from their officers to join the armed forces. Recruiting to these services had lapsed at the beginning of the war and the men had been needed where they were, administering the law, collecting the revenues, keeping order, preserving the civil peace. Perron judged the officer to be in his middle thirties. At that age he would normally have held a senior post in the police, which would have made a wartime transfer to the army even more difficult to arrange.

The officer got up. He tucked the briefcase under the left arm which he then adjusted until it was clamped to his waist. The arm must have been amputated above the elbow. He took the spare glove and swagger cane in his right hand.

'By the way, sergeant. I gather from your officer that you were at school at Chillingborough. When, exactly?'

Perron told him and after a moment added, 'Were you there as well, sir?'

The officer paused before replying. 'Hardly. I had quite other grounds for asking. Presumably you would know an Indian boy there, who called himself Harry Coomer. Actually Hari Kumar.'

'Harry Coomer? Yes, I remember him, sir.'

'He would have been a year or two your junior, I suppose? Did you know him closely? Closely enough to have learned much about his attitudes and interests?'

Perron was thinking back, attempting an image of the young Indian. The way Coomer came into focus was in white flannels making one of those sweeps to leg which even Perron who had been bored by cricket and played it badly recognized as elegant. The boy's actual presence was otherwise misty. Only an ambiance remained; and a detail or two.

'Actually,' Perron said, 'I don't remember him being interested in anything much except cricket.'

He was about to add, Why, sir? Do you know him? But the answer was self-evident.

Perron had not thought of Coomer for years. He realized he

had not even thought of him when he came out to India, perhaps because at school he had never really thought of Coomer in connection with any place but Chillingborough. Only a brown skin had distinguished him from the several hundred other boys undergoing the Chillingborough experience. Everything else, manners, behaviour, had so far as Perron could remember been utterly commonplace. Perron could not even recall Coomer speaking English with an Indian accent. What he did recall was asking Coomer a question about the difference between karma and dharma and being told politely that Coomer was afraid he didn't know because although born in India he had grown up in England and couldn't remember a thing about it and didn't know anything about its peculiar customs and odd ideas.

'Cricket,' the officer said, smiling at last. 'I'm afraid that his range of interests began to extend beyond cricket once he got back to this country. That expensive education turned out to be pretty much a waste. As so often happens in such cases. Did you know anything of his background?'

'Nothing at all, sir. Nothing I can remember.'

'No, well, I suppose you wouldn't. Not being a close friend of his.'

Perron's officer came back.

'We've unearthed your driver,' he said. 'He's waiting outside. I'm trying to whistle up some char. Would you like a mug before you tootle off?'

'No, thank you. And thank you for your help this evening. I'm sorry the havildar was so unforthcoming. It would have been more interesting for you if he'd been one of the talkative ones. But the object of the exercise was achieved from my point of view.' He seemed about to say goodnight and go but then stood his ground, as if thinking something out.

'It's interesting,' he began, and turned to Perron. 'There you have the havildar, whose father got a posthumous VC in the last war, and who I dare say was brought up to have his father's example rammed down his throat day after day. One thing it will be worth finding out is how he behaved in action, when it came to it. My guess is he showed up badly and couldn't face being shut in behind barbed wire for the rest of the war with men who'd seen how frightened he was. What do you think, sergeant? Psychologically, could it work that way?'

'I think it could, sir.'

'Well Kumar couldn't face it either. I mean face the fact that he wasn't what his father tried to make him and had led him to believe he was. You know nothing of this?'

'Nothing, sir.'

'When did you reach India?'

'In 1943, sir.'

'Ah well. It happened the year before. But I'm glad he wasn't a close friend of yours. He kept pretty poor company out here. He and five of his disreputable friends were arrested in '42 on a very serious criminal charge. They wriggled out of that, but we got them under the Defence of India Rules and locked them up as political detenus.'

As he spoke the officer kept his eyes firmly on Perron. And now continued so, as though demanding a comment or a question. The only thing Perron could think of to say was: 'Was it you who arrested him, sir?'

'Yes. It was. It was indeed.'

He nodded at Perron, and saluted Perron's officer by touching his cap with the swagger cane; and went.

Perron returned his officer's glance. He said, 'Who was that, sir?'

'Name's Merrick. Described himself as involved at a high level with this INA tamasha. Frosty sort of bugger, wasn't he?'

It was this man whom Perron saw first on re-entering the Maharanee's living-room.

He was, however, under observation by three. As well as the one-armed Punjab officer there was a tall elderly white man in white ducks who leant on an ebony cane and whose left eye was hidden by a black patch secured by a strip of elastic round his head, and – the only man of the three not suffering from any physical disability – a good-looking young Indian in well-cut civilian clothes.

Sometimes, since the night on the docks, in the moment before sleeping, the last conscious image in the blackness behind his lids had been of Coomer, driving, sweeping, cutting or blocking a rapid and relentless stream of deliveries from an invisible bowler, in an empty field that was green, sunstruck and elm-shaded; devoid of sound. The boy's face was never clear. The images conveyed little except a melancholy idea that they were a reproach of some kind, and by morning he had usually forgotten them. But the sight of the young Indian, combined with the shock of coming face to face with the Punjab officer, brought them back and for an instant he had an absurd notion that the young Indian was Coomer.

His hesitation on entering had been marked enough to be interpreted by the elderly man in the white ducks as shyness. The man smiled and said, 'Come in.'

Approaching them, avoiding a direct glance at the Punjab officer, Perron said good-evening and then, 'I'm afraid I'm an interloper. An officer sent me with a package for the Maharanee and she's very kindly invited me to stay for the party. My name's Perron. Sergeant Perron.'

'Perron? Perron? That is a most interesting name. Any ancient connection with the Sergeant Perron who became a general and Governor of Hindustan under Daulat Rao Sindia?'

Perron smiled. It was rarely that the question was asked.

'No, sir. In any case the Perron who served under Daulat Rao was really Pierre-Cuiller. Perron was his nickname.'

'That I either did not know or have forgotten. Anyway, Mr Perron, at Aimee's parties what you call interlopers are the rule rather than the exception. For instance I am the only one of us here with a personal invitation. But Aimee likes one to bring people along.' The accent was un-English but Perron could not place it.

'So let me initiate introductions,' the man continued. He placed a skeletal hand on his breast, indicating himself and bowing slightly. 'Dmitri Bronowsky. This is Mr Ronald Merrick, actually of the Indian Police but at the moment as you see employed as a major in the Punjab Regiment. And this is my secretary, Mr Ahmed Kasim, younger son of Mr Mohammed Ali Kasim, of whom you may have heard.' Bronowsky put a hand on Perron's shoulder, turned him round an inch or two, to read the shoulder tab. 'Ah, now what does this mean, A E C?'

'Army Education Corps, sir.'

The slight twisting of his shoulder enabled him to look directly at Major Merrick. In this harsh light the scar-tissue that disfigured the left side of the man's face was revealed more unkindly than it had been in the shed on the docks, and the blue of the eyes – now recollected – was intensified. The look Perron got in return gave nothing away.

Bronowsky's hand was still on Perron's shoulder. Letting him free now he said, 'How does one educate an army?'

'It's not so much a case of educating it, sir, but of finding ways of stopping it being bored.'

'Nevertheless, you need teaching qualifications?'

'Not always, sir.'

'But you have such qualifications?'

'Yes, sir.'

'A degree?'

'Yes, sir.'

Bronowsky asked in what subject. Perron told him. The bearer entered their midst with a tray of drinks but this did not halt the old man's catechism. Which university? Which college? Before that what school had he attended?

'A place called Chillingborough, sir.'

'Indeed?' Bronowsky hesitated. 'How interesting. And what will you do after the war, Mr Perron? Go on to a course of post-graduate studies?'

Perron nodded. But the flow of questions could not be stemmed. In what subject? What aspect of Indian history? Why that one? Perron attempted to deflect the question and open the conversation out with a general comment about the narrowing range and increasingly esoteric nature of study in the post-graduate field but Bronowsky was not to be put off.

'That is its charm and logic, surely. I expect you have found that being in India has encouraged you in your choice. Have you thought of staying on for a while after the war?'

'Not really, sir. One tends to lose ground so quickly. The academic world is as competitive as any other.'

'That is so. But one should perhaps sometimes ignore the professional competition and arrange matters in a way most advantageous to the scholar in oneself. You would easily find a temporary post in a university here and have plenty of opportunity to do original research. Either in a university or in one of the colleges. Our own college in the little state of Mirat is always short of well-qualified teachers. In history, for instance.'

'Are you its principal, sir?'

Major Merrick interrupted.

'Count Bronowsky is Chief Minister to the ruler, the Nawab of Mirat.'

'But emotionally I'm very attached to the college and always anxious to foster its interests because it was one of my first innovations. When I went to Mirat to advise Nawab Sahib, nearly a quarter of a century ago, there was no place of higher education in the state where clever young Hindus could go. There was only the Muslim Academy which taught boys to pray and recite the Koran and which turned out tax-collectors – if Ahmed here will forgive me for saying so, although he did not personally undergo such a traditional Islamic training, did you, Ahmed?'

'What?'

'Incorrigible!' Bronowsky exclaimed, but laughed and put three fingers of the hand that held the ebony cane on the young man's shoulder. 'He seldom listens to conversations. He comes to parties only to drink as much whisky as he can and to make up to the prettiest girls. That apart, as a secretary he is quite efficient. And here are two very pretty girls. Aneila, my dear, was I in error in supposing your aunt said seven-thirty on? Are we as conspicuously early as we feel?'

'Oh, no. Auntie's parties begin when the first people arrive. Have I omitted anything? Auntie will be very cross if I have, so please tell me. Oh! Nobody is smoking! What a bad beginning. Please help yourselves. I will tell Auntie to hurry.'

She ran out, and in the passage called instructions presumably to some of the servants. Perron, the only guest who knew without looking where the cigarettes were, picked up the box and went first to Miss Layton who was now standing next to Major Merrick. He arrived at her side a few seconds behind the bearer with the tray of drinks. He noted the gleam of her unfussily set fair hair and then her dress which was not the one she had on when they met outside the block of flats on the Oval, but was not obviously labelled 'party only'. A bag hung in the crook of her arm. The left hand was raised. She wore no engagement ring. She chose a gimlet and then, seeing the box, smiled at him and shook her head.

'Thank you, not just now.'

Merrick declined too. He made no attempt at an introduction. Perron passed on to Bronowsky. 'I always smoke these,'

Bronowsky said, opening a gold case and showing the contents: a row of oval-shaped pink gold-tipped cigarettes.

'But only in the evening,' Miss Layton said, from behind Perron.

'Ah, so you remember my little anecdote. By the way you know Mr Perron of the Education Corps?'

'Yes,' came her voice, 'we introduced ourselves in the hall.'

Perron offered the box to Ahmed Kasim but he declined. Bronowsky moved across to Miss Layton and Major Merrick, Perron put the box down, retrieved his drink and set about trying to make conversation with the young Indian.

'Your father must be the Congress statesman, M A K.'

Kasim nodded, then reapplied himself to his glass of whisky. So far as Perron knew it was the first time he had spoken to an Indian whose father had been imprisoned by the *raj*. He did not know quite what to say to him. He could hardly apologize. He would have liked to ask what truth there had been in newspaper reports that Mr Kasim senior was realigning himself politically, abandoning Congress in favour of the League and Jinnah's mad, divisive dream of a separate state for Muslims: Pakistan; but that was a tricky subject too. He wondered what on earth a son of a politician like M A K was doing acting as secretary to the Chief Minister to the Nawab of Mirat. There was generally no love lost between Congress and the autocratic rulers of the Princely states. But he could not ask that question either. He fell back on small talk.

'Are you in Bombay for long?'

'A few days.'

'It must be interesting working for a Nawab's Chief Minister.'

Ahmed Kasim nodded, but his attention was elsewhere. Hearing voices Perron glanced round. A group of English officers had come in, but they were obviously not the object of Mr Kasim's study. A stunningly attractive Eurasian girl and two pretty Indian girls had come in too and were talking excitedly to Aneila. Two more bearers joined the one already in the room. After a few seconds Perron turned back to Kasim.

'Is Mirat in relationship with the Crown through a Resident or through a provincial government?'

'A Resident. Except that he isn't.'

'A non-resident Resident.'

'It used to be through the provincial government but all that was altered some time ago.'

'Generally, or just in Mirat's case?'

'I think generally. Something to do with the federal scheme. But that's fallen through. Things do in this country.'

'Where does the non-resident Resident reside?'

'In Gopalakand.'

'Is that far from Mirat?'

'Far enough.'

'Is that a good thing, then?'

Mr Kasim looked into his glass.

'I'm sorry,' Perron said. 'Undiplomatic question. Is Count Bronowsky what we used to call a White Russian? A member of the emigration from the revolution?'

'Yes.'

'A soldier?'

'No, I don't think so.'

'I wondered about his loss of an eye.'

'He says his carriage was blown up by a revolutionary when he was on his way to the Winter Palace in St Petersburg. He's lame in the left leg for the same reason.'

'He mentioned being in Mirat for twenty-five years. Was he Chief Minister from the beginning?'

'Not officially. Not until the Political Department was mollified.'

'How was it mollified?'

'I believe when they saw he was a good influence on the Nawab. Then they allowed the appointment. Dmitri says that nowadays some of the senior members of the Political Department behave as if they invented him themselves. Before he came the state was quite feudal.'

'Does Miss Layton have any connection with Mirat? She and the Count seem quite old friends.'

'She visited once. Her sister got married there. They stayed at the Palace guest house.'

'She lives in Bombay?'

'No, in Pankot.'

'Pankot?'

'You know it?'

'Of it. Anyway, of its regiment, the Pankot Rifles.'

'Her father was CO of the 1st battalion. She's in Bombay to meet him. He's been a prisoner-of-war in Germany.'

Perron moved so that he could see her. Her back was to him. She stood in a group consisting of Count Bronowsky, two of the English officers, and Merrick. Merrick was watching him, still with that expression of giving nothing away although Perron fancied he now read into it an understanding that Miss Layton's name had just been mentioned and a warning to give nothing away himself, as if they both had something to hide: Perron his real identity and Merrick – what? Just the fact that they had met before or, primarily, the circumstances of that meeting? The interrogation of the Pankot Rifles havildar? Sarah Layton was one of Colonel Sahib's daughters. Although he now recognized the name Sarah in this connection he could not remember the name of the other daughter – the one presumably married in Mirat. Merrick had referred to them both when questioning the havildar. Sarah mem and — mem.

He turned back to Kasim.

'Is Colonel Layton back in India yet?'

Mr Kasim had to incline his head and ask him to repeat the question, but before he could do so there was a cry, 'Ahmed, darling!' and an elderly Indian woman in a green and gold saree brushed them apart to embrace the young man. 'What are you doing in Bombay? Is your father here? I wrote to him after the Simla fiasco but he never replied.'

Perron stood back to give them more room. She ignored him. 'Is it true what Lodi told me about your poor brother Sayed?' she shouted. Perron moved away and did not hear Kasim's reply. Gramophone music started up and the stunning Eurasian girl began dancing with one of the two Indian girls who had come in with her. The other rather reluctantly accepted a young English officer as a partner but talked to the Eurasian girl as they moved round in the limited space available. So far the services were represented entirely by officers. Perron was the only non-commissioned man in the room. Four Indian women, neither young nor handsome, had settled themselves on a long settee and were in conversation of the kind that did not invite inter-ruption. The servants had multiplied and the room was quite full. There was still no sign of the Maharanee.

He made his way through the room towards the hall. At the

door he stood aside to let in a middle-aged, portly, red-faced English civilian in open-necked shirt, white duck trousers and black cummerbund. The civilian said, 'Hello, Sergeant, where's the bloody bar, then?' and looked ready to talk but Perron, indicating the direction, went through. There were more people in the hall. A servant stood at the front door staring at the wall above it where there was what looked like a bell-box, which in a sense it turned out to be because an orange bulb inside it suddenly lit up and the servant promptly opened the door and admitted two more guests. Perhaps the same sort of signal was given in the servants' quarters. Perhaps there was a bell-light watcher on the staff. Perhaps the Maharanee didn't like the sound of bells ringing. He was glad to have the question basically cleared up.

'Hey, Sarge, what d'you reckon, then?'

The speaker was a REME corporal. He was standing against a wall with an AB of the Royal Navy.

'Reckon?'

'To all this.'

'Are you on your own?'

'No, with him.' The corporal nodded at the sailor then looked at Perron's glass. 'What they rush you for the booze?'

'They don't. It's free. It usually is at parties.'

'Parties? Isn't it Amy's?'

'Well the hostess's first name is Aimee.'

'Hostess?'

'The lady giving the party.'

Perron recited the Maharanee's full title. The corporal looked at his mate. The sailor said, 'The rotten sods.' The corporal felt in a pocket and produced a grubby piece of paper. He looked at it and then showed it to Perron. On it was written: 'Amy's', the address and flat number and a note at the bottom saying: 'Six chips.' Perron handed the paper back. He shook his head. 'I think someone's played a practical joke on you. It's not that kind of place. What did you say when the bearer opened the door?'

'I just said, "Amy's?" He didn't ask for names or nothing so it looked okay. At least it did until we saw the company. I mean, *women* — coming *in*. We'd better blow before we get chucked out.'

'I don't think you would be.'

'But we don't know anyone and from the look of this lot we aren't likely to.'

'Hey, have a dekko at that,' the sailor said. He nudged the corporal in the ribs. Perron turned round. Aneila was flowing down the corridor to her aunt's room.

'Yeah, that's better. Who's she, Sarge?'

'The Maharanee's niece.'

'Any more like her inside?'

'Yes, several.'

'Who are you with, Sarge?'

'No one in particular.'

'If anyone asks can we say we're with you?'

'You'd better say you're friends of Captain Purvis, but he hasn't turned up yet.'

'Suppose he does turn up?'

'He won't. He's ill in bed.' A bearer came by with a loaded tray. Perron stopped him. 'Have a drink anyway, then you won't look conspicuous. There's beer too if you want it. You only have to ask.'

The two lads gingerly took glasses from the tray.

'Okay?'

'Yeah, thanks. Thanks, Sarge. Captain *Purvis*?'

'Leonard Purvis. The economist.'

The corporal nodded, abstractedly.

'See you, corporal,' Perron said and turned away. Major Merrick had come out of the room and was waiting for him.

'I'd like a word.'

They moved to an uncluttered part of the passage.

'Are you on duty?'

'Yes, sir.'

'Are you expecting your officer?'

'No, sir.'

'I take it this disguise is permitted?'

'In certain circumstances, yes, sir.'

'Always a bit risky though, isn't it? However slight the chances of coming across someone who knows you. For instance, Miss Layton has just told me about your meeting earlier this afternoon. In your other uniform.'

'Not in anyone else's hearing I hope, sir.'

'No. But quite properly she thought I ought to know.'

'Did you tell her you knew already, sir?'

'Without going into detail, yes. This officer – Captain Purvis? Is he in your department too?'

'No, sir.'

'Are you going back to his flat?'

'I shall have to, sir. To change.'

For a while Merrick stared at him without speaking. In the living-room another record was put on and there was some loud laughter. Eventually Merrick said, 'What time do you expect to leave?'

'I'm not sure, sir.'

Merrick glanced at the other people in the passage. Three young Indian women sat on the settee chattering and giggling. The corporal and the sailor were now being talked to by the middle-aged Englishman in the cummerbund. Merrick continued: 'I've been thinking about making our excuses and taking Miss Layton home. Everything considered and in view of what you know, would you think that justified, to save her possible embarrassment?'

A movement near the doorway into the living-room caught his eye. The middle-aged civilian was shepherding the corporal and the sailor in. He gave the sailor an encouraging pat, low enough on the spine to rank as a slap on the buttocks. Perron returned his attention and saw that the gesture had not gone unnoticed by Merrick. Perron assumed as blank an expression as he could manage.

'I simply can't say, sir. It should be quite easy to slip away, I imagine, without giving offence.'

'Giving offence wouldn't bother me. What I'm asking you to tell me is whether in your view the reasons for your own presence here are likely to become apparent, through some kind of general or particular unpleasantness.'

'I'm not sure I understand you, sir,' Perron said. 'It's all fairly routine from my point of view.'

Merrick looked across Perron's shoulder in the direction of the settee where the three Indian girls were.

'Routine?' he said.

Perron lowered his voice although with no one in easy earshot there was no need. 'The reason for my presence, sir.'

Merrick continued staring at the girls on the carved sofa and then looked in the opposite direction at the main door of the flat which the bearer had just opened. Two tall white girls, exaggeratedly made up and wearing sarees, came in ahead of a couple of Air Force officers, an Englishman and an American. The taller of the girls, who seemed familiar with the flat, led her companion down the passage towards the room set aside for women. As she went by she gave Perron a dazzling smile. But heavy make-up – and pungent scents – had never much appealed to him, neither for that matter had white women in sarees. Their bones were usually too big – as in this case. He watched them go into the women's room. Apparently the three Indian girls thought them as incongruous as he did; they lowered their heads, covered their faces and laughed.

'I sympathize with you then, sergeant, if this is routine.'

'I don't mean the party, sir. The reason for my being at it.'

'You see nothing odd about the party, though? Nothing that would encourage you seriously to consider leaving if you were in my shoes and had Miss Layton to think of? Or even if you were by yourself and had no special reason for staying?'

'I suppose it is a bit noisy, sir. And of course it does have its unusual aspect.'

'What is that, in your opinion?'

'Other ranks mixing with officers, sir. But of course I knew beforehand, otherwise I should have had to come in civilian clothes and that leads to so many awkward questions, who does one work for, what does one do. A sergeant is more anonymous.'

'And better bait. Well, I won't ask you what you expect to hook but if you're thinking of this as routine I should advise you to be careful where and how you cast. In fact, although I think you're being less than frank with me I'll give you the benefit of the doubt and a friendly warning. I have a much longer experience of this country and its peculiarities, on most levels of its society. In Indian terms you may think this an example of the top level because the hostess is a Maharanee. That is as may be. But it's at the top you find the scum, isn't it? You can certainly see plenty of it here. I must give Count Bronowsky the benefit of the doubt too and assume he had no idea the particular kind of party the Maharanee is giving this evening. I shall know better about that in a moment when I go back in and tell him I intend to take Miss Layton home before things get worse.'

'Worse, sir?'

'Worse.' Merrick studied him. 'I begin to wonder about your powers of observation, sergeant. The two white girls in sarees who have just gone into the ladies' room – one of whom made a pass at you – are boys, probably airmen. The three Indian girls giggling on the sofa there are also boys, not professional trans-vestites, which as you may know is a special kind of Indian sect, and all right in its place, but not I assure you all right here. They will undoubtedly dance for the company later in the evening and manage to make it clear what they are, and what they are offering.'

Perron looked at the three figures on the settee. He studied their covered breasts, their ringed fingers and bare forearms, the sandalled feet and bangled ankles; the shapes of jaws, joints and noses. Because he had been told, he saw.

He turned back to Merrick.

'Yes, I see.'

'I'm glad to hear it. The English boys' get-up is very good but crude in comparison. That's why the Indian boys laughed at them. Tell me at least one thing. Are the REME corporal and the AB you were talking to also on duty, like you?'

'No, sir. Certainly not to my knowledge.'

'Do you know who they're with?'

'They're just with each other, sir. But the party's a bit of a surprise to them. They were expecting something rather different.'

'Meaning?'

'A place called Amy's at a cost of six rupees.'

'They weren't far wrong. Would you say that an ageing tea-planter wasn't what they hoped to find?'

'I should think it highly unlikely that they did, sir.'

'In that case, sergeant, I think your duties might conceivably extend to ordering them to leave, for their own good.'

Perron felt a twitch of irritation.

'I don't think I need interfere, sir.'

'Then you misjudge the degree of temptation.'

They broke off. The two white men in sarees had come out of the women's room. This time Perron got a smile from both of them. They wore wigs. Now that he had been told, the masquerade was obvious. When they had gone by he glanced up the corridor where the two officers they had come with were waiting for them, holding drinks ready. The draped hips swung rhythmically. As the men reached their escorts Perron caught the American officer's eye: a beefy-looking fellow, who winked at him.

He looked back at Merrick, thinking of the map room.

'Do I, sir? Misjudge the degree of temptation?'

'I think you do. A corporal and a sailor can't have found it easy to scrape together six rupees each for a visit to a prostitute. Some flattering attention, a taste of what they think of as the high life, an offer of a handsome tip or a present that they can sell in the bazaar aren't necessarily inadequate or unacceptable payment to very young fellows like that. Alternatively, the teaplanter might find himself badly beaten up and his money gone and there could then be two more young men who've discovered a way of making easy money and will end up in serious trouble. Either consequence is one it seems sensible to avoid.'

'I do see that point of view, sir. But I couldn't risk it.'

'Risk it?'

'Risk doing what you suggest. They might not go quietly.'

'They would if you took them on one side and dealt with it tactfully but firmly.'

'I'm sorry, sir.'

Merrick paused, but never let his glance fall.

'Have you a proper identity card with you?'

'Yes, sir.'

'Then you could show it to them on the quiet.'

'No, sir.'

'Why not?'

Perron's irritation was gone and his temper roused.

'You must know why not, sir.'

'Would you show it to me if I asked to see it?'

'No, sir.'

'If I ordered you to?'

'No, sir.'

'Let me put a hypothetical case, sergeant. I have seen you in one place, in one *persona*, apparently bona fide, but here I find you in another and in the most unsavoury surroundings. I have

suspicions about your true identity. I order you to show me the
card. You refuse. I call another officer to ring for the military
police. What then?'

'Presumably I would be arrested, sir.'

'And then?'

'And then, sir, we should see.'

Suddenly Merrick smiled.

'Your officer was right.'

'Right about what, sir?'

'About your being a tough nut to crack. I think I told you he
was singing your praises. But I wanted to find out how easy it
would be to force you to act against your better judgment and
the security of the job you're doing. I agree it would be quite
absurd to risk drawing attention to yourself by warning those
fellows off. If I'd looked like succeeding in browbeating you into
it I'd have had to stop you. I was only testing you out.'

'May I ask why, sir?'

'I can't tell you here. But if it's not too late when you get back
to Queen's Road and have collected your things from Captain
Purvis, ring the bell at Lieut.-Colonel Grace's door on your way
down and ask for me. Colonel Grace is Miss Layton's uncle. You
know, of course, who her father is.'

'Do I, sir?'

'Weren't you pumping young Kasim? I could have sworn you
were.'

'Yes, I know who her father is.'

'Well, if you call you may meet him. They're going back
to Pankot tomorrow. I should want you to say nothing about
Havildar Karim Muzzafir Khan, either to him or to Miss Layton.
In fact nothing at all about the circumstances in which we met
before. The other taboo subject, at least in front of Miss Layton,
is the subject of Hari Kumar. It might conceivably crop up
because Colonel Layton is an old Chillingburian too.'

Merrick broke off. The door of the Maharanee's room had
opened and Aneila was coming hastily towards them. Seeing
Perron she ran to him and grasped his arm.

'Oh thank goodness you are still here, Auntie is asking for
you. Please come quickly. She is in a terrible temper and won't
come out to her party. It is so embarrassing with all these
people here.'

Still holding his arm she turned back towards the room so that Perron was forced to follow. As he went Merrick said, 'We shall be here for another few minutes, I expect.'

Directly Aneila entered the room the Maharanee cried, 'Shut the door! I cannot stand it! Why do they hang around in the corridor when there are all the rooms to use? Why don't you organize things better? How am I going to rest for my party with all this noise going on?'

'Oh, Auntie, please don't shout, people will hear!'

'How can they hear? I cannot even hear myself speak!'

But it no longer mattered. Aneila had shut the door and stood, visibly trembling, leaning against it.

The Maharanee was still on the couch but by its side now was a small table holding a tray, the bottle of whisky and a glass.

Pointing at the bottle she said, 'Taste it! Taste it! What is this Purvis creature trying to do? Poison me?'

Perron went across to the couch and picked up the bottle. It was nearly a quarter empty. He glanced at the Maharanee and then at the label. Surprised, he put the uncapped top near his nose and sniffed. The label was genuine. He wondered where Purvis had managed to get hold of it. He hadn't seen a bottle since 1939. He had first tasted the particular brand of whisky it contained at the age of eighteen when it had had an elaborately erotic effect on him. He looked at the Maharanee again, warily.

'You see!' she shouted. 'It is disgusting! Taste it! The taste is even more disgusting than the smell. Aneila, why are you standing there doing nothing? Get Mr Perron a glass.'

Aneila ran into the adjoining bathroom.

'Actually, Your Highness, it's a very fine and rare old malt whisky, an acquired taste perhaps, admittedly –'

'It is disgusting! What is keeping you, Aneila? I said bring Mr Perron a glass.'

'I'm bringing it, Auntie.'

She ran in with a tumbler. It was wet from running water from the tap under which it had been rinsed.

'Pour him one!'

But Perron took the glass and reverently poured the whisky himself. It was too precious to waste. He sipped.

'Well? Is it not disgusting?'

'Not to my way of thinking, Your Highness. On first

acquaintance it could seem a little smoky but that's part of its charm to people who like it.'

'They must be depraved then. Who but people with depraved tastes could drink such disgusting stuff?'

'There's a very interesting story about it. They said it wasn't until the English learnt to drink and appreciate it that they managed to subdue the Scots.'

'Scots, English, what is the difference? You are all barbarians. Are there many of you at my party?'

'Yes, I'm afraid so.'

'Who else? Aneila is hopeless. She remembers nobody's name.'

'So far I've talked to only a few. I think you know one of them – Count Bronowsky.'

She waved a hand impatiently. 'Yes, I know. Even Aneila can tell me that. But why is he here? Why is Dmitri here tonight? I told him any time except tonight. Who is with him?'

'The secretary who's a son of Mr Mohammed Ali Kasim.'

'Politics!' she exclaimed. 'It is too boring.'

'And a Major Merrick with a charming girl called Sarah Layton. Count Bronowsky brought them.'

'He is mad! And how can Sarah Layton be charming? With a name like that she must be English. I detest English girls. They are always so stupid and rude. They come out here because in England they are nobody and wouldn't be looked at twice. It is impossible. The party is cancelled, Aneila. Tell the servants to lock up the drinks and stop preparing the food. Tell them to go to bed. I am ill. Poisoned by this Purvis creature. I wish to see no one, not even Mira if she arrives. We shall leave Bombay tomorrow. It is too full of spongers and hangers-on. I am tired of it. Tired of it.'

'Oh, Auntie, Auntie!'

'Is that all you can say? Is coming to Bombay and having a good time all you can think of nowadays? Isn't it time to consider my feelings in the matter?'

'Auntie, what can I *say* to everybody?'

'Why should you say anything? What right have they to an explanation? Do as I *say* and then go to bed. They will soon get fed up.'

She looked at Perron and indicated the bottle.

'Please return it to the Purvis creature or better still since you seem to like it drink it yourself and then you will not have come all this way for nothing. Only take it. I cannot bear even the smell.'

Perron bowed, retrieved the cap from the table, put it on the bottle. The paper in which the bottle had been wrapped was on the floor. He stooped and picked it up. As he did so the Maharanee reached across to the table on which the lamp stood and recovered the shade with the piece of crimson velvet. She went out like an illuminated picture that had been switched off.

'Goodnight, Your Highness,' Perron said. 'I regret being in any way the cause of your indisposition.'

'Goodnight, Mr Perron. You must visit me again when I come back to Bombay and give my next party. Some of my parties are very nice and go on for a day or two.'

He groped his way back to the door. Somewhere in the darkened room Aneila was crying quietly to herself.

There was ample room on the back seat of the limousine for Miss Layton, Major Merrick and Count Bronowsky, and for Perron and Mr Kasim on the bench that was let down to face it. Separated from the passengers by panes of glass set in panels of upholstery and figured walnut rode a chauffeur and a footman wearing what Perron assumed to be the livery of the Nawab of Mirat. The limousine had been waiting outside Ishshee Brizhish and now glided along Marine Drive towards the Oval.

'Mr Perron, may I thank you for your thoughtful tactic in tipping us off?' Count Bronowsky said, breaking a rather strained silence. 'It means I have a little less to apologize for to Miss Layton and Major Merrick. We were able to come away in fairly reasonable order.'

'Why *have* we come away?' Miss Layton asked. She seemed perfectly composed. She just wanted to know. He thought her behaviour admirable. When he came out of the Maharanee's room, found Merrick and warned him that the party was over it had been obvious that Merrick hadn't yet suggested leaving. Perron was surprised that during the time it had taken them to get away from the flat Merrick hadn't found an opportunity to tell her what had happened. It was a better excuse than the one he might have had to invent.

He waited for Merrick to tell her now but still the man said nothing. Street-lighting alternately illuminated the left and right sides of his face and it was not until the car turned a corner and a brief but total exposure of the whole head was made that it occurred to Perron that the disfigurement of the left side in a curious way reflected something otherwise inexpressible about the right. Realizing that an explanation was being left to him, he said, 'I have an unhappy feeling that a certain Captain Purvis is to blame.'

He told the story of the whisky.

'What's wrong with the whisky?' Miss Layton asked.

'In my opinion, nothing.' He mentioned its official name. She said, 'The genuine thing?'

He unwrapped the bottle sufficiently to expose the label.

'But it's extraordinary,' she said.

'You know it?'

'Great-grandfather had some in his cellar. My father was talking about it only the other day. He said great-grandfather had the sense to keep going until the last bottle was finished. Then he died.'

Perron wondered whether Miss Layton's great-grandfather had referred, as his own Uncle Charles always had, to this particular brand as Old Sporran. He said, 'The Maharanee called it a drink for barbarians but she'd had a glass or two before she decided to complain. I think the whisky was just an excuse to end a party she'd decided she didn't want to give after all.'

'A shrewd assessment,' Bronowsky said. 'Poor Aimee has never made up her mind what she wants in life. But perhaps the whisky was a blessing.' He turned to Merrick and Miss Layton. 'I was beginning to have doubts about the wisdom of having taken you along. May I in addition to most abject apologies for the failure of the first part of the evening offer some entertainment for what is left of it? For instance the supper I misled you to expect at the party?'

'That's very civil of you,' Merrick said, 'but Miss Layton has a tiring journey ahead of her tomorrow and all things considered an early night now would be a good thing.'

'I understand. Quite. So we have met again merely to part. But better briefly than not at all. What about you, Mr Perron?'

Unprepared for the invitation Perron hesitated. He would have liked the opportunity to talk to the old *wazir*.

'Well, thank you, sir, but . . .'

'What the sergeant means, Count,' Merrick interrupted, 'is that he hadn't expected to be asked to stay at the Maharanee's and he's been worried about getting back to his billet because he has no late pass. Isn't that what you were rather delicately avoiding telling me in so many words when we were talking in the corridor?'

Perron admired Merrick's inventiveness, but resented becoming the victim of it. He said, 'More or less, sir.'

Bronowsky was smiling. He said, 'I had no idea that in the education you were so regimented. Is the place where you suggested being dropped the most convenient or should we first deliver Miss Layton and Major Merrick at Queen's Road and drive you on? We have plenty of time.'

Merrick interrupted again. 'I'm afraid the sergeant is quartered quite a distance away but I think I can lay on transport for him. If that's all right by you, sergeant?'

'Thank you, sir.'

'At the same time you could take a document for me to the Major Beamish I mentioned. There'd be no need to deliver it until morning, but I'll give you a note as well if you like to satisfy anyone who might try to get you into trouble for being out late without permission.'

Beamish's name, so casually used, presumably served a double-purpose: to lend credibility to what was a complete fiction, and to alert him to the fact that Merrick had an intimate knowledge of that department. He said, 'It's very good of you, sir. I don't think a note will be necessary.'

'We'll see.' He turned to Miss Layton. 'It's all right if the sergeant comes in for a moment, I hope? The document's in the case I left.'

'Of course.'

Perron again offered his thanks. Merrick said, 'A lift back to camp seems the least we can do. Your warning saved Miss Layton the embarrassment of finding the drinks locked up under her nose and all the servants gone to bed, it seems. I find it quite inexplicable.'

After a moment Bronowsky said, 'It is India.' He stirred, as if to ease his lame leg and turned his face fully to Merrick who had the seat next to him.

'I hope you are not plagued still by incidents such as arose when you were in Mirat, Major Merrick? Has all that sort of thing died down?'

'Yes, thank you.'

'I'm glad. We for our part have not been revisited by the venerable Pandit who was using the boy's aunt on that occasion. You never met the girl's aunt, did you?'

'No.'

'Because I had that pleasure – perhaps I should say melancholy pleasure – last November in Gopalakand. She was staying, in a sense incognito, with the Resident, Sir Robert Conway, an old friend apparently. We didn't, of course, refer in any way to Mayapore. In fact our conversation was confined almost entirely to the safe subjects of the weather and the historical and architectural interest of the Residency. I did gather however that she had spent most of the recent hot weather in Pankot, but in what she called the seclusion of the unfashionable side. So I don't suppose any of you were aware of her presence, Miss Layton?'

Merrick moved abruptly as if trying to identify the stretch of road they were on. Miss Layton spoke across him:

'Are you talking about Lady Manners, Count Bronowsky?'

'Yes, the girl's aunt.'

'Actually she signed the book at Flagstaff House when she arrived.'

'Indeed?'

'And again when she left. She didn't write in an address.'

'How strange. I mean, signing the book. Does one interpret it as a gesture of submission or defiance, or simply an ironic observance of hill-station convention?'

'I don't know,' Miss Layton said.

'Strange. Very strange. But how interesting. And talking of this,' Bronowsky said, attracting Perron's attention by lightly touching Perron's right shin with the tip of the ebony cane, 'when you were at that school of yours you must have known a boy called Kumar.'

'Kumar?'

'An Indian boy, Hari Kumar.'

'I don't clearly recall, sir.'

'Coomer was the Anglicization, I believe. Harry Coomer.'

Merrick again leant forward.

'Does your driver remember the block? We're almost there. We ought to be slowing down.'

'I believe he does but I shall make sure.'

Bronowsky unhooked a speaking-tube and gave an order. The car which had already been slowing down just before he spoke now dropped to a crawl and came to a stop opposite the entrance to the flats.

'Didn't you know Coomer?' Bronowsky continued.

'We had an Indian boy or two but I don't recall the name, sir. They were rather junior to me.'

'Yes, I see.'

The footman or second chauffeur opened the nearside door and helped Count Bronowsky on to the pavement. Perron and Kasim stayed put on the bench until Merrick had followed and helped Miss Layton out.

'I should have liked you to meet my father, Count Bronowsky,' Miss Layton was saying, 'but Aunt Fenny and Uncle Arthur managed to persuade him to go out with them and they won't be back yet. Won't you and Mr Kasim come in for a drink, though?'

'My dear, how kind,' he said, taking her hand, 'but I couldn't claim your hospitality, having failed so badly in my own. And Mr Merrick is right. You have the journey tomorrow and your father to look after. I hope he'll be fit again very soon. My kindest regards to your mother and of course to your sister.' He raised her hand and kissed it. 'You accompany Miss Layton and her father as far as Delhi, Major Merrick?'

'Yes, I do that.'

'Then it is au revoir to you both. If you have time when you're in Delhi do call on Mohsin.'

'Mohsin?'

'Nawab Sahib's elder son. He is at the Kasim Mahal most of the year. He's rather a dull fellow but his wife is very hospitable. Mirat bores her. She likes to be in the swim, but *her* parties are beyond reproach. I shall write to them and mention you, so do send in your card.'

'Thank you,' Merrick said. 'And goodnight.' He shook the Count's hand and turned to wait for Miss Layton who was talking to Mr Kasim.

'I often think of it,' she was saying. 'And our ride that morning. Do you still go out regularly?'

Perron did not hear young Kasim's reply because Bronowsky had turned to him to say goodnight.

'If you are ever in Mirat, Mr Perron, a note to the Izzat Bagh Palace would always reach me even if we're up in Nanoora.' He gave Perron his card. 'The Izzat Bagh Palace was built in the eighteenth century. The interior has been much modernized but there's a lot there that would still interest you.'

Perron thanked him, shook hands with him and with Mr Kasim and as the two men returned to the limousine followed Merrick and Miss Layton into the block of flats. The lift was still out of order. At the foot of the stairs Merrick muttered something to Miss Layton. She nodded and began to climb.

'I think the form is, sergeant, for you to change into your other uniform and call in on your way down. There is, of course, no document for Major Beamish. Incidentally, *are* you going to need transport?'

'No, sir.'

'Where actually are you going?'

'Kalyan?'

'Tonight?'

'Yes, sir.'

They went up the stairs. The servant whom Purvis had nearly knocked over was just opening the door to Miss Layton who went in without looking at either of them.

'We'll see you presently, then.'

Perron went up to the next floor and rang the bell of Purvis's flat. This time he noticed the nameplate. Hapgood. Hapgood the Banker. Mrs Hapgood the Banker's wife and Miss Hapgood the Banker's daughter. One of the happy families currently relaxing in Ooty. He rang the bell again. From inside he heard men's voices. The door was opened by the servant who had originally met him on the stairs. He looked wildly at Perron and began to talk rapidly in what sounded to Perron like Tamil – of which he understood only a few words. At the first opportunity he interrupted, speaking in English.

'What's the matter? I don't understand what you're saying.'

There were two other servants at the dark end of the corridor, the cook and his boy, probably. The boy was grinning. Perron shut the door. The bearer had resumed his incomprehensible complaint but was clearly inviting Perron to follow him into the living-room.

Arrived there his first impression was that there had been a visit by thieves who had torn the place apart to find what they had come for. The drinks table lay on its side surrounded by broken glasses and bottles. Cushions from the settees were scattered at random. The glass protecting two of the priceless Moghul paintings was smashed and the paintings themselves damaged. Inspecting them Perron realized that a bottle of rum had been shied at them. He could smell it. Stains ran down the wall. On the settee beneath he found bottle-fragments.

The bearer was now referring repeatedly to 'Purvis Sahib'. The cook came into the dining-room. His responsibilities did not extend beyond the kitchen. What was a disaster for the bearer was for him an interesting break in routine. The scene fascinated him because he was not going to be blamed for it.

'What happened?' Perron asked him in English.

'Purvis Sahib,' the cook said. He waved his arms about then mimed a man drinking, staggering, throwing things. He tapped his forehead. Purvis Sahib had gone mad.

'Where is Purvis Sabib now?'

'Room.' He shut his eyes, put his head on one side, let his tongue loll, imaging a man in a drunken stupor.

Perron went back to the corridor. The cook came with him.

'Locked,' the cook said. 'Sahib ish-shleeping.'

Perron tried the handle. He knocked. He called, 'Captain Purvis? It's Sergeant Perron.'

The bearer joined them.

'How long has he been here?'

'Half-hour, Sahib.'

The cook said, 'Drunk. Ish-shleeping.'

'What happened?'

The bearer started to explain. Perron interrupted him, asked him to tell him in English.

A telegram had come. When? Soon after Sergeant Sahib had left with the bottle of whisky. A telegram from where?

The bearer went back to the dining-room. Perron followed. The telegram – actually an official military signal – was under the telephone on a side-table.

When Purvis Sahib read the telegram he was very angry. He used the telephone. He rang people. Nobody he wanted to talk to could be found. He tried to ring Delhi. While he waited for the call he drank. He kept ringing the operator. Because he could not get through he was shouting all the time and drinking; and swearing.

Perron asked the bearer to be quiet while he read the signal. It was prefixed Secret and Urgent. It informed Captain Purvis of his secondment to the department of Civil Affairs and ordered him to report to Headquarters, South-East Asia Command, by August 9. Copies had been sent to an impressive list of authorities. No explanation was given but that was hardly necessary. In Ceylon, Purvis would find himself attached to a group of Civil Affairs officers bound for Malaya either with or in the wake of Zipper.

'Did Captain Purvis Sahib eventually speak to Delhi?'

Yes. The call had come through. During the conversation Purvis Sahib had become like a wild man, shouting and screaming. Then the line had been disconnected. Purvis Sahib began to throw the cushions, and then the bottles. Finally he kicked the table over. No one had dared go near. They had watched from the corridor. When Purvis Sahib staggered to his room they ran into the kitchen. They heard the door slam. Then they heard him shouting and throwing things again. After a bit they heard him crying. Cook had tried to open the door but it was locked. Now he was unconscious with drink. What to do? What would happen when Hapgood Sahib returned from Ooty? What would Hapgood Sahib say when he saw the damage? Was the telegram not from the army sending Purvis Sahib to another station? Did not this mean that when Hapgood Sahib returned Purvis Sahib would not be here? Would the Sergeant Sahib write a chit to Purvis Sahib asking Purvis Sahib to write a chit to Hapgood Sahib offering to pay for the damage and making it clear that the servants were not to blame?

Perron, already on his way back to the locked door, did not answer. He knocked loudly and called Purvis again. He grasped the handle and rattled. There seemed to be only one bolt.

'I'm afraid I shall have to break in. I'll write a chit for the door.'

Perron launched himself left shoulder forward. The impact

was as bad as the jarring shock of walking into a tree or a lamp-post. The door remained shut. The bearer started shouting again. A broken door, apparently, would be the last straw.

'Is there another way in?'

The bearer did not understand but the cook did. He sent the boy for some keys and then opened the door into the adjoining room and switched on the light. The room must be Miss Hap-good's. It smelt of stale powder and self-satisfaction. There was a great deal of chintz and several numdah rugs on the stone floor. The french-doors on to the balcony were open to keep the room aired but the way out on to the balcony was blocked by a thick wire-mesh screen. This was padlocked. While they waited for the boy to bring the key the cook explained that between this balcony and the one outside Purvis's room there was a gap of only a foot or two. The Sergeant Sahib would find it easy to step from one parapet to the other. Perron hoped this would be so and that Purvis's wire screen was not closed and padlocked too. The bearer assured him it would not be; but this remained to be seen.

The boy came with the key and in a moment Perron was outside. The balcony overlooked a broad passage between the block of flats and its neighbour and also had a view of the backs of other blocks. It was a world of hot night air and lighted windows. From some of them music came. The gap between the balconies was as narrow as the cook had promised. The cook allowed his shoulder to be used as a support while Perron got up on the parapet, steadied himself and stepped across. Without pausing to lose momentum or balance he jumped on to the floor of Purvis's balcony, barely managing to avoid twisting his ankle. One foot had landed within an inch of a potted plant which looked both virile and belligerent. The curtains in Purvis's room were closed but the wire-mesh screen gave at a touch. He entered.

The room was unoccupied. He tapped at the bathroom door and called. There was no sound from inside. He tried the handle. This door was locked too. He unbolted and opened the one into the corridor. The three servants were waiting outside.

'Did Purvis Sahib have his bath before the telegram came?'

No. All Purvis Sahib had done after Sergeant Sahib left was to sit drinking.

'In the flat below,' Perron said, slowly and carefully, 'there is a Major Rajendra Singh of the IMS. A Doctor Sahib. Please go downstairs, ring his bell and ask him to come quickly if he is there. If not come back at once.'

The cook volunteered to take the message but Perron said, 'No, you help me.' The cook looked tougher than the bearer. 'Purvis Sahib may be very ill. We have to break into the bathroom.'

Perron did not wait to watch the bearer go. He rattled the bathroom door, kicked the bottom and punched the top. The bolt was at waist level. Again he launched himself, right shoulder this time. After three attempts he stood back.

'Together. Okay?'

The cook lined himself up. On Perron's count of three they attacked the door together. There wasn't really enough working surface. Two shoulders needed a wider door. But Perron thought he felt something give. He fingered one of the panels. The door was a good solid piece of carpentry; which was a pity because breaking in looked like a chopper or axe job.

'Once more.'

This time the sound and feel of cracking wood was unmistakable. The bolt-hole was being forced out of the door-frame. Some of the frame would come with it.

'I think I can manage now.'

He stood the cook aside, made an anchorage for his left arm on the cook's shoulder and kicked hard at the door just above the handle with the flat of his shoe. He did this four times. At the fifth kick the door gave, swung open and revealed their own reflections in the mirror above the hand-basin: an unlooked-for and disturbing confrontation.

Perron went in. The water in the bath-tub had a pink tinge. In it Purvis lay, fully clothed except for his shoes which were placed neatly on the cork mat. His body had slumped and the head, turned into one shoulder, was half submerged. The source of the pink tinge was a series of cuts on the inner side of the left arm which was bare to the elbow. From these cuts slicks of blood rose. In his right hand, which lay under the water, the fingers touching but not grasping it, was the broken-off bottle neck that he had used to inflict the wounds. Other fragments of the bottle were visible. The label – from the second of the two bottles of Old Sporran – floated on the surface.

There was space enough between the wash-basin and the head

end of the bath. From there Perron reached down, grasped the collar of Purvis's bush-shirt and heaved him up far enough to get the head out of the water and a hand under one arm. He had to struggle to get a grip under the other. He glanced round. The cook was standing in the doorway looking as if he had come to announce that the dinner was ruined through no fault of his own.

'Help me with his feet,' Perron said.

'Sahib dead?'

'I don't know. Help with his feet.'

Reluctantly the man came in. After one glance at Purvis's face he looked away, studied the feet and presently leant over and grasped them, none too firmly.

'Up.'

Shoulders and feet came clear but Purvis was a dead weight. He sagged in the middle. The feet fell back in. The cook was drenched. Perron's eyes began to sting with sweat. The bathroom was like a hothouse. By contrast Purvis's body felt alarmingly tepid through the sodden khaki material. Changing tactics, Perron heaved the shoulders further up and then began to turn Purvis over on to the rim of the bath. As the face disappeared from the cook's view his attention to the mechanics of the problem improved. He grabbed Purvis's knees and heaved. Purvis was now face down and half out of the bath at the top end. Perron readjusted his grip and began to pull. The cook got hold of the thigh and knee of the left leg. At one moment Purvis was balanced entirely on the rim and in danger of falling off it. Perron walked backwards to the door, dragging Purvis with him. The water sloshed out of Purvis's pockets. The cook now got a secure grip on both ankles. They carried Purvis through into the bedroom.

'Bed, Sahib?'

'No, here.' Perron lowered his end to the floor. The cook followed suit.

'Towel.'

While the cook went back for this Perron turned Purvis's face sideways and adjusted the arms, straddled the body and began the exhausting drill for first-aid to the drowned. While he did so he looked at the left arm. There didn't seem to be much blood on the floor. Perhaps the slashes on the arm were superficial. A towel dangled in his face. 'Sahib,' the cook said. Perron broke off, took the towel and wound it tightly round the slashed arm. Then he resumed. A thin trickle of water and what looked like vomit came from Purvis's mouth.

'Doctor Sahib not answering,' came the bearer's voice. The cook repeated the message. 'No answer, doctor sahib.'

Perron continued exerting and relaxing pressure. A large trickle of water came.

'Go downstairs,' Perron said, between pressures. 'Ring Colonel Grace Sahib's bell. Ask for Major Merrick. Anyone. Say: Doctor, ambulance, Purvis Sahib. Quick. Okay?'

The cook repeated the instructions to the bearer.

'Go with him,' Perron said. 'Doctor. Ambulance, Sergeant Perron's request.'

Alone, Perron paused to wipe sweat. He looked at his watch. Twenty minutes altogether was what was recommended. Say another fifteen yet to go. After that Purvis could be presumed dead. He was probably dead now. Perron was tempted to pause again and listen for heart and pulse beat but he supposed the most important thing now was to keep up the rhythm. He resumed. He had studied the drill but this was the first time he had had to put it into practice. The action he was performing suddenly struck him as distasteful. Not only was the body very likely dead, it was Purvis's. It would have been preferable if the inert figure, prone between his thighs, had been that of a complete stranger. The fact that he had sat and talked to Purvis strengthened the unpleasantness of their present positions. He wondered whether Purvis would thank him if he succeeded in reviving him. The suspicion that he would not made the task that much more objectionable. There was another ejaculation of water and vomit. Perron turned his head, closed his eyes. He began breathing in and out through his mouth, slowly, to the rhythm of his own body's movement. He breathed audibly, thinking that perhaps by some quirk of nature Purvis's moribund brain and water-logged lungs might be stimulated into action by an association of ideas.

From breathing just audibly he progressed to doing so hoarsely through a half-closed throat, and continued so after his throat had begun to ache; the point being that he wanted Purvis to *hear* what he himself now began to despair of hearing from Purvis.

His back hurt. His arms and shoulders hurt. Sweat poured unchecked over and around his closed eyes. His knees were numb from contact with the tiled floor. Pain stabbed through them down the shins and up the thighs with each forward and backward movement. Only his hands, pressing into Purvis's thin bony back and rib-cage, still seemed capable of doing their work indefinitely. He went on, exerting and relaxing pressure and breathing hoarsely until suddenly his throat dried up. He closed his mouth, swallowed and tried to make saliva. The effort put him off his stroke. He stopped for a moment and then, alerted, opened his eyes and stared down at Purvis. From Purvis's open mouth was coming a sound and under Perron's hands the rib-cage was moving. Purvis was breathing, or anyway fighting for breath.

'I think you can stop now, Sergeant,' someone said. He looked up and round. Merrick stood just behind him. 'I'll get another towel. We've rung for a doctor. He's just up the road so he'll be here in a tick.'

Perron nodded and looked down at Purvis. The struggle for breath seemed immense. Surprisingly it was not without a certain dignity. When Merrick returned with the towel Perron took it from him and spread it over the vomit and then, folding a clean section, tucked it under Purvis's cheek and stroked a lank bit of the mousy hair away from the closed eyes. As he did so Purvis's mouth shut and then opened again.

Merrick said, 'I think a blanket would be a good idea if there is such a thing.' He found one in the almirah and brought it over. Perron helped him cover Purvis with it.

'We'd better have a look at this.' He leant down and lifted Purvis's left arm. Perron unwound the towel. The inside was fairly bloody now but only one of the cuts was seeping seriously.

'I think just wrap the towel round again, Sergeant, until the doctor gets here,' Merrick said. 'It wasn't a very effective job, was it?'

'He was pretty drunk.'

'What on? More of the whisky the Maharanee didn't like?'

'To judge by the broken bottle.'

'And the smell in this room.'

'Is there a smell?'

'Very much so. Haven't you noticed?'

Perron sniffed. He noticed it now.

'Not the most prepossessing chap by the look of him, is he?' Merrick said. 'Do you know what was wrong?'

'I think he'd just had enough.'

'You look as if you have. Where did you leave the bottle you brought back from the Maharanee's?'

Perron told him he thought it must be in the living-room.

'I think you should have some. I'll bring it.'

Merrick went. Purvis's breathing was shallow but fairly regular. Perron got up stiffly. A man's voice in the corridor called 'Hello?' There was an exchange between Merrick and the new arrival. Merrick came back into the room with an English IMS officer. The officer knelt, lifted Purvis's eyelid and felt his temple.

'You're the chap who found him, are you, Sergeant?'

'Yes, sir.'

The doctor unwrapped the towel from the arm.

'Bath, I gather. Face completely submerged?'

'Right side, sir.'

'D'you know how long for, roughly?'

'No, sir.'

'How long were you resuscitating?'

'About ten minutes, sir.'

The doctor had his stethoscope out. When he had finished and slung the earpieces round his neck he glanced up.

'Well done. You'd better go next door and have a bloody strong drink and get out of that wet uniform. Major Merrick – perhaps a couple of the fellows outside will help me get him on to the bed while you ring for the blood-wagon?' He gave Merrick the number as Perron left the room.

After Purvis had been taken away Merrick came back from downstairs and into the wrecked living-room where Perron sat drinking some of the Maharanee's whisky and admiring the vivid and lively effect of the Guler-Basohli technique. The paintings were the only things he felt able to concentrate on. They were about one hundred and fifty years old. Even the two damaged ones maintained that air of detachment and self-sufficiency that went with a talent for survival.

Before Merrick could speak Perron said, 'Until I told Purvis what those pictures were he'd no idea. If I'd kept quiet he'd probably have left them alone.'

Merrick inspected them.

'It's what's called Kangra painting, isn't it?'

Perron nodded. Kangra was close enough.

Merrick said, 'Actually I find all oriental art unattractive.' He turned from the paintings. 'I don't think you need worry further about Captain Purvis unless he does the unexpected and dies, which would mean an inquest. But Simpson says he'll be all right. When he's recovered they'll hand him over to the psychiatric people. Are you going to be fit to drive back to Kalyan?'

'I should think so, sir.'

'Then get your other things and come downstairs and clean up. We'll give you something to eat. How much of that whisky have you had?'

'This is my third glass.'

'Rather a strong one, isn't it? When you're downstairs you'll remember which subjects are taboo, won't you?'

'The subjects of Havildar Karim Muzzafir Khan and Harry Coomer.'

'Good. Incidentally I liked the way you handled Count Bronowsky, but I was surprised he thought fit to raise the subject.'

Perron sipped whisky. He had not liked lying. He felt he was owed an explanation. 'Perhaps you'll tell me what Coomer did, sir?'

'He and five of his friends raped an English girl called Daphne Manners, the niece of the Lady Manners whose name also came up. It was a squalid and extremely nasty business and I find it inconceivable that a man should refer to it in front of a woman.'

Perron sipped more whisky. How old-fashioned. His inclination was to laugh. He wondered whether it was Merrick's intention to make him.

'Was a charge of rape the one you said he wriggled out of, sir?'

'Yes. But as I told you we got him and the others on political grounds.'

Perron drained the glass and stood up. 'It all sounds so melodramatic. I find it difficult to imagine Coomer raping anybody.'

'But then you didn't really know him, except with a bat and ball. Are you one of those people who think that if you teach an Indian the rules of cricket he'll become a perfect English gentleman?'

'Hardly, sir. Since I know quite a few Englishmen who play brilliantly and are absolute shits.'

'Do you?' Merrick said. He stared at Perron. 'What are you going to do about the Maharanee's whisky?'

'Keep it, I should think.'

'In view of what Miss Layton said about her father's fondness for that particular brand I was wondering whether it would be a nice gesture for you to leave it with her as a sort of thank you.'

'Thank you?'

'She's putting herself out to see that you have something to eat.'

'I didn't ask for anything to eat, sir.'

'I did that for you. I don't want you driving on a stomach full of nothing but liquor. And then there's the danger of delayed shock impairing your judgment and leading to an accident.'

'It's nice of you to have my welfare at heart, sir.'

'My concern is quite unaltruistic. I have a vested interest in your continuing capacity to perform efficiently. Now, let's go down and get you cleaned up and fed.'

'May I ask what vested interest, sir?'

'I'm arranging to have you attached to my department. The signal ordering you to report for an interview is probably waiting for you in Kalyan but the interview will be no more than a formality. You can assume you'll be working for me. You'll find it pretty interesting.'

'It's very kind of you, sir, but I imagine my department will think its present commitments much too important to allow me to go elsewhere.'

'You'll find they're overruled without much fuss.'

'The point is, sir, I shouldn't want them overruled.'

'Well that does you credit. One becomes attached to one's own unit. But I imagine you'll bow to the inevitable with more equanimity than our friend Purvis. Let's not keep Miss Layton waiting any longer.'

Perron picked up the bottle and went to Purvis's room to collect his pack. Back in the corridor he found Merrick instructing the bearer to leave everything as it was until morning. Perron preceded him through the open door, waited for him and then followed him downstairs. Just short of the door of the flat, which was ajar, Merrick said, 'I'll relieve you of that, shall I?' and took the bottle.

Going in, Merrick called, 'Sarah? I've got Sergeant Perron here.'

Perron followed. In layout the flat was a mirror-duplicate of the one upstairs. She was coming through the dining-room area towards them.

'Hello. Are you all right?'

'I think he's still a bit groggy,' Merrick said before Perron could answer.

'If you are I don't wonder. I'll show you where you can relax and freshen up. Ronald, you go and sit down.'

Her manner was brisk but sympathetic. The bedroom she took him to corresponded with the one Purvis had occupied upstairs but was properly furnished. The light and the ceiling fan were already on. There were two beds; between them a writing-table and a chair with an officer's bush-shirt draped over its back. The bush-shirt looked brand-new. The woven shoulder-tabs were those of a Lieutenant-Colonel of the Pankot Rifles.

The door to the bathroom was open and the light switched on. She said, 'Do bathe or shower if you want to. You'll find a large green towel on the rail that hasn't been used.' She had made simple but efficient preparations. She looked at his damp uniform. 'I know father wouldn't mind your borrowing his dressing-gown if you want to have anything dried out and pressed quickly.'

'It's very kind of you, Miss Layton, but I've got a change of clothes in here.' He indicated the pack. 'My correct uniform. The one you saw me in this afternoon.'

'Yes, of course. I'll leave you to it, then. How hungry are you?'

'I'm not at all hungry but I suppose I ought to eat something.'

'I think you ought to if you possibly can. Not that there's much to offer you. Aunt Fenny assumed we'd all be out so she gave cook the night off and Nazimuddin isn't very inventive.'

'Whatever's going will be fine.'

'I'm afraid it's only soup, cold chicken and salad, and what Aunt Fenny calls a shape. In other words, blancmange.'

'I'm rather partial to shape.'

'Good.'

They smiled at one another rather gravely.

'Well,' she said, 'come along whenever you're ready. I'll send Nazimuddin in with a drink. What would you like?'

'Major Merrick thinks I'd just better eat. I've had some of the Maharanee's whisky. Incidentally, he thought your father might like what's left of it. Will he be insulted, being offered left-overs?'

She hesitated. 'Not of that particular whisky. How very nice of you. Are you sure you wouldn't like a glass while you're changing?'

'Quite sure.'

'Did Major Merrick tell you I tipped him off that there was a Field Security man in disguise at the party?'

'Yes, he did.'

'I wasn't sure whether to tell him or not so it was a relief when he said you'd already met and were coming to work with him.'

'You were quite right to tell him. You weren't to know which uniform was the masquerade.'

'Actually that never crossed my mind.'

There was a knock on the open door. The curtains parted and Merrick looked in.

'What is it, Ronald?'

'You've been such a long time I thought our sergeant friend was suffering a reaction from his exertions and that you were having to minister.'

'Actually, sir,' Perron said, 'we've been discussing the attrac-tions and nutritive value of that homely pudding, the blancmange.'

'Oh,' Merrick said, not looking at Perron, speaking to Miss Layton. 'You're having shape again, then. Well, if it's one of the sergeant's favourite afters we'd better let him get changed.' He pushed the curtain further aside: a gesture of command rather than a mark of good manners. Miss Layton hesitated and then went through, murmuring 'Thank you, Ronald' as she did so. Still without looking at Perron Merrick followed her.

Perron put his pack on the nearest of the two beds. Taking out his carefully folded jungle-green issue uniform, spreading it, considering it, he said aloud suddenly, 'I'll be buggered if I will.'

The Zipper-bound boats out there in the roads riding the gentle swell of the Arabian Sea, patient in the night and the persistent rain, seemed infinitely welcoming; his working clothes (in comparison with the jacket that hung on the chair-back) purposeful, appropriate. Going into the bathroom he felt his chin. It could have done with a shave but he didn't go back for his razor and brush. A day's growth of bristle was appropriate too. He stripped off the damp harlequinade and stepped into the tub, on to Purvis who lay there invisibly entombed in the smooth white porcelain. Perron's feet went right through him; but when he turned the shower faucet and gasped under the impact of a needle-sharp cold spray he felt the sodden flesh of Purvis's left arm take shape against his shins and the hand take hold of his ankle. Be not afeared, Perron began to declaim, the Isle is full of noises, sounds and sweet airs that give delight and hurt not.

When Purvis had been half-drowned for the second time that evening and Perron had dried himself on the green towel (put out on the rail by Miss Layton's own charming hands?) he returned to the bedroom and put on a clean set of cellular cotton under-shorts and clean socks – the second of two changes care-fully packed that morning. Soldiers, he thought, acquired old-maidish habits – especially in the tropics. He got into the green trousers and bush-shirt, unrolled the sleeves and buttoned them at the wrists. Then he sat on the bed and put his boots on, folded the trouser-bottoms and secured them with the webbing anklets. All that remained in the pack now was his shaving kit, small towel, clean handkerchief, webbing belt, holster, pistol and lan-yard. If Purvis had known about the pistol would he have gone to the trouble of getting it out of the pack? He put these things on the bed and went round the room and bathroom collecting the stuff he had discarded and cramming it into the pack, so that the damp clothes were at the bottom. This done he replaced the stuff from the bed and secured the pack straps. He checked his breast pocket for the piece of paper on which before leaving for the Maharanee's he had got Purvis to write down the address of the place where they had left his jeep, and which he'd fortunately not put in the pocket of the khaki uniform. It might have been illegible now, from bath water. He looked at it, rememorized it.

Finished, he glanced round the room until his attention was again taken by the brand-new khaki bush-shirt that belonged to Sarah Layton's father. It was, Perron supposed, one of the first things Colonel Layton would do on his return from prison-camp in Europe: get himself fitted out afresh, no doubt from necessity but also to look trim for the arrival in Pankot with the regiment. How would they march in? With bags of swank to make up for the silence in the hills?

But there was nothing particularly swanky about the bush-shirt. It hung on the chair back without distinction, like a jacket on a coat-hanger too narrow for it. There were eyelets sewn on the left breast which showed where two broad bars of medal ribbons would be pinned, but these were not there, nor on the table, and their absence struck Perron as eloquent, as a clue to some special attribute the jacket had which he hadn't identified.

He identified it now. The jacket was new but the slip-on shoulder-tabs, although pressed and starched, were old, much laundered. The cream and brown cottons of the embroidered pip and crown, and the black cotton of the regimental name, were faded.

The attribute was twofold, a combination of economical habit and modest impulse. The way the bush-shirt hung on the chair back, shoulders drooped, ostensibly in possession of chair, room, suggested a claim to occupation, but – Perron thought – a claim made in awareness of the insecurity of any tenure. He tried to give the jacket a perkier look by twitching the shoulders back up. They slipped off again. This was because the chair was too narrow, not because Layton was a man of impressive build. Perhaps he had been, before years in prison camp wore him down.

The bush-shirt began to depress him; it was threatening to undermine his confidence in much the same way that the whole experience of being in India had so often seemed on the point of undermining it. Staring at the bush-shirt, on a perch it clung to which did not properly support it, he was struck by its mute indication of the grand irrelevance of history to the things that people wanted for themselves. As in Beamish's office, earlier, he again tuned in the inner ear, the one that could catch the whisper of the perpetually moving stream; but now caught nothing. It began to ache from the pressure of a marble silence so smooth and dense that the plop of a drop of water – the built-in residue in the nozzle of the bathroom shower hitting the porcelain – came as a relief, an excuse to tune back in to the world in which the most significant sound was that made by a hall full of men, ignorant of and indifferent to their history, and giving it the bird.

He got out his notebook and recorded Purvis's remark: 'Six

years' waste of the world's natural resources and human skills. I don't think I shall ever be able to forgive it.' That was at once a moral judgment and a revelation of thwarted ambition.

'Sahib?'

Perron looked up. The servant Nazimuddin stood in the doorway holding the curtain aside. He indicated a direction – that of the dining-room. Perron nodded – a little surprised to be invited to eat there. He let Nazimuddin go, put his notebook away, waited for a moment or two and then followed, carrying his pack, fighting an urge to open the front door when he got to it and leave without another word.

As though to forestall him Merrick was stationed near it. Through the dining-area, beyond the archway, Perron could see Miss Layton, in profile, seated, talking to someone in the living-room who was hidden from view.

'Leave your pack here, Sergeant.'

Perron put it down near the door. When he had straightened up Merrick continued. 'I told the servant to hurry you up because Miss Layton's father has come back unexpectedly. He's had dinner out and wants an early night but I've been telling him about you and he'll have a few words, so come along.'

Hearing them coming, she broke off what she was saying. Her father sat at one end of a large cretonne-covered sofa. Perron stopped and, briefly, held himself in an attitude akin to parade-ground attention.

'Father, this is Sergeant Perron. My father, Colonel Layton.'

'Good-evening, sir,' Perron said. He stayed where he was. The colonel got up but they were too far from each other to shake hands. He was tall, very thin, slightly stooped. He wore a replica of the bush-shirt in the bedroom. At the head of the row of medal ribbons was the MC.

'Hello,' he said. 'Hear you've been in the wars a bit tonight.' His voice was mild and pleasant. His upper lip was covered by the regulation bristly, cropped, moustache. His head was balding, his complexion pale; a washed-out, rather worn sort of face, but with the same bony structure as his daughter's and so perhaps once more resolute and attractive than it now appeared.

'The evening has been on the hectic side, sir.'

'Mine was too. Thought I'd give the rest of it a miss. Perron. Perron, is it?'

'Yes, sir.'

'Perron. Well, let's sit down again shall we, unless I'm holding the kitchen up.'

'It's only a question of heating the soup, the rest's cold so there's no hurry.'

'Splendid.' He turned to look behind him, as if the act of getting up had disoriented him, left him uncertain about the location or even the continuing existence of the sofa; then, remembering the other two, he indicated vacant places and waited until Merrick and Perron had chosen seats and settled in. There were two floral cretonne-covered sofas at right angles to each other, a small tapestry-covered wing chair in which Miss Layton was sitting, and a larger matching chair which Merrick took. Perron sat on the second sofa; in this way he faced the company. The furniture was arranged round an Indian carpet. There were Benares brass coffee-tables in front of each sofa. The room was not elegant like the banking Hapgoods' living-room, but comfortable, attractive in a homely English way. On the wall behind Colonel Layton hung a couple of faded portraits – conversation-pieces in the Zoffany style – with eighteenth-century ladies and gentlemen under trees, with attendant servants: in one case transfixed in expository attitudes and in the other restraining cheetahs on leashes.

'There are cigarettes in the box, Mr Perron,' Miss Layton said. 'And the lighter works. So do help yourself whenever you want.'

'Perron,' Colonel Layton repeated, as if trying to place the name.

Before Perron could speak Merrick said, 'There was a man called Pierre-Cuiller who was known as Perron. He became Governor of what was called Hindustan and commanded the armies under Daulat Rao Sindia. Originally he was a sergeant.'

'In the French Army?' Layton asked. The question was open to both of them but Merrick took it up. 'I can't recall the early origins exactly. But I seem to remember he began life as a pedlar as a result of his family losing all its money. It must be in Compton, but it's some time since I read him. Perron was certainly in the French navy and I think he was in the French Army before that. He came out on a French ship but I can't remember whether it was on the Coromandel or Malabar coast he deserted. Anyway he disappeared up country to seek his fortune with the mercenary Europeans who helped the Indian princes run their armies. What I do remember is that he was among the remnants of Lestineau's brigade when they were taken over by another mercenary, de Boigne, Mahdaji Sindia's chap. Perron was still a sergeant then but rose pretty rapidly and when de Boigne retired after Mahdaji's death and Daulat Rao's succession Perron took over. But of course the two Wellesleys were in control of British interests by then and the French were practically finished. The Mahratta power was fading out and Perron never acquired a reputation as high as de Boigne's. Would you agree, sergeant?'

After a moment Perron smiled, to convey his appreciation of the point Merrick had made: that he was to be reckoned with.

'Yes, I'd agree, sir. But compared with de Boigne Perron was second-rate. Of course he was handicapped –'

Perron stopped – silenced by the impact of one of those un-expected shock-waves, scarcely more than a ripple, of delayed response to a forgotten factor. He had meant that Perron was handicapped by political and military circumstances more com-plex and threatening than de Boigne had ever had to contend with, but in the split-second before he used the word handi-capped he recalled another impediment, one that he was always forgetting because it had seemed to play so insignificant a part in Perron's career. He looked at Merrick's left hand. The gloved artifact was at rest, just off the chair-arm.

Merrick said, 'I suppose you could call it a handicap but I don't remember it ever being said to worry him. Which hand was it by the way?'

Monsieur Perron had lost a hand while throwing a grenade that exploded prematurely. Perron said, 'The right, I imagine, unless he was left-handed or being particularly hard-pressed.'

Merrick said, 'I don't think it was important.' He turned to Colonel Layton. 'The real answer is that he didn't have de Boigne's luck and of course it's difficult stepping into the shoes of an outstandingly successful man. It's an interesting coincid-ence to come across a modern Sergeant Perron, especially one who's making a study of British-Indian history.'

'Are you connected?' Layton asked amiably. 'I mean des-cended?' Perron said he was not.

'But the mercenaries are what you'd call your subject?'

'No, sir.'

'What is?'

'At the moment, sir, Field Security in the Bombay Presidency.'

Layton waited a few seconds then put his head back against the sofa. 'Ha!' And then added, 'Jolly good answer.' He crossed his legs, glanced at Merrick, then returned his attention to Perron. 'All the same, war over and all that, what'll be your subject then?'

'Eighteen-thirty to the Mutiny, I think, sir.'

Layton narrowed his eyes. 'Good period. Bad too, I suppose. That your point?'

'I haven't got a point yet, sir. Choosing a period's rather like sticking a pin in a map of likely runners. Eighteen-thirty or eighteen-thirty-three to eighteen-fifty-eight is simply the period between the East India Company's loss of its trading charter and its metamorphosis into the Indian Civil Service. So it represents about thirty years' dress rehearsal for full imperial rule. Some of the clues to what eventually went wrong are probably there. That's an over-simplification but it's the neatest way I can put it.'

Colonel Layton was still observing him through those narrowed eyes, apparently paying close attention, but his next remark showed that his attention was on Perron himself and not on what he was saying.

'Perron. I've remembered now. There was a Perron at the school I was at. Younger than me, but a big boy. Remarkably fine athlete. Before the First World War. Place called Chillingborough.'

'That would have been my father, sir.'

'Would it now?' Did Layton's eyes stray to the stripes on his sleeve? Had the reference to Chillingborough been carefully prepared? Or had Merrick said nothing to Layton? On the whole Perron preferred to give him the benefit of the doubt.

'So you're Perron's son, then. Don't suppose I've thought of him since I left. Is he still going strong?'

'He was killed in 1918, sir.'

'Oh. I'm sorry.'

'Ironically enough, on November the tenth.'

'What awful luck. And your mother?'

'She died in 1919, of Spanish 'flu.'

'You poor fellow. Still, you'd be too young to know anything about it, I imagine.'

'Yes, sir. Actually I had a very pleasant childhood. I was brought up by some rather eccentric aunts and uncles.'

'Eccentric enough to send you to Chillingborough too?'

'Yes, sir.'

'Which house?'

'Bank's.'

'The same as your father.'

'No, sir. He was Coote's.'

'Ah. Yes. So he was.'

Layton turned his body rather awkwardly and put his left hand into the nearest of the two large side-pockets of his bush-jacket. Coote's was a nickname. Perron had used it quite unconsciously but it was the sort of thing only someone familiar with Chillingborough lore would be likely to know.

'Did you know someone called Clark?' Miss Layton asked.

'I knew two. One with an e and the other without.'

She sat back and folded her arms, cupping the elbows. She said, 'I've always thought of him as Clark without an e. But now you mention it I'm not sure. My aunt and uncle would know. I only met him once. His first name was James.'

'They were both James. So we called them Clarke-With and Clark-Without. Clark-Without otherwise lacked very little. I thought of him as someone who would go far in life.'

'Then the one I knew must have been Clark-Without. I met him on the sixth of June last year.' She had turned to speak to her father. 'I know it was the sixth of June because that's the day I visited Ronald in hospital in Calcutta and the day we heard about the second front.' She looked back at Perron. 'He was flying to Ceylon the next day to take up some glamorous-sounding job at South-East Asia Command Headquarters. I've not heard of him again, though.'

'Then it could only have been Clark-Without. Clarke-With wasn't what I'd call Command Headquarters material.'

He wondered about Miss Layton's brief acquaintance with Clark-Without. Clark-Without had not been officially expelled but, in Chillingborough's peculiar language, withdrawn by mutual consent. A Rolls had turned up and Clark-Without had driven away in style, not up-front with the chauffeur but at the back, smoking a cigarette. A mature boy for his age. Perhaps he had been excessively self-publicized in regard to his affairs with girls. Miss Layton did not look in the least embarrassed. In any case she had raised the subject herself. But why? To test for further proof that he himself had been at Chillingborough or to hear him speak the name of a man she had fancied?

'I think your father is tired, Sarah,' Merrick said.

'Ronald thinks you're tired, Father. Are you?'

'Not in the least. Tell you what I'd like, though. A peg of that whisky of Ronald's. Why don't we all do that?'

'It wasn't Ronald's whisky, Father. It was Sergeant Perron's. Before that it was the Maharanee's and before that Captain Purvis's. Nazimuddin!'

Colonel Layton looked from one to the other as if bemused by such a complicated history, and finally concentrated on Perron. 'Extraordinary thing,' he said, 'in the last conversation I had with a very civilized Oberleutnant at the camp I was at, the name of this particular brand came up. We were saying goodbye and he told me he'd be thinking of me in a week or two's time sitting in a comfortable chair in a cosy room, reading *Pride and Prejudice*, sipping a glass of special malt whisky and fondling the ears of my faithful black Labrador, Panther. Apparently one day months before he'd said, "What would you most like to be doing at this very moment?" and it seems that's what I told him. I hadn't the faintest recollection of it. Memory's a bit haywire. But it was pretty well in line with the sort of thing I'd often thought, so obviously I had done. Well, he got the names right. I didn't have the heart to tell him I never knew the dog except as a puppy and that I'd since heard the poor beast was dead anyway, that there wasn't a hope of getting a bottle of that particular whisky in India, so that the only accurate part of his picture could be the comfortable chair and Jane Austen. He'd remembered the detail so accurately. I must say I found that rather touching. Um? Something one says quite casually capturing another chap's imagination and staying in his mind. A nice fellow. Very formal. Very correct. But fair. Yes. Fair. Very fair.'

Nazimuddin who had come in while Colonel Layton was talking and had collected glasses and the bottle at Sarah's low-voiced instructions now brought them to her. She told him to put the tray on the coffee-table nearest her father.

'Will you join us for supper, Father?'

'What?'

'Supper.'

'No, no. Had my supper. Any case, got the unexpired portion of the day's rations if I get peckish.'

She told Nazimuddin they would eat in ten minutes. The man went. Her father leant forward and picked the bottle up. He stared at the label.

'Extraordinary,' he said. 'I've not held a bottle of this for years.'

He put his free hand above his eyes like a shield, as though there was too much light, then folded it until it was across his eyes; and seemed to become fixed in that position, still gripping the bottle.

Miss Layton got up and went to him, bent down, took the bottle, put it on the table and then took his hand in hers. 'Come on, daddy, you've had a long day.'

Perron got up and moved away, making for the folding glass doors that gave on to the balcony but which were closed to keep out the rain. Through the windows he could see little except the reflection of the lighted room, the dark bulk of the back of the wing chair in which Merrick was obviously still sitting, Sarah Layton's bent head, strongly lit by the lamp at the side of the sofa. He could still hear her voice but she was speaking too quietly for any words to reach him. He was glad; he did not want to hear; he did not want to see, either, but wherever he looked the room and its occupants were there in the window. He saw her help Colonel Layton to his feet and lead him out. The colonel still had one hand over his face. The other rested on his daughter's shoulder.

After they had gone Perron did not move. He stared at the reflection of Merrick's chair. He could see the top of Merrick's head and the elbow of the shattered arm. There was the click of a cigarette lighter. In a moment he saw the smoke spiralling gently through the diffused ray cast by the lamp and, after it had vanished, a thinner wisp, rising from about the level of the shattered elbow, which meant that Merrick must have stuck the cigarette between two fingers of the black-gloved artifact.

Perron re-entered the sitting area and did not look at Merrick until he had taken a cigarette from the box Miss Layton had invited him to use, lighted it and sat down. Merrick was supporting his chin in his good hand and holding the cigarette in the artificial one. The unblemished side of his face was comparatively in shade.

'How did you come by that arm, sir?' Perron asked.

'Pulling a certain Captain Bingham out of a burning jeep, under fire, near Imphal, in 1944.'

Such precision. 'Is that what you got the decoration for? Rescuing Captain Bingham?'

'There was an Indian driver to get out as well. He survived. Captain Bingham didn't. He was Miss Layton's brother-in-law.'

'Since when you've been a sort of friend of the family, sir?'

Merrick released his chin, reached across and retrieved the cigarette.

'I knew them before. I was Captain Bingham's best man when he married Susan Layton in nineteen-forty-three.'

'Susan. Yes, that was it. Susan-mem and Sarah-mem. And the wild dogs in the hills.'

'You have a memory for detail. Good.'

'Difficult to forget the wild dog bit, sir.'

'Why?'

'Well, you nearly had him there, sir, didn't you?'

'Had him?'

' "Your wife will not hold her head up and even the wild dogs in the hills will be silent." The chap nearly cried.'

Merrick drew on his cigarette, then rested his chin again on the free fingers of the good hand; arm supported at the elbow by the chair-arm; the smoke floating up.

'He cried later.'

'Yes, sir?'

'When we examined him a week or so ago in Delhi.' Merrick stroked the outer corner of his right eye with his little finger, as if to remove something that irritated it. 'The evidence of his possible complicity in the death of the sepoy in Königsberg is quite strong.' Merrick flicked ash and then put the cigarette back between the black-gloved fingers.

'Is that why the subject's taboo down here? Because it upsets Colonel Layton?'

'It's taboo because it would particularly upset him to know about Königsberg. Actually neither he nor Miss Layton yet know I've seen the man and questioned him. I've tried to give them the impression the man's case isn't a priority. You realize that these men's old officers aren't allowed to go anywhere near them, don't you?'

'No, I didn't, sir. Why aren't they?'

'Because we'd be inundated with requests for interviews. Colonel Layton is a good example. He's convinced he could straighten Havildar Muzzafir Khan out in ten minutes. The attitude is quite admirable, of course, but given half a chance a lot of these men's old officers would try to deal with their own cases at regimental level, and the only sensible course is to keep them firmly out of the picture, otherwise it will get hopelessly confused. And of course it increases the prisoners' sense of isolation, and readiness to talk.'

From behind, in the dining-room area, came the sounds of plates being set out on the table.

'So not a word about the Havildar. I shall break the news to Colonel Layton in my own good time.'

They heard her voice, calling Nazimuddin.

She came into the dining-room. 'Come on, Mr Perron. You must be starved now. Are you ready too, Ronald?'

She waited for them to join her. The table was laid with places at either end and a third in the middle, facing the living-room. She asked Perron to sit in the middle and took the place on his left. Merrick sat at the other end. While they waited for the soup she asked him how long he'd been in India, how much of the country he'd seen and whether it was all as he'd pictured it. After Nazimuddin had brought in the soup and served it he expected her to give Merrick some of her attention, but she did not. For a few moments they drank soup and did not talk at all. He broke the silence by asking her how long she'd been in India herself.

'I was born here. Up in Pankot. So was my sister. We came back out in the summer of 'thirty-nine.'

Perron asked how long the journey to Pankot would take. She said the train left Bombay at two o'clock the following afternoon and that they would be home early on Wednesday morning – unless they decided to break the journey at Delhi. She looked across at Merrick. 'He mentioned it again just now. I've done all I can. It's up to you, Ronald, I'm afraid.'

'It's quite pointless,' Merrick said. 'A complete waste of time.'

'I know. But it's for you to explain why.'

'I thought I had.'

'I mean again.'

'When?'

'Tonight, preferably. Tomorrow morning at the very latest. I want it cut and dried before we get on the train because if we're going to stop off at Delhi I must try to get through to mother and tell her. It's only fair.'

'Personally, I think it would be better to let things lie. Once he's on the train the idea of getting off it will have less appeal.'

'But we get off at Delhi anyway, to change. There's a wait of at least two hours for the Ranpur connection. I don't want to stand around there not knowing whether we're going on or staying. And I certainly don't want to find myself trying to get through to mother from there and telling her we won't be home next day after all.'

'Very well. I'll have a word with him tonight. Incidentally, sergeant, where and what is this transport of yours?'

Perron told him.

'Well that's just round the corner if we take a short cut. We can walk easily, then you could drop me off.'

'That's kind of you, sir, but I'm sure I can find it on my own if you give me directions.'

'Major Merrick isn't staying here, Mr Perron. He's at the Taj.'

'Oh, I see.'

Nazimuddin had cleared away the first course and now brought in the second. Miss Layton made her selection from the tray. Merrick was provided with a plate of pre-prepared chicken and salad that he could deal with single-handed. The servant now reached Perron's side.

'I'm sorry,' Miss Layton said. 'We were talking just now about something you probably don't know about. The point of getting off at Delhi is for father to try to see one of his NCOs who's in trouble. The only man in the regiment who joined the Frei Hind force in Germany. But Major Merrick says it's a waste of time because of an order prohibiting contact between INA prisoners and their old officers.'

'Yes. It seems rather hard.'

'Understandable in one way, but father's rather upset because he's known the man in question since he was a boy of six or seven. Father was present when the boy and his mother were given the posthumous VC the boy's father won in the last war and he says he showed up awfully well in the fighting in North Africa, so he simply can't understand what got into his head.'

'Presumably Subhas Chandra Bose got into it,' Merrick said. 'But why?'

'It's the sort of thing we'll have to find out.'

'Father thinks he could find out better and quicker than anyone.' For Perron's benefit she added, 'According to the other men in the regiment, Bose and some Indian officers from another regiment who'd already turned coat came to the camp they were in and told them it was their duty to fight with the Germans for India's freedom. Then over the next few days the VCOs and senior NCOs were taken off separately for interviews. Some didn't come back for quite a while but the only one who never came back was this man my father's concerned about. The others thought he'd been tortured and killed because some of the NCOs who were interviewed had a rough time if they told Bose's officers what they thought of them, and Havildar Muzzafir Khan had a reputation for being pretty outspoken. When another lot of Indian officers visited them a few months later and said Muzzafir Khan had joined the Frei Hind army and that they should all follow his example, one of them stood up and asked why Havildar Muzzafir Khan wasn't there to tell them himself. The poor man was carted off, didn't come back for a month and had a ghastly time. Now it seems that the officers were right, but most of the men in the regiment think as daddy does, that something awful must have been done to him to make him join Bose and that even then he'd only have joined to muck things up or escape to the allies at the first opportunity.'

'But he didn't escape,' Merrick said. 'He was among a group of Indians captured by the Free French when the Germans were on the run. The French were all for shooting them out of hand but an American army sergeant whistled up a helicopter and took them back to his unit as prisoners. The sergeant was a Negro, if that's relevant.'

'You've never mentioned that.'

'No. It's what drew my attention to his case, the discovery that one of the men listed in the report of the helicopter incident was a havildar from your father's regiment.'

'That will count against him, won't it? That he was actually fighting?'

'It's not clear whether he was fighting. The report didn't say. And he's just one man out of several hundred in the European and several thousand in the Eastern theatre.'

'Ought I to mention the helicopter incident to Father?'

'It's up to you. I'd prefer not. There's absolutely nothing he can do and the less he knows just now the easier it'll be for him to accept that.'

'Yes,' she said. 'I suppose so.'

'It's not as though your father's opinion of Havildar Karim Muzzafir Khan won't be asked for. When we reach the stage of dealing with the case someone will come up to Pankot to take statements from people who want to make them.'

'Will the person coming up be you, Ronald?'

'Possibly.'

They concentrated on their food.

Presently Perron said to her, 'I suppose it'll be quite a home-coming on Wednesday? Is there a special train laid on for the regiment?'

'There was hardly a train–load left. But they went back about three weeks ago. My father stayed on in Bombay because when the boat docked there were some men who had to go straight to hospital and he didn't want to leave them behind at this stage of the game.'

'That was very nice of him.'

'Yes, I thought so. The men appreciated it. A bit tough on my mother of course. She couldn't come to Bombay because my sister hasn't been well. But she's talked to the sick men's families and passed on messages and of course father's visited the hospital every day and been able to cheer them up.'

'How many sick men were there?'

'Only six. Five sepoys and a havildar.' She spoke across the table. 'If Father's obstinate about getting off at Delhi to get per-mission to see Havildar Muzzafir Khan we'll probably find the sick men obstinate about not going on alone to Pankot, espe-cially the havildar because he and Karim Muzzafir Khan were friends. In fact they're related.' She turned again to Perron. 'The first battalion is very close knit. Hill regiments often are. My father can look at the nominal roll and draw a family tree of nearly every man on it. I mean if Naik X is married to a daughter of ex-Havildar Y, he'd know. Does that strike you as silly?'

'No,' Perron said. 'As admirable.'

'Yes. Admirable. And sad. Wouldn't you say sad? Particularly if you'd watched most of them die and seen the rest carted off as prisoners, and felt responsible.'

Merrick put his fork down. Nazimuddin offered him the tray but he declined another helping. Throughout the meal the gloved hand and artificial arm had been disposed on the surface of the table. He leant back, hooked the good arm over the back of his chair and stared at his empty plate, waited for the others to finish. When they had done so Nazimuddin came in with the shape: shapes, rather – three of them, turned out into glass bowls from individual fluted moulds. The shapes were white and looked tasteless but there was a bowl of jam to liven them up. Having served Miss Layton Nazimuddin went across to Merrick.

'Since your Aunt Fenny isn't here to feel hurt, do you mind if I say no?' Without waiting for her answer he said to the servant, 'Give mine to the sergeant. It will build him up. Not that you look starved exactly, but then sergeants seldom do. You manage to do yourselves pretty well, I suppose.'

'Usually, sir.'

'Even in India?'

'I think rather better in India, sir. One doesn't depend so much on diverting rations meant for the officers as one does at home.'

Merrick looked at the mat that marked his place at table, and at the spoon and fork he was not going to use. Miss Layton said, 'I'm afraid there's no savoury, Ronald. Perhaps you'd like to go and talk to Father, then we could all have coffee and Mr Perron could be on his way.'

'Perhaps that will be as well.' He began to get up, rather awkwardly, tucking the artificial arm close to his body. When he had gone Miss Layton said, 'You must have known someone called Rowan, too.'

'Nigel Rowan?'

She nodded.

'Only as one of the minor figures on Olympus would know Zeus. He came out here to the army, didn't he? I remember, because he was always walking away with prizes for classics and I thought he'd carry on in that field or at least go into the ICS if he really wanted an Indian career.'

'Yes, he is in the army, but he was transferred to the political department in 'thirty-eight or 'thirty-nine. He had to go back to his regiment when the war started. He was in the first Burma campaign and got fever badly. At the moment he's ADC to the Governor in Ranpur. He told me he was trying to get back into the Political.'

'Does he still have what I recall as a very detached and patrician manner?'

She smiled. 'I think it is only a manner. Will you have the other shape?'

'No, thank you.'

'They weren't very good, were they? Shall we go in then?'

Nazimuddin had carried the coffee tray through into the living-room. Following her, he stood for a moment and studied the Zoffany-style pictures and then watched while she poured coffee from a silver-plated pot. He took the cup from her, sat down.

'What does your uncle do?'

'He runs a course about civil and military administration in India in peace time. To attract young officers into the ICS or the police when the war's over.'

'English officers?'

'Indians too. But mostly English.'

'Does he have much success?'

'More in Bombay than in Calcutta. He expects even more in view of the result of the election in England.'

'Yes, I suppose some people must think the prospects at home are now pretty bleak. But aren't the prospects for an Indian career even bleaker?'

She was stirring *ghur* into her coffee, occasionally stopping, tapping the spoon on the rim of the cup and then resuming. 'It's some years since anyone in their right mind thought of India as a career, if you mean India as a place where you could expect to spend the whole of your working life.'

'Is your father coming up to retiring age?'

'He hasn't long to go now. He'll be one of the lucky ones, I should think. The hardest hit will be men like Nigel Rowan, I mean men of his age. It depends on how power's eventually transferred. If there's a prolonged handing-over period, and if Uncle Arthur's right when he says the Indians will be glad to have experienced Englishmen working with them, then men like Nigel might have quite a few more years useful working life out here. But I don't think Uncle Arthur's right, do you? I don't think there'll be a prolonged handing-over period.'

'Why?'

'Because that would be the logical thing and I think the whole situation's become too emotional for logic to come into it.'

He waited for her to continue but she seemed to have come to a stop. He said, 'How will you feel about it, when it happens?'

'I shouldn't want to stay on.'

'Why, especially?'

'I don't think it's a country one can be happy in.'

'You'd be happy in England?'

'I didn't care for it much when I first went home as a child. But it's where I really grew up and started to think for myself. It's where I feel I belong. I know India much better, but ever since my sister and I came out again after going home to school I've only felt like a visitor.'

'Does your sister feel the same?'

'I think a bit the same. She tried not to. But it's difficult to say what she feels nowadays. She's had rather a bad time.'

'Major Merrick told me what happened to her husband. I'm sorry.'

'Did he mention his part in it?'

'Yes.'

She drank her coffee. She said, 'I'm sorry you don't remember Hari Kumar. Nigel does.'

He thought she intended to say more but just then they heard Merrick's footsteps.

'I think that's settled,' he said. She glanced at him as if to judge from his expression how gently he had dealt with her father. Perron glanced at him too but could tell nothing. As in the dockyard-hut the night of Karim Muzzafir Khan's interrogation, Merrick lifted his right hand and looked at the watch which he wore with the face on the inner side of the wrist.

'I'll skip coffee if you don't mind. I've got some work to finish back at the hotel. And before that, of course, I must help the sergeant to find his jeep.' He nodded at Perron. 'If you're ready.'

'There's surely time for a cup? Mr Perron, perhaps you'd like another? Or the drink you never got?'

'The sergeant has to drive.'

'Does he really have to? Weren't you on duty of some sort at the Maharanee's party, Mr Perron?'

'Yes, I was.'

'Well who's to say when it might have ended? If you don't really have to report back to Kalyan tonight we could always give you a shake-down here. Frankly I don't think you should go all that way after the sort of evening you've had. We can send Nazimuddin out scouting for a taxi if your work is all that urgent, Ronald. Or you could wait until Uncle Arthur's back. He's using the staff-car.'

'I think you're asking the sergeant to risk getting into trouble.'

'There'd be no risk of that, sir. I'm allowed to use my discretion to a great extent and there are a number of perfectly adequate reasons why I might stay in Bombay overnight if that's what I decided.'

'Good. Then you'll stay, Mr Perron?'

Momentarily he was tempted to accept, help her get rid of Merrick which is what it seemed she wanted, and be alone with her for a while. But very soon the flat would be invaded by its owners, her aunt and uncle, and there would be explanations to make, chat about Purvis, chat about the course, chat about staying on in India. *Raj* chat. And she would fade back into that dreary predictable background. He was sorry for her. He felt she deserved better of life. But so many of them did. There was nothing he could do. Their lives were not his affair. He had his own to live. Their dissatisfaction, their boredom, the strain they always seemed to be under, were largely their own fault. The real world was outside. Impatient, he stood up. If you allowed yourself to sympathize too much they would destroy you. You would lose what you valued most. Your objectivity.

He said, 'It's very kind of you, Miss Layton, but what I have to do in Kalyan tomorrow is more important than what I might do in Bombay, so the quicker I get back the better. In any case, I've already offered Major Merrick a lift to the Taj.'

'Then I won't press you. Incidentally, my father asked me to make sure you know how grateful he is for the whisky and how sorry he was to be so much under the weather.'

They were all on their feet now. Merrick began to go into details of the arrangements for getting to the station the following

day. Perron moved away since none of this concerned him. He
retrieved his pack and occupied himself pretending to check the
straps. That done he stood up and humped the pack on his left
shoulder and waited. Merrick was still talking as he and Miss
Layton came through to the archway between dining-room area
and passage, where Perron stood. Her arms were folded in the
manner Perron assumed was characteristic – hands gripping
elbows; one grip loose, the other tight. Too tight? An attitude
more of self-control than of self-possession?

Merrick said, 'Tomorrow, then,' and with his right hand
reached for and held her left shoulder and bent his head. Instinctively she bent hers away so that the kiss was placed somewhere
near her right ear. Her eyes were closed. She smiled, as if to
herself, and said, 'Tomorrow.' Merrick let her go. He nodded
at the closed door, mutely commanding its opening. Miss Layton
called Nazimuddin and then put out her hand.

'Goodbye, Mr Perron.'

The hand was cool and dry. The delicate aroma of the scent
she used added to his pleasure in holding it. He thanked her for
her hospitality and said goodbye. 'Perhaps we'll meet again,' she
said. From behind him Nazimuddin asked if a taxi were wanted.
Told that it wasn't he opened the door and salaamed to Perron
as he went out. Merrick said goodnight to Miss Layton. Just
before the door shut on them Perron caught her slight gestures:
a nod, a movement of one hand. They were meant for him.

The rain had stopped some time ago but there were no stars, no
breaks in the cloud-cover. Neither had the last downpour cooled
the air, although there was a hint of freshness in the warm intermittent breeze that played around the palm-fringed *maidan*. He
walked a pace or two behind Merrick until they reached an
intersection where Merrick stopped. A taxi had drawn up to
let its passengers out. 'We'll take this, sergeant, since it's here.
It might save us getting wet. I'll drop you and go on to the hotel.'
He got in after giving the driver instructions and Perron
followed, glad to be saved the walk and the prolonging of the
effort of being civil to Merrick which the walk and a jeep drive
would have involved. Escape was imminent.

'A very nice girl, Miss Layton, sir.'

Merrick took his time replying.

'She has many admirable qualities. Her father certainly has cause to be grateful to her.'

'Oh?'

'When a man leaves a family of women behind one of them has to assume responsibility for keeping things going. I think she assumed most of it. But of course it tends to develop a girl's domineering instinct. As perhaps you noticed.'

'No, I didn't notice that, sir.' He added, 'This looks familiar. It was somewhere about here.'

'The next road on the left, in fact. Did she refer at all to Kumar when you were alone?'

'Only to say she was sorry I didn't appear to remember him.'

'What did you say?'

'Nothing.'

As the taxi pulled up Merrick said, 'I'll wait until you've made sure of your jeep.'

The gates of the house at which the taxi stopped were shut, perhaps padlocked, and the house apparently in darkness. Perron was almost grateful for Merrick's suggestion. Arrangements made by Purvis were probably not very reliable.

But in this case they were, in all respects except that of security. Directly Perron reached the closed iron gates a lamp was shone on him and a cockney voice said, 'Come for your gharry, Sarge?' Perron said he had and went back to the taxi.

'Everything's in order, sir.'

Merrick was looking out of the other window. He did not move.

He said, 'One case you should find interesting when you join me is that of the brother of the young Indian you met tonight.'

'Ahmed Kasim?'

Merrick turned his head, put a finger to his lips, and nodded in the driver's direction. 'He went over to Bose in Malaya. We got him in Manipur last year. It is interesting when you think who the father is. Right. I'll see you in Delhi. In a couple of days or so, I expect.'

Perron shut the door and threw up a smart one which so far as he could make out Merrick acknowledged in the languid manner officers cultivated. The taxi drew away. Perron watched it go down the poorly lit tree-lined street.

'Oh no you won't. You bloody well won't,' he said aloud.

*

Half an hour later, soaked to the skin by the renewed downpour, he gave up trying to trace the fault in the brand-new jeep's electrical system and accepted the guard-commander's offer of a bed-down for the night. The guard-commander, a British corporal – seemed to welcome company. In the guardroom, keeping his voice low so as not to disturb the three huddled shapes disposed on charpoys in corners away from the dim light of a lamp that hung centrally above a trestle-table littered with mugs, playing-cards and worn copies of *Picture Post* and *Reader's Digest*, he offered Perron a shot of buckshee rum.

'Found its own way here, Sarge,' the corporal said, and winked. Outside, in the dark, he had called Perron sir at least twice but had got over any embarrassment this might have caused him. While they sat smoking and drinking rum the corporal explained that he and his bunch had been in India for a whole month and were still wondering what had hit them. They were part of a formation that had been under orders for France just before – as the corporal put it – old Hitler packed it in. For a while they'd been looking forward to becoming part of the army of occupation. There were chaps making fortunes there right now and from what he'd heard the frauleins would do it for a packet of cigarettes or even a Naafi sandwich. The corporal had been in the army for a year and some of the men in his unit less than that. They had reckoned Germany would be a cushy billet in which to see their time out and from the way 'old Slim's lot' had given the Japs 'the bum's rush out of Burma' the last thing any of them had expected was to be sent out East. When you looked at the map (the corporal said) you could see that the Japanese had had it. You could hardly see where places like Malaya were. But here *they* were. Had the Sarge ever known such a bleeding awful place. How long had the Sarge been out here?

'Two years,' Perron said.

'Christ.'

The corporal studied him, respectfully, but looking for signs of deterioration. 'I reckon I'd be round the twist if they kept me out here that long.' His tone became even lower; confidential. 'What's it like, Sarge. With these Indian bints?'

'The colour doesn't come off.'

The corporal shook his head. 'I couldn't fancy it somehow. Some of the half'n'halfs look okay but the ones who're white enough not to put you off are only interested in officers, aren't they? We been warned to watch it too. They say there's always a coal-black mum waiting in the parlour to get the banns read if you so much as touch the daughter. That true, d'you reckon, Sarge?'

'I've heard of cases.'

The corporal shook his head again. Perron glanced at the sleeping men. Only one of them had his face turned towards the light. He looked about nineteen; so, come to that, did the corporal. The faces were those of urban Londoners and belonged to streets of terraced houses that ended in one-man shops: newsagent-tobacconist, fish and chip shop, family grocer, and a pub at the corner where the high road was. What could such a face know of India? And yet India was there, in the skull, and the bones of the body. Its possession had helped nourish the flesh, warm the blood of every man in the room, sleeping and waking.

'Where do I turn in?' Perron asked.

'I'll show you.' The corporal looked at his watch. 'Then I got to change the guard.' He led the way out into a passage. 'There's a coupla wog clerks that sleep down that end, and there's a duty officer upstairs with the phone put through. He's a wog too. I think the officers that work here take it in turns to sleep in, not that anything ever happens, but there's a safe in the room the duty-officer sleeps in, so I reckon there's a lot of secret papers. There's a spare charpoy here, though –' he opened a door and switched on a light – 'and a bog through that door. You got a blanket, Sarge?'

'No.'

'I'll bring you one in.' He switched on the fan and went out. The room was an office, so sparsely furnished it looked like a monk's cell. Along one wall, under a shuttered window, stood a bare charpoy. Aslant one corner, there was a trestle-table covered by an army blanket, with one folding canvas chair behind it and a folding wooden chair in front of it for visitors. A neatly positioned telephone and blotting pad, a pen and pencil tray, an empty in-basket and an empty out-basket told a story of meticulous attention to work or of a complete absence of work to give attention to. Facing the visitor, parallel to the top edge of the blotter and the pen and pencil tray, was a triangular wedge of wood on which the name of the desk's occupant was painted in white.

Capt. L. Purvis.

Here behind the desk Purvis had sat, waiting for a call from Delhi that never came, and presumably here he had lain, on the charpoy, gazing at the alien geography of the ceiling, nursing his invaded gut and his invincible Englishness. And, on the wall behind the desk, he had marked off with a blue crayon the days of his martyrdom. Perron looked at his watch. Not yet midnight. Even if Purvis had learned to cheat by crossing a day off immediately before he left the office in the evening Perron did not feel he could cancel out August 5 for him until his watch showed 00.01.

'Here's your blanket, Sarge, and something for a pillow. Anything else?'

'No thank you, Corporal.'

'We brew up at 06.00. Okay for you?'

'Fine.'

'Pleasant dreams then, Sarge.'

After he had taken off his damp uniform, hung it over the chair back under the fan and mopped himself reasonably dry with the green handtowel from his pack, Perron sat in his underwear on the edge of the charpoy and slowly performed the nightly task of trying to obliterate from his mind all the disturbing residue of the day's malfunctioning and so leave it free to crystallize, to reveal the point reached in a continuum he was sure existed but, in India, found so difficult to trace.

He lit a cigarette and stared at his stockinged feet, then reached over to his jacket and got out the notebook and pencil. After a while he wrote: 'Two continua, perhaps, in this case? Ours, and the Indians'? An illusion that they ever coincided, coincide? A powerful illusion but still an illusion? If so, then the *raj* was, is, itself an illusion so far as the English are concerned. Is that what she meant when she said she did not think India was a country one could be happy in?'

Dissatisfied with this he drew a pencil line lightly across the entry and tried again.

'For at least a hundred years India has formed part of England's

idea about herself and for the same period India has been forced
into a position of being a reflection of that idea. Up to say 1900
the part India played in our idea about ourselves was the part
played by anything we possessed which we believed it was right
to possess (like a special relationship with God). Since 1900, certainly since 1918, the reverse has obtained. The part played since
then by India in the English idea of Englishness has been that of
something we feel it does us no credit to have. Our idea about
ourselves will now not accommodate any idea about India
except the idea of returning it to the Indians in order to prove
that we are English and have demonstrably English ideas. All this
is quite simply proven and amply demonstrated. But on either
side of that arbitrary date (1900) India itself, as itself, that is to
say India as not part of our idea of ourselves, has played no part
whatsoever in the lives of Englishmen in general (no part that
we are conscious of) and those who came out (those for whom
India had to play a real part) became detached both from English
life and from the English idea of life. Getting rid of India will
cause us at home no qualm of conscience because it will be like
getting rid of what is no longer reflected in our mirror of ourselves. The sad thing is that whereas in the English mirror there
is now no Indian reflection (think of Purvis, those men I lectured
to, and the corporal here in the guardroom), in the Indian mirror
the English reflection may be very hard to get rid of, because in
the Indian mind English possession has not been an idea but a
reality; often a harsh one. The other sad thing is that people like
the Laytons may now see nothing at all when looking in their
mirror. Not even themselves? Not even a mirror? I know that
getting rid of India, dismantling all this old imperial machinery
(which Purvis sees as hopelessly antiquated, a brake on economic
viability – his word) has become an article of faith with the intellectual minority of the party we have just voted into power. But
we haven't voted them into power to get rid of the machinery,
we've voted them into power to set up new machinery of our
own for our own benefit, and for the majority who voted India
does not even begin to exist. Odd that history may record as
pre-eminent among the Labour Party's post-war governmental
achievements the demission of power in countries like this?
Could it be that, in power now, and with a mandate to demit
power, the party will forget or omit to demit it? It could be. But

we shall see. The machinery for demission is wound up and there are, as Purvis knows, overriding economic arguments for setting it in motion as soon as the war's over. In England the war *is* over. It ended on May 6. In England the war's a dead letter except for people with sons, brothers and fathers and husbands out here. And the fact that they're still out here simply adds to an English sense of grievance that England ever got involved with anything or anywhere south or east of spitting distance of the white cliffs of Dover. Terrific insularity. Paradox! The most insular people in the world managed to establish the largest empire the world has ever seen. No, not paradox. Insularity, like empire-building, requires superb self-confidence, a conviction of one's moral superiority. And I suppose that when the war is really over the recollection that there was a time when we "stood alone" against Hitler will confirm us in our national sense of moral superiority. Will it be in those abstract terms and on those shifting grounds that we'll attempt to build a new empire whose cornerstone will be the act of relinquishing for "moral" reasons the empire we actually had?'

He hesitated, then added, 'Tonight I am a bit drunk.'

Then, looking at his watch he saw it was tonight no longer. He put pencil and notebook back in the jacket pocket. The evening at the Maharanee's was over. Standing, staring at that name, Purvis, he realized that curious and complex as it had been the evening had had shape. Beginning with Purvis, it had ended in Purvis's office. He appreciated the symmetry of that.

He visited the bathroom. Returning, he went over to the light switch, changed his mind and crossed to the desk, found the blue crayon and went to the wall calendar. He drew an X through the 5, stared at the 6 and said aloud, 'That, anyway, is the crystal-lization, the point reached in the *time* continuum.'

He turned the fan down to its slowest rate of revolutions, switched off the light, opened the shutters on the unglazed barred window and breathed in. Bombay. Bom-Bahia. Part of an inheritance. His monarch's. His own. The corporal's, Purvis's, the Maharanee's. The street beggar's. He lay, adjusted the cushion the corporal had brought as a pillow, and the blanket so that it just covered his abdomen, the most vulnerable part of the body when there was a fan going. For a while pictures of the day just ended flickered across the screen lowered by his eyelids, but all at once there was the disturbing invasion of shots of Coomer, from all angles, long, medium and close; Coomer opening his shoulders, hitting out at a sequence of balls whose pitch and pace were subtly varied by the invisible bowler, or team of bowlers; the deliveries were in too mercilessly rapid a succession for one man alone to send down.

The cameras of Perron's imagination began to tire. Presently only one remained, and this zoomed in close to re-create a memory of the boy's face. There was a face, an idea of a face, a man's rather than a boy's, and formed from a notion of an expression rather than from one of features: an expression of concentration, of hard-held determination, of awareness that to misjudge, to mistime, would lead to destruction. There was no sound. And suddenly the face vanished. A flurry of birds, crows, rooks, rose from the surrounding elms, startled by a sudden noise, although there had been no noise. And they were not elms, but palms; and the birds were kitehawks. They circled patiently above Perron's head, waiting for him to fall asleep.

I

IN VIEW OF what once happened there the countryside through which the mail train passes on the first stage of the journey from Mirat to Ranpur is surprisingly undramatic. The passenger who has what initially seems the good luck to be alone in a compartment soon grows restless as mile follows mile with nothing to catch the attention or work on the imagination other than what in India is common-place: the huddles of mud villages; buffalo wallowing in celebration of their survival from the primeval slime; men, women and children engaged in the fatal ritual of pre-ordained work.

Only the slow train stops at the wayside stations. On their single platforms people wait with bundles and a patience that has something exalted about it, although this impression could be the result of the express passing through too quickly for individual faces to be clearly noted. There are three such stations all of which are reached within thirty minutes of leaving Mirat cantonment. Thereafter, the villages become distant, but there is one, abandoned and ruinous, which appears suddenly and unexpectedly, close to the line.

Those ruins don't look old. For an instant the traveller conjures images of flames, of silhouetted human shapes running distractedly, stooped under burdens. But the moment of imaginative re-creation is a brief one. The crippled dwellings and crumbled walls slide quickly out of sight and the panorama of wasteland, scarred by dried-out nullahs and rocky outcrops, appears again and expands to the limit of the blurred horizon where the colourlessness of sky and earth merge and are distinguished only by a band of a different intensity of colourlessness which, gazed at long enough, gives an idea of blue and purple refraction. Everything is immense, but – lacking harmony or contrast – is diminished by its association with infinity.

The ruined village is explained. The land is eroded. The

exodus must have been slow, quite unremarkable. One by one the men would have gone, taking their women and children and driving their thin cattle, while inch by inch the soil was swept away and the implacable rock exposed until there was nothing but the empty waste; and the wind blowing hot in the telegraph wires that border the railway.

The land now seems to be at peace. It requires some effort to see such a place as a background to any sudden or violent event. Perhaps there was no bloodshed, no murder on this stretch of line. But, as if remembering violence the train slows and then draws to a stop. There is a clank under the carriage; cessation, immobility. The compartment – not air-conditioned, one fan not working – grows warmer. Presently there comes the hollow sound of unevenly clunking goatbells and in a moment or two the straggling herd comes into view, driven by a lean man and a naked urchin, in search of patches of impoverished grazing. They go by without a glance, drugged by the heat and the singleness of their purpose. When they have gone there is silence but their passing has disturbed the atmosphere. The body of the victim could have fallen just here.

A few moments before, he is said to have gestured at the shuttered window of the compartment door on which strangers outside were banging and said 'It seems to be me they want', and then smiled at his shocked fellow-passengers, as if he had recognized a brilliant and totally unexpected opportunity. In a flash he had unlocked the door and gone. Briefly, a turbanned head appeared, begged pardon for the inconvenience and then removed itself. The door banged to. One of the passengers stumbled across luggage and relocked it. After a moment he lowered the shutter and looked out. Those nearest to him might have seen his horrified expression.

Just then the engine driver up ahead obeyed an instruction and the train glided forward. It was the smooth gliding motion away from a violent situation which one witness never forgot. 'Suddenly you had the feeling that the train, the wheels, the lines, weren't made of metal but of something greasy and evasive.'

Without warning it glides forward now, from the place where the herd of goats has been, seeming to identify a spot marked with the x of an old killing by its mechanical anxiety to get away before blame is apportioned and responsibility felt. Increasing speed, the train puts distance between itself and the falling body and between one time and another so that in the mind of the traveller the body never quite achieves its final crumpled position on the ground at the feet of the attackers.

'It seems to be me they want,' the victim said. Perhaps he said no such thing but gave the impression of thinking it because of that look on his face of recognizing some kind of personal advantage. This look may have been due to nothing more than a desire to reassure the other occupants of the carriage that they had nothing to worry about themselves and that he would be quite safe so long as he went of his own free will. But all the evidence suggests that the witness was right about the words and the expression. The victim chose neither the time nor the place of his death but in going to it as he did he must have seen that he contributed something of his own to its manner; and this was probably his compensation; so that when the body falls it will seem to do so without protest and without asking for any explanation of the thing that has happened to it, as if all that has gone before is explanation enough, so that it will not fall to the ground so much as out of a history which began with a girl stumbling on steps at the end of a long journey through the dark.

The train is cautious in its approach to Premanagar. Tracks converge from the east, coming from Mayapore. To the left, some miles distant, is the fort, no longer a prison, infrequently visited by tourists; peripheral to the tale but a brooding point of reference and orientation. To the south, now, lies Mirat with its mosques and minarets. North, a few hours' journey, is Ranpur, where a grave was undug, and farther north still, amid hills, Pankot, where it was dug in too great a hurry for someone's peace of mind. Beyond the fort, the west lies open, admitting a chill draught. The erosive wind, perhaps. After a short halt the train moves on to its final destination.

It is dark by the time it clatters across the bridge and worms its way into the city of Ranpur, as it was dark on Tuesday August 7, 1945, when Sarah Layton and her father, and the handful of soldiers released from hospital, arrived from Delhi and dis-embarked to pick up the midnight connection to Pankot; and since the railway station has changed little it is easy to picture them, to pick them out of a crowd which behaves as crowds on platforms do (with a mixture of hysteria, impatience, gaiety and – in isolated cases – resignation). The platform is one of several protected by the vaulted, glassed and girdered roof that rests on steel ornamental pillars. At the base of these pillars people congregate, waiting for trains or inspiration. The lighting is yellow, intermittent. There are areas of light and half-light and areas of shadow. Through these areas passengers walk or run, and coolies trot barefoot, erect under head-loads, shouting warnings of approach. The grey paving is spattered with new and old spittings of betel-juice which a stranger to the country may confuse with bloodstains. There is a smell of coalsmoke, ripe fruit and of cotton cloth which human sweat has drenched and dried on and drenched again. It is a smell by no means peculiar to this station but for those to whom Ranpur represents a homecoming it has a subtle distinction, a pungency of special intensity, a benign and odorous warmth which even Sarah who had not been away for long was conscious of as she got down from the coupé and joined her father. Patiently he was choosing three coolies from the gang that had run alongside for fifty yards or more.

There had been no problem at Delhi. Ronald Merrick had waited to see them off on the Ranpur train, to be on hand if at the last moment Colonel Layton again had to be dissuaded from breaking the journey. But he had been docile, good-humoured, quietly intent on the morning papers with their latest reports of the significance of the bomb of 'devastating power' which the Americans had dropped on the Japanese city of Hiroshima on Monday morning.

News of the attack had reached them on the platform of the Victoria terminus in Bombay, half an hour before the train was due out. Some English people said they had just heard it on the lunch-time radio. Aunt Fenny sent Uncle Arthur off to see what more he could find out. He had put on weight and did not walk quickly, was away some time, nearly missed them, had to accompany the moving train shouting 'Seems to be true but I can't make head or tail of it. Have a good trip.' In the evening when they stopped to take on dinner-trays there was confirmation in the evening papers. It had been an atomic bomb. The ultimate weapon. The question was whether Hirohito would now surrender to save other cities, Tokyo itself, from devastation. Sarah thought: It might be over, then. And knew relief. Excitement even.

'The moral reservations' (she has said) 'came later. At the time you could only feel glad. Awestruck, I suppose, by the sheer size of the thing. And by the miracle. I never met anyone who felt otherwise until long after. If we had doubts about the wisdom of letting off bombs like that they were very long-term. Too long-term to bother us. The short-term was the important thing.'

In the short-term, above all, it might mean safety for her father. He'd said nothing about further active service. The prospects were shadowy but they existed. No one expected the liberation of Malaya and the conquest of the Japanese mainland to be accomplished quickly or cheaply. If the war continued he would probably manoeuvre for a command before he was fully fit. But now the chances were that it would not continue and, walking with him along the platform, with one coolie ahead and two behind, to rendezvous with the havildar and the five sepoys who had travelled in a compartment a long way separated from their own, she was able to entertain an illusion of serenity, of entering a period of life which by contrast with the one just ended might be described as free, uncluttered, open at last to endless possibilities.

II

For a few seconds she awaited confirmation that the child had whimpered, but there was no sound of Minnie stirring in the spare room to pick him up and comfort him. Wondering whether Susan was still asleep or up to something odd, she felt for the switch on the bed-side lamp. The shock of no contact brought her fully conscious. She sat up in unfamiliar surround-ings, a wall on one side, nothing on the other. She recalled, then, where she was; and because there was utter stillness, assumed that probably what had woken her was the jerk of the train coming to a halt. From her upper-berth she glanced down into the well of the coupé and saw her father – his shape, rather – standing at the carriage door. The window was lowered. She could smell the pine-trees – the scent of the hills. The air was chill. The light of Wednesday was just beginning to come.

'All right, Father?'

She spoke quietly but he drew his head in and glanced up at once, as if caught doing something forbidden.

'Did I wake you? I'm sorry.'

'No. It wasn't you. It must have been the train stopping.'

'Afraid that was ten minutes ago. I made a duff hand of open-ing the window. How about some tea? There's plenty in the flask.'

'I'll come down and get it for us.'

'No, no. You stay there.'

She felt for her dressing-gown. 'I'll come down anyway.'

'Do you want some light?'

'No,' she said. 'That would spoil it.'

He said nothing. She felt that he understood her mood. She climbed down and removed the steps from their hooks. He had his back turned, pouring tea from the thermos into the cups Aunt Fenny had packed in the hamper. The tea in the thermos had been bought the night before from the station restaurant at Ranpur. He handed her a cup. She stood near the lowered win-dow, warming her hands on it.

'In the old days,' he said, 'we used to stop round about here to get up a proper head of steam. Then we got the new locomo-tive and were able to get up the gradient in a brace of shakes. I suppose the new engine's getting old. Listen.'

There was a faint noise, an abrupt exhalation, followed by a clank. It came again, then again. It sounded far off. The coupé was in a carriage at the rear of the train which was halted on a curved stretch of line. The window her father had opened looked east towards the plains they had left, across a deep valley, at the moment full of mist – below eye-level so that it looked like the surface of a lake. On the other side of the carriage was the rock face. The road, which took steeper gradients, was above them. She turned her wrist until she was able to make out the position of the hands of her watch. He saw what she was doing and said, 'Just over two hours to go, or should be if we keep to the timetable.'

She moved away from the window so that he could resume his vigil if he wished to, and sat on the lower bunk. He went back to the window. She wanted a cigarette but resisted temptation. In Bombay he had said to Aunt Fenny, 'Isn't Sarah smoking rather a lot?' and Fenny had tipped her off. She had tried to cut down, not for fear of his disapproval but as part of her campaign to guard him from as many sources of irritation as was in her power. She had warned her mother by letter how easily he could be upset, of the prison-camp habit of saving 'the unexpired portion'; pocketing bits of bread to eat later; the mark of a man who had known hunger. The habit was dying hard, as hard – no doubt – as recollections of conditions of which he never spoke. And he had been uninquisitive about affairs she had been prepared for him to question her on.

He had never mentioned the death of Teddie Bingham, the son-in-law he had never seen, nor delved into the nature of Susan's illness. Neither had he referred directly to the death of his stepmother, Mabel, from whom Rose Cottage had been inherited. Sarah had once begun to warn him that her mother had made a few changes in the place, but he had interrupted, saying Fenny had mentioned 'something about a tennis-court'. He'd added: 'Pity about the roses, but I suppose they needed a lot of attention and the court's a good idea for you girls.'

What else had Fenny said 'something' about? She was the kind of woman who let things slip without necessarily meaning to or even knowing that she'd done so. But in the case of the destruction of the greater part of the rose garden to make room for the tennis-court, Sarah was grateful to be relieved of the job of telling him herself. She had feared doing so; unnecessarily, it seemed, judging by the casual way he had taken it.

But had he taken it *in*? From Germany after he got their letter telling him Mabel had died, he'd written: 'It's sad news but not a shock because she was getting on. I'm glad my last memory of her is in the garden the time I went up from Ranpur to say goodbye to her and to arrange your accommodation in Pankot once the regiment left for overseas. I'm sorry I wasn't able to fix up anything better than those cramped quarters in the lines, but Mabel was quite right. Even if she'd given marching orders to that PG of hers the three of you with Mabel would have been just as cramped at Rose Cottage, and however poky a place is there's nothing like having your own, is there Millie? Anyway I have this picture of you now, moving in to the cottage, all amid the roses and the pine trees. I long to be with you all again and not just have to picture it.'

It was possible that as he stood at the open window of the

coupé any picture he had of his homecoming was of the house
and garden as he remembered it and that the tennis-court had
not penetrated visually, as an idea. Even after all these months
Sarah could get a shock when she went through to the verandah
and instead of the rose-beds saw the high netting, the lime-
marked grass, the centre net or the bare posts if the net had been
taken down by the *mali*. The court was seldom used. Sarah didn't
play well and watching bored her. And the days were gone when
her younger sister used a tennis-court and a tennis outfit as two
more ways of ensuring that she was the centre of attention. That
role had been discarded and the new one precluded violent exercise. Only Mildred, their mother, seemed to get any pleasure out
of the court, not by playing, but by having it there as one might
have anything that made an invitation attractive. 'Come up
to the house at the weekend,' she might say to someone new
on station, of whom she approved, 'and if you're keen bring a
racquet and things. We've a sort of court you can get a game
on.' And there was usually someone there to protest: 'Don't be
deceived. Sort of court! Binky swears it's better than the number
one here at the club.' And then her mother would raise her eyebrows and smile, that characteristic downward-curving smile
that Sarah was afraid she might acquire, having once or twice
got a glimpse of herself in a mirror smiling in that way. There
was a way of sitting too and she had caught herself at that on
more than one occasion, on the verandah of Rose Cottage,
glancing from the tennis to her mother and recognizing her
mother's attitude as the origin of her own: well settled in a cane
chair, legs out-stretched and crossed at the ankles, elbows supported by the chair-arms, and the hands, drooping at the wrists,
bearing the burden of a glass of gin-sling. She had sat up, put
her glass down, leant forward and folded her arms, but that was
becoming a habitual attitude too, and just as defensive.

Up ahead the whistle sounded and presently the train moved,
taking the curve. The mist-filled valley flowed away and they
entered a cut where the rock-face loomed on both sides. Her
father stayed by the open window for a while, breathing in the
scent of damp stone, wild ferns and mosses. When the scent
became pungent with captive drifting smoke he ducked back
in and raised the window. There remained in the carriage an
opacity as if some of the eastern light had stayed inside.

He sat down. Unexpectedly he said, 'I haven't thanked you for coming to Bombay and for what you've done while I've been away. Your Aunt Fenny told me what a brick you've been, what a help to your mother and Susan. I just wanted you to know before we get in how grateful I am.'

As soon as he began she looked down at the cup in her hands. They had never been a demonstrative family. When he finished he put an arm round her shoulders, very briefly, just long enough for her to acknowledge the embrace by leaning into it for a moment.

'Shall I pour you another cup?'

'No thank you, daddy. Later perhaps. What about you?'

'I'll wait a while. Keep some in reserve in case we're held up again and get thirsty.'

'I'll rinse the cups then.'

'No, I'll do that. Unless you want to go in there.'

'Not yet.'

He took the cups into the w.c. cubicle, leaving the door ajar. The train was making slow time. She heard him humming. In the past three weeks she had learnt to interpret this as a sign of restlessness, of anxiety to be occupied. She wondered whether it was light enough for a game of chess. She looked for and found the travelling set which he had brought back from Germany and on which he had taught her to play in Bombay. She had a beginner's enthusiasm and in one case what had seemed like beginner's luck. No doubt he'd deliberately contrived that, to encourage her; but she felt she had learned enough at least to give him a bit of a game.

Unable to see it clearly she put the set away. She wondered how long it would be before they played again, or whether they ever would. Once home, the pattern of relationship established in Bombay would change. He came back with the cups. She took them from him and put them in the hamper, protecting them with a napkin from contact with the neck of Sergeant Perron's bottle of whisky; of which he had said, 'Let's save some for your mother.' She doubted that her mother would want any. Not whisky.

He said, 'If you're sure you don't want to go first I think I'll shave and get done.'

She nodded, watched him potter around – potter was the only

word for it – collecting sponge bag, shaving kit, towel, clothes, and finally his uniform from the hook on the wall. His movements were slow, thought out. Perhaps this had always been his habit. She did not remember it but not remembering was probably further evidence of how little she knew him, as little now as she had known him – and her mother – on her return to India in 1939 after the years of unavoidable separation. He switched the light on in the cubicle and this time closed the door but there was no sound of the bolt being shot. Had the Germans ever put him in solitary confinement? If so, for what crime? Attempting to escape? Eventually her mother would question him and get answers or he would regain confidence in his freedom and volunteer information, and then they would be able to put the story of the past few years of his life together piece by piece; as he would be able to put theirs together. But in neither case the whole stories. Probably never that.

She lit a cigarette now and settled closer to the window. In her imagination she had often rehearsed the circumstances of her father's return but had not pictured them like this, with the two of them travelling alone from Bombay to Pankot. He confessed he had rehearsed them too but said there had always been a moment when his imagination failed, the moment following the actual reunion, and that this was probably because the scene of reunion was not determinable in advance: a railway station, a dockside, even an airport, the old house in Kabul road in Ranpur, the front verandah of Rose Cottage, the compound of the grace and favour bungalow in the lines of the Pankot Rifles depot. The reunion itself was the important thing, one did not think beyond it. He told her of a fellow prisoner-of-war, a Catholic, who had shocked a padre by confessing that he had always wondered what after spending six days creating the world and then resting on the seventh God had done on the eighth. The day of reunion was like the seventh day. Today, Wednesday, was the seventh. She could not visualize tomorrow except as a continuation, an emotional perpetuation, of today which of course it could not be. One thought about a day of reunion but the reunion itself was only a moment in a day. She and her father had had that moment in Bombay. He had another to come this morning but of this she would be no more than a spectator; perhaps not that because he had asked that no one in the family should be at the station. His request that the families of the sepoys and havildar should also be dissuaded from coming to the station, his warning that the only reception committee he wished to find would be at most the depot adjutant, Kevin Coley, plus an NCO and a truck to take the men back to the lines and some kind of transport for himself and Sarah, was an indication of his fear of any kind of scene that might affect him.

It would be nice, he had said, just to drive from the station with her in whatever transport could be arranged and to arrive at Rose Cottage much as though he had simply come home for breakfast after early-morning parade. She had conveyed this wish to her mother and knew that it would be respected. She was prepared to let him go into the bungalow alone and busy herself outside in the garden or on the side verandah where probably little Edward would be, in Minnie's charge, playing with the new Labrador puppy.

Neither Sarah nor her mother had wanted the puppy. It was Susan's idea that they should have one, as like as possible to Panther who had been little more than a puppy himself when her father went abroad on active service. Susan said it would be a nice surprise for him and persisted until their mother said they'd see, but that black Labradors weren't to be had just like that. Susan then played her trump card. Maisie Trehearne knew some people down in Nansera who had some puppies ready.

The job of trying just once more to talk her out of it had fallen to Sarah, but when she tried she drew nothing except the look of hostility with which she was now familiar but had never got used to, so in the end she went down to Nansera with old Maisie Trehearne who loved dogs and had seen Panther die, and who made the morning's car journey down tense by continually referring to that episode, and the afternoon journey back exasperating by talking incessantly to the trembling little creature that was Panther's successor and had cost two hundred rupees and was guaranteed house-trained, a qualification which it showed evidence of being unaware it possessed by making a mess in its own basket, perhaps out of fright or a combination of fright and uncertainty about which of the two women abducting it was to be its new owner. Do pet it, Sarah, Maisie kept saying, in between bouts of petting it herself. But Sarah refused. 'It's Su's dog. I want Su to be the first to show it affection.'

'Of course, you're right. Isn't she, little fellow?'

And Susan had shown it affection. For a while the old Susan was there, on her knees, flushed and pretty, pushing a dark curl from her forehead with one finger and holding out her other hand, invitingly, caressingly, letting the puppy squirm up to her and sniff, bending down until her face was close, allowing it to lick her cheek, then hugging it and taking it to introduce it to Little Master who was sprawled on a rug on the verandah, dabbing at a toy dog, and who, after a moment's disbelief in this confrontation with a real one, screamed, so that the puppy – already named Panther the Second by Susan – backed away, puzzled, wholly at a loss until he found Sarah's by now familiar-smelling feet. He sat down against them and stared at the strangers. Susan stared back at him and then up at Sarah, so that on impulse Sarah pushed the puppy away with the side of her shoe and went to the verandah rail.

Ayah was comforting the child and Susan turned to help her. From the rail Sarah watched the puppy. Noting how it looked from the three on the rug to her and back again and then settled on its haunches on the spot where she had left it, ducked its head down and up again but made no sound, she realized that it had character and that she must harden her heart against it for both their sakes. She went indoors and called for Mahmoud to tell the bhishti to draw her bath. From the bedroom she heard Susan taking the little boy to task for being afraid of a puppy. The child had not yet learned to speak. Sometimes Sarah wondered whether he ever would, whether he knew whose child he was; his mother's, Ayah's or Sarah's. With the puppy it would be different. Dogs made their own decisions in such matters, as Panther 1 had done, choosing Susan as the owned and owning object of adoration despite her variable response to him and, finally, her absolute neglect.

She had always had that power, still had it, a power of immedi-ate attraction for animals and people, and Sarah understood her sister's own attitude to that power, her inability to believe that she truly possessed it and something of the terror she felt know-ing that she did. 'Come on, puppy,' she was calling. 'There. Nice puppy. Mummy's not afraid of puppy, see? Puppy loves mummy already. Come on now, stroke puppy. Show mummy what a brave boy you are.'

Gradually the boy had lost his terror and for a day or two the puppy was petted, played with, fed on the verandah by Susan and overseen by Minnie or Mahmoud during his periodic visits to urinate and defaecate, which he announced his intention of doing by going to the head of the steps into the garden and trying to get down them. The veterinary officer, Lieutenant Khan, came up from the Remount depot, examined his mouth and teeth and ears and gave him injections and powders which made him look miserable but did not dampen his playful spirit. Returning at lunch times and in the late afternoons from her work at Area Headquarters, Sarah noted the situation but knew that it would change.

On the fourth or fifth day (she could not remember which) she came back for lunch, was aware of the puppy's absence but said nothing until Susan went to their room for her afternoon nap and she and her mother were alone. 'I didn't see Panther Two,' she began. 'Is he all right?' Her mother supposed he was all right. Mahmoud had him in the servants' quarters. He had made a mess on the verandah. That's all her mother knew; that and that there had been a scene with Minnie crying and the child crying and Susan angry and then retreating into one of her moods. 'Do you *have* to go back to the daftar this afternoon?' her mother asked.

'I'm afraid I do. Why?'

Why didn't matter in that case, her mother said, and got up and left her alone. Sarah knew why and knew her mother knew she knew. But oppressed by the apparently unalterable rhythm of life at home she felt justified in pretending not to and it helped to get out for a few more hours. Nothing would happen during them. It took some time for a crisis to build up, if there was to be a crisis.

Her father came back into the compartment.

'There, all done.'

'How smart you look.'

'Dressed for the part.'

In the old days he would never have said that. He seemed to have acquired a sense of charade. He wore KD with Sam Browne, collar and tie. The rainbow ribbons above the left breast pocket added colour to his occasion. He had on one of the pairs of hand-made shoes which he had left behind in 1940 which

throughout the war Mahmoud had kept dubbined and had
recently polished to a deep conker-brown. She had taken two
pairs to Bombay. This was the first time he had worn them.

'Are they comfortable?'

'I think,' he said, 'my feet have lost weight too. But they're
good and soft.'

'I'll get dressed,' she said, 'then we'll have the other cup.
Unless you'd like it now.'

'No, I'll tidy up here, then we'll have more room.'

Tidy up was one of the new expressions. He had become used
to doing things for himself. In Bombay Nazimuddin had been
scandalized by the sight of Colonel Sahib cleaning his own shoes,
washing out pairs of socks, drawing his own bath, packing his
own cases. Rather than tell him that in England many Sahibs
were used to looking after themselves Sarah tried to explain that
doing such chores helped her father get well again after being so
long a prisoner in Germany.

He had left the w.c. cubicle immaculate. The hand-basin glis-
tened, the speckled mirror gleamed. The stone floor looked
newly swept. At Pankot the sweepers would have nothing to do
but clear up after her. She wondered how her father had achieved
such spotlessness. There was no brush or mop or cloth. Perhaps
he had used handfuls of toilet paper.

In her valise which she set down against the door she had her
civilian skirt and blouse and her WAC(I) uniform. While sitting
on the closet smoking another cigarette she wondered which to
wear. He had not seen her in uniform yet. She'd intended
to wear it this morning, partly as a compliment to him and partly
because she anticipated there being a moment when it might be
better for her to leave her mother and father and Susan together
and go down to the daftar to report back and arrange the day
and time to resume duties. Which were not onerous. Never
had been.

She decided on the uniform and emerging later and finding
him with his head out of the farther window stood waiting for
him to become aware of her, turn round and react. It was years
since she had considered to what extent two girls had been a
disappointment to him, years since she had been conscious as
the first-born of being under some sort of obligation to make
up to him for not being a boy; but standing there in uniform

she realized that putting it on, today, was also partly an act of contrition, a way of saying: It's the best I could do. She was seeking approval as a boy might have done and this embarrassed her suddenly. She heaved the valise up on to the upper-bunk, heard him move, felt his appraisal. She glanced round.

'I say,' he said.

She faced him, smiling, awkward.

'How nice,' he said. 'How very nice. But you didn't tell me about the third stripe.'

'It's very recent.'

'All the same. Sergeant. Jolly good.'

'I'll get the tea. Would you like a cold bacon sandwich?'

'Cold bacon?'

'Cold fried bacon. I got some last night in Ranpur from the station restaurant.'

'Did you, now! Then you ought to have a crown as well.'

She laughed and opened the hamper which he had lifted on to the seat in readiness for breakfast. She loved train journeys. In England as a child she had been disappointed to find how quickly they were over. In an Indian train one could put down roots, stake out claims, enjoy transitory possession for a day or so of a few cubic feet of carriage which even a change of trains did not seem to interrupt.

The hamper belonged to Aunt Fenny and was zinc-lined, with compartments for flasks, cups, knives, spoons, forks and food. The cold fried rashers for sandwiches were in greaseproof paper.

'And a new loaf!' her father said.

'I got them to slice it. I hope it isn't dry.'

'When was all this?'

'After we'd had dinner and you were seeing to the men. It's a surprise breakfast. Have a hard-boiled egg first?'

'Hard-boiled eggs too. Well done. No, I'll have a sandwich first.'

When she was a child and before the years of exile at school in England they had trekked on ponies through the Pankot hills, making camp at tea-time, striking camp at dawn; rather, the servants had made camp ahead of them and done all the striking. What's for breakfast? her father used to say. Hard-boiled eggs and cold bacon sandwiches. With mugs of hot sweet tea. Eaten and drunk before the sun had risen and scorched the mist away.

Night found her so tired that she slept before she had time to fix in her mind the position of the jackal packs in relation to the camp. That was the year of the map-reading lessons when she had been initiated into the mysteries of orientation, six point references and compass bearings; lessons begun on the verandah of Rose Cottage which had a view of the hills and distant peaks which he taught her to relate to the hatchings and contours of a map pinned to a board, under talc upon which the coloured chinagraph pencils left marks you could rub out with your finger and obliterate entirely with a rolled-up handkerchief. He taught her the tewt – the tactical exercise without troops – and she had seldom looked at a landscape since without being alerted to its topographical influence on what was or was not militarily feasible to perform in it. But she had never grasped as a man could do the points of weakness, the conditions that were favourable for the daring stroke that spelt success. Everything, hill, valley, hedge, tree, lake, river, bank, forest, seemed – militarily – overwhelmingly dangerous. So her military accomplishments really began and ended in the commissariat – providing hard-boiled eggs and cold fried bacon sandwiches. These she could understand, appreciate, hunger after; and happily leave to him and to men like him the things that sharpened different appetites. Preparing a bacon sandwich now she thought of how he had virtually lost a regiment. She handed the sandwich to him, as it were in compensation.

He waited until she had made one for herself and then, looking at each other like old conspirators, they bit in, holding their hands up to catch crumbs.

'They taste better on a train,' he said, after swallowing. 'Something to do with the smoke and soot.' She poured tea into the mugs. Because they both liked it sweet she'd had the milk and sugar added in the flask: a thick strong picnic brew. The regular puffing sound of the engine came and went as it negotiated the bends and gradients on the hillside. She looked at her watch. One hour to go. He was at the window again, mug in hand.

'There they are!'

He waved and made room for her. Several carriages along the sepoys had their heads stuck out of the window of the special compartment Movement Control had reserved for them. They were grinning and waving. She waved back. One of them pointed.

Perhaps his village was visible from here, or in this vicinity. But most of them came from the higher hills beyond Pankot. What a lot they had seen. What tales they could tell. In their villages they would be important men. They had seen the world and would be accounted wise in its ways. Their advice would be listened to. They would swagger a bit. The hands of the un-married ones would be sought by parents with dowries and daughters. And a special distinction attached to them because Colonel Sahib had waited in Bombay until they were all fit enough to travel. That tale would be told far into the future. It was something he had done for them. They would always remember.

She waved again and turned back in. He was on the bench looking up at her, smiling, as if proud of them, of her; as if happy. But she knew he was not; not deeply happy. She offered him an egg and a twist of pepper and salt to dip it in after he'd cracked and shelled it. He began this operation and she sat beside him similarly occupied. In India, yes, one could travel great distances. But the greatest distance was between people who were closely related. That distance was never easy to cover. Is Sarah heartfree still? he had asked Aunt Fenny in private, but Fenny had told her and added, Are you pet? So that for a moment it seemed that she would refer to what had never been referred to since it happened. And what had happened constituted the greatest distance there could be between her and her father. Or did it? She would have liked to tell him. She believed he would understand. But the train rattled on and she said nothing. They cracked eggs.

I particularly remember the eggs (Sarah has said), the moment when, simultaneously, he became conscious of the mess we were making and I became conscious that it irritated him.

There followed the moment of revelation, that in his valise her father had an old clothes brush. He used this to sweep the crumbs and sharp little fragments of shell into the *Times of India* – after they had brushed down their clothes and the seat with their hands. He carried the folded paper into the w.c. and poured the contents down the pan.

When he came back he made no comment. Gradually her embarrassment spent itself. She looked at him encouragingly, alert to the possibility that he had something special to say for

which the clearing up of the mess may have been a delaying
tactic as much as anything else; and looking at him, came up
against the barrier of his inarticulate affection, his restraint, his
inner reservations – as solid an edifice as the rock-face that marks
the end of the line from Ranpur to Pankot where the traveller
gets down from the train several hundred feet below the hill-
pass that leads into the Pankot valley.

Here there is a sound, neither far nor distant, but because the
arrival of a train is always noisy the traveller may not notice it
except perhaps as a faint singing in the ears or a gentle pressure
on the back of the neck, a sound that does not vary in intensity.
Full awareness may be delayed but when it comes identification
is immediate. It is the sound of the streams and waterfalls that
emerge from fissures and secret places in the rock: invisible from
any part of the station or the concourse, above and around which
the rock looms, softened by vegetation and (most mornings)
mists which may gradually reveal themselves as drizzle, or burn
away as the sun gets at them.

Somewhere along the road that winds up from the station the
sound of rushing water is lost, but to know precisely where you
would have to travel on foot, or order the taxi or the tonga to
halt at every likely turn and twist, and listen, and in the one place
where the driver would be prepared to obey such an order (the
brow of the hill, at the pass where in the turning between rocks
the whole panorama of the Pankot valley is suddenly disclosed)
the sound has already gone and the ear is blessed by the holy
silence that only the biblical clunk of goat-bells interrupts.

'*Thairo*,' her father said, at the same time leaning forward and
touching the shoulder of the lance-naik driver whom Captain
Coley had sent with the staff-car to meet the train. Ahead of
them the truck-load of ex-invalids careered on down the long
straight road that led into the valley, making for the depot where
some of their families waited for them. Her father's wishes had
been scrupulously carried out. The arrival had been unremarkable; departure from the concourse delayed until only the truck
and the staff-car remained. He had waited for a while in the
carriage and, later, on the platform, until – within twenty
minutes – the entire train-load of passengers had found or chosen
their transport and gone. The sounds of the streams and the water
were louder, then. Now on the brow of the hill, with the engine

switched off and the windows open, he sat for a moment and then got out. She did not follow him.

After a while he got back in. He said 'Everything seems so much closer together,' as if in his absence Pankot had shrunk, the three hills which enclosed the valley been edged towards one another and squeezed up against the bazaar whose upper storeys of wooden balconies under steep-pitched wooden roofs rose above the mist into the clear morning air (which, Sarah saw, made them look nearer than they were).

Ten minutes later the car entered the V-shaped bazaar, at the low point of that letter: the square, with its war memorial, the meeting place of the road up into West Hill and the steeper road that thrusts assertively into the other hill upon which the British had chosen to build when they discovered in Pankot an ideal retreat from the hot weather in Ranpur. The main street, flanked arcaded shops, probably looked narrower to him. Passing the general store he said, 'Jalal-ud-din', and smiled, shook his head, as if the store-sign was evidence of the indestructibility of Pankot's principal contractor. Jalal-ud-din's shutters were still up. The first servant with a chit would not appear until nine o'clock. It would be ten o'clock before the first memsahib arrived to give an order and inspect the new stock. At this present hour there were few people and the car was not obstructed by tongas, cylists or cows. It continued, making for the junction of Church and Club Roads where the driver changed gear for the long uphill climb and where Sarah (as nowadays she always did) saw what her father couldn't: Barbie Batchelor's overturned tonga, the horse struggling, its leg broken, and the tin trunk, the cause of the trouble, upended in the ditch where it had burst open on impact and scattered its contents of missionary relics. From this scene of disaster Barbie had walked away, up Church Road to the rectory bungalow, mud-stained, clothes torn, still dazed and, according to the chaplain's wife, Clarissa Peplow, demanding a spade, still apparently harping on that old question: whether Mildred had buried Mabel in the wrong place, in the churchyard of St John's in Pankot instead of by the side of her second husband, Colonel Layton's father, in the churchyard of St Luke's in Ranpur.

'What was that?'

Had she spoken? He seemed to think so. She had been thinking: Poor Barbie. She might have said it aloud. She smiled, shook her head, looked out across the golf-course which had played a part in a dream Barbie had had and had liked describing, a dream that had ended in St John's and which Barbie interpreted as heavenly reassurance that her old friend Edwina Crane had been forgiven for taking her own life. But that was three years ago, after the riots of 1942. Now Barbie's dreams were waking ones, lived behind barred windows in Ranpur. I have nothing to give you in exchange, she had written, not even a rose: written on a pad because she no longer spoke – which made it more difficult than ever to tell what she remembered, if anything. But 'not even a rose' had shown some grasp of the past, some stubbornly held recollection of the time when she had been happy, with Mabel, in Rose Cottage.

The car was getting near to the cottage now and she found herself suddenly short of breath, as though her heart had begun to beat for both of them, and this seemed extraordinary to her because at the same time she was conscious of having, just now, as they passed the entrance to the club, also passed the point of any further personal involvement in his homecoming. When she thought of the things to be done and said during the next quarter of an hour her skin prickled with irritation. The familiar names at the entrances to the bungalows in the last stretch of the road to Rose Cottage increased her uneasiness. Her body pressed back hard against the seat, ostensibly to give him a better view, but he was not leaning forward to look, in fact he was pressed back too, or so it seemed to her from the sense she had of his body's alignment with her own. So far as she could tell they both sat thus, wedged into their corners, staring straight ahead or gazing obliquely away from one another through the nearest window, passive and reluctant rather than active and eager, and it occurred to her that perhaps he was as aware as she that so much more could have been made of their time together and that now it was over and the opportunity to know each other better gone, perhaps for ever.

'I think,' he said suddenly, and then jerked forward, touched the driver's shoulder. 'Stop here.' And hesitated before saying to her, 'If you don't mind. I'll walk the rest.' She nodded. He got out. Before he shut the door he asked her, 'Will you give me time to cope? Say five minutes?'

'Of course.'

She understood. In this way he could achieve a small measure of surprise. It did not offend her that he wanted to achieve it alone. He set off, striding easily, alert and upright, already – as he had said – dressed for the part but now performing it. The driver was puzzled, glanced over his shoulder, uncertain whether he was supposed to drive on, follow slowly or stay put. She said in Urdu: Wait here for five minutes. He switched off. He was too new to the regiment to remember her father personally. He had not been overawed by the occasion; proud, rather, of the part he was playing in it. She wondered whether he felt cheated of its climax. This was the time when she should jolly him along, like a good colonel's daughter, but she was disinclined to ask the formal questions, which her father had also omitted to do: What is your name? What village do you come from? What other family members have served in the regiment? Instead she lit a cigarette. As she clicked the lighter off her eyes met his in the driving-mirror. He looked down immediately, too quickly for her to judge his reaction but she supposed that smoking was one of the things that made Englishwomen sexless to boys like this; smoking, short skirts, uniforms; and the white skin that probably made the body appear composed of a substance that was not flesh but an unsatisfactory substitute whose erotic qualities only men similarly endowed could appreciate.

As she exhaled, this notion seemed to take form in the smoke and hang with it until it was sucked through the open window, leaving her with a profound sense of her misplacement in these surroundings. But there was no compensating sense of release from them because she could not easily imagine alternatives: to Pankot, yes, but the alternative to Pankot was still an Indian alternative, a variation of Pankot, and Pankot was already crowd-ing in on her, threatening that illusion of serenity, of future possibilities, which had excited her the evening before, getting off the train at Ranpur. She was still in India, still of India. You could exchange one surrounding for another but not the occupa-tion, an occupation less and less easy to explain and to follow except by continuing to perform it and seize opportunities to demonstrate – like the artist who carved angels' faces in the dark-est recesses of a church roof and countered the charge that people couldn't see them by saying that God could – that dim as the light had grown it was still enough by which to see an obligation.

Five minutes had gone but she sat motionless, watching the smoke from her cigarette, unwilling to give the order to start up, unwilling to stir sufficiently to lift the cigarette to her mouth. From somewhere in the forested slopes a coppersmith-bird began its insistent high-pitched calling, a monotonous tapping sound of which she was usually only subconsciously aware but whose single rhythmically repeated note, coming just now, seemed to be counting the seconds away for her; and then, as it continued, encouraging her not to move but to listen, to surrender to its nagging persuasion until she entered a state of torpor or stupefaction, of which it might take some predatory advantage, reveal itself as a bird of more ominous intention, a bird of the species Barbie watched beyond the barred window, planing the sky above the invisible towers.

Abruptly it fell silent. The driver looked round.

'*Panch minute, memsahib?*'

'*Han*,' she said, '*lekin —*'

But what? Carefully she stubbed the cigarette in the chromium tray on the panel of the door, reluctant to bring the journey to a conclusion. Her capacity to feel or show family affection had diminished and in one area all but vanished. She felt closest now to Aunt Fenny who had seen her through the thing that happened to her. They had seen it through together, if such a lonely and loveless experience could ever be thought of as anything but solitary. Where there might have been recriminations between them there had been only a wounded but finally healing silence; healing because it had been warmed once by physical contact — Aunt Fenny's plump arm round her shoulders, Aunt Fenny's head against hers. Between herself and her mother there had been neither word nor gesture. Nothing. For her mother it had never happened. It was her mother's assumption of ignorance that hurt her most. Sometimes, holding Susan's baby and chancing to find her mother watching her, she felt she would have welcomed any response, even disgust, that showed her mother appreciated that the act of ministering to her sister's child was one that could fill her with the anguish of her own physical deprivation; and then, seeing no glimmer of recognition in that steady dispassionate gaze, she felt deprived again, of part of herself, of everything really except her guilt.

Her guilt was unquestionable but there was only one aspect

of it which she was truly ashamed of, and this she bitterly regretted. She knew that behind her longing to talk about it to her
mother lay a need for consolation and that this was a weakness,
a form of self-indulgence. Understanding this she could live with
her mother's silence, endless though it was as a punishment.
For her mother the silence was part of the code, the standard:
the angel's face in the dark. Or was it a demon's? Whichever it
was it helped her mother to preserve an attitude of composure
and fortitude and Sarah was able to admire her for it and see the
point. In this way Sarah carved angel faces of her own and only
at moments of acute distress had destructive impulses to tear the
fabric of the roof and expose the edifice to an empty sky.

I shall walk the rest of the way, too, she told herself. And
opened the door, got out, shut it, before she could change her
mind. She told the driver to go ahead to the bungalow and wait.
She stood in the road until the car had started then, following
slowly, watched it as it took the last section of the hill. Rose
Cottage was behind the next bend.

The coppersmith had resumed but from farther off, having
flown to try its luck elsewhere or to plot another point in the
boundary of its territory. She knew nothing of its habits, little
of the lives of wild creatures whose co-existence with her own
species created a mysterious world within a world; or rather,
worlds, a finite but to her uncountable number, self-sufficient,
separated, but intent on survival. She walked faster, to the tune
of the distant coppersmith, and recalled with clarity the night of
Susan's wedding in Mirat, wandering amidst the fireflies in the
grounds of the palace guest house and saying aloud to her absent
father: I hope you are well, I hope you are happy, I hope you
will come back soon: and then turning back towards the house
where Uncle Arthur sat alone on the lit verandah, a long way
away from her, in a pattern of light, a circle of safety. My family,
she had thought then. My family, my family.

She had said the words aloud and said them aloud again as she
approached the entrance to the front garden of Rose Cottage.
My family. My family. Before repeating the words she had not
expected anything of them but at once she felt the tug of an old
habit of affection and then a yearning for the powerful and
terrible enchantment of inherited identity, which she had spent
most of her adult years fighting to dispel; fighting as hard as Susan

had fought to feel herself touched by it; and drawn into it, to its very centre, where she would no longer feel, as she had once confessed to Sarah she felt, like a drawing that anyone who wanted to could come along and rub out; that there was nothing to her except this erasable image. The first psychiatrist, Captain Samuels, had shown no special interest when Sarah mentioned it. He had simply said, What do you think that means? But had turned away to arrange things on his desk as if uninterested in her amateur opinions. So she had not answered and the question of Susan's idea of herself as a drawing people could rub out had never come up again, either with Samuels or with his successor, Captain Richardson.

But it had stayed in Sarah's mind as an explanation of her sister's self-absorption and self-dramatization. She did not understand what it was that had made Susan feel so inadequate and the discovery that she did had been a shock. Until then, the self-absorption had seemed to her that of a girl who not doubting her attraction demanded that others should provide her with constant evidence of its existence, and paid obsessive attention to the smallest detail when setting the scenes for these necessary acts of recognition. But the sequence of scenes that had made up – still made up – Susan's life could no longer be thought of as Susan playing Susan. It was Susan drawing Susan, drawing and re-drawing, attempting that combination of shape and form which by fitting perfectly into its environment would not attract the hands of the erasers. What Sarah feared now was that the game had stopped being a game, had become a grim and conscious exercise in personal survival; that Susan now drew and re-drew herself attempting no more than a likeness that she herself could live with; and that she might tire of the effort.

When she reached the open gateway which was flanked by two stone pillars, she paused, convinced that her father had done so too a few minutes ago. In Mabel's day the name of the bungalow was set out in metal letters fixed to an unpainted wooden board planted in the high bank that bordered the road. Over the years the colour of the metal had become hardly distinguishable from the wood. They had faded into the background, as Mabel had faded into hers, and left the board with a look of being indifferent to the arrival of strangers. The board was still there but was partially hidden by the wild growth on the bank. To see

it at all you would have to know it existed. Its identifying function had been usurped by neat white boards, one on each of the
stone pillars, announcing respectively in bold black lettering the
name and number of the house and the name of its occupier:
Colonel J. Layton. Yes, he would have stopped, confronted
abruptly by this evidence of ownership, and then perhaps
searched for the old board until he found it, probably in a place
that didn't quite conform with the one he remembered.

She set off along the curved gravel drive between the rockeries
which were vivid with the blue, white, yellow and purple stars
of flowering plants. There had been rain in the night and the air
was fresh, chill in the shadows of trees and bushes, but the sky
was now cloudless and as she came to the end of the rockeries
the sun heated her face.

The staff-car was parked opposite the steps up to the square-
pillared verandah. There was no sign of the driver. The thick-
set white stuccoed bungalow looked deserted, but in the way a
place could do that had only just been abandoned. Again she
stopped. If she entered she would find the occupants gone, the
signs of their presence still fresh and warm, and a strong odour
of the danger from which they had fled. She had felt this once
or twice before, but this morning the sensation was particularly
strong.

And, looking at the bungalow, as it were through her father's
eyes, she thought she saw for the first time what it was that sometimes gave this impression. By stripping it of anything that made
it look 'cottage' – pots of plants on the balustrades, flowering
creepers round the square pillars – her mother had restored to it
not its elegance (it could never have had that) but its functional
solidity, an architectural integrity which belonged to a time when
the British built in a proper colonial fashion with their version of
India aggressively in mind and with a view to permanence.
Exposed by the cutting back of trees and plants, set off by the new
gravel on the drive and the widening of the forecourt (the rockeries were also earmarked for destruction) its squat rectangular bulk
was revealed, and with it its essential *soundness*. The secluded,
tentative air which Sarah had often associated with it in Aunt
Mabel's time had quite gone. The name, Rose Cottage, given to
it by a previous owner, a tea-planter, was now all too clearly,
absurdly, inappropriate, and only the difficulty there would be

with the *dak* had stopped her mother scrapping the name entirely
and identifying the bungalow as 12 Upper Club Road.

In restoring it to a likeness of its former self, Sarah knew her
mother had intended to create a setting that would speak for
itself and also for her and her family's claim on history through
long connection. The name Layton, and her mother's maiden
name, Muir, under portraits on the walls of Government House
in Ranpur and Flagstaff House and the Summer Residence in
Pankot, on the drunken headstones in the churchyards of St
John's and St Luke's, performed the same function of austere
advertisement. In their dumb immobility they avoided the
vulgarity of the words whose meanings they conveyed; but conveyed with so remote, so mute a self-awareness that even when
identified they seemed thinned by irony. Service, sacrifice,
integrity. And she had succeeded, but at a cost. By cutting away
inessentials, the accumulations of years, she had robbed the place
of a quality that belonged to that accumulation, the quality of
survival and the idea behind it – that survival meant change.
Restored, the bungalow no longer reflected the qualities of the
people living there, it no longer fitted them as they truly were,
so that – even when they were in it – from outside the bungalow
looked empty, like a place of historic interest, visited but not
inhabited. And, more than usually oppressed this morning by
the sensation that she had arrived at a moment when it was
deserted, she saw the bungalow in a sudden, shatteringly direct,
light – looking as it looked now but even starker, uncompromisingly new amid the raw wounds left by space having been
cleared for it; and on its verandah a white man in Indian clothes
at ease in a cane lounging chair, or on a charpoy, attended by
servants or by one of his Indian mistresses, and contemplating
through the mists of claret fumes and cheroot smoke the fortune
he had made or hoped to make out of private trade. The words
whose meanings her mother had wanted to convey belonged
to a later age, an age when the bungalow was already old.
Unwittingly she had exposed the opposites of those words: self-
interest, even corruption.

She made her way quickly, avoiding the steps, taking the path
round the side, then stepping off it because the new gravel
crunched, on to the new turf that had been put down on ground
cleared of shrubs. The side verandah was empty but there was a

spread blanket, a coloured ball and some bricks where the child had been playing. The doors to the room she shared with Susan were open. She hesitated. There was no sound of voices inside the house. Ahead she could see one side and corner of the high netting surrounding the tennis-court, and moving forward, widening the angle of vision, saw Minnie, the little ayah, inside the netting at the far end of the court, walking behind the child whose arms she held aloft by the wrists as he took faltering bandy-legged steps towards his mother. The centre net was not up and Susan sat on a blanket in the middle of the court at the point where the lime-marked centre lines met, with her back to the house, leaning on her right hip, her left arm stretched back, grasping one ankle, the other arm taut, hand palm down on the blanket, taking the weight. Close to this hand Panther 2 sat watching the child, scraping the blanket with his tail. Susan wore one of the full-skirted flowered cotton dresses that made her look eighteen still, too young to be a mother, touchingly too young to be a widow; and, round the shoulders, tied by its sleeves, a cardigan. The hairdresser had been – perhaps yesterday. The dark hair sported a crisp new set, a thick fringe of tight curls at the back that left her neck bare. When she spoke her voice carried. 'Come along then.' More faintly Sarah heard Edward's gurgling response. But suddenly he squealed. Minnie had picked him up and was running forward. She placed him on the blanket close to Susan and then retreated, ran to the opening at the side of the court and through it across the lawn towards the servants' quarters, as though this were part of a game of hide-and-seek.

But Sarah knew that it was not; guessed that the girl had seen Colonel Layton coming out into the garden and – partly out of shyness (for she was still very young and had never met the head of the household), partly out of unwillingness to intrude, or to receive yet the look or expression of gratitude which she had earned – put herself out of reach.

As if alerted by Minnie's sudden action, Susan had looked round, and now got to her knees, picked Edward up and stood facing the bungalow with her head down talking to the boy, holding his right hand out in the direction of his grandfather who now entered the court from the gate on the verandah side of the netting. At first Sarah thought he was alone, but presently she saw her mother following slowly, arms folded, one hand at her neck, pressing down her string of pearls. The hairdresser had attended her too. And Sarah did not recognize the jumper and skirt. Nor the shoes. They were new. Beside her mother and sister she felt travel-stained, dowdy in her uniform, excluded from the scene: from what she recognized *as* a scene – for all its appearance of evolving naturally from a sequence of haphazard events. It bore, for Sarah, the familiar mark of Susan's gift for pre-arrangement, or her continuing and frightening attempts to reduce reality to the manageable proportions of a series of tableaux which illustrated the particular crisis through which she was passing.

It would be better, she had said to her mother, *for you and daddy to be alone for a bit when he gets here, wouldn't it? So I'll be in the garden with ayah and Edward.*

In this way the true climax of his homecoming had been delayed, transferred from the scene with his wife to the scene with the daughter who had a grandson to present. And a dog. But no husband. Instead, the ghost of the soldier whom she had married. The ghost, and the living likeness of the man in the child. These were her gifts to her father and her current explanations to herself of what she was in the world's eyes and in his particularly: a promise for him of his continuity and in that promise perhaps she saw a dim reflection of promise for her own.

He stopped just short of mother and child, raised his arms, inviting a triple embrace. *It's grandpa,* Susan seemed to be saying. She held Edward up and after a moment's hesitation her father took him and holding him firmly under the arms raised him high. Edward gazed down at the stranger with an expression that from a distance struck Sarah as oddly dispassionate for a child so young. It was an expression she had seen before on Edward's face when confronted by men. He seemed to have a reserve, amounting to a vague antipathy, for grown members of his own sex. Almost alone among them, Ronald Merrick had inspired an early positive response, in spite of the burn-scars, the artificial hand. These had not frightened the child.

The one thing Edward seldom did when men touched him was cry; but his grandfather did not know this and perhaps interpreting Edward's failure to show pleasure or interest in being raised aloft as a warning that tears could quickly follow, put him carefully down on the nearest corner of the blanket and, straightening up, gazed at Susan.

Hello, daddy, she seemed to say. Then she covered her face with both hands and, standing so, was embraced. When she uncovered her face and raised her head to kiss and be kissed her eyes were closed and she was crying. Sarah could hear her. He began saying things to comfort and jolly her out of it. And although he must have noticed the puppy before he chose this moment to exclaim about it. They both looked down at Panther, broke apart and knelt together on the blanket. Introductions were made. Panther wagged his tail and skittered a bit, happy but cautious under the flurry of attention. Colonel Layton scratched the puppy's head, ruffled Edward's red curls, placed an arm round Susan's shoulders. She wiped her left cheek dry with the palm of her hand. The scene was over.

I can enter now, Sarah told herself.

III

By the time the car had negotiated the narrow lanes from the Samaritan Hospital of the Sisters of Our Lady of Mercy in the old city of Ranpur, through the Koti bazaar to the Elphinstone fountain, the street lighting was coming on.

Only one police squad remained of the force that had been out in the afternoon. The men were relaxed, awaiting the order to return to barracks. Traffic was flowing freely around the circus and access to the Mall and the Kandipat road was no longer restricted – signs that His Excellency the Governor had made the journey from the airfield out at Ranagunj back to Government House without incident and that news of Mr Mohammed Ali Kasim's brief stop in Ranpur, *en route* from Mirat to Pankot with the body of his secretary, Mr Mahsood, had not led to a popular demonstration in the latter case nor to an anti-government demonstration in the former – or certainly not one of the kind that got out of hand and at nightfall left the air charged with anxiety and irresolution.

As the driver turned into the Mall an Indian Sub-Inspector broke off conversation with a head constable, came to attention and saluted: the car rather than its occupant.

Rowan touched the peak of his cap then leant back and looked

ahead to the still distant bulk of Government House, dark against
the deep mauve northern sky and the grey pink-tipped storm
clouds. The avenue of approach was bordered on each side by
double rows of shade trees and the compounds of Ranpur's
oldest European houses and bungalows. The sidewalks were as
wide as the road. It was a processional route but seldom used for
such an occasion because the way from the airfield where people
usually arrived now lay to the east of Government House,
beyond the cantonment.

The Mall, running for a measured mile and a half from the
Elphinstone fountain to the Governor's residence, was bisected
midway by Old Fort Road. In the middle of this intersection
rose the bronze canopied statue of Queen Victoria. In 1890 that
statue had been the cause of serious deliberations by the committee of the Ranpur Gymkhana Club. Unwilling quite to believe
the story, since it seemed so perfectly apocryphal, Rowan had
tackled the club secretary and eventually been shown the faded
but still legible page of the committee's minute recording a bare
majority vote against a proposal to paint the statue white to meet
the criticism of members that, in bronze, Victoria – particularly
in profile – bore an unhappy resemblance to a Rajput warrior
lady of the kind who defied the British in the early decades of
the century. The motion had been lost on the grounds of
impracticability. A further motion that representations should be
made to the appropriate department to try to ensure that any
future replica of the Monarch should be executed in the best
white marble was carried unanimously.

Although the Civil Lines officially began at the Elphinstone
fountain, the Victoria statue was now regarded as the threshold.
She stood on permanent sentry duty, accoutred with orb and
sceptre, gazing with an air of abstraction towards the city. Behind
her back the Mall continued, but on this second stretch there
were no houses. The double lines of shade trees now bordered
areas of flat open ground on which the military and police
authorities could quickly establish command posts and hold
reserve forces at time of civil disturbance. The line (or front)
formed by Old Fort Road was considered the furthest that a
civil demonstration should be allowed to march on Government
House unless its intentions were clearly peaceful. Coming up
the Mall from the fountain, riotous marchers invariably found

the way blocked by squads of police, or soldiers, deployed across the road in front of the statue. The old houses and bungalows on the Mall between the statue and the fountain had long since been abandoned by the British and taken over by rich Indians. According to the British it was the inconvenience of places built in the late eighteenth and early nineteenth centuries which had caused their removal to the newer and better accommodation provided by subsequent building along Old Fort Road and on the cantonment side of Government House, although it was occasionally admitted that it would have been tedious to live on a route so frequently used by crowds of people making nuisances of themselves. The joke still current among the Indians, though, was that the British had lost their nerve and decamped, leaving their Queen behind.

To reach the Gymkhana Club Rowan would have to tell the driver to turn at the statue and go along the eastern arm of Old Fort Road. He was tempted to do so. Since 18.00 hours it had been his twenty-four hours off-duty. The prospect of beginning it with a dip in the club's pool, a drink or two on the terrace and a quiet supper alone in the annexe to the main dining-room, attracted him. He could send the driver back to Government House with a note for the duty-officer to say where he was. Or he could ring the duty-officer from the club to ask whether HE had asked for him, although that was unlikely. The twenty-four hours off-duty once a week was treated by Malcolm with rigorous respect.

But he gave the driver no instruction.

Having passed the sentries and the checkpoint inside the west gate they came out on to the forecourt of the west wing and pulled up at a certain point below the flight of steps leading to the great colonnaded terrace. Rowan signed the man's logbook, got out, went up and pushed through half-glazed double doors into the hall, full as usual with white-uniformed servants. He signed the duty book, marking himself OD, added his name to the mess list, went to check his pigeon-hole for letters and was handed two by the hall steward. Both felt like formal invitations. He went through the open half-glazed doors out on to an inner terrace, one of the four that flanked the inner courtyard: an immense rectangle laid out with intricate geometric precision and formality

with lawns, paved walks, ponds and fountains. On ceremonial
nights the fountains were floodlit but in the wet season were
usually not even turned on. This evening the courtyard was lit
only as far as the light from ornamental lanterns that hung from
the apex of each section of the vaulted ceilings of the terrace could
reach. Between the square pillars there were set great whitewashed tubs of hydrangea, geranium and bougainvillaea, and the
ubiquitous crimson canna lilies. To reach the entrance to the
staircase to his quarters Rowan had to walk past these almost to
the end of the terrace and past the offices which coped with the
routine work of the household. Most of these were shut and the
benches provided for messengers empty, except outside the telephone exchange and the signals office which were manned round
the clock, as was the cypher office, in the east wing, where Rowan
spent most of his working day. He glanced across the courtyard.
The first-floor windows of Malcolm's private rooms were lit.

Reaching the narrow door and the narrow staircase Rowan
began to climb. His quarters were high up, on the second floor
where the corridors were narrow, the rooms small, the ceilings
low and the windows perpetually grimy. He had a sitting-room,
a bedroom and a bathroom which suffered the drawback of
having no running hot water. This had to be brought up from
the basement in kerosene tins.

Without his bell, his telephone, and without the servants who
manned the corridor, he might have felt himself marooned in a
little oasis of inconvenience and for the first few weeks of his
temporary appointment as an aide he had in fact suffered mild
attacks of claustrophobia. But he had grown to see only the
advantages of the place, even to be fond of it, and when offered
something better on being transferred from temporary to official
duty he had elected to stay. The quarters were supposed to
provide short-term accommodation only and he was now the
corridor's oldest inhabitant. One of the advantages was that
the servants allotted to the corridor looked upon themselves now
as virtually in his personal employ. He knew their histories, their
weaknesses, their aspirations; helped them with their private
problems and settled their disputes. He had never felt himself
cut out to be a good regimental officer; but he was sufficient of
a soldier to miss contact with men for whose welfare he was
responsible. The servants were a surrogate.

Two of them greeted him now. One took a key from its hook on the board and another a sealed envelope from the pigeon-hole used for internal messages. Jaiprakash opened the door of his sitting-room and switched the lights and fan on. Rowan handed him the key to his drink cupboard and asked him to pour a whisky-soda. Jagram meanwhile went into the bedroom and bathroom, turning on lights and fans, then came back and went out to the corridor to call the bhishti. So it was, night after night.

To drink his whisky Rowan sat in his one comfortable chair. He opened the invitations, neither of interest to him, and then the envelope containing the internal mail. Two of the smaller envelopes inside contained bills. In addition there were various memoranda, the daily communiqué from the press office, a copy of a bread-and-butter letter from a senior officer of Eastern Command who had spent a few days at Government House and mentioned Rowan among those he thanked for making his stay comfortable. The largest envelope contained several cyclostyled pages: the general programme for the next few days, giving dates, times, functions, and the names of those members of the Governor's staff who were required to attend. Wherever his own name appeared the clerk had inked in an asterisk. Since Rowan had drafted most of the itinerary himself he glanced through it now mainly to refresh his memory and to check whether the Governor's private secretary, Hunter-Evans, had had to make any last-minute changes.

Tomorrow night at 19.30, when his day off was finished, he was to be at the reception in the state rooms for members of the Department of Education, the Municipal Board and the Ranpur Chamber of Commerce and at 21.00 at the dinner for Mr Kiran Shankar Chakravarti who in the past few years had made several crores of rupees out of army contracts and had donated a sufficient number of them to found a department of electrical engineering at Government College.

At 10 a.m. the day after, he and Priscilla Begge (representing Sir George and Lady Malcolm respectively) were to welcome and escort to Government House Lady Burke from Delhi, whose interests were the Red Cross, the WVS and the work of women's committees, and in the afternoon he had another reception committee at Ranagunj airport to collect a popular English entertainer who had been touring Burma and Bengal and who was to stay at Government House and give a concert at the Garrison Theatre in the cantonment. On the evening of the same day he was to accompany the indefatigable Lady Burke and Mrs Saparawala, the vice-chairman of the Ranpur Women's War Committee, back to the station to catch the night train for Calcutta where they were to attend a conference. The day after that there was a morning meeting of the Executive Council followed by a lunch party for HH the Maharajah of Puttipur, and an afternoon visit to the quarries out at Rangighat. That was new to him. He hesitated, then remembering that the Maharajah was greatly addicted to the sight and sound of dynamiting, he took up a pencil and marked Rangighat with a stroke, to remind himself to check that someone had thought not only to warn the Ranpur Quarry and Construction Company of the Maharajah's visit but to tell them to be sure to have a few decent bangs laid on, even if they weren't scheduled, and whatever the weather.

In the evening the job of helping to entertain His Highness fell to a fellow aide, Hugh Thackeray, who was to accompany HH and General Crawford to the mess of the Ranpur Regiment. HH's son and heir, the Maharajkumar, was an officer in the fourth battalion. He had served in Burma and was presently in Rangoon. Thackeray, a Ranpur Regiment man himself, was also to accompany HH the following morning to pick up his private aeroplane at the airfield. In the afternoon of that day Rowan was to go with the Governor, the Member for Finance and the Member for Education, to the foundation-stone laying ceremony at the site of the new Chakravarti extension in the Government College grounds.

He put the itinerary away and thought how narrow his life sounded when set out like this. Jagram came back and went through to the bathroom. The familiar click of bolts on the corridor door meant that the bhishti was on his way up with the hot water. He took his whisky over to the desk, emptied his pockets and then his briefcase of all the papers connected with the day's assignments: at General Crawford's office, at the CID, at old Chakravarti's house. And – a private visit – at the Samaritan Hospital of the Sisters of Our Lady of Mercy. Among these last was the letter from Sarah Layton which had been written two days ago, on Saturday August 11. She would not expect to hear from him so soon, nor perhaps when she did, by telephone. But it was to ring her, really, that he had come back and not gone to the club.

He unfolded the letter. The telephone number was there in the printed heading. He sat at the desk, spread the letter out and sipped whisky. This morning, because of its length and careful exposition, the letter had given him the impression of there being more urgency about the inquiry she asked him to make than she thought it fair to convey. He had already done what she asked. It would be nice to ring her to say so. But, exposed again to the letter's apparently casual tone he wasn't sure that he should.

Dear Nigel (she had written)

When we last met that time I was on my way to Bombay to meet my father you were generous enough to tell me never to hesitate to let you know if there were anything you could do for me in Ranpur. I hope you'll forgive me for taking you up on that so soon.

I think you'll remember my mentioning that whenever I came down to Ranpur I took the opportunity to visit a Miss Batchelor who used to live here at Rose Cottage as a PG of my father's step-mother, Mabel Layton. I'd just come away from seeing her that day you turned up at the Spendloves where I was staying a couple of nights before going on to Bombay. I was more grateful to you than you may have realized for persuading me to go along with you to those friends of Hugh Thackeray's, because seeing her in the state she'd reached was always discouraging. Her memory had gone, and so had her voice – she wrote everything down – but they said that was psychological. They assured me she was perfectly happy but it was such a depressing place I found that hard to believe.

Yesterday I heard in a roundabout way that she was dead and I confirmed this by ringing the Mother Superior at the Samaritan Hospital, where she was. I'd intended to ring ever since getting back from Bombay (just three days ago, on Wednesday) to find out how she was but kept putting it off. According to the Rev. Mother she died on Monday morning and was buried the following afternoon at St Luke's in Ranpur. She wasn't a Catholic, and was at the Samaritan because as you know theirs

is the only place in the city that caters for Europeans who are ill
in that way. All the arrangements both for her being there and for
the funeral were made by the Bishop Barnard Protestant Mission
Schools, which Barbie used to work for.

The line between Ranpur and Pankot is sometimes very bad
and was yesterday. On top of that the Rev. Mother has a habit
of not talking straight into the phone so she always sounds far
away and if you keep asking her to repeat things she gets nervous.
I mention this because I can't be sure whether the things I
gathered remain to be dealt with are things the Bishop Barnard
people have neglected or said they weren't interested in. She said
she'd been going to write to me, so I asked her to do that, but
she said she'd told me now and perhaps I'd call in (just like that,
from Pankot!). I've never found her anything but competent and
efficient but she has that curious nun's vagueness about anything
she's not dealing with on the spot, face to face.

The trouble is that in all the time Barbie was a patient there
I was the only person who knew her before she became ill who
visited her, and the staff got into the habit of thinking of me as
a sort of go-between if there was anything to settle between the
Samaritan and the Bishop Barnard who – I must say – did rather
keep their distance and seemed to think it was sufficient that
the bills were paid regularly although that was all done by their
lawyers who were also Barbie's. I didn't mind going to and fro,
whenever I was down there, settling odd things the Samaritan
had just let pile up until my next visit. I did rather want them
to feel that I had an interest in Miss Batchelor and that poor
Miss Batchelor had someone taking an interest in her. I'd always
assumed I'd be told if she suddenly became dangerously ill or
was dying. They had my Pankot address. The fact that I was in
Bombay when it happened doesn't alter the fact that neither the
hospital nor the Bishop Barnard seem to have tried to contact
me. I suppose the Reverend Mother would have written to me
eventually – all of which suggests mainly that whatever it is that
seems to be a loose end can't be very important.

I rang the Bishop Barnard too but the Superintendent is on
tour. Her deputy didn't know of anything still to be dealt with.
She said everything of Miss Batchelor's had been removed from
the Samaritan and signed for and was now in the Superintendent's room awaiting disposal. Since then she may have been in

touch with the Samaritan and sorted out whatever it is that seems to be a loose end. 'Things you should deal with,' is all I could really understand when I spoke to the Rev. Mother.

Unfortunately the only person I know in Ranpur well enough to ask to look into it is on holiday in Kashmir. (Mrs Fosdick, Mrs Spendlove's sister.) And perhaps it's not a place I'd want to put Mrs Fosdick to the trouble of getting in touch with. Here, the Peplows, the rector and his wife, who took Barbie in for a while after she had to leave Rose Cottage, are in Darjeeling. Clarissa Peplow is one of the very few people who know that I kept tabs on how poor Barbie Batchelor was making out, and I know if she'd been here she'd have rung the Vicar at St Luke's and asked him to clarify things with the Rev. Mother. So I turn to you. If you have a moment, could you ring the Rev. Mother (The Samaritan Hospital of the Sisters of Our Lady of Mercy, Latafat Hossain Lane, Tank Road, Lower Koti Bazaar, Tel. 3124) and try to find out what 'has to be dealt with' and then let me know — by letter? I'd be awfully grateful. The line between GH and the hospital will probably be clearer and you always sound so calm and collected and in control of things she may be encouraged out of her vagueness.

Since there's been a Governor's conference in Delhi I realize you may still be up there with HE, in any case I know you'll be busy. Anyway, there's absolutely no rush about this, so really don't worry if for some reason or another there's nothing you can do. I've dropped Rev. Mother a line mostly about Barbie but adding that I didn't quite get the hang of the query she raised and have asked a friend in Ranpur to get in touch with her, since I can't get away myself just now. I expect if it's anything important she might write to me, but she never has before.

I was longer in Bombay than I expected. I expect you know why because I gather Sir George Malcolm had a reception committee waiting to welcome back the main body of the regiment when it got back three or four weeks ago. Father wasn't in awfully good shape and as a few of the men had to go into hospital in Bombay we stayed on until they were fit enough to travel. Incidentally, on my last day in Bombay I met Count Bronowsky and Ahmed Kasim and so was vividly reminded of first meeting you on Ranpur station and the game pie and champagne. We went on to an interesting but rather odd party at a flat supposedly belonging to a Maharanee but had to come away before the hostess had all the drinks locked up and turned us all out. Ronald Merrick was with us – my reluctant escort. He'd turned up in Bombay. He didn't want to go to the party but I insisted on going so he insisted on coming. He warned me not to say anything to the Count or to Ahmed about the job he's doing. Perhaps he didn't trust me not to. Anyway it was quite an evening, I'll tell you all about it when next we meet.

It looks as if everything's more or less over now that the Americans have bombed Nagasaki too and Russia has come in (some caustic comments here, about that). It will seem odd not to be at war with anyone. Father is looking much better now. I go riding with him every morning and don't turn up at the daftar until eleven or so, so I'm having an easy time of it.

Love, Sarah.

He lay the letter aside, glanced at the package and envelope the Reverend Mother had given him and then at his watch. At 7.45 on a Monday evening there was a good chance of finding her at home. But in the second reading he had been struck by that phrase 'and let me know – by letter'. It occurred to him that the members of her family might not be among those few people who knew she had kept tabs on Miss Batchelor and that her concern for the old missionary's health was one they did not share and would not approve of. He thought it would be very like her to respect their lack of concern by keeping her own concern to herself; just as a year or so ago she had respected their reasons for not calling on Lady Manners when they found themselves on neighbouring houseboats in Srinagar, but had herself ignored the barrier the conventional world put up, by crossing the few yards of water on a day when she was alone and could do so without causing fuss or offence, and visited that old and enigmatic woman. She had attributed her action to curiosity. Initially she had used the word morbid, but then said, 'No, that's not right. But I was curious to see her, and the child.' Later she had said something odd, which interested him. 'In a way I think I envied her. But I'm not sure why.'

From the bathroom came the sound of water being poured into the tub. Deciding it would be better to relax in a tepid bath before making up his mind whether to ring her or write to her, he went into the bedroom and began to undress. While he did so he thought of their last meeting and of the time they had spent together; and of their first meeting, just over a year ago.

IV

Her quiet self-reliance had been the first of her qualities to impress and attract him. Her unexpected entrance ahead of Dmitri Bronowsky into the gilt and red plush railway carriage had caught him unprepared, caused him some difficulty – sitting as he was with briefcase on knee and a finger keeping the page of the file of documents he had been studying during Bronowsky's absence.

It was an intrusion he would have welcomed if she had brought into that baroque interior a classic air of feminine elegance. But she was in uniform, and this was crumpled. She looked travel-worn, hastily pulled together, like someone Bronowsky had just rescued from a crush on the platform, although the side platform where the Nawab's private train was drawn up was almost empty. It was not until she had taken her cap off and was sitting next to him on one of the ornate Louis XV-style salon chairs, in the light of the crimson-shaded lamps, drinking champagne and smoking one of Count Bronowsky's pink-papered and gold-tipped cigarettes, smiling at the old man's gay reminiscence of his earlier *émigré* life in the south of France, that the first impression was overtaken by another: that in her unusual, perhaps plain, way she was beautiful. The bone structure of her face was prominent but lacked the arresting emphasis which would have made it striking. Her face had to be studied before it revealed its natural and incontrovertible logic, and then one felt instinctively that it would endure, that in old age it would be marked by the serenity of understood experience and the vitality of undiminished appetite.

'What a sad story,' she said when Bronowsky finished the tale of the eighteen-year-old English boy who had loved and lost a Spanish girl; lost because he could talk to her only in English or in the schoolboy French Bronowsky had been hired to correct and improve. The story was subtly turned. Many girls would have laughed blankly – or, had they been aware of Bronowsky's reputation and hence of the fact that he was probably recounting the tale of a lost love of his own (the boy), not even smiled. But, 'What a sad story' was what she said and then glanced at Rowan. It was no more than a glance but to him extraordinarily eloquent, and continuing to watch her it struck him that she was in love herself, that she was sustained by that, protected from all malice and unkindness and shallowness by the intensity of her commitment to the man she had chosen and the depth of her conviction that her own life was now set on a course that would bring more happiness than sorrow. The expression on her face was like that on Laura's when Laura broke it to him that she had changed her mind and was going to marry a man called Ratcliff.

He believed that what Laura must have felt for Ratcliff this girl – whose first name he did not know – felt for an unnamed man. This was so clear to Rowan that his mind played the trick of confusing her with Laura and the unknown man with Ratcliff, and he recalled quite vividly the feeling of helplessness which had underlain the stronger emotions of jealousy and anger and which had come full circle when he heard that Laura and her planter husband had become prisoners of the Japanese in Malaya.

Bronowsky called for another bottle of champagne. It was his seventieth birthday, he explained. Spending it on duty, he had equipped himself with special comforts. The salon, got up to look like that of a travelling nineteenth-century European monarch with cosmopolitan tastes, was an appropriate setting for such a celebration.

'What news of your father?' Bronowsky asked, turning the conversation from himself to Miss Layton. All Rowan knew from Bronowsky's introduction was that Miss Layton was the sister of a girl who had been married in Mirat and that she had stayed with her family at the palace guest house before and after the wedding. Her father seemed to be away – at some distance – she had not heard from him recently. There was a mother. The sister was mentioned again. Miss Layton said they were both well. She herself had just been to Calcutta. She had an aunt and uncle there whose surname was Grace.

'And the officer who was best man at your sister's wedding,' Bronowsky went on. 'Captain Merrick. Have you had news of him? He interested me considerably. I thought him an unusual man.'

Spoken casually like that in these strange but civilized surroundings the familiar name, Merrick, had the same disconcert-
ing effect as a sudden change in the intensity of light. He found
himself concentrating on certain essentials. The girl was a
stranger, not Laura. The Merrick she and Bronowsky knew need
not be his Merrick. But her manner had altered. The prominence
of bone seemed more accentuated. This, perhaps, was imaginary.
She said that it was to visit this Merrick in hospital that she had
gone to Calcutta. This Merrick, her Merrick, had been wounded
and a Captain Bingham killed. Her Merrick had tried to help
someone called Teddie and had lost an arm. He had pulled Teddie
out of a blazing truck while they were under fire. He was in for
a decoration. Captain Bingham and Teddie must be one and the
same man. She had gone to see her Merrick in hospital because
her sister was anxious to find out if there were anything they
could do.

This Merrick had been best man at her sister's wedding.
Whose best man? Teddie's? It sounded like that. If so the sister
was already widowed; still prostrate, perhaps; well in health but
not fit to travel; which might explain why she had sent her sister
all the way to Calcutta to talk to the man who had lost an arm
trying to save her husband. 'Physical courage,' Bronowsky was
saying, 'you could see he had that.' Meaning *her* Merrick. On
asking which arm Merrick had lost and being told the left the
old man was quiet for a moment. 'That's something,' he said.
'I observed him picking up bits of confetti, also stubbing a
cigarette. He was right-handed.'

How painstakingly observant. Rowan glanced up and found
Bronowsky watching him through that one appraising eye.

'You may remember the man we're speaking of? Merrick?'

'No, I don't think so.'

'I don't mean you would remember him personally. He went
into the army from the Indian Police. He figured rather promi-
nently in the case involving an English girl, in Mayapore in 1942.
The Bibighar.'

Her Merrick. His Merrick. The same man.

'Oh yes. That case.'

'He was District Superintendent. In Mirat I had a long and
interesting talk to him and found him utterly convinced that the
men he arrested were truly guilty. I myself and I suppose most

people since have come to the conclusion that they couldn't have been.'

Bronowsky was wrong. At the top of the administrative hierarchy, yes, one could say that, but even there the suspicion that Merrick had blundered was tempered by a determination not to allow it to be officially admitted. Uncorroborated and inadmissible evidence that in the case of Hari Kumar the blunder was one of a peculiarly unpleasant kind looked like having to remain a haunting burden on the consciences of a few. The irony of Merrick's act of bravery and the recommendation for a decoration was not lost on Rowan. It would justify the opinion originally held by the rank and file of the administration, and never truly altered, that in the Manners rape case Merrick had acted with that forthright avenging speed which had once made the *raj* feared and respected, and India a place where men did not merely operate a machine of law and order, but ruled and damned the consequences of ruling.

'It would have been understandable,' Bronowsky went on, 'if Merrick had begun to waver in his opinion – unless you accept that he left the police temporarily under a cloud and harboured a grudge. But he had tried for years to get into the army. He was a very ordinary man on the surface but underneath, I suspect, a man of unusual talents. Are those boys still in prison?'

'Which boys are those?' Rowan asked.

'The ones arrested, not tried, but detained, as politicals.'

'I'm afraid I don't know, Count.'

The old man smiled, possibly to convey that his inquiries were made only out of general curiosity.

'I hope they are not forgotten and just being left to rot. The provincial authorities have an obligation in this matter, surely?'

'I'm sure they are not just forgotten.'

'The Indians remember. Unfortunately not only Indians of the right sort. There is a venerable gentleman of Mayapore who last year visited Mirat and engaged in some tortuous processes of intimidation.'

Another name clicked into place in Rowan's mind, but again, as in the case of Merrick whom he had never met, a name without a face. The name was Pandit Baba but the face was Harry Coomer's – Kumar's rather, quite unrecognizable, unidentifiable with the boy Rowan had known as Coomer: hollow-cheeked, prison-pale under the brown skin: the voice was Kumar's too, describing Pandit Baba of Mayapore in that halting staccato way: *I knew him as a man my aunt hired to try to teach me an Indian language – He smelt strongly of garlic – He was very unpunctual – the lessons weren't a success.*

Between each short sentence there had been a pause, as Kumar focused on an image, probably long forgotten. The manner in which he answered the question was what first suggested to Rowan that the documents he had studied and which were damning, damning to Kumar, were not going to stand up. It was the manner of a man talking to himself as well as to the two men on the other side of a table; searching his memory for certain details to convince himself of the reality of things he knew had happened to him but had preferred not to think about for a long time. For Rowan, this careful answer to his unimportant question about Pandit Baba had been the first of a series of answers, brief spoken meditations, which drove a persistent unwavering line through recurring doubt and uncertainty, until they culminated in that shatteringly casual remark which he believed he would never forget and which had finally convinced him Kumar must be telling the truth: *It's difficult to breathe in that position. It's all you think about in the end.*

Was Pandit Baba the man Bronowsky meant, the venerable gentleman from Mayapore who had been in Mirat? What he had gathered from Kumar of the Pandit's talent for avoiding trouble and leaving his young followers to carry the can made 'tortuous process of intimidation' sound right. But whom had he intimidated?

Bronowsky had turned to Miss Layton. 'The stone,' he said, 'you recall the stone – was certainly thrown at the instigation of this slippery customer. He is one of those on whom we keep a watchful eye. I am told he has recently left Mayapore, but I am not told where he has gone or why. Forgive me, it is an uncheerful subject.' Again he looked at Rowan and then began to rise. 'And Miss Layton must eat. We shan't wait for Ahmed. In any case he's probably only going to be interested in the champagne.'

Rowan looked at his watch. Young Kasim and his mother were already half an hour late. He hoped they wouldn't cut it too fine. After half-past midnight the line to Premanagar would be closed to them by the regular service. It would be 2 a.m. before it could be opened again for the Nawab's private train.

Bronowsky leant over him, lightly touched his arm. 'We shall be able to leave on the scheduled time. Ahmed will see to it. Come.'

As he followed Miss Layton in to the dining-salon he smelt the delicate scent of cologne and pictured her dabbing her wrists and neck and forehead with it to relieve the tensions and staleness of the journey from Calcutta. She turned round and spoke, saying something complimentary about the *fin-de-siècle* splendours of the Nawab's train, but he did not quite catch it. He bent his head inquiringly. He was very close to her. He was disturbed again, but in a way that did not become clear to him until later when they were eating game pie and drinking more champagne and she was telling them about her uncle's new job in Calcutta, which was to run courses of lectures to attract wartime officers to the post-war civil administration.

She discussed the logic of this. She spoke well and clearly, in control of a line of argument that was undogmatically developed. He suspected that she was not strong on small talk, that in company she found uncongenial she might even appear shy or withdrawn. The champagne helped perhaps, and Bronowsky was a skilful and encouraging listener, capable of charming anyone out of shyness, particularly good-natured and well brought up girls for whom he presumably felt the gallant, undemanding and guarded affection of the ageing homosexual.

As she spoke Rowan saw how, indirectly, she was making a point: that the situation of these men who attended her uncle's courses – those who would succumb to the obvious temptations and those who would take a calculated risk – was in exaggerated form the same situation in which she, every English person of her generation in India, Rowan himself, found themselves. The outlook was shadowy but one could not (she implied) make this an excuse for working at half-pressure, nor for standing back from a job that was there to be done. In the course of her argument she used the word Indianization, which suggested that the one criticism of her uncle's efforts she would accept as valid was that they were not officially directed as thoughtfully as they could have been to that end. In a girl of her type such a view was unusual. It was one he shared. It had lain immature and unformed behind his youthful decision to seek a military and not a civil career in India; a decision he had regretted and sought to remedy before the war by undergoing a probationary period in the Political Department, in the hope of transferring to it permanently and applying what talent he had to the problems of the constitutionally backward Princely states. It was in these that he still saw the most satisfactory opportunities, the chance, when he was fit again, to do some useful work.

The oval table was covered in white damask, it glittered with silver. From the centre-piece – a gilded wicker basket of white and scarlet carnations set amid ferns which trembled in the currents of air from the electric fans – came the dry delicate scent of the flowers. Watching her, still thinking yes she is in love, he put his finger on what it was that disturbed him. Had Kumar after all been lying? It didn't seem possible to place the image of Kumar's Merrick alongside Miss Layton and then see them in a relationship at all, let alone one of intimacy. She had not contradicted Bronowsky when he said that most people now assumed Merrick had made a mistake but she had not agreed either. She had said nothing. But Calcutta was a long way to go even on a mission of the kind he'd gathered it was – one involving the gratitude – in other words the honour – of the family. Her aunt and uncle could have undertaken it far more easily and just as effectively.

He sat patiently, talking little, awaiting an opportunity to find out more about her. Bronowsky was now telling stories of pre-revolutionary St Petersburg, of his *émigré* life in Berlin and Paris and Monte Carlo, but omitting (as he was reputed always to omit) the most interesting tale of all, which was perhaps apocryphal; the story of his successful negotiation between the Nawab, then a young man, and the European woman whom the Nawab had followed from India in a towering Oriental passion at being deceived: a negotiation for the return of jewellery the young prince had given her as any ordinary young man might give a girl a diamond engagement ring on the assumption that she would return it if she backed out. What pressure Bronowsky had brought to bear on the woman was a matter for conjecture (Rowan had heard several versions) but when the Prince returned to Mirat without the woman, according to the story, he had the jewellery, and he also had Bronowsky for whose tact and skill he was supposed ever since to have had the deepest admiration; an admiration that was not shared by the Political Department until they could deny no longer that under Bronowsky's guidance the wild and potentially dissolute young prince had become a model of rectitude and political wisdom.

The return to the salon for coffee brought no change of subject. The old man talked on and presently Rowan noticed that Miss Layton had become anxious about the time, about what was happening on the platform. Obviously she had a connection to make. It was twenty minutes to midnight. The only train he knew of due to leave Ranpur at that hour was the nightly train up to Pankot.

'I must go, I'm afraid,' she said, putting down her cup. Bronowsky pleaded for another five minutes but she said, 'If I stay another five minutes I shall never want to go, and I've got my compartment to get unlocked.'

They stood up. Bronowsky kissed her hand, thanked her for her company, asked her to visit Mirat again one day. She said she would like that, then turned to Rowan.

'Goodbye, Captain Rowan.'

He said, 'I'll see you to your compartment.'

But Bronowsky claimed that as his own privilege and there was nothing for it but to stand aside and let her go.

Just before midnight while Bronowsky was still absent young Kasim arrived with his mother, who was in purdah. He did not introduce her to Rowan but took her straight to the adjoining carriage where there were sleeping berths. At five past midnight Bronowsky came back. There were consultations with railway officials. Rowan settled in a corner, smoked, read documents, trying to reconcentrate on the matter in hand. The train left on time. He declined to join Bronowsky and young Kasim in the dining-saloon. From behind the closed curtains he heard Bronowsky's voice. He considered going to bed but the steward had brought him brandy and he sat on, drinking this, and doubting that he would sleep in the few hours it would take to reach Premanagar where he and Ahmed were to leave the train for the rendezvous at the Circuit House with Mohammed Ali Kasim, who was probably sleepless too, keeping watch through the small hours of his last night as a prisoner in the Fort.

Rowan did not envy young Kasim the task he had undertaken, that of breaking the news to his father that Sayed had been captured fighting in the INA and that the release from the Fort was only a partial release, that he was to live now under restriction, in the protection of his kinsman the Nawab. Rowan's own part in the affair was of minor importance. Officially he was merely representing the Governor, but it was the second time Malcolm had given him a job that fell outside the ordinary limits of the duties of an aide. The first had been the examination *in camera* of Hari Kumar at the Kandipat jail, little more than three weeks before. It interested him that tonight he should have found himself face to face with two people who knew Merrick.

But how well did they know him? He sipped his brandy, closed his eyes and put his head back. The kind of knowledge he had in mind was the sort one could describe as elusive; to her, perhaps, inaccessible; as obscure as the dark side of the moon. It irked him that he could do nothing to warn her of its existence. Its possible existence. Merrick was protected by shadows of doubt that could never be dispersed, and by the iron system of the *raj* itself. If there had been a weakness, a fissure through which rumour and conjecture could flow and adversely affect Merrick's future, it had now been sealed up by the heroic act.

Rowan smiled, but at the irony of it, and – opening his eyes – found Bronowsky sitting opposite him, smiling too. The carriage, well-carpeted and sprung, ran smoothly and quietly. Bronowsky must have come in at a moment when the train was crossing points.

'Have I woken you?' he asked, raising his voice just sufficiently above the muffled rhythmic clatter for Rowan to hear him clearly across the width of the carriage. 'If so I owe an apology. Your dreams were obviously pleasant ones.'

'Satisfying recollections. I hadn't expected such a splendid supper.'

'Nor such charming company? I met her but the once, in Mirat, when they were staying there for the wedding, and tonight out there on the platform I didn't recognize her in uniform. Many girls would have been piqued, at the same time thankful not to have to stop and exchange banalities with an elderly foreigner. But Miss Layton made herself known. In Mirat I underestimated her. I marked her down as shy, even as a trifle colourless in the

way – forgive me – that only well-bred English girls can be colourless. But I now see what it was. In Mirat she was taking a back-
seat because it was her sister's wedding and the sister is extremely
pretty and vivacious. Or was. Now she is expecting a baby, and
already a widow. She and Captain Bingham had such a brief time
together. He was killed in Imphal in April. I saw the notice and
wrote to them but I knew nothing of the dramatic circumstances
until tonight.'

Rowan nodded. A pregnancy could explain why Miss Layton
rather than her sister had travelled to Calcutta.

'I've not been in Ranpur long enough to know everybody,'
he said. 'Are they a Ranpur family?'

'Yes, but they've been in Pankot since the father went abroad
on active service. He commanded the 1st Pankots in North
Africa. He's a prisoner of the Germans. Then there was her grandfather, who was a distinguished civilian, Finance Member of
Council here in Ranpur during the previous war. And her maternal grandfather, General Muir, was General Officer commanding, also in Ranpur, early in the 'twenties.'

Rowan nodded.

'And you, Captain Rowan? I see you were in Burma, presumably during the retreat. But nevertheless effectively. Or do you
affect the traditional indifference to the Military Cross and
pretend that it came with the rations?'

'It sometimes seems the only satisfactory explanation.'

'Were you wounded?'

'Only exhausted. It was a long march.'

'You have been ill?'

'I think, rather, debilitated.'

'The malignant and endemic fevers that used to cut life short
but have learnt subtler methods of invasion. Quite. Our court
physician, who doubles that far from onerous rôle with the
slightly more exacting one of Minister of Health in our little
Council of State and runs a hospital in his spare time, has a theory
that it is only the lethargy induced in Englishmen by low but
persistent tropical fevers, the lethargy and its corollary, the concentration of mental and physical resources on a particular task,
that has kept the *raj* stubbornly intact. He says that the moment
medical science finds a way of rendering the English bloodstream
and the English bowel system immune to the attacks of Indian

microbes and amoeba, then the English will all perk up, look around and wonder what on earth they are doing out here, and as a consequence roar with laughter and resign. He cites as an example of depressive and obsessive behaviour the case of General Dyer, who shot all those unarmed Indians in Amritsar in nineteen-nineteen, believing that by doing so he was saving the Empire. Habbibullah is convinced that the poor old fellow's brain was inflamed by the accumulation in the bloodstream of the poisons of chronic amoebic infection. Of course he tells me all this because he is convinced that as a European I am similarly infected, in spite of my protests that for my age I am in vigorous good health and have never shot anyone, armed or unarmed.'

'Actually I believe General Dyer had arterial sclerosis and died of it quite a few years later, but it's one of the slow diseases, isn't it? Someone did once suggest to me that it could have affected his judgment at Jallianwallah.'

'I didn't know that. I must tell Habbibullah. How nice to meet a young Englishman who knows a bit about the country's history. Dyer was another man who made a mistake, or acted controversially, and remained convinced to the end that he had been absolutely right.'

Rowan did not reply immediately. He wondered whether the allusion to Merrick was intentional.

'It surprises me a little, sir. That you should feel that. Most Englishmen who work out here have to be pretty well informed, surely. Not that knowing about Dyer is much of a test.'

Bronowsky smiled at him and leant forward, with his hands one on top of the other, supported by the ebony cane that was probably not as necessary an aid to balance as he made it appear.

'I exaggerated, yes. But one meets so many young officers who turn out to be here only because of the war and who know nothing. Mention General Dyer to them and they say, Oh, which division is he? It's different with the hard core of the professionals, which I take it you belong to. Do you have family connections with India?'

'Only on my mother's side. My father was out here at one time, but in the British Army.'

'Ah. I have been uselessly sifting my old memory for a Rowan. What was your mother's maiden name?'

'Crawley.'

The old man lowered his head, raised one finger and placed it on his chin.

'Crawley,' he repeated. 'There was a Thomas Crawley who was Resident at Kotala. He ran things very successfully during the ruler's minority. Were he and your mother related?'

'He was her brother, but considerably older. Did you know him?'

'Only by reputation. In latter days he experienced some difficulties. It was a pity. Have you had anything to do with the Political Department yourself?'

'I worked a probationary year just before the war.'

'Indeed. Your ambitions lie in that direction? But the army reclaimed you for the war no doubt. Where were you? Presumably not in Kotala?'

'No, but I did meet the Maharajah in Delhi.'

'How did that go?'

'Not at all, at first. When I told him Crawley had been my uncle he sheered off.'

'You told him voluntarily?'

'It would have been unfair not to. He was in one of his expansive moods, inviting people at random.'

'Inviting them to what?'

'One of his famous parties at the palace in Kotala.'

'That must have been a temptation. To see the place where your uncle spent the best part of his working life.'

'Yes, it was. My mother lived with him at the Residency for two or three years before she went home to get married. I'd seen all the photographs and heard all the tales about how it was in those days, and quite a bit about what happened after the ruler came of age. But I felt I'd only get the best out of a visit if I went openly as Tommy Crawley's nephew.'

'You said the meeting with the Maharajah didn't go well at first, that he sheered off. Did he change his mind?'

'Yes but I don't know how quickly. He must have kept tabs on me through his grapevine, though, because a couple of months later when I was touring with the agent for a small group of states north of Kotala I got a letter from him inviting me to call. It was a bit of a poser because it meant getting clearance from the department as well as from the Resident in Ranikot.'

'Why Ranikot?'

'When Uncle Tommy left Kotala the agency was transferred to the group that came under Ranikot. The Resident there put an assistant in at Kotala but everything had to go through him.'

'That can't have pleased the Maharajah.'

'It wasn't meant to. By regrouping his state and severing his direct link with the Crown Representative, the department thought he'd be upset enough to withdraw the accusations he'd made, that my uncle was interfering in private and state matters to an intolerable degree, not only withdraw but beg to have him sent back. I think they were looking forward to telling him it was too late and were rather surprised when he made no complaint.'

'Why too late?'

'Well my uncle was getting on and the strain of their constant bickering had ruined his health. My mother came out to see him in Simla while he was on sick leave and tried to persuade him to retire at once and not wait the two or three years he still had to go. She wasn't at all surprised when we met her off the boat and told her Uncle Tommy had died while she was on the passage home. The Maharajah wrote to her offering his sympathies. She'd known him well when he was a boy but didn't feel up to sending him more than a formal acknowledgement. When I was coming out, though, she said that if ever I bumped into young Kotala I should give him her salaams.'

'And did you?'

'Yes. He was very touched.'

'You accepted his invitation, then, in spite of the red tape. Good.'

'I'm afraid I couldn't. The officer I was touring with was dead against it, and actually a private trip on the side would have been a bit much for him to agree to because I was dogsbodying for him in a fairly hectic programme and supposed to be learning the ropes. So I wrote begging off. But I gave him my mother's message and said I hoped there'd be another opportunity of meeting. A week later he turned up at our next stopping place. He'd driven more than a hundred miles.'

'Was he so anxious to apologize for his treatment of your uncle?'

'He apologized for sheering off. I was afraid of the other thing too. I'd worked it out years before, from all the things my mother told me or let slip that the fault had really been my uncle's. I think she'd reached the same conclusion. As you said, he virtually ran the state while the prince was a minor and apart from that they'd formed an extremely close and affectionate father-and-son relationship. When the prince came of age all that should have stopped. My uncle should have stood back and been content to let the young man assume full responsibility, but he made the error of continuing to treat him as a minor, of forgetting that he was a ruling Hindu prince. And, of course, that must have led to a situation in which the prince's relatives and his state officials made it clear that they despised him for letting the Resident browbeat him and that if he had an ounce of real spirit he'd start showing my uncle where to get off. Unfortunately he did that in a young man's over-exuberant way, spending money wildly on personal extravagances, drinking too much and womanizing, all the things that gave my uncle the opportunity to press his criticisms. In fact after a year or so you only needed evidence of cruelty and corruption and complete disregard for the welfare of his poorer subjects to have had a case to depose him.'

'And there was no such evidence.'

'I imagine the only harm the Maharajah ever did to anyone was to himself. And I think he felt that. I'd say it still rankled. I got the impression he would really have liked to be abstemious and upright, all the things my uncle no doubt represented to him as virtues when he was growing up, hated being unable to resist other temptations and blamed my uncle for that as well. Well as I say he apologized for sheering off when we first met but when it got to the point where it was obvious one of us ought to mention Uncle Tommy he became very edgy. He'd driven all that way so I felt the ball was in my court, but I was reluctant to play it. I'm ashamed to admit I thought there might be a price-tag on the whole thing, that the idea was to soften me up by a display of magnanimity or remorse so that I'd agree to put a word in for him over some scheme he might have going.'

'Well, you'd been in the country just long enough to suspect he might think you new enough to try it on. How did you play the ball?'

'I didn't. I shirked it. So just before he got into the car to go back he confronted me. It's the only word. Have you ever met him?'

'No. Not the maharajah. We've never been to Kotala and he's not in the Chamber. Insufficient guns.'

'Quite tall. Very plump. He uses scent and wears rings. Diamonds mostly. There was even a small jewelled cockade in the centre of his turban. I think you could call Kotala the walking effete-looking Indian potentate of popular English imagination. It isn't an image that conveys what *we* mean by dignity whatever it may convey to Indians, but ever since that day I've tried not to prejudge from appearances. I don't think anything could have been more dignified than his parting speech. He said he was glad to have met Tommy Crawley's nephew, trusted we'd meet again and have the opportunity to build a relationship on the friendly basis he hoped we'd established, but that this wouldn't be possible from his point of view unless I knew and accepted that although he had loved my uncle as a boy and had happy memories of those times, he had had a terrible time with him later, which he would never forget and could never forgive. He said, "When I was young your uncle was always saying, when you know you are in the right, fight for it, never give in, never retreat and never retract. My opinion is that in that matter I was right and he was wrong. If I regret anything it is the nature of the weapons he forced me to use and the nature of the balm he forced me to resort to to heal the wounds he inflicted." I was so impressed that when he'd gone I went straight to my room and wrote it down.'

'A prepared speech,' Bronowsky said, 'but effective. I should think sincere. Yes. Very English in its sentiment, but of course very Indian too. He was testing your mettle and temper as well as getting something off his chest. What did you say?'

'The first thing that came into my head. Afterwards I realized I was lucky he hadn't made a speech like that when I first met him. In the interval I'd been around and cottoned on to the system, the one that calls for the ruler to stand his ground and you yours but for you both to open up the ground between without committing yourself to occupy it. I said I personally knew very little of the quarrel between them except that my uncle had been deeply affected by it, had presumably felt as strongly about the correctness of his own behaviour, that I'd always regretted my uncle's career should have ended on such a note but would regret it far more had it seemed now that their differences after all hadn't been so serious that they couldn't somehow have been overcome, and was most grateful to His Highness for speaking so frankly and relieving my mind of any such supposition.'

'Were you alone with him?'

'Yes, why?'

'A pity. If your superior officer had heard that, I imagine you'd have received a most favourable report.'

'Actually I'm not at all sure it didn't raise a doubt about my fitness for political work. I was questioned pretty closely about what we'd said to each other and was made to feel I might do better if I applied myself more conscientiously to routine matters.'

'Young men with an aptitude usually excite caution rather than enthusiasm. It has ever been so. But you will probably survive. I trust so. If you have ambitions there still. Do you?'

Rowan smiled. He said, quoting, ' "The body's fever, dying like a fire, Sheds little light upon the heart's concerns." '

'Ah,' Bronowsky said after a moment. 'Gaffur. But a somewhat more elegant translation than the one in the existing English version. The fading fever in the blood is like a dying fire, de dum de dum etcetera. But how apt. Gaffur, recovering from a bout of malaria or dysentery. Is that other version your own? Yes? Then we have one vice in common, although my own translations from the Urdu come more under the heading of extra-curricular activities for Nawab Sahib. Of course you know the Gaffur connection?'

'He was court poet in Mirat, in the eighteenth century.'

'And connected to the ruling family. A Kasim. Nawab Sahib had never read Gaffur in English. But he has many exquisite volumes in the original. Whenever people feel they should give him a gift that shows forethought but not extravagance they usually hit upon the poems of his distinguished ancestor. For instance, the Laytons presented him with a copy when he offered them the hospitality of the guest house at the time of the wedding. But the habit is rarer in English people than in Indians. He was very pleased and expressed the wish to learn some of his favourite verses in English. He was horrified when he read Colonel Harvey-Fortescue's Victorian effusions and since then I have had to try my own hand. I shan't assume the false modesty of the complacent amateur and pretend I'm not highly satisfied with some of the results. In fact I've become quite addicted to the exercise of this latent skill and sometimes fancy myself quite a little Pushkin. But it is hard on the eye. Having only one it is sensible to take care of it, but difficult to remember to do so. One adjusts so easily to such a slight impediment and seldom thinks of oneself as handicapped, unless one sees or hears of someone in the same or worse condition.'

The stories of Bronowsky's blind left eye and lame left leg ranged from the possible to the scurrilously unlikely. It was Rowan's chance to hear one of them and his chance to approach the subject of disability, the subject of lost limbs, the subject of Merrick. A chance again deliberately contrived? It was worth taking up. He realized how much he was enjoying talking to the old wazir and it pleased him to think that the conversation was no more than a ritual, a courtly circumnavigation of a subject they were both interested in but both too skilled to raise directly. Each had stood his ground. The space between was wide open. One could step on to it now without giving much away.

'I notice,' Rowan said, 'that the blind eye and the lame leg are both on the left side. Does that mean there was a common cause or is it a coincidence?'

'Oh, common. And common enough in those days. St Petersburg. A makeshift bomb. An explosive little incident at dusk on the drive from the Winter Palace.' Bronowsky leant back in his chair. 'An explosion like a scarlet flower in black foliage, thrusting out of the snow. A little summer miracle in winter. That and the pressure. One did not recall a noise. Perhaps the snow muffled it. Such are one's recollections. Later the discomfort. And the strange remote satisfaction of knowing it was no worse. No limb lost. A mere eye. A bad leg. Growing pleasure. The distinction of a limp and an eye-patch. The poor young fellow who threw the bomb was the only fatal casualty. He mistook me for Another. I made a callous joke. That now I had only one eye to weep with and mourn his useless little death. But that was to disguise less insensitive feelings. I thought, How strange. He did not know me, nor I him, but all through his life, from birth, for twenty years, without realizing it he had been moving towards me, step by inevitable step, and I had been waiting for him, preparing to set out on that drive through the snow, to keep an appointment, wrapped in my furs, well muffled, well disguised, so that he would not recognize me at the very last moment as the agent of his death. I saw his photograph. They had it, of course. And one from the morgue of his remains. They showed me this too, as if it would please me. Extraordinarily his face was unmarked. Very pale against the blackness of his hair and the wispy adolescent growth of beard on cheeks and chin. A dark young man, I thought, of random destiny and private passions. It was a revelation. As I looked at the photograph I realized that *he* could have been *my* death, that perhaps fate had decreed this, but had wound the machinery up wrong and was now aghast at the error. It struck me that, well, I must watch out, that perhaps even now a birth was taking place in some remote village, to rectify things. It seemed to me that fate would work this way, that the destiny so apparently random must be shaped even so from the beginning, that I had at least twenty years' grace before I must keep the next appointment, this time with a young man who would complete the task. I pictured his life. How it would be. Not privileged like mine but harsh and sombre, so that his heart would grow into a habit of sadness which it pleased me to think of as also a sadness for me, because of what he must do that he did not know. I fell a little in love with him. And there were times when things were not good with me that I wished to hasten the consummation. This was in nineteen hundred. When I left Russia nearly twenty years later it was with the feelings almost of a deserter. By then, you see, he would have been in the prime of youth with only a few years to wait. In Berlin and in Paris I watched out for him, at first only among the young men of our emigration but then among young Germans too and young Frenchmen, because I realized that the appointed agent need not after all be of Russian nationality and that one of fate's little jokes might be that I should think myself secure merely because I had crossed a frontier. Even in India I used to watch.'

'But not any longer?'

'Oh, sometimes. India particularly is rich in possibilities. It is easy here to be a marked man. I spoke of this to our friend Merrick during the interesting conversation I had with him in Mirat.'

'Merrick? Oh, you mean the Mayapore case. Miss Layton's friend.'

'When I say spoke of it I mean spoke in general to him of being a marked man, of the part played by these young men of random destiny and private passions. I did not mention my own case. Mine after all is illusory. His was real. He had been a marked man ever since Mayapore. Persecuted even, but in subtle ways to remind him that he was not forgotten, that his transfer into the army had not shaken off whoever it was, whoever it is, who wished him to be under no delusion, but know that his actions in Mayapore will have to be answered for one day. To give him that uncomfortable impression, anyway. My own feeling was that these people were less interested in retribution than in the use that could be made of a controversial figure, such as Merrick's, to stir young men up to create trouble, to achieve some particular political or religious objective.'

'People like the venerable gentleman from Mayapore? The one you said was in Mirat last year engaged in some tortuous process of intimidation?'

The train passed over a network of points, rocking gently. The lights dimmed, then brightened, flickered out, came on again. In the very brief spasm of darkness it seemed to Rowan that Bronowsky had altered position. But there would not have been time for him to do so unobserved: a second or two. But he looked different. Rowan could not say in what way. It was strange.

'The venerable gentleman, yes.' Even his voice had altered, it seemed, but the whole thing must be a trick of the mind, or something to do with a change in the pressure in the carriage. Perhaps the country through which they were passing had altered. Or someone had opened a door or a window further down the coach.

'You mentioned a stone being thrown. Thrown at this man Merrick, did you mean?'

'Quite so.'

'At the instigation of this slippery customer?'

'How accurately you recall my words. Let us simplify things for each other. His name was Pandit Baba.'

'And he went all the way from Mayapore to Mirat to incite someone to throw a stone at poor Mr Merrick?'

Bronowsky laughed. He said, 'Precisely. Such a gesture would also strike me as excessive. The pandit, I think, would not expend energy on such an inconsiderable thing. Which was why

I took note. It is too long a story, the story of the stone and Mr Merrick. In itself irrelevant and in its wider context of concern only to me, in so far as it concerns me as well as our chief of police to protect Mirat from these tiresome infiltrations.'

'I'm not quite with you.'

'When you people in British India clamp down, when you have a sweep and clap subversives and firebrands into jails, proscribe political parties or in any way make things unhealthy for Indians who stand up to you, then those who escape your nets go to ground. And where better than in the self-governing princely states where your formal writ does not so easily run? When you had that grand round-up in nineteen-forty-two, at the time of the Quit India campaign, I do not know how many activists, terrorists, anarchists, militant communalists or simple Congress extremists hitched up their dhotis and hot-footed it to places like Mirat. I know which of them turned up *in* Mirat, because I saw to it that they quickly hitched their dhotis up again and hot-footed it back across our borders.'

'Your chief of police must be very efficient.'

Bronowsky glanced away, smiling to himself. 'I suppose one or two escaped our combined vigilance. But we were very vigilant. It is wise to be. The states offer a wide variety of opportunities for political intrigue and some states I think deserve what they get in that way. But I will not have political or communal disturbances stirred up in Mirat by people who do not belong to Mirat. Both the major Indian political parties have been guilty of attempting it in the past twenty years. I need not elaborate. Quite apart from the fact that Nawab Sahib is by definition an autocrat he is also a Muslim. The majority of his subjects are Hindu. My life in Mirat has been spent trying to ensure that the two communities have equal opportunities, which was not always so, that they live in amity and have reason to be perfectly content to live as subjects of the Nawab, and do not hanker after the democratic millennium promised by Gandhiji on the one hand or the theistic paradise-state on earth envisaged by Mr Jinnah on the other.'

For a while he was silent, looking now at the shoe on his left foot, which was thrust out, the heel on the thick carpet that helped to muffle the drumming of the wheels. He said, 'Eventually, of course, there can be no separate future for us, and latterly

I have been directing my thoughts to the problem of how best to ensure a smooth and advantageous transition.'

'No separate future?'

'When the British finally go. No freedom separate from India's freedom. No separate future for Mirat nor for any of the states, with the possible exception of the largest and most powerful such as Hyderabad or those whose territories merge into each other and who might combine administratively. The alternative is Balkanization, which of course even if permitted would be disastrous.'

'There is an obligation to the princes on our part. I should say that it's been made clear often enough that we recognize it.'

'Well. Come. Come. You are all going, aren't you? One day. When? In five years? Ten years? Even five is not long. Perhaps I shan't live to see it. On the whole I hope not, because when you go the princes will be abandoned. In spite of all your protestations to the contrary. They will be abandoned. I have told Nawab Sahib so. He pretends not to believe it. I show him the map. I point to the tiny isolated yellow speck that is Mirat and to the pink areas that surround it which are the provinces directly ruled by the British. Since India passed under the Crown, I say to him, you have relied on the pink bits to honour the treaty that allows the yellow speck to exist. But you cannot have a treaty with people who have disappeared and taken the crown with them. The treaty will not be torn up but it will have no validity. It will be a piece of paper. A new treaty will have to be made with the people who have taken the pink parts over from the British. You will have to negotiate a new treaty with Mr Gandhi and Mr Nehru. You can forget Mr Jinnah because even if he gets Pakistan it will be so far away from you that it will be meaningless. So you will have to bargain for the continuing existence of the yellow speck which is Mirat with Mr Nehru and the Congress High Command. Nawab Sahib smiles. He can see it as clearly as I can see it – the form such bargaining might take. But he smiles also at what he likes to persuade himself is my simplicity. No, Dmitri, he says, we have supplied the British with money and men in two world wars. And there are over five hundred little yellow specks, and some not so little. The British are pledged to protect our rights and our privileges and our authority. I nod my head. I say, this is true, Nawab Sahib. But they are pledged as well one day to hand over *their* rights and privileges and authority to Mr Gandhi and Mr Nehru. They are pledged in two directions but can only go in one. Nawab Sahib smiles again. That, Dmitri, is where they are so cunning. He does not say what cunning he sees. He knows that if he puts it into words his illusion of it will collapse. So the words will not come. But in his mind he tells himself that the pledge to Mr Gandhi and to Mr Nehru cannot be fulfilled because of the pledge to the princes, or that it can only be fulfilled if the princes agree that it should be and that the princes will only agree if their territories are first secured to them in perpetuity. Therefore, my dear Captain Rowan, with Nawab Sahib adopting this reverent attitude to his piece of paper, you will appreciate that I am very much alone in this business of working and planning for the most advantageous position for my prince. And because I need peace and quiet to work and plan I do not welcome venerable gentle-men from Mayapore, or any of their like from wheresoever, who seek to cause the sort of unrest which our future masters will point to as proof that Nawab Sahib's subjects groan under the yoke of an iron, archaic dictatorship. A Muslim dictatorship at that. I do not welcome venerable gentlemen from Mayapore, because in their wake, in their footsteps, springing up like sharp little teeth, are these dark young men of random destiny and private passions – destinies and passions that can be shaped and directed to violent ends.'

Rowan nodded, leaving Bronowsky to guess what opinion he himself held about the future of the states. Since he had accepted Malcolm's invitation to officiate at the transfer of Mohammed Ali Kasim to the protection of the Nawab, he had been checking on Mirat's status. There was no political agent actually resident in the state. Mirat's relationship with the crown was conducted through the Resident in Gopalakand and this was old Robert Conway, whom Rowan knew only by reputation. It had sur-prised him a bit when Lady Manners mentioned him as an old friend of hers. Holding a high opinion of Lady Manners he decided there was probably more warmth in Conway than people usually admitted, but even she had described him as an unemotional man with rigid views. Bronowsky would not find it easy to communicate with him, nor – Rowan imagined – was Conway a man who would encourage Bronowsky in what he called his search for the most advantageous position for his prince. From what Rowan heard of Conway he suspected the Nawab would be encouraged to believe that he would be abandoned only over Conway's dead body and the dead bodies of every member of the Political Department.

'Well,' he said, 'let's hope the venerable gentleman stays clear. Some other time you must tell me about the stone. It does seem a bit far-fetched to go to all that trouble. I suppose he's safe now.'

'Who?'

'Miss Layton's friend – Merrick.'

'Frankly I doubt he was ever in much danger. Harming a white man in this country is a hazardous occupation. But I agree he's probably safe from further persecution, if only because he's probably long since served his most useful purpose from Pandit Baba's point of view. His own purpose – well – that is another matter. And who can say what is the purpose of a man like that?'

Rowan stretched. 'Perhaps just to do his job.'

'Few men have aims as simple as that.'

'Are he and Miss Layton old friends?'

'As I remember they met only at the wedding. He wasn't even a close friend of the bridegroom. What you might call a last-minute substitute for a best man who was ill. No one knew he was the Merrick in the Bibighar Gardens case until the wedding-day. He'd kept it dark, but it came out then because of the stone and because I identified him at once directly I heard this Captain Merrick had been in the Indian Police. The stone, by the way, hit the poor bridegroom. Why do you ask?'

'Only that she seemed such a nice girl and that it would be tough on her if they're committed to one another.'

'Committed to one another?'

'Engaged, for instance.'

'Tough on her because of his lost left arm?'

'She didn't strike me as the sort of girl who would back out, and it would be hard on her, wouldn't it?'

'Oh, I agree. I doubt that Miss Layton would back out. But such a thing hadn't occurred to me.' With the ebony cane clasped in both hands he raised it to his chin and put his head back, gazed at the ornate ceiling. 'Committed. Such a thing hadn't occurred to me. There would hardly have been time for such a relationship to develop when they were in Mirat and no

opportunity for it to have done so since, except by correspondence. No. I doubt there could have been time for a relationship
of that nature even to begin, even if everything else had been
normal.'

Tapping his chin with the silver knob of the cane Bronowsky
continued to contemplate the view above his head. Rowan
waited.

'But I see why it might occur to you,' Bronowsky went on.
'That she was just back from a long journey undertaken for
the reasons she gave but also for her own private emotional
satisfaction.'

The ceiling ceased to interest him. He looked at Rowan but
still tapped his chin.

'Let us hope you are wrong. It would be a somewhat one-
sided affair, I should say. Unless, in Mirat, I was mistaken, which
is always possible.'

'Mistaken in what?'

'In my assumption that he didn't really like women.'

Rowan said nothing.

'It is what makes the Mayapore case interesting. It was interesting from the beginning but in a rather cliché-ridden way. Well,
there was this girl, this poor Miss Manners, recently out from
England, untutored in and unsympathetic to the rigid English
social system here. Good-natured and intelligent – a little like
Miss Layton but in comparison with her an innocent abroad, so
far as India was concerned. For a time she lives with her aunt
Lady Manners in Rawalpindi, a liberal-minded old lady whose
husband once governed Ranpur and incurred the hostility of the
die-hards with his pro-Indian policies. Nowadays the old lady
has almost more Indian friends than she has British, they say.
Her niece, this Miss Manners, is invited by one of them, a Lady
Chatterjee, to stay with her in Mayapore where the social structure is even tighter and more provincial than in Rawalpindi. And
in Mayapore she becomes friendly with an Indian boy. Not
one who moves in the small official circle of socially acceptable
Indians but one out of the black town. Cliché number one. The
princess and the pauper, but with a racial variation on the theme.
And then there is cliché number two: the boy although now a
pauper is really a gentleman, brought up in England entirely and
educated at an English public school. A family misfortune alone

accounts for his presence on the wrong side of the river, from which from time to time he ventures into the cantonment in the capacity of a humble reporter for the local English-language newspaper. The friendship with Miss Manners ripens but almost clandestinely because there are so few places where she can go that he can go. But she is impatient of these artificial barriers, so they are noticed together. She is warned against the association. She ignores the warning but the friendship is now under a strain. In other words, cliché number four. And then, what really is the boy after? Cliché number five. The warning proves more than merited, or so it would seem. One night she is attacked and assaulted. She swears she did not see her attackers. Later she swears that although she did not see them she knows who they were not – not in other words the kind of boys who have been arrested who of course include her young Indian friend. Who in Mayapore doubts though, or doesn't guess who led them? Certainly the head of the police does not doubt. Within an hour of her return home after the assault her boyfriend and his companions were in custody. But now comes cliché number six. The head of the police himself has a regard for Miss Manners of an even tenderer kind than he would feel for any girl of his own race who gets into trouble. How tender a regard? No one is sure but it is whispered that he loves her or loved her once and was spurned. He does not actually deny it. In confidence he will tell you that his erstwhile regard for Miss Manners made it that much more difficult for him to keep a properly detached view and ensure that all his actions are performed dispassionately in the service of justice. Such manly frankness is appealing. If in the past there were people who had marked him down as not quite pukka, as not really out of what you English call the top drawer, they admit that in this business his behaviour has been impeccable as well as energetic. So the story seems to go, proving yet again that if fact is no stranger than fiction it is just as predictable. But did the story go like that? I think not quite. When I met him I talked to him at length and as we talked I got this other impression that Miss Manners had never really interested him at all, that he had scarcely noticed her until her association with the Indian boy had begun, and that he could not avoid noticing her then because he had had his eye on the young man for a long time. The young man was an obsession, an absolute fixation.

Perhaps even Mr Merrick does not fully appreciate all the possible reasons why.' Bronowsky paused. 'Perhaps that is cliché number seven. At least in life if not in tales. Cliché number eight is that with a job to do in a few hours from now you should get some rest. I will ask the steward to wake you at 4.15, shall I?'

'Thank you.' Rowan reached for his briefcase.

'I hope it isn't only good manners that have kept you up. For me sleep is a waste of time, it being my seventieth birthday, although strictly speaking that was yesterday. I've enjoyed our talk. I shall cheat for a few hours more, drink some more champagne and read Pushkin.'

As Rowan got up Bronowsky said, 'You'd better disregard what I said, unless the question of those boys ever crops up at Government House. I hate to think of them lying forgotten in some inhospitable jail, if they were innocent. I do hope you are wrong, by the way.'

'Wrong?'

'About Miss Layton's reasons for going so many miles to see the wounded hero. I believe he has a number of admirable qualities but none of them strikes me as likely to promote the cause of anyone else's happiness. Not even his own. He is one of your hollow men. The outer casing is almost perfect and he carries it off almost to perfection. But, of course, it is a casing he has designed. This loss he has sustained – the left arm – even this fits. If he regrets the loss, presently he will see that he has lost nothing or anyway gained more in compensation. What an interesting thought. I am tempted to say that had he not suffered the loss he might one day have been forced to invent it.'

Rowan smiled. 'To the extent of removing part of a limb?'

Bronowsky laughed.

'But absolutely!'

For a while he gazed at Rowan and then said sedately: 'I speak metaphorically, naturally.'

V

Bathed and dressed Rowan went back to his sitting-room. Jaiprakash poured him the second routine whisky-soda, the one he used to wash down the evening dose of pills. He picked up the telephone and asked for the Pankot number. The operator said he would ring him back when a priority call on the Pankot line had been cleared: probably in ten minutes. He asked to be put through to the mess steward. He ordered a tray and a tankard of beer. He did not feel like going into the dining-room. He then rang the signals office and checked how long he had to get a package down to go in the night bag to Area Headquarters in Pankot. The answer was an hour and a half to be on the safe side.

The telephone rang almost as soon as he'd put down the receiver. He picked it up again. Through atmospherics he heard the male operator in the exchange downstairs saying that the Pankot number was on the line and distantly a woman's voice saying 'Hello? Hello?' The crackling ceased abruptly. The con-nection sounded a good one. He asked to speak to Miss Sarah Layton.

'Speaking.'

'Sarah, this is Nigel. Nigel Rowan.'

'Oh, hello.'

'I got your letter.'

'That was quick.'

'I've done what you asked.'

'Already? How good of you.'

'I'm sorry to ring. Is it inconvenient?'

'No, of course not.'

But she sounded a little guarded.

'I thought I should let you know what I intend to do. If it's all right just say yes. It was only a matter of collecting some envelopes and a package. I'll get them done up and sent in the bag tonight to Area Headquarters. I don't think there's anything important. The Reverend Mother said you may decide to throw the lot away. I've rung just to make sure you knew to be on the look-out for them. If I mark the package private and personal will it reach you without any problems?'

'Yes, that would be fine. I'm awfully grateful.'

'She's nice, isn't she? The Reverend Mother.'

'Yes. Just vague on the phone.'

'How are things?'

'Pretty good.'

'I'm longing to hear about the party. The one in Bombay where the drinks got locked up.'

'Oh, the Maharanee's.' She laughed, sounding relieved to get off the subject of Miss Batchelor. 'If there's such a person. She didn't put in an appearance.'

'Which Maharanee was she supposed to be?'

'I'm not sure Count Bronowsky ever told us. He referred to her as Aimee.'

'Aimee? Was this at a place called Sea Breezes on the Marine Drive?'

'Yes. Do you know her?'

'She's the ex-Maharanee of Kotala. Has Bronowsky known her long?'

'I got that impression.'

'The old Machiavelli.'

'Why?'

'We talked about the Maharajah in June last year, the night you and I first met. He never mentioned knowing the ex-wife. Kotala was the Maharajah I was telling you about a few weeks ago. The one my uncle had the trouble with.'

'Really? I wish I'd met her.'

'She's someone I try to avoid.'

'But you've been to the flat in Bombay?'

'No, only to her place in Delhi. I remember the name Sea Breezes because she was always sending notes from there when I was in Bombay with HE last Christmas. I thought Sea Breezes rather funny because she has a reputation for being hermetically sealed-in wherever she goes.'

'The flat was breezy enough.'

'Perhaps the room she was hiding in wasn't. She told me in Delhi she hated fresh air, light, the sound of doorbells and talking on the telephone and that her idea of true repose would be to have a magic wand to conjure up a party and make it disappear when she was fed up with it. You were lucky only having the drinks locked up. When she was Kotala's wife they say she kept a tame leopard and made it snarl to order. It could empty the palace of unwanted guests in one minute flat. When it bit one of his favourite girlfriends he sued for divorce. He wanted to cite the leopard as co-respondent but decided not to because it was a female leopard and people said he'd only be able to accuse it of alienation of affections.'

'Oh, Nigel.'

He smiled. 'It's true.'

'You're making me think your uncle was right after all. Actually she did have a sort of leopard, but he was on our side and warned us about the drinks being locked up. So we beat a dignified retreat before it happened. He was rather nice. His name was Perron.'

'Perron? Don't tell me he was a sergeant in the French Army.'

'He had two different uniforms, but he was a sergeant in both of them, yes.'

'Whatever is she up to? Raising an army? Anyway she's got her history mixed up. She's a Rajput not a Mahratta. The Rajputs weren't a bit keen on Sergeant Perron.'

'You know all about him too?'

'The Perron who succeeded De Boigne.'

'His real name was Pierre-Cuiller.'

'Was it? I don't think I knew that. Oddly enough we had a Perron at school. I was told to chastise him once for persistent slackness at games. The consensus of House opinion was that his incompetence on the playing field was a deliberate exhibition of eccentricity and the unpleasant task of persuading him to conform fell to me.'

'You mean you had to cane him?'

'I'm afraid so.'

'He was in Bank's, then?'

'That's right.' Rowan hesitated. 'I don't remember telling you which house I was in. What are you laughing at?'

'The picture of you caning Perron.'

'He thought it was rather funny too.'

'Did it improve his games?'

'No. He warned me it wouldn't. Actually I'm exaggerating. Violence wasn't necessary. I was supposed to apply corrective methods but he and I decided the best thing would be to talk it over. He told me he found team sports awfully depressing, all that waiting around at cricket on the one hand and what he called the incomprehensible hurly-burly of football on the other. Fortunately I'd discovered through another source that he rowed quite a bit during the holidays. We weren't a rowing school but there was a local canoeing and sculling club in the town so I got permission for him to join and that suited him down to the ground because it got him out of the school and off by himself on the river. When I last saw him he would have been about seventeen, but nearly six feet tall and with shoulders like an ox.'

'When was that, Nigel?'

'The same occasion I was telling you about at the party Hugh Thackeray took us to – when I visited the school between finishing at Sandhurst and coming out here.'

'And watched Hari Kumar playing cricket?'

'Yes.'

'He said he didn't remember Kumar.'

'Who said he didn't remember Kumar?'

'Sergeant Perron.'

'Sergeant Perron?'

'The Sergeant Perron who was at the Maharanee's party. The one who tipped us off about the drinks being locked up. I was only joking when I called him the Maharanee's leopard. He's a sergeant in Field Security. He came back with us and met my father and they talked about Bank's and Coote's. He remembered you but pretended not to remember Kumar.'

'A sergeant in Field Security?'

'At the Maharanee's he was a sergeant in Education. But when I first met him he was in Field Security.'

'You've met him twice?'

'Twice on the same day.'

'In one day he switched from Field Security to Education?'

'Education was only a disguise. I suppose I oughtn't to talk about it on the phone.' She sounded amused.

'Sarah, what *are* you talking about?'

'About your old friend Perron.'

'It can't be the same one.'

'Well he was over six foot. He looked like an oarsman. He remembered you. He remembered your first name. In fact he remembered you quite clearly. And still being only a sergeant is rather eccentric so obviously he hasn't changed. Does that convince you?'

'But he didn't remember Coomer.'

'Pretended not to.'

'Why should he do that?'

'I think probably Ronald could tell you.'

'Ronald? Ronald Merrick?' After a moment he said, 'Where does he fit in?'

'Sergeant Perron is going to work for him.' She added, 'I got the impression he wasn't very keen.'

'What made you think so?'

'The look on his face whenever Ronald ordered him to do anything. In fact I think he'll try to get out of it. I'm sorry. He was nice. He would have been an asset in that particular sphere. I'd better let you get on. I may get down to Ranpur again in a few weeks because daddy says he may be going. I'll let you know shall I? Unless you've gone by then. Have you had any news?'

'No. None.'

'It was awfully good of you to see the nuns. You must have been pretty busy if the *daftar* here is anything to go by. They've been at sixes and sevens ever since they heard Mr Kasim's coming up to attend his old secretary's funeral.'

'Oh, why, particularly?'

'In case he takes the opportunity to make some sort of political announcement. There are quite a lot of people crowding in. Some are already camping out near the station.'

'Old Mahsood was a Pankot man.'

'But the police think it's M A K they're coming to see.'

'A popular demonstration or just taking *darshan*?'

'Taking *darshan*, we hope. Has there been any trouble in Ranpur?'

'Just a few crowds, directly it leaked that he was on his way from Mirat with old Mahsood's coffin.'

'Is Ahmed with him?'

'Not to my knowledge. Isn't he still in Bombay?'

'That was a week ago. The police here think it's going to be more like a political meeting than a Muslim funeral. They've drafted in men from Nansera.'

'I don't think they need worry. He was very devoted to old Mahsood. Bringing the body home is a mark of respect, I should say. If not he wouldn't have been at such pains to tell us what he was doing and ask for what amounts to official protection from excessive curiosity. That's probably the real reason why there are extra police.'

'Oh well. So much for that rumour. But people here are so used to nothing happening they'll probably be disappointed when it doesn't. I shan't be. It suits father as it is.'

'I'm glad he's better. Is there anything else I can do for you?
Anything for your father, for instance?'

'Nothing I can think of, but thank you.'

'Let me know if there is. I'm afraid I've been keeping you.
Look after yourself.'

'And you. Oh, and remember me to Hugh Thackeray.'

'I will.'

When they had rung off he collected together the envelope and
package the Reverend Mother had given him. It seemed absurd
to think of her actually having them in her hands tomorrow
morning. The package, which contained something hard like a
book and something soft, some sort of material, was inscribed:
In the event of my death: Dear Sarah. The envelope, inscribed by
a different hand, probably the Reverend Mother's, was marked
'Oddments' and seemed to contain papers and other envelopes.

He put both the package and the envelope into a large manila
envelope, sealed it and addressed it to Sarah at Area Headquarters,
Pankot. The telephone rang. He picked it up immediately,
thinking she might have remembered something important and
rung back.

'Nigel?' It was Hugh Thackeray on the internal line.

'Oh, hello. Well. How was Delhi?'

'Like Delhi. More to the point, how is Pankot? I've been trying to get you but they said you were talking to Pankot. The fair
Miss Layton, would it be?'

Hugh was still very young.

'It would. She asked to be remembered to you.'

'Very nice of her but quite unnecessary. I was thinking about
her anyway. On your behalf, I hasten to add. What are you
doing?'

'Nothing right now. I'm off-duty.'

'I know. But you're not under the weather, are you?'

'Not in the least. Why?'

'They tell me you've ordered a tray.'

'And a tankard of beer.'

'They kept that dark. I was a bit worried. I imagined something more on invalid lines. HE would like a word.'

'Right.'

'I mean over here in the study. Shall I tell him five minutes?'

'Yes, I'll come right over.' He hesitated. 'Any news?'

'What news did you have in mind?

'From Tokyo, say?'

'We think they're still agonizing about how to surrender unconditionally on condition that the Emperor remains sacrosanct. I can't think why he doesn't commit *hara-kiri*.'

'I don't think sons of heaven can. Any suggestions about which subject I could usefully mull over on the way down?'

A moment's silence. Then: 'M A K perhaps?'

'Right.'

He replaced the phone. He had hoped for something else, something more personal. He called Jaiprakash, told him where he was going. He took the envelope down to the signals office and then crossed over to the east wing. Here there were several people in the main hall: General Crawford and his aide – a slim and handsome Sikh in a pale blue turban – the Deputy Inspector-General of Police; old MacRoberts, the senior Member of Council, with Henderson of the Finance Department and his pale and angular wife who caught his eye and smiled; Mrs Saparawala and Doctor Bannerji, the Member for Education, and another fellow aide of Rowan's, Bunny Mehta. Some of them had been at Ranagunj airfield to meet the Governor. All except Bunny were on their way home, awaiting cars, calm among the servants who were coming and going intermittently. Rowan made for the narrow corridor to the private staircase: a spiral enclosed by wrought-iron that took him up to the small landing on the first floor and a green baize door through which he passed into the lobby of the air-conditioned private quarters. Here the public grandeur of pillars and black and white tiled floors, of busts on plinths and of immense potted palms in brass bowls, gave way to homelier oak-panelling and thick Turkey carpeting. With its magazine-cluttered central table, leather chairs and sofas set around the walls, it always reminded him of a doctor's waiting-room.

Priscilla Begge, looking both competent and harassed (he had never quite worked out how she managed to convey at one and the same time such apparently mutually exclusive qualities) was standing with her hockey-player's legs astride next to the little corner desk, talking on the telephone, watched by the two duty-bearers whose job was to ensure that the lobby was never unmanned. She gave Rowan a smile of welcome and a frown of pained exasperation, put her hand over the mouthpiece and stage-whispered, 'You can cross off —' then uncovered the mouthpiece and went on with her conversation but made a pleading (also commanding) gesture with her free hand, which he supposed meant she wanted him to wait. The door to the room of private audience opened and Hugh Thackeray looked in. He grinned at Rowan and then mouthed something at Priscilla who turned her back irritably and said, 'Will you repeat that please?' as if Hugh had distracted her.

'Poor old Bully-Off,' Hugh said when he and Rowan were alone in the empty audience room. 'Lady M's not well again and HE wants her to go down to Ooty to decide what's best to be done. Hang on here a moment. I'll just make sure he's ready.'

Thackeray went back into the study and shut the door. Rowan stood by the uncurtained window, looked down into the darkened grounds. He felt sorry for Priscilla. Much as she adored Lady Malcolm whose cousin she was, as well as secretary, and much as she loved the crisp healthy air of Ootacamund, her sense of duty, and the obligation she felt she was under to hold the fort during Lady Malcolm's frequent illnesses and absences, always made an order such as Malcolm had just given her seem to her like an instruction to abandon her post. Not that she saw herself as indispensable. Priscilla only lost her harassed look when Lady Malcolm was in residence and then it was replaced by one of thankfulness and hearty devotion. Rowan liked her because she had virtually no notion of her own capabilities. It was as if she could never quite credit it that she got anything right. The senior women in Ranpur who found themselves co-opted to act as hostess at Government House when poor Louise Malcolm struggled asthmatically for breath or retired to the one place in India that turned out to suit her affected to be amused by but never impatient of old Bully-Off's indefatigable efforts to help them to endure a rôle that actually gave them pleasure to assume. Malcolm had once said to him, 'If Priscilla could only stop thinking of herself as a prefect and start seeing herself as Head Girl what a good Governor's wife she would make.' But that Priscilla could never do. It was against her nature. On the night she was told that her name was on the next Honours List for an MBE all the colour left her face and for a day or two she had seemed preoccupied, as by intimations of some kind of lost innocence.

He turned from the window at the moment Thackeray opened the Library door. He nodded. As Rowan passed through Thackeray whispered, 'See you later, maybe. I'm going to hold Priscilla's hand and assure her that everything will be all right so long as we remember we're a team. Aren't I a tease?'

The Governor was at the far end of the room where the desk – already cluttered – was angled to take light from one of the tall windows. The desk-lamp was on but Malcolm was standing gazing out of the window, as Rowan had been a few moments before, hands behind back, holding his horn-rimmed spectacles. He was in dressing-gown, slacks and slippers.

Rowan said good-evening. Malcolm turned round and smiled and went to the desk, putting on his spectacles.

'How was New Delhi, sir?'

'New Delhi?' He sat and rummaged. 'New Delhi. Here we are.' But whatever he had looked for and found he then seemed to lose interest in. He sat back, removed the glasses and rubbed the bridge of his nose. 'New Delhi. Very bad for one's sense of proportion, New Delhi.' He put the glasses back on and started making notes on a memorandum pad. 'Have a drink, Nigel. I'll have one too if you'd be so kind.'

Rowan crossed over to the area in front of the fireplace. Three sofas were arranged round it. The live-coal effect was on below the unused elements of an ornate electric fire. The drinks tray was set out on the main sofa-table. The light from the fire was caught in the facets of the cut-glass decanters. An illusion of cosiness. The air-conditioning hummed gently. The private rooms could strike uncomfortably chilly. The imaginary live fire was Priscilla Begge's idea. She said it cheered one up. He poured whisky for himself and Malcolm his usual brandy. No ice for either of them. Not too much soda. He took the drinks to the desk and set the Governor's on a cork mat next to a square cut ashtray. Malcolm nodded his thanks but continued writing his memorandum.

'Be with you in a tick,' he said presently. 'Do sit down. I'm sorry about this by the way, you're supposed to be off, aren't you? Off. Making hay. That's it, then.' He threw down the pencil, looked at what he had written, pushed the pad aside, reached for his glass and said, 'Cheers.'

'Cheers.'

'Well now. New Delhi.'

'Interesting developments, sir?'

'Confirmation of assumptions.'

'Elections?'

'Yes. War virtually over, so – elections. To the central legislature first, then in the provinces.'

'When sir?'

'When do we do anything in this country if there's a choice?'

'In the cold weather?'

Malcolm was playing with the horn-rimmed spectacles. 'The cold weather. How comforting it always sounds. Never do today what you can put off until the weather cools down.'

'I suppose it's soon enough in this case. And elections are what everybody seems to want.'

'Quite. Jinnah wants them. Nehru wants them. Even we poor overworked provincial Governors want them. Some of course more than others. Most important of all the fount of all wisdom in Whitehall wants them. I suppose we ought to be worried. Such universal agreement.'

'And the Viceroy, sir?'

'Oh, yes. Wavell wants them. What man could fail to seize the opportunity of at last doing something which everyone approves of? He'll announce the decision to hold elections in a week or two, and then pop off back to London to make sure everyone is talking about the same thing, and that the British Government understands that an election in India is rather different from one at home at any time of year.'

'Will there be an extended franchise?'

Malcolm smiled and put the spectacles back on. 'Heaven forbid. That would take two cold weathers. Central legislature first, then the provinces that have responsible ministries, after that our kind, in Section 93. How does that strike you?'

After a moment Rowan replied, 'It strikes me as rather problematical in regard to Section 93 provinces.'

'Elucidate.'

'Constitutionally, you'll have to dissolve the existing legislature before calling for new elections. It wasn't the elected legislature that resigned in 1939. Only Mr Kasim and his colleagues resigned. From the ministry.'

'Quite. What's your point?'

'Only that constitutionally there's no difference between provinces where ministries still exist as a result of the 1937 elections – most of them Muslim majority and Muslim League provinces – and provinces where ministries don't exist because they were Congress ministries and resigned when Congress told them to resign. In the provinces where ministries as well as legislatures still exist the assemblies will be dissolved by due process, prior to new elections. In Section 93 provinces the Governors will have to order dissolution.'

'Well, that's because Section 93 provinces are under Governor's rule. Are you suggesting that I can't dissolve the existing assembly which exists virtually only on paper, without inviting Mr Mohammed Ali Kasim kindly to reform his ministry first?'

'I'm not saying you can't, sir, obviously. I'm wondering whether it's wise.'

'I'm under no constitutional obligation to recall Mr Kasim.'

'The Viceroy was under no obligation to release certain political leaders from jail last June. But he could hardly have held the Simla conference without doing so.'

'A thoroughly bad analogy. But of course, I thoroughly agree with you.'

'Oh.' Used as he had become to Malcolm's habit of arguing aloud for the opposition he was often uncertain what the Governor actually believed himself. 'May I ask why you agree, sir?'

'I'd prefer to hear your own reasons first.'

Rowan smiled. 'Well, I suppose the idea of elections at this stage is to inspire confidence and create an atmosphere of letting bygones be bygones.'

'One can do that without reverting to a bygone status quo.'

'But if you don't revert to it the Congress will be at a disadvantage.'

'They may think so . . .'

'Isn't it what they may think that will count? It's not our fault their ministries resigned in the provinces and not our fault that the ministries that stayed were predominantly Muslim, nor our fault that nowadays that virtually means Muslim League. But the fact is that the League will go into the elections with all the advantages usually enjoyed by a party already in ministerial power while the Congress will have to fight from scratch with all the disadvantages of a party that has been proscribed, its members imprisoned and its funds largely sequestrated. They might interpret the failure to invite them to reform provincial ministries as a first step to new elections as proof that we secretly sympathize with the Muslims and the idea of Pakistan and are still set on punishing Congress for non-co-operation in the war.'

Malcolm pushed the spectacles down his nose and looked at Rowan over the rims. 'I advanced the same arguments myself but with more tactful allowance for the hostility they were bound to arouse. Unfortunately I couldn't answer the logical and inevitable question.'

'What question, sir?'

'The question what I thought Mr Kasim's response to such an invitation would be in the unlikely event of it being agreed I should extend one.' He pushed the glasses back on. 'How would you have answered that?'

'I suppose by saying I'd find out the moment it was agreed I should try.'

'That wouldn't have been an answer. The question was, what do you *think* he would say? And the answer is that one simply doesn't know. One has so little idea that one suspects he might decline as easily as accept and that he would decline because an invitation like that would force him to show his hand, and that he isn't ready to do that yet. And if one is the least anxious, as I am, to see Mohammed Ali Kasim again heading a Congress ministry in Ranpur one is disinclined to do anything that will force him into a false position. So I am perfectly content to fall in with consensus opinion and let provinces under Governor's rule remain so until after the elections. One doesn't even know whether M A K will stand again, or for which party, or if he stands for his old constituency he now has a chance of holding it against the League. One knows absolutely nothing of his present intentions, let alone of his future prospects. One knows nothing about his attitude to his elder son, either.'

Malcolm took the glasses off, picked up his brandy and held it at eye-level as if examining the colour and clarity of the liquid. Then he drank it down.

'And not knowing has become onerous. By the way, I'm losing you.'

'What, sir?'

'They're taking you back into the Political Department. One

of the Crown Rep's people mentioned it and said I could tell you. I won't say I'm sorry because I know you'll be pleased. I'll miss you though. You'll get instructions in about a week's time.'

'Did he say anything about where?'

'No. You've done your probation so I should think they'll put you in as assistant at one of the Residencies, wouldn't you?'

'So long as it isn't Frontier Tribes.'

'He asked how fit you honestly were now. So I said you were blooming. Are you? Young Thackeray seems to think you ought to have a spot of leave before you go. He was under the very odd impression that a few days in Pankot would have a thera-peutic effect on your liver.'

'Oh?'

'But I suppose he only said that because he was afraid of being sent himself.'

'Sent himself? To Pankot?'

'Pankot's where I'm told Mr Kasim is to be found in the next day or so. I want you to go up tonight, see him as soon as you can and give him the letter I've written. After that I want you to do whatever is necessary to persuade him to arrange the earliest possible private meeting with me, preferably here, but I shan't absolutely insist. I'm sending V. R. Gopal with you. They're rooting him out now. Don't worry about the bandobast, it's being coped with. All you have to do is pack and be ready by eleven-thirty. Is that all right?'

'Of course, sir.'

'Sorry it's such short notice but I don't want him slipping the net and turning up in Bombay or 'Pindi or Lahore or even back in Mirat before I've had a chance to talk to him.'

'I take it you rule out exerting official pressure?'

'To cause him to appear? Yes, I do.'

'Is he expecting the letter?'

'Possibly. I got Hunter-Evans to ring his house. His new secre-tary said he was resting because he was going up by car tonight.'

'The car's a new idea. Presumably the coffin still goes by train.'

'Yes, I think Hunter-Evans said it did.'

'And Mr Kasim wouldn't come to the phone himself.'

'He was resting.'

'Perhaps he'll ring back once he's rested.'

'Aren't you keen to go?'

'Perfectly keen, sir. I was just thinking of short-cuts. Obviously there aren't any. How do I and Gopal travel?'

'By train. They're putting on the special coach so you should have every comfort. A car from Area Headquarters will meet you in Pankot and take you up to the Summer Residence guest house. All that's laid on.'

'What's Gopal's rôle exactly?'

'Go-between. He and Kasim have always had a great respect for one another as you know. You'd better wear mufti incidentally.'

'I take it I don't hand the letter to anyone but M A K?'

'Preferably not. I leave it to your discretion. If Kasim can't or won't see you then Gopal will have to give it to him. He'll be involved with the funeral most of tomorrow, but get Gopal off to try and contact him directly you arrive. Gopal was an old friend of Mahsood's too. He can melt into the background without arousing anyone's curiosity. I shan't provide you with a copy of the letter but you'll have a separate sheet of notes for guidance which might help if M A K asks questions you feel you have to answer to get him to agree to a meeting.'

'Will Gopal be as fully informed?'

'No. My approach to Kasim is personal and in one way I may be sticking my neck out. It's nothing to do with inviting him to form a ministry before the elections, though.'

Rowan looked at his watch.

Malcolm said, 'You'd better go and get packed. I'll send the letter and notes up. Ring down if there's anything you want clarifying. And ring me from Pankot tomorrow night to say how things look.'

'You'll be rather busy tomorrow night, sir. You've got the reception and dinner for Chakravarti.'

'So I have. And the foundation stone ceremony later in the week. You'd better take a copy of the days' arrangements in case M A K asks you to suggest a time. I'll try to fit in but I'd prefer not to cancel the Chakravarti ceremony.'

'The stone-laying? Perhaps Mr Kasim would like to attend, sir.'

'Which day is it?'

'Friday, in the afternoon.'

'Would Chakravarti be offended?'

'Not so long as M A K doesn't steal the scene. Chak's been contributing heavily to secret party funds.'

'And hedging his bets by contributing to the Hindu Mahasabha too, so they say. Perhaps the odd lakh finds its way to the Muslim League as well. After all he's a business man with interests all over India. It's a possibility. By all means suggest it. And ring me tomorrow night however late. If Kasim drives down from Pankot on Thursday, say, I could meet him here on the Friday morning.'

'You have HH of Puttipur until mid-morning.'

'But not for lunch?'

'No, Hugh takes him to the airfield just before midday.'

'Then Kasim and I could lunch here and go on to the ceremony at the college. Separately, naturally.'

'Should I come back with him by car?'

'No.' Malcolm smiled. 'Your job's finished the moment he agrees to a time and place. He'll keep his word. The special coach can be held up there until you ask for it to be coupled on. But let Gopal come back directly neither of you sees any further point in his staying. He can use the coach if you like. You can stay on and relax for a few days. I think you should, don't you? Get some hill air into your lungs. Let's say I shan't expect to see you until a week today. By then instructions ought to be through from Simla or Delhi.'

'That's very good of you, sir.'

'You'd better get a move on, then.'

Rowan stood up. Malcolm had never welcomed references to his wife's frailty but he felt he couldn't leave without saying something.

'Thackeray tells me Lady Malcolm isn't well, I'm very sorry.'

'Yes. Thank you.' He took off his spectacles again and put them down. 'I'm sending Priscilla down.' He stood up and, unexpectedly, came round the desk and put out his hand. Surprised, Rowan clasped it briefly.

'I won't actually say goodbye but I suppose there's always a chance of our not coinciding again. One gets punted around like a bloody football in this job. Thank you for everything you've done, Nigel.'

'Thank you, sir. It's been a very happy and very useful experience.'

'Good. I hope things pan out. Today's rather one of those days when I can't quite see how anything pans out for anybody. It was a real horror, I'm told.'

'What?'

'Hiroshima. Absolutely and inconceivably bloody awful.'

'Unexpectedly so?'

'We shan't have the answer for quite a while. Someone said twenty years. That's food for thought, isn't it? And so is the idea that if a high-ranking Japanese delegation had been persuaded over to the States under a flag of truce to watch them test the thing, they'd have gone back and forced the Emperor to surrender then and there.'

'As impressive as that?'

'According to observers God knows how many miles away from the test area in the middle of the New Mexican desert. It leaves one with a rather humiliating sense of the essential parochialism of one's own concerns.'

'Yes. I suppose. I'd better go and get on with mine. Goodnight, sir.'

'One thing before you go.'

Malcolm thrust his hands into his dressing-gown pockets.

'I've always intended to say this when the time came. In my opinion you're admirably suited for the job you've done and even more for the one you're going to do. We have the same sort of views and much the same sort of way of expressing them to each other. We can gauge each other's thoughts and feelings pretty accurately. But the Indians can't, so easily. Sometimes not at all. I know it's a wretchedly difficult thing and nothing's worse than going to the opposite extreme, relaxing and unbending so much that you don't even convince yourself, let alone them.'

'But you think I need to unbend more than I do, sir?'

'It might help. The English manner is a formidable obstacle to mutual understanding between the races. As a young man of your age I used to believe precisely the opposite. But I was confusing mutual understanding with mutual respect and lack of understanding with lack of respect. Take young Thackeray.'

'In what way?'

'He's an awfully kind-hearted boy. Full of fun. Splendid with visiting brass from Eastern Command or GHQ and with young Indian officers like Bunny Mehta. But put him with a handful of senior Indian civilians, any distinguished Indian who's not in uniform, and he's a different fellow. Actually he's terrified of upsetting them or putting a foot wrong. But they don't know that. They look at what to me and you is his rather touching but sometimes exasperating expression of boyish concentration and they interpret it as one of a fully mature sense of racial and class superiority. I don't honestly think he feels that. But the English manner has never been much of a medium for communicating feeling. Sometimes I think that's at the bottom of half our troubles. Wavell's a good example. One of the sincerest and best disposed men who's ever held that wretched post. But also one of the most silent and unbending and outwardly austere. It's the English manner come to perfection. It won't do. And the irony is, Nigel, that at home it's been going out of fashion for years. Rather like one of those strains of indigenous plants that turns out to flower more profusely abroad and withers away in its home soil. Anyway. It's worth bearing in mind.'

He began moving away from the desk to the centre of the room. Level with the sofa table he came to a halt.

'One other thing. This girl in Pankot young Thackeray assured me would make a few days up there quite an attractive proposition for you. Miss Layton.'

'Miss Layton. Yes.'

'The same Miss Layton?'

Rowan nodded.

'Have you heard from her recently?'

'Actually we were on the phone this evening.'

'Anything to do with a havildar of her father's regiment who went over to Bose in Germany?'

'No, sir?'

'He's now with a batch of prisoners that came over from Bordeaux, in a camp near Delhi. General Crawford has a letter from Colonel Layton asking to be allowed to see him. Apparently he's the son of a Pankot Rifles subedar who won the VC in the last war.'

'No, she said nothing about that.'

'Did she refer at all to our friend Merrick?'

'Only in passing. He was in Bombay when she was. I don't know why or for how long.'

'Has Colonel Layton met him?'

'She didn't say so. I imagine he must have done.'

'Is Merrick still in the department that's working up these INA cases?'

'Yes. He hadn't been in it long when she told me about it. That's only six weeks ago. And she and Merrick were at a party in Bombay last week. Ahmed Kasim was there. Merrick told her not to let Ahmed know he was connected in any way with the brother's case.'

'Ah. Well that's one thing. The other thing is Merrick's bound to know about the Pankot Rifles havildar too, presumably. Is he sufficiently in with the family to want to help Colonel Layton have an interview with the man?'

'Probably. In with the family, yes. I don't know about the other thing.'

'No. Perhaps Layton's letter to Crawford indicates he's tried that string and Merrick wouldn't play. Perhaps you'd try to find out. Crawford was going to write back and say there was nothing doing but I've asked him to sit on it for a few days. If Merrick's playing along and pulling strings, let me know. We could pull a few from here. If he's not there isn't a hope. But in that case tell her how sorry I am her father can't see his havildar. He may appreciate knowing that I've been consulted personally by Crawford.'

'Right, sir.'

Malcolm hesitated.

'Is young Thackeray barking up the wrong tree? Perhaps I shouldn't ask. But I can't help wondering. The only times you've mentioned her to me have been to pass on what she's told you about Merrick. Very helpful on that first occasion. Interesting on the second. But I've assumed your interest in her was, what, limited to that subject? The way Thackeray spoke made me feel I've been insensitive.'

'I can't think why you should feel that.'

'No. Well. How much have you told her – about our view of Merrick?'

'Nothing, sir. Nothing specific.'

'Well, that would be difficult. Even if one disregards the element of doubt. But what impression do you have of her attitude?'

'I know she believes he made a mistake in the Kumar case.'

'How did the subject come up?'

'I asked her how the chap she'd visited in hospital was. And she told me he was all right and had gone to Delhi to deal with the INA cases –'

'Yes, I remember that. We were both struck by the idea of Merrick conducting a whole series of interrogations. How did she happen to mention the Kumar case?'

'She said she hoped he wouldn't start every examination of INA men with a preconceived conviction of the man's guilt. We went on from there.'

'Did you tell her you knew Kumar?'

'I only mentioned the school part of it. It interested her because her father went to the same one. She knew Kumar had been brought up and educated in England but hadn't heard definitely where.'

'Why is she so interested in Kumar?'

Rowan had asked himself the same question. He did not know the answer. He could only base an answer on Gopal's: that Kumar was really an English boy with a brown skin and that the combination was hopeless.

'I think she sees him as a man who couldn't have existed without our help and deliberate encouragement. I should say that in quite an impersonal way she thinks of him as a charge to our account — guilty or not guilty. But believing him not guilty makes the charge heavier.'

'She sounds an unusually thoughtful person.'

'Yes, I think she is.'

'Did you tell her he's free?'

'No.'

'So she doesn't know you keep an eye.'

'No.'

'I imagine she'd approve? Well —,' Malcolm smiled, '— I expect you have more than one reason for hiding that particular light. I take it Kumar remains in ignorance too?'

'I hope so.'

'Does he still suspect Gopal's man of being CID?'

'That, or one of Pandit Baba's creatures.'

'The CID still keeps tabs, presumably?'

'Very much so. On Gopal's man, too.'

'Does he mind?'

'Gopal says not.'

'What will you do when you've left Ranpur? Leave everything to Gopal?'

'I shall have to. There's not much to leave.'

'Yes, well, it's a minor matter. How are things with him though?'

'He lives much as you'd expect. Coaching a few students at a few rupees a time.'

'How is the aunt?'

'She still looks after him.'

'Is he as devoted as she deserves?'

'According to Gopal's man, yes.'

'Good.' Malcolm paused. 'I hope we did the right thing, that's all.'

VI

The car, which had been sent first to pick up Vallabhai Rama-swamy Gopal at his home, reached Government House a few minutes after eleven-thirty. Rowan had retrieved the envelope from the Signals Office and had it packed in his case. As he got into the car the old man said, 'Keep away, Nigel. I have a cold you see.' There was a smell of eucalyptus. Having spoken, Gopal clamped a square-folded handkerchief to his nose. He was wearing a grey flannel suit and had a woollen scarf round his neck.

'How did you manage that, VR?'

'I am catching cold easily nowadays. My wife tells me to keep an onion in my pocket. She has these outdated ideas.'

'How is Mrs Gopal?'

Gopal jerked his head. 'Okay. Very angry because I am not taking her to Pankot. She says what is the use of being married to a man who is always rushing off.'

'Are you always rushing off?'

'It is what I ask. When was I rushing off last? To Pun, isn't it, two years ago and who was that with me? But it is useless to talk fact and logic to Lila when she is angry. Please excuse me for bringing so many things.'

Mr Gopal's feet were hidden behind an assortment of luggage and oddments, among them an aluminium tiffin set. Outside on the roof rack he had already noticed a bed-roll and a wooden chest. His own suitcase was being put on.

'While she quarrels with me also she gets the servant to pack this and that. It is best not to argue.'

Rowan had visited the house once. The Gopals' quarrelling

was not to be taken seriously. Jaiprakash announced through the open window that the suitcase was safely stowed. As the driver got in Mr Gopal spoke to someone on the other side of the car: a youth. He got in too and sat next to the driver.

'It is my nephew Ashok coming to see me off. Making sure for Lila I am not rushing somewhere I shouldn't be. Ashok, say how do you do to Captain Rowan.'

The boy turned round, ducked his head shyly but formally.

'Ashok is doing his BA here, isn't it, Ashok? But now he is talking of going to Calcutta for BSc.'

'Why Calcutta?'

'It is what we are asking. From Government College he can get BSc also, but no, he is insisting Calcutta. Ashok, tell Captain Rowan what you told Auntie Lila.'

Judging that the boy was too embarrassed to speak Rowan said, 'Perhaps the real question is why not Calcutta?'

'No, no, the question was definitely why Calcutta.' Mr Gopal sometimes took a very literal line. 'And the answer is for physics. Isn't it, Ashok? In Ranpur he tells his Auntie there is no decent teacher in physics. For the past few days it has been physics, physics. You know what the trouble is with him, Nigel? He wishes to be the first Indian to make an atomic bomb. He says only for power and energy but I know what is in his mind. He will blow us all up. And only last week it was Wordsworth and daffodils.'

They were through the west gate heading for the Mall and the western arm of Old Fort Road which would take them the longer but less congested way to the station. The car was now accompanied by two motor-cycle outriders – military police who had been waiting one hundred yards beyond the gate.

'Look Ashok, what a story you will tell your mother and father. Driving from Government House with a motor-cycle escort.' He turned to Rowan. 'Lila said I should not bring him but I said you would not mind.'

'Of course not. But what about getting back?'

'He lives near the station. He is Lila's sister's youngest boy. He was only visiting us. It is a lift home for him very nearly, otherwise I would not have brought him.'

'It's very late.'

'I'm often out as late as this, sir,' the boy said, turning round. 'I shall be perfectly all right.'

Rowan glanced at Gopal, but Gopal had the squared handker-chief covering the lower part of his face.

'You speak English very well, Ashok.'

'Thank you, sir.' He faced front. Again Rowan glanced at Gopal who jerked his head slightly, an affirmative answer to Rowan's unspoken question. 'He has found a very good coach and visits him two three times a week after classes. Other evenings he is attending YMCA and doing Ju-Jitsu. *Mens sana in corpore sano.* Ashok? You know the meaning of this?'

'Yes, uncle.'

'What a bright boy. Now physics. What will be the use of mind or body if you blow us all up? Will your physics cure my cold? What a state we are in. In one pocket the formula for splitting the atom and in the other an onion.'

'Do you know the English cure for cramp, VR?'

'No?'

'A raw potato in the bed.'

Gopal laughed. Ashok looked round, smiling. Rowan thought: I unbend easily enough with Gopal.

He looked out of the window. He remembered the time when neither of them had quite trusted the other. Now they were friends. Before that Rowan had known of him only as a shrewd and conscientious civil servant who was said to owe his position in the Department for Home and Law to Mohammed Ali Kasim. A member of the uncovenanted provincial civil service his advancement might otherwise have been blocked by the preference given to British and Indian members of the august ICS. Rowan didn't know in just what way he had caught M A K's eye when M A K was chief minister but he had been a good choice for the senior position he now held in the secretariat.

They had turned off Old Fort Road and were headed south down the ill-lit Upper Tank Road with the barrack-like PWD buildings in darkness on their left and on their right the grounds of Government College – the principal's bungalow, the playing field, the building-site for the Chakravarti extension, and finally, at the intersection with the brightly lit thoroughfare of Elphinstone Road, the old Victorian Gothic building of the College itself.

The car turned right into Elphinstone Road and was filled

with sliding slanting bars of light and shadow. The motor-cycle escort shortened the distance between themselves and the car to mother it through the crowds that walked freely on the road. At the Lux Cinema they were still showing *Jawab*.

'Did you know old Mahsood well, VR?'

'He was not so old. He came to see us when MAK was released from Premanagar and sent to Nanoora in Mirat. He was very upset because he wanted to go too, and Mrs Kasim would not take him because she was afraid he would tell Kasim how ill she had been. When he went Lila said "He says Mrs Kasim is ill, but he is ill also." Then of course Kasim sent for him, so he closed the house up and joined them.'

'He lived in the Kasim household didn't he?'

'Since many years. He was never married. "What do I need with wife and children?" he used to say to Lila. "MAK and Mrs MAK are like brother and sister to me and Sayed and Ahmed are like sons or nephews." It was from Mahsood that Lila and I first heard about Sayed and INA. He said he suspected MAK would not forgive the boy and that this would be terrible for Mrs Kasim.'

'How much do you think is generally known now about Sayed?'

'How much? Or by how many people? Everyone is knowing something. No one is officially knowing anything. This is why the press keeps quiet. It is afraid of libel. Ask Ashok here what the students are saying. Tell Captain Rowan, Ashok, what the students are saying about Lieutenant Sayed Kasim. No? He does not want to say in front of you. The students are calling Sayed a hero because he fought with Netaji's army against the British. They know he has been kept in prison-camp awaiting court-martial ever since he was recaptured in Manipur, but they say he will never be tried because the British are afraid that MAK will conduct the defence himself and bring proof that Indian King's commissioned officers were left in the lurch by their English colleagues when the Japanese invaded Burma. And all things of that sort, isn't it, Ashok?'

'Not all students say this, uncle. Some concentrate on their studies. They aren't interested in Bose. He is only a Bengali.'

'Only a Bengali? You say this, Ashok? Are the physics teachers in Calcutta all non-Bengalis, then?'

'It's not what I say, uncle.'

'Who is saying, then? Your friend Vidyar Awal for one, isn't it? Ashok's friend Vidyar is very anti-Bengali, very anti-Bose. His father is a major in the Engineers and comes from UP. You see how these distinctions arise.'

'Yes, I do.'

Gopal sat forward suddenly.

'What are they doing? They should have gone down Chowpatti. This is the old way to the special shed.'

'That's where we're heading.'

'To avoid crowds? There will be no crowds. Everyone knows M A K has gone up by road now.'

'But you and I are going in the special coach, VR. Didn't they tell you?'

'The special coach? Oh, dear God.'

'HE wanted us to be comfortable.'

'Then we should go third class or in the wagon with poor old Mahsood's coffin. Ashok, you must say nothing to your mother and father about this. Say nothing to anyone. Above all say nothing to your Auntie Lila.'

The boy was grinning. 'Why, uncle?'

'Oh, dear God.'

Rowan smiled, judging that Gopal was not really displeased. The little convoy turned left into the road that would bring them out at the coal and goods-yard area. They were already going past go-downs and repair sheds. Cyclists and car-driver had dipped head-lamps on. The road was not lit except where light fell from the high arc-lamps in the yards of the warehouses. There was a warm smell of drains, the acrid odour of coal and oil. They bumped over an uneven level-crossing. 'Oh dear God,' Gopal said again as if every spasm of discomfort were an indication of sustained discomfort to come. They approached a white post-barrier guarded by railway police. This was raised and the convoy entered an arc-lit cinder-yard and drew up at the entrance to a covered stairway to a covered footbridge. An English officer and an Indian station official were waiting for them. There was a batch of coolies to carry the baggage. The Englishman wore the armband of Movement Control. The Indian wore a sola topee. Rowan got out first. The MCO, not Captain Carter, but a man Rowan didn't know, addressed him as sir and announced that everything was laid on. Gopal was still in the car directing the removal of his hand-luggage. The MCO spoke to his Indian colleague. 'See to that lot, old son.' Then he turned to the staircase as if he expected Rowan to go on ahead.

'Okay, sir?'

'Yes, fine.' Rowan remained where he was. 'Incidentally I'm not a civilian and I don't outrank you. Has it been a problem getting the coach ready at such short notice?'

The MCO looked wary. 'All we had to do was see the thing shunted out of the shed to the side platform. I didn't know what the message meant at first because I didn't know there was a special Government House coach. I've only been here three weeks.'

'There used to be several.'

'Just for the Governor?'

'Governor, staff, secretaries, clerks, files. Government used to go up *en masse* to Pankot every hot weather.'

'What happened to the other coaches, then?'

'You've got them in general service. You'd probably have this one too if the interior would adapt.'

'Yes. I looked inside. If you don't mind me saying so I thought it was bloody ridiculous nowadays.'

'It was built for an earlier age.'

'And there's really just the two of you tonight?'

'That's right.'

'The message said two but about four or five servants turned up.'

'That would be about the normal complement.'

'They've been making beds and putting flowers in vases. I thought probably some ladies were coming along.'

'I think the flowers are the usual drill.'

'There's a drill is there?'

'It simplifies things.'

Gopal had emerged now. He carried an umbrella. Ashok held the tiffin set. The coolies were dividing the luggage up among themselves. Gopal called out to one of them to be very careful with the box because the clasps were unreliable and the box was heavier than it looked. To anyone not knowing Hindi it probably sounded like a complaint. The MCO looked at his watch. On his face was that familiar English expression of utter detachment from an Indian activity. As Gopal and Ashok approached he said to no one in particular, 'Right then.'

He led the way up the staircase to the covered bridge. Their footsteps sounded hollow on the worn and grimy boards. Rowan had never travelled on the special coach himself but he had accompanied Pankot-bound guests from Government House to catch the train on several occasions. The previous MCO, Carter, had appreciated the fact that there *was* a special coach. Most of those who travelled on it had priority passages. Without the coach Movement Control would have found itself turfing passengers out of the ordinary first-class compartments to make room for them.

The covered bridge always reminded him of his schooldays. There had been one at Chadford where he changed trains on the journey between London and Chillingborough. This one smelt much the same, impregnated with decades of engine smoke. Briefly, above the undoubted Indianness of the station at Ranpur, he could imagine himself back at Chadford.

As they came down the stairs the station that was not Chadford presented itself, raw and uncompromising. They were at the front of the train. The special coach stood directly opposite the exit from the covered bridge. It was flanked by two guard's vans, one separating it from the engine, the other from the first of the first-class carriages. Beyond this the train stretched back a couple of hundred yards or more. The platform was crowded but a rope barrier guarded by police kept the area in front of the Governor's coach clear of everyone except people who had business there. Of these there did seem rather a large number.

Gopal was talking to the MCO's Indian colleague, apparently putting Ashok into his care. Two Government House servants stood at the foot of the steps that led to the coach's observation platform, which was also the point of entrance. They saluted Rowan when they caught his eye. The MCO was talking to a British sergeant who had a clipboard of papers. The luggage was going up into the coach. Beyond the barrier charwallahs were collecting money and taking back mugs from hands at windows. Further beyond where the crowds were greatest Rowan could still make out bouncing headloads – the luggage of late arrivals. He wondered where the coffin was and eyed the guard's van-like coaches which flanked the one he and Gopal were to travel in. And had his suspicions.

'You could help me out, maybe,' the MCO said, arriving with his clipboard at Rowan's elbow. 'I know it's supposed to be sacred territory but I've got six officers in three of the four-persons-only compartments and three officers in most of the coupés. Now I've got a GHQ priority who's just come in on the Delhi train.'

'The one due in at 21.30?'

'It was ninety minutes late.'

'And you want to put him in the special coach?'

'According to my calculations after you and the Indian gentle-man are settled in the two single-berths there's a couple of coupés going spare. Unless of course the servants are travelling in style.'

'What rank is your GHQ priority?'

'Lieut.-Colonel.'

'That's not senior enough to qualify as a possible exception. But I'll ask Mr Gopal if he has any objection and then see how we're placed. Has Captain Carter been transferred?'

'Carter?'

'The MCO here.'

'I'm the MCO here. The previous chap's name was Carter.'

'Did he hand over to you?'

'He'd gone when I got here. Why?'

'He would have explained the uses and abuses of the special coach.'

'I don't know where abuses comes in.'

'Abuses come in if the coach kept to save Movement Control inconvenience from sudden Government House priorities is treated as a convenient way of solving routine problems of overcrowding. lf Mr Gopal and I weren't going up to Pankot tonight the coach wouldn't be on the train.'

'It is on the train.'

'Because we're going up.' Rowan looked at the top paper on the clipboard. 'Is that a copy of the GHQ priority?'

The MCO pulled it from the clip and handed it to Rowan. 'See for yourself.'

Rowan took the paper, the usual carbon copy of a movement order, with an illegible signature – someone signing for an officer of the Advocate-General's branch. Rowan read the text. Then read it again and handed the paper back.

'It says Colonel Merrick is accompanied by a sergeant and a servant. Where are they all at the moment?'

The MCO referred to his own sergeant, who said there was no problem about the servant and that the colonel's sergeant had been 'fixed up'. But the colonel himself was waiting, hoping for something better than a third place in a coupé. He had a disability. The MCO said, 'What sort of disability?'

Rowan broke in. 'I know the officer in question. Just a moment.' He went to Gopal who was lecturing Ashok. 'May I have a word, VR? Let's go in.'

From the observation platform one entered directly into the sitting compartment. The coach had been equipped to look as much like a houseboat on the Dal lake as was possible. The sofa and over-stuffed chairs were covered in chintz. Numdah rugs added to the thickness of an Indian carpet. There were chintz curtains at the windows. A faint smell of sandalwood.

'Oh dear God,' Gopal said yet again. He had brought the tiffin set with him and the umbrella.

Rowan put his briefcase on one of the chairs. 'An interesting situation has arisen,' he began.

'We are to travel in an ordinary compartment?'

'No, they're all full up. The MCO wants us to take some of the overflow.'

'To me this sounds like a confusion. Why do you call it interesting?'

'The overflow happens to be Merrick.'

Slowly the smile and frown of pretended exasperation left Gopal's face. He seemed to take a firmer grip on the umbrella and the tiffin set, making them look like defensive weapons. Offensive, even.

'Merrick? Ex-Superintendent of Police? Now Major?'

'Major no longer apparently. Lieut.-Colonel.'

'You have seen him?'

'Not yet. I wouldn't know him by sight anyway. But there's no doubt it's Merrick. Would you object?'

'Object to him travelling with us? Is that open to me? You are His Excellency's chief emissary. It is for you to say.'

'It could be useful.'

'Useful? What could be useful about being with this man?'

'Aren't you in the least curious to see him?'

'Not in the least curious, Nigel. I will have nothing to do with it, but please don't bother about me. They can make up my bunk and I can nurse my cold.'

'The beds are already made up in the two main single berths.'

'No, no. I must have my own bedding. I have it with me. They can put it in one of the old aide's coupés. Your Mr Merrick can sleep in His or Her Excellency's berth.'

'We'll have to talk about what we do tomorrow before you go to bed. I'd better tell the MCO it's no go. Obviously you feel strongly.' It surprised Rowan a bit that he did.

'And obviously you want him. You say useful. You are the better judge of this. So let him in. But first let me sort out my sleeping quarters and disappear. If we must talk let us do so in there. And please send Ashok in to say goodbye.'

Gopal went through into the dining-compartment. Rowan returned to the platform and gave Ashok his uncle's message. The MCO was standing with arms folded, his weight on one leg, advertising his patent amusement.

'We'll take Colonel Merrick and his party. The servant will have to muck in with our own but I don't suppose he'll be any less comfortable.'

'You mean you're offering two berths?'

'For Colonel Merrick and his sergeant, yes.'

The MCO's assistant said, 'There's that Major Hemming sir, the one who kicked up a fuss.'

The MCO nodded. 'If it's two berths going spare the answer is two officers, surely. Colonel Merrick and this Major Hemming.'

'The berth's aren't going spare. There's one for Colonel Merrick and one for Sergeant Perron.'

'Is that his name?'

'So it says on the movement order.'

'The sergeant's settled in.'

'Then you'll have to unsettle him or squeeze his officer into a coupé.'

'We're due out now.'

'That's up to you. But there'd be no point in bringing Colonel Merrick without the party specified in the movement order. The officer, the sergeant and the servant.'

'You're saying all or nothing?'

'Yes.'

'It beats me.'

As the MCO and his sergeant set off Ashok came down from the coach. Rowan spoke to the Indian official to confirm that he would see the boy safely out of the station. He bade Ashok goodbye, wished him luck in his exams and returned to the sitting-room compartment. The head bearer was putting out bottles and glasses on the marble top of a waist-high mahogany corner cabinet. A miniature brass rail held them secure. He ordered a brandy and soda and presently carried the glass out to the observation platform and placed himself where he could see fairly far down the train. The rope barrier was still in position but a section of it had been opened up. There was a sound of warning whistles. The platform was still crowded. The only Englishwomen he could see were in a group: girls in uniform, QAs, seeing someone off, probably on short leave or on posting up to the General Hospital in Pankot. They had some RAF and American officers in tow and looked merry.

Then they moved in closer to the carriage making room for people to pass: the MCO and an officer whose left arm hung stiffly by his side. Behind them Rowan just made out the tall jungle-green clad figure of a man wearing a green slouch hat and, next to him, someone in a pugree. Luggage bobbed on the heads of the coolies in the rear.

Rowan went back into the coach and drank his brandy down and returned to the observation platform. He went down the steps as the party passed through the opening in the rope barrier.

'Colonel Merrick?'

The man tucked a swagger cane under his left arm. Momentarily Rowan was appalled by the scar-tissue that disfigured the left side of Merrick's face. Sarah had never mentioned that. He took Merrick's right hand, briefly.

'My name is Rowan.' He had been steeling himself to say 'sir'. The word did not come. But he managed the rest of what he'd rehearsed. 'I think we have a mutual friend in Sarah Layton. I already know your sergeant.' Before Merrick could react he turned to Perron. Yes. No mistake. He offered his hand. 'How are you, Guy?'

A little muscle ridged itself on Perron's cheek.

'Fine, thank you, Nigel.'

They shook hands. Rowan readdressed himself to Merrick.

'We'd better sort things out so that the luggage can go in. There's a spare coupé which has its own bath cubicle, and then there's a single berther that's probably more comfortable but it shares washing arrangements with another. There's no one using the coupé.'

'I should be more than content with either,' Merrick said. 'But I do have a certain handicap. The coupé would suit me very well if it's really not wanted. Then I could have my servant in with me. In any case, it's very civil of you.'

'I'll have the luggage put in then. Is this your servant?'

Rowan glanced at the man who stood to one side of Guy Perron. Extraordinary. A cap of gold thread swathed with stiff white muslin, an embroidered waistcoat over a white tunic gathered at the waist by a belt, and baggy white trousers. Into the belt was tucked a miniature axe on a long shaft decorated with silver filigree. The face was clean-shaven but pock-marked. The eyes looked as though they were rimmed with kohl. A bazaar Pathan: handsome, predatory; the kind of man Rowan instinctively distrusted.

'Yes, that's Suleiman,' Merrick said. 'There isn't much luggage. We came in a hurry and fairly light.'

Rowan called over one of the servants from the coach. He gave orders for Merrick's luggage to be placed in whichever coupé wasn't occupied by Mr Gopal.

'What have you got, Guy?'

Perron indicated a kit-bag by his side and a briefcase in his hand. 'Just these.'

'Well we can sort you out later.' He told another bearer to put Perron's kit-bag in the sitting-room. 'I expect you could both do with a drink. Let's go up.' He led the way to the observation platform and stood aside to let Merrick up. Perron waited. Rowan waved him on. When they had both gone up he watched the Pathan follow the porters into the coach at the other end. Then he smiled at Ashok, nodded to the MCO and went into the sitting-room.

Merrick had removed his cap and placed it with the swagger cane on the small table between the two armchairs. He looked younger than Rowan had expected and, by Perron's side, curiously unimpressive. Perron, in this confined area, appeared large and heavily built. The jungle-green uniform added a special note of aggressiveness. His hair was fairer than Rowan remembered and the face, in maturity, less mobile in expression. As a youth Perron had smiled constantly.

'Thank you for taking us in,' Merrick said. 'I imagine it's meant bending the rules a bit.'

'Imperceptibly. What will you have, Colonel Merrick?'

'A whisky would do very nicely, thank you. And perhaps Perron may have one too. Then I think he'd like to get his head down. He's spent most of the past week travelling.'

'There'll be a light supper next door in ten minutes or so,' Rowan said. Warning whistles were being blown. 'What about it, Guy? The MCO said the Delhi train was very late in. Haven't you missed dinner?'

'I haven't had it but I haven't missed it.' Perron's tone was edgy and abrasive. 'Incidentally; no whisky for me. Unless it's Scotch.'

'It is.'

'Really? Well, that fits.'

'Fits what?'

Perron didn't answer. He stiffened his trunk and limbs as if coming to attention. 'With your permission, sir,' he said to Merrick, 'I should like to do as you suggest and get my head down.'

'Of course.'

'Shall I continue in custody of the bag, sir?'

'No, leave that here.'

Rowan signalled to a servant in the dining-room and pointed at Perron's kit-bag.

'If you want to tuck down I'll show you where you can settle in.'

The bearer was handing Perron a glass of whisky and soda as Rowan went past him. In the dining-room he paused, heard Perron say, 'Goodnight, sir', and Merrick's reply, 'Goodnight, Sergeant.' The train began to glide forward. When Perron came in, holding his glass, Rowan went to the far door at the right-hand side of the dining compartment and passed through it into the corridor. Merrick's Pathan, on guard outside the farthest coupé, watched him. Rowan slid open the door of No. 1 compartment. The lights were on. His case was on the luggage rack. Perron followed him in.

'Which would you like, Guy? This one with the bed arranged so that your head faces away from the engine?' He opened the door into the shower and BC cubicles and then another door into a duplicate berth. 'Or this one where the head faces towards?'

Perron looked round the rosily-lit compartment.

'Have you nothing in between?'

'I'm afraid not.'

'Then I'll make do with this.'

'I'm told the last Governor's lady preferred it.'

'What about the present Governor's lady?'

'She never comes up to Pankot. If HE has to he goes by road.'

'The coach is something of an anachronism?'

'You could say that.'

'That fits too.'

'Like Scotch. Why? Fits what?'

'The generally hallucinatory atmosphere I currently exist in. Your health.'

The servant came in with the kit-bag, stowed it on the rack and left by the sliding door that gave on to the corridor. When he had gone Perron shot the bolt.

'Guard your property and your life,' he said, as though it were a quotation. In one corner of the compartment there was a diminutive armchair, chintz-covered. He squeezed himself into it. 'The Red Shadow is at large. Did you ever see anything quite as camp?'

'Camp?'

'Suleiman.' Perron hesitated. 'Never mind.' Then, 'Sandhurst, wasn't it? Chillingborough and Sandhurst. Now this. ADC to HE. The Governor in Ranpur. Unless I've been imagining it all and still am, which seems likely. I believe something may have happened to me a week ago tonight. It *is* Sunday?'

'No. Monday. The thirteenth. What happened to you a week ago on Sunday?'

'There was a Maharanee mixed up in it somewhere. And then there was poor Purvis. Are you sure it's the thirteenth? I could swear it was still Sunday.'

Rowan looked at his watch. 'Actually we're both wrong. It's now Tuesday the fourteenth.'

'Good,' Perron said. 'Two days nearer.'

'Nearer what?'

'The successful conclusion of Operation Bunbury. She'll have had my telegram by now. She will have given the first little tug to the first little string. What should we allow? A month, conservatively? Can I hold out even for a month? Or shall I commit murder? What do they do to sergeants who murder their officers?'

'Hang them, I think.'

'Very degrading. A firing squad would be different. Aunt Charlotte would approve of a firing squad.'

The train clacked over a series of points. Rowan steadied himself. Perron produced a hip flask from a sidepocket of his jacket and topped up his whisky and soda. 'Scotch,' he said. 'A parting gift from my previous officer. A pleasant enough but finally very ineffectual man. The only alternative he had to propose was that I apply at once for a commission. He thought it likely it could have been immediate but I said immediate or delayed made no difference because accepting a commission at this stage of the game would simply be a policy of despair.'

'There's no need to drink your own whisky, Guy. Just press the bell.'

'I don't suppose you have the slightest idea what I'm drivelling on about, have you, Nigel?'

'Some of the details are a bit obscure but oddly enough I get the general drift.'

'Do you? I wish I did. I find the general drift elusive. So here's to Aunt Charlotte and Operation Bunbury. I hope you're not going to ask me to explain Bunbury as well as camp.'

'No. But how will an imaginary sick friend solve your problem?'

'He died. At least he did according to the telegram I sent Aunt Charlotte. You remember Aunt Charlotte?'

'The sister of your balloonist uncle?'

'That's the one. The one who got on awfully well with that stunning girl you were with at School versus Old Boys. I can't remember her name. Did you marry her, by the way?'

'No.'

'Are you married?'

'No, go on about Bunbury.'

'Bunbury was Aunt Charlotte's idea. When I told her I couldn't delay my call-up any longer she said I obviously wasn't trying and that it was most unpatriotic of me because it wasn't going to be fair on the men for whose lives and welfare I so thoughtlessly intended to accept responsibility. She only became resigned to it when I got it through to her that I intended to serve anonymously in the ranks and when I agreed to tip her off the moment I wanted her to pull strings to get me out. Throughout my relatively short but not uneventful military career, from Salisbury Plain to Kalyan, I've kept her informed of my state of mind by reporting on our friend Bunbury's state of health. His death last week will have galvanized her into action.'

'What sort of action?'

'She has several friends in what are called high places. Permanent establishment, not politicians. And fortunately I have a pleasant little niche awaiting me in what poor Purvis's benefactor called the groves of Academe. Perhaps more fortunately, our new government is both anti-imperialist and pro-education. In every graduate they will discern a future pillar of an expanded state school system. Not that I intend to be one. But I have the utmost confidence in Aunt Charlotte's ability to arrange a priority demobilization especially if she works in unison with a certain professor of modern history.'

'Who is this Purvis you keep mentioning?'

'Was. Not is. He's dead too.' Perron drank deeply, not quite finishing what was in his glass. 'I don't think I want to talk about Leonard Purvis. I'd rather talk about Bunbury. I had to follow up the telegram to Aunt Charlotte with a letter just in case the cable went astray. Would you like to know what I told her about how Bunbury died?'

'How did Bunbury die?'

'He committed suicide. Twice.'

'Twice.'

'The first time he did it in the bath-tub but I managed to revive him but when he did it again I wasn't there. They'd put him in an upstairs ward and when they weren't looking he threw himself out of the window and broke his neck.'

'A very determined Bunbury.'

'I'm glad you appreciate that. It's what I feel. In determination of that calibre there is something heroic. The thought first struck me at the hurried little inquest which they dragged me up from Kalyan to attend. They made out it was suicide while of unsound mind but you could tell they knew he was as sane as they were. On the other hand what *I* knew was that there wasn't a man in the room with anything like so profound a sense of what he was in the world to do, nor anything like so profound a sense of the criminal waste of human energy that we've seen in the last six years. I'm glad he didn't survive to hear about the new bomb.'

'Are you sure about not eating, Guy?'

'Could I have something in here?'

'Of course.'

'Then I'd better.' He poured more neat Scotch into the over-rich mixture. 'Normally, you know, I'm quite abstemious, but I've spent the past few days discreetly stoned to the eyeballs, a condition which the Red Shadow observes with envy and malicious longing to get his corrupt and filthy thieving hands into my kit-bag to see how many bottles I have left. I for my part long to catch him at it, so that I can boot him in the arse. And believe me, Nigel, before I leave, boot him I shall, with or without provocation. It's a point of honour. The arses of the Suleimans of India exist to be booted by British sergeants. It's traditional. One for the sergeant, two for the regiment and three for the *raj*. And then the women of the Suleimans of India will laugh like drains, the wild dogs of the hills will yelp their satisfaction and there will be peace again on the Khyber. I think you'd better go, because Suleiman will be making a note of the time you and I have been alone in a locked compartment and will make his report accordingly to Major Merrick. I beg his pardon. Colonel. But it's difficult to keep up. He was a major when I saw him in Bombay on Bunbury Sunday. A colonel when I reported at his office in Delhi on Thursday. I entertain this illusion now that it's dangerous to be parted from him for more than a day or two. Every night I go to sleep terrified that in the morning he'll be a full colonel or even a brigadier.'

'I take it you're not enamoured. Why, particularly?'

Perron sipped.

' "I do not love thee, Dr Fell, the reason why I cannot tell".' He sipped again. 'On the other hand I've been working out why. He's the man who comes too late and invents himself to make up for it. Even that arm, you know, is an invention. You needn't think it happened in a flash, with a bang, or even on an operating table. It appeared quite gradually, like the stigmata on a saint's hands and feet and side. So that the world would notice, and pause. The pause is very important. I think you'd better join him. He doesn't like being neglected or kept waiting.'

'What takes him to Pankot?'

'The case of one Havildar Karim Muzzafir Khan, late of the Pankot Rifles.'

'I think I may know a bit about that.'

'You were always insufferably well-informed. About rowing for example. What bit do you know?'

'If it's the one who joined Bose's people in Germany' – Perron nodded – 'then Miss Layton's father has put in a request for permission to see him. Is Merrick arranging it?'

Perron drank more whisky.

'No. We're going up to take statements from the havildar's former fellow NCOs.'

'No chance of an exception being made.'

'An exception?'

'No chance of Colonel Layton being allowed to see him?'

'None at all. What's so special about Colonel Layton?'

'Nothing. But what's so special about Havildar Karim Muzzafir Khan that Delhi sends a half-colonel all the way to Pankot to take statements?'

'Oh, that's easily answered. The havildar was special because Merrick chose him.'

'You mean as an example?'

'I mean he was a chosen one. It's part of the technique of the self-invented man. Merrick looks round, his eye lights on someone and he says, Right, I want *him*. Why else do you think I'm here. I'm a chosen one. I expect Coomer was.'

'Coomer?'

'Coomer. Kumar. Harry. Hari. Don't tell me you don't remember him. Miss Layton said you did. It puzzled her when I said I didn't. It aroused her suspicions. Very embarrassing. It made her wonder whether I was only pretending to have gone to Chillingborough. So she dropped a name or two. Yours was one. And then there was Clark-Without.'

'Clark-Without? How did she come to know him?'

'I think she said they met in Calcutta. You remember his reputation, I expect. Hasn't she ever mentioned him?'

'There's no reason why she should.'

'But of course she's told you about meeting me. Obviously.'

'Not all about it. Why did you say you didn't remember Coomer, by the way?'

'The subject was taboo. Not fit for mixed company. Merrick ordered me not to discuss it. The easiest way to avoid being drawn into a discussion was to pretend I didn't know him. Did you know our friend Coomer put cricket behind him and went in for rape and that our friend Merrick caught him at it?'

'Is that what he told you?'

'Has he got it wrong?'

'There are two schools of thought. How did you come across Merrick? Just by being posted to his department?'

'Attached. Not posted yet, thank God. But no. I met him one warm night. On the docks. At Bombay. It sounds romantic, doesn't it? Then I didn't meet him again until the evening at the Maharanee's. But, already I was chosen. Fate. It has driven me to drink, to Bunbury and Aunt Charlotte, and to a refutation of Emerson.'

'Emerson?'

' "Society is a wave. The wave moves onward, but the water of which it is composed does not. The same particle does not rise from the valley to the ridge. Its unity is only phenomenal. The persons who make up a nation today, next year die, and their experience with them." Emerson failed to see that there were exceptions. People like you and me.'

Rowan smiled. He made neither head nor tail of it and on the whole saw no reason to try. But a penny had just dropped.

'Did you meet a Count Bronowsky at the Maharanee's? Sarah told me he was there.'

'He was certainly there. Why do you ask?'

'He put that idea into your head, didn't he? About Merrick inventing himself and the arm?'

'He certainly didn't. It's my copyright.'

'Coincidence then. He has much the same idea. I'd better leave you to it, Guy, and get them to bring you in some supper. By the way, when I was still out on the platform just now did Merrick take the opportunity to ask you how you and I knew one another?'

'He did.'

'What did you say?'

'I said we knew one another quite well before the war. I don't think it satisfied him. He probably thinks we've been in touch recently because neither of us showed any surprise at meeting.'

'You didn't mention Chillingborough?'

'I had a feeling it wasn't necessary.'

'It doesn't matter either way but one likes to be prepared.'

'Because of Coomer? What interests you and Sarah Layton about Coomer? The fact that he's an old Chillingburian who has been in what used to be called a Spot of Bother?'

'I suppose that provides a very rough basis for an interest.'

'As for everything else? This, for instance?' He gestured round the compartment. 'I imagine Colonel Merrick's coupé isn't half as comfortable. This cosy little compartment is symbolic, don't you find?'

'I hadn't thought of it. What is it symbolic of?'

'Of our isolation and insulation, our inner conviction of class rights and class privileges, of our permanence and of our capacity to trim, to insure against any major kind of upheaval affecting our interests, and of course of our fundamental indifference to the problems towards which we adopt attitudes of responsibility. Not moral responsibility, ownership responsibility. A moral responsibility would be too trying. Even poor underprivileged Purvis was clearheaded enough to admit that. Property on the other hand can always be got rid of and new property acquired. New property, new responsibility, but the same manner, the same deep inner conviction and the same snug cosy sense of insulation. I know where I shall find mine when I'm back home. Where will you find yours, Nigel, I mean when India is got rid of?'

'I've really not thought about that, Guy. It's just a shade too far ahead.'

'You haven't thought about it. But of course you don't need to. Neither of us does. Nothing can erode our ingrained sense of class security. Your face has taken on that remote patrician look that tells me you would find what I say offensive if you thought for one moment I meant it. Well I do. Every bloody word. Emerson was obviously too much of a peasant to appreciate the significance of you and me. Society is a wave. The wave moves onward. You and I move along with it. Emerson was writing for the Merricks and Purvises of the world. The ones who get drowned. Merrick hopes not to be. But he will be.

Can't the fool see that nobody of the class he aspires to belong to has ever cared a damn about the empire and that all that God-the-Father God-the-*raj* was a lot of insular middle- and lower-class shit?'

'An uncle of mine took God-the-father God-the-*raj* quite seriously, I should say.'

'You mean he had principles?'

'Yes, I think so.'

'I bet that if you cut right through the principles you'd find all he took seriously was his unassailable right to deploy things and people to his uttermost personal advantage and private satisfaction.'

'Is Merrick a principled man?'

'Principled as a rock. He thinks people like you and me are scum. He believes we've abandoned the principles we used to live by, what he would call the English upper- and ruling-class principle of knowing oneself superior to all other races especially black and having a duty to guide and correct them. He's been sucked in by all that Kiplingesque double-talk that transformed India from a place where plain ordinary greedy Englishmen carved something out for themselves to balance out the more tedious consequences of the law of primogeniture, into one where they appeared to go voluntarily into exile for the good of their souls and the uplift of the native. The transformation was illusory of course. A middle-class misconception of upper-class *mores*. But a man like Merrick can't be expected to see that. He's spent too long inventing himself in the image to have energy left to realize that as an image it is and always was hollow. He only notices it has become rarer. Poor Coomer obviously never stood a chance. An English public school education and manner, but black as your hat.'

'Not so black.'

'Black enough for Merrick. But most of us are as bad as black to him. There aren't many real white men left. And the odd thing is that when he comes across any he despises them. Colonel Layton for instance.'

'He despises Colonel Layton? Why?'

'White man gone soft. Guide *and* correct, remember? The two pillars of wisdom. Despises because Layton has and is every-thing Merrick covets. But Layton hasn't the nerve or guts to live up to it. He'd clasp the Bose-tainted havildar to his bosom, for instance. Tears of sorrow rather than the lash of anger. Too many bloody tears altogether. Even over a half-empty bottle of Old Sporran. So God help us tomorrow. Have you got any by the way?'

'Got any what?'

'Old Sporran. Doesn't Government House run to it?'

'Not nowadays. Why God help you tomorrow?'

'Not nowadays. No. Nowadays Old Sporran is reserved for the Purvises. Damned proletariat getting in everywhere. He hanged himself.'

'Who hanged himself? Purvis?'

'No, Purvis fell. The havildar hanged himself. Havildar Karim Muzzafir Khan, son of subedar Muzzafir Khan VC.'

'Oh. When?'

'Tuesday you said? So, a few minutes ago it was Monday. Sunday morning, then. Some time on Sunday morning. Before daylight. Which is why there's no chance of Colonel Layton being allowed to talk to him. There's no poor weary shagged-out shamed and insulted havildar to talk to.'

'Shamed and insulted by whom?'

'Merrick of course.'

'You witnessed it?'

'Only the beginning and the end. Bombay in June and Delhi on Friday. I expect I missed the best bits in the middle.'

'What happened in the middle?'

'I don't know. The real working-over I expect.'

'Physical working-over?'

'No sign of that on the body. I don't think that's Merrick's style.'

Perron emptied the flask into his glass. The liquor was now neat.

'You saw the body, then.'

'Oh yes. "Come over to D block, will you, sergeant? There has been an interesting development." At four o'clock in the morning.'

'Interesting?'

'That's what he said. It was quite deliberate. So that I should be unprepared. He presented the scene like a *tableau vivant*, well not so vivant, but one he'd set up which he wanted me to react

to. I'm surprised he let them cut him down before I got there.'
Perron swigged whisky. 'The whole thing was unspeakably ugly
and sordid.'

'What did he use?'

'The havildar? You mean for rope? Torn strips of shirt and
vest knotted together. He'd tried to cut his throat first with a
broken bit of mess-tin. I'd prefer not to talk about it. I'll just tell
you what Merrick said. "Not a very prepossessing-looking chap,
was he, sergeant?"'

'Yes, I see. So the real reason for the journey is to report the
death to Colonel Layton?'

'No. The real reason is to sustain the connection. The role
of friend of the family. Nothing brash of course. Nothing pushing. Just a persistent air of quiet competence and capacity and
authority. Occasional sudden concentration of effort and flurry
of activity that show the range and depth of feeling and concern.
Like this visit. The human touch. And all these statements to be
taken from the havildar's ex-comrades. As if anything that can
be recorded now in the havildar's favour is not only welcome
but a white man's duty to discover and put on the file.' Perron
closed one eye and stared at Rowan as if he suddenly found it
difficult to focus. Then he nodded and said:

'He's chosen the Laytons, too.'

Perron opened the closed eye and added: 'But don't worry.
I mean if you do worry, don't.'

'Worry about what?'

'His choosing the Laytons. I said Laytons; not any one Layton
in particular. At least I shouldn't think so. So don't worry. What
was her name?'

'Whose?'

'The stunning girl Aunt Charlotte took a shine to.'

'Laura Elliott.'

'Laura Elliott.' Perron put his head back as if tired. 'What a
sad name. What happened?'

'She married someone else.'

'Anyone I know?'

'I shouldn't think so. She met him in Rangoon. His name was
Ratcliff. He planted rubber in Malaya.'

'What was she doing in Rangoon?'

'Visiting me.'

'When was this?'

'Nineteen-forty-one.'

'How did she get to Rangoon in nineteen-forty-one?'

'Her parents were in Mandalay. Civil service.'

'I always thought of her as army.'

'Her brother was.'

'Sandhurst together?'

'Yes.'

'Same regiment?'

'Yes. The three of us came out on the same boat.'

'Were you and Laura Elliott ever engaged?'

'Eventually.'

'When you went to Burma.'

'No, we became unengaged in Burma.'

'Were you in the Burma show in 'forty-two?'

'I never think of it as a show. Just as a retreat. I was in that.'

'Well, show or retreat, you survived. Did Laura Elliott's brother?'

'No.'

'Did Laura and her rubber-planter get out of Malaya?'

'The parents got out of Burma but only Mrs Elliott's still alive. She lives in Darjeeling and writes to me occasionally. She heard from Laura once early on, after she'd been interned by the Japanese. There was no news of Tony and Laura's never written again. At least nothing's been received.'

'Poor Laura. I said it was a sad name.' Perron brought his head back level. 'Does it upset you still?'

'Not any more.'

'What about Sarah Layton?'

'What about her?'

'She referred to you with what I'd call respect and admiration. Mutual?'

'Yes.'

'Pity. I mean for me. Given half an opportunity making a bit of a pass at Sarah Layton was the one thing that made the prospect of several days in Pankot bearable. But I expect I'd better behave, hadn't I? Yes. Well. Incidentally, do you mind very much if in future I call you sir in front of other people? You can go on calling me Guy if you like but it offends my sense of military decorum to call you Nigel in public.'

Smiling, otherwise ignoring this, Rowan said, 'Do you know where you're putting up?'

'You mean quartered. No, but I have every confidence in my officer. He's the kind of man who knows it's good form to look to the needs of horse, groom and self in that order, although his own comfort is assured, naturally, so it can always be safely left until last. Why? Were you thinking of keeping in touch?'

'We ought to arrange an evening if we can. You can reach me by ringing Two Hundred.'

'The Governor's hill palace?'

'It's the guest house attached to what used to be the summer residence.'

'Used to be? Has the weather deteriorated?'

'I mean it's shut up.'

'With accommodation so short?'

'People complain, but like this coach it doesn't convert very easily. And the next Governor may revive the old seasonal system of six months in the hills and six on the plain. Anyway ring me there. We'll fix something.'

Perron nodded.

Rowan said, 'I'll send a bearer in with the menu. He'll bring you a drink too if you want another. I'll leave that to your discretion. And feel free to ring the bell at any time.'

Again Perron nodded.

'Sleep well,' Rowan said, and began to go.

'Thanks for the bed, Nigel. I'm very grateful.'

The corridor was empty. No Red Shadow. In the dining-room two tables were laid and were being set out with chafing dishes. He smelt, fleetingly, carnations. And the scent of cologne. But there were only marigolds. He told one of the bearers to attend to the guest in compartment number two and then went through into the saloon.

Suleiman was kneeling, easing one of Merrick's feet into crimson leather slippers. Between the stiff first and second fingers of Merrick's black-gloved left hand was a lighted cigarette. Merrick and Suleiman both turned their heads. Suleiman grinned, showing handsome teeth. Merrick smiled, an odd lopsided smile – or so the scar tissue made it appear; and Rowan, in spite of everything, felt touched and under an odd kind of compulsion to forget what he knew, what he thought he knew; what it was unfair, after all, to allow himself to be affected by when he had scarcely said more than a few words to the man. As he took his seat on the sofa and nodded to the bearer indicating that he wanted another drink before eating, and listened to what Merrick was saying about Suleiman's theory that it was bad for the circulation to wear walking shoes when one wasn't walking, he also felt himself being supported, braced up almost, by an unexpected sensation of being once more – away from Guy Perron – in control of things, of himself, and in surroundings that matched his mood. And presently when Suleiman had gone, taking Merrick's shoes with him, and he and Merrick were alone, eyeing one another with what Rowan supposed an observer would interpret as cautious interest, it struck him as being odd that the one man he might have expected to be a disruptive or abrasive presence was not, but seemed to fit in and to share with him this feeling of repose, or anyway of momentary relief from the pressures which had been piling up, undermining his confidence: a feeling accentuated, perhaps, by the way the coach absorbed and muffled the vibration and clatter of the wheels without diminishing the flattering sensation of a speed and movement forward that were absolutely effortless.

THE MOGHUL ROOM

I

MY AUNT CHARLOTTE's knowledge of India and Indian affairs was very limited but her enthusiasm for any subject that interested another member of the family was quickly stirred and once it had been stirred it was difficult to moderate. For example, the technique and mystique of ballooning continued to exert a fascination for her long after her brother, my Uncle Charles, had abandoned it as a sport (having come down near Cobh in Ireland after setting out from Kent for Essex). For years, subsequently, she maintained a scrap-book into which she pasted cuttings of anything she could find that was connected with the subject of unpowered aerial navigation.

Flattering as her sharing of one's interests was it could be a little tiresome even if one's own enthusiasm remained unflagging. The clippings of newspaper articles and reports about India which she sent or saved for me until her first and fatal illness were, in a sense, an unnecessary duplication. However it is to her I owe a comparison between Operation Bunbury and the last Viceroyalty.

'Your viceroys are all Bunburyists,' she declared. (From the moment of my return home in 1945 all Indian personalities, policies and problems, were referred to as mine: your Mr Gandhi, your Mr Nehru, your Kashmir problem, your non-alignment policy, your confrontation with the Chinese, your application for foreign aid, your green revolution, your family planning.) 'Your viceroys' in 'Your viceroys are all Bunburyists' was just one of many examples of this habit of placing everything Indian as it were in my gift. Asked to justify this statement, though, she pointed out the regularity with which at certain climactic moments in talks and negotiations my viceroys withdrew, packed their bags and came home for consultation.

This, she said, was 'pure Bunburyism', clear evidence of pre-arrangements between my viceroys and my Secretary of State for India in Whitehall to ensure the continuation of whatever policy the British Government was currently pursuing in regard to the sub-continent. 'Take your present policy,' she said once, when Wavell was still Viceroy (I always kept notes of our conversations), 'this is clearly a policy of conducting serious talks about a future constitutional change within a general framework of an assumption on our part that the existing status quo will be maintained. Which means that when your Lord Wavell detects that the serious talks are about to break down – or look like continuing so successfully that the status quo is actually at risk – he has himself called from the conference room as if to the telephone and returns a few minutes later to announce that there has been a development in London that requires his immediate presence there. It is merely another way of saying as Mr Worthing would have done, "I'm afraid my poor friend Bunbury has taken a turn for the worse and that I must catch the 3.15."'

I thought this a bit unfair to Wavell but on reflection saw that there was something in it in regard to viceroys in general, and said so. Thereafter whenever the Viceroy – Wavell, and then his successor, Mountbatten – arrived back in London, Aunt Charlotte sent me a postcard (usually of aerial views of the countryside) with a brief message: 'Bunbury unwell again.' 'Poor Bunbury giving cause for anxiety,' etc. The Mountbatten vice-royalty, though, produced this (an extract from one of the many letters of hers which I have preserved):

'If Attlee *means* that power is to be transferred as early as 1948, then Bunbury's ill-health has undergone a change. I don't mean he's better or worse, merely unwell in a different way. If our policy now *is* to get out, then you will begin to see that Bunbury's delicate constitution will respond admirably to every turn of events which advances our policy of demission of power by 1948 but suffer serious setbacks on any occasion when impediments to it are put in our way.'

In reply I pointed out that for the first time a viceroy of mine (Mountbatten) appeared to have plenipotentiary powers and that although this was advantageous administratively it meant that the Bunbury gambit might well have had its day. Aunt Charlotte declared at once that a viceroy with plenipotentiary powers would be the greatest Bunburyist of the lot, because it meant he would have taken Bunbury to India with him. This was not clear to me. I asked her to elucidate. She wrote:

'I mean that Bunbury has at last emerged in his true colours as The British Presence in India – traditionally seated (I mean bedridden) in Whitehall, but at last visiting with Dickie (how well that boy has done) the scene of his hitherto only vicarious triumphs and failures. Attlee has said (it is so plain to me I wish it were to you) that a holiday in India until 1948 might be beneficial to him. A valedictory tour, so to speak, like the personal appearance of a famous film-star known to millions but only as a shadow on the silver screen. After the valedictory tour he will return home, retire and be content to fade away to look at his press-cuttings. So henceforth any deterioration in Bunbury's health will occur only when it looks to the Viceroy as if your Indians aren't going to let Bunbury leave as planned.'

The force of her argument was driven home early in June 1947 when the Viceroy – having had what the papers revealed day after day as the greatest difficulty in finding someone among the contenders both able and willing to relieve us of Indian responsibility and letting Bunbury go (I recalled Purvis's warning) announced that power would be transferred not in 1948 but in ten weeks' time.

Telegrams between Aunt Charlotte and myself crossed. Mine read: Bunbury stop looks like experience of personal appearance proved too much. Hers: Doctors here have re-examined Bunbury X-rays stop condition worse than thought stop vital expedite his return otherwise fear worst in that climate stop Dickie coping but suggest you fly out observe and supervise stop will arrange passage and underwrite reasonable expenses.

Reading this I realized that Aunt Charlotte had become a convinced Purvisite. 'Condition worse than thought' argued that a British Presence in India was as Purvis might have said no longer viable economically or administratively. 'Vital to expedite his return' was a hint that the members of the Labour Government after nearly two years in office were getting desperate at the prospect of having to continue to support this presence. Considering the complexity of the moral, political and historical issues which surrounded the attempted transfer of power in India and considering that these were the only issues ever publicly discussed I think Aunt Charlotte showed remarkable perspicacity. She thought so herself and as the years passed took undisguised pleasure in heavily underlining confirmatory passages in the articles and books she sent me – the writings of soldiers, states-men and civil servants, journalists and historians – to draw my attention to admissions of the kind that supported what, mis-understanding me slightly, she claimed with my authority as her own entirely original opinion: that as a result of the war, the policy of Indianization, the running down of the machinery of British recruitment to the civil service and police, and as a result of the infiltration of political, communal and nationalistic modes of thought into the Indian armed services (the Naval Mutiny in Bombay in 1946 was always cited as an example) it would have been difficult, even impossible, to maintain in India any form of stable government with a responsibility to Parliament at home and for law and order and national defence in India, except at a cost which even if the will and the means were available would have been excessive and just not on from the British taxpayer's point of view.

In the delirium of pneumonia (at an advanced age she unwisely took an interest – an active interest – in her grand-nephew's pas-sion for duck-shooting at dawn on the marshes) she spoke of many things which made sense to a member of the family. 'What, there, the penny black. Who would have thought it had so much blood in it?' Such a statement, sinister from the point of view of the medical staff, was perfectly rational if you remembered Aunt Hester's craze for philately and Uncle William's frustrated theat-rical ambitions which dated from his appearance in a school production of *Macbeth*. Other remarks, obscure to the nurses, clear to me, showed that she was thinking turn and turn about of the things that had interested or obsessed her brothers and sisters. I should explain that my father was the only Perron of his generation who got married. The other brothers and sisters paired off: George (who was the eldest and who inherited) and Harriet, William and Hester, Charles and Charlotte. Cousins Henry and Sophie were my grandfather Perron's only brother's children. They paired off too. My father, Aunt Charlotte used to say, only got married because he was the odd boy out. Insisting on being sent to Chillingborough with a view to an Indian career, joining the army at the outbreak of the great war and getting married (not even to a relation) were, I suppose, the forms which

Perron eccentricity took in his case. I was sent to Chillingborough really as an act of devotion to my father's memory. It
was felt that he had never had a chance to show what – as a Perron
– he could do – but that being killed on November 10, 1918,
suggested he had been on the right lines. His brothers – who all
had brilliant minds but unadaptable personalities – were in the
main privately tutored between expulsions from a number of
establishments of varying reputations and competence.

I am trying to convey as clearly and economically as I can
something of the background of the last surviving member of
that generation of Perrons who as she lay dying revealed herself
to me as a woman whose life, so apparently full, had been in so
far as original enthusiasms and direct experience were concerned
(with that single and fatal exception) empty. A croaked reference
to speed bonny boat could have been related either to my rowing
or to the punt in which she had set out with her great-nephew
to see for herself what so enthralled him about shooting duck.
Drugs succeeded in reducing her temperature and there was a
lucid interval before she relapsed into sleep, unconsciousness and
coma. Opening her eyes and finding me there she said – indicating what she obviously recognized as a private room – 'Well I see
that I am dying beyond my means' – closed her eyes and never
opened them again, nor communicated, except by smiling intermittently at thoughts she did not share with me. That explicit
reference to Bunbury's creator was the nearest she came to
touching on a subject that had been a bond between us ever
since I first set sail for India; but in making it she was just as likely
to have been thinking of her Thespian brother as of her 'Indian'
nephew, or even of neither but of her late brother George who,
inheriting the bulk of the Perron estate, had made a number of
foolish investments.

She was such an unegotistical person, such a champion of
other people's causes, that it seems grossly unfair to connect her
in any way with responsibility for a death roll that was never
accurately counted but which has become widely accepted as
reaching the one-quarter million mark.

'Your Punjabis,' she said when I got back from the euphoric
and bloodstained country after taking the trip to 'observe and
supervise' which she had subsidized in 1947, 'Your Punjabis
would appear to have taken leave of their senses.'

She was referring to the massacres that accompanied the migrations of communities after the decision to partition. I told her that the murders of Hindus and Sikhs by Muslims and of Muslims by Hindus and Sikhs had by no stretch of the imagination been confined to the land of the five rivers, but Punjab was a word which had always had a strong appeal for people like Aunt Charlotte and she probably felt that once you had pronounced it (particularly as she pronounced it, with a rotundity of mouth and emphasis of jaw – Poonjawb) then you had said all that needed to be said about the golden land below Afghanistan. She therefore continued to demarcate the zone of violence on this provincial basis and I think succeeded too in mentally reducing the slaughter to the manageable proportions of an isolated act of insurrection which was the result of allowing things to get a bit out of hand.

It would never have occurred to her to examine her conscience in regard to those one-quarter million deaths, although she had, in fact, as I had done – voted for them. It would not have occurred to her because she held single-mindedly to the Purvis principle, the view that a British presence in India was an economic and administrative burden whose quick offloading was an essential feature of post-war policy in the welfare state. I'll give her this, though: in adhering to this principle she never once introduced the ethical argument that colonialism was immoral – an argument that supported so many of us. I don't think the ethical argument ever entered her head. She was essentially a pragmatist. The only moral argument I ever remember her advancing was the one she used to try to convince me that my joining up would be unfair to the men she assumed I would accept responsibility for.

Needless to say, I never told Aunt Charlotte that she, as well as I, was responsible for the one-quarter million deaths in the Punjab and elsewhere. But I did once ask her who, in her opinion, *was* responsible. She said, 'But that is obvious. The people who attacked and killed each other.' There was no arguing with this, but it confirmed my impression of her historical significance (and mine), of the overwhelming importance of the part that had been played in British–Indian affairs by the indifference and the ignorance of the English at home – whom Aunt Charlotte, in an especially poignant way had in my mind come to represent;

and upsetting though I found it, nothing was more appropriate than that in that delirium, when images of all the acquired and borrowed interests of her life flowed swiftly through her heated imagination, images of India were totally forgotten.

In investing someone with historical significance one should proceed cautiously but I think the conclusion I came to about her share of responsibility for disorder and bloodshed can be traced back to that grey humid morning in Kalyan when I stood up and spoke for half an hour to a hall full of restless and inattentive men about the territorial ambitions of Mahdaji and Daulat Rao Sindia, and realized how little any of us knew or cared about a country whose history had been that of our own for more than three hundred years and which had contributed more than any other to our wealth, our well-being.

Less than a month later I was passing through Deolali to embark at Bombay on a homeward-bound ship in a mood alternating between the exhilaration of a man released to follow his own bent and the depression of one who retires from a situation gratefully but with some doubts about the means he's adopted to extricate himself. There were as well some unexpected regrets.

If I had been with Ronald Merrick right up to the time when the signal came ordering me to report to Deolali, I doubt that I should have felt anything except relief and grateful astonishment at the speed with which Aunt Charlotte had apparently worked. But I wasn't with him; rather, he wasn't with me and the signal happened to arrive at a moment when I was aware of being comfortably situated and pleasantly occupied.

In the morning, after that night journey from Ranpur in the Governor's special coach, when Rowan and I bumped into each other in the narrow passage between Their Excellencies' compartments (w.c. on one side, shower on the other) he was polite but (I thought) a little cool. I think he assumed I was lying when I told him I had no hangover, or assumed that I had already started on one of the bottles in my kit-bag so that I could face up to another day with Merrick and the Red Shadow.

He may have been right about the hangover because my recollections of the arrival in Pankot aren't very clear. But there could be another reason for that. To have travelled on the same train as a coffin without knowing it is one thing. To be greeted by a large crowd banging on drums another. I don't recall how soon it was before I connected the crowds and the drums with a funeral, or the funeral with a coffin that had come in on the train, or the coffin with the body of Mr Kasim's secretary, and I'm not sure whether it was Merrick's information alone, or Merrick's and the Red Shadow's plus other people's that helped me to fit the pieces together. What I do remember is that it was nothing Nigel Rowan said because he said very little. An impression I had that morning was of not inspiring his confidence; another was that as a result of whatever conversation he'd had with Merrick the night before there was an amiability between them now which seemed, on Rowan's part, advertised to show me that he discounted everything I had told him about that officer's behaviour. Without caring much what the answer was I wondered whether Nigel had said anything to Merrick about my attitude to him, and whether Merrick's silence in the 15 cwt that Area HQ had sent to the station for us was especially ominous.

Nigel's detachment, Merrick's silence, the distracting crowds at the station, the drums and the shouting, the revolting stink of the Red Shadow's stale breath and unwashed body in the confined luggage-loaded space at the tarpaulin-covered back of the truck: these have stayed with me as parts of the jigsaw. Another part of it is waiting, in several places; keeping upwind of the Pathan if on the same verandah with him and moving if he came too near. The waiting was done in the complex of old Victorian barracks and huts of more recent origin that was Area Headquarters. A dry sunny morning? Something cool but hard – metallic – in the air, the smell of a century or more of Pankot's experience of military occupation. A late breakfast in a British NCOs' mess. Eating it alone at a long table as yet uncleared of used plates and cups and saucers. The depredations of white ants in wooden window frames set in crumbling plaster. Views from these windows of the hills. The sound of a coppersmith. Shafts of sunlight? A padlocked glass-fronted cupboard that displayed a few silver cups, sporting-trophies. A dartboard and last night's chalked scores. A little bit of Salisbury Plain in the Indian hills. I had never hated the army so much as I did in this hour or two

in this drearily familiar and horribly anonymous area of roads
and pathways, directional signs, inhospitable huts and character-
less rooms – the makeshift impermanent jerry-built structures
that seem to rest for sole support on the implacable and rigid
authority of military hierarchy. The fire of hatred (so intense, so
unexpected, so out of character) was stoked and fanned by a
sudden and utter lack of confidence in the machine I thought
I had set in motion with the telegram and letter to Aunt Charlotte. The illusion of imminent escape withered away in this
uncompromising and heartless reality.

Another piece of the jigsaw: as I sat beneath the dartboard,
stupefied by this misery, there was a distant crackling fusillade of
shots whose echoes bounced from one hill to another. When
the echoes were finally spent I heard the uninterrupted song of
the coppersmith. No barking. The birds and dogs of Pankot –
wild or tame – were used to the sound of range practice.

And I remember relief when the truck came back from wherever it had been with Merrick and the Red Shadow and I was
taken by the driver (a surly, solitary man) from the NCOs' mess;
relief that was short-lived because it ended in another anonymous room, an annexe in the grounds of the General Hospital
(military wing) which I later discovered lay approximately half-
way between Area Headquarters and the lines of the Pankot
Rifles depot.

From the window of this room there was no view at all. The
hospital was well provided with shade trees and the annexe was
half-hidden in bushes. I didn't bother to ask the driver why I was
to be quartered there, nor did I ask where Merrick and the Red
Shadow were. One of the pleasures of being a sergeant is of feeling under no obligation to satisfy your curiosity about the background to events. You don't originate *anything* if you can help
it. Delivered by the driver, admitted by a servant (who must have
had an instruction from somewhere) I entered the room in the
annexe and because it had a bed had no difficulty in assuming
that this was where I was to sleep while in Pankot. I dumped
pack and kit-bag and lay down.

Out of this phase (morning of August 14 to morning of
August 16) one important minor figure emerges: that of an
RAMC corporal, a young man from Bermondsey. I shall call
him Corporal Dixon. The British NCOs on the hospital staff

messed together and formed a little clique. It was a very un-military set-up: sergeants, corporals, but not lance-corporals. Driven by hunger to leave the room in the annexe and find the mess-hut I found I was expected, but I think only as a man with a name and the barest identification. I was received in a friendly easy-going fashion and given a beer. The mess conveyed an idea of intellectual superiority. There was a Van Gogh reproduction on one wall and the sound of Mozart from the portable gramo-phone. A few of the NCOs had seen service in the field. For them, Pankot was a relief station. Among these front-line veterans was Corporal Dixon, known affectionately as Sophie, or Miss Dixon, or Mum.

I was told that he kept the patients in the wards in stitches and that he had tamed the QA nursing sisters and the medical officers. I was also told that a wounded officer who had watched him at work at a casualty clearing station in the Arakan and listened to the stream of morale-boosting queenly chat – a mock-ing commentary on the sounds of battle near by – had said: 'You deserve the MM, Corporal.' Sophie had said, 'Oh that would never do, sir, I wouldn't presume, and where would they pin it, the cheeky things?'

But these tales came later when I set about trying to find out how I had offended, what had caused the temperature to drop. Between the friendly reception and the freezing up no more than a few hours passed. Dixon's first appearance was at lunch. 'A copper!' he said, fingering my green armband. 'Has someone been at the drugs? It's no good looking here, sergeant, we're all clean-living boys. It's that Matron over at Private. She's never been the same since she visited Cox's Bazaar looking for a bargain and found it closed for stocktaking.'

I laughed and was introduced. Dixon was rather welcome comic relief. Perhaps if I hadn't laughed he would have been tipped the wink to quieten down. Lunch was at a long table. White cloth. A vase or two of marigolds. I was at one end, as I remember, and Dixon at the other. The atmosphere was amiable. Once it was established that I wasn't at the hospital on duty but only quartered temporarily in the annexe I don't think any further questions were asked. I remember that towards the end of the meal all conversation died away because Dixon had taken the stage and was recounting a series of scurrilous but very funny stories, most of them delivered in a tone of prim outrage, of astonishment at the trickery and under-handedness of the world. It took me some time to sort out the code. After failing to see the point several times I realized that 'she' almost invariably meant 'he'. A sentence such as 'Well you should have seen her, got up to the nines in her new frock, preening she was, poor old thing, well she doesn't often have one does she?' didn't, I discovered, refer to a matron at a hospital dance but to a senior officer of the RAMC or the IMS who was wearing a new uniform, hadn't been looking where he was going and had bumped into and knocked Corporal Dixon over at a moment when he happened to be carrying a bedpan full of urine. 'So there she was, drenched with Private Thingummy's piss, new dress ruined, and there was me flat on me bum and covered in piss too, thinking I'd really ask for me cards this time. But you can't beat breeding, can you? "Is that Corporal Dixon?" she says to Matron looking down her nose, oh very ladylike. "I'm afraid it is," Matron says. "I see," she says. "I suppose it was not entirely his fault so we won't hold it against him." Well as to *that*, I thinks to meself, chance would be a fine thing.'

How much of Dixon's tale was true one could only guess. (Did RAMC corporals carry bedpans in India?) What was clear was his rôle. He was the safety-valve. How well-timed and sustained his performances were over a period I could not judge except from the behaviour of his companions in the mess. Presumably he knew when to play up and when to give it a rest. I detected no signs either of boredom or aggression. Before the meal was quite over the steward brought in a note. It was for me; from Merrick. The truck-driver had brought it. I got up to leave.

'Are you with us for long, Sergeant?' Sophie Dixon called out. I told him probably for a day or two; added that I'd see them tonight anyway.

'Coppers,' he said for my benefit before I reached the door. 'The competition's been something cruel since they started sending them to college.'

A row of men, smiling, interested to see how I took it. Still smiling when I left. The next time I saw them they were not even civil; as though in the interval the gloom that began to settle on me during the long irritating afternoon had conveyed itself to them. I was deprived of the comic relief, of an antidote to Merrick who had surpassed himself to the extent when for two pins I would have set about undermining the whole subtly balanced structure of mystification and intimidation which was what he erected to get what he wanted.

From the medical NCOs' mess I was translated to a world of old barracks and hutments, parade grounds, flagpoles in beds of white-washed stones, the smell of creosoted wood warmed by the sun; a hot breeze blowing in from hills which were rigid in the torpor of an Indian afternoon. The distant coppersmith. I was delivered to the adjutant's office in the lines of the Pankot Rifles and conducted from there to a low block – square stuccoed whitewashed pillars of brick supporting the overhang of a steep-pitched roof to form a verandah – into a room that was being emptied of benches by a squad of sepoys. A school- or lecture-room. The walls were hung with posters, aids to recognition of enemy planes, tanks and personnel. At a table on the daïs sat Merrick. Three officers stood round him: a pale middle-aged Englishman (who was the adjutant, Coley), a youngish Indian captain and a very young English subaltern, smart as paint, stiff as starch with a lot of fine blond hair showing on his arms between immaculately turned up and laundered sleeves and on his legs between the hem of knife-edged khaki shorts and the tops of stockings worn with puttees and brown boots. Of the four only Merrick failed to respond to my ener- getic entrance and salute. But he was facing the door and although he didn't look up from the file he was reading he knew who it was. There were a couple of jemadars, a havildar who looked like a clerk and a naik in charge of the sepoy work-squad.

When the last bench had been taken out Merrick said, 'We shan't need the daïs either.' The three officers got down from it. Merrick remained. 'And if it's not too much trouble, Coley, I'd like this table placed where the light falls as fully as possible on whoever's sitting behind it.'

'Of course.'

No one asked why he wanted this light. He had the trick of directing people's minds from strategy to tactics. The table was tried several ways while Merrick stayed enthroned on the daïs. The subaltern was used as a stand-in to test for the light. When the right place was found Merrick got up to allow the chair to be taken over and placed behind the table. Then he went across and sat down again. The sepoys took the daïs out. 'We shall want another table and several more chairs,' he said, 'including another one with arms to go in front of *this* table.' All this was attended to. Then a medium-scale map of the Pankot District was sent for. A box of pins with different-coloured heads. A pair of compasses. The maps were brought. The jemadars pinned them to the wall in sequence. Mugs of tea arrived, followed by the compasses and pins which turned out to be my cue.

'This is where you can make yourself useful, sergeant,' he said. He gave me a copy of the list of VCOs, NCOs and men who had been prisoners-of-war in Germany. Against each man's name was the name of his village. With the compasses a circle was described on the map with its centre at the depot and with a radius equal to five miles on the ground. Then, as I read out the men's names and villages the jemadar stuck a pin in the map, a different-coloured pin for each different rank. Whenever a pin was stuck inside the pencilled circle I had to mark the name on the list with an asterisk.

We must have been occupied thus for well over an hour. Merrick came and went, sometimes with Coley, sometimes with the Indian officer. The subaltern remained with me and the jemadar, absolutely enthralled because he had no idea what we were up to. By the time we had finished the map showed at a glance how many of the ex-prisoners-of-war, now on leave, could be fairly easily got hold of; how many of them, in other words, lived within five miles of the depot. When I explained this to the subaltern he seemed quite bowled over at such an efficient – and humane – bit of staff-work. No one liked to inter-rupt such well-earned leave, so the first set of interviews would be with men who could be collected from and returned to their villages in the course of a single day.

He also saw why the table had been placed so that the light fell on the faces of the officers asking for statements and not on the faces of men who were to be encouraged to make them. The table tops had already been covered by blankets, and there was a vase of flowers on one of them. From Delhi Merrick had brought with him poster-size blow-ups of smiling victorious generals: Monty, Alex and Wavell (chosen for their connections with the Middle East where the 1st Pankots had fought). There were also posters of Bill Slim and Dickie Mountbatten as

Supremo. These were all pinned in strategic places on the walls. The master-stroke was the inclusion of a much enlarged photograph of a group of Indian officers leaning out of tanks and shaking hands with Americans, and of VCOs, NCOs and sepoys being matey with European other ranks in what looked like a street in devastated Berlin or Cologne. Everything in the room now conspired to make the ex-prisoners-of-war who had been true to the salt and not gone over to Bose – proud and helpfully talkative. The subaltern, so obviously newly commissioned, and perhaps secretly relieved that he would now never have to lead his men into battle, was almost visibly moved. He interpreted the whole *mise en scène* as a compliment to men of a fine regiment and as a stroke of genius on the part of the one-armed Lieut.- Colonel who, although coming from Delhi, obviously knew a thing or two and respected what he knew.

What the subaltern didn't know (how could he?) was that the whole business of the interviews and statements was utterly pointless. The Indian lieutenant suspected of being implicated in the death of a sepoy in Königsberg was himself dead – so I had discovered from the files in Delhi. Karim Muzzafir Khan's name, far from 'cropping up several times' in depositions taken in Germany about the dead sepoy had cropped up once. Moreover, the death of the sepoy might well have been due to natural causes. Suspicions had arisen solely from accusations and counter-accusations among Frei Hind sepoys who had been questioned after the Germans collapsed and who had no connections with the Pankot Rifles and one of whom may well have chosen to cast doubts on Havildar Karim Muzzafir Khan's conduct simply because he was an infantryman from a stuck-up regiment. There was no statement to be taken from any of the returned Pankot Rifles prisoners that could have any bearing on the dead sepoy, the dead lieutenant or on the dead Karim Muzzafir Khan's behaviour. The only things the ex-POWs would be able to tell us were the things they had already told Colonel Layton and their other officers directly they were reunited: their experiences of being talked to or intimidated by Bose's officers. Brief statements were already on the file. Eventually these might have to be elaborated but the cases against the Frei Hind officers were a long way down on the list of priorities.

I said the arrangements being made for these interviews were utterly pointless. That's not quite accurate. They weren't point-less in terms of Merrick's passionate exploration outwards from the hollow centre of his self-invented personality, and in these terms they were in every detail an exposition of his determining will and of his profound contempt for anything, for anybody, that crumbled without resisting. Some hindsight here; but when-ever I think of him nowadays this little *mise en scène* comes back to me as a vivid illustration of the extraordinary care he took to manipulate things, people and objects, into some kind of signifi-cant objective/subjective order with himself at the dominating and controlling centre.

What arguments he used to convince senior officers in his department in Delhi that he should leave at once on a statement-taking mission, accompanied by his newly acquired sergeant, I don't know. If there was opposition I wasn't aware of it; the operation was mounted smoothly, swiftly – as if Merrick had anticipated the havildar's suicide and planned in advance so that the only impediment to the scheme had been the havildar's tire-some stubbornness in staying alive. I certainly had no doubt that one of the chief reasons for the sudden journey was his desire to tell Colonel Layton to his face that the havildar was dead.

He had this effect on me. I attributed to him the grossest motives and the darkest intentions without a scrap of real evi-dence. The interesting thing is that I was convinced that he knew this, that my instinct to hold him in such intense dislike and suspicion was clear to him from the beginning and was one of the reasons why he had chosen me. I believe he found it necessary to be close to someone whose antagonism he knew he could depend on and that without this antagonism he had nothing really satisfactory by which to measure the effect of his behav-iour. My antagonism was like an acid acting on a blank photo-graphic plate which had been exposed to his powerful and inventive imagination. It made the picture emerge for him. This excited him, the more so because my antagonism could not be expressed openly without risk to myself of being guilty of insub-ordination. There were moments in our association when I felt that my animosity inspired in him a gratitude and a contempt both so overwhelming that he felt for me the same tender com-passion that is often said to overcome the inveterate slaughterer of game in the split second before he squeezes the trigger.

*

Pankot, then: the evening of August 14, 1945. On this same evening things were taking place of much greater consequence; for instance, in Tokyo, where the Japanese War Cabinet, persuaded by the Emperor, had finally decided to 'bear the unbearable'. In the past week since the incident in Hiroshima and its follow-up in Nagasaki it had become obvious to them that when the bomb-owning governments said Unconditional Surrender this was precisely what was meant. No trimming; no understanding even as between gentlemen that there would be no allied occupation of the Japanese mainland (that had been tried). No promise that the Emperor's person would be respected (that had been sought). So, on this evening the decision to surrender unconditionally was made, and perhaps as Merrick and I were driven away from the Pankot Rifles depot, having left the *mise en scène* in a state of readiness for the commencement of the charade the next day – the Emperor of Japan was at his desk recording the edict which was to be broadcast to his weeping subjects at midday tomorrow August 15, well before which time the decision would have been conveyed to us through the Swiss.

And at the very moment Merrick and I drove out into Rifle Range Road heading for Cantonment Approach Road and the Pankot General Hospital, it is probable that the handful of dissenting Japanese officers who tried to break into the Emperor's palace later that night to destroy the recorded edict before it could be broadcast were already gathering and working out ways and means and the odds against the success of this last-ditch Samurai act of patriotic defiance.

In Pankot the height of the surrounding hills made for a longer evening than one was accustomed to down on the plains and instead of encroaching from the east night seemed to lap slowly down the inner slope of west hill (where rich Indians had built their hill-station houses) and glide across the valley and then inch its way up east hill where the English lived and on whose peak, amid conifers, one could make out the roofs and upper-windows (last reflectors of the light of day) of the Summer Residence. Once the light had gone from the roof of this dominant but unoccupied building night fell – you might say – with the Government's permission. Sarah smiled when I suggested this

to her. She knew the view well from the lines of the Pankot
Rifles but its symbolism had not struck her before.

My recollection is of seeing it first when waiting on the verandah outside the room that had been got ready for the interviews
with the ex-POWs, because I'm sure I retained a visual impression of it on the journey back and that when Merrick turned
round and said, 'You know where to reach me?' I pictured him
standing at the window of one of those blazing upper rooms of
the Summer Residence, getting burnt on the other side of his
face but feeling nothing. The real answer to the question where
he could be reached was only slightly less impressive. He was
staying at Flagstaff House with the Area Commander.

One question I longed to ask him was how Colonel Layton
had taken the news of Karim Muzzafir Khan's death. I assumed
the news had been passed on and that by the afternoon it was
generally known by the other Pankot Rifles officers and the
senior NCOs and VCOs, and that this had accounted for the
heavy pause – the brief but significant silence that followed my
intentionally clear announcement of his name and village when
I got to it on the list and the jemadar fumbled with the coloured
pins as if looking for a black one.

But I restrained my curiosity and said nothing; even when the
truck drove inexplicably *past* the hospital entrance and made for
the bazaar. The crowds who must have attended the funeral
seemed to have gone but left hostages, groups of people still
en fête and bunches of idle police. We stopped outside a general
store. The driver got out and walked down the crowded road
towards War Memorial Square – by prearrangement, obviously,
since Merrick didn't question him. In fact he lit a cigarette.
Without turning – addressing the windscreen – he said, 'Do you
expect to see your friend Captain Rowan again while he's in
Pankot?'

I told him we had no actual arrangement.

'It might be useful,' he said, 'for us to know just what he's
up to.'

It was typical of Merrick that he should describe Rowan as
being 'up to' something – and 'up to' something that had or
might have a bearing on what Merrick himself was up to. It so
happened that Nigel was in fact up to something, on the Governor's behalf, but I wasn't aware of this until later when Rowan

– stung by certain developments – dropped his guard and disclosed that his distrust and dislike of Merrick were almost as great as my own. Discounting what he called an element of doubt, he had cogent reasons but wouldn't at first say what they were.

But it irritated me that because I now worked with Merrick he thought I could be used to pump an old friend for information which he hinted I not only could but ought to get for him. My polite but thick sergeant act (the NCO equivalent of what is known as dumb-insolence in private soldiers) saved me from actually promising something I had no intention of performing. And it may have sufficiently served Merrick's purpose to observe the effect his suggestion had on me. There was no reason why he shouldn't ask Rowan himself what brought him to Pankot. He had more opportunity, officially and socially. I discovered later that he and Nigel had both accepted an invitation to dine that night at the Laytons' and that each knew that the other would be there.

The driver came back; not alone. He had the Red Shadow in tow. The Red Shadow climbed into the back, disposed some parcels (presumably bought for Merrick) and gave me one of his malevolent grins. I never worked out the significance of these grins. More often than not he stared at me unsmiling. But since it was clear that he wished me no good in either case I never gave much thought to the matter, and on this occasion responded as usual with a gaze as blank as I could make it.

The truck was now reversed and we drove back to the hospital. The manoeuvre that had taken me past the hospital, to the bazaar, and now back again, seemed quite pointless, but it was all part of Merrick's mystification technique and I was becoming used to it. We drove through the gates of the hospital and for a sickening moment I thought that the Red Shadow was to be quartered where he could keep an eye on me. This suspicion hardened when we stopped outside the medical NCOs' mess and the Red Shadow vaulted over the tailboard and arrived on the asphalt, legs apart, like an acrobat fetching up in a standing position at the end of a sequence of spectacular leaps and somersaults. He was, thank God, only making room for me to make a less agile descent. He climbed back in again directly I was out. But now Merrick also got out. He came round to where I stood dusting my hands.

'I can't guarantee transport in the morning, sergeant.'

'No, of course not, sir.'

'The Pankot's adjutant says he can produce two of the men we want to interview by 10.30 tomorrow morning. I shall get to the office by ten so if nothing's come to pick you up by 09.30 you'd better get a tonga down to the depot or scrounge some transport from one of the NCOs here. Are you quite comfortably situated, by the way?'

I told him very.

'I ran into one of the medical officers who helps me from time to time with this arm. He said his NCOs had a spare billet or two. I thought you'd find it more congenial than any of the alternatives.'

'It was very thoughtful of you, sir.'

He stared at me for rather longer than seemed necessary. Then he said, 'Tomorrow will be rather interesting. Goodnight, sergeant.'

I stamped on the asphalt and threw one up. I thought he blinked but couldn't be sure. A really good salute requires one's eyes to be fixed fair and square on the bridge of the officer's nose. He touched the peak of his cap with the tip of his swagger cane. Before the truck had started up I was off down the path past the mess to my quarters feeling in my pocket for the key to the padlocked steel ring that secured my kit-bag. In the bag there was the last of two bottles of Scotch and one of rum: sweeteners from my previous officer – a man whose experience of Poona had in my opinion had a dampening effect on his initiative. Otherwise he would have fought for me.

So far I have said nothing about my private life in India and the time has come when it ought perhaps to be dealt with. I should describe it as moderately satisfactory, as achieving its peak (perhaps appropriately) in Agra with the wife of an officer who was having an affair with the wife of another and its nadir in a massage parlour in Bombay which had been recommended and which I had first visited after a rough journey through warm rain on a 500 c.c. Norton, had vowed never to visit again but dropped in on during the afternoon following the inquest on Leonard Purvis, which was the same afternoon Beamish told me I was to go to Delhi to join Merrick. Otherwise the graph of satisfaction, while giving me no cause for smug self-congratulation at the time, does not in retrospect go quite so far as to suggest positive deprivation.

I mention it because, while sitting in my tin tub, drinking whisky, the cool invigorating air of the Pankot hills suddenly hit me and twenty minutes later I was setting off for the mess, turning over in my mind the interesting possibility that the friendly senior NCO (whom I shall call Sergeant Potter) might turn out accommodating in regard to whatever arrangements there were to maintain a good relationship with the Eurasian nurses (or even with the less snobbish of the QAs). Not caring much for rum I took the bottle with me, to present it to the mess, and arrived there, matily, full of good intentions. These very quickly withered.

To begin with the rum was declined on the grounds that the drinking of anything but beer in the mess was strictly regulated and that mess rules did not allow members, let alone guests, to bring bottles in. Then there turned out to be a non-treating rule which, broken on my first appearance at lunch-time, was now rigidly reapplied and meant that I couldn't sign a chit to repay earlier hospitality but only for whatever beer I wanted myself. All this was explained by Potter as the others drifted away from the bar to the sitting area. He stayed with me, but less out of friendliness than a determination to protect his colleagues from me, or so it began to seem.

But it wasn't until Sophie Dixon arrived that I really came to the conclusion that for all practical purposes I was in Coventry. He swept in, came to the bar, ordered a beer, signed a chit, acknowledged Potter, ignored me and then went over to the others. Then he started.

There was a smell in the room, he said. Had anyone let wind? If not, was it the drains? Or something in the cookhouse? It really was a very peculiar smell. But vaguely familiar. Given time he'd identify it. Meanwhile it quite turned him up. It made him feel very queer. He didn't think he'd last out. Especially after the day he'd had. Guess whom he'd seen? Her very self. Miss Khyber Pass of 1935. Prancing around like a two-year-old. Positively cavorting. She'd do herself an injury if she didn't look out. In fact he wondered how she had the energy considering she had two of them in tow this time. Count Dracula again, but also a new one, Golden Boy. Very superior, Golden Boy. Very posh.

In fact you might say regal. But smart. Oh yes, very smart. Full
of bull. When he came to attention it fair went through you. In
fact you thought yours would drop off and you wondered why
his hadn't. Well you did if you thought he had any in the first
place, which you couldn't take for granted nowadays when they
were letting anybody in and not even bothering to say cough.

At dinner, Potter who sat at the head of the table indicated
I should sit on his right again but this time the place on my
own right and the place opposite were left empty. The others
crowded together and talked shop. Potter looked unhappy. Our
conversation petered out. The others left the table as and when
they'd finished. Eventually I was alone with Potter at our end.
Dixon and another corporal remained at the other.

Potter said, 'Breakfast's a bit of a moveable feast. You could
have yours in your room if you like.'

I said, 'I will if it's more convenient and what you'd prefer.'

Dixon muttered something. It sounded like, ' 'ark at 'er.'

Potter, playing with the spoon and fork on his pudding plate,
said, 'Just tell the boy.' Then he said, 'There's not a bad Chinese
restaurant in the bazaar. We sometimes go there of an evening.'

'Actually,' I said, 'I'm not awfully keen on Chinese cooking.'

'Oh, Christ,' Dixon said, almost loudly.

'But I suppose they do egg and chips?' I added. For the first
time Potter met my glance, pitifully grateful. He hated being
rude. He said there was a good film on at the Electric Cinema.
They'd all seen it themselves and enjoyed it. If I wanted to go
tonight I could catch the second house.

I didn't go that night. I went the following night – after eating
at the Chinese restaurant. August 15. Sergeant Perron's lonely
VJ day celebration. But it *was* a celebration. I began the day by
having breakfast in my room, and so heard nothing about Japan's
formal surrender until I arrived at the Pankot Rifles depot by
tonga and went to the hut we'd set up the day before. Merrick
wasn't there. I was told about the Japanese by the adjutant, Coley.
He assumed that the interviews would be postponed. The depot
commandant, Colonel Trehearne, had declared a holiday from
all parades. The truck that was to have collected the two men
chosen for interview hadn't yet set off.

The depot lines had a look of a Sunday-morning make and

mend. The air was bright. Things sparkled. The hills were in clear definition. There had been no rain for a day or two. Depot sweepers were sprinkling water to lay the dust on the road outside the hut and on the earthen floor of the verandah. The young subaltern arrived and was chatty. We walked up and down in the sunshine and he confided in me his intention to stay in India as long as he could. By eleven o'clock the truck still hadn't left and Merrick still hadn't appeared. Maintaining my policy of initiating nothing I hung round, talking to whoever turned up.

Merrick arrived at midday. He saw the adjutant first and then came out to talk to me. As a result of Japan's surrender Merrick had been recalled. He was to fly that evening from Ranpur to Delhi and thence to Ceylon – from where, providing the Japanese forces in Malaya laid down their arms, he would fly on to Singapore where he would be busy with the initial sifting of blacks, greys and whites among the INA men who had co-operated with the enemy. I never discovered how hard he had tried on the phone that morning to persuade Delhi to order me to accompany him. I'm sure he did try because his attitude was unmistakably begrudging. He didn't want to leave me behind in Pankot. Delhi must have told him to. Another officer would be sent to replace him. Meanwhile I was to stay and get the interviews started with an interviewing board of a couple of Pankot Rifles officers and myself with a watching brief.

You will understand my euphoria. It became difficult to sustain my dumb-insolence act. This did not escape Merrick's notice. The unblemished side of his face acquired, just under the skin a tremor.

'I may send for you in Singapore,' he said. He was about to take his leave. We were strolling up and down the road outside the hut where the truck was parked. He was giving me instructions about the conduct of the interviews and the importance of keeping them strictly within the terms of reference and not letting the Pankot officers get lost in irrelevancies. Then he stopped, and said, 'I suppose that is all.' We were by the truck. The Red Shadow was in the back, grinning. I affected not to notice him.

'Incidentally,' Merrick said. 'I saw Captain Rowan last night. We dined at Colonel Layton's house. Has he contacted you at all?'

I said he had not.

'I'm sure he will. So be careful what you say if he raises the subject of Mr Kasim's INA son. He was pumping me rather. I'd have liked to be more forthcoming because it was rather a special evening, but the department isn't so sure now that it would be at all helpful, whatever Government says, so I didn't want to raise his hopes. It would be better if you pretended to know nothing.'

He was back on form. I told him it wouldn't be difficult to pretend I knew nothing because I didn't.

'But you've read the file on Sayed Kasim.'

'No, sir.'

'I thought you would have done. I told you in Bombay it was one of our most interesting cases.'

I didn't answer.

He said, 'Perhaps it's just as well you didn't, though. Otherwise your old school-friend might have cross-examined you more successfully than he did me. He's been well trained to find out a lot and give little away. But so have I. Although in a different school.'

The time had come to say goodbye. Had he been about to offer his good hand? Was he aware of the possibility that we would not meet again? I gave myself no chance to find out. Smart step back. Stamp. One two three, up. The combination of muscular tension and emotional relief caused me to grunt. He smiled, tipped his cap peak with the cane and got in.

As he did so – and as I took in this *mise en scène* – the skin on the back of my neck and above my ears seemed to contract. Perhaps the hair stood up. Whatever the effect the cause was that I had apprehended not only the significance of Sophie Dixon's monologue of the evening before but the significance of the back-to-the-hospital-via-the-bazaar routine. In a different setting we had just re-enacted the end of that seemingly pointless journey. But it had been far from pointless. We had gone first to the bazaar because he wanted the Red Shadow in on the act. We had then driven to the hospital and into the grounds and stopped in view of the NCOs' mess because Merrick wished us – if possible – all to be seen together by the members of that mess. And obviously we had been. The three of us. Count Dracula, Miss Khyber Pass of 1935 and Golden Boy. Dracula and

Miss Khyber Pass were known figures. Golden Boy was new. Accepted for myself on my first appearance – once identified as belonging to Merrick and the Red Shadow and transformed by some sinister magic flowing from them into Golden Boy, I was at once rejected. I did not know why. All I knew was that this rejection had been deliberately engineered by Merrick. He had sent me, unidentified and unaccompanied, into a nest of his enemies. And having established me there he had with meticulous attention to detail arranged to have me exposed as an enemy too. Nothing has ever convinced me otherwise.

He beckoned me to come closer.

'By the way, sergeant. I'm leaving Suleiman in your care. At least for a day or two. He'll continue to be quartered with the servants at Flagstaff House but I've told him to report to you here every morning. He has his month's wages and his return travel warrant. The officer who comes up to replace me may want to borrow him. If not I'll send word and then I rely on you to get him on to a train and send him back to Delhi. Meanwhile, make whatever use of him you think fit. He knows his way round Pankot pretty well now.'

It was Merrick's parting gift to me, the only one he had available that he calculated would cast a blight on my day of liberation. But in this case he had miscalculated. The Red Shadow was still grinning at me. I grinned back at the Red Shadow, making calculations of my own. If the grin surprised the Red Shadow he gave no sign of it, but I think it surprised Merrick. Puzzled him? Interested him? Suggested to him a new line of attack for future dealings with me? It was difficult to say. When I turned from the Red Shadow to Merrick and snapped out, 'Right, sir,' there was a look on the looking side of his face that I can only describe as one of triumph and no-triumph, of contempt and no-contempt. And the scarred side was immobile and expressionless as if it had long since grown tired of living with its enigmatic counterpart.

Merrick left Pankot on the morning of VJ day. I had my midday meal with VCOs at the depot, and spent the evening at the Chinese restaurant and the cinema. Apart from breakfasts in my room, an evening bath and a night's sleep, I kept clear of the hospital set-up and could have done so more or less indefinitely.

But Rowan came to the rescue. I'm fairly sure that he did so on Thursday, August 16.

He turned up at the Pankot Rifles depot, inquiring for me. He knew that Merrick had gone. He had finished his own job in Pankot but was staying on for a while. The Indian civilian who had come up with him, Gopal, had gone back to Ranpur. Nigel was alone at the guest house. He suggested I should join him. I said I'd be glad to. So it was arranged that I should transfer my stuff up there in the evening. He offered to send a car but I told him not to bother. He said he'd inform the billeting officer at area headquarters.

One reason for choosing Thursday as the day I moved in with Rowan is my recollection of the timing of certain events concerning the Red Shadow. Merrick left on the Wednesday, having told me that the Pathan would report to me every morning at the depot. I was prepared to find these instructions disobeyed so I was surprised when he turned up on – as it must have been – the first morning of Merrick's absence. He was waiting at the stick-guard post that controlled entry to the administrative block when I got there at 10 a.m. The first thing he asked for was a pass so that he could come and go freely on any errands I sent him on. I said I would think about it but not today because I had no errands for him to run. It would be enough for me if he reported again the following morning.

Seeing that I was about to pass through the gate he plucked my sleeve and held on and began to murmur at me confidentially. Presently it became apparent to me that he was offering to perform a particular service, that of procuring, and was anxious to hear what my special preferences were.

I put on a puzzled look and said, 'What do you mean?' and at the same time pulled my arm free of the grip. His kohl-rimmed eyes glittered and a sort of redness emanated from them – a rush of blood, but not I think of anger at my brushing him off so much as of irrepressible delight at the prospect now before us. He began to rehearse the range of Pankot's sex-life. The astonishing range. The impact on my imaginative sense and the smell of garlic which came in waves from behind his gleaming tombstone teeth combined to translate me momentarily from the prosaicness of white pole, sentry-box and wire fence (the charm and orderliness of the military lines of an old-established

British hill station: monument to imperial rectitude and proper conduct) to a vantage point from which I had a sneaky glimpse in to the world within a world, hermetically sealed and composed entirely of a nest of boxes (Kama Sutra rather than Chinese), each offering successively its revelation of the inventive means by which one might secure release from the pressure of the biological urge. Could all that be available here? In Pankot? By comparison the Bombay massage parlour positively glinted as with a clinical aseptic light.

When the Red Shadow had exhausted either the list or his own imagination and fell expectantly silent, I said, 'Anything else?' Logic indicated that there could not *be* anything else but he took the question as seriously as I had seemed to ask it and looked put out, even alarmed at the thought that there might be avenues of delectable exploration which he had never heard or dreamt of.

'Whatever Sahib desires,' he said at last and then smiled, pop-eyed, as if stunned by the elegance and ingenuity of his reply.

In the many barrack-rooms and sergeants' messes I'd lived in since getting into uniform – I might say in all of them – the one thing I'd be willing to admit had always distinguished me from my companions was my failure to acquire a *habit* of bad language. I don't mean that the soldier's words weren't in my vocabulary, they were; but they were reserved for special occasions. Like this one.

'What the Sahib desires,' I said, smiling generously, 'is that you should **** ***.' [I use asterisks because it always seems to me that written and printed the dignity of such phrases is lost and the pure metal of offensive *speech* debased.]

I did not wait to study the final effect of my remark. The immediate effect was sufficient – that is to say I was satisfied that his knowledge of the English language hadn't been put under any kind of strain and that what I said might even have had, for him, a ring of familiarity. Showing my own pass to the stick-guard (a very young but intelligent-looking lad) I indicated the Red Shadow (now some ten yards away, staring, wagging his head at me) and explained that he was a notorious thief, cur-rently on parole, but not to be trusted and under no circum-stances allowed into the lines unless accompanied by myself. Any credentials he offered could be assumed to be forged or stolen

and in any case better not touched by hand because he was suffering from a venereal disease now in an advanced, irreversible and
highly infectious stage, a situation which made him reckless of
his own life and the lives of others, especially the lives of young
people (of either sex) under the age of twenty. I said twenty
because the stick-guard looked like a raw recruit aged eighteen.
A lot of what I said probably passed over his head, his military
Urdu not yet being up to scratch and my knowledge of the local
dialect being nil. But I think he got the general drift.

Thus, I had got rid of the Red Shadow for another twenty-
four hours; but not, I admit, got rid of some of the impressions
he had left me with of the arcane aspects of life in Pankot. Images
tended to obtrude. Sometimes an odalisque appeared, scattering
rose-petals for one to walk over in one's ammunition boots.
Coley, languidly using a fly-swatter, appeared to me occasionally
to be a eunuch dispensing attar from a silver shaker. A female
sweeper, bent over her gently swishing broom, might have been
performing a more delicate task; excitation of the dust the last
thing in her mind, or in mine. The tea tasted odd. Goat's milk
or bromide? And which, I wondered, of these men behind the
blanket-covered tables, were sitting there satiated, just about
getting through the day after a night's sampling of one or several
of Pankot's erotic specialities? Coley? Yes, Coley perhaps. Not
a eunuch after all. He had that remote washed-out look of a man
whose secret life absorbed nine-tenths of his energy.

Having lunched with the VCOs the day before, today
I lunched with the havildars, and in the afternoon Nigel Rowan
turned up and invited me to move into the Summer Residence
guest house. As a consequence I spent the rest of the afternoon
with a clearer and more practical focus for my wandering
thoughts. The odalisque took on more and more the outward
appearance of Sarah Layton whose part of Pankot I was about
to enter, disguised in my fleece, shepherded by Rowan. By 4.30
or so when the second interview of the day petered out in cosy
military reminiscences of the questioned man's experiences in
North Africa, the transformation of the odalisque into colonel's
daughter was virtually complete; the room, the hut, the whole
precise military complex had reasserted itself and when I walked
out past the stick-guard post the perfumed midnight garden of
secret Pankot seemed as far away as the memory of the Red

Shadow importuning that morning. I climbed into a tonga and felt the blessing of the ramshackle motion, the pine scent of the hills and the ancient smell of dung and wood smoke that hung in the invigorating air and mellow light. It had been my intention to keep the tonga waiting while I crammed into the kit-bag the few things I'd taken out, but as we got near the hospital I remembered I owed some money in the mess and would have to find someone competent to accept it. Realizing that this might take a bit of time my inclination became to bathe and change, postpone my arrival at the guest house and extract from the hospital the last ounce of the pleasure I would have in leaving it.

So I paid the man off at the gates and walked through the leafy grounds to the mess and to the hut where I had my quarters. It would have been about 5 p.m. The only men around were the servants. The room allotted to me was one of four or five under a single roof and sharing the same verandah, with its own bath-house and w.c. cubicle at the back, overlooking a courtyard or compound. At this time, apart from one sergeant (of whom I'd only seen the back view as he left in the morning for duty: it wasn't Potter) I was the only occupant of this particular block but there seemed to be plenty of bearers and bhishtis about. I never had any trouble getting what I wanted. The servants probably also looked after other huts and I was fortunate to be close to where they lived.

I had a key to padlock the front door from outside and the back door from inside. The drill was, once you were inside, to unlock the back door in the bath-house and then shout for the bearer or the bhishti. Actually to shout was seldom necessary. Directly you opened the back door bodies tended to converge and enter, the sweeper to sweep out (even if he had swept out in the morning), the bearer either to make your bed or to get it ready for the night, and the bhishti with the kerosene tins of hot water for bathing. If you waited for anyone it was usually the bhishti.

I told the bearer I was leaving, hustled the sweeper-boy out (giving him his bhaksheesh) and ordered a bath. Having unpadlocked my kit-bag I settled down to enjoy a Scotch and wait for the hot water to arrive. I decided to wear civvies and set them out on the bed with a change of underwear. The hot water came while I was undressing. I took the bottle of Scotch, my glass and

another bottle of soda into the bath-house and settled in the tub
for a leisurely soak.

The dénouement, after such careful scene-setting, is I suppose
as obvious to you as it became to me before it actually occurred.
Do you believe in a sixth sense? I don't think I heard a sound
other than the noise the servants were making in the compound,
shouting at one another, and the sound I was making myself,
gently splashing water and humming a popular tune called 'Do
I Worry?' But at one moment I was listening to the servants
shouting and my own humming and at the next continuing to
listen but, as it were, against a background of a soundless presence,
a vibrating sense of intrusion.

Someone was in my bedroom and it needed no special gift of
intuition to conclude that it was the Red Shadow. I went on
humming and splashing, and kept my eyes well away from the
door which, although closed, probably gave a man with an eye
close to one of the hair-line gaps between door and frame, a
view. I had little doubt – so strong was the sensation of being
observed – that the Red Shadow was at the moment applying
one kohl-rimmed eye to this gap, reassuring himself that I was
doing what it sounded as if I was doing. I waited for the sensation
of being watched to go away. When after yet another verse of
'Do I Worry?' it still hadn't I felt a powerful urge to grab the
towel and hold it up like a purdah screen. I hadn't so far associated the Red Shadow with voyeurism, at least not when the
observed object was a grown man long since past the peach-
bloom of youth. Just, though, as embarrassment was giving way
to simple outrage the eye stopped looking through the crack
and its owner tiptoed towards the real objectives: my discarded
uniform (wallet) and my kit-bag (bottles). This, you understand,
was what my sixth sense told me. At the same time this sixth
sense took control of my physical actions. It brought me, still
humming, still scooping water, very slowly from the squatting
to the crouching position. It kept me in the latter to minimize
the change of level from which the hum was coming. Then it
picked one of my feet slowly out of the tin tub on to the duckboard and then the other. It kept the water-scooping hand and
arm going.

It then ceased to be inventive. There I was, stark naked,
crouched and scooping and humming. The door was within

leaping distance. But could one, should one, emerge, however furious, however vengeful, in a state of such wretched naked-ness? Particularly after that voyeuristic interlude? The towel near by was not the kind one could wrap round with much confi-dence in its staying put during the energetic demonstration I had in mind. It was now that I noticed my discarded underpants. Still scooping, still humming, I hooked them with a toe and gathered them in and pulled them on. I leapt for the door, grabbed the handle and opened it.

The wallet was going back into the breast-pocket of my jacket. A ten-rupee note from it had stuck to his fingers and (how dextrous he was) was disappearing into his belt at the same time that the wallet was disappearing back where it had come from. But both movements were now frozen at the point of com-pletion and his head (looking stuck on his neck at a not quite convincing angle) was twisted round and presenting to me an O-shaped mouth.

I roared for the bearer – instinctively calling a witness – and this galvanized the Red Shadow.

'Sahib,' he said, opening his innocent arms, showing his empty hands and backing away, making for the door. As he backed I advanced and pronounced anathema.

'Rejected seed of a diseased pig-eater,' I began. 'Despised dropping from a dead vulture's crutch. Eater of sweeper's turds and feeder on after-birth. Fart in the holy silence of the universe and limp pudenda on the body of the false prophet.'

With each phrase I pushed him in the chest, out of the room, on to the verandah and then along its length. At each phrase he shook his head, wagged it rather in the Indian way, from side to side, an ambiguous movement suggesting both agreement and disagreement but striking a balance which seemed to mean: What the Sahib says, the Sahib says. And the Sahib continued saying, astonishing himself with a richness of imagery and flu-ency of Urdu he had never achieved before and has never matched since. Why didn't I write it down immediately after-wards? I've often wished that when finished the Red Shadow and I could have sat together and gone through it. But it has gone – like the Red Shadow but less precipitately and without my prompting. The verandah, elevated two feet from the ground but without a balustrade and giving on to a gravel path, made a perfect launching pad. And the Red Shadow when it came to it did not lack a certain grace and elegance of line. I've always felt that recognizing the inevitable the artist in him rejected resistance and settled for co-operation. Our combined movements were balletic, slightly rough and ready and under-rehearsed but cumulatively not without poetry.

As we approached the edge of the verandah my flat-palmed pushes became closed-fist prods – not punches; but they brought his arms and hands from the appealing to the protective position. We established a rhythm of prod and jerk and presently I grabbed his shoulders (this was the moment when he seemed to decide to go along with me) steadied him, removed the ten-rupee note from his belt, and swung him round to face the way he was about to go, which he did, borrowing rather than receiving thrust from the sole of my bare foot, and adding some thrust of his own in an attempt to jump that wasn't made quite soon enough but contributed to the angle of flight and the arc of descent. He fell, rather heavily, spreadeagled, his lower body on the gravel and his upper on the grass on the other side of the path. And lay there; winded or pretending to be.

The sequence at an end and my week-old ambition fulfilled, I turned and found that there had indeed been witnesses. Apart from the bearer, the sweeper, the bhishti, and an unidentified person (no doubt of the kind who always turn up when there is an accident or act of God to contemplate with serene detachment – a freelance extra, as it were) there was Sergeant Potter.

What odd things one says to people, post-crisis. Seeing Potter I called out, 'Just the man I wanted. Will this cover everything? I'm leaving.'

'So I gathered,' Potter said, ignoring the ten rupees and looking down at the Red Shadow. 'But presumably not together?'

What Merrick had done was unforgivable. I had the story from Potter whose curiosity about my relationship with Merrick had been aroused by watching me deal violently with Merrick's servant. Ten minutes later he came to my room with my bar chits and the change from the ten rupees. By this time I was dressed and packed and I'd sent the bearer down to the gates to get a tonga. The Red Shadow had gone; where, I neither knew nor cared. Potter asked what it had all been about so I told him.

I bore Potter no ill-will because I was convinced that the NCOs' sudden change in attitude to me was entirely due to having seen me with a man they'd met before and had cause to dislike. But what cause? I wanted to know. Finding I was still friendly, Potter began to open up.

He said, 'Will that fellow make trouble for you with Colonel Merrick?'

I said it wouldn't bother me, but that as Merrick had gone to Ceylon and as I expected to be repatriated almost any day I'd probably be back in England before Merrick knew what had hit him or rather what had hit Suleiman. But I didn't refer to them as Merrick or Suleiman. I called them Count Dracula and Miss Khyber Pass. Potter blushed. He said, 'Look, I'm sorry. We thought he'd had the nerve to plant you on us.'

Potter didn't take much more persuasion to spill the beans.

It concerned a medical NCO. Potter didn't give me his name, but let's call him Lance-Corporal Pinker, Pinky for short, and let us imagine him as a reserved, studious and hard-working young man who had lived an institutional life with other men in uniform without ever seriously arousing the suspicion that he was what is called abnormal. Even Sophie Dixon wasn't absolutely clear on this score, or particularly interested. He liked Pinky because Pinky was harmless and friendly, quite intelligent and very conscientious. He had never served in the field, always at base hospitals. He had been in India for a few months and in Pankot for most of them. He was already in Pankot when Corporal Dixon and Sergeant Potter returned from Burma and were posted to the hospital's military wing.

At that time Pinky was working on the wards. His transfer to the office of Captain Richardson, the psychiatrist, came later. Pinky and Sophie were on the same officers' ward when Colonel Merrick (then Major) used to turn up for treatment and adjustment of his artificial hand and arm. He did this whenever he visited Pankot and on one occasion was admitted for two or three days because the chafing of the harness had set up inflammation and there was some question of infection.

It was now that Potter filled me in on Sophie Dixon's record in the field. His compassion for sick or wounded men sprang from the feminine side of his nature and he never left anyone in doubt about his physical preferences, but these were made entirely acceptable to the men he tended because it was his compassion and care – his dignified ministration to a sick man's needs that they were made to feel, never the other thing. They knew the other thing was there, they had only to listen to him camping it up in the casualty station tent or basha – but (as Potter put it) 'when he touched a man you could see that nothing was being conveyed except clinical reassurance'. In Potter's mind there was even an idea that Sophie's overt posture was a form of sublimation and that in fact he lived like a monk, on and off duty.

According to Sophie, the officer with the burnt face and artificial arm 'must have been quite a dish'. This was the irony; originally Sophie had liked Merrick, so had Pinky. Whenever he came for treatment, Sophie mothered him. He thought the wounded hero brave, patient and well-disposed. Merrick never seemed at all put out when Sophie put on his act. 'Sometimes I wonder about the Major,' Potter remembered Sophie saying. 'When I give him the bedpan this morning he looked at me ever so thoughtful. I nearly come out in one of me hot flushes. Watch it, Dixon, I says to meself. Hands off the tiller and leave it to the Navy.'

It would have repaid him to have listened to his own advice or rather to have watched not 'it' but Pinky. If he had watched Pinky closer he might have seen when the time came that Pinky was in trouble or heading for it. But by then Pinky was off the wards and in the psychiatrist's office. When Merrick next turned up for treatment he said to Sophie, 'I see your old colleague's working for Captain Richardson. Isn't that a waste of nursing skill?'

It didn't surprise Dixon that Merrick had visited the psychiatrist. Considering the nature of his wounds a chat with the psychiatrist would not have been in the least remarkable. Six weeks later Merrick was again in Pankot. He visited the hospital. This time he was accompanied by the Red Shadow. Sophie saw them together and at once nicknamed Suleiman Miss Khyber Pass of 1935. A few days after Merrick had gone back to Delhi, taking the Red Shadow with him, Sophie found Pinky crying and packing his kit. It took Sophie some time to find out why.

*

Working in Richardson's office Pinky (so it would seem) had had his eyes opened for the first time in his young life to the fact that his inclinations were not nearly as uncommon as he had supposed. His was a typical case. Over-protected as a boy he had preferred the company of girls until he reached the age of puberty. After that he found himself attracted, mysteriously, to his own sex. He felt unique. Later he learned that to be like this was wrong, and later still that it was not so unique as to have escaped being a criminal offence. As he grew older he also discovered that it made ordinary men laugh. He knew he couldn't help being what he was and he didn't hate himself, but he couldn't have borne to be found out. He told Sophie that when he came to Pankot at the age of twenty he had had no sexual experience with anyone except himself.

His job in Richardson's office was clerical and highly confidential. It wasn't a hard job because the number of cases in the hospital needing serious psychiatric treatment was never high. There were a few disturbed men in one ward and, now and again, in another, an officer or two whose 'equilibrium' had been upset. Psychiatry was still a bit of a joke in Pankot but it had become vaguely fashionable in the army. Just as potential officer-cadets in England had a routine chat with a psychiatrist at the war-office selection boards so, now, in Pankot's military wing, convalescent men had chats with Richardson. It was almost a branch of welfare.

Richardson had a lot of time on his hands and Pinky discovered that he made use of it by keeping separate sets of private and confidential files for personal reference in his future civilian career. As Richardson's confidence in Pinky grew so did Pinky's opportunity to satisfy his curiosity about the contents of these private files. Richardson told him that psychiatry was a very inexact science and that there were judgments it was wiser not to record officially because the army simply didn't understand the complexity of a man's emotional life and it was grossly unfair to penalize someone by recording an informed professional but far from conclusive opinion that might be interpreted subsequently in the naïvest manner and block a man's promotion. When Richardson found that Pinky was genuinely interested in psychiatric method he sometimes lent him 'closed files' of men who had been discharged and, during slack times, even discussed them with him. He never showed him files on men which were

still 'open' and all the files, both the official and the separate
private files, were kept under lock and key. If Pinky was lent a
file he had to return it to Richardson before Richardson left
the office.

What fascinated Pinky was the revelation that in Richardson's
view (and who was Pinky to argue?) 'repressed homosexual
tendencies' were not infrequently the cause or one of several
causes of what – up there in the wards – might look simply like
depression or apathy or a temporary inability to cope. He
became intensely curious about the notes Richardson had made
or was making about the men currently undergoing treatment
– in particular one man around whom Pinky had been spinning
private fantasies: a tough, good-looking corporal who had been
in Burma with Wingate's expedition.

A timid boy, his obsession gave him courage. He stole Richardson's key – easy enough because the key was kept in a drawer
of the desk which Richardson did not always remember to lock.
What took nerve was getting a copy of it made in the bazaar and
putting the original key back. Thereafter, night after night, he
sat at his desk with one of the current confidential files, risking
discovery but taking the risk because what he read absorbed him.
The files changed his whole attitude to himself. The man in the
ward, for instance, the one whom Pinky fancied, had admitted
to Richardson that he had 'mucked about' with a fellow Chindit,
still preferred women but wasn't ashamed of the mucking about
because he thought of it as something that had 'just happened
quite natural', just 'part of the business of being stuck in the
jungle and being shot at' and if he were back there he'd probably
do it again. What amazed Pinky was Richardson's diagnosis that
this man was 'intelligent and well-balanced' with a 'healthy attitude towards sex', and that his depression was almost certainly
due to a combination of the physical after-effects of the dysentery for which he had already been treated and an understandable
but by him unacknowledged conviction that he'd had enough of
combat. The note on the official file, which mentioned nothing
about 'mucking about' closed with the comment, 'Fit for active
duty from the point of view of this department but recommend
further analysis of faeces'.

Intelligent and well-balanced. A healthy attitude towards sex.
Pinky seized on the phrases as if they were lifebuoys. He acquired

nerve. When he went down to the canteen or into the bazaar he looked about him, eyes open, newly confident. When he sat in the downstairs room of the Chinese restaurant (the floor reserved for other ranks) he glanced more boldly at men he liked the look of. Any one of them, judging by the files, might be willing to 'muck about'.

It was during this first extrovert phase that Merrick came back into his life, arriving at the office one evening after Richardson had gone and just at the moment when Pinky was at the filing cabinet selecting his evening's reading. He hadn't heard Merrick knock or come in but, looking up, saw him in the open doorway between Richardson's office and his own. Pinky's alarm was short-lived. Merrick was not to know that the cabinet was private. When Merrick spoke to him in a friendly manner, remarking on his transfer from the wards, Pinky stopped feeling guilty and asked Merrick what he could do for him. Merrick said he was in Pankot for a day or two and hoped he would be able to have a word with Captain Richardson. Pinky looked at the diary and made an appointment for the following afternoon. 'Merrick?' Richardson said next day, 'Isn't that the officer with the burnt face and amputated arm?'

When Merrick arrived Pinky sent him straight in. Presently he was called in himself. Richardson handed him the key and asked for a particular file. Without thinking – because he was now so used to handling them – Pinky brought him the official buff file and the private green one. Richardson handed back the latter and Pinky put it away. Merrick was in Richardson's office for about twenty minutes. When he had gone Pinky went in with some incoming mail and found Richardson studying the private green file. He gave both files back to Pinky. Pinky asked whether he should open a file for Major Merrick. He was told that Merrick wasn't a client. The files that had been got out in connection with Merrick's visit were known to Pinky. They weren't among those that interested him. They concerned a woman. He wondered what Merrick had been asking that caused the files to be got out, but did not inquire. The only other point of interest about this episode was that Pinky learnt for the first time that Merrick's peacetime job was in the Indian Police. The subject came up because Pinky said he supposed when the war was over the amputated arm would mean an end of

Merrick's military career. Richardson said he'd no doubt go back into the police with a desk job and added, 'CID I shouldn't wonder. He's dealing with these INA cases already.' Pinky thought perhaps the woman's file was also connected with the INA business. He wasn't interested in the INA either.

Thus, lulled, Pinky rode for his fall. Several nights a week he went to the Chinese restaurant. Twice he thought he would have made it if he'd had the final ounce of courage it seemed to need to convey to a table companion that more than chat was on offer. After eating he often lingered in the bazaar, venturing beyond the area of light into the shadows and walking home, anticipating that longed-for voice calling out, Hey, soldier. And in the bazaar, during these patrols of his from shop to shop, he no longer shooed away the small urchins who pimped for their so-called sisters offering jig-a-jig, but grinned at them, shaking his head, listening for the miraculous change of tune from You want Girl, to You want Boy? Once, he heard it, but coward-like ignored it. It wasn't a boy he wanted, anyway, but someone of his own age.

Between Merrick's interview with Richardson and Pinky's next sight of him, several weeks passed, weeks which Pinky spent in the way I've described but which now culminated in what, had the consequences not been so terrible, he would probably have remembered ever afterwards as his unforgettable night. For a day or two before this memorable occasion, wandering in the bazaar he had been aware of the possibility that a young Indian lad was as interested in him as he – because this possibility was there – had become interested in the lad. He had never seen him in Pankot before but now they seemed to keep passing each other. The Indian was dressed western-style. He looked clean. He also looked vigorous: a dark-skinned version of the athletic kind of young Englishman Pinky was attracted to. On one occasion Pinky and the Indian were both looking at the window display in Gulab Singh's, the chemist, which was opposite the Chinese restaurant. The display was of clocks and watches. The next night Pinky stood outside the shop again. Again, as if from nowhere, the Indian turned up. They did not speak. Pinky wanted to but his mouth was too dry. When the Indian left Pinky stayed a moment longer and then left too. As he stepped into the road between a couple of parked tongas a man touched his arm and said, 'Sahib, you want woman?' Pinky shook his head. The man bent closer. 'Sahib, you want boy? That boy looking at watches? That boy very good boy. Like English soldier very much. He like you. He is telling me. Sahib wait here. Boy come.'

The man went – a turbanned white-clothed figure, wearing an embroidered waistcoat and baggy trousers, walking quickly up the road openly and jauntily, stopping only once to make sure Pinky was waiting. Pinky began to tremble with excitement. To Pinky, this man looked manly and virile. East of Suez no shame attached to wanting boys. The man understood and casually accepted Pinky's need.

Pinky moved away from the tongas and went back to the arcaded pavement and strolled slowly along looking at the shop windows. When he came to an alley he stopped and looked back. The boy was coming, walking briskly. As he went past Pinky he smiled and walked up the alley. The alley was dark. For a few seconds Pinky was afraid. Sometimes alleys like this were patrolled by the military police and the west side of the bazaar, to which the alley led, was out of bounds to other ranks. Well, if the MPs stopped him and asked why he was following a boy he would say the boy had offered to introduce him to a college girl. Then he'd get off with a warning and an approving laugh. The blood began to pound in his chest. Pinky marched on.

'What was it like, love?' Sophie quite naturally had thought to ask Pinky, when he got to this part of his story. No go, apparently. He'd been over-excited. One gathers there was an encounter of some kind, prolonged but obstinately unsatisfactory. The Indian had explained his own failure by saying it made him unhappy to see Pinky so nervous. Then he had said it would be all right next time. He said, 'Come back tomorrow. Meet me outside Gulab Singh's at half-past nine and we will come to my room again.' When they were dressed the Indian became miserable and said he didn't think Pinky would come back. Pinky said nothing would stop him. 'Leave me a token then,' the Indian said. 'Lend me your wristwatch. Then I'll know that you like and trust me.' Pinky gave him the watch and told him to keep it. The Indian had already refused money. He refused to accept

the watch except as a token of Pinky's intention to return the
next evening. He took Pinky back down the rickety stairs into
the alley and went with him until the light from the bazaar lit
Pinky's way.

When I left for the summer residence guest house we got the
tonga-wallah to drive through the hospital grounds along a path
that led past Richardson's office. By we, I mean myself and
Potter. He pointed the office out and then got off and walked
back. After studying the place I gave the driver orders to move on.

The office was in a low building isolated from other blocks.
It had the usual steep-pitched roof, the overhang supported by
pillars to form a verandah. A small signboard outside announced
Richardson's name. One entered by a door at one end. This led
to a passage. A window to one side of the door lit what had been
Pinky's office. A window beyond lit Richardson's. The hut was
presumably isolated to encourage patients to feel that anything
they said to the psychiatrist went no further than here. Both
Pinky and Richardson had had keys to the main door. The last
to leave locked up. Outside the door, on the verandah, was a
bench, a fire bucket and a cycle rack.

At about 6 p.m. on the evening of the day following Pinky's
meeting with the Indian lad, he was alone in the office reading
Richardson's private notes on the case of an ordnance officer
who had collapsed under the strain of 'feeding the guns'. He
kept looking at his watch and, because thrillingly it wasn't there,
having to judge by the fall of the light outside how much longer
he could afford to spend on this fascinating stuff before locking
up, going to his billet to shower and shave and set out on his
journey to bliss. He had just decided to call it a day and was
closing the file when the door opened and Merrick walked in.

Pinky gave him a cheerful good-evening. Merrick asked if
Captain Richardson was in. Pinky told him he had gone for the
day but would be in the office tomorrow as usual and that if
Major Merrick wanted an appointment he would be glad to look
at the diary and write one in.

Merrick said that would be good of him. Pinky went into
Richardson's office and came back with the diary. Merrick was
now sitting. An hour was agreed and written in. Pinky took the
diary back and put it on Richardson's desk. When he returned

Merrick had the green folder and was examining the cover. For an instant Pinky was alert but Merrick didn't open the file and when Pinky was back at his desk he put the folder down. Then, smiling in a friendly way, he adjusted his artificial arm, as if it needed easing. The black-gloved artefact was held out, closed. He prised the fingers open. In the palm of the glove lay Pinky's watch.

He said, 'I think this is yours.'

Pinky did not remember with any clarity what happened next. On the whole he thought he just stared at the watch while Merrick sat waiting for him to react. The next thing Pinky was fully conscious of was Merrick standing with the watch in the artificial hand and the green file in the other saying: 'My understanding from Captain Richardson was that these files were always kept under lock and key and were available to no one when he was not in the office himself.'

And then:

'I take it you have managed to obtain a key. You were at the filing cabinet the last time I came at this time of evening. If you have such a key you would be well advised to hand it over now.'

Pinky did so.

'Is this the only file you have removed tonight?'

Pinky nodded.

'Does this telephone go through to the hospital or the civil exchange?'

Pinky mumbled through dehydrated lips that it went through to the hospital exchange but that the hospital exchange could get any number.

'Right,' Merrick said. 'Wait outside. You will be wise to wait and do nothing foolish.'

Pinky stumbled into the passage. Merrick closed the door behind him. He found himself out on the verandah without knowing how he got there. Shock had affected his ability to co-ordinate what he did and saw with any sort of understanding of it. For instance he was aware of a figure leaning against a pillar, gazing at him, but the figure to him was simply a deformation of the pillar. When he realized it *was* a figure he assumed he must be hallucinating because it was a copy of the figure of the man who had procured the Indian for him the night before.

After a period of time, borrowed from and never repaid to him, he heard Merrick closing the door of the office. He got unsteadily to his feet, knowing the real shame began *now*, waiting somewhere for the military police, whom Merrick had obviously been phoning, to come and escort him to a guard-room.

But what happened was quite different. Without even a glance in Pinky's direction Merrick walked away up the path, followed by the procurer – or, let's give him his proper name, the Red Shadow. When they were out of sight Pinky began running. Then, wondering where he was running he ran back where it was safe. But it wasn't safe. So he was sick. After he had been sick he ran off again. Again he ran back and covered the vomit with sand. After he had done that he felt like a visitor, a stranger to the scene. Lights were coming on in windows of other huts that he could see through the trees. The evening was real. *He* wasn't real, but the evening was, and this unreal self had to lock Captain Richardson's office up. Before that he had to close Captain Richardson's office windows.

The green file was still on the desk. Automatically he went with it into Richardson's office. The cabinet wouldn't open. He felt for his key. Merrick had it. Or had he? Pinky turned on lights and started hunting for the key. There was no key; only the locked cabinet and the rogue file that couldn't be put back into it. If he could only get the file back into the cabinet and lock it he might be able to say he hadn't done it and that Merrick was lying. He knew this was impossible but that's the way his mind was working. Then he remembered that the key and the file were quite unimportant in comparison with the wrist-watch. Perhaps he could find the watch. If Merrick had left the file lying round perhaps he had left the watch. There wasn't a watch, though. Merrick had the key and the watch and he, Pinky, had the file. He hid the file in a drawer in his own desk. He shut all the windows and turned off the lights, locked the doors and ran back to his quarters. He went to the latrine. What he evacuated was liquid. He sat in the latrine in the dark with the liquid streaming from him. Then he did a very odd thing. He manipulated himself into a state of excitement and then out of it and leaned back exhausted. Subsequently this puzzled him. He asked Sophie if Sophie could explain why he did a thing like that. Sophie couldn't but remembered later and told Potter that he'd read somewhere that when a man was being executed by the rope he sometimes suffered an involuntary emission as though that part of him too was saying good-bye.

In the morning, unable to face what had to be faced, Pinky reported sick. The duty MO couldn't find anything wrong with him but he looked so terrible that to be on the safe side the MO sent him to the staff sick-bay for observation. There was no one in sick-bay except an Indian orderly. Pinky lay on a bed fully clothed. He was given a nimbopani and drank it gratefully but immediately afterwards brought it up. A QA sister arrived to chart his temperature and pulse. The temperature was slightly above normal and the pulse was rapid. An hour later he brought up another nimbopani. The duty MO came over. Specimens of urine and blood were taken. Pinky was put into hospital pyjamas and bedded down. He lay curled in the embryonic position. He hadn't slept at all the previous night. Mercifully he slept now, shutting the world out. He slept right through the most trau-matic part of the day – the hour of Merrick's appointment with Richardson. When he woke in the late afternoon Richardson was sitting on his bed.

'My green file on the ordnance officer, Captain Moberley,' Richardson said, quite gently. 'Can you tell me where I might find it? I have an interview with him this evening.'

'Yes, sir,' Pinky said. He felt calm now. 'It's in the bottom left-hand drawer of my desk.'

'Thank you, Pinker.' Richardson stayed on the bed. Pinky could see that he was considering a number of alternative state-ments. Richardson was not a great talker. He was so used to listen-ing. 'All things considered, Pinker,' he said eventually, 'I think you'd better remain here for a day or two, even though there is nothing physically wrong with you. I don't mean that you're malingering. I mean that your illness is psychosomatic. I take it you yourself are in no doubt of that?'

Pinky nodded. There was nothing Richardson could do for him but Pinky felt at least he understood. Richardson's was the last friendly face he was likely to see until he came out of prison. But he did not think he would ever come out. He would die of terror and humiliation. He hoped so. How could he ever face his parents again if he survived to be sent home? Two years. In an Indian prison. For a crime he hadn't committed and had never intended to commit. He had only wanted a bit of love.

The next morning he felt not better but somehow purged. The QA sister said she was pleased with him. He had expected that by now everyone would have heard about him and he had steeled himself to bear their contempt. So he guessed that whatever Richardson was doing he was doing as discreetly as he could.

Allowed up, he sat on the sun-verandah of the sick-bay and opened his mind slowly to his 'case' – the strange and puzzling aspects of it. The business of the files was of minor importance, surely. What Merrick was after was the nailing of men like him: queers. Probably Merrick had taken one look at him months ago and thought 'Ah.' His discovery that Pinky was sneaking looks at confidential files – gloating over them – would simply have reinforced a poor opinion of his character. And yet. And how long had Merrick had him watched and followed? When Pinky thought back to those weeks patrolling the bazaar he went cold.

Pinky had never seen the Indian procurer before but he must have seen Pinky. Was he in Merrick's pay or a fellow-victim of Merrick's cleaning-up operation? And what had happened to Tommy, the Indian lad? Had he been working with the procurer or had he been pounced on afterwards and made to hand the watch over? And then what happened? Had Merrick pounced on the procurer? Pinky became dizzy trying to work out the permutations. So he closed his mind to his case and lay on the sun-verandah all day trying hard to think of other things like home and times when he had been happy.

But throughout the day one question kept nagging at him. *Why me?*

After two days in sick-bay he reported for duty at Richardson's office. He had already packed a military criminal's kit – his small pack. When he arrived he found another NCO at his desk. The new lance-corporal said it would be helpful if Pinky could show him the ropes. He asked Pinky where he was going. All Richardson had told him was that he was to take over Pinky's job. Pinky said he didn't know yet but thought he'd better not interfere unless Richardson gave him official permission to hand over.

He waited outside. Richardson arrived. Pinky saluted smartly. Richardson told him that since he was up and about he might as well show the new NCO some of the routine. A spark of hope was kindled. Logic said he should have been in a guard-room long ago. It was very odd. He spent the morning and afternoon helping his successor. Richardson came and went. He was neither friendly nor unfriendly. About five o'clock he came back and as he went into his office he told Pinky to come in.

When Pinky was inside with the door shut Richardson handed him a piece of paper. Pinky read it. He read it twice. It was a posting order to a Field Ambulance in a division that was preparing for something called Operation Zipper. When Pinky finally understood what this meant he sat down without asking permission and cried.

He cried from relief and out of gratitude. The only explanation he could find for his escape was that somehow Richardson had managed to suppress the terrible charge. How, he could not begin to imagine. For a moment he did not care.

Richardson let him cry the cry out. It didn't last long and wasn't noisy. The lance-corporal in the other room could not have heard it. Richardson poured him a glass of water and then went and stood in a characteristic position, with his back to the room, looking out of the window, his hands in his trouser pockets.

When Pinky had quietened down he stood up, ready to leave. He said that before he went he wanted to apologize for having abused Captain Richardson's confidence in the matter of the files. He knew it had been very wrong and he was very sorry. He didn't know what else to say because he couldn't bring himself to mention the thing that Richardson had only referred to obliquely – so obliquely that it was almost as if he hadn't referred to it at all.

Richardson said, 'Yes, I suppose it was an abuse. Between us we might have overlooked it, but in all the circumstances I decided you would have to go. If it's any comfort to you, Pinker, although I suppose I ought not to say this, I think you were extremely unfortunate to have come up against that particular officer. However, there it is. You did. And no experience, how-ever disagreeable, is ever wasted.'

Richardson left the window, smiling, as if nothing much had

happened. 'Also, if it's any comfort to you, from observation I'd say that you'll actually be much happier in the field than in a place like this. Your conduct sheet is clean, there's no reason why it shouldn't stay like that, is there?'

Richardson offered his hand. Dumbly, Pinky took it.

'Tell me,' Richardson added, putting his hand back in his trouser pocket. 'How long was Major Merrick trying to get me on the telephone the other evening?'

'Get you on the telephone, sir?'

'He said he tried to ring me so that I could come over and deal with – this problem. He said he tried there and then, from this office.'

'He sent me outside, sir.'

'Yes. I see. How long were you outside?'

'I honestly don't know, sir.'

'Quite. Well, never mind, but actually I was in my quarters the whole evening. You didn't by any chance palm him off with a dud number?'

'He didn't ask for a number, sir. Just whether the phone was on hospital or civil exchange.'

'Well I only wondered, because my phone never rang. But it's of no importance. The operators probably ballsed the call up. That wouldn't be new, would it, Pinker? But perhaps it was as well they did. These things are much better discussed in the cold light of the day after. Wouldn't you say? Goodbye, Pinker. Good luck.'

Pinker said goodbye and thanked him. He tried to say more but couldn't. He had the impression that Richardson was really asking him to say more. But he shirked it. Just before he reached the door Richardson said:

'Oh, Pinker, I nearly forgot. This is yours, isn't it?'

He was holding out Pinky's watch.

'I think it must need a new strap otherwise you'll lose it again.'

Slowly, disbelievingly, Pinky took the watch. His face was burning. He mumbled something like thank you sir and goodbye sir, and then, remembering, came to attention. He was still at attention when Richardson said:

'If it's any interest to you, I found it among the Ms. I suppose it slipped off your wrist when you helped yourself to Captain Moberley's file.'

That evening, in the midst of his packing, Pinky stopped, sat down and looked at the watch: the gift of his parents when he joined up. Then he threw it on the floor and stamped on it with the heel of his boot until it was in pieces. This was what he had done with his life so far. He resumed packing, pausing every so often to wipe his eyes and cheeks. He kept telling himself to be a man. But that didn't help. Thus, Sophie found him.

There were only two explanations for the returned wrist-watch. The first was that Merrick had given it to Richardson and told him how it had come into his possession and that Richardson had persuaded him not to take the matter further but leave him to deal with it. This was the explanation Pinky believed was the correct one – the only one that made sense to him and which bore out his opinion of Richardson's stout character. It didn't make sense to anyone who knew Merrick as I knew him. It didn't make sense to Sophie and Potter but neither had an alternative explanation.

From their point of view here was an officer who had gone to a great deal of trouble to nail Pinky on a charge of gross immorality. Without compunction he had used another man (obviously, according to Pinky's description, his own servant) to act as agent provocateur and perhaps even a third man, the Indian lad, in order to get incontrovertible evidence. Sophie said he was familiar enough with British police methods in dealing with homosexuals not to find anything in the least remarkable about an officer of the Indian police using similar methods to shop a soldier. If Pinky had ever been charged and tried, Sophie said, we'd have been amazed at the transformation from fact to fiction in the statement made about how the evidence was obtained.

But then, after all this trouble, Merrick had done nothing more. Why? Had Richardson given Merrick a bad time? Had he seen through whatever story Merrick told him and warned Merrick that he would kick up a stink about the deliberate pro-vocation he could see had been used? Had Merrick been scared off, been persuaded to hand over the prime bit of evidence – the wrist-watch – even been glad to get rid of it and slink off none the richer but wiser?

Pinky accepted this as the explanation because he wanted to. Sophie and Potter didn't accept it but couldn't conscientiously refute it. At one time after Pinky had gone Sophie was prepared to see Richardson and ask, but Potter dissuaded him. So, failing a revelation, they had both settled for the fact that Merrick had set Pinky up, sadistically using powers which were his but which finally he hadn't exercised to the full extent open to him – just possibly because after talking to Richardson (but why had he waited to do that and not called the MPs then and there?) he dared not take that risk.

Not dare take the risk? They didn't know Merrick. He certainly set Pinky up and having set him up used him. If there had been any further advantage to be had out of persecuting Pinky he would have taken it. He was the kind of man who worked for preference within a very narrow margin of safety where his own reputation was concerned. He courted disaster. Deep down, I think, he had a death wish. It came out in this way, pushing his credibility to the limit, sometimes beyond it.

But once he had got what he wanted – in the Pinky affair as in any other – he was no longer interested except to the extent that it pleased him to see his victim suffer. What he wanted in this case was not, I think in one sense, very important to him, but he had made up his mind to have it and had seen how he might get it. He had a talent, one that amounted to genius, for seeing the key or combination of keys that would open a situation up so that he could twist it to suit his purpose.

Originally Merrick went to see Richardson to discuss someone who had been one of Richardson's patients. This may have taken Richardson by surprise and like any psychiatrist he would have been reluctant to discuss the case in any detail. He would not have told Merrick much, only as much as an ordinary man would have realized he had to be satisfied with. But during that interview Merrick realized that there were files – a green one in particular – which would tell him far more, tell him as much as Richardson knew himself and which he was absolutely determined to have a look at. Sheer luck, coming upon Pinky at the filing cabinet the night before, acute observation and shrewd deductive powers, had already shown him the way in which to get that look.

So what Merrick wanted, *all* that Merrick wanted, was a look at the green file, the private file about the patient he went to discuss. It was as simple, as absurd as this. Even while Potter was telling me the sordid little story I was – because I knew Merrick

– casting about for the unconsidered trifle, but the significance of the file did not really emerge until later when I talked to Rowan.

While Pinky was outside on the verandah counting the grains of sand in the fire bucket or whatever he subconsciously did when in the grip of that sense of unreality, Merrick telephoned nobody. He opened the cabinet with the key he had guessed Pinky had and which he had terrified him into handing over and at his leisure looked through the file. The Red Shadow was there to continue terrorizing Pinky but also on sentry-go to warn Merrick if someone not in the little *mise en scène* approached. When Merrick finished, he placed Pinky's watch in the cabinet – not in the Bs where the file he had been reading belonged but with the Ms which was the section to which he knew the file on Pinky's desk belonged, because he had looked at and memorized the name on the cover. He had then locked the cabinet and come away leaving Pinky sitting outside. He must have enjoyed that, leaving his victim in that sort of sickening suspense. He kept his appointment the following day, gave Richardson the key and shopped Pinky – not for sodomy but for abusing Richardson's trust. Precisely what Merrick said nobody knew, except Richardson.

In telling the story of Pinky, in trying to give an impression of my idea of what happened, I have filled the story out with some imaginative detail and also placed events in the order in which they occurred – not in the order in which they emerged during my talk with Potter. For instance, when Potter referred early on to Merrick's first visit to Richardson I said at once, 'What did he go to see Richardson about?' Potter said Pinky assumed he went to see him about the patient whose file Richardson asked for. I said, 'What patient?' Potter said, 'Pinky said it was a woman, he'd had the file out at one time but put it back when he found out it was not about a man.' I said, 'Do you know what woman?' Potter said the answer was a woman called Bingham, but neither Pinky, Potter nor Sophie had ever heard of her.

I then asked him to continue with the story, but from there on I was on the alert because there was unlikely to be more than one Bingham in Pankot and surely Bingham was the name of the officer Merrick had tried to rescue from the blazing jeep, the officer Sarah Layton's sister married, who hadn't been well enough to go to Bombay to meet her father and whom Sarah had described as having had a bad time: obviously, in view of Richardson's file on her, not just a bad time physically but psychologically. And there was Merrick visiting Richardson to talk about her and becoming determined to have a look at her private file. Why?

It was rather late when I got to the Summer Residence guest house. This was a two-storeyed brick and timber building; appearing from the outside a cross between a shooting-lodge and the kind of villa you see half-hidden by fir trees and rhododendrons in the hills around Caterham. Inside, it was straightforward Anglo-Indian hill station stuff and smelt of damp and of aromatic wood. Rowan sat me down on a verandah whose floorboards sounded hollow underfoot so that it was rather like moving around in a sports pavilion or boat-house, except that the view was across an acre or so of rising ground to the Summer Residence (a dark hulk which in daylight proved to have been the inspiration for the guest house, architecturally speaking). On this verandah there were a lot of palms in brass pots and a set of white lacquered cane lounging chairs well upholstered by heavy cushions covered in durable royal blue cloth; and there was a smell of incense which presently I tracked down to a couple of joss-sticks smouldering away on a carved side-table. It struck me that if he went on like this and didn't get married soon Rowan might end up wearing Indian pyjamas indoors and eating pan prepared by himself from ingredients kept in little silver boxes, and discussing the Bhagavad Gita with a gentle down-at-heel professor from some nearby Hindu college; but only during his leisure hours. And even then, in pyjamas, preparing pan and discussing the significance, say, of Krishna's remark to Arjuna that 'Learned men do not grieve for the living' no one would ever mistake him for anything other than an Englishman – one, moreover, of the kind it took a long time to get to know sufficiently well to be sure whether the amiable expression on his face was there for the benefit of the present company or for his own in dealing, as he constantly had to, with so many pressing and troublesome affairs.

For instance, having invited me there, having brushed aside my apology for lateness and sat me down, told the highly distinguished-looking bearer to bring a whisky-soda for me and a gin-fizz for himself, he looked at me as if he wondered where I'd sprung from and what advantage I might expect to wrest out of this sudden and unexpected intimacy. He couldn't help it. It was an effect India had on a man whose manner was already naturally remote and uncommitted.

I said, 'Well, Nigel, tell me all about Merrick and Hari Kumar.'

His expression didn't alter. He said. 'Why?'

'I thought it would be a good way to bring the subject up. The subject of Merrick.'

'Why do you want to do that?'

'I thought you did. If we start right away wouldn't it make it easier for you to ask about Merrick and Mr Mohammed Ali Kasim's INA son?'

The bearer came with the drinks. Mine had far too much soda and ice in it. The coldness burnt my lips.

When the bearer had gone he said, 'I don't follow you.'

'Then I'd better start again. By the way, if anyone comes to put me under arrest would you be prepared to say that we spent the whole day together?'

Fractionally his eyebrows went up. 'I think that would depend on what they came to arrest you for.'

'Common assault?'

'On whom?'

'The Red Shadow.'

'Merrick's servant? Didn't he go back with him?'

'No. I just caught him pinching ten chips from my jacket.'

'If assault followed attempted theft I imagine you're safe enough.'

'In ordinary circumstances.'

'Were these not?'

'Are they ever where Merrick or one of his creatures is concerned? Who is Mrs Bingham?'

He picked up his gin-fizz. 'Sarah Layton's widowed sister. Why?' He sipped.

'Tell me about Merrick and Hari Kumar first.'

'I'd rather you told me what you meant about Merrick and Mohammed Ali Kasim's INA son. Unless that would take you longer than we've got. We're dining out, if that's all right.'

'Should I change?'

'What you're in will do very well. If you could add a jacket.

What gave you the idea I'd be interested in talking about Sayed Kasim?'

'Merrick told me to pretend not to know anything if you asked. But, as I said to him, that won't be difficult because I don't.'

'When was this?'

'Yesterday, just before we parted.'

'I saw him the night before. We discussed the case of Sayed Kasim – or rather a situation arising out of it – as fully as was necessary I'd have thought. So I really don't know what he means.'

'Weren't you pumping him?'

'Not at all. I asked a question and he answered it. Quite satisfactorily. It's all quite simple, Guy, but rather confidential. The thing is that since he was let out of prison M A K has consistently refused to see the son who fought with the INA and was taken prisoner last year. Government was prepared to let him but he said no. At least, he never took the offer up. All I wanted to know from Merrick, now that there's this department dealing with these cases, was whether he thought they'd co-operate about arranging a meeting if M A K suddenly changes his mind.'

'Has he?'

'Perhaps. But I didn't see Kasim until last night. When I spoke to Merrick the night before, the question was still rather hypothetical.'

'What did Merrick say?'

'That he didn't think his department would be keen now and might put up objections, but he was quite clear that Government might override them and could persuade the C.-in-C. it would be a good thing. He accepted that because his department doesn't initiate policy.'

'Well that's it, then. That settles it. Merrick's as mad as a hatter.'

Rowan watched me a while. He said, 'I hope not,' and drank more gin-fizz.

'What advantage does Government see in arranging a meeting between father and son? I take it it *is* a question of advantage. I met the other son, incidentally, at the Maharanee's.'

'So Sarah told me. I'm not sure there is much advantage now. But then I'm not personally in a position to judge. You know Kasim headed the pre-war Congress ministry in this province?'

'Yes.'

'He's in rather an unenviable position just now. Confidentially, Malcolm would like to see him back one day as chief minister, possibly because the alternatives to M A K are rather bleak. So anything one can do to help him solve his problems and clarify his position is done with that end in view. Does that surprise you? That a provincial Governor should have a soft spot for an Indian politician?'

'Why should it?'

'I thought perhaps it might. The *raj* is obviously not your favourite animal.' He looked at his watch and at my almost empty glass then glanced over his shoulder and summoned the bearer. 'Have the other half before we go.'

'May I have less soda and no ice this time?'

Rowan passed the instruction on but I sensed his disapproval.

'Is Mrs Bingham fully recovered?' I asked.

'Recovered?'

'Miss Layton told me her sister had had a bad time. What was wrong?'

'I think some kind of breakdown. She was pregnant when her husband was killed. Then she had the unpleasant experience of being alone in the house when Colonel Layton's stepmother died there. The baby was born prematurely. But it's quite some time ago. She seems all right now.' He added after a moment, 'You'll see for yourself. That's where we're dining.'

'At Mrs Bingham's?'

'At the Laytons'. They all live together. Mrs Layton rang earlier and asked me to go round. I said you were now staying with me and she said she'd be delighted if you'd come along too. I didn't think you'd mind so I said yes for both of us.'

The other half arrived. Nigel had ordered nothing for himself. He still had some gin-fizz left. There was no ice in my whisky but the soda was over-generous. I thought perhaps this was just as well after all, if we were dining at the Laytons'. Rowan said, 'Merrick told you then?'

'Told me what?'

'About Mrs Bingham.'

'He told me he was best man when she married the officer he tried to save.'

'Nothing else.'

'No.'

'Then what made you ask about her?'

'It's too long a story.'

'Oh.' He sipped gin-fizz. 'If she asks you tonight how you like working with Colonel Merrick you'd better tell her a lie and say you find it extraordinarily interesting.'

'Must I? My inclination would be to say I couldn't stop working for him soon enough.'

'I know. But she's going to marry him. It was announced at dinner the other evening.'

He studied me, as if for a particular reaction, then looked at his watch and got up. 'I've got a call to make. I'll be about five minutes, then we ought to go.'

I remained on the verandah, drinking my soda and whisky and considering the significance – the now clear and peculiarly distasteful significance – of Merrick and Mrs Bingham's file. I thought: Well. It's none of my business. A few minutes later Nigel came back. 'I'm ready when you are,' he said.

I told him I was begging off because I didn't feel up to it.

'Aren't you well?'

'I don't think I would be if I had to spend the rest of the evening dissembling.'

He said, 'You wouldn't be the only one.'

'No. Miss Layton doesn't like him either, does she? But I suppose she'll have to learn to now. I won't. I'd rather not pretend otherwise to her poor sister.'

Rowan had propped himself against the balustrade, arms folded, ankles crossed. He said, 'When I said you wouldn't be the only one dissembling I really meant myself.'

'I thought you'd only just met him.'

'I've known about him, quite a while. But you guessed that, surely. Otherwise why ask me to tell you about him and Hari Kumar?'

'Is it what you've known about him or what you've just seen of him that puts you off?'

'Known was wrong. I'm sorry. *Heard*. One must be fair.'

'My Uncle George once said that the only reward in life for being fair is an obscure death.'

'He might well be right. Is he the balloonist?'

'No, that was Uncle Charles. Uncle George spends his life

reading balance sheets and share prospectuses. We rely on him absolutely because he's the only member of the family who can count.'

'I never know when to take you seriously. I never did. How much time did you actually spend rowing on those Saturdays you got off?'

'Very little. The thing was to go about a mile up river to a place where a fellow-member of the club had found what he called a lot of spare local talent. We called it Knocker's Reach.'

'You mean that unwittingly I put you in the way of what Bagshaw called the temptations of the town?'

'Yes.'

Unexpectedly, Rowan smiled. 'Colonel Layton mentioned Bagshaw the other evening. He remembers him as a very junior maths master. I think it does him good to talk about things like that. Won't you change your mind?'

'An old boys' after-dinner session?'

'Would that bore you?'

'It would add no charm to the evening.'

'It would from his point of view, I think.'

'Does he find much charm in the prospect of having Colonel Merrick for a son-in-law?'

'Presumably he's not tried to stop it. The announcement was made in a friendly enough atmosphere.'

'What about Mrs Layton?'

'I expect her main concern is with Susan's welfare.' Rowan hesitated. 'The thing is, Merrick's extraordinarily good with the child.'

'How old a child?'

'Just over a year.'

'Boy or girl?'

'Boy.'

'In what way is he extraordinarily good with him?'

'He inspires the boy's confidence. I've seen it for myself. Watched them playing together with a box of bricks. They were both totally absorbed. Creatively absorbed. He has the knack of making a game seem important. Incidentally the child's not the least afraid of the artificial hand, or of the burn scars. I'm not much good with children so that the fact that I got no change at all out of young Edward is no guide, but Sarah says Merrick's the only man, more or less the only person of either sex who does. If Susan's main reason for marrying him is to give the child a father she'd have to look a long way before she found anyone more capable.'

'Do you think that is her main reason?'

'Wouldn't you agree it's a perfectly sound one?'

'So far as it goes. But I should say the important thing for a child is a sense of security. What's the point of having Merrick as an effective father-figure if the mother is unhappy?'

'Unhappy? One can't prejudge that.'

'You accept the possibility?'

'Susan's not a happy person by nature. But I feel quite incompetent even to hazard a guess about how a marriage like this will work out emotionally.'

'Or physically?'

He ignored this. He said, 'My worry really is about what might happen to affect Merrick's career adversely and make life difficult for her. When he was involved in the Mayapore rape case in nineteen-forty-two he went on the Indians' list of officials who were thought to have exceeded their authority in putting down the Quit India riots. If there's still such a list and I'm sure there is it would be remarkable if he's not still on it.'

'Were repressive measures taken?'

'The mood of the country was highly volatile.'

'In other words some officials acted beyond the limit allowed by law.'

'Well, yes. I think one has to admit it.'

'I can't think why you're bothered. They'll be well protected. They always have been.'

'But things have changed a bit, haven't they? The people now in Westminster know as little as their predecessors did about India, but I imagine they'll be more disposed to believe the very worst about the way India's been governed. I shouldn't think it will need more than a couple of ministers, men like Cripps, to come out here and hobnob with the Mahatma and the disciples of Annie Besant for the new Secretary of State to be rushed into setting up a commission of inquiry. The signs are that the Congress High Command may press for it.'

'Anything wrong in appointing a commission?'

'I think a very great deal. It might look like a genuine British attempt to see justice done impartially but the motive would be entirely political, a bit of window dressing in Westminster and damn the consequences in Delhi. And from the point of view of the morale of a frankly already overstretched Indian administration an inquiry of that sort would be pretty well disastrous. If there were cases of unduly repressive measures there were an infinitely greater number of cases of intense and by no means invariably non-violent provocation. You have to put both the provocation and the methods used to meet it in the context of the atmosphere prevailing at the time, and that was a pretty tricky one. The Japanese were on the Chindwin, Singapore had gone and Burma had gone. Most of Europe had gone and North Africa was a mess. The plain fact is that strategically and I'm sure morally, India had to be hung on to. And I honestly don't see that any Indian leader who incited people to rebel against the *raj* and obstruct or sabotage its war effort has any right whatsoever to complain if quite a few of them got harshly treated. What else I see is that both sides would be wise to forget both the provocation and the reaction. Settling old scores is a fairly useless exercise at any time. When there's something else at stake as serious as trying to reach a sane and sensible agreement about the country's future government and constitution then it's worse than useless. It's damned stupid.'

'I owe you an apology.'

'Oh?'

'For thinking of you the other night as indifferent – how did I put it? – indifferent to affairs over which we adopt attitudes of concern and responsibility? So. My apology.'

'I don't actually feel owed an apology. But if you want to make one, the car's waiting at the front. We'd be no more than a minute or two late even if you want to wash your hands and comb your hair. But in any case, I must go.'

When Rowan told the driver to take us to Rose Cottage, Colonel Layton Sahib's place, I had a picture of what I must be in for, one so vivid that it depressed me. As a name, Rose Cottage wasn't quite as bad as say Mon Repos or Dunromin but I could not imagine anything much worse than dining there, among the cosy souvenirs of a lifetime of exile on the King's business. I pictured the Laytons surrounded by Benares brass and sweet

briar, floral cretonnes and bronze gods; a Buddha smiling back
at a yawning tiger-skin, and – above the mantelpiece – a water-
colour of the Western Ghats and – on it – photographs of Sarah
and Susan as little girls on ponies in Gulmarg. There might even
be an imitation Chinese vase filled with dry bulrushes in a corner
or on a grand piano; a standard lamp with a tasselled shade and
dinner mats painted with hunting scenes from the English shires:
Taking a Fence; The Water Jump; The Whipper-in; In Full Cry.

But directly we drove between two rather gaunt pillars my
spirits rose. Had I heard right? Rose Cottage? One illuminated
board simply announced '12' and the other 'Colonel J. Layton'.
A moment of hiatus followed, a dark transit past dim ugly shapes
which I feared might be rockeries, but then – lit from arc-lamps
in the forecourt – I saw the beautiful proportions of an early-
nineteenth-century Anglo-Indian bungalow: squat, functional
and aggressive, as well anchored to the ground as a Hindu
temple.

'Good Heavens.'

'What's wrong?' Nigel asked.

'I hadn't expected anything so fine.'

'It's one of the oldest buildings in Pankot, I'm told. Is it your
period?' He was smiling, taking something of a rise out of me
but pleased that I was pleased. The verandah showed signs of
vandalism: a wooden balustrade, obviously a later addition, but
not recent; but apart from this the whole area was free of ornament, with one exception: a hanging lantern of iron and glass,
plain, ugly and perfectly in keeping. In a niche near the door
there was a handbell but the bearer, simply dressed in white linen
tunic and trousers, was already receiving us. Nigel called him
Mahmoud and told him I was Perron Sabib. The square hall was
beautifully proportioned but mined by oak panelling. I noted,
though, that there were no wall hangings – no pictures, or trays.
It looked as if something had persuaded the owner to leave the
panelling to make its own vulgar statement. On the tiled floor
there was a large Persian rug of a lovely silky texture. Heavy
mahogany doors marked the positions of the rooms surrounding
the hall. The one facing us was open. Mahmoud led us in.

I have tried to recapture events in some kind of sequence to give
a lucid picture of my evening with the Laytons but it is as though

after the shocks and surprises of that day I suffered a reaction of such intensity that I might have been hard put to it to write a coherent account the following morning let alone twenty-five years later.

Moreover, it was an evening during which nothing happened which contributed to what *you* would call a narrative line and which left me with nothing more useful from your point of view than impressions of members of the family – first impressions of the two I'd not met before and changed ones of the two whom I had. The most vivid impression of all was made by Mrs Layton, a woman whose personal distinction was heightened by an icy stoicism and by what was overlain but not disguised by that coldness: an unmistakable human sexual warmth, which I judged would be strong when aroused. Her air of detachment, the economy of movement and expression, the hard outer casing of the memsahib – so often tiresome in other members of that monstrous regiment – were, in her, peculiar graces. You felt that through them she was protected against the shock of life in general, and with them ready to meet the shock of her own head-on.

Rowan, in introducing us, told her how impressed I was with the house. She said something uncompromisingly direct like, 'Oh. Why?' My reply, whatever it was, helped to establish a tenuous bond between us. I understood that she had been making alterations both to the outside and inside and that there was still a lot to do which she was quite determined on in spite (was it?) of opposition from people who preferred it as it had been in Colonel Layton's stepmother's day. It must have been much later, probably when Nigel and I were leaving, that the question of the oak panels in the entrance hall was raised. She described them as 'a pity', the more so because the damage done by removing the panelling might be considerable and the expense, in consequence, perhaps incalculable.

I describe the bond between us as tenuous because although I often felt a mutual empathy whenever we spoke to one another or when our glances happened to coincide, there were as many if not more occasions when a remark I made which she might easily have taken up was utterly ignored. She fascinated me. I observed with solicitude the portents of physical decline, the areas of flesh between eyebrow, cheek and ear, from which the

resilience had gone, leaving the skin to find its own salvation, which it could only do with the help (presumably) of
astringents which might, but didn't, never do shrink it sufficiently to arrest the development of a network of minute folds
and fissures which show up as lines and wrinkles and lend to the
eyes a sad and perplexing beauty and luminosity, for the eyes do
not age in the way that the flesh does, or do not when they are
the eyes of a woman who is still handsome and armed with a
proper measure of self-respect.

When she lifted her head – she had a habit of doing so and at
the same time touching the necklace she was wearing – the pad
of flesh under the chin was tautened and, for an instant, this and
a consequent firmness of throat and neck created an illusion of
youth, until you saw one, then two, obtrusive tendons and a
faint blotchy discoloration in the region of the thyroid. On one
occasion when my conscious critical self observed these marks
of ageing, the other self, the self that weighed rather than noted
evidence, was moved by a tender curiosity and a bold impulse
to touch the skin as if to verify that what the eye saw was real,
and as if, too, to communicate an opinion that it was virtuous
in her to own such marks and that they inspired admiration, not
pity. Perhaps it was her sensitivity to this reaction that caused her
every so often to switch herself off from me, as a precaution
against an unnecessary complication.

Possibly my reaction was an effect of the invigorating Pankot
air acting in conjunction with the effect of that empathy, my
recognition of Mildred Layton as an attractive older woman, one
who, while conscious of the fact that one was borne along on
the ever-flowing tide whose sound I sometimes listened for, did
not allow the angle of her vision to be restricted to the view of
here and now. She had, I believed, a vigorous sense of history,
vigorous because it pruned ruthlessly that other weakening sense
so often found with the first, the sense of nostalgia, the desire to
live in the past. Throughout that evening she impressed me more
and more as a woman who instinctively rejected the claims of
years gone by if – unlike 12 Upper Club Road as I discovered
she preferred to call it and to which she was in the process of
restoring only what it could properly claim – these claims con-
flicted with her own claims, her determination both to survive
and to defeat any force that currently threatened her.

Such strength of mind and character I attributed to her, and I judged it had probably not been sustained without effort and some assistance. She drank fairly heavily, like one accustomed (one might say disciplined) to it. One thing I noticed, the switching off became more frequent towards the end of the evening and was signalled by a lowering of the lids, a partial hooding of the eyes; but this was the only sign I could detect of the working of the alcohol.

Susan was the first of the two daughters to put in an appearance. If I had met her somewhere else and spoken to her for any length of time without knowing who she was, no familiar note would have been struck. Between this conventionally pretty girl and her sister there seemed to me to be no resemblance. Dark, carefully dressed hair and a high complexion, eyes that slid away from contact with your own and seemed emotionally disconnected from the smile of the neatly lipsticked mouth. The mouth alone performed the function of doing its social duty. Or was I *looking* for signs of disorientation? Her breasts were full, freckled above the deep cleft between them. She would be buxom in middle-age in spite of that narrow little waist (accentuated, I think, by a belt and a flared skirt). She was encumbered, distracted rather, by a Labrador puppy which had hectic manners which suddenly deserted it as if it had seen a ghost or had recollected some standing order about behaviour indoors. It retreated into a corner and sat awaiting a command or inspiration. It had the Labrador trait of looking at you in a way that revealed the white of its eyes – or so I think, having seen a similar animal recently that evoked these memories. Between Susan and this puppy there was a curious tension – a febrile acknowledgement both of the importance and unreliability of the other's presence. It did not take me long to recognize that for each the other was a symbol of a security desired but not felt. It took me a little longer to see that Susan Bingham felt no security in anything and longer still to work out one of the reasons why this insecurity made itself felt so strongly. The room was wrong for her, the room, the whole house. If the house had been as I'd expected, she would have fitted it. As it was it deprived her of the safety of a proper background. I noted how her mother kept watch, alert for any sign Susan might give of not intending to go through with something she had promised to perform. This is not hindsight. I was not at ease. Susan was difficult to talk to. I felt that the only way to break through to her would be to say: Tell me all about *yourself*. Her self-centredness was like an extra thickness of skin. Without it, I believe, she would have died of panic or exposure. What she needed – the sense of human correspondence – was precisely what she protected herself from experiencing. I was appalled at the idea of the proposed marriage. As a victim, she was ready-made.

But it was – I reminded myself again – none of my business. None of this was. I was merely a spectator; as much but no more involved than someone in the audience of a theatre. The play had Chekhovian undertones. For all the general air of easiness, the uneven co-operative effort to perform, *en famille*, each member of the cast was enclosed, one felt, by his own private little drama. Rowan, surprisingly talkative, did well – I thought rather too well – in his part of cheerful friend of the family. He wasn't cut out for it.

When Sarah came in at last it was as if someone had strayed on to the stage through error. She looked nondescript and her behaviour was colourless. She was quite unlike the girl I met in Bombay. My disappointment was profound. I assumed that in Bombay I must have been in a very uncritical mood where women were concerned. She was wearing the same dress, the one she had worn at the Maharanee's, but this time it did nothing for her. Her hair was dressed in the same way but lacked lustre. She did not even walk well. She had little to say to any of us. The one pleasant effect of her arrival was that Susan became a little more communicative and Rowan much less so. He had acquired the tentative air of a man who hadn't quite decided whether he was as fond of someone as he had imagined. Sarah gave him little encouragement. To me she gave none.

It was at dinner that it occurred to me that the evening had a motif; neither planned for nor consciously acknowledged. It was suddenly in the air. The motif was the forthcoming marriage and the part which I might or might not play in frustrating it. Only Susan and Colonel Layton, I thought, were completely unaware of this.

The motif first became apparent to me in the table arrangement. Mrs Layton put Rowan on her right and me on her left.

Colonel Layton, at the other end, had his married daughter on his right and Sarah on his left, which meant that Susan was next to me and Sarah next to Nigel. This strict adherence to an order of precedence that gave the married daughter seniority over her elder unmarried sister was, I thought, nevertheless open to more subtle interpretation, for there would have to come a point when I deliberately engaged Mrs Bingham in one of those table conversations which – even at so small and intimate a gathering – assume a semi-private character; and it would undoubtedly be my duty to mention her engagement to the officer I worked for and to offer my good wishes.

The subject of Susan's engagement hadn't arisen yet. After dealing with soup and responding to Mrs Layton's questions about the places I had visited in India, about the origins of the name Perron, about my balloonist uncle and my other eccentric relatives (Nigel must have briefed her well) I became very conscious that Susan was not communicating with her father nor (I felt) listening either to Nigel and Sarah or to her mother and me; that she was, in fact, waiting, self-contained, embattled; waiting for me to turn round and say: Well, tell me all about yourself.

This is the one moment in the evening I clearly remember. The soup plates were being cleared. Mrs Layton transferred her hostess's attention to Nigel, giving me the cue to transfer my own to Mrs Bingham. Protected, as I thought, by the conversation between Nigel and Mrs Layton I turned to Mrs Bingham and said Nigel had told me about her engagement to Colonel Merrick and that I should like to offer her my best wishes for their future happiness.

In the sudden silence in which I found myself ending it, my quiet little speech splashed as loudly as a stone thrown into a placid pond on a summer night.

After the ripples had died away Mrs Bingham looked round and smiled. 'Thank you,' she said. 'That is most kind of you. I'm sure we shall be. Very happy.'

Then she turned away, resuming contemplation of her place at table. I noticed Colonel Layton's left hand was occupied moving bits of bread from the middle of his side-plate to the outer rim and back again, as if he were counting cherry-stones that told his future. I imagine I tried several times to engage

Susan Bingham in something approximating to conversation.
I have no recollection of succeeding; instead I recall, chiefly, a
sense of other people's resignation – particularly Mrs Layton's.
Neither she nor Nigel (nor Sarah) could possibly have expected
me to say anything except what I did say. Perhaps it was only
when I said nothing more that they recognized their own subconscious expectations; resigned themselves to the inevitability
of the marriage. Only Colonel Layton seemed unaware, unaffected. He smiled; ate sparingly. His demeanour suggested
thoughts passing through his mind: How extraordinary – how
nice – how lucky I am – whatever will happen to me next? The
emotional instability of Bombay had gone. Rather, it lay hidden
under the carapace, the hardening shell of reaffirmation.

When the women withdrew the servant brought a couple of
decanters. One of them contained the remains of that much-
travelled bottle of Old Sporran. I declined the whisky and had
brandy; an act of self-denial which I followed up by mentioning
Bagshaw and inviting what I would least welcome: a claustrophobic conversation about the hermetic world of school, that
alchemy in reverse which transmutes the gold of life into the
lead of tiresome recollections of immaturity. But Colonel
Layton showed no enthusiasm for Bagshaw. He smiled benignly,
uncommitted. He was suffering, I thought, from delayed reaction to the shock of homecoming. Here for him, briefly, was a
likeness of the world he had just escaped from, a room occupied
entirely by men. I don't think he liked it, suddenly. He raised
his glass of malt whisky in a rather shaky hand and said, 'Strange
thing. There was a young Oberleutnant at the last camp I was
at –' and retold the story for – I assumed – Rowan's benefit, but
when he had finished and I glanced at Rowan I fancied Rowan
too had heard it before but assumed I hadn't.

'Extraordinarily kind of you, Perron,' Layton said, nodding
at his glass. 'I feel it would be civil to write to the Oberleutnant
and tell him it came true. Haven't actually sat down to Jane
Austen yet, though. So mustn't deceive him. Not that one would
know where to write. By the way, my future son-in-law told me
that officer you rescued from the bath succeeded on his second
attempt. Sorry about that. It was his whisky originally, wasn't it?'

I agreed that originally it was.

'Odd thing,' he said, 'the compulsion to suicide.' Layton was studying the pale liquid in his glass, perhaps seeing in the whisky of one dead man the face of another. 'What do you say, Rowan? Odd? To be quite so at the end of the tether?'

Rowan said he was inclined to think there was a certain dignity in taking one's own life. Layton said he supposed the Japanese would agree but that it was wretched for the family and that that was what a man should think about. In the case he'd just had, the case of Havildar Karim Muzzafir Khan, it was the plight of the widow and her children that most concerned him. The regiment would have to make sure she didn't suffer unduly. But she had left her dead husband's village and gone back to her own. He feared that her neighbours had made life impossible for her when they heard what he'd done, in Germany. He turned to me. 'Perron, is anything that's worth knowing coming out of these interviews?'

The briskness of the military manner flared up in that one question and then went out again. I decided that he would prefer the truth so replied that so far as I was qualified to judge I should say nothing worth knowing whatsoever. He nodded.

'That's rather the conclusion I've been coming to,' he said. And nodded again. The images of the evening at Rose Cottage end there.

In my bedroom at the guest house I found on the bedside table a copy of Emerson's essays – heavily underlined and marked in the margins. Its owner, or one of its owners (it had obviously been handled a great deal) had written her name on the fly-leaf. Barbara Batchelor. The underlining began with the first familiar and sonorous paragraph of the essay on History: *There is one mind common to all individual men*: and continued intermittently. I flicked the pages to find the other familiar passage in the essay on self-reliance and found that marked too: *Society is a wave. . . .*

'You've found the book, then,' Rowan said when I took it out on to the verandah to join him over what he called a night-cap. 'I'm sorry, I ought to have mentioned it, but forgot. It was among some things I brought up from Ranpur for Sarah. We thought you'd like it.'

Barbara Batchelor was an old missionary who'd once lived at

Rose Cottage as companion to Mabel Layton, Layton's step-mother, now dead. Miss Batchelor was dead too. The book was among some things she'd left for Sarah.

When I was settled Rowan said, 'Incidentally, it needn't make any difference to you, but I've decided to go back to Ranpur tomorrow.'

I felt bewildered. 'Whenever did you decide that?'

'I suppose in the last half-hour or so.'

Recalling the tentative arrangement I'd overheard him making with Mrs Layton to play some tennis over the weekend I realized he was telling the truth. I didn't press for an explanation.

'I can't very well stay here once you've gone,' I said. 'I'd better see the accommodation people tomorrow.'

'That'll only confuse them. They know you're here. If I were you I'd hang on at least until an officer comes up to take Merrick's place, or you get ordered back to Delhi. I've signed you in as my guest. I'll mark it *sine die*, so all you'll have to do is sign any chit the servant asks for and sign the steward's register before you leave.'

'Who pays? Government or you?'

'Government. So long as you don't dine the station or do anything the auditors might think odd, like drinking three bottles of whisky before breakfast. They'd apply to me in that case.'

'You pay for the drinks anyway, don't you?'

'Don't let it inhibit you. You can drink to my future if you like. I'm going back into the Political. HE warned me about it before I came up. That's why I've been having these few days off. I rang him tonight before we left though and he told me the signal had come in. I fly to Delhi on Tuesday and then get told where I'm going.'

'It's only Thursday.'

'Oh, well. Clearing things up, packing. Better to get on with it.'

'Does Miss Layton know you're going?'

'She knows I'm expecting the posting.'

'Didn't you tell her it had come?'

'No.' He hesitated. 'Somehow the atmosphere tonight didn't seem right. I'm sorry it wasn't all that successful an evening.'

I asked him what time he intended leaving. He said the private coach was still in Pankot. It was just a question of getting it coupled on to the midday train. Gopal had gone back by car, with Mohammed Ali Kasim. He said, 'Perhaps there'll be a signal for you tomorrow too, from your Aunt Charlotte. Then we could go back together.'

'It's a shade early for my signal.'

'You were serious, though, about Bunbury?'

'Deadly serious.'

'What happens if it doesn't work?'

'A court-martial, I should think. Are you positive it's hanging and not shooting?'

But this irritated him. He stopped looking at me. He seemed to find the dark beyond the verandah the most rewarding of anything within his range of vision. I waited. Presently he glanced back at me. He said, 'Was it a surprise to see me the other night at Ranpur station?'

'Totally unexpected.'

'But you recognized me.'

'Easily.'

'Would you, if you hadn't met Sarah in Bombay and she hadn't mentioned I was in Ranpur, working as an aide to HE?'

'Perhaps not so instantaneously.'

'Even if we'd been contemporaries at school, same house, same year, and close friends. It wouldn't necessarily follow would it that we'd recognize each other if we met years later in a public place?'

'It could follow. Why do you ask?'

'Do you remember a boy called Colin Lindsey?'

'It rings a vague bell. Who was Colin Lindsey?'

'Harry Coomer's closest friend.'

'Then I may. I once asked Coomer to tell me the difference between karma and dharma but he said he didn't know. I suggested he might ask his father during the summer holiday but he said he probably wouldn't see him because he was spending the holiday with – well – "Lindsay, here"?'

That was the picture: Coomer and 'Lindsey, here', standing together, the brown boy and the white boy, resisting an inquisitive prefect's invasion of their solidarity and privacy.

Rowan said, 'He saw more of the Lindseys than of anyone. His father encouraged it and kept himself in the background.

He wanted Harry to grow up as much like an English boy as he could.'

I was about to say: How much like was that? But checked myself. Rowan was too delicately poised between confession and characteristic silence for me to take the risk of upsetting him with that kind of facile question. For a while neither of us said anything but he began to lose interest in the dark beyond the verandah, as if Kumar were no longer out there but had come in to shelter in our recollections of him. A third, empty, white cane chair might have been his. Well, not his, not Coomer's; but Kumar's, whatever Kumar was or had become; whatever he would look like now, sitting there, no longer interested in cricket, but rape. White women. It meant nothing to me. But I wondered how deep Rowan's prejudice lay. Of the depth of Merrick's I had no doubt.

He said, 'I suppose we ought to take into consideration the distinct possibility of our not meeting again for at least as long as it's been since we last did. What, ten years ago?'

'Next time it won't seem so long. I'm told the older you get the quicker time goes.'

Such cliché simplicity also seemed to irritate him. He asked me what it was that amused me. I told him that what amused me was the awful seriousness that seemed to overcome people who worked in India. He said he thought I'd only just stopped accusing him of not being serious enough. I said that wasn't quite what I meant. There was a difference between taking a situation seriously and taking oneself seriously.

He became interested again in the dark beyond the verandah. I thought I had done it this time and that soon he would drink up and say goodnight. Instead he said, 'Yes, but out here there are penalties for appearing not to. At least, that's one's earliest understanding. One is wrapped up in the cocoon of a corporate integrity. It's a bit like being issued with a straitjacket as well as a topee. It makes it difficult to act spontaneously and you become so used to wearing it that you find it difficult to do without it.'

'They used to issue spinepads too.'

'I know.'

'But they went out. Like topees are doing.'

'I don't think the straitjacket ever will.' But he was smiling again. He said, 'Sarah puts it well. She says that in India English people feel they are always on show. I think that's true and on the whole that nothing worries us more.'

'Why do you say that?'

'Perhaps because we feel that fundamentally there's so little to see?'

'The *raj* with a superior manner hiding an inferiority complex? I can't say I've come across much evidence of that.'

'You could begin with me. I've very little real confidence. But it would be dangerous to give that impression. I expect I overcompensate. Most of us do. It's probably what happened to Colin Lindsey.'

It was my cue but I didn't take it up. I wanted him to tell me about Kumar and Merrick but I suspected that any further prompting would result in my getting a watered-down account and that I would only get a reasonably full one if I left the initiative to him. He hesitated again. But whatever it was that made him want to tell me finally won the struggle with whatever it was that made him reluctant to do so.

In May of the previous year (1944) on the day Rowan resumed his duties as ADC after one of several spells in hospital, the Governor called him into his study, said, 'You're an old Chillingburian, aren't you?' and asked him if he remembered a boy called Hari Kumar or Harry Coomer. Rowan said he did. The Governor handed him the confidential file on a man currently detained under the Defence of India Rules. This was Kumar. Rowan found it surprising that the boy he had known should have developed into a political activist. The real shock came when he read further and realized that Kumar had not been arrested on political grounds but on suspicion of leading a criminal assault by several Indians on an English girl called Daphne Manners in Mayapore in August 1942.

Rowan remembered the Bibighar Gardens case quite well. He had been in hospital in Shillong still recovering from illness contracted during the long march out of Burma with what remained of his regiment. The Bibighar Gardens affair was something out of the common rut among the reported incidents of rioting, arson and sabotage that followed the arrest of political leaders, because it involved what in spite of that cautious phrase 'criminal assault' had clearly been the rape of a white woman.

Rowan also recollected the sense of anti-climax when nothing further happened. A report that the men arrested had not after all been charged but sent to prison as political detenus was taken up by the Calcutta *Statesman*. It seemed odd, the *Statesman* suggested, that all six men originally reported arrested with such promptness, while presumably turning out to be the wrong men (since no charges had been made) should also all turn out to be politically active in a way that caused the authorities such concern that detention orders had had to be issued.

The *Statesman*'s interest in the case provoked no official comment; and when the riots were over, the Bibighar Gardens affair like so many others that had marked that period of violent confrontation between the *raj* and the population, simply passed into history together with the rumours that had added colour to it, the chief of which was that the girl herself had scotched the charges by denying that the arrested men were those who had attacked her and threatening to say such extraordinary things about colonial justice and colonial prejudices, if a trial were held, that it was decided there would be no point in attempting to hold one.

Rowan had heard these rumours, the accompanying explanation that one of the men arrested had been her lover and that she was so besotted or terrified that she had willingly perjured herself to save him, in fact had only admitted to being attacked because she couldn't disguise the awful state she came home in. She'd cooked up a story about the men being of the badmash or criminal type, not young educated boys like the ones in custody. He also heard the story that later she returned pregnant to her aunt in Rawalpindi and in the March of 1943 he had seen the notice in the *Times of India* of her death in Kashmir and of the birth of a child on the same day. The child, a girl, had been given an Indian name, and the notice had been inserted by her aunt, Lady Manners, the widow of Sir Henry Manners, one-time Governor of the province of Ranpur. At this time Rowan was again in hospital, in Calcutta. From there he went back to his regimental depot. Later he was in Delhi for a while. Early in 1944 he was appointed to Malcolm's staff at Government House, where Sir Henry and Lady Manners had lived during the late 'twenties and early 'thirties. But when Malcolm gave him the file on Hari Kumar he had not thought of the Manners case for months.

The next point of interest to emerge from the file was that Kumar was the man Daphne Manners was supposed to have been infatuated with. The longer Rowan studied the file the stronger the evidence seemed to him to be that Kumar, having formed an association with Miss Manners, had then plotted with several Indian friends of his to attack and rape her. In custody after the rape he had virtually given the game away according to the police report by mentioning Miss Manners's name before her name had been mentioned by the police. Moreover when arrested at the house where he lived with his aunt he had been bathing scratches and bruises on his face such as might have been given by a girl fighting her attackers in the dark; and the clothes out of which he had just changed were mud-stained. Throughout his interrogation he stated repeatedly, mechanically, that he had not seen Miss Manners since a night some weeks before when they visited a temple. (Miss Manners had used virtually the same words.) But he refused to account for his movements on the night of the rape or for the state of his clothes and the marks on his face. His almost invariable answer to questions was: I have nothing to say.

The one document in the file that caused Rowan uneasiness was one relating to the alleged discovery by a junior police officer of Miss Manners's bicycle in a ditch outside Kumar's house, and an accompanying document, attested by the District Superintendent of Police, stating that this curious piece of evidence (with its ridiculous implication that Kumar had cockily ridden Miss Manners's bicycle home from the Bibighar and then left it outside his own home) had been the result of a misunderstanding. The bicycle had actually been found by the superintendent in the Bibighar Gardens when the site was searched after the assault had been reported. It had been put into a police truck. The truck had then been driven to Kumar's house – to Kumar's house because of the known association between Kumar and Miss Manners and because the District Superintendent had called there earlier in the evening after Miss Manners had been reported missing by a Lady Chatterjee, at whose house Miss Manners was staying, and found Kumar not at home, and his aunt unable to say where he was. On the way to Kumar's house this second time (with the cycle in the back of the truck) the police's attention had been attracted by a lighted hut in some waste ground not far from the Bibighar. Inside the hut they had found five young men, all of them 'known to the police' for 'political affiliations' and several of them 'known to the police as friends of Kumar'. These men were 'fairly intoxicated' and were drinking home-made liquor, itself an offence that warranted arrest, but also in the District Superintendent's opinion certainly deserving investigation on a night when the authorities were on the alert for demonstrations against the government for its imprisonment of Congress leaders and when a European woman had been assaulted by five or six Indians. In arresting these young men, in putting them into one truck, in the continuation of the journey to Kumar's house, in the 'change of police personnel' from one truck to the other and the despatch of the five arrested men back to the police headquarters, 'a misunderstanding' had arisen. The inspector finding the bicycle on the road outside Kumar's house where 'it must have been temporarily placed, again as a result of a misunderstanding' had 'assumed that this was where the bicycle was found' and had accordingly put in a report which, even if that was not his intention, might certainly have led to 'this erroneous conclusion'.

The District Superintendent was Merrick. This was the first time Rowan came across his name. Someone, either in the Inspector-General's department or the Secretariat had minuted in the margin of this disclaimer about the bicycle, 'Pity about this'; an ambiguous phrase which did little to subdue Rowan's uneasiness; but initially the disclaimer gave him a favourable impression, not of the Mayapore police, but of the superintend-ent as a man who had not hesitated to sort out a muddle which would have been helpful in bringing Kumar to trial if left as it was. Subsequently, he was uneasy for a different reason. He could not help wondering whether the evidence of the bicycle had been planted by Merrick or with Merrick's blind-eye approval and then refuted by Merrick when he saw that it was too danger-ous a piece of falsification.

Two other points of interest arose in the account of the actual arrest. In Kumar's room there were found (a) a photograph of Miss Manners and (b) a letter from England signed 'Colin' which referred to a letter Kumar had written to *him* but which he'd been unable to read because his father had opened and then destroyed it as one unsuitable for his officer son to receive – a letter, so it seemed, of a political and anti-British nature. The letter from Colin dated back to the post-Dunkirk era.

But, Rowan said, apart from this hearsay evidence of anti-Britishness, and unless the assault on Miss Manners could be interpreted as political, the evidence on the file of Kumar's political commitment was thin to the point of non-existence. He had – just once – been taken in for questioning because his attitude to a police officer had been unsatisfactory and arrogant.

The officer was Merrick. This incident occurred some six months prior to the rape. Searching an area of the native town for an escaped political prisoner called Moti Lal, Merrick had visited a place known as The Sanctuary, a clinic and feeding centre for the homeless and destitute run by a Mrs Ludmila Smith. Mrs Smith (also known as Sister Ludmila) went out every night with stretcher-bearers, searching for men and women who had come into Mayapore to beg, or to die. On the night before Merrick arrived looking for the escaped Moti Lal, she had picked up a young man found lying unconscious near the banks of the river.

This was Kumar, and all that was wrong with him was that he was dead drunk. When Merrick arrived in the morning he asked Kumar who he was, where he lived, what he had been doing. Kumar had a hangover. The interview went badly. Merrick decided to continue it at the nearest police station.

At this point in the file, Rowan said, there was a brief summary of Kumar's background. Kumar (according to Merrick) had not been frank about his identity but had 'finally admitted' that his name was Kumar, that he knew Moti Lal because Moti Lal had once been employed by Romesh Chand Gupta Sen, a contractor. Kumar had himself been employed by Romesh Chand who was in fact Kumar's aunt's brother-in-law. Romesh Chand had sacked Moti Lal because he didn't like his clerks to concern themselves with anything except the business, and that included not concerning themselves with politics. Kumar had left Romesh Chand later, when offered a job as a sub-editor and occasional reporter on the Indian-owned English-language newspaper, the *Mayapore Gazette*.

There was then a statement that 'the man Kumar claimed to

have been brought up in England by his father, Duleep Kumar, since deceased, and to have been educated at a public school which he named as Chillingborough College'.

Subsequent notes suggested that Merrick had investigated Kumar's claim and had got further information; that Kumar was born in the UP, that his mother died while he was still an infant and that aged two he had been taken to England by his father, who had sold his land to his brothers and now set up in business, anglicizing the name to Coomer. But in 1938 Duleep Kumar's businesses failed. He committed suicide. Hari was penniless. At the age of eighteen, through arrangements made between lawyers in London and his Aunt Shalini, widowed sister-in-law of Romesh Chand, and his own father's sister, Hari came out to India.

From the date Kumar was first questioned by Merrick he was under surveillance. Kumar never explained why he was drunk but the names of his drinking companions were obtained and there were cross-references to other files kept on these young men. The surveillance seemed to have been fairly casual, but Merrick had been thorough in recording what was known locally about this English public-school-educated Indian reporter. He'd discovered that Kumar had once applied to an English firm, British–Indian Electric, for a post as a trainee but been turned down on the recommendation of the technical training manager who thought him not intelligent enough.

A young man whose place Kumar had taken on the *Mayapore Gazette*, one Vidyasagar, was also under surveillance. Vidyasagar was now working on a nationalist local, *Mayapore Hindu*. There were notes of several occasions when Kurnar and Vidyasagar had been 'seen together', but these couldn't strike a reader as very significant because the occasions were invariably those when they had simply been in the same place at the same time, as reporters (at District and Sessions Court, for example, and local functions on the *maidan*).

The most important items in Merrick's notes were those concerning Kumar's friendship with the English girl, Daphne Manners, who had come to Mayapore to stay with a Lady Chatterjee – a friend of Lady Manners in Rawalpindi. Miss Manners's parents were dead. She had lost her brother in the war and had come out to India quite recently to stay with her surviving relative, her aunt, Lady Manners. Since coming to Mayapore she had been doing voluntary work at the Mayapore General Hospital.

The notes about her association with Kumar began with one dated in April 1942. 'At the War Week exhibition on the *maidan* Miss M left her party to speak to K who was hovering in the vicinity.' The next note suggested that Merrick had taken the trouble to find out how Miss M and K had previously met. 'It seems K was invited to Lady Chatterjees's place, the MacGregor House, where Miss M was staying, shortly after K was questioned in the matter of Moti Lal, probably through the suggestion of the lawyer Srinivasan who was sent to police headquarters to inquire why I'd had K taken to the kotwali for questioning. Srinivasan is Romesh C's lawyer.'

There were several further notes giving dates when K and Miss M were seen in one another's company, one of which – 'Miss M dined with K and his aunt at their house in the Chillian-wallah Bagh extension' – Rowan found particularly distasteful since it indicated that Kumar could not even have someone to dinner without the fact being reported.

Finally, among the documents, there were two statements and a report from the Divisional Commissioner. The first statement, by Merrick, described how Kumar had first come to his notice and the opinion he had formed of him as a result of this, what was known locally about the characters of the young men in whose company he had been on the night he got drunk, how Merrick eventually thought it his duty to warn Miss Manners 'that the young Indian with whom she had struck up a friend-ship, which few Europeans on station had failed to notice, was not the kind of man one could recommend her to take into her confidence'.

Merrick's statements ended with an account of his own actions on the night when he had called on Lady Chatterjee and found her 'alarmed' at Miss Manners's failure to arrive home, and of his second visit when he found Miss M arrived at last but 'in a distressed condition as a result of having been attacked and crim-inally used by five or six men in the Bibighar Gardens'. He con-tinued with a description of his discovery of the young men in the hut near by, of the state in which he found Kumar when call-ing again at the house in Chillianwallah Bagh and of the obstinate but suspicious behaviour of Kumar when taken into custody.

The second statement was a report made by three officers of the civil administration after a private interview with Miss Manners. According to this report, Miss Manners had not confirmed her earlier verbal statement that the men had come at her in the dark, covered her with her own raincape, dragged her off her bicycle and into the Bibighar, and that she had therefore not been able to identify them. She now stated that she had been *in* the Bibighar, alone, and that although it was dark, and the men came at her suddenly, and did cover her head with the raincape, she had had just sufficient glimpse and smell of them to swear on oath that they were all of the badmash or criminal type, not educated or westernized boys of the kind who had been arrested; that it would be ridiculous to bring such boys into court, that she could not fail to deny that they were the men involved, and that it would be just as reasonable to bring in a group of young British soldiers and accuse them of having blacked their faces in order to attack her.

The report from the Divisional Commissioner was simply to the effect that he had studied the files on the arrested men and all the statements and while agreeing that in view of Miss Manners's attitude the evidence against them in the matter of criminal assault was insufficient on which to charge them and bring them to trial, he agreed with the opinion that quite apart from suspicion of criminal assault the evidence obtained over several months of their conduct and political affiliations warranted their detention under Rule 26 of the Defence of India Rules.

When Rowan had studied all this material he returned the file to Malcolm who asked him whether he thought Kumar wrongfully imprisoned. Rowan said he thought so, technically, but that suspicion of complicity in rape was strong enough to take the view that he may have got off extremely lightly. The Governor then asked him whether there was any doubt about this Kumar being the Kumar Rowan had known at school – and handed him a police photograph; full face and profile. He hadn't seen Kumar since Kumar was about fifteen, but he thought the features were like those of the boy he remembered; apart from which everything on the file about Kumar's history fitted what he had known of Kumar's background. The Kumar he knew *had* spent all his life in England, was known as Harry Coomer. His accent had been as English as Colin Lindsey's and Rowan's own.

You would only have to hear him speak to know whether they were one and the same man.

The Governor said Rowan would have an opportunity to confirm this. He was to arrange and lead a private examination of the prisoner at the Kandipat jail, in a room known as Room O. He would have a shorthand writer and an official from the Department of Home and Law to assist him. There would also be a fourth person, a woman, who would watch and listen to the interview from a specially equipped adjoining room. The Governor had had many pleas from Kumar's aunt, Shalini Gupta Sen, to review the case against her nephew, and the poor woman had in fact come to Ranpur to be near by in case some steps were taken. But the request for this examination and the request to be present were from Lady Manners. Her visit was to be kept secret. Of the members of the examining board only Rowan was to know of her presence. The examination would not be made under oath and the entire affair was to be conducted in as discreet and confidential manner as possible.

With this Rowan had to be content. For the moment Malcolm would discuss it no further. Rowan made the arrangements at the Kandipat and on the day he met Lady Manners at Government House he was already hating the whole business. Kumar had been in jail for more than eighteen months and Rowan had decided that the only explanation for Lady Manners's sudden emergence from the obscurity in which she had lived since the tragedy of the assault and the tragedy of her niece's death in childbirth was that she had been biding her time, perhaps obtaining further evidence against Kumar and now wanted vengeance.

The impression did not survive his first short meeting with her the day before the examination; and on the day itself driving with her to the Kandipat, observing her physical frailty, noting her gentleness of manner, it struck him rather forcibly that here was a woman who felt that her life was coming to an end and that there were dispositions to make. He knew from Malcolm that she was staying under an assumed name at an hotel in Ranpur and that the child and its ayah were with her. To minimize the risk of being recognized by old servants at Government House she wore a deep veil over an old-fashioned sola topee, which she only raised in the car to look at the photograph of Kumar, whom she had never in her life seen.

But – Rowan wondered – if the object of the examination was to secure the release of a man she felt, or knew, to be wrongfully imprisoned, why had she waited so long? Or was it so long? More than eighteen months since the assault, but only half that time since her niece died. As they drew near Kandipat, Rowan began to pull down the blinds of the car. They entered the jail precincts in semi-darkness.

The deeply subjective feelings, like joy, fear, love, are the most difficult to convey. One has to make do, more often than not, with the crutch of the words themselves. Very occasionally if an experience has been vivid enough, the quality of it comes through without there being much conscious attempt to communicate it. This was the way Rowan conveyed to me what the examination in the Kandipat jail had been like, for him. It had been a claustrophobic experience. I have thought of Rowan's experience of the Kandipat often, tried to shed light on it, as a scene, but the light coming out from the scene always seems stronger. One ends up a bit dazzled by it. The eyes hurt. You glance away, to rest them, and then momentarily there's the illusion of blindness, blankness. You feel shut in. I hit on the word claustrophobic while Rowan was describing it to me. Directly I hit on it I knew I had also hit on a description of the effect Merrick had on me.

That light I mentioned, the one coming out from the scene, was actually a real light: a light bright enough to interrogate by, but nothing crude; subtly balanced, tilted, as if haphazardly, but in fact shining on the examinee at an angle that would only worry him if he chanced to look up above the level of Rowan's head and wonder about the grille in the wall behind. But had he done so he would have assumed that it was part of the air-conditioning plant.

Another thing Rowan managed to communicate to me without putting it into so many words was the shock of this initiation into one of the *raj*'s obscurer rites, the kind conducted in a windowless room with artificial light and air, an early form of bugging system and spy-system, and making an uncompromising statement about itself as the ominously still centre of the world of moral and political power which hitherto he had known as one revolving openly in the alternating light of good intentions and the dark of doubts and errors. The room in the Kandipat emitted nothing but its own steady glare. It illuminated nothing except the consequences of an action already performed and a decision taken long ago. These could never be undone or retracted. In the world outside new action could be taken and new decisions made. But the light of what had been performed would glow on unblinkingly, like radium in a closed and undiscovered mine.

When the prisoner entered Rowan thought: No, that's not the man, the whole thing is a ludicrous mistake. The man is an impostor. It was not even the man in the police photographs. He had expected some change but not such a devastating one. This man looked middle-aged. He seemed not to understand English. Rowan asked him to sit down but it wasn't until the assistant examiner from the Home and Law Department, an Indian, said '*Baitho*' that he did so; and then the contours of the chair seemed to puzzle him, as if he lacked physical co-ordination. Rowan asked him whether he wished to have the examination conducted in English or in Hindi. He asked him this question in Hindi. The prisoner answered in Hindi, using the single word *Angrezi*, meaning 'in English'. As he answered he looked directly at Rowan for the first time and the conviction that the man was the wrong man weakened.

The eyes, Rowan said, were those 'of one man looking out of the eye-sockets of another' and the man looking out could have been Kumar; his answers to the routine opening questions whose object was identification all added up to an admission that he was, but still the answers came in Hindi – the abbreviated word *hān*, repeated tonelessly. Hān. Hān.

At this point Rowan reminded the prisoner that he had elected to have the examination conducted in English. Questions had been put in English. So far he had answered in Hindi. Did this mean that he had changed his mind and would prefer the questions to be put in Hindi too? He hoped that the answer would come again, hān; then the onus of putting questions would fall on his colleague, and for him the whole thing would become a semantic exercise. For Lady Manners in the adjoining room it would become an exercise in patience. He doubted that her Hindi was even as good as his. But that didn't matter. He would prefer to take a back seat. He didn't want this gaunt shambling creature to be Hari Kumar; certainly not Coomer, whom he remembered Laura Elliott describing as 'that good-looking boy who caught you before you even scored'. Old Boys versus School. Rowan had approached him after stumps, congratulated him; asked him what he intended doing. The boy had said, 'Try for the ICS, I suppose, sir.' And gone out of Rowan's life.

To emerge here? It wasn't possible. The physical evidence was against such a transmigration. The eyes could have been Coomer's; they showed no recognition of Rowan but Rowan wouldn't have expected it. But he had expected something far more telling. A manner.

Rowan waited for the prisoner to respond. He seemed not to have understood the question and Rowan wondered whether he should repeat it in Hindi. He was about to do so when the man spoke. He said he was sorry, answering the questions in Hindi had been a slip; he seldom had the chance of speaking English, except to himself.

Rowan described the effect of this casual statement in straight-forward English as electrifying. It was as though there were two men in the chair, the one you could see and the one you could hear. The one you could hear was undoubtedly Coomer and once you were aware that he was Coomer the unfavourable impression made by the shambling body and hollow-cheeked face began to fade. The English voice, released from its inner prison, seemed to have taken control of the face and limbs, to be infusing them with something of its own firmness and authority.

'I felt,' Rowan said, 'that quite unexpectedly our rôles were reversed or at least levelled up and that it wasn't Coomer who was being examined so much as a system that had ostensibly given us equal opportunities but had ended like this with me on the comfortable side of a green baize-covered table and him on the unpleasant one. And one of the interesting questions was, where precisely did this leave my Indian colleague and co-examiner?'

The Indian colleague was the same Mr Gopal who accompanied Rowan up to Pankot and just gone back to Ranpur with Mr Kasim. Before Kumar's examination Rowan and Gopal were no more than casual acquaintances and one of the ironies of that examination, Rowan had always felt, was that whereas he himself had a common bond of sympathy with Kumar but could not absolve him from suspicion of some kind of connection with the attack on Daphne Manners, Gopal – as became obvious – believed him innocent on every count, believed that he had been victimized by the Mayapore authorities because he was an Indian, but at the same time disliked him for being the kind of Indian he actually was. Quite early in the questioning Gopal elicited from Kumar the fact that Kumar's father had admired the British and the British form of administration in India and that he had deliberately brought Kumar up in a way that should have enabled him to enter the administration with the same qualities and advantages an English boy had. At the same time, Gopal's form of questioning made it clear he believed this could only have been done at the cost of Kumar senior turning his back on his own people – which in fact had been the case and a major cause of the ensuing tragedy.

Kumar senior had been exposed as a man with an obsession that had cost his son dearly. One of Gopal's objectives in this line of questioning about Kumar's background was of course to establish that with an upbringing such as he'd had the very idea of his ever becoming a danger to the British was nonsensical. To Gopal, Kumar/Coomer *was* British. During the recess when Kumar had been taken outside for a while, Rowan admitted that he and Kumar had been at the same school but that Kumar didn't realize this, didn't recognize him. Gopal then described Kumar as 'an English boy with a brown skin' and said, 'the combination is hopeless'.

Rowan called the recess because he'd felt the examination was getting out of hand. He had tried unsuccessfully to keep it strictly to the question of Kumar's political affiliations. These, he believed, had been virtually non-existent and had now been shown to be non-existent. The only occasion when Kumar had consorted with any of the young Indians who were found drinking in the derelict hut on the night of the rape was that other night, six months before, when he got drunk himself and was picked up by Sister Ludmila's stretcher-bearers. Until then and after then he had kept fairly clear of them. He felt no animosity towards them but they weren't young men whose interests he could share, whose experiences he had shared, or whose aspirations he could regard with anything except a detached kind of understanding. They were all young nationalists but, he said, why shouldn't they be? In examination he made no bones about that, but no bones either about his view of the limited form their nationalism ordinarily took. They were young, therefore inconsistent, laughing at the British, talking against them, but fond of wearing western-style clothes and with a tendency to copy British manners. They were friendly, at times deeply depressed, at times euphoric. They were educated to a standard a peg or so above the level on which society determined they could live.

The truth which Coomer had had to face was that this was a level on which he now had to live too: that of one young Indian among countless others who could never expect to achieve any kind of position of authority; young men doomed, it seemed, to spend their lives as members of a literate but obscure and powerless middle class, thankful for jobs as ill-paid clerks in shops and offices and banks – a life infinitely poorer than the one he would have led if he had grown up in his father's ancestral village, or if Kumar senior's obsession about the value of an English upbringing had not been so deeply felt and so uncompromisingly followed that he had sacrificed his own security and – with that single exception of his young widowed sister – the regard of his family.

Hari never knew much about his father's business affairs in England but for many years these must have prospered. Hari's childhood was spent in security and considerable comfort. There had been housekeepers, governesses, tutors, a private school and then Chillingborough. In the spring of 1938 he had been looking forward to his last term, the prospect of university and of preparation for the ICS examinations. Qualified, he would eventually have come out to India on terms of parity with young Englishmen entering the covenanted civil service and so fulfilled his father's ambitions. Duleep Kumar's death would not in itself have altered these prospects but pennilessness did. Probably it was the elder Kumar's realization of what his complete financial failure would mean to his son that led him to take his own life. As a boy himself Duleep Kumar had had to wear down his own father's opposition before getting himself a college education in

India and wear it down again as a young man before going to England to study law. When he returned, unqualified, an academic failure, he had had no alternative but to settle down with the child-wife to whom he'd agreed to be betrothed before leaving England. The Kumars were well-to-do landowners, orthodox, rigidly opposed to any change in status quo. Their power and authority flowed from their wealth and possessions. With this they were content. The men were semi-literate, the women quite illiterate. The sole exception was Shalini, Duleep Kumar's youngest sister, whom he taught to read and write in both Hindi and English. India could hold more for an Indian than this, he knew. If he could not get it for himself then he would do so for the son his wife presently bore. She made it easier for him by dying. But still he wasn't free. His father, having divided the inheritance among the sons, left his family to earn merit by relinquishing his earthly ties and become *sannyasi*. Commending their mother to the sons' care he departed, with staff and begging-bowl. They never saw him again. The mother, living the life of a widow in the family house, survived two years. Shalini had gone to Mayapore as the child-bride of one Prakash Gupta Sen. After his mother's death there was nothing to keep Duleep Kumar in India. He sold his interest to his brothers and departed, presumably quite well-off, and took Hari to England. Probably he still had friends and acquaintances in England from his law-student days, and such connections would have been helpful, but he must also have been enterprising and skilful. Just what eventually went wrong, Hari Kumar did not know.

What he knew was that his father was dead from an overdose of sleeping pills and that the lawyers said there was no money because the creditors would take everything. The only Indian relative he knew of, the only one his father had ever written to, was his Aunt Shalini. The lawyers wrote to her. The assumption was that money to keep him at school, at least, might be forthcoming. It was not. Shalini, widowed and childless, was a dependant of her Mayapore brother-in-law, Romesh Chand. She borrowed money from him to pay for Hari's passage. He would live with her. And still the assumption was that Hari would continue his studies and become an ICS candidate in India. His ignorance of India was as great as the lawyers' ignorance. When he sailed he had not the smallest

conception of the devastating change made to his life by his
father's failure and suicide.

Rowan told me that these facts emerged in the first five or ten
minutes of the examination but that he had been able to build
for himself a far more complex and disturbing picture, indeed
had been unable to get it out of his mind since. He said that
Hari's old life must have ended and the new one begun the
moment he stepped off the ship in Bombay. His link with
England would have snapped, then, with shocking abruptness.

Rowan said, 'Well. You know. Whatever kind of shock India
is, pleasant or horrid, if you're a young Englishman coming out
to the civil or military or to any kind of job, you're cushioned
from the shock the moment you step off the gangplank because
metaphorically you step off into a covered-way that extends from
the dock – however many hundreds of miles – to your first
station. When Elliott and I and Laura stepped off we were met
by friends of Elliott's parents. I've forgotten who, people I never
saw again, but I remember that within an hour or two we were
at the Gymkhana Club having a drink and everything was very
English and reassuring. Everything was done for us. We didn't
have to lift a finger. I remember thinking, How good this is. But
even if we'd not been met there would have been people to see
us through, an agent to take charge of us, or people going up to
the same station. And in any case we had our white faces and
our official standing.'

Think, Rowan said, of Harry Coomer's arrival. The bewilderment he must have felt was scarcely imaginable. It was to be
hoped that if no one met him he had at least fallen in with some
people on the boat who were helpful. Perhaps the bewilderment
had started on the boat. Rowan doubted that he would have had
a first-class passage. And when it came to the train to Mayapore,
he suspected he would have had to travel third but sincerely
hoped not. The boy spoke nothing but English and the kind of
people who spoke his kind of English would have been, suddenly, on the other side of the fence. He would have been one
more face in the multitude. And the graver revelation was still
to come.

A few months ago Rowan had accompanied Malcolm on a
tour that included a three-hour visit to Mayapore. He had not

been in Mayapore before and thought the cantonment charming. But the cantonment had not been where Kumar was bound
seven years earlier, in 1938. Rowan would have liked to slip away
from the Governor's entourage but this had been impossible. At
one moment, though, the entourage was in the vicinity of the
Mandir Gate Bridge, scene of one of the worst of the Mayapore
civil riots in 1942, and there, across the river, he had a view and
needed no further evidence.

Somewhere in that noisome mass Kumar had lived with his
Aunt Shalini, had found himself put to work in his uncle's
warehouse in the Chillianwallah bazaar, had been regarded as a
man who had lost caste, who ought to undergo ritual purification to rid himself of the stain of having lived abroad. There
was to be no more education, no degree, no ICS, no entry even
into the lower levels of the provincial administration. This was
the orthodox urban middle-class Hindu India which hoarded
its profits and kept itself to itself, and served no interests but its
own and existed, quite unmoved, side by side with the India of
unspeakable poverty and squalor. And this was the India in
which Hari was expected to settle, grateful for the charity
bestowed.

Rowan said, 'I think if it had happened to me, once I'd realized
that it was real and that there seemed no way out, I'd have cried
myself to sleep every night. Perhaps he did, old as he was.'

His Aunt Shalini had adored her brother, Hari's father. They
had kept up a correspondence through all the years of separation.
She was proud of her 'English' nephew as she called Hari and
there's no doubt that she loved him and did her best for him,
her best to help him to adjust; but as a childless widow of
Romesh Chand's brother she herself was little more than one
of Romesh's chattels and the means she had to help were limited.
How long Kumar worked in his uncle's warehouse Rowan
didn't know, but in the examination he had found out more
about Hari's attempt to get a job with British–Indian Electric.
The technical training manager who had turned him down as
'not intelligent enough' was obviously the sort of man – self-
conscious about his own education and background – who
disliked his own English bosses and despised all Indians on principle. Hari Kumar, with his brown skin and public school voice

and manner, was a sitting duck. Ignoring Hari's statement that he had no technical knowledge but was willing to learn he asked him a series of technical questions and when he'd finished and Hari had been unable to answer, he said, 'Where are you from, laddie? Straight down off the tree?'

Hari walked out. A mistake, perhaps, but Rowan thought it showed how deep his instinct still was, how automatic his response to any threat to what he still possessed and still prized; prized because it was all he did possess: his sense of what he owed himself and had to keep on paying to himself, even at the expense of a lost job; the debt incurred by his English upbringing.

He got his job on the *Mayapore Gazette* because of his knowledge of the language in which the paper was supposed to be printed. He had no ambition to be a journalist. By this time he must have picked up some Hindi, but he had abandoned attempts to learn it systematically. For a while his aunt had paid for him to have lessons from a local pandit, one Pandit Baba Sahib – apparently an unfortunate choice since Baba Sahib was known by the police to recruit young men to the cause of Hindu extremism under cover of having scholarly discussions with them about Hindu mythology. From Hari's point of view the lessons weren't a success. Baba Sahib was always late and always smelt strongly of garlic. After a while Hari told him not to bother to come again. His association with this tiresome old man was brief but it probably counted against him eventually. Rowan imagined that Hari gave up learning Hindi because he did not want to pick it up sufficiently to start thinking in it, or to acquire an Indian tone of voice.

His knowledge of English was the one asset he had that could be put to practical use. When he joined the *Mayapore Gazette* as a sub-editor his uncle reduced his Aunt Shalini's allowance. Rowan imagined he'd been paid little or nothing for working in his uncle's warehouse. There couldn't have been any overall financial gain from the change of jobs but the offices of the *Gazette* were far more congenial. They were in the cantonment.

Hari crossed the river from the native to the English quarter. The new job brought him into closer physical contact with the kind of people he thought he knew because he had once been one of them. He realized he no longer was and that he had become invisible to them. But there was always Colin to write to and Colin to get letters from although Colin's letters changed in tone as he responded to the political crisis in Europe. To Hari, Europe seemed so far away that he could not share Colin's concern. He was aware of growing areas of estrangement. Colin might have been aware of them too had Hari ever described the kind of life he was living now. This he never did. He allowed Colin to go on thinking of India as a glamorous sort of place. He didn't want to appeal to Colin for pity and he wanted to keep in touch.

Colin joined the Territorial Army and thereafter wrote of nothing else. When war broke out he at once became a full-time soldier. It was between the outbreak of war and the defeat of the BEF and its evacuation from Dunkirk that Hari wrote the letter Colin's father destroyed because it was full of what he later described to his wounded son as 'a lot of hot-headed political stuff'. According to Hari, this letter had just been an attempt to discuss the pros and cons of the Congress resignation from the provincial ministries in protest against India's automatic involvement in the war against Germany. If the British Government could not declare war on behalf of dominions like Canada and Australia, but had to leave them to come in voluntarily, why should war be declared on India's behalf through the Viceroy, without consultation even? That was the basis of the Congress argument. Legally, of course, this was the only way war could be declared; but a point which Hari must have made (after the liberal education which men like Bagshaw had ensured remained a Chillingborough tradition) was that with Dominion status ranking as a declared principal aim of the British for India, the outbreak of war had been as good a moment as any to show that the spirit rather than the letter of the law was to be the guiding factor in the British–Indian relationship. But there hadn't been even a pretence of consultation between the Viceroy and his provincial ministers and central legislative assembly. Piqued, the Congress had resigned, declaring that a war against the European dictator could only be waged by free men.

Rowan said it must have been the kind of letter 'one old Chillingburian would have written to another', as strong in its arguments for the Viceroy as in those against him. It was unfortunate that it had reached Colin's home at a time when Colin was in hospital recovering from wounds and when – as Mr Lindsey probably put it – Britain was 'standing alone'. One could imagine all too easily the sort of man Lindsey was or had become; the sort who, if he had tenants or male servants would have liked to round them up and march them to the nearest recruiting office; the sort who stuck pins in maps and nursed a sense of personal injury if anyone, man or nation, cast any doubt whatsoever on the conduct of those whom God had raised to positions of power and responsibility. The attitude of Indian politicians since 1939 wouldn't have endeared any Indian to him. Deliberately opening Hari's letter he would have had his suspicions of that country's population confirmed.

'A lot of hot-headed political nonsense'. A thoughtless, empty phrase. But how damaging it had seemed two years later when the police found the letter from Colin in which it was repeated and apologized for. It was the only letter from Colin which Hari kept. That was unfortunate. It was like preserving the one real piece of evidence against oneself. Hari kept it because it was the only letter he had had from Colin which struck him as coming from the fair-minded boy he had known. Young Lindsey's baptism of fire had knocked some of the jingoism out of him. He had stopped flag-wagging. The war had become too real for that. Perhaps for the first time since Hari left for India Colin wondered what *Hari's* reality was like.

In 1941 he was to find out. His regiment came out to India. He wrote to Hari in Mayapore saying he hoped he would get down to see him or that somehow they could meet. He wrote again from another station, this time saying how difficult such a trip would be. Then he stopped writing. Hari told himself that the regiment had probably been sent down into Burma or Malaya; and at the turn of the year when the Japanese attacked, he felt sorry for him, in the thick again, having a bad war.

Rowan hesitated. I took the opportunity to interrupt, to ask a question that had been nagging for the past few minutes.

'He could have joined up himself, couldn't he? He'd have got in at once as an officer-cadet.'

'I know. It's a question I intended to ask him, but didn't, because I realized he'd have been quite justified in saying something like, "Why the hell should I have? Why should one pip on my shoulder have made me visible and acceptable to English people all of a sudden?'' An answer like that, however justified, would have looked bad on the record.'

'Evidence of anti-Britishness?'

'On paper, yes. But I haven't told you the other thing that technical training manager said to him. "I don't like bolshie black laddies on my side of the business." If you have a thing like that said to you by a member of a firm like British–Indian Electric in Mayapore, I think it follows that you don't rush to join the colours when their country goes to war in Europe. What I don't think followed in Hari's case was a rush to join the opposition. I don't believe he saw any *political* significance in what was happening to him.'

As a reporter on the *Gazette* he often attended English social functions such as flower-shows, gymkhanas, cricket matches. Occasionally an Englishman would compliment him on his English accent, ask him where he'd acquired it, and show such disbelief when told that Hari stopped saying 'Chillingborough'. A Chillingborough man didn't end up as a tuppenny-hapenny reporter on a fifth-rate local Indian newspaper. So he steered clear of these embarrassing confrontations.

And then early in 1942 he saw officers and men of Colin's regiment in the cantonment. The battalion had come into Mayapore. He wondered whether he would arrive home one night and find that Colin had visited him. He rather hoped not. It was unlikely anyway. The city on his side of the river was out-of-bounds to troops and although an officer could always get an official pass Hari thought it more likely that Colin would write, or perhaps turn up at the office of the *Gazette*. No letter came. He never saw Colin among the officers who shopped in the cantonment bazaar. It was possible, he realized, that Colin was no longer with the battalion, but in his heart he must have suspected that a few months in India had shown Colin the truth about the kind of life a young Indian with no official position would have to lead. A glance at the map of Mayapore would have shown him how close they were, how far they were separated socially.

But Colin was in Mayapore. On the *maidan* – to report a cricket match – Hari saw him. They were within a few feet of one another. They looked at one another. Neither spoke. The

kindest construction Hari could put on Colin's failure to speak
was that he didn't recognize one brown face among so many.
This, at least, was the suggestion he made when Rowan was
examining him. Kumar described the incident in the course of
answering the board's question, why – on a date in February
1942 – he had been found on waste ground near the river, dead
drunk, and taken to Sister Ludmila's Sanctuary.

He said he'd always avoided intimacy with young men like
Vidyasagar and his companions, always refused invitations to go
with them to coffee-houses. After the meeting with Colin on
the *maidan* he'd met Vidyasagar and on the spur of the moment
accepted an invitation to go home with him. It was as if he knew
that his one true link with the past had now been snapped, as if
he could see no reason to go on deceiving himself that he was
any different from these semi-westernized youths. That night he
discovered that they distilled or had access to illicit liquor. They
were used to it. He was not. He got very drunk. They took him
home but after they had gone he wandered off again, across the
derelict ground where destitutes and untouchables camped out
and where Sister Ludmila and her stretcher-bearers found him.

You could begin with me, Rowan had said, *I have very little real confidence. But it would be dangerous to give that impression. I expect I overcompensate. Most of us do. It's probably what happened to Colin Lindsey.*
Assuming mutual recognition, over-compensation for lack of
confidence seemed to me a curious way of describing Lindsey's
behaviour. Could one assume mutual recognition? Could one
even assume that the man Kumar thought he recognized as
Lindsey had been Lindsey? Apparently he must have been. Subsequently Rowan checked, through the military secretary's
department. A Captain Colin Lindsey had been in Mayapore,
not actually with his battalion but on the staff of the formation
with which the battalion had been brigaded for training, and had
then been transferred at his own request away from Mayapore to
divisional headquarters.

Still; mutual recognition remains an assumption. But, if there
was mutual recognition, one has to assume that Lindsey saw
nothing so clearly as the embarrassment that would follow any
attempt to renew an old acquaintance in such very different circumstances. His transfer to Division suggests that he probably

applied for it directly he heard that he was going to Brigade, in Mayapore. Little to do with over-compensation for lack of confidence, but a lot to do with straightforward self-protection from the consequences of having a friend who was no longer socially acceptable and who might turn out to be a pest, the sort of Indian who as the *raj* so often said would try to take advantage, make demands it would be impossible to satisfy and which it would be wiser and more comfortable not to lay oneself open to.

Where I agree with Rowan is in pinpointing the meeting with Lindsey as the one meeting in Kumar's life which, leading directly to the other from which all his true misfortunes flowed, must bear a special significance: no Lindsey on the *maidan* that day, no drinking bout with young Vidyasagar and friends; no wandering on to waste-ground, no stretcher-bearers, no Sister Ludmila, no Sanctuary; no morning waking there, hungover, resentful and unco-operative.

No Merrick.

And yet how logical that meeting was, between Kumar – one of Macaulay's 'brown-skinned Englishmen' – and Merrick, English-born and English-bred, but a man whose country's social and economic structure had denied him advantages and privileges which Kumar had initially enjoyed; a man, moreover, who lacked entirely that liberal instinct which is so dear to historians that they lay it out like a guideline through the unmapped forests of prejudice and self-interest as though this line, and not the forest, is our history.

Place Merrick at home, in England, and Harry Coomer abroad, in England, and it is Coomer on whom the historian's eye lovingly falls; he is a symbol of our virtue. In England it is Merrick who is invisible. Place them there, in India, and the historian cannot see either of them. They have wandered off the guideline, into the jungle. But throw a spotlight on them and it is Merrick on whom it falls. There he is, the unrecorded man, one of the kind of men we really are (as Sarah would say). Yes, their meeting was logical. And they had met before, countless times. You can say they are still meeting, that their meeting reveals the real animus, the one that historians won't recognize, or which we relegate to our margins

Neither Rowan nor I saw it like this, then. I doubt that he

would see it like this now. Simply, he would remain appalled and puzzled, a man with a conscience that worked in favour of both men; more in favour of Kumar than of Merrick; but Merrick was given sufficient benefit of the liberal doubt to leave Rowan inert. What Rowan was doing, in telling me all this, was trying to set off against his own inertia someone else's positive action: mine. He wanted me to do what he could not do: help Kumar. His ideas on the subject, it goes without saying, were woolly.

Kumar had been washing under a tap, trying to clear his head, when Merrick arrived at the Sanctuary looking for the escaped prisoner, Moti Lal. The first ball of the over. The merciless succession of deliveries after all came from the same hand. Merrick saw him, a young man of twenty-two, washing under a tap; and chose him. I wondered how 'prepossessing' Hari Kumar had been before prison had had its effect and made him look like one man peering out of the eye-sockets of another. Self-punishment being out of the question, Merrick punished the men he chose. After Karim Muzzafir Khan's suicide I was never in any doubt about Merrick's repressed homosexuality. Rowan always evaded this issue, and the result was that for him I think it assumed a graver importance than it merited, except perhaps in regard to the proposed marriage to Susan Bingham. But he had found it quite impossible, obviously, to convey any suspicion of this kind to Colonel Layton, or to anyone whom it might concern. One can understand this. It was no business of his, just as it was no business of mine.

For not answering Merrick's questions smartly and respectfully, Kumar was taken forcibly from the Sanctuary, pushed, punched and thrown into a police truck; not by Merrick but by one of Merrick's sub-inspectors (the same one, perhaps, who made an 'erroneous' report about the bicycle?).

But Merrick saw him being punched. So did Sister Ludmila. After the truck had driven away she sent word to Hari's uncle Romesh Chand. Romesh sent the lawyer Srinivasan to inquire why young Kumar had been 'arrested', but by the time he got there Kumar had been released. The word got round, though, that a young Indian of good character and good education had been roughed-up by the police and taken in for questioning – got round in those circles of Indian society which formed a link between the rulers and the ruled; Indians with a foot in both camps.

Four years after his arrival in Mayapore this world became aware of him. He had to be hauled into a kotwali first. It must have intrigued Merrick that this world now took note of Kumar. Srinivasan, first; and then, no doubt through Srinivasan, no less a person than the District and Sessions Judge, an Indian, who apparently inquired gently why this young Indian had been taken to the kotwali with no obvious justification. For Srinivasan and the judge Merrick can only have had contempt.

The *doyenne* of this official Indian society in Mayapore was Lady Chatterjee, a woman of cultured and cosmopolitan tastes, one imagines, since she was a friend of Lady Manners. *Persona grata* with the Deputy Commissioner, with whom she played bridge, she was neither blind nor deaf to evidence of the *raj*'s high-handedness even if (as one supposes) she often had to be to its frequent vulgarities. What Srinivasan, the lawyer, or Menen, the judge, told her about the young Kumar, interested her sufficiently to cause her to invite him to a party at her house.

He went, one imagines, out of curiosity; prickly curiosity, as resentful of the interest his 'case' had aroused as he was resentful of the fact that it had taken so long for this privileged section of Indian society to notice him. Rowan gathered it had been a mixed party – a further irony. Kumar would have been under observation by both sides. Admitting to Rowan that from his point of view the party wasn't a success (nor, he thought, from Lady Chatterjee's, whom he failed to thank), he said he had forgotten how to behave in this sort of company.

One questions that until remembering that he had never been in that sort of company before, and realizes that what he really meant was that he had no idea how to behave in a gathering of people, white and brown, who even when they mingled were observing certain rules which hinted at segregation. These were rules which only Miss Manners seemed unaware of. At first he thought she was merely trying over-hard to put him at his ease. It was a long time since an English person had talked to him without either condescension or self-consciousness, which was what Miss Manners *seemed* to be doing and what subsequent events suggested she *had* been doing. And that would make her the first Englishwoman to have talked to him on the simple human level of woman to man. When last in England he had still been a schoolboy. One wonders about the effect this would have on him. Rowan had never seen a photograph of her. The one the police found in Kumar's room was not in the file. But he had heard her described as not much to look at; but this was afterwards, when people had no time for her and assumed she had rigged the evidence to save a man she was infatuated with or terrified of.

One really knew nothing about Daphne Manners except that she was in some degree or other attracted to Kumar. One knew nothing about Kumar's feelings. The history of their relationship could be made to fit almost any theory one could have of Kumar's character and intentions. Here he was, for instance, doing as little as he could to encourage her because he found her embarrassing. Or here, doing that same little in order to excite her more. Or here, genuinely fond of her, perhaps falling in love with her, but seeing no future for either of them and doing his best to make her see that there was no future. The theory most people had was that he egged her on, made her chase after him, to humiliate her, but subtly, so that she did not realize that she was being humiliated.

'Which theory do you subscribe to?' I asked Rowan.

'I think he was fond of her. I don't believe he meant her any harm. I think she fell in love with him quite early on. And eventually I think they started making love. I think they were making love in the Bibighar Gardens. It's the only explanation that makes sense of all the rest. They were making love and were interrupted by the men who assaulted her.'

'His friends?'

'They weren't his friends. He'd only been out with them once, the night he got drunk. They weren't his enemies either. And they were really only kids. If Hari and Miss Manners were making love in the Bibighar that night then I think the men who attacked them and assaulted her really were the kind she described later when she had to admit she'd had a glimpse of them. Badmashes who'd come into Mayapore to pick up what they could in the riots everyone was expecting and which had already started down in districts like Dibrapur. The Bibighar Gardens sounds like a public place but it was a derelict site. The kind of place men like that would collect in, waiting for dark.

And the kind of place Kumar and Miss Manners would go to, to be on their own.'

'Didn't you ask Kumar whether this is what happened?'

'It only occurred to me later. Quite recently, in fact. In any case Kumar wouldn't have admitted it. He refused to say anything about her. He went on insisting he'd not seen her for something like three weeks, after the night they visited the temple. Exactly the same as he insisted when Merrick arrested him. And then of course don't forget I was trying not to examine him about the rape. I was taking a very literal view of the terms of reference, which were for the examination of a political detenu. But the rape couldn't be avoided. Everything came back to it because everything came back to Merrick. Kumar seemed to want it to come back to Merrick. So did Gopal. So for that matter did Lady Manners. Gopal started asking him about his first interrogation – I don't mean the one in February – I mean after Merrick had carted him away from his home on the night of the rape. He told Gopal Merrick had had him stripped and that his genitals had been examined. Lady Manners was listening in and watching through the grille. The microphone was in a telephone on my desk but she and I could use the telephone to communicate. When she realized I was trying to stop things going along these lines she rang through and told me I mustn't bother about her hearing unpleasant things. The other thing she wanted to know was whether Kumar knew her niece had died in childbirth. I pretended it was an outside call, naturally, and took that opportunity to call a break and send Kumar out. I tried to explain to Gopal that if we started concentrating on the alleged rape the record of the examination might be thrown out as irrelevant. But he insisted. I thought it pretty dangerous. You have to realize, Guy, that at this time I was fairly convinced that Kumar was mixed up in the assault somehow or other and that Gopal was being very naïve, over-anxious to show that Kumar had been a victim of *raj* terrorism. And, well, to be quite frank, it went against the grain to hear Kumar beginning to accuse an English police officer, a man who wasn't there to defend himself.

'Kumar wasn't on oath, the examination was private. The police officer couldn't legally be affected by anything Kumar decided to say or make up. And I wondered why he was suddenly so co-operative about answering questions he'd previously refused to answer. In 1942 his reply to every question according to the file had been that he had nothing to say. The only thing he still had nothing to say about was what he'd been doing between leaving the *Gazette* office as usual about six in the evening and arriving home about 9.30 in mud-stained clothes and with scratches and abrasions on his face. On the other hand –'

I waited.

'On the other hand, if he'd spent his time in prison making up fantasies about Merrick's treatment of him I felt he could have made up a plausible story to cover that ominous gap. But he hadn't. And whatever he said *sounded* like the truth. I didn't know what to think. But I felt like a defending lawyer who knows he can get his client off so long as he sticks to the point – the minor legal issue – and avoids anything controversial. I think I could have stuck to that and overridden Gopal if Kumar had co-operated. But he kept on saying that the real situation couldn't be avoided. He didn't mean the rape, he said he meant the situation between Merrick and himself. So when he came back after the recess I let everyone pull out the stops. I felt I'd exchanged briefs and was now prosecuting. If I let him talk about what he called the situation I thought he'd inadvertently give something away. It wasn't what I wanted. It was what I felt I couldn't resist any more. Do you see that? Or do I sound like someone covering up a prejudice and pretending the prejudice was never there?'

It was a difficult question. I couldn't answer it. I didn't try. What worried Rowan was the thought that after all his suspicion of Hari's complicity in the rape was not based so much on the evidence in the file as on the fact that Hari was an Indian and the colour of his skin coloured one's attitude to him, and that in fact it was a relief to exchange his brief, throw off the mask and let Hari condemn himself while he was trying to condemn Merrick.

And I think it was then, with Rowan sitting opposite me, showing not a trace of anxiety (carve him in stone and nothing would have emerged so clearly as his rigid pro-consular self-assurance, remoteness and dignity), that I understood the comic dilemma of the *raj* – the dilemma of men who hoped to inspire trust but couldn't even trust themselves. The air around us and in the grounds of the summer residence was soft, pungent with aromatic gums, but melancholy – charged with this self-mistrust and the odour of an unreality which only exile made seem real. I had an almost irrepressible urge to burst out laughing. I fought it because he would have misinterpreted it. But I would have been laughing *for* him. I suppose that to laugh for people, to see the comic side of their lives when they can't see it for themselves, is a way of expressing affection for them; and even admiration – of a kind – for the lives they try so seriously to lead.

It was Gopal's theory that the cuts and abrasions Kumar was said to have been bathing when the police turned up at his house hadn't been there until after the police turned up, or until he arrived at police headquarters, or even until later; that is, not there until they started getting rough with him and needed a report on the file that would explain the state of his face and at the same time harden the evidence against him. When the examination got under way again Rowan read out to him Merrick's statement about his arrival at Kumar's house and his discovery of Kumar, bathing his face, which was cut and bruised, and of the discarded muddy clothes.

Was that an accurate report? Rowan asked.

Yes, Kumar replied. It was.

Gopal was deflated but bided his time. There was another report on Kumar's file, quite a brief one, a copy of a statement by a magistrate who'd been asked by the Deputy Commissioner to question Kumar on two rather unpleasant aspects of the handling of the case. Word had got round in Mayapore that to try to make them confess the arrested boys, all Hindus, had been forced to eat beef. Also that they'd been whipped. The magistrate's name was Iyenagar. Rowan hadn't seen the files on the five other boys; he'd only been shown Kumar's. According to this file Kumar told Iyenagar that he had no complaint to make about his treatment, a simple enough refutation of the rumours and one that seemed to be borne out by the report from the medical officer at the Kandipat jail who examined Kumar physically the day he was sent there as a detenu – more than two weeks later. The only mark of physical violence noted down by the prison doctor was a contusion on his cheek. But that had been there when Merrick found him bathing his face.

The bruise, however, gave Mr Gopal an argument which he tried to turn to Kumar's advantage. He said that the marks on Hari's face, which Hari himself refused to explain, had been interpreted by the police as marks got from Miss Manners in the struggle with her attackers. He said that in a court of law a lawyer might reasonably have asked whether a woman could hit a man hard enough for a bruise to stay on his cheek for as long as two weeks. He was still trying to get Hari to say that the police had beaten him up. But Hari wouldn't say this. He said it was a good point but that in a court a prosecuting counsel might well have turned it against him by suggesting that the men who attacked Miss Manners also fought with each other.

'I saw an opening there,' Rowan told me. 'I asked him casually if that was what had happened. I remember how he looked at me. He said he'd no idea what happened among the men who attacked her. But he realized I'd exchanged briefs. I tried again to get him to say what had happened to him that night, gave him the chance to go back over the ground, back to the question of Colin, back to his relationship with Miss Manners, but all I got out of him was the information that sometimes he and Miss Manners had helped Sister Ludmila at the Sanctuary, occasionally visited one another's homes, and sometimes on a Sunday morning met in the Bibighar Gardens, the kind of places where they could go without attracting what he called abusive attention, but that all this ended on the night they visited the temple, when they had some sort of tiff.

'I saw another opening. I said, "But you made the quarrel up later." He didn't fall for that. He pointed out that I was forgetting he and Miss Manners hadn't seen each other since that night – the night they visited the temple. So I let Gopal take over, which meant letting Gopal get Hari to say what happened after Merrick arrested him.'

Almost at once they were in what Rowan called very murky waters. While they'd concentrated on the political evidence it had been possible to show that the conflict was not a conflict of evidence so much as of interpretation. Directly Hari began to describe what happened after he'd passed through the room in which the five other boys were being held behind bars, euphoric with liquor, and down into the air-conditioned basement of Merrick's headquarters, it became a question of setting Merrick's official statements about the interrogation against Hari's recollections of it. Recollections, or fantasies?

For example, from the police file: this – 'At 22.45 hours the prisoner Kumar having continually refused to answer questions relating to his activities that evening asked for what reason he had been taken into custody. Upon being told it was believed he could help the police with inquiries they were making into the criminal assault in the Bibighar Gardens earlier that evening he said: I have not seen Miss Manners since the night we visited the temple. On being asked why he named Miss Manners he refused to answer and showed signs of distress.'

When Hari was asked to say whether this was accurate he said it wasn't. He had refused to answer questions but the statement left out the fact that he'd said he would refuse to do so while he was left in ignorance of why he'd been arrested. It may have been 22.45 hours before Merrick finally said he was making an inquiry, but he described it first as an inquiry about an Englishwoman who was missing, then added, 'You know which one,' and then made what Hari called an obscene remark. He didn't know what was meant by a distressed condition unless this was a reference to the fact that he was shivering as a result of being kept standing for a long time, naked, in an air-conditioned room, after Merrick had inspected his genitals. After that inspection Merrick had said, 'So you've been clever enough to wash?' and later, 'But she wasn't a virgin, was she, and you were the first fellow to ram her.' After that, according to Hari, Merrick had sat on his desk, drinking whisky, and talked to him about the history of the British in India, every so often interjecting remarks about the boys in the cell upstairs, suggesting that they looked on him as a leader, that they'd do anything he said, and again making the comment that 'she hadn't been a virgin' and that Hari had 'been the first to ram her'. From this sequence of events, Hari claimed, he gathered that he and the others were suspected of rape. He claimed that he didn't mention Miss Manners until Merrick finally told him, at 22.45 hours – a time he didn't dispute – that an Englishwoman had been criminally assaulted, and added, 'you know which one' and then made an obscene remark. He refused to say what the remark was but admitted that he now told Merrick he hadn't seen Miss Manners since the night of the visit to the temple.

Gopal pointed out to him that unless he repeated the obscene remark his explanation for naming her remained unsatisfactory. But he would not repeat it.

It annoyed Gopal that he wouldn't. He went on pressing. Hari went on refusing. Gopal became heated, as if he were suddenly on *Merrick's* side and intended to show that if Kumar wouldn't repeat the remark that was because he couldn't; it had never been made; everything he had said about Merrick's behaviour was a pack of lies.

Hari remained unmoved. Rowan joined in again. He went over Merrick's statement point by point, forcing Hari to agree that in a number of details it was correct. Hari *had* named Miss Manners. The time was not in dispute. And he *had* been showing signs of distress if only because he was shivering.

The rhythm of question and answer quickened. How long had Hari been kept standing naked? He couldn't remember. Why? He lost track of things like time. One hour? Two hours? Perhaps. Was he alone with Merrick? Not all the time, other people came in. Who? Two constables. Anyone else? Yes, there may have been others. Couldn't he remember? Why couldn't he remember? Was he saying he was confused, giddy and cold from standing all that time? He wasn't standing all the time. He was allowed to sit then? No, he wasn't allowed to sit.

Gopal said he didn't understand. If Kumar wasn't standing and wasn't sitting, what was he doing, lying down?

Hari said, 'I was bent over a trestle, tied to it. For the persuasive phase of interrogation. A cane was used.'

Rowan said, 'I read out Iyenagar's report and asked him whether that was an accurate record of his interview with the magistrate. He said it was. In a way I was prepared for that answer because when I began reading Iyenagar's report *aloud* it struck me for the first time how very carefully the questions had been framed. They were the kind of questions a cautious authority would ask if it was suspected that a man would be too frightened to say he'd been ill-treated and if it was felt that a denial would be better for everybody's sake. "Have you any complaint to make about your treatment in custody?" was the first question. Hari said "No." Most of the questions were like that. And if Hari couldn't actually reply "no" he just said he had nothing to add to his first answer. Before I began reading it I thought I'd make it impossible for him to explain why he now accused the police of physical violence when he'd had the opportunity to do that at the time. He'd agreed that the Iyenagar report was accurate. I intended to show that he was being inconsistent. But he wasn't. I knew the answer to this before he gave it. He'd told Iyenagar the truth. He had no *complaint* to make. Just that. No complaint.

'The question wasn't so much why he didn't complain then as why he was complaining now. And was he telling the truth? I read out the prison doctor's report, the one that didn't note any visible marks of physical violence apart from the bruise on his face. But I couldn't shake him. He implied that the doctor had seen other marks but hadn't recorded them. We asked how many times he'd been hit. He said he couldn't remember. Whenever they stopped hitting him Merrick talked to him to encourage him to confess. He said Merrick told him Miss Manners had already named him but that he didn't believe her story. He believed she'd egged Hari and the others on and then got more than she bargained for and wanted them punished. Hari said that every time Merrick felt he was getting nowhere he told the constables to start again. I asked how long they had gone on. I still didn't really believe him. He said he didn't remember. Gopal asked if he was implying he lost consciousness. He said he never lost consciousness. He simply couldn't remember how long he was on the trestle.'

Rowan paused. 'Then he explained why he couldn't remember. He said it was difficult to breathe in that position and that breathing was all you thought about. I believed him then. It's not the sort of thing a man could easily make up, is it? And the trouble was that believing him made the next bit that much more difficult to write off as pure invention. He said Merrick sent the constables out of the room and spoke and acted even more obscenely. I asked him what he meant. I rather wish I hadn't. He said Merrick – fondled him.'

'Fondled him.'

'I told the shorthand writer to strike that out, leave his notebook on my desk and wait outside until I called him back. Then I really started on Hari. I put it to him that he was lying, taking advantage of the examination of his case as a political detenu to make baseless accusations in the mistaken belief that these would protect him if a charge of rape were made even as late in the day as this. I really pitched into him. I told him he had the chance to retract and advised him to think very carefully before passing the chance up.'

'Did he retract?'

'No. He apologized.'

'What for?'

'For what he called misunderstanding the reason why he was being examined.'

'What had he thought was the reason?'

'He thought Miss Manners had managed to persuade someone at last that he'd done nothing to deserve being locked up and that this had been his chance to prove it.'

'He wasn't far out, was he?'

'No, but I should have stuck to the political evidence. As soon as we went into the business of the rape I couldn't hide my suspicions and so he thought no one had really been persuaded of anything except that it was time to interrogate him again. Either that or that we were trying to salve bad consciences. He asked outright if something had happened to her. He'd had no news of her of any kind. I told him what had happened, that she'd died of peritonitis a year before, after a Caesarean operation. He asked whether she had married. She hadn't of course. He didn't ask if the child survived. At first I thought he was quite unmoved. Then I saw he wasn't. I asked if he wanted time to compose himself. He said he didn't but that we should have told him. It was very odd. His voice was quite unaffected. Physically he was composed. But he was crying. I asked him whether what he meant when he said we should have told him was that he would have answered the questions differently if he'd known she was dead. He said he only answered them because he thought she must have wanted us to ask them. If he'd known she was dead he wouldn't have answered them at all. I reminded him there was one important question he still hadn't answered. He knew I meant the question about where he was when she was being attacked. He said he'd never answer it. I was ready to bring things to an end but Gopal began again about the situation between Hari and Merrick. The clerk was no longer in the room. Officially the examination was over. He realized that. He seemed willing to talk – about that situation – even anxious. I didn't stop him. I believed he'd told the truth about the caning. I accepted that. I think you have to. I don't condone it. I'm not sure I can condemn it. It would be unfair to single Merrick out. Caning's a normal judicial punishment in this country. There were a lot of such sentences dished out in 1942 and I don't doubt a fair number of beatings-up in cells to get confessions. What I didn't accept, don't accept, without question, is – well the other thing. He could have imagined it. By his own admission he wasn't in full possession of his senses. I see you don't agree.'

'The violence makes more sense if you do accept what you call the other thing. Was Merrick kind to him at any point?'

Rowan stared at me. 'Kind to him?'

'Afterwards.'

'He gave him water. But he made him thank him for it.'

'It's the sort of thing I mean. Tell me about it.'

'I can only tell you what Hari said. It doesn't mean it happened.'

'Well tell me what Hari said.'

'He said he was taken into another room and manacled to a charpoy. Merrick was alone with him. He gave him a drink of water and made him say thank you. He bathed the cuts. He told him there'd be no more questions until morning. He said the whole evening had been an enactment of the real situation between them and that now they both knew how matters stood and what that situation was.' Rowan paused. 'It was a master and man situation, a simplified way of putting it, but near enough. At one point Merrick said, What price Chillingborough now? At another point he told Hari that there were only two basic human emotions, contempt and envy, and that a man's personality existed at his point of equilibrium between the two. But when I met Merrick the other day I simply couldn't imagine him behaving and talking like that.'

'I'm sure he did.'

'Yes, I thought you'd believe it. It's one of the reasons I'm telling you.' Again he hesitated. 'Hari said that it was to punish himself for thanking Merrick for the water that he decided to answer no more questions. He said the situation between himself and Merrick wouldn't exist if he dissociated himself from it and refused to say anything more to Merrick or to anyone else. Does that make sense to you?'

'It makes very good sense. It's what I've been trying to do. Dissociate myself from the situation that arises out of being chosen.'

Rowan was silent for a while. Then he said, 'Has he chosen Sarah Layton's sister?'

'I don't know. I don't think so.'

'Just the Laytons as a family?'

That suddenly didn't fit entirely either. But I saw what did. I said: 'In the way I mean by choose I should say he's chosen the child.'

'The child,' Lady Manners had said (meaning that other child fathered by a person unknown). 'The child. But even now I can't be sure, only surer. She was so sure.' The other thing she said was, 'He spoke the truth', but qualified it later as they drove through Kandipat, blinds down. She said, 'One has to make do with approximations' and that this was what one meant when one said he spoke the truth. When Rowan left Room O he too was sure he had heard the truth. He told Lady Manners that Kumar would be released but regretted this later when various impediments to such a release had all contributed to a partial revival of disbelief, to a renewed conviction that Kumar *had* somehow been involved in the assault. Lady Manners had asked to be taken back to her hotel and not to Government House. As they parted she thanked him for having undertaken such a distasteful task and asked him to give Malcolm a message: a very short one. 'I know my niece did not lie, that he never harmed her and is very wrongfully imprisoned.'

When he gave the message to the Governor, Malcolm said they would discuss it when the record of the examination was typed up and he'd had the chance to read it. He was going to Calcutta for a few days and preoccupied with other matters. He told Rowan to give the confiscated shorthand book to Cynthia, His Excellency's private secretary. He thought it unwise to have it transcribed by the shorthand writer at the Secretariat. 'Don't worry,' Malcolm said. 'Cynthia's pretty broad-minded.' All the same, Rowan tore out the page which the shorthand writer had drawn a line through before handing it to her.

She must have worked late. The following morning she sent him a sealed envelope containing the notebook and a top and two carbons of an impeccable typescript. When he rang through to thank her she merely said, 'Oh, well. Press on you know. Only way to get round the course.' When he read the typescript through he was astonished at her apparent equanimity. It sounded even worse in print. He kept notebook and typescripts in a locked drawer until Malcolm returned, and hourly expected Gopal to ring him and ask when the shorthand writer could complete his job by typing the record. But Gopal didn't ring.

When Malcolm had read the typescript he told Rowan it was a pity he hadn't been able to stick to the political evidence. The transcript showed that he had tried and also why he hadn't succeeded. But it was a pity. He explained that although senior police officers had always stood by Merrick, and that included the Inspector-General, the Inspector-General's private opinion was that Merrick had botched the evidence by being over-anxious and emotionally involved because he had been fond of the girl himself. If the IG saw this transcript he would be so shocked by Kumar's accusations that he would write them off as pure fantasy and point out that the only result of the examina-tion had been to revive suspicion of Kumar's guilt, and that this would be sufficient reason to keep the fellow locked up until the end of the war. The IG would say that to release Kumar now would be as good as recording a reprimand on Merrick's per-sonal file and that this could count against him, very unfairly, when he returned to the police after his army service.

'Then the best thing,' Rowan had said, 'will be to file the transcript away and forget all about it.'

But Malcolm said he didn't think he could allow that. In Kumar's case Rule 26 had fairly clearly been abused. The abuse was less obvious in the case of the other boys. If they had had a political leader at all it would have been Vidyasagar who wasn't among those arrested for rape but who was arrested a couple of days later for printing seditious literature on the press in the *Mayapore Hindu* office. In comparison with Vidyasagar even the others might be thought of as lambs led to the slaughter. Kumar, Malcolm was sure, hadn't even been a member of the flock. 'By the way,' he said, 'why did you confiscate the book and end the examination so abruptly?'

Rowan told him.

'It isn't in the transcript.'

'I removed the offending page.'

'And deprived Cynthia of the dénouement? What happened after you sent the shorthand writer out?'

Again Rowan told him.

'And Lady Manners heard *all* this?'

'Yes.'

'Did she make any other comment in the car coming home apart from giving you that message?'

'I gathered she was now surer Kumar was the father of the Manners child, but not as sure as her niece had been.'

'What did you infer from that?'

'That Miss Manners told her aunt she and Kumar had been lovers.'

'Her niece told her nothing. She left a written statement absolving Kumar completely. The old lady found it after her death, but she wouldn't show it even to me.'

Rowan felt like exploding with irritation.

'If we'd had Miss Manners's statement we might have had a more successful examination,' he told the Governor. But the Governor pointed out that the examination had been of a man detained for political reasons. Miss Manners's statement, presumably, dealt entirely with her emotional involvement with Kumar. The only value a statement like that would ever have would be in the event, now highly unlikely, of a charge being brought against Kumar for rape, when defending counsel might construct his case from it. In Malcolm's view, Lady Manners was perfectly justified in otherwise keeping it to herself. Neither she – nor her niece – had ever had any answer to the political charges, which lay outside their competence, however deep the conviction was that political detention had been imposed out of sheer frustration; the frustration felt by the civil authority which had wanted to nail Kumar much more effectively. And in *that* regard, in the matter of the charge of rape, Malcolm suggested, Miss Manners's silence, Kumar's refusal to answer questions, during the period when a charge of rape might so easily have been brought, had not only been effective then but was eloquent now. Just how eloquent, Malcolm wasn't sure. Except that he believed it suggested that they had loved one another and that, loving him, she had been afraid for him.

Just as eloquent, he thought, was the fact that Lady Manners had let a certain amount of time elapse before trying to hoist the civil authority with its own petard: Kumar's 'political' crimes. Clearly non-existent. He could order Kumar's immediate release simply on the basis of the transcript of the examination but was reluctant to do so without the approval of both the member for Home and Law and the Inspector-General. That approval, he thought, wouldn't automatically flow from the transcript of the examination.

'He left it to me,' Rowan said, 'to find a *modus operandi*.'

The first thing Rowan did was to edit a copy of the transcript to isolate the political content. When he'd done this he persuaded Cynthia to type copies of the revised version. 'Very neat', she said, when she handed the revised version to him. He thought so himself. It was now the kind of transcript that could be shown — for instance to the Inspector-General — without much fear of blood-pressures rising or of waking departmental sensitivities.

However, there was one man who might upset the applecart. Both Rowan and Gopal would have to initial the transcript before it went on file. Gopal could wreck everything by refusing to put his initials to a document that was obviously rigged. The question was, in what was Gopal most interested? In the release of an unjustly imprisoned Indian detenu or in the eventual exposure of a British police officer? Rowan rang Gopal at the Secretariat. He asked if they could meet somewhere, unofficially. Gopal didn't bite. Rowan had no option but to go to the Secretariat. He took with him a carbon of the full typescript and a carbon of the edited version. He asked Gopal to read both documents and then get in touch with him so that they could discuss the problem.

The following day Gopal rang. He asked Rowan to have dinner with him at his home that evening and gave instructions how to get there. It was the beginning of an association that ripened into friendship and affection. Gopal had seen the point of the edited typescript at once. He was on Kumar's side. He said he would be prepared to initial the edited typescript at once, with one proviso, that the title of the document should include the word Abstract and that the general heading should make it clear that the examination was in regard to a warrant issued under the Defence of India Rules. He produced a draft of the kind of heading he had in mind. Rowan accepted it at once.

'Are we doing the right thing, though?' Gopal asked as they parted. 'In prison at least he has an identity.'

But even with the edited typescript in front of him, the Inspector-General threatened to prove stubborn. An unexpected nigger in the woodpile was Pandit Baba. Since 1942 this man had become much more actively involved in affairs which attracted the CID's attention. Kumar's disclosure that he had been taught Hindi by Baba interested the IG considerably. Kumar had refused to answer questions about the Pandit at the time of his arrest. His admission now surely showed how well-informed Merrick had been, how right to suspect a connection, how right to ask questions about a connection. Until now it hadn't been clear why he did. At the time the Pandit's activities had been too unimportant for one's attention to have been attracted to his name on the file. But he was nowadays believed to be a subtle and potentially dangerous leader of Hindu youth, anti-Congress, anti-Gandhi, anti-British, with affiliations with the Hindu Mahasabha and its activist group, the Rashtriya Swayam Sevak Sangh. And what was the connection between the pandit and the detenu's aunt – who had bombarded Government with pleas for her nephew's release and was now in Ranpur without visible means of support? The examination showed that the aunt had paid for the Hindi lessons, and that it was she who had chosen Baba as Kumar's teacher. Did her persistence, her constant pleas, suggest prompting by Baba Sahib? Was she being used by this man? He had always been much too clever to get into trouble himself. Currently he had disappeared from the scene. But if one released Kumar mightn't he be the very type of young man the Pandit would find it useful to have as a disciple?

Rowan suggested to Malcolm that if the main obstacle to Kumar's release was the suspicion that he would fall at once into the Pandit's net of eager young disciples perhaps the thing to suggest to the IG was that if the CID wanted to nab the Pandit a free Kumar might be more helpful than an imprisoned Kumar.

But Malcolm said, 'Either we believe Kumar and his aunt have no political commitments or we don't. If we don't believe it we're not justified in releasing him. Frankly I do believe it. The

Pandit's just a red herring the IG's suddenly noticed. So, let it lie. Have you ever understood Einstein?'

Rowan said he hadn't. Malcolm said he hadn't either, but that sometimes when faced with this apparently insoluble and intricate problem of reaching a solution through the thickets of departmental vanities he applied his own theory of relativity, which was that although people seldom argued a point but argued round it, they sometimes found the solution to the problem they were evading by going round in ever *increasing* circles and disappearing into the centre of *those*, which, relatively speaking, coincided with the centre of the circle from whose periphery they had evasively spiralled outwards.

So Rowan let it lie. His belief in Kumar's innocence or guilt was like a pendulum. He wished he could get that to lie too, wished he could stop it at the vertical point which represented non-commitment. It was a relief when a couple of weeks later Malcolm gave him another confidential assignment – one which called for him to officiate on the Governor's behalf at the transfer of another detenu – Mohammed Ali Kasim – from imprisonment in the fort at Premanager to the protection of his kinsman, the Nawab of Mirat; a form of parole, an ostensibly compassionate act but not without its element of political shrewdness.

And it was on this assignment that he'd met Sarah Layton – changing trains on her way back to Pankot from Calcutta where she had visited the wounded hero, the best man at Susan's wedding. There she was, a rather travel-stained *Deus ex machina*, bringing news about wounds and decorations which might solve the problem of departmental concern for Merrick's reputation and Merrick's future; but for Rowan, I thought, rather more than that. Was he, by the time I met him on the same station, more than just rather fond of her?

I thought so. His decision to go back to Ranpur the next day suggested he had had hopes which he had suddenly given up. I should have liked to see them together, not as I had done that evening, but in Ranpur during two or three days of what I judged to have been a tentative exploration of airier regions that promised to be in common ownership. Mutual antipathy to Merrick was no more than a way in to those regions. Rowan, of course had not – and never would have – disclosed to her what he knew, and she had nothing to disclose except her instinctive

woman's prejudice. These meetings between them had taken
place during the brief time she spent in Ranpur before going
down to Bombay to meet her father. Before then, they had met
only that once when she had just come in from Calcutta and her
visit to Merrick. He hadn't been sure what her relationship with
Merrick was. It was a relief to him, he said, to discover that in
one sense there was no relationship. Another discovery was that
she had once met Lady Manners in Kashmir, had seen the child;
believed Merrick had made a terrible mistake. It was now that
he told her he'd known Kumar as a boy, at school. But that was
all. He might have told her more this time, on this visit to Pankot,
but naturally hadn't done so.

'Naturally?' I asked.

He said, 'Well, of course.'

It was silly to have questioned it. Merrick was to be Miss
Layton's brother-in-law. That being so, from Rowan's point of
view the subject of Merrick and Kumar was utterly closed as one
he felt able to discuss with her. I wondered when she had first
heard or suspected that Merrick planned to marry her sister.
Almost certainly the answer must be that she'd suspected nothing
until she and her father got back to Pankot. Most certain of all
was that it had been a shock to Rowan. I began to see the fullness
of Rowan's little tragi-comedy. He had, after all, had hopes of
her. The brief holiday in Pankot had been intended as an opportunity to convey to her that his resumed career in the political
was one he hoped she might share with him. Perhaps his hopes
had only finally been dashed, or shelved for future exploration,
during the few hours we'd spent that night at Rose Cottage.
Perhaps, with Merrick gone, he had hoped to find her recovered
from the shock, less weighed down, looking and acting like the
girl he knew (the girl I remembered). Had he at any time said
anything to her at all about his hopes? Had she rebuffed him?

His attention was again directed to the darkness beyond the
verandah; and suddenly I saw this other, faintly ludicrous aspect
of the affair; one that inclined me to believe that because Rowan
was the kind of man he was he had said nothing to her at all. He
would have taken his time anyway, and before an opportunity
arose the wind had been knocked out of his sails by the announcement of Susan's engagement. Well, imagine it: imagine, for
instance, Rowan shaving, brushing his hair, facing up to his

reflection; thinking what he *must* have thought because every man would. Imagine him thinking this: Could I honestly spend the rest of my life knowing what I think I know about the man who would be my brother-in-law and say nothing?

And the answer would be, no. The other answer would be that knowing himself incapable of saying anything he knew that his own hopes had to be abandoned.

Malcolm was on the point of leaving for Delhi when Rowan got back from the Kasim assignment and told him the news about Merrick's gallantry in the field. 'I'll check it,' Malcolm said. 'Meanwhile we'll say nothing. It would be best if the Inspector-General got to know through his own sources.' It meant another delay, the possibility too of this development making the IG even more stubbornly opposed to any course of action that belittled Merrick's earlier performance as a guardian of the law. But the farce was coming to an end. Quite suddenly, without fuss, it was over. The IG withdrew his objections to Kumar's release. Kumar was informed and told the date on which he would be free and instructed to report to the police in Ranpur once a week for six months. He was allowed to write to his aunt to prepare her for his return.

The aunt was living in rooms above a shop in the Koti bazaar. So Gopal told Rowan. They met the night the order of release was signed – a form of gentle celebration by two conspirators. Rowan was thinking: Yes, but release to what? Gopal had already formed a plan. He said it would be possible to put Kumar in the way of beginning to earn a living as a private teacher of English. He knew a reliable young man who would help him and who had already made contact with the aunt. The poor woman was very nervous and suspicious. It had been difficult for Gopal's young man to gain her confidence. He had had to ask her to trust him when he said the authorities had at last taken an interest in her nephew's case, trust him when he said there was every reason to hope that Hari would be released, and trust him again when he said he would help him to find work and keep out of the way of people who might want to exploit him.

'I suppose I was sticking my neck out,' Gopal said, 'but that is what necks are for.'

*

It was ironic, Rowan said, and salutary, that of the two of them
it was old Gopal, who had begun by not liking Hari, who had
put his mind to the question of Hari's rehabilitation.

Kumar had been free for over a year now. Rowan hadn't seen
him, neither had Gopal. He relied on Gopal for news and Gopal
relied on his reliable young man. Kumar no longer had to report
to the police but the CID still kept an eye on him. It had been
weeks before Kumar trusted Gopal's young man enough to fall
in with the scheme for teaching English. He made the excuse
that he would himself have to learn Hindi properly, first. But
eventually, probably when it occurred to him to wonder what
they lived on and he realized that his aunt had come to the end
of her small resources and had always been too proud to beg help
from her brother's family and only too anxious to cut herself off
completely from her dead husband's, and had now sold the last
bit of her jewellery, he agreed to help cram a couple of candidates for entrance to the Government College. Their success
brought him other boys, including a nephew of Gopal's. He
seldom visited their homes. He seldom left the apartment. He was
paid very badly but he refused anything that smelt of financial
help. The reliable young man, when he could do so without
Kumar knowing, gave the aunt small gifts, as if in return for the
cups of tea and coffee he had when he visited them; gifts of a few
vegetables, flour, ghi. The young man's own means were limited.
Some of these gifts, Rowan suspected, came from Mrs Gopal.

Rowan had been able to do very little. He knew no Indians
of the kind whose sons would go to an anonymous private
teacher in the Koti bazaar. Rowan's Indian friends were rich.
Gopal was the exception – the only middle-class Indian with
whom he had ever become on intimate terms. At the same time
perhaps the only Indian with whom he had ever been on such
terms.

And now Rowan was leaving Ranpur. He had no idea where
he would be sent. Even that little which it had been open to him
to contribute, so vaguely, so anonymously, would come to an
end, now. He would keep in touch with Gopal as far as that was
possible. Gopal and he had always had an idea that as circumstances changed, politically, it would be in their power unobtru-
sively to guide Kumar back into life. What he was living now
was hardly a life. The reliable young man reported that Kumar

seemed to have no ambition and that it was distressing to listen to the aunt painting an optimistic picture of a happy future when you only had to look at Kumar's face to see that Kumar's window on to the world was still closed and darkened. And once, coming on her alone, the young man had found Aunt Shalini crying. 'Why should he hope?' she asked, 'when there is nothing for him to hope for? He understands only English people and they will never forgive him because of the girl. The doors will always be closed to him.'

She meant the doors Hari had been brought up to open – the doors into the Administration. And what she said was true. Rowan himself was in possession of no key that would enable Hari to enter. Neither was Gopal. Even the way in to a junior teaching post in a Government College was barred.

'I've often thought of writing to old Bagshaw,' Rowan said. 'I don't really know why. One couldn't put it all in a letter anyway. And perhaps the old boy's dead now.'

'Is that where you see a future for Kumar? Back home?'

'I don't see much of a future for him here. I'm just broadening the perspective. It occurred to me that back home, if that's really where you're going, you might chance on something that could help. Anyway, I'd appreciate it if you'd write to me sometimes. Would you like another drink?'

I said I would, but that I'd take it to my room. It was nearly one o'clock.

'I'll send it in.' I imagined him sitting up for a while yet.

He didn't send it in. He brought it himself, calling to me through the half-open bathroom door. With a glass of brandy he gave me a large manila envelope.

'It's a carbon of the full typescript. I thought you might like to keep it. Take it home with you. To the groves of Academe. Officially it doesn't exist. HE told me to lose the copies of the full record. I destroyed the top and the shorthand book. I kept the carbons. I still have one.'

'Do you always carry this around?'

'No. I thought of giving it to Mr Gopal as a parting gift but thought better of it. Sleep well.'

On the way out he stopped.

'You'd better destroy it if you find Operation Bunbury snarled up and you're still stuck with Merrick. I mean in view of his light-fingered servant. Incidentally, you've never told me why you asked who Mrs Bingham was.'

'It's still too long a story.'

'But connected in some way?'

'Where Merrick's concerned everything's connected.'

'Yes. I suppose it is.'

When Rowan left me I opened the envelope meaning just to glance through it while I drank the brandy, but it was two o'clock before I'd finished reading and except for a sip or two the brandy was untouched. Far more than when Rowan described the examination I was attracted, appalled, riveted, firmly convinced of Kumar's innocence but deeply puzzled by his stubborn refusal to answer that vital question. If Rowan's object had been to ensure that I would find it difficult to get Kumar out of my mind then he had probably succeeded.

I put the transcript in my kit-bag and padlocked it, drank the brandy and went to bed.

I'd read the transcript using Rowan's final interpretation like a sieve, to isolate scraps of gritty evidence – the interpretation he'd only recently arrived at, the only one he thought made sense. I agreed. Kumar and Miss Manners had become lovers. They had been making love in the Bibighar. The marks on his face were got in a scuffle with men who pulled them apart, beat him up, knocked him unconscious or sat on him while one by one they raped the girl.

That, I thought, made sense; but thereafter there was no sense – only a silence which however hard I listened to it seemed incomprehensible. Nothing emerged from it after I turned the light out except pictures of Kumar: the man I had never seen not the boy whose face I couldn't clearly remember; but sweeping and cutting and blocking that merciless succession of contemptuous deliveries. Elms and rooks; but then again, not these, but palms and crows: the view from the flat which Purvis contemplated, retreated from, saying, 'I'm an economist', then coming in and pushing me further and further back into that elegant room with its priceless paintings in the Ghuler-Basohli style. Standing there, drink in hand, I lurched into sleep and Purvis was Kumar, seated, looking up at me through the eyes of this other man who kept saying: I don't think I'll ever forgive it.

*

Rowan had left a note. The steward brought it with my breakfast and the morning papers at 8.30. Rowan wrote that he'd had to make an early start to Area Headquarters to arrange about the special coach. He would have to go down to the station too. A tonga could be got to take me to the Pankot Rifles depot and he'd try to call in there to say goodbye. In case he couldn't he gave me an address in Delhi (that of a bank) for future correspondence. Very thoughtfully he gave me the name of the officer at Area HQ who would know of any signal arriving for me.

I got to the Pankots' depot at ten o'clock. They had suspended the interviews. I waited an hour but Rowan didn't turn up. I went to Area Headquarters. He had been there but had gone (I imagined) to say goodbye to the Laytons. In the signals office I introduced myself to the signals sergeant and made sure he had my telephone number. I went back to the guest house and was told that Rowan had just rung to say goodbye. For the rest of the day and throughout the evening, Ulysses-like I lashed myself to the mast of my quarters, deaf to every seduction except that of the sirens of the telephone exchange and signals office; afraid to go out, just in case a miracle had speeded Operation Bunbury up and a movement order was already on its way to me, one that required immediate action to be considered valid.

Saturday is a blank. All I remember is a reduction in the guest house staff. An invisible garrison commander had issued orders to reduce the rations and send the cooks and bhishtis, every able-bodied man, to fill the gaps at firing-ports and listening posts, leaving me attended by one shabby fellow who scavenged somewhere for pallid meals of thin gravy soup, dried meat and miserly salad and got steadily drunker, deafer and more difficult to conjure either by electric bell, handclap or parade-ground order. His name was Salaam'a. One yelled this greeting at empty space unoptimistic of his filling it. It puzzled him that I wore a sergeant's uniform. He thought it was some kind of disguise.

Sunday: the first Sunday of the peace. When I woke I knew I couldn't spend another day cooped up. I persuaded myself that Aunt Charlotte couldn't have moved quickly enough to justify my absurd expectations unless she had pre-empted the situation some weeks ago and decided that since the war in Europe was thoroughly over there was no reason for me to carry eccentricity to the absurd length of staying out East and eating the rice needed by starving natives.

Among the notices in the guest house was one from St John's (C. of E.). Communion at 8 a.m.; morning service at 11. I had missed the first but felt I ought to attend the second. I got out my best khaki. I polished a pair of brown shoes and rubbed up the dazzle on the badge of my side-cap. I darned a small hole in the heel of a clean pair of socks. Then I shaved – twice – until the lower half of my face looked properly baked and glazed.

These were acts of contrition for the destructive and mutinous mood of the morning of my arrival in Pankot; gestures of voluntary submission to the military system. At ten-thirty I set off and marched myself to church at heavy infantry pace.

St John's was packed. It was like poppy day at Chillingborough; hymns and prayers in chapel. All that lacked was an old boy to give an ambiguous address about the obscenity and waste of war. I glanced round, looking as it were for Harry Coomer; but met only the mass of pale and ruddy complexions of an all-white congregation. Were there no Indian Christians in Pankot? No Eurasians at St John's on this Sunday of all Sundays? Perhaps there were. My view, from one of the back pews, and to the wall side of it, close to an exit, was limited. I was among the soldiery, a lone volunteer among the pressed men. Far ahead, towards the pulpit, shoulders glittered with pips and crowns making angular shapes between decorative hats.

But no dark face that I could see. I began to feel oppressed, slightly agitated, and glanced at the nearby door. The chaplain was reading a lesson. In a moment there would be another hymn. I checked the advertised number in the borrowed hymn book. From Greenland's Icy Mountains, From India's coral strand, They call us to deliver, Their land from error's chain. When the congregation got up to sing it I slid out of the pew and in a moment was in the open, going down a gravel path between ancient drunken gravestones. Outside on the road under shade trees tongas waited, their drivers slumped in their seats or disposed on the ground in twos and threes smoking bidis. I flashed a two-rupee note and commandeered someone's equipage. It could be back at the church by the time the service was over.

I only wanted to go to Area Headquarters. As I climbed in I thought I heard a voice from the church saying: That's right. Aunt Charlotte's voice.

The signals sergeant was leaving his office as I approached it. Seeing me, he stopped dead. He ignored my courteous greeting. He stared at me as if I were his worst enemy. I followed him into the office where without a word he handed me a signal.

Bunbury.

After I'd read it, twice, he said, 'How d'you manage it, then? That's all I ask. How?'

But there was no vice in him. He just envied my luck. Where had I been, he wanted to know. He'd rung Pankot 200 only ten minutes ago and got no answer. I told him I'd been to church. He said, as if this explained the signal, 'I must try it some time.' Then he became very helpful. He took me and my AB 64 and the precious piece of flimsy paper ordering Sergeant Perron to proceed immediately to Deolali for onward transmission to UK for demobilization (War Office instruction Number Such and Such and Stroke This Stroke That) to the Admin office where he enlisted the help of a havildar-clerk who, having no axe to grind about speeding an English soldier out of the country, set to work with detached efficiency.

Interpreting a string of references at the end of the signal he told me that I ought to arrive in Deolali in possession of certain important documents including a medical on my fitness to be allowed back into the UK at all. He checked my AB 64. So recently Zipper-bound my jabs were up to date. He told me other things I would need. He seemed quite happy telling me. I wasn't much interested. Nothing worried me. Somewhere just behind my eyes were rosy vistas, shimmering images of a world that had become benign. Area Headquarters was full of this benevolence. It was at low-pressure, staffed by nice people who seemed to have lent themselves voluntarily to the idea of simply keeping it going between Saturday and Monday. I felt the clerk was relieved to have something to do that he could put his mind to. I could rely on him utterly. I could rely on the Signals sergeant too. He kept close to me as if he thought some of my luck might rub off.

'Let's find the Duty Officer,' he said. We walked along shady verandahs. The fire-buckets, I noted, were painted an enchanting shade of red. The sand in them sparkled. We went into a semi-darkened airy room where the desks and empty chairs were waiting for tomorrow and then through into a room whose windows were unshuttered. A girl in WAC(1) uniform was at a filing cabinet.

'Morning, Sarge,' my sergeant said.

She had three stripes. She turned round. It was Sarah Layton.

But the original Sarah, the friendly one. I said, 'Good Lord, you're a sergeant too.'

'Well I am when I'm playing soldiers.'

'Is that what you're doing?'

'Yes. I'm glad you looked in. I've just tried to get you on the phone.'

'You know each other,' the Signals sergeant accused us. We agreed that we did. He gave me an odd look but said that would make it easier. He told Sarah what I represented: a problem which Area Headquarters had to solve. He explained what the problem was, how much of it was already being tackled and what remained to be done.

While he spoke I watched her, on the look-out for any sign of disappointment that the chances of knowing each other better were limited to here and now. I thought there was such a sign but couldn't be sure. If she had been anticipating a quiet morning on duty with nothing much to do, the expression I marked (a slight darkening of the eyes) could just as well have been irritation at the interruption as of sorrow at my departure.

'The duty officer's gone off somewhere, but I'll cope,' she said. 'You can leave Sergeant Perron to me.'

The sergeant caught my eye, nodded in her direction. 'You're lucky. Most of the others slope off at the first smell of anything like work. O.K. Miss Layton. Buzz me if you get stuck.'

She spent a lot of time on the telephone. I sat watching her, wondering at the change in her. Probably it was only life at home that got her down. Eventually she said, 'Right, that's tied up so far. Let's go.' I followed her out of the office. She locked the door.

'Where to?'

'Just relax. The army's taking care of you.'

'What about your office? Can you just leave it?'

'I was only sorting things out for tomorrow. I'm not officially on duty. But everyone at home has gone to church.'

We went back to the havildar-clerk. She went through documents with him, collected a batch. We went to another block. She told me to wait outside. Ten minutes later she came out with more documents. Then to another office. She came out with another batch. I said, 'You're making me feel redundant, that I exist only on paper.'

'The next bit is more personal.'

She hailed a 15 cwt that was driving towards the exit. She told me to get in the back. Five minutes later I recognized the grounds of the hospital but when I got out I didn't recognize the building. She explained it was the private wing. The duty MO had promised to 'do me' if we came to the private wing at midday. It was five to. This time it was she who waited outside. The MO was a pleasant fellow. 'Feeling all right?' he asked. I said I was, really. 'Silly question,' he muttered, filling in spaces on the form. We worked out my height and weight without the aid of scales and measures. 'They'll do you in Deolali, too,' he warned, 'but if you arrive without a medical sheet you could be held up.' He signed the sheet and handed it to me. 'Lucky chap,' he said. 'Just try not to get clap between here and Deolali. It sometimes happens.'

He came out with me and chatted to Sarah. He said if she'd finished repatriating Sergeant Perron he'd take her up to the club. She said there was still some documentation to do but that she'd probably see him there later.

Back in the havildar-clerk's office she gave him all the documents we'd collected. They checked through them, detaching copies for different files. Finally he handed me all that I apparently required from this storm of paper: a few sheets which went into an envelope.

Outside she said, 'Well, that's it. All you have to do is to be at the station before midday tomorrow – unless –'

Without another word she led the way to the signals office. The sergeant was just coming out, going to lunch.

'Is there any transport going into Ranpur tonight?' she asked him. He said there probably was. She turned to me. 'If you could get down to Ranpur during the night you could get the train that leaves at 8 a.m. You'd gain over twelve hours, and that might make a lot of difference at the Deolali end.'

I said it was a good idea. She said to the sergeant, 'I'll ask at

the club. Perhaps you'd have a look round too, Joe, and ring
Sergeant Perron at 200 if there's anything going in.'

He said he'd have a word with a Sub-Conductor Pearson in
the mess. I could go along with him now, if I wanted. I made
an excuse about having food laid on and packing to do. We
shook hands in case we didn't meet again.

Sarah and I shared a tonga back up the hill. I thanked her for
everything she'd done and said the food at the guest house wasn't
much cop since Nigel had gone but that it would be nice if she
could have lunch with me. She said there was a lunch party at
the club which she couldn't get out of. I asked her what she'd
tried to ring me about earlier. She'd rung because she knew I was
on my own and wondered if I was all right, since I hadn't rung
her. I asked her whether she could manage tea. She wasn't sure.
She'd be in touch some time, though.

As she got out of the tonga at the club entrance she looked at
me and said: 'I envy you, Guy. But I'm glad for you. And I'm not
at all sure you don't deserve a medal. Ronald Merrick's going to
be furious.'

I told Salaam'a to bring beer to the verandah. I sat studying the
precious documents. For the first time I noticed that the signal
hadn't come via Delhi, via Merrick's department, but had originated in Poona. The first War Office instruction must have been
signalled from Delhi to Poona and my old officer must have rung
Delhi, been told where I was and then copy-signalled direct to
Area Headquarters in Pankot. I went to my room and wrote him
a note of thanks, added a PS, to the effect that my tin trunk
which had been left in Poona could either be repatriated too or
broken open and its contents (a greatcoat and winter uniform)
disposed among the needy. Then I had a couple of gins, a pallid
replica of yesterday's pallid lunch, and composed myself to sleep,
having first told Salaam'a to attend to the telephone and in any
case wake me with tea at four.

Zipper was coming to grief. Speeding towards the beaches in
landing craft on the September tides near Port Swettenham we
were opened fire on by rogue Japanese who had opted out of the
Emperor's peace, chosen to die, but to take us with them. For a
moment I listened, aghast, at the guns and the water rushing

against the steel hulls of the boats, aghast because of the danger and of the miserable realization that Bunbury had been only an Indian ocean dream.

I raised my wrist to check the time of landing and, doing so, woke to the reality of Pankot time which said ten to five, a thunderstorm, but all well. But not wholly all well. From the bedroom I wouldn't have heard the telephone and it looked as if Salaam'a wouldn't have been hearing it either, being either asleep or dead drunk at last. I pressed the bell-button. Like those at Ishshee Brizhish one could never tell what effect pressing the button had unless someone turned up. No one did inside the half-minute I allowed before getting out of bed, tying a towel round my waist and going in search.

I went through the living-room shouting that ridiculous name and then out on to the verandah from whose roof water was cascading from an invisible pipe or leaking gutter on to the gravel path. Beyond, vertical rods of water obscured the view of the Summer Residence.

From contemplation of this same scene Sarah Layton turned her head, to glance up from the cane lounging chair where she rested, smoking. A tray of guest house tea was on the table by her side.

She said something that I couldn't hear and I was too conscious of my near-nakedness to go closer and cup an ear. She indicated an unused cup. In dumb show I told her I'd be out again in a minute, and went back, splashed my face, combed my hair, and got into a shirt and slacks and sandals.

'I hope you don't mind,' she said when I joined her. 'The boy was just going to wake you when I got here. I told him to leave you for a bit.' She felt the pot. 'We'd better ring for some more.'

I did so. I asked her when she'd arrived. She thought it must have been nearly an hour ago. I wondered whether she had been waiting for me to wake or for the rain to stop, but didn't ask. She said, 'You'll be glad later, I mean to have slept on a bit because I'm afraid you won't have a very comfortable trip if you decide to go tonight. The best we could do is the back of a fifteen hundredweight that's leading a convoy down. But it'll take you right to the station in Ranpur.'

She opened her bag and gave me a slip of paper with a name – Sub-Conductor Pearson – and a telephone number written on it. 'The convoy leaves at ten this evening. Call him just before seven. He'll tell you where to go to get it. I'm afraid I drew a blank at the club, so I liaised again with Joe Baker. He was going to ring you but I said I'd call and tell you.'

Our hands touched as the paper was transferred. The softness and gentleness of her fingers balanced out the impression of hardness, of military efficiency. It occurred to me that the time she'd devoted to me could perhaps best be repaid by giving her the chance to take up some of mine if she wanted to. I didn't *have* to leave Pankot tonight. And now that it came to it I wasn't sure that I wanted to.

'On the whole,' she said, as if reading my thoughts, 'I'd settle for the discomfort if I were you. Joe Baker's had another signal. There's a Major Foster arriving tomorrow morning on the night train. You're asked to meet him, so I suppose he's Ronald's replacement.'

I'd met Major Foster. He was a ditherer, the kind of well-meaning chap whom it could be fatal to get near. If I met him and told him I had to leave on the midday train, on repatriation, he might out of sheer good intention invent so many problems that we would still be solving them two hours after the train had gone.

I said, 'Yes, he is the replacement. I'll settle for a night's discomfort. I may as well ring Sub-Conductor Pearson now. Then we'll know how long I've got.'

'I shouldn't if I were you. Not for a while. Joe Baker said six-thirty or so.'

For some reason she reddened slightly and returned her attention to the rain, which was stopping.

Salaam'a appeared.

'Would you prefer a drink to more tea? Nigel said I could make free so long as I didn't dine the station. You're not quite the station.'

'No, I'm not, am I? I'd like a drink very much.'

I told Salaam'a to bring out the drinks trolley. When we were alone I said, 'Can you stay and have an early meal with me?'

She didn't answer. She must have heard. The rain had now stopped entirely. She continued to stare ahead of her. Her cigarette was nearly finished. I glanced over my shoulder to see what apparently held her attention. The sun was just coming out. The

Summer Residence rose – base to roof – out of the fast-moving shadow of a retreating cloud. Sunshine had already flowed across the garden. It pressed hard against the line of the balustrade, warmed my back and made me conscious of the hastiness with which I'd put clothes on.

'You've seen the house, I suppose,' she said. 'I expect Nigel showed you over.'

'No. Isn't it shut up?'

'The servants will always let you in.'

'There seems to be only one servant left.'

'They live in the main quarters. They only come down if there are people at the guest house. The house itself was built in 1890. Most of it's plain Anglo-Indian but there's a Moghul suite where they used to put up pet princes. The throne room's very ordinary, just a couple of chairs on a daïs, and the ball-room's quite small. But they danced on the terrace too. There used to be coloured lights in the trees.'

'That must have been nice.'

'It was all rather stiff and starchy. At least on the surface. And that's about all you see when you're young and just back out from home. Not that I'm really competent to judge. People here sigh for what they used to call the full season when the Governor and his wife moved up for the hot weather. But there hasn't been a full season since 'thirty-nine, and Susan and I missed that. I remember it best as part of childhood. We had ghastly parties here.' She smiled at a memory. 'When the new Governor took over in 'forty-one he was rather unpopular at first for not continuing the tradition of six months in the hills. Mother says the dances Susan and I have been to were very scratch affairs by comparison, but people get used to anything. At Flagstaff House we used to rate a major-general but since the beginning of the year we've only had a brigadier. People complain but they're getting used to that too. And now that the war's over I suppose it'll alter even more, with people whose retirement's been postponed upping sticks and going home, or settling here and growing old and tiresome and complaining that their pensions don't go far.'

'When does your father retire?'

'In about three years. But I've no idea what they'll do.'

'Rose Cottage belongs to them?'

'Yes, they're luckier than some. The army stopped people buying or building property in Pankot years ago – I don't mean on West Hill, only Indians build there. But father's stepmother got hold of Rose Cottage a few years before the embargo. She left it to him along with everything else she had. I expect you could see what a lot of money's been spent on it recently. I've always imagined father and mother spending the rest of their lives there, but now I don't know.'

Salaam'a wheeled the trolley out. We both chose gin. While he prepared the drinks I excused myself and went inside to wait for him. When he came in I told him I was leaving for Ranpur that evening, that he should arrange supper for two because the memsahib might be staying. I gave him his baksheesh and an extra few rupees to tip his invisible assistants. Then I told him the memsahib and I wanted to look at the house, that we would go over in about fifteen minutes. How did we get in? He said the head chaukidar would let us in. He would go now and make sure the head chaukidar was there.

She was waiting, glass poised to drink. I faced her, leaning against the balustrade. We toasted the space between us. After drinking we remained silent. I gave her a full minute by my watch and the same full minute to myself to prove beyond reasonable doubt that my idea about the immediate future was not all that different from hers.

The minute gone the silence continued, but delivered us slowly from any sense of the strain that slightly marked its beginning. Eventually I said to her, 'I never thanked you for Emerson.' She put her head back against the cushion, studied me, as if she knew the passage which had come into my mind and which had caused me to mention the book:

The world rolls: the circumstances vary every hour. All the angels that inhabit this temple of the body appear at the windows, and all the gnomes and vices also. By all the virtues they are united. If there be virtue, all the vices are known as such; they confess and flee.

On the way there I looked for them but they must have scattered; but remembering the distant view of the upper storey from the lines of the Pankot Rifles depot I asked her whether she had ever noticed how the sun setting behind West Hill seemed to have to pause until the upper windows of the Summer Residence released its last reflection, and the *raj* allowed night to fall. Well, she said, she was familiar with the effect but had never identified its cause. She was smiling, her head up, one hand shielding her eyes, neck curving from the brave little angles of jaw and chin. Something dazzled her – the suddenly exposed sky, sunshine on wet surfaces, or the drops of rain strung in the trees to dry. We had left the path, chosen the director way across the lawns for which she was more suitably shod than I. My feet and trouser bottoms were wet, the chappals clung to my bare soles. A week later, unpacking and repacking my kit-bag in Deolali, the chappals, still slightly damp to the touch, smelt of grass, and the trouser bottoms were tide-marked. The chappals were in my possession for a number of years, and – even after a long time unused – discovered in a cupboard, dried, cracked, the buckles rusty, the smell of dampness and the smell of grass still seemed to be in them like a perfume of their own recollection of that occasion; their recollection of the persistence of damp when moving across dry flagged terraces and interior floors of stone and parquet and carpet, through chill shadow and hot streaks of filtered light when shutters were opened like doors on the tombs of flies and moths whose mummified bodies lay on dusty sills; taking the weight of the wearer's heels as he gazed upward at vast chandeliers enveloped in balloons of muslin; or substituting for weight the stickiness of suction when the ankles were crossed for the enthronement of the substitute Governor and his Lady on two shrouded chairs; the weight redistributed again, concentrated on the toes as the sightless painted eyes of Muirs and Laytons and fellow members of a pro-consular dynasty were met by live eyes in a head thrust forward – the body canted to achieve a position where the light on dark varnish less obscured the detail and colour of pigment underneath.

Stairs, corridors; doors opened by keys obtained earlier for a consideration from the ancient chaukidar who was lost below in a dream of opium and the vanished splendour of which he was the guardian and we no more than observers. Sensibly and more drily shod she moved through the Summer Residence like a visitor who had been before and had little to gain except the satisfaction of her companion's curiosity, which was minimal, overriden by preoccupation with the way she walked through this maze of imperial history, or stood revealed by the chance

falling of light and shade, responding to changes in the pressures
that different rooms imposed on her recollections which seemed
to be of a time she no longer recognized as real.

And yet, turning from some object pointed out in one particular room, an object that had failed like so many in so many
rooms to recommend itself to me as having continuing substance
or sustained meaning, she seemed to me to have only this unreality in her possession and to belong to it like a prisoner would
belong, after a time, to a cell his imagination had escaped but
whose door he was not permitted to open.

We chose this particular room, I think, because at first glance it
represented in itself a form of release: release from the stupefying
weight of nearly a century of disconnection from the source. But
the Moghul suite was no less burdened by that weight; it was the
inner box of a nest of boxes. Through one unshuttered window,
westering sun filtered through the intricate fretwork of a screen
on to the tiled floor where the chappals lay, temporarily set aside.
A smell of old incense permeated the fabrics of the covers and
cushions of an immense divan such as might have been used
by court-musicians. One fancied that dust rose from it, gently
enveloping us in a dry benevolent mist in which hung minute
particles of the leaves and petals of garlands of flowers: jasmine,
roses, frangipani and marigold, and all the names of Allah. One
observer: a mouse. Are you afraid? I asked. No, she said, I'm
not afraid. Eyes closed, at rest, I realized that we had been both
observed and accompanied. The distant coppersmith still continued, beating out his thin, endless, strip of metal into the
alternating shapes of the sounds and silence of the Pankot hills.

Returning the keys to the chaukidar, I make my own way out
and look for her; and, mistaking the place, think for a moment
she has taken the opportunity I gave her (out of delicacy, thinking she might prefer not to have to bid the chaukidar goodnight)
to abandon me too; but she is waiting, out there on the lawn,
gazing up at the highest windows where the day awaits permission to end. Joining her, I glance up and find that it is already
ended. There are no faces, either, unless they are our own,
watching us go – not only as we do, across the lawn back to the
guest house – but further, much further, on separate roads that
may never cross again.

Having poured her another drink I go inside to telephone Sub-Conductor Pearson. A woman answers. Her voice has a Eurasian lilt. She leaves the phone. I hear her calling for 'Leonard'. Pearson, not Purvis. Calling him from his Sunday afternoon in married quarters? Waiting, I wonder what Sergeant Baker said to make Sarah blush when she recommended not disturbing the Sub-Conductor until 6.30 or 7 (until an appetite for beer and curry and Sunday love had been appeased and been slept off?). His voice is full of nuts and bolts, of oil and graphite; and sober irritation at being reminded of a promise given earlier when all the Sunday pleasures were ahead. But he is a man of his word. He tells me where to go and when to be there and whom to ask for. I have about two hours.

She said she would not stay to supper. She would have liked to but she had left it too late to ring and say she had made other arrangements. She ought to get back soon.

'Then let me take you.'

'No. You've too much to do. I'll wait while you pack and change. Then I must go and you must eat.'

My packing was a hit and miss business. First I had to change back into uniform. In doing so I seemed to change my flesh. I was a sergeant again. She, in her uniform, remained a colonel's daughter. Theoretically a rule had been broken. I began searching in the kit-bag for some tissue-paper packages – scarves and stoles for the Perron women (and a few for non-Perron women). My hand kept touching the transcript of the examination.

'Guy?'

She was standing just inside the bedroom door.

'I just wanted to say I'll make sure that someone meets Major Foster tomorrow. Is that servant of Ronald's still around? Nigel told me you caught him thieving.'

'I've not seen him.'

'Major Foster will probably ask. Where was he quartered?'

'At Flagstaff House, I think, with the other servants.'

'I'll make sure. I'm going now.'

'Going *now*?'

'Yes, I must. Write to me some time. Let me know how you get on.'

There are situations in which it is very difficult to know what to say. One of the tissue-packages was in my hand.

'I bought a few things for people back home. I've nothing else.'

She took the package because I really gave her no alternative. 'It's only a scarf. At least I think it is. Perhaps we'd better open it in case it's something like a tie for one of my uncles.'

'Whatever it is I shall like it.'

We went back to the verandah.

'One more drink.'

Her back and shoulders felt so much thinner than they really were.

She shook her head and said there wasn't time. She must go. She didn't need a tonga. It was only a short walk up the hill. I went with her to the front of the guest house. The light had almost gone. I said I couldn't let her go home alone.

'I shall be perfectly all right. It's what I'd prefer. Honestly. Goodbye, Guy.'

She turned and set off down the narrow drive. I called after her. She glanced round, waved the package. I began to follow her, but stopped, understanding that her wish to go now and go alone was genuine. In a moment the curve of the drive had taken her away. I went back to finish packing my kit-bag. As I shoved the typescript well in to make room for the slacks and shirt and chappals I remembered that particular line: *We haven't seen each other since the night we visited the temple*. I rolled down my sergeant's sleeves, the drill for night-time. While buttoning the cuffs a trick of light made my hands seem brown.

They had emerged, erupted violently, from the shadows of the Moghul Room, attacked me, pulled me away, hit me in the face. Later when they had gone and we held each other again I said: Let me take you home. She said, No. No. We haven't seen each other. We haven't seen each other since the night we visited the temple. She saw the danger I would be in if I dared to go with her, dared to mutter to someone, a white man, an official, any of the men who would ask questions, 'We were making love. These men attacked us.' She had seen the danger of implicating me in any way, but she hadn't seen the marks on my face, because it was too dark. And I hadn't thought of them until I got home.

*

I don't remember eating. I remember sitting on the verandah drinking the last of the ADC's brandy and staring out into the dangerous Indian night until it was time to send Salaam'a to fetch a tonga to take me to the rendezvous with Sub-Conductor Pearson's convoy and the first leg of the journey back to the source, where all these things, becoming distant again, would count for little and seem to belong to another world entirely.

THE DAK BUNGALOW

I

THE SCENE WAS OVER. I can enter now, Sarah told herself.

But I did not enter. None of us did. I thought I saw the reason. What had held us together as a family was father's absence; his return showed how deeply we were divided. You could feel him making the attempt to come to terms with each of us separately. There was a time for mother, a time for Susan and Edward, and a time for me; and a different kind of time for the servants, for Pankot, for the regiment.

My time was before breakfast. Between seven and eight-thirty every morning father and I rode. He associated me with these early hours of the day and during them treated me with a special solicitude, as if the pattern of intimacy which had been established on the journey from Ranpur when we shared tea and bacon sandwiches and were careful with crumbs, might develop through repetition into something complex, mysterious and satisfying. At times he had the look of a man with a secret he was patiently waiting to share; at others that of a man empty of knowledge and recollection.

After a couple of days I noticed on these morning rides that we were taking the same route – down the northern slope of East Hill into the valley – and stopping at the same place. The view wasn't spectacular. About a mile ahead you could see a village. That was all. But he reined in and sat motionless, gazed at the distant huddle of huts and the terraced fields that traced the contours of the hill. The earth was tawny. There was always a mist. You could smell the smoke of wood and dung fires. After five minutes or so he would look at his wrist-watch and say, 'Well, better get back.' Apart from this single comment he kept silent during the halt.

An obvious explanation of the choice of turning point was that it was fixed according to a formula involving time available, distance to be covered, expected time of return. But we did not always take the same route home and got back to Rose Cottage anywhere between say 8.15 and 8.45. The only part of the ride I could be absolutely sure of – the part that I began to feel was plotted by an obsession – was the route out and the halt and the five minutes' silent contemplation of a village whose name I wasn't certain of but checked on one of the large-scale maps at Area Headquarters. It was called Muddarabad.

We had never kept horses at Rose Cottage. Such stabling as there had been had – long before Aunt Mabel's time even – become merged with the servants' quarters and store-rooms. A syce brought horses up from the depot. In the past year or two I had ridden seldom, mother less and Susan not at all. In Bombay father had said that one of the things he was looking forward to was getting accustomed again to the saddle. He hadn't ridden for nearly five years. I assumed that it might be a week or two before he felt fit enough to go out and that in any case it would be mother who went with him, but on his first evening at home he said, 'What about riding tomorrow?' and he said it to me. He rang Kevin Coley and I looked out my things but didn't discover until I put them on in the morning that my jodhpurs were uncomfortably tight round the waist. Mounting, I was as nervous as I had been as a small girl. He wore slacks and chukka boots. He led off as though he had been going out every morning of his life.

This would have been Thursday, August 9. He rode a few paces ahead of me. We spoke very little. I felt some reserve – embarrassment – in regard to his physical presence – imagining mother still lying in their bed considering through half-shut eyes the pillow beside her which bore an impression of the head of the man who kept looking back at me, smiling, as if in delight in rediscovery. Do children, when grown up, even nowadays, quite believe in the reality of their parents' sexual life?

Logic told me that in the past few years there must have been moments when my father lay in his bed in prison-camp and thought, God, God, I must have a woman. Suspicion rather than logic told me that in my father's absence my mother had had an affair. Logic in fact didn't come into it. Kevin Coley looked incapable of physical passion; a dry desiccated creature whom nothing would arouse except a threat to the professional obscurity in which he'd been content to live since his wife's death in the

Quetta earthquake. But, nursing my suspicion – and my growing understanding of the complexity of physical needs and physical responses – I had to throw out the idea of non-capability, non-culpability, and – in consequence – try to suppress every emotion except that of ironic acceptance, which wasn't easy – so difficult in fact that I couldn't sustain it for long and had to try to counter-act suspicion by telling myself that it was based on nothing more reliable than poor Barbie Batchelor's delirious imagination, coupled with the workings of my own which, alerted by Barbie's at first incomprehensible ramblings in the Pankot hospital, had since stretched the evidence (things seen, overheard, intuited) to make a case which the strictly rational side of my nature rejected, because even if adultery were the kind of game I could imagine my mother playing, adultery with Kevin Coley struck me as ludicrously out of character. So, I was back at the beginning of the circle of conjecture, and beginning to go round again, all the time conscious, naturally, that what chiefly nourished the retaliatory instinct to suspect her was her treatment of me, her utter disregard, her pretence of knowing nothing while knowing everything about the sordid abortion in Calcutta – everything except the name of the man who would have been the child's father, which she could have found out easily enough not from me but from Aunt Fenny who couldn't have been in much doubt but respected my silence and was fondly and foolishly guilt-ridden at the thought that she had been initially responsible for putting me in his way, or putting him in mine (it came to the same thing).

It was on the Friday – after our second ride to Muddarabad – that I heard poor Barbie was dead. Major Smalley mentioned it to me at the daftar, having heard it from his wife, and she was invariably well-informed. When I rang the Reverend Mother of the Samaritan Hospital in Ranpur and she talked vaguely of papers meant for me or my family I feared some kind of revela-tion, a written statement, a letter to my father whom Barbie had hardly known but on whom I knew she relied to settle once and for all the question whether mother had buried Aunt Mabel in the wrong place – a letter perhaps referring to mother's associa-tion with Coley. I didn't believe Barbie capable of malice. What I feared was an unintentional accusation by a woman whose wits were scattered – as scattered as the contents of the trunk she'd left at Rose Cottage where she'd been Aunt Mabel's companion, and which she removed on the morning of the accident – the trunk that was the cause of the accident because it was too heavy for the tonga.

The trunk was full of things connected with Barbie's work as a mission teacher, old textbooks, exercise books she'd kept to remember special pupils, gifts from the children and their parents, and a copy of the picture her old mission friend Edwina Crane had been given as a reward for heroism in the North West Frontier Province during the Great War. Barbie told me that the trunk wasn't particularly important but it was 'her history and without it according to Emerson she wasn't explained'. When Mabel died she had to move into a small room at the rectory bungalow. She'd taken things down there bit by bit during the week or so mother gave her to give us vacant possession of Rose Cottage. The rectory wasn't a permanent arrangement and Clarissa Peplow was worried about the amount of stuff she seemed to have. Barbie asked me if she could leave the trunk with the *mali*. I offered to take care of it myself. Susan and I would be sharing the room that had been Barbie's and I saw no reason why I shouldn't look after the trunk until she found a permanent home. But she knew mother would object. She said that if the *mali* put the trunk in his shed then providing I knew it was there that would be good enough. So that's what was done.

Muddarabad was the village Havildar Karim Muzzafir Khan came from. We stopped there because father couldn't bring himself to ride on and enter it and confront the havildar's wife and family. Each morning, I think, he set off with that intention and then, reaching the halting-place, found the intention collapsing under the weight of his notion of its futility. *Man-Bap.* I am your father and your mother. This traditional idea of his position, this idea of himself in relationship to his regiment, to the men and the men's families, had not survived his imprisonment; or, if it had survived, the effort of living up to it had become too much for him. Was it lack of energy or lack of conviction, I wondered, that caused him to rein in and sit straight-backed as if posing for his portrait as a military officer watching the course of a battle for whose outcome he would be held responsible, or studying the ground over which, tomorrow, conclusions would be tried?

And, watching *him*, it struck me how very rare after all were men whose genius lay in active warfare. For one genius there would be almost countless plodders who were commanders in name only, men to whom the structure of a landscape would present almost as great a problem in military understanding as it had always done to me, but who had been taught to apply a set of ready-made formulas so that it was upon these and not the terrifyingly wide margins of error that their minds were concentrated. As a child he had seemed godlike to me, revealing some of the secrets of his profession. I had the feeling now that he believed himself dishonoured – not by anything he had done but by his talent, which turning out limited had narrowed the whole area of his self-regard.

Waiting at the halting-place on the third morning, the Saturday, I recalled my mother's words overheard the night before, when I came home late, having stayed on at the daftar to telephone the Reverend Mother at the Samaritan. 'It's a question of your presence more than anything. It was the same for me when you all went into the bag.' And in retrospect it seemed scarcely any time at all since she had ridden out with Kevin Coley from one village to another to talk to the women whose husbands, sons and grandsons and brothers were either dead or captured in North Africa.

For her to visit every village would have been impossible but on other occasions she talked to women who came in from outlying districts for confirmation of the news, receiving them outside the adjutant's office and even in the compound of the grace and favour bungalow where we lived in those days. Colonel Sahib, Colonel Memsahib. Two aspects of the one godhead. My mother was not built to look like a woman another woman could be comforted by – but at these meetings her very stiffness seemed right. The important thing was that she was there, in the shell of her flesh which if hard seemed trustworthy. She told these women the truth always, for instance that as prisoners of war the men would be separated from their officers and that it would be virtually impossible for father himself to ensure their welfare. But, subsequently, in many unobtrusive ways, she had kept an eye on the widows, and the wives who like herself could only wait patiently for their men's return. She did this entirely out of her sense of duty. It was an act, but she played the part with a perfect sense of what would be extraneous to it. She did not make the mistake of identifying herself too closely with it. When she came back into the bungalow she shed it, or seemed to shed it. And called for gin.

So, 'Why don't you?' she had said the night before, meaning why didn't he ride on into Muddarabad. But it was different for father. *Man-Bap.* That act had been an inseparable part of his life as a commander of Indian troops. *He* had to identify himself closely with it. It was supposed to go deep into him, right down to the source of his inspiration. Every morning, when we stopped after riding down the northern slope of East Hill, it was as though he waited there for the inspiration to return and lead him down into the village. But, 'Well', he would say, and said it again that Saturday, 'Better get back'. On the way home we usually rode abreast and talked about the things that had happened yesterday and the plans there were for today.

After riding we had breakfast and then I went down to the daftar. Officially he was on station leave but sometimes he went down to the Pankot Rifles lines. The immediate future was very uncertain. There was a question of long leave, the possibility of taking it at home; but the more important questions for him were of his fitness and of his next appointment. Long though I did for home leave the prospect wasn't one I considered likely even if the war ended as people expected. He was too close to retirement to waste time in England. He had too much time to make up. He and mother were now well enough off, having inherited Mabel's money, not to go after promotion simply to earn a higher pension, but he would go after it, I believed, to redress the balance. And it would be something to put his mind to. The obvious job for him was that of commandant of the depot which Colonel Trehearne had held throughout the war, postponing his own retirement. But now I got the impression that mother had set her sights higher and that she wanted to get out of the station. I couldn't blame her. The expense she had gone to in altering Rose Cottage couldn't in her case be seen as evidence of an intention to make it a permanent home. Even the prospect of final retirement there now seemed questionable.

*

Feeling I must do something about whatever it was Barbie had left which the Bishop Barnard Mission hadn't collected or didn't want and about which the Reverend Mother was so vague and yet so insistent, I wrote to Nigel Rowan to ask him whether he'd ring her and get the facts clearer. That was on the Saturday. On that evening we dined with the Trehearnes.

Maisie Trehearne was tall, pale and stately, and so upright that it was rumoured she was supported by a steel corset. Lately she had taken to wearing flowing dinner gowns of grey or blue georgette which gave her the appearance of a metallic ghost. When she moved she created the illusion of cooling breezes which weren't necessary because the Commandant's house was the draughtiest in Pankot and wretched to dine at on a winter evening. The Trehearnes were the last people to order fires lit and the first to order the hearths to be cleared and guarded by brass trays. And never, in the rainy season, when the evening could be chilly – which fortunately it wasn't on this occasion – was an electric fire brought in and switched on. Her husband, Patrick, now sixty, had the same frail, febrile but inflexible look: highly tempered steel worn to the thickness of a wafer. There was scarcely a line on their faces. They were the faces of people who had never had a sleepless night or a moment's worry, or, if they had, had somehow acquired an almost oriental sense of spiritual detachment from the cares of life.

The other obstacle to comfort at the Trehearnes was the pack of dogs, a strange hybrid collection ranging from puppies to full-grown brutes, seldom less than three altogether; raw, savage, the terror of servants, cause of concern to timid guests; obstinate, disobedient; objects of Maisie's devotion and her husband's sufferance. The dogs seemed natural victims of the disasters that were always befalling them. Ruling the roost at Commandant House they seemed disinclined to learn that the world outside was a hostile place. One, attacking a tonga horse, was kicked to death; another was bitten by a krait; yet another run over by a staff-car from Area Headquarters which it had thought had no business on the same road as itself. One, straying, was shot on the rifle-range. Others simply succumbed to one of the diseases domestic animals in India were always dying of. You would have thought that a woman so genuinely fond of animals, particularly of dogs, would have lost heart, but Maisie never did, she was always acquiring replacements for those that had fallen, and you always felt that her attachment was deep, her sense of duty to them strong, her horrified reaction to any tale of cruelty to animals of any kind absolutely real. You could still feel this about Maisie even when sitting in their dining-room under the glazed eyes of the creditable number of mounted shikar trophies for whose deaths she and Patrick were just about equally responsible. The trophies were seldom referred to. Perhaps they were there merely as relics of youthful exuberance which had long since been grown out of. I once heard Lucy Smalley say she wondered that Maisie didn't mount the heads of the dogs too: a typical Smalley remark but not (which was also typical) wholly unjustified.

'Watch out for the dogs, John,' mother had warned father when we set out in the car Colonel Trehearne had sent up. The warning was unnecessary. Perhaps for once Patrick Trehearne had put his foot down, or Maisie and Patrick had both had the foresight to see that the usual kind of welcome you got at Commandant House didn't sort well with greeting a man who had been locked up for several years. Instead, the dogs had been locked up and we entered unmolested.

It was father's first dinner out and Maisie had promised mother to keep the party small. It turned out even smaller than planned because Kevin Coley's servant rang just before we arrived to say that the Adjutant Sahib had gone to bed with a temperature. 'Actually,' Maisie said, 'we're rather worried about Kevin. He suddenly seems restless. After all these years resisting any attempt to move and promote him he's acting as though he thought it was time something was done about him.'

The Trehearnes' bedroom where we left our stoles, exposing necks, shoulders and arms, like Spartan women, to the chilly rigours of the interior, was immense. In it the twin beds looked diminutive, mere sparrows' nests. High above them, suspended from the raftered ceiling, were circular frames for the mosquito nets which were hardly ever necessary but which Maisie had a fondness for. It was the kind of room, sparsely furnished, which always looked camped-out in rather than occupied, and where you wouldn't have been surprised to find bird-droppings on the floor.

It was while we were in the bedroom that the subject of Barbie came up and I discovered that mother also knew she was dead. Susan was momentarily out of the room, powdering her nose in the adjoining bathroom (people in Pankot had learned not to refer to death and disaster in front of her, if they could help it). Maisie said, 'Mrs Stewart at the Library tells me that according to Lucy Smalley, Miss Batchelor died the other day. Did you know?'

She addressed the question to both of us. I was standing at the foot of one of the beds. Mother was peering into the glass of the dressing-table, making a minor repair with her lipstick. Perhaps this provided her with an excuse not to speak. But she didn't react at all, her expression remained constant, concentrated. I was forced to answer. I said that Major Smalley had mentioned it to me at the daftar.

'There was nothing in the *Ranpur Gazette*,' Maisie said. 'And the death columns are the first thing I read. It used to be the births and marriages but you seem to reach a time of life when you know only the people who die. How did Lucy hear?'

'I don't know,' I said, truthfully.

'Do you, Mildred?'

'Do I what?'

'Know how Lucy Smalley heard Miss Batchelor was dead.'

'All I know is what Mrs Smalley told me when she rang, but I suppose in this case one can take it as more or less true.'

'What did she say?'

'Only that the Bishop Barnard people had written to Arthur Peplow and that the chaplain who's filling in for him opened the letter and asked her who Miss Batchelor was. Mrs Smalley, it goes without saying, had only dropped into the rectory bungalow to see if she could help with any little problem.'

'Had the Peplows kept in touch with the Mission, then?'

'I don't know about keeping in touch. But the rectory was the woman's last address. I expect the Mission wanted to be sure she's left nothing here that they ought to have and I'm sure their solicitors will be already on to ours making a fuss about the annuity Mabel willed her. I suppose the estate will have to cough up what she'd have received if we'd ever got round to buying it. Thank God I had the presence of mind at the time to tell our own solicitors in London to drag their feet, and thank God she went off her head as soon as she did because that gave them a good excuse to drag their feet even harder. Mabel must have been off *her* head, making that sort of provision for an elderly spinster.'

'I've never really understood about annuities,' Maisie said.

'You buy the damned things to provide an income for life which is all right if the person the annuity's bought for lives a long time. The catch is, once it's bought, the capital sum has gone for ever. Even if you die the next day. I must say it would amuse me if the Bishop Barnard people think they've got several thousand rupees coming to them. They have complete control of her estate, apparently, for what it's worth.'

'Poor Miss Batchelor,' Maisie said. 'I sometimes think she had a sad life.'

Mother put away her lipstick. As she did so she glanced up, regarding me through the mirror. Then she snapped her handbag and turned round.

'I don't think you'd feel so sympathetic, Maisie, if you'd had to watch her encouraging Mabel's eccentricities and anti-social instincts and at the same time be pretty sure she was feathering her own nest pretty neatly, and then making all that macabre fuss about where Mabel should have been buried. I had Mabel's funeral to cope with and Susan's premature labour to cope with and I had to cope with them virtually alone because Sarah was down in Calcutta visiting that man Merrick in hospital. And on top of it all I had this damned silly woman running all over Pankot saying I was shoving Mabel into the ground at St John's when she'd wanted to be buried at St Luke's in Ranpur, next to John's father. Even that elderly admirer of hers, Mr Maybrick, thought it was a bit much. And of course John tells me he never heard Mabel say a single thing about where she wanted to be put. I took him to see the grave this morning. He thought it very suitable.'

Susan came out of the bathroom and the subject was dropped.

'How pretty you look,' Maisie said, which was no less than the truth, the kind of thing Susan still needed to hear but which was nowadays inspired more by the obligation people felt under to encourage her back to life and happiness than by spontaneous admiration. I imagined that Susan herself was aware of this not very subtle undercurrent of intention, and that she responded to praise in the same way that someone who is enjoying remission from the pain of a disease they know they're not yet cured of must respond to being told how well they're looking. And, because it had happened before, I was now prepared to wake up that night and hear the sound of her crying. Her crying was terrible, because when she cried and I tried to comfort her we seemed very close, closer than we had ever been as children; but within a day or two we were farther apart than ever. Every measure of love and affection had to be paid for by a larger measure of antagonism.

'How pretty you look,' Maisie had said, and then as if by an association of ideas, and leading us out, she said, 'We have invited young Mr Drew.'

Edgar Drew. Eager Edgar. I tried to catch Susan's eye but she had assumed her party rôle. Eager Edgar had been to Rose Cottage once or twice. In a rare conspiratorial moment between us Susan and I had christened him thus.

'We thought,' Maisie was saying to mother, 'it would be nice for him to meet John.' By which she really meant he would be suitable young company for Susan and me.

He had obviously arrived before us because Maisie didn't greet him when we went into the sitting-room where he stood with Colonel Trehearne and father, one hand behind his back, the other clutching his sherry glass, his head adjusted to a slant of attentiveness and inquiry, the wary look of a young man whose heart wasn't quite in what he had been taught he had to do to get on; of a man who having no inner resources of strength and energy – at least none he dared trust – saw no alternative to the perplexing business of flattering his elders. His father was an insurance broker in Byfleet and he had been to a public school of which I think he'd just reached the stage of feeling slightly ashamed because he realized it ranked as 'minor'. Physically he was attractive but he nullified this attraction every time he opened his mouth. His conversation was excruciatingly dull and he seemed to have no opinions of his own. He worked hard to sound self-confident, so hard that one became aware of the effort it cost him.

The Trehearnes had taken to him because they thought him a cut or two above most of the last year or so's intake of newly-commissioned English subalterns from Belgaum and Bangalore who had arrived at the depot, stayed a few weeks and then departed to join the 4/5th and the 2nd battalions in Burma. Moreover, Second-Lieutenant Drew had expressed interest in the idea of applying for a regular commission and this ambition counted in his favour when it came to comparing him with some of the rougher-spoken and rougher-mannered men who had got into the regiment with (I suspected) higher qualifications from OTS as potential leaders of infantry. He was what was never actually called but certainly thought of as regimental depot material which meant it was thought he would eventually prove to be perfectly adequate for active regimental duty but was meanwhile presentable enough in the mess and at dinner parties such as this to be put temporarily by and employed more pacifically.

I could tell that he had had little or no experience of women; his attentiveness betrayed anxiety. Someone, his mother probably, may have told him that a gentleman never looked lower than a girl's nose. The result was that when he talked to you he kept his chin up and head back and made you feel disembodied below the neck. He had beautiful hands; not fine and elegant but firm and shapely. But you seldom had a chance to admire them. They were usually clasped behind his back or bunched into fists. Even at table they tended to disappear between mouthfuls, presumably to clutch one another or be wiped surreptitiously on his napkin. When you had the opportunity to touch or be touched by them – that is, when he danced with you – they were uncomfortably moist, but at least they were a connection; although a distant connection because he danced with you at arm's length – which made it seem like dancing with a draught. I admit I had occasional fantasies about Mr Drew's hands, and after seeing him in the club swimming pool I also had occasional fantasies about the rest of him. Perhaps I should have told him, not for my own good, but for his. He can't have been unaware of his physical appearance, but I think he probably needed confirmation from outside before he could relate his own awareness to other people's. I had a distinct impression that he might be the only child of elderly parents. He seemed to belong to a generation earlier than his own – that of the Edwardians, say – which would explain his enthusiasm for the outward forms of Anglo-Indian life.

He was, of course, more directed towards Susan than to me

(interested or attracted would be the wrong words). She aroused his masculine instinct to protect. Confronted by me he was always on the defensive. It was I who reminded him that fundamentally he was a bit afraid of all of us. Sometimes when talking to him I heard in my own voice tones like those Clark-Without had used when talking to me, tones calculated to provoke; and then I stopped, a bit appalled at the ease with which one followed disreputable examples, and at the ease with which bitterness, once felt, lodged itself, dug itself in and hardened all the edges of your personality.

When we went into dinner Maisie put him between mother and Susan. I had been intended to sit between Colonel Trehearne and Kevin Coley, which would have been rather like sitting between a couple of posts. As it was, I sat between Colonel Trehearne and my father, which while not greatly different was more comfortable. And from here I was able to watch Mr Drew more or less undistracted and, while mother talked to Colonel Trehearne, attend to what Susan and Mr Drew were jointly building that might rank as a conversation; and occasionally contribute to it myself, talking across the table when Mr Drew found himself at a loss. One advantage Mr Drew had in making a go of sitting next to Susan was that he took the shy man's way out; he kept the ball rolling by asking her questions about herself; about what she had been doing, about whether she had enjoyed that, about what she thought she might do next week and about the chances she saw of enjoying that too or enjoying it more. I suppose it was really due to her that the conversation was a success, because once he had got on to the subject of what she had done or had thought, she was able to take an interest of a kind that encouraged him to go on feeding her with questions, scraping the bottom of the barrel of his imagination, but managing. When a change of course signalled a change in talking duties and mother turned to him he became at once less articulate. A faint flush of anxiety spread across his face and stayed there. You could see the gleam of perspiration on his forehead.

I don't remember what she talked to him about nor, now that Colonel Trehearne was free, what subject or subjects he and I chose in order to avoid talking about others. What I do remember clearly is the way in which I suddenly became conscious of the yelping and whining of the dogs. While Maisie talked to Susan and mother talked to Mr Drew and Colonel Trehearne and I exchanged trivial bits of information, the imprisoned dogs moaned and barked and snarled somewhere at the back of the compound. If Maisie heard this distant accompaniment of protest she gave no sign of it. The talk continued. The noise never stopped except to change key.

Father was the only person at the table not talking, and at the moment I became conscious of the dogs I became conscious of this too; aware of the nervous intensity of the silence in which he listened to the cries of those chained animals. He stopped eating. Maisie glanced at him and then very quickly turned back to Susan; which made it plain that mother had warned her to take no notice of anything he did which she thought odd, like putting his fork down, covering a piece of bread with a napkin; staring at the plate.

But this was different. It was the effect of the barking of the dogs that left him unable to eat another mouthful, unable to speak (I felt) or even to move, because of what the dogs reminded him; what, locked up, they represented. I was afraid of what he might do. I took an opportunity to say something to him. He looked at me. His smile was benign. Beneath the table his right hand was trembling. Perhaps my speaking broke the spell. He resumed eating. But sometimes when the sound of the dogs reached a crescendo his knife and fork shook.

'If I were you, Maisie,' my mother said, when we were out of earshot of the men, having left them to drink their whisky in the draughty dining-room, 'I'd let those hounds loose. It's worrying John, hearing them yelp.'

Intermittently she had this capacity to astonish me with unexpected proof of having noticed things she'd seemed protected from or unconcerned about; but on this occasion my reaction to the revelation was very strong. Waiting my turn for the lavatory and my turn at the looking-glass, it struck me that there was now absolutely nothing to keep me living where I was living, doing what I was doing. It had all come suddenly to an end. I sat on Maisie's bed and opened my mind to the prospects, the joyful prospects of being free because there was no further family duty for me to perform, no one it was necessary to keep an eye on, or stand by, see through a crisis, make excuses for as I'd had to do in the early days at the grace and favour bungalow before there was Mabel's money to be extravagant with and bills ran up, card debts were being forgotten, and too much gin was being drunk (so elegantly, so discreetly); no one now for whose return I had to wait. Even Susan no longer needed me. She only needed everyone.

So I could go home, stay with Aunt Lydia in Bayswater, find myself a job, a place of my own, and a man I could look at and not feel that he was tortured by an affection for the country I'd not been happy in and to which he would always be longing to return, as if to prove something to himself. I could finish with India before it had quite finished with me, rusted me up, corroded me, corrupted me utterly with a false sense of duty and a false sense of superiority.

I emerged (a little over-painted I think – I noticed mother look at me) and determined to be nice to Mr Drew. I tried to get him to talk about Surrey (where great-grandfather had lived and where, walking with Aunt Mabel to show her the stream where Susan and I played together I had been stung by a wasp at the moment of one of what I called my funny turns, which might have been growing pains and made me feel immense in a diminutive landscape); but when Mr Drew did talk about Surrey it sounded to me like a different country – a foreign place – so I made him dance with me to Maisie's portable, out on the verandah where it was no draughtier than indoors, while Susan sat inside, not watching us, but with an expression on her face that I recognized but tonight refused to do anything about. Then the dogs came in and there was pandemonium. Susan's coffee cup somehow got knocked over (or was deliberately spilled to distract attention from the dogs). Her new dress was stained down the front and before you could turn round the pieces on the board had been rearranged and Susan was there in the middle of the scene, with people sponging her, inviting her to have another cup, while she tried to embrace the hound that had caused the trouble; and Mr Drew got down on his knees to collect bits of broken china, and then realized he'd made a gaffe because what else were all these servants for? Still outside, I re-wound the gramophone and played another record of which no one took any notice except towards the end when father came out and said, 'Years since I did this,' and shuffled round with me for the last few bars. Then we went inside where two of the dogs had their devoted heads on Maisie's and Patrick's knees and the third was lolling, tongue out, enfolded by one of Susan's arms: the two of them leaning against one another, squatting in the centre-piece of the rug, in front of the empty hearth.

But those intimations of freedom continued. My limbs felt as though they were made out of a substance that wasn't always obedient to the law of gravity. I seemed buoyant, almost on the verge of levitation; to have become in relation to Pankot a dominant but disinterested force. I was no longer ashamed of the dreams I had and had considered shameful, dreams in which I also played a dominant rôle, loving a man who was an amalgam of Major Clark and the young American officer in Darjeeling who was Clark-Without's only successor so far, and who had so impressed Aunt Fenny with his courtly Boston manners that she never suspected him of having other than a brotherly interest in the girl she was supposed to be chaperoning, the girl who was supposed to be convalescing from a spell in a nursing-home in Calcutta, and whose problem was no longer emotional but physical, and who let him into her room three nights in a row, because unlike her Aunt Fenny she hadn't been deceived; had recognized in the American the same single-minded and powerful sexual drive that had distinguished Clark-Without and which she wanted – perhaps for a number of reasons – to appease and be appeased by.

For not least among those reasons was the need to satisfy again her own fully awoken physical desires. I oughtn't to say 'not least'. The need was pre-eminent. An almost unbearable ache. Perhaps I should leave it at that and perhaps it is only some lingering old-fashioned idea that desire without love needs excusing in a woman that makes me not want to refer to this episode without also groping for other explanations. The danger of doing so is that one could come up with another idea, equally false; the idea that I was deliberately debasing myself, paying myself out, being consciously promiscuous because that was now all I was fit to be; a well brought up young woman who had betrayed her upbringing by lying on her back for the first man with the power to persuade her on to it, and who had then had to get rid of the result in the usual sordid way, going in for a d and c and coming out foetus-free but permanently stained, soiled.

Well, I was not debasing myself with John J. Bellenger III but I was not in love with him either. Nor was I hoping that he would fall in love with me so that I could laugh in his face and have my own back on Clark-Without, on men in general. Perhaps all these possibilities were there, in my mind, like echoes of explanations, other people's explanations, but fundamentally there was only the desire, and if it was enclosed by a kind of anguish that anguish was for the loss of a scarcely begun life, the destruction of a child I had conceived, should have carried, loved and looked after. Appeasing the ache of physical desire, I was – yes, I think so – also comforting that anguish, trying to numb it.

But I do not know. The American told me with some understandable pride that I was the twenty-third girl he had had, not counting the ones he had had to pay for. I wasn't sure whether he wanted to amuse or shock me, hurt me or excite my admiration. It could have been that he was unsure himself because when I asked him which of these reactions he expected he looked confused, then laughed and said I had struck him as a girl who was naturally inquisitive and who would be interested in statistics, and that he'd never told a girl before which statistic she represented. I didn't believe him. Afterwards, when he had gone back to what he called States-side (he was in Darjeeling getting in some leave at the end of a tour of flying duties) and Fenny and I went back to Calcutta where mother and Susan were to join us, I worried rather about the possibility of having caught a disease, which would have been the last straw as far as mother was concerned (if I was unable to keep it as secret from her as she was determined the other business officially had to be).

The anguish had been part of the dreams, but now it had gone, or been sublimated in images of extraordinary sensuous tranquillity. One's moral sense sleeps while the subconscious mind works out its logic. Here we were, in perfect amity, revealing to one another the purity of a simple physical connection, myself active, they supine, eyes closed, mouths smiling faintly, free of that grim alignment which in real life reflected tensions. I now woke up from these dreams gradually enough to suffer no shock. For a few moments the tangible quality of pleasure lingered, so that the pleasure seemed to come with me into the actual world and colour all my responses, even my response to the knowledge that I'd only dreamt. Lying in the dark I luxuriated in my own ability to smile. And when up and about, getting on with the dull repetitious routine of coping with things and with other people, I had the idea of this smile in my head, in my whole body, as if a smile were a newly developed faculty.

Saturday, Sunday night, Monday. On the Monday night, because he had unexpectedly rung me, Nigel Rowan came into the dream too, not centrally, but on its misty periphery, as if he were waiting for me to finish and resume some kind of moral responsibility.

'Who was that?' my mother had asked when I'd put the phone down in the hall and joined her and father in the living-room. I told her. 'Is he in Pankot, then?' she asked.

No, I said, he was ringing from Ranpur. She expected to be told more than that and when she wasn't told she said, 'Was he ringing to say he's coming up?'

She'd heard more about Nigel Rowan from Clara Fosdick than she had ever heard from me. Clara Fosdick had probably given her a good report of him and exaggerated the amount of time Nigel and I spent together in Ranpur before I continued on to Bombay to await father's arrival.

'No,' I said. 'He's not coming up.'

'Did we ever know any Rowans, John?' she asked father.

'I don't remember. Why?'

'Sarah's met a Rowan who's one of Malcolm's aides. According to Clara Fosdick he had a relative in the Political but the name Rowan doesn't ring a bell. Did you know a Rowan at school?'

'I don't remember one.'

'Clara said this Rowan was at Chillingborough. Perhaps his father was too.'

'Do you mean Perron?'

'No. Not your eccentric sergeant. A Captain Rowan.' She looked at me again. 'What did he ring about?'

'About something I asked him to do.' I turned to father. 'Nigel Rowan's uncle was Resident at Kotala. He's just told me.'

My father nodded. He wasn't taking it in. But mother said,

'Then he must be Tom Crawley's nephew. You remember, don't you, John? All the fuss there was? How interesting. Are you sure he's not coming up?'

'He didn't say he was.'

'Did you tell him about your eccentric sergeant?'

'I mentioned Mr Perron. Yes.'

'Did he remember him?'

'Yes. Very well.'

'Not an impostor, then.'

'No, mother. Not an impostor.'

'He won't go to sleep,' Susan said, coming in with Edward in her arms and the ayah just behind her. 'He won't go to sleep until he's said goodnight again to grandpa.'

The child was as good as asleep, but this scene was part of the day's programme. I had delayed it a bit by being so long on the telephone. The child turned his head into Susan's breast when his grandfather dutifully leant over him and said, 'Goodnight, old chap.' Satisfied, Susan transferred him to Minnie's arms.

'Is there time for me to have a drink, or have I held things up too long already?' Susan asked.

'We couldn't have gone in before because Sarah's been on the phone,' mother explained.

'Oh. I'll take it in shall I then?'

'There's no hurry,' father said. He went to the side table where Mahmoud as instructed had set out the bottles and glasses so that Colonel Sahib could mix the drinks himself.

'Do you know,' he said, 'I realized today that I've put up a fearful black? I'm not sure I shan't have to send in my papers.'

'What dreadful thing have you done, John?'

'I've been on station very nearly a week and I've neither sent up my card to Flagstaff House nor signed the book. Back in 'thirteen, in Ranpur, it took me the best part of two weeks, doing nothing else, just leaving my card, ticking off the names on the list that Mabel gave me. Had to dress right for it too, and it cost a fortune in tonga-fares and shoe-leather.'

My mother smiled. She said that in the circumstances she imagined his failure to call at Flagstaff House might be over-looked.

'Really?' he said. 'Things have changed.' He caught my eye. 'Not sure I approve.'

It was the first joke he had made. I laughed. I said we could ride past Flagstaff House the next morning.

'So we could.'

But we didn't. On that Tuesday morning he was late joining me on the front verandah where I waited, smoking, watched by the two syces who had brought the horses up. Usually only one syce came, riding one horse and leading the other. When I first came out it was drizzling slightly but now it was clearing rapidly in that way which foretold a hot sunny morning. Remembering the funeral I asked the syces whether the bazaar was very crowded. The syce I knew said no, but it was said there were many people at the station, and he had seen people making for there. The bazaar would be crowded later, with people who had nothing better to do than look at a Congresswallah. That was why he had brought a companion; in case when they went back the crowds were big enough to worry the horses.

I said that was wise, and smiled because almost invariably the people who served us spoke contemptuously of politicians. A form of flattery. It was nearly twenty-past seven before father came out. The syces stood to attention and salaamed him.

'Well done,' he said. 'Well done,' as if bringing the horses up on time stretched their mental and physical resources. He said this every morning. And every morning he kissed me lightly on the cheek. This morning he did not kiss me. He put his arm round my shoulders and exerted faint pressure but did not look at me. He looked at his watch instead and apologized for being late. I asked him whether he had got his cards with him. I had to explain what I meant.

'Oh, lots of time for that. Lots of time.'

He led off as usual and once out on the road turned to the north, towards Muddarabad.

As I trailed behind him (the wisest thing to do on this narrow twisting section of road whose high-banked bends could mask the noise of trucks that sometimes used it) I felt vaguely disappointed. A change of route would have suited my buoyant mood. I had hoped that this morning would be different but obviously it was going to be like all the others unless I could force a variation, persuade him past the halt, into the village.

But it was he who forced the variation. About a quarter of a mile before we reached the halting-place we came to a road that led in from our right. We had taken this road once or twice on the way home. Now, without more warning than a glance behind to check my position, he led into it, then reined in to let me come up and said, 'I thought we'd take a look at that.'

That was the old dak bungalow, wedged in the hillside, about a quarter of a mile away. A track would take us up to it. The bungalow hadn't been used for years, to my knowledge. It had always looked derelict to me. But this morning as we approached I saw the figure of a boy on the verandah. I said, 'There's someone there.'

'So there is. Good Lord.'

He was a poor actor. And getting closer I now recognized the *mali*'s boy. He had on the blue mazri shirt that had originally been one of father's, which mother had handed on to the gardener who had since had it cut down to fit his son.

'Isn't that *mali*'s boy?' father asked, forcing his tone. 'Well I never. What's the young scamp doing here?'

The boy had begun to unpack a haversack. I said, 'Playing truant I expect. It looks as if he's brought food for the day. Wouldn't it be nice if he'd got sandwiches and coffee and offered us some?'

'Shouldn't think much hope. All the same. Jove. Yes, wouldn't it, just? Still, mustn't count our chickens.'

We came up the steep and partially overgrown track in file. Far off I could hear the coppersmith. The sun had got up well into a clear sky. The old bungalow looked as if it were resting on the vapour which clung to the green hillside. Beneath my horse's rather clumsily placed hooves small wet pebbles slithered and crunched.

What is all this? my father called to the grinning urchin, in Urdu. *What are you doing here? Making arrangements for breakfast, Sahib*, the boy called back. Father laughed. He shouted up, *Will there be breakfast for us also? For Sahib and Memsahib-miss*, the boy called back.

'I say, we're in luck. Free scoff.'

Another urchin appeared to hold the horses. A well-bred urchin. Ignoring the burra sahib he stood first by me while I dismounted. I thanked him and asked him whether he was Fariqua's friend. He said he was. I asked him his name. He said,

'Ashok.' Ashok and Fariqua. A Hindu boy and a Muslim boy. Ashok led the horses round to the back. We went up the rickety steps to the ruinous-looking but in fact still quite stout verandah. On the wooden table Fariqua had spread out the feast on a coloured cloth: thermos, cups, pot of sugar, pot of salt, spoons, plates, unnecessary knives and forks, stacks of sandwiches wrapped in paper already appetizingly stained with what looked like bacon-fat.

'Well done,' father said. '*Bus.*'

The boy saluted and ran off to join his friend. (Later they came and squatted on their hunkers at some distance, in silence, observing us gravely.)

We sat side by side on the old bench. I reached for the thermos. 'No, let me,' he said. Pouring tea his hand scarcely trembled. He said, 'Better than leaving one's card.'

'Much better.'

He'd woken early, he explained, and had the idea, had got the servants moving, but it had taken longer than he imagined. The boy hadn't been able to leave with the picnic breakfast until ten to seven, so he'd hung around, made a long business of shaving and dressing, to guard against our catching the boy up. He'd wanted it to be a surprise.

'It's a lovely surprise.'

I'd never been to the old dak bungalow before. There had never been a reason to – even as a child. It was too close to home, wherever home had variously been in Pankot, a different home every summer, practically. The dak bungalow (open in those days, now declined, neglected) had been a point of reference in a familiar landscape. From it I now had a view of Pankot new enough to make the place look oddly unfamiliar.

He opened the first package of sandwiches.

'They won't be a patch on those we had on the train,' he said. 'Bacon sandwiches have to mature a bit, don't they? Crisp but not brittle. Not too moist, not too dry. I'm afraid this batch only got put down an hour ago. All the same, they don't smell too bad.'

And they tasted good. We munched for a while, content. It must have been now that the two boys came back to watch us.

'Did you know about our young supernumerary?'

'Fariqua's friend? Is he a supernumerary?'

'Well, I think he's attached himself to our strength. I caught sight of him the other day when I went round the servants' quarters. Thought he was just visiting because he dodged out of the way. But this morning I found him and Fariqua curled up in the goat-shed.'

'Hasn't he a home?'

'Probably several. None permanent. Orphan. Ambitious boy, though. Tells me he's going to Rajputana one day, to become a mahout, ride an elephant for a maharajah. Meanwhile he scrapes a living running errands in the bazaar and sleeping where he can, I suppose. I should have told *mali* to boot him out but hadn't the heart. Trouble is, once you've recognized the existence of a boy like that you're in a fair way to having to pay for services rendered but not wanted. *Mali* doesn't need two boys to help him, does he? Not with the little he has to do nowadays.'

What he meant was: now that the rose beds are gone. He missed the garden more than he would ever admit. From where we sat I could see the fold near the peak of East Hill behind which Rose Cottage lay. I tried to make out the fir tree that stood at the farthest point of the grounds. I said, 'Well, the tennis-court needs some keeping up.'

'I expect it does.'

I waited. I thought he was going to talk about Mabel. The roses. Or the grave. It hardly mattered which. They were all connected. But he went on, 'We must have a game presently. Bit strenuous for me at the moment though. But don't you and Susan give it up just because I'm back. I'd enjoy watching. You could get up a foursome. Young Drew maybe. And some other young fellow.'

He hesitated. 'I expect there *are* other young fellows? Been up before, waiting for a chance to come up again?'

'It shouldn't be difficult to make up a four.'

'With anyone in particular?'

I pretended not to understand, tilted my head at him, filling my mouth with bacon sandwich.

'Any young fellow who'd be particularly keen? This young ADC for example. Nigel Rowan?'

'Nigel Rowan's down in Ranpur.'

'What I mean is, well, forget tennis. Any young fellow in particular, special from your point of view, that I don't know about?'

I continued munching sandwich and considered the situation from what I imagined must be *his* point of view, looked at a woman, now twenty-five, who had been back in India for six years, and who must surely long since have worn out the excuse that of two sisters she was the less obviously attractive. Statistically, the odds against her remaining single or unattached must have been higher than in any comparable period. India had been jam-packed with eligible young men, and proportionately shorter than ever of eligible women. There were several possible explanations, none of them comforting to anyone who had her happiness at heart: she was frightened of men, she was one of the world's born old maids, she was consumed by a passion for a man who hadn't noticed her or who was married or for some other reason unattainable; or, she preferred women. Of these possibilities the consuming and unrequited passion was the one that most fathers would find the least disturbing and I wished badly that I could have confessed such a thing to him. Being unable to, being unable to confess to any of these things, I felt unsatisfactory and inadequate. I said, 'There's no one in particular so far, daddy.'

We went on, munching bacon sandwiches and Ashok and Fariqua continued to observe us, as though we were exhibits which it was only part of their job to look after, the other part being to watch us closely for clues to the trick we were performing to sustain an illusion of our ordinariness, the illusion that the Sahib-log too liked to eat and take a rest and did not live like birds of paradise, perpetually in flight, feeding on celestial dew.

'Has there never been anyone in particular?'

'You mean someone I wanted to many?'

'Yes. That sort of in particular.'

I shook my head, pushed the sandwiches closer to him. He took one – seemed to think about it – and then placed it on one side. 'Tell me,' he said, 'what are your feelings towards Ronald Merrick?'

I stopped chewing and stared at him. I remember that: just staring at him, and suddenly wondering whether there was a plot to try to pair me off with the only man I could easily think of who appalled me. To avoid answering I turned the question. I asked him what *his* feelings were.

He regarded me rather sombrely.

'He wasn't what I expected. Being a friend of Teddie's – the same rank – I'd expected a younger man.'

'He wasn't a friend of Teddie's. They only shared the same quarters in Mirat.'

'But he was best man.'

'A last-minute substitute.'

'Yes, I see. Not that it matters.'

'I think it mattered to Teddie.'

'What makes you say that?'

'Well, I was there. I think Teddie regretted it. If I'd been in Teddie's shoes I'd have regretted it too. Hasn't mother or Aunt Fenny told you what happened at the wedding?'

'I know about the stone some chap threw that hit Teddie and delayed the ceremony.'

'The stone was thrown at Ronald but nobody realized that at the time, or why a stone had been thrown at all. The only explanation seemed to be that it was intended for the Nawab. The Nawab had lent us cars and the cars had crests on them. So we imagined the stone was thrown in error by someone who didn't like the people at the palace. We ended up guarded by MPs. That was a mess too. When the Nawab and his party turned up at the Gymkhana Club for the reception, the MPs didn't know who he was and tried to stop him coming in because he was an Indian. Then when we were seeing Teddie and Susan off at the station we were bothered by a poor old woman who prostrated herself at Ronald's feet. The whole thing was a mess but by then we knew who Ronald was. We knew the name of the district where he'd been superintendent of police.'

'Yes, I know all that. Ronald's told me himself. But I shouldn't think Teddie held it against him for long. It was hardly Ronald's fault.'

My father picked up the sandwich now and bit into it. I poured us more tea.

'What was Teddie Bingham like?' he asked.

'A bit like young Mr Drew. But not so shy.'

'Your Aunt Fenny told me he was rather attentive to you, at one time, before his engagement to Susan.'

'Yes. Actually it got to the stage where I was afraid he might propose.'

'Why afraid?'

'I realized how easy it would be just to say yes. A girl can, you know. It's a kind of inertia. You think well, why not? It's what's expected. Getting married to a fairly presentable man. Decent background. Good regiment. Nothing known against. And it's very flattering to be wooed a bit. Even by someone as automatic and predictable as Teddie.'

I should have liked to tell him about the night things came to a head, with Teddie obviously thinking the wooing drill had gone on long enough and that it was time to clarify things between us; the night he shifted gear and became fastidiously amorous, kissing me for so long that it was like a breath-holding contest and we both longed to come up for air, and then knew beyond any doubt that we were both bored with one another. But I felt you couldn't tell your father a thing like that about the man who had gone on to marry your sister. So instead I said, 'Why did you ask about my feelings towards Ronald Merrick?'

'I asked because – well, I've been given to understand that you had some special – no, that's wrong – that you *might* have some special regard for him.'

'Who gave you to understand, daddy?'

'Your Aunt Fenny. She's very fond of you, you know. She has your happiness very much at heart.'

'And I'm fond of her. But I can't think why she should think that. I told her a long time ago what I felt about Ronald Merrick.'

'Yes, but she wondered whether there might have been a change of heart. No, I'm exaggerating again. She said a change of heart couldn't be ruled out.'

'Well it can. I can't imagine how Aunt Fenny could get such an idea. She saw us together often enough when he turned up in Bombay. So did you, daddy. I don't like him. It must show.'

'I wouldn't actually say that.'

'Well whether it shows or not, that's the situation. Furthermore he knows I don't like him.'

'Oh?' He hesitated. 'I don't think he does.' He leant back. 'Neither does your mother. She has much the same impression as Fenny. That you might have a special regard for him.'

'*Mother* told you I might have a special regard for Ronald Merrick?'

He studied me very seriously.

'Yes. Have you?'

'No, daddy.'

'I didn't really think so, but I wouldn't hold out as an expert, you know, not against Fenny and your mother. So I wanted to be sure. Can I be sure?'

'Absolutely sure.'

'Why don't you like him?'

'I can't easily explain why.'

'I know he's not, well – how stuffy it sounds – but not quite our class.'

'It doesn't sound stuffy at all. It's true. He's not quite our class. Class has always been important to us. Why should it suddenly stop being important?'

He had leant forward, arms on the table. He was smoothing one side of the close-cropped moustache with his knuckles. He seemed puzzled. It wasn't the kind of reaction he expected. Not from the rebel of the family.

He said, 'It's only important over quite a narrow area of life, although I agree it's an important area. The private bit. It's easier to be intimate with someone who comes out of the same box. But there are other areas where it's not important at all. Areas where it's actually harmful, I'd say. Anyway, in Ronald Merrick's case, does it honestly arise? Unless we insist on looking only at the background?'

'You mean he's our class now? That he's made the effort to raise himself to our level and if he keeps quiet about his origins no one will know they weren't much cop. Is that what you mean?'

'He doesn't try to hide them. That's one thing in his favour.'

'One thing? All right. One thing.'

'Surely he has a lot of admirable qualities?'

'Like what, daddy?'

'Like physical courage, moral too, I dare say. No, I don't dare say, I do say. Don't you agree?'

'I prefer a bit of moral cowardice myself.'

'Oh?'

'Or whatever it is that makes you admit there can be two sides to a question, other points of view as good as your own.'

'That's not moral cowardice.'

'I said moral cowardice because you said moral courage. And

moral courage is so often what you say people have who really only have their minds rigidly made up to suit themselves.'

'Yes,' he said. He smoothed the other side of the moustache. 'I suppose it can be. I'd not thought of it like that. And I grant you in Ronald's case a certain inflexibility. But you often find it in men who've had to fight their way up the ladder. They have to work so much harder. Did you know he lost both parents when he was only fifteen?'

'He mentioned it once.'

'You know what they were?'

'He said they were in a very small way. I didn't inquire how small or what way.'

'They had a small shop in North London. Newsagent, tobacconist. That sort of thing. I got the impression that before the First World War they were both in service. The shop did pretty well and they took over a larger one. Ronald began at a local boardschool but got scholarships and ended at quite a good grammar. Then the parents were killed in a motor-accident. There was a country uncle somewhere but he wasn't interested in the boy. The assistant headmaster of the school was, though. He took him in to live as a ward and to stay on and matriculate. This fellow had some sort of Indian connections or interests. Socially it was a leg up. Ronald said he imagined if his parents hadn't died he'd have been shoved into something like insurance or accountancy. He knows he owes everything to the schoolmaster. Not just the chance to complete his education but the chance of a better background as well. A good enough one to scrape him into the Indian Police. Physically and academically he must have been more than good enough.'

'You've learnt a lot. More than any of us.'

'Only what he openly volunteered.'

'I realize that. What puzzles me is why he volunteered it.'

'Does it puzzle you? Really? You've no idea?'

'None.'

'Yes, I see. And I'm sorry. I mean sorry you don't much like him. But at least that's better than the other thing. He told me all this because he wants to marry Susan. He said Susan had given him reason to believe she wasn't averse to the idea but that no decision could be made until I got home. Fenny and your mother were surprised. Very surprised. They thought that if he had that kind of regard for either one of you it must be for you. I wanted to be sure how you felt. But it's taken me a bit of time to pluck up the nerve to mention it to you. I was afraid of it hurting you. . . .'

'It doesn't hurt me.'

He took my hand. I said: 'It doesn't hurt me, it appals me. I don't honestly believe it. She's said absolutely nothing, but if he's right, if she's thinking on these lines, you've got to stop it. Really. She's not fit to marry anyone yet, let alone Ronald Merrick.'

'The psychiatrist apparently says she is.'

'Which psychiatrist?'

'The one here.'

'Who told you that?'

'Ronald. He saw the fellow a few weeks ago.'

'With Susan's approval?'

'No. He saw him before he spoke to Susan. He wanted to know what effect a proposal of marriage might have on her, whether it would set her back at all. Whether he should wait a bit before saying anything even to me.'

'What a bloody nerve.'

'I thought it rather sensible.'

'Well of course – you thought exactly what he planned you should think. I hope Captain Richardson gave him bloody short shrift.'

'Oh? Why? If you were Richardson and a man who's short of an arm and has half his face burnt off came to you and said, Look I want to marry one of your patients, what are the problems likely to be from her and your point of view?'

'I know, I know. It's all beautifully logical. Absolutely square and above-board. Admirable. On the surface. On the *surface*, daddy.'

'He's very good with young Edward.'

'Yes. He's very good with young Edward.'

'Better than I.'

'Better than you. Better than any of us. Better than anyone. Better than Susan. But he wouldn't be marrying Edward. He'd be marrying Susan. How good will he be with her?'

Directly I'd said that the blood came to my face. I guessed what he probably thought. For one wild moment I wondered whether it could be true, wondered whether if I went to Richardson and described the situation to him he would say, It's clear of course, Merrick appals you because he attracts you and your exaggerated concern for your sister is simply a reflection of your fury at being rejected in her favour.

But it wasn't true. What I believed *was* true was that my mother had deliberately tried to manipulate things. She couldn't possibly want Susan to marry Ronald Merrick, but rather than say so she had grasped the opportunity offered by Aunt Fenny's foolish but well-meaning hint to make father believe that it might break my heart. It could even have been in her mind that in time if the idea of having Ronald Merrick in the family persisted he could be paired off with me because neither of us deserved any better.

'What I don't understand,' father said, 'is your having no idea how the land lay. From Susan's point of view.'

'Did mother?'

'No. But sisters share confidences, surely. You've been very close to her. I know that. At least I know what your Aunt Fenny says.'

'What does Aunt Fenny say?'

'If it hadn't been for you Susan would have had a complete breakdown.'

'She had a complete breakdown, daddy.'

'I meant, might have had to be put somewhere.'

'She was put somewhere.'

'But only in the nursing home, here.'

'In a room with barred windows. They thought she might hurt herself. They were afraid of violence. She'd put the baby at risk. Hasn't mother told you that?'

After a while he said, 'I suppose I've been told just as much as it's thought I can take in. Fair enough. Anyway, that's all over, isn't it? She's quite better now, surely. And quite capable of weighing things up and making a decision she'd have no reason to expect to regret?'

'What does that mean? That she's decided?'

'Yes, I think she has.'

'You've actually discussed it with her?'

'Yes.'

'Did *Susan* say I might be upset?'

'She seemed to think you were expecting it. She was surprised her mother wasn't. She thought it must have been obvious to everyone for a long time that if she married again it would be to Ronald. She's given it a lot of thought, you know. She said she couldn't expect to fall in love more than once in her life, but she does respect him and she knows she's got to think of the boy's future. She assured me there wasn't any element of pity or gratitude in her decision – I mean gratitude to Ronald for what he tried to do to save Teddie. And she's also not blind to the fact that his disabilities make his future career a bit chancy. All in all, I was rather impressed by the way she's thought it all out.'

'Was mother impressed?'

'Your mother was chiefly concerned about the effect it might have on you.'

'She raised no objections on her own account? She hasn't gone so far as to say she doesn't want Ronald in the family?'

I could have phrased that better. Again he regarded me seriously, still not entirely convinced that I was being frank about my own interests in the matter. But I let it go at that. I had to become used to the idea that I no longer had responsibilities. It was no business of mine whom Susan married. He had much the same thought, apparently. He said, 'Well when you come down to it Susan's free to marry whoever she likes. It would be nice if we all liked him too. Your mother hasn't actually said she doesn't. Being the mother she's obviously not too happy about one of her daughters marrying a partially disabled man. Come to that neither am I. It is a liability. He's very conscious of it himself. If for any reason you think he and Susan have been over-secretive, do take the disability into account. A girl's got to think pretty hard before she commits herself in a case like this. Think it out on her own. So does the man.'

'He's ten years older than Su, at least.'

'It's not much.'

'Why hasn't he married before? Have you asked yourself that?'

'My dear, what's that supposed to mean?'

'It's not supposed to mean anything. It's just a question.'

Eventually father said, 'I don't see anything in particular to question. I'll admit he's probably been keen to make the sort of marriage that, well, he could congratulate himself on making, but I see nothing wrong in that. Good luck to him. Why not?

Senior police appointment, the guts to pester his department for a wartime commission, a DSO. It's not a meagre record, not as though he's bringing nothing worth while. I suppose you can say India's made him what he is, but after all isn't it India that's given *us* whatever distinction we have? Without India, I wonder what we'd have been? Lawyers like my grandfather? Merchants like his father? And on the Muir side – Scottish crofters? A long way back, but not all that long way. It's only a difference in timing. India's always been an opportunity for quite ordinary English people – it's given us the chance to live and work like, well, a ruling class that few of us could really claim to belong to.'

'It's no longer an opportunity.'

'That's hardly Ronald's fault.'

'I didn't mean it that way. I meant it's no longer any use looking at Susan's future from that angle. It's all finished. She ought to go home. Ronald's the kind of man who'll never let her. He's worked too hard to get here. It would be different if they were in love. But they're not. They can't be. I don't believe he's capable of feeling that for anybody.'

My father leant back, folded his arms.

'It's not his first proposal, though, is it?'

'Isn't it?'

'Didn't you know?'

'Know what?'

'That he was very fond of the girl in that wretched case that caused him so much trouble.'

Again I stared at him. I could tell from his expression that he was still ready to believe that any reference to Ronald and another woman hurt me. 'Daphne Manners? Ronald told you he was very fond of Daphne Manners? Fond enough to propose to her?'

'Yes. He did.'

'It's not the impression he originally gave me. All he said was that he once thought he liked her but that he went off her pretty quickly when he realized she wasn't sound.'

'Sound?'

'He may not have said sound. It's what he meant. Not sound. Meaning bluntly too friendly with Indians.'

'He told me he proposed marriage to her. I don't see it as a thing a man would invent.'

'And I don't see it as a thing a man would talk about. Why did he?'

'I suppose I asked him. I don't mean directly. It just came up. We were discussing the case. Talking about his future. He said his Inspector-General had supported him but he wasn't sure what the long-term effects would be on his career as a whole. He was very frank.'

'He thinks he made a mistake?'

'No. I didn't get that impression. Rather the reverse. But I believe it's often worried him that his feelings for the girl might have influenced him, made him act too hastily, not wrongly, just too hastily. Well, I don't wonder. Wretched case altogether. Wretched to talk about.' He hesitated. 'I'd really prefer not to.'

'All right, daddy, we won't talk about it. That doesn't mean we may not have to live with it, Susan especially, if people start pressing for inquiries into some of the things that were done at the time. But I mustn't say that, must I? The mere prospect might make you feel sorry for him. You should never feel sorry for Ronald.'

'I'd feel sorry for any man who was victimized.'

'Victimized, yes. So would I.'

I'd started to fold the paper in which the sandwiches had been packed. Noticing some still ungathered crumbs I unfolded it again, swept them in, and refolded. I had repaid him badly for the care and trouble he'd taken, for the love and affection he'd shown, making arrangements like these before telling me something he thought might upset me. I'd neither set his mind at rest nor, in the last few minutes, even spoken kindly to him.

'It was such a lovely breakfast,' I said. 'I'm sorry if I've spoilt it. I honestly didn't mean to. Now I suppose we ought to be getting back.'

'You haven't spoilt it. What is the time?'

'Eight-thirty.'

'Are you on duty again?'

'Yes, I'm afraid so.' I remembered the Government House bag, with stuff in for me from Nigel. I'd meant to get to the daftar quite early to round up Sergeant Baker to make sure I got the packages.

'What will you say to Susan?' father asked.

'Nothing. She won't ask my opinion. The thing has been for

me to be there when she's wanted me to be there. To be there and go along with whatever she's decided to do. Oddly enough, I've been quite good at that. If marrying Ronald is her new interest she'll be all right so long as she's making plans and seeing everything in terms of the next step ahead.'

'If she stops seeing things like that, would you know?'

'Yes.'

'Sooner than your mother?'

'Probably.'

'Would you tell me?'

'If I'm here, daddy.'

'Might you not be?'

'I can't live at home indefinitely.'

'I do understand that. But – well, for a while. At least until after the wedding.'

'That might depend on when the wedding is.'

'I'd not imagined anything impulsive.' He felt for my hand again. 'Don't *you* be impulsive. What had you in mind?'

'Going home, really. I'd like to get myself a job of some kind. Aunt Julia would take me in for a bit, I expect.'

'Going home? But that's a long-term plan, surely?'

'I thought of going to Aunt Fenny in Bombay for a while. Then on from there when I've really decided. I can pay my own passage. Aunt Mabel left us each five hundred pounds of our own. Susan and me, I mean. And I've got a bit more.'

'That's your nest-egg. There's no question of forking out your own fare, if going home's really what you want. But I hope not yet. Not yet, Sarah. Give me a bit of time to enjoy my whole family.'

I felt the net closing in again. I said, 'Well the war's not quite over yet.'

'No, but if it is, try not to be in too much of a hurry or think me too selfish. It'll be easier for us all to make plans when we know what's to happen to me. The Trehearnes will be going after Christmas. It looks as if I'll take over. But there's just a chance of my getting the Area. Your mother's a bit restless, she'd really like a change of scene, but if we got the Area that would rather please her. Flagstaff House. All that goes with it. And it would probably see out my time.'

'You'd like it too, wouldn't you?'

'Yes, I would. As a young man I assumed I'd end up a general. Small chance of that now. I'd settle for brigadier. Or just full colonel doing Trehearne's job.'

'Then I'll cross my fingers, daddy.'

'Would it make any difference to your plans?'

'Flagstaff House?'

'You were practically born there. And, well, if it happens I'd be sorry to think of your missing it altogether. You've had your share of stale gingerbread. Opportunity for a bit of gilt. But perhaps I shouldn't have mentioned it. Raising hopes.'

He would never understand how little the idea of moving into Flagstaff House raised my hopes. And just then they needed raising. Looking at that oddly unfamiliar view of East Hill it seemed to me that once long ago I'd been marooned there and that now the flood had receded, receded so far that you would have to walk miles to find water and even then have to wade on, endlesssly, without coming to a depth sufficient to swim in.

For one moment I believed, perhaps illogically, my only hope of getting away lay in confessing to my father what had happened to me. I could say: Look, I'm no longer a virgin. I was bedded by one of those officers Uncle Arthur's paid to make enthusiastic about having a career in India, only this chap turned out only to be enthusiastic about what Uncle Arthur would call the wrong things, and I was left in the club, also the wrong one, like any tiresome little skivvy, but unlike her we were able to arrange to have it brought off, and boringly unconventional though I've always been from most people's point of view, I simply didn't have the nerve to walk round pregnant and unmarried in Pankot. I know I'm not by a long chalk the first colonel's daughter to wander down the primrose path, but the catch is that I would never marry a man without first telling him what had happened, which mother knows. I made it clear to Aunt Fenny and if Aunt Fenny's run to form she's obviously told mother that I'd never marry under false pretences. Mother's probably guessed it anyway. And she doesn't really mind because it would go against her patrician scale of values to let me marry a man she really approved of and she thinks the ones she'd approve of are the ones who'd turn tail once they knew. So she's written me off. You'd better too.'

I glanced at him, and then, summoning the nerve, I began to tell him. I got as far as 'Look –' and then, after a second or two, departing from script, 'There's something I want you to know, something I must tell you,' but I got no further because he suddenly grabbed my hand and, not looking at me, said, 'No,' quite sharply, and then repeated it more gently.

'No. Nothing to tell me. Better be off.'

Still without looking he let go of my hand; briefly but quite strongly put his arm round me and then let go altogether and stood up and shouted something to the boys who scrambled up and ran round to get the horses. Then he went to the head of the steps and down them. He was calling something to me, pointing, perhaps at the fir tree high up on East Hill which his better-trained eye had sighted; but half-keeping his back to me, giving me time to let the reason for his reaction sink in.

He knew about the pregnancy and the abortion. Fenny or my mother had told him. Fenny probably; perhaps only hinting at a cause of unhappiness which my mother had more coldly identified. I went to the head of the steps, pretended to look where he was pointing, shading my eyes.

The boys brought the horses. Ashok helped me to mount. When he'd done so I thanked him and led off without waiting for father, heading down the stony track. Half-way down my horse began to miss his footing. The effort of keeping control, slight as it was, seemed immense; the last shameful straw. By the time I reached the road I couldn't see clearly. I waited until he came up. We could go one of two ways. He chose the shorter, and I fell in behind him. But presently he moved over to his right, waited until I was level and, apart from having to drop back a couple of times when a vehicle went by, stayed silently abreast of me until we reached home.

Susan was in the bathroom which meant I didn't have to talk to her. I changed quickly into uniform and to avoid seeing anyone set off for the daftar without even washing the smell of horse off my hands. Momentarily I'd forgotten the reason for wanting to be early on duty, but recalled it when the tonga approached the spot where Barbie's accident had been, the spot Clarissa Peplow once pointed out to me, where after careering down Club Road out of control the tonga had overturned, spilling them all into the ditch. From this point Barbie had walked, mud- and blood-stained, presumably refusing assistance from passers-by, making for the rectory bungalow into which she strode, calling for a spade and announcing that she had seen the Devil. The spade was for resurrecting Mabel. The devil was Ronald Merrick.

Rose Cottage had been shut. Mother, Susan, the baby and ayah had gone down to Calcutta to join Fenny and me after our holiday in Darjeeling, a reunion intended to maintain the illusion that everything was well with everybody. In the family's absence Mahmoud had discovered the trunk in the *mali*'s shed and complained about it to the man mother had asked to keep an eye on things – Kevin Coley. And Kevin had gone down to the rectory to ask Barbie to remove it.

According to Clarissa, Barbie didn't mind. When she went up to the cottage to collect the trunk she found a stranger there. Ronald. He'd come up to the Pankot hospital to have the artificial hand fitted and had called at the cottage to see us. According to Ronald he and Barbie sat and talked, mainly about her missionary friend, Edwina Crane, whom he'd known in Mayapore. She insisted on giving him the copy of the picture which she associated with Edwina. Then she asked him to supervise the loading and securing of the trunk in the back of the tonga. He said he'd advised her against it; it was too cumbersome, too heavy. But she wouldn't listen. He said she struck him as over-excited, in fact, he said, 'Exalted might be the better word.'

It was quite a while before I talked to Ronald about his meeting with Barbie. He had left Pankot before we returned from Calcutta. At that time I'd only met him twice. I'd not liked him. But the real animosity came later when he began to turn up in Pankot on the excuse of visiting the hospital, but in fact it seemed to me to attach himself to us. I realized that he was a very lonely man in the ordinary sense of the word and without my realizing quite how it happened I found myself more often in his company than seemed explainable. At the pictures, for instance, or eating out at the Chinese restaurant when it was inconvenient to entertain him at home (when Susan wasn't well, or had taken too much of her sedative). Going out with him when he was in Pankot, so far as I was concerned, was no more than a duty, one more duty to add to the many I'd got lumbered with or stupidly volunteered for and I assumed that this was understood by the family as a whole. What he assumed about it had been beyond me to work out. He knew I disliked him. Knowing he knew made me feel that we were all safe from him.

When we went to the Chinese restaurant he always ordered a particular table, the one in the window on the first floor (officers only) which looked out on to the bazaar, and which at least provided him with the view to which my silences too often forced him to give attention. I never felt that my being poor company upset him. We were at the Chinese restaurant when I first asked him to describe in detail his meeting with Barbie. I didn't tell him I'd just seen her, in the Samaritan in Ranpur, but I think he guessed. When he said, 'She struck me as being over-excited when she set off, in fact exalted might be the better word,' he studied me closely as if checking for the effect of that word exalted. The exaltation began (he said) when she opened the trunk to give him the picture and found a lace shawl which she said didn't belong to her but which she thought Mabel's old servant Aziz must have put in the trunk when he temporarily had the key to it.

I knew which lace he meant, lace which Mabel had been given by her first husband's mother – lace like a web of butter-flies, worked by a blind old French woman, some of which had been used for Susan's baby's christening, and some, years before, for my own. I had recognized it only a couple of days before at the Samaritan hospital, draped round Barbie's head and shoul-ders, stained brown with dried blood.

Ronald said, 'She put it on when she got into the tonga, like a bridal veil.'

The lace shawl, with its rusty stains, was among the packages that Nigel had been given by the Reverend Mother to hand over to me.

But of course there was nothing waiting for me at the daftar, nothing – Sergeant Baker told me – addressed to me in the over-night bag from Government House. I thought of ringing Nigel up but delayed doing so, finding an excuse not to do that until after five, because he would be busy, but in fact shirking it because the main reason for ringing him would be to tell him about Ronald and Susan and to try to coerce him into helping me to stop it; which seemed a bit unfair.

I remember sitting at the typewriter in the daftar, cutting a stencil from a holograph order written out by Major Smalley, and using so much red-sealer to obliterate mistakes that the wax paper began to look like a piece of the lace shawl Barbie had worn, seated at her window. She had on that occasion seemed to have found peace, the peace of absorption in a wholly demanding God, a God of love and wrath who had no connection with the messianic principles of Christian forgiveness, and it was like that I preferred to remember her, not – as at other times when I had visited her – unanchored, unweighted, withershins, attempting to communicate with the doomed world of inquiry and compromise.

When I was midway through the stencil the phone rang. The operator told me a Captain Rowan was on the line. It was as though I'd conjured him. I said, 'Nigel? I'm afraid there was nothing in the bag. Is that why you're ringing?'

'Partly,' he said. 'Actually I brought the stuff up with me.'

He explained the situation but I wasn't being very bright and it took me some time to understand that he was in Pankot, that he'd travelled up on the overnight train, was staying at the Summer Residence guest house and in the last few minutes had spoken to my mother on the phone and been given my Area HQ number and extension.

'Has she rung you at all?' he asked.

'No, yours is the first call I've had. Why?'

He said, 'In which case you probably won't know Ronald Merrick's here too. By chance I travelled up with him. He had our mutual friend Guy Perron in tow. Merrick's with your parents now. He's come to break some rather sad news to your father. A havildar from your father's regiment who was in the Frei Hind force in Germany committed suicide the other day. Merrick thought your father might be very upset. He wanted to break the news to him himself.'

'Yes. I see. I think he will be. Upset.'

'Merrick's now a half-colonel.'

'What?'

'He's been promoted to Lieut.-Colonel. Did you know?'

'No, I didn't, Nigel. The other thing I didn't know was that he might also become my brother-in-law. Father told me this morning. He wants to marry Susan. And Susan wants to marry him.'

I may have got that wrong: the order in which things were said; but I plainly recollect then a very long silence. We were both trying to assimilate wholly unexpected bits of information: on my part, the poor havildar's death, Ronald's sudden and to me ominous presence in Pankot.

'What do you think of him now that you've met him?' I asked.

'He wasn't quite what I imagined.'

'How long are you here for? I'd love to see you. Is today possible, or is HE in control?'

'The Governor's not here. There's only a Mr Gopal. Actually your mother's just asked me to have dinner at Rose Cottage tonight. I'd like that but I'm not sure whether I can make it. I've got a thing to do for HE. I'm free once I've done it but I'm not sure when that will be. Could you lunch here?'

'You mean today?'

'Yes. Come up as soon as you like.'

I could do that now, I said; and did – leaving the wounded stencil in the machine and looking in on Major Smalley to make the excuse that I was feeling off-colour but hoped to be back in the afternoon.

A man came down the steps as the tonga pulled up in front of the guest house. I hadn't seen Nigel in mufti before and for a moment scarcely recognized him. A suit disguised some of the thinness which his uniform accentuated; he looked fitter, more relaxed, like a man released from some kind of duty which he'd found more and more difficult to do. We had never embraced. Just here, just now, an embrace would have seemed right, but we did as we'd done when parting in Ranpur; shook hands rather solemnly. He held my elbow as a token of support while we climbed the steps but at the top he let go. We went through to the rear verandah which had the view I knew best – across the lawns to the closed Summer Residence – although I couldn't recall just when I'd last seen it.

On a table between two white cane blue upholstered chairs were the several packages he'd brought up from the Samaritan. I thanked him but for the moment didn't want to deal with them or even look at them. He ordered drinks, offered me a cigarette. While I smoked he told me something about the special job he had to do in Pankot. For the moment, at least until he'd had some word from Mr Gopal, he was more or less a prisoner at the guest house, since he might have to make himself available at any moment. He doubted, though, that this would be earlier than the following day.

'So you might be able to come to dinner tonight?'

'Yes, it's very likely.'

'And you might be here for a day or two at least?'

'A day or two certainly.'

The drinks came. While he dealt with the steward I settled back in the cane chair considering how in two days Nigel and I might effectively collaborate to stop a marriage I was sure ought to be stopped. He could talk to my father. I would talk to Susan. The main problem was that Ronald was in Pankot too. So far I'd hardly taken in that fact and now that I did so and had time to consider the excuse Ronald had found to come up from Delhi, the havildar's death seemed like something he had invented to suit his own ends; so that then I began to wonder what it could be that Barbie's death had been invented for. My mind was racing, but I could feel my body settling into a posture of embattled indolence and could hear a voice warning me: Don't say too much. Go carefully.

I'm trying to reproduce for you an occasion of awful disorientation. Failing probably. God knows how one could succeed.

'Well when did all this happen?' he asked. 'Your sister and Ronald Merrick?'

'I wish I knew. She's never said anything to me. Not the slightest hint. But there it seems to be. According to father. I've not talked to Susan yet but father has. And apparently Ronald's talked to him.'

'Your sister is serious, then?'

'So father believes.'

'Does he approve?'

'Let's say he doesn't know Ronald well enough not to.'

'Nor well enough to give his consent immediately?'

'The drawback is, consent's not actually needed.'

'No. Of course. So you have the impression it may be more or less fixed?'

'If it is, I want to unfix it. I hoped you might help me.'

He said nothing. But his expression was kind. I went on: 'It's a lot to ask. But if there's anything you can do to help, I'd be very grateful.'

He didn't answer at once. Then he said it was difficult to see on what grounds he could. He didn't know Susan at all. He and I had talked about Ronald only in general terms. He added, 'Now that I've met him I can't say he's the kind of man I'd want to go out of my way to have much to do with. I suppose one has to assume some serious emotional involvement on your sister's part. One's instinct isn't much to go on, if it comes to thinking of interfering.'

'Is it only instinct, Nigel?'

He thought for several moments and then said, 'From the family's point of view I'd be concerned mainly about the possibility – I don't say probability – the possibility of his name cropping up in any future fuss the politicians make about officers suspected of exceeding their duty in nineteen forty-two. Of course, there's no need even to anticipate a fuss. But if there is a fuss, Merrick might be involved. Not that that would make the slightest difference to Susan, I imagine. Assuming a fondness. Nor to the family. But that's all I can offer – as a practical argument against. Perhaps your father should be warned. About the possibility.'

'I've already warned him. But it didn't have much effect because Ronald's already discussed that aspect of things with him. I was hoping you might dot a few i's and cross a few t's.'

He frowned, not at me but at his glass. He said, 'Well there's also the history of persecution, isn't there, but you know more about that than I do. If it's resumed, your sister could be hurt by it.'

'I've told father about the persecution, but I think it just makes him feel sorry for the man. And Ronald naturally has been very frank about the effect the Manners case could have on his career. It's part of his technique. What I meant was being able to tell father something I don't know. But which you might know. Something on a confidential file, for instance? I may be wrong, but whenever we've talked about Ronald you've always left me with the idea that you know far more than could be expected of a man who'd never met him. So. A file?'

After a while Nigel said, 'I should think all a file would tell you about Colonel Merrick is that he left the comparative safety of the police for active service in the army and was decorated with the Distinguished Service Order, since when there has been a history of regular promotion, no doubt well-deserved.'

'In which case there would be nothing much to fear from a political fuss later, would there, if the files show him as such a paragon?'

Hearing the sharp edge to my voice I suddenly pictured what perhaps I looked like – a hard-bitten little memsahib interfering in other people's lives to stop herself shrieking with the boredom and frustration of her own – or (and perhaps Nigel wondered about this too) trying to stop a marriage because she coveted the man for herself, in spite of all she had ever said to the contrary about her attitude to him.

'I'm sorry, Nigel, I shouldn't try to involve you. It's not your problem. I'd better ring home and tell them I won't be back for lunch. Then I'll go through this stuff of poor Barbie's.'

He accompanied me inside, showed me where a telephone was and a bedroom-bathroom suite that I could use, should I want to; in fact, he said, the phone could be switched through to the one in the bedroom if I preferred that. The steward could get the number. I said that might be best and went into the bedroom, sat on the bed, waiting. The phone rang. Mother was at the other end. She said, 'Where are you?' I told her.

'Good,' she said. Apparently she had rung the daftar and had been expecting me to arrive at any moment, 'off-colour'. She had rung to tell me Nigel Rowan was in Pankot and that if he got in touch I should do my best to persuade him to accept the invitation to dinner at Rose Cottage. She added, 'Presumably you know by now who else is here.'

'Yes. Nigel told me. I'm sorry about the havildar. Is daddy very upset?'

'Not too upset not to have invited Ronald Merrick to dinner this evening. I don't want just a family dinner. I want Captain Rowan here too.'

'He'll come if he can.'

'I want you to make sure he does. I must have another man at the table.'

'If you want to make sure you'd better invite someone else. Nigel's not definitely free. There's always Edgar Drew.'

'I said man, not boy. And a man of our own sort.'

'Then ask Ronald to bring Guy Perron. I gather he's brought him up to Pankot.'

'So we've all gathered. We've all been having to admire the

invisible feather in Colonel Merrick's cap. Colonel! But you can hardly ask a colonel to bring his sergeant along even if there was a chance of his agreeing to. Which in this case there isn't. What a pity the ranks aren't the other way round. I want Captain Rowan.'

'I can't promise.'

'I'm asking you to do so. I'm saying that the least you can do for me is to guarantee he'll be here.'

'The least?'

'The least. He sounds to me the most presentable man you've ever bothered to get to know. In the circumstances, in *all* the circumstances, I should prefer it if you brought him into the open and remembered that this isn't Calcutta, but Pankot.'

I said, very quietly, 'Why do you want that, mother? So that Susan can take one look at him and decide he's for her? I suppose that would solve everything from your point of view.'

'Not quite everything,' mother said. She put the phone down. A meaningless retort; the kind someone is stung into making out of sheer exasperation. I went into the bathroom so that I could calm down and stop shaking. I heard the telephone ringing again in the bedroom but before I could reach it – thinking it was mother calling back to apologize – it stopped, presumably because the call had been taken elsewhere. Going through into the living-room I found Nigel taking the receiver from the steward. I indicated that I would go out to the terrace and did so. The steward followed and asked if I would have another drink. While waiting for it I stood by the balustrade and smoked and then, remembering the packages on the table, decided I might as well look at some of them. The first and bulkiest (containing something solid, like a book, and something soft) was marked: *In the Event of my Death: Dear Sarah.*

Inside I found the butterfly lace which I hastily put down. The solid object was a book of Emerson's essays. I remembered her fondness for them. A quick flip through the pages showed that many of the passages were underlined. I read several of these but found them tiresome and self-righteous. I put the lace back in the wrapping and left the book on the table. The other package, an envelope, contained several smaller envelopes, variously marked: To Sarah: Not to be Opened Before My Death. Private and Personal: To Colonel Layton's daughter. To the Girl who

Visits me. To the Girl with the fair helmet of Hair. To Whom it Might Concern. To Gillian Waller from a Friend.

Every glance – I found it too painful to give much more just then – and subsequent study showed heart-breakingly little except her continuing concern over the question of Mabel's grave – evoked images of her distraction and how, as time went on, she seemed not to have recognized me. In the end she had even given me another name, Gillian Waller. It rang a bell, but I couldn't remember why.

I stuffed the envelopes into my shoulder-bag and managed to push the lace in too. I didn't want the lace for one particular reason. For the same reason I couldn't throw it away. There remained the book. I picked it up again and was glancing through it when Nigel came out.

He said, 'Good, that's settled.' He looked pleased. 'Tomorrow. Probably in the evening.'

'Which leaves you free for tonight?'

'Yes.'

'You know Ronald Merrick's invited too?'

'I wasn't sure.'

'I'll make your excuses if that's what you'd prefer.'

'Would you prefer to dine here?'

'I think that's ruled out, Nigel. I'm not inventive enough to think of an excuse that would cover both of us.'

'In which case I'll come to Rose Cottage. Have the other half before we go into lunch.'

'I'm having the other half.'

'Well, have the next.'

'No, this is fine. I've a stencil to finish this afternoon. But you're one drink behind. You'd better catch up.'

He gave an order to the steward; then noticing that the packages had gone from the table leaving an unidentified book in their place he said, 'Mystery cleared up?'

'I don't think there was much of a mystery after all but I haven't looked through everything yet. I really am grateful though. Are you keen on Emerson?'

'I don't know him I'm afraid. Guy Perron's the Emerson expert. He was quoting him last night.'

'Oh? Barbara Batchelor was an expert too I should think, judging by the homework she seems to have done on him.

I thought you might like to keep the book as a reminder of a pretty odd sort of mission.'

'I shan't need reminding. If you don't want it why not give it to Guy? It might cheer him up.'

'Is he very down-in-the-mouth?'

'I shouldn't say that. Fighting mad might be nearer the mark. He told me he has a scheme to wangle his repatriation. But I never did know when Guy was being serious.'

'I should say he's serious when it's necessary. For instance in Bombay he saved a man from drowning himself in the bath.'

'But not – I gathered – from chucking himself out of a hospital window later and breaking his neck. So Guy said.'

'I didn't know that. Poor Captain Purvis.'

I felt suddenly like laughing. Such a useless, farcical death.

Nigel had been leafing through the book. 'Here it is. "Society is a wave." One of Miss Batchelor's favourite passages too if the markings are anything to go by.' He handed the book back to me. I read the passage. It meant nothing to me. I put the book on the table.

'I think Sergeant Perron should have it if you don't want it, although a sermon on self-reliance is hardly what he needs. Will you be seeing him?'

'I'm not sure. I've given him this number to ring. He didn't know where he'd be billeted. Poor Guy. Two suicides in one week and an order attaching him to Ronald Merrick's department. Incidentally, coming up last night he told me you'd met another old Chillingburian, Jimmy Clark, or Clark-Without as we called him.'

'Yes, that's right.'

'Where was this?'

'In Calcutta.'

'What was he doing there?'

'Oh, passing through on his way to Kandy, looking up old acquaintances, including Uncle Arthur and Aunt Fenny. He'd been on one of Uncle Arthur's courses and was quite the blue-eyed boy.'

'Was that the only time you met him?'

'Yes, he flew to Kandy next day to take up some glamorous-sounding appointment. Or perhaps he was just swanning around.'

'Probably. What did you make of him?'

'I thought he talked a lot of sense. He had us all sized up pretty well.'

'Us?'

'People like us. English people in India. Except that he didn't think we were really English any more. He said we got left behind. Preserved in some kind of perpetual Edwardian sunlight.'

Nigel laughed. 'Let's eat,' he said.

'Game pie of a kind,' he pointed out. 'And champagne also of a kind. Compliments of Government House. It came up in the ice-box.'

'Who are they meant for, though? Not me. Could it be the elusive congressman, Mr Kasim?'

'No, for me, I think, from HE. This is my last assignment for him. They're taking me back into the political.'

'When? When are you going?'

'I'm probably leaving Ranpur some time next week.'

'It's what you wanted.'

'Yes, it is.'

'Where will you go? Kotala?'

'I shouldn't think Kotala.'

'What's your ambition? The Residency at Hyderabad?'

'Too late for that. I'd need another ten or fifteen years.'

'Then why go on? Why not just get out?'

'I thought we talked about that when we first met over Count Bronowsky's champagne. I thought you said nothing was an excuse for working at half-pressure, or standing back from a job while it's still there to be done.'

'Did I say that?'

'Yes.'

'And you've remembered. It doesn't sound like me at all.'

'I thought it did. Anyway. It's what you said.'

'I can't have been thinking straight.'

'Have some more game pie.'

'I can't even get through this.'

Suddenly I felt nauseated. Irregularity was one of my problems these days, so I was usually prepared; and it was better than the punctual but protracted miseries I'd once endured. I murmured an excuse, got up and went back to the guest bathroom and scrabbled in my crammed shoulder-bag for what I needed; panicking when for a moment I couldn't find it among all the things from Barbie's room at the Samaritan. But once I'd un-covered it the sensation of sickness seemed to change its nature. I found myself shivering, as if from a slight fever. But it wasn't fever, it was delayed shock, a physical response to the emotional strain of the ride home from the dak bungalow after the realiza-tion that either my mother or Aunt Fenny had told father about the abortion in Calcutta. It had been for me to tell him; no one else. I seemed to have his forgiveness. If I wanted anything it was understanding.

Plugging myself against the unseasonable but likely menstrual flow I found myself weeping as I'd never done before, not even at that time Aunt Fenny took me in her arms in the hospital room and warned me that mother would never refer to what had happened because for her it hadn't, and that anything I wanted to get over should be got over there and then.

To muffle the sound of my crying I ran the taps hard, and bathed my face. The cold water was like a series of slaps. I stared at my ruined self, hating every pore, every line, every bone. But, ruined or not, as a face it was indestructible. A Layton more than a Muir face. Built to last.

The thought was not new, and thinking it again I recalled the last time I'd thought it: in the garden of Rose Cottage, bending my head to take the scent of a red rose. That was all. The garden. The rose. Barbie and I. And this conviction of being built to survive. But I couldn't recall the context. It might have been before or after Mabel's death.

I began to repair my Layton face; doing it with care and deliberation as if the end-result had to represent my conscious projection of myself into a particular future. And then the con-text came back: the context of the rose and Barbie and of Gillian Waller. It had been before Mabel's death, when Susan was still pregnant. Who is Gillian Waller? Barbie had asked me. We were walking in the garden, the garden as it had been before the time of the tennis court. Who is Gillian Waller? I don't know, I'd said. Why? And unwittingly Barbie disclosed that at night some-times she went into Mabel's room, took off her spectacles, put away the book she'd fallen asleep over, tucked her up and turned off the light, and then waited until she could be sure the sleep hadn't been interrupted. In this sleep, this half-sleep, Mabel had sometimes muttered to herself, as old people do. Gillian Waller, she had said. So it sounded. So: Who was Gillian Waller? 'I'm afraid to ask,' Barbie explained. 'I hate to seem to pry. She's such a self-contained person. There are people like that. She's one. Is Susan more cheerful?'

Not cheerful, I said. Holding on.

I could feel Barbie's hand on my arm as she said, 'To what? Would you say she's dangerously withdrawn?'

I leant over the basin, stared at the white porcelain; smelt the rose. 'We endure,' I said. 'We're built for it. In a strange way we're built for it.' But at this point the context changed, led me to another similar occasion when Barbie and I were in the garden and she grasped my arm again and said, 'They say the child should have a father. I'd encourage it if I were you. If she doesn't marry again you'll never get away. Some people are made to live and others are made to help them. If you stay you'll end up like that, like me.'

'Are you all right, Sarah?' Nigel called from the bedroom.

'Yes, thank you,' I called back.

I waited until I heard the click made by the bedroom door as he went back into the main living-room. Then I considered my reflection very seriously and understood, slowly, the full irony of the situation. I said to my reflection: 'There goes a man I might have been happy with and who up to the time he rang me at the daftar and I told him about Susan and Ronald probably thought he could be happy with me.'

I completed the mask, exaggerating the lipstick and, before opening the bathroom door, smiled, to prepare for the entrance.

But I did not have to enter. I had entered already, long ago.

THE CIRCUIT HOUSE

I

THE ONLY LIGHT entering the compartment came from one of
the arc-lamps that lit the siding, but a dim light was on in the
corridor and when the door slid open he saw that it was Ahmed,
not Hosain, who had come to wake him.

'It's time, father.'

'Has Mr Mehboob arrived?'

'Yes, half an hour ago. But Hosain said you hadn't bothered
to go to bed and were only dozing, so I left you until the last
moment.'

'Even on stationary trains I don't sleep. Just for me we could
all have come by car and not bothered with this.' He wound his
scarf round his neck and put on his cap. 'How far is the Circuit
House? I've forgotten.'

'About half an hour's drive.'

'So near?' On that previous occasion, coming from the Circuit
House, the journey seemed endless. But that had been a journey
with a joyful reunion, not a painful one, at the end, and they
had driven all the way to the station at Mirat, not this station.
He made a mental note: I am not fully awake – guard against
these muddles.

Outside in the carpeted corridor Hosain was waiting and took
the briefcase from him, to relieve him both of the weight and
of the supposed indignity of having to carry anything himself.
Unencumbered he went to the door. The last time he got off a
railway coach at this particular siding it had been with difficulty,
climbing down backwards because there was no platform, the
distance between the level of the coach floor and the level of the
cinder-yard great, the steps perpendicular. He had had to beg
help with his luggage from one of the conducting officers. That
was three years ago, almost to the day. 'Where is this?' he had
asked. The receiving officer had said, 'Premanagar'. Which
meant they were imprisoning him in the fort. After that he had

had to climb unassisted into the back of a police truck. He had barked his shins. But this morning – for it was nearly five o'clock – there were special steps already in position and two railway employees to steady them and him against every eventuality.

Mr Mehboob came fussily across the dimly lit and deserted cinder-yard to greet him and conduct him to the waiting limousine, whose driver held the door open. *Everything has meaning for you, Gaffur,* he quoted silently to himself, *the petal's fall, the change of seasons.*

The railway coach and the limousine both belonged to the Nawab. But this was the last time he would find himself in his kinsman's and Count Bronowsky's debt; or very nearly the last. When what had to be done at the Circuit House had been done he would return to the coach, which was filled with all the accumulated stuff of his life under restriction at Nanoora, and travel on by rail to Ranpur to reoccupy his home permanently. The limousine would return to Mirat. Mehboob had been right. There would have been no point in coming from Nanoora to Premanagar by car when the coach had to come anyway, would leave Nanoora earlier, and offer him a chance to sleep during the hours it was parked in the siding.

The secretary followed him into the Daimler and settled ponderously beside him on the softly cushioned back seat. He had wanted Ahmed beside him. But Mehboob was jealous of his own prerogatives. As a secretary he wasn't a patch on poor old Mahsood and as a man Mr Kasim found him irritatingly like an English caricature of an Indian – possessive towards people with power, arrogant to those with none. Even his physical characteristics now fitted him for the part he played with such breathless intensity. His plumpness was only just short of obesity. His nickname was Booby or Booby-Sahib – a kindly enough invention of Mahsood's (who towards the end when he was losing his grip but refusing to let go was always saying, 'I will ask Booby. I will tell Booby') but which was now used behind Booby's back and sometimes even to his face with less charitable intention. As Mahsood's assistant Booby's liabilities had been less apparent than his assets, chief among which was what had seemed an unrivalled knowledge of party political machinery acquired at grass-root level on the local sub-committees and in the corridors of the provincial legislative assembly. He had first come to

Kasim's notice in 1937 as the backroom man largely responsible for the election campaign that had sent to the assembly another Muslim Congressman, Fariqua Hamidullah Khan. Khan had defeated a Muslim Leaguist whom the League had thought would walk away with the seat – a lean hawk of a man whose expression in defeat had been a sight to see.

In those days Mehboob had been lean too. Kasim had met him in old Hamidullah Khan's house on the painful occasion when he had had to tell the old war-horse that his name wouldn't be going forward to the Governor as a candidate for a portfolio in the first Congress Ministry in Ranpur. He had expected to be given the department of education and there were times, subsequently, when Kasim regretted not having given the old man his chance. A Muslim minister for education might have been quicker (even a man as slowed up by age, vicissitudes and disappointments as Hamidullah Khan) to pounce on or defy the hard-line Hindus who had made it compulsory in the district schools to salute the Congress flag, sing songs which had a Hindu rather than an Indian national connotation, and to teach history in a religious rather than a political context. It had been this more than anything throughout the country that had alerted the Muslims to the dangers of a Hindu-*raj* succeeding a British-*raj* and which had provided Jinnah with the kind of political ammunition he'd been so short of. But Kasim hadn't given Hamidullah Khan his chance and in July 1942 the old man died while on a visit to his ancestral home near Rawalpindi. The next month Kasim was imprisoned in the fort at Premanagar. Released in 1944 to the protective custody of the Nawab, joined by his wife, and presently by old Mahsood, he had looked at his ageing secretary and seen the unmistakable signs of deterioration. 'You need a young assistant,' he had said. 'Perhaps so, Mac-Sahib.' And a day or two later Mahsood had come to him. 'There is a man, poor young Mehboob who got Hamidullah Khan into the assembly. Doing nothing since Khan Sahib died. Like Othello. Occupation gone.' 'Get him,' Kasim had said, recalling the lean young man.

And here he was, Mehboob, Booby, Booby-Sahib, sitting beside him, weighing the Daimler down at the left-hand side.

'Were there any letters after I left?' Mr Kasim asked, turning his attention from the window.

'I have them here,' Mr Mehboob said. 'Three are marked personal so I have not opened them. One of them is from Bapu. Another from your daughter, Mrs Hydyatullah.'

'And the third?'

'From our indefatigable suppliant, Pandit Baba Sahib.'

'You could have looked at that. After all CID will already have done so.'

The door on Mehboob's side opened. Ahmed leaned in.

'Everything is ready,' he said.

'Then come along.'

'I'm going in the escort vehicle.'

'You would be more comfortable here.'

'It's all arranged. An alteration would create confusion.'

Kasim nodded. Ahmed shut the door. The driver got in. Presently the car moved. Kasim closed his eyes and didn't respond when Mehboob said, 'Premanagar very depressed area. Here too much erosion, too much poverty, no industry. Government has just abandoned it as hopeless. Here presently we shall have communists, isn't it? Everyone very bolshie. Why else are they giving us an armed escort?'

Kasim didn't answer. It was mainly Mehboob's fault that Ahmed had elected to go in the other vehicle. His younger son and his new secretary had never pulled on well together. Mehboob despised Ahmed for having no political sense; Ahmed was simply indifferent to Mehboob. He was indifferent to everybody. He lived his own life. He was dutiful when it was necessary to be dutiful. But there was no affection. He had seemed to love only his mother. When she died he had acted as if her death need not have happened, and as if he blamed his father for the fact that she died without having seen Sayed again.

'Give me my daughter's letter, then,' he told Mehboob.

'Light! Light!' Mehboob instructed the driver.

'No, no, no light. Just give me the letter. I'll read it later.'

Mehboob opened his own briefcase, got out some envelopes, leaned forward, putting his face close to them, and eventually handed one to him.

'Did you notice the post-mark?'

'Yes, it is from Lahore.'

'Good. Then she is back from Srinagar.'

'Also I noticed it had been opened. You can always tell.'

'And Bapu's?'

'This too.'

'Achchha.'

He held the letter at an angle to the window getting what light he could to confirm his daughter's handwriting. Politically it didn't bother him that the Lahore Government had intercepted, opened and read the letter and reported its contents to Delhi. Any letter from his daughter could only strengthen the impression Government had that he was being tempted over to the League. Her husband, Hydyatullah, was now an ardent Leaguist and separatist. She had become one too and a potentially staunch supporter of the INA, therefore of Sayed. But privately Kasim was outraged to think that strangers had read the letter. He had never got used to the idea that his personal life was also government property. He folded the letter carefully so that it would fit neatly into the breast pocket of his coat.

'Did anything else of interest happen after I left Nanoora?'

'Government House in Ranpur rang confirming your appointment tomorrow, but I think really to make sure that you had left for Premanagar. Also there was a call from the *Statesman*'s man in Ranpur. He asked if it was true that you were now coming back to Ranpur. I told him that if he was exercising patience the truth or otherwise of this rumour would be revealed to him in due course.'

'You are beginning to talk like Bapu. Was he content with this evasive reply?'

'He wasn't pursuing it further at the moment. He said his paper was very much anxious to obtain an exclusive interview. I said exclusive interviews had never been the Minister's policy.'

'Did he comment on your using that title?'

'No. He called you Minister himself, and was seeking favours. He said, "Has the Minister said anything about the Viceroy's broadcast announcing elections?" I said obviously the Minister has said things about it, all India is saying things and also wondering why really the Viceroy has now flown back to London. So he switched subject. He said, "What is Minister's view of the reports of the death in an air crash of Subhas Chandra Bose?"'

'What did you say?'

'I said the Minister had read these reports and assumed that they were probably correct.'

'And his response?'

'His response was that not everybody assumed this. But he did not pursue it. He was anxious to maintain cordiality and the prospects of an exclusive interview when you get back to Ranpur.'

After a while Kasim said, 'He did not mention Sayed?'

'No, Minister. He did not mention him but of course was thinking and wondering. The newspapers are still saying nothing for the moment.'

When Booby called him Minister to his face he always felt himself being flattered in a way that amounted to a rebuke.

Light was just beginning to come when they reached the Circuit House. Deliberately he kept his eyes lowered so that he would not inadvertently catch a glimpse of the fort. The compound and the Circuit House itself seemed smaller than he remembered them. A year – nearly fifteen months ago – after imprisonment in the fort the whole landscape and everything in it had looked immense. When the car stopped he said, 'I wish to see no one for some time. Ask Ahmed to come and collect me when it is confirmed that there is a room for me to go to and be alone. Then I shall wish to bathe and have breakfast.'

'All that is arranged, Minister. No, no, no, no, no! Wait! Wait!'

Someone had opened the door on Mehboob's side. The door shut again. In the compound Mr Kasim could see figures of men, waiting, one of them with a slung rifle. The sight of the man with the rifle unnerved him. The presence of such a man suggested that they had already brought Sayed from the fort.

'Something is wrong,' he began.

'Nothing is wrong, Minister. All arrangements have been checked, double-checked. It is simply that the British always like to put on a show. Here is Ahmed now.'

Mehboob lowered the window and said, 'Your father is waiting here. Tell them to show you the room and tell them that the Minister will see no one for some time, isn't it? Also that all these people should disperse. It is like a bloody circus.'

'Ahmed –' Kasim said, but Mehboob held up a hand.

'Your father is not wanting anybody. I am waiting here with him until you tell us everything is as he wishes. Private room and no damned reception committee or all that nonsense.'

Ahmed went. Mehboob rolled the window back up and began to complain about the English weakness for making a *tamasha* of everything. 'Take all this show away from them and what is left? Look at all these people milling around in the name of security.'

But, Kasim thought, *tamasha* was precisely what the British could most easily dispense with; and presently when the shadowy figures in the compound had mostly disappeared and the man with the rifle had made himself scarce, going down towards the culvert-entrance, when the compound was quiet, unpopulated, he felt more than ever the weight of the *raj*'s authority; and, feeling it, allowed himself to focus clearly on the dawn-image of the fort – on the place, rather, where the silhouette should be, some miles distant but elevated commandingly above the plain on a hill.

He did not at first identify it. And then did, and stared, fascinated by the evidence of its relatively diminutive proportions. It had originally been a Rajput fort. The Muslims had conquered it. It was they who had built the mosque and the zenana house in the inner courtyard where Kasim had spent his imprisonment. The Mahrattas had invested it. The British had acquired it. So much history in so insignificant a monument? Insignificant, that was to say, in relation to the vast stretches of the Indian plain.

II

Everything has meaning for you, Gaffur: the petal's fall, the change of seasons. New clothes to celebrate the Îd.
    The regard of princes.
    Rocks. These are not impediments. All water flows towards uneasy distances. Life also –

He had bathed and shaved. He had prayed. He had had a light breakfast. Now he had read for the planned ten minutes from the works of Gaffur. He put the book away, retained his spectacles and took his daughter's letter from the table where he had placed it ready. It was dated August 20, six days ago.

'We reached home yesterday and found your letter which of course had been opened. Guzzy suggests that we should send all our letters unsealed to save them this bother but I said why should we save them bother? If they want to pry into our private

affairs let them go to whatever trouble is necessary. Tomorrow
we are having a party to listen to Wavell on the radio which
I expect will be the usual guff, everyone knows he is going to
announce elections. Guzzy says he has no alternative but that the
results will surprise him and force him to recognize the reality of
the problems that divide the country. We were glad to get away
from Kashmir. On VJ day people excelled themselves. The place
was packed with British and Americans and the drunkenness
and vulgarity had to be seen to be believed. I am sorry, daddy,
that we could not break off to go down to Pankot. Poor old
Mahsoodi. I cried all night after getting your telegram (I hope
you got mine? Your letter does not say).

'Poor Sayed has at last been allowed to answer my last letter
to him but of course it tells me nothing that is necessary to hear.
He writes mostly of childhood recollections. Please, daddy,
write to him. He says little but I know he is hurt never to have
heard from you and blames Government since this is the only
explanation he can find as a dutiful and loving son much
devoted to his father. He asks me to tell you to thank Ahmed
for his last note. Soon I hope you will write and tell me you are
back home for good in Ranpur. Then perhaps Guzzy and I can
visit you and bring the children. I never liked coming to
Nanoora since I knew you didn't like being there but stuck it
out. Also it was bad having to get permission, even when darling
mummy was so ill. Guzzy and I were much amused by the
picture in the newspaper of the Governor's stonelaying ceremony in Ranpur. You looked very bored and distinguished, as
Guzzy said "Like a man keeping his own counsel." I was very
proud. In pictures so many people just look like hangers on.
Your loving daughter.'

He refolded the letter and returned it to its envelope, opened
his briefcase and put the envelope inside, then the book of
Gaffur's poems, then his Astrakhan cap. From the briefcase he
took the white Congress cap. In the old days he had been criticized for wearing it. It had not been worn for months. It was
necessary to wear it now. He placed it on his head. The crown of
thorns. It was nearly eight o'clock. At eight, promptly, Mehboob
knocked and came in and stood arrested. Mehboob had never
seen him wearing the cap, except presumably years ago before
they were closely associated.

'It is eight o'clock, Minister,' Booby said. 'They are here.'

'And Sayed?'

'I have not seen Sayed, but they assure me he is here. He is probably still in the compound.'

'Has he breakfasted?'

'I will go and ask, Minister.'

'Please! Do not call me that. And by all means go and ask. It should not be necessary but do it now. You should think of these things. You should anticipate my questions. They have probably pulled him from his bed and brought him here without even asking him if he wants a cup of tea.'

'I will find out –'

'Yes, yes! Find out! I will see nobody until I am assured he has breakfasted. It should all have been thought of.'

Mehboob went. Kasim, after a moment, covered his face with his hands and whispered: 'Glory be to You who made Your servant go by night from the Sacred Mosque to the Farther mosque. Praise be to Allah who has never begotten a son, who has no partner in His Kingdom, who needs none to defend Him from humiliation.'

When Mehboob came back his pale copper-coloured face was flushed. 'I am unable to find out whether Sayed has breakfasted,' he announced.

'What has made you so angry?'

'It is impossible dealing with such people. They cannot answer even civil questions. They treat everybody like dirt.'

'Who are they?'

'Two English subalterns wearing revolvers. They are in the court-room, feet on the table and smirking and hardly bothering to reply.'

'Only these two?'

'There are also the people who were here when we arrived, a police inspector and another young Englishman who is assistant to the Divisional Commissioner. But they are only local, in charge of the general arrangements. They have nothing to do with the party coming from the fort.'

There was a knock on the door. Mehboob opened it just sufficiently to see who it was.

An English voice said, 'The party is fully present now but the senior conducting officer would appreciate a preliminary word with Mr Kasim.'

'Who is that?' Kasim called out. Mehboob opened the door wider. A young English civilian stepped in.

'Good-morning, sir. My name's Everett. I'm assistant to Mr Harding, the Divisional Commissioner. He asked me to apologize for not being here himself. I hope the arrangements have been all right, so far?'

'Thank you, Mr Everett. Perfectly satisfactory. Is Lieutenant Kasim here now?'

'Yes, sir.'

'He was not a moment ago and my secretary had difficulty in getting an answer to the question whether he had breakfasted properly.'

'Yes, I know. That was unfortunate. But I've just asked the senior conducting officer myself and he assures me your son had a good breakfast.'

'And the senior conducting officer wants to have a word with me?'

'Yes, if that's all right −', Everett broke off because Ahmed tapped at the open door and now came in − , 'and if it might be in private.'

'I'll let you know. I'll send word.'

Everett went out, closing the door.

'Have you seen your brother, Ahmed?'

'No, but I've seen the conducting officer. I thought I'd better warn you. It's Merrick.'

'Merrick?'

'The ex-police officer in the Manners case, the one Pandit Baba's been pestering you about. I didn't know Merrick had anything to do with the INA, but he was in the army in intelligence when we met him in Mirat. Actually I saw him again in Bombay about three weeks ago. He said he was working in Delhi.'

'Ah, yes. That Merrick. The one Dmitri told me was badly wounded. You never told me you saw him again so recently.'

'I haven't seen much of you since getting back. And the case didn't seem to interest you.'

'No,' Kasim said. 'But perhaps it will. He knows you know him in connection with that old case?'

'Yes.'

'So he will assume that by now I know too. In fact he would probably assume that you would be here with me to meet your brother, which means that he does not in the least mind my knowing who he is. But he must know, mustn't he, Booby, that he is on the List?'

'It is clear, Minister. He hopes to ingratiate himself somehow. You could always say you will meet nobody except Sayed.'

'What is his rank, Ahmed?'

'Major, I think.'

'Since you know him it would be a good idea if you went now and brought him along personally. Go with Ahmed, Booby. I shan't want you again until all this is over. Meanwhile open and read the letter from Bapu so that we can discuss it later. Ahmed – give me one minute, please, before you bring Major Merrick.'

When they had gone Kasim went to the single window, which overlooked the inner courtyard. A policeman with a rifle was posted nearby facing towards him. There were bars but no glass in the window frame. Kasim closed the inner shutters. The only light in the room now came from the single naked bulb in the centre and from the high fanlight on the wall that faced the front compound. The furniture was sparse: a string charpoy with a mattress, two wooden armchairs and two smaller chairs, a table. He made a move to sit at the chair behind the table but then decided to remain standing.

'Major Merrick? Please come in.'

Ahmed, who had opened the door and stood aside without entering, let Merrick through and then closed it. Kasim offered his hand and felt a twinge of pity for a man with such a badly disfigured face and such an obviously useless left arm, clamped to his body with the cap tucked under it at elbow level and a briefcase suspended from the gloved fingers of an artificial hand. The man said, 'Actually Lieut.-Colonel, since I and your younger son last met, Mr Kasim.'

The grip of the right hand was strong, like the voice. Kasim indicated a seat and sat down himself. He now noted the pip and crown on each shoulder tab, the regimental name and the ribbon of the DSO. He watched while Merrick dealt with his cap by removing it from under the left arm, placing it on the table, and with his briefcase by removing it from the artificial hand and placing it on the table too, next to the hat. He glanced at the inner side of his right wrist, checking the time.

'I'm sorry about the few minutes' delay, but when we arrived your elder son asked for a few minutes alone before he came in. So I sent the others along and waited near the car. But I assure you his reason was not because he felt unwell as a result of not having had an adequate breakfast –' Merrick smiled. The effect was strange, lopsided. He continued – 'Nor as a result of in-adequate sleep. We reached the fort early enough yesterday even-ing to let him rest up after the journey from Delhi. The journey itself was not very taxing. We flew to Ranagunj and came on by road. In fact I believe you'll be much tireder than he because I gather you travelled down overnight and only got here an hour or so ago. Incidentally, Mr Everett tells me your secretary may have been upset by the two young officers' apparently unhelpful attitude over the question of what kind of breakfast your son had. The explanation is that they had no idea what he had, since I breakfasted with him alone. They are only temporary escorts. They reported to me at Ranagunj in exchange for two other officers who came with me on the plane. They have no informa-tion about any of us. All they know is that the Indian officer is in custody.'

'The question of Sayed's breakfast has already been satisfac-torily answered, Colonel Merrick. So far as I'm concerned it is a closed subject. Incidentally, my younger son Ahmed had no idea you were in any way connected with Sayed. Does Sayed know that you know his brother?'

'The one is a social acquaintance. The other is not. So the answer is, no.'

'Please tell me what is the purpose of this preliminary private word?'

'The purpose is to tell you as much as possible about the charges which Lieutenant Sayed Kasim will probably have to face.'

Kasim hoped that he betrayed no surprise. But he was sur-prised. He said: 'I have not asked for this. I'm not sure that I wish to be told anything about such matters. My son must himself have a good idea what charges there may be. What can you tell me that he cannot?'

Merrick said, 'Naturally, Mr Kasim, it's entirely up to you whether we have a preliminary word. It wasn't my own department's idea, but Government seemed to think it fair.'

'Fair?'

'The charges and evidence in these cases aren't fully prepared yet by any means. But Government feels that your son would be much more at ease if he doesn't have to tell you everything himself.' Merrick paused. 'It could after all be a bit painful for him.'

'Painful?'

Merrick kept him waiting for a reply. He seemed utterly composed and in command. 'He has never struck me as being among those who are unrepentantly proud of the situation they find themselves in.'

For the first time Kasim was unable to keep his eyes unwaveringly on the man. He glanced down and carefully covered his right hand with his left to control the familiar tremor before it began.

'Very well,' he said. 'Tell me what you wish. But as briefly as possible.'

'A charge of waging war against the King-Emperor is of course going to be the almost unavoidable common charge to be faced in these cases and in your son's case the evidence is incontrovertible since he was captured fighting in one of the INA units that accompanied the Japanese when they tried to invade India in 1944 and got as far as Manipur and Kohima. The unit he commanded surrendered voluntarily and seemed to have been abandoned in an untenable position by the Japanese, without access to any supplies or lines of communication. I'm afraid one often found that. Voluntary surrender or no, however, he was in arms, waging war.'

'You were in that theatre of war yourself, Colonel?'

'I was on the staff of one of the divisions that were brought up to mount the counter-attack. As an intelligence officer the INA became my special concern.'

'Were you present when Sayed was brought in?'

'No, I was out of the line by then.'

'Wounded you mean, thus?' Kasim indicated the arm.

'Yes. Thus.'

'By INA action?'

'There were INA about. Japanese as well. Why do you ask?'

'The reason is obvious, surely? A man wounded as badly as you could be forgiven for accepting a job that gave him an opportunity to redress the balance.'

'One does the job one is given. But I take your point. The INA were involved in the incident but I was wounded entirely by my own fault.'

'How was it your own fault?'

'I was trying to stop a fellow officer acting thoughtlessly.' Merrick paused. 'You asked me to be brief –'

'I know, but I should like to hear about this other matter. It is all relevant to my rather sparse knowledge of the INA.'

'Very briefly, then. I'd gone forward to collect an INA prisoner. At that time they were rather a rare species. The sepoys of the Indian Army tended to shoot them out of hand. This prisoner was originally from the Muzzafirabad Guides. The officer who was on the same divisional staff as myself was also Muzzafirabad Guides. He insisted on going with me and when the man said there were two other INA ex–Muzzy Guides soldiers hiding in the jungle near by waiting to give themselves up the officer suggested we went to collect them. I said we shouldn't, but the next thing I knew was he'd taken our jeep, and the prisoner, and gone forward to do just that. I borrowed another jeep and went after them. When I found them the jeep was under fire and on fire. The prisoner had decamped, presumably to rejoin the enemy, and the officer was burning to death. I pulled him and the driver out but it was too late to save the officer.'

'Was he a friend of yours?'

'We knew one another pretty well. At least since I acted as his best man. At his wedding in Mirat. I expect Ahmed will have told you about the wedding. Ahmed, or Count Bronowsky.'

'The wedding. Ah, yes.'

'But I think it fair to say I went after the officer only to secure the prisoner, who was my responsibility. The result was hardly the prisoner's fault, nor was it really the officer's. I needn't have followed. He was one of those men with the not un-common idea that any sepoy who'd been in the regiment would only have to come face to face with one of the officers of that regiment to throw his gun down and return contrite to the fold. I took the less romantic view that guns only got thrown down when the alternative was hunger and no other escape-route.'

'As in Sayed's case?'

'I don't think you'll find he pretends otherwise. And being an officer he was responsible for the lives of the men in what remained of his unit.'

'You've interrogated Sayed often?'

'Since joining the department several months ago I have talked to him quite frequently, yes.'

'Forgive these questions. An old lawyer's habit. Please go on. He was captured originally by the Japanese in Kuala Lumpur in ninteen forty-two when the Japanese defeated the British Army there.'

'The British Army and the Indian Army. Yes. Of course you know he asserts he didn't join the INA until after August nineteen forty-two when he heard of the arrests in India after the Congress Quit India resolution – arrests which included your own. He told you this in his first letter home, after we'd re-captured him. I'm afraid copies of all his letters in and out have had to be made.'

'Don't apologize, Colonel. I am used to that sort of thing. In the same letter to my late wife he apologized for having failed in the march on Delhi.'

'It was probably the same letter. I remember the phrase from my study of his file.'

'Tell me, Colonel Merrick. How does this apology for having failed in the march on Delhi balance with your view that he is not among those unrepentantly proud of the situation he finds himself in? Which situation do you mean? His situation as a Lieutenant of the Ranpur Regiment, now your prisoner awaiting trial for waging war against the King, or his situation as a Major in the INA who failed in his march on Delhi to free India from the British but lives to tell the tale?'

'It's more than a year since he wrote that letter.'

'You mean he has had second thoughts?'

'Frankly, Mr Kasim, I should say he had had a great number of thoughts. For the past year he hasn't had much to occupy his mind except the single subject of why he decided to switch his allegiance.'

'And wage war against the King. Yes.' Kasim waited, then said, 'What other charges?'

'Incitement? Abetment? Bringing aid and comfort to the

enemy? As I said, charges aren't framed. But your son has admitted to helping to recruit other Indian POWs into the INA and also
to helping devise propaganda about the INA and broadcasting on
one occasion to India, incognito.'

'Is there any more serious factor that may have to be considered?'

'More serious factor, Mr Kasim?'

'One hears gossip, tales, possibly exaggerated, or so one hopes,
that recruitment was not always voluntary, that in a few cases
certain methods were used to persuade sepoy prisoners-of-war
to join.'

'You mean brutal methods?'

'Yes, I mean that.'

'And what you want to know is whether this is a factor that
may have to be considered in your son's case and might lead to
a charge that he used such methods himself?'

'Yes.'

After some moments Merrick glanced at the table. The one
good eyebrow contracted slightly. Kasim wondered whether the
full ramifications of the question of brutality were lost on him.
They could not be if his reputation from the time of the Bibighar
was deserved. But perhaps that reputation was simply the result
of rumour too.

'A factor that may have to be considered?' Merrick repeated
to himself. He looked at Kasim again. 'The only answer I can give
you, Mr Kasim, is that I don't know. I can assure you it hasn't
arisen yet but it would be quite unrealistic of me to assure you that
it can't arise.'

'You mean there are indications that such accusations may be
made against Sayed?'

'On the contrary. A lot of evidence has been collected of
cases of torture and brutal behaviour and several officers and
NCOs have been named, but your son's name has never been
among them. In fact the men who surrendered with him have
invariably spoken of him with great respect, particularly in
regard to his care for their welfare and for the way he stood up
to Japanese officers when this was necessary. No, my point is
that the men we have access to, those already recaptured, represent only a percentage of the eventual sources of evidence. There
are all those still in Malaya for instance. I can't vouch for what
some of them may or may not say about your son's conduct

once we've got hold of them. It was a very large army.' He hesitated, then added, 'I'm exceeding my brief expressing a personal opinion, but I shall express it none the less since you seem concerned. I should be very surprised if at any time between now and the completion of the collection of all the evidence in all the cases your son is implicated in any charges other than those I've mentioned.'

'Yes. I see. Thank you. And this is all you have to tell me?'

'I think so. I hope it's helped you in a general way.'

'Yes.' He made a snap decision. 'Tell me, Colonel Merrick – are you still troubled as I understood from Ahmed you were – I mean troubled by incidents devised to remind you that your conduct as Superintendent of Police in Mayapore – I should say suspected conduct – had made you unpopular in certain quarters and wasn't going to be forgotten?'

Merrick smiled. A cheerful smile, Kasim thought.

'Not until recently.'

'Another stone?'

Merrick reached for his briefcase and began to manipulate the artificial hand back round the handle while he continued speaking. 'No, there's only been the one stone. Chucking stones at British officers *is* rather a hazardous operation. They've reverted to the subtle approach. The bicycle again.'

'Bicycle?'

'A bicycle. Left on my verandah. Rusty and useless, naturally.'

'A rusty bicycle left on your verandah, Colonel Merrick? What purpose does this serve?'

'It's obviously a symbol of the bicycle I'm supposed to have planted outside the house of one of the boys who assaulted Miss Manners. Miss Manners's bicycle.' He stood up. So, after a moment, did Kasim. 'The bicycle's rather a good touch. They began after I'd left Mayapore just by chalking inauspicious signs outside the door of my bungalow. Then one day there was this rusty old bicycle outside my quarters. That was in Mirat, just before someone chucked the stone. The incidents have a twofold purpose, of course – to let me know it's known where I'm currently living and working – which they do – and to undermine me psychologically – which they don't.'

'When and where was this new incident, this second bicycle?'

'According to my cook, about a week ago in Delhi. I've been

down in Ceylon and Rangoon and got back only just in time to accompany your son here. My cook said he found it leaning against the verandah rail one morning. He got the sweeper to take it to the back of the compound because there was a bad smell which he traced to the saddle-bag. He wouldn't touch it himself after that because the smell was that of a putrid pork chop. Since he's a Muslim I've had some difficulty in persuading him to stay. He's a very good cook. He cooks fresh pork chops for me quite happily. Just seems to draw the line at putrid ones in the saddle-bags of rusty bikes.'

Kasim averted his face to disguise his own revulsion.

'You should report such things to the police.'

'I always do. It doesn't bother me personally but then whoever is responsible for this kind of childish persecution isn't really in the least concerned either about me or about what are no doubt still called the innocent victims of the Bibighar. The Bibighar affair was used as an excuse to stir up trouble generally and it rather looks to me as if it's going to be given another innings in conjunction with the INA cases because it's been discovered I'm connected with them.'

'Given another innings by whom, Colonel Merrick?'

'By whoever prefers anarchy to law and order. Has Count Bronowsky never talked to you while you've been living in Nanoora, about the power exercised in India by uncommitted and irresponsible forces? He was very eloquent about it on the first occasion I met him.'

'Count Bronowsky and I don't have an intimate relationship, in spite of my younger son's connection with him. He and I are politically opposed. He is dedicated to the continuing autocratic authority of the Nawab. I am dedicated to the diminution and final extinction of the autocratic authority of *all* the Indian princes. My respect for Count Bronowsky has become quite strong since I've lived under restriction at the Nawab's court, but we are still political opponents and seldom exchange views.'

'I suppose you and I are potentially opponents too, Mr Kasim.'

'You and I?'

'I and your party. Surely I'm on the list?'

'What list, Colonel Merrick?'

'The list of officials whose conduct in nineteen forty-two may be inquired into. I'm told it looks as if I'm likely to be on it.'

'Told by whom?'

'The CID officer I reported the new incident to. Not that it surprised me. The fact that the subject has come up at a political level is sufficient warning. Anyway, if I'm not on it yet I imagine from what I'm told that my old friend Pandit Baba of Mayapore won't be happy until I am. Of course it's he who's responsible for the childish persecution, but there's never been any clear evidence to connect him with it. He's not a very connectable man. You can't pin him down with any certainty even as a member of the militant wing of the Hindu Mahasabah. But he has a genius for inspiring young men to sacrifice themselves in whatever cause he's currently taken up. I admired him rather. In Mayapore whenever we caught one of his disciples as they called themselves breaking the law they always swore the only thing they discussed with the Pandit was the Bhagavad Gita and went willingly to prison. What I admired was his power to inspire such loyalty. In those days his activities were more tiresome than dangerous but I should say he's capable of graduating to better things. Assassination, for instance. You know the man I mean, Mr Kasim?'

Kasim smiled.

'I have never met him. I think now I must see Sayed. You are due to take him back to the fort when?'

'When your meeting is finished.'

'And when do you take him back to Delhi?'

'This evening.'

'By road to Ranagunj and then by aeroplane?'

'Yes. I must be in Delhi tomorrow. I have to fly back to Kandy and from there probably to Singapore.'

'Then I will say good-bye to you now, Colonel Merrick.' Again he made a snap decision. 'I don't think we shall ever be opposed in the sense you mean. Not you and I personally. I am not interested in past quarrels, only in solving present and future problems. It is the only way any of us will ever make progress.'

'Quite. Quite.'

For the first time Merrick looked uncertain of himself, disappointed, if the unscarred side of his face was anything to go by. Kasim thought: He's proud to be on the list, in which case what people said about his conduct in Mayapore is probably true.

The man reached for his cap. Kasim did not watch him go through the awkward motions of tucking it under his left arm.

'I'll bring Sayed now,' Merrick said. He hesitated then went towards the door.

'No, please do not bring him. I wish our meeting to be completely in private and in any case it would offend me to see him physically in the custody of anyone. And there is another thing –'

He went over to the window. 'This room is very hot and dark. It is like a cell. I closed these shutters because there is a guard outside whose presence disturbs me. I know that guards are necessary – if only as a formality since Sayed could hardly effect a credible escape in the middle of this desert.' He opened the shutters and breathed deeply. The guard was still there, just out of earshot. 'So I apologize for any inconvenience but I think I should prefer to see Sayed in the court-room. At least it will be larger and airier and they can post as many men outside as they wish. That should take only a few minutes to arrange, shouldn't it? Just a question of clearing the other people out. Perhaps you'd be so kind as to send someone to let me know when everything is ready.'

'I'll come myself, Mr Kasim.'

'That is kind of you.'

III

He realized how little he could have seen of the Circuit House on that previous visit fifteen months ago. He did not recognize the corridor that Merrick now led him along. They stopped at a door. Merrick opened it on to a small room.

'This isn't the court-room,' Kasim said. 'It's the magistrate's room.'

'It's the best way in.'

'No! The worst! How can I enter the court-room through the judge's door? Where have you put Sayed? In the dock?'

'I can bring him here if that's what you'd prefer.'

'I wish no one to *bring* him anywhere.' He felt ill. He turned back into the corridor whose series of grimy windows gave on to the verandah of the inner courtyard. The place stank of unresolved cases, of the acrid odour of legal millstones grinding fine and slow between sessions; and of his youth, pleading interminable cases in court-houses such as this. After all, interviewing

Sayed in the court-room would be a mistake. It would be like putting him on trial. But then, for Kasim, what was about to follow *was* Sayed's trial.

'Mr Kasim, are you all right?'

'I am perfectly all right. It is just that –'

He broke off. There was a third man whom Merrick was urging forward from the open doorway; a tall man, taller than himself, broad-boned, well-fleshed, dressed like an active-service officer in dark green cotton uniform; pale brown skin, dark-browed, brown-eyed. Between the nostrils and the lip a moustache grew, close-cropped in the British style. The hair was cropped too, but not too close. A fine-looking man. Only the eyes betrayed a weakness: the weakness that accompanied an uncertainty about the warmth of his reception.

But Sayed did not wait to find out what kind of reception he would get. Silently, effortlessly, in one flowing movement he knelt at Kasim's feet, placed his hands on Kasim's shoes, lowered his head to his hands and then raised it, at the same time removing his hands. As he rose Kasim instinctively performed his own task, putting his arms round him. So, for a moment, they remained.

'Come, let us go through,' Kasim said, and released his son. Merrick was walking down the corridor, his back to them; but he had been a witness. Kasim led the way through the magistrate's room, out on to the daïs in the court-room and down into the well of the court. He stopped by one of the pleaders' tables; that table at which Sayed must have been sitting. There were an empty coffee cup and a used cigarette tray. The smell of tobacco smoke hung in the air. He still drank too, probably, like Ahmed, but with at least the excuse that it was a habit acquired in army messes, just to prove equal capacity with British officers. But the smoking was new and despite himself Kasim found the dirty ashtray repugnant. He said nothing, but Sayed, also without a word, removed it, took it across to the other table.

'Please, there is no need. If smoking has become necessary to you, smoke by all means. It doesn't bother me.'

But Sayed left the ashtray where he had put it and came back, stood; the weakness was still discernible, the uncertainty was still there, in the eyes. Kasim sat. From this angle his elder son looked even taller and broader. Both Ahmed and Sayed dwarfed him but Sayed would make even Ahmed look slenderly built. The periods of privation must have been of short duration, unless the British had been feeding him up.

'Come, sit.'

Sayed did so.

'Have you seen Ahmed yet?'

'Not yet, father. But Ronald told me he's here.'

'Ronald?'

'Ronald Merrick. The chap you've been talking to. He said he'd make sure Ahmed and I had a word afterwards. He's quite a good fellow really. Very decent to me.'

The voice was strong too, the accent clipped, more clipped than Kasim remembered from their last meeting, certainly more clipped than it had been after Sayed had passed out of the Indian military academy when Kasim had told him, 'You sound like a British officer.' They had both laughed. He could have stopped Sayed choosing the army as a career. He had been criticized for not stopping him. It hadn't always been easy for him to explain why he had a son who held the King-Emperor's Commission. It couldn't always have been easy for Sayed when young Englishmen, fellow members of the mess, learnt who his father was. But Sayed had never complained and when Kasim became Chief Minister in Ranpur any embarrassment Sayed might have felt vanished. He remembered Sayed saying, 'You are a Minister. I am an officer. We are both necessary.' He had meant necessary to India and Kasim had been moved.

'How are you treated then? You look well. Put on an inch or two. Like Ahmed. As you see, I have taken off. Who is commandant at the fort nowadays? Still Major Tippet?'

'I don't know, father. I was only there overnight. You were there too?'

'Oh yes. Better than the Kandipat although boring after a bit. They gave me a room in the old Zenana House. I wonder whether my bed of onions is still flourishing? It was in a courtyard a few feet from the steps to the Zenana. I watered them mostly with the water from my shaving mug. So this is how they tasted. Of soap. What one will do to keep oneself occupied. But onions are good for warding off colds. So your mother always said.'

The muscular geography of his son's face momentarily revealed itself: an intricate map. The eyes hardened. Kasim folded his hands on the table. He said, 'When I was released to go to Mirat they brought me here first of all to meet Ahmed. Now that I'm going back home it seemed a convenient place to tell them to bring you. If I had come to Delhi the world and his wife would have been watching. Anyway, it gives you an outing. What did they tell you? Anything?'

'First they just told me to get ready for a trip. But then Ronnie Merrick got back from Rangoon and put me in the picture. He said Government had given permission for us to meet and that he was coming with me.'

'The impression was that I had petitioned Government and that Government had decided to be magnanimous?'

'Yes.'

'It is not entirely accurate.'

'Oh, I didn't swallow it whole. I know how devious they can be.'

'In this case devious to what end?'

Kasim waited. Sayed said nothing.

'Come. Don't hold back. Just because I am your father.'

Sayed looked down at the table. 'They know you've never written to me. They think this shows you disapprove of what I've done.' He glanced up. 'It would be very useful to them to have someone like you on their side. A member of Congress, ex-Chief Minister. And a Muslim. Someone to denounce us all as traitors. They realize such people will be in short supply.'

'Quite so. Both major parties will stand behind the INA. The true nature and extent of INA came as a surprise to many of us. But people who are locked up a long time have a lot of surprises in store when they mingle freely again and find out what has been going on. So among us at Simla it was generally agreed that INA would be supported.'

'Generally, not unanimously?'

'Quite clearly all parties will combine to organize the defence if these cases ever come to trial. Whether they will do so is up to the Viceroy and the Commander-in-Chief. It will be interesting to see how they solve the problem of who should be tried and who should not. From a legal point of view the entire matter is without precedent. Administratively it is farcical. Some kind of legal strategy will have to be evolved to uphold the spirit if not the letter of the law. But I am sure the British will find a way.

They have considerable experience of how to deal pragmatically with situations which pose profound questions. They cannot just say, You have sinned, go home and repent, without running the risk of their entire Indian Army resigning *en masse* by way of protest and going home also. On the other hand they cannot court-martial every INA soldier because it would take several years to do so. On top of that, it is not in them to find a solution such as the Germans might have found. Or the Japanese. It is not in them to line you all up in a concentration camp and shoot you out of hand. It is not in them politically and it is not in them emotionally. What can they do? The answer is fairly clear. They must establish a scale of priorities. In such a scale every King's Commissioned Officer who joined INA will be at the top. He cannot hope to escape being cashiered at the very least. Your military career is finished, Sayed. You must make up your mind to that. Even if the British left India tomorrow it would be finished. Because whatever we politicians say and however stoutly we defend you, the loyal Indian members of the Indian Army will not defend you. Why should they? It is against their interests. They are on the winning side. Whatever military plums there are to pick when we are independent they will claim properly as theirs. Why should they share them with Subhas Chandra Bose's defeated people? Of course it would be different if the British had lost the war. Then you'd be in clover. But they've won it. Your first error, a very pardonable one, was perhaps to have assumed in nineteen forty-two they'd already lost it. Isn't this so, Sayed? Isn't it this more than anything else that persuaded you to join INA? Isn't it this more than the fact that you heard I and most other Congressmen had been imprisoned and that the whole country was in turmoil that decided you?'

'No, father. It was entirely because you were arrested along with everybody else and that the whole of India was rising and telling the British to quit.'

'Who told you I was arrested?'

'Shah Nawaz Khan. General Shah Nawaz Khan. Originally a captain in the Punjab Regiment. But so far as I'm concerned, *General*. He came up to Kuala Lumpur in nineteen forty-two as commander of all Indian prisoners-of-war parties. I knew him slightly. He was a very good officer. He stopped the Japanese doing all sorts of things to us.'

'But he was INA?'

'He had joined, yes, but only to stop the Japs exploiting Indian prisoners and to wreck the INA from inside if necessary. I am talking of first INA, under Mohan Singh. But you must know all this.'

'No, tell me.'

'Mohan Singh was also Punjab Regiment. Shah Nawaz said he thought him a very average officer. Mohan Singh was captured somewhere like Alor Star. People say he had a bad time with his British officers and that they left him to face the Japanese alone. He started organizing the prisoners. When the British surrendered at Singapore all the Indian officers were separated from the British and made to assemble with all the Indian troops at Farrer Park and handed over by the representative of the British Government, to an intelligence officer called Fujiwara and given orders to obey the Japanese. Then Fujiwara handed them over to Mohan Singh. Fujiwara said Mohan Singh was their GOC and had power of life and death over them. I was not in Singapore then. But this is what I was told.'

'Who are you saying gave the prisoners orders to obey the Japanese?'

'The British Government representative.'

'All prisoners of course must obey the lawful orders of their captors. There is nothing much to be made of that. More interesting is the order for the separation of British King's Commissioned Officers from Indian King's Commissioned Officers. By whose order was this separation?'

'The Japanese, presumably. But I never heard any protests from the British. They were too interested in saving their own skins. As at Kuala Lumpur. "Hold this position, Kasim old chap," Colonel Barker said. So I held it while the rest of the battalion and all the British officers disappeared. I held it for four days. Nothing happened for three of them. In three days Colonel Barker and the others got down to Johore. He got one of the last ships out of Singapore or Malacca, I don't know which. All I know is that on the fourth day the Japs came and that on the fifth we couldn't hold them off any longer. We had nothing. Nothing to eat. No ammunition. At the time I said, Well, it is war. Somebody has to carry the can. Since then I thought there was another explanation. Here in India, father, the army looks very sound, very pukka, very good form and very secure, very gentlemanly. In Burma and Malaya you realized a lot of it was eyewash. They never wanted us. They never trusted us.'

He took his father's hand, leaning forward, lowering his voice. 'But I have seen senior British officers in Singapore and in Rangoon bowing to Japanese sentries. And I have seen senior British officers slapped and kicked for not bowing, and *then* bowing.' He leant back. 'So much for the *raj*. They too can be made to act like peons. I shall never forget.'

Hand free, Kasim held it out, palm towards Sayed and shut his eyes. 'Please. Forget all this. I have heard all this sort of thing before. It is of no importance. It will not help you in any way whatsoever. It's your conduct that is in question not the conduct or misconduct of this British officer or that British officer. Let us speak no more of disparities between British officers and Indian officers. If you try to do this in court-martial prosecuting counsel will eat you alive and spit you out as a silly boy with a grudge.'

'I wanted you to know —'

'I know. I *do* know. But when you are court-martialled you will be well advised to give quite a different picture and pretend it has never entered your head that your commanding officer treated his white officers in one way and his Indian subaltern in another. If necessary praise him. Adopt a soldierly attitude to this matter. Do not antagonize the court. It will be a military court. Even if one of its members is an Indian officer — which is almost bound to be so to preserve the idea of impartiality — do not be tempted to raise the question of this disparity. Secretly he might agree with you but it will embarrass him and put him further against you. He will be already against you because he will be thinking: Here is this young fellow who is only a lieutenant but calling himself major and also being called a hero by the politicians and the people and here am I, still a captain after twenty years of loyal service to the *raj*.'

He hesitated, then said, 'What is wrong, Sayed?'

Sayed's eyes had become tearful. He bent his head. He said, 'I'm sorry, father. I prepared myself to find that you weren't going to help me. I was wrong. I'm ashamed to have thought it. All this is very good. Very helpful.'

Kasim felt himself begin to tremble. He said, 'Clearly I must help you. I'm not only your father but a man who happens to know something about the law and the way the law works. You are to clear your mind of every consideration except that of your defence. Neither of us can wish to see you sent to rigorous imprisonment or transportation for life. That you will be cashiered and finished for ever with the army is sufficient punishment.'

'Finished for ever?'

'For ever. It is my opinion. I have told you why. So. As I say. Clear your mind. Shah Nawaz Khan told you in Kuala Lumpur that Congress Party leaders in India had been arrested and that I was among them and that the country was rising against the British. This led to your decision to join INA. What you call first INA. Why did it? Let me suggest why. Naturally you were angry that your father had been put in prison simply because he was a leading member of Congress. But then you calmed down. You sat back and considered the situation. The British had been defeated in France. They had been defeated in Burma and Malaya. The Japanese held the Chindwin. Beyond the Chindwin lay India. In India the population appeared to have been driven to desperation and had risen against the *raj*. Although your father was a politician you yourself were politically uneducated. Like Ahmed you have never bothered much about such matters. You did not fully understand why Congress passed a resolution calling on the British to quit but broadly you understood it was because in a war for freedom India should also be free. Also you understood that everyone felt that so long as the British remained in Delhi the Japanese were bound to attack your country. Now. The Japanese were pretending to be friendly towards the Indians as fellow-Asians, but you did not trust them. If they invaded India and as seemed likely again defeated the British the very clear danger was that far from gaining the independence which the British themselves had promised, India would again become subject to a foreign government, this time a Japanese government. A Japanese *raj*. And what could you do about that, sitting in Kuala Lumpur as their prisoners-of-war?'

'What indeed?'

'It was a terrible problem. On the one hand you felt you could not just sit in Kuala Lumpur waiting to be told that Hirohito was now the titular ruler of Hindustan. On the other hand not to sit around would mean appearing to kowtow to the Japanese and disregarding your oath to the King-Emperor. To escape from prison-camp was one thing – virtually impossible though that was in the Far East. To secure your release by throwing in your lot with an organization which the Japanese had helped to bring into being was another. Moreover, should the INA ever march with the Japanese into India, march with whatsoever patriotic intention, there would be the inevitable armed confrontation with those of your own countrymen who were still serving under the British flag.

'How could these problems be resolved? The answer was they could *not* be resolved. You had to choose. And you could not see into the future. You had no crystal ball. You had to weigh one possibility against another possibility and make a decision. And then one day you looked around and perhaps remembered some of the things the Japanese had done. And you remembered how this Shah Nawaz Khan had stopped them doing such things in this place or that place. And you thought of the Japanese doing or trying to do these things in India and how it was necessary to stop them doing them.

'Then for the first time you saw clearly what the problem was, that it was a question of choosing between your own integrity and your country's integrity. Only an officer who was a national of a country already under foreign rule could ever face this dilemma. But this is an explanation, Sayed, not an excuse. Legally it isn't even a mitigating circumstance, so put that out of your mind. Go back to Kuala Lumpur and your decision to join Shah Nawaz Khan. You asked to see him and told him you'd made your mind up to join INA?'

'Not quite like that. And he made a point of never persuading anybody against their own judgment. I didn't decide until the end of September. He'd gone back to Singapore then. While he was in KL things improved for us but after he'd gone there were several incidents.'

'What kind of incidents?'

'For example. Before Shah Nawaz came to KL the Japanese were forcing our jawans to learn Japanese foot drill, things like that. He stopped them. He told me it was what the English prisoners in Rangoon were having to do and that it showed the Japanese intended to make us all puppets if they could. When he had gone it started again. I protested, but it made no difference.

One sepoy who refused became very ill. The Japanese must have beaten him up pretty badly.'

'The sepoy's name?'

'I don't remember. It was happening too often.'

'More than one sepoy, then.'

'Yes, more than one.'

'And you took a risk, protesting?'

'That didn't matter.'

'You were in some kind of position of authority in this camp?'

'Only a section of the camp. And as a prisoner oneself one's power was limited. I was responsible for this section, though.'

'But you were only a lieutenant.'

Sayed glanced up.

'Shah Nawaz and Mohan Singh were only captains. How many Indian majors, colonels and brigadiers do you know of, father? Do you personally know any Indian generals? The British have always been careful to see that no Indian officer rises high enough to be in a position of much authority.'

'Again I must warn you not to say such things at your court-martial. Please try to concentrate. What steps did you take at the end of September when you came to the decision to join INA?'

'I spoke to two INA officers who visited the camp.'

'Officers visiting for recruitment purposes?'

'Only partly. Mainly to make sure for Shah Nawaz Khan that we were not being exploited. I told them about the sepoy who had been hurt. They got permission to take him to their house. They gave him good food and medical attention.'

'But you don't remember his name?'

'Perhaps it was a name like Laksham. He was a non-combatant. A sweeper, I think. I'm not sure.'

'I ask because if this man has survived his testimony might be useful to you.'

'I understand that, father. I don't know whether he survived.'

'Well, go on. You told these two INA officers that you'd thought about it very hard and had decided to join the INA.'

'Yes.'

'They were pleased of course.'

'Yes, but they advised caution and to say nothing to the Japanese. They promised to speak to Shah Nawaz Khan and Mohan Singh in Singapore.'

'Why this caution?'

'Things were very difficult just then. The INA faced a crisis. Mohan Singh was not strong enough. Many officers were afraid he would let the Japanese use the INA for their own purposes. Also there were many different opinions among INA officers about legality and such-like. They told me that at one time an INA party had even been sent to infiltrate across the Chindwin and contact Congress in India.'

'Seeking Indian political approval of the INA?'

'Yes.'

'I did not know this. This is new to me. What happened to the infiltrating party?'

'It failed. But one of them deserted and got through to the British and presumably told them everything that was going on. Meanwhile you were all being locked up so there was no one left to contact even if another party had been sent.'

'Good. Good. So you were all still in the dark and had no crystal ball. It supports the argument I am outlining. And here there is an attempt to act constitutionally in some way. Democratically. Patriotically certainly. What INA were pondering then is the question what is the will of the people of India in this matter? Do they want an INA? And now getting no answer and realizing that it will not be possible now to get an answer. Go on.'

'The two officers said I would be a useful officer in a properly constituted free Indian Army. They said they'd have a word with Shah Nawaz Khan and Mohan Singh but that I should be patient meanwhile and say nothing. They said Shah Nawaz had had a very disagreeable experience down in Singapore opening a new officers' training school and then having to close it almost at once because the Japanese told Mohan Singh it couldn't be tolerated or something like that. The Japs wanted complete control. In their hearts some of their officers despised us and Mohan Singh was unable to resist them effectively.'

'So you continued a prisoner?'

'Yes.'

'Taking care of your men. Good. Did you ever discuss these matters with them?'

'Sometimes I talked to the NCOs so that they could tell the sepoys and give them some hope for the future, poor fellows.'

'Then what happened?'

'Then I became quite unwell for a time.'

'Why was this?'

'A Japanese officer humiliated me in front of the jawans.'

'Tell me about this humiliation.'

'He assembled all my men and stood me in front of them. He said Lieutenant Kasim would now have personal lessons in Japanese drill and words of command so that he in turn could teach these lessons himself.'

'So you had these lessons. In front of your own men?'

'No, I refused.'

'You said you were humiliated. If you refused what humiliation existed?'

'The humiliation existed because of what he said in front of everybody after I'd refused.'

'What did he say?'

'He said, "Here is a Lieutenant called Kasim. The British have put his father in prison. What sort of man is this who so loves the British that he will not take up arms with us against them?" Then he spat between my feet. Then he slapped my face and then I was taken away and beaten up.'

'This man's name?'

'Hakinawa.'

'Of course you will say nothing of this at your court-martial. You understand this? Only with the greatest reluctance should you answer questions about it if counsel happens to press for information of this kind. Then only should you give a hint and then leave it to him whether to go on pressing. However much he presses and however much you are inclined to speak out, you will discover your answers are of no importance to your defence. You understand? Try to let prosecuting counsel alone stand convicted of raising this kind of emotional subject in evidence. Only if the prosecution can be seen and heard to squeeze it out of you must you mention such a thing.' Kasim paused. 'Of course a clever defence counsel, knowing of this, might manipulate the prosecution into the mistake of pressing such a point. Now, go on. You were beaten up. What afterwards was the attitude towards you of your men, who had seen what you call this humiliation?'

'I don't know. I was separated from them.'

'How separated?'

'First I was put in solitary confinement for a week or two. Then I was sent to another camp.'

'How were you treated there?'

'All right, I suppose.'

'All right, merely, or very well? Well, which? Come, keep alert, do not think of me as your father but as your prosecutor. How were you treated? All right or very well? Let me suggest you were treated very well. Let me put it to you that a Japanese officer apologized to you and spoke of Hakinawa with contempt, also that perhaps he hinted you might find yourself back with Hakinawa unless you showed yourself more co-operative. Which month was this, by the way. October? November?'

'November, I suppose.'

'November, nineteen forty-two?'

'Yes.'

'In November, nineteen forty-two, then, you began to be treated well. Thank you, Lieutenant Kasim.'

Sayed stared at him.

Kasim said, 'You see? You see the dangers of this line of evidence and argument? At this point prosecuting counsel sits down. He asks no more questions so you cannot answer them. The court looks at you and thinks perhaps it sees a man who wanted no more beating up. Every other consideration goes by the board, swept off by this one emotional consideration. The court looks at you and thinks, Well he is a coward –'

'Father –'

'Coward! Coward! This is what they are thinking. At this point defence counsel rises and tries to demolish this unfortunate impression by going back over all that old ground when you were supposed to be thinking seriously and objectively about this matter and that matter, about what is constitutional and what is not, and what is for India's good and what is not. But he does not find it easy. Prosecution has tricked you into raising this emotional question of to what extent Lieutenant Sayed Kasim was thinking of his country and to what extent thinking of his own skin. Defence Counsel's voice begins to carry less conviction. He knows that nothing can obliterate that impression, that Lieutenant Kasim is a man who joined the INA to avoid being beaten up again by a Japanese officer called Hakinawa. Nevertheless he has his brief and must go on to the bitter end.'

Kasim took out his squared handkerchief and dabbed his forehead. 'I remember the first case I pleaded in front of a British
magistrate. A very minor case to do with a land dispute between
two brothers. In private consultation my client made much of
the emotional rift in family feeling. Presumably his brother, the
claimant, had been doing likewise because when we got into
court his counsel began to present the case as though it were a
dispute between Cain and Abel, with my client cast as Cain.
I had to listen to many of my excellent pleas and arguments being
turned against me before even I had a chance to speak. I looked
at the young magistrate. For a moment I could not interpret his
expression. Then it suddenly struck me that he was wanting to
hear none of this. It embarrassed and disturbed him. He was
keeping his eye on his papers and trying to get it all down in
writing. So when my turn came to stand up I proceeded very
haltingly – at first actually because I had no alternative. I had lost
all inspiration. I fell back on legal precedents, almost automatically, and he kept interrupting me, getting his clerk to show
him this reference and that reference from this book and that
book. While he did this I stood silent. At first I thought his
interruptions were his way of accusing me of incomplete preparation. And then we happened to glance at one another at the
same time and instinctively I knew that he was grateful just to
be referred to points of law and the land records. Instinctively
I knew I had provided him with a way out of this emotional
situation that claimant's counsel had tried to establish. So then
I became deliberately even more dry and boring, boring to the
court but not to this boy-magistrate. And to make sure of this
I sometimes made an old legal joke, old to the court, but new
to him in the sense that while he had probably already heard the
jokes from his tutors this was probably the first time he had heard
them repeated in a court-room. My client was in despair. The
claimant and the claimant's counsel were looking very smug. So
I stopped looking at them. I looked only at the boy-magistrate
and his expression was sufficient to encourage me to continue
along these lines. I could see him beginning to feel that it was
exactly for this that he had been trained for so long and so expen-
sively. I could see him recognizing that this training had some
point after all. I began to refer to the very old cases I knew he
must have studied for his initial examinations. He became very

confident, almost peremptory. Sometimes he rebuked me for getting a reference wrong. Mostly he rebuked the claimant's pleader for interrupting. His table became piled with books and documents. Sometimes he said, "What is your point in regard to such and such a sub-section, Mr Kasim?" I would tell him and at the same time refer him to another sub-section which I guessed he had had to answer questions about more recently. The public benches began to empty. The claimant's pleader pretended to go to sleep. People were yawning. It was the most boring case of the year. But it was the one the boy-magistrate will probably never forget and the one I must always remember, Sayed. From this case I removed every last speck of emotion. I made him see that Indians too are capable of detachment. There was practically nobody left in the court when he found in favour of the counter-claimant, my client.'

'Yes, I remember all that, father. You told us many years ago. Many times.'

'Oh, did I?' He dabbed his forehead again and suddenly felt very old. 'The reason I tell you again —' he began.

'I know the reason, father. You've always believed that the English are very emotional but unwilling to show it in public.'

'This is so, isn't it?'

'I can't take it into consideration. What the English feel or don't feel is no longer important. We've finished with them, whether you like it or not.'

'Why do you say whether I like it or not? What has my life been, then? What have I been doing? Asking them to stay?'

'No. Not asking. But perhaps making it possible because you believe so much in the power of the law. Their law.'

'In this case you'll be well advised to rely on it too. You will be finished if you persist in making emotional appeals. Now, go back to November, nineteen forty-two. How long were you in this new camp where you were treated all right, as you put it?'

'Until the following February. One of the two officers I'd already spoken to came to see me. He said Mohan Singh had been arrested by the Japanese in December for withholding full co-operation and trying to insist that only the INA should deal with India. But now they'd had word that Subhas Chandra Bose was coming from Germany to take charge. Shah Nawaz was raising a new INA and determined that the Japs wouldn't be allowed to interfere, but made to treat us as equals and not as a puppet army they could do what they liked with.'

'So you yourself now joined?'

'Yes. I went down to Singapore.'

'Taking some men with you, other recruits?'

'Yes, I visited my old camp. I told the men my decision. I left it to them to make up their own minds. A few NCOs volunteered immediately. I took them to Singapore with me.'

'Was Bose there already?'

'No, he didn't come for several months. We concentrated on training and on stopping the Japanese from interfering. Someone in the Japanese Government had told them to treat us with more respect and when Bose did come it was a revelation. You only had to see and listen to him once to know that at last we had a real leader. And then of course he put everything on a pukka footing.'

'By pukka footing you mean his establishment of a so-called Government of Free India in exile?'

'Why so-called, father? What was de Gaulle's Free French Government, then? You don't hear people referring to that as so-called.'

'You know the difference between de Gaulle's and Bose's governments. There is no need for me to tell you. That sort of statement would be very smartly thrown out or sneered at as a quibble by the president of the court.'

'It wasn't a quibble to us. It made us independent of the Japanese. The Azad Hind Fauji became a properly constituted army, the armed force of a properly constituted and independent government.'

'You joined the INA before Bose took over. You would be sensible to say nothing on these lines. Tell me, why did you do this broadcast? Colonel Merrick says you admit to helping with propaganda generally and to doing a broadcast. I knew about the broadcast quite a long time ago. Someone listening in Ranpur thought they recognized your voice. I of course was in prison so heard nothing, but I was told about it afterwards. This *was* your voice?'

'Probably. I did one broadcast. Early last year. January, I think. After that I moved up into Burma in command of a battalion for the advance into Manipur.'

'What sort of thing did you say in the broadcast?'

'I just spoke in general terms, about the fight for India's freedom and the choice that had to be made by someone like myself, an officer in the Indian Army. They have a copy of the broadcast on their files in Delhi. All these broadcasts were monitored.'

'What was the main purpose of these broadcasts?'

'To encourage people here at home who had opportunities to listen. It was important for them to know that if the Japanese invaded, Indians would be with them. One couldn't say anything about not trusting the Japanese, but people listening could read between the lines. They'd realize that we'd be doing our best to stop the Japs giving them trouble.'

'Very well. Then you moved into Burma, you said. And then across the Chindwin and into Manipur.'

'Eventually, yes.'

'And waged war against the King.'

'Yes, I suppose so.'

'Not "yes, I suppose", Sayed. Just yes. Yes. Yes. You waged war against the king. It was the unavoidable result of the decision you made. We have already dealt with that. What remains to be dealt with is your attitude at this time to the Japanese.'

'It was the same as Netaji's.'

'Netaji? You mean Bose. What was Bose's attitude?'

'For him it was a question of wait and see. Under Netaji the lives of thousands of Indians in Asia were made better and the Japanese said repeatedly that we were allies, they'd no quarrel with India. But Netaji said many times to us in private that we must be prepared to fight them too if necessary. We should never fully trust them. Also he said they were perhaps afraid of us. I think this was why they kept us short of supplies and equipment and why in Burma they stopped us operating as a fully independent and major force. Whatever the Japanese Government said, we knew there were many Japanese officers who had their own ideas and way of dealing which wasn't in line with the official policy. They were the ones who didn't agree that India should be Netaji's sphere of influence. They only wanted to see the Rising Sun hoisted in Delhi in place of the Union Jack.'

'Good. Remember that. That could be a helpful point. But what does this mean, sphere of influence?'

'Surely it is obvious, it was fundamental. Netaji said –'

'I want it in your own words, not Netaji's.'

Sayed again hesitated. He said, 'What have you against Netaji? He spoke to me about you with much warmth and admiration.'

'What did you expect? For him to tell you he thought I was a bloody fool? No matter. Just that he and I never got on. Anyway he's dead –'

'Perhaps –'

'Perhaps, perhaps. Perhaps Hitler did not die in the bunker. Perhaps Bose did not die in a plane crash. The world must always have its myths. Let us get back to spheres of influence. You should avoid that phrase. It is one used by journalists when they are really talking about a political carve-up. You must try not to give this impression, that Bose sat down with Togo and said, right, you keep Burma and Malaya, and all the rest. We'll have India.'

'What is wrong with that? It's our own country.'

'The British still happen to think that legally it is theirs. Just do not use that phrase. Rely more on what you said about the Rising Sun and the Union Jack. Rely entirely on the question not of what appeared to be agreed between your Netaji and the Japanese within a framework of spurious legality, but on the underlying distrust, the fear that if and when the British were defeated, which seemed imminent, the Japanese would run riot in the country, looting and raping and enslaving, and that the best way to try to stop them doing this was unfortunately to march with them.'

Sayed said nothing.

'So now there comes the question, of whether there was any deepening of your distrust as a result of your experience of marching with them into India. Did the distrust increase?'

'Yes, because they dealt with us unfairly.'

'How?'

'Over things like rations, supplies, arms and ammunition. In not giving us proper operational information. They tried to palm us off with coolie work. The men were getting browned off. I was always having to dispute with Japanese officers mostly junior to me in rank to get the men a proper deal.'

'Morale in your battalion was not as high as you would have liked?'

'Morale was always high. We were fed up only with the Japanese. Among ourselves things were okay. I tried to share their hardships with them.'

'Sometimes no doubt you had to punish some of them.'

'Never to appease the Japanese. If a Japanese officer complained of any of my men's behaviour I told him to shove off.'

'I did not mean this. You were what you call a properly constituted army. You had a disciplinary code, no doubt, an army act laying down rules and regulations and punishments for infringement.'

'Everybody accepts this necessity. Our regulations were based completely on the Indian Army Act.'

'You cannot use the words based and completely together. Either they were a duplicate or based merely. Based with variations for local conditions and circumstances.'

'Yes, I see. You've been listening to all these rumours of ill-treatment. But where do such rumours come from except from men who joined us and have been recaptured like me but are hoping to suck up to the British with tales of tortures. I know nothing of such things. The only barbarity I have ever witnessed was in my old regiment in Kuala Lumpur when the officers' mess cook was ordered by Colonel Barker to receive six strokes of the rattan for stealing rum and selling it in the bazaar. We were all made to assemble and watch.'

'Under the pukka Indian Army Act such punishments are prescribed for menials. I am questioning you about punishments of combatant soldiers.'

'And I've already answered. I know nothing of brutal punishments. In Rangoon I ordered such things as extra fatigues, confinement to barracks, forfeiture of pay. And in the field, extra guard duties or heavy pack drill. I am not a monster. I am not a barbarian.'

'And you know nothing of this kind and worse kinds of violence in forcing men to *join* the INA?'

'Nothing.'

'You never had a case of desertion in your battalion?'

'No.'

'If you had, what would have happened if the man had been caught? Come. Think of me still as your prosecutor. What punishment did your INA prescribe for desertion, for instance in the face of the enemy, meaning in the face of the British and the Indian armies? Death?'

'That would have been the maximum.'

'In the eyes of the British who are not interested in INA acts or regulations, to execute such a sentence on an Indian soldier, even a traitorous Indian soldier, would amount to murder under the Indian Penal Code. You realize this? I am sorry to press you on the subject. Were such a sentence ever passed and executed, everyone concerned would be guilty at least of abetment to murder. You see how difficult things become when there is no political let alone legal recognition of the losing side by the winning side? I want to be absolutely sure there is no problem of this kind attaching to your case.'

'I've told you, father. You can be sure.'

'Because if there is any doubt, all my advice to you so far is valueless. You would have to work your case up on lines that would seek to establish the legality of what I have called Subhas Chandra Bose's spurious constitutional framework. You would need the services of an expert on Constitutional and International Law. On full consideration, do you think after all you might require such services?'

'All I know is that I've only told you the truth. What I understand of it. I am merely a professional soldier. I don't follow all these technicalities.'

'They are not just technicalities, Sayed. Never mind. Go back now and concentrate your mind on the situation that ended in your surrender in Manipur. But let me lead you a little. In court your counsel would not be allowed too much licence in that respect.'

He smiled, attempting to make Sayed smile too.

'In Manipur,' he went on, 'you find yourself in a difficult, perhaps untenable military position. No supplies, no ammunition, no lines of communication. You are somewhere in the hills near Imphal. The Japanese are suddenly nowhere. The British and the Indian armies are uncomfortably close. Now – were there among your men any who said, Major Sahib, this is our chance. Now we can do what we really joined the INA to do – escape from prison-camp and return to duty at the earliest possible moment?'

Presently Sayed said, 'Yes, there were some men who pretended to think like that.'

'How did you deal with them?'

'I tried to make them see what folly it was.'

'Folly? Why folly?'

'Folly to expect the British to swallow a story like that.'

'Folly is not a good word. I suggest you do not use it. It would make it sound as if you were thinking what was wise and what was foolish and not of what your position really was – that you had all made a certain decision as prisoners-of-war, with a certain idea at its end, and here was the idea in ruins, with the Japanese being beaten back and not any longer looking likely to march on Delhi to hoist the Rising Sun in place of the Union Jack. Which meant that all of you were in ruins too, unless you abandoned whatever post the Japanese had left you to hold before leaving you in the lurch, abandoned it and retreated and ran back after the Japanese to share their defeat with them. Perhaps to fight another day. Perhaps not. It seems to me, Sayed, that the one thing your INA never took into account was what was to happen if the Japanese *were* defeated. Or were you so convinced of their superiority that the eventuality never occurred to you? Were you by any chance relying on the defection of the Indian Army, the moment they saw Indians marching shoulder to shoulder with the Japanese? Did you think the Indian Army would at once turn on its British officers and join with you and the Japanese to massacre the British Army?'

Sayed did not reply. But he got up and went towards the other pleader's table. 'Yes,' Kasim said, misunderstanding. 'Smoke if you want to. And then tell me how you tried to convince these men of yours of their folly. But I hope you were thinking not of folly but of dishonour.'

But Sayed had gone on past the table, hands behind back. For a moment he stood near the rail behind which when the court was in session the public sat. Then he came back and stood looking down at his father.

'No,' he said. 'I asked them, "What folly is this? What mercy do you expect from the British or even from our own fellows who are commanded by them and dare not disobey? You will all be shot like dogs just as so many of our people have always been treated like dogs. Isn't it better to die here?" Then one of them said, "Major Sahib, we do not care. To surrender is our only chance now of seeing our families again, so let the British and our own old comrades shoot us if they want to, it no more matters. We do not care either about the British or the Japanese. Staying here we shall all be killed anyway, and our women and children will starve, no one will see to them or bother about them and it will all be up with them." Then another said, "Here we are only so many, but most of us are thinking like this, that we must risk being shot, because it is our only chance. You have only to ask the others. We are all thinking the same. That it is all finished with us!"'

'Please sit. I cannot speak to you while you are standing up.'

'It's easier for me to stand, father. So let me tell you. I sent these men away and assembled the others. There weren't many of us left anyway. I said, Well what is the decision of the majority? Who is for surrendering and chancing being shot? One hand went up and then another until there were only a few hands not up. Including mine. Then I went away to be alone for a bit. Perhaps you would have preferred me to do what it was in my mind to do. Shoot myself. A very honourable solution. But what is the good to India of a dead Indian just now? And perhaps also I wished to see my family again, only it was not even that I was allowed to see my own mother before she died.'

'Sayed –'

'No. Let me speak please. You are talking about a world that exists only in a court of law and I am not. In the world as it is it is necessary to act sometimes according to the heart –'

'I do not advise this, Sayed. It is pure emotional rhetoric. It will not get you anywhere.'

'Will not get me anywhere? Where is this place I am supposed to be going? Where is all this supposed to be leading, this advice you are giving me? The truth is that after all you don't intend to help me. You are giving me a lot of ideas about how to placate the British. Why should they be placated? What right have they to say what I shall do and what I shall not do?'

'I am helping you in the only way I can. I must make it clear to you that I don't intend to make political capital out of this. I cannot advise you to present your own case in a political framework. I do not intend to take that road. I advise you not to. I do not approve of what you have done. I do not approve of INA. I shall not identify myself with any committee set up for the defence nor shall I defend you in court, although to do so would be a very popular thing in the country generally. On the other hand I shall not criticize you, nor the INA, to anyone, which is perhaps what Government has been hoping I would do. I do not intend to commit political suicide, although you will appreciate that the situation I find myself in does not augur well for my immediate political future.'

Kasim paused; went on before Sayed had a chance to speak: 'If you plead guilty I will continue to help you. I will help to choose and to instruct your defence counsel, but in a wholly private and confidential manner. Everything I have been trying to put into your mind this morning as the proper way to conduct your case has been to this end: that you should plead guilty to waging war against the King, and then submit a reasoned state-ment setting out the considerations that led you to do so. Pleading guilty is the only way you can come out of court with any kind of personal integrity left.'

Sayed, still standing, had looked away, but now turned on Kasim. 'Integrity? What else have you ever done, father, except wage war against the King? Hasn't this been your whole life, to get rid of the British? What is the difference between you and me except that you went to prison now and again and I carried a gun?'

'You have just explained the difference, Sayed. If you cannot see it, then it is pointless to discuss it any further. So yes, come, come. Let us finish. We are simply aggravating one another.'

He got up.

'You are throwing everything away,' Sayed said.

'Not everything.'

'No one will trust or respect you if you don't stand up for us along with other political leaders.'

'I hope it is not my fear of this that you have been relying on?' He made to go, but stopped, unable to part with his son on such terms. 'It is you who have thrown away everything, Sayed. The men who did not are the Indian soldiers and officers who are still in prison-camp, who resisted all these perhaps understand-able and pardonable temptations and suffered infinitely greater hardship, and who will now be coming home. In a year or so, if you are not in prison, where will you be? For a time yes, you will all be heroes. But when there is no longer any reason to treat you as heroes, then you will be forgotten or if you are remembered at all it will be with mistrust, as men who broke their contracts, men who voluntarily took an oath of loyalty and then disregarded it, men who treated their commissions as mere scraps of paper to be used or thrown away as they thought fit. And if you *do* go to prison for this meanwhile, I beg of you do not try to console yourself with the thought that you and your father have both in your time suffered the same punishment for the same crime. It will not be so. The only contract I have ever made of this kind is with myself, to do what I could to obtain the independence and freedom and unity and strength of this country. Whenever in earlier days I defied the law it was in performance of that contract, and I defied it knowing full well the penalty and indeed inviting the penalty and proudly admitting that I had incurred it. The last time I went to prison was because I would not repudiate my membership of a party that Government lawfully suppressed. Unjustly but lawfully suppressed. It is true that at one time I was sworn in as a minister and it is true that I and all my colleagues resigned when we felt we could not any longer participate in an administration under the British. But a soldier cannot resign in wartime. When you became a soldier, Sayed, this fact should have been clearly in your mind as defining the difference between us. I did not interfere with your decision to become a soldier because I asked myself what kind of independent country will India be if we do not have a properly trained and experienced professional army to defend that independence. That the British allowed Indians to become officers I have always taken as a sign of their good faith in the matter of eventually bowing to our demands to rule ourselves. But that is by the way. What is not by the way is that now you can no longer be a soldier, you can no longer help your country. And this is what angers me. Your life so far has been wasted.'

Sayed stared at him.

'It is not a country. It is two countries. Perhaps it is many countries, but primarily it is two. If I'm not wanted in one perhaps I shall be wanted in the other.'

'Ah!' Kasim exclaimed. And sat down. 'So this also has happened to you. Then we are even more deeply divided.'

'We're only divided by your refusal to face facts, father, and by your reliance on this and that legal interpretation, also I begin to think by your reliance on the British to act as gentlemen. I no longer believe in such concepts. I have seen too much of life. It is no good relying on principles and no good relying on the British who themselves have no principles that can't be trimmed to suit *them*. In any case, they are finished. They are no longer of importance and will drag us down with them if we aren't careful. They are only interested in themselves and always have been. But now they are afraid of the Americans and the Russians and will try to get rid of India as quick as they can, both to curry favour with the USA and USSR and not to have any longer the responsibility. They will hand us over to Gandhi and Nehru and Patel – and then where will you be, father? How can you trust Congress as a whole? How can you imagine that just because you've been useful to them in the past you – a Muslim – will be allowed to remain useful when they have power? They will squeeze you out at the first convenient opportunity. Congress is a Hindu party whatever they pretend. They will exploit us as badly as the British have done, probably worse. There's only one answer and that is to seize what we can for ourselves and run things our own way from there.'

Sayed leaned over the table.

'When you say my military career is finished, I would agree with you. It would be finished if the British stay and finished if we merely substitute a Hindu for a British *raj*. It would be finished because I'm a Muslim and they hate us. Also they hate each other. A Hindu from UP hates a Hindu from Bengal and both hate a Hindu from the South. A Hindu *raj* would be a catastrophe. They have nothing to hold them together. They hate and envy us mostly because we have such a thing. We have Islam. It will be madness not to resist them. The only thing that matters in this world, father, is power. We must grasp our own. Surely it is true you have been thinking of this too? Please, do not be too proud? I do not want to see you become neglected and bitter in your old age.'

Kasim kept his attention on his son's hands: good, square capable hands. No sign of a tremor. Nor perhaps of sensitivity. He kept his own clasped.

'You are asking me to throw everything away and go over to the League?'

'It wouldn't be throwing anything away. Guzzy and Nita are very keen on this, I think. Their letters are full of hints. Jinnah would welcome you. Almost I imagine he is expecting it, because you have been so difficult for people to get hold of.'

'And Ahmed? Is he keen?'

'What does Ahmed know about anything? He is still a child.'

'No,' Kasim said. 'He is not a child.'

'Well, no, no, not in that way. A man with a reputation I gather.'

'A reputation?'

'For liking the things a man likes.'

'Women? Drinking? This is so.'

'He should be careful. It must worry you.'

Kasim did not reply. He noted the solicitous tone in his son's voice. Which verged on condescension. Sayed added, 'Perhaps he is like this because he feels himself to be without chance or opportunity.'

'You mean he does not agree with the things I stand for?'

'How can I say, father? He is a good boy at heart, I'm sure. I shall try to find out what he thinks, shall I?'

'He does not think about much. Except these things you mentioned. And hawking.'

'Hawking?'

'He was always very keen on riding. Now he has trained a falcon. It is very difficult, you know. It demands much attention and concentration. Sleepless nights. All that sort of thing. But he is much attached to her. He goes out whenever he can.'

'But that is good! A good manly sport. I am glad. I should not like him to become dissipated.'

Sayed placed one hand on his father's coupled ones. Kasim did not look up. But he felt, as a physical pressure, the steady way his elder son watched him.

'Perhaps we should say goodbye now, father. Thank you for coming to see me.'

'It is you who have come the greater distance.'

'That is my duty.'

Kasim stood up. Dutifully too, he held his arms out. They embraced. Speaking into his son's shoulder he said, 'Do not rely too much on this Colonel Merrick. He has known Ahmed for some time. He has told neither of you that he knew the other.'

'He told me just before he brought you in, father. But don't worry. I rely on no Englishman. He is of no importance either.'

'They will be waiting for you outside, no doubt. No doubt you can see Ahmed alone in here also, but you had better go out now. It would offend me to see you in custody of any kind. By the time they bring you back in I shall be gone.'

'You will write to me?'

Kasim nodded. He murmured: Allah be with you. Then released him and moved away. He heard his son's firm, heavy footsteps; and in a while the opening and closing of a door. He looked round the empty court-room and, familiar though it was, as such rooms went, it seemed to him lacking in the quality that gave such rooms meaning or even the dimensions of reality. Then he walked out by way of the daïs and the magistrate's room, through the corridor and along it in search of the room that had been set aside for him.

By the time they drove into the siding at Premanagar it was nearly half-past ten. There was barely an hour before the night train from Mirat to Ranpur was due to stop and pick them up. The stationmaster was fussing because the coach had to be shunted to a more convenient place for coupling and he had expected them by ten o'clock.

A puncture had delayed them. For half an hour Kasim had waited on the roadside, listening to the wind in the telegraph wires. The night sky had no luminosity. The wind held the smell of approaching rain; a small rain; but better than a heavy rain in country like this which the wet monsoon either avoided or flooded, first drying the top-soil for a couple of years, then sweeping it away. He welcomed the rain and the darkness of the sky. The fort, unsilhouetted, had entirely disappeared. He welcomed the wind and the air. It was good to feel braced and chilled after the heat and humidity of the room in the Circuit House; but he knew he might catch cold. Instinctively he had felt in his pocket for the onion that was supposed to ward colds off. There was no onion. He had given that up when his wife died.

Now to the stationmaster's fussing, Booby was adding his own. Where were the steps by which to mount? 'We don't need steps,' Kasim said and reached for the handgrips, heaved himself up only to find himself steadied unexpectedly from inside by Ahmed who had been in the coach collecting the small suitcase he'd brought from Mirat and was now going to take back to Mirat in the Nawab's Daimler.

'Surely you're not going yet?'

'Not for a moment or two, father. I didn't want to forget it though.'

'Well give it to one of the people to take to the car then come and talk to me for a moment.' He was conscious of the peremptory tone in his voice and wasn't encouraged by it. He went down the corridor. Hosain was waiting. He slid the door open.

'Tell them to bring tea or something.'

He entered the compartment. Before he could sit Mr Mehboob followed him in and put the briefcase on a seat.

'Where is Ahmed? I want to see him alone for a moment. And please shut the door. I've been standing all that time in the open.'

'You shouldn't have got out on to the road, Minister, when we had the puncture.'

'How can they change a wheel with two people like us sitting at ease in the back? It is bad for the springs, Ahmed says, and it is the Nawab's car and must be returned in good condition.'

Hurt, Booby left the compartment and began to close the door but opened it again for Ahmed. Sulkily he shut it when Ahmed was inside.

'Come, sit, they are bringing tea.'

Ahmed looked at his watch but sat down. 'I've not time for tea, father, it's a long drive and the chauffeur wants to go to a garage to get the punctured wheel repaired so that we have a spare.'

'There will be no garage open at this hour.'

'He knows of one.'

'It will take hours. You will get cold standing around.'

'What he advises is best, father. So I mustn't be long. Anyway they're going to move the carriage at any moment.'

'I don't like you travelling alone in a car at night all the way to Mirat. It is a bad area round here. And the escort van has gone.'

'I shan't be alone, father. There's the driver. Anyway, Booby came down at night. I can take care of myself just as well as he can.'

'Booby is paid to risk his life,' Kasim said. But smiled. Encouraged by Ahmed's answering smile he said, 'We have had no opportunity to talk today.' That was untrue. He had deliberately avoided being alone with Ahmed. 'What I want to suggest is that you come back now to Ranpur. Come back for a few days. There is a great deal to do and a great deal you can help me with. Poor Booby is such a muddler. Ring Dmitri in the morning and explain the necessity. If you like, send a note back with the driver too.'

'I promised Dmitri I'd be away only two nights. There's a meeting of Council tomorrow.'

'Council, council. He doesn't need you. The Council is Dmitri. Anyway, you do not attend these meetings personally.'

His heart sank. It was so badly said. He wished he could withdraw the imputation that Ahmed's official duties in Mirat were negligible; although he knew they were. He should never have agreed to Ahmed going to work in Mirat – but then he should never have let his elder son go into the army. Both had seemed acceptable enough solutions at the time. He had found adequate explanations: that India would need experienced officers; that it could be useful to have a son experienced in the administration of feudal survivals like the princely states. But for months now he had found these explanations less convincing than the other explanation – that in his heart he had felt at the time that neither son was capable of contributing much more. Neither son had inherited the spark. Neither son cared deeply about the things he cared for himself. The only thing he could still convince himself of was that he had believed, hoped, that in time they would, that their occupations would help to nourish in them the necessary passion, determination, and restraint.

'Well,' he said, 'if you must go back, you must.' He was not going to beg. Nor was he going to admit that he could not bear the thought of returning to the empty old house in the Kandipat road alone; although he believed that Ahmed understood this. When he had said to Sayed, *No, Ahmed is not a child*, he had not meant what Sayed thought he meant. He had been thinking of the occasion when Ahmed startled him with a shrewd assessment of the situation in which he might find himself – indeed now found himself; startled him into realizing it at a moment when he had been incapable of thinking clearly; the previous occasion at the Circuit House when they had brought him unprepared, without breakfast, from the fort, telling him nothing, so that he had feared the worst, that his wife was ill or dead and that they were releasing him on compassionate grounds as they had released Bapu when Kasturba was dying. He had nearly disgraced himself – finding Ahmed there – pathetically crying out 'Then God is good!' when Ahmed reassured him. Relief had been followed by bitter resignation when the truth came out, that his release was only partial, that he must suffer the humiliation of living under restriction at Mirat, and the bitter-sweet humiliation of learning that his wife was to share that restriction with him. And after the relief, the resignation and the humiliation, had come the shock of hearing Ahmed speak so calmly of Sayed's capture in Manipur. Outraged, he had not only called his first-born son a traitor, but had insulted Ahmed. It had been unforgiveable, yet Ahmed had seemed to forgive it, had gone on, speaking calmly still, intelligently, about the motives Government might have in releasing him from the fort. It could have been the turning point in their relationship. His own stubbornness, his peremptoriness, his coldness of manner – carefully nurtured defences against the Islamic sin of betraying emotion – had perhaps been the chief impediments to closer understanding. And yet after that one moment, that opportunity they had had to be closer to one another, Ahmed had seemed to withdraw again. It was as if the spark of involvement and commitment had failed to ignite. Subsequently, Kasim had tried tentatively to kindle it again and sometimes Ahmed had seemed to respond, but when his mother became ill, fatally ill, the capacity to respond had seemed to be deliberately smothered, and he had become again merely dutiful in matters where dutifulness seemed obligatory. As now, when he was dutifully sitting on the opposite seat, but leaning forward, hands clasped, indicating imminent departure.

'Well tell me, Ahmed, how *you* found things with Sayed?'

'He looked very fit and cheerful, I thought. He says he's treated pretty well.'

'I know. I know. Did he say anything you feel you should tell me?'

'We talked about hawking mostly. We weren't alone. One of the subalterns sat in the room.'

'But why was this?'

'Major Merrick said his instructions were that only you could be alone with him. But he made the subaltern sit where he couldn't hear easily. It didn't matter really. It was amusing if anything.'

'He is now Colonel Merrick. Didn't you notice? Also he is either equally unobservant or deceitful. He told me Sayed was not among those he'd classify as unrepentantly proud of what he has done. It wasn't my impression. Was it yours?'

'I'd no impression either way. We didn't talk about that kind of thing.'

'Just about hawking?'

'No, but mostly about me. I'm afraid I couldn't think what to ask him about himself. One day must seem to him much like another, after all.'

'What things about you, other than hawking?'

'Oh, personal things.' Ahmed grinned. 'He said Merrick saw me drinking whisky in Bombay. He said I should stop that.'

And, Kasim thought, they had probably talked about their mother's illness and death, the temporary burial at Nanoora that would have to be gone through again so that she could rest finally in the Kasim tomb in Ranpur.

'He said nothing about Jinnah, then?'

'Oh, yes. He said he thought Nita was becoming very pro-Jinnah.'

'Only that?'

'Well he said Nita was probably pro-Jinnah because Guzzy was, and that wives usually follow their husbands in such things.'

The steward knocked, slid back the door and brought in tea.

'You'll change your mind, Ahmed?'

'No, I haven't time. I must go in a minute.'

'Then bring it later,' Kasim told the steward. The steward went. 'Sayed did not ask you your own view of Jinnah?'

'No.'

'He did not tell you he had strongly recommended me to go over? And that he had undertaken to find out your own feelings?'

'No. Nothing like that at all.'

'Obviously he had begun to when he mentioned Nita. Were you interrupted soon after?'

'Yes, they came and said time was up. We'd had our ten minutes or whatever it was.'

'That's all they allowed? It doesn't matter. What matters is that he attempted to do what he said he'd do. So let me settle the question – what your feelings would be if I went over to the League. The League is very strongly placed. In the last few years while most of the Congress was in prison they have paved the way to divide the country. In the elections they are likely to win most of the seats reserved for Muslims. Even my own is not safe. If I offered myself to the League Jinnah would welcome me. I might even get a portfolio in whatever central government he's able to set up in whatever kind of Pakistan he is able to wrest out of us. To make sure of a portfolio I could also do what perhaps a father should. Publicly defend my son against charges of treason. I put it to you in these crude terms because for once, Ahmed, for once I am asking you to tell me what your honest opinion would be if I did these things. You said a moment ago that women always followed their husbands in such matters. Your mother always followed me. It was not easy for her eventually because her own family became very Pakistan conscious and very Jinnah conscious, just as Nita and Guzzy have become. What I am asking you is whether you and Sayed and Nita and your mother were thinking that I was wrong all the time, and that you were all conforming and saying nothing out of family loyalty. Whether it is your view that now I should in turn conform for everybody's sake, including my own.'

Beneath them the coach wheels clanked. The coach had been coupled to a shunting engine.

'I've got no view, father,' Ahmed said, getting up. 'You know I don't understand all these ins and outs. They don't seem to me to have anything to do with ordinary problems, though I suppose they must. But however many solutions are found people are still always dying of starvation. All that kind of thing. Or if they aren't dying of starvation they're killing one another senselessly. It all means nothing to me, parties and such-like.'

Kasim got up too.

'Then it means you don't care either way? That is one question out of the way at least. I shan't have to consider your feelings, or rather shan't have to feel conscience-stricken about you as well as Sayed. That is a relief. You see I made my mind up long ago what I would have to do. I have only been waiting for the moment when I was forced to take action. Let me just say this to you, Ahmed, that whatever your answer had been, my mind would not have been altered. But one likes to know where one stands with one's own family. To me Sayed is a man whose actions remain indefensible because he broke his word, he broke his contract. It follows that I cannot break mine. Never in my life shall I go over to Jinnah. I did not say so to Sayed because I felt he did not deserve an answer either way –'

The train shoved forward a yard or two and stopped abruptly. They avoided being thrown together by reaching for different handholds to steady themselves.

'So that is the position,' he said, righting himself. 'You, I think, deserve to know. You had better go now, if you're not coming to Ranpur.'

He slid the door open and led the way down the deserted corridor. The train, after the clanking and jerking was un-naturally still; as if it had died. The carpet muffled the sound of footsteps. When he turned round, near the exit, it was almost a shock to find Ahmed so close behind him.

Formally he embraced him.

'Do not hang around too long in that garage. Find yourself some coffee or something.'

'Yes, father, I'll do that.'

'And something stronger, no doubt, I expect you have your flask.' He could smell the whisky behind the scent of garlic on his son's breath. He let the boy go, then stopped him.

'What I have said about Sayed, please never repeat. It might make things worse for him. The other thing, about Jinnah, is in confidence. It will become public knowledge soon, though. Since you profess political detachment I can't expect you to approve or disapprove, but I'm sorry if I've spoken roughly. I haven't meant to upset you.'

Again the train jerked and this time began moving slowly forward. Ahmed grasped one handrail and began to get down. 'Why should I be upset?' he asked. 'I've won my bet with Dmitri. He bet me you'd go over to Jinnah. I bet him you wouldn't.' The shunting engine's whistle pierced. He raised his voice. 'He wouldn't offer stakes, though. We both expected me to win really.'

Ahmed jumped and ran for several paces to maintain momentum.

'Ahmed!' Kasim cried, wanting him back.

'Mind yourself! Shut the door!' Ahmed shouted, coming to a halt in the cinder-yard.

'Ahmed! What do you mean? Expected, or wanted? Ahmed!'

But the cinder-yard had got up speed, taking Ahmed with it, taking him out of earshot, revealing more of its detail in the shape of coal bunkers and godowns, the sudden glare of an arc-lamp, and then a suffocating smoky darkness which drove him in, back almost into Booby Sahib's arms.

'Minister, what are you doing? Why is the door open? Why isn't someone here looking after things in a proper way? It is getting so that no one can be relied on to look after you at all.'

'No, Booby,' he said, placing a hand on the fat pudgy shoulder. 'I am well looked after.'

IV

They paused in the ante-room while the aide who had called for him and Booby with a car at the Kandipat road knocked at the door, opened it, and then with a slight bow indicated that Kasim should go in and that Booby Sahib should stay where he was.

When Kasim entered, the Governor was half-way across the long high-ceilinged room. He had on what looked like the same crumpled chalk-striped suit he'd worn on the day of the laying of the Chakravarti foundation-stone. He carried his spectacles in his left hand; the right was being offered.

'Mr Kasim. Prompt as usual. How are you?'

'Very well, thank you, Governor-ji. But this time the prompt-ness is due chiefly to your Captain Thackeray who brought the car on time.'

'The car didn't embarrass you? I'm told your house has been pretty well besieged all day.'

'Chiefly by well-wishers, fortunately.'

'Good. I thought we'd sit here. The fire's not really on. Just the imaginary coal bit. Say if you're cold.'

Without Malcolm having done anything visible to command it, the Government House magic worked, in the shape of doors opening and servants bringing in tea. There were five of them. Malcolm ignored them. They simply operated.

'How is Lady Malcolm, Governor? I hope better?'

'Somewhat better, thank you.'

'Not as good as you hoped?'

'No. I'm trying to get her to go home to see a particular chap. It's just a question of finding a way of persuading her to leave Ootacamund. Then we'll see.'

They were now surrounded by an English-Indian tea. Kasim could smell the curry-puffs without even looking for them. The servants vanished as smoothly as they had appeared. When the last one had gone, Kasim said:

'I shall not be contesting the elections.'

'Yes, I see.' Only the voice betrayed disappointment. The face remained calm.

'I shall recommend to my colleagues in the Congress Party that a man called Fazal Huq Rahman should stand in my old constituency. He is still very anti-Jinnah, very competent, and in my opinion stands the best chance of holding this Muslim seat for Congress, although undoubtedly my old sparring partner Nawaz Shah will leap at the opportunity to pass his own seat on to someone else and contest mine on behalf of the League.'

They sipped the tea which the servants had poured.

'Nawaz Shah?'

'Abdul Nawaz Shah. Not to be confused with Shah Nawaz Khan.'

The Governor smiled. He said, 'I wasn't Governor at the time, but I seem to remember you wanted Abdul Nawaz Shah in your nineteen thirty-seven Ministry.'

'He is an able and dedicated man and in nineteen thirty-seven there were constitutional grounds for forming a coalition, as well as reasonable hopes of satisfying the League that our policies were not after all anti-Muslim. Now of course such hopes are very slender.'

'Yes. I'm afraid they are.' Malcolm put his cup down. 'All this means that you're also not going to align yourself with the defence of the INA?'

'Yes. It means that.'

'Does it help if I point out that elections in this province won't take place until some time in the New Year? By which time the subject of the INA might not be so delicate?'

'Not really, Governor. The election *campaigns* will begin almost at once. It is clear that the subject of the INA will be taken up strongly by both major parties and just as clear that unless

I align myself with the defence of INA personnel I should lose an important Muslim seat for Congress. The electorate would say, Who is this man who won't defend even his own son?'

'But my dear Mr Kasim, no one would blame you for defending your son, for defending the INA. I least of all.'

'I have imagined you would not. It is what you were delicately hinting when we had lunch a couple of weeks ago. On earlier occasions I detected from Government rather less delicate hints that it was hoped I might lead an attack on these fellows.'

'Is it your intention to lead an attack?'

'No. I do not have a suicidal turn of mind.'

'Well that's one good piece of news at least. On the other hand, if you don't publicly defend the INA and your son, how can you survive, politically?'

'I do not know whether I can survive. But I am an old enough professional to know that when you do not know how, you bide your time. I will do nothing to help nourish this idea that the INA are heroes. Eventually other people may agree with me. A free and independent India may not want to employ such officers. But personally I should not like to feel that at one time I defended them, and then refused to employ them. So for me it is simply a question of refusing now. Many of them had perhaps understandable and excusable reasons. But how can you judge which man had what reason? Let into your army one man of the suspect kind I have in mind and you plant the seed of a military dictatorship, you nurture a man who will throw away his commission again and challenge and even overthrow a properly constituted civil authority. I do not want a government of generals. I do not want to see such an India. I do not believe there will be such an India. But too much adulation of INA seems to me the best way of getting such an India. So, for the moment, I must be what you call *hors de combat* because I am out of rhythm with my country's temporary emotional feelings, and the country's temporary emotional feelings are out of rhythm with my own. I should be, as you also say, rusticated, for everybody's sake. So, Kasim, I tell myself. Go and cultivate your garden for a while.' He smiled. 'At Premanagar I had plenty of practice.'

Malcolm smiled too. He said, 'Not everyone has the taste for martyrdom, Mr Kasim. It rather surprises me to sense it in you.'

'Martyrdom? Oh, no, you've got me all wrong! A martyr is the last thing I'm cut out for. I am a very practical man, even a pragmatist. The equal of any Englishman in that respect. But I have trained myself to take the long view also and taking the long view has taught me that you have to live for ever with a single moment of short-sightedness.'

'Well let's not say martyrdom. Just let's say you're putting a very high price on your conscience, your moral sense. Does it follow you've put a low one on the ultimate good of this province?'

'Governor, you know that this is a Congress majority province. Whoever you invite to form a government will be a Congress-man. The price I exact for my moral sense is one Muslim seat, one minority seat in the assembly. So. My temporary rustication is bought very cheaply. I could not possibly win it in all the circumstances.'

'Temporary rustication? What have you in mind?'

'At the moment only cultivating my garden. Doing every-thing I can to promote the claims of Fazal Huq Rahman and disputing the claims of Jinnah and his League for partition. Oh, they will soon see that I am not in his camp. And, if I am asked my views about INA, I shall take – forgive me – the line of the English gentleman. I shall say, "How can I comment on such matters when I, my son, my whole family are involved? It is for others to speak." Also I shall fall back on the time-honoured excuse that certain family misfortunes and personal health do not make me a suitable candidate for elections in the coming cold weather. Now, what do you give me for my moral sense? You see what a Machiavellian viper you have been harbouring in your bosom?'

Malcolm put his head back, closed his eyes and laughed.

'So, Governor. May we have just another word about Fazal Huq Rahman?'

Malcolm put his spectacles on and looked at Kasim. He said, 'What more of Fazal Huq Rahman?'

'Should he defeat Nawaz Shah in the elections, which is very unlikely, and a misfortune for India which we can attribute to the late Lord Minto. . . .'

'Why Lord Minto?'

'It was during his viceroyalty that the decision to provide sepa-rate electorates for Muslims was taken –'

'Entirely as a result of Muslim pressure –'

'That is technically so, but Minto need not have agreed. He and the British wanted to agree, he was unconsciously dividing and ruling. Lady Minto was dividing and ruling quite con-sciously. You never should have allowed your memsahibs into the country. It was she who greeted the arrangement for separate electorates with cries of amazon joy, because what she called Indian national subversion had been effectively blocked. It is to people like the Mintos we owe Jinnah.'

Malcolm was smiling. 'Go back to Fazal Huq Rahman,' he said.

'I was about to. I was merely reminding you, Sir George, of the political background to these constitutional absurdities. It is as though, Sir George, at home you had separate electorates for Protestants, Catholics, non-conformists, evangelists and Christian-Scientists. Communalism has been written into our political structure by the *raj*. The cold weather elections will be fought on a religious not a political issue. However, should Fazal Huq Rahman persuade his Muslim majority constituency that unity and not separation is the answer, which is doubtful, let me first of all say that he is not yet of ministerial calibre, and then reassure you that he is neither relative nor friend nor the friend of a cousin to whom I owe some favour –'

Again Malcolm put his head back. He took off his spectacles and wiped his eyes. He said, 'What should I do about Fazal Huq Rahman?'

'When you discuss portfolios with your new chief-minister designate, he will suggest a man for Education and no doubt like all good Governors you will raise no objection. But having raised no objection it would be useful if you could introduce Fazal Huq Rahman's name into the conversation and indicate some interest in seeing him in that department with a brief of some kind.'

'I'll keep my eye open, Mr Kasim. Perhaps nearer the time you'll help to guide it finally in the right direction?'

'I don't think that would be very wise. I don't think, you know, that we ought to see each other again except in public, socially.'

The Governor gazed at him steadily. He said, 'I should be sorry for that. But I must leave it to you. Are you going back to practise the law?'

'No, no. I am a fortunate man. I don't have to earn a living, as you know.'

'I really meant, interest yourself in legal matters?'

'One never loses one's interest.'

'No, quite. What I meant was identify yourself with what I might call quasi-legal committees set up to look into matters involving possible legal processes or inquiries?'

'You are referring to matters that might arise from the civil disturbances that followed Government's arrests of Con-gressmen like myself?'

'Yes.'

'And the way they were put down?'

'And the way they were put down.'

'No, I am not interested in anything like that. To me it is all water under the bridge. Turbulent water at the time but to me it is foolish to re-disturb it. Now I think I must go.' He got up. Malcolm got up too. Kasim said, 'Thank you for what you arranged, and hoped to arrange. Next year you can forget all these things. I hope Lady Malcolm will soon be fully recovered.'

'Thank you.'

They began to walk slowly towards the doors that led to the ante-room. Then Malcolm stopped. He said, 'Mr Kasim, do you remember the last thing I said to you in this room, just before you went off to the Premanagar Fort?'

'Yes, I remember it very well. You said you would leave a thought in my mind, that one day this room might be mine.'

'Is it what you'd like? If so, I think I might almost guarantee it. It's not the same as heading a Ministry, but it has its compensa-tions. Ranpur hasn't had an Indian Governor before but you wouldn't be the first Indian Governor appointed in the country.'

'You mean sworn in, not appointed.'

'Well, yes.'

Kasim felt the tremor beginning again in his right arm and hand. Almost unconsciously he steadied it by clasping the right wrist. For a moment the temptations of the peak – that splendid heady upper air, that immensity of landscape – made his head sing.

He heard himself saying, 'Well you see how difficult that would be, unless the Viceroy had been succeeded by a Governor-General of a self-governing dominion, and unless his executive council had been superseded by an Indian cabinet responsible to

a freely elected central Indian assembly. And in that context a provincial governorship, if such a thing survives which I suppose it
will, will be a job for an old man. Please don't misunderstand me.'

'I don't misunderstand.'

'Furthermore, for me to be sworn in, when you retire, would
necessitate severing my active party political connections.'

'I understand that too. I suppose I was looking for a way of
ensuring that your rustication isn't too permanent.'

'Well that is my problem but it is kind of you to involve yourself in it.'

'Not kind, Mr Kasim. I am involved whether I like it or not.
But I prefer to like it. How serious were you when you said we
oughtn't to see each other again in private?'

'Oh, very serious. I try not to say things lightly.'

'In that case is there anything I can do apart from saying goodbye and wishing you good luck?'

'Oh yes, one small thing. I am almost ashamed to mention it.'

'But please –'

'I know that any letters Sayed writes to members of his family
and any letters members of his family write to Sayed must be
opened and censored. That is quite correct in all the circumstances. But it has become onerous to feel that one can neither
write nor receive letters from whomsoever on whatsoever
subject that have not been looked at by strangers – no doubt
perfectly disinterested fellows just doing their jobs. But it tends
to limit one's sense of one's right to proper self-expression, and
is so ridiculous when by contrast I know I can come here and
frankly and freely speak my mind.'

'I attended to that a couple of days ago when a particular point
was brought to my notice and I realized it was still going on. But
give it a day or two –' Malcolm smiled – 'you know how slowly
any administration works.'

'Oh yes. I know, only too well. Thank you. Good-night,
Governor.'

'Good-night, Mr Kasim.'

The crowds were still there in the Kandipat road, in the dark,
patient, waiting to welcome him back from whatever great
occasion he had gone out on. At the entrance to the house the
progress of the car was interrupted. Thackeray was not in the car

and there was nothing to identify it as one from Government House, but tomorrow it would be all round Ranpur where he had been. By then it would not matter and tonight it did not matter, to the patient crowds, where he had been or what he had done. It was enough for them that he had been out and done something in this sort of style, challenging the *raj*. With such crowds Booby was a different man. He beamed, he smiled, he rolled the window down and said cheerfully, 'Okay, okay, what is all this, what are you waiting for, he is tired can't you see, please let us pass. Tomorrow is another day. He will have something to say then. *Hān, hān! Jai Hind. Jai Hind.* All people go home now. Everything is okay.'

And rolled the window up as the crowd divided like a Red Sea and the car swept in through the iron gates. 'You see, Minister,' Booby said enthusiastically, 'here we are finally at home.'

Booby had even arranged that the fountain should play in the shallow pool in the miniature inner courtyard. Kasim leant on the railing that protected the second-floor balcony and watched the dimly lit aquarium-effect for a while. Then he went back to the room he had asked should be set aside for him – the room his father had studied and meditated in during his own widowerhood – a room without ornament, with cream-washed walls, fretted windows, a simple bed, a desk, a chair, two lamps (oil-lit in his father's day, now electric). He sat at the desk and again opened Bapu's letter.

'Minister?'

'What is it, Booby?'

'Can I get you anything?'

'No, no, but come in, sit down.'

There was nowhere for Booby to sit so Kasim vacated the chair and sat on the bed. Still Booby did not sit.

'You must sleep,' he said, 'you did not sleep all night again.'

'I am not tired. I must draft a letter to Bapu.'

'Please, dictate it. I have my pad and pencil.'

'No. I shall draft it. Then we can discuss it. Then it can be typed.' Booby's shorthand left a lot to be desired. Old Mahsood had had no shorthand. Somehow this had not seemed to matter.

'Very well,' Booby said. 'Then there is for the moment only the question of the letter from Pandit Baba.'

Kasim shut his eyes and flicked his hand, negatively. 'Oh, throw it away, Booby. It is all water under the bridge. We have never answered him before. Why should we answer now? We do not even know, only guess, what he is bothering me personally for. He is a tiresome man and of no account.'

'Yes, Minister. I will throw it away then. Mr Chakravarti has rung. Inviting you to dinner next week.'

'I cannot go to dinner with Chakravarti next week.'

'I will tell him so.'

'No, do not tell him. Accept and then decline later. The day before. It is so much less complicated. What else?'

'Mrs Nawaz Shah also rang.'

'So she can ring.'

Kasim looked up. Booby nodded. Expressionless. But somehow approving. Perhaps Booby would do after all.

'And?'

'Ahmed rang from Mirat this afternoon while we were out.'

'Saying what?'

'I couldn't get hang of it. We need more intelligent staff, Minister.'

'Perhaps. Tomorrow we'll discuss this, but primarily I shall leave it to you. What did the message say?'

'It is completely without meaning.' Booby referred to a note. 'Three words only. "Expected and wanted." '

'That is all?'

'That is all, Minister.'

Kasim smiled. 'It is enough. Thank you, Booby. That is all for tonight.'

After a while he got up from the bed and sat at the desk and began drafting the letter to Bapu. He inscribed the heading: To Mr Mohandas Karamchand Gandhi.

Dear Bapu, (he wrote)

Thank you for your letter and your kind expression of sympathy in the loss of my old friend Mahsood. As you know he was with me for many years and now all that is over. One feels such a loss. I am grateful for your letter because it helps me knowing the loss is shared.

It has, however, been a particular blow, coming on top of others and frankly I am in low spirits and prey to all kinds of doubts and uncertainties. Please do not misunderstand. I have no doubts whatsoever about our commitment to the cause of freedom and unity and non-violence to which you have given not only your life's work but also inspiration to the rest of us. This cause I shall never abandon. The uncertainties I spoke of arise from many different sources. For instance –

Momentarily Kasim's inspiration failed. Then he continued: For instance, I find myself uncertain which of two recent events – the election of a socialist government in London and the destruction of Hiroshima by a single atomic bomb – will have the profounder effect on India's future. It is this pressure from the world outside India that perhaps creates these uncertainties in my mind, although I am sure these outside pressures are reflected in pressures from within. On the one hand, there is the element that one might call purely political, and on the other an element one cannot but see as rooted in or flowing from a power that goes beyond the norm of what we morally understand by power –

Kasim broke off. He stared at the paper for a while. The words meant so little. What was in his mind seemed to mean so little too. It was the world outside his mind, the world he felt he couldn't encompass that meant much. Tonight, it couldn't be reached.

Coda for Operation Zipper

Early that September, coming into the harbour of Georgetown on the island of Penang, where the tide was presumably low, the first detachment of re-occupying British troops observed what looked like an uncomfortably large number of Japanese soldiers assembled along the harbour wall, so that for a moment it wasn't clear to them whether they faced a reception committee or something less welcoming, whether Zipper which had begun life as an offensive operation and then been rescaled as an expedition of liberation of the people of Malaya wouldn't now become an operation again.

The matter was cleared up satisfactorily when a young Marine officer, attempting to mount the perpendicular iron ladder on the harbour wall from the light assault vessel that rocked up and down in the low-lying water, got into difficulties and the Japanese soldier nearest above him got down on his knees, stretched out an arm, and said, 'I help you, Johnnie?' Subsequently, most of the men, mounting at other points, found themselves momentarily relieved of their rifles, which certainly made the climb easier for them, but rather nullified the impression they'd had that the Nips were among the least accommodating people you'd be likely to find East of Suez (which was saying something). And Penang looked much more promising than Kalyan. Behind the line of Japanese soldiers were groups of pretty Chinese girls, grinning and waving.

Further down the coast, on one of what Leonard Purvis once heard fellow guests of the Maharanee's call the beaches around Port Swettenham, there was no harbour wall to scale, instead, an idyllic scene, an immense stretch of golden sand backed by elegantly disposed palm-trees. The senior officer riding in on a swift shallow-draughted landing craft was sardonically amused by the sight of three diminutive Japanese officers waiting for him on the sand, holding their swords in a manner that indicated submission. Beautifully uniformed and shod, the Englishman had himself carried ashore through a few inches of water by two stalwart marines who placed him gently on dry land in front of the Japanese commander. After an exchange of polite formalities, the English officer said, 'Perhaps you'd like to see how we would have come in in less peaceful circumstances?'

He gave an order. A junior officer in the landing craft blew a whistle and raised a flag. From half a mile out, where waited a formidable line of heavy landing craft (and further behind still, the big ships that had formed part of the Zipper convoys) there at once came the growling sound of marine engines starting up. Almost, one could smell the oily fumes. They came in, making impressive waves and wakes with their blunt bows and sterns: ten, twenty, thirty of them; and then stopped, crashed down their single fronts or dramatically opened their double ones. Being so heavy they had not come in further because it was known (through intelligence) that for the last two hundred yards the water was barely wading depth, not more than eighteen inches, insufficient to get way astern for putting back to the ships for more loads. They had stopped about four hundred yards out where there were three feet beneath them, sufficient for their purpose, and no obstacle either for the green-clad infantry or for the water-proofed trucks, carriers and armoured vehicles which now spewed out of them and began to advance, remorselessly shortening the distance between themselves and the observers on the sands.

After going fifty yards, though, something odd happened. The leaders of the files of soldiers in the centre suddenly disappeared beneath the bland, scarcely rippling surface, and on one of the flanks the line of vehicles sank equally suddenly – not completely like the men but up to their superstructures. Whistles blew, men shouted and thrashed around. Only on the other flank was the operation of landing going smoothly but in that sector there was no treacherous and unexpected sandbank, nor any of the quick-sand which nearly cost a life or two and claimed more than one armoured vehicle.

The senior officer on the beach, having run instinctively forward, was standing now, bemused, with his beautiful boots in several inches of water. He was concerned for his troops and had no opportunity of observing the Japanese officers behind him; but his aide did, and later – whenever he recounted the tale – said he had never until that moment really understood what was meant by the inscrutability of the Orient.

He also said he hoped that if his commander felt he'd suffered any kind of humiliation from this incident he'd been more than compensated a few days later when he went down to Singapore, freshly laundered, to watch the simple, precise, efficient and impeccably organized formal surrender by the Japanese in Malaya to the brisk and handsome naval officer, the Supremo, who in less than eighteen months' time was to mount a far less simple but equally precise, efficient and impeccably organized operation – not for receiving power back but for handing it over.

BOOK TWO 1947

PANDORA'S BOX

I

1947

IT WAS JUNE, and there was a full year to go before the date the British Government had proposed as one by which it could be assumed that a satisfactory constitutional settlement would have been reached and the *raj* could withdraw in honour of its undertakings, and the long struggle for independence could be considered over.

But the bustling new Viceroy was back in Delhi. He had returned from consultations in London on the last day of May. Scarcely pausing to get his feet back under the desk, on June 2 he held meetings with Indian leaders and told them in confidence of the new plan proposed by him and approved by the British cabinet. On June 3 he broadcast to the Indian nation and said it was now clear that the division of India into two self-governing dominions, India and Pakistan, was inevitable, and added that the British Parliament would pass the necessary legislation to demit power on this basis during the present parliamentary session.

On June 4 he held a press conference (a feature of his vice-royalty which some old hands thought unnecessarily showy) and in answer to a question confirmed that this hastening through of legislation in Whitehall meant that Government would transfer power not next year but this year. He said, 'I think the transfer could be about the fifteenth of August.'

The astonished questioner did a rapid calculation. Ten weeks to go. Ten weeks. Ten *weeks*? It may have been that on this occasion several members of the Bengal Club at least looked like dying of apoplexy, but there is no reliable evidence, and they must by now have become inured to such rude shocks, however terminally rude this one seemed. It is far more likely that in other places where a more sophisticated response was to be expected, people simply said, 'I wonder what Halki will make of it?'

Halki was the new pseudonym of a young Brahmin, Shankar

Lal, a shy retiring man who had left his orthodox family in the Punjab to earn his living as a cartoonist in Bombay. *Halki* meant 'light-weight or counterfeit' and replaced an earlier pseudonym, *Bhopa* (a priest possessed by the spirit of the god he worships). The new pseudonym wasn't intended to hide his identity; his style was unmistakable; even the CID recognized it when his cartoons began to reappear after the several months of un-employment that followed the publication of the still-famous Churchill two-finger cartoon. As to that unemployment, the one or two close friends in whom he confided explained to others that his silence was not due to editorial cowardice so much as to Shankar Lal's strength of character. Lal had refused several offers from editors only too willing to uphold the freedom of the press. He had gone into seclusion to think about the nature of his political commitment and to perfect his style; but he had made a verbal agreement with the editor of a popular Indian-controlled English-language newspaper to offer his work exclu-sively to him directly he felt ready to publish again.

During this interim period his editor-designate sometimes went out to Juhu, where Lal lived in great simplicity, to look at his work and try to persuade him to start publishing right away. Lal declined, with his usual courtesy, but often gave the editor whichever of the private cartoons he had most admired, and these the editor framed and arranged round the walls of his office (which was where Perron now saw them).

Halki's most devoted admirers used to – and still – say that a retrospective exhibition would show how Shankar Lal's youthful political adherence to Congress's aims of unity and freedom had shaded off into a generally humanist view of life. Among the unpublished work from the watershed period between the Churchill two-finger cartoon and an equally famous cartoon that marked his reappearance was one drawn in late August, 1945, after Wavell's announcement of cold-weather elections. This depicted the then-Viceroy, statue-naked on a plinth (inscribed 'Vote!') in the attitude of Rodin's Thinker, his bronze shoulders caked with snow. Actually, there were two versions of this unpub-lished work. The first included in the distant background a hot and sweaty affray between Muslims and Hindus and was cap-tioned 'The Solution?'. The second version, still featuring Wavell as the snow-clad Thinker, omitted the affray but substituted the figure of an undernourished child asleep at the base of the plinth, with one hand grasping his begging bowl. The word 'Vote!' had disappeared from the plinth but reappeared on the side of the empty bowl. This was Perron's favourite of the two.

A successor to this unpublished cartoon (also unpublished) was dated September 20, 1945, the day after Wavell's report to the nation on his return from London, where he had attempted (unsuccessfully) to wrest from Attlee's government the kind of clear statement of policy that would have given the already announced cold-weather elections the special significance which all political parties in India felt was lacking: a clear state-ment about independence. This cartoon was captioned 'Box-Wallah', and portrayed Wavell in the garb of an itinerant Indian merchant and purveyor of ladies' dress materials, squatting on his hunkers on the verandah of a European bungalow, recom-mending his wares to a gathering of memsahibs who bore remarkable resemblances to Bapu, Nehru, Patel, Tara Singh, Maulana Azad and Mohammed Ali Jinnah. Jinnah was sitting somewhat apart from 'her' colleagues, consulting a glossy maga-zine marked 'The Pakistan Ladies' Home Journal'; but none of them was responding to the pleas of the box-wallah or to the sight of the avalanche of silks and woollens he was flinging hope-fully in all directions (lengths marked: 'New Executive Council – Indian patterns'; 'Central Assembly Dress Lengths (for Cold Weather Wear)'; 'Constituent Assembly Fashion Designs, For All Seasons'. 'Provincial Election Lengths: Graded Prices'; 'Dominion Status Fabrics (Slightly Soiled)'.

Why didn't Halki want to publish this one? Perron asked. Oh, the editor said, Halki wanted to. It was he, the editor, who had refused. One couldn't dress such eminent men up in women's clothes, like so many transvestites, especially when the women's clothes were European-style. Look at Gandhi's legs, (the editor said) and at those flapper's shoes.

The next significant cartoon was the one with which Halki had made his public reappearance, in December 1945, when (after an adjournment) the 'showpiece' trials of three INA officers began at the Red Fort in Delhi. Perron had already seen this one, because his old officer from Poona days had sent it to him. It was with this cartoon that Perron's interest in Halki had begun.

The trials were described as showpieces because they seemed to have less to do with the seriousness of the cases chosen to begin the long legal process of bringing to justice men who had waged war against the king than they had to do with proving GHQ's and the C.-in-C.'s determination not to show partiality (or, conversely, to attack the three main communities simultaneously). The officers chosen for the grand opening trial at the Red Fort had been Shah Nawaz Khan (a Muslim), Captain P. K. Sahgal (a Hindu) and Lieutenant G. Dhillon (a Sikh).

Halki's cartoon was very simple. It consisted merely in a beautifully sombre and perfectly proportioned drawing of the Red Fort, and carried the bleak caption, 'The King-Emperor's Tomb'. That was all. From that day, the editor told Perron, circulation began to rise. The cartoonist had caught the right new mood and Halki became famous overnight. But he had remained shy, enigmatic. Some of his cartoons occasionally seemed almost pro-British, or anti-party. For instance there was this one, in 1946, at the time of the short-lived but tricky mutiny at Bombay in the Royal Indian Navy, a mutiny which had surely convinced the British, if they weren't convinced already, that their time had expired. But the cartoon had taken editorial courage to publish because it showed an Indian frigate, controlled by mutinous ratings who had trained the ship's guns on the Royal Yacht Club and were about to open fire. Bursting through the roped-off gangway to stop them was Patel, in full Congress garb, waving his arms hysterically. The caption ran, 'What are you doing, for God's sake? One day we may want it ourselves.'*

Perron did not remember this one. Neither Bob Chalmers, his old officer from Poona, nor Aunt Charlotte had sent it to him. Nor did he remember the next two or three the editor showed him. The first of these pre-dated the naval mutiny joke and made a pair with the Red Fort cartoon. It was a meticulous drawing of a famous building, the Central Assembly in Delhi, in which in the first phase of the cold-weather elections the Congress had captured all the general seats but the Muslim League had won every one of the seats reserved for Muslims. Both parties had claimed a landslide victory and Halki's cartoon

*Royal Yacht Club – traditionally the most exclusive in India – was actually closed down after independence.

was captioned *Jai Hind*! Closer inspection revealed a fissure in the foundation of the building and a crack spreading right up through one side of the fabric. Reluctantly, the editor hadn't published this, but he published the two-part cartoon in which Halki satirized the climax and anti-climax of the INA trials at the Red Fort.

The first frame showed a senior British officer mounted on a dome in the attitude of the statue of justice above the Old Bailey in London. Although blindfolded, the officer was recognizable as the C.-in-C. His scales were unusual since instead of two suspended trays there were three, each occupied by a mannikin figure representing the religion of each of the three accused, a Hindu, a Sikh and a Muslim. The C.-in-C.'s sword was held firmly aloft. In the second frame, which celebrated the anti-climax after the verdicts of Guilty and the C.-in-C.'s reduction of the sentences of life transportation, cashiering and forfeiture of pay to cashiering and forfeiture only, the scales were empty and his sword lacking its blade (it looked as if it must have fallen off through faulty workmanship). Beneath the blindfold the C.-in-C.'s expression remained unchanged: austere, determined and disapproving.

Yet one more cartoon was devoted to the subject of the INA, but Perron had to get the editor to explain it After the anti-climax to the Red Fort trials it had become clear that except in several serious cases involving murder or brutality the *raj* could do nothing except cashier the officers and discharge the approximately 7,000 sepoys and NCOs who, classified as 'black', had not already been discharged as 'greys', or, as 'whites', returned to their units in semi-disgrace. The bulk of these 'black' discharges (after which the subject of the INA could conveniently be considered closed) occurred at Holi, 1946, the spring fertility festival, traditionally celebrated by crowds roaming the streets throwing coloured powders and squirting coloured inks at everyone in sight. Halki's cartoon, captioned 'Holi', depicted a crowd of the discharged men emerging from a detention centre, being greeted by their families and throwing immense quantities of powder into the air and at one another. It took some time to discern in the distant background the plight of a loyal Indian Army sepoy still on guard-duty at the camp who had been sprayed with coloured ink by the departing prisoners and who was obviously being put on a charge by an immaculately dressed and irate British officer for being unkempt on duty. The editor published this cartoon too and received several threatening letters as well as a formal protest from the committee of the All-India Congress.

The next cartoon was one that Perron had also seen. Rowan had sent it to him as an enclosure with the only letter he had ever written. It illustrated a meeting of the Cabinet Mission of 1946 which had come out to India in the hot weather after the elections to seek an agreement on the major constitutional issue arising out of the continuing difficulty the British Government seemed to be having in establishing to whom to hand over when the time eventually came. The cartoon showed the three sweating members of the Mission: Cripps (merely President of the Board of Trade, but difficult to detach from Indian affairs), the Secretary of State (Pethick-Lawrence) and the First Lord of the Admiralty (Alexander). They were sitting staring at a large map of India which showed the country's provincial boundaries. A legend at one side of the map provided the clue to the different hatchings: perpendicular lines for Hindu majority provinces and horizontal lines for Muslim majority provinces (with a few areas of cross-hatching in the Punjab and Bengal). But nearly one-third of the map remained unhatched. The main caption was: 'A Paramount Question' and this was followed by a sub-caption in the form of a dialogue between the three ministers:

Sec. of State: I say, Cripps, what do the blanks represent?
Cripps: God knows.
Alexander: Perhaps the fellow ran out of ink.

Rowan's comment when sending this cartoon to Perron had been: 'Confidentially, it's said to be quite true, that three senior cabinet ministers between them had no idea that the self-ruling princely states, who have individual treaties with the paramount power (the Crown) respecting their rights to their own independence, cover so much of India.'

Another cartoon, which Perron hadn't seen, dated June 29, 1946, showed the cabinet mission returning disconsolately to London, climbing aboard a plane labelled 'Imperial Shuttle Service'. The Secretary of State was carrying the Imperial Crown and Cripps was surreptitiously handing him back a large diamond and saying, 'You'd better stick it back in, already.'

Halki's inventiveness here lay chiefly in the way he made the three British ministers look like three shady Jews from Amsterdam, and Nehru, Jinnah and Tara Singh look like three equally shady Arab merchants who had come to wave them off but were eyeing each other suspiciously, wondering if the jewel from the crown had been secretly handed over to whichever one of them had offered the highest number of piastres. Perron hadn't seen the cartoon because the editor hadn't dared publish it.

After this light-hearted cartoon came a series of tragic ones, every one of which the editor had published. They belonged to the period following Congress's decision to accept Wavell's invitation to join a new executive council which became known as the interim government, and to do this without the League. With governments formed in all the British-ruled provinces after the elections, some with League ministries but the majority with Congress ministries, the vital gap in government lay at the disputed and potentially federal centre. One of Halki's cartoons portrayed this enigmatically. It was the one in which he first reintroduced a characteristic figure from his 'Bhopa' days – the struggling and emaciated figure of Indian freedom and unity, last seen clenched in Churchill's two-fingered fist. Here he was now, the emaciated figure, stretched on a pavement asleep, but in two sections. Nothing connected the trunk to the lower limbs. You could see pavement between them. The majority of its Congress admirers interpreted it as a criticism of the Muslim principle of partition, of a separate Muslim state as a *sine qua non* of independence. The editor told Perron that it was really Halki's criticism of the men who had it in their power to join the two portions of the body together by at least attempting to work together at the centre.

'And these,' he said, leading Perron to another wall, 'are what I call Halki's Henry Moore cartoons, all inspired by those drawings your artist did of English people living like troglodytes in the underground railway stations during the Blitz. I published all these and became very unpopular with the proprietors. A cartoon should make people laugh, they said, even if it is only to laugh at themselves. But I said, What is there to laugh about now? Well – look at this!'

'This' was a sombre pen and ink drawing of Calcutta, captioned 'Direct Action Day', August 16, 1946 and celebrated the
result of Jinnah's decision to resort to violence in the belief that
the Viceroy had betrayed him by allowing Congress to enter
the central interim government without him. In this picture,
though, it was difficult to distinguish Muslim dead from Hindu
dead. Halki had just drawn a pile of bodies, such as might be
seen on the streets of Calcutta on any night of the week, except
that these were obviously dead, not sleeping, but ordered in
rows, like sleepers, in diminishing perspective from a lit to an
unlit area.

There were several variations on this theme, but it was always
night-time and the street was always the same street, the fore-
ground lamp-post the same lamp-post. The most striking
(Perron thought) was the one that showed the street all but
empty. There were no bodies on the pavement, blood-stains
adumbrated the shapes of bodies cleared away. In the background you could just see Bapu, with his staff, accompanied by
Jinnah (hands behind back) walking down the road towards the
lit area. This carried no caption and was the last of the pictorially
sombre cartoons. Sombreness, though, continued in the jokey
ones that followed.

A cartoon dated September 3, 1946 marked the occasion of
the swearing in of the interim central government headed by
Nehru, ostracized by Jinnah and overshadowed by the assassination of one of the nominated non-League Muslims, Shafaat
Ahmed Khan, which caused riots in Bombay and Ahmedabad.
Another, in mid-October, celebrated Jinnah's about-face, his
decision to co-operate and enter the interim government to protect Muslim interests. To accommodate him three non-League
Muslims had to resign. A third cartoon, dated in November,
represented Halki's satirical view of this armed collaborative
truce, a drawing of Wavell presiding over a round-table conference of his brawling Indian ministers (whose briefcases, leaning
against their chairs, were bulging with fused bombs). A window
gave a view of a rioting mob. A doorway was marked as the way
into the Constituent Assembly where the future constitution of
free India would eventually have to be settled. The door was
wide open but clearly no one was prepared to enter. In this
cartoon Wavell was drawn in diminutive proportions, crouched

in an overwhelming viceregal chair, and with two heads – or rather one head drawn twice, with connecting lines denoting its swift turning to and fro, as he listened first to one argument and then to another. The caption ran: 'I see' and only readers who knew that this brief sentence was said to be the Viceroy's most frequent contribution to every conversation really appreciated the joke.

One of the unpublished Halki cartoons of the last phase of Wavell's viceroyalty was drawn early in December when Wavell had persuaded the British Government to invite a delegation (headed by himself) of Hindu, Muslim and Sikh leaders, to a consultation in London, which he hoped would break the dead-lock. Once again there was the waiting aeroplane ('Imperial Shuttle Service'). The pilot, looking out of his window, was Attlee and the co-pilot Cripps. Advancing across the tarmac were Nehru, Baldev Singh and Jinnah and Liaquat Ali Khan. At the head was Wavell, but whereas the four Indian leaders were depicted as free agents merely prodding each other forward with a peremptory finger digging into the back of the man in front, Wavell's hands were manacled behind his back and the finger pressing into *him* was Nehru's. It was captioned 'The Invitation'. The editor had not published it because he thought it a shade too sympathetic to the Viceroy and potentially troublesome. Later he regretted his decision.

He had missed the point of the leer Halki had drawn on Attlee's face and only fully appreciated Halki's interpretation when in the following February (1947) after a further couple of months' variations on the theme of incompatibility (with the constituent assembly assembling without the League, and then the Congress threatening to withdraw from the interim gov-ernment if the League insisted on remaining in it), Attlee announced his government's intention of transferring power peacefully and responsibly by June 1948 and hinted that if the constitutional issue hadn't been solved by then an award would have to be made and power transferred to whatever authority Britain felt would govern in India's best interests. This (as the editor pointed out to Perron, who agreed) was exactly the kind of clear statement that Wavell had always tried to get. But it was accompanied by another, to the effect that Wavell's 'wartime appointment as Viceroy' (which was the first anyone had heard about such a limitation to a traditional five-year term of office) would end in March and that his successor would be Louis Mountbatten, the victorious Supremo of South-East Asia Command in the recent war, a relation of the King's, but patently a man of the new world.

Halki celebrated this news with a cartoon which the editor published against considerable internal opposition but with popular acclaim. Again, it was a two-frame cartoon, each frame showing a different aspect of one of those old-fashioned cottage-style barometers: a little rustic house from which a male figure emerged in poor conditions and a female one in summery.

Halki's rustic house was a simplified version of the main entrance to Viceregal House. Frame one showed Wavell outside the first of the twin doors. The sky above was black. Bulging monsoon clouds were pierced by a fork of lightning coming from the mouth of a heraldic, rather ancient, winged lion, labelled 'Imperialism, circa 1857'. In the second frame the sky was bland, lit by a sparkling little sun held aloft by a frisky airborne lamb (with Attlee's face) labelled 'Imperialism, circa 1947'. Below this bland sky the gaunt figure of Wavell had retired into the gloom of Viceregal House and out of the other door had come the fine-weather figure of a smart toy-soldier (Mountbatten), magnificently uniformed, taking the salute, smiling excessively and exuding sweetness and light.

Subsequently, Halki had found his cottage-barometer theme a useful one to hark back to during the first month or so of Mountbatten's appointment, weeks spent in seemingly inexhaustible rounds of conferences and counter-conferences. These later cartoons portrayed the various problems the new Viceroy had had to contend with and (perhaps) his growing exasperation at his inability to solve them to his own satisfaction. Political intransigence (from whichsoever party) was portrayed in the shape of the stormy figure (for example Jinnah, but not invariably; there was once even Gandhi) emerging from the dark door while the toy-soldier retreated into his, and the bland sky was threatened by clouds that never quite covered the frisky lamb (although the smile on the lamb's face tended to get more and more strained).

'But that first barometer cartoon,' the editor said, referring back to the Wavell/Mountbatten version, 'is the prime example of Halki's gift for foreseeing the inner nature of events before they have actually taken place.'

'When will Mr Shankar Lal be back in Bombay?' Perron asked. The editor shrugged. 'He went almost without notice. He came to see me just two weeks ago and said he must go to the Punjab to try to persuade his parents to come down here, because otherwise they would find themselves living in bloody Pakistan. He said he had been working two or three days on a cartoon for publication on August 15, in case he isn't back by then.'

'But there's still a fortnight to go.'

'I know. But he said his parents are very stubborn people. Anyway, I have the cartoon. It is terrible. I may not dare publish it. It is in the safe at home so I cannot show it to you. But you saw his June 3 cartoon? People say it is his masterpiece.'

'No, I haven't seen that.'

'Oh you must, Mr Perron. It is very funny. I have the original at home because even my wife laughed. Everybody laughed. They rang me from Delhi and told me Mountbatten had laughed.' The editor banged his desk bell. 'I will get a copy of the relevant issue.'

For the June 5 issue, commemorating Mountbatten's announcement that Pakistan was now inevitable, and that the British would withdraw 'probably by August 15' Halki had worked throughout June 4 and drawn a picture of an immense Gothic building, or rather a structure which the architect had planned as one only to be frustrated (one had to imagine) over certain details of land acquisition. The attempt to create an illusion of a single façade, although admirably conceived and executed, hadn't quite worked, although it took several moments of close study of Halki's exemplary drawing to discern this. The cartoon occupied a whole page.

The main building, one such as citizens of Bombay were especially familiar with, was a huge emporium bearing some basic resemblance to the local army and navy shop. Across the façade the name ran: *Imperial Stores*. Between the word *Imperial* and the word *Stores* were the royal coat of arms and the announcement: *By Self-Appointment*. The building was several storeys high and drawn so as to show the main street frontage and one side-street elevation. The main entrance, curiously, was on the side-street. Above this side-street entrance there was another sign: *Proprietor: Albert George Windsor; Manager:* Clem Attlee.

At ground level, front and side, there were display windows crammed with goods but across each banners had been pasted proclaiming: *Grand Closing Down Sale. Expiry of Lease. Starts June 3. Bargains in Every Department. All Stock must be Sold by August 15.* Above this building the lamb held the sparkling sun aloft.

Outside the main entrance on the side-street stood a tall, splendidly uniformed commissionaire who was looking at his watch, awaiting the moment to open the doors. Halki had caught Mountbatten's expression of detachment and self-confidence perfectly. All round the building there were queues of eager bargain hunters, mostly civilians but also soldiers and police. Each queue was separated from the others by its own 'Queue Here' sign – and these were variously inscribed, Congress, League, Sikhs, Hindu Mahasabah, Liberals, Europeans, Anglo-Indians, Tribes, Scheduled Castes; and at the head of each queue was a clearly identifiable leader who was consulting his shopping list.

The queues were orderly and well drilled – you felt that the commissionaire had disciplined them to be so and that he knew, they knew, he would stand no nonsense. One of these queues stretched right round the side-street and along the main frontage. This was the one headed by Mr Nehru and Mr Gandhi and was by far the longest. But exactly mid-way along the main frontage this queue was interrupted to allow passageway from the road into the building, and it was this visual break that confirmed (or originated) the impression that the building was not really an architectural whole.

Sandwiched between what could now be seen as two interrupted halves was an older building, obviously still in the ownership of a small shopkeeper who had been surrounded, propped up, pressed up against and down upon, by the giant concern, but never wholly absorbed. A great deal of ingenuity had been shown in creating the illusion that the smaller shop was part of the bigger one, that the older structure was a mere decorative flourish that did nothing to diminish the architectural integrity of the whole edifice. The older building announced itself as 'The Princes' Emporium' and was labelled, 'Imperial Stores (Paramountcy, 1857) Ltd'. The sticker across its one narrow window said, 'Business as Usual' and its narrow little Moghul door was guarded by a commissionaire whom the editor told Perron was recognizable as the head of the British Political Department.

Free access to this door from the road was secured by ropes that separated the orderly Congress queue, and Halki had depicted a very old-fashioned Rolls Royce drawn up at the pavement. Emerging from this limousine were a Maharajah and the first two or three of what looked like a car-full of wives arriving on a shopping expedition. Standing in the road just behind the car was a policeman – looking exactly like Patel, the chief enemy in the Congress camp of the Indian princely states. He was noting down the car's registration number in a book labelled 'Traffic Offences (Obstructions)'.

The fun did not end there. Facing the main frontage on the other side of the road there was work in progress on a giant multi-storeyed building, only the ground floor of which was completed and occupied. A placard announced: *Anglo-American Atomic and Commercial Enterprises Inc. and Ltd (Successors to Box-Wallah and Co.)*. Through the ground-floor windows you could see men at work in the offices. An American executive sat with his feet on a desk, smoking a cigar and using three telephones. A British executive sat with his feet under the desk, smoking a pipe and talking into only one. Queueing to enter the building was a hybrid collection of Indian businessmen consulting attend-ant lawyers who were in turn consulting draft contracts. Already in the building too, were figures representing the great Indian industrialists (Tata and Birla). A separate side-street entrance gave access to a queue of Muslim (Pakistan) businessmen, most of whom seemed destined to end up at the desk of the American executive.

And still the fun did not end. In distant perspective, on a con-tinuation of the main frontage of Imperial Stores, was a Labour Exchange, and here there were four queues of Englishmen and Englishwomen whose children were being comforted by faithful bearers and ayahs: a queue each for ICS, IMS, army and police. The queuers were going into and coming out of doors marked 'Pension' and 'Compensation'. Some of those who had collected their dues were walking across the road, holding moneybags, to join the queue waiting to enter the offices of Anglo-American Enterprises Inc. and Ltd. Some, obviously elderly, were trekking in another direction, to the office of a travel agent whose windows were bannered: Cheap One Way Retirement Tickets. Bilaiti and All Best Hill Stations.

There was no caption. A caption would have been excessive.

'Tomorrow I have a party,' the editor said. 'Come and see the original. At my house.'

'I'm afraid I can't. I'm leaving Bombay tomorrow morning,' Perron said.

'Then take this copy. I have never yet had in my office an Englishman all the way from London who comes to see me entirely to discuss Halki. He will be very flattered. No, no, that is wrong. I have never yet succeeded myself even in flattering him.'

'Thank you,' Perron said. He felt rather moved. It was the special gift Indians had, to move you unexpectedly; unexpectedly because you felt that historically you did not deserve any consideration or any kindness.

Leaving the newspaper office he walked for a while along the crowded Bombay pavement, then saw and hailed a taxi. He told the man to go in the direction of the Gateway and the Taj. When the taxi reached the spot where he had drawn up his jeep just two years ago he told the driver to stop but wait for him. He walked the few yards to the wall of the esplanade, with its view on to the Arabian Sea; and its smell. Disgusting. Peaceful. I shall never go back home, one Perron cried. The other said: Take me back, for God's sake. When he returned to the taxi he threw annas at the little crowd of children and told the driver to go to Queen's Road.

He paid the wallah off, tipping excessively as though this munificence had become obligatory since Mountbatten had removed the last doubt that the British intended to go and so made them the only people left in India who were universally popular. He studied the blocks of flats. He couldn't be certain which block he wanted, but then – believing he recognized the forecourt – he entered it, imagining Purvis ahead of him barging into the servant and the girl. He climbed the few steps to the dark entrance and went along an unfamiliar passage to the lift-shaft. This convincingly announced itself as out of order and on either side the name plates stirred other recollections. Desai?

Tractorwallah? He climbed the steps to the first floor and stood, perplexed, facing the door whose name plate should be Grace but wasn't. He went to the door opposite. Major Rajendra Singh, IMS. That, surely, was right? He climbed the next flight and arrived at the flat above Rajendra Singh's.

Hapgood. Mr Hapgood, the banker, Mrs Hapgood, the banker's wife and Miss Hapgood, the banker's daughter. One of the few remaining happy families in Bombay? He pressed the bell. Would the servant be the same servant? Would they recognize one another? The door opened. He did not recognize the servant. The boy was (God help us all, Perron thought) Japanese.

'Is Mr Hapgood in?' he asked. He handed in his card. The boy studied it carefully, ridging eyebrows as beautifully shaped as Aneila's. Not quite Japanese; a mixed-blood oriental from Sumatra? Singapore? Jakarta? A handsome, poisonous-looking young man who sported a gold wrist-watch. One could smell the starch on his arrogantly spotless white steward's jacket and trousers. He wore black shoes with pointed toes. 'I will see if Master is in.'

Perron thought: Master, now, is it? The British will always be safe.

The boy let him in, then shut the door and went in the direction of the living-room. Perron glanced down the corridor towards Purvis's old room. The door was shut, so was the door of the adjoining room. And the flat looked as if it had not been redecorated since then.

'Master says come.'

Perron followed the boy through the dining-room area and into the living-room which had once struck him as elegant, which now looked just a little disorganized. A quick glance at the wall behind the long settee confirmed the continuing existence of the Guler-Basohli paintings. A man stood on the balcony, as Purvis had done, holding a glass, looking out at the Oval. It was a clear evening, the sun not yet down. The man was tall and thin. For some reason Perron had always imagined Hapgood as short, rotund and red-faced; like the tea-planter at the Maharanee's. Hearing footsteps, Hapgood turned round.

'Mr Perron?'

'Yes. Mr Hapgood?'

'What can I do for you?'

'I'm sorry to bother you. I called downstairs on the off-chance of seeing Colonel and Mrs Grace. I see they've gone, but I thought I'd take the opportunity to come up, because I feel I owe you an apology.'

'Oh?' Hapgood was a man with formidable eyebrows. His face was yellow and very creased. His jaw and chin suggested firmness of opinion. 'Have we met?' he asked.

'No. You and your family were away, in Ootacamund I think. But there was an officer called Leonard Purvis billeted here – a couple of years ago. I was here the day things rather got on top of him. I wasn't here when he smashed things up, but I saw the results, and I've always felt it was partly my fault that two of your Kangra paintings were damaged.'

Hapgood's eyebrows twitched. He glanced at the wall.

'Oh?' Then, 'Actually they're Guler-Basohli school. But Kangra covers it.'

The servant had come in with a glass on a tray. He put this down on the drinks table.

'Scotch? Gin?' Hapgood asked.

'Gin, thank you.'

'Master will have gin,' Hapgood told the boy without looking at him. 'Why do you feel it was partly your fault?'

'Purvis had no idea what they were, until I admired them and told him how valuable they were. So it was probably my fault that he singled them out when he was throwing bottles.'

'Oh,' Hapgood said. 'Was that why? We often wondered. He never seemed to notice them.' He strolled across the room towards the paintings. 'But as you see, the damage has been fairly well disguised. They are exquisite, aren't they? My wife was pretty upset at the time. But as I told her, it needs more than a bottle of rum to destroy a work of art.'

Perron had forgotten it was rum. Hapgood hadn't. He turned to Perron suddenly. 'Did you know the man my old bearer told me about? The man who had to climb the balcony and pull Purvis out of the bath?'

Perron admitted that he was the man.

Hapgood said, 'Good heavens.' Then, 'My dear chap. How nice of you to call – to have remembered the paintings. My wife will be sorry to have missed you. She was awfully touched that you bothered to leave the servant a chit about the bathroom door.'

Perron recalled that the servant had asked for a chit. He didn't actually remember writing one. Obviously he had done, probably while sitting in this room afterwards, drinking Old Sporran.

'Perron,' Hapgood was saying. 'Perron. Yes, I remember now. But ...'

'*Sergeant* Perron,' Perron said, to clear up any doubts. 'Field Security, Poona.'

'Field Security? I see. Somehow we'd always imagined the Sergeant Perron who pulled Purvis out of the bath was something to do with his so-called economic advisory staff.' Hapgood led the way back to the balcony. 'Field Security, Poona. Did you know a fellow who's now in pharmaceuticals here? What's his name –'

'Bob Chalmers?'

'That's it. Chalmers. His firm banks with us. I don't know him well. I remember he said he was Field Security in Poona and liked it so much he stayed on.'

'Chalmers was my officer. Actually I'm staying in his flat here in Bombay. We kept up, after the war.'

'Well bless my soul. Have you come out to join his firm?'

'No, I'm only on a visit. Quite a short one. And I've not seen Bob yet and probably won't now. He had to go to Calcutta just before I arrived, but left everything laid on so that I could stay at his place.'

'Yes, I see. And you knew the Graces?'

'No, I knew their niece, and their niece's father.'

'I'm afraid Mrs Grace has left. Poor old Arthur Grace died last year. Very suddenly. My wife and I were quite upset. He'd had dinner with us only the night before. Mrs Grace had gone up country to see her sister. The niece was getting married. Yes, I remember now. She was here to meet her father, wasn't she, when we were in Ooty?'

'The elder niece was here. There was a younger one.'

'I don't remember that. Anyway, one of them got married. Which was why Fenny Grace was away and poor old Arthur was on his own for a couple of weeks. We used to have him up. I thought he was perfectly all right but my wife said she wasn't happy about him. She said he looked as if he didn't know what anything was about any longer. Curious phrase. But women have these intuitions. He had a heart attack. Went, just like that.'

Hapgood snapped his fingers, but to call the servant's attention to his empty glass. Perron's was still half-full.

'This was last year?'

'Last year, yes. Middle of February. When the Indian ratings here mutinied. Things were a bit of a mess, but Fenny came back the moment we wired. Actually we thought it a bit thick that no one from her family came with her to help her get through it. But you're right. There must have been two nieces. I remember her saying her niece wanted to come with her. She couldn't have meant the niece who'd just got married. Must have been the other.'

'Sarah, I should think. The one who got married must have been Susan.'

'It rings a bell.'

'Susan must have married a man called Merrick.'

'I think that was it. Chap with something wrong with him?'

'He lost an arm in the war.'

'That's it. Yes. Fenny left us some snaps she took at the wedding. She had them printed here once she'd dealt with the funeral. Pity my wife's away. She'd have details like this much clearer in her mind. If you're anxious for news of the family I'm sure I could turn up the sister's address. Pankot, wasn't it? Fenny must have given it to my wife, and my wife's very efficient keeping her address book written up.'

'I have the Pankot address. It's just that I've not heard since the end of 'forty-five. My fault really. One somehow lets things slide.'

'True. True. One lets things slide. The last we saw of Fenny was when she left for Delhi after the funeral. She was going to fly home to another sister in London. I expect the London address is in my wife's book too, but I don't think they wrote to one another because Fenny said it would only be a short trip and that she'd be back again. Then our daughter married an awfully nice Canadian Air Force chap we met in Ooty. We were in Montreal last year for the wedding. Pretty killing expense. But once in a lifetime. Now my wife's back in Montreal waiting to become a grandmother. I'm expecting a telegram almost any day.'

Perron lifted his glass. 'Good luck.'

'Thank you.' After drinking Hapgood said, 'Are you committed this evening?'

Perron lied. 'I'm afraid so, yes.'

'Tomorrow, perhaps?'

'Unfortunately I've left this call very late. I'm off tomorrow.'

'Oh. Where are you off to? Not home?'

'No, a little state called Mirat.'

'A long journey. They had some trouble there recently. Is that why you're going?'

'I didn't know that. What sort of trouble?'

'Usual thing. Communal riots. I think it's died down. Anyway, it's in the Punjab things are getting tricky. Too many people on the move in the hope of ending up in the right place. But what can you expect when you draw an imaginary line through a province and say that from August fifteen one side is Pakistan and the other side's India? The same applies to Bengal.'

'It is rather drastic, isn't it?'

Hapgood gave Perron a penetrating glance. He said, 'It's what an important minority felt they had to have and in the long term it's probably for the best.'

Perron nodded. Hapgood was probably more in sympathy with the Muslims than with the Hindus.

'Do you have press connections, then, Mr Perron?'

'Only rather marginal ones. Sufficient to help me move about and get seats on planes.'

'I asked because nearly every stranger from home you come across nowadays is either a journalist or a member of parliament swanning around ostensibly to observe the democratic process of dismantling the empire but actually making soundings for his private business interests. Nothing wrong with that, of course. India's going to be an expanding dominion market once it settles down. The thing is, we'll have to meet more outside and inside competition. Do you have business interests as well as marginal press ones, Mr Perron?'

'My interests are primarily academic.'

Again Hapgood snapped his fingers and again while they continued talking his glass was taken and replenished and returned. This time Perron had his own glass topped up. The Oval was under the spell of pink and turquoise light, fading into indigo shadows.

'If you have press connections, though, I suppose you're here to be in at the kill, if I may put it that way. Forgive me, but Mirat seems such an unlikely little place to go. If you want to be in at the kill you should go up into the Punjab and try to accredit yourself to the wretched chaps who've been formed into the boundary force and have the job of protecting the refugees and stopping them tearing at one another's throats.'

'Well as I said. My interests are primarily academic. And at the moment primarily concerned with the relationship between the Crown and the Indian states.'

'Well you could go up to Bahawalpur. They've had some high jinks there. Or down to Hyderabad. That's the one princely state large and powerful enough to prolong its independence for a while. Have you seen Patel? He's in charge of what I call the coercing operation. Have you seen the head of the British Political Department? He'd give you the other side of the picture. They say his department has been burning private papers for weeks now, all the scandalous stuff we've collected over the years about the way some of the Princes behaved. Couldn't let Patel get his hands on those, could you?'

'Well I have a definite invitation to Mirat. I think it will suit me very well, especially if it's had its troubles.'

'What sort of invitation, Mr Perron? I ask because I might be able to help you.'

'That's very kind of you. Actually the invitation's from the Chief Minister, Count Bronowsky. I met him here in Bombay during the war. He was kind enough to say I'd be welcome in Mirat at any time.'

'Then there's nothing I could do to smooth your way better. It was Bronowsky I had in mind. I don't know him socially, but he's had an account with us for years, and we usually meet in my office when he comes to Bombay. I haven't seen him for some time. Probably because of the troubles they've had there. How is he?'

'I've no idea, but well, I imagine. I wrote to him just before coming out from England and there was a telegram waiting for me at Bob Chalmers's flat, inviting me to turn up whenever I wanted.'

'Well. Give him my regards.'

Perron looked at his watch, and prepared to finish his drink.

'Are you absolutely committed this evening? I've got a few people coming in, couple of chaps from the bank and their wives. Friends. Not all that boring. Actually it's buffet. Nowadays in Bombay you never know who'll turn up or who they'll bring. Being alone just now I encourage it.'

Perron was tempted. He had a brief and flaming image of the Maharanee floating in on the arms of a couple of English bankers, in her scarlet saree, subsiding on to the long settee under the Guler-Basohli paintings, showing her nipples; and of Aneila offering chairs, cigarettes, and dewy tumblers which she had rinsed under the tap in Purvis's bathroom to help the sinister little servant cope. And an image, then, of all the lights going out, because the light had virtually gone now from the forgiving Bombay sky, leaving only a gleam in the fretted edges of the palm fronds. And the sweet, grave, unforgettable unforgotten smell, drifting across from Back Bay.

'I'm afraid I am committed, sir,' Perron said. 'Perhaps if I come back this way I could give you a ring.'

'Of course,' Hapgood said, pleased to be called sir. But it was *now* Hapgood wanted. A new face to ease the ache of boredom. Hapgood's own face went out, as the nearby street-lamp came on, below and behind him. A trick of illumination.

'You have a new servant, I see.'

'Young Gerard? Yes. Bit of a mongrel. We inherited him from a chap who retired last year. Our agent in Ipoh. Gerard kept things going for him while he was in prison-camp. Very efficient fellow. Not like poor old Nadar, the one you'd remember. Trouble with Nadar, he couldn't keep his hands off stuff that got left around. We had to let him go. Mistake, probably. My wife says it's better to employ a dishonest servant you know inside out than one you'll never get on any sort of terms with. Not that it's going to matter either way to us next year. Our time will be up then. Learn to do our own cooking and washing up, I shouldn't wonder. Neither of us fancies Montreal. So it looks like Ewell or Sutton. Know anything about mushrooms?'

Automatically Perron thought of cloud formations.

'Mushrooms?'

'A friend of our Canadian son-in-law, an ex-RAF type who lives in Surrey, has gone in for mushrooms. Grows them in his garage. Making a fortune, I'm told. Not that we'll be looking to do that. But you need to put your mind to something, so preferably something with a saleable end-product. I don't fancy chickens. Mushrooms are quieter.'

Hapgood smiled. His face, re-illuminated as he guided Perron back into the living-room where Gerard had switched on some of the table-lamps, looked composed. And resigned. 'Well,' he said, 'if you change your mind, just arrive. Meanwhile I'd better get myself ready for the invasion.' Perhaps Gerard had run his bath (with the same imperturbable expression he had shown when running baths for Japanese officers in his previous master's house in Ipoh?).

Perron was about to say, 'Do you still have the same cook?' but realized in time that this might sound like an inquiry into the quality of the food to be expected. So he left not knowing whether that happy, co-operative, and sturdy little man still presided over the hot stoves in the Hapgood kitchen. On the whole, Perron thought, it was unlikely that he did. The bearer, the cook, and the cook's boy, had been a happy family too, in spite of the rivalry and the demarcation of zones of responsibility. When the bearer went they had probably followed him.

As Gerard held the door open, Perron glanced once again down the corridor, to get his last glimpse of Purvis's still-closed door.

Back in Bob Chalmers's rather odd flat he made a few notes about his visit to Hapgood. The oddness of Bob's flat consisted not merely in the unexpected situation of the house (in one of the narrow rather squalid roads behind the Gateway; not far, surely, from where the massage parlour had been?) but in the admixture of traditional and emergent Anglo-Indianism in its appointments. The rooms where basic European needs were scrupulously met (bathroom, bedrooms, dining-room) were furnished in the old dependable style. But in the living-room there was nowhere to sit comfortably. There were imitation Persian rugs on the floor, sparkling cushions from Rajputana, mattresses covered by dur-ries or printed cotton bedspreads, a pair of tablas, a harmonium, and in a conker-coloured leather case – a tamboura, probably from Bengal. On the walls there were modern paintings by modern Indian painters. Impressionism had arrived (and a poin-tilliste school, after Seurat, to judge by a disturbing view of the

burning ghats at Benares). Scattered round the room on cushions, on floor, on mattresses and in a unit-style bookcase, were
the things that showed Bob Chalmers to be perhaps a little
uncertain where his tastes lay. There were trade magazines
dealing with pharmaceuticals and other light and heavy industrial subjects. There were literary magazines published in
Calcutta and pale blue stiff-boarded editions of works by Radak-
rishnan about *karma* and *dharma* and the Hindu way of life. The
bookcase held several volumes from the Left Book Club, a row
of old *Readers' Digests* and the latest novel by Nevil Shute. On
a very low coffee-table, among pottery ashtrays, were a translation of the poems of Gaffur by a Major Tippet, and the March
1947 issue of *The New English Forum* which Perron had sent him.
This was an issue containing one of Perron's articles, the article
originally entitled *Daulat Rao Sindia and the British Other Rank*,
but subsequently retitled (for publication) *An Evening at the
Maharanee's*, which title Perron had tossed out from the top of
his head at the end of a rather drunken lunch at Prunier's with
the young Tory MP who published the magazine and whose
personal assistant in the publishing firm he directed had recommended Perron as a likely contributor, after reading Perron's
review (in the *New English University Monthly*) of a book called
My Memories of INA and its Netaji, by Major-General Shahnawaz
Khan, Foreword by Pt Jawahar Lal Nehru [*sic*], which Bob
Chalmers had sent him from Bombay after its publication in
Delhi in 1946 with a letter of which the only passage Perron
clearly remembered was: 'Remember Bombay and Bordeaux?
Well, this is connected. And get that last paragraph of "Jawahar
Lal's" foreword, I quote: "I must confess that I have not been
able, through lack of time, to read through this record, but I have
read parts of it and it seems to me that this account is far the best
we have at present." Unquote. How's that for shrewd fence-
sitting, now that the trials are over?'

But then, Perron thought, putting his notebook away, and
nodding assent to Bob Chalmers's bearer who was standing in
the doorway indicating that supper was ready (which he could
already tell, smelling the delicious scent of turmeric) where else
can one sit, and remain in balance?

II

Perron woke. The silence was solid; as if he had been spun off the world into space. There were no echoes, not a glimmer of light in the primeval dark. Then he heard the engine breathe in the distance and re-identified himself as the lucky lone occupant of a coupé on the night train from Ranpur to Mirat. He sat up, reached for his cigarettes. The lighter illuminated his watch. Five a.m. He twisted his body round and raised the blind and then the shutter and gazed out at the pale frozen landscape. So vast a country. Its beauty unnerved him. The engine breathed again, sounding nearer. He held his own breath and listened to another sound: the cries of dogs hunting the plain in packs.

When he woke again light was streaming through the un-shuttered window and the train was moving slowly, clacking its wheels rhythmically, reluctantly. The landscape was eroded. Nothing could live here, he thought.

He was cold. He got up, slipped his feet into chappals and reached for his robe. Enfolded in silk he rasped one hand against his cheeks. His eyes were gummy. They felt raw from the specks of sand and soot that had entered the compartment. Pushing through the door into the lavatory he felt the chill coming up through the hole in the pan. He wanted hot coffee. Comfort. There was none. In an hour or two it would seem impossible that he had ever felt cold.

Shaved, washed, dressed, he went to the sunny side of the compartment to warm himself. It was 7 a.m. He should have been in Mirat by now and drinking coffee or tea in the station restaurant, getting some bacon and egg. He had lost the knack of travelling in India. He hadn't even brought a flask of water. All he had was yesterday's papers, bought in Ranpur: the *Times of India* and the *Ranpur Gazette*. He now read through the *Gazette*, scarcely taking it in, flicking the pages. The only pieces worth reading were a waspish editorial and a quiet essay by someone calling himself Philoctetes. He couldn't remember who Philoctetes was. In this case, probably, the editor, exercising a gentle taste for *belles-lettres*.

He went back to the window. The train was passing a village. Water buffalo wallowed in the local tank. Women walked with baskets of cow-dung on their heads. Men drove skeletal goats and horned cattle. There was a smell of smoke. It would be a hot dry day.

It was gone nine o'clock when the train drew into Mirat (Cantonment): two hours late according to the new schedule. He was glad that he hadn't announced his arrival in advance and put anyone to the trouble of meeting him.

The platform was crowded. Officers, wives, mounds of luggage. Departing British. A train seemed to be expected in the other direction, from Mirat to Ranpur. The restaurant was crowded too. There wasn't a vacant table and he didn't want to share. He decided to push on and told the coolie to take him to where tongas were to be had.

The concourse was also crowded, mostly by squads of British troops squatting on piles of kit-bags, smoking. Perron's suitcase and hold-all were put on to a tonga. He told the man to go to the club. The tonga set off through the cantonment bazaar. Perron breathed in the familiar smell: an oily, spicy scent mingling with that of burning charcoal. And then they were out on to the first of the wide geometrically laid out roads of a military station, metalled roads with khatcha edges, shade trees, and lime-washed stones marking the culvert crossings over monsoon ditches, which gave access to the compounds of the old bungalows. The tonga passed neat white-shirted Indian clerks on cycles and was passed in turn by military trucks. Once you had seen one cantonment, it was said, you had seen them all.

It took twenty minutes to reach the club. The way in was by a broad gravel drive that curved through a compound darkened and cooled by trees and shrubs. The colonnaded façade was dazzling white. Against the white the sprays of red and purple bougainvillaea stood out exuberantly. After the tonga wallah had taken the luggage into the vestibule Perron paid him off.

There was no one in the vestibule. The hall beyond led to a terrace set with wicker chairs and tables. The vestibule was dark, high ceilinged. There were palms in brass pots. He banged a bell on the desk (which was discreetly positioned behind a pillar). A servant appeared from behind another pillar. Perron asked for the secretary. While he waited he studied some of the framed photographs that hung on the white-washed walls. These were

mostly of victorious teams from old tournaments in the 1920s.
Tennis, polo, cricket, golf. There was a photograph of Edward
VIII when he was Prince of Wales.

A young Indian in European clothes came into the vestibule,
asked if he could help, explained that the secretary was still
having breakfast. Perron gave him his card and said he would be
in Mirat for a little while and wondered whether the club could
offer temporary membership, and if so whether it might include
accommodation, say for tonight, and some breakfast now. The
card he offered was the one that gave his London club address.
The man glanced at it and said he was sure this could be arranged
but that he would speak to the secretary. The bearer came back.
The clerk told him to show the sahib out on to the terrace and
serve him breakfast.

The terrace was longer and wider than the view from the
vestibule suggested. Apart from the wicker chairs and tables
which were arranged close to the balustrade to give occupants a
view directly on to a long sweep of lawn and flowerbeds (with,
beyond, behind a white painted fence, rougher ground set out
for jumping and riding displays), there was also a line of club
dining-tables and chairs ranged along the length of the inner
wall. The tables were free of napery, their mahogany surfaces
highly polished. Each had a silk-shaded lamp. There were probably a dozen of these tables and, between each pair, casement
doors which led into the interior. Half-way along the terrace
one of the tables was occupied by two Indian officers and an
Indian civilian (or an officer in civilian clothes). The rest were
empty. At the far end of the line of wicker chairs and tables sat
a European woman. She wore sunglasses and was drinking
coffee. The Indian officers and the civilian were finishing breakfast. The bearer guided Perron to the first of the empty dining-
tables.

He was a grizzled old man, white-uniformed, sashed, bare-
foot, gloved and turbanned. Having seated Perron he went away,
returned almost at once with a tray from which he took things
to lay a single place on the gleaming surface. Having done this
he produced the final item − a menu secured in a silver-plated
stand. 'Sahib,' he said, and went, leaving Perron to consult the
bill of fare. Perron, picking the card up by its stand, suddenly
leant back, gazed out at the sweep of lawn, the canna-lilies, the

immense earthen pots of delicately tinted and scented flowers that stood sentinel between each batch of wicker chairs and tables. India, he thought. India. I'm back. *Really* back. Why, he wondered, was the Mirat Gymkhana Club so familiar? And then saw why. Once, both wearing civilian clothes, Bob Chalmers had breakfasted him at the Turf Club in Poona. The Mirat Gymkhana might have been a duplicate. The bearer came out again with a wooden contraption which he opened up and set behind the side-plate. A newspaper rest. Upon this he placed a folded newspaper called the *Mirat Courier.*

'No *Times of India?*'

'Not until midday, Sahib. Yesterday's is available.'

'I think not yesterday's. What is Fish Soufflé Izzat Bagh?'

'Local fish, Sahib. Caught daily in Izzat Bagh lake. Cooked with spice and served with rice. Today not recommended.'

'Oh, why?'

'Today not fresh, Sahib. Fish too long on ice. Fishermen not going out two day now.'

Perron ordered eggs and bacon and, when the old man had gone turned to watch the belligerent shining blue-black crows making hungry sorties on to the wet lawn. The Indian officers suddenly laughed aloud and slapped their napkins down. The European woman wearing the sunglasses was getting up, gathering her things. She went through one of the open casement windows at the far end of the terrace. The civilian with the officers went on talking. Perhaps he was telling them funny stories.

'Mr Perron?'

An elderly man, short, stout, bald, stood by Perron's table. Perron got up, took the offered hand.

'Macpherson,' the man said. 'I'm the secretary. Please –' But Perron remained standing until, accepting his invitation Macpherson sat too. 'I hope you're being looked after all right.' Perron assured him he was. 'Don't have the fish, incidentally.'

'Your chap's already warned me off it.'

'That must be old Ghulam. Thank God for him anyway. Staff's difficult nowadays. Night train from Ranpur?' Perron nodded. 'Should have been in at seven. It gets worse every year. I see from your card you're from home. Been out here long?'

'About ten days. Can you put me up for the night?'

'For as long as you like. Nowadays we have more departures

than arrivals. All the same, even for a night I'm afraid you'll have to pay temporary membership and I'm afraid the fee's for a minimum of one calendar month. War-time rule, dating from when young officers were coming and going and being posted overnight.'

'And forgetting to pay their bills?'

'That's about it. Still, a lot of them are dead long since, I expect. You've been out here before haven't you?'

'Yes, but not for long. A couple of years during the war.'

The Indian officers and the civilian had got up and were approaching. Macpherson looked up. 'Everything all right, Bubli?'

'Everything's fine, Mac.'

'Are you dining tonight?'

'Who can tell, with one thing and the other?'

'If you don't tell you're likely to get Fish Soufflé Izzat Bagh.'

'Oh, God help us. I'll let you know. See you, Mac.'

'See you, Bubli.'

'Nice fellow,' Macpherson said when they were alone again. 'Gentleman. But then most of them are. Which I can't say for some of our fellows.'

'How long have you been secretary, Mr Macpherson?'

'About ten years. Mirat was my first station. Oh, years ago before the other war. Artillery. I got a chance to come back in nineteen thirty. Jumped at it. Retired in 'thirty-five. Took this on. Don't regret a single day. Look forward to many more. No ties at home anyway.'

Perron nodded. He understood that here was where Macpherson would prefer to die.

'I had a job, though, back in 'thirty-seven, opening membership to Indian officers. It split the committee right down the middle. But I said if a man's got the King's Commission what does it matter what his complexion is. During the war the old members agreed I was right. It damned well disgusted us. We were damned well ashamed, I mean of some of our own countrymen. Do you know what they did once? Emptied all the chamber pots from the men's room into the swimming pool, because they'd seen a couple of Indian subalterns swimming there. I marched them out pretty smartly. Chamber pots in the swimming pool were just about their Kingston Bypass style. Of course, that was wartime, 'forty-two, when the Indian politicians were kicking up a fuss. But do you know what happened here a few weeks ago?'

'No?'

'Swimming pool again. Someone excreted into a Gandhi cap and floated it. I never found out who. But I had my suspicions. Had to drain the pool, have it scraped, and get a Brahmin priest along to do a purification ritual before it was refilled. No Indian's been in it since. It'll be all right though.'

'Whom did you suspect?'

'The leader of what I called Mirat's second-fifteen rugger club. The English officer who let wind when I took Mirat's Chief Minister into the men's bar one evening.'

'Did the Chief Minister comment?'

'Not directly. He's not an Indian. If he had been he wouldn't have commented at all. But he couldn't resist saying, Shall we get some fresh air?' Macpherson waved a hand, indicating the terrace. Perron's breakfast began to arrive. 'Sorry, Mr Perron. Unpleasant subject. Enjoy your breakfast.'

Perron stood to acknowledge the secretary's leave-taking. He said, 'I know the man you mean, Dmitri Bronowsky? Actually I'm in Mirat to see him. Perhaps I can telephone from here and leave a message that I've arrived?'

Macpherson hesitated. 'Is he expecting you?'

'In general, yes.' Perron explained about the telegram that had awaited his arrival in Bombay. 'But I didn't wire back. I thought I'd just turn up.'

'I know he was here a few days ago but he may have gone to Gopalakand. I can find out easily enough. He's got a full plate just now. Not just Patel and company. Things haven't been too good here the past week or so.'

'It all looked quiet enough this morning.'

'Oh, in the cantonment. But across the lake, in the city. Not so good. That's why we don't recommend the Fish Soufflé Izzat Bagh. The fishermen are Muslims. They've fished the Nawab's lake since the eighteenth century. Tradition. Special sect. But they haven't dared go out the last couple of days since a couple of them were found drowned. They call it murder and blame the Hindus. So it looks as if we may be back to how it was last year and earlier this. There's a curfew in the old city. But we can always make you comfortable here, Mr Perron. I'll send my clerk along with the temporary members' book.'

Macpherson went. Perron drank his orange juice. The clerk came with the book. Perron filled in the columns at the top of the clean page at which the book was open. He resisted the temptation to turn back and check how long it had been since the club had last received a temporary member.

The front page of the *Mirat Courier* for today, Monday August 4, featured a muddily reproduced photograph of the Viceroy in Delhi with some of India's leading princes, which Perron had already seen in the *Times of India*. There was no reference in the accompanying article to Mirat's own prince, the Nawab, but the tone of the article suggested that the editor was anxious to convey an impression that the relationship between the princes and the Viceroy was of the friendliest kind; which, however true, was largely irrelevant to the political issue. The front page was, in fact, all sweetness and light. There was no follow-up to the rumour Perron had heard that Jinnah was accusing the Sikh leader Tara Singh of planning to assassinate him and sabotage the partition of the Punjab.

The bearer brought his bacon and egg and, glancing up, Perron saw that the woman in the sunglasses had come out of the further casement doorway and was walking slowly along the central strip of coconut matting. From a distance he'd assumed that she was middle-aged, perhaps because her hair looked dull, colourless, and because the sunglasses accentuated the rather disagreeable set of the mouth. Nearer to, he saw that she was quite a young woman, thin but well-shaped, with a good bust, and a graceful walk of the kind that suggested she had always been proud of her carriage and had worked at perfecting it: an acquired good carriage, rather than the natural good carriage that he remembered as characteristic, for example, of Sarah Layton. As she came nearly level with his table Perron smiled and said, 'Good morning.' She smiled too and murmured good morning and went slowly on. She reminded him (he realized) of a younger *Mrs* Layton. She had that kind of composure: indolence almost. She left behind her a whiff of scent just heavy enough to suggest that it was expensive.

Before starting on his breakfast Perron turned the *Mirat Courier* over to its back page. Here was another muddy photograph, illustrating a report headed 'Happy Occasion in Ranpur', and by-lined 'From our Ranpur Correspondent'. He settled to eat and read.

'The grounds of Government College in Ranpur were the scene of a happy occasion on Saturday when His Excellency the Governor, Sir Leonard Perkin, opened the new college building in which a future generation of Indian engineers will receive their education. "Let us hope," Sir Leonard said, "that these young men, on whose shoulders India places great responsibility, as she moves forward into a new industrial age, will look back on the times they spent here, in this handsome building, with a gratitude at least as great as we here feel today to its inspirer and founder and principal benefactor, Mr Chakravarti."

'Sir Leonard went on to recall how, just two years ago, when the future seemed less certain, his distinguished predecessor, Sir George Malcolm, laid the first stone for the new wing. "Many of you," Sir Leonard said, "will remember that occasion and perhaps regret as I do that Sir George is not here to open the splendid college that has arisen from that single stone. Be assured that I shall send him an account and appropriate photographs of it."

'Sir Leonard went on to speak of the gratitude he himself had always felt to the evening technical institute he had attended as a youth after a hard day's work in the industrial north of England. He then referred to the "grave doubts" he had had when, in 1946, Prime Minister Attlee had proposed to put his name forward as Governor in Ranpur. "Well, Len, the PM said to me, we've already sent Fred Burrowes to Bengal and he's an old railwayman too and not doing too badly. Unfortunately," Sir Leonard continued, "Fred has stolen my best joke, which was that while I knew nothing about shootin' and huntin' I knew quite a bit about tootin' and shuntin', so perhaps after all I could be of some service in the brief period I hoped it might take, which indeed it has taken, for us to climb down from the foot-plate and make way for you chaps, of whose skill and devotion and confidence in the future this college is both proof and symbol."

'Amid popular acclaim, Sir Leonard then led the way from the platform to the main entrance of the new building. Receiving the key he made a characteristically generous gesture, placing the key in the door and then inviting Mr Chakravarti to turn it so that he would be the first to enter the college which Mr Chakravarti described later as "the fulfilment of an old dream".

'Present among the guests was Mr Mohammed Ali Kasim, obviously recovered from the recent chill that prevented his attendance at the Chamber of Commerce dinner two weeks ago. Until the announcement also two weeks ago that Mr Trivurdi would succeed Sir Leonard Perkin, Mr Kasim had been widely tipped as the new Governor-designate. Answering your reporter's questions, Mr Kasim said he had no particular plans for the immediate future but that Mr Trivurdi's appointment as Governor was one that would have his whole-hearted approval. He declined to answer our question whether the Governorship had been offered to him first, and whether such a refusal was an indication that presently Mr Kasim intends to return actively to politics in the province.'

The article about the Chakravarti building had seen Perron through his bacon and egg and part of his toast and marmalade. The bearer asked if the sahib desired a fresh pot of coffee. Perron said he did. He took another piece of toast and folded the *Mirat Courier* to pages two and three. A glance at page two showed that it was taken up entirely by box-advertising, so he placed the paper on the stand with page three towards him.

Another muddy photograph; but suddenly he paused, a piece of toast on its way to his mouth, but never getting there. He pushed back his chair and took the *Courier* over to the stronger light near the balustrade. The face in the photograph was virtually unrecognizable. The heading alone made identification possible:

Lieutenant-Colonel Merrick, DSO
A moving ceremony

'The funeral service for the late Lieut.-Colonel (Ronnie) Merrick, DSO, whose tragic death we reported last week, was held last Saturday here at St Mary's, in a simple but moving ceremony conducted by The Reverend Martin Gilmour who, in his short address to a large congregation, spoke of Colonel Merrick as "a man who came into our midst, a stranger, and inspired us all by his devotion to duty, and has now gone, leaving us not poorer but richer for the example he set".'

The same Merrick? The three-quarter profile photograph did not itself confirm so. Perron scanned quickly down to the smaller print where the names of the chief mourners might be found.

'Supporting the widow were members and close friends of the family, Colonel John Layton, Mrs F. Grace, Captain Nigel Rowan (AAGG) and Mrs Rowan. Among the representatives of the cantonment were the station commander and his wife, Colonel and Mrs Rossiter and the Misses Rossiter, Brigadier and Mrs Thorpe, Colonel and Mrs S. K. Srinivasan, Major Thwaite and Miss Drusilla Thwaite, Major and Mrs Peabody, Captain and Mrs P. L. Mehta.'

So, then, yes. Merrick. But who was Mrs Rowan? Sarah? She wasn't otherwise named. And what were they all doing in Mirat? AAGG meant assistant to the agent to the Governor-General. Was Rowan political agent in Mirat? He went back to the larger print.

'Referring briefly to Colonel Merrick's skilful handling of the far from easy task entrusted to him some months ago, the chaplain pointed out that the man whom they had gathered together to mourn and honour was one who had a disability that would probably have persuaded many men to feel that the period of their useful active employment and service had ended. "Ronnie," he said, "never felt this. Some of you have seen, many of us have heard, how this gallant officer who had taught himself to ride again, led his detachment of States Police during times of trouble, patiently and humanely but firmly restoring order and securing the peace of the state in whose service he was for all too short a time."

' "Today," he continued, "our hearts and prayers should be offered to Colonel Merrick's widow, in thanksgiving for a life so well lived, so abruptly ended, so sadly lost."

'After the singing of the hymn "Abide with Me" there was a moment's silence and then from outside the church came the clear sombre notes of the Last Post, sounded off by a bugler of the Mirat Artillery. An equally moving last touch to the simple service was made when the Chief Minister of State in Mirat, the Count Bronowsky, stepped forward and assisted the widow from the church.

'A few days earlier a post-mortem confirmed that Colonel Merrick died as a result of injuries sustained in a riding accident.

The funeral was delayed to enable the widow and other members of the family to attend. The remains were cremated.'

'Sahib?'

The bearer had brought the tray of fresh coffee. He was asking Perron whether he wanted it at the breakfast table or at the verandah table where Perron was leaning against the balustrade. Perron nodded at the verandah table and then read the report again. And now the muddy photograph began to take on a sinister likeness to the Merrick he had known. He sat down, poured more coffee, and continued to study both the photograph and the report.

'I didn't know,' a woman's voice said, 'that the local rag could be so absorbing.'

Startled, he looked up. The woman in the sunglasses had come back and was sitting two tables away. Her voice was low-keyed, a bit hoarse, but attractive. He smiled, put the paper away and said, 'I'm sorry, I didn't see you.'

'That's what I mean. You are Guy Perron, aren't you?'

'Yes —?'

'You've been expected. So I did wonder when I saw you arrive. I've been nosey and had a look at the book you signed. No, please don't move.' She got up herself and came to join him. She took the sunglasses off, revealing rather pale eyes, blue-grey with a tinge of violet. A tiny scar, about an inch long, white, showed clearly beneath the left one. In spite of this blemish she was in a sad, rather exhausted way, beautiful.

'You won't recognize me. But you might remember me as Laura Elliott. At least Nigel told me you did.'

After a few seconds Perron said, 'Yes. Laura Elliott.' He offered his hand. Hers was rather clammy. He said, 'The coffee's fresh. Let me ask the bearer for another cup.'

'Thank you.' She sat down. He rang the handbell. When the old man came out he saw at once what was wanted and went back in. Perron sat. She was gazing steadily at him.

'I *think* I remember you,' she said. 'I mean I know I remember you but think I recognize you.'

'And I you.'

'No. I shouldn't think so.'

She had a directness that wasn't unpleasant, but having made this denial there was a hint of confusion in the way she replaced the sunglasses. He thought it possible that Nigel might also have said to her: Guy called you that stunning girl. She was stunning no longer.

The bearer brought another cup and another pot of coffee. She poured for them both. 'Why have you come to the club, Mr Perron? Nigel said they were expecting you at the Izzat Bagh.'

'I never got round to wiring the day and time I'd get here. After a night on the train I thought it would be a good idea at least to get some breakfast and even make sure of a bed for the night without putting people out.'

'Well, and it's nice to be on your own for a while. Before putting on one's visiting face. Is Nigel going to be disappointed?'

'Why disappointed?'

'He said you'd be surprised to find him in Mirat. But you don't seem surprised. You haven't even asked me who I mean by Nigel. Did Dmitri give the game away after all?'

'No. And I am surprised. But the edge has been knocked off by what I've just read in the *Mirat Courier.*'

'Oh, have they said something about him? I never read it.'

'His name's included in a list of people who went to a funeral on Saturday. Mr Nigel Rowan, AAGG. And then the other names clinched it. The only person I don't know about is Mrs Nigel Rowan.'

Laura Elliott smiled. Her mouth went down with the smile. 'That's me, I'm afraid. Was I mentioned too? Nigel will be pleased. It worries him a bit that printed guest lists seldom refer to us both. But then how can they if I'm always making excuses or just not turning up? It's Dmitri Bronowsky who's expecting you really, isn't it? Are you going to ring him up?'

'The secretary said he mightn't be in Mirat but that he could easily find out.'

'In which case he's probably looking for me. Dmitri was in Mirat yesterday. He must still be. But you needn't ring. Nigel will either be ringing me here or arriving here some time this morning. You could go back with him. In any case I'll let him know you're here.'

'It's well over a year since Nigel and I were in touch. How long have you been married?'

'Rather less than a year. But do you mind if we don't talk

about it? I was always very fond of Nigel and still am, but I'm afraid his marriage hasn't been a success.'

Perron studied Laura Elliott's face – turned, for once, away from him as she watched the swooping crows; and thought he saw a woman who had had a bad time and was trying to pick up the pieces. She had rejected Nigel originally for a planter in Malaya. He remembered Nigel referring to a surviving Elliott parent in Darjeeling, who had only heard from Laura once, after she had ended up in a Japanese prison-camp. Presumably, unless there had been a divorce, the planter-husband hadn't survived. He felt he couldn't ask. He felt she would welcome a discussion about her and her first husband's captivity as little as she welcomed discussion of her marriage to Nigel. He said:

'Are you staying here at the club?'

'Yes, temporarily.' The sunglasses were redirected at him. 'I've just remembered.' She took the glasses off. 'You had a delightful but rather dotty aunt. Is she still alive?'

'She's paying for most of the cost of this trip and she's pulled most of the strings that make things easy when I want them easy.'

'I'm glad she's still alive. People like that deserve a long life.'

'People like what?'

'People who take an interest in other people, especially in young people. I felt that. I felt her reacting to me as if I were a person, not just another good-looking girl.'

'I'll tell her what you say.'

'Oh, she won't remember me.'

'But she does.'

A moment of nakedness. Then the glasses went back on. There was the sound of a telephone ringing. Perron said, 'Perhaps that's Nigel now.'

'We shall soon know. You'd like some more coffee?'

'Thank you.'

She began to pour. Hearing footsteps, Perron looked round. It was Macpherson. He said:

'Ah, there you both are. Already introduced yourselves. Good. Your husband is on the line, Mrs Rowan.'

She thanked Macpherson, pushed the glasses hard against the bridge of her nose and got up and went without another word or a glance in Perron's direction.

Macpherson said, 'It looks as if you're in luck and I lose an overnight guest.'

She did not come back. The clerk came ten minutes later with a message from her. A car would call for Perron at midday to take him to the Izzat Bagh. He stayed on the terrace for another half-hour or so. But still she did not return.

The car slowed to pass through a sentry-guarded checkpoint marked by a notice: *End of Cantonment Limits* and then headed along a straight road slightly below the level of the railway. He put on his own dark glasses and took out Rowan's note and re-read it.

'My dear Guy, I'm sorry I can't come to collect you personally. It's one of those pressing official mornings. I've not had the chance yet to tell Dmitri you've arrived, but will. Meanwhile, the best thing is for you to come to my bungalow. It's next to the Dewani Bhavan, Dmitri's house, where you'll be staying, but a lot has happened since he wired you in Bombay and you may find dossing down with me at least a good temporary solution. You're very welcome. Laura tells me you and she met and that you've seen the *Courier*, so know something of the score. Colonel Layton went back to Pankot this morning but Susan and her aunt are still here. They're staying at the palace guest house. Sarah's here too, of course, and has promised to be at my bungalow to welcome you and to see you settled in. I may have to stay at the palace for lunch, but I've organized things for you to lunch at my place. I expect you'll want to relax anyway. The bungalow is tucked between the Dewani Bhavan and the bungalow that was Susan's and Ronald's.

'You'll get a good view of the Izzat Bagh Palace and the guest house directly you fork right from the railway and the road starts to lead you round our side of the lake. Once you've passed the walls of the palace grounds you're at the Dewani Bhavan (and our bungalow which overlooks the waste ground between the palace and the city). See you soon. Nigel.'

The fork was ahead. He moved to the left-hand side of the car. Presently he saw the palace at the other end of the dazzling stretch of water: a rose-coloured structure with little towers, and on the lake-shore a white domed mosque with one slim minaret reflected. To one side, amidst trees, a palladian-style mansion. The guest house presumably.

At this upper end of the lake there were huts and boats (beached). A detachment of armed police patrolled the area. The lake seemed to be separated almost into two by an isthmus and an area of reeds. Where the reeds began the road curved away from the bank as though everything beyond the reeds was private property. The car became cooler, shaded by banyan trees. And to the left there suddenly appeared a brick wall mercilessly topped by spears of broken bottle-glass. The palace grounds. The wall continued for half a mile. Perhaps more. But suddenly ended, at a right angle, and the road was now edged on that side by an immense stretch of open ground, broken by nullahs. The car slowed. Just ahead on the right there was a grey stucco wall, a glimpse of a substantial bungalow, the Dewani Bhavan. But his attention was taken by a more distant view, the view of what lay at the far end of the waste ground, about a mile away: the blur of the old walled and minareted city of Mirat.

The car turned, across a culvert, into the compound of a small bungalow, a very old, squat building with square pillars to its verandah. The compound was rough and untended.

Standing in the shadow of the deep verandah was a woman wearing a blouse and skirt. Sarah. She had her arms folded (hands, as he remembered, clasping the elbows). As the car drew up she came down the steps ahead of a servant.

The first thing he noticed as he pushed the door open and looked up at her was a little pad of flesh beneath her chin.

'Hello, Guy.' She offered her hand. He took it and could not tell whether a warmer embrace had been expected, or would be welcome. Free, she folded her arms again and led the way on to the verandah which at this central point was deep, set out with tables and lounging chairs. There was a dusty uncared-for look about it. Whether this was Laura's fault or one of the reasons why Laura wasn't living here were questions whose answers might become clearer.

The interior hall was dark, sombre. You could smell damp. Sarah moved through it unaffected, he felt, by the oppressive weight of masonry, the brooding pressure of the thick square pillars that rose from the tiled floor up, up, into a remote raftered roof. She opened a door and the scale diminished to one that was more accommodating to the human ego. But this room was long, too narrow for its length. Here, he sensed the presence of hidden fungus, a sweet heavy smell which, mixed with the light dry scent of some kind of antiseptic, immediately depressed him. A white mosquito-net shrouded a narrow little bed. The main source of light was from the open bathroom door. It was probably from the bathroom that the smell of antiseptic came.

'It's rather spartan,' she said. 'Nigel asked me to apologize. But I probably don't need to. I expect Laura warned you they've not been here long and won't be staying.'

Perron let that go. He said, 'What date do you think? 1830? 1850?'

'I don't know. Shut up too long anyway. Watch out for scorpions. And I don't want to alarm you but there was a snake not long ago, on the verandah at the back. They had a good hunt after it was killed so I don't think you need worry, in any case Nigel says snakes are very misunderstood creatures and that the thing to do if you meet one is bow politely and ask it to go its way in peace.'

'I shall probably just yell the place down.'

She laughed, standing there, in front of him, arms still folded. He moved forward, put one arm lightly round her. She didn't move but in a moment briefly leant her head so that her hair brushed his chin.

'It's nice to see you again, Guy. You always made me laugh.'

She moved away. The servants were bringing in his suitcase and holdall. She said, 'I don't think Nigel will be back for lunch, but it's all organized for you to have directly you want it. So let's have a drink. Then I'll leave you to settle in.'

'Do you have to leave?'

'Yes. But I've got time for a drink.'

They returned to the verandah. She called out to the driver that she'd be ready in fifteen minutes. He went away, round the side of the bungalow. A servant had already placed a tray and bottles and glasses on a side-table. She told him to go and then asked Perron what he'd have.

'Out here I still like the gin.'

She poured, added ice and fizz and brought the glasses over. She said, 'I'd ask you to lunch at the guest house in ordinary circumstances but today I think you'd be happier eating here alone.'

'If you think so.'

He offered her a cigarette. She hesitated then took one. 'I've been trying to cut down, which means I've joined that boring gang of cadging non-smokers who never have their own. Thank you.' Bending forward to give her a light he noticed that the hand holding the cigarette was a bit unsteady; and that her hair, once so smooth and gleaming, looked less well cared-for. He felt this suited her rather better. She seemed more marked by experience. He said, 'I've come at rather a bad moment, haven't I?'

'Up to a week ago we'd certainly thought of your arrival rather differently.'

'How differently?'

'Nigel and I and Ahmed were going to meet you at the station. It was Dmitri's idea. I expect he'd have come too, because he likes surprising people. That's why when he got your letter from home he didn't answer but waited until there was just time to send you a welcoming telegram in Bombay. He thought he couldn't very well write a letter without mentioning the fact that Nigel and I were here. And Ronald of course.'

'You were here when my letter arrived then? I thought you'd probably come down just now. From Pankot.'

'No, I've been here for quite a time. It was Susan who had to come down. With father and Aunt Fenny. Father went back this morning. Did you come in on the night train?'

'Yes.'

'Then you must have been on the station at roughly the same time as father.'

'There was quite a crowd. Were you there, seeing him off?'

'No, but Aunt Fenny was. He has to get back to Pankot to go on handing over his command at the depot. He wanted us to go with him but at the last moment Susan wouldn't. So Fenny felt she had to stay too.'

'What about your mother?'

'Oh, mother went home last month to start house-hunting.'

'So no retirement to Rose Cottage?'

'No. Actually we moved down to Commandant House quite a while ago and rented the cottage to people called Smalley. We can't sell it, except to the army, but that's what will happen now. I expect the Smalleys will stay there a while because they're staying on under contract with the Indian Government. At least for a year or two. He's a bit too young to retire. A bit too old to fancy his chances at home. Father of course would have retired next year anyway. Neither of them wants to stay out here, though.'

'So back home for you too?'

'I don't know about me. Aunt Fenny and I went back for a month or two last year, after Uncle Arthur died. You never met them, did you?'

'No, but I know about Colonel Grace dying. I called at Queen's Road the other day and saw Mr Hapgood.'

'Hapgood?'

'The people upstairs. Captain Purvis's billet.'

'Oh.' She leant back, shutting her eyes. 'How long ago all that seems.'

'You never got in touch with me.'

'What?'

'When you were in England last year, with your Aunt Fenny.'

'No.'

'Nor answered my second letter.'

'No, I'm sorry. But that was a long time ago too.'

'Was the visit home a disappointment?'

'I don't suppose I gave it a proper chance. It might have been different if Aunt Fenny had gone home for good. But she had her return passage booked. And when the time came I felt I had to come back too.'

'You told me once that India wasn't a place you felt you could be happy in.'

'Did I? Yes, I remember thinking that.' She looked at him. 'I've been very happy since.'

'Has Susan been happy?'

Sarah didn't answer at once. Then she said, 'At the moment she's in rather a bad way, probably worse than the family realizes. I can't remember what you knew about her history, but she's never been what is called really stable.'

'Didn't Ronald Merrick give her stability?'

Again she didn't answer at once.

'He's provided it now. You'll see what I mean if she talks to you about him, which is fairly likely. He's all she talks about.'

'It was a successful marriage, then?'

'I expected it to be disastrous. Of course, he adored the boy, and the boy adored him. Edward doesn't know Ronnie's dead, by the way. I ought to warn you.'

'Is the boy here?'

'Yes.' Sarah stubbed her cigarette. 'Su wouldn't leave him in Pankot, which is partly why Fenny had to come. Anyway, it's no bad thing for her to have him with her, but it's had its awkward side. I looked after him while the others went to the funeral. It was difficult explaining to him why mummy kept crying and why they'd come all the way back to daddy's house and not seen daddy. He said daddy had promised he'd still be here when their holiday in the hills was over and he'd made everything safe again. So of course I said that things were quite safe now but that daddy had had to go away for a while to make them safe somewhere else.'

'Ronald sent them back to Pankot because of trouble here?'

'Partly that, but to get them into the hills for the hot weather as well. Su wanted just to go up to Nanoora, but Ronald said if there was any more trouble Nanoora would be just as bad.'

'Has there been much trouble?'

'Off and on, yes. Quite a lot. That's why he was sent here in the first place. They were up in Rajputana. He'd become temporarily attached to the States Police. You know? The reserve pool that sends officers and men to states where the rulers' own police forces need helping out? He packed Su and Edward back to Pankot and came down here alone. They say he did a marvellous job. The Nawab's own police are practically all Muslims, and that was part of the problem, because they took sides in communal disturbances, lashing out at Hindu crowds and mobs and turning a blind eye if the Muslims were having a go. Ronnie stopped all that. He pretended it was easy. He said all he'd had to do was make the Muslim Chief of Police see he had a duty to the whole community, but it can't have been as simple as that.'

'When was all this?'

'Last December. He didn't expect the job to last long. But Dmitri was so impressed by the way he handled it he persuaded the States Police to let him stay on and help overhaul the whole Mirat Police Department and devise a new training and recruiting programme. It suited Ronnie very well. At one time there was an idea he might retire officially from the service and make a contract with the Nawab. Su and he set up house early last

March. Then in May when the hot weather was really cooking up he sent her and Edward back to Pankot. As I said, partly because of the heat and partly because there was another outbreak of communal riots.'

'That was their bungalow next door, wasn't it?'

'Yes. It's not nearly as dilapidated as this. In fact he made it very comfortable. I stayed with them for a while after I helped Su move down from Pankot. But since April I've been living either at Dmitri's or the palace. Now, of course, I'll have to go back with Su. Fenny can't cope with the journey alone. And I don't know how badly Su'll take it when the reaction sets in.'

'I see there was a post-mortem.'

'Yes.' She got up. 'I really must go.'

Perron, getting up too, said, 'How long has Nigel been in Mirat?'

'About six weeks. The Political Department sent him down to try and sort things out. Actually Dmitri asked for him. Mirat comes under the Resident at Gopalakand and things got rather difficult. Nigel will tell you all about it. I'll be in touch, Guy. Probably this evening.'

The driver had come back. But just as she began to go down the steps another car came into the compound. 'You're in luck,' she said. 'Here's Nigel now.'

She went down to meet him. Perron stayed on the verandah. The car stopped several yards away from the one already parked. The driver got out and opened the door. A man emerged. If it was Rowan then he had lost even more weight. This man's skin was pale yellow and looked almost translucent, stretched over the cheek-bones. The man raised a welcoming hand to Perron, then said something to Sarah. They came towards the steps. Only now was the man's face recognizable as Rowan's.

'Hello, Guy,' he said. 'I'm sorry but I'm afraid I'm only here to pack a case.' They clasped hands.

'I'll see to the case,' Sarah said. 'How many nights?'

'Two at the most. I ought to be back tomorrow evening. And don't bother. Tippoo can do it.'

'Does it include black tie?'

'I've got all that in Gopalakand. Just one other suit. Isn't Tippoo here?'

'Yes, but I'll see he gets it right.' She went inside calling for someone named Tippoo. From the far end of one of the narrow wings of the verandah a middle-aged Indian in European clothes came out of a casement doorway: a clerk, not a servant. Rowan said, 'Just a second, Guy,' and went to meet him. They talked for a while. Then Nigel came back.

'Have you got a drink?'

Perron indicated his glass.

'Let me freshen it for you. I really do apologize. We're in the middle of what I suppose you'd call a flap. I've got to go up to Gopalakand.' He handed Perron the refilled glass. 'You're looking very fit. I'll be back in a moment.'

He went inside. Perron heard him calling Tippoo and Sarah calling something back. The clerk came out again, with a couple of files, but seeing Perron alone he went back inside, presumably to look for Rowan indoors. A telephone rang and was quickly answered. The two drivers were gossiping. Perron sat down and composed himself, to let the tide of India flow over him; presently it would ebb and leave him revealed: a visitor who was excluded from the mystery, the vital secret. I have been happy since, Sarah had said; as a woman might say if she were in love. In love with whom? Nigel? But he had been in Mirat only six weeks and she had been here since March, obviously content. Merrick? No, that was impossible. And Merrick's death didn't seem to have disturbed her in the way she would have been disturbed by the death of a man she had loved. The only answer seemed to be: in love with the land itself, after all; yes, in love with that, and content to be here whatever happened. A strange but perhaps logical reversal of her old attitude.

'I won't apologize again,' Rowan said, coming back and sitting opposite, glancing at his watch. 'But I have to be off in five or ten minutes, so let's work out what's best for you. There are three possibilities. You're more than welcome to stay here, and you could rely on Tippoo to look after you. Dmitri asked me to tell you you're equally welcome to move into the Dewani Bhavan, but he's unlikely to be around much if at all in the next day or two. We've got a couple of States Department people over at the palace –'

'Waving the standstill agreement and the instrument of accession to Congress India, and asking for the Nawab's signature before August fifteen?'

'Good, you know about that. That cuts out a lot of tedious explanation. The other alternative for you while I'm away is the Gymkhana Club if you'd prefer that sort of atmosphere. If you opt for the club I could take you there now, as my guest it goes without saying. I've got to collect Laura. Sarah would keep in touch with you of course and there'd always be a car available to take you anywhere you want to go. But don't feel I'm pushing you out. My clerk will be here too most of the time and he'd help you in any way he can. Otherwise you can just forget about him. He has his own domestic arrangements. So, Guy, I leave it to you and in spite of what I said about not apologizing again, I do.'

'It's entirely my fault. I ought to have sent a wire. Checked that it was convenient.'

'The flap would have occurred anyway. It's not inconvenient for us. We're just worried about you.'

'I'd like to stay here, if that's all right.'

'Good. Actually it'll make things easier for Sarah, not that she ever complains, but we do all tend to load her with extra jobs. She could help look after you better here than at the club.'

'Tell me one thing, is the Resident at Gopalakand in what I call the entrenched opposition camp that's encouraging the princes to stand firm on their own independence?'

'Fundamentally, that is the problem.'

'What does Dmitri want?'

'Honourable integration.'

'And the Nawab?'

'I don't think the poor old man knows. But after all these years he's suddenly resisting Dmitri's advice. The Resident's trying to persuade the Maharajah in Gopalakand to sign nothing and reserve his position until paramountcy automatically lapses on August fifteen and leaves him technically independent. As a result the Nawab's taking that line too. It's quite hopeless of course. He knows it, but he's being very stubborn and the Resident isn't being in the least helpful. He's never really been interested in Mirat. Mirat should have had its own agent long ago.'

'Are you on Dmitri's side, then?'

'Let's say I agree that the only sensible course for Mirat is to accede to the new Indian Union on the three main subjects, sign the standstill agreement and then get the best deal possible.

Mirat's entirely surrounded by what's been British-Indian territory and overnight becomes Indian Union territory. The Nawab
can't live in a vacuum.'

Perron nodded. He said, 'How have things been for you,
Nigel, this past two years?'

'I've moved around a lot. Little else. Perhaps I ought to have
stayed in the army. It turned out to be the wrong time to come
back into the Political. Still, the end would have been the same
in either case.'

'What do you hope to achieve in Gopalakand, or is that
confidential?'

'If I can come back with a letter from Conway to the Nawab
making it clear that Mirat's on its own and that Conway can't
advise either way, then we should be able to persuade the old
chap to sign. And sign he must. There's no sensible alternative.
Except chaos, if that's sensible. From what I've seen going on in
the past few weeks I sometimes wonder whether the Political
Department cares, so long as it can close itself down convinced
that it's upheld the principles of the whole past relationship
between the States and the Crown.'

' "Nothing can bring you peace but yourself," ' Perron quoted.
' "Nothing can bring you peace but the triumph of principles." '

'What?'

'Emerson.'

'Oh.' Nigel smiled. 'Did he say that? How apt. That sums up
my department's attitude admirably.'

'Not just your department's. I think it sums up the attitude
of everybody who's concerned in what happens on August
fifteenth.' Perron took a sip of his gin. 'I'm sorry about Merrick,'
he said. 'Not that I ever liked the man. Still, he seemed to have
made good in Mirat.'

'Yes.' Rowan looked at his watch again.

'And Harry Coomer? Any news of him? I'm sorry I decided
there was nothing to be done at my end.'

'I don't think I really expected it, but I appreciated your giving
thought to it, and appreciated your letter. One becomes involved
for a time, and then the involvement ends. In any case, I don't
think there was anything Kumar wanted.'

'Why do you think that?'

'He implied as much. We exchanged letters after Gopal died,
last year. Poor old Gopal. He was always getting colds. He took

his wife down to Puri for a holiday and caught cold and got pneumonia. I asked Mrs Gopal to put me in touch with the man who'd been helping Kumar rehabilitate himself. Got Kumar's address out of him, so wrote. Difficult letter to write. I didn't hear for ages. He'd moved, so my letter followed him around. When he wrote he didn't give me his new address but the letter was postmarked Ranpur so he must still have been there, I imagine. Probably still is.'

'What did he say?'

'What it added up to was that he was quite content doing what he was doing, coaching students privately.'

'A defensive attitude?'

'I don't think so. He seemed very grateful for the one or two things I'd suggested.'

'What sort of things?'

'Just general ideas about how he could make best use of his talents.'

'Commerce for instance?'

'Yes, but that would be open to him at almost any time.'

'Would it, Nigel? The kind of commerce we think of as commerce? I seem to remember he failed to get into it once, with British–Indian Electric.'

'Once.'

'Has British–Indian Electric changed?'

Rowan said nothing.

'Will anything ever really change in India, for him? Isn't Harry Coomer the permanent loose end? Too English for the Indians, too Indian for the English?'

'That, rather, is Sarah's view. Frankly, I think he's more interested in being just his own kind of Indian.'

'Have you told her you tried to help him?'

'Yes, but only quite recently.'

'I don't suppose you ever showed her a transcript of the examination?'

'Good God, no. She knows nothing about that.' He lowered his voice. 'Few people do now, except you. Everything in connection with the examination was destroyed, except the orders for Kumar's release.'

'To protect Merrick's reputation?'

'The issues involved ranged far wider than that. I imagine quite a lot of files were vetted, and rearranged.'

'To make it more difficult for an incoming Congress ministry to smell out witches?'

'A witch-hunt was what certain sections of Congress wanted. An inquiry could have aggravated racial tension to an intolerable degree, coming as it would have done on top of the INA trials. If it interests you as a student of history, there was no inquiry because between them Nehru and Wavell put a stop to it. They both saw what it could lead to.'

'And Merrick got off scot-free.'

'Actually, I think it annoyed him. I believe he felt slighted. There were only a few individual inquiries into serious cases involving rather senior officials. It was all done very quietly. One or two people got retired, prematurely.'

'What happened to Kasim's son, Sayed?'

'He was cashiered. That's all.'

'What's he doing now?'

'I'm not sure. Living in Lahore, I believe, with his Muslim League sister and brother-in-law. In some kind of business. Ahmed will tell you.'

'No splendid appointment for one of the INA heroes?'

'They were only heroes for a while. In a way they still are. But folk-heroes. People in a story or legend. When it comes to finding places for them in the world of affairs it's a bit different.'

Sarah came out. Behind her were a couple of servants with bags and the clerk with a briefcase. They went down to the car while Sarah said: 'You're all set, Nigel. If Laura asks, her green taffeta's in the blue case, along with other things she might need.'

'That's good of you.'

'Give Sir Robert my kind regards.'

'I will. Guy's going to stay here, by the way.'

'Good. Do you ride?'

'Off and on. Fortunately more on than off. But it's pure luck.'

She laughed. 'Perhaps we could go out tomorrow morning. I'll ring you later today, anyway.'

The three of them went down into the compound but after he and Nigel had said goodbye Perron stayed near the bottom step while Nigel saw Sarah into her car and then got into his own. He waved them both off.

'Sahib,' Tippoo said, behind him. 'Gin'n'fizz?'

*

Rain. Geckos. Clack-clack-clack. On the walls. Heraldic lizard shapes, pale yellow on the grey-white wash. Chasing one another, intent on copulation. He had woken erect himself – and, half-asleep, smiled, reassured both by this and the realization that the faint discomfort in his bowels had gone, that he was acclimatized. He peered at his wrist-watch. It was only half-past four. He had slept for two hours, after a lunch of chicken pulao, mutton curry lightly spiced in the northern Indian style, and Murree beer. Somewhere a gutter was overflowing. On the bas-ket-work bed-side teapoy there was a tray of tea and a plate of bananas and bread and butter. It must have been the slight clatter of the tray that had woken him. He began to open the mosquito-net and, swinging himself up and round was about to get out when he remembered scorpions and paused, his feet well away from the floor. He reached down, tapped his slippers, and then thrust his feet into them. He grabbed a towel from the bedside chair, wound it round his middle and went into the bathroom.

But, returning, he paused on the threshold of the bedroom, alert. There was a smell he hadn't noticed before. A foul, sweet smell. He glanced around. In a moment or two the smell seemed to have gone. He sat down and poured tea. He glanced up at the sloping rafters; then lit a cigarette, smoked the recollection of the smell away. The shrouded bed looked like a catafalque. There was a sudden flash of lightning that lit the bathroom and momentarily distorted the shape of the bed. After that, the thunder. And then the humdrum sound of continuing but gradually diminishing rain.

As he finished his tea the bathroom was flooded in sunshine. He called for Tippoo.

By five-thirty he was bathed and dressed. He went out into the compound. The shadow of the bungalow thrust itself across the drive. He walked round the side, seeking the sunshine and warmth. At the back the compound stretched for perhaps one hundred yards. There must once have been a lawn and flower beds, but the latter were overgrown. The grass needed scything. An immense banyan tree, its main trunk on this side of the wall dividing Rowan's bungalow from Merrick's, connected the two gardens through its aerial roots. From the other side of the wall

Perron heard the high-pitched voice of a young child, a boy, and lower-pitched woman's laughter.

'Catch, Minnie!' the boy shouted. But the throw was too high. A ball sailed over and came to rest some thirty or forty yards away from where Perron was standing; but the ground was too rough for it to bounce. It died, disappeared. He moved off the path and struck out across the grass, wetting his shoes, the bottoms of his slacks. He cast to and fro. Eventually he found it: a grey, soggy tennis ball.

He picked it up, then turned and saw an Indian woman and the child standing near the banyan tree. Beyond the tree a gate between the two compounds which he hadn't noticed before stood open. The child made a commanding gesture to the woman, as if bidding her stay where she was and then advanced towards Perron: a Pathan child dressed in baggy white pantaloons and shirt, sash, embroidered waistcoat, and cocks-comb pugree. Stuck in the sash was a toy dagger. A miniature Red Shadow. As he got nearer Perron saw that he was of course an English boy, dressed up. His eyes were bright blue, his eyelashes very pale. From under the turban emerged a lick of sandy red hair. He stopped and stuck his little fist round the handle of the toy dagger.

'Who are you?' the boy asked.

'I'm just a visitor. Who are you?'

'I live next door. Is that my ball?'

Perron stooped and showed it to him.

'It looks like mine. Has it got MGC on it?'

Perron inspected it. 'Yes, you can just see MGC.'

'Then it must be mine. MGC means Mirat Gymkhana Club. Mr Macpherson always used to give me used tennis balls.'

Perron nodded, handed the ball over. The child spoke with the assurance of a boy far older.

'It was Minnie's fault. Women can't catch. Thank you for finding it. If you hadn't, Minnie would have had to look and she didn't want to because she's afraid of snakes.'

'Aren't you?'

'No. At least, not very afraid. There were snakes here when Uncle Nigel came. He's not my uncle really. I don't have an uncle because my father didn't have a brother and my mother only has a sister. My stepfather doesn't have a brother either. I've got a stepfather because my real father was killed in the war.'

'You're Edward, aren't you?'

'Yes. My full name is Edward Arthur David Bingham.'

'My name's Guy. My other name is Perron.'

'They're both rather funny names, but I like Perron best. So I'll call you Perron.'

'Then I shall probably have to call you Bingham.'

'Okay.' A minor matter had been satisfactorily settled. A more important one was coming up. 'Can you throw, Perron?'

'Yes.'

'Which arm do you use?'

'The right arm.'

'I throw with my left arm because I'm left-handed. My step-father has to throw with his right arm because his left arm was cut off. But he's a very good thrower.'

'What do you call your stepfather?'

'Ronald. At least, I do mostly. My mother likes me to call him daddy, so sometimes I do. But he likes me to call him Ronald.'

'Do you know what Ronald means?'

'It means it's his name.'

'Most names have meanings. My name means wide. On the other hand it might mean wood. So you'd better go on calling me Perron which is probably just the place where we lived once. And I shall call you Edward after all. Ronald means the same as Rex or Reginald. It means someone with power who rules. Edward means a rich guard.'

'But I'm not very rich. At the moment I've only got one rupee and four annas.'

'I don't think it's a question of money. Anyway you're guarding the fort while Ronald's away. You're looking after your mother, aren't you?'

'Yes. My mother's name is Susan. What does Susan mean?'

'It means a very beautiful flower called a lily. Not the red ones you see here. White ones.'

'She is quite beautiful. Except when she cries. She's crying now. That's why they sent me out to play in the garden. She may have stopped crying though, if you want to see her. Come on. If she's still crying we can play in our garden. It's a nicer garden than this one.'

Perron got up. The child led the way. As he drew near the ayah he held the ball up and said, 'Here's the ball, ayah. We may

want to play with it again.' The girl took the ball in one hand
and with the other half-covered her face with the free end of
her saree, to protect herself from Perron's gaze.

The Merrick garden was certainly 'nicer'. The lawns were
well-cut, and there were signs of work-in-progress, in the form
of beds recently dug into ovals, circles and rectangles. Edward
pointed them out.

'That's where Ronald's going to try to grow roses.'

Beyond the beds, at the far end of the Merrick compound,
was a tennis-court. A thick hedge of shrubs and bushes hid
the servants' quarters. The bungalow itself had been re-stuccoed
and painted. The rear verandah formed an elegant whitewashed
colonnaded semi-circle which embraced the central set of steps
leading to the house. Between the columns hung green tattis,
some lowered, others at half-mast. Tubs of canna lilies stood
sentinel. The bungalow had the slightly raw look of having been
stripped recently of ancient creepers to allow redecoration.

The little Pathan marched across the lawn towards the verandah and then at the bottom step kicked off his chappals and
climbed barefoot. Perron decided that this was part of a private
game, not obligatory, so he climbed shod. The boy waited for
him at the top, legs apart, fist on the handle of the toy dagger.

'Would you like to see my room first, Perron?'

'Very much.'

The boy strode off to the right, along the verandah and round
the corner. At the side of the bungalow he pulled open a wire-
screen door, held it, and let Perron enter first.

A small room, austere, remarkably unboylike. That was
Perron's impression until he remembered that Edward hadn't
slept or played here for several months. The narrow little charpoy was unmade, its mattress rolled, the net folded. Across the
exposed webbing were the clothes he had taken off – diminutive
khaki shorts, a blue shirt and grey socks. A cane chair, an almirah
and a chest of drawers were the only other furnishings. The door
of the almirah was ajar, which suggested that the first thing
Edward had done was seek out his Pathan outfit and hasten to
get into it.

'Do you like my room?'

'Yes, I do. Where does ayah sleep?'

'There of course.' He pointed at the floor near the casement door. 'Except neither of us sleeps here just now. We're staying at the palace guest house. I'll show you the palace if you like, but not today. Do you like my picture?'

Perron looked at the wall where the child was pointing. Above the chest of drawers was a coloured print in a gilt frame. He went to inspect it.

'Daddy gave it to me. It's called "The Jewel in Her Crown" and it's about Queen Victoria.'

Perron saw that indeed it was. It was the kind of picture whose awfulness gave it a kind of distinction. The old Queen was enthroned, beneath a canopy, receiving tribute from a motley gathering of her Indian subjects, chief among whom was a prince, bearing a crown on a cushion. Ranged on either side of the throne were representatives of the *raj* in statuesque pro-consular positions. Disraeli was there, indicating a parchment. In the background, plump angels peered from behind fat clouds, and looked ready to blow their long golden trumpets. The print was blemished by little speckles of brown damp.

'But it isn't the jewel in the crown the prince is holding. The jewel's India,' the boy explained.

'Yes, I see.'

'It's an alle-gory.'

'What's an alle-gory?'

'Don't you know? It means telling a story that's really two stories. The Queen's dead now of course. I should think they're all dead, except the angels. Angels never die.'

'No. So I'm told.'

'Have you ever seen an angel, Perron?'

'No.'

'Nor've I. Daddy says mummy saw an angel once, an angel in a circle of fire, but I mustn't talk about it because it upsets her. Come on. Let's see if she's still crying.'

Reluctantly, Perron followed him to a closed door. The boy opened it, put his head out and listened. The silence coming from the other side was peculiarly oppressive. But Edward obviously found it reassuring.

'I think she's stopped.'

He opened the door wide. Beyond was the main entrance-hall, as encumbered with square pillars as the hall in Rowan's bungalow; but the tiled floor shone – except in the area exposed by the taking up of a carpet which had been rolled and corded and now awaited disposal.

Edward pattered across the hall on his bare feet, entered a room whose door stood open. There was a pause, and then a woman's shriek; a pause, a repetition of the shriek, longer drawn out, and then continuing.

The boy emerged, levitated. Simultaneously a magenta-coloured shape flowed past Perron – the ayah. The ayah grasped the boy out of the air, and so revealed the source of the levitation; Sarah, who turned immediately back into the room from which the shrieks were still coming. As the ayah carried Edward away he began to wail. A white-clad, sashed and turbanned servant ran in from the front porch, across the hall and into the room.

Then the shrieking stopped. Slowly, Perron approached the wide-open doors, uncertain what to do. The doors were double and from the threshold he could see that the room was a bedroom, but a very large bedroom, dominated by a bed which was centrally placed, raised on a stone-stepped daïs. Sarah was sitting on the edge of this bed cradling and rocking Susan in her arms. The servant stood nearby. Perhaps he had spoken because Sarah seemed to be shaking her head at him. Presently the servant took a few steps back, then turned, saw Perron, and came out, went past without a word.

Below the daïs there was an open tin trunk and scattered all around it what must be Ronald Merrick's relics: KD uniforms, Sam Brownes, leather cases, hairbrushes, a sword in a black and silver scabbard, mess dress, leather gloves, swagger canes, a Field Service cap, riding boots, jodhpurs, Harris tweed jacket, checked flannel shirts, a Gurkha's kukri, grey slacks, brown shoes, chukka boots: the detritus of a man's life in India.

Three tall casement windows, facing west, had been un-shuttered. The evening light filtered through. The shafts of this light were alive with mobile particles of dust. He turned to leave. He didn't think Sarah had seen him, but just then she said, 'Don't go away altogether, Guy.'

He said, 'I'll be outside.'

He sat on the front verandah. The trees and bushes in the front compound were in a similar state of decay as those in Rowan's, but thick enough to screen the bungalow from the road. The servant was talking to the chauffeur of one of the palace limousines, parked near the foot of the steps. The servant came up and asked if the sahib wished anything. Perron shook his head.

He smoked. He thought: Why should she scream? It was her own son. He sat on the balustrade. As he finished his cigarette the ayah and Edward came out. Edward was now wearing his ordinary clothes. His little chappals clattered. He looked what he was – a small boy scarcely out of infancy, three or four years old. But when he spoke he was still the little Pathan.

'Hello, Perron. Are you coming to the guest house?'

'Afraid not, old chap. Not today, anyway.'

'If you do I can show you the palace after all.'

'I'd like that. Tomorrow, perhaps.'

The boy offered his hand. Perron reached down and shook it.

'Goodbye, Perron.'

Edward clattered down the steps and ran to the car. The ayah hastened after him. He shouted at the driver, 'Jeldi, jeldi. Ham ek dam Guest House wapas-jane-wale hain. Chalo!'

The driver, approaching, wagged his head and called back, 'Thik hai, Sahib.' He helped Edward get up on the running-board and open the rear door. The ayah followed him in but must have been told to go to the farther seat because when the door was shut Edward put his head out of the open window and shouted:

'I can show you the white peacock too, Perron.'

Perron made an appreciative sideways nod of his head. The boy sat back. The car set off.

'You've made a hit.'

Sarah had come out and was standing behind him. She said, 'The white peacock's his special secret. But why does he call you Perron?'

'We agreed to be informal. He's a remarkable boy, isn't he? How old?'

'He was three last June. I remember wondering whether he'd ever learn to talk.'

'Is Susan all right now?'

'Yes, perfectly. She'd like it if you came in and had a word. She may ask you to dinner at the guest house this evening. That was originally my idea too but I'd prefer it if you made an excuse. These upsets sometimes have repercussions later. So I'd rather we left anything like that until tomorrow.'

'What upset her?'

Sarah, arms folded in the characteristic way, shrugged slightly. She didn't look at him. Her manner struck him as evasive. He realized that this was not the first time today that it had. She said, 'Oh, the whole afternoon mainly. She insisted on coming over and sorting out some of Ronald's things, so I had to come too because Aunt Fenny's not feeling very bright. Then Edward insisted on coming with us. The whole thing was a mistake from the start.'

'Could you have dinner with me, at Nigel's?'

'I'd like to but I'd better not. Let's go out tomorrow morning, though. I'll try and rope Ahmed in too.'

'What time?'

'Could you be ready by seven? That's the best time.'

'Rain or shine?'

'At this time of year it only rains in the afternoon, if it rains at all.'

'I've got nothing special to ride in.'

'That doesn't matter. Well, let's go in. The guest house is only a few minutes away so the car will be back soon and I want to get Susan away before the light goes.'

'We met didn't we, Mr Perron? That time in Pankot just after Ronnie and I became engaged and you were working with him.'

She had on a cotton print dress with a full skirt, which was disposed to envelop her legs while she knelt on the floor by the tin trunk, her weight centred on her left hip, supported by a stiffened left arm. After they'd shaken hands she placed her right hand back on her left shoulder. The light which twenty minutes before had streamed through the unshuttered windows had diminished, but what was left of it lit one side of her pretty flushed face and picked out the red-brown tones of hair which in full daylight would look dark, almost black. She seemed perfectly composed now.

She said, 'Of course, you know that I've lost him. My son doesn't know. It's really a question of working out a way of how and what to tell him.' She reached out and touched the Field Service cap.

Sarah said, 'Why don't you leave it all, Su? Khansamar will

put it away. Then we could all have a drink outside while we wait for the car.'

'No, I don't want a drink. But you both have one. I've still got a lot to sort out and I don't want Khansamar touching anything.'

'Then I'll help you start putting things back.' Sarah knelt and began to fold the tweed jacket.

'How little there is,' Susan said. 'I mean when you think of the years a man spends out here. So little he would want to keep. Will daddy have as little as this?'

'I don't expect there'll be much more.'

Susan fingered the pommel of the sword. 'And even the things they do have look like toys, don't they? I suppose that's because the things they play with when they're young are just smaller versions of the things they'll have to use later. It's different for us. A doll's house isn't at all like a real house. And a doll not in the least like a real baby. You didn't know my husband well, did you, Mr Perron? You were hardly with him at all, were you?'

'No. A very short time.'

'Ask anyone here in Mirat and they'll tell you what a fine man he was. I don't yet think of him as dead.'

Sarah gently withdrew the sword from her sister's touch and placed it in the trunk.

'And then my not being here at the time makes it seem it hasn't happened, and when I tell Edward we'll be seeing daddy again soon, that's what it seems like. That we will be seeing him. Please stop putting things back, Sarah. It's all that's left of Ronald and it's not even all here.'

'Oh?' Sarah said, not looking at her sister. 'What's missing?'

'His arm for one thing.'

Sarah pushed hair away from her right cheek and didn't comment.

'I mean the artificial one, Mr Perron. His harness. But we always called it his arm. It was one of the ways we made light of it. Where's my arm? he used to say. He took it off every night. Nobody knows the discomfort he was in, from the chafing. The first time I saw his poor shoulder and his poor stump, I cried. They were so inflamed and raw. That's because he never spared himself. He learned to ride again, you know. Getting up on what he called the wrong side. He played tennis too. He called it patball because he had to serve underarm by dropping the ball and hitting it on the bounce but he played a strong game otherwise.'

Sarah had got up and was opening a chest of drawers. Susan said, 'It's no good. I've looked in all the drawers and cupboards. I've looked everywhere, but I can't find it.'

'What's this, then?' Sarah held up a contraption of webbing and metal.

Without even looking Susan said, 'That's the one he couldn't wear. The new one. The one they said was much better, a much more modern design. But if you look at it you'll see it can't have been worn more than a few times.'

Sarah thrust it back into the chest and closed the drawer.

'I hope this doesn't embarrass you, Mr Perron. Talking about his arm. But you see he never, never, wore it in bed. He took it off every night. He had to be very careful not to let the stump get too inflamed. I know what a relief it was to him to get out of the harness, and sometimes what torture it was to put it back on in the morning. He wouldn't have worn it while he was laid up after his riding accident.'

Perron said, 'Perhaps the accident explains why it's not here, Mrs Merrick. It could have been damaged and sent away for repair.'

'Oh.' She considered him gravely. 'I hadn't thought of that.' She smiled. 'Ronnie was quite right. He always was. He said women have instincts, they know when something is wrong or not properly explained. But men work things out logically much better. It struck me as odd when I couldn't find it, because to put it brutally I couldn't see them putting the arm on, just to take – just to take his body to the mortuary for the post-mortem. And there had to be a post-mortem because he was found dead in bed and people thought he was getting better. I blame Dr Habbibullah, but daddy says I shouldn't. He said no one can foresee a clot of blood. But why was there a clot of blood? Unless there was an internal injury from the riding accident that Dr Habbibullah hadn't diagnosed?'

'Well you know, you can seem in perfect health one minute, and then –'

'Drop dead the next. Oh, I know. But all these doctors protect themselves and each other don't you think, Mr Perron? I mean whether they're English or Indian. And I do blame Dr

Habbibullah even though Ronnie himself once said he was one of the best doctors he'd ever come across.' She looked round at Sarah. 'Khansamar would know about Ronnie's harness, Sarah. Whether it was damaged.'

'I don't think we should worry Khansamar over a thing like that, Su.'

'Why?'

'Because he's a servant. When you ask servants what's happened to something it always sounds as if you're accusing them of stealing. I'll ask Dr Habbibullah if you really want me to.'

'Yes, I do. But what about the other things that are missing? Where are his Pathan clothes? He was very fond of his Pathan clothes.' She turned to Perron again. 'He had to choose Pathan clothes because of his blue eyes. He had two sets but only one pugree and only one embroidered waistcoat.' She looked at the scattered stuff. 'There's only one set here, these trousers and this shirt. The other set's missing, and so are the pugree and the waistcoat. And the sash. And the little axe.'

'He probably gave them away,' Sarah said. 'It must be years since he used them.'

'Oh no. He went out in them in Mirat too. With one of his spies. He had to have spies, Mr Perron. I'm sorry if it sounds melodramatic, but this is a very melodramatic and violent country. If you're a police officer and take your job seriously you can't just sit in an office like a deputy commissioner. You have to get out into the bazaars and listen to what people are saying. You have to do all sorts of things that so-called pukka members of the *raj* pretend don't have to be done. Of course if you like you can leave it entirely to subordinates, but Ronnie wasn't like that. He knew it was his duty to get out and see and hear for himself. I expect a lot of people who sing his praises now for what he did to settle Mirat when he first came here would pretend to be shocked if they knew he ever had to go out at night dressed as an Indian servant. But he was prepared to do that for the job's sake. It was very dangerous. That goes without saying. That's why he never told me. But I found out. Shall I tell you how I found out, Mr Perron?'

'Only if you want to.'

'Yes. I think I do. I don't know whether you know, but I haven't been very well. For quite a long time. I can't sleep without taking something. He was so understanding about that. And sometimes when there was any kind of trouble brewing or crisis or flap on, anything that kept him working late or might mean his being called out, he'd sleep in another room, so as not to disturb me, once I'd taken my pills. But the pills don't always work. And then I go through phases of not wanting to take them at all because you can't spend the rest of your life taking pills just to get to sleep. And one night I didn't take any pills at all, and Ronnie was working late and sleeping in this other room, and I just lay here trying and trying to get to sleep naturally. And that's terrible. When you're so tired, but can't sleep and you toss and turn and the night just seems to be slipping away and you start imagining all kinds of silly ridiculous things and there's this awful temptation to take not just one or two of the pills but enough to make you sleep for ever. So I went to Ronnie's room to see whether he was still awake, so that I could tell him I had this awful temptation, and when I got to the door I saw the light was on. And at four o'clock in the morning that was just as if he'd stayed awake in case I needed him and I felt terribly beholden to him. But when I opened the door it didn't seem to be Ronnie there at all, but this terrifying Indian just standing there staring at me. But of course it was Ronnie. That's why I lost my nerve though, a while ago, when Edward ran in dressed just the same way. I don't mean I didn't know Edward had the same little kind of outfit, I only mean it was like seeing Ronnie again, and just at the moment I was wondering where his own Pathan clothes were.' She turned to Sarah. 'Can't we ask Khansamar even about the clothes?'

'No, we can't. That would be worse than asking him about the harness. The car must be here. I'll go and see. Then we ought to be getting back. Khansamar can put all this away.'

Sarah went.

Susan said, 'My sister isn't very intuitive.'

'No?'

'No. You see, Mr Perron, Ronnie's missing arm and Ronnie's missing clothes are like the dog that didn't bark in the night.'

'Conan Doyle?'

She smiled brilliantly.

'My favourite as a child was *The Speckled Band*. I used to read it by torchlight under the bedclothes at the school Sarah and

I went to at home. *The Speckled Band* reminded me of India. Because of the snake. When Aunt Fenny told me last week that Ronnie was dead I thought first of a snake. Or of a scorpion. I've always been terrified of scorpions.'

'I'm terrified of both.'

'Oh, men always say terrified. But they're only pretending. Ronnie was afraid of nothing.'

'I imagine not.'

'I depended on him, Mr Perron. You see, I've always been terrified of almost everything.'

To his alarm he saw that quite suddenly tears were falling down her cheeks. But they fell as if her eyes were at a different season from the rest of her. She still smiled. Her voice altered not at all. She remained physically still. She said, 'I'll never meet another man who understands – I mean who understood me so well. He seemed to guess things about me that no one else in the family ever guessed, not even my sister. It was like living with someone who'd lived with you always, even in your secret life and knew the nice things and the not so nice things. Even things you'd forgotten and even the things you'd dreamt. Until I met Ronald I'd no idea a man could be so patient and understanding. It was a long time before I could help him with his arm. I mean help him to put it on and take it off, and help him with the salves and powders. He understood that. When I'd learned how to help him we became very close. Very close. Closer than at any other time. I've never been so close to anyone before. He realized that. I think he realized that helping him with his arm was a way of helping me to become close to people. Which is what I'd never been. Never felt. His arm was very important to me, Mr Perron. I prefer to think of it being damaged, not just thrown away. Although if it was damaged in the accident I expect it has been thrown away because people don't understand the importance of symbols. But wherever we went, he was admired and respected. Especially here in Mirat. You see, he never *pretended*. He always said what he thought, so people knew where they stood with him. Some of them didn't like where they found themselves standing, but they couldn't blame him, or accuse him of being two-faced. He wasn't always easy on people. At one time I used to get upset when he was angry or disapproving or cold. But he was only angry when he found

people out cheating or lying or pretending. And it was good for
me. I'm not nearly as afraid as I used to be. I don't know what
will happen now, though, but at least he's left me with Edward.
When you look at Edward now you wouldn't credit what a poor
miserable little boy he used to be. With nothing to say to anyone.
Terrified of animals.'

The tears had dried. 'At least, at first. He grew out of that.
Perhaps that's my one contribution. We had a labrador puppy
and Edward became quite fond of him. But we had to get rid of
him in Rajputana. Ronnie didn't like animals in the house.'

'Your son's certainly a friendly little boy.'

'I'm glad you think that.' Briefly she made that gesture more
familiar in her sister: one hand reaching out to clutch the elbow
of the other arm. 'But it's time he went home. He's very preco-
cious. It's what happens out here. And you shouldn't order other
people about like that. I remember doing it myself as a child.
But that was because I was afraid of them.'

'I don't think Edward's in the least afraid.'

'No. But you can't tell. Aggression can be a sign of insecurity.
Ronnie was never able to help me over that sort of thing. He was
the most secure person I've ever known and when Edward talks
to servants the way he does I sometimes think he's just copying
Ronnie. Ronnie was always very firm. But fair. Don't misunderstand. The servants always adored him. What is it, Sarah?'

'The car's here,' Sarah said from behind. Perron wondered
how long she had been standing there. 'We ought to go.'

'Yes, I suppose so. If Khansamar bolts the shutters and locks
the door we can leave all this just as it is until tomorrow. I know
in my heart he's trustworthy really, because Ronnie always said
how reliable he was and he was a good judge. I was just telling
Mr Perron, Sarah, how good Ronnie was with the servants.'

She stirred. Perron got up. He helped her to rise. As she came
level and stood near him he felt that she was as taut as a bent bow.

'When we first came here,' she said, accepting his arm, and
allowing herself to be led out, 'that's to say when I and Edward
came down from Pankot to join Ronnie, he'd already had the
old bungalow cleared and decorated. He'd started furnishing it,
with Dmitri's help of course. Everything except the hall-carpet
belongs to Dmitri. The whole compound at the back had been
cleared too. Of course at that time it looked as if we might be

here for quite a while but in any case that was the way Ronnie worked, to make a home wherever it was, however impermanent. He was so much better at that sort of thing than I'll ever be. He said it was a terrible mess when he first got here. Nobody had lived here for ages and at that time he only had Khansamar. Well. There was a cook and a sweeper, and a bhishti and a mali, but only as temporary people. He said it was for me to decide how permanent they should be. But I couldn't fault his choice. He had that knack of looking at people and knowing whether they'd be any good or not. So really from the start we had a full complement. But unemployment in the state is a terrible problem and I remember how week after week these young men and boys used to turn up, begging for a job. Ronald had such a good reputation for paying a fair wage and treating servants properly that they came here first rather than anywhere else. You'd have thought that eventually they'd have given up. But they never did.'

She stopped abruptly, in the dim entrance hall.

'Where *are* all the servants, Sarah? I've only seen Khansamar.' But she did not seem to need a reply. She placed one hand just below her throat. A theatrical little gesture, Perron thought. But in Susan, all such gestures were probably mute cries for help. 'The whole place is so quiet. As though everyone has gone.' She turned, offered her hand. 'Thank you for your kindness, Mr Perron. For being so logical. For being here. For knowing Ronald.'

It was an exit line. She went quickly across the hall out on to the verandah and then down the steps to the car. For a moment Sarah stayed with Perron in the hall. Then she murmured, 'Thank you, Guy,' and went out too.

III

He was dressed by five to seven and on the verandah as the second-hand of his watch ticked up the hour. It was a clear sunny morning.

At ten past he heard the growl of a vehicle being changed down to enter the compound. A jeep swept in. A khaki-clad figure was riding shot-gun on the high rear seat. Sarah was driving. Her head was bound in a silk scarf. She wore khaki too. She braked but kept the engine running and smiled up at him. This was the old Sarah of Area Headquarters who knew a thing or two about getting a move-on.

'Where's the horse?' he asked. She patted the seat on her right as though it were a saddle. He climbed in over the low port. She wore a khaki skirt too. In fact she had on her old WAC(I) uniform. He could see where the stripes had been. The Indian with the rifle was a soldier. His shoulder tab said *Mirat Artillery.* His face was pitted by smallpox. He looked cheerful. Sarah re-engaged gear, gave a burst of power and drove the jeep down to the exit.

Coming out on to the road he saw that the *maidan* opposite – the rough ground that stretched from the walls of the palace grounds to the walls of the old city – was now populated by military vehicles and groups of soldiers and armed police. He expected her to turn right, imagining that the horses were wait-ing somewhere on the *maidan*. But she turned left, passing the Dewani Bhavan and then the palace wall, going in the direction of the lake, but suddenly turning left again into a rough un-metalled road. The wind flicked her scarf and the collar of her khaki shirt. She drove very well. A bumpy road, but a smooth ride. Clearly she was familiar with the route.

Coming in from the right, a little way ahead, and from the left, were the spurs of two low wooded hills. Otherwise the country-side was open, poor, unfertile. There was no visible habitation. The land was tawny, flecked with patches of dusty olive green scrub. As the jeep entered the section of road enclosed by the two wooded spurs, Sarah slowed. The road was straight and there seemed no reason for her caution; until, a long way ahead, he saw an elephant plodding rhythmically towards them. As they drove nearer he saw the elephant was pushing or urging some-thing ahead of it with swings of its trunk. Sarah slowed almost to a crawl. Behind the elephant were two men and ahead of it, its calf, an absurdly small creature. Seeing the jeep the mother elephant advanced protectively and the calf went under the shadow of its huge head. Now that they were close Perron saw that the animal's hide was almost black, but red from the dust of the tawny earth. Just before they came level the elephant swung into a side-track, followed by the men. And Sarah drove on.

She said, 'They're the Nawab's. They belong to his forestry

department. No one can build here. A hundred years ago it was all forest.'

The road began to descend into an area of scrub-jungle. The horizon was already blurred and violet with the day's promise of heat. A twist in the road brought them to an area of rising land, almost devoid of trees. On the brow of the hill Perron saw two horsemen, as still as statues. Sarah drove a little further and then pulled in behind an army truck and a large closed-in van: a horse-box. A couple of soldiers, with rifles slung, were standing on the opposite side of the road.

'We can watch from here,' she said, getting out. From the dash-board she took a pair of binoculars and handed them to him. 'Here,' she said. 'Now you can see something of the old India.'

Even in close focus the horsemen seemed perfectly still. The lenses blurred the colours slightly, isolated purple refraction so that the profiles of the men's faces seemed to be outlined by a dim reddish-blue glow. They were brown faces. What was so extraordinary was the lack of movement, the intensity of concentration. One of the men was turbanned, the other bare-headed. The turbanned man was dressed in what looked like a studded leather jerkin and tight dark pantaloons. The younger man with the bare head (Ahmed surely?) wore an ordinary pale blue shirt, corduroy breeches and riding boots. Around his raised left forearm was a leather shield which ended in a glove. Upon the forearm sat a hawk. Perron fancied that he could see the feathered shift of its neck, the gleam of its fierce eye.

Then the vision in the binoculars suddenly blurred and Perron lowered them and just caught the end of the fighting movement of Ahmed Kasim's arm, citing the hawk at its prey – a movement that produced in the bird apparent momentary lack of co-ordination, quickly righted, and developing into a powerful and breath-taking ascent, a great arc, the beginning of a spiral of such formal beauty that Perron caught his breath and held it until he discerned in the empty heavens, through the planned geometry of the hawk's attack, the objective, the intended point of killing contact: a dark speck intent on escape.

He felt Sarah's hand groping for his. But she only wanted the binoculars. He let them go and then gave all his attention back to the aerial hunt, one that left no vapour trails but reminded him of a summer that had mapped them. The hawk plummeted. Its shape merged with the speck. Sarah cried out, with pleasure and pain. He looked at her. All he could see was her hand gripping the binoculars, her slightly open mouth, the brave little thrust of chin and the tautened throat.

She gave the glasses back to him and said without looking at him, 'You must watch this.'

He took the binoculars and readjusted the focus. The horsemen had put their mounts forward at a slow walk. He searched the lower sky in the direction they were heading and, almost too late, picked up the image of the hawk just descending. The prey was invisible. The hawk's wings were still at stretch, but folding back in slow motion, in satisfaction. And then they were at stretch again, beating against gravity, intent on ascent. He followed its course, saw Ahmed throw something. It swooped down, clawed at ground level, attacking something with its beak. The older horseman was riding in the direction of the kill. Ahmed, motionless, watched the hawk swallow its gift – presumably an appetizing and bloody piece of raw meat. Presently there came the far-off sound of Ahmed's voice, a sound like Tek, Tek, Tek-Allahallahallah. The hawk was now beating at the air again, rising, circling once round Ahmed, flirting at the lure of his leathered forearm, and then gently turning and coming in to alight. It ducked its head, arched its wings, then allowed itself to be brought near to Ahmed's face: the likeness of a kiss.

Unexpectedly, Ahmed flighted the hawk again, but not at prey, unless he himself were the prey. He cantered to and fro, round and round, gradually descending the hill, spiralling at ground level as the hawk had spiralled the sky, while the bird flew to and fro as well, sometimes swooping in mock attack.

'I wish he wouldn't do this,' Sarah said. 'But he trusts her utterly.'

It was like a game of love. Sometimes Ahmed called out and when he did the hawk seemed to turn away, spurning him, only to meet him again at the end of another swerving course. About one hundred yards from the road, Ahmed reined in. The hawk planed above him for a while and then as if breathless too, ready to call it a day, came in and settled gently on his proffered arm. Perron saw that Ahmed was securing the jesses. Again he brought the bird close to his face, then he sat erect and came the rest of the way at a sedate walk. Some distance behind, the falconer was following slowly down. He had a canvas bag slung over his shoulder. The kill.

'Hello,' Ahmed called. He kicked his stirrups away, brought his right leg up and across the saddle and slid down. The bird stayed rock-still on his forearm. He tickled her stomach. She glared at him and then at the strangers. But what else, Perron wondered, could a hawk do but glare?

'Her name's Mumtaz,' Sarah said. 'Come and meet her. Incidentally, don't offer to shake hands with Ahmed. She's very jealous and protective. Aren't you, Mumtaz? I'm not allowed to touch her at all, because she senses I'm female. But if Ahmed tells her it's all right she'll allow you to tickle her throat.'

Ahmed said, in Urdu: *Here is Perron Sahib, from across the black water. He is a friend. Say hello.* He stroked her breast feathers, then said in English, 'You can touch her now, Mr Perron.'

Perron extended a finger. The head turned. A glaring eye observed the finger. Risking the loss, he placed the finger on her breast and smoothed downwards. When he withdrew the finger the hawk's wing stirred slightly.

'Ah,' Sarah said. 'She liked that. Ahmed, you'd better keep your eye on her. I think she's a bit of a rover.'

Ahmed laughed, then, noticing her skirt said, 'Aren't you going to ride?'

'No, I thought not today.'

'What about you, Mr Perron? You can have Begum here. She's still quite fresh.'

'I'm more than content to watch you hawk.'

'Oh, no more of that. I'm glad you were just in time. We can have a run after breakfast if you like. Come, Mumtaz. You can go to sleep now.' The falconer had come up and dismounted. Rather tetchily Mumtaz hopped from Ahmed's arm to the falconer's. The falconer took her down to the truck and Perron now noticed that there was an awning attached to the truck's side and, under the awning, a table laid for breakfast. Nearby, in the shade of a tree, a portable perch had been set up, with a silver chain attached to its cross-pole. The falconer transferred Mumtaz to this, secured her and clapped a little scarlet velvet hood on her head.

'Come,' Ahmed said. 'I hope everybody is hungry.'

They went down to the table under the awning. Ahmed absented himself for a while. As Perron and Sarah sat she said, 'Are you glad you came?'

'Not glad. Enchanted.'

'I meant back to India.'

'The answer's the same.'

She smiled.

The convoy home was headed by the army truck. The soldiers sat in the back of it, the falconer up front, with Mumtaz. Behind, Ahmed drove the jeep with Sarah next to him and Perron in the back seat. Bringing up the rear was the horse-box which gradually got left behind. Perron, shouting against the noise of the engine and the currents of air asked what the bird thought of mechanical transport. Sarah leaned back and said: 'Ahmed thinks it's her favourite part of the proceedings. But she's very blasé. She goes to sleep.'

'What do the soldiers make of it all?'

'I think they get a bit of a kick out of it. It's still quite new to them.'

No one had explained the presence of the soldiers. If the hawking was quite new to them then presumably a military escort was a recent innovation. But how recent? And why was it necessary? Sarah turned round again and shouted, 'We're going to the palace if that's all right. I've got to visit Shiraz, but Ahmed will take you round and show you the interesting bits.'

Ahmed said something to her which he didn't catch. She laughed.

'Who is Shiraz?' Perron shouted.

'The Nawab's daughter.'

Perron nodded. He did not know the Nawab had a daughter. But he thought that between Ahmed and Sarah there was a special kind of empathy, the kind that two people betray in small gestures and in the way they have of dealing with one another in public. Well, if that was how the land lay he could only wish her good luck, slightly deflating though it was to his own ego.

He looked at Ahmed's back. He remembered him as a pleasant but rather unsociable young man, given apparently to whisky and women, a combination which might by now have begun to show signs of taking toll. Instead, young Kasim looked (as Uncle

George would say) well set-up. Mounted, and flying his hawk, Perron appreciated that to Sarah he would even cut a heroic figure. And she was the kind of girl who would defy the convention that a white woman didn't fall in love with an Indian.

When they came close to the end of the unmetalled road Sarah called out, 'Go in through the guest house entrance, Ahmed, and drop me there. I've got a few things to do. I'll join you at the palace later.'

Ahmed nodded and then hooted and drew ahead of the truck, paused at the T-junction and raised his arm to indicate that the truck should turn right. Turning left himself he came to a halt to make sure the driver had understood. Perron looked back. As the truck came into view he saw the falconer's arm which was resting by the elbow on the open window frame, and upon the arm, Mumtaz, hooded, head slightly inclined –

(*Extract from Perron's diaries*)
(Tuesday August 5) – asleep, dreaming of what? The palace wall is backed by trees. You can see nothing from the road. We turned in at an unexpected culvert. Twin iron gates. Closed. A smart sepoy opened them at once and we went in, past two more who were armed and came to attention. The gates were closed again once we'd passed through. The path is bordered by rhododendron. Just where it forked (giving on the left a glimpse of the guest house) Sarah made Ahmed stop. She insisted on walking from there. We continued along the right-hand fork and came out after a hundred yards into a large formal park, with the extraordinary pink palace on the left. To the right, half a mile away, was the main entrance gate and frontage, facing on to the *maidan*. The park was laid out with avenues, terraces and fountains. As we got close to the palace. you could see that parts of the pink stucco needed replastering. The palace bears some resemblance to the Wind Palace in Jaipur. We drove to a side entrance. Sentries again. Steps up. The smell of ancient damp masonry. A long terrace, a lot of servants and officials coming and going. Obviously the business side of the place. Then through a narrow Moghul arch into a dark stone corridor – the kind in which you feel the weight of India: a heavy darkness which is a protection from glare and heat but reminiscent of tombs and dungeons.

But the inner courtyard was beautiful. At the far end, facing the paths and fountains was the old Hall of Public Audience, a deep terrace with a high roof supported by convoluted pink columns; and, with a marble canopy and daïs centrally placed, the stone seat on which in the old days the Nawab was enthroned on cushions: the *gaddi*. Behind the Hall of Public Audience (Ahmed said) was a smaller courtyard overlooked by the present Nawab's private apartments. Avoiding this other courtyard we crossed and went out through another series of dark passages to the other side of the palace. Lawns swept down to the lake and the little white mosque which was enclosed in its own railed courtyard. We went down to the lake shore. The glare was intense. Ahmed said they were fishing again this morning. Beyond the distant reeds you could just see a couple of boats and men casting large shimmering nets. Ahmed took me back inside the palace to see what he called the modern rooms. These were at the front. The old Moghul passages gave way to corridors, Victorian in style (dark lincrusta, hundreds of pictures cluttering the walls, as thick as postage stamps in an album) and then – fascinating! – a kind of salon which reminded you of the public lounge of a Ritzy Edwardian hotel, all gilt and plush and potted palms in gilt wicker baskets, ornate draught screens and a circular padded bench around a central marble column. Dmitri Bronowsky's influence, one would imagine.

It was in this *fin-de-siècle* foyer that Ahmed left him, to change out of his riding gear. He promised to be back shortly. He said, 'Would you like a swim later? There's an outdoor pool. We can provide towels and costumes.'

'Yes, I'd like that very much.'

'It can't be for about an hour, though. Sarah usually gives Shiraz her swimming lesson between eleven and twelve. I'll tell them to send you coffee and the papers.'

The coffee and papers came. Today's *Times of India* and the *Statesman* (which obviously reached the palace earlier than they reached the club), the *Mirat Courier* and the *Ranpur Gazette*. This morning in the national newspapers some play was being made with the latest difficulties Jinnah was said to be raising: questions about the precise status Mountbatten would have in Karachi when he made his last appearance there as Viceroy on August 13. Two days later Jinnah would become Governor-General of the new dominion of Pakistan (moth-eaten Pakistan as he had called it, when he found he wasn't getting either the whole of the Punjab or the whole of Bengal – least of all Kashmir or a corridor connecting the west with the east).

It seemed that Jinnah had been gently reminded that the Viceroy would still be Viceroy on August 13 and he himself only Governor-General designate, just as Mountbatten was also Governor-General designate of the new Dominion of India. There was no question of Jinnah taking precedence before the date of independence, and Mountbatten couldn't be in both Karachi and Delhi on August Fifteen.

There were depressingly familiar reports from Lahore, Amritsar and Calcutta of troubles with the Sikhs and of murders and arson, and equally depressing commentaries on the harrowing experiences of some of the refugees already making their way from what would be Pakistan to what would be India, and vice versa. But the photographs in the papers were only of smiling statesmen's faces.

The *Mirat Courier*, predictably, published similar photographs and gave up its front page to preliminary details of the official programme for independence day celebrations. A Muslim firm in the cantonment called Mir Khan Military Tailors and Outfitters had taken half a page to announce a grand cut-price sale of all items of uniform and sporting equipment. At the rear pages were brief details of a number of farewell parties held the previous week.

He turned more expectantly to the waspish *Ranpur Gazette*, and was not unrewarded. The editorial – a long one – was headed: Pandora's Box. It read:

'The pocket-kingdom of Mirat was, until 1937, except for a brief period in the early 'twenties, in direct relationship with the Crown through the agency of the Governor in Ranpur, which suited all parties and conformed with the geographical and political facts of life. Geographically and politically Mirat has always existed and can only exist in future as part of the geographical and political territory by which it is surrounded.

'That it exists at all as a separate political unit is due to the pure luck and chance of the fall of the dice of history. Long drawn-out though the battle for power was between the European merchants and the ruling Indian powers in the seventeenth,

eighteenth and nineteenth centuries, there came a point when
the dominant European power, the British, made a settlement
with what was left of the scattered remnants of Moghul India.
That point was reached in 1857.

'Dare one say that as a result of the Mutiny the Crown feared
it had gone far enough with its policies of expansion or that it
simply decided that the status quo, then existing, would prove
the most profitable, if maintained? Be that as it may, with two-
thirds of the sub-continent now under the direct rule of
Whitehall and the real power of the remnants of Princely India
reduced virtually to impotence, a declaration was made of "no
further territorial ambitions" (what a sinister ring that phrase has
nowadays!) – and treaties were made with the rulers of the nearly
600 remaining states, widely scattered and varying in size from
mere estates to provinces the size of Ireland, treaties which
secured to the rulers and to their successors their princely rights,
revenues, privileges and territories, assured them of autonomy in
all but the major subjects of external affairs and national defence,
treaties which undertook to protect the princes from each other,
from attack both internal and external.

'Separate though these treaties were – a series of private formal
individual contracts between rulers and crown, they have nevertheless always been part of a larger unwritten treaty – or doctrine:
the doctrine of the paramountcy of the British Crown over all
the rulers; the paramountcy of the King-Emperor or Queen-
Empress who, through the Crown Representative, could depose
an unruly prince, withhold recognition from a prince's heir, and
generally take steps to ensure the peace, prosperity and well-
being of a prince's subjects.

'But none of the doctrinal powers of "paramountcy" could
abrogate the treaty made with a state. From time to time the
Crown has taken over a state's administration, but only in trust.
The declaration of "no further territorial ambitions" has been,
one may feel, upheld.

'Unfortunately, the doctrine of paramountcy has run counter
to the doctrine of eventual self-government for those provinces
ruled directly by the British parliament, through the Government of India. Paramountcy has always been illogical in the
long run, and this illogicality is best exemplified by the dual
rôle assigned to the Viceroy. In his rôle as Governor-General it

has been his duty to govern and guide and encourage the British-Indian provinces towards democratic parliamentary self-rule. As Crown Representative, it has been his duty to uphold, secure, oversee and defend the autocratic rule of several hundred princes.

'Many princes have therefore assumed, or pretended to assume, or felt entitled to assume, that the demission by the Governor-General of power into Indian hands in provinces directly ruled by the British, could not absolve the British from treaty obligations to uphold, secure and defend the integrity of the territories the princes have ruled, for better or worse, and which they believe they have every right to continue to rule, irrespective of who rules the rest of India.

'It is fair to say that until quite recently they have been encouraged in this assumption by statements from Whitehall and New Delhi, and by the behaviour and attitude of senior members of the Political Department. Their chief fear was that "paramountcy" would be transferred by the Crown to the Crown's successors in British India (in this case, the Congress Party, which for years has made it clear that the survival of autocratic states, some quite feudal in their administration, could not be tolerated). But they were reassured. Paramountcy was a doctrine. You could not transfer a doctrine.

'But if you can't transfer it what can you do with it? The answer is, nothing. It simply lapses when the paramount "power" disappears. But what about the treaties? Can treaties lapse unless both parties agree to the lapse? Indeed they can. They lapse when one party no longer has the power (or the presence) to perform its part of the bargain. By abdicating in British-India, the British Crown no longer has the power to protect and secure and uphold the territorial integrity of Princely India, without running the risk of going to war with the new Dominion. One prince rumoured to be consulting his lawyers in Switzerland with a view to suing the British Government in London for nonperformance of contract. Another is rumoured to have gone to Delhi armed with a revolver. Other princes, of course, see the lapsing of paramountcy and of treaty obligations as the opportunity to declare their complete independence.

'What the British Crown has really done for the past hundred years is advance the territories it ruled directly to full democratic and parliamentary self-government, and maintain the territories it did not rule directly, but was paramount over, in forms of autocratic government alien in nature to the form of government itself advocates and which the British people themselves enjoy at home and seem convinced is everyone's birthright. You can hardly wonder that this left-hand/right-hand policy was entrusted to one man, the Viceroy, in order to create the illusion that there was a unity of purpose.

'Our new Viceroy has been, as ever, quick to grasp the irreconcilable details and see the immense political vacuum that technically follows the removal of British power in British-India. The new States Department is his efficient answer to nature's abhorrence of such a vacuum. You could say that Whitehall foresaw the situation in 1935. You could say that the princes themselves are largely to blame for refusing at that time to co-operate in the Federal Scheme for a united and self-governing India (but they were not the only people who were suspicious of the scheme and refused to co-operate). You could blame the princes for many things, including their haughty distrust of one another, or of anybody. You cannot in principle blame them for standing by their treaties, for acting out the Ruritanian farce currently playing up and down India (and Pakistan); a farce all too frequently encouraged by senior members of the Political Department who have served in India for years and have been brought up to take the treaties as serious and sacrosanct documents.

'This is a farce in which Muslim rulers of predominantly Hindu states which are hedged about on all sides by territory which from August 15 will be ruled by the Congress from Delhi, elect to join one of the two distant arms of Pakistan; or in which Hindu rulers of predominantly Muslim states in or contiguous to Pakistan declare allegiance to Congress India, or in which rulers of immense landlocked states declare their independence of everything and everybody. You cannot blame them because not only is the farce implicit in the treaties and the doctrines but these declarations and intentions do not in any single case contravene either the spirit or the letter of the law. They are simply devoid of any means of reasonable implementation. From the princes' point of view, the long years of British power and influence have left them in possession of preserved but unpossessable goods. Geographically and politically they cannot survive individually once the Crown abdicates and twentieth-century India (or Pakistan) takes over.

'All this, and the terrible reports of the breakdown of civil authority in many areas of the Punjab, must make it seem that to achieve the objective of a political transformation scene in the long pantomime of the British-Indian Empire, the Viceroy, obeying the wishes of a well-meaning but ignorant British electorate, has found himself in the unenviable position of opening Pandora's Box and letting out all the evils that have afflicted this country probably since time began but which have been imprisoned, under a lid shut and locked by the single rule of British Power and British Law; evils which have not died of asphyxiation, but multiplied.

'Which brings us back to the small but not unimportant state of Mirat, which is not only geographically part of this province but traditionally and politically part of it.

'Under the present ruler, His Highness Sir Ahmed Ali Guffur Kasim Bahadur, and his Chief Minister, Count Dmitri Bronowsky, Mirat has made notable strides forward. A predominantly Hindu state, the administration used to be the almost exclusive preserve of Muslims, a situation common enough where the ruling family is Muslim, but one that always causes dissatisfaction and unrest. For the past two or three decades, official posts, including senior official posts have been open to Hindus. There are Hindus on the Council of State and for many years now there has been a Hindu College of Higher Education.

'The existence in the state capital of a large military cantonment and training area for troops of the British and the Indian armies has contributed (for nearly a hundred years) to Mirat's prosperity and no doubt to its peace and security. For the past year or two, however, there has been a great deal of unrest. Both the main Indian political parties must be held partly responsible for this because neither has been slow to take political advantage of the problems posed for India as a whole by the continuing existence of states whose rule, however benevolent, can hardly be called truly democratic.

'The Nawab is now faced with the problem of what action to take now that his treaty with the Crown and the doctrine of the Crown's paramountcy are lapsing. One may think it a pity that since 1937 his relationship with the Crown has been conducted through the Resident at the distant court of a much larger state, Gopalakand. Whatever advice Sir Robert Conway is giving the Maharajah of Gopalakand ought not, one may suggest, to be the same advice he should give to the Nawab of Mirat. But that is by the way. At this juncture, advice from the Political Department is largely irrelevant. The consideration that should be uppermost in the Nawab's mind is the well-being of his subjects.

'It is important to remember the tradition of intense loyalty and reverence felt by the subjects of a princely state for their ruler, the tradition of dependence on him to make wise decisions. The main Indian political parties may scoff at these traditions as outmoded and feudal, but they exist. And already we have reports of the first effects on the people of Mirat of rumours of indecision at the palace.

'For instance, the rumour that the Nawab has not been co-operative with representatives of the States Department of the government of the new Indian dominion and may declare himself an independent Islamic state, affiliated to Pakistan, has led to the murder of Muslims in the city of Mirat and in the villages by extremist Hindus, and to burning and looting of Muslim shops. Retaliation, by Muslim extremists, has led to the murder of Hindus and the burning and looting of Hindu houses and shops. In all this, the position of such British troops as remain in the cantonment is, to say the least, delicate, and that of Indian troops equally delicate since they are in the main troops allocated to the new dominion of India and most of the Muslim elements of regiments that are to be divided have already left the area.

'Nevertheless it is to the cantonment, which might itself turn out to be the scene of awkward confrontations, that Muslim refugees from the villages and from the city have gone, seeking temporary refuge. Some of these refugees are no doubt bona fide travellers *en route* to Pakistan. Most, one suspects, are there temporarily, simply to protect their lives, having lost their property.

'We cannot afford to have in this province of British India which in ten days' time will become a province of the new Indian dominion, a pocket of such potential communal and political danger.

'The Nawab could defuse the bomb in an instant, by taking the logical, the only practical step, which is to sign the instrument of accession to the new Dominion of India on the three subjects of external affairs, defence and communications and the standstill agreement which will allow him time to negotiate a settlement with India on all the complex and vitally important points arising from the lapse of paramountcy and the end of his treaty with the Crown.

'If he signs, his subjects will then know where they stand. Since the majority is Hindu, one might say that the majority would approve such a step. The Muslim minority who until recently have lived in comparative harmony with the Hindus of Mirat would also accept his decision, as that of their ruler and co-religionist, but those of them who see a better future for themselves in Jinnah's new Islamic state could then peacefully wind up their businesses and affairs and leave – just as peacefully.

'One can sympathize with the Nawab. One should sympathize with any man whose traditional assurances and traditional courses of action are suddenly removed or closed to him. But it is *his* sympathies, not our own, which are under test and examination. One is fairly confident that the outcome will show them firmly placed with the present and future welfare of all his people.

'So at least one must hope. Classical scholars will recall that Hope was the only thing that didn't fly out of Pandora's Box but remained obstinately at the bottom.'

'Guy?'

It was Sarah. She had changed into a cotton frock.

'Ahmed asks me to apologize. He's got something urgent to attend to. But Dmitri would like to have a few words and present you to HH, if you're agreeable.'

'Of course. Have you had your swim yet?'

'I can't this morning. I've got to go back to the guest house soon. But I can take you back to Nigel's bungalow after you've met HH. I'm sorry if we seem to be messing you about again.'

'Hardly that.'

She led him by a new way into the inner courtyard and then along one of the paths between the lawns and fountains.

Strolling up and down the colonnaded terrace on their left were four men; one of them in full Congress garb, another in a lounge suit, the other two in long-skirted high-necked coats.

'States Department?' Perron murmured.

'The two on this side are. The others are members of the Nawab's council. Finance member and food member.'

One of them called out, 'Good-morning, Miss Layton.'

She called good-morning back.

'That's the food member. He's an expert on agrarian economy. Dmitri pinched him from Calcutta before the war. I wish you could have gone to Biranpur and seen the model farm and village he set up. Perhaps you'll be able to, if you're staying for a while and things settle down.'

'Perhaps you'll go with me?'

'I wish I could. I'd like to see it again. But I can't think when that'll be. Susan's decided to go back to Pankot right away and I'll have to go with her. I don't know what will happen after that.'

'What does right away mean?'

'The day after tomorrow, I think. Ahmed's looking into the arrangements now.'

She moved ahead of him, through the Hall of Public Audience, to a narrow archway that gave on to the courtyard Ahmed hadn't shown him, the one overlooked by the private apartments. Going through the archway she suddenly stopped and said, 'Oh. Wait. Do you mind?' She went down into the courtyard leaving him alone, in the shadow of the archway.

Seated on the rim of a fountain at the centre of the courtyard was a young Indian girl dressed – how odd – in slacks and blouse. As Sarah approached her Perron saw two older women, in sarees, getting up from squatting positions on the terrace and making *namaste*. The Indian girl's back was towards Sarah but the movements of the women alerted her and she looked round, then down again, head bowed. Sarah sat beside her and after a moment put her arm round her.

Perron turned away and considered the Nawab's eye-view of the main courtyard. From here there was nothing that oppressed him. The courtyard was brilliant with sunshine and colour and splashing water. Then he saw the white peacock – at least, *a* white peacock – strutting across one of the lawns, its breast carved like the prow of a Viking ship, its long trailing tail quills making stern and wake. The quills were in moult. Should it erect them now they would look like the spokes of a moth-eaten fan. But the proud statement of the bird's slow stalking was only marginally impaired.

He went back to the archway in time to see Sarah and the girl walking slowly arm in arm, climbing up to the terrace. The women followed some distance behind. Then the girl broke away and ran in through a doorway. Sarah returned to the court-yard. The two women hastened after their charge.

He went down and waited.

'Shiraz?' he asked.

'Yes. Shiraz.' Then she took him up to the private apartments.

'My dear Mr Perron,' Count Bronowsky said, limping across the darkened, almost completely shuttered, room. 'How can I sufficiently apologize for not having greeted you before? I don't mean that Sarah and Nigel haven't tried their best to cover up for me, but I'm very conscious of my personal failure in the matter of hospitality. Please forgive me.'

A single shaft of light from the louvres of a shutter exposed the half-blind face and the parchment texture of the skin. The offered hand seemed made of nothing but frail bone. There was a faint smell of eau-de-cologne. A stronger shaft of light fell on to a couch near a window. It was to this that Dmitri led him, skeletal hand lightly resting on his shoulder. 'When I had your letter from England, I thought – Ah! Mr Perron may be per-suaded to lecture at our college on the subject of the European mercenaries and the history of the Mahrattas. But in the event the college is temporarily closed owing to what one calls circum-stances beyond one's control. The students are on strike.' They sat on the couch. 'In any case this was just a thing I selfishly thought you might agree to do for us. The important question is what we can do for you. You mentioned the possibility of writing and publishing something on the subject of the transfer of power as it affects states like this. I've forgotten the name of the paper.'

'It's a new quarterly review called *The New English Forum*. It probably won't survive more than a few issues. I'm afraid my journalistic credentials are entirely spurious.'

'I see you have this morning's *Ranpur Gazette*.'

Perron realized he still carried the folded newspaper.

'I hope you won't think it very discourteous of me, Mr Perron, if I ask you to hide it away. His Highness hasn't read this morning's issue and there's a long editorial in it which from my point of view has come out a shade prematurely. You've read it? What did you think of it?'

'I thought it quite well-argued.'

'The editor of the *Ranpur Gazette*, an elderly Englishman incidentally, does have quite an effective style. I suppose Nigel told you what he was hoping to achieve in Gopalakand?'

'Yes, he gave me a rough outline.'

'He's been on the telephone this morning and will be back some time later today with the necessary letter from the Resident. In other words his mission was a success. But I haven't told Nawab Sahib yet. I don't intend to do so until after the morning audiences and petitions. He was hoping Conway would encourage him to stand firm on independence, but Nigel has persuaded him not to encourage him. If Nawab Sahib reads that article now it will put his back up. I don't want him with his back up when I tell him that Conway is washing his hands of Mirat and that he should sign the instrument of accession if he so wishes.'

Perron handed Bronowsky the newspaper and said, 'Perhaps you'd better dispose of it. Thank you for warning me. I might have referred to it.'

'It was Miss Layton who warned me you might have been reading it. That is why I came out for a private word. She is a remarkably shrewd and thoughtful young woman. We shall miss her at the palace. Nawab Sahib's daughter is heart-broken and begs her to come back soon. Miss Layton is the only person who has ever succeeded in bringing poor little Shiraz out of her shell. For years I tried. Nawab Sahib tried. I tried to get Ahmed to try. But the influence of the late Begum, her mother, seemed indestructible. Shiraz threatened to go into full purdah, can you believe it? Now she is riding and swimming and wearing modern clothes and even sometimes talking to men. Even Ahmed is showing an interest in her at last. And it is all Sarah's doing. She is with Nawab Sahib now, saying goodbye. He too has become very fond of her. It is a piquant situation. She treats him like a father, but I sometimes think he looks at her and vaguely resents that for the past twenty years I have kept him on such a strait and narrow path. As a young prince, you know, when his father ruled, the Political Department was in two minds about recognizing him as the heir. Their files would reveal some scandalous things about him in his wild youth. Perhaps about me too. Thank God these files are all being destroyed before Patel can get his hands on them.'

'Is Shiraz the Nawab's heir?'

'Oh, no. He has two sons, both older. The younger is in the Indian Air Force, not a pilot, they never succeeded in teaching him to fly, poor boy. The elder is Mohsin, but Mohsin and his wife live mostly in Delhi. He is much involved with business affairs and his wife does not like Mirat at all. She hates coming here. But finally this has had one advantage. She insisted on a swimming-pool being built in the grounds for her to bathe in. It has been very useful to Sarah, in educating Shiraz.'

'The succession is secure, then.'

Bronowsky nodded, but did not otherwise reply. Instead he said, 'Tomorrow I hope that these States Department people will be on their way back to Delhi with their signed bits of paper and that I shall be able to leave the palace and go back across the road to my own home. Then perhaps you will be my guest and in any case come to dinner tomorrow evening, if all goes well. I don't know whether Sarah will be able to come if they are to travel the next day. But I hope Nigel can be there. And Ahmed. Ahmed has promised his father to be in Ranpur for the August fifteen celebrations and I cannot deny him that. Since the Laytons have decided to go back to Pankot he may as well accompany them as far as Ranpur. It is a good opportunity.'

He stood and placed a hand on Perron's shoulder and indicated a double set of doors.

'Nawab Sahib is in there with Sarah. I'm afraid you will not find him very communicative. He is shy with strangers. So do not be offended if I intervene quite quickly and take him through to see his petitioners. The morning audiences are a relic of the past. All the real business is done by members of council and their staffs, but the tradition is important. I shall have to go in with him but Sarah will then look after you and take you back to Nigel's.'

Bronowsky went to an ornate desk, opened a drawer and pushed the *Ranpur Gazette* into it. As he rejoined Perron he said, 'Did you by any chance call on our old friend Aimee when you were in Bombay?'

'No, I didn't. I called on Mr Hapgood though. He sent his regards.'

'Hapgood? Oh, the bank official. But how well I remember that evening at Aimee's. What a terrible disaster you averted – what a terrible mistake I made, taking Miss Layton and poor Ronald there! The previous time I visited her everything was beyond criticism. You made an impression on her, did you know? The next time I saw her, I think in Delhi, she was a bit confused about the precise circumstances but she said, "Where is that British sergeant you brought to one of my parties, who gave me a lovely bottle of whisky, and then took it away with him, the crook?" So, you see? Come. Let us go in.'

Extract from Perron's diary, Tuesday August 5.
– to a smaller room, a salon, decorated and furnished in the Empire style. The Nawab stood at the window indicating something to Sarah (it turned out to be the view of the fishermen on the Izzat Bagh Lake – so-called because an earlier Nawab had declared that the *izzat*, the honour of the ruling house, would be maintained for as long as the lake didn't dry up). Dmitri left me near the door, said something to the Nawab, a small man in comparison with Dmitri. The Nawab came across. I advanced a step or two and bowed. The offer to shake hands was slightly delayed. One sensed that today he distrusted all Englishmen. His long-skirted coat was amazingly shabby. The cuffs were frayed and the material was very thin around the button-holes. (He is a rich man, generous and not mean. His austerities are wholly personal, Sarah tells me.) The face is narrow, lined, quite a deep brown, curiously anonymous. The kind of face you easily forget. But he has the sort of presence you remember, self-containment, suggesting restraint of packed nervous energy and intensity of feeling – suitable in the descendant of men who were feared, before whom Mirat trembled, years ago.

An exchange of compliments. A bleak pause. Dmitri hovering in the background, a gaunt one-eyed guardian, smiling but alert. Then the Nawab offered some samples from his stock of small-talk. I replied in kind. Suddenly he frowned. Perron? he asked. A descendant of the successor to Benoit de Boigne? His ancestors could have had no love for either of them. Relief, when I disclaimed connection. Then the preliminary to courtly dismissal. I must be sure to inform Count Bronowsky of anything necessary to my comfort and to my researches. A friendly, shy, smile.

No handshake in parting. He turns to Dmitri as if wondering whether he has omitted anything. One realized his dependence and his current distraction. Before he went he silently pressed both Sarah's hands. Then he and Dmitri went out through another set of doors. A glimpse of a much larger chamber with about a dozen people in it, who bowed deeply; one even making full obeisance.

Sarah and I leave in solemn but not too solemn silence. We run the gauntlet of servants making *namaste* (to her, not to me, I think). Then she drove me back to Nigel's bungalow. Tippoo was waiting on the verandah. She wouldn't stay for a drink. I didn't press her. She seemed preoccupied.

But before I let her go I said, 'What *did* happen to Ronald?' She said, 'Don't ask me, Guy. Ask Nigel. Or Dmitri. Or better still, nobody.'

IV

After lunch he slept again. But sleep was intermittent. There was another storm, brief but disturbing, and the rain brought out that smell of damp, of decay. He woke between dozes with a persistent sense of ill-being and was thankful when Tippoo brought in his tea at four o'clock. He thought of starting a letter to Aunt Charlotte, but the room was suddenly intolerable. He dressed and went out to the rear compound to get air and sunshine. There was no sound from Merrick's compound. He inspected the banyan tree. How old would it be? One hundred years at least? So fine a specimen would be especially holy. But its holiness lent no tranquillity to the bungalows in whose compounds it grew.

He found the gate in the compound wall unlocked so went through. Today Merrick's garden looked less well-tended. Overnight the grass seemed to have grown an inch. All the green tattis between the white columns had been rolled up, exposing windows obviously locked and shuttered. One could visualize indoors the shrouded shapes of furniture draped in dust-covers, signs that the occupants had gone and that no one knew when they might be back.

He went towards the house intending to go up on to the verandah but then decided he shouldn't intrude on so much absence, so much impending absence, so much darkness, so much loss. He took the path that skirted the side of the bungalow and came out into the front and stood still, hackles rising.

A van was drawn up. Down the steps from the front verandah two men were carrying a black coffin. The coffin was tilted downwards, resting on their shoulders. When they reached ground level they jog-trotted to the van, then shoved the coffin into the back.

Not a coffin. Merrick's trunk. Another man was bringing down the long sagging sausage of the rolled hall carpet. This went into the truck too. Then the rear flap was put up and fixed. Two of the men got in the back, the other went to the front. Khansamar came down the steps carrying an object that glinted. A picture in a frame. The boy's picture of the old Queen. He handed it to the driver and then went back indoors.

When Perron returned to his own room he paused on the threshold, convinced that in the few seconds it had taken him to open the door someone who had been in there had got away, only just in time.

By nine o'clock that night Rowan still hadn't arrived back and Sarah hadn't rung. Tippoo persuaded him not to wait any longer so once again he ate alone. Afterwards he sat on the front verandah with his notebook, his file of newspaper cuttings, a pair of scissors and the day's papers which Tippoo assured him Rowan wouldn't mind him cutting up. A light shone from the clerk's office. He hadn't seen the clerk except on some of the occasions when the telephone rang or the *dak* came, or a despatch rider turned up. Otherwise the little man kept to his room, so far as Perron could tell.

He sat with notebook and files and papers untouched, drinking brandy and soda. He was half-inclined to knock at the clerk's door, invite him to join him, get him to talk about the routine of keeping records for a political agent, or about his life; about anything. Instead he continued drinking alone, watching the moths and insects dance round the dim depressingly yellow verandah lights. The lights were too dim to work by. The light in his own room was better. He didn't want to go back to his room. The room undermined his confidence. The whole bungalow undermined it. Perhaps Mirat undermined it. Perhaps Mirat was a mistake.

He opened the *Ranpur Gazette*, began to read 'Pandora's Box' again but grew tired of it within a paragraph or two. He turned pages, holding the newspaper at an angle to get some light on it. There was no cartoon, but, on the middle pages, boxed, was a piece called 'Alma Mater' by Philoctetes. He folded the newspaper so that he could read this.

'On Sunday when the happy occasion at Government College was over, when the inaugural daïs for the opening of the Chakravarti wing had been stripped of its bunting, of its red carpet and striped awning, the raw timber scaffolding exposed (and already under the destructive hammers of carpenters) I visited the new extension hoping I would pass as someone with business to do there.

'I need not have worried. No one challenged me. The carpenters and the workmen assumed I was a member of the college staff and such members of the staff as I encountered assumed I was connected with the builders.

'Assured of anonymity I had a free run of the college-to-be. Occasionally I faced dangers in the shape either of planks and ladders where walls are still being whitewashed or plastered, or of piles of tins, canvas sheets and tools of humbler trades than will be learned here. But unmolested I visited class and lecture-rooms (a few with window panes already cracked or broken) and found no desks, no chairs, and rectangular spaces where blackboards have yet to be installed. The laboratory looked like the ward of a hospital or clinic from which all the beds had been removed and replaced by long pinewood tables and benches which awaited the decision of someone who might say to what use they should be put.

'The present emptiness was not (for me) diminished by anything the imagination could invent about the future. Accompanied only by my own echoing footsteps it seemed unlikely somehow that in a month or two the desks would be in place and students at their places at the desks, teachers standing on these bare platforms and the as yet invisible blackboards already becoming grey from the wiped-off chalkmarks of demonstrated equations.

'Subdued, I left the building and walked down the asphalt path that connects the new building with the old. A few shade trees have already been planted. The old college buildings from here look serene, weathered. I turn, and try to picture the Chakravarti extension as it will be, ten, twenty, fifty years from now, and am glad really, that few if any of those who will then remember it as the benign mother will have seen it quite as I am seeing it now; raw, uncompromising, so clearly dependent on what as yet unproven teachers and as yet unadmitted students must make of it and give to it before they can take anything lasting away from it.

'I walk home, thinking of another place, of seemingly long endless summers and the shade of different kinds of trees; and then of winters when the branches of the trees were bare, so bare that, recalling them now, it seems inconceivable to me that I looked at them and did not think of the summer just gone, and the spring soon to come, as illusions; as dreams, never fulfilled, never to be fulfilled.'

Philoctetes

He read the piece again and coming to that final paragraph for the second time found himself moved. The brandy probably. He poured himself another. He got up. His nervous system seemed suddenly awry. He would have to take some action, if it were only to begin packing, or better (because packing meant going into that bedroom), to ring Sarah and tell her he thought he might as well go back with her as far as Ranpur. He went into the hall, consulted the short list of important telephone numbers and asked the operator for 234, the guest house. A servant answered. He asked for Miss Layton and gave his name which was one servants often failed to get right.

After half a minute or so, a woman said, 'Is that Mr Perron?' An older woman.

'Yes. Mrs Grace?'

'Yes, hello. I'm afraid Sarah's not here.'

'I'm sorry to be calling so late.'

'Oh, not late really. I don't suppose she'll be long. She's out to dinner. When shall I meet you? I've heard so much about you. Sarah tells me you called on dear old Archie Hapgood. How was he?'

Mrs Grace had a fine contralto voice. He imagined (not without reason) a comfortable-looking bosom, fullish jowls, carefully set hair and once sharp eyes that were now dimmed a little. He liked the sound of her. He told her he thought Archie Hapgood looked well, then said:

'I rang to tell Sarah I'm thinking of going back to Ranpur, and I wondered whether we might make a party of it. There's not a great deal for me to do in Mirat now, and I do have to be back in Delhi by the fifteenth. I suppose the main problem is getting a reservation.'

'It shouldn't be a problem on the day train because nobody needs a sleeper. The trouble is we're going on Thursday. You mustn't cut your visit short, unless it really suits you.'

'It would suit me very well.'

'I'll tell Sarah what you suggest, or leave her a message. How late can she ring you back?'

'No restrictions at this end.'

'Well thank you, Mr Perron. Mr Kasim is coming to Ranpur with us, and perhaps some people called Peabody, but they're not absolutely sure. An extra man would be rather nice. I suppose it's awfully foolish of me but since Colonel Layton went back to Pankot I've been feeling a bit out of my depth.'

There spoke the widow, with one widowed niece, one un-married niece, a grand-nephew and an ayah, all to look after and feel responsible for. They said goodnight to one another, and having made the decision to go he now felt better. He went back to the verandah to pour himself another drink, and wait for Sarah's call.

There was no call but just before midnight a car turned into the compound. When it stopped, Tippoo – who had heard it – was already down there, opening the door. Rowan got out. He was alone. Laura's absence was somehow eloquent. 'Hello, Guy,' he said, coming up, 'I hope you've eaten.'

'Yes, I have. What about you?'

'I've had something at the palace.'

'Well, have a brandy.'

Rowan glanced at the bottle. 'You shouldn't be drinking your own.' The clerk came out of his office. 'Guy, I'll be with you in ten minutes or so. Unless you'd rather go to bed.'

'The last thing.'

Rowan went towards the office, then turned round, 'I nearly forgot. Sarah says she'll ring you in the morning about your Thursday plan.'

Alone, Perron poured himself another brandy and soda.

Tippoo came past him with Rowan's suitcase. Ten minutes later he reappeared and said, 'Sahib?' Perron found himself being taken indoors, to a room similar in shape to his own bedroom but on the other side of the hall, and furnished as a study, with a desk, and three easy chairs set round a low table on which there were glasses and a decanter. A connecting door, open, gave a glimpse of a larger room – Nigel's and Laura's bedroom, presumably. Tippoo went in. Presently Nigel called, 'With you in a moment, Guy. Help yourself.'

But he didn't help himself. He was thinking: Odd – I've been here before. And then remembered when and where, and smiled. He looked round the study for the cricket-stump and wondered which of the chairs Rowan would suggest as the best for a slacker at games to kneel on. He was still smiling when Rowan came in. Rowan was smiling too, but at a more recent memory.

'Well, it's done.'

'The Nawab's signed? Congratulations.'

Rowan poured deep amber liquid. 'Soda?'

'To the top.'

They raised glasses, drank; then sat. Settled, Rowan said, 'Well then. I gather you feel you've learnt as much as you need in Mirat.'

'I shouldn't mind having a chat with Dmitri. I gathered that might be possible tomorrow night.'

'But you want to go when the others go, the day after.'

'It would fit in. And I do want to be in Delhi before August fifteen. But I suppose whether I go on Thursday depends on what Sarah and her aunt decide.'

'They'd both welcome you.'

'I gather you've seen Sarah tonight?'

'I looked in at the guest house on my way from the palace. She'd just got back and felt it really was too late to ring you.'

'I'm glad she was able to get out somewhere.'

'She was only over at the women's hospital, saying goodbye to the staff. But they made her stay to supper.'

'In the cantonment?'

'No. The Mirat women's hospital. Just over the other side of the *maidan*, here. She's done a lot of voluntary work for them. Didn't you know?'

'No, I didn't.'

'It used to be a purdah hospital for Muslim women only, but Dmitri got it extended some years ago. She's been very popular with the patients and the nurses. She even got Shiraz to take an interest. The hospital's one of the main reasons she's stayed in Mirat all through the hot weather. If Dmitri had let her she'd have gone out to work at the Biranpur leper colony too. Are you thinking of going all the way up to Pankot with them?'

'Only to Ranpur. I'm rather hoping Ahmed can wangle an interview for me with his father.'

'I'd forgotten your journalistic assignment.'

'It's hardly that.'

'If you're not going back to England from Delhi, you could always come down to Gopalakand. I've left Laura there. I'll be closing down here in the next day or two and joining her. Officially I'm still assistant to the resident in Gopalakand – at least until midnight on August fourteen, when we all become redundant. But Conway won't be going immediately. Laura and I will be there for a week or so as his and the Maharajah's guests, while we decide about the future. Gopalakand might interest you. Just send me a wire at the Residency if you think it would.'

'It might. Thank you. Is it a very tricky situation?'

'Perhaps only tricky for me. The Maharajkumar told me his father's going to sign the instrument of accession too. But he's known Conway a very long time and doesn't want to hurt him by appearing to disregard his advice completely. I think my last few days in the Political Department are going to be spent as pig-in-the-middle. Smoothing things between Conway and the Maharajah. Gopalakand is a Hindu majority state with a Hindu ruler. The only things at stake are the pride of the ruling family and the pride of the Resident. It's much larger than Mirat but self-supporting independence is just as much out of the question. If you do come down everything should be peacefully settled by then, and the Maharajah is very hospitable.'

'Perhaps I'll take you up, then.'

'An old friend of Conway's is coming down too. She's lived in Rawalpindi for years but doesn't want to stay on now that it's becoming part of Pakistan.'

'Who is that?'

'Lady Manners.'

'Have you kept up with her?'

'Not kept up. I visited her a few months ago when we were in that area.'

'Did you tell her you'd heard from Hari?'

'I began to. She asked me not to tell her. It's a subject she doesn't discuss.'

'Why?'

'I think she feels she did what she had to do and that anything else would be an invasion of his privacy and would smack of condescension.'

'You feel that too?'

'I think so.'

'Does she still have the child?'

'Yes.'

'What will happen to it when Lady Manners dies?'

'I imagine she'll be looked after by one of Lady Manners's Indian friends. She's been brought up to think of herself as Indian. She's an enchanting little girl.' Rowan leaned forward and filled their glasses. Perron said:

'How did you meet Laura again?'

'She wrote to me when she got back from prison-camp in Malaya. I'd always kept in touch with her mother. We corresponded for a while. Then we met in Simla. And married.'

'What happened to her first husband?'

'The Japanese killed him. She said it was probably his own fault. He had a bit of a temper. When the Japs first arrived at his rubber estate he put up some sort of show and got knocked about in front of her. They took him to one camp and her to another, of course. Later they sent her his personal effects and a letter of regret informing her that he'd died of fever. She didn't believe it, it goes without saying. She spent some time in Singapore when the war was over, finding out the truth from fellow prisoners of Tony's. Some of the truth. It all went to make up further evidence against a Japanese officer who was tried and hanged as a war criminal.'

'Poor Laura.'

'Yes.' Rowan glanced at him. 'But I don't think her first marriage was much of a success either. I gather she made it clear to you yesterday that ours hasn't been. I don't know why it hasn't. But there you are. She hated it here. That's why I've left her in Gopalakand. She said this bungalow reminded her of the one she and Tony lived in in Malaya. It was one of the things she didn't like about it. So after a week or two we decided she'd better go to the club.'

'*One* of the things she didn't like?'

'It's a bit depressing, isn't it? And I had to leave her on her own a great deal. After three years in a crowded prison-camp she doesn't at all mind being alone, but she needs space and air and light. The Residency at Gopalakand works better for her. This place is very closed in. Damp and dark. I'll be quite glad to get out of it myself. The business of the snake was the last straw. Sarah warned you there'd been one, didn't she? I asked her to.'

'Yes. Was it Laura who found it?'

'Yes, it was.'

'And you who had to kill it?'

'No. I should have hated that. It was Merrick who killed the snake.'

Yes, Perron thought. Merrick was bound to come into the picture. 'What kind of snake?' he asked.

'A young cobra. It was asleep in the bath-tub.'

'The bath-tub? My bath-tub?'

'No. Ours. Through there.' He indicated his bedroom.

'Sarah said it was found under the verandah at the back.'

'I expect she said that to reassure you. No. It was in the bath. Laura happened to go in. She didn't panic. She just came out and shut the door and told Ronald. I was over at the palace, but fortunately Ronald had dropped in. I don't think Tippoo would have been much use. He really *is* terrified of them.'

'How did Ronald kill it?'

The question seemed to put Rowan slightly off his stroke.

'What makes you ask?'

'I imagine he got the last ounce of drama out of it. Unless he'd changed considerably. Which I find difficult to believe. In spite of the funeral oration. And the Last Post. Whose idea was that?'

'Susan's. She said the only time she'd ever seen Ronald moved was at a beating of the retreat in Rajputana. It was a bit embarrassing for us. But the oration was no more than he actually deserved. And he gave Susan a sense of security.'

'Well tell me,' Perron said, 'how he killed the snake.'

*

Does Nigel have a revolver? Merrick had asked. The answer had been, no. *Then I'll have to go next door for a moment*, he said. While he did this Laura went into the compound at the back. She knew the snake had to be killed, but was as much against killing snakes as Nigel was, unless it couldn't be avoided. She walked up and down waiting for the sound of the shot. She visualized, perhaps, the shaft of sunlight in the bathroom slowly and dangerously shifting, leaving the snake in shadow, cooling it, waking it; and wondered whether snakes had thoughts and if so what they thought about. What manner of sleep they slept. What dreams they had. (What dreams do falcons have, under those scarlet hoods? And how different those dreams must be – on the one hand of limitless sky, on the other of endless, endless earth.)

Well here it is, Merrick said. She hadn't heard him approach. She swung round and there he was, a kukri in his good hand, the cobra suspended from the artificial one. At first she thought the cobra was whole but then the head end slipped out of the black glove and fell on the grass, leaving the tail end behind; and Laura cried out and was at once sick, all over her elegant shoes.

'He was very contrite,' Rowan said. 'He kept on apologizing. To me, I mean. He said he'd decided he couldn't shoot it because he wasn't sure what the ricochet would do if he missed the snake and hit the tub. In any case he didn't want to puncture the bath.'

If Merrick's story was to be believed he had used his artificial arm as a lure and, when the cobra struck and sank its fangs into the gloved hand, had swung the kukri and cut it neatly into two. A gash in the porcelain was evidence.

'He was taking a risk,' Rowan ended.

'He always did. Had Laura quite liked him up until then?'

'I don't know.'

'I was wondering, you see, as I used to put it, whether you ever felt that he had chosen her.'

'I remembered the phrase.'

'When, exactly?'

'I expect it would be more accurate to say I'd never forgotten it, but I certainly remembered it when Laura and I first got here and found him living alone next door. Susan and the boy were up in the hills.'

'Didn't you know he was in Mirat?'

'Yes, I knew. Sarah and I have always written to one another. I hadn't expected – such close proximity. I didn't tell Laura much about him, just that we'd met. It amused her when he started turning up at odd moments when I happened to be out. It reminded her of the rubber estate, when Tony went down to KL or Singapore and left her alone, and all the local bachelors and grass-widowers homed in on her bungalow, making feeble excuses, or no excuses at all. When you remember what Laura looked like in those days, it's no wonder. But it used to annoy her. She said it made her feel like an object, because if they didn't come to make a pass they just came to stare. Anyway, she made a joke of it at first, of Ronald turning up whenever I was out. She has this idea that she's now physically repulsive. She said Merrick probably thought he was physically repulsive too.'

Rowan stopped. Perron waited. After a while Rowan said, 'But I came home one night and found her in a very odd mood. She started talking to me about her life in prison-camp, and that was something she'd never done. I'd tried to get her to talk about it, but she always shied off. Did you happen to see the scar under her left eye?'

'Yes.'

'I ask because with strangers she normally keeps those sun-glasses on, even indoors. And you may find this difficult to believe, but I've never found out how she came by it.'

'But she told Ronald.'

Rowan looked away. 'Apparently, yes. I got home and found her in this odd mood. Over dinner she started talking about prison-camp. Then she asked me whether I didn't want to know about the scar. We had a bit of a scene. She asked me why she could talk to Ronald about it but not to me, why Ronald was the only person she'd ever met who could get her to talk as she wanted to talk. Spill out the whole awful bloody business. The only thing I could think of to say – and it came out quite un-rehearsed – was that she couldn't talk to me about it because she knew I loved her but had to talk to Ronald because he'd chosen her. As a victim.'

'What did Laura say?'

'Nothing. And we didn't mention Ronald again until a few days later when I got back and found her packing, the day he'd

killed the snake. She said she was going back to Gopalakand.
That would have been best but I talked her out of it and we
decided she should go to the club. As soon as she'd gone the
whole situation seemed absurd. There was nothing I could
accuse him of. But whenever I saw him he started explaining
and apologizing. He wouldn't let it alone. He turned up at the
club once or twice, trying to see her, but she says she kept out
of his way.'

'But went to the funeral. What was that? A mark of respect
or of celebration?'

'She went to the funeral because I asked her to.'

'Why did you do that?'

'The thing was –'

'Yes?'

'To remove anything that didn't fit into the picture.'

'What picture?'

'Of an Englishman who'd earned respect and admiration from
most sections of the community.'

'Why did Laura have to fit into that?'

'You know what people are like in places like this. The kind
of people who wondered why she'd left the bungalow. It didn't
go unnoticed that she wouldn't see him when he called at the
club. I had to ask him to stop calling.'

'Did he stop?'

'At once. But he seemed quite hurt. He said he hated mis-
understandings. He'd only been anxious to find out why he'd
upset her. He implied as well that he hated feeling responsible
for any misunderstanding between Laura and me. At the same
time –'

'What?'

'I had an idea it didn't worry him and might even please him
that people were beginning to link their names.'

'It flattered him to be thought of as the Other Man?'

Rowan glanced at him. 'I see what you mean. I hadn't thought
of it in quite such a general way. I just wondered whether he
was trying to get his own back on me by making people wonder
about Laura and him. I'm positive he knew that Kumar had been
privately examined and that I was the one who'd done the examining. Why not? He still had friends in the Inspector-General's
department. Someone probably told him.'

'Very probably.'

'Sometimes he actually seemed to be daring me to come out with it. We had a very odd relationship. On the one hand mutual goodwill and respect between a visiting political agent and a police officer who'd done a good job, and on the other this subtle sort of antagonism.'

'How long was he in Singapore?'

'Singapore? He *was* in Singapore. Why?'

'I wondered whether he was ever involved in the case against the Japanese officer who was hanged as a war criminal. The one who murdered Laura's first husband, no doubt among several scores of others.'

'Wouldn't he have said?'

'Not necessarily. But knowing something about the Japanese officer could have been the way he got Laura to talk.'

'It sounds pretty far-fetched.'

'Nigel – for me, nothing was far-fetched with Merrick. I believe he had a photographic memory. He'd only have to look through a file to have a whole situation at his fingertips. And he was quite clever at getting his hands on files. He got his hands on Susan's confidential psychiatric file. Did you know that?'

'No, you've remembered incorrectly. He had an interview with the psychiatrist, that's all. So Sarah said.'

'He did more than that. He saw her confidential file. So when Susan talks about Ronald being the only man she'd ever met who understood her and seemed to know things about her she'd never told anyone inside the family, that's the explanation. He could have tried something like the same technique with Laura, but I imagine she's tougher. What happened to the Red Shadow?'

'The what?'

'That disgusting bazaar Pathan he had trailing round with him in Pankot. The one I kicked up the backside. The one who had his hands on my wallet.'

'I don't know. But Merrick must have got rid of him. He gave up having personal servants when he got married.'

'Why?'

'He was always on the move. They never had a permanent home.'

'He hired and fired as it suited him?'

'No, I think he just accepted what was available. Like Khan-samar next door.'

'Who of course is Dmitri's man?'

'Everything here is Dmitri's. All three bungalows. The Dewani Bhavan, this one, and Merrick's. Dmitri lived in this bungalow when he first came to Mirat. He built the Dewani Bhavan round about nineteen twenty-five.'

'Did Merrick ever live here?'

'Yes, I think for a month or two when he first arrived. Before Susan joined him.'

'I imagine he slept in my room.'

'What makes you think that?'

'It has a resonance.' Perron hesitated, and then came out with it. 'What did he do, Nigel? Commit suicide? Cut his wrist and die in the bath?'

'He didn't die in the bath.'

'Nor as a result of a riding accident?'

Rowan said nothing for a while. Then: 'The fall wasn't serious. But he said someone deliberately scared the horse. He was out on the *maidan*. According to Ahmed and Sarah there was no one within half a mile, except them.'

'They were all together? What were they doing, hawking?'

'No. Merrick was always trying to scrounge an invitation to watch Ahmed out with Mumtaz. Ahmed's very particular about who gets to watch and who doesn't. He was running out of excuses. They were supposed to go hawking that morning and Merrick was pretty upset when they turned up with horses and no falcon. When they got to the *maidan* he galloped off on his own. They saw him jumping the main nullah. It's pretty wide where he attempted it and he came a cropper. When they got to him the first thing he said was "Did you see the blighter?" He made out that someone who'd been in the nullah had suddenly stood up. Later on he said someone must have thrown a stone. Sarah says there was nothing like that. But Dmitri got rather worried.'

'Why?'

'The last thing he wanted, the last thing any of us wants just at the moment is an attack on an Englishman. It really could have the most tragic consequences. One dead English official, one English official attacked, and that could be it. You'd get some hard-bitten British sergeant in the cantonment belting an Indian and calling all Indians murdering bastards and then who knows what would happen?'

'Perhaps what Merrick wanted to happen.'

'That was rather the conclusion we came to, that he would have liked some of the stops pulled out, some sort of showdown. So it seems would other people.'

'What other people?'

'Whoever it was who arranged his death.'

Perron's heart sank. He had known it, instinctively. Rowan watched him. He said, 'Dmitri and I feel you ought to know. Sarah agrees. And in view of the way you handled an awkward question of Susan's yesterday, she thinks you're to be relied on not to say anything. She's the only member of her family who knows that Ronald was murdered.'

Absurd, really, Perron thought, that he should now feel shocked, outraged on Merrick's behalf. Perhaps he had hated the man too much not to feel guilty now for a violent death. It was as though he had contributed to it.

'Well tell me,' Perron said.

Rowan poured more brandy. This time he topped his own glass up with soda, as well as Perron's. He said, 'After the riding accident he refused to go into hospital but Habbibullah insisted on him going to bed and keeping to his room. He suspected concussion. Ronald was a very bad patient. And of course there was all this business about the imaginary man in the nullah and the imaginary stone. He went on about it whenever I or Sarah or Dmitri visited him. We did that as often as we could. I was the last one of us to see him alive. Sarah asked me to go and talk to him because he'd been on the phone to her saying he was better and asking to be taken out next morning in the jeep and watch Ahmed hawk. He couldn't ride but wanted some fresh air and something interesting to do. So I went across and had a drink with him. He was sitting up in his dressing-gown – smoking in that way he had – do you remember? Sticking the cigarette in his artificial hand. He seemed perfectly all right to me. And for once he didn't mention Laura. He talked about getting a job in Calcutta or Bombay, or of offering his services to Pakistan. He was quite frank about not wanting to go home to England. And he thought he stood a better chance of a job among Muslims. He said he'd like to live somewhere like Peshawar, near the old North-West Frontier, where administration was much more a question of off-the-cuff decisions and not of just going by the book. We really got on quite well, rather like the first time we met, on the train to Pankot. He asked me to ring Sarah then and there and fix the morning programme. So I did. I asked her to come round with the jeep at seven. She said she'd have a word with Habbibullah but I didn't tell Merrick that. And I didn't tell him she thought Ahmed wouldn't play. I pretended it was all fixed. He told Khansamar to wake him at six next day. When I got back here I rang Sarah again. She said Habbibullah wouldn't allow it, which was a blessing because Ahmed felt he couldn't refuse any longer. We agreed that she and Ahmed would turn up at seven, but with Habbibullah, and that they'd take it from there. So that's how we left it.

'Tippoo woke me at six and then the phone rang and Tippoo said Khansamar wanted a word, which struck me as odd. Khansamar's one of the best trained servants I've come across, but that's Dmitri's influence. He said something had happened which he couldn't deal with and would I come over right away. So I put on a dressing-gown and went across. When I got to the front of the house Khansamar was sitting on the front steps smoking. There was nothing to suggest anything wrong.

'But then he took me indoors and said, "Sahib is dead. I've locked everything up." He took me into Merrick's bedroom. What I expected was just the sight of Merrick dead in bed but the whole place was an absolute shambles. The mosquito net was ripped to ribbons, the bedsheets were all over the place and stained with blood and Merrick was lying on the floor, dressed in his Pathan clothes, but hacked about with his own ornamental axe and strangled with his own sash. And all over the floor there were chalked cabalistic signs. And someone had scrawled the word Bibighar across Susan's dressing-table mirror with the same brown make-up stick that had been used to daub his face.'

'Did Sarah see this?'

'No. And she doesn't know the details. She turned up with Habbibullah and Ahmed, but we kept her out. Dmitri saw it, so did the Chief of Police in Mirat and the commander of the military police in the cantonment. The station commander was consulted too. The one thing that was agreed was that a murdered Englishman at this stage of affairs is the last thing anybody wants. Particularly when it looks as if the murder was intended to cause disorder and racial conflict.'

'What about the law?'

'Everything is properly recorded, right the way down from Habbibullah's real post-mortem, through the private inquest and the sworn statements of witnesses like myself and Khansamar. And the police and CID haven't been inactive. I doubt that the man or men who murdered Ronald will ever be tracked down though. The operation seems to have been carefully planned and patiently seen through to the end.'

'By whom? Pandit Baba?'

'It was Dmitri's first thought. But the Pandit runs true to form. The CID say that for the past month he's been on a pilgrimage to the Himalayas, and still is.'

'And the Bibighar suspects?'

'Two who're still in Mayapore have been cleared by the police there. One is reported dead of tuberculosis in Benares a year ago, and two more are working as clerks in Calcutta. There's nothing to connect any of them.'

'They got a very rapid clearance.'

'It was a rapid clearance because I gave Dmitri their names. I can still recite them from memory. All Dmitri had to do was get his police chief to liaise with the police in Mayapore.'

'Did he ask how you knew the names?'

'Yes.'

'And you told him you'd examined Kumar?'

'Yes.'

'And what about Kumar? What about Hari?'

'He's still in Ranpur. And also in the clear. Dmitri told me this evening.'

'Not such a rapid clearance.'

'We didn't go through the police in Hari's case. Ahmed got his father's secretary to ask Mrs Gopal to find out what she could through the young man who used to help him. We got the reply today. He's still coaching students. He never leaves Ranpur. He was there the whole of last week. One of his pupils is the youngest son of a Congress minister and he's been at the minister's house every evening for the past month coaching the boy for his matriculation.'

'Things have improved for him, then.'

'A little, I suppose. But it must be a poor enough livelihood.'

'Perhaps he supplements it.'

'How?'

'A bit of free-lance journalism? He used to be a reporter and sub-editor.'

'Perhaps. Incidentally, we now have an address. If you want it.'

'Yes, I'd like his address.'

'I'll get it for you. Then I'll have to go to bed, Guy. I've got to see the States Department people off on the morning train.' He got up, went into the adjoining room, came back and handed Perron a slip of paper with Kumar's address scribbled on it. 'Be careful what you say to Sarah, won't you? She doesn't know the worst details. We had Merrick's bedroom cleared up before she saw it. None of the other servants was allowed to see it either.'

'Presumably they were questioned, though.'

'Yes, but the Chief of Police did that himself, without saying exactly why. Khansamar was put through the hoop too.'

'Where are the other servants?'

'Back at the Dewani Bhavan, where they came from.'

'There must be rumours, surely.'

'Rumours, yes. Too many people had to be involved, and eventually it'll become more or less common knowledge, but the thing has been to counteract the rumours, especially in the cantonment, and keep up the fiction that Merrick died as a result of the riding accident.'

'Who has his clothes? And his arm?'

'The Chief of Police. I must turn in, Guy. If you see Dmitri tomorrow, he can probably answer any questions better than I.'

Perron said goodnight and made to go, then paused.

He said, 'Who was Philoctetes?'

'What?'

'Philoctetes.'

Rowan rubbed his forehead. He looked so tired that Perron was about to leave the question until morning. But then Rowan said, 'The great archer.'

'A great *archer*?'

'Friend of Hercules. One of the heroes of the Trojan war. Sophocles wrote a play about him, but it's one I never read. They had to set him ashore, abandon him on the voyage out. Lemnos, I think.'

'Why?'

'He was hurt in some way. Wounded by one of his own poisoned arrows. Or perhaps he just developed boils and sup-purating sores from a vitamin deficiency. Anyway, he stank, and the others couldn't stand the smell. So they set him ashore, and went on.'

'Yes,' Perron said. That fitted. 'Did he ever get to Troy?'

'Eventually. If I remember rightly they decided they needed him after all. What interests you about Philoctetes?'

'I came across the name recently and wondered, that's all.'

When he got back to his room he found that Tippoo had brought in all the stuff he'd left on the verandah, the scissors, notebook, the newspapers, and his own bottle of brandy. He had a final drink and read the essay *Alma Mater* once again. That night, fearful of snakes, of ghosts, he cocooned himself in a sheet, within the security of his mosquito-net shrouded bed. He lulled himself to sleep by counting arrows, flying from the bow, at first slowly, well-aimed, and then quicker, until they were flying incredibly fast as the archer stood, holding his ground, intent on survival. Just before he slept he thought: The smell in the room is not after all just Merrick's smell, but also the smell of the archer's wound.

He woke while it was still dark, from a nightmare that had transformed him into a huge butterfly that beat and beat and fragmented its wings against the imprisoning mesh of the net.

V

Extract from Perron's Diary, Wednesday August 6
11 p.m.

An ominous day, ending with the reflection of fires in the night sky above the city. This afternoon, news of the Nawab's acces-sion to India brought out a crowd of Congress supporters who assembled on the *maidan* for speeches and cheers. The police and military kept them away from the palace, and from a convoy of Muslim families making their way in trucks, carts, dhoolies and on foot to the collecting point in the cantonment. Tonight there were repercussions, angry Muslims attacking Hindus. Attack. Counter-attack. The sky glows. Police and military patrol the road outside this bungalow and presumably make forays into the city. They say there will again be no fishing on the Izzat Bagh lake tomorrow.

Beyond the lake you can just see the paler glow of the cantonment bazaar. The *raj* rests quietly in the darkness behind. In bungalows here and there there must be lights and laughter, parties. (The departing Peabodys are giving one.) Here, where I am, a strange feeling of being suspended between these two worlds. On other similar occasions when the situation became difficult, Merrick would be found touring the city, by jeep, or sometimes during daylight on horseback. 'Tonight I miss him,' Dmitri said. He hadn't mentioned Merrick until then. Dmitri and I had champagne. We smoked pink gold-tipped cigarettes. He told me something about St Petersburg (between interruptions, of which there were many). At ten-thirty our meeting ended. The Nawab had sent for him. 'Poor old dear,' Dmitri said. 'He's looked at the sky and wonders what he has done wrong, or what I have ever done right.'

This ominous day began early. She did not ring but arrived with horses shortly after Nigel had gone across to the palace to take the States Department people to the station. They were to travel in the Nawab's salon coach so as (Dmitri said) to give them a taste for princely luxury as a 'frail insurance against any future diminution of it'. Tomorrow we are to travel by ordinary first-class passenger coach. Dmitri has cancelled the arrangement to send us by another of the Nawab's coaches in case after today's troubles it becomes a target for attack by Muslims who feel that the Nawab has let them down. He has got the movement control officer to guarantee a compartment for us. We shall be 9. The old-fashioned first-class compartments seat 8 comfortably and one of the 9 is little Edward and another is the ayah who will probably sit on the luggage. Which leaves only 7 adults: Sarah, Susan, Mrs Grace, the two Peabodys, Ahmed and me. We should be comfortable enough and are due at Ranpur at 7 p.m. The Peabodys are reported upset, though, that they aren't to travel in a palace coach. Dmitri said: 'Don't stand any nonsense with them if they start objecting to the ayah or to Ahmed. Times have changed.' He seems very insistent on this. The number in the compartment won't worry me. It sounds like being a good party. Mrs Grace is fun.

The horses Sarah brought were a pleasant surprise. She was

dressed for riding. There was no Ahmed. No Mumtaz. We trotted out to the *maidan* and across to the other side. She showed me (at a distance behind shade trees) the barracks of the Mirat Artillery, the police barracks, and the hospital and told me about the first time she got Shiraz to go with her, how nervous the girl was, how over-awed the staff and the patients were at this manifestation from the Palace: the Nawab's daughter, rumoured to be cross and difficult and haughty. Sarah had broken the ice, in the maternity ward, by picking up a baby she'd become used to handling (whose mother wasn't recovering as quickly as she should) and then placing it in Shiraz's arms. The first contact Shiraz had ever had with a commoner outside the palace. It worked. And of course the mother would never forget it: that the Nawab's daughter had held her son. 'What made you give so much time to this girl?' I asked. 'Her unhappiness,' was all Sarah said. Then she cantered away, towards the open ground beyond the military tents and horse-lines.

Suddenly she cries out and thrashes her reins, left, right, and gallops off, making for the distant city wall, or what is left of it. The gateway alone is intact. I try to catch up but she is by far the better and more confident horseman, and she knows the lie of the nullahs, which I don't. But, behind her as I am, we seem to career together towards that implacable pink stone. Then she suddenly veers and shouts again, loudly, savagely, and races her horse back at a pace I really can't match: thrashing the reins in that way, left, right, as if charging cannon in some desperate enterprise. And there is nothing there except the pale blue sky, the green of the shade trees, the tawny stain of the scrubby earth. I let her go, ease my own horse's pace, watch her; small white-shirted figure, going like a little demon into the distance, leaping the nullahs. I think it was her way of saying goodbye to a place where she has been free and happy. She rides in a wide circle, coming round now and galloping towards me. At first I assume she will ride right up, but just ahead of me she moves in a tight turn and then brings her mount to a canter, a trot, a walk, to a stand. As I reach her she puts it at a sedate walk. We say nothing. It isn't necessary. But as we near the road again, outside my bungalow, she says, 'Come to the guest house and meet Aunt Fenny. We'll have breakfast there.'

Neither of us has mentioned Merrick.

Mrs Grace is a plump rather florid woman (much as one thought). A bit breathless, but very talkative. Susan not up for breakfast. We have ours on the terrace. This is where the Laytons stayed when Susan came to Mirat to marry Teddie Bingham. I asked about Colonel Layton. Since early in 1946 he has been Colonel Commandant at the Pankot Rifles training depot. A disappointment. He had hoped for the area command. He is handing over now to a man called Chaudhuri, who was only a major a few months ago. The new 1st battalion goes to a Sikh who has been in Pankot for some years, Chatab Singh. For a while there was a problem about the regiment's future. Officially, the Pankot people are predominantly Muslims, as a result of conversion in the days of the Moghuls. The regiment, mixed, but reflecting this predominance, has such a good reputation that Jinnah wanted it and offered it a home near Peshawar. How he thought he could keep it recruited from men who lived in the Pankot hills, one does not know. Some English people in Pankot have raised the question of the silver in the mess and suggest that the new Indian Government should buy all the knives, forks, spoons and trophies, everything of value, and that the proceeds should be shared out among the families of the men who had contributed to their cost. 'So you see we all end up like carpet-sellers in Cairo,' Mrs Grace said. 'John gets hot under the collar when he hears people talking like that.'

Edward comes out. He takes me to see the white peacock. Not the one I saw myself. This one is carved out of marble and is secluded in a secret place among the trees. Fear snakes. When we get back Nigel has arrived from the station, seeing the States Department people off. The Peabodys were seeing off the Rossiters and told Nigel that this evening it would be open house at their bungalow. Mrs Grace said, 'Those awful people. Do we have to travel with them? Can't we rustle up an extra body or two and crowd them out?'

Interesting, this. Universally popular as the English are in India just now, among themselves there emerges this dissension. The old solidarity has gone because the need for it has gone.

'But of course,' Bronowsky said, 'now we are all *émigrés*. Have some more champagne and a cigarette.'

Perron nodded. The servant came to his side and refilled his glass. In the Dewani Bhavan there was the dry dusty scent of potpourri. The lighting was rose-coloured. It glowed on ormulu and gilt chair-arms. In this light Dmitri Bronowsky looked twenty years younger. His lame left leg rested on a gilt and plush footstool. The ebony cane and the black eye-patch accentuated the white of his tropical suit which was faintly tinged by the glow of the lights. He wore a tie of the same pink as the cigarettes.

The invitation to dinner had reached Perron at five o'clock. Leaving Rowan working on his written report to the Resident at Gopalakand, it had surprised him to find no other guests. By eight-thirty, after a number of interruptions by messengers and telephone calls, he realized that he and Dmitri were to spend the evening alone. He had hoped for Sarah. As if recognizing a source of disappointment, Bronowsky – leading him into a grand dining-room – said he asked Sarah but that she felt she couldn't leave Susan alone on their last night in Mirat. 'And failing Sarah, I felt we might dine alone. It is a little selfish of me to subject you to my unadulterated company, but not entirely so. If we had another guest or two then I could not tell you the things you have come to Mirat to learn about – how princes rule and live in this country. Anyway, I feel I deserve an evening off myself, with just one sympathetic listener.'

The table was long enough for twenty or thirty guests and the room was lit as if there were that number needing to see what they ate. Perron and Bronowsky sat at one end, where great bowls of flowers gave off heady scents. Bronowsky ate little, seemed to be content with a bite or two of each course and a glass of each of the wines that accompanied them. He talked with skill and good humour. The range of the old wazir's knowledge and experience and the clarity of his memory were remarkable. It struck Perron, too, that he talked vividly because he knew that the opportunities to hold court, while he still had power, were becoming fewer. The last thing Dmitri Bronowsky would ever be was an old and tiresome man living on his memories and boring other people with them. On the day he had to retire, he would probably retire quite happily into himself.

'What is Mirat's future, then?' Perron asked, when the right moment came, between sips of the champagne with which, along with the *pêche flambée*, the meal was delightfully ending.

'We shall be absorbed into the provincial administration of Ranpur. Our executive and our judiciary will be superseded by those of Ranpur. We shall be ruled from Ranpur and from Delhi. We shall have a deputy commissioner sent down to control us. Some of our younger men will be lucky and secure official appointments. Our revenues will go to Government and Government in turn will accept certain responsibilities for us. Also, and this is so interesting, we shall become a constituency or several constituencies and elect and send members to the legislative assembly. All this I have told and constantly tell Nawab Sahib. I remind him how years ago I foretold it. If either of his sons had political talent, ah then, that would have been one way of maintaining *izzat* under a new dispensation. For in a world where a ruling prince becomes redundant isn't there an opportunity for one of his heirs, someone in his family, to sit not on the *gaddi* but in the assembly, or even in a ministerial chair at the Secretariat?'

'And neither son has political talent?'

'In confidence, my dear Mr Perron, neither talent nor wit. It did not take me long to see that this was and would be so. So. I cast around. And my eye lighted on another member of the house of Kasim. The Ranpur branch. The rebellious political branch.'

'Ahmed?'

'Many people have wondered what I am doing employing the son of Mohammed Ali Kasim who is, by nature, opposed to princes. Many people have wondered what Mr Mohammed Ali Kasim can have been thinking of to allow his younger son to take service in a feudal little state. I do not know what Mr Kasim had in mind. Perhaps he was just pessimistic about the boy in those days. I have always been optimistic. Scratch me a very little and you will find an eternal optimist. Scratch a little deeper and you will no doubt uncover a great intriguer, but I hope a well-intentioned one. Scratch deeper still, never minding the blood, and perhaps you will find an old White Russian of liberal sympathies but intent even now on rescuing his Tsar from the cellar in Ekaterinburg, or failing his Tsar, the little Tsarevich. An English lady in the cantonment who had psychological perceptions once described me so. Your glass is empty, Mr Perron.'

It was refilled.

'It was my intention to arrange, if it could be done without undue pressure, an alliance between the princely Kasims of Mirat and the political Kasims of Ranpur. I had hoped that Ahmed and Shiraz would fall in love one day. They say that when a man falls in love, with a woman, he becomes aware of all his worldly responsibilities. If there is one thing I do most sincerely wish just now it is that Ahmed and Shiraz were man and wife and that marriage had awakened in him all those political instincts he must have inherited from his father, no matter what he says to the contrary. I wish this because just now when Nawab Sahib is in the doldrums, when he summons me at midnight or early in the morning because he cannot sleep or hasn't slept, and stares at me, it would be so nice to say: What are you bothered about? I have always warned you that there may be nothing for your sons to inherit except the remnants of a purely formal dignity, but here is your daughter Shiraz and here is your son-in-law Ahmed, son of a famous and respected Indian politician who still has great influence behind the scenes. When you begged me to come back to India with you because of the little service I had done for you, you said, "I must be a modern state. Make me modern." So, admit it, I have made you modern in every way I can. Moreover you have a son with business interests in Delhi and who has a wife who builds swimming pools and has money in Zurich. You have another son in the air force. Above all you have a son-in-law who may one day represent Mirat in the pro-vincial assembly and, who knows, end as a minister of central government, perhaps even as Prime Minister. Isn't that modern enough for you? Unfortunately, I cannot tell him this because he has no son-in-law. Man can only propose. But given another year or two's grace and perhaps God would have disposed, as I so devoutly wished. For my prince's benefit, you understand, Mr Perron. For my prince. Perhaps a little for myself. As it is I have to go and sit with him, late at night or early morning, and try to prepare him just to face the moment when the States Department people will descend on us again, this time with their scales and abacuses and weights and measures and arithmetical tables, their meticulously devised formula for separating what belongs to the people and what belongs to Nawab Sahib, what is a proper charge on Government and what is a charge on Nawab's personal household, asking how many palaces have you, then, and what are they used for, and who pays for all *this* –'

Bronowsky indicated the room, the table, the silver and the glass and the patient silent servants.

'Who pays, the people or the occupier? And who is Dmitri Bronowsky? Who pays him? How much is he paid? How much pension does he expect from you? How much pension can the people of India afford to pay you so that you can go on paying all these pensions to which you say you are already committed? And I know what Nawab Sahib will say, because he has already begun saying it. He will say, "Dmitri, what have I to do with these people or they with me? What are all these facts and figures and percentages and bureaucratic mumbo-jumbo? If you load my head with all this, how can I hold it up?" Come, let us have coffee.'

As they went Perron said, 'As Mrs Grace said this morning, now we've all got to get used to living like carpet-sellers in Cairo.'

'But of course!' Bronowsky said, delighted. 'Now we are *all émigrés*. Have some more champagne and a cigarette.'

The servant came to his side and refilled his glass, offered the open silver box. Dmitri settled his left foot on the stool. He told the servant to leave the champagne in the ice-bucket, to bring in the brandy and then to leave them.

'The thing that holds the members of an emigration together is only their recollection of a mutually shared past, Mr Perron, but they are divided by a deep distrust of one another's present intentions. So there is no creative coherence. And individually they feel guilty of desertion. An emigration is possibly the loneliest experience a man can suffer. In a way it is not a country he has lost but a home, or even just a part of a home, a room perhaps, or something in that room that he has had to leave behind, and which haunts him. I remember a window-seat I used to sit in as a youth, reading Pushkin and teaching myself to smoke scented cigarettes. That window is one I am always knocking at, asking to be let in.'

A steward brought a note. To read it Bronowsky took out a gold rimmed monocle. 'Forgive me, I must leave you for just a moment to attend to this.'

Alone, Perron went out on to the terrace. The garden was flood-lit. At its centre was a fountain whose jets sprayed inward from the rim. In a moment Bronowsky was back. 'There are other illuminations at the front, it seems, not of my devising.'

From the front compound they could see the glow of the fires in the city. 'They are burning each other's shops,' Bronowsky said. 'In the past eight months, whenever I saw a sight like this, I was comforted by the thought that Colonel Merrick was coping with it. Tonight I miss him. So perhaps will the police. All I can do is to ensure that what should be done is being done and what shouldn't be isn't. The cost is counted in the morning. Meanwhile one feels a bit like Nero, in need of a fiddle. Perhaps I should send for the court-musicians. But let us go back and finish the champagne.'

They strolled up and down the terrace. The fountain kept changing colour. Perron was struck by the irony of the situation. Here, luxury, elegance. A mile away, everything a man possessed in the world was perhaps going up in smoke.

'Until the war,' Bronowsky was saying, 'there was almost no civil disturbance in Mirat. Such communal dissatisfaction as there was arose from the feeling the educated Hindus had that in spite of all my efforts they were still at a disadvantage, and from the counter-feeling high-ranking Muslims had that Hindus had been encouraged to compete too well. But by and large there was peace, particularly in the rural districts where the things that mattered to people were to enjoy prosperity when it was there to be enjoyed and to feel they could trust their Nawab to look after them when it wasn't. Before the war, Mr Perron, I could tour the state and talk to a Mirati farmer out there in the *mofussil*, a Hindu or a Muslim, and he would prove to have but the vaguest idea of who Gandhi was, or who Jinnah was. For him the world began and ended in his fields, and with his landlord, and with the tax-collectors, and with Nawab Sahib who sat here in Mirat, Lord of the world, Giver of Grain. Out there it is not so very different now but in our towns and in our city they have become affected by what Congress is saying, what the Muslim League is saying, up there in Delhi, in Calcutta and Bombay. This began during the war. Mirat was also affected by the realization that the British *raj* had proved far from invincible in Burma and

Malaya and in Europe. On top of that we had all these people who fell foul of the British and scurried to places like this where it was not so easy for your police to get hold of them. It was left to our own. Well, you can pick a man up and send him back where he came from, but you cannot send ideas back, especially if there is an element of truth and justice in them.'

'What led to your applying for help from the States Police?'

'A virtual breakdown in our own police department and a danger of mutiny in our State Armed Force, which consists of one regiment only, the Mirat Artillery. That was last November – but the trouble began earlier when men of the regiment who had been prisoners of the Japanese returned home and it became generally known that some of their comrades had joined the INA and were now prisoners of the *raj*. No one knew at the time quite what to make of this. The prisoners who had stayed loyal came back to a heroes' welcome, naturally. Men of the Nawab's artillery have served in both world wars, in France in 'fourteen–'eighteen. In Malaya this time. The artillery is a Mirati tradition. In the old days they used to make some of those huge old cannon you'll know about from your study of eighteenth-century Indian history and the men from this region have always been adept at gunnery. So. It has always been a proud regiment, too. Unfortunately by the time the men came back, to their heroes' welcome, Congress and the League had already taken the cudgels up on behalf of the INA. Our gunners found themselves in bad odour when they said what they thought of Bose. Some of the most outspoken were beaten up one night in the bazaar, probably by the same people who beat poor Ahmed up when it became known that his father wasn't going to defend Sayed. Perhaps that was a blessing in disguise because it stopped him going into the bazaar to visit what in my youth were called ladies of easy virtue. For a long time afterwards he was faithful only to Mumtaz. But the worst situation arose in the spring of last year, when the officers and men of the Mirat Artillery who had been in the INA came back, the officers cashiered and the men released –'

'At Holi.'

'Ah, yes, at Holi. Almost as stupid a decision as the decision to try the Sikh, the Muslim and the Hindu at the Red Fort.'

'Did the INA men get a heroes' welcome too?'

'It was unofficial, but warmer if anything. There were only two officers and nineteen men. The officers' careers were finished, not that they needed careers, they both came from well-to-do families. The main question was what was to happen to the nineteen gunners. In Mirat, political parties do not officially exist, since the state proscribes them, but there are shadow parties and shadow committees and of course one has always known who belongs to them and who the leaders are and who will therefore emerge presently as the men with local political power in Mirat. The nineteen gunners were being persuaded by both these shadow parties, Congress and League, that they should be reinstated by a grateful Nawab for having tried to help Bose rid the country of the British.'

'Which didn't please the loyal men of the Mirat Artillery?'

'To put it mildly. The cumulative effect of all this purely political propaganda was that on the Muslim League's All-India Direct Action Day, the Mirat Artillery refused duty to stand by in aid of the civil power, and their officers were powerless. The men took a very simple view, Mr Perron. They thought that Direct Action Day was simply a ruse to reinstate the nineteen gunners and they would have nothing to do with it, either way. They sat in their barracks while the civil population ran riot. The Mirat Police were entirely ineffective because they were in sympathy with the League. We had to get aid from the cantonment, British troops, and the officer commanding those troops knew his men were so fed up with India and Indian politics that he dared only issue one man in twelve with live ammunition. I remember standing with Nawab Sahib in one of the upper rooms at the front of the palace and watching the pall of smoke above the city and thinking, My life has been wasted.'

Bronowsky rested against the balustrade, sipped his champagne.

'But one always feels better next day. All the same I have never seen Nawab Sahib so angry. He blamed the poor regiment. He said his grandfather would have had the officers trampled to death by elephants and every mutineer blown from the guns. He raved against Gandhi and Jinnah and then against the Viceroy and the Commander-in-Chief, and then because he knew there was only one head he could effectively roll, he turned on me and accused me of ruining him with all this modernity. It took me a day or two to persuade him that the artillery only needed

his personal assurance that the INA gunners would not be reinstated. The police were a graver problem. It took me longer
to persuade him that we needed assistance from outside, from
the States Police. He felt we could rely entirely on help from the
cantonment. But you know, Mr Perron, too much reliance of
that kind sours the relationship between city and cantonment.
Well. In the end he let me go to Delhi and put the position to
them. And so – some weeks later – Ronald.' Bronowsky paused.
'I am a little chilly. It's the fountains. They cool the air amazingly.
Let us go in and have brandy.'

He had dismissed the servants and served the brandy himself.
Now he settled opposite Perron and rested his foot on the stool.
   'When I heard who was coming in command of a States
Police detachment and in an advisory capacity to the Nawab
and myself, it was my instinct to say no, no, no, no, he is a man
with too controversial a reputation and the last time he was in
Mirat he was subject to the attention of people who seemed
determined to persecute him for his behaviour in Mayapore.
What are they doing sending him here? What are they doing
employing him again in the police? Then I wondered what
business that was of mine. And remembered that I had on very
first acquaintance found him an interesting and impressive man.
Impressive in some ways. You know that he had certain qualities,
Mr Perron?'
   'I saw only the bad side, I'm afraid.'
   'That I think is because in spite of your interest in the past
you are a man of the present, as I have always tried not very
successfully to be. Merrick without question was a man of the
past, so much so that he believed implicitly both in its real virtues
and in what he imagined had been its virtues. And you know,
in the situation that has existed here in Mirat this past year or so,
where few people know what they are doing or why they are
doing it, the presence of such a man comes almost as a relief.
He treated the whole thing as though it were just a silly quarrel
between naughty children. And in a way he was right. He
inspired confidence with his impartiality and his absolutely
inflexible and unshakable sense of his own authority. It can be a
very dangerous combination. But there was one thing about him
this time that seemed to me to be new. He struck me now as an

inwardly melancholy man. I would never have said that about him before. The only time I saw him, how shall I put it, glow with the old *conviction*, was when he was with the child.'

'Not when he was with his wife?'

'I am no judge, Mr Perron. Unless a man and a woman are obviously and tiresomely publicly wrapped up in one another I find it difficult to judge the degree of warmth between them. That is a warmth I have never enjoyed. One eventually withdraws. Perhaps becomes insensitive. I was, I admit, sensitive to what I thought might be certain tendencies in Merrick when I first met him in Mirat at the time of Susan's first wedding. I wish now that I had been more sensitive to the possibility of these tendencies having become, how shall I say, in no way lessened by his experience of marriage. Even at my age one assumes – well – what it is easiest to assume. So when he first arrived to take up his appointment I said, Are you still being persecuted by people making melodramatic demonstrations, throwing stones and chalking inauspicious signs on your doorstep? We made a joke of it. But he said what he had said in Bombay, that all that had ended. I knew that could be only partly true because Ahmed had told me there was a revival of persecution when he was in Delhi dealing with his brother's and other INA cases. But I decided to take his word for it and there was no reason to suppose that persecution would start up again simply because he was back in Mirat. Unfortunately it did begin again, but in a much subtler way. It may seem a little odd to you, Mr Perron, that whoever wished to persecute him for what he did in Mayapore in nineteen forty-two should have waited so long to bring the operation to its logical conclusion? There must have been many opportunities to kill him in the past five years.'

'It was twenty years before someone assassinated the ex-Governor of the Punjab. Ostensibly for supporting General Dyer over the Jallianwallah Bagh massacres.'

'That's true. Why do you say ostensibly?'

'I shouldn't think the Governor was shot for that at all. It was a conveniently dramatic form of protest against India being dragged into another European war.' Perron smiled. 'I gather from Nigel you have an idea Merrick was a convenient victim too. That killing him was intended to aggravate racial tension as much as anything.'

'Yes.' The old man studied him for a moment or two. 'Not everyone feels the British have earned the immunity you all seem to be currently enjoying. I myself am not entirely convinced that it is fully deserved. But if it's the last thing I do in Mirat, I'll take every step necessary to ensure that this immunity continues, even if it means suppressing evidence and issuing false statements. Do you disapprove?'

'A little.'

'So do I. But I balance my disapproval with the thought of what might be happening now if we had shouted murder, also with the thought that the murder was so subtly planned and executed that the prospect of ever seeing justice done is infinitely remote. Then of course there's the thought of the distress and pain Susan would have been caused by any open investigation. It's a good thing, in her unstable state of mind and health, that she doesn't know in what strange and unsavoury circumstances her husband died.'

'Strange and unsavoury?'

'I don't mean just the manner of death but what made him vulnerable to such a death.'

'Yes, I see. Do his spies come into the picture?'

'Who mentioned spies to you?'

'Susan. She also mentioned Indian clothes. The ones he wore to go out with his spies.'

'Mr Perron, he had no spies. Nor did he ever go out in these clothes. Perhaps in his younger days he used to get up to that romantic sort of trick, colouring his face and disguising himself as a Pathan and going out into the bazaars. And of course in his time he must have employed spies in his department, just as our own police chief employs them. But Ronald and spies and Indian clothes, in Mirat, no, no, these were mere bits of play-acting. Khansamar never believed in the spies. He is a good servant, though, and not given to gossiping. I wish he had been. If I had known about so-called spies then I would have been alerted and I could have warned Khansamar to be more on his guard. And although it would have been a rather delicate thing to do I might have warned Ronald too. He may not have needed a warning, though. It is quite possible that he knew what was going on. In which case his murder might be seen as a form of suicide. Unfortunately I only knew about spies when it was already too late and Khansamar was questioned and told us about these visitors.'

'Visitors as distinct from people coming asking for jobs?'

'Why do you ask that?'

'Susan said people were always coming looking for jobs.'

'That was how it would have seemed to her. Originally that was how it seemed to Khansamar. But with the benefit of hindsight one begins to understand that it was all part of a new subtle form of persecution. At that time, Merrick was living alone, in Nigel's bungalow. The other one was being got ready. According to Khansamar these young fellows began to turn up soon after Merrick arrived. Khansamar turned them all away. He knew they were not Miratis. They span the same tale, of coming long distances to seek work and always offered little chits of references. Khansamar is illiterate. Chits mean nothing to him. Then one day Merrick found him shooing one of them off, a persistent fellow who had come several times. Merrick looked at the boy's references, which may or may not have been genuine, probably not, not that it mattered. Merrick told him there was no work to offer him. But he was back again next day. He stood at the gate and salaamed Merrick whenever he passed in and out until in the end Merrick told Khansamar he was fed up with the sight of him and that he might as well be given a job for a day or two, helping one of the malis repair and lay out the tennis-court in the compound of the bigger bungalow. So this is what Khansamar did. He told the mali to work the boy hard, so hard that he would give up. But he worked so well that in a day or two the tennis-court was nearly finished.'

Moreover, so the story went, the mali's wife had taken to the boy and had begun to mother him. He was a handsome young fellow and very well-mannered. After working all day in the compound he would make himself useful in the servants' compound. The mali was keen to keep him on but after three days Khansamar went to Merrick and reminded him that the day or two was up. Merrick went to inspect the tennis-court. They were just laying out the lines of lime-wash. Merrick watched for a while, then said, 'He is obviously used to hard work. Put him to cutting all the long grass.'

Khansamar was quite pleased. There was a lot to be done in

both compounds. Many odd jobs. And the boy was very respectful to him. When he had cut all the grass in one compound
Khansamar set him to work in the other. In the evenings he
worked on a new vegetable patch behind the servants' quarters,
work which the mali himself had been putting off day after day.
On one such evening Khansamar asked him, 'Do you never rest,
Aziz?' And the boy said, 'I am alone in the world, father. Work
is all I have.'

Old Khansamar had had three wives, ten daughters and no
son, ever. It touched him to be called father by a boy like this.
He began to give him less strenuous jobs. A week, two weeks,
a month went by. Sometimes Merrick would say, 'Well, Khansamar, how is that young fellow of yours? I see you have made
something of a carpenter and decorator of him too. What is a
farmer's son doing with so many accomplishments? Can he also
read and write? If so he can put my books in order, once he has
put up the shelves and painted them.'

The answer was, yes, Aziz could read, a little slowly. But every
night, now, he read to the servants from the newspapers. He had
had to give up school when both his parents died. At an early
age, he said, he had left his village to find work in the nearest
town. But he had always tried to keep up his reading.

So Aziz was put to the task of finishing the shelves in the
bigger bungalow and then of transferring the books from the
packing cases and putting them on the shelves in alphabetical
order of authors' names.

And one day, when Khansamar was going towards the room
where Aziz was working, to tell him it was time for his evening
meal, he heard the boy laughing. He looked into the room
and saw Aziz sitting on the floor, with his back to the door,
reading a book, and turning the pages, turning them rapidly
for someone who normally read with difficulty. But, that evening, when Khansamar went to the servants' quarters, he found
Aziz stumbling, reading aloud, with difficulty, from the morning newspaper.

'You must understand, Mr Perron, that Khansamar had come to
regard the boy with affection, as a son almost, and that it was not
easy for him to admit to himself that there was something a bit
suspicious, that the young man he had seen quickly reading

through one of the Sahib's books and laughing was rather a different young man from the one who worked in the compound like a farmer's son. And now he also remembered that when the boy had first scythed the grass he had had to wear rags round his hands the next day and in the evening Khansamar had noticed the blisters, on his palms and fingers. At the time he had merely been touched that Aziz had worked so hard and hadn't complained of his sore hands. But now he was troubled. Troubled by the thought that the boy was not the sort of boy he pretended to be. And that night when he went to bed he couldn't sleep. He found himself tossing and turning and wondering and puzzling. And then something else odd struck him. He realized that since Aziz had turned up looking for a job, and had been employed, no one else had arrived at the gate, waving their little chits and begging to see Colonel Sahib.

'So he got dressed and went to the hut Aziz slept in. The door was bolted on the outside, which meant Aziz was out. It was very late, one or two o'clock in the morning. He went round to the front of the house and found the chaukidar fast asleep on the verandah.'

'Which bungalow was this?'

'The one which Nigel has. The one at which you are staying. The bigger bungalow was nearly ready, but not quite ready. Chaukidar should have been patrolling between the two, but he was fast asleep on the verandah. The front gates were closed but anyone can climb these things. It was simply a peaceful Indian night, Mr Perron, and Khansamar thought, well, Aziz was a strong active young fellow. He was probably in the bazaar, making love to a girl whose husband was away. Reprehensible, but understandable. So Khansamar woke chaukidar up and told him off for sleeping. Then he went back to his quarters but found himself more wide awake than ever, and listening for the sound of Aziz coming back. This, he heard, only a little sound, the sound of the bolt on the door of Aziz's hut being opened. He got up and put on his shawl and went over to the hut and saw there was a light on. So he knocked. When Aziz opened the door Khansamar began saying things like, What foolishness is this? Where have you been? Aziz said he had been at the back relieving himself. So Khansamar said, What, for two hours? Are you ill or something?

'Then he noticed that there were marks on the boy's face and that he had been bathing them. He said, What happened? Did the husband come back? Or have you been brawling in the bazaar? He was talking to him like an angry father who is not really angry. Probably Aziz understood this because he became contrite. He said it was true he had been in the bazaar, but there had been no angry husband and no brawling. He had fallen and grazed himself climbing back in over the locked gate and in the morning he would no doubt have a black eye.

'Khansamar said, Wasn't Chaukidar there to help you over? And Aziz laughed and said Chaukidar was no doubt asleep on the front verandah as usual and that nothing would ever wake him.

'Khansamar did not believe Chaukidar could have gone to sleep again, after being told off, but he realized that with two bungalows to look after it would have been possible for Aziz to slip in over one of the gates, and not be seen. So he just gave the boy a telling off too and warned him that Merrick Sahib might have to be informed.

'When he got up in the morning, which was always before anyone else, to make Colonel Sahib's *chota hazri*, he looked for the chaukidar and asked him whether he had stayed awake and if so whether he had seen anything unusual. The chaukidar said he had certainly stayed awake after being woken but that there had been nothing unusual. Khansamar asked him whether he wouldn't call it unusual to see Aziz climbing over a gate and missing his footing and falling on the gravel so heavily that he had grazed his face badly. Chaukidar agreed that that would be unusual.

'In which case, Khansamar said, chaukidar had neglected to see something unusual, because this was what had happened, and that in the circumstances he could only believe that chaukidar had fallen asleep again, and that this would have to be reported to Colonel Sahib.'

Bronowsky lit another pink cigarette.

'Chaukidar said, I do not advise that. You can accuse me to Colonel Sahib of nodding off for a few moments if you like, but you should not say you know I did because I failed to see Aziz climb over the gate. Colonel Sahib will think you are trying to make trouble for him. For two nights – last night and the night before – Aziz was with Colonel Sahib. I saw Aziz go in through the door of the *gusl-khana* just as I saw him go in the night before. The only difference was that the night before I stayed on watch, expecting to see him come out like a thief, in which case I would have pounced on him. But he came out after some time by the same door, and this time Colonel Sahib was with him, dressed in the clothes he sometimes wears when he is alone. He is at heart a Pathan, and Aziz is a fine sturdy boy. If I were not a dried-up old man I would be tempted myself and it does not surprise me that Colonel Sahib has been tempted because for weeks I have sometimes seen him watching the boy at work in the compound. When he went into the bungalow again last night I thought, It is none of my business, but since Colonel Sahib is not alone in the house I can nod off for a moment.'

Dmitri drew on the cigarette, exhaled, stubbed it out as if already tired of it. He took the ebony cane in both hands and leaned forward, chin resting on the hands that rested on the cane.

'So,' he said, 'Khansamar thought it was no business of his either. But he had seen the mess that had been made of Aziz's face and when he took in Colonel Sahib's *chota hazri* he found him already up, sitting in front of the dressing-table, and wearing his harness. The knuckles of his right hand were grazed. He had beaten the boy with his fist. And at that moment, you know, Khansamar conceived for Merrick a dislike. Not a violent dislike. A cold dislike. Contempt. And of course he wondered why a boy like Aziz submitted to that kind of treatment. Do you wonder, Mr Perron?'

'Tell me why you don't.'

Bronowsky smiled and leant back, swirled his brandy in the glass, sipped and put the glass down.

'I think it is clear he had been so instructed. Instructed to present himself, to stand there at the gate until Merrick had seen him. Also instructed to submit, without complaint, to whatever Merrick did once he had accepted the lure of this terrible attraction, of this terrible temptation which young men like Aziz represented.'

'Instructed by whom?'

'I think not Pandit Baba, don't you agree? If it was the Pandit then he must have studied more than the Bhagavad-Gita. He must also have studied Freud. So I do not think the Pandit. The Pandit has probably long ago been superseded by someone with a more modern and intelligent approach. There are always plenty of gurus waiting in the wings, and many of these young men willing and ready to serve and submit and suffer in the belief that what they do is done for a cause. In their death-photographs they look so pale, so insecure. But not in life. Whoever instructed Aziz, and his predecessors, and those who followed him, had come to know of these tendencies in Merrick. How? Always known? I doubt that. More likely through some later indiscretion or lapse. That he had always been kept track of as a potentially useful instrument goes without saying. And this was the new and subtle form of persecution. Young men like Aziz, turning up, with no instructions I imagine other than to tempt, submit, and not complain, not accuse, perhaps to go, so that they could be replaced, gradually, by young men of steelier temperament, young men capable of taking the ultimate step when the victim was properly lulled.

'But what other instructions the boy who called himself Aziz might have had, one does not know. In the event, Merrick sacked him. He told Khansamar there was no further work for Aziz to do. So Aziz was sent packing. And a week or two later another boy arrived, begging for a job, and coming back day after day, standing at the gate. The same kind of boy. But Merrick resisted the bait. And the boy gave up. Only to be replaced by another. And another. And then Susan and Sarah arrived, with the child and the ayah and the bigger bungalow was occupied. But still they came, these young fellows. Perhaps some of them were genuinely looking for employment. Khansamar thought this was so, because they were not all of them boys like Aziz. But among them, from time to time, there would be one like that.

'And then the tactics changed. Khansamar did not at first connect the one thing with the other. A young Pathan arrived quite late one night, sometime towards the end of April, when the heat was getting bad but Susan was still here and Merrick was often working late, often slept in a room on the other side of the house. The Pathan insisted on seeing Merrick personally. He said he had an official and confidential message. He was alone with Merrick for only a short while. I wonder what was said? What services were offered? What services implied? In May Susan and the child and ayah went back up to Pankot. A few days after they had gone Merrick told Khansamar that he was expecting a messenger, probably quite late, and that the chau-kidar shouldn't lock the gates. The Pathan arrived just before midnight. This time he had a companion. Merrick had them taken to his study, then ten minutes later called for Khansamar and told him that one of these men should be given a bed for the night. The Pathan left and the chaukidar locked the gates after him. The companion who stayed was the younger man. He had a bedroll and said he could sleep anywhere. The verandah would do very well. It was very hot. He would be glad if he could be woken at five o'clock. Khansamar said he was a boy like Aziz but probably better educated. He wore European clothes. He was grateful for the charpoy Khansamar put out on the verandah and for the cup of tea he was given. He said he came from Lahore originally and asked a lot of questions about Mirat, so many that Khansamar said, Why do you ask so many questions? The boy laughed and apologized and said it was a habit got from the kind of work he did. Khansamar asked what kind of work that was and the boy looked surprised and said confidential work for the police, what else?

'Khansamar believed it in one part of his mind but not in another. He didn't worry very much either way. It was the Sahib's affair if he slept with boys when his wife was away, not his. But in the morning when he took the boy some tea he was quite innocently asleep where Khansamar had left him and in half an hour he had washed and dressed and gone. Khansamar didn't ask the chaukidar whether the boy had ever left his bed and chaukidar didn't volunteer anything, which might have meant that there was nothing to say or that he had been asleep again – perhaps the latter because Khansamar was sure he smelt the boy's hair-oil on one of the pillows in Merrick's bed when he was making it up.

'And so it continued, Mr Perron, about every two or three weeks, always two young men arriving, one going, one staying. Sometimes the one who had stayed the previous time accompan-ied the new boy. Sometimes Khansamar had seen neither of them before. None of them was a Mirati and Khansamar never noticed the smell of hair-oil on the pillow again. He questioned chaukidar once who said that yes, on one occasion when he patrolled, the boy's bed on the verandah was empty but that when he waited expecting to see him come out of Merrick's *ghusl-khana* he saw him instead coming back from the compound, as if he had been relieving himself and that when he went over and greeted him the young man acted quite naturally and offered him a cigarette and sat and smoked and talked to him for a while.

'So, one wonders. And one wonders what really was in Merrick's mind, whether there was some reality behind this illusion of spies or whether he had simply agreed with the Pathan to have boys procured for him. And in the latter case one wonders again whether he saw a connection between this arrangement and the older forms of persecution, and deliberately put himself in the way of it. I'm afraid we shall never know, Mr Perron. And in a country as vast as this all these young fellows have just disappeared, as if they never existed.

'But consider it this way. And discard the evidence of the hair-oil on the pillow. The smell of the oil could have been in Khansamar's imagination. He never smelt it again. Not even when the rains came and the boys no longer slept on the verandah but on Merrick's instructions indoors in an empty room, where they were free to go to him at any time. Did they go? Perhaps. But if they went, did anything occur? Or did they just sit there discussing with him the information they had pretended to collect or actually collected for him? Was there any such information? Perhaps. On the night he was murdered the private drawer in his desk was forced open, so something might have been removed. But what? A slowly collected dossier about the subversive activities of real or imaginary political activists in Mirat, or a dossier about the scandalous activities, real or imaginary, of Mirat police officers and Mirati officials? If so, had Merrick ever believed in any of it? When he was going on and on about the man in the nullah and the imaginary stone he never referred to the existence of such dossiers, although he said the chief of police should start investigating what he called subversive elements. So, if he had any dossiers, files containing information collected from these so-called spies, had he believed in any of it, or had he just sat there, listening to these young men, pretending to accept their reports, pretending to need their reports but waiting for them to make it clear what else they were offering, and puzzling them by blandly ignoring every hint, every temptation. You knew him, Mr Perron. Would you say that was possible?'

'I should have thought very possible, but in view of the Aziz business, not very probable.'

'And there I disagree. I think perhaps it was probable precisely because of the Aziz business. I think it likely that what he did with, and to, Aziz revealed something to him about himself that utterly appalled him . . .'

'Appalled him?'

'I don't mean the revelation of his latent homosexuality and his sado-masochism. These must have been apparent to him for many many years and every now and again given some form of expression. What I mean by a revelation is revelation of the connection between the homosexuality, the sado-masochism, the sense of social inferiority and the grinding defensive belief in his racial superiority. I believe – although you may not – that Aziz was the first young man he had actually ever made love to, and that this gave him a moment of profound peace, but in the next the kind he knew he couldn't bear, knew he couldn't bear because to admit this peace meant discarding every belief he had. I think he realized that, when he woke up after his first night with the boy. And I think that when the boy turned up the following night he just found himself punished and humiliated. And I believe that when Merrick beat him with his fist he was inviting retaliation. I believe he knew why Aziz had arrived. I am sure that finally, Mr Perron, he sought the occasion of his own death and that he grew impatient for it. He *wanted* there to be a man in the nullah. He wanted there to be a stone thrown at his horse. He wanted what happened to happen. Perhaps he hoped that his murder would be avenged in some splendidly spectacular way, in a kind of Wagnerian climax, the *raj* emerging from the twilight and sweeping down from the hills with flaming swords –'

A steward interrupted, approached, leant close, murmured something to him. Bronowsky nodded. The steward went.

'Nawab Sahib?' Perron asked.

'Yes. He has seen the fires in the city. Forgive me, Mr Perron. It is a summons I can't disobey. But really it is just that he cannot sleep, and wants company.'

They both rose.

'The car can drop you next door and take me on to the palace,' Bronowsky said.

'It's only a step or two.'

'But the car has to take me anyway. Come.'

Bronowsky led him out on to the terrace, taking the long way round to the front. He placed his left hand on Perron's right shoulder. 'But let me tell you what did happen. Or all that one knows. Which isn't much. There was no apparent difference between all the previous nights of the spies and the fatal night. Two young men turn up. Neither has visited before. One goes. The other stays. Perhaps the one who went did not really go, but came back and stayed hidden, to assist, when the time came. It was a lot for one man to do alone. But all that is a mystery, a little event between midnight and six o'clock in the morning when Khansamar went in with the *chota hazri*. The visitor who was to stay the night had gone. Chaukidar had seen nothing, heard nothing. The fact that he did not see them going does not necessarily mean that he was asleep. When the boys made off they might have gone over the wall at the back. No. The real mystery is what happened in the room. Did Merrick dress himself in those clothes, do you think? Habbibullah says that he was strangled before he was hacked about with the little axe and that he was dressed in the clothes before being hacked. One wonders why this was the chosen night, whether it was because time was running out or because the time was now exactly right for leaving on our doorstep as it were, one dead Englishman.'

Bronowsky stopped, released Perron's shoulder, leant for a moment on his stick. 'I wonder – was the thing done in the old Thuggee way?'

'Not unless the neck was broken and a grave already dug.'

'Ah. I had forgotten that. But it was something else I had in mind – the many days the Thugs sometimes travelled with their chosen victims, to lull suspicion. Isn't there a resemblance between this and the long period of preparation? And then it is said, isn't it, that when it came to it they were mercifully quick. Compassionate, even.'

The fountains rose, changed colour, subsided and then murmured on. Bronowsky took Perron's shoulder again and began to walk forward. 'Perhaps it is there, in the compassion, that I have been hoping to see the real resemblance.'

VI

'I hadn't thought that we were to be quite so large a party,' Mrs Peabody said.

She had to raise her voice because the platform was crowded and noisy even where the first-class coaches stood and where the usually sober British were being determinedly cheerful and jolly, seeing off and being seen off. Even Mrs Peabody was smiling so Perron wasn't sure whether she was making a comment or a complaint.

'I expect we'll all fit in easily enough,' he shouted back. Mrs Peabody was thin, but tall, so tall that her greatest problem looked like being lack of head-space rather than of elbow-room. Peabody was the same height and not much better fleshed. It would be like travelling with two bean poles. The Peabodys were, as people put it, 'staying on', but were going to do that in Rawalpindi. So much Perron had gathered. They had an immense amount of luggage whose stowing in the compartment Peabody was overseeing. It had already been going into the compartment when Perron and the party from palace and guest house arrived, and still was. It was a good thing that everyone else was travelling fairly light – as Mrs Grace had pointed out after greeting Mrs Peabody and discovering in answer to her question that, yes, all this stuff was going into the compartment because years and years of travelling in India had inspired no confidence in either Peabody, in the luggage vans, even on a daytime trip. For instance one would not, Mrs Peabody pointed out, like to have some of one's things off-loaded by mistake at Premanagar.

After this exchange Mrs Grace had dissociated herself from the Peabodys and their luggage and engaged herself in conversation with Bronowsky and Ahmed while Sarah and Nigel helped Susan and ayah to keep Edward entertained. This had left Perron under an obligation to make himself pleasant to Mrs Peabody, but it was up-hill work. The Peabodys were working in unison, he inside, she out. Their joint efficiency suggested years of practice. Every few moments she broke off the exchange of small-talk to point a coolie at a piece of luggage, or if she didn't break it off herself Peabody did by coming to the open compartment door and reminding her that such or such a piece ought to be stowed next.

'Well I don't know about fitting in easily,' she said eventually, 'but no doubt we shall manage, since there are only six of us.'

'Eight,' Perron said.

'Dora,' Peabody called from the carriage door. 'We'd better have the guns now.'

'There's still the tiffin-box.'

'I think the guns first, then the tiffin-box.'

'As you wish, Reginald.' She pointed a coolie at canvas-shrouded packages, long and thin enough to be Peabody guns.

'Eight,' she said, not having lost the thread. 'How do you make eight?'

'Eight and a half, actually, if you include both me *and* the little boy.'

'Well naturally one includes you both.'

'Right-o, Dora. Tiffin-box now.'

She pointed a coolie at the tiffin-box. It was a wooden box, of majestic proportions, presumably zinc-lined, with air-holes on one side. Watching it go in Perron thought that at least none of them would starve if the train broke down and the Peabodys unbent sufficiently to share out.

'I still make it only six and a half, unless Captain Rowan is coming to Ranpur instead of joining Laura in Gopalakand. But I think that would still make it only seven and a half. Not that mathematics were ever my strong point. Once the thermoses have gone in we can leave the field clear.' She moved to the compartment door and shouted, 'Reginald? I hope the upper berths are let down. They'll need them to stow *their* few things.'

Perron joined Sarah and Nigel. 'I have a feeling that at least two members of the departing *raj* aren't going to leave without standing by their old rights. Or anyway making a fuss about Ahmed and ayah travelling in a first-class compartment.'

'Oh, for God's sake,' Sarah said.

'The Peabodys?' Nigel asked. 'They'd better start getting used to it. He's making a contract with Pakistan for a couple of years. Actually I don't blame him. He's a brilliant military administrator.'

'Brilliant and only a major? Or hasn't he been quite pukka enough to make it to half-colonel?'

Rowan smiled. 'Originally, no. And she's half-Jewish and very anti-semitic. But she's now the Honourable Dora.'

'The Honourable Dora? What a terrible combination.'

'She's furious that it always gets omitted in newspapers. But it came rather late, when her father was made a law baron. It's never got into the Indian lists.'

'Shall I start stowing our luggage?'

'You mean they've finished?' Sarah asked.

Perron rounded up their own coolies and entered the compartment. It smelt of Peabody's bay rum.

In these old first-class compartments there were no corridors. There was no need of them and one was better without them. Each compartment, coupé or four-berther, had its private lavatory. The compartments were broad enough and the berths long enough to suit the tallest man at full stretch and hold the combined luggage of four long-distance travellers. Normally the luggage could be piled up against what might be called the bulkhead between the sleeping compartment and the lavatory; and there was sufficient space down the centre between the two fixed lower benches to stow ice- and tiffin-boxes without restricting foot room.

But when Perron entered he saw that the Peabodys had commandeered all this space and more. Luggage was piled against the bulkhead, blocking the farther exit and coming within an inch or two of the door to the lavatory. He hoped that the exit at Ranpur was on the same side as the entrance at Mirat. Presumably the Peabodys knew. Stretching from the pile of bulkhead luggage was a line of trunks and cases down the centre of the compartment. Even some of the luggage-space provided by the lowered upper sleeping berths was taken up. He ordered his own party's suitcases to be stowed above, and then remembered Merrick's relics. Were they out on the platform? The answer was at once given – by the appearance in the doorway of a coolie holding one end of the black tin coffin, the battered old trunk, with the stencilled name, Lieut.-Colonel R. Merrick, DSO, still visible, still eloquent.

'You'd better put it here,' he said, indicating a place that would leave barely sufficient room for people to get from one side of the compartment to another. He hoped the carpet wouldn't come too. But it did. It looked smaller, though. It had been doubled up and tied with string. He had it placed on top of the trunk.

He clambered out, and down on to the platform. The Peabodys were bidding farewell to an elderly servant who was placing garlands round their thin necks. He reported to Sarah. A warning whistle blew. She turned to Bronowsky who took off his rakish little panama hat. Beyond the first-class compartment area the platform had begun to seethe. Perron could hear the mournful voice of the man selling tea. Cha-ay Wall-*ah*, Garam cha-*ay*. Black hands stretched down from open third-class compartments grasping those stretched up to bid goodbye. A woman shrieked.

'Goodbye, my dear,' Bronowsky was saying to Sarah. 'Don't be too long before coming back.' He bent to embrace her.

Perron clasped Nigel's hand. 'I'll wire you,' he said.

'Do. I'll be a better host in Gopalakand. Have a good journey.'

A hand fell on Perron's shoulder. Bronowsky's. The one eye observed him. 'Thank you for coming to Mirat. Here is a little token of your visit.'

He found himself presented with a little package. A book by the feel of it. Then Edward intervened.

'Goodbye, Chief Minister. Thank you for letting us stay at the Nawab's guest house, while daddy's away.'

One by one they entered the compartment. Another blow on the whistle. Distantly the woman shrieked again.

'Mrs Merrick, there is room for your tiffin basket on top of ours,' Mrs Peabody said.

'Please don't worry,' Susan replied. She sat at the far end of the compartment opposite Mrs Peabody, divorced from her by the black tin trunk and the folded carpet. On her lap she held a basket.

'Has your ayah a compartment quite close?'

'Oh, very close, Mrs Peabody. In fact here. Ayah will sit with me, in case I doze off and Edward needs attending to. It's the best thing.'

After a moment Mrs Peabody said, 'Reginald, let me sit at the other end. It is a little close here.' They changed places.

'Are you sure about that basket, Mrs Merrick?' Peabody asked.

'Absolutely sure, Major Peabody.'

Perron, at the doorway, received Edward from Dmitri's arms. 'I don't want to sit down yet, Perron,' the boy said. 'I want to wave from this window.'

'Okay, but let the troops on first.'

Mrs Grace came next. She looked at the compartment and then at the Peabodys and said, 'Good Heavens, it looks as though we're being delivered from Egypt,' and went to sit next to Susan. Sarah kissed Nigel and came up next. She went down and round over the baggage and sat between Major and Mrs Peabody.

'Ayah!' Edward shouted. 'Hurry up! You're going to miss the train.'

Ahmed helped ayah up.

'Come on, ayah,' Mrs Grace said, and patted the seat next to her. '*Baitho.*'

The girl tried to take Edward with her but he resisted. So she went and sat, alert, on the edge of the green leather-upholstered bench. A pretty girl, Perron realized; this morning not covering her face with the edge of her saree. Ahmed came next. He seemed to have no luggage except a small canvas bag.

Another whistle-blow. Ahmed shut the door, turned, lifted Edward up to the open window.

'Goodbye Dmitri!' the child called. 'Goodbye Uncle Nigel!'

Abruptly, the carriage began to glide away. Perron steadied himself against the piled Peabody luggage and bent, peering through the other windows to watch the unfolding tapestry of the departure from Mirat.

I remember (he has said) dark faces taking over from the white faces. I remember the woman who ran trying to keep up with the train.

'Are you really sure about the basket, Mrs Merrick?' Mrs Peabody said. 'Couldn't your ayah look after it?'

Susan didn't reply this time. When Perron had climbed over the luggage and settled himself next to Mrs Peabody, Sarah whispered to him, 'Try to get her to shut up about the basket. It's the urn. Susan won't let anyone else touch it.'

At a suitable moment, when Edward was shouting playfully at ayah, Perron passed the message on. Mrs Peabody opened her mouth, then shut it. Presently she opened her handbag and brought out a little lace handkerchief, moist with eau-de-cologne. She wiped it gently over her dry yellow skin.

They were sitting in this order:

On the bench that ended close to the one unencumbered door – first, Ahmed, then ayah, then Mrs Grace and Susan. The child used this side of the compartment as his roving territory. Opposite Susan sat Peabody, then Sarah, then Perron and Mrs Peabody. At Perron's and Mrs Peabody's end there was almost total luggage block, with Ahmed and ayah visible only from chest height. Ahmed got up and went into the lavatory. Perron heard Mrs Peabody draw in her breath and then slowly exhale. He had the impression that however badly she might need to she would now avoid going to the lavatory for the rest of the day, or get out at the only stop (Premanagar) whether she needed to or not, as a form of insurance against too great a desperation later. She remained tense throughout the few minutes Ahmed was absent, probably counting them, in order to work out whether he was urinating or doing something of a graver nature. When Ahmed came out she continued silent, and Perron began to feel that she was holding *him* responsible for everything, from the overcrowded compartment right down through the urn to the use of the lavatory by natives.

'Bang!' Edward shouted. After they had been going for about half an hour (and all, one by one, except Perron and the Peabodys had used the lavatory – Perron because he didn't want to go badly enough to feel it worth his while fighting the way over that mound of luggage) Edward had found the perfect use for the piled trunks and cases. He shot them from behind this entrenchment until they were all dead. Except Mrs Peabody, who was resistant to imaginary bullets.

But the 'Bang!' obviously stirred thoughts. 'Do you hunt, Mr Perron?' she asked. These were not the first words she had spoken to him, simply the first she had volunteered.

Perron said he didn't.

'Do you shoot?'

'No. I watched Ahmed hawking the other day.'

'Who?'

'Ahmed. Mr Kasim. Over there.'

'Hawking?'

'With a hawk.'

'Oh. I see. Yes. Really? I don't think I should care for that. It seems to me rather cruel to tame a wild creature. But I like a day out with hounds and a day out with the guns. We hope to get in a few days at Bharatpur before going on up to 'Pindi.

You've been to Bharatpur, I suppose? Oh, you should. The jhils there are famous.'

She talked on for a while, about Bharatpur, about Kashmir, about the boundless number of places she and Reginald had been in India. 'We've never been south though, except of course through it to Ooty. There's some good going in Ooty. But the south always depresses me. I never think of it as India at all. We're northern India people by temperament, I suppose. Tell me, what is your regiment?'

Perron admitted that he did not own a regiment and had never served in one except for a few months during the war as a private, after which he had transferred to Intelligence and then to Field Security.

'But you were in India?'

'For a while.'

'In Field Security?'

'Yes. With a man called Bob Chalmers.'

'Chalmers. Chalmers. No, I'm afraid I don't know that name.'

'He's now in pharmaceuticals in Bombay.'

'Really. How interesting. He stayed on, then. Reggie was awfully tempted to go into pharmaceuticals himself, after all one of the few things we can do for this country now is help them fight the battle of disease.'

'And poverty.'

She smiled. 'I sometimes think the poverty is very exaggerated. Most of the Indians one knows could buy one up lock stock and barrel.'

'There are the ones one doesn't know.'

'In the villages, Mr Perron, every peasant woman has her gold bangles. No, no. It is not the poverty. It is the disease. The superstition. The *inertia*.'

'Bang!' Edward said.

Perron died again.

And then so did the train. The luggage juddered from the vibration of the braking. Minnie grabbed the child. They all rocked to and fro for a moment and then steadied themselves. The train came to a halt.

'Probably a cow on the line,' Mrs Peabody said. 'Reggie – see what you can see if you can manage to climb over that carpet.'

But Ahmed was already up. He lowered the window of the door and leant out.

'I remember a cow on the line,' Susan said in the dead silence. 'Don't you, Sarah?'

'Yes, I remember.'

'But where? All I remember is the train stopping and daddy saying just what Mrs Peabody just said. "Probably a cow on the line." And there was. But where was it, Sarah?'

'Between Ranpur and Delhi. Nineteen-thirty.'

'Ranpur and Delhi. What lovely names. There's so much poetry in Indian names. Ronnie used to say that. Where is your home at home, Mrs Peabody?'

'We are in Northamptonshire. Just outside Norby.'

'Norby. That's what I mean. And mother says she's found a house in Epsom. It sounds like an aperient.'

'Major Peabody?' Ahmed called out. 'Would you please put up the windows and close the shutters on your side? Mrs Grace? Please? On yours?'

He was locking the compartment door. Now he pulled the window up and closed the wooden shutter.

'What is it, Ahmed?' Mrs Grace asked.

'Oh, nothing much. Just some kind of silly nuisance. Mr Perron, please, on your side?'

'What's the chap say?' Peabody asked.

'He seems to want the windows closed and the shutters pulled down,' Mrs Peabody said. 'I can't think why. It's hot enough and there's one fan not working.'

Peabody stood up. 'What are you doing? Baking us alive or something?'

Ahmed was helping Mrs Grace to close windows and pull down shutters on the other side of the compartment. Perron started doing the same on the Peabody side.

'What's wrong, Ahmed?' Sarah asked.

'Just some silly people making a nuisance. Don't worry.'

There was nothing to be seen through the windows except a vast hot dry eroded landscape. 'Do you mind?' Perron asked, leaning in behind Mrs Peabody and dealing with her window and shutter.

'Yes I do. I do mind. For heaven's sake!'

'Just shut the windows please and pull down the shutters,'

Ahmed repeated. 'Mrs Grace, I think ayah shouldn't sit here. Let her get under the seat just for a while. Come, Minnie.' He got hold of her and forced her gently to the floor. 'Play hide and seek with chokrasahib. Come on, Edward. Look, ayah is hiding.'

Edward shouted, 'Why is she hiding? I don't want to play hide and seek. It's a silly girl's game.'

'No, it isn't silly,' Ahmed insisted. 'Come on, help hide ayah. Pretend bad men are looking for her.'

'Look here, Kasim,' Peabody began – but just then there was a long drawn-out wail, rising in pitch, from up ahead. There was a grumble of voices from the adjacent compartment, then a shout, and the sound of windows and shutters being closed. The wailing continued as an accompaniment now to sudden screams.

They remained, as if transfixed. From under the bench came a low moan from the little ayah. The boy bent down. 'What's wrong, ayah?' he asked. Ahmed got hold of him and said, 'Okay, it's only a game. Ayah's pretending to hide from bad people. Major Peabody, please come to this side and take ayah's seat so that no one can see her.'

Peabody hesitated, then began to clamber over the luggage. As he did so something hit the compartment, something soft. And again. The sound of a hand slapping the side of the carriage. Behind it all the continuing sound of wailing and screaming.

'Take the boy,' Ahmed said, and lifted him over into Sarah's arms. Peabody was still straddled across the luggage.

'Reggie, what are you *doing*?' his wife asked him. He looked at her as if he thought her a perfect fool but said, 'God knows what anyone's doing, it must be some kind of damned silly demonstration,' and completed the movement of stepping over the luggage, lost his footing and fell against Mrs Grace and Susan. 'Oh, damn it,' he said and just then people outside began to pound heavily on the door and the side of the compartment and then there was a little crack and an explosion of broken glass and Susan shrieked. Another explosion; another shattering of glass. She shrieked again. As if by old instinct, Peabody remained ducked down, forgetting that the glass couldn't fly in through the lowered shutters. It was dark in the compartment. Little wires of light lay along the edges of the wooden louvres. The occupants of the seats were ducked down too, including Ahmed. Mrs Grace had her arm round Susan. Sarah held the boy. This was the

tableau Perron saw when after a sudden silence had lasted a few
seconds he looked up and round.

There was a bang on the door. Then a hammering that went on
for some while. When it stopped a man's voice came quite clearly:
'Come on, Kasim Sahib.' More bangs on the door. Susan gasped.
Mrs Peabody cried out, 'What are they doing, what are they
doing?' Then the voice from outside could be heard again. 'Come
on out. Kasim? Kasim Sahib? Come on. Or do we have to break
in and annoy all the sirs and ladies? Kasim? Kasim Sahib?' When
the voice stopped the hammering on the door began again.

Silence suddenly. Then another shattered window. This time
Edward began to cry. Sarah cradled him. Perron got up – to do
what he didn't know: climb over to the door, open the shutter
and shout that there was no Kasim there?

But Ahmed had got up too. Because of the noise of Edward
crying and Susan shrieking Perron did not clearly hear what
Ahmed said, but it sounded like, 'It seems to be me they want.'
It could have been, 'Be ready to re-lock the door.' But he smiled,
shrugged, and had suddenly unlocked it. As he did so Peabody
lunged forward, as if to stop him. But he was too late. Ahmed
opened the door and went.

A turbanned head appeared. Peabody must have seen the head
at eye-level. Perron saw it from above. The head rose. The man
must have been getting purchase on steps and handgrip. It looked
as if he was coming in. He got one hand on the door-handle. In
his other was something that looked like a sword but surely
couldn't have been. He said, 'Sorry to have disturbed you, sirs
and ladies. On to Ranpur, isn't it?'and then let himself fall away,
dragging the door shut. Peabody lunged forward again and
locked it.

A feeling of terrible relief swept over Perron. At the time it
was just relief. It was terrible subsequently; when it sank in that
it had been the relief a man feels when his self-protective
instinct tells him he has personally survived a passing danger.
Perhaps Peabody felt the same relief. And perhaps it was this
that presently made him push up the shutter and look out.

Then he lowered it quickly, stood for a moment, staring at
the shutter, checked the lock on the door, and turned round and
sat on the bench in the place Ahmed had vacated without saying
a word.

And as he did so the train began to glide forward – slowly, silkily, smoothly; as if getting stealthily away from a dangerous and incomprehensible situation. Except for Peabody, who had looked out, none of the people in the compartment could quite visualize the scene of this second departure. Later they must all have done so. In Perron's mind it remains so vivid that it sometimes seems to him that he raised a shutter himself and watched as the train drifted away along this stretch of line, on whose embankment bodies lay; some close, some farther off as though they had tried to run away and then been caught and struck down – men, women, youths, young girls, babies, in death looking all the same, like dummies stuffed for some kind of strange fertility festival.

It took three-quarters of an hour to get to Premanagar. At first it seemed as if they would cover the entire distance in the semi-darkness of lowered shutters and in total silence apart from the rhythmic clack of wheels hastily putting distance between the living travellers and the abandoned dead, but after five minutes or so Mrs Peabody said, 'Reggie, do you think we might have some light and air? I think otherwise I might be going to faint.'

'Only on your side,' Mrs Grace said. 'Here we have a great deal of trapped broken glass.'

'It was my side I was thinking of. Perhaps you'd help me, Mr Perron, since you're here.'

Perron lent a hand.

'I didn't like that game, Auntie Sarah,' Edward said. 'Is it finished?'

The child's tear-stained face was revealed as the shutters went up. He climbed off Sarah's lap and then up and over the piled luggage. 'You can come out now, ayah,' he shouted. 'We've stopped playing that game. Where's Ahmed? Has he gone to pee again? I want to pee too.' He had to say it several times and then staggered towards the door of the w.c. His unsteadiness suddenly impressed itself on Major Peabody's eye.

'Come on, old chap, then. I'll take you.'

'What's *your* name?' Edward asked as he was taken in.

'Never mind my name,' Peabody said; and shut the door on them both.

Sarah was now leaning forward, both elbows clasped in her

hands, her head bowed. Ayah had got up and was standing against the luggage. When the door of the lavatory opened and Edward came out alone she took charge of him and sat with him in the place that had been Ahmed's and then Peabody's and was now anybody's or nobody's. Peabody was in the cubicle for nearly ten minutes. Perhaps he was being sick. He looked very pale when he came out. Finding his new place gone he clambered over the luggage and sat once more in the far corner opposite Susan who still cradled the basket and was still cradled in Mrs Grace's arms.

'Is mummy crying again?' Edward asked.

Nobody answered. But then Sarah said, 'We just let him go. We all of us sat here and let him go.' After that none of them spoke. In this way they came into Premanagar.

Before the train actually stopped Peabody got up. Perron got up too. At the door Peabody said in a whisper, 'Keep them in here, Perron. They mustn't come out on to the platform.'

'But I must.'

Peabody said, 'I think not.'

'I'm sorry, Peabody. But I've got to go back to where Ahmed got out.'

Peabody frowned. Perhaps at the use of his surname. 'There's nothing to go back for. He was hacked to pieces.'

Perron didn't really take this in. He said, 'I must get to a phone and ring the palace. We can't just leave it like that. Someone's got to go back.'

From outside, suddenly, as the train came to a halt, came the renewed sound of wailing and shouting. Peabody's breath smelt acid. He said, 'They might turn on us when they take it in. They might decide it's our fault. You'd be better advised to stay here and look after the women. I'm going to find out what's happening.'

'It's all right, Major Peabody,' Sarah called. 'Mr Perron knows what he must do. I'll stand by the door if that's what you want.' She clambered over. Reluctantly Peabody opened the door. An English voice outside exclaimed, 'My God.' Peabody and Perron went down. 'Lock it,' Peabody told Sarah. She said, 'There's no need to lock it now.'

Other English passengers had come down from the adjacent compartments – two of them women. Two Indian officers ran through asking them to make way. Automatically they stood back, as if accepting that this was an Indian affair, not theirs. They stood pale-faced, shocked.

Some of the dead were already being brought out of the third-class carriages. The nearest of these was a purdah-coach and out of this white and black bundles of veiled women were being lowered. Most lay motionless when put down, one or two seemed to be trying to crawl back in. Among the dead from the purdah-coach were the bodies of small children. And beyond the purdah-coach the platform was becoming littered with blood-stained bundles of white cloth, with black limbs sticking out of the cloth. One body lay on the roof of the coach. No one seemed to have noticed it. From some of the windows of the coaches heads and arms hung down. Blood slowly made shapes on the dirty grey concrete of the platform. Ahead, the locomotive suddenly let off steam, as if about to haul the train out again. People began to shout. A wave of panic swept along the platform and then because the train didn't move died away and left only the wailing of those searching among the rows of dead and dying passengers.

'I'm sorry,' the MCO said, 'I cannot allow private calls of any nature. I am trying to raise Mirat. The lines may be down. Please go away.'

The MCO was a Sikh. Sikhs, people were saying, had been among the gang that stopped the train and slashed Muslim passengers to death with swords. But if he feared for his own life he didn't show it. He had moved freely up and down the platform. Perron had waylaid him on one of his brief visits to the office where a havildar-clerk was constantly on the telephone.

'If you get Mirat, would you please tell them that Ahmed Kasim, the son of Mohammed Ali Kasim may have to be presumed dead and that the Nawab of Mirat's Chief Minister should be informed?'

'Ahmed Kasim? Ahmed Kasim? Who is Ahmed Kasim?'

'He was travelling with us.'

'Then why is he presumed dead? You are first-class, surely. Please go away. What is one man among so many?'

'Mirat, sir,' the clerk shouted, and handed the phone over.

The MCO grabbed the receiver, at the same time saying,

'Please all of you go away.' He began talking rapidly in a mixture of English and Hindi. Perron was not the only unauthorized visitor. There were about six crowded into the tiny office. But all of them were English – people who were anxious to contact friends left behind in Mirat or waiting for them in Ranpur, friends who some time during the day might hear what had happened and start worrying.

'Let's try the stationmaster,' one of them said.

'He's worse than this chap.'

They had absorbed the shock. The old reactions were already setting back in, but the impulse to take charge had gone. It was the kind of situation that had always been bubbling under the surface trying to break out, the kind that the *raj* had had to try to control. Now the worst had happened.

'God knows how they're going to cope in this place,' one of the officers told Perron as they went back on to the platform. 'Premanagar's always been a dead-alive hole. No proper troops and no pukka hospital.'

The MCO's office was next to the first-class restaurant. The trains always drew up so that the first-class compartments were opposite the places that first-class passengers needed. In this area, then, the platform was an isolated little island, bordered on both sides by the horrors. Perron noticed that armed police had turned up. It was twenty minutes since the train's arrival. He went to the compartment. The door was open. Inside there were only the two Peabodys – he kneeling by an open bag, she lying full length on the bench, hand over her eyes.

'Where are the others?' Perron asked.

'Women's rest room.'

From the bag Peabody was taking a webbing belt and holster. The holster had a revolver in it. Perron got down again and went to the women's rest room. It was crowded. There were several men among the women, looking pale, dignified and protective. At one end of the room he saw Mrs Grace, ayah and Edward, and Susan. He made his way to them, passing from under one area of fanned air to another. 'Where's Sarah?' he asked Mrs Grace.

'She's gone to see what she can do to help. I let her. It's what she wanted.'

Perron pushed his way out again. 'Savages,' a woman was

saying. And a man, 'What do you expect? It's only the beginning. Once we've gone they'll all cut each other's bloody throats. Non-violence. Makes you laugh, doesn't it?' But it didn't make Perron laugh. Once out on the platform he forced his way through a little cordon of armed police into the place where the kind of help Sarah had to offer might be needed. He couldn't see her, so went back again, passing through the area of safety and certainty, out to the other side, through another cordon of police, to another place of horror. Here he saw two Indian nurses, and a stretcher-bearer. A nun. Two nuns. However unpukka the nearest hospital was it had begun to operate. And there were two white women, one elderly, one quite young. A middle-aged Indian in European clothes stopped him. 'Are you a doctor?' 'No,' Perron said. 'I wish to God I were.' And passed on. The two white women were nursing children. The nuns, both Indians, were binding wounds, staunching the flow of blood from terrible-looking cuts which revealed the whiteness of the bone, the redness of the flesh under the brown skin. Another middle-aged man, an English-man this time, looked up and said, 'Are you the doctor?' 'No,' Perron said. The man said, 'Never mind. Water's the problem. Could you help with that? But it's got to come from the tap down there. Not the one for caste-Hindus. But a lot of these wretches are dying of thirst if nothing else.'

It was at the tap 'down there' that he found Sarah. She was on her knees, in the filth and the muck, her skirt wet through, handing up little brass vessels to the man controlling the tap, reaching out for empty ones without looking, placing the filled vessels on the other side. The vessels, mugs, glasses were being brought and taken away by men and women and youths. He knelt by her. 'Come on,' he said, 'let me take over.'

'No,' she said. 'I'm all right doing this. I can't do the other thing. But if you can, please do.'

So Perron picked up one of the brass jugs and turned and went among the dying. Or the dead. It wasn't always easy to tell. He knelt first by an old grey-beard who seemed to be smiling up at him gratefully, joyfully, but who did not respond when he put his hand under the man's neck to try to raise him. The eyes were glazed and the smile was merely a death-smile.

*

The train had been the 10 a.m. express to Ranpur, its only scheduled stop Premanagar, normally reached at 11.15. The ambush
had been laid at a point on the line some miles from the last of
three wayside halts, all of which were reached and passed by the
express within half an hour of leaving Mirat, and beyond which
there was no habitation, nothing but desert, until you reached
Premanagar.

As the train came out of a curve on to a straight level embankment, the driver had indeed seen a cow, apparently ruminating.
He did not remember seeing more than two or three men asleep
on the embankment, but at this point there were a few shade trees
growing in the dips on either side, and when he brought the train
to a stop he realized there were very many more men. They came
up on both sides. Two – armed with swords – climbed on to the
footplate. The others began running down the track and climbing
into the carriages.

Some passengers said that the attackers were joined by men
who had travelled on the train from Mirat and who now produced knives and cudgels and joined the raiders. It must have
been one of these men who had noted the compartment Ahmed
Kasim got into. Opinions varied about the length of time the
train was halted while the men went through it, dragging
Muslims out or killing them on the spot. Some said only five
minutes, others remembered the slaughter continuing for perhaps half an hour. The truth was that it lasted no more than
ten or fifteen minutes. At the end of that time, getting a signal,
one man released the cow (which had been tethered) and
slapped it away to find its own salvation. The two intruders on
the footplate ordered the driver to resume his journey and then
jumped off. He needed no persuasion. He believed himself
lucky to get away with his life and that of his young apprentice.
He didn't look back until the locomotive had got up speed.
Then he saw men scattering across the rough rocky ground
towards a huddle of mined huts. He saw no vehicles, got no
indication of how the men had congregated in this place, or
how they hoped to get away. But there probably were vehicles,
an old carrier-truck, perhaps, an ancient bus. It was forty-five
minutes before the train reached Premanagar, perhaps another
fifteen before the Premanagar authorities had contacted Mirat,
perhaps another half-hour before troops, police and medical

units from Mirat arrived at the scene of the ambush, having dropped search parties off at the villages served by the wayside halts. At the scene itself there was only the terrible evidence: the dead and the dying. By then, the attackers had had nearly two hours in which to scatter.

By road, the journey from Mirat to Premanagar could be accomplished in one and a half hours, only fifteen minutes longer than the journey by rail. The first contingent of troops and medical staff and armed police from Mirat arrived at about one-thirty in the afternoon, fifteen minutes later than the scheduled time of the express train's normally delayed departure for Ranpur, after a leisurely stop for early first-class restaurant lunches. By then, the deputy commissioner and the district superintendent of police had been on the scene since midday. The transfer of dead and wounded to an emergency casualty station set up in the goods-yard area was nearly complete. Some kind of order had been restored. The carriages and the platform were being washed down. The rumour was that the train would leave for Ranpur at about 3 p.m., this time under armed guard, and mightn't be more than an hour or so late reaching its destination that evening. About a dozen of the first-class passengers went into the restaurant. The bar had been in use for some time.

Perron's trousers and shirt were spattered with blood. He had lost sight of Sarah. He made his way from the goods-yard back to the platform and the compartment.

Mrs Peabody was still stretched out on the bench. Peabody was bending over the tiffin-box, pouring a drink from a thermos. The carriage was otherwise empty. The garlands which had been presented to the Peabodys in Mirat lay on the floor.

'Have you seen Miss Layton?'

Peabody nodded at the lavatory cubicle. 'She's in there, changing. The others are still in the women's room I suppose. You'd better change too. Will you have some malted milk? It's very fortifying.'

'No thank you.'

'There's a spare sandwich or two here. Or have you got your own tuck?'

'I don't want anything to eat, thank you.'

'You ought to eat. Especially if you're going back. I've just been having a word with Bob Blake. He'll take you if you still want to.'

'Who's Bob Blake?'

'He's OC the refugee protection force in the cantonment. They got here a little while ago. I told him what happened to Kasim. He's ringing the station commander in Mirat. There can't be anything you can do but you seemed keen, so I told Bob. He knew Kasim slightly. He'll be here to have a word presently, I shouldn't wonder.'

Sarah came out of the cubicle. She carried a hold-all. The dress she had on was creased but unstained. And dry. She glanced at his shirt and trousers. She said:

'Have you had a drink yet?'

Peabody said, 'I offered him one but he didn't want it.'

'I meant a real drink.'

Perron shook his head. 'I don't want a real drink, either.' He felt now as if he was going to be sick. He went down on to the platform. Sarah came down too. She said, 'Sorry to scrounge. Have you a cigarette?'

He got out his case. He found it difficult to open. She tried to steady his hand while he helped her light up, but they were both trembling.

She said, 'Are you really going back?'

'Are you asking me not to? Do you want help in Ranpur?'

'No. No, thank you. I want to go back too. But I can't. I can't let Aunt Fenny cope alone. But they'll soon know at the palace what happened to Ahmed. Someone ought to go back and try to say how it did.'

'Mr Perron?'

Perron turned. A stout, rather red-faced middle-aged English officer had come up. Sarah said, 'Guy, this is Major Blake.' They shook hands. Blake said, 'I'm going back in about fifteen minutes. If you want to come with me can you be ready by then?'

'Yes, I've only got to change.'

'I'm leaving my subaltern in charge of the train, Miss Layton,' Blake explained. 'You'll be quite safe for the rest of the journey. I'm putting on a whole platoon.'

He took Perron's arm, guided him a few steps away and said, 'I've been on to the station commander in Mirat. He told me Count Bronowsky's already phoned him. The news got round

fairly fast. I'm afraid the station commander told him that only
Muslims in third-class compartments were killed, but that's what
he assumed. He's going now to the place where the bodies are
being brought in. Is there any possibility that Kasim wasn't
killed?'

'I don't think so. He just opened the door and went, Peabody
saw the rest.'

'The station commander said that if young Kasim is dead he'd
be very grateful if you do come back. Where were you going,
Mr Perron, Pankot?'

'Just to Ranpur, then on to Delhi.'

'Any urgency?'

'None.'

'All the same, I'll help you in any way I can to get you away
again. Did you see the chalk-mark on the door?'

'Chalk-mark?'

'Miss Layton noticed it a little while ago. Someone had
chalked a moon low on the door of your compartment. It must
have been done in Mirat by whoever was watching which part
of the train Kasim got into. Yours was the only first-class compartment attacked. All they had to do was look for the chalk-
mark. Well. I'll send a chap to help you sort out your bags and
bring them over.'

Blake went back to Sarah. They spoke for a few moments.
Then he touched his cap and went. From the bar there came a
sudden roar of laughter. Perron went back into the carriage to
get his bags down and change. As he did so he noticed a fresh
smear low down on the door, where the chalk-mark had been
wiped off.

Mrs Grace and Susan, Edward and ayah, were still in the rest
room. He didn't want to intrude on them. He said goodbye to
Peabody. Mrs Peabody was still prostrate. There was only Sarah
to see him off. One coolie had his suitcase, another his hold-all.
A lance-naik sent by Blake was in charge of them, waiting to
take Perron to the truck, whatever kind of vehicle it was he and
Blake would travel in.

'Are these yours, old man?' Peabody called, offering something
from the open carriage door: a little package and a canvas bag.

The package was certainly his. Dmitri's gift. Unopened. A

book, presumably. Perhaps a translation of the poetry of Pushkin. The canvas bag, for a moment, was unrecognizable. Then was. He came away from the door holding both. Sarah looked away from the bag.

'Shall I see you again?' he asked.

'I don't know.' She was still shivering. 'What is there to see?'

He touched her shoulder. 'A great deal,' he said. Then leant down and kissed her. He let her go. She turned and climbed back into the carriage. He smiled at her, then followed the naik. At the exit he looked back; she was at the carriage door, holding her elbows in that way, watching him. Briefly she released one hand and raised it. And then went in.

I'm sure (Sarah has written) that he did say, 'It seems to be me they want.' It's what Guy heard, what I heard, what we heard at the time, and it made sense. And the fact that he smiled encouraged me to think that if he went out to the people who called out to him everything would be all right. This is what it was like at the time. I can't justify it now except by saying that there were so many conflicting claims; how to stop Edward crying, how to stop Susan shrieking, how to explain even to myself just why ayah was hiding under the bench. When he first looked out of the window when the train stopped he must have seen them dragging Muslims out. If we'd been travelling only a week or two later we'd have been prepared for it, because by then the business of stopping trains and slaughtering people had become part of life. No English were ever harmed. And it became quite the ordinary thing to hide Indians, friends and servants, under the seats – Hindus if it was the Muslims who were attacking, Muslims if it was Hindus. And if people hammered on the doors you just told them to go away. But we didn't know that. We weren't prepared for it. I suppose Ahmed was, or saw at once how things were. And whoever wanted to kill him knew he was travelling that day. The massacre itself must have been a retaliation for the killings and burnings the night before in Mirat when Muslims attacked Hindus because Mirat was going under Congress rule. I suppose Ahmed was marked out as a victim not just because he was a Muslim but because the people who killed him didn't want Muslims in the Congress, or didn't trust Muslims in Congress and his father was still in Congress. And perhaps because they knew his brother was a rabid Pakistani and perhaps because on top of that they hadn't forgotten that Ahmed's father hadn't stood by the INA, which made it senseless anyway because Sayed had been INA. But it was all so senseless. Such a damned bloody senseless mess. The kind which Ahmed tried to shut himself off from, the mess the *raj* had never been able to sort out. The only difference between Ahmed and me was that he didn't take the mess seriously and I did. I felt it was our responsibility, our fault that after a hundred years or more it still existed.

Ahmed and I weren't in love. But we loved one another. We recognized in each other the compulsion to break away from what I can only call a *received* life. When I knelt at the tap, filling up those somehow meaningless little brass jugs and lotas and pots, whatever there was, it was driven home to me that what I was doing was just as useless as what he'd just done. I've never hated myself so much as I did then. I felt like throwing the jugs down and saying, Well, get on with it. And I hated Ahmed for not keeping the door locked and telling us he damned well wasn't going to die unless they smashed right through the windows and climbed in with their swords and slaughtered the lot of us, or started a fire under the compartment to smoke us out, so that they could cut us down one by one. All those possibilities must have been in his mind. But when it came to it he didn't let any of it even begin to happen to us. And *I* couldn't stop filling the bloody jars, going through my brave little memsahib act.

I'm sure he smiled just before he went, and I'm sure he said, 'It seems to be me they want.' Major Peabody said he thought he said, 'Make sure you lock it after me.' But I think that's what Major Peabody wanted to hear. Perhaps we all heard only what we wanted to hear. Perhaps there was nothing to hear because he said nothing, but just smiled and went, in which case I suppose that meant he knew there was nothing to say because there wasn't any alternative, because everyone else in the carriage automatically knew what he had to do. It was part of the bloody code. The moment he got into the carriage *he* sub-consciously knew that sub-consciously *we* had cast lots even before there was any question of lots having to be cast to see who would survive and who wouldn't.

No. I don't know what was in the canvas bag. And Guy never looked. A bottle of whisky, perhaps, and a clove or two of garlic.

Coda

Ranagunj airfield (Ranpur). Saturday August 9, 1947.

The tannoy system crackled. An Indian voice speaking in English told the few people sitting on the hard benches of the little airfield lounge that the plane from Mayapore was now landing and that departure for Delhi would be in twenty minutes.

The English officer sitting next to Perron closed the *Reader's Digest* and said, 'How civilized we make it sound. Do you know an extraordinary thing? As far back as December in nineteen forty-five when I flew from Singapore to Rangoon and on to Calcutta on an RAF plane and we landed for fuel in the middle of Burma, the door opened and an erk in white dungarees looked in and said, "You've now landed in Meiktila." '

'Meiktila?'

'Yes. I'd lost quite a lot of good men there scarcely more than six months before in the battle for the airstrip. But here we were, practising for the courteous world of civil aviation. I thought, How quickly the grass grows.'

The plane was delayed, delayed by storms. It was nearly midnight. It had rained throughout most of the day. The old Dakota was parked about a hundred yards from the airfield buildings. An immense puddle had to be negotiated by the six or seven people who having taken leave of friends walked ahead of or behind Perron towards the steps leading to the open port. Inside, bucket seats, thinly cushioned, had replaced the old port and starboard benches. About ten passengers were already seated. Passengers from Mayapore. Officers. Officers' wives. A blue-rinsed grey-haired woman who was probably Red Cross. Two beefy-looking fellows in shorts and shirts who might have been Australians but turned out to be English: technicians, perhaps, from the British–Indian Electric Company. Their shirts were black with sweat. They were drinking beer from the bottle.

Perron found a single seat on the port side. He stowed his hand luggage. Sat. Closed his eyes.

Mayapore, Ranpur, Delhi. He wondered how many of the passengers from Mayapore had been in the town in nineteen forty-two; at the time of the Bibighar. Perhaps none. The *raj* had always led a nomadic existence. And these little airfields, relics of the war, now merely hastened their movements from place to place. Some of them were moving out for the last time.

He opened his eyes and stared out of the window at what remained for him of Ranpur: an illuminated puddle. The airfield building. A petrol tanker, now hauling away. Beyond this darkness and this light – after these absurd little marks and portents of human occupation – the adventure. The port engine fired, exploding the silence. The port airscrew began to spin. Little ripples showed on the surface of the puddle, as though the fishermen on the Izzat Bagh lake had cast a net. Another small explosion, on the starboard side. He shut his eyes again. Whenever he travelled by air he prayed just before take-off and just before landing. These were nowadays his only offerings to God. It was inconceivable to him that the prayers could be heard because he felt that if there were a God, God would be praying too, watching these extraordinary machines shudder and flutter their frail way along the tarmac towards the lit runway.

And there was always that moment as the aeroplane squared up and seemed to pause; the moment of dying intention, and then the moment when defiance set in again and the paper-tiger roared and vibrated. It was like being drawn back and then shot in slow motion from a bow, so slowly that sometimes you felt that the pilot's inspiration had run out and left him with nothing but a grinding determination to prove against all evidence that the thing could be done.

The sensation of being no longer ground-borne always came as a shock. The extraordinary thing had again been achieved. Following which, even at night, when there was no visible horizon, there was this sense of exultation.

He opened Bronowsky's gift, the book, not of Pushkin poems but Bronowsky's own translations of Gaffur (privately printed, in Bombay, dedicated to the Nawab). From its leaves he took out and read what he had begun writing to Sarah in the airport lounge.

'I'm waiting for a plane that should have come in an hour ago but is delayed by storms. My watch says 10.45 so by now you'll be back and have had the message from your father that I rang. I hope Susan will be better soon. Please give her my best wishes. Your father said you'd all be staying at Commandant House for a few weeks because the new Indian commandant's wife isn't joining him yet and he's making other temporary arrangements. But after that? I didn't ask all the questions I wanted to, questions like where are you going when the few weeks are up? Back home? How absurd it is that suddenly there is this question of a roof over one's head. I gathered Susan was only suffering reaction and shock and should be out of hospital in a day or two.

'A false alarm. Someone said the plane had landed. It hadn't. But I shall have to finish this letter in Delhi. I gave your father my address there. I don't know whether I shall go down to Gopalakand as Nigel suggested. Wire me if you want me to come back to Ranpur, or up to Pankot. Your father said you'd had Nigel's telegram, the one he sent from Mirat on Thursday night, finally confirming what was never really in doubt. I tried to ring you that night, and yesterday, but the lines were hopeless. I came up to Ranpur on the night train and got in about 8 a.m. this morning and tried to ring you again from the airforce mess where Major Blake arranged for me to put up during the day. He's arranged this flight for me, too. I left Mirat because there was nothing more for me to do there. Ahmed's father arrived there yesterday morning. I met him for a few moments. An impressive man. Hiding his grief.

'When I got back to Mirat from Premanagar last Thursday, and to the place where all the bodies had been taken, Dmitri and Nigel were already there, and had identified and made some of the necessary arrangements. Nigel told me – and perhaps I should tell you – that the only person Dmitri blames is himself for letting Ahmed go on that particular day and for not anticipating that something like that might happen. Before I left last night Dmitri asked me to give you his love, then made us sit down for a moment on a couch and say nothing. It was like a Chekhov play. But shall I ever return to Mirat?'

The letter ended there.

But I thought (he said silently to Sarah, putting the letter away as the lights of Ranpur performed geometrical movements as if they were man-made constellations) I thought – today in Ranpur – of solving once and for all the mystery of Hari, if he is a mystery. Before I came to the airport I went with that little piece of paper on which Nigel had written words and numbers which established an idea of an address, a place where Hari might be found, where he might actually live, exist, eat, perform duties, make love perhaps, follow a life through, be content, be happy, or at least survive and be contacted by strangers, visitors, people carrying messages, and words from Rome. I found the place but it wasn't easy. The taxi-driver demanded more money when he reached the street he said led to Hari's. He wanted to go no further. Taxis, he said, did not go into such places. So I paid him off and went on foot. Immediately, I was appalled, and then frightened. I had to remind myself that this was where Hari lived, where he *had* survived. Three or four small beggar boys accompanied me, demanding money. The street was very narrow. Perhaps no Englishman had ever walked down it. To the beggar boys were added a beggar-man and three beggar-women. Other people called out to me from dirty-looking open shops. The smell of animal and human ordure and human sweat was overpowering. I almost turned back. But in the midst of all this squalor a boy of twelve or fourteen confronted me. He was so clean, neat shorts and neat white shirt, anxious to be of service, anxious to speak English to the Englishman. I trusted him. I stopped being frightened. I showed him the piece of paper. He walked ahead, saying: Come, sir, this way, sir. Within a hundred yards or so he turned into a narrow stairway. It led up between two shop fronts to a kind of tenement. The walls of the stairway were stained and greasy. The boy stopped at the second landing. But by now other people were crowding the stairs.

The door the boy and I stood at was bolted outside and pad-locked. But there was a card pinned to the jamb on which was typed the name. H. Kumar. The people on the stairs were shout-ing to the boy. I thought perhaps they were warning him not to disclose anything. I couldn't translate the bazaar dialect. But then the boy said the people were saying that Kumar Sahib was out, visiting a pupil. His aunt was out at the market in the Koti bazaar. She would be back soon. Kumar Sahib would be back later. The boy added: 'Please sir, meanwhile come and have coffee, clean shop. Brahmin shop.'

But I told him I hadn't time. I began to get out a card to give to the boy to give to Hari. But when I looked at the card it seemed like a cruel intrusion. I remembered saying to Hari: What is the difference between *karma* and *dharma*? He didn't know. I had learned the answer long ago. So had Hari. He was living it.

I went down the stairs, passing through that crowd of inquisitive people. Some of them followed us out. The boy eventually gave up pressing his invitation to drink coffee with him and said he would take me to the place where I could find a taxi. We went back through the narrow street, still followed by several youths and men and women. But now that I was out in the open I believed they were only people who wished Hari well, people who merely hoped to keep me there until he got back, so that they could offer me to him as a gift.

But it would have been a cruel gift, wouldn't it? Everything about my presence was cruel. My leaving without a word to him was cruel. When we got to the place where taxis were to be had the boy hailed one. I got out a card again and a pencil, but then wrote nothing on it. I gave the card to the boy. I offered him money. He took the card but refused the money. I told the taxi-driver to take me to the cantonment.

I don't know whether I'm glad that I did what I did or whether I bitterly regret it. In the taxi back I consoled myself with the thought that if ever he needed help he had the card, a little rectangle of pasteboard. I got my wallet out and looked at another of them, imagined him receiving one like it from the boy, in an hour or two, only half-listening to the description the boy would give of the man who had come to visit, the man who had left it, the visitor from another world. I didn't know, I don't know, what harm or good I'd done. Have done. The other thing I had in my wallet was the little essay by Philoctetes which I'd cut out with Nigel's scissors. I'd intended to show it to him, intended to say, You wrote this, didn't you, Hari? I have by heart the passage that comes at the end.

'I walk home, thinking of another place, of seemingly long endless summers and the shade of different kinds of trees, and then of winters when the branches of the trees were so bare, that recalling them now, it seems inconceivable to me that I looked at them and did not think of the summer just gone, and the spring soon to come, as illusions; as dreams, never fulfilled, never to be fulfilled.'

Perron replaced the unfinished letter between the pages of the book Dmitri had given him. He stared out of the port. Far below, dim isolated points of light marked the villages of India – the

India his countrymen were leaving, the India that was being given up. Along with what else?

He returned his attention to the book, to the poem at the end which was said to be the last Gaffur had ever written; dictated rather. But by now he had this by heart too. So he closed the book, shut his eyes, rested his head against the back of the bucket seat.

Everything means something to you; dying flowers,
The different times of year.
The new clothes you wear at the end of Ramadan.
A prince's trust. The way that water flows,
Too impetuous to pause, breaking over
Stones, rushing towards distant objects,
Places you can't see but which you also flow
Outward to.

Today you slept long. When you woke your old blood stirred.
This too meant something. The girl who woke you
Touched your brow.
She called you Lord. You smiled,
Put up a trembling hand. But she had gone,
As seasons go, as a night-flower closes in the day,
As a hawk flies into the sun or as the cheetah runs; as
The deer pauses, sun-dappled in long grass,
But does not stay.

Fleeting moments: these are held a long time in the eye,
The blind eye of the ageing poet,
So that even you, Gaffur, can imagine
In this darkening landscape
The bowman lovingly choosing his arrow,
The hawk outpacing the cheetah,
(The fountain splashing lazily in the courtyard),
The girl running with the deer.

AUTHOR'S NOTE AND ACKNOWLEDGEMENTS

A Division of the Spoils is the last in a sequence of four novels about the closing years of British rule in India. The characters were imaginary. So were the events. The framework was as historically accurate as I could make it. Three return visits to India during the time the sequence has taken to write have left me indebted to many people there for information, for help, for hospitality; and I gratefully acknowledge that debt. I am indebted, too, to the Arts Council for an award in 1969.

Above all, I am indebted to seven people who must be named because without their combined encouragement and practical help I doubt that the enterprise could have been brought to a conclusion. Each novel in the sequence has already been dedicated, for reasons that they know, to someone who seemed to be particularly connected with it. I dedicate the sequence as a whole, if I may, to (in New York) Dorothy Olding, John Willey, Larry Hughes and Ivan von Auw, and (in London) David Higham, Roland Gant and Charles Pick.

Facta non verba.   P.S.

This book is set in BEMBO which was cut
by the punch-cutter Francesco Griffo
for the Venetian printer-publisher
Aldus Manutius in early 1495
and first used in a pamphlet
by a young scholar
named Pietro
Bembo.